SCIENCE FICTION, FANTASY, & HORROR: 1987

SCIENCE FICTION, FANTASY, & HORROR: 1987

A Comprehensive Bibliography of
Books and Short Fiction Published
in the English Language

Charles N. Brown
William G. Contento

LOCUS PRESS
Oakland, California
1988

Locus Press
P.O. Box 13305
Oakland CA 94661

ISBN: 0-9616629-4-8

Printed in the United States.

Contents

Preface

The data in this book is based upon the monthly Books Received columns in *Locus,* and includes books and magazines seen between January and December 1987. The information has been checked and corrected, and comments have been expanded. In addition the contents of all new anthologies, collections, and magazines are listed. Appendices contain Book, Cinema, and Short Fiction Summaries, Recommended Reading, and a Publisher Directory.

The only major format change from previous books in this series is the elimination of the use of terse abbreviations for story sources. The title of the source publication is now either listed in full or a commonly used abbreviation is given, such as *IASFM* for *Isaac Asimov's Science Fiction Magazine* or *F&SF* for *The Magazine of Fantasy and Science Fiction.* This makes for a longer index, but makes it much easier to use.

The book contains seven main sections in the following formats:

1. **Author List: Books** This section lists by author full publication information for each book seen in 1987 and includes notes about each book. format:

Edition, Book Author(s), **Book Title**, (Publisher & ISBN, Publication Date, [Date First Seen], Price, Length, Binding) Notes

example:

*Bear, Greg **The Forge of God** (Tor 0-312-93021-6, Sep,87 [Aug,87], $17.95, 474pp, hc) Hard sf novel of the destruction of Earth. Fast-paced and well-written; highly recommended. (TM)

2. **Title List: Books** A listing by title of all books entered in the Author List. format:

Edition, **Book Title**, Author(s), Type

3. **1987 Original Publications** This section lists by author all books and stories that first appeared in 1987. format:

Author(s)
   Book Title/Story Title, Type, Source

4. **Subject List** This section lists by subject all books first published in 1987. A book may be listed under more than one subject. For example, all "Star Trek" novels are listed under both Science Fiction Novels and Novelizations. For an accurate count of the types of books published see the Book Summary. The "Type" entry following the Book Title is given only if it differs from the type implied by the subject. For example, under Anthologies, a book type "an" for "anthology" would not show the type code, but a book type "oa" for "original anthology"

would have the code listed. format:

Author(s)
   Book Title, Type

5. **Author List: Stories** This section lists by author the contents of all new anthologies, collections, and magazines. Included is information on the length and original source of each story, and a list by publication date of all books and magazines reprinting the story. A "+" following the Book Author indicates that there are additional co-authors for the book. format:

Story Author(s)
   Story Title, Type, Source
      Story Notes
      Book/*Magazine* reprinting the story, Book Editor, Source

example:

Bear, Greg
   Tangents, ss *Omni*, Jan,1986
      The Year's Best Science Fiction, Fourth Annual Collection, Gardner R. Dozois, an, St. Martin's, 1987
      Mathenauts, Rudy Rucker, an, Arbor House, 1987
   The Visitation, vi *Omni* Jun,1987

6. **Title List: Stories** A listing by title of all stories entered in the Author List. format:

Story Title, Author(s), Type, Source

7. **Contents List** A listing by title of all new anthologies, collections, and magazines. The story author is not listed for collections. An asterisk (*) for Source indicates the story is original to this publication. format:

Edition, **Book Title**, Book Author(s), (Publisher & ISBN, Publication Date, [Date First Seen], Price, Length, Binding) Notes
Contents:
Page#, Story Title, Story Author(s), Type, Source
      Story Notes

example:

*Isaac Asimov's Magical Worlds of Fantasy #9: Atlantis**
Asimov, Isaac, Martin H. Greenberg & Charles G. Waugh, eds. (NAL/Signet 0-451-15144-5, Jan,88 [Dec,87], $3.95, 349pp, pb) Anthology of 11 fantasy stories.
Contents:
   9 Introduction: The Lost City, Isaac Asimov, in
  15 Treaty in Tartessos, Karen Anderson, ss *F&SF* May,1963
  23 The Vengeance of Ulios, Edmond Hamilton, nv *Weird Tales* Jul,1935
  61 Scar-Tissue, Henry S. Whitehead, ss *Amazing* Jul,1946
      ....

Definitions

Edition: A one character code indication the edition of the listed book. * = first edition, + = first U.S. edition. No code indicates a reprint or reissue.

Date First Seen: Most books are in stores a month before their publication date, some are not available until months later. Date First Seen is when we were first able to examine a copy of the book. This is omitted if the same as Publication Date.

Book Type: A code indicating the content of a book.

examples:

```
n.  = novel
an  = anthology
nf  = non-fiction
```

Story Type: Story Type is an indication of story length or type of entry if other than a story. Story lengths are determined from the page count of the story according to the following formula:

3 or fewer pages ..	vi	- vignette	< 1000 words
4-20 pages	ss	- short story	1000 - 7,499
21-45 pages	nv	- novelette	7,500 - 17,499
46-100 pages	na	- novella	17,500 - 39,999
over 100 pages	n.	- novel	40,000+ words

examples of non-story entries:

```
ar  = article
in  = introduction
pm  = poem
```

Source: The earliest found printing of a story. This may additionally contain information on significant reprints of the story. Reprint information follows the source information separated by a semi-colon (;).

example:

Bradbury, Ray
　　The Gift, ss *Esquire* Dec,1952; *Fantastic* Jul,1959

Book Source information includes the book publisher and date of publication.

Novelizations: Novels written from a play, screenplay, teleplay, or based on a background developed by another author. This includes *Star Trek* and *Doctor Who* novels, Conan novels *not* written by Robert E. Howard, Thieves' World novels, and any other novels written to fit into a set background.

Special Considerations

Sorting Rules: All data is sorted character by character in the following sequence:

1. Blank or space.
2. Special characters (except where they appear as the first characters of a title, in which case they are ignored).
3. Numbers.
4. Letters (upper and lower case are considered equal).

Format: Book titles are printed in **bold**, magazine titles are printed in *italics*, and movie titles are printed in ***bold italics***.

Names: Prefixes to family names such as "de", "del", "Fitz", "van", etc. are listed according to the sorting rules with the position of spaces determined by the common spelling of the name. Therefore "de la Mare" appears before "deFord". Names beginning with "Mc" and "Mac" are sorted as other names.

Collaborations: All collaborators are listed for each book and story. The main entry for a book will be under the author listed first on the book. Collaborations are listed after solo appearances for each author in the Author Lists. If one book lists a story as a collaboration, while another book lists the same story as by only one author, the story will have entries for each version.

Pseudonyms: Each book and story is listed under the author given in that book. As a result some books and stories may appear under the author's real name and under a pseudonym.

Story Titles: Each story title is the same as that given in the book containing the story, except for corrections made for minor punctuation or capitalization differences. If the original story title is different, or if the story also appears under a different title, that information is given in brackets after the story title. Other information that may appear after the story title includes pseudonym the author used for the original publication of the story, author of the screenplay that the story is based upon, notes about the story, or alternate source for the story.

Abbreviations: Abbreviations are used for book type, story type, binding, and for some story source entries. They are listed in alphabetical order as folows:

an	....	anthology
hc	....	hard cover
F&SF	....	*The Magazine of Fantasy & Science Fiction*
IASFM	......	*Isaac Asimov's Science Fiction Magazine*
ss	....	short story

—William G. Contento

Introduction

This newest edition of **Science Fiction, Fantasy, & Horror** lists 2954 books from 530 publishers and indexes 5782 shorter works -- a record amount which will probably be unsurpassed until next year. This current edition also includes a complete list of awards presented, a necrology, a recommended reading list, a discussion of the books, magazines, movies, etc. which appeared druing the subject year.

From a commercial point of view, 1987 was the best year yet. The general bestseller lists had novels by Piers Anthony, Isaac Asimov, Arthur C. Clarke, David Brin, David Eddings, Robert A. Heinlein, Larry Niven, L. Ron Hubbard, Marion Zimmer Bradley, Katherine Kurtz, Stephen R., Donaldson, Philip K. Dick (!) and many others as well as many Star Trek Books, DragonLance Books, etc.

Various publishers expanded or started new lines including a new imprint, Pageant Books, a partnership between Crown Books and the chain bookstore Waldenbooks — vertical integration with a vengeance. There were also the usual number of publishers or conglomerates buying other publishers.

Carl Sagan moved into Stephen King's range with a $3 million advance for his next sf novel; Arthur C. Clarke managed a million dollar advance for **2010** *plus* $3 million for collaborations with Gentry Lee; David Eddings got a couple of million for his next series; Dean Koontz got $3 million for his next three books — no plots, outlines, etc. — just whatever he does. Clive Barker managed a million for a package of books and input.

There was a dramatic upsurge in horror novels during 1987. Unfortunately, most were pure schlock. There were some outstanding books, notably Stephen King's psychological novel **Misery**, Robert McCammon's sf horror books, **Swan Song**, and Dean Koontz' cross genre **Watchers**.

There was also, unfortunately, a dramatic upsurge in sharecropping novels — books written by newer writers set in fictional universes created by famous writers. Such books bring little credit to either famous or newer writer.

Death claimed sf great Alfred Bester, 73, whose two novels of the fifties, **The Demolished Man** and **The Stars My Destination** proved seminal works. Terry Carr, 50, one of the most influential editors of the last two decades also died, as did Alice Sheldon, 71, who, as James Tiptree, Jr., gave us nearly two decades of great stories. C.L. Moore, 76, and Randall Garrett, 60, whose bodies survived, alas, without their minds for several years, also were finally laid to rest.

The 45th World Science Fiction convention, Conspiracy, was held in Brighton, England, August 27-31, 1987 with an attendance of 5,000 from 36 different countries. Famed Soviet authors Arkady and Boris Strugatsky, English writer Doris Lessing, and American writer Alfred Bester (unfortunately *in absentia*) were the Professional Guests of Honour. The Strugatskys, making their first trip to the West, were the hit of the convention. The 1987 Hugos (see page 409) were presented.

All in all, it was a good year for sf, fantasy, and horror — and I hope next year will be too.

—Charles N. Brown

Author List: Books

AB HUGH, DAFYDD　　　　　　　　　　　　　　　　　　　　　　　**ALDISS, BRIAN W.**

*ab Hugh, Dafydd **Heroing** (Baen 0-671-65344-X, Oct,87 [Sep,87], $3.50, 346pp, pb) Heroic fantasy novel featuring a woman warrior. A first novel.

*Abbey, Lynn **Unicorn & Dragon** (Avon 0-380-75061-9, Feb,87 [Jan,87], $5.95, 230pp, tp) Historical fantasy novel, with illustrations by Robert Gould. A "Byron Preiss Visual Publication."

*Abbey, Lynn, Robert Lynn Asprin & Tim Sale **Thieves' World Graphics 4** Main listing under Tim Sale.

*Abbey, Lynn & Robert Lynn Asprin, eds. **Thieves' World 10: Aftermath** Main listing under Robert Lynn Asprin.

Abbey, Lynn, Robert Lynn Asprin & Richard Pini, eds. **Elfquest, Vol.1: The Blood of Ten Chiefs** Main listing under Richard Pini.

Abbott, Edwin A. **Flatland** (Penguin 0-14-007615-8, Jan,87, £2.50, 91pp, tp) Reprint (Seely 1884) fantasy novel about two-dimensional world. In the "Penguin Science Fiction Classics" series.

Abdullah, Achmed **The Thief of Bagdad** (Donning/Starblaze 0-89865-523-4, Oct,87 [Nov,87], $12.95, 121pp, tp) Reprint (H.K. Fly 1924) fantasy, novelization of the Douglas Fairbanks movies, newly illustrated by P. Craig Russell.

Ackroyd, Peter **Hawksmoor** (Harper & Row/Perennial Library 0-06-091390-8, Jan,87 [Mar,87], $8.95, 290pp, tp) Reissue (Hamish Hamilton 1985) mystery/horror novel.

*Adams, Douglas **Dirk Gently's Holistic Detective Agency** (Simon & Schuster 0-671-62582-9, May,87, $14.95, 247pp, hc) A "ghost-horror-detective-time travel-romantic comedy epic," according to the blurb. It ends with a "to be continued" line. Simultaneous with the British edition.

Adams, Douglas **Dirk Gently's Holistic Detective Agency** (Heinemann 0-434-00900-8, Jun,87 [Apr,87], £9.95, 247pp, hc) Reprint (Simon & Schuster 1987) humourous sf novel. [First U.K. edition]

*Adams, Douglas, [ref.] **Don't Panic: The Official Hitch Hiker's Guide to the Galaxy Companion** Main listing under Neil Gaiman.

*Adams, Pamela Crippen & Robert Adams, eds. **Friends of the Horseclans** Main listing under Robert Adams.

*Adams, Pamela Crippen, Robert Adams & Martin H. Greenberg, eds. **Robert Adams' Book of Alternate Worlds** Main listing under Robert Adams.

*Adams, Robert **Horseclans #16: Trumpets of War** (NAL/Signet 0-451-14715-4, Feb,87 [Jan,87], $3.50, 223pp, pb) Sf novel, latest in the post-holocaust series.

*Adams, Robert **Horseclans #17: Madman's Army** (NAL/Signet 0-451-14968-8, Sep,87 [Aug,87], $3.50, 222pp, pb) Latest in the series, a flashback novel.

*Adams, Robert **Of Chiefs and Champions** (NAL/Signet 0-451-15110-0, Dec,87 [Nov,87], $3.50, 238pp, pb) Sf novel, #4 in the "Castaways in Time" series.

*Adams, Robert & Pamela Crippen Adams, eds. **Friends of the Horseclans** (NAL/Signet 0-451-14789-8, Apr,87 [Mar,87], $3.50, 284pp, pb) Shared-world original sf anthology set in Robert Adams' world of the Horseclans. 12 stories.

*Adams, Robert, Pamela Crippen Adams & Martin H. Greenberg, eds. **Robert Adams' Book of Alternate Worlds** (NAL/Signet 0-451-14894-0, Jul,87 [Jun,87], $3.95, 366pp, pb) Anthology of 9 alternate-world stories, both sf and fantasy.

*Adams, Robert & Andre Norton, eds. **Magic in Ithkar 4** Main listing under Andre Norton.

*Adkins, Patrick H. **Lord of the Crooked Paths** (Ace 0-441-49036-0, Oct,87 [Sep,87], $2.95, 216pp, pb) Fantasy novel set in the era of the Greek Titans and elder gods. A first novel.

Ahern, Jerry **The Survivalist #13: Pursuit** (NEL 0-450-40577-X, Mar,87, £1.95, 240pp, pb) Reprint (Zebra 1986) post-holocaust adventure novel. [First U.K. edition]

Ahern, Jerry **The Survivalist #14: Terror** (NEL 0-450-41123-0, Jul,87, £1.95, 222pp, pb) Reprint (Zebra 1977) post-holocaust adventure novel. [First U.K. edition]

*Ahern, Jerry **The Survivalist #15: Overlord** (Zebra 0-8217-2070-8, May,87, $2.50, 252pp, pb) Post-holocaust survivalist sf novel.

Ahern, Jerry **The Survivalist #15: Overlord** (NEL 0-450-41348-9, Dec,87, £1.95, 252pp, pb) Reprint (Zebra 1987) sf novel. [First U.K. edition]

*Ahern, Jerry & Sharon Ahern **Miamigrad** (Pocket 0-671-62667-1, May,87, $3.95, 373pp, pb) Near-future sf novel. Russia invades Miami.

*Ahern, Sharon & Jerry Ahern **Miamigrad** Main listing under Jerry Ahern.

*Aickman, Robert **The Model** (Arbor House 0-87795-878-5, Apr,87 [Mar,87], $14.95, 138pp, hc) Fantasy novel set in early 20th century Russia.

Aiken, Joan **Black Hearts in Battersea** (Dell/Yearling 0-440-40904-7, Dec,87 [Nov,87], $3.25, 240pp, pb) Young adult alternate world historical fantasy novel.

Aiken, Joan **Fog Hounds, Wind Cat, Sea Mice** (Piccolo 0-330-29511-X, Mar,87, £1.75, 75pp, pb) Reprint (Macmillan 1984) collection of three juvenile tales of magic and the supernatural.

*Aiken, Joan **A Goose on Your Grave** (Gollancz 0-575-03985-X, May,87 [Dec,87], £6.95, 159pp, hc) Collection of stories, many of them fantasy or supernatural.

*Aiken, Joan **The Moon's Revenge** (Knopf 0-394-89380-8, Oct,87, $12.95, unpaginated, hc) Children's fantasy tale, illustrated by Alan Lee.

*Aiken, Joan **The Moon's Revenge** (Cape 0-224-02477-9, Oct,87 [Nov,87], £5.95, 32pp, hc) Juvenile fantasy novelette. Illustrated throughout by Alan Lee.

Aiken, Joan **Night Birds on Nantucket** (Puffin 0-14-030346-4, Mar,87, £1.95, 172pp, pb) Reissue (Cape 1966) juvenile alternate history novel. Volume 3 in the "Alternate England" series.

Aiken, Joan **Nightbirds on Nantucket** (Dell/Laurel-Leaf 0-440-46370-X, Jan,88 [Dec,87], $3.25, 215pp, pb) Reissue (Cape 1966) young adult alternate world novel, part of the adventure/humorous series featuring Dido Twite. Recommended. (FCM)

Aiken, Joan **The Shadow Guests** (Dell/Yearling 0-440-48226-7, Dec,86 [Jan,87], $2.95, 150pp, tp) Reprint (Cape 1980) young-adult fantasy. A boy from Australia goes to England and learns of his family's curse.

Aiken, Joan **The Wolves of Willoughby Chase** (Dell/Yearling 0-440-49603-9, Nov,87 [Oct,87], $3.95, 168pp, pb) Reissue (Cape 1962) young adult alternate world novel, first of a long, very fine series. Recommended. (CNB)

*Albano, Peter **Return of the Seventh Carrier** (Zebra 0-8217-2093-7, Jun,87 [May,87], $3.95, 397pp, pb) Sf novel of China, with a working SDI and western civilization's fate hinging on an old WWII carrier and samurai warriors. Sequel to **The Seventh Carrier**.

+Alcock, Vivian **Ghostly Companions** (Delacorte 0-385-29559-6, May,87, $13.95, 132pp, hc) Young-adult fantasy/horror collection. First U.S. edition (Methuen 1984).

Aldiss, Brian W. **Cracken at Critical** (Kerosina 0-948893-11-7, Aug,87, £12.50, 192pp, hc) Reprint (Franklin Watts 1987, as **The Year Before Yesterday**) sf novel. The book has been revised for this edition. [First U.K. edition]

Aldiss, Brian W. **Cracken at Critical/The Magic of the Past** (Kerosina 0-948893-10-9, Aug,87, £35.00, 192+48pp, hc) Deluxe collector's edition of the above, including a hardbound copy of **The Magic of the Past** (0-948893-12-5). [First U.K. edition]

Aldiss, Brian W. **Cryptozoic!** (Avon 0-380-01672-9, Jan,88 [Dec,87], $2.95, 191pp, pb) Reissue (Doubleday 1967) sf novel; 6th printing.

Aldiss, Brian W. **Helliconia Winter** (Berkley 0-425-08994-0, Apr,87 [Mar,87], $3.95, 281pp, pb) Reprint (Atheneum 1985) sf novel, conclusion of the "Helliconia" trilogy. First mass market edition.

*Aldiss, Brian W. **The Magic of the Past** (Kerosina 0-948893-13-3, Aug,87, £4.50, 48pp, tp) Original sf collection.

Aldiss, Brian W. **Non-Stop** (Grafton 0-586-06817-1, Dec,87 [Nov,87], £2.95, 269pp, pb) Reprint (Faber & Faber 1958) sf novel.

*Aldiss, Brian W. **Ruins** (Hutchinson 0-09-167860-9, Sep,87, £7.95, 85pp, hc) Mainstream novella, billed as "a modern parable".

*Aldiss, Brian W. **The Year Before Yesterday** (Franklin Watts 0-531-15040-2, Apr,87 [Mar,87], $16.95, 227pp, hc) Sf alternate world novel composed of **Equator** (Brown, Watson 1958) and "The Impossible Smile" (*Science Fantasy* May & June 1965 as by Jael Cracken) plus a new framework.

+Aldiss, Brian W. & Sam J. Lundwall, eds. **The Penguin World Omnibus of Science Fiction** (Penguin 0-14-008067-8, Oct,87 [Sep,87], $4.95, 320pp, pb) Anthology of international sf stories from 26 countries. First U.S. edition (Penguin 1986). This is actually a reissue of the original, distributed for the first time in the U.S. with a $4.95 American price on the back.

Alexander, David **Dark Messiah** (Star 0-352-32152-0, Nov,87, £1.95, 221pp, pb) Reprint (Leisure 1987) post-holocaust adventure novel. Volume 1 in the "Phoenix" series. [First U.K. edition]

*Alexander, David **Phoenix #1: Dark Messiah** (Leisure 0-8439-2462-4, May,87 [Aug,87], $2.95, 221pp, pb) Post-holocaust adventure novel.

*Alexander, David **Phoenix #2: Ground Zero** (Leisure 0-8439-2517-5, Aug,87 [Jul,87], $2.95, 224pp, pb) Post-holocaust sf adventure novel.

*Alexander, Lloyd **The El Dorado Adventure** (Dutton 0-525-44313-4, Apr,87, $12.95, 164pp, hc) Young-adult adventure novel, sequel to **The Illyrian Adventure**. There isn't any actual fantasy, but the Victorian world it takes place in, with unknown countries and lost races *a la* H. Rider Haggard, is definitely an alternate world. The young female adventurer and her bumbling professor escort are great fun. (CNB)

Alexander, Lloyd **The Illyrian Adventure** (Dell/Laurel Leaf 0-440-94018-4, Mar,87 [Feb,87], $2.50, 132pp, pb) Reprint (Dutton 1986) juvenile fantasy novel set in a Graustarkian country.

*Alkon, Paul K. **Origins of Futuristic Fiction** (Univ. of Georgia Press 0-8203-0932-X, Dec,87, $30.00, 341pp, hc) Non-fiction, critical study of early futuristic fiction (1659-1834).

*Almquist, Gregg **Beast Rising** (Pocket 0-671-63497-6, Sep,87 [Aug,87], $3.50, 256pp, pb) Horror novel.

*Amis, Kingsley **Collected Short Stories** (Hutchinson 0-09-172737-5, Apr,87, £11.95, 321pp, hc) Collection of most of Amis's short fiction, including some sf.

Amis, Kingsley **Russian Hide-and-Seek** (Penguin 0-14-005738-2, Jul,87, £2.95, 251pp, pb) Reissue (Hutchinson 1980) literary sf novel.

*Amis, Martin **Einstein's Monsters** (Cape 0-224-02435-3, Apr,87 [May,87], £5.95, 127pp, hc) Collection of stories, including some sf. Simultaneous with American edition.

*Amis, Martin **Einstein's Monsters** (Crown/Harmony 0-517-56520-X, May,87, $14.95, 149pp, hc) Collection of 5 pre- and post-holocaust stories on the folly of war. There's a simultaneous British edition.

Andersen, Hans Christian **Andersen's Fairy Tales** (NAL/Signet Classic 0-451-52107-2, Jun,87 [May,87], $3.95, 381pp, pb) Reissue (NAL/Signet 1966) selection from **The Snow Queen and Other Tales**; selected, translated, and with an afterword by Pat Shaw Iverson. Illustrations by Sheila Greenwald.

*Anderson, C. Dean **Torture Tomb** (Popular Library 0-445-20370-6, May,87 [Apr,87], $3.50, 325pp, pb) Horror novel of good witches vs. "an evil dynasty built upon the unspeakable secrets of the damned." The author writes heroic fantasy as Asa Drake.

*Anderson, Karen & Poul Anderson **The King of Ys 2: Gallicenae** Main listing under Poul Anderson.

*Anderson, Karen & Poul Anderson **The King of Ys: Dahut** Main listing under Poul Anderson.

*Anderson, Mary **The Leipzig Vampire** (Dell/Yearling 0-440-44719-4, Oct,87, $2.50, 122pp, pb) Juvenile horror novel, second in the "Mostly Ghosts" series.

*Anderson, Mary **Terror Under the Tent** (Dell/Yearling 0-440-48633-5, Nov,87 [Oct,87], $2.50, 123pp, pb) Juvenile fantasy novel, "Mostly Ghosts" #3.

*Anderson, Michael Falconer **God of a Thousand Faces** (Robert Hale 0-7090-3064-9, Oct,87 [1987], £10.50, 192pp, hc) Horror novel. [Not seen]

*Anderson, Michael Falconer **The Unholy** (Robert Hale 0-7090-2877-6, Feb,87, £10.95, 192pp, hc) Horror novel. [Not seen]

+Anderson, Michael Falconer **The Unholy** (St. Martin's 0-312-00699-3, Jun,87 [Apr,87], $15.95, 223pp, hc) Reprint (Hale 1987) supernatural horror novel. First U.S. publication.

Anderson, Poul **The Broken Sword** (Baen 0-671-65382-2, Jan,88 [Dec,87], $2.95, 266pp, pb) Reprint (Abelard-Schuman 1954, Ballantine 1971) fantasy novel. A fine Norse saga. This edition follows the 1971 revised text. One of Anderson's best fantasies. Highly recommended. (CNB)

Anderson, Poul **A Circus of Hells** (Sphere 0-7221-1147-9, Dec,87, £2.50, 189pp, pb) Reissue (Signet 1970) sf novel.

Anderson, Poul **The Dancer from Atlantis** (NAL/Signet 0-451-15354-5, Jan,88 [Dec,87], $2.95, 192pp, pb) Reissue (SFBC 1971) sf time travel novel; 6th printing.

Anderson, Poul **The Earth Book of Stormgate - 1** (NEL 0-450-04796-2, Aug,87, £1.95, 144pp, pb) Reissue (Putnam 1978) sf collection.

Anderson, Poul **The Earth Book of Stormgate - 2** (NEL 0-450-04800-4, Aug,87, £2.25, 159pp, pb) Reissue (Putnam 1978) sf collection.

Anderson, Poul **The Earth Book of Stormgate - 3** (NEL 0-450-04926-4, Aug,87, £2.25, 173pp, pb) Reissue (Putnam 1978) sf collection.

*Anderson, Poul **The Enemy Stars** (Baen 0-671-65339-3, Jul,87 [Jun,87], $2.95, 218pp, pb) Contains the novel **The Enemy Stars** (Lippincott 1959) plus a novelette coda, "The Ways of Love" (1979).

Anderson, Poul **A Knight of Ghosts and Shadows** (NAL/Signet 0-451-15057-0, Nov,87 [Oct,87], $2.95, 222pp, pb) Reissue (SFBC 1975) sf novel in the Dominic Flandry series; 3rd Signet printing.

Anderson, Poul **Past Times** (Sphere 0-7221-1291-2, Jan,87, £2.50, 212pp, pb) Reprint (Tor 1984) collection of 7 stories and an article. [First U.K. edition]

Anderson, Poul **Strangers From Earth** (Baen 0-671-65627-9, Mar,87 [Feb,87], $2.95, 211pp, pb) Reprint (Ballantine 1961) collection of 8 stories.

Anderson, Poul **There Will Be Time** (Sphere 0-7221-1148-7, Dec,87 [Nov,87], £2.50, 189pp, pb) Reissue (SFBC 1972) sf novel.

ANDERSON, POUL

ANTHONY, PIERS

Anderson, Poul **Twilight World** (Sphere 0-7221-1288-2, Jan,87 [May,87], £2.50, 180pp, pb) Reprint (Torquil 1961) sf novel. Dated 1986.

*Anderson, Poul & Karen Anderson **The King of Ys 2: Gallicenae** (Baen 0-671-65342-3, Sep,87 [Aug,87], $3.95, 374pp, pb) Historical/fantasy novel, second in the "King of Ys" tetralogy.

*Anderson, Poul & Karen Anderson **The King of Ys: Dahut** (Baen 0-671-65371-7, Jan,88 [Dec,87], $3.95, 398pp, pb) Historical fantasy novel, part III of a single novel in four volumes.

Andrews, V.C. **Flowers in the Attic** (Pocket 0-671-64045-3, Oct,87, $4.95, 411pp, pb) Reissue (Pocket 1979) horror novel, 41st printing. This contains the first chapter of **Garden of Shadows** as a teaser at the end.

*Andrews, V.C. **Garden of Shadows** (S&S Poseidon 0-671-64259-6, Oct,87 [Dec,87], $18.95, 376pp, hc) Horror novel, prequel to **Flowers in the Attic**. Issued simultaneously in paperback by Pocket Books. Although he isn't credited, this was finished by Andrew Neiderman.

*Andrews, V.C. **Garden of Shadows** (Pocket 0-671-64257-X, Nov,87 [Oct,87], $4.95, 376pp, pb) Horror novel, prequel to **Flowers in the Attic**.

Andrews, Virginia **Dark Angel** (Fontana Overseas 0-00-617418-3, 1986 [Apr,87], £2.95, 443pp, pb) Reprint (Pocket 1986) horror novel. Sequel to **Heaven**. Special "open market" edition.

Andrews, Virginia **Dark Angel** (Collins 0-00-223190-5, Feb,87, £9.95, 443pp, hc) Reprint (Pocket 1986) horror novel. Sequel to **Heaven**. [First U.K. edition]

Andrews, Virginia **Dark Angel** (Fontana 0-00-617418-3, May,87, £2.95, 443pp, pb) Reprint (Pocket 1986) horror novel. Sequel to **Heaven**.

Andrews, Virginia **Dark Angel** (Ulverscroft Large Print 0-7089-8438-X, Nov,87, £9.25, 544pp, hc) Reprint (Pocket 1986) horror novel. Sequel to **Heaven**. [Not seen]

*Angadi, Patricia **The Highly Flavoured Ladies** (Gollancz 0-575-04001-7, Jul,87 [Dec,87], £10.95, 219pp, hc) Historical novel with touches of fantasy.

*Angell, Judie **The Weird Disappearance of Jordan Hall** (Franklin Watts Orchard 0-531-05727-5, Sep,87 [Dec,87], $11.95, 121pp, hc) Juvenile fantasy novel. Magic turns a boy invisible.

+Anonymous, ed. **Gollancz/Sunday Times SF Competition Stories** (David & Charles/Gollancz 0-575-04074-2, 1987 [Nov,87], $19.95, 200pp, hc) Original anthology of 25 stories. This book was published in Great Britain (Gollancz 1987) and is being distributed in the U.S. by David & Charles, Inc., North Pomfret VT 05053.

*Anonymous, ed. **Gollancz/Sunday Times SF Competition Stories** (Gollancz 0-575-04074-2, Aug,87, £10.95, 200pp, hc) Collection of best stories entered for the recent Gollancz & Sunday Times SF Short Story Competition. Actually edited by Malcolm Edwards.

*Anonymous, ed. **Mad and Bad Fairies** (Attic Press 0-946211-40-X, Jul,87 [Oct,87], £3.50, 60pp, tp) Anthology of feminist fairy tales. Volume 3 in the "Fairytales for Feminists" series.

*Anonymous, ed. **Night Visions 4** (Dark Harvest 0-913165-20-4, Oct,87, $49.94, 275pp, hc) Original anthology with horror stories by Dean R. Koontz, Edward Bryant, and Robert McCammon (several stories each), plus an introduction by Clive Barker, and illustrations by Kevin Davies. Signed, boxed, limited edition of 500 copies.

*Anonymous, ed. **Night Visions 4** (Dark Harvest 0-913165-21-2, Oct,87, $18.95, 275pp, hc) Trade edition of the above.

*Anonymous, ed. **The Orbit Poster Book** (Orbit 0-7088-8247-1, Aug,87, £6.95, 32pp, tp) Collection of covers from 16 recent Orbit books.

*Anonymous, ed. **Rhysling Anthology 1987** (SF Poetry Assc. no ISBN, Sep,87, $2.00, 30pp, ph) Anthology of sf poetry, finalists for the 1987 Rhysling Awards.

Anstey, F. **Tourmalin's Time Cheques** (Greenhill 0-947898-48-4, Jan,87 [1987], £8.95, 184pp, hc) Reprint (Arrowsmith 1891) time-travel novel. [Not seen]

Anthony, Piers **Bearing an Hourglass** (Ballantine/Del Rey 0-345-31315-1, Dec,87 [Nov,87], $3.95, 372pp, pb) Reissue (Del Rey 1984) fantasy novel, "Incarnations of Immortality" #2; 5th printing, with 424,000 paperbacks in print.

*Anthony, Piers **Being a Green Mother** (Ballantine/Del Rey 0-345-32222-3, Dec,87 [Nov,87], $16.95, 313pp, hc) Fantasy novel, Book 5 in the "Incarnations of Immortality" series.

Anthony, Piers **Blue Adept** (Grafton 0-586-05445-6, Feb,87, £2.50, 383pp, pb) Reissue (Del Rey 1981) sf/fantasy novel. Volume 2 in the Apprentice Adept series.

Anthony, Piers **Chthon** (Ace 0-441-11880-1, Mar,87 [Feb,87], $3.50, 236pp, pb) Reprint (Ballantine 1967) sf novel.

Anthony, Piers **Ghost** (Tor 0-812-53127-2, Dec,87 [Nov,87], $3.95, 279pp, pb) Reprint (Tor 1986) sf/fantasy novel.

Anthony, Piers **Mute** (NEL 0-450-05696-1, Jul,87 [Aug,87], £3.50, 441pp, pb) Reissue (Avon 1981) sf novel.

Anthony, Piers **On a Pale Horse** (Ballantine/Del Rey 0-345-33858-8, Dec,87 [Nov,87], $3.95, 325pp, pb) Reissue (Del Rey 1983) fantasy novel, "Incarnations of Immortality" #1; 10th printing, with 526,000 paperbacks in print.

*Anthony, Piers **Out of Phaze** (Ace/Putnam 0-399-13272-4, Jun,87 [Apr,87], $17.95, 288pp, hc) Fantasy novel, Book 4 of the "Apprentice Adept" series.

Anthony, Piers **Phthor** (Ace 0-441-66238-2, Jun,87 [May,87], $2.95, 198pp, pb) Reprint (Berkley 1975) sf novel, sequel to **Chthon**.

Anthony, Piers **Rings of Ice** (Avon 0-380-00036-9, Nov,87 [Oct,87], $3.50, 191pp, pb) Reissue (Avon 1974) sf disaster novel; 4th printing.

Anthony, Piers **Shade of the Tree** (Tor 0-812-53103-5, May,87 [Apr,87], $3.95, 348pp, pb) Reprint (Tor 1986) dark fantasy novel.

Anthony, Piers **Shade of the Tree** (Grafton 0-586-07304-3, Nov,87 [Oct,87], £2.95, 352pp, pb) Reprint (Tor 1986) horror novel. [First U.K. edition]

Anthony, Piers **Statesman** (Grafton 0-586-06272-6, Oct,87 [Sep,87], £2.95, 367pp, pb) Reprint (Avon 1986) sf novel. This edition is dated 1988. Volume 5 in the "Bio of a Space Tyrant" series. [First U.K. edition]

*Anthony, Piers **Tarot** (Ace 0-441-79841-1, Nov,87 [Oct,87], $8.95, 616pp, tp) Omnibus edition of a fantasy trilogy: **God of Tarot** (Jove 1979), **Vision of Tarot** (Berkley 1980), and **Faith of Tarot** (Berkley 1980); they're combined, with new, continuous chapter numbering.

*Anthony, Piers **Vale of the Vole** (Avon 0-380-75287-5, Oct,87 [Sep,87], $3.95, 324pp, pb) Humorous fantasy novel in the "Xanth" series, first in a new trilogy.

Anthony, Piers **Wielding a Red Sword** (SFBC #104927, Apr,87, $5.98, 276pp, hc) Reprint (Del Rey 1986) fantasy novel, Book 4 of "Incarnations of Immortality".

Anthony, Piers **Wielding a Red Sword** (Grafton 0-586-07093-1, Jul,87, £2.95, 368pp, pb) Reprint (Del Rey 1986) fantasy novel. Volume 4 in the "Incarnations of Immortality" series. [First U.K. edition]

Anthony, Piers **Wielding a Red Sword** (Severn House 0-7278-1462-1, Oct,87 [Sep,87], £10.95, 368pp, hc) Reprint (Del Rey 1986) fantasy novel. Volume 4 in the "Incarnations of Immortality" series. [Not seen]

Anthony, Piers **Wielding a Red Sword** (Ballantine/Del Rey 0-345-32221-5, Dec,87 [Nov,87], $4.50, 313pp, pb) Reprint (Del Rey 1986) fantasy novel, #4 in the "Incarnations of Immortality" series.

ANTHONY, PIERS

ASIMOV, ISAAC

Anthony, Piers **With a Tangled Skein** (Severn House 0-7278-1397-8, Mar,87, £9.95, 416pp, hc) Reprint (Del Rey 1985) fantasy novel. Volume 3 in the "Incarnations of Immortality" series. [Not seen]

Anthony, Piers **With a Tangled Skein** (Ballantine/Del Rey 0-345-31885-4, Dec,87 [Nov,87], $3.95, 404pp, pb) Reissue (Del Rey 1985) fantasy novel, "Incarnations of Immortality" #3; 4th printing, with 385,000 paperbacks in print.

*Anthony, Piers & Robert E. Margroff **Dragon's Gold** (Tor 0-812-53125-6, Jul,87 [Jun,87], $3.95, 282pp, pb) Fantasy novel.

*Apel, D. Scott, ed. **Philip K. Dick: The Dream Connection** (Permanent Press no ISBN, Mar,87 [May,87], $19.95, 296pp, hc) Mostly non-fiction, a collection of memoirs and essays on Dick, an interview with him, and a Dick short story. It's a handsome, well printed book and a useful addition to collections, among the Dick flood. (CNB) Available only by mail (add $2.00 postage/handling) from D. Scott Apel, Box 700305, San Jose CA 95170.

Appel, Allen **Time After Time** (Dell/Laurel Leaf 0-440-59116-3, Mar,87 [Jan,87], $6.95, 372pp, tp) Reprint (Carroll & Graf 1975) time travel fantasy novel about a history professor who is projected back to the Russian Revolution by mysterious forces.

Arensberg, Ann **Sister Wolf** (S&S Washington Square Press 0-671-64507-2, Sep,87 [Aug,87], $5.75, 191pp, tp) Reprint (Knopf 1980) contemporary novel with fantasy elements.

*Armstrong, F.W. **The Devouring** (Tor 0-812-52758-5, Apr,87 [Mar,87], $3.95, 283pp, pb) Horror novel.

*Armstrong, Michael **After the Zap** (Popular Library Questar 0-445-20438-9, Jun,87 [May,87], $3.50, 246pp, pb) Post-Electro-Magnetic-Pulse sf catastrophe novel (of a quirky sort); a first novel. Witty and thoroughly eccentric, it's an entertaining work. Meet the Wonder Blimp and the bush punks! (FCM)

*Arnason, Eleanor **Daughter of the Bear King** (Avon 0-380-75109-7, Aug,87 [Jul,87], $3.50, 239pp, pb) Fantasy novel. Monday morning, she's a housewife doing her wash in Minneapolis. Monday night she is battling a slimy/feathered monster and enjoying it. By Tuesday, the two worlds merge.

Arnason, Eleanor **Daughter of the Bear King** (Headline 0-7472-3052-8, Dec,87, £2.95, 239pp, pb) Reprint (Avon 1987) fantasy novel. [First U.K. edition]

*Aronovitz, David **Ballantine Books: The First Decade** (Bailiwick Books 0-9618295-0-8, Sep,87, price unknown, 107pp, hc) Non-fiction, subtitled "A Bibliographical History & Guide of the Publisher's Early Years." This is a bibliography of all the Ballantine hardcover editions -- sf and otherwise -- from 1952 to 1957. Order from David Aronovitz, 781 E. Snell Rd., Rochester MI 48064.

Ashe, Geoffrey & Debrett's Peerage **The Discovery of King Arthur** (Holt 0-8050-0115-8, Jan,87, $8.95, 224pp, tp) Reprint (Doubleday/Anchor 1985) non-fiction, historical research into another candidate for the "real" Arthur. Associational.

*Ashe, Rosalind **The Laying of the Noone Walker** (Bantam UK 0-593-01168-6, Feb,87 [Jun,87], £9.95, 314pp, hc) Supernatural novel.

Asher, Marty **Shelter** (Faber & Faber (US) 0-571-12953-6, May,87, $6.95, 136pp, tp) Reprint (Arbor House 1986) fantasy novella about an obsessed man and a rock concert that saves the world.

Asherman, Allan **The Star Trek Compendium** (Titan 0-907610-99-4, Aug,87 [Dec,87], £7.95, 184pp, tp) Reprint (Pocket 1981) associational book about *Star Trek*. Revised edition. [First U.K. edition]

Asimov, Isaac **Alternate Asimovs** (Grafton 0-586-07162-8, Jun,87, £3.50, 349pp, pb) Reprint (Doubleday 1985) collection of previously unpublished drafts of three of Asimov's stories. [First U.K. edition]

Asimov, Isaac **The Best Mysteries of Isaac Asimov** (Grafton 0-246-13186-1, Aug,87 [Jul,87], £10.95, 345pp, hc) Reprint (Doubleday 1986) mostly non-sf/fantasy, associational. Collection of 31 stories including some sf mysteries. 7 of the stories have not been collected before. [First U.K. edition]

Asimov, Isaac **The Best Mysteries of Isaac Asimov** (Ballantine Fawcett 0-449-13287-0, Sep,87 [Aug,87], $4.50, 400pp, pb) Reprint (Doubleday 1987) collection, associational with some sf elements.

Asimov, Isaac **The Best Science Fiction of Isaac Asimov** (Grafton 0-246-13180-2, Feb,87 [Jan,87], £10.95, 320pp, hc) Reprint (Doubleday 1986) collection of Asimov's selection of his best sf stories and poems (excluding any Robot stories). [First U.K. edition]

*Asimov, Isaac **Fantastic Voyage II: Destination Brain** (Doubleday 0-385-23926-2, Sep,87 [Aug,87], $18.95, 332pp, hc) Sf novel, not a sequel to **Fantastic Voyage** but another book using the same basic idea, in a more plausible manner.

*Asimov, Isaac **Fantastic Voyage II: Destination Brain** (Doubleday 0-385-24392-8, Oct,87 [Sep,87], $125.00, 332pp, hc) This is the signed limited edition. We listed the regular last month.

Asimov, Isaac **Fantastic Voyage II: Destination Brain** (Grafton 0-246-13210-8, Oct,87, £10.95, 392pp, hc) Reprint (Doubleday 1987). Amazingly enough, this reprise of (rather than sequel to) **Fantastic Voyage** makes the original version look scientifically realistic and plausible by comparison. [First U.K. edition]

Asimov, Isaac **Foundation** (Ballantine/Del Rey 0-345-33627-5, Oct,87 [Sep,87], $3.95, 285pp, pb) Reissue (Gnome 1951) sf novel, first in the "Foundation" series; 17th Del Rey printing. Contains the 1982 introduction "The Story Behind the Foundation" by Asimov.

Asimov, Isaac **Foundation and Earth** (QPB no ISBN, Jun,87, $8.95, 356pp, tp) Reprint (Doubleday 1986) sf novel. Reproduction of the hardcover in a soft cover the same as the jacket; no ISBN number.

Asimov, Isaac **Foundation and Earth** (Grafton 0-586-07110-5, Jul,87, £3.50, 510pp, pb) Reprint (Doubleday 1986) sf novel. Volume 5 in the "Foundation" series.

Asimov, Isaac **Foundation and Earth** (Ballantine/Del Rey 0-345-35142-8, Aug,87, $4.95, 494pp, pb) Reprint (Doubleday 1986) sf novel, #5 in the "Foundation" series. International edition.

Asimov, Isaac **Foundation and Earth** (Ballantine/Del Rey 0-345-33996-7, Oct,87 [Sep,87], $4.95, 494pp, pb) Reprint (Doubleday 1986) sf novel, #5 in the "Foundation" series.

Asimov, Isaac **Foundation and Empire** (Ballantine/Del Rey 0-345-33628-3, Oct,87 [Sep,87], $3.95, 285pp, pb) Reissue (Gnome 1952) sf novel, second in the "Foundation" series; 13th Del Rey printing, with the 1982 intro (same as in **Foundation**).

Asimov, Isaac **Foundation's Edge** (Ballantine/Del Rey 0-345-30898-0, Oct,87 [Sep,87], $3.95, 426pp, pb) Reissue (Doubleday 1982) sf novel, #4 in the "Foundation" series; 12th Del Rey printing.

Asimov, Isaac **New Guide To Science** (Penguin 0-14-007621-2, Mar,87, £8.95, 880pp, tp) Reprint (Basic 1984) layman's guide to science. Fourth edition.

Asimov, Isaac **Pebble in the Sky** (Grafton 0-586-06952-6, Sep,87, £2.95, 226pp, pb) Reprint (Doubleday 1950) sf novel. Volume 3 in the "Galactic Empire" series.

Asimov, Isaac **Robot Dreams** (Gollancz 0-575-04021-1, Apr,87, £10.95, 349pp, hc) Reprint (Berkley 1986) sf collection, including one original story, illustrated by Ralph McQuarrie. [First U.K. edition]

Asimov, Isaac **The Roving Mind** (Oxford Univ. Press 0-19-286077-1, Feb,87, £5.95, 350pp, tp) Associational interest. Reprint (Prometheus 1983) collection of Asimov's essays.

ASIMOV, ISAAC　　　　　　　　　　　　　　　　　　　　　　　**ATWOOD, MARGARET**

Asimov, Isaac **Second Foundation** (Ballantine/Del Rey 0-345-33629-1, Oct,87 [Sep,87], $3.95, 282pp, pb) Reissue (Gnome 1953) sf novel, third in the "Foundation" series; 12th Del Rey printing, with the 1982 introduction (same as in **Foundation**).

Asimov, Isaac **The Stars, Like Dust** (SFBC #10814, Apr,87 [May,87], $4.98, 185pp, hc) Reissue (Doubleday 1951) sf novel.

Asimov, Isaac **The Subatomic Monster** (Grafton 0-586-05844-3, Mar,87, £2.95, 288pp, pb) Reprint (Doubleday 1985) collection of science columns from *F&SF*.

Asimov, Isaac **A Whiff of Death** (Ballantine Fawcett 0-449-21461-3, Dec,87 [Nov,87], $3.50, 222pp, pb) Reprint (Avon 1958 as **The Death Dealers**) mystery novel; associational.

*Asimov, Isaac & Janet Asimov **How to Enjoy Writing: A Book of Aid and Comfort** Main listing under Janet Asimov.

*Asimov, Isaac & Janet Asimov **Norby and the Queen's Necklace** Main listing under Janet Asimov.

*Asimov, Isaac & Janet Asimov **Norby Finds a Villain** Main listing under Janet Asimov.

*Asimov, Isaac & Janet Asimov **Norby: Robot for Hire** Main listing under Janet Asimov.

Asimov, Isaac, ed. **Beyond the Stars** (Severn House 0-7278-1374-9, Feb,87, £8.95, 320pp, hc) Reprint (Doubleday 1985 as first half of **The Hugo Winners: Volume 4**) sf anthology. [First U.K. edition]

Asimov, Isaac, ed. **The Dark Void** (Severn House 0-7278-1424-9, Jun,87 [Jul,87], £9.95, 239pp, hc) Reprint (Doubleday 1985 as second half of **The Hugo Winners: Volume 4**) sf anthology. [First U.K. edition]

*Asimov, Isaac & Martin H. Greenberg, eds. **Isaac Asimov Presents the Great SF Stories: 16 (1954)** (DAW 0-88677-200-1, May,87 [Apr,87], $3.50, 350pp, pb) Anthology of 17 stories from 1954.

*Asimov, Isaac & Martin H. Greenberg, eds. **Isaac Asimov Presents the Great SF Stories: 17 (1955)** (DAW 0-88677-256-7, Jan,88 [Dec,87], $3.95, 349pp, pb) Anthology of 14 sf stories.

Asimov, Isaac, Martin H. Greenberg & Charles G. Waugh, eds. **Cosmic Knights** (Robinson 0-948164-41-7, Jul,87, £2.95, 339pp, tp) Reprint (Signet 1985) fantasy anthology. [First U.K. edition]

Asimov, Isaac, Martin H. Greenberg & Charles G. Waugh, eds. **Flying Saucers** (Ballantine Fawcett 0-449-21400-1, Aug,87 [Jul,87], $3.95, 349pp, pb) Reprint (Fawcwtt 1982) anthology of 26 stories.

Asimov, Isaac, Martin H. Greenberg & Charles G. Waugh, eds. **Giants** (Robinson 0-948164-42-5, Jul,87, £2.95, 351pp, tp) Reprint (Signet 1985) fantasy anthology. [First U.K. edition]

*Asimov, Isaac, Martin H. Greenberg & Charles G. Waugh, eds. **Isaac Asimov's Magical Worlds of Fantasy #8: Devils** (NAL/Signet 0-451-14865-7, Jun,87 [May,87], $3.50, 351pp, pb) Anthology of 18 fantasy stories.

*Asimov, Isaac, Martin H. Greenberg & Charles G. Waugh, eds. **Isaac Asimov's Magical Worlds of Fantasy #9: Atlantis** (NAL/Signet 0-451-15144-5, Jan,88 [Dec,87], $3.95, 349pp, pb) Anthology of 11 fantasy stories.

*Asimov, Isaac, Martin H. Greenberg & Charles G. Waugh, eds. **Isaac Asimov's Wonderful Worlds of Science Fiction #6: Neanderthals** (NAL/Signet 0-451-14716-2, Feb,87 [Jan,87], $3.95, 351pp, pb) Anthology of 11 stories and an article.

*Asimov, Isaac, Martin H. Greenberg & Charles G. Waugh, eds. **Isaac Asimov's Wonderful Worlds of Science Fiction #7: Space Shuttles** (NAL/Signet 0-451-15017-1, Oct,87 [Sep,87], $3.95, 384pp, pb) Anthology of 14 stories.

*Asimov, Isaac, Martin H. Greenberg & Charles G. Waugh, eds. **Young Witches & Warlocks** (Harper & Row 0-06-020183-5, Jul,87, $11.95, 207pp, hc) Juvenile anthology of fantasy stories.

*Asimov, Janet & Isaac Asimov **How to Enjoy Writing: A Book of Aid and Comfort** (Walker 0-8027-0945-1, Jul,87 [Jun,87], $15.95, 163pp, hc) Non-fiction, book on writing, of associational interest.

*Asimov, Janet & Isaac Asimov **Norby and the Queen's Necklace** (Walker 0-8027-6659-5, Dec,86 [Jan,87], $11.95, 144pp, hc) Juvenile robot novel, latest in a series. Published in 1986; missed.

*Asimov, Janet & Isaac Asimov **Norby Finds a Villain** (Walker 0-8027-6710-9, Sep,87 [Aug,87], $12.95, 102pp, hc) Juvenile sf novel, part of a long series.

*Asimov, Janet & Isaac Asimov **Norby: Robot for Hire** (Ace 0-441-58635-X, Feb,87 [Jan,87], $2.95, 203pp, pb) Omnibus edition of two juvenile sf tales in the "Norby" series.

*Asire, Nancy **Twilight's Kingdoms** (Baen 0-671-65362-8, Nov,87 [Oct,87], $3.50, 376pp, pb) Fantasy novel of Light vs. Darkness. A first novel.

Asprin, Robert Lynn **Little Myth Marker** (Ace 0-441-48499-9, Jul,87 [Jun,87], $2.95, 167pp, pb) Reprint (Donning 1985) humorous fantasy novel, sixth in the "Myth" series.

*Asprin, Robert Lynn **M.Y.T.H. Inc. Link** (Donning 0-89865-470-X, Feb,87, $30.00, 151pp, hc) Humorous fantasy novel, latest in the "Myth" series. Limited edition of 1200 hardcover copies with a special numbered bookplate signed by author and artist (Phil Foglio). We've already listed the trade paperback, which apparently came out first. The pages and copyright page are identical.

Asprin, Robert Lynn **M.Y.T.H. Inc. Link** (Ace 0-441-55277-3, Jan,88 [Dec,87], $2.95, 159pp, pb) Reprint (Donning Starblaze 1986) humorous fantasy novel, 7th in the "Myth" series.

*Asprin, Robert Lynn **Myth Alliances** (SFBC #11114, Jul,87 [Aug,87], $6.98, 375pp, hc) Omnibus edition of three books in the humorous fantasy series.

*Asprin, Robert Lynn **Myth-Nomers and Im-pervections** (Donning/Starblaze 0-89865-529-3, Oct,87 [Nov,87], $7.95, 189pp, tp) Humorous fantasy novel, latest in the "Myth" series, illustrated by Phil Foglio. A hardcover limited edition of 1200(!) copies was announced, but not seen.

*Asprin, Robert Lynn, Lynn Abbey & Tim Sale **Thieves' World Graphics 4** Main listing under Tim Sale.

*Asprin, Robert Lynn & Phil Foglio **Myth Adventures Two** Main listing under Phil Foglio.

*Asprin, Robert Lynn & Mel White **Duncan and Mallory: The Bar-None Ranch** (Donning/Starblaze 0-89865-506-4, Sep,87, $6.95, unpaginated, tp) Humorous fantasy graphic novel, second in a series.

*Asprin, Robert Lynn & Lynn Abbey, eds. **Thieves' World 10: Aftermath** (Ace 0-441-80597-3, Nov,87 [Oct,87], $3.50, 273pp, pb) Original anthology of 6 stories, latest in the "Thieves' World" fantasy shared world series.

Asprin, Robert Lynn, Lynn Abbey & Richard Pini, eds. **Elfquest, Vol.1: The Blood of Ten Chiefs** Main listing under Richard Pini.

*Atwood, Margaret **Bluebeard's Egg** (Cape 0-224-02245-8, Jun,87, £10.95, 281pp, hc) Collection of stories, some with elements of fantasy.

Atwood, Margaret **The Handmaid's Tale** (Ballantine Fawcett 0-449-21260-2, Feb,87 [Jan,87], $4.95, 395pp, pb) Reprint (Canadian 1985) near-future dystopian sf novel.

Atwood, Margaret **The Handmaid's Tale** (Virago 0-86068-866-6, Jun,87, £3.95, 324pp, tp) Reprint (Canada 1985) sf novel.

Atwood, Margaret **The Handmaid's Tale** (Chivers Press 0-8161-4172-X, Aug,87 [Sep,87], £10.95, 456pp, hc) Reprint (Canada 1985) dystopian sf novel. [Not seen]

AUEL, JEAN M.   **BARKER, CLIVE**

Auel, Jean M. **The Clan of the Cave Bear** (Hodder & Stoughton 0-340-25967-1, Oct,87 [Dec,87], £13.95, 491pp, hc) Reissue (Crown 1980) fantasy novel. Volume 1 in the "Earth's Children" series.

*Auel, Jean M. **Earth's Children** (Hodder & Stoughton 0-340-41759-5, Oct,87 [Dec,87], £42.95, 491+571+639pp, hc) Fantasy omnibus. Boxed set of the three novels in the "Earth's Children" series.

Auel, Jean M. **The Mammoth Hunters** (Hodder & Stoughton 0-340-34934-4, Oct,87 [Dec,87], £13.95, 639pp, hc) Reissue (Crown 1985) fantasy novel. Volume 3 in the "Earth's Children" series.

Auel, Jean M. **The Valley of Horses** (Hodder & Stoughton 0-340-28134-0, Oct,87 [Dec,87], £13.95, 571pp, hc) Reissue (Crown 1982) fantasy novel. Volume 2 in the "Earth's Children" series.

*Auster, Paul **In the Country of the Last Things** (Viking 0-670-81445-8, Apr,87 [Mar,87], £14.95, 188pp, hc) Sf novel of a future nightmare New York.

*Austin, Richard **The Guardians #8: Desolation Road** (Jove 0-515-09004-2, Jun,87 [May,87], $2.95, 219pp, pb) Post-holocaust sf adventure novel, latest in the series.

*Austin, Richard **The Guardians #9: Vengeance Day** (Jove 0-515-09321-1, Nov,87 [Oct,87], $2.95, 201pp, pb) Post-holocaust men's sf adventure novel.

Avi **Devil's Race** (Avon/Flare 0-380-70406-4, Oct,87, $2.75, 118pp, pb) Reprint (Lippincott/Harper & Row 1984) young adult horror novel.

*Axler, James **Deathlands #3: Neutron Solstice** (Worldwide Library 0-373-62503-0, Mar,87 [Feb,87], $2.95, 252pp, pb) Post-holocaust sf adventure novel.

*Axler, James **Deathlands #4: Crater Lake** (Gold Eagle 0-373-62504-9, Aug,87 [Jul,87], $2.95, 250pp, pb) Post-holocaust sf adventure novel.

*Baen, Jim, ed. **New Destinies, Vol. 1/Spring 1987** (Baen 0-671-65628-7, Mar,87 [Feb,87], $2.95, 288pp, pb) Original anthology/magazine, Vol.1/Spring 1987, incorporating the preceding Baen anthology **Far Frontiers** and concluding a Poul Anderson novella serialized there; it also has other fiction and non-fiction, including an unsigned review column.

*Baen, Jim, ed. **New Destinies, Vol. 2/Fall 1987** (Baen 0-671-65346-6, Aug,87 [Jul,87], $2.95, 232pp, pb) Original anthology of stories and essays.

Bailey, Robin Wayne **Frost** (Tor 0-812-53143-4, Feb,87 [Jan,87], $2.95, 208pp, pb) Reprint (Pocket 1983) fantasy novel, Vol. 1 in the "Frost" series about a swordswoman.

*Baker, Jane & Pip Baker **Terror of the Vervoids** Main listing under Pip Baker.

*Baker, Pip & Jane Baker **Terror of the Vervoids** (W.H. Allen 0-491-03056-8, Sep,87, £7.95, 144pp, hc) Juvenile sf novel. Volume 125 in the Doctor Who series.

*Baker, Pip & Jane Baker **Time and the Rani** Main listing under Pip Baker.

*Baker, Pip & Jane Baker **Time and the Rani** (W.H. Allen 0-491-03186-6, Dec,87, £7.95, 144pp, hc) Juvenile sf novel. Volume 128 in the "Doctor Who" series. [Not seen]

*Baker, Scott **Drink the Fire From the Flames** (Tor 0-812-53147-7, Aug,87 [Jul,87], $3.95, 343pp, pb) Fantasy novel, sequel to **Firedance**.

*Baker, Sharon **Journey to Membliar** (Avon 0-380-75114-3, Jul,87 [Jun,87], $3.50, 247pp, pb) Sf novel, set in the same world as **Quarreling, They Met the Dragon**.

*Baldwin, Bill **Galactic Convoy** (Popular Library Questar 0-445-20408-7, Dec,87 [Nov,87], $3.50, 332pp, pb) Sf novel, space opera, sequel to **The Helmsman**.

*Ball, Duncan **The Ghost and the Gory Story** (Angus & Robertson 0-207-15501-1, Nov,87, £5.95, 120pp, hc) Juvenile ghost novel. Sequel to **The Ghost and the Gogglebox**. [Not seen]

*Ballard, J.G. **The Day of Creation** (Gollancz 0-575-04152-8, Sep,87, £10.95, 254pp, hc) Mainstream novel.

*Ballard, J.G. **The Day of Creation** (Gollancz 0-575-04192-7, Sep,87, £50.00, 256pp, hc) Limited (100 copy) signed edition of the above. [Not seen]

Ballard, J.G. **The Drowned World** (Carroll & Graf 0-88184-324-5, Jun,87 [May,87], $3.95, 175pp, pb) Reprint (Berkley 1962) surreal sf novel. This was Ballard's first novel.

Ballard, J.G. **Empire of the Sun** (Pocket 0-671-64877-2, Nov,87 [Oct,87], $4.50, 384pp, pb) Reprint (Gollancz 1985). Non-sf, associational -- autobiographical novel.

Ballard, J.G. **The Terminal Beach** (Carroll & Graf 0-88184-370-9, Nov,87 [Oct,87], $3.50, 224pp, pb) Reprint (Gollancz 1964) collection of 12 stories. This differs from the earlier Berkley edition, **Terminal Beach** (no *The*) in contents.

Banerji, Sara **Cobwebwalking** (Black Swan 0-552-99220-8, Jul,87, £3.95, 143pp, tp) Reprint (Gollancz 1986) literary fantasy novel.

+Banerji, Sara **Cobwebwalking** (Adler & Adler 0-917561-40-6, Oct,87, $15.95, 155pp, hc) Literary sf/fantasy novel of a girl's special bond with nature, and what she does after the holocaust. First U.S. edition (Gollancz 1986).

Banks, Iain **The Bridge** (Pan 0-330-30075-X, Jul,87, £2.95, 286pp, pb) Reprint (Macmillan UK 1986) novel with sf touches.

*Banks, Iain **Consider Phlebas** (Macmillan 0-333-44138-9, Apr,87, £10.95, 471pp, hc) Sf novel. Rousing space opera, a change of pace from Banks.

*Banks, Iain **Espedair Street** (Macmillan 0-333-44916-9, Sep,87, £10.95, 249pp, hc) Novel of "Sex, Drugs and Rock-and-Roll". Listed for Banks fans.

Banks, Lynne Reid **The Indian in the Cupboard** (Avon/Camelot 0-380-60012-9, Oct,87 [Sep,87], $2.95, 181pp, pb) Reissue (UK 1980) juvenile fantasy novel.

Banks, Lynne Reid **The Return of the Indian** (Avon/Camelot 0-380-70284-3, Oct,87 [Sep,87], $2.95, 189pp, pb) Reprint (Doubleday 1986) juvenile fantasy novel, sequel to **The Indian in the Cupboard**.

*Barbour, Douglas & Phyllis Gotlieb, eds. **Tesseracts 2** Main listing under Phyllis Gotlieb.

Barker, Clive **Books of Blood** (Weidenfeld & Nicolson 0-297-79251-2, Oct,87 [Nov,87], £12.95, 500pp, hc) Reprint (Scream/Press 1985) omnibus of the first three Books of Blood collections.

+Barker, Clive **The Damnation Game** (Ace/Putnam 0-399-13278-3, May,87 [Apr,87], $18.95, 379pp, hc) Horror novel, a first novel. First U.S. edition (Weidenfeld & Nicholson 1985).

Barker, Clive **The Damnation Game** (SFBC #10878, Oct,87 [Nov,87], $4.98, 368pp, hc) Reprint (Weidenfield & Nicolsen 1985) horror novel.

Barker, Clive **In the Flesh** (SFBC #10653, Jun,87, $4.98, 187pp, hc) Reprint (Sphere 1985 as **Clive Barker's Books of Blood, Volume 5**) collection of original horror stories.

Barker, Clive **In the Flesh** (Pocket 0-671-61269-7, Jan,88 [Dec,87], $3.95, 255pp, pb) Reprint (Sphere 1986 as **Clive Barker's Books of Blood, Vol. 5**) original collection of 4 horror tales.

Barker, Clive **The Inhuman Condition** (SFBC #10329, Feb,87, $4.98, 179pp, hc) Reprint (Sphere 1985 as **Clive Barker's Books of Blood, Vol. 4**) horror collection.

BARKER, CLIVE   **BEAGLE, PETER S.**

Barker, Clive **The Inhuman Condition** (Pocket 0-671-61269-7, Aug,87 [Jul,87], $3.95, 254pp, pb) Reprint (Sphere 1985 as **Clive Barker's Books of Blood, Vol. 4**) original collection.

*Barker, Clive **Weaveworld** (Simon & Schuster Poseidon 0-671-61268-9, Oct,87 [Sep,87], $19.95, 584pp, hc) Fantasy/horror novel. There's also supposed to be a limited edition, -64839-X, $85.00.

*Barker, Clive **Weaveworld** (Collins 0-00-223254-5, Oct,87, £10.95, 722pp, hc) Fantasy/horror novel. Simultaneous with the US (Simon & Schuster) edition.

Barker, Clive **Weaveworld** (Collins 0-00-223372-X, Dec,87, £80.00, 722pp, hc) Reprint (Simon & Schuster 1987) fantasy/horror novel. Limited (to 500 copies), signed and slip-cased edition with illustrations by the author.

*Barker, Dennis **Winston Three Three Three** (Grafton 0-586-07089-3, Aug,87, £2.95, 267pp, pb) Thriller set in Great Britain in 2089.

Barlowe, Wayne Douglas, Beth Meacham & Ian Summers **Barlowe's Guide to Extraterrestrials** (Workman 0-89480-324-7, Sep,87 [Oct,87], $10.95, 146pp, tp) Reissue (Workman 1979) sf art book, 2nd Edition, 4th printing, with a new foreword by Robert Silverberg.

Barlowe, Wayne Douglas, Beth Meacham & Ian Summers **Barlowe's Guide to Extraterrestrials** (Workman 0-89480-500-2, Oct,87 [Dec,87], $16.95, 112pp, hc) Reissue (Workman 1979) book of art and text on aliens from sf novels. New introduction by Robert Silverberg. The hardcover is the same as the new trade paperback.

*Barnes, John **The Man Who Pulled Down the Sky** (Congdon & Weed/Contemporary 0-86553-185-4, Apr,87, $15.95, 256pp, hc) Sf novel. Solar system intrigue, politics, and war *a la* **The Moon is A Harsh Mistress**. A first novel.

Barnes, Julian **Staring at the Sun** (Picador 0-330-29930-1, Sep,87, £3.50, 195pp, tp) Reprint (Cape 1986) literary sf novel.

*Barnes, Steven, Larry Niven & Jerry E. Pournelle **The Legacy of Heorot** Main listing under Larry Niven.

Baron, Mike **Robotech: The Graphic Novel** (Comico 0-938965-00-X, Dec,86 [Jun,87], $5.95, 48pp, tp) Reissue (Comico 1986) "graphic novel" version of a plot by Carl Macek, from the tv sf cartoon show. Second printing dated December '86, not seen until 1987.

*Barr, Marleen S. **Alien to Femininity** (Greenwood 0-313-23634-8, Jul,87 [Oct,87], $32.95, 189pp, hc) Non-fiction, critical study of feminism in sf. Available in UK for £30.75.

*Barr, Marleen S., Richard Law & Ruth Salvaggio **Suzy McKee Charnas, Joan Vinge, Octavia Butler** (Starmont House 0-916732-91-6, Dec,86 [Jan,87], $9.95, 72pp, tp) Non-fiction, 3 critical studies with chronologies and bibliographies.

*Barratt, David **C.S. Lewis and His World** (Eerdman's 0-8028-3639-9, Aug,87 [Oct,87], $9.95, 46pp, hc) Non-fiction, short, heavily illustrated critical/biographical study. It looks like a school textbook.

*Barrett, Neal, Jr. **Through Darkest America** (Congdon & Weed/Contemporary 0-86553-184-6, Apr,87, $15.95, 275pp, hc) Sf novel set in a bleak and bitter post-holocaust America.

Barrie, J.M. **Peter Pan** (NAL/Signet Classic 0-451-52088-2, May,87 [Apr,87], $2.50, 200pp, pb) Classic juvenile fantasy novel with new illustrations by Sergio Martinez. New afterword by Alison Lurie.

Barrie, J.M. **Peter Pan** (Unicorn 0-88101-069-3, Oct,87, $16.95, 179pp, hc) Reprint (Hodder & Stoughton 1911) juvenile fantasy novel, with new illustrations by Greg Hildebrandt.

*Barron, Neil **Anatomy of Wonder, Third Edition** (R.R. Bowker 0-8352-2313-2, Aug,87 [Oct,87], $39.95, 874pp, hc) Non-fiction, critical/bibliographical/reference work on sf. A major one-volume reference, especially on modern sf, and the standard work for libraries. Highly recommended. (CNB)

Barry, Jonathan & Whitley Strieber **Catmagic** (SFBC #10534, May,87, $4.98, 376pp, hc) Reprint (Tor 1986) dark fantasy novel.

Barth, John **Giles Goat Boy** (Doubleday Anchor 0-385-24086-4, Sep,87, $9.95, 710pp, tp) Reprint (Doubleday 1966) quasi-sf literary novel.

Bauer, Steven **Steven Spielberg's Amazing Stories** (Futura 0-7088-8230-7, Jul,87, £2.50, 234pp, pb) Reprint (Charter 1986) collection of stories adapted from Spielberg's television series. [First U.K. edition]

Bauer, Steven **Volume II of Steven Spielberg's Amazing Stories** (Futura 0-7088-3671-2, Nov,87, £2.50, 225pp, pb) Reprint (Charter 1986) collection of 11 stories adapted from the teleplays. [First U.K. edition]

Baum, L. Frank **The Classical Wizard/Magus Mirabilis in Oz** (Scolar Press 0-85967-723-0, Aug,87 [Nov,87], $19.95, 295pp, hc) First Latin edition of **The Wizard of Oz**, translated by C.J. Hinke and George Van Buren. An excellent way to study Latin. A special English-Latin word list is available from the publisher. The original W.W. Denslow illustrations are included, and the layout is the same as the first edition. (CNB)

Baum, L. Frank **Dorothy and the Wizard in Oz** (Dover 0-486-24714-7, Jul,87, £4.20, 256pp, tp) Reissue (Reilly & Britton 1904) juvenile fantasy novel. Volume 4 in the "Oz" series. [Not seen]

Baum, L. Frank **The Marvellous Land Of Oz** (Treasure Press 1-85051-206-X, Jan,87 [1987], £3.99, 240pp, pb) Reprint (Reilly & Britton 1904) juvenile fantasy novel. Volume 2 in the "Oz" series. [Not seen]

Baum, L. Frank **Wizard of Oz** (Chancellor Press 1-85152-068-6, Oct,87 [Nov,87], £7.99, 208pp, hc) Reprint (George Hill 1900, as **The Wonderful Wizard of Oz**) juvenile fantasy novel. Volume 1 in the "Oz" series. [Not seen]

Baum, L. Frank **The Wizard of Oz** (Isis Large Print 1-55763-013-8, Oct,87 [Dec,87], £8.70, 200pp, hc) Reissue (George Hill 1900, as **The Wonderful Wizard of Oz**) juvenile fantasy novel. [Not seen]

Baum, L. Frank **The Wonderful Wizard of Oz** (Pavilion 1-85145-135-8, Jul,87, £9.95, 308pp, hc) Reprint (George Hill 1900) juvenile fantasy novel. This is a facsimile of of the original edition, with a new afterword by Peter Glassman. Volume 1 in the "Oz" series.

Baum, L. Frank **The Wonderful Wizard of Oz** (Morrow/Books of Wonder 0-688-06944-4, Aug,87 [Oct,87], $17.00, 267pp, hc) Reprint (Hill 1900) classic juvenile fantasy novel, facsimile of the original edition, with illustrations by W.W. Denslow.

Baum, L. Frank **The Wonderful Wizard of Oz** (Cornerstone 1-55736-013-8, Sep,87 [Oct,87], $12.95, 188pp, hc) Reprint (Hill 1900) juvenile fantasy novel, large print edition with the original W.W. Denslow illustrations.

+Bayley, Barrington J. **The Rod of Light** (Arbor House 0-87795-935-8, Dec,87 [Nov,87], $15.95, 193pp, hc) Sf novel, sequel to **The Soul of the Robot**. First American edition (Methuen 1985).

Beagle, Peter S. **A Fine and Private Place** (Ballantine/Del Rey 0-345-35156-8, Jan,88 [Dec,87], $3.95, 273pp, pb) Reissue (Viking Press 1960) fantasy novel; 11th printing. A warm, funny ghost story. Recommended. (CNB)

Beagle, Peter S. **The Folk of the Air** (Headline 0-7472-3068-4, Sep,87, £4.95, 330pp, tp) Reprint (Del Rey 1987) fantasy novel. [First U.K. edition]

Beagle, Peter S. **The Folk of the Air** (SFBC #11279, Sep,87, $5.50, 279pp, hc) Reprint (Del Rey 1986) fantasy novel.

Beagle, Peter S. **The Folk of the Air** (Headline 0-7472-0052-1, Oct,87, £10.95, 336pp, hc) Reprint (Del Rey 1987) fantasy novel. [Not seen]

Beagle, Peter S. **The Folk of the Air** (Ballantine/Del Rey 0-345-34699-8, Jan,88 [Dec,87], $4.50, 375pp, pb) Reprint (Del Rey 1986) fantasy novel set in a thinly-disguised Berkeley, about a thinly-disguised Society of Creative Anachronism. Recommended. (FCM)

BEAGLE, PETER S.

BERMAN, MITCH

Beagle, Peter S. **The Last Unicorn** (Ballantine/Del Rey 0-345-35367-6, Jan,88 [Dec,87], $3.95, 248pp, pb) Reissue (Viking Press 1968) fantasy novel; 27th printing.

Bear, Greg **Eon** (Legend 0-09-952350-7, Nov,87 [Oct,87], £4.95, 503pp, tp) Reprint (Bluejay 1985) sf novel. Distinctly 'hard' sf, reminiscent of Clarke at his best. Recommended.

*Bear, Greg **The Forge of God** (Gollancz 0-575-04101-3, Aug,87, £11.95, 473pp, hc) Sf novel. Simultaneous with US (Tor) edition.

*Bear, Greg **The Forge of God** (Tor 0-312-93021-6, Sep,87 [Aug,87], $17.95, 474pp, hc) Hard sf novel of the destruction of the Earth. Fast-paced and well-written; highly recommended. (TM)

*Bear, Greg **Hegira** (Gollancz 0-575-04008-4, May,87, £2.95, 222pp, pb) Sf novel, revised from earlier version (Dell 1979).

*Bearne, Betsy **Eli's Ghost** (Macmillan McElderry 0-689-50420-9, Mar,87, $10.95, 104pp, hc) Juvenile fantasy novel about a boy who leaves his unpleasant father to find his mother, a reputed witch. He almost dies in a swamp, and as a result a poltergeist is created, which does all the things the boy wants to do but doesn't because he's too timid.

*Beauchamp, Gorman, Kenneth Roemer & Nicholas D. Smith, eds. **Utopian Studies 1** (Univ. Press of America 0-8191-6165-9, May,87 [Apr,87], $12.75, 197pp, tp) Non-fiction, anthology of scholarly essays, co-published with the Society for Utopian Studies. (Hardcover and library binding editions have been announced; not seen.)

*Bedard, Michael **A Darker Magic** (Atheneum 0-689-31342-X, Oct,87 [Sep,87], $13.95, 183pp, hc) Young-adult novel of magic and horror. A first novel.

*Beebee, Chris **The Hub** (Macdonald 0-356-14800-9, Aug,87, £10.95, 249pp, hc) Sf novel.

*Belden, Wilanne Schneider **Mind-Hold** (HBJ/Gulliver 0-15-254280-9, Mar,87, $14.95, 242pp, hc) Post-disaster young-adult sf novel of psi powers and survival, a sequel to **Mind-Call** (1981).

Bell, Clare **Clan Ground** (Dell/Laurel-Leaf 0-440-91287-3, Dec,87 [Nov,87], $2.95, 258pp, pb) Reprint (Atheneum 1984) young adult sf novel, second in the "Ratha" duology.

Bell, Clare **Ratha's Creature** (Dell/Laurel Leaf 0-440-97298-1, Nov,87 [Oct,87], $2.95, 259pp, pb) Reprint (Atheneum 1983) sf novel, first in a duology set in an alternate world where evolution diverged and cats gained intelligence.

Bellairs, John **The Eyes of the Killer Robot** (Bantam Skylark 0-553-15552-0, Dec,87 [Nov,87], $2.95, 167pp, pb) Reprint (Dial 1986) young adult fantasy novel in the "Johnny Dixon" series; illustrations by Edward Gorey.

Bellairs, John **Spell of the Sorcerer's Skull** (Corgi 0-552-52366-6, Jan,87, £1.75, 143pp, pb) Reprint (Dial 1984) juvenile fantasy novel. [First U.K. edition]

+Bemmann, Hans **The Stone and the Flute** (Viking 0-670-80186-0, May,87 [Jan,87], $19.95, 855pp, hc) Fantasy novel, translated from the German **Stein und Floete** (1983) by Anthea Bell. This edition has both American and British prices and copyrights. The UK edition appeared 9/86.

Bemmann, Hans **The Stone and the Flute** (Penguin 0-14-007445-7, Aug,87 [Jul,87], £4.95, 855pp, tp) Reprint (Viking UK 1986) fantasy novel. Translated from the German (Verlag 1983) by Anthea Bell.

Bendixen, Alfred, ed. **Haunted Women: The Best Supernatural Tales by American Women Writers** (Ungar 0-8044-6101-5, 1987 [Oct,87], $10.95, 276pp, tp) Reprint (Ungar 1985) anthology. First paperback edition.

*Benford, Gregory **Across the Sea of Suns** (Bantam Spectra 0-553-26664-0, Aug,87 [Jul,87], $3.95, 353pp, pb) Sf novel; the sequel to **In the Ocean of Night**. Mostly a reprint (Simon & Schuster 1983), but the last chapter of the original has been rewritten and another chapter added to tie it in with the next thematic book in the series, **Great Sky River**. The changes are not mentioned on the copyright page, but are important enough for us to consider it a revised (and therefore new) book. It's one of Benford's best in his continuous exploration of man/machine civilizations. Highly recommended. (CNB)

Benford, Gregory **Against Infinity** (NEL 0-450-05719-4, Aug,87, £1.95, 251pp, pb) Reissue (Timescape 1983) sf novel.

*Benford, Gregory **Great Sky River** (Bantam Spectra 0-553-05238-1, Dec,87 [Nov,87], $17.95, 326pp, hc) Sf novel, a thematic sequel to **Across the Sea of Suns** and the start of a new series taking place at the center of the galaxy. The science doesn't get any harder than this exploration of new man/machine interfaces. Highly recommended. (CNB)

Benford, Gregory **In Alien Flesh** (Tor 0-812-53176-0, Jan,88 [Dec,87], $3.95, 280pp, pb) Reprint (Tor 1986) collection of 14 sf stories plus comments on each.

Benford, Gregory **In the Ocean of Night** (Bantam Spectra 0-553-26578-4, Jul,87 [Jun,87], $3.95, 321pp, pb) Reprint (Dial 1977) sf novel, first in a series; a Nebula nominee. Highly recommended. (CNB)

Benford, Gregory **Timescape** (Pocket 0-671-50632-3, Mar,87 [Apr,87], $3.95, 384pp, pb) Reissue (Simon & Schuster 1980) sf novel; 5th Pocket printing.

Benford, Gregory **Timescape** (Sphere 0-7221-1630-6, Dec,87, £3.50, 412pp, pb) Reissue (Simon & Schuster 1980) sf novel.

Benford, Gregory & David Brin **Heart of the Comet** (Bantam Spectra 0-553-25839-7, Mar,87 [Feb,87], $4.50, 477pp, pb) Reprint (Bantam 1986) sf novel.

Benford, Gregory & David Brin **Heart of the Comet** (Bantam UK 0-553-17291-3, Apr,87 [Mar,87], £2.95, 478pp, pb) Reprint (Bantam 1986) sf novel.

Benford, Gregory & Martin H. Greenberg, eds. **Hitler Victorious** (Berkley 0-425-10137-1, Aug,87 [Jul,87], $3.95, 323pp, pb) Reprint (Garland 1986) anthology of 12 stories set in alternate realities where Hitler prevailed. Some of the stories, including *Locus* poll winner "Thor Meets Captain America" by David Brin, are originals. Recommended. (TM)

*Benjamin, Michele & Jim Ridgway, eds. **PsiFi: Psychological Theories and Science Fictions** For main entry see under Jim Ridgway.

*Bennett, Thea **The Gemini Factor** (Magnet 0-423-02300-4, Nov,87, £1.75, 169pp, pb) Novelization of children's TV series about telepathic children. Based on script by Paula Milne.

Benson, E.F. **The Luck of the Vails** (Salem House/Hogarth Press 0-7012-0722-1, Apr,87 [Mar,87], $6.95, 320pp, pb) Reprint (Heinemann 1901) fantasy suspense novel. This is the 1986 Hogarth Press British edition, imported by Salem House.

Bentine, Michael **Lords of the Levels** (Grafton 0-586-06643-8, Aug,87, £2.95, 302pp, pb) Reprint (Grafton 1986) occult novel.

*Berger, Thomas **Being Invisible** (Little, Brown 0-316-09158-8, Apr,87, $16.95, 262pp, hc) Literary fantasy novel about a man who can disappear at will.

Berger, Thomas **Nowhere** (Methuen 0-413-14200-0, Feb,87 [Mar,87], £2.50, 186pp, pb) Reprint (Methuen 1986) literary fantasy novel.

*Berman, Mitch **Time Capsule** (Putnam 0-399-13197-3, Jan,87, $18.95, 295pp, hc) Sf novel, "a postnuclear Huckleberry Finn" with two characters traveling across a devastated America; a first novel.

BERRY, STEPHEN AMES

BLOCH, ROBERT

*Berry, Stephen Ames **The AI War** (Tor 0-812-53193-0, May,87 [Apr,87], $2.95, 249pp, pb) Military sf novel.

Bester, Alfred **The Deceivers** (Pan 0-330-26969-0, May,87, £2.95, 255pp, pb) Reissue (Wallaby 1981) sf novel.

Bester, Alfred **The Deceivers** (Tor 0-812-53186-8, Nov,87 [Oct,87], $3.50, 304pp, pb) Reissue (Pocket/Wallaby 1981) sf novel, with (uncredited) artwork by DeMarco. 2nd printing.

Bester, Alfred **The Demolished Man** (SFBC #02237, Apr,87 [May,87], $3.98, 183pp, hc) Reprint (Shasta 1953) classic sf novel.

Bester, Alfred **The Stars My Destination** (Franklin Watts 0-531-15050-X, Apr,87 [Mar,87], $15.95, 197pp, hc) Reprint (NAL 1957) sf novel. This classic of sf is now available again in hardcover. The text is offset from the 1975 Gregg Press edition, which was itself offset from the 1957 NAL edition. It's getting fuzzy around the edges. (CNB)

Bester, Alfred **Tiger! Tiger!** (Penguin 0-14-010122-5, Nov,87, £3.95, 249pp, tp) Reissue (Sidgwick & Jackson 1956) sf novel. One of Bester's best books, back in print again. More famous under its American title **The Stars My Destination**. In the Penguin Science Fiction Classics series.

*Betancourt, John Gregory **Rogue Pirate** (TSR/Windwalker 0-88038-456-5, Jun,87 [May,87], $2.95, 219pp, pb) Fantasy adventure novel.

*Bierce, Ambrose **The Devil's Advocate: An Ambrose Bierce Reader** (Chronicle 0-87701-401-9, Dec,87 [Nov,87], $22.50, 327pp, hc) A selection of stories, newspaper columns, letters, poetry, and excerpts from books. Edited by Brian St. Pierre. A Trade paperback edition (0-87701-476-0, $12.95) was announced but not seen. Stories indexed are from the section "Stories of the Supernatural."

*Biggle, Lloyd, Jr. **Interface for Murder** (Doubleday Crime Club 0-385-24310-3, Nov,87 [Oct,87], $12.95, 185pp, hc) Associational. Mystery novel by an sf writer.

Biggle, Lloyd, Jr. **The Quallsford Inheritance** (Penguin 0-14-010007-5, May,87, $3.95, 278pp, pb) Reprint (St. Martin's 1986) Sherlock Holmes novel. Associational.

*Billias, Stephen **The American Book of the Dead** (Popular Library Questar 0-445-20335-8, May,87 [Apr,87], $3.50, 214pp, pb) Picaresque sf novel of Zen and the threat of nuclear war. A first novel.

+Bingley, Margaret **Devil's Child** (Popular Library 0-445-20472-9, Dec,87 [Nov,87], $3.50, 253pp, pb) Horror novel. First American edition (Piatkus 1983).

*Bingley, Margaret **The Unquiet Dead** (Piatkus 0-86188-601-1, Jan,87 [Oct,87], £9.95, 215pp, hc) "A chilling story of psychic children."

*Bird, Antoinette Kelsall **The Daughters of Megwyn** (Headline 0-7472-0039-4, Aug,87 [Nov,87], £10.95, 250pp, hc) Novel set in 15th century England, with fantasy touches.

Bishop, Michael **Ancient of Days** (Paladin 0-586-08618-8, Nov,87, £4.95, 368pp, tp) Reprint (Arbor House 1985) sf novel. [First U.K. edition]

*Bishop, Michael **The Secret Ascension** (Tor 0-312-93031-3, Nov,87 [Oct,87], $16.95, 341pp, hc) Sf novel of an alternate U.S., a Philip K. Dick pastiche, starring Philip K. Dick as a character.

Bishop, Michael **Who Made Stevie Crye?** (Headline 0-7472-3043-9, Nov,87, £4.95, 309pp, tp) Reprint (Arkham House 1984) horror novel. Contains the original illustrations by J.K. Potter. [First U.K. edition]

Bisson, Terry **Talking Man** (Avon 0-380-75141-0, Aug,87 [Jul,87], $2.95, 192pp, pb) Reprint (Arbor House 1986) contemporary fantasy novel. God lives in a junkyard, and he has some enemies. Wild, witty, and very entertaining. (FCM)

Bisson, Terry **Talking Man** (Headline 0-7472-3011-0, Aug,87, £2.50, 192pp, pb) Reprint (Arbor House 1986) fantasy novel. [First U.K. edition]

Black, Campbell **Letters from the Dead** (Grafton 0-586-07033-8, Jan,87 [Dec,86], £2.95, 317pp, pb) Reprint (Villard 1985) horror novel. [First U.K. edition]

Black, Campbell **Letters from the Dead** (Severn House 0-7278-1515-6, Nov,87, £9.95, 320pp, hc) Reprint (Villard 1985) horror novel. [Not seen]

Black, Campbell **The Wanting** (Jove 0-515-09177-4, Aug,87 [Jul,87], $3.95, 347pp, pb) Reprint (McGraw-Hill 1986) horror novel.

*Black, Ian Stuart **The Macra Terror** (W.H. Allen 0-491-03227-7, Jul,87 [Sep,87], £7.95, 139pp, hc) Juvenile sf novel. Volume 123 in the Doctor Who series.

Black, Ian Stuart **The Macra Terror** (Target 0-426-20307-0, Dec,87, £1.95, 139pp, pb) Reprint (W.H. Allen 1987) juvenile sf novel. Volume 123 in the "Doctor Who" series.

Blackwood, Algernon **A Mysterious House** (Tragara Press 0-948189-15-0, Jul,87 [Aug,87], £9.00, 24pp, tp) Reprint (*Belgravia* July 1889) of Blackwood's first published short story, with an introduction by Richard Dalby. A limited edition of 125 copies, of which 100 are for sale. [Not seen]

*Blakeney, Jay D. **The Omcri Matrix** (Ace 0-441-62353-0, Mar,87 [Feb,87], $2.95, 203pp, pb) Sf novel of an officer in the Planetary Patrol vs. alien assassins.

Blatty, William Peter **The Exorcist** (Bantam 0-553-27010-9, Sep,87, $4.50, 403pp, pb) Reissue (Harper & Row 1971) horror novel; 45th Bantam printing.

*Blaylock, James P. **Land of Dreams** (Arbor House 0-87795-898-X, Aug,87 [Jul,87], $16.95, 264pp, hc) Contemporary surreal/alternate world fantasy set in the same world as his award-winning "Paper Dragons". This is Blaylock's best book yet; recommended. (FCM)

*Blaylock, James P. & Edward Bryant **The Shadow on the Doorstep/Trilobyte** (Axolotl 0-939879-16-6, Aug,87, $30.00, 14 + 27pp, hc) Back-to-back "double" with a short story by Blaylock (originally published in *Asimov's*) and 3 very short stories by Bryant (these appear to be original despite a 1986 copyright). Signed, limited edition of 300 copies; a deluxe leatherbound was also announced at $65.00.

*Blaylock, James P. & Edward Bryant **The Shadow on the Doorstep/Trilobyte** (Axolotl 0-939879-18-2, Sep,87 [Aug,87], $6.00, 14 + 27pp, tp) Trade paperback of the above.

Blish, James **A Case of Conscience** (Ballantine/Del Rey 0-345-34125-2, Aug,87 [Jul,87], $3.50, 240pp, pb) Reissue (Ballantine 1958) sf novel. One of the classics of sf, and one of the few successful religious/sf works. Highly recommended. (CNB)

*Blish, James **The Tale That Wags the God** (Advent 0-911682-29-5, Jul,87 [Sep,87], $15.00, 290pp, hc) Non-fiction, collection of essays about sf; edited by Cy Chauvin.

*Blish, James, [ref.] **Imprisoned in a Tesseract: The Life and Work of James Blish** Main listing under David Ketterer.

Bloch, Robert **American Gothic** (Tor 0-812-51572-2, Jul,87 [Jun,87], $3.95, 246pp, pb) Reprint (Simon & Schuster 1974) psychological horror novel; no fantasy. Listed for Bloch enthusiasts.

*Bloch, Robert **Lost in Time and Space with Lefty Feep** (Creatures at Large 0-940064-01-4, Apr,87 [Mar,87], $12.95, 258pp, tp) Collection of 9 humorous sf stories, one original, about a racetrack tout. Introduction by Chelsea Quinn Yarbro. The paperback is limited to 5,000 copies, and a 250-copy hardcover edition (-02-2, $40) was announced but not seen.

*Bloch, Robert **Midnight Pleasures** (Doubleday 0-385-19439-0, Apr 17,87 [Mar,87], $12.95, 177pp, hc) Collection of 14 stories.

Bloch, Robert **Psycho 2** (Lythway Large Print 0-7451-0525-4, Jun,87, £9.50, 312pp, hc) Reprint (Warner 1982) horror novel. [Not seen]

*Bloch, Robert, [ref.] **The Complete Robert Bloch: An Illustrated, Comprehensive Bibliography** Main listing under Randall D. Larson.

*Bloch, Robert, [ref.] **Robert Bloch** Main listing under Randall D. Larson.

*Block, Bob **Galloping Galaxies** (Target 0-426-20296-1, Jun,87, £1.80, 124pp, pb) Novelization of children's TV spoof sf serial.

*Blumlein, Michael **The Movement of Mountains** (St. Martin's 0-312-00621-7, Aug,87 [Jul,87], $17.95, 289pp, hc) Sf novel of future medicine and a virus affecting bio-engineered slaves. A first novel.

Bonanno, Margaret Wander **Dwellers in the Crucible** (Firecrest 0-85997-922-9, Jul,87 [1987], £7.95, 320pp, hc) Reprint (Pocket 1985) sf novel. Volume 40 in the Star Trek Novels series. [First U.K. edition, not seen]

*Bonanno, Margaret Wander **Star Trek: Strangers From the Sky** (Pocket 0-671-64049-6, Jul,87 [Jun,87], $3.95, 402pp, pb) New Star Trek novel, not part of the numbered series; it's the second "giant Star Trek novel" -- an "epic novel of first contact between man and Vulcan", part flashback, part alternate-history of the Federation.

Bonanno, Margaret Wander **Star Trek: Strangers From the Sky** (SFBC #10882, Aug,87, $5.98, 310pp, hc) Reprint (Pocket 1987) Star Trek novel. Kirk and Spock found the Federation in this time travel story.

Bonanno, Margaret Wander **Strangers From the Sky** (Titan 1-85286-008-1, Sep,87, £3.95, 402pp, pb) Reprint (Pocket 1987) sf novel. Volume 50 in the Star Trek Novels series. [First U.K. edition]

Bond, Nancy **A String in the Harp** (Puffin 0-14-032376-7, Nov,87 [Oct,87], $5.95, 370pp, tp) Reissue (Atheneum 1976) young adult Welsh fantasy novel set part in the present and part in the past. A Newbery Honor Book. Recommended. (CNB)

*Bosshardt, Robert **Whom the Gods Destroy** (Maverick 0-89288-157-7, 1987 [May,87], C$8.95, 305pp, tp) Sf novel about UFOs and "alien emissaries from another dimension." A Canadian original.

*Boston, Bruce **Alchemical Texts** (Ocean View no ISBN, 1985, $3.00, 18pp, ph) Poetry collection chapbook. In **The Bruce Boston Omnibus**.

*Boston, Bruce **All the Clocks Are Melting** (Velocities Chapbook Series 0-930231-00-7, 1984, $3.00, 40pp, ph) Poetry collection chapbook. In **The Bruce Boston Omnibus**.

*Boston, Bruce **The Bruce Boston Omnibus** (Ocean View 0-938075-06-3, Dec,87 [Oct,87], $12.95, "210", bx) Despite the title, this is not really an omnibus, but a boxed set containing 5 earlier books of sf stories and poetry: **Jackbird, She Comes When You're Leaving, All the Clocks are Melting, Alchemical Texts**, and **Nuclear Futures**.

*Boston, Bruce **Jackbird: Tales of Illusion & Identity** (Berkeley Poets' Workshop & Press no ISBN, 1976, $2.00, 88pp, tp) Collection of six stories. In **The Bruce Boston Omnibus**.

*Boston, Bruce **Nuclear Futures** (Velocities Chapbook Series 0-930231-02-3, 1987, $3.00, 18pp, ph) Poetry collection chapbook. Graphics by Robert Frazier. In **The Bruce Boston Omnibus**.

*Boston, Bruce **She Comes When You're Leaving & Other Stories** (Berkeley Poets' Workshop & Press 0-917658-14-0, 1982, $3.95, 64pp, tp) Collection of eight stories. In **The Bruce Boston Omnibus**.

*Bova, Ben **Battle Station** (Tor 0-812-53202-3, Oct,87 [Sep,87], $3.50, 304pp, pb) Collection of fiction and non-fiction.

*Bova, Ben **The Kinsman Saga** (Tor 0-312-93028-3, Oct,87 [Sep,87], $17.95, 566pp, hc) Sf novel. A slight rewrite of Bova's two best books, **Millennium** (1976) and **Kinsman** (1979), his excellent series about the space program, near-future politics, and SDI(!). The rewrite adds more characterization and motivation, but events have turned these into parallel world books, destroying most of their original power. (CNB)

Bova, Ben **The Multiple Man** (Tor 0-812-53225-2, Dec,87 [Nov,87], $2.95, 250pp, pb) Reprint (Bobbs-Merril 1976) near-future political/sf novel.

Bova, Ben **Voyagers** (Methuen 0-417-07280-5, Aug,87 [Dec,87], £2.95, 391pp, pb) Reissue (Doubleday 1981) sf novel.

Bova, Ben **Voyagers** (Severn House 0-7278-1502-4, Oct,87, £10.95, 400pp, hc) Reprint (Doubleday 1981) sf novel. [Not seen]

Bova, Ben **Voyagers II: The Alien Within** (Severn House 0-7278-1405-2, Jan,87, £9.95, 352pp, hc) Reprint (Tor 1986) sf novel. Volume 2 in the "Voyager" series. [First U.K. edition, not seen]

Bova, Ben **Voyagers II: The Alien Within** (Methuen 0-413-14130-6, Aug,87, £2.95, 344pp, pb) Reprint (Tor 1986) sf novel.

*Bova, Ben **Welcome to Moonbase** (Ballantine 0-345-32859-0, Nov,87 [Oct,87], $9.95, 254pp, tp) Associational item. "Non-fiction" guide to a future moon base, with illustrations by Pat Rawlings.

Bova, Ben **The Winds of Altair** (Tor 0-812-53227-9, Jan,88 [Dec,87], $3.95, 317pp, pb) Reprint (Tor 1983) sf novel, rewritten from a 1973 Dutton juvenile.

*Bowes, Richard **Feral Cell** (Popular Library Questar 0-445-20352-8, May,87 [Apr,87], $3.50, 220pp, pb) Contemporary fantasy novel of parallel worlds. It's uneven and quirky, but often fascinating, with powerfully strange images of the places where worlds meet. (FCM)

*Bowker, Richard **Dover Beach** (Bantam Spectra 0-553-26810-4, Oct,87 [Sep,87], $3.95, 265pp, pb) Sf novel of a self-styled private eye from a war-devastated America. Offbeat and effective -- recommended. (FCM)

*Bowker, Richard **Marlborough Street** (Doubleday 0-385-19753-5, Feb,87 [Jan,87], $12.95, 182pp, hc) Occult fantasy novel. A good psychic (Red Sox fan) vs. a bad psychic (Yankee fan); illusions and delusions.

*Bowkett, Stephen **Dualists** (Gollancz 0-575-04106-4, Sep,87, £7.95, 152pp, hc) Juvenile sf novel.

Boyer, Elizabeth H. **The Troll's Grindstone** (Corgi 0-552-13201-2, Dec,87 [Nov,87], £2.95, 393pp, pb) Reprint (Del Rey 1986) fantasy novel. Volume 5 in the "World of the Alfar" series. [First U.K. edition]

Boyer, Elizabeth H. **The Wizard and the Warlord** (Corgi 0-552-12761-2, Jan,87, £2.50, 332pp, pb) Reprint (Ballantine 1983) fantasy novel. Volume 4 in the "World of the Alfar" series. [First U.K. edition]

Brackett, Leigh **The Big Jump** (Tor 0-812-53229-5, Oct,87 [Sep,87], $2.95, 182pp, pb) Reprint (Ace 1955) sf novel.

Bradbury, Ray **The Day It Rained Forever** (Penguin 0-14-010120-9, Oct,87, £3.95, 233pp, tp) Reissue (Hart-Davis 1959) sf/fantasy collection. In the Penguin Classic Science Fiction series.

Bradbury, Ray **Death Is a Lonely Business** (Bantam 0-553-26447-8, Feb,87 [Jan,87], $3.95, 216pp, pb) Reprint (Knopf 1985); associational, mystery novel.

Bradbury, Ray **Fahrenheit 451** (Ballantine/Del Rey 0-345-34296-8, Sep,87 [Aug,87], $3.50, 179pp, pb) Reissue (Ballantine 1953) classic sf novel; 70th(!) printing. This contains the novel only; the original edition had 2 additional stories.

+Bradbury, Ray **Fahrenheit 451/The Illustrated Man/Dandelion Wine/The Golden Apples of the Sun/The Martian Chronicles** (Octopus/Heinemann 1-85256-023-1, 1987 [Nov,87], $11.98, 798pp, hc) Omnibus edition of 5 novels. First U.S. edition.

*Bradbury, Ray **Fever Dream** (St. Martin's 0-312-57285-9, Nov,87 [Oct,87], $6.95, 32pp, hc) Juvenile fantasy story. A 1948 Bradbury fantasy tale with new illustrations by Darrel Anderson (each with a "glow in the dark" detail).

BRADBURY, RAY   **BRIN, DAVID**

Bradbury, Ray **The Martian Chronicles** (SFBC #02150, Apr,87 [May,87], $4.50, 222pp, hc) Reissue (Doubleday 1950) sf classic collection/novel.

Bradley, Marion Zimmer **The Bloody Sun** (Arrow 0-09-917820-6, Aug,87, £3.50, 372pp, pb) Reissue (Ace 1964) sf novel. This version has the revised (1979) text but omits the short story "To Keep the Oath". In the "Darkover" series.

Bradley, Marion Zimmer **City of Sorcery** (Legend 0-09-944870-X, Dec,87, £3.50, 423pp, pb) Reissue (DAW 1984) sf novel in the "Darkover" series.

Bradley, Marion Zimmer **Darkover Landfall** (Arrow 0-09-915410-2, Aug,87, £2.50, 188pp, pb) Reissue (DAW 1972) sf novel in the "Darkover" series.

Bradley, Marion Zimmer **Darkover Landfall** (DAW 0-88677-234-6, Nov,87 [Oct,87], $3.95, 160pp, pb) Reissue (DAW 1972) sf novel in the "Darkover" series; 12th printing.

+ Bradley, Marion Zimmer **The Fall of Atlantis** (Baen 0-671-65615-5, Feb,87 [Jan,87], $3.95, 502pp, pb) Omnibus edition of fantasy duology **Web of Light** (1983) and **Web of Darkness** (1984). First American edition of the omnibus (Richard Drew 1985 as **Web of Darkness**).

*Bradley, Marion Zimmer **The Firebrand** (Simon & Schuster 0-671-64177-8, Oct,87, $19.95, 608pp, hc) Historical fantasy novel of Cassandra and the Trojan War.

Bradley, Marion Zimmer **The Forbidden Tower** (Arrow 0-09-921430-X, Apr,87, £3.50, 416pp, pb) Reissue (DAW 1977) sf novel in the "Darkover" series.

Bradley, Marion Zimmer **The Forbidden Tower** (DAW 0-88677-235-4, Nov,87 [Oct,87], $3.95, 364pp, pb) Reissue (DAW 1977) sf novel in the "Darkover" series; 9th printing.

Bradley, Marion Zimmer **The Heritage of Hastur** (Arrow 0-09-919190-3, Oct,87, £2.95, 428pp, pb) Reissue (DAW 1975) sf novel in the "Darkover" series.

Bradley, Marion Zimmer **The Heritage of Hastur** (DAW 0-88677-238-9, Dec,87 [Nov,87], $3.95, 381pp, pb) Reissue (DAW 1975) sf novel in the "Darkover" series; 13th printing.

Bradley, Marion Zimmer **The Ruins of Isis** (Pocket 0-671-46843-X, Oct,87 [Sep,87], $3.50, 298pp, pb) Reissue (Donning Starblaze 1978) sf novel of an ancient planet ruled by women; 4th Pocket printing.

Bradley, Marion Zimmer **The Shattered Chain** (Arrow 0-09-916710-7, Apr,87, £2.50, 272pp, pb) Reissue (DAW 1976) sf novel in the "Darkover" series.

Bradley, Marion Zimmer **The Spell Sword** (Arrow 0-09-915950-3, Oct,87, £2.50, 171pp, pb) Reissue (DAW 1974) sf novel in the "Darkover" series.

Bradley, Marion Zimmer **The Spell Sword** (DAW 0-88677-237-0, Dec,87 [Nov,87], $3.95, 158pp, pb) Reissue (DAW 1974) sf novel in the "Darkover" series; 11th printing.

Bradley, Marion Zimmer **Thendara House** (Legend 0-09-942390-1, Dec,87, £3.50, 414pp, pb) Reissue (DAW 1983) sf novel in the "Darkover" series.

Bradley, Marion Zimmer **Two to Conquer** (DAW 0-88677-174-9, Feb,87 [Jan,87], $3.50, 335pp, pb) Reissue (DAW 1980) "Darkover" novel; 7th printing.

Bradley, Marion Zimmer **Warrior Woman** (Arrow 0-09-949310-1, Aug,87, £2.50, 205pp, pb) Reprint (DAW 1985) fantasy novel. [First U.K. edition]

Bradley, Marion Zimmer **The Winds of Darkover** (Arrow 0-09-917810-9, Apr,87, £2.25, 155pp, pb) Reissue (Ace 1970) sf novel in the "Darkover" series.

Bradley, Marion Zimmer **The World Wreckers** (Arrow 0-09-919950-5, Apr,87, £2.25, 190pp, pb) Reissue (Ace 1971) sf novel in the "Darkover" series.

Bradley, Marion Zimmer **The World Wreckers** (Ace 0-441-91178-1, Jan,88 [Dec,87], $2.95, 215pp, pb) Reissue (Ace 1971) sf novel in the "Darkover" series; 8th printing.

Bradley, Marion Zimmer & The Friends of Darkover **The Keeper's Price** (DAW 0-88677-236-2, Nov,87 [Oct,87], $3.95, 206pp, pb) Reissue (DAW 1980) original anthology of "Darkover" stories; 6th printing.

*Bradley, Marion Zimmer & The Friends of Darkover **The Other Side of the Mirror** (DAW 0-88677-185-4, Feb,87 [Jan,87], $3.50, 303pp, pb) Shared-world anthology of "Darkover" stories. There are 5 stories here. Three of them are by Bradley and apparently appear for the first time. One is a 40,000 word novella. This is the most interesting and best of the "Darkover" anthologies. (CNB)

*Bradley, Marion Zimmer & The Friends of Darkover **Red Sun of Darkover** (DAW 0-88677-230-3, Nov,87 [Oct,87], $3.95, 287pp, pb) Original shared world anthology of Darkover stories including two pieces by Bradley.

Bradley, Marion Zimmer & The Friends of Darkover **Sword of Chaos** (DAW 0-88677-172-2, Feb,87 [Jan,87], $3.50, 240pp, pb) Reissue (DAW 1982) shared-world sf anthology; 6th printing.

*Bradley, Marion Zimmer, ed. **Sword and Sorceress IV** (DAW 0-88677-210-9, Jul,87 [Jun,87], $3.50, 285pp, pb) Original anthology of 18 fantasy stories, by both seasoned professionals and new writers.

*Bradman, Tony, ed. **The Magic Kiss and Other Tales of Princes and Princesses** (Blackie 0-216-92015-9, Aug,87 [Dec,87], £6.95, 94pp, hc) Anthology of short stories about princes and princesses.

*Brady, John Paul **A Voyage to Inishneefa** (John Daniel 0-936784-31-8, Jul,87 [Oct,87], $8.95, 103pp, tp) Satiric fantasy novel, Swiftian pastiche -- a "5th voyage" of Lemuel Gulliver.

*Brandner, Gary **Cameron's Closet** (Ballantine Fawcett 0-449-13068-1, Feb,87 [Jan,87], $3.50, 314pp, pb) Horror novel. The monster in a boy's closet becomes frighteningly real.

Brandner, Gary **Carrion** (Arrow 0-09-944440-2, Apr,87, £2.25, 265pp, pb) Reprint (Fawcett 1986) horror novel.

Brandner, Gary **Hellborn** (Arrow 0-09-938540-6, Sep,87, £2.50, 187pp, pb) Reprint (Fawcett 1986) horror novel.

Brandner, Gary **The Howling III: Echoes** (Severn House 0-7278-1509-1, Oct,87, £9.95, 256pp, hc) Reprint (Fawcett 1985) horror novel. Volume 3 in the "Howling" series. [First U.K. edition, not seen]

Brandner, Gary **Return of the Howling** (Severn House 0-7278-1423-0, Apr,87, £8.95, 208pp, hc) Reprint (Fawcett 1982 as **The Howling II**) horror novel. [Not seen]

Brautigan, Richard **The Hawkline Monster** (Arena 0-09-939120-1, Apr,87 [Sep,87], £2.95, 142pp, pb) Reissue (Simon & Schuster 1974) gothic western novel with fantasy touches.

*Brians, Paul **Nuclear Holocausts: Atomic War in Fiction, 1895-1984** (Kent State Univ. Press 0-87338-335-4, Aug,87 [Jul,87], $29.50, 398pp, hc) Non-fiction, bibliographic study. History and criticism of literary works which depict nuclear war or its aftermath, followed by a detailed annotated bibliography.

*Bricusse, Leslie **Christmas 1993** (Faber & Faber 0-571-14651-1, Sep,87 [Dec,87], £7.95, 32pp, hc) Story in verse about Father Christmas's battle with bureaucracy. Illustrated throughout by Errol Le Cain.

*Brin, David **Earthclan** (SFBC #11624, Dec,87, $9.98, 985pp, hc) Omnibus edition of **Startide Rising** and **The Uplift War**.

Brin, David **The Postman** (Bantam UK 0-553-17193-3, Jan,87, £2.95, 321pp, pb) Reprint (Bantam 1986) sf novel.

BRIN, DAVID   **BRUNNER, JOHN**

Brin, David **The Practice Effect** (Bantam Spectra 0-553-25593-2, Jul,87, $3.50, 277pp, pb) Reissue (Bantam 1984) light-hearted science fantasy novel in the *Unknown* style with robots, wizards, strange creatures, and a beautiful princess. 6th printing, with a new cover by Jim Burns.

Brin, David **The River of Time** (Bantam Spectra 0-553-26281-5, Feb,87 [Jan,87], $3.50, 295pp, pb) Reprint (Dark Harvest 1986) collection.

Brin, David **The River of Time** (Bantam UK 0-553-17398-7, Aug,87 [Jul,87], £2.50, 295pp, pb) Reprint (Dark Harvest 1986) sf collection, including four original stories. [First U.K. edition]

Brin, David **Sundiver** (Bantam Spectra 0-553-25594-0, Jul,87, $3.50, 341pp, pb) Reissue (Bantam 1980) sf novel. This was Brin's first novel, and the prequel to **Startide Rising**. Recommended (CNB). 9th printing, with a new cover by Jim Burns.

*Brin, David **The Uplift War** (Phantasia Press 0-932096-44-1, Apr,87, $22.00, 506pp, hc) Sf novel, indirect sequel to **Startide Rising** and the latest in Brin's future history series. This one features intelligent chimpanzees as lead characters. Recommended. (CNB) There is also a 475-copy signed, limited, boxed edition at $60.00.

Brin, David **The Uplift War** (Bantam Spectra 0-553-25121-X, Jul,87 [Jun,87], $4.50, 638pp, pb) Reprint (Phantasia 1987) sf novel. An indirect sequel to **Startide Rising**. Very highly recommended. (TM)

Brin, David **The Uplift War** (Bantam UK 0-553-17452-5, Aug,87, £3.50, 638pp, pb) Reprint (Phantasia 1987) sf novel. Sequel to **Startide Rising**. [First U.K. edition]

Brin, David & Gregory Benford **Heart of the Comet** Main listing under Gregory Benford.

*Brittain, Bill **Dr. Dredd's Wagon of Wonders** (Harper & Row 0-06-020713-2, Jul,87 [Aug,87], $11.50, 179pp, hc) Juvenile fantasy novel, part of the "Coven Tree" series, with illustrations by Andrew Glass.

Brittain, Bill **The Wish Giver** (Harper & Row/Trophy 0-06-440168-5, Apr,86 [Jan,87], $2.95, 181pp, tp) Reissue (Harper & Row 1983) connected group of three juvenile fantasy stories. Published in 1986; missed.

*Broderick, Pat, George R.R. Martin, Neal McPheeters & Doug Moench **Sandkings** Main listing under George R.R. Martin.

Brooke-Rose, Christine **Xorander** (Paladin 0-586-08654-4, Apr,87, £3.95, 211pp, tp) Reprint (Carcanet 1986) literary fantasy novel about a sentient boulder.

Brookins, Dana **Soul-Eater** (Futura 0-7088-3263-6, May,87, £2.50, 308pp, pb) Reprint (US 1985) horror novel. [First U.K. edition]

Brookins, Dana **Soul-Eater** (Macdonald 0-356-14562-X, Sep,87, £11.95, 320pp, hc) Reprint (US 1985) horror novel. [Not seen]

*Brooks, Cuyler W., Jr. & Michael T. Shoemaker, eds. **Guinevere and Lancelot & Others** Main listing under Arthur Machen.

*Brooks, Terry **The Black Unicorn** (Ballantine/Del Rey 0-345-33527-9, Oct,87 [Sep,87], $16.95, 286pp, hc) Fantasy novel, sequel to **Magic Kingdom for Sale--Sold** (which had 15,000 hardcover copies in print and made the *New York Times* Bestseller List).

Brooks, Terry **The Black Unicorn** (Macdonald 0-356-14926-9, Dec,87, £10.95, 352pp, hc) Reprint (Del Rey 1987) fantasy novel. Volume 2 in the "Magic Kingdom" series. [First U.K. edition, not seen]

Brooks, Terry **The Black Unicorn** (Orbit 0-7088-3587-2, Dec,87, £4.95, 286pp, tp) Reprint (Del Rey 1987) fantasy novel. Volume 2 in the "Magic Kingdom" series. [First U.K. edition]

Brooks, Terry **Magic Kingdom for Sale--Sold!** (Ballantine/Del Rey 0-345-31758-0, Apr,87 [Mar,87], $4.50, 373pp, pb) Reprint (Del Rey 1986) fantasy novel, first of a new series.

Brooks, Terry **Magic Kingdom for Sale--Sold!** (Orbit 0-7088-8240-4, Dec,87 [Nov,87], £2.95, 350pp, pb) Reprint (Del Rey 1986) fantasy novel. Volume 1 in the "Magic Kingdom" series.

*Brown, Charles N. & William G. Contento **Science Fiction, Fantasy, & Horror: 1986** (Locus Press 0-9616629-3-X, Sep,87, $35.00, xiii + 347pp, hc) Non-fiction, reference book. Lists all material, both books and shorter fiction, published in English in 1986. Limited to 600 copies.

*Brown, Fredric **And the Gods Laughed** (Phantasia Press 0-932096-47-6, Oct,87 [Sep,87], $19.00, 431pp, hc) Collection of fantasy and sf stories, with an introduction by Richard A. Lupoff. Over 70 stories -- 6 written in collaboration with Mack Reynolds. It contains the complete text of two earlier collections, **Nightmares and Geezenstacks** (1961) and **Honeymoon in Hell** (1958), plus additional stories. There is a signed, limited, boxed 475-copy edition ($50) with bound signed sheets left over from an earlier book.

Brown, Fredric **Martians Go Home** (Grafton 0-586-07164-4, Nov,87, £2.95, 203pp, pb) Reprint (Dutton 1955) hilarious sf novel, available in the UK for the first time. [First U.K. edition]

Brown, Fredric **Pardon My Ghoulish Laughter** (Dennis McMillan 0-9609986-6-7, Oct,87, $5.95, 163pp, tp) Reprint (Dennis McMillan 1986) collection of mystery stories, all involving vampires, voodoo, etc.; but only one is actually sf or fantasy. There is an introduction by Donald E. Westlake.

Brown, Fredric **What Mad Universe** (Grafton 0-586-07163-6, Aug,87 [Jul,87], £2.95, 238pp, pb) Reprint (Dutton 1949) humourous sf novel. [First U.K. edition]

Brown, Mary **The Unlikely Ones** (SFBC #105403, Mar,87, $5.50, 409pp, hc) Reprint (Century Hutchinson 1986) fantasy novel.

Brown, Mary **The Unlikely Ones** (Arrow 0-09-950400-6, May,87, £3.50, 426pp, pb) Reprint (Century 1986) fantasy novel.

Brown, Mary **The Unlikely Ones** (Baen 0-671-65361-X, Nov,87 [Oct,87], $3.95, 426pp, pb) Reprint (Century-Hutchinson 1986) fantasy novel, an inventive new take on familiar motifs. You've never read a "talking animal" book like this one. Recommended. (FCM)

Brown, Rebecca **The Haunted House** (Picador 0-330-29174-2, Apr,87 [Dec,87], £2.95, 139pp, tp) Reprint (Picador 1986) literary occult novel.

Brown, Rosel George & Keith Laumer **Earthblood** Main listing under Keith Laumer.

Browne, Gerald A. **Stone 588** (Chivers Press 0-86220-178-0, Feb,87, £9.95, 640pp, hc) Reprint (Arbor House 1986) thriller with super-natural elements. Large Print edition.

Browne, Gerald A. **Stone 588** (Penguin 0-14-009223-4, Aug,87, £3.50, 496pp, pb) Reprint (Arbor House 1986) thriller with super-natural elements. [Not seen]

Brunner, John **The Compleat Traveller in Black** (Methuen 0-413-14910-2, Apr,87, £2.50, 232pp, pb) Reprint (Bluejay 1986) fantasy collection. [First U.K. edition]

Brunner, John **Interstellar Empire** (Arrow 0-09-938870-7, Aug,87, £2.50, 256pp, pb) Reissue (DAW 1976) sf collection. Volume 4 in the Venture SF series.

Brunner, John **More Things in Heaven** (DAW 0-88677-187-0, Feb,87 [Jan,87], $2.95, 221pp, pb) Reprint (Dell 1973) of a revision of **The Astronauts Must Not Land** (Ace 1963); sf novel.

*Brunner, John **The Shift Key** (Methuen 0-413-14920-X, May,87, £2.50, 227pp, pb) Borderline sf novel.

Brunner, John **Stand on Zanzibar** (Easton Press no ISBN, 1987 [May,87], price unknown, 507pp, hc) Reprint (Doubleday 1968) classic sf novel. Leatherbound "Collector's Edition," part of Easton's "The Masterpieces of Science Fiction", with a new introduction by David Brin and several illustrations (one full-color) by Vincent DiFate. Available by subscription only from The Easton Press; call 1-800-243-5160.

BRUSH, KAREN A.

CALDECOTT, MOYRA

*Brush, Karen A. **The Pig, the Prince & the Unicorn** (Avon 0-380-75062-7, Jun,87 [May,87], $2.95, 216pp, pb) Fantasy novel. With the aid of a prince/bard, a witch, and a moray eel, the pig Quadroped must save the world from the evil Black Unicorn. Something of a satire, but it gets more serious than the scenario suggests.

*Brust, Steven **The Sun, the Moon, and the Stars** (Ace 0-441-08410-9, May,87 [Apr,87], $16.95, 210pp, hc) Fantasy novel, first in a series (by various authors), "Fairy Tales", using classic stories as a jumping-off point for original novels. These are not just retellings of the original stories.

*Bryant, Edward & James P. Blaylock **Trilobyte/The Shadow on the Doorstep** Contents listed under James P. Blaylock.

Budrys, Algis **Rogue Moon** (Gollancz 0-575-03979-5, Apr,87 [May,87], £2.95, 173pp, tp) Reprint (Fawcett 1960) sf novel. Volume 11 of the Gollancz Classic SF series.

Budrys, Algis **Who?** (Popular Library Questar 0-445-20314-5, Feb,87 [Jan,87], $3.50, 212pp, pb) Reprint (Pyramid 1958) sf novel. One of the classics of sf. This political novel of the cold war is still undated and powerful. (CNB)

*Budrys, Algis, ed. **L. Ron Hubbard Presents Writers of the Future, Vol. III** (Bridge 0-88404-245-6, Apr,87, $4.50, 429pp, pb) Original anthology of 14 stories plus essays by Pohl, Benford, Pournelle, and Hubbard. Later releases of the first edition have a sticker on the back cover correcting a typo in the ISBN.

*Bujold, Lois McMaster **Test of Honor** (SFBC #10681, May,87, $7.98, 473pp, hc) Omnibus edition of related sf adventure novels.

Bulgakov, Mikhail **The Master and Margarita** (Grove Press 0-802-13011-9, Sep,87 [Nov,87], $6.95, 402pp, tp) Reprint (Grove Press 1967) satanic/ironic fantasy novel, translated from the Russian by Mirra Ginsburg. This edition has a new biographical introduction by the translator. This is a different translation from the one issued by Harper & Row in 1967 and now available from the Science Fiction Book Club.

*Bull, Emma **War for the Oaks** (Ace 0-441-87073-2, Jul,87 [Jun,87], $3.50, 309pp, pb) Fantasy novel, the first Ace Fantasy Special and a first novel.

*Bull, Emma & Will Shetterly, eds. **Liavek: Wizard's Row** Main listing under Will Shetterly.

*Bulmer, Ken, [ref.] **The Writings of Henry Kenneth Bulmer** Main listing under Roger Robinson.

*Burgess, Anthony **A Clockwork Orange** (Hutchinson 0-09-168381-5, Feb,87, £5.95, 64pp, tp) Adaptation of the classic sf novel as a play with music (both by Burgess). [Not seen]

Burgess, Anthony **The Eve of Saint Venus** (Arena 0-09-941680-8, Sep,87, £2.95, 125pp, tp) Reprint (Sidgwick & Jackson 1964) literary fantasy novel.

*Burgess, Mason **Graveyard** (Leisure 0-8439-2534-5, Oct,87, $3.75, 320pp, pb) Horror novel. A one-time wimp returns from the grave to get revenge.

*Burkholz, Herbert **The Sensitives** (Atheneum 0-689-11842-2, Jul,87 [Aug,87], $18.95, 278pp, hc) Thriller about telepathic espionage agents.

Burnett, Frances Hodgson **The Secret Garden** (Windrush 1-85089-908-8, 1987 [Oct,87], $12.95, 331pp, hc) Reprint (Heinemann 1911) juvenile fantasy novel, large print edition. U.S. distribution of British edition from Oxford Windrush.

+ Burroughs, William S. **The Adding Machine: Collected Essays** (Seaver 0-7145-4073-0, Jul,86 [Jan,87], $16.95, 205pp, hc) Reprint (UK 1985) collection of essays including autobiography, literary criticism, and "far-out fantasy." Published in 1986; missed.

Burroughs, William S. **The Place of Dead Roads** (Paladin 0-586-08592-0, Apr,87, £3.95, 268pp, tp) Reprint (John Calder 1983) of associational interest: Burroughs' foray into the Western.

Burroughs, William S. **The Ticket That Exploded** (Paladin 0-586-08591-2, Jan,87, £3.50, 159pp, pb) Reprint (Grove Press 1967) literary novel with sf elements.

Busby, F.M. **The Demu Trilogy** (Pocket 0-671-53229-4, Jan,87, $3.95, 522pp, pb) Reissue (Pocket 1980) omnibus of sf novels **Cage a Man** (1973), **The Proud Enemy** (1975), and **End of the Line** (1980), plus a short story.

*Busby, F.M. **Getting Home** (Ace 0-441-28267-9, Aug,87 [Jul,87], $2.95, 195pp, pb) Collection of 20 stories.

*Busby, F.M. **The Rebel Dynasty, Volume I** (Bantam Spectra 0-553-26954-2, Dec,87 [Nov,87], $4.95, 443pp, pb) Omnibus of two space opera novels, **Star Rebel** (Bantam 1984) and **Rebel's Quest** (Bantam 1984), in the "Holzein Dynasty" series. Busby writes some of the best modern space opera. Recommended. (CNB)

*Busby, F.M. **The Rebel Dynasty, Volume II** (Bantam Spectra 0-553-26988-7, Jan,88 [Dec,87], $4.95, 475pp, pb) Omnibus edition of **The Alien Debt** (Bantam 1984) and **Rebel's Seed** (Bantam 1986), two parts of the "Holzein Dynasty" space opera series.

Busby, F.M. **Rebel's Quest** (Orbit 0-7088-3578-3, Nov,87, £2.50, 243pp, pb) Reprint (Bantam 1985) sf novel. Volume 2 in the "Hulzein" series. [First U.K. edition]

Busby, F.M. **Star Rebel** (Orbit 0-7088-8236-6, Aug,87, £2.50, 216pp, pb) Reprint (Bantam 1984) sf novel. Volume 1 in the "Hulzein" series. [First U.K. edition]

*Bussing, Sabine **Aliens in the Home: The Child in Horror Fiction** (Greenwood 0-313-25420-6, Mar,87 [May,87], $32.95, xxi + 203pp, hc) Non-fiction, critical study; there's an appendix on horror films. "Contributions to the Study of Childhood and Youth, No. 4."

Bussing, Sabine **Aliens in the Home: The Child in Horror Fiction** (Greenwood 0-313-25426-5, May,87 [Jun,87], £31.95, 232pp, hc) Associational non-fiction study. [First U.K. edition, not seen]

*Butler, Octavia E. **Dawn** (Warner 0-446-51363-6, May,87 [Apr,87], $15.95, 264pp, hc) Sf novel of the far future.

Butler, Octavia E. **Dawn** (Gollancz 0-575-04190-0, Oct,87, £11.95, 272pp, hc) Reprint (Warner 1987) sf novel. Volume 1 in the "Xenogenesis" trilogy. [First U.K. edition, not seen]

*Butler, Octavia E., [ref.] **Suzy McKee Charnas, Joan Vinge, Octavia Butler** Main listing under Marleen S. Barr.

Buzzati, Dino **Restless Nights: Selected Stories of Dino Buzzati** (Carcanet 0-85635-684-0, Feb,87, £4.95, 180pp, tp) Reprint (North Point Press 1984) collection including some sf. [Not seen]

*Byatt, Antonia **Sugar and Other Stories** (Scribner's 0-684-18786-8, Jul,87 [Aug,87], $16.95, 248pp, hc) Collection of stories, some of which deal with ghosts and the afterlife.

*Cadigan, Pat **Mindplayers** (Bantam Spectra 0-553-26585-7, Aug,87 [Jul,87], $3.50, 276pp, pb) Sf novel on the border of cyberpunk (mostly cyber without the punk). A first novel about mind and technology. Recommended. (CNB)

*Caidin, Martin **Exit Earth** (Baen 0-671-65630-9, Apr,87 [Mar,87], $4.50, 638pp, pb) Sf near-future disaster novel. The cover says, "Soon to be a Major Motion Picture."

*Caldecott, Moyra **Etheldreda** (Arkana 1-85063-070-4, Sep,87, £4.95, 215pp, tp) Historical novel with fantasy elements. Distributed in the U.S. by Methuen at $8.95.

Caldecott, Moyra **Guardians of the Tall Stones** (Arrow 0-09-942810-5, May,87, £3.50, 630pp, tp) Reissue (Arrow 1986) fantasy omnibus.

*Caldecott, Moyra **The Silver Vortex** (Arrow 0-09-943840-2, May,87, £3.50, 281pp, tp) Fantasy novel. A sequel to **Guardians of the Tall Stones**.

CALLIN, GRANT D.   **CARR, TERRY**

*Callin, Grant D. **A Lion on Tharthee** (Baen 0-671-65357-1, Oct,87 [Sep,87], $3.50, 342pp, pb) Sf novel, sequel to **Saturnalia**.

Calvino, Italo **Castle of Crossed Destinies** (Picador 0-330-25586-X, May,87, £3.50, 122pp, tp) Reissue (Secker & Warburg 1977) literary fantasy collection.

Calvino, Italo **Cosmicomics** (Abacus 0-349-10484-0, Nov,87 [Dec,87], £3.50, 153pp, tp) Reissue (Harcourt, Brace & World 1968) literary fantasy collection.

Calvino, Italo **Time and the Hunter** (Abacus 0-349-10485-9, Nov,87 [Dec,87], £3.50, 152pp, tp) Reissue (Harcourt, Brace & World 1969) literary fantasy collection.

*Campbell, Hope **Looking for Hamlet** (Macmillan 0-02-716400-4, Oct,87, $14.95, 238pp, hc) Young-adult ghost story/romance/detective, subtitled "A Haunting at Deeping Lake".

Campbell, Ramsey **Cold Print** (Grafton 0-586-06364-1, Jun,87, £2.95, 365pp, pb) Reprint (Scream/Press 1985) collection of horror stories related to the Cthulhu Mythos. [First U.K. edition]

*Campbell, Ramsey **Cold Print** (Tor 0-812-51661-3, Nov,87 [Oct,87], $4.50, 331pp, pb) Horror collection. This is an expanded version (adds 3 stories) of the 1985 Scream/Press edition. It drops the J.K. Potter illustrations.

*Campbell, Ramsey **Dark Feasts** (Robinson 0-948164-47-6, Sep,87 [Aug,87], £9.95, 339pp, hc) Horror collection.

*Campbell, Ramsey **Dark Feasts** (Robinson 0-948164-37-9, Sep,87, £3.95, 339pp, tp) Trade paperback edition of the above.

Campbell, Ramsey **The Doll Who Ate His Mother** (Arrow 0-09-953300-6, Oct,87 [Sep,87], £2.95, 284pp, pb) Reprint (Bobbs-Merrill 1976) horror novel. [First U.K. edition]

Campbell, Ramsey **The Doll Who Ate His Mother** (Century 0-7126-1156-8, Dec,87, £10.95, 284pp, hc) Reprint (Bobbs-Merril 1976) horror novel.

Campbell, Ramsey **The Hungry Moon** (Century 0-7126-1441-9, Jan,87 [Jun,87], £9.95, 293pp, hc) Reprint (Macmillan 1986) horror novel.

Campbell, Ramsey **The Hungry Moon** (Tor 0-812-51662-1, Jun,87 [May,87], $4.50, 360pp, pb) Reprint (Macmillan 1986) horror novel.

Campbell, Ramsey **The Hungry Moon** (Arrow 0-09-949190-7, Oct,87, £2.95, 428pp, pb) Reprint (Macmillan 1986) horror novel.

*Campbell, Ramsey **Scared Stiff: Tales of Sex and Death** (Scream/Press 0-910489-17-3, Jul,87 [Jun,87], $25.00, 173pp, hc) Collection of Campbell's most outrageous "adult horror" stories (two original), illustrated by J.K. Potter. A boxed, signed edition of 250 copies was announced, but not seen.

*Campton, David & Mary W. Shelley **Frankenstein** (Beaver 0-09-949770-0, Oct,87, £1.75, 143pp, pb) Juvenile horror novel. Volume 5 in the Fleshcreepers series.

*Campton, David & Mary W. Shelley **Frankenstein** (Hutchinson 0-09-173483-5, Oct,87, £5.95, 144pp, hc) Hardcover edition of the above. [Not seen]

*Cantrell, Lisa W. **The Manse** (Tor 0-812-51674-5, Nov,87 [Oct,87], $3.95, 341pp, pb) Horror novel of evil on Halloween.

*Caraker, Mary **Water Song** (Popular Library Questar 0-445-20512-1, Sep,87 [Aug,87], $2.95, 214pp, pb) Sf novel of a water planet threatened by a changing climate.

*Card, Orson Scott **Cardography** (Hypatia Press 0-940-84102-9, Mar,87, $17.95, 183pp, hc) Collection of 5 fantasy stories plus an introduction by David Hartwell plus a new afterword (and maps) by Card. Limited to 750 + 194 + 56 copies in various limited, signed states.

Card, Orson Scott **Ender's Game** (Arrow 0-09-949610-0, Feb,87, £2.95, 357pp, pb) Reissue (Tor 1985) Hugo and Nebula Award winning sf novel.

*Card, Orson Scott **Red Prophet** (Tor 0-312-93043-7, Jan,88 [Dec,87], $17.95, 311pp, hc) Fantasy novel set in an alternate historical America, Book 2 in the "Tales of Alvin Maker".

*Card, Orson Scott **Seventh Son** (Tor 0-312-93019-4, Jul,87 [Jun,87], $17.95, 241pp, hc) Fantasy novel set in an alternate 19th-century America, "The Tales of Alvin Maker", Book 1. Recommended. (FCM)

Card, Orson Scott **Songmaster** (Tor 0-812-53255-4, Oct,87 [Sep,87], $3.95, 377pp, pb) Reprint (Dial 1980) sf novel. This edition has a 1987 copyright in addition to earlier ones, which might or might not indicate some rewriting.

Card, Orson Scott **Speaker for the Dead** (Tor 0-812-53257-0, Feb,87 [Jan,87], $3.95, 415pp, pb) Reprint (Tor 1986) sf novel, sequel to **Ender's Game**. Nebula award winner.

Card, Orson Scott **Speaker for the Dead** (Arrow 0-09-950320-4, Feb,87, £2.95, 415pp, pb) Reprint (Tor 1986) sf novel. Sequel to **Ender's Game**. This year's Hugo & Nebula Award winner. [First U.K. edition]

Card, Orson Scott **Speaker for the Dead** (Century 0-7126-1516-4, May,87 [Sep,87], £10.95, 415pp, hc) Reprint (Tor 1986) sf novel. Sequel to **Ender's Game**. This year's Hugo & Nebula Award winner.

*Card, Orson Scott **Wyrms** (Arbor House 0-87795-894-7, Jul,87 [Jun,87], $16.95, 263pp, hc) Sf novel, a grotesque fable of a planet with regressed politics and mutated flora and fauna.

Card, Orson Scott **Wyrms** (SFBC #11344, Oct,87, $4.98, 246pp, hc) Reprint (Arbor House 1987) sf novel.

*Carey, Diane **Star Trek: Final Frontier** (Pocket 0-671-64752-0, Jan,88 [Dec,87], $4.50, 435pp, pb) A Star Trek novel not in the numbered series, third "Giant" Star Trek novel. Tells the "real" first voyage of the *Enterprise* under the command of Capt. Robert April and First Officer George Kirk.

*Carl, Lillian Stewart **Shadow Dancers** (Ace 0-441-75988-2, Nov,87 [Oct,87], $2.95, 283pp, pb) Fantasy novel, third in the "Sabazel" series.

*Carlisle, Anne **Liquid Sky** (Doubleday 0-385-23930-0, Nov,87 [Oct,87], $8.95, 186pp, tp) Novelization of the very strange cult sf movie, by the co-writer and co-star (in the two leading roles) of the original script.

*Carlock, Lynn **First Love From Silhouette #176: Daughter of the Moon** (Silhouette 0-373-06176-5, Feb,86 [Feb,87], $1.95, 155pp, pb) Romance/fantasy novel. Psychic teen must come to terms with her heritage and powers, and her new love for an "ordinary" boy. Published last year, but just seen.

Carpenter, Christopher **The Twilight Realm** (Berkley Pacer 0-425-09574-6, Mar,87 [Feb,87], $2.50, 237pp, pb) Reprint (UK 1985) young-adult fantasy novel of a role-playing game turned real.

Carpenter, Leonard **Conan the Raider** (Tor 0-812-54262-2, Sep,87 [Aug,87], $3.50, 276pp, pb) Reprint (Tor 1986) heroic fantasy novel, based on the Robert E. Howard character.

Carr, John Dickson **The Devil in Velvet** (Carroll & Graf 0-88184-328-8, Aug,87 [Jul,87], $3.95, pb) Reprint (Harper & Row 1957) historical fantasy/time travel novel. A modern man makes a pact with the devil and becomes his own ancestor in 1675, in order to solve a murder. Brilliant novel of the Restoration, plus some excellent changes on the deal with the devil story. Recommended. (CNB)

Carr, John Dickson **Fire, Burn!** (Carroll & Graf 0-88184-336-9, Sep,87 [Aug,87], $3.50, pb) Reprint (Harper & Row 1957) classic time travel fantasy/mystery novel set in 1829.

Carr, Terry **Cirque** (Doubleday 0-385-13140-2, Sep,87, $12.95, 180pp, hc) Reprint (Bobbs Merrill 1977) sf novel.

CARR, TERRY, ED.　　　　　　　　　　　　　　　　　　**CHALKER, JACK L.**

Carr, Terry, ed. **Best SF of the Year 16** (Gollancz 0-575-04085-8, Dec,87, £3.95, 388pp, tp) Reprint (Tor 1987, as **Terry Carr's Best Science Fiction and Fantasy of the Year #16**) SF/fantasy anthology. This edition omits the summary of the sf year by *Locus* editor Charles N. Brown. [First U.K. edition]

Carr, Terry, ed. **Science Fiction Hall of Fame, Vol. 4** (SFBC #11628, Dec,87, $6.98, 462pp, hc) Reprint (Avon 1986) anthology of the Nebula Award winners, 1970-1974.

*Carr, Terry, ed. **Terry Carr's Best Science Fiction and Fantasy of the Year #16** (Tor 0-312-93025-9, Sep,87 [Aug,87], $17.95, 402pp, hc) Anthology of 11 stories, plus a summary of the sf year by *Locus* editor Charles N. Brown.

Carr, Terry, ed. **Universe 15** (Tor 0-812-53265-1, Dec,87 [Nov,87], $3.50, 244pp, pb) Reprint (Doubleday 1985) original anthology of 10 sf stories.

*Carr, Terry, ed. **Universe 17** (Doubleday 0-385-23853-3, Jun,87 [May,87], $12.95, 180pp, hc) Original anthology of 6 stories, by Tiptree, McDevitt, Randall, and others. The last of the **Universes**.

*Carroll, Jonathan **Bones of the Moon** (Century 0-7126-1504-0, May,87 [Aug,87], £9.95, 216pp, hc) Sf/fantasy novel.

Carroll, Jonathan **Bones of the Moon** (Arrow 0-09-949870-7, Nov,87, £2.50, 217pp, pb) Reprint (Century 1987) sf/fantasy novel.

+Carroll, Jonathan **Bones of the Moon** (Arbor House/Morrow 0-87795-937-4, Jan,88 [Dec,87], $15.95, 217pp, hc) Fantasy novel about a dream world which becomes real. First American edition (Century 1987). Recommended. (FCM)

Carroll, Jonathan **The Land of Laughs** (Arrow 0-09-939260-7, Nov,87, £2.50, 241pp, pb) Reissue (Viking 1980) fantasy novel.

Carroll, Lewis **Alice in Wonderland** (Longman 0-582-52278-1, Apr,87 [Jun,87], £1.25, 64pp, pb) Reprint of a classic juvenile fantasy novel. Abridged by D.K. Swan. [Not seen]

Carroll, Lewis **Alice's Adventures in Wonderland** (Simon & Schuster 0-671-63565-4, Sep,87 [Jul,87], $14.95, 158pp, hc) New edition, illustrated by David Hall, with an afterword by Brian Sibley.

*Carroll, Lewis **The Complete Alice and The Hunting of the Snark** (Salem House 0-88162-228-1, Apr,87 [Mar,87], $24.95, 344pp, hc) Omnibus art book. Although the text is not new, the interest here is in the profuse illustrations by Ralph Steadman. The 8.5" x 11" size helps too. The three illustrated volumes have appeared separately: **Alice in Wonderland** (1967), **Through the Looking Glass** (1972), and **The Hunting of the Snark** (1978).

Carroll, Lewis **Complete Illustrated Works** (Crown 0-517-38566-X, Apr,87 [1987], £7.95, 869pp, hc) Reprint juvenile fantasy collection. Edited by Edward Guiliamo. [Not seen]

Carter, Angela **The Bloody Chamber** (Penguin 0-14-005404-9, Dec,87, $5.95, 126pp, tp) Reprint (Gollancz 1979) collection of 10 re-takes on fairytales. One of Carter's best. Recommended. (FCM)

Carter, Angela **Fireworks** (Chatto 0-7011-3215-9, Apr,87 [May,87], £10.95, 120pp, hc) Reprint (Quartet 1974) collection of stories with fantasy elements. This is a 'revised' edition.

Carter, Angela **Fireworks: Nine Profane Pieces** (Penguin 0-14-010588-3, Dec,87, $5.95, 133pp, tp) Reprint (Quartet Books 1974) collection of 10 stories.

Carter, Angela **Saints and Strangers** (Penguin 0-14-778215-5, Dec,87, $5.95, 126pp, tp) Reprint (Chatto & Windus 1985 as **Black Venus**) collection of 8 stories. The text follows the slightly revised 1986 Viking edition, also published as **Saints and Strangers**. Some fantasy, all darkly witty tales. Recommended. (FCM)

*Carter, Bruce **Nightworld** (Century 0-7126-1660-8, Jul,87 [Aug,87], £11.95, 354pp, hc) Animal fantasy novel.

Carter, Carmen **Dreams of the Raven** (Titan 0-907610-93-5, Jul,87, £2.95, 255pp, pb) Reprint (Pocket 1987) sf novel. Volume 34 in the Star Trek Novels series. Includes an extract from Margaret Bonanno's **Stranger From the Sky**. [First U.K. edition]

*Carter, Carmen **Star Trek #34: Dreams of the Raven** (Pocket 0-671-64500-5, Jun,87 [May,87], $3.50, 255pp, pb) Star Trek novel.

*Carter, Lin **Horror Wears Blue** (Doubleday 0-385-12504-6, Nov,87 [Oct,87], $12.95, 174pp, hc) Pulpish sf/crime novel in the "Zarkon" series; Carter's version of Doc Savage.

Carter, Lin & L. Sprague de Camp **Conan the Liberator** Main listing under L. Sprague de Camp.

Carter, Lin & L. Sprague de Camp **Conan the Liberator** Main listing under L. Sprague de Camp.

Carter, Lin, L. Sprague de Camp & Robert E. Howard **Conan of Cimmeria** For main entry see under Robert E. Howard.

Carter, Lin, L. Sprague de Camp, Robert E. Howard & Bjorn Nyberg **Conan the Swordsman** Main listing under Robert E. Howard.

*Carter, Margaret L. **Specter or Delusion? The Supernatural in Gothic Fiction** (UMI 0-8357-1822-0, Aug,87 [Jul,87], price unknown, 131pp, hc) Literary criticism, written in straight academic style.

*Carver, Jeffrey A. **The Rapture Effect** (Tor 0-312-94381-4, Feb,87, $18.95, 371pp, hc) Sf novel.

Carver, Jeffrey A. **The Rapture Effect** (SFBC #10613, May,87, $4.98, 310pp, hc) Reprint (Tor 1987) sf novel.

*Carver, Jeffrey A. **Roger Zelazny's Alien Speedway 1: Clypsis** (Bantam Spectra 0-553-26536-9, Oct,87 [Sep,87], $3.50, 163pp, pb) Sf novel based on a concept by Zelazny, first in a series. It includes racing ship designs drawn by Hayashi. A Byron Preiss Productions packaged book.

*Cassutt, Michael **Who's Who in Space: The First 25 Years** (G.K. Hall 0-8161-8801-7, Apr,87, $35.00, 310pp, hc) Non-fiction, associational. Biographies and photos of astronauts, cosmonauts, and "international space travelers," by space buff/sf writer Cassutt.

*Catley, Melanie **Candlelight Ecstasy Supreme #125: Moonlight & Magic** (Dell 0-440-15822-2, Jun,86 [Feb,87], $2.75, 283pp, pb) Romance/fantasy novel. A contemporary witch faces a choice between her magic and the man she loves. Published last year, but not seen until now.

*Cerasini, Marc A. & Charles Hoffman **Robert E. Howard** (Starmont House 0-930261-27-5, Apr,87, $9.95, 156pp, tp) Non-fiction, critical survey. "Starmont Reader's Guide #35".

Chalker, Jack L. **A Jungle of Stars** (Ballantine/Del Rey 0-345-33958-4, Feb,87 [Jan,87], $2.95, 217pp, pb) Reissue (Del Rey 1976) sf novel; 6th printing.

*Chalker, Jack L. **The Labyrinth of Dreams** (Tor 0-812-53306-2, Mar,87 [Feb,87], $3.50, 320pp, pb) Sf detective novel, "G.O.D. Inc" No. 1.

*Chalker, Jack L. **Pirates of the Thunder** (Ballantine/Del Rey 0-345-32561-3, Mar,87 [Feb,87], $3.50, 307pp, pb) Sf novel, Book Two of "The Rings of the Master".

*Chalker, Jack L. **The Shadow Dancers** (Tor 0-812-53308-9, Jul,87 [Jun,87], $3.95, 284pp, pb) Sf novel, "G.O.D. Inc." #2.

*Chalker, Jack L. **Warriors of the Storm** (Ballantine/Del Rey 0-345-32562-1, Aug,87 [Jul,87], $3.95, 338pp, pb) Book 3 in "The Rings of the Master", an sf adventure series.

Chalker, Jack L. **The Web of the Chozen** (Ballantine/Del Rey 0-345-33959-2, Feb,87 [Jan,87], $2.95, 210pp, pb) Reissue (Del Rey 1978) sf novel; 5th printing.

CHALKER, JACK L.

CHESBRO, GEORGE C.

*Chalker, Jack L. **When the Changewinds Blow** (Ace 0-441-88081-9, Sep,87 [Aug,87], $3.50, 293pp, pb) Fantasy novel, first in the "Changewinds" series.

Chambers, Aidan, ed. **Ghost After Ghost** (Puffin 0-14-031461-X, Dec,87, £1.95, 173pp, pb) Reissue (Kestrel 1982) original juvenile ghost anthology.

*Chambers, Aidan, ed. **A Quiver Of Ghosts** (Bodley Head 0-370-31008-X, Mar,87 [Sep,87], £3.95, 137pp, tp) Original juvenile ghost anthology.

Chant, Joy **The High Kings** (Unwin 0-04-823389-7, Jul,87, £3.50, 197pp, tp) Reprint (Bantam 1983) non-fiction study of the Arthurian legends. This edition omits the illustrations.

*Chapman, Vera **Miranty and the Alchemist** (Marilyn Malin 0-233-98042-3, Jun,87, £5.50, 112pp, hc) Fantasy novel? [Not seen]

*Charles, Steven **Private School #6: The Last Alien** (Pocket 0-671-60331-0, Feb,87 [Jan,87], $2.50, 137pp, pb) Latest in a young-adult sf series about alien invaders (and supposedly the conclusion); this one features a werewolf. A Byron Preiss Visual Production.

Charnas, Suzy McKee **The Bronze King** (Bantam Skylark 0-553-15493-1, Apr,87 [Mar,87], $2.95, 189pp, pb) Reprint (Houghton Mifflin 1985) young adult fantasy novel.

*Charnas, Suzy McKee, [ref.] **Suzy McKee Charnas, Joan Vinge, Octavia Butler** Main listing under Marleen S. Barr.

Cheetham, Ann **The Beggar's Curse** (Dell/Laurel Leaf 0-440-91024-2, Mar,87 [May,87], $2.50, 192pp, pb) Reprint (Fontana 1984) young-adult horror novel, in the "Dark Powers" series.

Cheetham, Ann **Black Harvest** (Dell/Laurel Leaf 0-440-91039-0, Jan,87 [May,87], $2.50, 143pp, pb) Reprint (Fontana 1983) young-adult horror novel in the "Dark Powers" series.

*Cheetham, Ann **The Pit** (Armada 0-00-692531-6, Jun,87, £1.95, 154pp, pb) Juvenile horror novel.

Cheetham, Ann **The Witch of Lagg** (Dell/Laurel Leaf 0-440-99412-8, May,87, $2.50, 160pp, pb) Reprint (Fontana 1985) young-adult horror novel in the "Dark Powers" series.

Cherryh, C.J. **Angel With the Sword** (Gollancz 0-575-04009-2, May,87, £2.95, 302pp, pb) Reprint (DAW 1985) sf novel. [First U.K. edition]

Cherryh, C.J. **Chanur's Homecoming** (SFBC #10580, Feb,87, $4.98, 349pp, hc) Reprint (Phantasia 1986) sf novel, conclusion of the "Chanur" series.

Cherryh, C.J. **Cuckoo's Egg** (Methuen 0-413-40370-X, Feb,87 [Jan,87], £2.50, 319pp, pb) Reprint (Phantasia 1985) sf novel. [First U.K. edition]

Cherryh, C.J. **Downbelow Station** (DAW 0-88677-227-3, Oct,87 [Sep,87], $3.95, 432pp, pb) Reissue (DAW 1981) Hugo-winning sf novel; 7th printing.

Cherryh, C.J. **The Dreamstone** (DAW 0-88677-013-0, Oct,87 [Sep,87], $2.95, 285pp, pb) Reissue (DAW 1983) fantasy novel; 5th printing.

Cherryh, C.J. **The Dreamstone** (Gollancz 0-575-04044-0, Oct,87, £2.50, 192pp, pb) Reprint (DAW 1983) fantasy novel. Volume 1 in the "Arafel's Saga" series. [First U.K. edition]

*Cherryh, C.J. **Exile's Gate** (DAW 0-88677-254-0, Jan,88 [Dec,87], $3.95, 414pp, pb) Sf/fantasy novel, Book IV in the "Gate of Ivrel" series.

*Cherryh, C.J. **The Faded Sun Trilogy** (Methuen 0-413-14310-4, Apr,87, £3.95, 756pp, pb) Omnibus of three sf novels.

Cherryh, C.J. **Fires of Azeroth** (DAW 0-88677-259-1, Jan,88 [Dec,87], $3.50, 236pp, pb) Reissue (DAW 1979) science fantasy novel, Book III in the "Morgaine" series.

Cherryh, C.J. **Gate of Ivrel** (DAW 0-88677-257-5, Jan,88 [Dec,87], $3.50, 191pp, pb) Reissue (DAW 1976) science fantasy novel in the Andre Norton tradition. This was Cherryh's first published novel. Tenth printing.

*Cherryh, C.J. **Glass and Amber** (NESFA 0-915368-34-X, Feb,87, 212pp, hc) Collection of minor stories and articles, some original. Issued to commemorate Cherryh's appearance as Boskone 24 Guest of Honor. Limited to 1,000 copies, of which the first 225 are signed and boxed (and sold out at the con -- ISBN -89-7). The regular post-con list price has apparently not been set yet.

Cherryh, C.J. **Hestia** (DAW 0-88677-208-7, May,87 [Apr,87], $2.95, 160pp, pb) Reissue (DAW 1979) sf novel; 6th printing.

Cherryh, C.J. **Hunter of Worlds** (DAW 0-88677-217-6, May,87 [Apr,87], $2.95, 254pp, pb) Reissue (DAW 1977) sf novel; 5th printing.

*Cherryh, C.J. **Legions of Hell** (Baen 0-671-65653-8, Jul,87 [Jun,87], $3.95, 407pp, pb) Fantasy novel in the "Heroes in Hell" shared world series. Portions of this book previously appeared as short stories.

Cherryh, C.J. **Port Eternity** (DAW 0-88677-206-0, May,87 [Apr,87], $2.95, 191pp, pb) Reissue (DAW 1982) sf novel; 3rd printing.

Cherryh, C.J. **The Pride of Chanur** (Phantasia Press 0-932096-45-X, Mar,87, $17.00, 207pp, hc) Reprint (DAW 1982) sf novel. First trade hardcover of the first in the tetralogy. Phantasia now has matching editions available of the set. This edition is limited to 1200 copies, with the first 350 specially bound, signed, and boxed ($40.00). This edition has a corrected text and a new introduction.

Cherryh, C.J. **The Tree of Swords and Jewels** (DAW 0-87997-850-3, Oct,87 [Sep,87], $2.95, 254pp, pb) Reissue (DAW 1983) fantasy novel; 5th printing.

Cherryh, C.J. **Well of Shiuan** (DAW 0-88677-258-3, Jan,88 [Dec,87], $3.50, 253pp, pb) Reissue (DAW 1973) science fantasy novel, Book II in the "Morgaine" series.

*Cherryh, C.J. & Janet Morris **Kings in Hell** (Baen 0-671-65614-7, Feb,87 [Jan,87], $3.95, 377pp, pb) Fantasy novel in the "Heroes in Hell" series. Alexander, Caesar, Cleopatra, and others refight the Trojan War.

*Cherryh, C.J., ed. **Fever Season: Merovingen Nights #2** (DAW 0-88677-224-9, Oct,87 [Sep,87], $3.50, 297pp, pb) Shared world original anthology, second in the series. C.J. Cherryh writes all the connections between the stories, weaving them into a quasi-novel.

*Cherryh, C.J., ed. **Merovingen Nights: Festival Moon** (DAW 0-88677-192-7, Apr,87 [Mar,87], $3.50, 300pp, pb) Shared-world sf original anthology based on the background of Cherryh's **Angel With the Sword**.

Chesbro, George C. **The Beasts of Valhalla** (Dell 0-440-10484-X, Nov,87 [Oct,87], $3.95, 327pp, pb) Reprint (Atheneum 1985) sf/mystery novel in the "Mongo" series, with our dwarf detective thrown into a manufactured **Lord of the Rings**.

Chesbro, George C. **The Golden Child** (Futura 0-7088-3269-5, Jan,87, £2.50, 205pp, pb) Reprint (Pocket 1986) novelization of film with fantasy elements. [First U.K. edition]

Chesbro, George C. **The Golden Child** (Severn House 0-7278-1447-8, Apr,87, £8.95, 208pp, hc) Reprint (Pocket 1986) novelization of fantasy film. [Not seen]

Chesbro, George C. **Shadow of a Broken Man** (Dell 0-440-17761-8, Dec,87 [Nov,87], $3.50, 252pp, pb) Reprint (Simon & Schuster 1977) mystery novel with fantasy elements; first in the "Mongo the Dwarf" series.

Chesbro, George C. **Veil** (Mysterious Press 0-445-40523-6, Sep,87 [Aug,87], $3.95, 228pp, pb) Reprint (Mysterious Press 1986) mystery novel of a parapsychic spy.

CHESTER, MICHAEL

CLARKE, ARTHUR C.

*Chester, Michael **The Shores of the Near Past** (School Street Press 0-939105-50-0, 1986 [Feb,87], 181pp, hc) Young-adult sf time travel novel. This appeared in 1986, but we did not see it until 1987.

Chesterton, G.K. **The Essential G.K. Chesterton** (Oxford Univ. Press 0-19-282056-7, May,87, £5.95, 489pp, tp) Reprint (Bodley Head 1985) collection of stories including some fantasy, edited by P.J. Kavanagh.

Chesterton, G.K. **The Man Who Was Thursday** (Dover 0-486-25121-7, Jun,86 [Jan,87], $4.95, 120pp, tp) Reprint (Dodd, Mead 1908) fantasy novel. Published in 1986; missed.

Chesterton, G.K. **The Man Who Was Thursday** (Lythway Large Print 0-7451-0603-X, Oct,87 [Dec,87], £8.95, 286pp, hc) Reprint (Dodd, Mead 1908) fantasy novel.

Chetwin, Grace **Out of the Dark World** (NAL/Signet 0-451-15148-8, Jan,88 [Dec,87], $2.50, 154pp, pb) Reprint (Lothrop, Lee & Shepard 1985) juvenile fantasy novel.

*Chetwin, Grace **The Riddle and the Rune** (Macmillan Bradbury 0-02-718312-2, Sep,87 [Oct,87], $13.95, 257pp, hc) Young adult fantasy quest novel, first in a new trilogy featuring Gom, a boy with a strange destiny and the hero of **Gom on Windy Mountain**, a prequel to the trilogy.

*Chetwynd-Hayes, R. **Dracula's Children** (Kimber 0-7183-0649-X, May,87, £8.95, 208pp, hc) Original collection of vampire stories.

*Chetwynd-Hayes, R. **The House of Dracula** (Kimber 0-7183-0668-6, Oct,87, £9.50, 206pp, hc) Original horror collection.

*Child, Lincoln, ed. **Tales of the Dark** (St. Martin's 0-312-90339-1, Jul,87 [Jun,87], $3.50, 184pp, pb) Anthology of 10 horror stories.

*Child, Lincoln, ed. **Tales of the Dark 2** (St. Martin's 0-312-90769-9, Sep,87 [Aug,87], $3.50, 181pp, pb) Anthology of 9 late-19th and early-20th-century supernatural stories.

*Childer, Simon Ian **Worm** (Grafton 0-586-06945-3, May,87, £2.50, 189pp, pb) Horror novel. This is a pseudonym for John Brosnan & Leroy Kettle.

*Choyce, Lesley **The Dream Auditor** (Ragweed Press/Indivisible Books 0-920304-63-X, 1986 [Feb,87], C$9.95, 87pp, tp) Very short story collection of 10 sf stories, 6 of them original. This small press edition has a 1986 copyright date, but we did not see it until now.

*Christopher, Joe R. **C.S. Lewis** (G.K. Hall/Twayne 0-8057-6944-7, Apr,87, $16.95, 150pp, hc) Non-fiction, critical study which concentrates on the fantasy novels.

Christopher, John **City of Gold and Lead** (Puffin 0-14-031685-X, Mar,87, £1.75, 159pp, pb) Reissue (Hamish Hamilton 1967) juvenile sf novel. Volume 2 in the "Tripods" series. This is a pseudonym for C.S. Youd.

Christopher, John **The White Mountains** (Puffin 0-14-031684-1, Mar,87, £1.75, 155pp, pb) Reissue (Hamish Hamilton 1967) juvenile sf novel. Volume 1 in the "Tripods" series. This is a pseudonym for C.S. Youd.

*Christopher, Paul **Beyond that River** (Pal Books 3-925942-00-9, Nov,87 [Dec,87], £4.95, 288pp, pb) Original horror collection.

*Christopher, Paul **Galactic Chronicles** (Pal Books 3-925942-5, Nov,87, £2.50, 128pp, pb) Sf novel. [Not seen]

*Chronister, Alan B. **Cry Wolf** (Zebra 0-8217-2094-5, Jun,87 [May,87], $3.95, 320pp, pb) Horror novel.

*Citro, Joseph **Shadow Child** (Zebra 0-8217-2117-8, Jul,87 [Jun,87], $3.95, 366pp, pb) Horror novel.

Clancy, Tom **Red Storm Rising** (Collins 0-00-223078-X, Jan,87, £10.95, 652pp, hc) Near future thriller about war with Russia. [First U.K. edition]

*Claremont, Chris **FirstFlight** (Ace 0-441-23584-0, Dec,87 [Nov,87], $2.95, 243pp, pb) Sf space opera novel, a first novel by a famed comic writer.

*Claremont, Chris, et al **The Uncanny X-Men** (Marvel Comics 0-939766-96-5, 1987 [Nov,87], $6.95, 185pp, tp) Graphic novel made up of issues #129-137 of the comic book series, with full-color illustrations.

*Clareson, Thomas D. **Frederik Pohl** (Starmont House 0-930261-33-X, Nov,87 [Oct,87], $9.95, 173pp, tp) Non-fiction, critical study.

+Clark, Joan **Wild Man of the Woods** (Viking Kestrel 0-670-80015-5, May,86 [Feb,87], $11.95, 171pp, hc) Young-adult fantasy novel of Indian masks that give a boy the spirits' powers. This appeared in 1986, but we did not see it until now. It's the first U.S. edition of a 1985 release from Penguin-Canada.

Clark, Mary Higgins **The Cradle will Fall** (Fontana 0-00-617086-2, Sep,87, £2.95, 286pp, pb) Reissue (Collins 1980) horror novel.

Clark, Mary Higgins **A Cry in the Night** (Fontana 0-00-616654-7, Aug,87 [Sep,87], £2.95, 295pp, pb) Reissue (Simon & Schuster 1982) horror novel.

Clark, Mary Higgins **A Stranger is Watching** (Fontana 0-00-617188-5, Aug,87 [Sep,87], £2.50, 222pp, pb) Reissue (Collins 1978) horror novel.

Clark, Mary Higgins **Where are the Children?** (Fontana 0-00-616127-8, Sep,87, £2.50, 176pp, pb) Reissue (Talmy Franklin 1975) horror novel.

+Clarke, Arthur C. **2001: A Space Odyssey/The City and the Stars/The Deep Range/A Fall of Moondust/Rendezvous With Rama** (Octopus/Heinemann 0-905712-82-X, 1987 [Nov,87], £11.98, 747pp, hc) Omnibus edition of the above titles. First U.S. edition.

*Clarke, Arthur C. **2061: Odyssey Three** (Ballantine/Del Rey 0-345-35173-8, Jan,88 [Nov,87], $17.95, 279pp, hc) Sf novel, sequel to **2010: Odyssey Two**.

Clarke, Arthur C. **Childhood's End** (Ballantine/Del Rey 0-345-34795-1, Jan,88 [Dec,87], $3.50, 218pp, pb) Reissue (Ballantine 1953) sf novel; 55th printing. One of the classics of sf. Highly recommended. (CNB)

Clarke, Arthur C. **The City and the Stars** (NAL/Signet 0-451-14822-3, May,87 [Apr,87], $3.50, 256pp, pb) Reissue (Harcourt Brace 1956) sf novel, with a new introduction by the author.

Clarke, Arthur C. **The Deep Range** (NAL/Signet 0-451-14753-7, Apr,87 [Mar,87], $3.50, 254pp, pb) Reprint (Harcourt Brace 1957) sf novel with a new introduction by the author; 11th printing.

Clarke, Arthur C. **Dolphin Island** (Ace 0-441-15220-1, Dec,87 [Nov,87], $2.95, 188pp, pb) Reprint (Holt, Rinehart & Winston 1963) young adult sf novel.

Clarke, Arthur C. **Expedition to Earth** (Sidgwick & Jackson/NEL 0-283-98623-9, Jan,87, £1.95, 175pp, pb) Reissue (Ballantine 1953) sf collection.

Clarke, Arthur C. **A Fall of Moondust** (Gollancz 0-575-03978-7, Feb,87, £3.50, 224pp, tp) Reprint (Harcourt, Brace & World 1961) sf novel. Volume 9 of the Gollancz Classic SF series.

Clarke, Arthur C. **A Fall of Moondust** (NAL/Signet 0-451-14717-0, Mar,87 [Feb,87], $3.50, 254pp, pb) Reissue (Harcourt Brace & World 1961) sf novel with a new introduction by the author. Tenth NAL printing.

Clarke, Arthur C. **Glide Path** (NAL/Signet 0-451-14866-5, Sep,87 [Aug,87], $3.50, 252pp, pb) Reissue (Harcourt Brace 1963), 9th NAL printing. Non-sf, associational, a novel of WWII and the first use of radar. New intro by Clarke.

Clarke, Arthur C. **Islands in the Sky** (NAL/Signet 0-451-14895-9, Jul,87, $3.50, 256pp, pb) Reissue (Winston 1952) young adult sf novel, 15th printing; has a new introduction by Clarke.

CLARKE, ARTHUR C.

Clarke, Arthur C. **The Lion of Comarre & Against the Fall of Night** (Harcourt Brace Jovanovich 0-15-652517-8, Aug,87 [Jul,87], $9.95, 214pp, tp) Reprint (Harcourt Brace & World 1968) omnibus edition of 2 novels.

Clarke, Arthur C. **The Nine Billion Names of God** (NAL/Signet 0-451-14755-3, Mar,87, $3.50, 253pp, pb) Reissue (Harcourt Brace World 1967) collection with a new introduction by the author; 11th Signet printing.

Clarke, Arthur C. **The Other Side of the Sky** (Gollancz 0-575-03988-4, May,87, £2.95, 245pp, pb) Reprint (Harcourt Brace 1958) sf collection. Contains a new introduction by Clarke.

Clarke, Arthur C. **The Other Side of the Sky** (NAL/Signet 0-451-14937-8, Aug,87 [Jul,87], $4.50, 254pp, pb) Reissue (Harcourt Brace 1958) collection, 13th printing.

Clarke, Arthur C. **Rendezvous With Rama** (Ballantine/Del Rey 0-345-35056-1, Jan,88 [Dec,87], $3.50, 274pp, pb) Reissue (Harcourt Brace Jovanovich 1973) sf novel, winner of both the Hugo and Nebula; 20th printing.

Clarke, Arthur C. **The Sands of Mars** (NAL/Signet 0-451-14790-1, Mar,87 [Feb,87], $3.50, 246pp, pb) Reissue (Sidgwick & Jackson 1951) sf novel with the 1967 introduction by the author; 10th Signet printing. Clarke's 35-year-old vision of Mars is still evocative, mostly undated, and a classic. Highly recommended. (CNB)

Clarke, Arthur C. **The Songs of Distant Earth** (Grafton Overseas 0-586-06623-3, 1986 [Apr,87], £2.50, 238pp, pb) Reprint (Del Rey 1986) sf novel. Special "open market" edition.

Clarke, Arthur C. **The Songs of Distant Earth** (Ballantine/Del Rey 0-345-32240-1, May,87 [Apr,87], $4.95, 319pp, pb) Reprint (Del Rey 1986) sf novel.

Clarke, Arthur C. **The Songs of Distant Earth** (Grafton 0-586-06623-3, Aug,87, £2.50, 238pp, pb) Reprint (Del Rey 1986) sf novel.

Clarke, Arthur C. **Tales of Ten Worlds** (NAL/Signet 0-451-14978-5, Jun,87 [May,87], $3.50, 252pp, pb) Reissue (Harcourt Brace & World 1962) collection, with a new introduction by Clarke. 11th printing.

*Clarke, Arthur C. **The Wind From the Sun** (NAL/Signet 0-451-14754-5, Mar,87 [Feb,87], $3.50, 244pp, pb) A slightly revised edition (3 new vignettes plus a new introduction) of the earlier collection (Harcourt Brace Jovanovich 1972). Even NAL doesn't really consider it a new book, and lists it as the 9th printing of the earlier work. Nevertheless, Clarke completists should note the three new "stories."

Clarke, Arthur C., ed. **Arthur C. Clarke's July 20, 2019** (Grafton 0-246-12980-8, Apr,87 [Mar,87], £14.95, 282pp, hc) Reprint (Macmillan 1986) non-fiction of associational interest. A look at a day in the life of the 21st Century. Clarke contributes an Introduction and Afterword and did some editing, the remainder is by assorted *Omni* editors. [First U.K. edition]

*Clarke, Arthur C., [ref.] **Against the Night, the Stars: The Science Fiction of Arthur C. Clarke** Main listing under John Hollow.

Clayton, Jo **Ghosthunt** (DAW 0-88677-220-6, Jun,87 [May,87], $2.95, 221pp, pb) Reissue (DAW 1983) sf novel, "Diadem" #7. 5th printing.

Clayton, Jo **Skeen's Leap** (DAW 0-88677-169-2, Jun,87 [May,87], $3.50, 320pp, pb) Reissue (DAW 1986) sf novel, first in a trilogy. 3rd printing.

*Clayton, Jo **Skeen's Return** (DAW 0-88677-202-8, Jun,87 [May,87], $3.50, 320pp, pb) Sf novel, second in the "Skeen" trilogy.

*Clayton, Jo **Skeen's Search** (DAW 0-88677-241-9, Dec,87 [Nov,87], $3.50, 303pp, pb) Final novel in the "Skeen" trilogy, science fantasy in the Leigh Brackett tradition.

Clayton, Jo **Star Hunters** (DAW 0-88677-219-2, Jun,87 [May,87], $2.95, 207pp, pb) Reissue (DAW 1980) sf novel, "Diadem" #5. 4th printing.

COLLINGS, MICHAEL R., ED.

*Clement, Hal **Intuit** (NESFA 0-915368-35-8, Sep,87, price unknown, 164pp, hc) Collection of 4 "Laird Cunningham" sf stories, one original. Issued for the 1987 NASFiC where Clement was Guest of Honor. There are 820 copies, with 225 available in a signed, slipcased edition (-90-0).

Clement, Hal **Mission of Gravity** (Gollancz 0-575-04022-X, May,87, £2.50, 203pp, pb) Reprint (Doubleday 1954) sf novel.

*Clement, Hal **Still River** (Ballantine/Del Rey 0-345-32916-3, Jun,87 [May,87], $16.95, 279pp, hc) Sf novel about a final exam on a VERY strange planet. Classic Clement problem story. Recommended. (CNB)

Clement, Hal **Still River** (SFBC #11626, Dec,87, $5.98, 245pp, hc) Reprint (Del Rey 1987) very hard sf novel.

*Clendenen, Bill **Stigma** (Bantam 0-553-27077-X, Jan,88 [Dec,87], $3.50, 227pp, pb) Supernatural horror novel.

*Clute, John, David Pringle & Simon Ounsley, eds. **Interzone: The 2nd Anthology** (Simon & Schuster UK 0-671-65450-0, Aug,87, £10.95, 208pp, hc) Anthology of 15 stories. Published in Britain by the British arm of S&S only. Available in U.S. as an import.

Cobban, J. MacLaren **Master of His Fate** (Greenhill 0-947898-56-5, May,87 [Mar,87], £8.95, 256pp, hc) Reprint (Blackwood 1890) classic sf novel. [Not seen]

*Coburn, Anthony **The Tribe of Gum** (Titan 1-85286-012-X, Dec,87, £2.95, 125pp, tp) Script of the first *Doctor Who* TV series.

*Cochran, Molly & Warren Murphy **High Priest** Main listing under Warren Murphy.

*Coffman, Virginia **The Devil's Mistress** (Piatkus 0-86188-602-X, Feb,87 [May,87], £9.95, 190pp, hc) Reprint (Lancer 1970) occult novel. Volume 1 in the "Lucifer Cove" series.

Coffman, Virginia **The Devil's Virgin** (Piatkus 0-86188-654-2, Aug,87 [1987], £9.50, 192pp, hc) Reprint (Lancer 1970) occult novel. Volume 3 in the "Lucifer Cove" series. [Not seen]

Coffman, Virginia **Priestess of the Damned** (Lythway Large Print 0-7451-0500-9, Apr,87 [1987], £8.95, 248pp, hc) Reprint (Lancer 1970) occult novel. Volume 2 in the "Lucifer Cove" series. [Not seen]

Cohen, Daniel **The Encyclopedia of Ghosts** (Dodd, Mead 0-396-09050-8, Apr,87, $7.95, 307pp, tp) Reissue (Dodd, Mead 1984); non-fiction, reference work on famous hauntings, etc.

Cohen, Daniel **The Encyclopedia of Monsters** (Dodd, Mead 0-396-09051-6, Apr,87 [Mar,87], $7.95, 287pp, tp) Reprint (Dodd, Mead 1982) reference book on both natural and supernatural monsters. Although the book has not appeared in paperback before, the interior seems to be the same as the 1982 edition (with only a 1982 copyright listing) and is probably from returned hardcovers rebound.

+Cole, Adrian **A Place Among the Fallen** (Arbor House 0-87795-883-1, May,87 [Apr,87], $17.95, 352pp, hc) Epic quest fantasy novel. First U.S. edition (Unwin/Unicorn 1986).

Cole, Adrian **A Place Among the Fallen** (Unwin 0-04-823366-8, Aug,87, £2.95, 352pp, pb) Reprint (Unwin 1986) fantasy novel. Volume 1 in the "Omaran Saga" series.

*Cole, Adrian **Throne of Fools** (Unwin 0-04-823384-6, Nov,87, £3.50, 410pp, pb) Fantasy novel. Volume 2 in the "Omaran Saga" series.

*Collings, Michael R. **The Stephen King Phenomenon** (Starmont House 0-930261-12-7, Apr,87, $9.95, 144pp, tp) Non-fiction, critical study of Stephen King as a bestselling author and his effect on publishing, etc.

*Collings, Michael R., ed. **Reflections on the Fantastic: Selected Essays from the Fourth International Conference on the Fantastic in the Arts** (Greenwood 0-313-25555-5, Oct,86 [Feb,87], $29.95, 109pp, hc) Non-fiction, critical studies. Collection of articles from the Conference on the Fantastic. This has a 1986 date, but we did not see it until 1987. UK price £27.00.

COMBES, SHARON

CORNWILL, SUE

Combes, Sharon **Caly** (Zebra 0-8217-1996-3, Feb,87 [Jan,87], $3.50, 282pp, pb) Reissue (Zebra 1980) novel of supernatural horror -- ghosts haunt a couple in an old Maine house. Third printing.

Combes, Sharon **Cherron** (Zebra 0-8217-2043-0, Apr,87 [Mar,87], $3.50, 344pp, pb) Reprint (Zebra 1980) horror novel.

Coney, Michael G. **Cat Karina** (Orbit 0-7088-3014-5, Feb,87, £2.50, 241pp, pb) Reprint (Ace 1982) sf novel. Related to the "Song of the Earth" series. [First U.K. edition]

Conly, Jane Leslie **Racso and the Rats of NIMH** (Puffin 0-14-032333-3, Dec,87, £2.25, 189pp, pb) Reprint (Gollancz 1986) juvenile fantasy novel.

*Conner, Jeff **Stephen King Goes to Hollywood** (NAL 0-453-00552-7, Jul,87 [Sep,87], $19.50, 144pp, hc) Non-fiction book on King and the movies, with lots of photos. Packaged and produced by Tim Underwood and Chuck Miller.

*Conner, Jeff **Stephen King Goes to Hollywood** (NAL Plume 0-452-25937-1, Aug,87, $9.95, 144pp, tp) Non-fiction guide to King's movies, with a reprinted interview of King. The book is written by Conner, but Tim Underwood and Chuck Miller appear on the cover as "producers," and the book is copyright in their name.

*Constantine, Storm **The Enchantments of Flesh and Spirit** (Macdonald 0-356-14548-4, Aug,87, £11.95, 318pp, hc) Sf novel. Volume 1 in the "Wraeththu" series.

*Contento, William G. & Charles N. Brown **Science Fiction, Fantasy, & Horror: 1986** Main listing under Charles N. Brown.

*Cook, Glen **An Ill Fate Marshalling** (Tor 0-812-53379-8, Jan,88 [Dec,87], $3.50, 313pp, pb) Fantasy novel in the "Dread Empire" series.

*Cook, Glen **Reap the East Wind** (Tor 0-812-53376-3, Jun,87 [May,87], $2.95, 213pp, pb) Fantasy novel, new addition to the "Dread Empire" series.

*Cook, Glen **Sweet Silver Blues** (NAL/Signet 0-451-15061-9, Aug,87 [Jul,87], $3.50, 255pp, pb) Fantasy/alternate magical world/ hardboiled detective novel. Tougher than most examples of this odd sub-genre, this one works well. (FCM)

*Cook, Hugh **The Shift** (Cape 0-224-02389-6, Jan,87, £9.95, 215pp, hc) Humourous sf novel.

+Cook, Hugh **The Shift** (Random Vintage 0-394-74739-9, Jun,87, $6.95, 215pp, tp) Literary sf novel set after the first thermonuclear war. A wild blend of sex, power-lust, and aliens. First U.S. edition (Jonathan Cape 1986).

+Cook, Hugh **Wizard War** (Popular Library Questar 0-445-20422-2, Jun,87 [May,87], $3.50, 447pp, pb) Fantasy novel, a retitling of **The Wizards and the Warriors** (Colin Smythe 1986), first in a new British fantasy series. This is its first American edition.

Cook, Hugh **The Wizards & the Warriors** (Dufour Editions/Colin Smyth 0-86140-203-0, Jul,87, $18.95, 351pp, hc) Fantasy novel. This is actually the original 1986 Colin Smythe edition, distributed in the U.S. by Dufour. To compound the confusion, it has also appeared in America as **Wizard War** (Popular Library 1987).

*Cook, Hugh **The Women and the Warlords** (Corgi 0-552-13131-8, Dec,87 [Nov,87], £2.95, 429pp, pb) Fantasy novel. Volume 3 in the "Chronicles of an Age of Darkness" series.

*Cook, Hugh **The Wordsmiths and the Warguild** (Corgi 0-552-13130-X, Jun,87, £2.95, 316pp, pb) Fantasy novel. Volume 2 in the "Chronicles of an Age of Darkness" series.

*Cook, Hugh **The Wordsmiths and the Warguild** (Colin Smythe 0-86140-267-6, Nov,87 [Dec,87], £9.95, 202pp, hc) Fantasy novel. Volume 2 in the "Chronicles of an Age of Darkness" series. Available in the US from Dufour Editions for $18.95.

*Cook, Paul **On the Rim of the Mandala** (Bantam Spectra 0-553-26582-2, Jun,87 [May,87], $3.95, 246pp, pb) Sf novel of a vulnerable immortal vs. genetically engineered saboteurs.

*Cook, Robin **Outbreak** (Putnam 0-399-13187-6, Jan,87, $17.95, 366pp, hc) Sf medical horror novel.

Cook, Robin **Outbreak** (Macmillan 0-333-44861-8, Aug,87, £9.95, 366pp, hc) Reprint (Putnam 1987) sf medical horror novel. [First U.K. edition]

*Cooke, Catherine **The Winged Assassin** (Ace 0-441-89425-9, Jun,87 [May,87], $2.95, 279pp, pb) Middle-eastern fantasy novel. A young man, the destined lover/sacrifice of a forbidden goddess, becomes involved with demons, gods, emperors, and spies, in his attempts to escape his fate.

*Cooper, Clare **The Settlement on Planet B** (Hodder & Stoughton 0-340-40257-1, Jun,87, £6.95, 158pp, hc) Juvenile sf novel. [Not seen]

Cooper, Jeffrey **The Nightmares on Elm Street** (Futura 0-7088-3575-9, Sep,87, £2.50, 216pp, pb) Reprint (St. Martin's 1987) horror novel. [First U.K. edition]

*Cooper, Jeffrey **The Nightmares on Elm Street, Parts 1, 2, 3: The Continuing Story** (St. Martin's 0-312-90517-3, Feb,87 [Jan,87], $3.95, 216pp, pb) Novelization of the three films, including "over 25 photographs" from the film series. Supernatural horror.

*Cooper, Louise **The Master** (Unicorn 0-04-823298-X, Apr,87, £2.95, 249pp, pb) Fantasy novel. Volume 3 in the "Time Master" series.

*Cooper, Louise **The Master** (Tor 0-812-53396-8, May,87 [Apr,87], $2.95, 285pp, pb) Fantasy novel, third in the "Time Master" trilogy.

*Cooper, Louise **Mirage** (Unwin 0-04-823382-X, Sep,87 [Aug,87], £2.95, 343pp, pb) Fantasy novel.

*Cooper, Richard **Knights of God** (Lions 0-00-672534-1, Sep,87, £2.25, 228pp, pb) Novelization of new children's television serial set in a near-future England ruled by a theocracy.

Cooper, Susan **The Dark Is Rising Sequence** (Puffin 0-14-031688-4, Jan,87, £5.95, 786pp, tp) Reissue (Penguin 1984) omnibus of the five novels in the "Dark is Rising" fantasy series.

Cooper, Susan **Seaward** (Macmillan/Collier 0-02-042190-7, Apr,87, $3.95, 167pp, pb) Reprint (Atheneum 1983) young-adult fantasy novel.

*Cooper, Tom **War*Moon** (Worldwide Library 0-373-97031-5, Feb,87, $3.50, 381pp, pb) Near-future thriller about a Soviet space battle station.

*Copeland, Lori **Candlelight Ecstasy Romance #462: Out of This World** (Dell 0-440-16764-7, Oct,86 [Feb,87], $2.50, 189pp, pb) Romance/sf novel. Toni watches a UFO steal the neighborhood hunk's barbecue grill. He thinks she's crazy, but falls in love anyway. As the book ends, they watch together as the UFO returns the grill. Published in 1986.

+Corbett, W.J. **Pentecost and the Chosen One** (Delacorte 0-385-29549-9, Jun,87 [May,87], $14.95, 238pp, hc) Young-adult fantasy novel, the further adventures of the talking mice in **The Song of Pentecost** (which won the 1982 Whitbread Award). First U.S. edition (Methuen 1984). The illustrations by Martin Ursell are apparently new.

Corelli, Marie **Romance of Two Worlds** (Society of Metaphysicians 1-85228-562-1, Feb,87, £6.00, 370pp, tp) Reprint (Bentley 1886) occult novel. [Not seen]

Corelli, Marie **Strange Visitation** (Society of Metaphysicians 1-85228-565-6, Mar,87, £6.50, 188pp, hc) Reprint (Newnes 1904) occult novel. [Not seen]

*Cornwill, Sue & Mike Kott **The Official Price Guide to Star Trek and Star Wars Collectibles, Second Edition** (Ballantine/House of Collectibles 0-876-37358-9, Jan,88 [Dec,87], $8.95, 415pp, tp) Non-fiction, reference. A list of prices for various books and other paraphernalia.

*Corydon, Bent & L. Ron Hubbard, Jr. **L. Ron Hubbard: Messiah or Madman?** (Lyle Stuart 0-8184-0444-2, Aug,87, $20.00, 402pp, hc) Non-fiction, biography of sorts -- not really a biography or an expose, but a tirade about Hubbard by a scientology believer on the outs with The Church of Scientology and Hubbard. There are some interesting tidbits, but it's badly written and mostly incoherent. It doesn't really address the issue of Hubbard as confidence man or sincere believer, and should probably be titled "Messiah *and* Madman" for its conclusions. (CNB)

*Costello, Matthew **Sleep Tight** (Zebra 0-8217-2121-6, Jul,87 [Jun,87], $3.95, 302pp, pb) Horror novel.

*Cotton, Donald **The Romans** (W.H. Allen 0-491-03833-X, Apr,87 [May,87], £7.50, 128pp, hc) Juvenile sf novel. Volume 120 in the Doctor Who series.

Cotton, Donald **The Romans** (Target 0-426-20288-0, Sep,87, £1.95, 128pp, pb) Reprint (W.H. Allen 1987) juvenile sf novel. Volume 120 in the Doctor Who series.

*Cover, Arthur Byron **Isaac Asimov's Robot City, Book 4: Prodigy** (Ace 0-441-37384-4, Jan,88 [Dec,87], $2.95, 176pp, pb) Sf novelization in the "Robot City" shared world series.

*Coville, Bruce **Murder in Orbit** (Dragon 0-583-31096-6, Aug,87, £2.25, 187pp, pb) Juvenile sf novel. Volume 2 in the "Omni Odysseys" series.

*Cox, Michael, ed. **The Ghost Stories of M.R. James** Main listing under M.R. James.

Cox, Michael & R.A. Gilbert, eds. **The Oxford Book of English Ghost Stories** (Oxford Univ. Press 0-19-214163-5, May,87 [Aug,87], $18.95, 504pp, hc) Reissue (Oxford 1986) anthology of 42 stories; 2nd printing. This same edition is available in the U.K., at £12.95.

*Coyle, H.W. **Team Yankee** (Presidio Press 0-89141-290-5, Sep,87 [Aug,87], $15.95, 313pp, hc) A novel set in the near-future world of Sir John Hackett's books on World War III.

*Coyne, John **The Hunting Season** (Macmillan 0-02-528590-4, Sep,87 [Oct,87], $15.95, 245pp, hc) Associational. Horror novel, but not supernatural even though it has quotes from both King and Straub on the back.

Coyne, John **The Legacy** (Ace Charter 0-441-47852-2, Apr,87 [Mar,87], $3.50, 246pp, pb) Reprint (Berkley 1979) fantasy horror novel "based on a story by Jimmy Sangster."

Coyne, John **The Shroud** (Ace Charter 0-441-76225-5, Jun,87 [May,87], $3.50, 297pp, pb) Reprint (Berkley 1983) horror novel.

Crace, Jim **Continent** (Picador 0-330-29964-6, Nov,87, £2.95, 154pp, tp) Reprint (Heinemann 1986) collection of seven loosely-connected stories set on an imaginary continent.

Craik, Dinah Maria, ed. **Classic Book of Fairy Stories** (Lamboll 1-85170-107-9, Jun,87 [Jul,87], £9.95, 379pp, hc) Reprint (Smith, Elder 1863, as **The Fairy Book**) collection of fairy stories. Illustrated throughout by Warwick Goble.

*Cramer, Kathryn & David G. Hartwell, eds. **Christmas Ghosts** (Arbor House 0-87795-873-4, Sep,87 [Aug,87], $17.95, 284pp, hc) Anthology of 17 "classic ghost stories of Christmas."

*Cramer, Kathryn & Peter D. Pautz, eds. **The Architecture of Fear** (Arbor House 0-87795-921-8, Oct,87 [Sep,87], $18.95, 304pp, hc) Original anthology with 14 horror stories by Gene Wolfe, Ramsey Campbell, Charles L. Grant, and others.

+Cresswell, Helen **Moondial** (Macmillan 0-02-725370-8, Oct,87, $13.95, 202pp, hc) Young adult time travel novel, a ghost story. First U.S. edition (UK 1987).

*Cresswell, Helen **Moondial** (Faber & Faber 0-571-14805-0, Oct,87 [Dec,87], £6.95, 214pp, hc) Juvenile ghost/occult novel.

Cresswell, Helen **Time Out** (Lutterworth 0-7188-2658-2, Jun,87 [Dec,87], £5.95, 73pp, hc) Juvenile time-travel novella.

*Crichton, Michael **Sphere** (Knopf 0-394-56110-4, Jun,87 [May,87], $17.95, 385pp, hc) Science fiction thriller novel. An alien spacecraft on the floor of the Pacific involves the explorers in time travel, black holes, giant squids, etc., and a real dumb ending.

Crichton, Michael **Sphere** (Macmillan 0-333-45298-4, Sep,87 [Aug,87], £10.95, 384pp, hc) Reprint (Knopf 1987) sf novel. [First U.K. edition]

Crispin, A.C. **Star Trek #11: Yesterday's Son** (Pocket 0-671-60550-X, Mar,87 [Feb,87], $3.50, 192pp, pb) Reissue (Pocket 1985); 4th printing.

Cross, Gillian **Born of the Sun** (Dell/Laurel Leaf 0-440-90710-1, Nov,87 [Oct,87], $2.95, 218pp, pb) Reprint (Holiday House 1983) young adult sf/adventure novel of a lost race in the Andes.

*Crossley, Robert, ed. **Talking Across the World** (Univ. Press of New England 0-87451-423-1, Dec,87 [Nov,87], $27.95, 383pp, hc) Non-fiction, autobiography. The love letters of Olaf Stapledon and Agnes Miller, 1913-1919. They touch on the philosophical themes later used in his sf and other writing.

*Crowley, John **AEgypt** (Bantam Spectra 0-553-05194-6, Apr,87 [Feb,87], $17.95, 390pp, hc) Literary fantasy novel.

Crowley, John **AEgypt** (Gollancz 0-575-04108-0, Sep,87, £11.95, 390pp, hc) Reprint (Bantam 1987) literary fantasy novel. Volume 1 in a new quartet. [First U.K. edition]

Crowley, John **Beasts** (Gollancz 0-575-04134-X, Dec,87, £3.95, 184pp, tp) Reprint (Doubleday 1976) fantasy novel. Volume 20 in the "Gollancz Classic SF" series.

Crowley, John **The Deep** (Unwin 0-04-823318-8, Jul,87, £2.95, 176pp, pb) Reprint (Doubleday 1975) sf/fantasy novel.

Crowley, John **Little, Big** (Bantam Spectra 0-553-26586-5, Apr,87 [Mar,87], $4.95, 625pp, pb) Reissue (Bantam 1981) fantasy novel, winner of the World Fantasy Award. Third printing. Highly recommended. (FCM)

Cuddon, J, ed. **The Penguin Book of Ghost Stories** (Penguin 0-14-006800-7, Oct,87, £5.95, 512pp, tp) Reissue (Penguin 1984) ghost anthology.

Cuddon, J, ed. **The Penguin Book of Horror Stories** (Penguin 0-14-006799-X, Oct,87, £5.95, 607pp, tp) Reissue (Penguin 1984) horror anthology.

Cudlip, David R. **Comprador** (Grafton 0-586-06886-4, May,87, £3.50, 475pp, pb) Reprint (Secker & Warburg 1984) near-future thriller.

*Curtis, Jack **Crows' Parliament** (Bantam UK 0-593-01215-1, Mar,87, £10.95, 349pp, hc) A thriller involving the use of ESP. A first novel.

Curtis, Philip **A Gift From Another Galaxy** (Andersen Press 0-86264-166-7, May,87, £5.95, 124pp, hc) Juvenile sf novel. [Not seen]

*Cush, Geoffrey **God Help the Queen** (Abacus 0-349-10670-3, Apr,87 [May,87], £8.95, 148pp, hc) Satirical novel about England in 2003. A first novel.

Cush, Geoffrey **God Help the Queen** (Abacus 0-349-10668-1, Oct,87, £2.99, 148pp, tp) Reprint (Abacus 1987) literary sf novel.

Cussler, Clive **Cyclops** (Sphere 0-7221-2756-1, Apr,87, £3.50, 500pp, pb) Reprint (Simon & Schuster 1986) sf novel.

Cussler, Clive **Cyclops** (Chivers Press 0-86220-196-9, Jul,87 [Aug,87], £9.95, 664pp, hc) Reprint (Simon & Schuster 1986) sf novel. Large Print edition. [Not seen]

*D'Ambrosio, Margaret **Meggie's Journeys** (Polygon 0-948275-44-8, Dec,87, £4.95, 175pp, tp) Celtic fantasy novel.

*da Cruz, Daniel **F-Cubed** (Ballantine/Del Rey 0-345-33644-5, Jun,87 [May,87], $3.50, 291pp, pb) Sf/spy novel of the U.S. vs. a Soviet chemical weapon.

DA CRUZ, DANIEL

da Cruz, Daniel **The Grotto of the Formigans** (Ballantine/Del Rey 0-345-34760-9, Sep,87 [Aug,87], $2.95, 185pp, pb) Reissue (Del Rey 1980) sf novel of strange creatures in the African jungle; 2nd printing.

*da Cruz, Daniel **Texas Triumphant** (Ballantine/Del Rey 0-345-34340-9, Dec,87 [Nov,87], $15.95, 301pp, hc) Sf novel, third in a series about an independent Republic of Texas at odds with the Soviet Union.

Dahl, Roald **Charlie and the Chocolate Factory** (Windrush 1-85089-902-9, Mar,87 [Oct,87], $12.95, 174pp, hc) Reprint (Knopf 1964) juvenile fantasy novel, large print edition. U.S. distribution of the British edition from Oxford Windrush. Order from ABC-Clio.

Dahl, Roald **Charlie and the Great Glass Elevator** (Windrush 1-85089-907-X, Mar,87 [Oct,87], $12.95, 178pp, hc) Reprint (Knopf 1977) juvenile fantasy novel, large print edition. U.S. distribution of the British edition from Oxford Windrush. Order from ABC-Clio.

*Dahl, Roald **The Complete Adventures of Charlie and Mr. Willy Wonka** (Unwin Hyman 0-04-440074-8, Oct,87 [Nov,87], £9.95, 316pp, hc) Omnibus of the two Charlie books. This is the first omnibus edition that includes the Michael Foreman illustration

*Dahl, Roald **Fantastic Mr. Fox: A Play** (Puffin 0-14-032208-6, May,87 [Nov,87], £1.50, 74pp, pb) Juvenile fantasy play, adapted by Sally Reid.

Dahl, Roald, ed. **Roald Dahl's Book of Ghost Stories** (Isis Large Print 1-85089-178-8, May,87 [Jun,87], £10.75, 339pp, hc) Reprint (Cape 1983) ghost story anthology. [Not seen]

*Dalby, Richard, ed. **Dracula's Brood** (Crucible 0-85030-594-2, May,87, £8.99, 348pp, tp) Anthology of 30 'rare' vampire stories, one original to this collection. Distributed in the U.S. by Inner Traditions International at $10.95.

*Dalby, Richard, ed. **The Virago Book of Ghost Stories** (Virago 0-86068-810-0, Nov,87 [Oct,87], £12.95, 331pp, hc) Wide-ranging slection of twentieth-century ghost stories written by women, including three stories commissioned especially for this volume.

*Dalby, Richard & Rosemary Pardoe, eds. **Ghosts and Scholars** For main entry see under Rosemary Pardoe.

*Dalmas, John **The Regiment** (Baen 0-671-65626-0, Mar,87 [Feb,87], $3.50, 404pp, pb) Military sf novel.

*Dalmas, John **Return to Fanglith** (Baen 0-671-65343-1, Aug,87 [Jul,87], $2.95, 280pp, pb) Science fiction novel, sequel to **Fanglith**. Straightforward sf adventure without Dalmas' usual mystical element. Recommended. (TM)

Dalmas, John **The Varkaus Conspiracy** (Tor 0-812-53477-8, Jul,87 [Jun,87], $2.95, 285pp, pb) Reissue (Tor 1983) sf novel, 2nd printing.

Dalmas, John **The Yngling** (Tor 0-812-53473-5, Apr,87 [Mar,87], $2.95, 254pp, pb) Reissue (Pyramid 1971) sf novel about post-catastrophe neo-vikings. First in a series.

Danby, Mary, ed. **Nightmares 2** (Swift 0-85997-692-0, Jul,87, £5.95, 160pp, hc) Juvenile horror anthology. [Not seen]

Dann, Colin **The Ram of Sweetriver** (Beaver 0-09-951240-8, May,87, £1.95, 214pp, pb) Reprint (Hutchinson 1986) juvenile animal fantasy.

*Dann, Jack M. & Jeanne Van Buren Dann, eds. **In the Field of Fire** Main listing under Jeanne Van Buren Dann.

*Dann, Jack M. & Gardner R. Dozois, eds. **Demons!** (Ace 0-441-14264-8, Jul,87 [Jun,87], $3.50, 283pp, pb) Anthology of 14 fantasy stories about demons.

*Dann, Jeanne Van Buren & Jack M. Dann, eds. **In the Field of Fire** (Tor 0-312-93000-3, Feb,87 [Jan,87], $17.95, 416pp, hc) Mostly original anthology of sf and fantasy stories dealing with Vietnam. The hardcover is a fairly limited edition -- probably 750 copies.

DE CAMP, L. SPRAGUE

*Dann, Jeanne Van Buren & Jack M. Dann, eds. **In the Field of Fire** (Tor 0-312-93008-9, Feb,87 [Jan,87], $8.95, 416pp, tp) Trade paperback edition of the above.

Dann, Jeanne Van Buren & Jack M. Dann, eds. **In the Field of Fire** (Tor 0-812-53487-5, Nov,87 [Oct,87], $3.95, 415pp, pb) Reprint (Tor 1987) sf/Vietnam anthology.

*Danziger, Paula **This Place Has No Atmosphere** (Delacorte 0-385-29489-1, Oct,86 [Jan,87], $14.95, 156pp, hc) Young-adult sf novel of a teenager who moves to a moon settlement. "There are only 750 people on the moon -- what if none of them is a boy her age?" The author flunked Earth Science in college, believing only diamonds and amethysts were worth identifying. Published in 1986; missed.

Danziger, Paula **This Place Has No Atmosphere** (Dell/Laurel Leaf 0-440-98726-1, Oct,87 [Sep,87], $2.95, 156pp, pb) Reprint (Delacorte 1986) young-adult sf novel.

*Datlow, Ellen, ed. **The Fifth Omni Book of Science Fiction** (Zebra 0-8217-2050-3, Apr,87 [Mar,87], $3.95, 381pp, pb) Anthology of sf from *Omni* plus one original story by Pat Cadigan.

*David, Peter **Knight Life** (Ace 0-441-45130-6, Apr,87 [Mar,87], $2.95, 195pp, pb) Humorous fantasy novel. King Arthur returns to modern Manhattan and, advised by Merlin, seeks modern rulership as mayor of New York. A first novel.

*Davids, Hollace & Paul Davids **The Fires of Pele** (Pictorial Legends 0-939031-00-0, 1986 [May,87], $9.95, 56pp, tp) Hawaiian fantasy story, "Mark Twain's Legendary Lost Journal", with color illustrations -- an odd combination of photocollage, paintings and cartoons, and Harryhausen-like 3-D figures. This has a 1986 copyright, but we had not seen it until now.

*Davids, Paul & Hollace Davids **The Fires of Pele** Main listing under Hollace Davids.

*Davidson, Alan **Bewitching of Alison Allbright** (Hutchinson 0-09-171861-9, May,87 [1987], £5.95, 192pp, hc) Juvenile horror novel. [Not seen]

*Davies, Paul **Fireball** (Heinemann 0-434-17701-6, Aug,87 [Sep,87], £10.95, 178pp, hc) Sf novel.

Davies, Pete **The Last Election** (King Penguin 0-14-009748-1, Apr,87, £3.95, 234pp, tp) Reprint (Andre Deutsch 1986) novel set in a nightmarish future England.

Davis, Richard, ed. **Encyclopaedia of Horror** (Hamlyn 0-600-55359-0, May,87, £4.99, 192pp, tp) Reprint (Octopus 1981) collection of essays on the horror genre, with particular emphasis on films.

*Day, Chet **Halo** (Pocket 0-671-64333-9, Oct,87, $3.95, 368pp, pb) Horror novel.

*de Camp, Catherine Crook & L. Sprague de Camp **The Incorporated Knight** Main listing under L. Sprague de Camp.

de Camp, L. Sprague **The Goblin Tower** (Grafton 0-586-07212-8, Nov,87, £2.95, 320pp, pb) Reprint (Pyramid 1968) fantasy novel. Although billed as a "UK Paperback Original", this has previously appeared from Sphere. Volume 1 in the "Reluctant King" series.

de Camp, L. Sprague & Lin Carter **Conan the Liberator** (Ace 0-441-11617-5, Jul,87 [Jun,87], $2.95, 191pp, pb) Reprint (Bantam 1979) fantasy novel based on a character by Robert E. Howard; "Conan" #14.

de Camp, L. Sprague & Lin Carter **Conan the Liberator** (Sphere 0-7221-2942-4, Jul,87, £2.50, 191pp, pb) Reissue (Bantam 1979) fantasy novel based on the character created by Robert E. Howard. Volume 14 in the "Conan" series.

de Camp, L. Sprague, Lin Carter & Robert E. Howard **Conan of Cimmeria** For main entry see under Robert E. Howard.

de Camp, L. Sprague, Lin Carter, Robert E. Howard & Bjorn Nyberg **Conan the Swordsman** Main listing under Robert E. Howard.

DE CAMP, L. SPRAGUE   **DICK, PHILIP K.**

*de Camp, L. Sprague & Catherine Crook de Camp **The Incorporated Knight** (Phantasia Press 0-932096-46-8, Aug,87, $17.00, 191pp, hc) Humorous fantasy novel. The first 5 chapters appeared as short stories in slightly different form. Also available in a signed/numbered/boxed edition of 275 copies, at $40 (same ISBN).

*de Lint, Charles **Ascian in Rose** (Axolotl 0-939879-10-7, Apr,87 [Mar,87], $30.00, 84pp, hc) Fantasy novella set in the same world as the novel **Moonheart**. Limited to 300 signed copies (also fifty leatherbound, $65.00).

*de Lint, Charles **Ascian in Rose** (Axolotl 0-939879-11-5, Apr,87 [Mar,87], $6.00, 84pp, tp) Trade paperback of the above. Limited to 500 copies.

*de Lint, Charles **Jack the Giant Killer** (Ace 0-441-37969-9, Nov,87 [Oct,87], $16.95, 202pp, hc) Contemporary fantasy novel, loosely based on the fairytale of the same name.

Debrett's Peerage & Geoffrey Ashe **The Discovery of King Arthur** Main listing under Geoffrey Ashe.

*DeChancie, John & Thomas F. Monteleone **Crooked House** Main listing under Thomas F. Monteleone.

*DeClements, Barthe & Christopher Greimes **Double Trouble** (Viking 0-670-81567-5, Apr,87 [Dec,87], $11.95, 168pp, hc) Young adult fantasy novel about twins sent to different foster homes; they have to save each other by using their telepathic abilities.

*DeCles, Jon **The Particolored Unicorn** (Ace 0-441-65192-5, Dec,87 [Nov,87], $2.95, 230pp, pb) Humorous fantasy novel; a first novel.

*DeHaven, Tom **U.S.S.A. Book 1** (Avon 0-380-75180-1, Feb,87 [Jan,87], $2.95, 185pp, pb) Near-future sf novel of students vs. a military dictatorship that has taken over America; first of a series, packaged by Byron Preiss and Dan Weiss.

Deighton, Len **SS-GB** (Grafton 0-586-05002-7, Jul,87, £2.95, 367pp, pb) Reissue (Jonathan Cape 1978) thriller set in alternate Britain.

Deighton, Len **SS-GB** (Grafton 0-586-07406-6, Jul,87, £3.50, 403pp, pb) Reissue (Jonathan Cape 1978) thriller set in alternate Britain. This special "Silver Jubilee" edition has a new foreword by the author.

*Deitz, Tom **Fireshaper's Doom** (Avon 0-380-75329-4, Dec,87 [Nov,87], $3.50, 306pp, pb) Fantasy novel, sequel to **Windmaster's Bane**.

Deitz, Tom **Windmaster's Bane** (Avon 0-380-75029-5, Dec,87 [Nov,87], $3.50, 279pp, pb) Reissue (Avon 1986) fantasy novel, 2nd printing.

Delany, Samuel R. **Babel 17** (Gollancz 0-575-04123-4, Oct,87, £3.95, 193pp, tp) Reprint (Ace 1966) sf novel. This edition follows the revised (Sphere 1969) text. Volume 17 in the Gollancz Classic SF series.

*Delany, Samuel R. **The Bridge of Lost Desire** (Arbor House 0-87795-931-5, Nov,87 [Oct,87], $17.95, 310pp, hc) Collection of 2 original stories and one extensively revised piece, in the "Neveryona" fantasy series, plus an appendix by the author's alter ego, K. Leslie Steiner.

*Delap, Richard & Walt Lee **Shapes** (Ace Charter 0-441-76103-8, Feb,87 [Jan,87], $3.95, 324pp, pb) Sf horror novel with a shape-changing alien that absorbs people.

*Denis, John **Goliath** (Fontana 0-00-617351-9, Mar,87, £2.95, 284pp, pb) Futuristic thriller. Author is a pseudonym of John Edwards & Denis Frost.

Denis, John **Goliath** (Collins 0-00-223159-X, Apr,87, £10.95, 256pp, hc) Reprint (Fontana 1987) futuristic thriller. Author is a pseudonym of John Edwards & Denis Frost. [Not seen]

Dennis, Ian **Bagdad** (Unwin 0-04-823307-2, Oct,87, £2.95, 210pp, pb) Reprint (Macmillan Canada 1986) fantasy novel. Volume 1 in the Prince of Stars in the "Cavern of Time" series.

*Dennis, Ian **The Prince of Stars** (Unwin 0-04-823306-4, Nov,87, £2.95, 221pp, pb) Fantasy novel. Volume 2 in the "Prince of Stars in the Cavern of Time" series.

*Dent, Lester **The Sinister Ray** (Gryphon 0-936071-04-4, Oct,87, $9.95, 175pp, tp) Collection of three scientific detective stories, originally published in the old pulps.

Denton, Bradley **Wrack and Roll** (Headline 0-7472-3009-9, Jul,87, £3.50, 406pp, pb) Reprint (Questar 1986) sf novel. [First U.K. edition]

Denton, Bradley **Wrack and Roll** (Headline 0-7472-0016-5, Aug,87, £10.95, 406pp, hc) Reprint (Questar 1986) sf novel.

*DeWeese, Gene **The Calvin Nullifier** (Putnam Philomel 0-399-21466-6, Nov,87 [Oct,87], $13.95, 142pp, hc) Juvenile sf novel. A UFO lands in Calvin's backyard. The alien is a cat. And the kids are saved by chocolate chip cookies. Third in the "Black Suits from Outer Space" humorous series.

DeWeese, Gene **Chain of Attack** (Titan 0-907610-85-4, Mar,87, £2.95, 251pp, pb) Reprint (Pocket 1987) sf novel. Volume 32 in the Star Trek Novels series. [First U.K. edition]

*DeWeese, Gene **The Dandelion Caper** (Putnam 0-399-21326-0, Nov,86 [Jan,87], $13.95, 159pp, hc) Young-adult sf novel, sequel to **Black Suits From Outer Space**. Published in 1986; missed.

*DeWeese, Gene **Star Trek #32: Chain of Attack** (Pocket 0-671-63269-8, Feb,87 [Jan,87], $3.50, 251pp, pb) Sf novel based on the tv series.

Dexter, Susan **The Mountains of Channadran** (Fontana 0-00-617430-2, Sep,87, £2.95, 367pp, pb) Reprint (Del Rey 1986) fantasy novel. Volume 3 in the "Winter King's War" trilogy. [First U.K. edition]

Dexter, Susan **The Mountains of Channadran** (Collins 0-00-223228-6, Oct,87, £10.95, 384pp, hc) Reprint (Del Rey 1986) fantasy novel. Volume 3 in the "Winter King's War" trilogy. [Not seen]

Dexter, Susan **The Ring of Allaire** (Fontana 0-00-617428-0, Jun,87, £2.50, 231pp, pb) Reprint (Ballantine/Del Rey 1981) fantasy novel. Volume 1 in the "Winter King's War" trilogy. [First U.K. edition]

Dexter, Susan **The Ring of Allaire** (Collins 0-00-223229-4, Jun,87, £10.95, 231pp, hc) Hardback edition of the above. [First U.K. edition, not seen]

Dexter, Susan **The Sword of Calandra** (Fontana 0-00-617429-9, Jul,87, £2.95, 341pp, pb) Reprint (Del Rey 1985) fantasy novel. Volume 2 in the "Winter King's War" trilogy. [First U.K. edition]

Dexter, Susan **The Sword of Calandra** (Collins 0-00-223230-8, Jul,87 [Oct,87], £10.95, 341pp, hc) Hardback edition of the above. [First U.K. edition]

*DiCarlantonio, Martin **Motherland** (Ansunda Publications no ISBN, Apr,87 [Mar,87], $6.50, 112pp, tp) Fantasy allegory of Mu, Atlantis, and nuclear war.

*Dick, Philip K. **The Collected Stories of Philip K. Dick, Vol. Five: The Little Black Box** (Underwood-Miller 0-88733-053-3, May,87, $125.00 [5 vols.], 395pp, hc) Introduction by Thomas M. Disch. 25 stories written 1964-1981, including three never before published plus several from fanzines and very obscure sources.

*Dick, Philip K. **The Collected Stories of Philip K. Dick, Vol. Four: The Days of Perky Pat** (Underwood-Miller 0-88733-053-3, May,87, $125.00 [5 vols.], 380pp, hc) 18 stories, written 1954-1964. Introduction by James Tiptree, Jr.

*Dick, Philip K. **The Collected Stories of Philip K. Dick, Vol. One: Beyond Lies the Wub** (Underwood-Miller 0-88733-053-3, May,87, $125.00 [5 vols], 404pp, hc) This volume has an introduction by Roger Zelazny. The stories are arranged chronologically and have an appendix on date of writing and of publication, plus notes by Dick. Volume One has work from 1947 to 1952, 25 stories including one early original. There is also a slipcased deluxe edition of the **Collected Stories** with signatures from Dick's checks; it has already sold out.

*Dick, Philip K. **The Collected Stories of Philip K. Dick, Vol. Three: The Father Thing** (Underwood-Miller 0-88733-053-3, May,87, $125.00 [5 vols.], 376pp, hc) 23 stories, written 1953-1954. Introduction by John Brunner.

DICK, PHILIP K.   **DICKSON, GORDON R.**

*Dick, Philip K. **The Collected Stories of Philip K. Dick, Vol. Two: Second Variety** (Underwood-Miller 0-88733-053-3, May,87, $125.00 [5 vols.], 393pp, hc) 27 stories, written 1952-1953. This volume has an introduction by Norman Spinrad.

Dick, Philip K. **The Cosmic Puppets** (Grafton 0-586-06331-5, Mar,87 [May,87], £2.50, 143pp, pb) Reissue (Ace 1957) sf novel. Dated 1986.

*Dick, Philip K. **Cosmogony and Cosmology** (Kerosina 0-948893-18-4, Nov,87, £4.50, 45pp, tp) Extracts from Dick's Exegesis writings, with an introduction by Paul Williams.

Dick, Philip K. **Dr. Bloodmoney** (Arrow 0-09-914960-5, Sep,87, £2.50, 290pp, pb) Reissue (Ace 1965) sf novel.

Dick, Philip K. **Eye in the Sky** (Arrow 0-09-920760-5, Mar,87, £2.50, 256pp, pb) Reissue (Ace 1957) sf novel.

Dick, Philip K. **Galactic Pot-Healer** (Grafton 0-586-06937-2, Mar,87, £2.50, 189pp, pb) Reprint (Berkley 1969) sf novel.

Dick, Philip K. **I Hope I Shall Arrive Soon** (St. Martin's 0-312-90838-5, Sep,87 [Aug,87], $3.50, 201pp, pb) Reprint (Doubleday 1985) collection of 10 stories and a speech.

Dick, Philip K. **In Milton Lumky Territory** (Paladin 0-586-08602-1, Feb,87, £3.95, 213pp, tp) Reprint (Dragon Press 1985) mainstream novel of associational interest.

Dick, Philip K. **The Man in the High Castle** (Penguin 0-14-008875-X, Mar,87, £3.95, 249pp, tp) Reissue (Putnams 1962) sf novel. In the Penguin Classic sf series.

*Dick, Philip K. **Mary and the Giant** (Arbor House 0-87795-850-5, Mar,87 [Apr,87], $16.95, 230pp, hc) Non-sf/fantasy, associational; mainstream novel set in the Fifties. Most reviewers agree this is Dick's best non-sf novel.

Dick, Philip K. **A Maze of Death** (Grafton 0-586-05897-4, Feb,87, £2.50, 191pp, n.) Reissue (Doubleday 1970) sf novel.

Dick, Philip K. **The Preserving Machine** (Grafton 0-586-06938-0, Oct,87 [Sep,87], £3.50, 413pp, pb) Reprint (Ace 1969) sf collection. Restores "What the Dead Men Say", dropped from all previous UK editions.

Dick, Philip K. **Puttering About in a Small Land** (Paladin 0-586-08604-8, Aug,87, £3.95, 286pp, tp) Reprint (Academy Chicago 1985) mainstream novel. Listed for Dick collectors. [First U.K. edition]

Dick, Philip K. **Radio Free Albemuth** (Grafton 0-586-06936-4, May,87, £2.95, 286pp, pb) Reprint (Arbor House 1985) sf novel. [First U.K. edition]

Dick, Philip K. **Radio Free Albemuth** (Avon 0-380-70288-6, Jun,87 [May,87], $3.50, 212pp, pb) Reprint (Arbor House 1985) dystopian/visionary sf novel. This was an earlier and different version of **Valis** found among Dick's unpublished work after his death.

Dick, Philip K. **Radio Free Albemuth** (Severn House 0-7278-1537-7, Oct,87, £9.95, 288pp, hc) Reprint (Arbor House 1985) sf novel. [Not seen]

Dick, Philip K. **Solar Lottery** (Arrow 0-09-905700-X, Mar,87, £2.50, 188pp, pb) Reissue (Ace 1955) sf novel.

Dick, Philip K. **Time Out of Joint** (Carroll & Graf 0-88184-352-0, Dec,87, $3.95, 263pp, pb) Reprint (Lippincott 1959) sf novel; this has the afterword by Lou Stathis, from the 1984 Bluejay edition.

Dick, Philip K. **The Transmigration of Timothy Archer** (Grafton 0-586-05886-9, Mar,87, £2.50, 252pp, pb) Reissue (Timescape 1982) sf novel.

Dick, Philip K. **Valis** (Kerosina 0-948893-15-X, Nov,87, £37.50, 256pp, hc) Cloth-bound version of **Valis** plus a hardcover edition of **Cosmogony and Cosmology** (0-948893-17-6). [Not seen]

Dick, Philip K. **Valis** (Kerosina 0-948893-16-8, Nov,87, £13.95, 256pp, hc) Reprint (Bantam 1981) sf novel, first hardcover edition, with a new afterword by Kim Stanley Robinson. Distributed in the U.S. by the publisher.

Dick, Philip K. & Ray Nelson **The Ganymede Takeover** (Arrow 0-09-921490-3, Sep,87, £2.50, 192pp, pb) Reissue (Ace 1967) sf novel.

*Dick, Philip K., [ref.] **Mind in Motion: The Fiction of Philip K. Dick** Main listing under Patricia S. Warrick.

*Dick, Philip K., [ref.] **Philip K. Dick: The Dream Connection** Main listing under D. Scott Apel.

*Dick, Philip K., [ref.] **The Secret Ascension** Main listing under Michael Bishop.

Dickinson, Peter **Annerton Pit** (Puffin 0-14-031042-8, Mar,87, £1.95, 172pp, pb) Reprint (Gollancz 1977) juvenile sf novel.

Dickinson, Peter **A Box of Nothing** (Magnet 0-416-96630-6, Feb,87, £1.75, 128pp, pb) Reprint (Gollancz 1985) juvenile fantasy novel who wants nothing and gets a box full of it. Illustrated throughout by Ian Newsham. Strongly recommended. (PS-P)

Dickinson, Peter **A Box of Nothing** (Lythway Large Print 0-7451-0547-5, Jul,87, £6.95, 208pp, hc) Reprint (Gollancz 1985) juvenile fantasy novel. [Not seen]

Dickinson, Peter **Healer** (Dell/Laurel Leaf 0-440-93377-3, Sep,87 [Aug,87], $2.95, 184pp, pb) Reprint (Gollancz 1983) young-adult fantasy novel of a girl with special powers. As always, Dickinson is quirky, intelligent, and a pleasure to read. Recommended. (FCM)

*Dicks, Terrance **The Ambassadors of Death** (W.H. Allen 0-491-03712-0, May,87, £7.50, 144pp, hc) Juvenile sf novel. Volume 121 in the Doctor Who series.

Dicks, Terrance **The Ambassadors of Death** (Target 0-426-20305-4, Oct,87, £1.95, 144pp, pb) Reprint (W.H. Allen 1987) juvenile sf novel. Volume 121 in the Doctor Who series.

Dicks, Terrance **The Faceless Ones** (Target 0-426-20294-5, May,87, £1.75, 140pp, pb) Reprint (W.H. Allen 1986) juvenile sf novel. Volume 116 in the Doctor Who series.

Dicks, Terrance **Junior Doctor Who and the Brain of Morbius** (Target 0-426-20063-2, Jan,87, £1.60, 80pp, pb) Reissue (Target 1980) juvenile sf novel based on the tv series.

*Dicks, Terrance **The Mysterious Planet** (W.H. Allen 0-491-03096-7, Nov,87 [Dec,87], £7.95, 127pp, hc) Juvenile sf novel. Volume 127 in the Doctor Who series.

Dickson, Gordon R. **The Forever Man** (Sphere 0-7221-3077-5, Sep,87, £3.50, 375pp, tp) Reprint (Ace 1986) sf novel. [First U.K. edition]

*Dickson, Gordon R. **In the Bone: The Best Science Fiction of Gordon R. Dickson** (Ace 0-441-37049-7, Mar,87 [Feb,87], $2.95, 228pp, pb) Collection of 11 stories. This reprints the fiction contents of **Gordon R. Dickson's SF Best** (Dell 1978) and adds two stories instead of the appreciations/bibliography.

Dickson, Gordon R. **The Man from Earth** (Tor 0-812-53581-2, Apr,87 [Mar,87], $2.95, 288pp, pb) Reissue (Tor 1983) collection.

*Dickson, Gordon R. **Secrets of the Deep** (Critic's Choice 0-931773-29-6, Oct,85 [Apr,87], $2.95, 288pp, pb) Omnibus of 3 juvenile sf adventure books. This actually first appeared in 10/85, but we missed listing it.

Dickson, Gordon R. **The Space Swimmers** (Tor 0-812-53584-7, Nov,87 [Oct,87], $2.95, 247pp, pb) Reprint (Berkley 1967) sf novel, with uncredited illustrations by Steve Fabian from the 1979 Ace edition.

Dickson, Gordon R. **Spacial Delivery** (Tor 0-812-53548-0, May,87 [Apr,87], $2.95, 155pp, pb) Reprint (Ace 1961) sf novel.

DICKSON, GORDON R.   **DRUMM, D.B.**

*Dickson, Gordon R. **The Stranger** (Tor 0-812-53579-0, Mar,87 [Feb,87], $2.95, 254pp, pb) Sf collection of 14 stories, mostly from the Fifties and early Sixties.

*Dickson, Gordon R. **Way of the Pilgrim** (Ace 0-441-87486-X, May,87 [Apr,87], $16.95, 341pp, hc) Sf novel of Earth conquered by giant aliens.

Dickson, Gordon R. **Way of the Pilgrim** (SFBC #11445, Oct,87 [Nov,87], $5.98, 436pp, hc) Reprint (Ace 1987) sf novel.

*Dietz, William C. **Freehold** (Ace 0-441-25186-2, Mar,87 [Feb,87], $2.95, 212pp, pb) Military sf adventure novel.

*Dillard, J.M. **Bloodthirst** (Titan 1-85286-039-1, Dec,87, £2.95, 264pp, pb) Sf novel. Includes an extract from the forthcoming **Final Frontier** by Diane Carey. Simultaneous with US (Pocket Books) edition. Volume 52 in the "Star Trek Novels" series.

Dillard, J.M. **Mindshadow** (Firecrest 0-85997-923-7, Jul,87 [1987], £7.95, 256pp, hc) Reprint (Pocket 1985) sf novel. Volume 42 in the Star Trek Novels series. [First U.K. edition, not seen]

*Dillard, J.M. **Star Trek #37: Bloodthirst** (Pocket 0-671-64489-0, Dec,87 [Nov,87], $3.95, 264pp, pb) Sf novel in the "Star Trek" series; it contains the first chapter of **Star Trek: The Final Frontier** at the end.

Disch, Thomas M. **334** (Carroll & Graf 0-88184-340-7, Sep,87 [Aug,87], $3.95, 269pp, pb) Reprint (MacGibbon & Kee 1972) sf novel of future New York. This may be Disch's best -- recommended. (FCM)

Donaldson, Stephen R. **Daughter of Regals** (Fontana 0-00-617554-6, Dec,87, £3.50, 366pp, pb) Reissue (Del Rey 1984) SF/fantasy collection. This is the first UK edition to contain "Gilden-Fire", previously published separately.

Donaldson, Stephen R. **The Illearth War** (Ballantine/Del Rey 0-345-34866-4, Nov,87 [Oct,87], $4.95, 528pp, pb) Reissue (Holt, Rinehart & Winston 1977) fantasy novel, second in the First Chronicles of Thomas Covenant. 22nd printing.

Donaldson, Stephen R. **Lord Foul's Bane** (Ballantine/Del Rey 0-345-34865-6, Nov,87 [Oct,87], $4.95, 480pp, pb) Reissue (SFBC 1977) fantasy novel, first book in the First Chronicles of Thomas Covenant. 29th printing.

*Donaldson, Stephen R. **A Man Rides Through** (Ballantine/Del Rey 0-345-33299-7, Nov,87, $19.95, 661pp, hc) Fantasy novel, conclusion of the "Mordant's Need" duology.

Donaldson, Stephen R. **The Mirror of Her Dreams** (SFBC #10530, 1987 [Jun,87], $6.98, 626pp, hc) Reprint (Del Rey 1986) fantasy novel, first of a duology.

Donaldson, Stephen R. **The Mirror of Her Dreams** (Ballantine/Del Rey 0-345-34715-3, Mar,87, $4.50, 627pp, pb) Reprint (Del Rey 1986), first volume of the two-book fantasy "Mordant's Need." International edition.

Donaldson, Stephen R. **The Mirror of Her Dreams** (Fontana 0-00-617399-3, Jul,87 [Jun,87], £2.95, 658pp, pb) Reprint (Collins 1986) fantasy novel. Volume 1 in the Mordant's Need duology.

Donaldson, Stephen R. **The Mirror of Her Dreams** (Ballantine/Del Rey 0-345-34697-1, Nov,87 [Oct,87], $4.95, 622pp, pb) Reprint (Del Rey 1986), first volume of the two-book fantasy "Mordant's Need."

Donaldson, Stephen R. **The One Tree** (Ballantine/Del Rey 0-345-34869-9, Nov,87 [Oct,87], $4.95, 475pp, pb) Reissue (Del Rey 1982) fantasy novel, second book in the Second Chronicles of Thomas Covenant. 11th printing.

Donaldson, Stephen R. **The Power That Preserves** (Ballantine/Del Rey 0-345-34867-2, Nov,87 [Oct,87], $4.95, 489pp, pb) Reissue (Holt, Rinehart & Winston 1977) fantasy novel, third book in the First Chronicles of Thomas Covenant. 21st printing.

Donaldson, Stephen R. **White Gold Wielder** (Ballantine/Del Rey 0-345-34870-2, Nov,87 [Oct,87], $4.95, 485pp, pb) Reissue (Del Rey 1983) fantasy novel, third book in the Second Chronicles of Thomas Covenant. 9th printing.

Donaldson, Stephen R. **The Wounded Land** (Ballantine/Del Rey 0-345-34868-0, Nov,87 [Oct,87], $4.95, 497pp, pb) Reissue (Del Rey 1981) fantasy novel, first book in the Second Chronicles of Thomas Covenant. 16th printing.

*Dooley, Dennis & Gary Engle **Superman at Fifty: The Persistence of a Legend** (Octavia 0-940601-00-1, Oct,87, $16.95, 189pp, hc) Non-fiction, essays exploring all aspects of Superman.

*Doran, Colleen **A Distant Soil** (Donning/Starblaze 0-89865-514-5, Sep,87, $6.95, unpaginated, tp) Sf/fantasy graphic novel, first in a series. It's compiled from a series of comics.

*Douglas, Carole Nelson **Keepers of Edanvant** (Tor 0-312-93012-7, May,87 [Apr,87], $15.95, 346pp, hc) Fantasy novel, both the end of the "Rynth" series and the beginning of the "Sword & Circlet" series.

Douglas, Drake **Undertow** (Leisure 0-8439-2495-0, Aug,87 [Jul,87], $3.95, 398pp, pb) Reprint (1984) horror novel.

Douglas, Gregory A. **The Nest** (Zebra 0-8217-2166-6, Sep,87 [Aug,87], $3.95, 448pp, pb) Reissue (Zebra 1980) horror novel; 2nd printing.

*Dowling, David **Fictions of Nuclear Disaster** (Univ. of Iowa Press 0-87745-142-7, Feb,87, $20.00, 239pp, hc) Non-fiction, critical study.

*Downer, Ann **The Spellkey** (Atheneum 0-689-31329-2, Oct,87, $13.95, 217pp, hc) Young adult fantasy quest novel, a first novel.

*Downie, Jill **The Raven in the Glass** (Paperjacks 0-7701-0699-4, Oct,87, $3.95, 471pp, pb) Historical/horror novel of an American woman and her Viennese double at the turn of the century.

Dozois, Gardner R., ed. **The Mammoth Book of Best New Science Fiction** (Robinson 0-948164-31-X, Aug,87, £4.95, 615pp, tp) Reprint (St. Martin's 1987, as **Year's Best Science Fiction, Fourth Annual Collection**) sf/fantasy anthology. [First U.K. edition]

*Dozois, Gardner R., ed. **The Year's Best Science Fiction, Fourth Annual Collection** (St. Martin's 0-312-00709-4, May,87 [Apr,87], $19.95, 602pp, hc) Anthology of 27 of the best stories of 1986. Dozois does an excellent job. Recommended. (CNB)

*Dozois, Gardner R., ed. **The Year's Best Science Fiction, Fourth Annual Collection** (St. Martin's 0-312-00710-8, May,87 [Apr,87], $11.95, 602pp, tp) Trade paperback edition of the above.

*Dozois, Gardner R. & Jack M. Dann, eds. **Demons!** Main listing under Jack M. Dann.

*Drake, David **Counting the Cost** (Baen 0-671-65355-5, Nov,87 [Oct,87], $3.50, 267pp, pb) Military sf novel, latest in the "Hammer's Slammers" series.

*Drake, David **Hammer's Slammers** (Baen 0-671-65632-5, Apr,87 [Mar,87], $3.50, 318pp, pb) Collection with **Hammer's Slammers** (Ace 1979) plus the short novel "The Tank Lords".

*Drake, David & Janet Morris **Kill Ratio** (Ace 0-441-44116-5, Oct,87 [Sep,87], $3.50, 268pp, pb) Sf novel of interstellar terrorism via a deadly plague. "Only Sam Yates can stop it."

*Drake, David, ed. **Cthulhu: The Mythos and Kindred Horrors** Main listing under Robert E. Howard.

*Drew, Wayland **Batteries Not Included** (Berkley 0-425-10105-3, Dec,87 [Nov,87], $2.95, 213pp, pb) Novelization of a movie about robot aliens.

*Drumm, D.B. **Traveler # 9: The Stalking Time** (Dell 0-440-18235-2, Jun,86 [Jan,87], $2.50, 174pp, pb) Post-holocaust sf novel, part of an adventure series. Published in 1986 but missed.

DRUMM, D.B.   **EISNER, JOEL**

*Drumm, D.B. **Traveler #10: Hell on Earth** (Dell 0-440-13612-1, Oct,86 [Jan,87], $2.50, 171pp, pb) Post-holocaust adventure novel in a series; published in 1986, missed until now.

*Drumm, D.B. **Traveler #11: The Children's Crusade** (Dell 0-440-11529-9, Feb,87 [Jan,87], $2.75, 172pp, pb) Post-holocaust adventure novel. Traveler turns a group of kids into a guerilla force to save post-WWIII America.

*Drumm, D.B. **Traveler #12: The Prey** (Dell 0-440-16958-5, Sep,87 [Aug,87], $2.95, 170pp, pb) Post-holocaust adventure novel, latest in the series.

*Drumm, D.B. **Traveler #13: Ghost Dancers** (Dell 0-440-12841-2, Dec,87 [Nov,87], $2.75, 171pp, pb) Post-holocaust adventure novel.

*du Maurier, Daphne **Classics of the Macabre** (Gollancz 0-575-04050-5, Sep,87 [Oct,87], £10.95, 284pp, hc) Ghost/occult collection. Illustrated throughout by Michael Foreman.

*du Maurier, Daphne **Classics of the Macabre** (Gollancz 0-575-04191-9, Sep,87 [Oct,87], £25.00, 284pp, hc) Limited (250 copies) signed edition of the above. [Not seen]

*du Maurier, Daphne **Daphne Du Maurier's Classics of the Macabre** (Doubleday 0-385-24302-2, Nov,87 [Oct,87], $18.95, 284pp, hc) Collection of 6 tales of terror (including "The Birds"), with new color illustrations by Michael Foreman. There is a simultaneous British edition from Gollancz.

du Maurier, Daphne **Kiss Me Again, Stranger** (Dell 0-440-14576-7, May,87 [Apr,87], $3.95, 318pp, pb) Reprint (Doubleday 1952) collection of 8 stories, including "The Birds".

Duane, Diane E. **Star Trek #13: The Wounded Sky** (Pocket 0-671-60061-3, May,87, $3.50, 256pp, pb) Reissue (Pocket 1983) Star Trek novel; 4th printing.

*Duane, Diane E. & Peter Morwood **The Romulan Way** (Titan 1-85286-002-2, Aug,87, £2.95, 254pp, pb) Sf novel, Simultaneous with US (Pocket) edition. Volume 35 in the Star Trek Novels series.

*Duane, Diane E. & Peter Morwood **Star Trek #35: The Romulan Way** (Pocket 0-671-63498-4, Aug,87 [Jul,87], $3.50, 254pp, pb) Star Trek novel.

Dubbs, Chris **Ms. Faust** (Popular Library 0-445-20416-8, Jul,87 [Jun,87], $3.50, 296pp, pb) Reprint (Richardson & Steirman 1985) horror novel about a woman executive's deal with the devil.

Dudley, Terence **Black Orchid** (Target 0-426-20254-6, Feb,87, £1.75, 143pp, pb) Reprint (W.H. Allen 1986) juvenile sf novel. Volume 113 in the Doctor Who series.

*Dudley, Terence **K9 and Company** (Target 0-426-20309-7, Oct,87, £1.95, 160pp, pb) Juvenile sf novel. Volume 3 in the "Companions of Doctor Who" series.

Duncan, Dave **A Rose-Red City** (Ballantine/Del Rey 0-345-34098-1, Apr,87 [Mar,87], $2.95, 227pp, pb) Fantasy novel, a first novel.

*Duncan, Dave **Shadow** (Ballantine/Del Rey 0-345-34274-7, Nov,87 [Oct,87], $2.95, 276pp, pb) Sf novel; though it reads more like fantasy, it's an unusually dark and ironic adventure. Recommended. (FCM)

Dunmore, Spencer **The Sound of Wings** (Tor 0-812-51714-8, Jan,88 [Dec,87], $3.95, 347pp, pb) Reprint (Macmillan 1984) aviator's ghost story.

*Dvorkin, David **Budspy** (Franklin Watts 0-531-15053-4, Oct,87 [Sep,87], $17.95, 259pp, hc) Alternate-America sf novel, set 40 years after the Nazis won WWII.

*Earnshaw, Brian **Starclipper and the Galactic Final** (Pied Piper 0-416-00802-X, Mar,87, £5.95, 128pp, hc) Juvenile sf novel. Volume 3 in the "Star Jam Pack" series. [Not seen]

*Easton, M. Coleman **The Fisherman's Curse** (Popular Library Questar 0-445-20332-3, Feb,87 [Jan,87], $3.50, 236pp, pb) Fantasy novel, sequel to **Masters of Glass**.

*Easton, M. Coleman **Swimmers Beneath the Bright** (Popular Library Questar 0-445-20456-7, Sep,87 [Aug,87], $2.95, 236pp, pb) Anti-technological sf novel set on a water planet with bioengineered inhabitants.

Eddings, David **Enchanters' End Game** (Corgi 0-552-12447-8, Aug,87, £2.95, 372pp, pb) Reissue (Del Rey 1984) fantasy novel. Volume 5 in the "Belgariad" series.

*Eddings, David **Guardians of the West** (Ballantine/Del Rey 0-345-33000-5, Apr,87 [Mar,87], $16.95, 454pp, hc) Fantasy novel, Book One of "The Malloreon", the sequel to his pentalogy "The Belgariad". The book takes up shortly after "The Belgariad" left off, with the same complex set of characters, only with a new focus on the child Errand. Time passes quickly as a new evil appears, and old comrades re-arm to oppose it. An enjoyable meeting with old friends for those who have read the previous series, this might be over-involved for the newcomer. (CFC)

*Eddings, David **Guardians of the West** (Bantam UK 0-593-01195-3, Apr,87 [Mar,87], £9.95, 429pp, hc) Fantasy novel, simultaneous with US (Del Rey) edition. Volume 1 in the "Malloreon" series.

Eddings, David **Guardians of the West** (Corgi 0-552-13017-6, Aug,87 [Jul,87], £2.95, 429pp, pb) Reprint (Bantam UK/Del Rey 1987) fantasy novel. Volume 1 in the "Malloreon" series.

Eddings, David **Guardians of the West** (SFBC #11483, Nov,87, $6.98, 369pp, hc) Reprint (Del Rey 1986) fantasy novel, Book One of "The Mallorean".

Edmondson, G.C. & C.M. Kotlan **The Black Magician** (Ballantine/Del Rey 0-345-33221-0, Nov,87 [Oct,87], $2.95, 298pp, pb) Reissue (Del Rey 1986) sf novel, second in the "Cunningham Equations" trilogy. 2nd printing.

Edmondson, G.C. & C.M. Kotlan **The Cunningham Equations** (Ballantine/Del Rey 0-345-33037-4, Nov,87 [Oct,87], $2.95, 295pp, pb) Reissue (Del Rey 1986) sf novel, first in a trilogy; 3rd printing.

*Edmondson, G.C. & C.M. Kotlan **Maximum Effort** (Ballantine/Del Rey 0-345-33222-9, Nov,87 [Oct,87], $3.50, 299pp, pb) Sf novel, third in the "Cunningham Equations" trilogy.

*Edward, Ames J. **The Force** (Leisure 0-8439-2480-2, Apr,87 [Jul,87], $3.95, 400pp, pb) Horror novel.

*Edwards, Claudia J. **Bright and Shining Tiger** (Popular Library Questar 0-445-20626-8, Jan,88 [Dec,87], $2.95, 218pp, pb) Fantasy novel, set in the same universe as **Taming the Forest King** and **A Horsewoman in Godsland**.

*Edwards, Claudia J. **A Horsewoman in Godsland** (Popular Library Questar 0-445-20310-2, Jul,87 [Jun,87], $2.95, 219pp, pb) Fantasy novel of a powerful bishop and an outland woman horse trainer, at odds in a land of supernatural forces.

Edwards, Claudia J. **Taming the Forest King** (Headline 0-7472-3060-9, Oct,87, £2.50, 215pp, pb) Reprint (Popular Library 1986) fantasy novel. [First U.K. edition]

Effinger, George Alec **The Nick of Time** (NEL 0-450-41736-0, Dec,87 [Nov,87], £2.50, 244pp, pb) Reprint (Doubleday 1985) hilarious time-travel romp, complete with its own puzzle for the reader to solve. Great fun. [First U.K. edition]

Effinger, George Alec **When Gravity Fails** (Bantam Spectra 0-553-25555-X, Jan,88 [Dec,87], $3.95, 276pp, pb) Reprint (Arbor House 1987) hardboiled near-future cyberpunk sf novel, set in an Arab-controlled city. Highly recommended. (CNB)

Eisner, Joel **The Official Batman Batbook** (Titan 0-907610-97-8, Jul,87, £6.95, 184pp, tp) Associational. A guidebook to the *Batman* TV series. [First U.K. edition]

Elgin, Suzette Haden **Native Tongue** (DAW 0-88677-121-8, Feb,87 [Jan,87], $3.95, 301pp, pb) Reissue (DAW 1984) sf novel; 3rd printing.

*Elgin, Suzette Haden **Native Tongue II: The Judas Rose** (DAW 0-88677-186-2, Feb,87 [Jan,87], $3.50, 363pp, pb) Sf novel, sequel to **Native Tongue**. "The secret language of women is their one hope for regaining their freedom -- and for saving humankind."

*Eliot, Marc **How Dear the Dawn** (Ballantine 0-345-34315-8, Aug,87, $3.50, 284pp, pb) Horror novel.

*Elliott, Janice **The King Awakes** (Walker 0-7445-0804-5, Aug,87 [Oct,87], £6.95, 188pp, hc) Juvenile fantasy novel about King Arthur in a post-nuclear-holocaust Britain.

*Elliott, Nathan **Innerspace** (Dragon 0-583-31274-8, Dec,87, £1.95, 141pp, pb) Sf film novelization, based on a screenplay by Jeffrey Boam and Chip Proser. This is a pseudonym for Christopher Evans.

*Elliott, Nathan **Kidnap in Space** (Dragon 0-583-31114-8, Oct,87, £1.95, 155pp, pb) Juvenile sf novel. Volume 1 in the "Star Pirates" trilogy. This is a pseudonym for Christopher Evans.

*Elliott, Nathan **Plague Moon** (Dragon 0-583-31115-6, Oct,87, £1.95, 160pp, pb) Juvenile sf novel. Volume 2 in the "Star Pirates" trilogy. This is a pseudonym for Christopher Evans.

*Elliott, Nathan **Treasure Planet** (Dragon 0-583-31116-4, Oct,87, £1.95, 156pp, pb) Juvenile sf novel. Volume 3 in the "Star Pirates" trilogy. This is a pseudonym for Christopher Evans.

*Elliott, Richard **The Einstein Legacy** (Ballantine Fawcett 0-449-13180-7, Dec,87 [Nov,87], $3.50, 281pp, pb) Sf novel. The authors are Richard Geis and Elton Elliott.

Ellison, Harlan **An Edge in My Voice** (Donning 0-89865-341-X, Jul,87, $10.95, 548pp, tp) Reissue (Donning 1985); associational, a collection of essays, mostly on movies and tv. This second printing has a sticker that says it's revised, but "corrected" is probably closer. The ISBN is the same, although it's supposed to change when the price goes up and the text changes.

*Ellison, Harlan **The Essential Ellison** (Nemo Press 0-914261-01-0, Aug,87 [Jul,87], $29.95, 1019pp, hc) Collection of many, many stories and essays, edited by Terry Dowling, Richard Delap, and Gil Lamont. This is ment as a 35-year retrospective (it's taken 3 years to publish) of Ellison's work, from his early 1949 juvenilia to his work in the '80s. It's not a "best of", but a "warts and all" collection, divided into 15 sections with introductions to each one by one of the various editors. The texts of every item have been "corrected", but not rewritten. It isn't a book you sit down and *read* as much as you browse in. It isn't even reviewable except as a book-length study of Ellison's life. It's a well made book despite its size, and should stand up to years of use -- even throwing across a room. A bargain at twice the price. Recommended. (CNB) A limited edition ($60) was announced, but has apparently not appeared yet.

Ellison, Harlan, ed. **Dangerous Visions** (Gollancz 0-575-04144-7, Aug,87, £6.95, 544pp, tp) Reprint (Doubleday 1967) original sf anthology. Volume 16 in the Gollancz Classic SF series.

*Elphinstone, Margaret **The Incomer** (The Women's Press 0-7043-4070-4, May,87, £3.95, 229pp, tp) Post-holocaust novel.

*Ely, Scott **Starlight** (Weidenfeld & Nicolson 1-55584-047-7, Apr,87 [May,87], $15.95, 195pp, hc) This is being advertised as a straight Vietnam war novel, but it apparently develops into sf/fantasy -- or maybe just hallucination.

*Emerson, Ru **In the Caves of Exile** (Ace 0-441-37050-0, Jan,88 [Dec,87], $2.95, 310pp, pb) Fantasy novel, second in the "Tales of Nedao" series.

Emerson, Ru **The Princess of Flames** (Unicorn 0-04-823359-5, Jan,87, £2.95, 327pp, pb) Reprint (Ace 1986) fantasy novel. [First U.K. edition]

*Emerson, Ru **To the Haunted Mountains** (Ace 0-441-79558-7, Feb,87 [Jan,87], $2.95, 314pp, pb) Fantasy novel, "The First Tale of Nedao." Princess Ylia becomes queen with the help of her magic cat Misana.

Ende, Michael **The Neverending Story** (Puffin 0-14-031793-7, Dec,87, £2.95, 445pp, pb) Reissue (Doubleday 1983) juvenile fantasy novel.

*Enderle, Judith **First Love From Silhouette #174: Adrienne and the Blob** (Silhouette 0-373-06174-9, Feb,86 [Feb,87], $1.95, 155pp, pb) Teen romance/sf novel. Adrienne finds a strange growing glob on a biology class field trip. Published last year; just seen.

Engh, M.J. **Arslan** (Arbor House 0-87795-884-X, May,87 [Apr,87], $17.95, 296pp, hc) Reprint (Warner 1976) sf novel. First hardcover edition. It's set in a U.S. taken over by an outside dictatorship.

*Engh, M.J. **The House in the Snow** (Franklin Watts Orchard 0-531-08317-9, Aug,87, $11.95, 132pp, hc) Juvenile fantasy novel about invisible robbers and the boys who oppose them; illustrations by Leslie Bowman.

*Engle, Gary & Dennis Dooley **Superman at Fifty: The Persistence of a Legend** Main listing under Dennis Dooley.

Erickson, Paul **The Ark** (Target 0-426-20253-8, Mar,87, £1.75, 144pp, pb) Reprint (W.H. Allen 1986) juvenile sf novel. Volume 114 in the Doctor Who series.

Erskine, Barbara **Lady of Hay** (Sphere Overseas 0-7221-3359-6, 1987 [Apr,87], £3.95, 760pp, pb) Reprint (Michael Joseph 1986) sf/historical romance novel. Special "open market" edition.

+ Erskine, Barbara **Lady of Hay** (Delacorte 0-385-29539-1, Jun,87 [May,87], $17.95, 545pp, hc) A psychic time travel novel. A skeptical journalist researches hypnotic past-life regression and relives a medieval life that becomes entangled in her present love-life. A dramatic, well-written first novel. (CFC) First U.S. edition (Michael Joseph 1986).

Erskine, Barbara **Lady of Hay** (Sphere 0-7221-3359-6, Jul,87, £3.95, 760pp, pb) Reprint (Michael Joseph 1986) sf/historical romance novel.

*Estes, Rose **Greyhawk Adventures #3: Master Wolf** (TSR 0-88038-457-3, Apr,87 [Mar,87], $3.95, 314pp, pb) Novel taking place in the World of Greyhawk fantasy game setting. The first two books were written by Gary Gygax.

*Estes, Rose **Greyhawk Adventures #4: The Price of Power** (TSR 0-88038-458-1, Aug,87 [Nov,87], $3.95, 316pp, pb) Fantasy novel based on a game.

*Estes, Rose **Saga of the Lost Lands, Volume 1: Blood of the Tiger** (Bantam Spectra 0-553-26411-7, Dec,87 [Nov,87], $3.50, 198pp, pb) Fantasy novel, first in a new prehistoric trilogy.

Etchison, Dennis **Darkside** (Futura 0-7088-3399-3, Aug,87, £2.50, 246pp, pb) Reprint (Charter 1986) horror novel. [First U.K. edition]

Etchison, Dennis **Darkside** (Macdonald 0-356-14746-0, Oct,87, £10.95, 208pp, hc) Reprint (Charter 1986) horror novel. [Not seen]

Etchison, Dennis **Red Dreams** (Berkley 0-425-10398-6, Sep,87 [Aug,87], $3.50, 309pp, pb) Reprint (Scream/Press 1984) collection of 13 horror stories.

Etchison, Dennis, ed. **Cutting Edge** (St. Martin's 0-312-90772-9, Oct,87 [Sep,87], $3.95, 299pp, pb) Reprint (Doubleday 1986) anthology of horror stories, mostly original to this book.

Etchison, Dennis, ed. **Cutting Edge** (Futura 0-7088-3608-9, Dec,87, £2.95, 290pp, pb) Reprint (Doubleday 1986) original horror anthology. [First U.K. edition]

*Etchison, Dennis, ed. **Masters of Darkness II** (Tor 0-812-51764-4, Jan,88 [Dec,87], $3.95, 338pp, pb) Anthology of 15 horror stories, an "author's choice" selection with afterwords by the authors.

*Evans, Christopher & Robert Holdstock, eds. **Other Edens** (Unwin 0-04-823378-1, Jul,87, £2.95, 237pp, pb) Original sf/fantasy anthology.

FAIRLEY, JOHN

FERGUSSON, BRUCE

*Fairley, John & Simon Welfare **Arthur C. Clarke's Chronicles of the Strange and Mysterious** (Collins 0-00-217618-1, Dec,87, £15.00, 191pp, hc) Another collection of unexplained mysteries and oddities, written by Fairley and Welfare, with the occasional note by Clarke.

*Falconer, Sovereign **To Make Death Love Us** (Doubleday 0-385-17628-7, Jul,87, $12.95, 181pp, hc) Psychic horror fantasy novel. The author is listed in the advance publicity as Craig Strete.

*Fancher, Jane **Gate of Ivrel: Claiming Rites** (Donning/Starblaze 0-89865-515-3, Sep,87 [Oct,87], $6.95, unpaginated, tp) Graphic novel, adapted from the "Ivrel" sf books by C.J. Cherryh.

Farmer, Penelope **Charlotte Sometimes** (Dell/Yearling 0-440-41261-7, Mar,87 [Feb,87], $4.95, 174pp, tp) Reprint (Harcourt 1969) juvenile fantasy time travel novel; new afterword by Eleanor Cameron.

+Farmer, Penelope **Emma in Winter** (Dell/Yearling 0-440-42308-2, Nov,87, $2.95, 138pp, pb) Young adult fantasy novel, first U.S. edition (Chatto & Windus 1986).

Farmer, Penelope **The Summer Birds** (Dell/Yearling 0-440-47737-9, Jun,87 [May,87], $2.50, 102pp, tp) Reprint (Bodley Head 1985) juvenile fantasy novel in which village children learn to fly.

Farmer, Philip Jose **The Dark Design** (Severn House 0-7278-1448-6, Jun,87, £10.95, 464pp, hc) Reprint (Putnams 1977) sf novel. Volume 3 in the "Riverworld" series. [Not seen]

*Farmer, Philip Jose **Dayworld Rebel** (Ace/Putnam 0-399-13230-9, Jun,87 [Apr,87], $17.95, 317pp, hc) Sf novel, sequel to **Dayworld**.

Farmer, Philip Jose **Dayworld Rebel** (SFBC #11116, Jul,87 [Aug,87], $5.98, 256pp, hc) Reprint (Ace/Putnam 1987) sf novel, "Dayworld" #2.

Farmer, Philip Jose **Dayworld Rebel** (Ace 0-441-14002-5, Jan,88 [Dec,87], $3.95, 314pp, pb) Reprint (Ace/Putnam 1987) sf novel, second in the "Dayworld" series.

Farren, Mick **Protectorate** (NEL 0-450-05708-9, Aug,87, $2.95, 251pp, pb) Reissue (NEL 1984) sf novel.

Farren, Mick **The Song of Phaid the Gambler** (NEL 0-450-05343-1, Aug,87, £3.95, 537pp, pb) Reissue (NEL 1981) sf novel.

*Farren, Mick **Their Master's War** (Ballantine/Del Rey 0-345-34554-1, Jan,88 [Dec,87], $3.50, 295pp, pb) Sf novel about human soldiers a la **Starship Troopers** fighting alien wars.

*Farris, John **Nightfall** (Tor 0-812-51778-4, Apr,87 [Mar,87], $3.95, 311pp, pb) Horror novel.

Farris, John **Nightfall** (NEL 0-450-41729-8, Dec,87 [Nov,87], £2.95, 311pp, pb) Reprint (Tor 1987) horror novel. [First U.K. edition]

Farris, John **Son of the Endless Night** (NEL 0-450-40575-3, Mar,87 [Feb,87], £3.50, 550pp, pb) Reprint (St. Martin's 1985) horror novel.

Farris, John **The Uninvited** (Tor 0-812-51776-8, Jun,87 [May,87], $3.95, 276pp, pb) Reprint (Dell 1982) horror novel.

Farris, John **Wildwood** (Hodder & Stoughton 0-340-37734-8, Jul,87, £11.95, 445pp, hc) Reprint (Tor 1986) horror novel. [First U.K. edition, not seen]

*Faulcon, Robert **The Ghost Dance** (Arrow 0-09-931790-7, Jul,87, £3.50, 411pp, pb) Omnibus edition of the third and fourth books in the "Night Hunter" series. Billed as "Robert Holdstock writing as Robert Faulcon".

Faulcon, Robert **The Ghost Dance** (Century 0-7126-1747-7, Aug,87, £11.95, 411pp, hc) Reprint (Arrow 1987) omnibus edition of the third and fourth books in the "Night Hunter" series. Billed as "Robert Holdstock writing as Robert Faulcon".

*Faulcon, Robert **The Labyrinth** (Arrow 0-09-952160-1, Jun,87, £2.50, 283pp, pb) Horror novel. Volume 6 (and last) in the "Night Hunter" series. Billed as "Robert Holdstock writing as Robert Faulcon".

+Faulcon, Robert **Night Hunter** (Ace Charter 0-441-57469-6, Jul,87 [Jun,87], $2.95, 184pp, pb) Horror novel, first in a series. The author is Robert Holdstock. First U.S. edition (Arrow 1983).

+Faulcon, Robert **Night Hunter 2: The Talisman** (Ace Charter 0-441-57475-0, Sep,87 [Aug,87], $2.50, 183pp, pb) Occult horror novel, second in the series. Faulcon is a pseudonym for Robert Holdstock. First U.S. edition (Arrow 1983).

+Faulcon, Robert **Night Hunter 3: The Ghost Dance** (Ace Charter 0-441-57478-5, Nov,87 [Oct,87], $2.95, 184pp, pb) Horror novel, third in a series. "Faulcon" is actually Robert Holdstock. First U.S. edition (Arrow 1983).

*Faulcon, Robert **The Stalking** (Arrow 0-09-930440-6, Jul,87, £3.50, 400pp, pb) Omnibus edition of the first two books in the "Night Hunter" series. Billed as "Robert Holdstock writing as Robert Faulcon".

Faulcon, Robert **The Stalking** (Century 0-7126-1742-6, Aug,87, £11.95, 400pp, hc) Reprint (Arrow 1987) omnibus edition of the first two books in the "Night Hunter" series. Billed as "Robert Holdstock writing as Robert Faulcon".

*Faust, Joe Clifford **A Death of Honor** (Ballantine/Del Rey 0-345-34026-4, Feb,87 [Jan,87], $3.50, 326pp, pb) Sf/murder mystery novel. A first novel.

Faust, Joe Clifford **A Death of Honor** (SFBC #11010, Jun,87, $4.98, 275pp, hc) Reprint (Del Rey 1987) sf/mystery novel, a first novel. Recommended. (CNB)

Feist, Raymond E. **A Darkness at Sethanon** (Grafton Overseas 0-586-06688-8, 1987 [Apr,87], £3.50, 527pp, pb) Reprint (Doubleday 1986) fantasy novel. Special "open market" edition.

Feist, Raymond E. **A Darkness at Sethanon** (Bantam Spectra 0-553-26328-5, Feb,87 [Jan,87], $3.95, 430pp, pb) Reprint (Doubleday 1986) fantasy novel, conclusion of the "Riftwar Saga".

Feist, Raymond E. **A Darkness at Sethanon** (Grafton 0-586-06688-8, Oct,87 [Sep,87], £3.50, 527pp, pb) Reprint (Doubleday 1986) fantasy novel. Volume 3 in the "Riftwar Saga" series.

*Feist, Raymond E. & Janny Wurts **Daughter of the Empire** (Doubleday 0-385-23393-0, Jun,87 [May,87], $17.95, 394pp, hc) Fantasy novel running concurrently in the same universe as Feist's "Magician" series. Study of a woman with a single goal and what she will do to achieve it. Highly recommended. (TM)

Feist, Raymond E. & Janny Wurts **Daughter of the Empire** (Grafton 0-246-13226-4, Aug,87 [Jul,87], £10.95, 409pp, hc) Reprint (Doubleday 1987) fantasy novel. [First U.K. edition]

Feist, Raymond E. & Janny Wurts **Daughter of the Empire** (Grafton 0-246-13232-9, Aug,87, £6.95, 409pp, tp) Trade paperback edition of the above. [First U.K. edition]

Feist, Raymond E. & Janny Wurts **Daughter of the Empire** (SFBC #11627, Dec,87, $6.98, 367pp, hc) Reprint (Doubleday 1987) fantasy novel.

Felice, Cynthia **Double Nocturne** (DAW 0-88677-211-7, Jul,87 [Jun,87], $3.50, 330pp, pb) Reprint (Bluejay 1986) sf novel.

*Fenn, Lionel **Agnes Day** (Tor 0-812-53789-0, Aug,87 [Jul,87], $2.95, 248pp, pb) Fantasy novel, third in the "Quest for the White Duck" trilogy. Silly baseball bat and sorcery series. The author is Charles L. Grant.

*Fenn, Lionel **Web of Defeat** (Tor 0-812-53787-4, Feb,87 [Jan,87], $2.95, 284pp, pb) Humorous fantasy novel featuring a magic baseball bat. Sequel to **Blood River Down**. Fenn is a pseudonym for Charles L. Grant.

*Fergusson, Bruce **The Shadow of His Wings** (Arbor House 0-87795-852-1, Feb,87 [Jan,87], $16.95, 278pp, hc) Gritty fantasy novel set in the medieval kingdom of Myrcia, telling of a young man's quest. A first novel.

FERGUSSON, BRUCE

Fergusson, Bruce **The Shadow of His Wings** (Grafton 0-246-13251-5, Oct,87, £10.95, 300pp, hc) Reprint (Arbor House 1987) fantasy novel. [First U.K. edition]

Fergusson, Bruce **The Shadow of His Wings** (Grafton 0-246-13252-3, Oct,87, £6.95, 300pp, tp) Paperback edition of the above. [First U.K. edition]

*Finch, Sheila **The Garden of the Shaped** (Bantam Spectra 0-553-26801-5, Sep,87 [Aug,87], $3.50, 217pp, pb) Sf novel of genetically altered humans on an isolated planet. With its royalty and shape-shifting, this reads more like fantasy. (FCM)

Findley, Timothy **Not Wanted on the Voyage** (Dell/Laurel Leaf 0-440-36499-X, May,87, $4.95, 343pp, tp) Reprint (Delacorte 1986) fantasy novel set on Noah's Ark. Recommended. (FCM)

*Finlay, D.G. **Graven Image** (Century 0-7126-1650-0, Jun,87 [Sep,87], £10.95, 254pp, hc) Occult novel, volume 4 in the "Lavenham" series.

*Finney, Jack **3 By Finney** (Simon & Schuster Fireside 0-671-64048-8, Jul,87, $10.95, 416pp, tp) Omnibus edition of **The Woodrow Wilson Dime** (1968), **Marion's Wall** (1973), and **The Night People** (1977).

Finney, Jack **Invasion of the Body Snatchers** (Sphere 0-7221-3502-5, Apr,87, £1.95, 170pp, pb) Reissue (Dell 1961) sf novel.

Fisher, R.L. **The Prince of Whales** (Tor 0-812-56635-1, Oct,87 [Sep,87], $2.50, 151pp, pb) Reprint (Carroll & Graf 1985) fantasy novel, with illustrations by an uncredited artist.

*Fisk, Nicholas **Living Fire and Other S.F. Stories** (Corgi 0-552-52453-0, Aug,87, £1.95, 188pp, pb) Original sf collection.

*Fisk, Nicholas **Mindbenders** (Viking Kestrel 0-670-81244-7, Apr,87, £5.95, 128pp, hc) Juvenile sf novel. [Not seen]

Fisk, Nicholas **On the Flip Side** (Lythway Large Print 0-7451-0587-4, Sep,87, £6.95, 200pp, hc) Reprint (Kestrel 1983) juvenile novel. [Not seen]

Fisk, Nicholas **On the Flip Side** (Puffin 0-14-031556-X, Oct,87, £1.75, 121pp, pb) Reissue (Kestrel 1983) juvenile sf novel.

Fisk, Nicholas **Time Trap** (Puffin 0-14-031064-9, Jan,87, £1.50, 96pp, pb) Reissue (Gollancz 1976) juvenile sf novel.

*Fletcher, Adrian & Ryder Syvertsen **Psychic Spawn** Main listing under Ryder Syvertsen.

Flint, Homer Eon & Austin Hall **The Blind Spot** For main listing see under Austin Hall.

Flint, Kenneth C. **Challenge of the Clans** (Bantam UK 0-553-17384-7, Sep,87, £2.95, 328pp, pb) Reprint (Bantam 1986) fantasy novel. Volume 5 in the "Sidhe Legends" series. [First U.K. edition]

Flint, Kenneth C. **Champions of the Sidhe** (Bantam UK 0-553-17256-5, Feb,87, £2.50, 277pp, pb) Reprint (Bantam 1984) fantasy novel. Volume 3 in the "Sidhe Legends" series. [First U.K. edition]

*Flint, Kenneth C. **The Dark Druid** (Bantam Spectra 0-553-26715-9, Aug,87 [Jul,87], $3.50, 326pp, pb) Celtic fantasy novel, conclusion to the "Challenge of the Clans" trilogy.

Flint, Kenneth C. **Master of the Sidhe** (Bantam UK 0-553-17292-1, May,87, £2.50, 248pp, pb) Reprint (Bantam 1985) fantasy novel. Volume 4 in the "Sidhe Legends" series. [First U.K. edition]

*Foglio, Phil & Robert Lynn Asprin **Myth Adventures Two** (Donning/Starblaze 0-89865-473-4, Jan,87, $12.95, 110pp, tp) Graphic novel, a gathering of issues 5 through 8 of the "Myth Adventures" comic, with art by Foglio (now in a color version) and captions by Asprin, based on his humorous fantasy series. There is also supposed to be a 2,000-copy "limited" hardcover (0-89865-414-2, $40.00) but we have not seen it.

FOSTER, ALAN DEAN

*Fonstad, Karen Wynn **Atlas of the Dragonlance World** (TSR 0-88038-448-4, Nov,87, $15.95, 168pp, tp) Maps and description of the "Dragonlance" world.

*Ford, John M. **How Much for Just the Planet?** (Titan 1-85286-018-9, Oct,87 [Nov,87], £2.95, 253pp, pb) Sf novel. Simultaneous with the US edition. Volume 51 in the Star Trek Novels series.

*Ford, John M. **Star Trek #36: How Much for Just the Planet?** (Pocket 0-671-62998-0, Oct,87 [Sep,87], $3.95, 253pp, pb) Latest in the series based on characters from the original tv show.

*Ford, Paul F. **Companion to Narnia** (Macmillan/Collier 0-02-084940-0, Sep,86 [Feb,87], $10.95, 450pp, tp) Non-fiction, critical study. Revised third edition of an index to the "Narnia" fantasies of C.S. Lewis. The earlier editions (Harper & Row 1980, 1983) are essentially the same and are probably just as useful, unless you are a true detail fan. This came out in 1986, but we did not see it until 1987.

Ford, Richard **Melvaig's Vision** (Grafton 0-586-05885-0, Feb,87, £2.95, 446pp, pb) Reissue (Granada 1984) fantasy novel. Volume 2 in the "Faradawn" trilogy.

Forrest, Katherine V. **Daughters of a Coral Dawn** (Naiad 0-930044-50-9, Jan,86 [May,87], $7.95, 226pp, tp) Reissue (Naiad 1984) feminist/lesbian sf novel. This second edition is dated January 1986, but we had not seen it until now.

*Forrest, Katherine V. **Dreams and Swords** (Naiad 0-941483-03-7, Sep,87, $8.95, 175pp, tp) Collection of 10 lesbian-oriented stories, mostly sf and horror. 9 of the stories are apparently originals.

Forrester, John **Bestiary Mountain** (Harper & Row/Starwanderer 0-694-05606-5, Jun,87, $2.75, 140pp, pb) Reprint (Bradbury Press 1985) young-adult sf novel.

*Forrester, John **The Secret of the Round Beast** (Bradbury 0-02-735380-X, Oct,86 [Jan,87], $12.95, 145pp, hc) Young-adult sf novel, sequel to **Bestiary Mountain**. This appeared in 1986; not seen until now.

*Forstchen, William R. **The Alexandrian Ring** (Ballantine/Del Rey 0-345-33581-3, Oct,87 [Sep,87], $3.50, 295pp, pb) Sf/military gaming novel, Book One of "The Gamester Wars". Alexander the Great is a character.

Forstchen, William R. **Into the Sea of Stars** (Futura 0-345-32426-9, Oct,87, £1.95, 231pp, pb) Reprint sf novel. This is the US edition (Del Rey 1986) with a UK price sticker. [First U.K. edition]

*Fortier, Ron & Ardath Mayhar **Trail of the Seahawks** Main listing under Ardath Mayhar.

Forward, Robert L. **The Flight of the Dragonfly** (NEL 0-450-05823-9, Aug,87, £2.95, 318pp, pb) Reissue (Timescape 1984) sf novel.

Fosburgh, Liza **Bella Arabella** (Bantam Skylark 0-553-15484-2, Apr,87 [Mar,87], $2.50, 102pp, tp) Reprint (Four Winds 1985) juvenile fantasy novel.

Foster, Alan Dean **Aliens** (Severn House 0-7278-1433-8, Jan,87, £8.95, 247pp, hc) Reprint (Warner 1986) sf film novelization.

Foster, Alan Dean **Bloodhype** (NEL 0-450-04339-8, Jul,87, £2.50, 206pp, pb) Reissue (Ballantine 1973) sf novel.

Foster, Alan Dean **Cachalot** (NEL 0-450-05193-5, Jul,87, £2.95, 275pp, pb) Reissue (Ballantine 1980) sf novel.

*Foster, Alan Dean **The Deluge Drivers** (Ballantine/Del Rey 0-345-33330-6, Jun,87 [May,87], $3.95, 311pp, pb) Sf novel, Book Three of the "Icerigger" trilogy.

*Foster, Alan Dean **Glory Lane** (Ace 0-441-51664-5, Aug,87 [Jul,87], $3.50, 295pp, pb) Humorous science fiction novel.

Foster, Alan Dean **Icerigger** (Ballantine/Del Rey 0-345-33395-0, Jun,87 [May,87], $2.95, 313pp, pb) Reissue (Del Rey 1974) sf novel, first in the "Icerigger" trilogy. 11th printing, with 385,000 copies in print.

FOSTER, ALAN DEAN   **GARDNER, CRAIG SHAW**

Foster, Alan Dean **Icerigger** (NEL 0-450-05423-3, Jul,87, £2.95, 319pp, pb) Reissue (Ballantine 1974) sf novel.

Foster, Alan Dean **Into the Out Of** (Warner 0-446-34559-8, Aug,87 [Jul,87], $3.95, 376pp, pb) Reprint (Warner 1986) horror novel.

Foster, Alan Dean **Into the Out Of** (NEL 0-450-41013-7, Aug,87, £10.95, 293pp, hc) Reprint (Warner 1986) fantasy/horror novel. [First U.K. edition]

Foster, Alan Dean **The Man Who Used the Universe** (Severn House 0-7278-1485-0, Jul,87, £9.95, 320pp, hc) Reprint (SFBC 1983) sf novel. [Not seen]

Foster, Alan Dean **Mission to Moulokin** (Ballantine/Del Rey 0-345-33322-5, Jun,87 [May,87], $2.95, 294pp, pb) Reissue (Del Rey 1979) sf novel, second in the "Icerigger" trilogy. 7th printing, with 238,000 copies in print.

Foster, Alan Dean **Nor Crystal Tears** (NEL 0-450-05594-9, Aug,87, £1.95, 231pp, pb) Reissue (Ballantine 1982) sf novel.

Foster, Alan Dean **Pale Rider** (Ulverscroft Large Print 0-7089-6341-2, Jan,87, £4.75, 400pp, hc) Associational. Western film novelization by sf author. [Not seen]

*Foster, Alan Dean **Spellsinger's Scherzo** (SFBC #10611, May,87, $7.98, 661pp, hc) Second omnibus of three novels in the "Spellsinger" fantasy series.

Foster, Alan Dean **The Time of the Transference** (Orbit 0-7088-8246-3, Oct,87, £2.95, 280pp, pb) Reprint (Phantasia 1986) fantasy novel. Volume 6 in the "Spellsinger" series. [First U.K. edition]

Foster, Alan Dean **Voyage to the City of the Dead** (NEL 0-450-39874-9, Aug,87, £2.50, 243pp, pb) Reissue (Del Rey 1984) sf novel.

+Foster, John, ed. **Spaceways** (Salem House/Oxford 0-19-276068-8, Apr,87 [Mar,87], $5.95, 128pp, tp) Juvenile sf poetry anthology. This is actually the 1986 British edition (Oxford) with distribution through Salem House.

Fox, Peter **Downtime** (Coronet 0-340-41366-2, Dec,87, £2.95, 254pp, pb) Reprint (Hodder & Stoughton 1986) near-future thriller.

*Franklin, Cheryl J. **Fire Get** (DAW 0-88677-231-1, Nov,87 [Oct,87], $3.50, 338pp, pb) Fantasy novel. "Could Rhianna survive the magical dangers of a Power quest?" Probably a first novel.

*Frankowski, Leo A. **Copernick's Rebellion** (Ballantine/Del Rey 0-345-34033-7, Apr,87 [Mar,87], $2.95, 202pp, pb) Near-future genetic/economic sf novel.

*Frazier, Robert **Perception Barriers** (BPW&P 0-917658-25-6, Aug,87, $5.95, 46pp, tp) Book of poetry, much of it sf-oriented.

Freeman, Maggie **Danger! Space Pirates** (Hodder & Stoughton 0-340-39307-6, Jan,87, £5.95, 112pp, hc) Juvenile sf novel. [Not seen]

Freeman, Mary E. Wilkins **The Wind in the Rosebush and Other Tales of the Supernatural** (Academy Chicago 0-89733-233-4, Jan,87, $15.95, 258pp, hc) Reprint (Doubleday 1903) collection. The paperback appeared in 1986; this hardcover is an instant binding of it.

Friedell, Egon **The Return of the Time Machine** (Starmont House 1-55742-045-9, Nov,87 [Dec,87], $19/95, 127pp, hc) Reprint (DAW 1972) sf novel, originally published in Germany in 1946. Sequel to the H.G. Wells classic by one of his contemporaries; translated by Eddy C. Bertin. This first hardcover edition is offset from the DAW plates and has a laminated cover without d/w. It's aimed at a library market.

*Friedman, C.S. **In Conquest Born** (DAW 0-88677-198-6, May,87 [Apr,87], $3.95, 511pp, pb) Sf novel about two generals, one from a race of telepaths, one from a race of "ultimate warriors," who are personal rivals in a war between the races. A first novel.

Friedman, C.S. **In Conquest Born** (SFBC #11589, Nov,87, $6.98, 440pp, hc) Reprint (DAW 1987) sf novel; first hardcover edition.

*Friedman, Michael Jan **The Glove of Maiden's Hair** (Popular Library Questar 0-445-20406-0, Mar,87 [Feb,87], $3.50, 234pp, pb) Fantasy novel of elves, magic, and modern New York.

Friends of Darkover, The & Marion Zimmer Bradley **The Keeper's Price** Main listing under Marion Zimmer Bradley.

*Friends of Darkover, The & Marion Zimmer Bradley **The Other Side of the Mirror** Main listing under Marion Zimmer Bradley.

*Friends of Darkover, The & Marion Zimmer Bradley **Red Sun of Darkover** Main listing under Marion Zimmer Bradley.

Friends of Darkover, The & Marion Zimmer Bradley **Sword of Chaos** Main listing under Marion Zimmer Bradley.

Friesner, Esther M. **New York by Knight** (Headline 0-7472-3054-4, Sep,87, £2.95, 252pp, pb) Reprint (Signet 1986) fantasy novel. [First U.K. edition]

*Friesner, Esther M. **The Witchwood Cradle** (Avon 0-380-75100-3, Mar,87 [Feb,87], $3.50, 241pp, pb) Fantasy novel, third in the "Chronicles of the Twelve Kingdoms".

*Frith, Nigel **Dragon** (Unwin 0-04-823351-X, Jul,87, £2.95, 305pp, pb) Fantasy novel.

Fuller, John G. **The Ghost of 29 Megacycles** (Grafton 0-586-06869-4, Jan,87, £2.95, 351pp, pb) Reprint (Souvenir Press 1985) occult non-fiction.

Furlong, Monica **Wise Child** (Gollancz 0-575-04046-7, Jun,87 [May,87], £7.95, 192pp, hc) Juvenile fantasy novel. [Not seen]

*Furlong, Monica **Wise Child** (Knopf 0-394-89105-8, Oct,87, $11.95, 228pp, hc) Young-adult Arthurian fantasy novel.

*Gadallah, Leslie **Cat's Pawn** (Ballantine/Del Rey 0-345-33742-5, Mar,87 [Feb,87], $2.95, 262pp, pb) Sf novel with cat-like aliens. A decent first novel about the first human to get to know an alien cat-people and their shameful secret. Though the "disgusting" quality of the secret is overplayed badly, it's an otherwise interesting picture of cat people and the human underworld of a "spaceport" ghetto. (CFC)

*Gaiman, Neil **Don't Panic: The Official Hitch Hiker's Guide to the Galaxy Companion** (Titan 1-85286-013-8, Jan,88 [Dec,87], £3.95, 182pp, tp) Associational book.

*Gallagher, Stephen **Valley of Lights** (NEL 0-450-40664-4, Jun,87 [Nov,87], £9.95, 191pp, hc) Horror novel.

Gallico, Paul **The Abandoned** (IPL 0-930330-64-1, Jun,87 [May,87], $5.95, 256pp, pb) Reprint (Knopf 1950; UK title **Jennie**) novel of cats in London, with fantasy elements (the cats talk to each other).

*Garcia Marquez, Gabriel, [ref.] **Garcia Marquez: Writer of Colombia** Main listing under Stephen Minta.

+Gardam, Jane **Through the Dolls' House Door** (Morrow/Greenwillow 0-688-07447-2, Oct,87, $10.25, 121pp, hc) Juvenile fantasy novel of children and the life of dolls. (The publisher bills it as "for all ages.") First U.S. edition (Macrae 1987).

*Garden, Nancy **The Door Between** (Farrar, Straus & Giroux 0-374-31833-6, Aug,87 [Oct,87], $13.95, 184pp, hc) Young adult fantasy novel, in the "Fours Crossing" series.

*Garden, Nancy **Mystery of the Night Raiders** (Farrar, Straus & Giroux 0-374-35221-6, Oct,87 [Nov,87], $11.95, 167pp, hc) Juvenile vampire/monster-hunting mystery novel, first in a series.

Garden, Nancy **Prisoner of Vampires** (Corgi 0-552-52368-2, Nov,87, £1.95, 191pp, pb) Reprint (Farrar Strauss Giroux 1984) juvenile horror novel. [First U.K. edition]

*Gardner, Craig Shaw **A Difficulty With Dwarves** (Ace 0-441-14779-8, Dec,87 [Nov,87], $2.95, 188pp, pb) Humorous fantasy novel, fourth in the "Ebenezvm Trilogy".

GARDNER, CRAIG SHAW

GLADNEY, HEATHER

*Gardner, Craig Shaw **The Exploits of Ebenezvm** (SFBC #11588, Nov,87, $6.98, 437pp, hc) Humorous fantasy omnibus of **A Malady of Magics**, **A Multitude of Monsters**, and **A Night in the Netherhells**.

*Gardner, Craig Shaw **The Lost Boys** (Berkley 0-425-10044-8, Jul,87, $3.50, 220pp, pb) Novelization of a film script, featuring teenage vampire bikers.

*Gardner, Craig Shaw **A Night in the Netherhells** (Ace 0-441-02314-2, Jun,87 [May,87], $2.95, 185pp, pb) Humorous fantasy novel, third in the "Ebenezum Trilogy".

Gardner, John **Golgotha** (Crescent Large Print 0-427-00075-0, Mar,87, £3.95, 325pp, tp) Reprint (W.H. Allen 1980) near-future thriller.

*Gardner, Martin **The No-Sided Professor** (Prometheus 0-87975-390-0, Apr 15,87 [Mar,87], $16.95, 220pp, hc) Collection of 26 stories -- fantasy, humor, and associational.

Garner, Alan **The Owl Service** (Windrush Large Print 1-85089-909-6, Mar,87 [1987], £7.65, 217pp, hc) Reprint (Collins 1967) fantasy novel. [Not seen]

+Garnett, Bill **The Crone** (St. Martin's 0-312-90747-8, Aug,87 [Jul,87], $3.50, 215pp, pb) Horror novel. First American edition (Sphere 1984).

*Garrett, Randall **Takeoff Too!** (Donning/Starblaze 0-89865-455-6, Apr,87, $7.95, 311pp, tp) A second volume of sf parodies and pastiches, following **Takeoff**. Introduction and afterword by Vicki Ann Heydron, who made the selections and tells why.

*Garrido, Mar **Eileen Goudge's Swept Away #6: Once Upon a Kiss** (Avon/Flare 0-380-75133-X, May,87 [Apr,87], $2.50, 170pp, pb) Teenage romance/sf novel, latest in a series about time travel by computer. This one takes the heroine back to the days of King Arthur.

Garton, Ray **Live Girls** (Futura 0-7088-8239-0, Oct,87, £2.95, 311pp, pb) Reprint (Pocket 1987) vampire novel. [First U.K. edition]

Garton, Ray **Live Girls** (Macdonald 0-356-14799-1, Nov,87, £11.95, 320pp, hc) Reprint (Pocket 1987) vampire novel. [Not seen]

*Gauger, Rick **Charon's Ark** (Ballantine/Del Rey 0-345-31773-4, Aug,87 [Jul,87], $3.50, 375pp, pb) Sf novel. Aliens kidnap a planeload of high school students, ranging from nerdy sf fan to airheaded prom queen type, to become exhibits/staff for a doomed space ark. Complex action and interesting situations get bogged down somewhat by a large cast of unlikeable characters, but this is a promising first novel. (CFC)

Geary, Patricia **Living in Ether** (Bantam Spectra 0-553-26329-3, Mar,87 [Feb,87], $3.50, 214pp, pb) Geary, Patricia free-associational life, is haunted by the ghosts (at least one of them real) of her past. Quirky and amusing. (CFC)

*Geary, Patricia **Strange Toys** (Bantam Spectra 0-553-26872-4, Jul,87 [Jun,87], $3.50, 348pp, pb) Fantasy novel of a girl growing up, and encountering the supernatural.

Geasland, Jack & Bari Wood **Twins** Main listing under Bari Wood.

*Geduld, Harry M. **The Definitive Time Machine: A Critical Edition of H.G. Wells' Scientific Romance** (Indiana Univ. Press 0-253-20427-5, Sep,87, $10.95, 218pp, tp) Critical edition with introduction and notes by Geduld, plus extensive appendices. Also announced in a hardcover edition (-31611-1, $27.50).

Gee, Morris **The Priests of Ferris** (Puffin 0-14-032061-X, Sep,87, £1.95, 180pp, pb) Reprint (Oxford University Press 1984) juvenile sf novel. Volume 2 in the "World of O" series.

*Gemmell, David **Wolf in Shadow** (Century 0-7126-1821-X, Aug,87, £5.95, 326pp, tp) Fantasy novel.

*Gemmell, David **Wolf in Shadow** (Century 0-7126-1559-8, Aug,87, £10.95, 326pp, hc) Hardback edition of the above.

Gemmell, David **Wolf in Shadow** (Legend 0-09-953470-3, Dec,87, £3.50, 326pp, pb) Reprint (Century 1987) fantasy novel. Despite the overtones of **Shane** this remains a very enjoyable book - distinctly less *twee* than most fantasy novels around.

*Gentle, Mary **Ancient Light** (Gollancz 0-575-03629-X, Aug,87, £11.95, 539pp, hc) Fantasy novel. Sequel to **Golden Witchbreed**.

Gentle, Mary **A Hawk in Silver** (Gollancz 0-575-02386-4, Sep,87, £8.95, 192pp, hc) Reissue (Gollancz 1977) juvenile fantasy novel. [Not seen]

Gerani, Gary & Paul H. Schulman **Fantastic Television** (Titan 0-907610-98-6, Jul,87, £7.95, 192pp, tp) Reprint (Harmony 1977) of associational interest. A rather dated guide to sf/fantasy TV series. [First U.K. edition]

Gerrold, David **Space Skimmer** (Arrow 0-09-950660-2, Apr,87, £2.50, 218pp, pb) Reprint (Ballantine 1972) sf novel. Volume 12 in the Venture SF series. [First U.K. edition]

*Gerrold, David **Star Trek, The Next Generation: Encounter at Farpoint** (Pocket 0-671-65241-9, Oct,87 [Sep,87], $3.95, 192pp, pb) Novelization of the first episode of the new series.

Gerrold, David **Starhunt** (Legend 0-09-940900-3, Dec,87, £2.50, 252pp, pb) Reissue (Dell 1972, as **Yesterday's Children**) sf novel. Volume 6 in the "Venture SF" series.

Gibson, William **Burning Chrome** (Ace 0-441-08934-8, Oct,87 [Sep,87], $2.95, 191pp, pb) Reprint (Arbor House 1986) collection.

Gibson, William **Count Zero** (Ace 0-441-11773-2, Apr,87 [Mar,87], $2.95, 246pp, pb) Reprint (Gollancz 1986) sf novel set in the same world as **Neuromancer** but not exactly a sequel.

Gibson, William **Count Zero** (Grafton 0-586-07121-0, Jul,87, £2.95, 335pp, pb) Reprint (Gollancz 1986) sf novel. Volume 2 in the "Cyberspace" series.

*Gilbert, Harry **Ghost's Playground** (Piccadilly 0-946826-81-1, Jun,87 [Jul,87], £4.95, 52pp, hc) Juvenile supernatural novella. [Not seen]

Gilbert, John **Aiki** (Pocket 0-671-61498-0, Jan,88 [Dec,87], $3.95, 278pp, pb) Reprint (Donald Fine 1986) futuristic martial arts/gladiator/drug novel.

*Gilden, Mel **Born to Howl** (Avon/Camelot 0-380-75425-8, Dec,87 [Nov,87], $2.50, 90pp, pb) Humorous juvenile fantasy/horror novel, sequel to **M is for Monster**. Fifth grade werewolf wants to be a "real" boy.

*Gilden, Mel **M. Is for Monster** (Avon/Camelot 0-380-75423-1, Nov,87 [Oct,87], $2.50, 89pp, pb) Humorous juvenile fantasy novella.

*Gilluly, Sheila **Greenbriar Queen** (NAL/Signet 0-451-15143-7, Jan,88 [Dec,87], $3.50, 330pp, pb) Fantasy novel based on a D&D game. A first novel.

*Giraud, Jean "Moebius" **Arzach and Other Fantasy Stories** (Marvel/Epic 0-87135-279-6, Aug,87 [Dec,87], $9.95, unpaginated, tp) Graphic collection.

*Giraud, Jean "Moebius" **The Long Tomorrow and Other Science Fiction Stories** (Marvel/Epic 0-87135-281-8, Dec,87, $9.95, unpaginated, tp) Graphic collection.

*Giraud, Jean "Moebius" **Moebius 1: Upon a Star** (Marvel/Epic 0-87135-278-8, Jun,87, $9.95, unpaginated, tp) Graphic novel, first in a planned series by illustrator Jean "Moebius" Giraud.

Giroux, Leo, Jr. **The Rishi** (Ballantine Ivy 0-8041-0111-6, Mar,87 [Feb,87], $4.50, 459pp, pb) Reprint (Evans 1985) fantasy novel. "The ancient cult of thuggee rises again...."

Giroux, Leo, Jr. **The Rishi** (Grafton 0-586-06934-8, Oct,87, £3.50, 560pp, pb) Reprint (Evans 1985) fantasy/horror novel.

*Gladney, Heather **Teot's War** (Ace 0-441-80083-1, May,87 [Apr,87], $2.95, 264pp, pb) Fantasy novel, a first novel.

GLOVER, JULIAN

GRANT, CHARLES L., ED.

*Glover, Julian **Beowulf** (Alan Sutton 0-86299-337-7, Nov,87, £14.95, 137pp, hc) This is the adaptation that Julian Glover did for his one-man show, based mainly on Michael Alexander's translation, and with an introduction by Magnus Magnusson. Probably not for the purist, but the glorious illustrations by Sheila Mackie are worth the price of admission on their own.

*Glut, Donald F., George Lucas & James Kahn **The Star Wars Trilogy** Main listing under George Lucas.

*Goddin, Jeffrey **The Living Dead** (Leisure 0-8439-2470-5, Apr,87 [Aug,87], $3.95, 383pp, pb) Horror novel. "They returned from the grave to drag the living back to hell."

Godwin, Parke & Marvin Kaye **Wintermind** (Orbit 0-7088-8249-8, Jun,87, £3.50, 297pp, pb) Reprint (Doubleday 1982) fantasy novel. [First U.K. edition]

Goldin, Stephen **Assault on the Gods** (Arrow 0-09-952770-7, Dec,87, £2.50, 189pp, pb) Reprint (Doubleday 1977) sf novel. Volume 16 in the "Venture SF" series. [First U.K. edition]

*Goldman, William **Brothers** (Warner 0-446-51279-6, Feb,87 [Jan,87], $17.95, 310pp, hc) Near-future thriller with elements of sf (inventions and mad scientists), sequel to **The Marathon Man**.

Goldman, William **The Princess Bride** (Ballantine/Del Rey 0-345-34803-6, Oct,87 [Sep,87], $3.95, 283pp, pb) Reissue (Harcourt Brace Jovanovich 1973) humorous fantasy novel; 17th printing. Movie tie-in edition, with a still on the cover and a new fold-out color map.

*Goldstein, Lisa **A Mask for the General** (Bantam Spectra 0-553-05239-X, Nov,87 [Oct,87], $14.95, 199pp, hc) Near-future sf novel. Recommended. (FCM)

*Goldstein, Lisa **The Red Magician** (Unicorn 0-04-823323-4, Feb,87, £2.95, 156pp, tp) Fantasy novel.

*Gordon, Jeffie Ross **First Love From Silhouette #198: A Touch of Genius** (Silhouette 0-373-06198-6, Aug,86 [Feb,87], $0.99, 157pp, pb) Fantasy romance novel. Teenage girl finds a handsome bottled genie, who falls in love with her high-school-cheerleader rival. Published in 1986, but not seen until 1987.

*Gordon, Stuart **Archon!** (Macdonald 0-356-14335-X, Aug,87, £11.95, 316pp, hc) Fantasy novel. Volume 1 in the "Watchers" trilogy.

*Gorey, Edward **The Raging Tide** (Beaufort 0-8253-0437-7, Nov,87, $9.95, 30pp, hc) A "choose-your-own" fantasy/art book as only Edward Gorey could produce.

Gormley, Beatrice **The Ghastly Glasses** (Avon/Camelot 0-380-70262-2, Feb,87, $2.50, 117pp, pb) Reprint (Dutton 1985) juvenile fantasy novel about a girl whose new glasses distort her vision and give her strange powers.

Gormley, Beatrice **Mail-Order Wings** (Avon/Camelot 0-380-67421-1, Feb,87, $2.50, 164pp, pb) Reprint (Dutton 1981) juvenile fantasy novel about a girl who gets mail-order wings.

*Gormley, Beatrice **Richard and the Vratch** (Avon/Camelot 0-380-75207-7, Oct,87 [Sep,87], $3.75, 133pp, pb) Juvenile sf novel about a tribe of prehistoric creatures.

Gorog, Judith **When Flesh Begins to Creep** (Lions 0-00-672777-8, Dec,87, £1.95, 142pp, pb) Reprint (Philomel 1982, as **A Taste for Quiet**) original juvenile fantasy/occult collection.

*Gotlieb, Phyllis & Douglas Barbour, eds. **Tesseracts 2** (Porcepic 0-88878-270-5, Nov,87, C$9.95, 295pp, tp) Mostly original anthology of 23 Canadian sf stories, including some appearing in English for the first time.

*Goudge, Eileen **Eileen Goudge's Swept Away #1: Gone With the Wish** (Avon Flare 0-380-75128-3, Sep,86 [Feb,87], $2.50, 166pp, pb) Young adult sf/romance novel, first in a series about time-traveling teens. Issued in 1986; not seen until now.

*Goudge, Eileen **Eileen Goudge's Swept Away #4: Star Struck** (Avon Flare 0-380-75131-3, Jan,87, $2.50, 202pp, pb) Latest in a series of teenage time travel romances; a computer makes Kiki Wynkowski's wildest dreams come true, and she's back in the '30s starring in a major movie.

*Goulart, Ron **The Curse of the Obelisk** (Avon 0-380-89858-6, Nov,87 [Oct,87], $2.95, 139pp, pb) Humorous fantasy novel.

*Goulart, Ron **Daredevils, Ltd.** (St. Martin's 0-312-90140-2, Jun,87 [May,87], $2.95, 185pp, pb) Sf novel of a future private investigator, part of the humorous "Ben Jolson" series.

*Goulart, Ron **Starpirate's Brain** (St. Martin's 0-312-90053-8, Oct,87 [Sep,87], $2.95, 184pp, pb) Sf adventure novel, Book 2 of "The Exchameleon series."

*Gowar, Mick, ed. **Twisted Circuits** (Beaver 0-09-943400-8, Jan,87, £1.75, 144pp, pb) Original juvenile sf anthology.

Grant, Charles L. **The Dark Cry of the Moon** (Berkley 0-425-10502-4, Dec,87 [Nov,87], $2.95, 184pp, pb) Reprint (Grant 1985) horror novel, part of the "Oxrun Station" series.

Grant, Charles L. **The Hour of the Oxrun Dead** (Tor 0-812-51862-4, Feb,87 [Jan,87], $3.50, 284pp, pb) Reprint (Doubleday 1977) horror novel, first in the series set in Oxrun Station. This was a finalist for the World Fantasy Award. The copyright page does not acknowledge earlier editions.

Grant, Charles L. **The Pet** (Tor 0-812-51848-9, May,87 [Apr,87], $3.95, 343pp, pb) Reprint (Tor 1986) horror novel.

Grant, Charles L. **The Pet** (Futura 0-7088-8229-3, Jul,87, £2.95, 343pp, pb) Reprint (Tor 1986) horror novel. [First U.K. edition]

Grant, Charles L. **The Pet** (Macdonald 0-356-14568-9, Sep,87, £11.95, 352pp, hc) Reprint (Tor 1986) horror novel. [Not seen]

Grant, Charles L. **The Soft Whisper of the Dead** (Berkley 0-425-10481-8, Oct,87 [Sep,87], $2.95, 159pp, pb) Reprint (Donald M. Grant 1982) horror novel in the "Oxrun Station" series.

Grant, Charles L. **The Sound of Midnight** (Tor 0-812-51864-0, Aug,87 [Jul,87], $3.95, 249pp, pb) Reprint (Doubleday 1978) horror novel in the "Oxrun Station" series.

*Grant, Charles L., ed. **Doom City** (Tor 0-812-51866-7, Dec,87 [Nov,87], $3.95, 307pp, pb) Original shared world horror anthology with 16 stories, sequel to **Greystone Bay**.

Grant, Charles L., ed. **Night Visions: Dead Image** (Berkley 0-425-10182-7, Sep,87 [Aug,87], $3.95, 309pp, pb) Reprint (Dark Harvest 1985 as **Night Visions 2**) original anthology of 12 horror stories, by David Morrell, Joseph Payne Brennan, and Karl Edward Wagner.

Grant, Charles L., ed. **Shadows** (Headline 0-7472-3002-1, Jun,87, £2.50, 216pp, pb) Reprint (Doubleday 1981 as **Shadows 4**) original horror anthology. [First U.K. edition]

Grant, Charles L., ed. **Shadows** (Headline 0-7472-0009-2, Jun,87, £10.95, 216pp, hc) Hardback edition of the above. [First U.K. edition, not seen]

Grant, Charles L., ed. **Shadows 7** (Berkley 0-425-09564-9, Feb,87 [Jan,87], $2.95, 183pp, pb) Reprint (Doubleday 1984) original horror anthology of 14 stories.

Grant, Charles L., ed. **Shadows 8** (Berkley 0-425-09890-7, May,87 [Apr,87], $2.95, 181pp, pb) Reprint (Doubleday 1985) original horror anthology.

*Grant, Charles L., ed. **Shadows 10** (Doubleday 0-385-23893-2, Oct,87, $12.95, 178pp, hc) Original anthology of 14 horror stories.

Grant, Charles L., ed. **Shadows II** (Headline 0-7472-3014-5, Oct,87, £2.50, 223pp, pb) Reprint (Doubleday 1978, as **Shadows**) original horror anthology. [First U.K. edition]

GRANT, CHARLES L., ED.

Grant, Charles L., ed. **Shadows II** (Headline 0-7472-0018-1, Nov,87, £9.95, 224pp, hc) Reprint (Doubleday 1978, as **Shadows**) original horror anthology. [Not seen]

*Grant, Gwen **Bonny Starr and the Riddles of Time** (Heinemann 0-434-94135-2, Jun,87 [1987], £6.95, 144pp, hc) Juvenile fantasy novel. [Not seen]

*Grant, John & David Langford **Earthdoom!** For main listing see under David Langford.

*Grant, Kathryn **The Phoenix Bells** (Ace 0-441-66227-7, Mar,87 [Feb,87], $2.95, 182pp, pb) Historical fantasy novel of old China, first in the "Land of Ten Thousand Willows" trilogy. To fulfill a prophecy, the Emperor seeks a wife in foreign lands.

*Grant, Richard **Rumors of Spring** (Bantam Spectra 0-553-05190-3, Mar,87 [Feb,87], $18.95, 439pp, hc) Witty sf/fantasy novel of mutated wild woods and offbeat romance. Recommended. (FCM)

*Grant, Richard **Rumors of Spring** (Bantam Spectra 0-553-34369-6, Mar,87 [Feb,87], $9.95, 439pp, tp) Trade paperback edition of the above.

Grant, Richard **Saraband of Lost Time** (Bantam UK 0-553-17280-8, Jun,87, £2.50, 327pp, pb) Reprint (Avon 1985) humourous sf/fantasy novel. [First U.K. edition]

*Grass, Gunter **The Rat** (Harcourt Brace Jovanovich 0-15-175920-0, May,87, $17.95, 371pp, hc) Literary fantasy novel. The title creature engages in dialogues with the author. First English language edition. Translated from the German (Hermann Luchterhand Verlag 1986).

Gray, Alasdair **Lanark** (Paladin 0-586-08613-7, Aug,87, £4.95, 560pp, tp) Reissue (Canongate 1981) literary fantasy novel.

*Gray, Linda Crockett **Scryer** (Tor 0-812-51872-1, Mar,87 [Feb,87], $3.95, 346pp, pb) Horror novel.

*Gray, Nicholas Stuart **The Sorcerer's Apprentices** (St. Martin's 0-312-57282-4, Nov,87 [Oct,87], $6.95, 32pp, hc) A 1965 fantasy story with new illustrations (including "glow in the dark" bits) by Martin Springett.

*Greeley, Andrew M. **The Final Planet** (Warner 0-446-51265-6, Jun,87 [May,87], $16.95, 302pp, hc) Sf novel "on the themes of love and faith," featuring a pilgrim colony ship on its last planetfall.

Greeley, Andrew M. **God Game** (Tor 0-812-58336-1, May,87 [Apr,87], $4.50, 310pp, pb) Reprint (Warner 1986) metaphysical fantasy novel.

Greeley, Andrew M. **God Game** (Arrow 0-09-948580-X, May,87, £2.95, 308pp, pb) Reprint (Warner 1986) fantasy novel.

+Green, Jen & Sarah Lefanu, eds. **Despatches from the Frontiers of the Female Mind** (Salem House/Women's Press 0-7043-3973-0, Mar,87, $4.95, 248pp, pb) Anthology of feminist sf stories. This is actually an American distribution by Salem House of the original British edition (Women's Press 1985).

*Green, Roland J. **These Green Foreign Hills** (Ace 0-441-65741-9, Dec,87 [Nov,87], $2.95, 188pp, pb) Military sf novel, Volume 2 in the "Peace Company" series.

*Green, Sharon **The Far Side of Forever** (DAW 0-88677-212-5, Jul,87, $3.50, 383pp, pb) Fantasy novel of 6 adventurers on a quest for a magical focus to save their world.

*Green, Sharon **Lady Blade, Lord Fighter** (DAW 0-88677-251-6, Dec,87 [Nov,87], $3.50, 366pp, pb) Fantasy novel, first in a new series.

*Green, Sharon **The Rebel Prince** (DAW 0-88677-199-4, May,87 [Apr,87], $3.50, 367pp, pb) Sf novel.

*Green, Terence M. **The Woman Who Is the Midnight Wind** (Pottersfield Press 0-919001-33-5, Apr,87 [Mar,87], C$9.95, 137pp, tp) Collection of 10 stories by a Canadian sf writer.

GREENBERG, MARTIN H.

*Greenberg, Martin H., ed. **Amazing Science Fiction Stories: The War Years 1936-1945** (TSR 0-88038-440-9, May,87, $3.95, 331pp, pb) Anthology of 10 sf stories, with an introduction by Isaac Asimov. Available in the UK for £2.50.

*Greenberg, Martin H., ed. **Amazing Science Fiction Stories: The Wild Years 1946-1955** (TSR 0-88038-441-7, Aug,87, $3.95, 318pp, pb) Anthology of 12 stories from *Amazing*.

*Greenberg, Martin H., ed. **Amazing Science Fiction Stories: The Wonder Years 1926-1935** (TSR 0-88038-439-5, Mar,87 [Feb,87], $3.95, 316pp, pb) Anthology of stories from the first decade of *Amazing*, with an introduction by Jack Williamson. UK price £2.50.

*Greenberg, Martin H., ed. **The Best of Pamela Sargent** Main listing under Pamela Sargent.

*Greenberg, Martin H., ed. **Cinemonsters** (TSR 0-88038-504-9, Nov,87, $7.95, 319pp, tp) Anthology of stories on which famous monster movies were based.

*Greenberg, Martin H., Pamela Crippen Adams & Robert Adams, eds. **Robert Adams' Book of Alternate Worlds** Main listing under Robert Adams.

*Greenberg, Martin H. & Isaac Asimov, eds. **Isaac Asimov Presents the Great SF Stories: 16 (1954)** Main listing under Isaac Asimov.

*Greenberg, Martin H. & Isaac Asimov, eds. **Isaac Asimov Presents the Great SF Stories: 17 (1955)** Main listing under Isaac Asimov.

Greenberg, Martin H., Isaac Asimov & Charles G. Waugh, eds. **Cosmic Knights** For main entry see under Isaac Asimov.

*Greenberg, Martin H., Isaac Asimov & Charles G. Waugh, eds. **Flying Saucers** Main listing under Isaac Asimov.

Greenberg, Martin H., Isaac Asimov & Charles G. Waugh, eds. **Giants** For main entry see under Isaac Asimov.

*Greenberg, Martin H., Isaac Asimov & Charles G. Waugh, eds. **Isaac Asimov's Magical Worlds of Fantasy #8: Devils** Main listing under Isaac Asimov.

*Greenberg, Martin H., Isaac Asimov & Charles G. Waugh, eds. **Isaac Asimov's Magical Worlds of Fantasy #9: Atlantis** Main listing under Isaac Asimov.

*Greenberg, Martin H., Isaac Asimov & Charles G. Waugh, eds. **Isaac Asimov's Wonderful Worlds of Science Fiction #6: Neanderthals** Main listing under Isaac Asimov.

*Greenberg, Martin H., Isaac Asimov & Charles G. Waugh, eds. **Isaac Asimov's Wonderful Worlds of Science Fiction #7: Space Shuttles** Main listing under Isaac Asimov.

*Greenberg, Martin H., Isaac Asimov & Charles G. Waugh, eds. **Young Witches & Warlocks** Main listing under Isaac Asimov.

Greenberg, Martin H. & Gregory Benford, eds. **Hitler Victorious** Main listing under Gregory Benford.

*Greenberg, Martin H., Joe W. Haldeman & Charles G. Waugh, eds. **Supertanks** Main listing under Joe W. Haldeman.

*Greenberg, Martin H., Frank D. McSherry, Jr. & Charles G. Waugh, eds. **Strange Maine** Main listing under Charles G. Waugh.

Greenberg, Martin H. & Walter M. Miller, Jr., eds. **Beyond Armageddon** For main listing see under Walter M. Miller, Jr.

*Greenberg, Martin H. & Patrick L. Price, eds. **Fantastic Stories: Tales of the Weird and Wondrous** (TSR 0-88038-521-9, May,87, $7.95, 253pp, tp) Anthology of 16 stories from the magazine, with an introduction by James E. Gunn plus a selection of color cover reproductions.

*Greenberg, Martin H., Carol Serling & Charles G. Waugh, eds. **Rod Serling's Night Gallery Reader** Main listing under Carol Serling.

GREENBERG, MARTIN H.

HAINING, PETER, ED.

Greenberg, Martin H. & Robert Silverberg, eds. **Great Science Fiction of the 20th Century** Main listing under Robert Silverberg.

*Greenberg, Martin H. & Charles G. Waugh, eds. **Battlefields Beyond Tomorrow: Science Fiction War Stories** Main listing under Charles G. Waugh.

*Greenberg, Martin H. & Charles G. Waugh, eds. **House Shudders** (DAW 0-88677-223-0, Sep,87 [Aug,87], $3.50, 332pp, pb) Anthology of 17 horror stories of haunted houses, etc.

*Greenberg, Martin H. & Charles G. Waugh, eds. **Vamps** (DAW 0-88677-190-0, Mar,87 [Feb,87], $3.50, 365pp, pb) Horror anthology of 16 stories featuring female vampires, plus an introductory essay on what it all means.

*Greenberg, Martin H., Charles G. Waugh & Frank D. McSherry, Jr., eds. **Nightmares in Dixie: Thirteen Horror Tales From the American South** Main listing under Frank D. McSherry, Jr.

*Greenberg, Martin H., Charles G. Waugh & Jane Yolen, eds. **Spaceships and Spells** Main listing under Jane Yolen.

*Greenburg, Dan **The Nanny** (Macmillan 0-02-545440-4, Nov,87 [Dec,87], $17.95, 229pp, hc) Horror novel of an ancient evil.

*Greene, Liz **Puppet Master: A Novel** (Arkana 1-85063-057-7, Mar,87 [Oct,87], £5.95, 306pp, tp) Occult novel.

*Greenland, Colin **The Hour of the Thin Ox** (Allen & Unwin 0-04-823341-2, Mar,87, £9.95, 186pp, hc) A fantasy novel set in the world of **Daybreak on a Different Mountain**, emphasizing character over fantasy trappings. Low-key but very well written -- recommended. (FCM)

Greenland, Colin **The Hour of the Thin Ox** (Unwin 0-04-440002-0, Sep,87, £2.95, 186pp, tp) Reprint (Allen & Unwin 1987) fantasy novel.

*Greenland, Colin, George E. Slusser & Eric S. Rabkin, eds. **Storm Warnings: Science Fiction Confronts the Future** Main listing under George E. Slusser.

*Greenleaf, William **Starjacked!** (Ace 0-441-78213-2, Apr,87 [Mar,87], $2.95, 187pp, pb) Sf novel. Space opera.

*Gregorian, Joyce Ballou **The Great Wheel** (Ace 0-441-30257-2, Apr,87 [Mar,87], $3.50, 307pp, pb) Fantasy novel, conclusion of the "Tredana" trilogy. Sibby returns to the magic middle-eastern land she visited as child and adolescent in the previous books, this time to aid a conqueror overrunning the lands of her forgotten husband, daughter, and lover.

*Greimes, Christopher & Barthe DeClements **Double Trouble** Main listing under Barthe DeClements.

*Gresham, Stephen **Midnight Boy** (Zebra 0-8217-2065-1, May,87 [Aug,87], 396pp, pb) Horror novel.

*Griffin, P.M. **Star Commandos: Colony in Peril** (Ace 0-441-78043-1, Jun,87 [May,87], $2.95, 199pp, pb) Sf novel, sequel to **Star Commandos**. An off-duty visit to a colony planet involves the husband and wife team of commandos in a plot to destroy the colonists for their planet's minerals. Aided by the cute, telepathic fauna of the planet, Sogen and Connor hold off the raiders in fierce battle.

*Grimwade, Peter **Robot** (Star 0-352-32036-2, Jul,87, £2.25, 144pp, pb) Sf novel. Volume 1 in a new series.

Grimwood, Ken **Replay** (SFBC #106203, Apr,87, $4.98, 249pp, hc) Reprint (Arbor House 1987) fantasy novel about replaying your life.

Grimwood, Ken **Replay** (Grafton 0-246-13191-8, Jun,87 [Jul,87], £9.95, 272pp, hc) Reprint (Arbor House 1986) novel about a man who has a chance to relive his life. [First U.K. edition]

Grimwood, Ken **Replay** (Berkley 0-425-10640-3, Jan,88 [Dec,87], $3.95, 313pp, pb) Reprint (Arbor House 1987) literary fantasy novel; a man lives his life over and over.

*Grocott, Ann **Danni's Desperate Journey** (Angus & Robertson 0-207-15568-2, Oct,87, £5.95, 176pp, hc) Juvenile sf novel.

*Guadalupi, Gianni & Alberto Manguel **The Dictionary of Imaginary Places, Expanded Edition** Main listing under Alberto Manguel.

*Gunnarsson, Thorarinn **The Starwolves** (Popular Library Questar 0-445-20643-8, Jan,88 [Dec,87], $2.95, 281pp, pb) Sf novel, a space opera with an alien created race as the "good guys" vs. humans.

Gunther, Max **Doom Wind** (Paperjacks 0-7701-0660-9, Oct,87, $4.50, 346pp, pb) Reprint (Contemporary 1986) sf/disaster novel.

*Gygax, Gary **City of Hawks** (Ace/New Infinities 0-441-10636-6, Nov,87 [Oct,87], $3.95, 400pp, pb) Fantasy adventure novel in the "Gord the Rogue" series, based on a fantasy game.

*Gygax, Gary **Night Arrant** (Ace/New Infinities 0-441-29863-X, Sep,87 [Aug,87], $3.95, 398pp, pb) Collection of 9 fantasy stories based on a gaming character, "Gord the Rogue," and friends. Illustrations by Jerry Tiritilli.

*Gygax, Gary **Sea of Death** (Ace/New Infinities 0-441-75676-X, Jun,87 [May,87], $3.95, 394pp, pb) Fantasy novel in the "Gord the Rogue" series, with illustrations by Jerry Tiritilli. It's set in the world of the "Greyhawk" books and games, which are being continued by other authors for TSR, and the copyright page notes the use of the terms "Greyhawk" and D&D in this product has not been approved by TSR.

*Gysin, Brion **The Last Museum** (Grove Press 0-394-55555-4, Nov,86 [Jan,87], $17.95, 186pp, hc) Surreal literary fantasy novel of the Paris Beat Hotel, dismantled and shipped to California, where it becomes a Tibetan realm of the dead. Introduction by William S. Burroughs. Published in 1986; not seen until 1987.

*Gysin, Brion **The Last Museum** (Grove/Evergreen 0-394-62263-4, Nov,86 [Jan,87], $7.95, 186pp, tp) Paperback edition of the above.

Hagberg, David **Last Come the Children** (Tor 0-812-53987-7, Dec,87 [Nov,87], $3.95, 347pp, pb) Reissue (Tor 1982) horror novel; 2nd printing.

*Hague, Michael **Michael Hague's World of Unicorns** (Holt 0-8050-0070-4, Sep,86 [Jan,87], $16.95, unpaginated, hc) Pop-up fantasy art book. Published in 1986; missed.

Hahn, Mary Dowing **Wait Till Helen Comes** (Avon/Camelot 0-380-70442-0, Nov,87 [Oct,87], $2.75, 184pp, pb) Reprint (Houghton Mifflin 1986) juvenile ghostly novel.

Haining, Peter **The Art of Horror Stories** (Chartwell 1-5521-091-0, 1986 [Feb,87], $8.95, 176pp, hc) Reprint (Souvenir Press 1976) of a non-fiction study of horror illustrating, originally published in Britain as **Terror!**. An instant remainder. Appeared in 1986; not seen until now.

Haining, Peter **Doctor Who: The Key to Time** (Comet 0-86379-153-0, Oct,87 [Sep,87], £5.95, 264pp, tp) Reprint (W.H. Allen 1984) of associational interest. A year-by-year guide to the **Doctor Who** TV series.

*Haining, Peter **Doctor Who: The Time-Travellers' Guide** (W.H. Allen 0-491-03497-0, Sep,87, £14.95, 272pp, hc) Associational book.

*Haining, Peter **The Dracula Centenary Book** (Souvenir Press 0-285-62822-4, Oct,87, £10.95, 160pp, hc) Associational book about Dracula.

*Haining, Peter, ed. **Poltergeist: Tales of Deadly Ghosts** (Severn House 0-7278-1474-5, Dec,87, £9.95, 249pp, hc) Anthology of stories about poltergeists. As usual, Haining has located some rar and interesting stories.

+Haining, Peter, ed. **Tales of Dungeons and Dragons** (Century 0-7126-9542-7, 1986 [Jun,87], $24.95, 406pp, hc) Anthology of 30 stories of horror and fantasy having nothing to do with "Dungeons and Dragons". There is a 4-page introduction by Ray Bradbury. This is an American edition of a 1986 British book, with an American price sticker and a title page listing David & Charles, North Pomfret VT 05053, as the distributor.

HAINING, PETER, ED.   **HARRIS, DEBORAH TURNER**

*Haining, Peter, ed. **Werewolf: Horror Stories of the Man Beast** (Severn House 0-7278-1465-6, Sep,87 [Oct,87], £9.95, 250pp, hc) Horror anthology.

*Halam, Ann **The Daymaker** (Orchard 1-85213-019-9, May,87, £7.50, 173pp, hc) "A stunning future worlds fantasy with a feminist slant." This is a pseudonym for Gwyneth Jones.

*Halam, Ann **The Daymaker** (Franklin Watts Orchard 0-531-08310-1, Aug,87, $11.95, 173pp, hc) Juvenile fantasy novel, published simultaneously in Britain. Halam is a pseudonym for Gwyneth Jones.

Halam, Ann **King Death's Garden** (Orchard 1-85213-115-2, Nov,87, £4.50, 128pp, tp) Reprint (Orchard 1986) juvenile fantasy novel. This is a pseudonym for Gwyneth Jones

*Haldeman, Joe W. **Tool of the Trade** (Morrow 0-688-07245-3, Apr,87, $15.95, 261pp, hc) Sf/suspense novel.

Haldeman, Joe W. **Tool of the Trade** (Gollancz 0-575-04118-8, Aug,87, £10.95, 261pp, hc) Reprint (Morrow 1987) sf novel. [First U.K. edition]

*Haldeman, Joe W., Martin H. Greenberg & Charles G. Waugh, eds. **Supertanks** (Ace 0-441-79106-9, Apr,87 [Mar,87], $3.50, 262pp, pb) Anthology of 10 sf tank stories including the shorter (and better) version of **Damnation Alley** by Roger Zelazny.

*Hale, Andrew **2020: Vision of the Future** (Ada Press 1-870734-00-9, Oct,87, £4.50, 48pp, tp) Sf novel. [Not seen]

*Halkin, John **Bloodworm** (Arrow 0-09-944880-7, Aug,87, £1.95, 251pp, pb) Horror novel.

*Halkin, John **Fangs of the Werewolf** (Century 0-09-173488-6, Nov,87, £5.95, 144pp, hc) Juvenile horror novel. Volume 6 in the "Fleshcreepers" series. [Not seen]

*Halkin, John **Fangs of the Werewolf** (Beaver 0-09-949760-3, Dec,87, £1.95, 160pp, pb) Juvenile horror novel. Volume 6 in the "Fleshcreepers" series. [Not seen]

Hall, Angus **The Scars of Dracula** (Severn House 0-7278-1382-X, Mar,87, £8.95, 144pp, hc) Reprint (Sphere 1971) horror novel. [Not seen]

Hall, Austin & Homer Eon Flint **The Blind Spot** (Greenhill 0-947898-57-3, May,87, £8.95, 256pp, hc) Reprint (Prime 1951) sf novel. [Not seen]

*Hall, Hal W. **Science Fiction and Fantasy Reference Index, 1878-1985** (Gale 0-8103-2129-7, Apr,87 [May,87], $175.00/set, 1460pp [2 vols], hc) Non-fiction, bibliography. An exhaustive data base index of as many articles about science fiction as the author could find. It has 16,000 citations by author (vol. 1) and 27,000 by subject (vol. 2). This has certainly become the new standard reference on sf, replacing all others. Anyone doing any sf research has to have access to a copy. Highly recommended, of course. (CNB)

*Hall, Sandi **Wingwomen of Hera** (Spinsters/Aunt Lute 0-933216-26-2, May,87, $8.95, 180pp, tp) Feminist sf novel. Cultures from two planets -- the parthenogenetic wingwomen of Hera and the rigid, ice-bound, male-dominated people of Maladar -- meet through an epidemic disease. The novel's strength lies in its swift-moving plot and characterization; its weakness in its overuse of poetic language and poor science (e.g. a city "far west of the axis" of Maladar). Book One of "The Cosmic Botanists" trilogy. (CFC)

*Hall, Willis **The Antelope Company at Large** (Bodley Head 0-370-31151-5, Oct,87, £6.95, 160pp, hc) Juvenile fantasy novel. Volume 3 in the "Antelope Company" series. [Not seen]

*Halliwell, Leslie **A Demon Close Behind** (Robert Hale 0-7090-2932-2, Apr,87 [Jul,87], £10.95, 240pp, hc) Original ghost collection.

*Halliwell, Leslie **Return to Shangri-La** (Grafton 0-586-07081-8, Dec,87, £2.95, 304pp, pb) Fantasy novel.

Hallworth, Grace **Mouth Open, Story Jump Out** (Magnet 0-416-07542-8, Dec,87 [Nov,87], £1.75, 119pp, pb) Reprint (Methuen 1984) collection of supernatural stories based on Trinidadian folklore.

Hambly, Barbara **Ishmael** (Firecrest 0-85997-924-5, Jul,87 [1987], £7.95, 256pp, hc) Reprint (Pocket 1985) sf novel. Volume 38 in the Star Trek Novels series. [First U.K. edition, not seen]

Hambly, Barbara **The Ladies of Mandrigyn** (Ballantine/Del Rey 0-345-30919-7, Jul,87 [Jun,87], $2.95, 311pp, pb) Reissue (Del Rey 1984) fantasy novel; 6th printing.

Hambly, Barbara **Search the Seven Hills** (Ballantine 0-345-34438-3, Nov,87 [Oct,87], $3.95, 309pp, pb) Reprint (St. Martin's 1983 as **The Quirinal Hill Affair**). Associational: historical mystery novel set in ancient Rome.

Hambly, Barbara **The Silent Tower** (Unwin 0-04-823377-3, Jul,87, £2.95, 349pp, pb) Reprint (Del Rey 1986) fantasy novel. Volume 1 in a new series. [First U.K. edition]

*Hambly, Barbara **The Unschooled Wizard** (SFBC #11009, Jun,87, $7.50, 600pp, hc) Omnibus edition of two fantasy novels: **The Ladies of Mandrigyn** (Del Rey 1984) and its sequel **The Witches of Wenshar** (Del Rey 1987).

*Hambly, Barbara **The Witches of Wenshar** (Ballantine/Del Rey 0-345-32934-1, Jul,87 [Jun,87], $3.95, 339pp, pb) Fantasy novel, an excellent sequel to **The Ladies of Mandrigyn**. Recommended. (FCM)

*Hambly, Barbara **The Witches of Wenshar** (Unwin 0-04-823381-1, Sep,87 [Aug,87], £2.95, 339pp, pb) Fantasy novel. Sequel to **The Ladies of Mandrigyn**.

Hamley, Dennis **The Fourth Plane at the Flypast** (Fontana Lion 0-00-672766-2, May,87, £1.95, 127pp, pb) Reprint (Andre Deutsch 1985) juvenile ghost story.

Hancock, Niel **The Fires of Windameir** (Popular Library Questar 0-445-20563-6, Dec,87 [Nov,87], $3.50, 407pp, pb) Reprint (Warner 1985) fantasy novel, first book in the "Windameir" quartet, sequel to the "Wilderness of Four" quartet, sequel to the "Circle of Light" quartet.

*Hancock, Niel **The Sea of Silence** (Popular Library Questar 0-445-20565-2, Dec,87 [Nov,87], $3.50, 374pp, pb) Fantasy novel, Book 2 of the "Windameir Circle" quartet and the 10th book in the overall series.

*Hanratty, Peter **The Book of Mordred** (Ace/New Infinities 0-441-07018-3, Jan,88 [Dec,87], $3.50, 256pp, pb) Fantasy novel, an Arthurian fantasy detailing the early life of Arthur's son, Mordred. Second in an Arthurian series.

Hanratty, Peter **The Last Knight of Albion** (Ace/New Infinities 0-441-47121-8, Sep,87 [Aug,87], $3.50, 267pp, pb) Reprint (Bluejay 1986) Arthurian fantasy novel.

+Harbinson, W.A. **Eden** (Dell 0-440-12212-0, May,87 [Apr,87], $3.95, 367pp, pb) Occult fantasy novel. First American edition (Corgi 1987 as **The Light of Eden**.)

*Harbinson, W.A. **The Light of Eden** (Corgi 0-552-12650-0, Mar,87, £2.95, 440pp, pb) Mystical fantasy novel.

*Hardie, Raymond **Abyssos** (Tor 0-51892-6, Sep,87 [Aug,87], $3.95, 344pp, pb) Horror novel of an evil cult.

+Hardy, Phil **The Encyclopedia of Horror Movies** (Harper & Row/Perennial Library 0-06-096146-5, Mar,87 [Feb,87], $16.95, 424pp, tp) Reference book on horror films. First U.S. edition (UK 1986).

+Hardy, Phil **The Encyclopedia of Horror Movies** (Harper & Row/Perennial Library 0-06-055050-3, Mar,87 [May,87], $34.50, 424pp, hc) Reference book on horror films. Listed earlier in trade paperback. It appeared in Britain in 1986.

*Harrington, Barbara **A Crock of Clear Water** (Robert Hale 0-7090-2913-6, Apr,87, £10.95, 192pp, hc) Supernatural thriller set in Victorian England. [Not seen]

*Harris, Deborah Turner **The Gauntlet of Malice** (Tor 0-812-53952-4, Jan,88 [Dec,87], $7.95, 334pp, tp) Fantasy novel, Book II of "The Mages of Garrillon".

HARRIS, GERALDINE

HARTWELL, DAVID G.

Harris, Geraldine **Seven Citadels: Prince of the Godborn** (Dell/Laurel Leaf 0-440-95407-X, Aug,87 [Jul,87], $2.50, 186pp, pb) Reprint (Macmillan UK 1982) fantasy novel, first of a 4-book series.

Harris, Geraldine **Seven Citadels: The Children of the Wind** (Dell/Laurel Leaf 0-440-91210-5, Sep,87 [Aug,87], $2.50, 196pp, pb) Reprint (Macmillan UK 1982) young-adult fantasy novel, "Seven Citadels" #2.

Harris, Geraldine **Seven Citadels: The Dead Kingdom** (Dell/Laurel Leaf 0-440-91810-3, Oct,87 [Sep,87], $2.50, 182pp, pb) Reissue (Macmillan UK 1983) fantasy novel, third in the "Seven Citadels" series.

Harris, Geraldine **Seven Citadels: The Seventh Gate** (Dell/Laurel Leaf 0-440-97747-9, Nov,87 [Oct,87], $2.95, 243pp, pb) Reprint (Macmillan UK 1983) young adult fantasy novel, fourth in the "Seven Citadels" series.

*Harris, Marilyn **Night Games** (Doubleday 0-385-18817-X, Sep,87 [Oct,87], $15.95, 302pp, hc) Occult horror novel.

Harrison, Harry **The California Iceberg** (Dragon 0-583-31140-7, Sep,87, £1.75, 92pp, pb) Reprint (Faber & Faber 1975) juvenile sf novel.

Harrison, Harry **Captive Universe** (Grafton 0-586-05677-7, Mar,87 [May,87], £2.50, 206pp, pb) Reissue (Putnam 1969) sf novel. Dated 1986.

Harrison, Harry **Deathworld** (Ace 0-441-14210-9, Apr,87 [Mar,87], $2.95, 137pp, pb) Reprint (Bantam 1960) sf novel, first of a trilogy also available as **The Deathworld Trilogy**.

Harrison, Harry **Deathworld 1** (Sphere 0-7221-4485-7, Feb,87, £1.95, 157pp, pb) Reissue (Bantam 1960) sf novel.

Harrison, Harry **Deathworld 2** (Sphere 0-7221-4484-9, Feb,87, £1.95, 160pp, pb) Reissue (Bantam 1964) sf novel.

Harrison, Harry **Deathworld 2** (Ace 0-441-14269-9, Jun,87 [May,87], $2.95, 136pp, pb) Reprint (Bantam 1964) sf novel, #2 in the "Deathworld" trilogy. Also published in England as **The Ethical Engineer** and as part of the omnibus **The Deathworld Trilogy**.

Harrison, Harry **Deathworld 3** (Sphere 0-7221-4506-3, Feb,87, £1.95, 157pp, pb) Reissue (Dell 1968) sf novel.

Harrison, Harry **Deathworld 3** (Ace 0-441-14266-4, Sep,87 [Aug,87], $2.95, 160pp, pb) Reprint (Dell 1968) sf novel, third in the "Deathworld" trilogy. Also available in the one-volume edition, **The Deathworld Trilogy**.

Harrison, Harry **Invasion: Earth** (Sphere 0-7221-4532-2, Feb,87, £1.95, 150pp, pb) Reissue (Ace 1982) sf novel.

Harrison, Harry **The Jupiter Plague** (Tor 0-812-53975-3, Mar,87 [Feb,87], $2.95, 280pp, pb) Reissue (Tor 1982) sf novel. A revised, expanded version of **The Plague From Space** (1965). Second Tor printing.

Harrison, Harry **Montezuma's Revenge** (Tor 0-812-50444-5, Sep,87 [Aug,87], $3.50, 243pp, pb) Reprint (Doubleday 1972) humorous suspense/spy novel; associational.

Harrison, Harry **Plague From Space** (Sphere 0-7221-4443-1, Feb,87, £1.95, 153pp, pb) Reissue (Doubleday 1965) sf novel.

Harrison, Harry **Planet of No Return** (Sphere 0-7221-4537-3, Feb,87, £1.95, 155pp, pb) Reissue (Simon & Schuster 1981) sf novel.

Harrison, Harry **Planet of No Return** (Tor 0-812-53981-8, Oct,87 [Sep,87], $2.95, 232pp, pb) Reissue (Wallaby 1981) sf novel, with illustrations by Rick DeMarco.

Harrison, Harry **Planet of the Damned** (Tor 0-812-53978-8, Sep,87 [Aug,87], $2.95, 250pp, pb) Reissue (Bantam 1962) sf novel; 4th Tor printing.

Harrison, Harry **Prime Number** (Sphere 0-7221-4435-0, Feb,87, £1.95, 191pp, pb) Reissue (Berkely 1970) sf collection.

Harrison, Harry **Queen Victorica's Revenge** (Tor 0-812-50446-1, Dec,87 [Nov,87], $3.50, 279pp, pb) Reprint (Doubleday 1974) humorous suspense novel; associational.

*Harrison, Harry **The Stainless Steel Rat Gets Drafted** (Bantam UK 0-593-01233-X, Aug,87, £9.95, 256pp, hc) Sf novel. Volume 7 in the "Stainless Steel Rat" series.

*Harrison, Harry **The Stainless Steel Rat Gets Drafted** (Bantam Spectra 0-553-05220-9, Oct,87 [Sep,87], $14.95, 256pp, hc) Humorous sf novel, in the "Rat" series. Simultaneous with Bantam U.K. edition.

Harrison, Harry **The Stainless Steel Rat Gets Drafted** (SFBC #11444, Oct,87 [Nov,87], $4.98, 214pp, hc) Reprint (Bantam 1987) sf novel in the humorous adventure series.

Harrison, Harry **To the Stars** (Bantam Spectra 0-553-26453-2, Mar,87 [Feb,87], $4.95, 472pp, pb) Reprint (SFBC 1981) omnibus edition of **Homeworld** (Bantam 1980), **Wheelworld** (Bantam 1981), and **Starworld** (Bantam 1981); sf trilogy.

Harrison, Harry **Two Tales and Eight Tomorrows** (Sphere 0-7221-4433-4, Feb,87, £1.95, 157pp, pb) Reissue (Gollancz 1965) sf collection; omits introduction by Brian Aldiss.

Harrison, Harry **Winter in Eden** (SFBC #105189, Jan,87, $5.98, 399pp, hc) Reprint (Grafton 1986) sf novel, sequel to **West of Eden**.

Harrison, Harry **Winter in Eden** (Bantam Spectra 0-553-26820-1, May,87 [Apr,87], $4.50, 430pp, pb) Reprint (Bantam Spectra 1986) sf novel, sequel to **West of Eden**.

Harrison, Harry **Winter in Eden** (Bantam Spectra 0-553-26628-4, Sep,87 [Aug,87], $4.50, 430pp, pb) Reprint (Bantam Spectra 1986) prehistoric alternate world novel of intelligent dinosaurs, sequel to **West of Eden**.

Harrison, Harry **Winter in Eden** (Grafton 0-586-06479-6, Sep,87, £3.50, 486pp, pb) Reprint (Grafton 1986) sf novel. Volume 2 in the "West of Eden" trilogy.

Harrison, M. John **The Pastel City** (Unwin 0-04-823333-1, Apr,87, £2.50, 142pp, pb) Reprint (NEL 1971) fantasy novel. Volume 1 in the "Viriconium" series.

Harrison, M. John **A Storm of Wings** (Unwin 0-04-823334-X, Jul,87, £2.95, 189pp, pb) Reprint (Doubleday 1980) fantasy novel. Volume 2 in the "Viriconium" series.

+Hartley, L.P. **The Complete Short Stories of L.P. Hartley** (Beaufort 0-8253-0353-2, 1986 [Oct,87], $24.95, 760pp, hc) Omnibus edition of a novella plus four earlier collections: "Simonetta Perkins" (1925); **The Travelling Grave** (1948); **The White Wand** (1954); **Two for the River** (1961); and **Mrs. Carteret Receives** (1971). Many of the 51 stories are fantasy. (**The Travelling Grave** was originally published by Arkham House). This edition has a 1986 date, but was not seen until 1987. First U.S. edition (Hamilton 1973).

Hartley, L.P. **The Complete Short Stories of L.P. Hartley** (QPB no ISBN, Nov,87 [Oct,87], $12.95, 760pp, tp) Reprint (UK 1973) omnibus of 51 stories, some fantasy. This is the same as the Beaufort hardcover except for the binding and lack of ISBN.

Hartley, L.P. **Facial Justice** (Oxford Univ. Press 0-19-282057-5, May,87, £3.95, 256pp, tp) Reprint (Hamish Hamilton 1960) dystopian sf novel, with a new introduction by Peter Quennell.

*Hartwell, David G., ed. **The Dark Descent** (Tor 0-312-93035-6, Oct,87, $29.95, 1011pp, hc) Massive anthology of horror stories. It attempts to trace the history of horror short fiction as well as covering the contemporary field. There is also a long, insightful introduction, and the head notes to each story actually try to say something about the literature and the author's place in it. This should be considered *the* reference work on horror short fiction, and will probably remain so for many years. Highly recommended. (CNB)

*Hartwell, David G. & Kathryn Cramer, eds. **Christmas Ghosts** Main listing under Kathryn Cramer.

HARVEY, M. ELAYN

*Harvey, M. Elayn **Warhaven** (Franklin Watts 0-531-15068-2, Oct,87, $15.95, 266pp, hc) Anti-war sf novel with fantasy elements, a first novel and the announced first of a trilogy.

*Hatchigan, Jessica **Count Dracula, Me and Norma D.** (Avon/Camelot 0-380-75414-2, Nov,87 [Oct,87], $2.50, 116pp, pb) Humorous juvenile novel of a young girl with ESP.

*Hawke, Douglas D. **Moonslasher** (Critic's Choice 1-55547-170-6, Jun,87 [May,87], $3.95, 352pp, pb) Horror novel.

*Hawke, Simon **Friday the 13th, Part I** (NAL/Signet 0-451-15089-9, Sep,87 [Aug,87], $2.95, 190pp, pb) Novelization of the first movie in the horror series.

Hawke, Simon **The Ivanhoe Gambit** (Headline 0-7472-3059-5, Aug,87, £2.50, 209pp, pb) Reprint (Ace 1984) fantasy novel. Volume 1 in the "Time Wars" series. This is a pseudonym for Nicholas Yermakov [First U.K. edition]

*Hawke, Simon **Spychodrome** (Ace 0-441-68791-1, Jul,87 [Jun,87], $2.95, 220pp, pb) Sf novel of a 25th-century game, first in a series. The author writes under his real name, Nick Yermakov.

*Hawke, Simon **Time Wars #7: The Arbonaut Affair** (Ace 0-441-02911-6, Aug,87 [Jul,87], $2.95, 195pp, pb) Time travel adventure novel.

Hawke, Simon **The Timekeeper Conspiracy** (Headline 0-7472-3058-7, Nov,87, £2.50, 215pp, pb) Reprint (Ace 1984) sf novel. Volume 2 in the "Time Wars" series. This is a pseudonym for Nicholas Yermakov. [First U.K. edition]

*Hawke, Simon **The Wizard of 4th Street** (Popular Library Questar 0-445-20302-1, Oct,87 [Sep,87], $2.95, 247pp, pb) Contemporary/Arthurian fantasy novel. Merlin & co. in New York.

Hawkins, Ward **Red Flame Burning** (Ballantine/Del Rey 0-345-32121-9, May,87 [Apr,87], $2.95, 280pp, pb) Reissue (Del Rey 1985) sf novel in the "Harry Borg" series; 2nd printing.

Hawkins, Ward **Sword of Fire** (Ballantine/Del Rey 0-345-32348-3, May,87 [Apr,87], $2.95, 297pp, pb) Reissue (Del Rey 1985) sf novel in the "Harry Borg" series; 3rd printing.

*Hawkins, Ward **Torch of Fear** (Ballantine/Del Rey 0-345-33612-7, May,87 [Apr,87], $2.95, 297pp, pb) Sf novel, latest in the "Harry Borg" series.

*Hayes, Barbara & Robert Ingpen **Folk Tales and Fables of the World** (Paper Tiger 1-85028-034-7, Jun,87, £14.95, 286pp, hc) Reprint (David Bateman Ltd.: Australia, 1987) collection of sixty classic folk tales and fables, retold by Barbara Hayes & illustrated by Robert Ingpen. [First U.K. edition]

Hayes, Michael, ed. **The Supernatural Short Stories of Sir Walter Scott** Main listing under Sir Walter Scott.

*Haynes, Mary **Raider's Sky** (Morrow/Lothrop, Lee & Shepard 0-688-06455-8, May,87 [Apr,87], $11.75, 166pp, hc) Juvenile sf novel of a devastated Earth where most of the survivors are children.

Hazel, Paul E. **Undersea** (Bantam Spectra 0-553-26697-7, Sep,87 [Aug,87], $3.50, 212pp, pb) Reprint (Atlantic/Little, Brown 1982) fantasy novel, Vol. 2 of the "Finnbranch Trilogy".

Hazel, Paul E. **Winterking** (Bantam Spectra 0-553-26945-3, Dec,87 [Nov,87], $3.50, 259pp, pb) Reprint (Atlantic Monthly 1985) fantasy novel, Book 3 of "The Finnbranch Trilogy".

Hazel, Paul E. **Yearwood** (Bantam Spectra 0-553-26681-0, May,87 [Apr,87], $3.95, 261pp, pb) Reprint (Atlantic-Little Brown 1980) fantasy novel, first in the "Finnbranch Trilogy".

Heinlein, Robert A. **Assignment in Eternity** (Baen 0-671-65350-4, Sep,87 [Aug,87], $3.50, 276pp, pb) Reprint (Fantasy Press 1953) collection with the short novels "Gulf" and "Lost Legacy" plus two short stories.

Heinlein, Robert A. **Between Planets** (NEL 0-450-03584-0, Nov,87, £2.25, 174pp, pb) Reissue (Scribners 1951) sf novel.

Heinlein, Robert A. **Citizen of the Galaxy** (Scribner's 0-684-18818-X, Mar,87, $12.95, 302pp, hc) Reissue (Scribners 1957) sf novel.

Heinlein, Robert A. **The Man Who Sold the Moon** (Baen 0-671-65623-6, Mar,87 [Feb,87], $3.50, 295pp, pb) Reprint (Shasta 1950) collection of 6 stories. The first book in Heinlein's "Future History" series.

Heinlein, Robert A. **The Menace From Earth** (Baen 0-671-65640-6, May,87 [Apr,87], $3.50, 271pp, pb) Reprint (Gnome Press 1959) collection of 8 stories.

Heinlein, Robert A. **The Moon is a Harsh Mistress** (NEL 0-450-00231-4, Sep,87, £2.50, 288pp, pb) Reissue (Putnam 1966) sf novel.

Heinlein, Robert A. **The Number of the Beast** (NEL 0-450-04675-3, Oct,87, £3.95, 556pp, pb) Reissue (Fawcett 1980) sf novel.

Heinlein, Robert A. **Orphans of the Sky** (NEL 0-586-04204-0, Jan,87, £2.50, 143pp, pb) Reissue (Gollancz 1963) sf collection. Part of the "Future History" series.

Heinlein, Robert A. **The Past Through Tomorrow Vol. 1** (NEL 0-450-05463-2, Sep,87, £2.95, 320pp, pb) Reissue (Putnam 1967, in one volume) sf collection. Part of the "Future History" series.

Heinlein, Robert A. **The Past Through Tomorrow Vol. 2** (NEL 0-450-04005-4, Sep,87, £2.95, 347pp, pb) Reissue (Putnam 1967, in one volume) sf collection. Part of the "Future History" series.

Heinlein, Robert A. **The Puppet Masters** (NEL 0-450-40578-8, Mar,87, £2.50, 224pp, pb) Reprint (Doubleday 1951) sf novel.

Heinlein, Robert A. **Red Planet** (Pan 0-330-10712-7, Feb,87, £1.95, 173pp, pb) Reissue (Scribner's 1949) sf novel.

Heinlein, Robert A. **Rocketship Galileo** (NEL 0-450-00695-6, Aug,87, £1.95, 159pp, pb) Reissue (Scribner's 1947) sf novel.

Heinlein, Robert A. **Sixth Column** (Baen 0-671-65374-1, Jan,88 [Dec,87], $3.50, 248pp, pb) Reprint (Grove Press 1949) sf novel; also issued as **The Day After Tomorrow**.

Heinlein, Robert A. **Space Family Stone** (NEL 0-450-04223-5, Oct,87, £2.25, 171pp, pb) Reissue (Scribner's 1952 as **The Rolling Stones**) sf novel.

Heinlein, Robert A. **Star Beast** (NEL 0-450-00829-0, Oct,87, £2.25, 173pp, pb) Reissue (Scribner's 1954) sf novel.

Heinlein, Robert A. **Starman Jones** (NEL 0-450-03040-7, Aug,87, £2.50, 207pp, pb) Reissue (Scribner's 1953) sf novel.

Heinlein, Robert A. **Starship Troopers** (NEL 0-450-00573-9, Aug,87, £2.50, 222pp, pb) Reissue (Putnam 1959) sf novel.

Heinlein, Robert A. **Starship Troopers** (Ace 0-441-78358-9, Nov,87 [Oct,87], $3.50, 208pp, pb) Reprint (Putnam's 1959) classic military sf novel. Hugo winner (1960).

Heinlein, Robert A. **Stranger in a Strange Land** (Ace 0-441-79034-8, Aug,87 [Jul,87], $3.95, 438pp, pb) Reprint (Putnam 1961) science fiction novel. Umpteenth printing (it hasn't been out of print since 1961) of one of the most famous of sf novels. Highly recommended. (CNB)

Heinlein, Robert A. **Stranger in a Strange Land** (NEL 0-450-00403-1, Aug,87, £3.50, 400pp, pb) Reissue (Putnam 1961) sf novel. 17th printing.

Heinlein, Robert A. **Time for the Stars** (Pan 0-330-02028-5, Feb,87, £1.95, 190pp, pb) Reissue (Scribners 1956) sf novel.

*Heinlein, Robert A. **To Sail Beyond the Sunset** (Ace/Putnam 0-399-13267-8, Jul,87 [Jun,87], $18.95, 416pp, hc) Sf novel, the "autobiography" of Maureen Johnson, Lazarus Long's mother. Recommended. (TM)

HEINLEIN, ROBERT A.

HICKMAN, TRACY

Heinlein, Robert A. **To Sail Beyond the Sunset** (Michael Joseph 0-7181-2950-4, Nov,87, £11.95, 446pp, hc) Reprint (Putnam 1987) sf novel. [First U.K. edition]

Heinlein, Robert A. **The Unpleasant Profession of Jonathan Hoag** (NEL 0-450-04798-9, Sep,87, £2.50, 191pp, pb) Reissue (Gnome 1959) sf collection.

*Heinlein, Robert A., [ref.] **Robert A. Heinlein** Main listing under Professor Leon Stover.

*Heller, Terry **The Delights of Terror: An Aesthetics of the Tale of Terror** (Univ. of Illinois Press 0-252-01475-8, Sep,87, $10.95, 218pp, tp) Non-fiction, critical study. Also announced in hardcover (-01412-X, $27.50).

Henderson, Zenna **The People: No Different Flesh** (Avon 0-380-01506-4, Aug,87 [Jul,87], $3.50, 221pp, pb) Reissue (Gollancz 1966) collection of 6 stories of the People; sequel to **Pilgrimage**. 13th printing.

Henderson, Zenna **Pilgrimage** (Avon 0-380-01507-2, Sep,87 [Aug,87], $3.50, 255pp, pb) Reissue (Doubleday 1961) novel of The People; 16th Avon printing.

Hendry, Frances **Quest for a Kelpie** (Kelpies 0-86241-136-X, Apr,87, £1.95, 154pp, pb) Reprint (Canongate 1986) juvenile fantasy novel.

*Henry, Laurie **1987 Fiction Writer's Market** (Writer's Digest Books 0-89879-267-3, Apr,87 [Mar,87], $18.95, 555pp, hc) Non-fiction, reference. A list of writers' markets including sf magazines. It has an article on science fiction by Rudy Rucker.

*Henry, Maeve **The Witch King** (Orchard 1-85213-024-5, Jun,87 [Nov,87], £6.95, 126pp, hc) A juvenile fantasy quest novel.

Henstell, Diana **Deadly Friend** (Bantam UK 0-553-17241-7, Mar,87 [Apr,87], £2.50, 323pp, pb) Reprint (Bantam 1986 as **Friend**) horror novel, now filmed.

*Henstell, Diana **New Morning Dragon** (Bantam 0-553-26323-4, Oct,87 [Sep,87], $4.50, 352pp, pb) Fantasy/horror novel. The Devil comes to New England.

*Herbert, Brian **Prisoners of Arionn** (Arbor House 0-87795-886-6, Jun,87 [May,87], $17.95, 356pp, hc) Sf novel of the San Francisco Bay Area kidnapped by aliens.

Herbert, Brian & Frank Herbert **Man of Two Worlds** For main entry see under Frank Herbert.

Herbert, Brian & Frank Herbert **Man of Two Worlds** Main listing under Frank Herbert.

Herbert, Frank **Chapterhouse: Dune** (Ace 0-441-10267-0, Jul,87 [Jun,87], $4.50, 436pp, pb) Reprint (Gollancz 1985, as **Chapter House Dune**) sf novel, sixth in the "Dune" series.

Herbert, Frank **Dune** (Easton Press no ISBN, Sep,87, price unknown, hc) Reprint (Chilton 1965) sf novel; leatherbound limited edition, illustrated in color by John Schoenherr. There is also a section of appreciations reprinted from *Locus* and other sources. Available only as part of the Easton Press set of sf volumes.

Herbert, Frank **Eye** (Ace 0-441-22374-5, Nov,87 [Oct,87], $3.95, 328pp, pb) Reprint (Berkley 1985) collection with illustrations by Jim Burns.

Herbert, Frank **The Heaven Makers** (Ballantine/Del Rey 0-345-34458-8, Aug,87 [Jul,87], $3.95, 230pp, pb) Reissue (Avon 1968) sf novel, 7th printing. This edition follows the text of the slightly revised 1977 Ballantine edition.

*Herbert, Frank **The Maker of Dune: Insights of a Master of Science Fiction** (Berkley 0-425-09785-4, May,87 [Apr,87], $7.95, 279pp, tp) edited by Tim O'Reilly. Compilation of articles and essays by Frank Herbert, edited and with introductions by O'Reilly. Some of the pieces are from unpublished interviews.

Herbert, Frank **The Santaroga Barrier** (NEL 0-450-04376-2, Feb,87, £2.50, 205pp, pb) Reissue (Berkley 1968) sf novel.

*Herbert, Frank **The Second Great Dune Trilogy** (Gollancz 0-575-04018-1, Apr,87, £10.95, 1111pp, hc) Omnibus edition of the last three "Dune" novels.

Herbert, Frank & Brian Herbert **Man of Two Worlds** (Orbit 0-7088-8224-2, Aug,87, £3.50, 397pp, pb) Reprint (Gollancz/Putnam 1986) sf novel.

Herbert, Frank & Brian Herbert **Man of Two Worlds** (Ace 0-441-51857-5, Oct,87 [Sep,87], $3.95, 426pp, pb) Reprint (Putnam 1986) sf novel.

Herbert, James **Fluke** (NEL 0-450-03828-9, Nov,87, £2.50, 224pp, pb) Reissue (NEL 1977) horror novel.

Herbert, James **The Fog** (NEL 0-450-03045-8, Nov,87, £2.50, 284pp, pb) Reissue (NEL 1975) horror novel.

Herbert, James **The Magic Cottage** (NEL 0-450-40937-6, May,87, £2.95, 351pp, pb) Reprint (Hodder & Stoughton 1986) horror novel.

+Herbert, James **The Magic Cottage** (NAL 0-453-00574-8, Sep,87, $17.95, 325pp, hc) Horror novel about an evil cottage's effect on the couple living there. First American edition (Hodder & Stoughton 1986).

Herbert, James **Moon** (NAL Onyx 0-451-40056-9, Dec,87 [Nov,87], $4.50, 316pp, pb) Reprint (NEL 1985) horror novel.

*Herbert, James **Sepulchre** (Hodder & Stoughton 0-340-39472-2, Jul,87, £10.95, 316pp, hc) Horror novel.

Herbert, Kathleen **Ghost in the Sunlight** (Corgi 0-552-12896-1, May,87, £2.95, 335pp, pb) Reprint (Bodley Head 1986) Dark Ages fantasy. Sequel to **Queen of the Lightning**.

Herbert, Kathleen **Queen of the Lightning** (Corgi 0-552-12438-9, May,87, £2.95, 252pp, pb) Reissue (Bodley Head 1983) Dark Ages fantasy.

Herley, Richard **The Earth Goddess** (Ballantine 0-345-34327-1, Dec,87 [Nov,87], $3.50, 260pp, pb) Reprint (Heinemann 1984) novel, conclusion to the "Pagans" trilogy about prehistoric England.

Herley, Richard **The Flint Lord** (Ballantine 0-345-34325-5, Oct,87 [Sep,87], $3.50, pb) Reprint (Heinemann 1981) prehistoric sf novel of the Stone Age. Second in "The Pagans Trilogy".

Herley, Richard **The Stone Arrow** (Ballantine, Aug,87 [Jul,87], $3.50, 281pp, pb) Reprint (Peter Davies 1978) first novel in "The Pagans", a historical fantasy series.

*Hernandez, Gilbert, Jaime Hernandez, Mario Hernandez & Dean Motter **The Return of Mister X** (Warner 0-446-38698-7, Dec,87, $8.95, unpaginated, tp) Graphic novel.

*Hernandez, Jaime, Gilbert Hernandez, Mario Hernandez & Dean Motter **The Return of Mister X** Main listing under Gilbert Hernandez.

*Hernandez, Mario, Gilbert Hernandez, Jaime Hernandez & Dean Motter **The Return of Mister X** Main listing under Gilbert Hernandez.

*Hickman, Tracy & Margaret Weis **The Darksword Trilogy, Volume 1: Forging the Darksword** Main listing under Margaret Weis.

Hickman, Tracy & Margaret Weis **DragonLance Legends, Vol. 1: Time of the Twins** For main listing see under Margaret Weis.

Hickman, Tracy & Margaret Weis **DragonLance Legends, Vol. 2: War of the Twins** For main listing, see under Margaret Weis.

Hickman, Tracy & Margaret Weis **DragonLance Legends, Vol. 3: Test of the Twins** For main entry see under Margaret Weis.

*Hickman, Tracy & Margaret Weis, eds. **DragonLance Tales Vol. 1: The Magic of Krynn** Main listing under Margaret Weis.

HICKMAN, TRACY   **HOLDSTOCK, ROBERT P.**

*Hickman, Tracy & Margaret Weis, eds. **DragonLance Tales Vol. 2: Kender, Gully Dwarves, and Gnomes** Main listing under Margaret Weis.

*Hickman, Tracy & Margaret Weis, eds. **DragonLance Tales Vol. 3: Love and War** Main listing under Margaret Weis.

*Hickman, Tracy & Margaret Weis, eds. **Leaves from the Inn of the Last Home** Main listing under Margaret Weis.

*Higgs, Eric C. **Doppelganger** (St. Martin's 0-312-00121-5, Mar,87, $14.95, 229pp, hc) Horror novel of an evil double.

Higgs, Eric C. **Doppelganger** (St. Martin's 0-312-90837-7, Jan,88 [Dec,87], $3.50, 229pp, pb) Reprint (St. Martin's 1987) horror novel.

High, Philip E. **Come Hunt an Earthman** (Arrow 0-09-938890-1, Jul,87, £2.25, 176pp, pb) Reissue (Hale 1973) sf novel. Volume 2 in the Venture SF series.

High, Philip E. **Speaking of Dinosaurs** (Arrow 0-09-950450-2, Jun,87, £2.50, 192pp, pb) Reprint (Hale 1974) sf novel. Volume 13 in the Venture SF series.

*Highsmith, Patricia **Tales of Natural and Unnatural Catastrophes** (Bloomsbury 0-7475-0097-5, Dec,87, £11.95, 189pp, hc) Original literary sf/occult collection.

*Hildick, E.W. **The Ghost Squad and the Prowling Hermits** (Dutton 0-525-44330-4, Nov,87, $12.95, 212pp, hc) Young adult fantasy novel, fifth in the "Ghost Squad" series.

*Hill, Douglas **Blade of the Poisoner** (Gollancz 0-575-03954-X, Jun,87 [Dec,87], £6.95, 192pp, hc) Juvenile fantasy novel. Volume 1 in the "Talents" series.

+Hill, Douglas **Blade of the Poisoner** (Macmillan McElderry 0-689-50418-7, Oct,87, $12.95, 192pp, hc) Young adult Middle to High Fantasy novel. First U.S. edition (Gollancz 1987).

Hill, Douglas **Day of the Starwind** (Dell/Laurel Leaf 0-440-91762-X, May,87, $2.50, 138pp, pb) Reprint (Gollancz 1980) young-adult sf novel, "The Last Legionary" #3.

Hill, Douglas **Deathwing Over Veynaa** (Dell/Laurel Leaf 0-440-91743-3, Apr,87 [May,87], $2.50, 144pp, pb) Reprint (Gollancz 1980) young-adult sf novel, "The Last Legionary" #2.

Hill, Douglas **Exiles of Colsec** (Bantam Starfire 0-553-27233-0, Jan,88 [Dec,87], $2.95, 164pp, pb) Reissue (Gollancz 1984) young adult sf novel, first in a trilogy.

Hill, Douglas **Galactic Warlord** (Dell/Laurel Leaf 0-440-92787-0, Mar,87 [Feb,87], $2.50, 144pp, pb) Reprint (Gollancz 1980) juvenile sf novel, Book One of "The Last Legionary" tetralogy.

*Hill, Douglas **Master of Fiends** (Gollancz 0-575-04095-5, Nov,87 [Dec,87], £7.95, 184pp, hc) Juvenile fantasy novel. Volume 2 in the "Talents" series.

Hill, Douglas **Planet of the Warlord** (Dell/Laurel Leaf 0-440-97126-8, Jun,87 [May,87], $2.50, 139pp, pb) Reprint (Gollancz 1981) young-adult sf novel, "The Last Legionary" #4.

Hill, Douglas **Young Legionary** (Dell/Laurel Leaf 0-440-99910-3, Jul,87 [Jun,87], $2.50, 142pp, pb) Reprint (Gollancz 1983) young-adult sf adventure novel, Book 5 in "The Last Legionary" series.

Hill, Susan **The Woman in Black** (Godine 0-87923-576-4, Aug,87, $15.95, 160pp, hc) Reissue (Hamish Hamilton 1983) ghost story; 2nd Godine printing.

*Hiller, B.B. **Superman IV** (Scholastic Point 0-590-41195-0, Jul,87 [Jun,87], $2.75, 140pp, pb) Novelization of the screenplay (by Lawrence Konner & Mark Rosenthal) of the latest movie in the series; includes 8 pages of stills.

*Hinz, Christopher **Liege-Killer** (St. Martin's 0-312-00065-0, Mar,87 [Feb,87], $19.95, 458pp, hc) Post-apocalypse sf novel. Though the sf motifs are familiar, this is an excellent first novel of deadly warriors and the hunters who pursue them. (FCM)

Hinz, Christopher **Liege-Killer** (SFBC #11280, Sep,87, $7.98, 378pp, hc) Reprint (St. Martin's 1987) sf novel.

Hinz, Christopher **Liege-Killer** (St. Martin's 0-312-90056-2, Jan,88 [Dec,87], $3.95, 458pp, pb) Reprint (St. Martin's 1987) sf novel.

Hitchcock, Alfred, ed. **Alfred Hitchcock's Book of Horror Stories: Book 6** (Coronet 0-340-41115-5, Jul,87, £2.25, 190pp, pb) Reprint (Davis 1981, as 1st half of **Tales to Make Your Hair Stand on End**) horror anthology. Actually edited by Eleanor Sullivan.

Hitchcock, Alfred, ed. **Alfred Hitchcock's Murderers' Row** (Severn House 0-7278-1385-4, Feb,87, £8.95, 208pp, hc) Reprint (Dell 1975) anthology of mystery/horror stories. [First U.K. edition, not seen]

Hjortsberg, William **Falling Angel** (Mysterious Press 0-09-921510-1, Oct,87 [Nov,87], £2.50, 243pp, pb) Reprint (HBJ 1978) thriller with occult touches.

+Hoban, Russell **The Medusa Frequency** (Atlantic Monthly Press 0-87113-165-X, Oct,87, $16.95, 142pp, hc) Contemporary literary fantasy novel, a take-off on the Orpheus myth. First U.S. edition (Jonathan Cape 1987).

Hodgell, P.C. **Dark of the Moon** (Berkley 0-425-09561-4, Feb,87 [Jan,87], $3.50, 351pp, pb) Reprint (Atheneum 1985) fantasy novel, sequel to **God Stalk**.

*Hodgman, Ann **Galaxy High School** (Bantam Skylark 0-553-15545-8, Sep,87, $2.50, 85pp, pb) Juvenile sf short novel based on the morning tv series.

*Hodgson, Amanda **Romances of William Morris** (Cambridge Univ. Press 0-521-32075-5, Feb,87 [1987], £22.50, 219pp, hc) Critical book. [Not seen]

*Hoffman, Charles & Marc A. Cerasini **Robert E. Howard** Main listing under Marc A. Cerasini.

*Hoffman, Curtis H. **Project: Millennium** (Ace 0-441-68312-6, Feb,87 [Jan,87], $2.95, 199pp, pb) Sf novel of "the ultimate war game" on distant planets. Richard III vs. the Norse gods.

Hogan, David J. **Dark Romance: Sexuality in the Horror Film** (MacFarland UK 0-89950-190-7, Jun,87 [Dec,87], £25.95, 334pp, hc) Reprint (MacFarland 1986) associational study of horror films. [First U.K. edition]

*Hogan, James P. **Endgame Enigma** (Bantam Spectra 0-553-05169-5, Aug,87 [Jul,87], $16.95, 408pp, hc) Sf novel set on a space station, a near-future espionage thriller with a surprise near the end. Recommended. (TM)

Hogan, James P. **The Proteus Operation** (Arrow 0-09-948200-2, Jul,87, £3.50, 496pp, pb) Reprint (Bantam 1985) sf novel.

*Hoklin, Lonn **The Hourglass Crisis** (Warner 0-446-34620-9, Nov,87 [Oct,87], $3.95, 374pp, pb) Sf/suspense novel of an attempt to restore the Third Reich through time travel.

Holden, Ursula **Tin Toys** (Methuen 0-413-15850-0, Jul,87, £3.95, 132pp, pb) Reprint (Methuen 1986) literary horror novel.

Holdstock, Robert P. **Earthwind** (Gollancz 0-575-04011-4, Sep,87, £2.95, 245pp, pb) Reprint (Faber & Faber 1977) sf novel.

Holdstock, Robert P. **Eye Among the Blind** (Gollancz 0-575-04010-6, Jun,87, £2.50, 219pp, pb) Reprint (Faber & Faber 1976) sf novel.

*Holdstock, Robert P. & Christopher Evans, eds. **Other Edens** For main entry see under Christopher Evans.

HOLLAND, CECILIA   **HUBBARD, L. RON**

Holland, Cecilia **Pillar of the Sky** (Arrow 0-09-945170-0, Jul,87, £3.50, 633pp, pb) Reprint (Gollancz 1985) historical novel with fantasy elements.

*Hollow, John **Against the Night, the Stars: The Science Fiction of Arthur C. Clarke** (Ohio Univ. Press 0-8214-0862-3, Apr,87 [Jul,87], $9.95, 217pp, tp) Non-fiction, slightly expanded edition of an excellent study of Clarke's fiction (Harcourt Brace Jovanovich 1983). The new 19-page essay on **The Songs of Distant Earth** and the movie version of **2010** are the weakest part of the book. (The bibliography and other lists have not been updated.) If you have the earlier edition, it's probably enough. If not, this one is recommended -- and a bargain at the price. (CNB)

*Hoobler, Thomas **Dr. Chill's Project** (Putnam 0-399-21480-1, Oct,87, $13.95, 188pp, hc) Young adult sf novel of teenagers with psi powers.

Hoover, H.M. **Children of Morrow** (Puffin 0-14-031873-9, May,87, £1.95, 229pp, pb) Reprint (Four Winds Press 1973) juvenile sf novel.

Hoover, H.M. **The Delikon** (Puffin 0-14-032167-5, Sep,86 [Jan,87], $3.95, 148pp, pb) Reprint (Penguin 1977) juvenile sf novel of a revolution on future Earth. Published in 1986; missed.

Hoover, H.M. **The Lost Star** (Puffin 0-14-032166-7, Sep,86 [Jan,87], £1.75, 150pp, pb) Reprint (Penguin 1979) juvenile sf novel about an archaeological expedition on a strange planet. Published in 1986; missed. US price $3.95.

*Hoover, H.M. **Orvis** (Viking Kestrel 0-670-81117-3, Aug,87 [Dec,87], $12.95, 186pp, hc) Young adult sf adventure novel of two people trying to survive on an abandoned Earth with the help of a robot.

Hoover, H.M. **This Time of Darkness** (Puffin 0-14-031872-0, Aug,87 [Oct,87], £1.75, 161pp, pb) Reissue (Viking Penguin 1980) juvenile sf novel.

*Hopkins, Mariane S. **Fandom Directory No. 9 (1987-1988)** (Fandata 0-933215-09-6, Mar,87 [Aug,87], $10.95, 480pp, tp) Non-fiction, latest update of this reference book with listings of fan publications, conventions, specialty stores, etc. Order from Hopkins, 7761 Asterella Ct., Springfield VA 22152.

Horowitz, Anthony **The Silver Citadel** (Methuen 0-416-97000-1, Feb,87, £7.95, 150pp, hc) Reprint (Berkley 1986) young-adult horror novel. Volume 3 in the "Power of Five" series. [First U.K. edition]

Horowitz, Anthony **The Silver Citadel** (Magnet 0-416-02572-2, Nov,87, £1.75, 150pp, pb) Reprint (Berkley 1986) young-adult horror novel. Volume 3 in the "Power of Five" series.

*Horvitz, Leslie **Blood Moon** (Pocket 0-671-61169-0, Feb,87 [Jan,87], $3.50, 309pp, pb) Medical horror novel of a plague of violence.

*Horwood, William **Skallagrigg** (Viking UK 0-670-80132-1, Oct,87, £11.95, 572pp, hc) Sf/fantasy novel.

*Hosken, John **Meet Mr. Majimpsey** (Pavilion 1-85145-095-5, Nov,87, £8.95, 176pp, hc) Juvenile fantasy novel. Illustrated throughout by Dave Eastbury.

Howard, Robert E. **Black Vulmea's Vengeance** (Ace 0-441-06661-5, Jun,87 [May,87], $2.95, 183pp, pb) Reprint (Zebra 1976) pirate adventure book of 3 related novelettes; associational.

*Howard, Robert E. **Cthulhu: The Mythos and Kindred Horrors** (Baen 0-671-65641-4, May,87 [Apr,87], $2.95, 245pp, pb) David Drake, ed. Collection of 13 pieces. One seems to be an original poem from the inexhaustible Howard trunk. I don't know what, if any, editing in the actual stories was done by Drake. The author in all cases seems to be Howard alone.

Howard, Robert E. **Swords of Shahrazar** (Ace 0-441-79237-5, Nov,87 [Oct,87], $2.95, 165pp, pb) Reprint (Berkley 1978) collection of 5 quasi-fantasy/adventure stories. An expansion of an earlier 3-story collection under the same title (Orbit 1976).

Howard, Robert E. **Three-Bladed Doom** (Ace 0-441-80781-X, Mar,87 [Feb,87], $2.95, 154pp, pb) Reissue (Zebra 1977) desert fantasy "novel". Second Ace printing.

Howard, Robert E. **Worms of the Earth** (Ace 0-441-91771-2, Sep,87 [Aug,87], $2.95, 233pp, pb) Reissue (Dell 1969 as **Bran Mak Morn**) collection of fantasy/historical stories with Bran as hero; second Ace printing.

Howard, Robert E., Lin Carter, L. Sprague de Camp & Bjorn Nyberg **Conan the Swordsman** (Ace 0-441-11479-2, Apr,87 [Mar,87], $2.95, 216pp, pb) Reprint (Bantam 1978) collection based on a character by Robert E. Howard. This was the first of a new Conan series which Ace has rebilled as Conan #13.

Howard, Robert E., L. Sprague de Camp & Lin Carter **Conan of Cimmeria** (Sphere 0-7221-4740-6, Jul,87, £2.50, 192pp, pb) Reissue (Lancer 1969) fantasy collection. Volume 6 in the "Conan" series.

*Howard, Robert E., [ref.] **Conan the Defiant** Main listing under Steve Perry.

*Howard, Robert E., [ref.] **Robert E. Howard** Main listing under Marc A. Cerasini.

Howe, James **The Celery Stalks at Midnight** (Dragon 0-583-30906-2, Mar,87 [May,87], £1.75, 96pp, pb) Reprint (Atheneum 1983) juvenile 'horror' novel about a vampire rabbit.

Howe, James **Howliday Inn** (Dragon 0-583-31104-0, Mar,87 [May,87], £1.75, 159pp, pb) Reprint (Atheneum 1982) juvenile 'horror' novel.

*Howe, James **Nighty-Nightmare** (Atheneum 0-689-31207-5, Mar,87, $11.95, 90pp, hc) Humorous juvenile fantasy short novel, part of the "Bunnicula" series.

*Howett, Dicky & Tim Quinn **The Doctor Who Fun Book** For main entry see under Tim Quinn.

*Howlett, Winston A. & Jean Lorrah **Wulfston's Odyssey** Main listing under Jean Lorrah.

*Hoyle, Trevor **K.I.D.S.** (Sphere 0-7221-4803-8, Jan,87, £2.95, 309pp, pb) Horror thriller.

Hoyt, Richard **The Manna Enzyme** (Tor 0-812-50493-3, Feb,87 [Jan,87], $3.95, 308pp, pb) Reprint (Morrow 1982) near-future thriller about an invention that could feed the world. Castro is a good guy vs. the CIA and KGB.

Hubbard, L. Ron **Battlefield Earth** (New Era 1-870451-17-1, Sep,87, £3.50, 1064pp, pb) Reissue (Bridge 1982) sf novel.

Hubbard, L. Ron **Buckskin Brigades** (Jameson 0-915463-46-6, Apr,87 [May,87], $5.95, 275pp, pb) Reprint (Macaulay 1937). Associational -- historical western adventure novel, Hubbard's first novel, with a new introduction by Winfred Blevins. Distributed by Kampmann & Co. A cloth edition is listed on the copyright page, but probably doesn't exist.

*Hubbard, L. Ron **Buckskin Brigades** (Bridge 0-88404-280-4, Jul,87, $3.95, 312pp, pb) Western novel; associational. Contains considerable text which didn't appear in the original edition (Macaulay 1937) and is different from the other re-edited edition (Jameson 1987). The newspaper quotes on the back are 50 years old!

Hubbard, L. Ron **Mission Earth, Vol. 3: The Enemy Within** (New Era 87-7336-485-1, Jan,87, £10.95, 393pp, hc) Reprint (Bridge 1986) sf novel. [First U.K. edition]

Hubbard, L. Ron **Mission Earth, Vol. 4: An Alien Affair** (New Era 1-870451-00-7, Apr,87, £10.95, 329pp, hc) Reprint (Bridge 1986) sf novel. [First U.K. edition]

Hubbard, L. Ron **Mission Earth, Vol. 5: Fortune of Fear** (New Era 1-870451-01-5, Jul,87, £10.95, 365pp, hc) Reprint (Bridge 1986) sf novel. [First U.K. edition]

*Hubbard, L. Ron **Mission Earth, Vol. 6: Death Quest** (Bridge 0-88404-212-X, Jan,87, $18.95, 351pp, hc) Sf novel, sixth in a dekalogy. As usual, this is marked as a second printing of the first edition, with the first sheets apparently held for a special binding. Since this appears first, it leads to confusion.

Hubbard, L. Ron **Mission Earth, Vol. 6: Death Quest** (New Era 1-870451-02-3, Nov,87, £10.95, 351pp, hc) Reprint (Bridge 1987) sf novel. [First U.K. edition]

*Hubbard, L. Ron **Mission Earth, Vol. 7: Voyage of Vengeance** (Bridge 0-88404-213-8, May,87, $18.95, 381pp, hc) Sf novel, 7th in a dekalogy.

*Hubbard, L. Ron **Mission Earth, Vol. 8: Disaster** (Bridge 0-88404-214-6, Jul,87, $18.95, 337pp, hc) Sf serial continues -- only two more to go!

*Hubbard, L. Ron **Mission Earth, Vol. 9: Villainy Victorious** (Bridge 0-88404-215-4, Oct,87 [Sep,87], $18.95, 419pp, hc) Sf novel. The dekalogy is almost over.

*Hubbard, L. Ron **Mission Earth, Vol.10: The Doomed Planet** (Bridge 0-88404-216-2, Nov,87 [Oct,87], $18.95, 329pp, hc) Sf novel, last in the dekalogy.

*Hubbard, L. Ron, Jr. & Bent Corydon **L. Ron Hubbard: Messiah or Madman?** Main listing under Bent Corydon.

*Hubbard, L. Ron, [ref.] **L. Ron Hubbard: Messiah or Madman?** Main listing under Bent Corydon.

*Hudson, Michael **Photon: Thieves of Light** (Berkley 0-425-09810-9, Apr,87 [Mar,87], $3.50, 215pp, pb) Sf novel based on the "laser-blasting" game. The author is actually Michael Kube-McDowell.

*Huffman-Klinkowitz, Julie, Jerome Klinkowitz & Asa Pieratt, eds. **Kurt Vonnegut: A Comprehensive Bibliography** Main listing under Asa Pieratt.

Hughes, Monica **Devil on My Back** (Bantam Starfire 0-553-26698-5, Sep,87 [Aug,87], $2.95, 196pp, pb) Reissue (UK 1984) young-adult sf novel; 2nd Starfire printing.

+Hughes, Monica **The Dream Catcher** (Atheneum/Argo 0-689-31331-4, Mar,87 [Jun,87], $11.95, 171pp, hc) Young-adult sf novel, sequel to **Devil on My Back**. First U.S. edition (Julia MacRae 1986).

Hughes, Robert Don **The Power and the Prophet** (Fontana 0-00-617345-4, Oct,87, £2.95, 339pp, pb) Reprint (Del Rey 1985) fantasy novel. Volume 3 in the "Pelmen the Powershaper" series. [First U.K. edition]

Hughes, Robert Don **The Prophet of Lamath** (Fontana 0-00-617343-8, Jun,87, £2.95, 357pp, pb) Reprint (Ballantine/Del Rey 1979) fantasy novel. Volume 1 in the "Pelmen the Powershaper" series. [First U.K. edition]

Hughes, Robert Don **The Wizard in Waiting** (Fontana 0-00-617344-6, Aug,87, £2.95, 357pp, pb) Reprint (Del Rey 1982) fantasy novel. Volume 2 in the "Pelmen the Powershaper" series. [First U.K. edition]

Hughes, Zach **Closed System** (NAL/Signet 0-451-15256-5, Dec,87 [Nov,87], $2.95, 222pp, pb) Reissue (NAL 1986) sf novel; 3rd printing.

*Hughes, Zach **The Dark Side** (NAL/Signet 0-451-15111-9, Dec,87 [Nov,87], $2.95, 207pp, pb) Sf novel, space opera.

Hughes, Zach **Gold Star** (NAL/Signet 0-451-15212-3, Dec,87 [Nov,87], $2.95, 173pp, pb) Reissue (NAL 1983) sf novel; 4th printing.

*Hughes, Zach **Sundrinker** (DAW 0-88677-213-3, Jul,87, $3.50, 269pp, pb) Sf novel set on an alien planet with various alien races. The lead characters are humanoids evolved from plantlife.

Hull, Elizabeth Anne & Frederik Pohl, eds. **Tales from the Planet Earth** Main listing under Frederik Pohl.

+Hutson, Shaun **Breeding Ground** (Leisure 0-8439-2544-2, Nov,87 [Oct,87], $3.95, 367pp, pb) Horror novel, sequel to **Slugs**. Almost a large print edition. First U.S. edition (W.H. Allen 1985).

*Hutson, Shaun **Deathday** (Star 0-352-32050-8, Apr,87, £2.75, 383pp, pb) Horror novel.

Hutson, Shaun **Relics** (Star 0-352-31797-3, Nov,87, £2.95, 269pp, pb) Reprint (W.H. Allen 1986) horror novel.

Hutson, Shaun **Shadows** (Star 0-352-31637-3, Nov,87 [Dec,87], £3.50, 325pp, pb) Reprint (W.H. Allen 1985) horror novel.

+Hutson, Shaun **Slugs** (Leisure 0-8439-2511-6, Aug,87 [Jul,87], $3.95, 380pp, pb) Reprint (Uk 1982) horror novel.

Hutson, Shaun **Slugs** (Star 0-352-31201-7, Nov,87, £2.50, 208pp, pb) Reissue (Star 1982) horror novel.

Hutson, Shaun **The Terminator** (Star 0-352-31645-4, Feb,87, £2.50, 172pp, pb) Reissue (Star 1984) novelization of sf film.

*Hutson, Shaun **Victims** (W.H. Allen 0-491-03027-4, Jul,87, £11.95, 288pp, hc) Horror novel.

Ing, Dean **Anasazi** (Baen 0-671-65629-5, Mar,87 [Feb,87], $2.95, 270pp, pb) Reprint (Ace 1980) collection of 3 somewhat connected stories including the title short novel. This edition has new introductions to each piece.

*Ing, Dean **Blood of Eagles** (Tor 0-312-93010-0, Apr,87 [Mar,87], $16.95, 280pp, hc) Suspense novel, associational; non-fantasy by an sf author.

*Ing, Dean **Firefight 2000** (Baen 0-671-65648-1, Jun,87 [May,87], $2.95, 247pp, pb) Collection of stories and speculative articles.

*Ingpen, Robert **The Voyage of the Poppykettle** (Paper Tiger 1-85028-054-1, Sep,87, £5.95, 48pp, hc) Juvenile fantasy novelette. Fully ilustrated by Ingpen. [Not seen]

*Ingpen, Robert & Barbara Hayes **Folk Tales and Fables of the World** Main listing under Barbara Hayes.

*Ingrid, Charles **Solar Kill** (DAW 0-88677-209-5, Jul,87 [Jun,87], $3.50, 301pp, pb) Sf novel, first in the "Sand Wars" series.

*Innes, Evan **America 2040 #3: The City in the Mist** (Bantam 0-553-26204-1, Apr,87 [Mar,87], $3.95, 374pp, pb) Science fiction series novel. "Wagons West" in space.

*Ironside, Virginia **Vampire Master** (Walker 0-7445-0805-3, Aug,87 [Oct,87], £6.95, 176pp, hc) Juvenile horror spoof.

Irving, Washington **Rip Van Winkle** (Morrow/Books of Wonder 0-688-07459-6, Sep,87 [Oct,87], $15.00, 94pp, hc) Reprint of the 1921 edition of the classic fantasy tale, with color illustrations by N.C. Wyeth.

*Irwin, Walter & G.B. Love, eds. **The Best of Trek #12** (NAL/Signet 0-451-14935-1, Aug,87 [Jul,87], $2.95, 206pp, pb) Non-fiction, collection of essays on Star Trek.

Jackson, Shirley **The Haunting of Hill House** (Robinson 0-948164-35-2, Sep,87 [Aug,87], £2.95, 246pp, tp) Reprint (Viking 1959) horror novel.

Jackson, Shirley **We Have Always Lived in the Castle** (Robinson 0-948164-36-0, Sep,87 [Aug,87], £2.95, 190pp, tp) Reprint (Viking 1962) horror novel.

*Jackson, Sir William **Alternative Third World War, 1985 - 2035: A Personal History** (Pergamon 0-08-034740-1, Sep,87 [Oct,87], £14.95, 268pp, hc) Another 'future history' book. [Not seen]

*Jacobson, Dan **Her Story** (Andre Deutsch 0-233-98116-0, Aug,87 [Dec,87], £8.95, 141pp, hc) Literary sf novel.

+Jacques, Brian **Redwall** (Putnam Philomel 0-399-21424-0, Jun,87 [May,87], $15.95, 351pp, hc) Juvenile fantasy novel. The good mice of Redwall Abbey and their woodland friends fight the rat and ferret horde of Cluny the Scourge. Despite a legendary sword, this is more a medieval adventure a la Disney than a fantasy. A charming, exciting, and intelligent juvenile -- if you don't mind talking animals. A first novel, but the second book in a trilogy! (CFC)

Jacques, Brian **Redwall** (Beaver 0-09-951200-9, Aug,87, £2.50, 416pp, pb) Reprint (Hutchinson 1986) juvenile fantasy novel.

*Jaffery, Sheldon R., ed. **Selected Tales of Grim and Grue from the Horror Pulps** (Bowling Green Popular Press 0-87972-392-0, Aug,87 [Oct,87], $15.95, 195pp, tp) Anthology of 8 stories from the horror pulps, offset from the magazines -- including illos and ads. There is also an index to Weird Menace pulps and an article about them. Also announced in hardcover; not seen.

*Jaffery, Sheldon R., ed. **The Weirds** (Starmont House 0-930261-92-5, Apr,87, $9.95, 173pp, tp) Anthology of facsimiles of stories, illustrations, and some ads from "the era of the shudder-pulps." These have all been taken from *Terror Stories* and *Horror Stories*. There is a historical introduction on the era.

Jakes, John **Brak the Barbarian** (Star 0-352-32116-4, Dec,87 [Nov,87], £1.95, 160pp, pb) Reprint (Avon 1968) fantasy novel. Volume 1 in the "Brak the Barbarian" series.

James, Henry **The Turn of the Screw & Other Stories** (Everyman 0-460-11912-5, May,87 [1987], £1.95, 312pp, pb) Reprint collection including the famous ghost story. [Not seen]

James, John **Votan** (Bantam UK 0-553-17358-8, Nov,87 [Oct,87], £2.75, 240pp, pb) Reprint (Cassell 1966) fantasy novel.

*James, M.R. **Casting the Runes and Other Ghost Stories** (World's Classics 0-19-281719-1, Apr,87 [Jun,87], £3.95, 352pp, pb) Collection of ghost stories, edited by Michael Cox.

James, M.R. **Ghost Stories** (Brompton Books 1-870774-00-0, Sep,87 [Oct,87], £8.95, 362pp, hc) Reprint ghost story collection. [Not seen]

+James, M.R. **The Ghost Stories of M.R. James** (Oxford Univ. Press 0-19-212255-X, 1986 [Jun,87], $18.95, 224pp, hc) A selection of James' ghostly tales, chosen by Michael Cox, with illustrations by Rosalind Caldecott. This is the 1986 British edition, (printed in Australia!) now distributed in the U.S. by Oxford University Press/U.S. It includes a long introduction with background material and photos. It's printed on coated stock and is a beautiful book. (CNB)

*James, M.R. **Masters of Fantasy 3: M.R. James** (British Fantasy Society no ISBN, May,87 [1987], £0.90, 24pp, pb) Ghost collection. Edited by Richard Dalby. Volume 10 in the BFS Booklet series. [Not seen]

James, M.R. **The Penguin Complete Ghost Stories of M.R. James** (Penguin 0-14-010226-4, Oct,87 [Nov,87], £3.95, 362pp, tp) Reissue (Edward Arnold 1931, as **The Collected Ghost Stories of M.R. James**) ghost collection.

James, M.R. **A Warning to the Curious** (Isis Large Print 1-85089-154-0, Oct,87, £9.50, 140pp, hc) Reprint (Hutchinson 1987) ghost story collection, edited by Ruth Rendell. [Not seen]

*James, M.R. **A Warning to the Curious: The Ghost Stories of M.R. James** (Hutchinson 0-09-170080-9, Feb,87, £9.95, 257pp, hc) Ghost story collection, selected and edited by Ruth Rendell.

*James, Robert **Blood Mist** (Leisure 0-8439-2523-X, Sep,87, $3.95, 365pp, pb) Horror novel.

*Janifer, Laurence M. **Knave & the Game** (Doubleday 0-385-15238-8, Aug,87, $12.95, 173pp, hc) Collection of 9 sf stories about adventurer Gerald Knave.

*Jarman, Julia **Ollie and the Bogle** (Andersen Press 0-86264-163-2, Apr,87 [Dec,87], £5.95, 135pp, hc) Juvenile fantasy novel about a tree-sprite.

*Jay, Peter & Michael Stewart **Apocalypse 2000: Economic Breakdown and the Suicide of Democracy** (Sidgwick & Jackson 0-283-99440-1, Jun,87 [Jul,87], £12.95, 254pp, hc) Future history novel.

*Jefferies, Mike **Palace of Kings** (Fontana 0-00-617467-1, Nov,87, £2.95, 314pp, pb) Fantasy novel. Volume 2 in the "Loremasters of Elundium" series.

Jefferies, Mike **Palace of Kings** (Collins 0-00-223239-1, Dec,87, £10.95, 288pp, hc) Reprint (Fontana 1987) fantasy novel. Volume 2 in the "Loremasters of Elundium" series. [Not seen]

Jefferies, Mike **The Road to Underfall** (Collins 0-00-223307-X, Nov,87, £10.95, 352pp, hc) Reprint (Fontana 1986) fantasy novel. Volume 1 in the "Loremasters of Elundium" series. [Not seen]

*Jensen, Ruby Jean **Annabelle** (Zebra 0-8217-2011-2, Mar,87 [Aug,87], $3.95, 332pp, pb) Horror novel.

*Jensen, Ruby Jean **Chain Letter** (Zebra 0-8217-2162-3, Sep,87 [Aug,87], $3.95, 382pp, pb) Horror novel.

*Jensen, Ruby Jean **Smoke** (Zebra 0-8217-2255-7, Jan,88 [Dec,87], $3.95, 366pp, pb) Horror novel.

*Jeter, K.W. **Dark Seeker** (Tor 0-812-52007-6, Feb,87 [Jan,87], $3.95, 317pp, pb) Sf horror novel about a drug which gives shared consciousness and creates monsters.

*Jeter, K.W. **Death's Arms** (Morrigan 1-870338-00-6, May,87, £10.95, 183pp, hc) Sf novel, third in the "thematic trilogy" which began with **Dr. Adder** and **The Glass Hammer**. This small press edition for a new publisher is limited to 1,000 copies in various confusing states.

*Jeter, K.W. **Death's Arms** (Morrigan 1-870338-05-7, May,87, £27.50, 183pp, hc) Signed, limited (250 copies) edition of the above. [Not seen]

Jeter, K.W. **Dr. Adder** (Grafton 0-586-07076-1, Apr,87, £2.95, 252pp, pb) Reprint (Bluejay 1984) sf novel. [First U.K. edition]

Jeter, K.W. **The Glass Hammer** (Grafton 0-586-07078-8, Aug,87, £2.95, 238pp, pb) Reprint (Bluejay 1985) sf novel. [First U.K. edition]

*Jeter, K.W. **Infernal Devices** (St. Martin's 0-312-00706-X, Apr,87 [Mar,87], $16.95, 282pp, hc) "The curious tale of a most unusual array of clockwork automations," this is set in a Victorian scene that's part-Lovecraftian, part-gonzo 19th century a la Powers and Blaylock ("steam punk"). It's one of the best works this sub-genre has produced, a wildly entertaining fantasy. Recommended. (FCM)

Jeter, K.W. **Infernal Devices** (NAL/Signet 0-451-14934-3, Nov,87 [Oct,87], $2.95, 239pp, pb) Reprint (St. Martin's 1987) Victorian fantasy novel. Recommended. (FCM)

*Jeter, K.W. **Mantis** (Tor 0-812-52009-2, Oct,87 [Sep,87], $3.95, 279pp, pb) Horror novel.

Jeter, K.W. **Soul Eater** (Tor 0-812-52011-4, Oct,87 [Sep,87], $3.95, 314pp, pb) Reissue (Tor 1983) horror novel. It still says "first edition" inside, but advertises Jeter's next book, **Mantis**, on the cover.

Johnson, Annabel & Edgar Johnson **The Danger Quotient** (Harper & Row/Starwanderer 0-694-05607-3, Jun,87, $2.95, 201pp, pb) Reprint (Harper & Row 1984) young adult post-holocaust sf novel: test tube genius invents time machine to save the world.

Johnson, Edgar & Annabel Johnson **The Danger Quotient** Main listing under Annabel Johnson.

*Johnson, James B. **Trekmaster** (DAW 0-88677-221-4, Sep,87 [Aug,87], $3.50, 397pp, pb) Sf/political novel with a war thrown in.

*Johnson, Shane **Mr. Scott's Guide to the Enterprise** (Pocket 0-671-63576-X, Jul,87 [Jun,87], $10.95, 127pp, tp) Pictorial, starship plans and associated material, written and illustrated by Johnson, based on "Star Trek" designs.

Johnson, Shane **Mr. Scott's Guide to the Enterprise** (Titan 0-671-63576-X, Jul,87, £6.95, 127pp, tp) Reprint (Pocket 1987) of associational interest. [First U.K. edition]

Johnson, Shane **Mr. Scott's Guide to the Enterprise** (SFBC #11347, Oct,87, $9.98, 128pp, hc) Reprint (Pocket 1987) "Star Trek" tie-in. First hardcover edition.

*Johnstone, William W. **The Devil's Cat** (Zebra 0-8217-2091-0, May,87, $3.95, 380pp, pb) Horror novel.

*Johnstone, William W. **Smoke from the Ashes** (Zebra 0-8217-2191-7, Oct,87 [Sep,87], $3.50, 348pp, pb) Post-holocaust adventure novel. (Part of a series?)

Johnstone, William W. **The Uninvited** (Zebra 0-8217-2258-1, Jan,88 [Dec,87], $3.95, 301pp, pb) Reissue (Zebra 1982) horror novel; 2nd printing.

Johnstone, William W. **Wolfsbane** (Zebra 0-8217-2019-8, Mar,87 [Feb,87], $3.50, 268pp, pb) Reissue (Zebra 1982) horror novel; 2nd printing.

*Johnstone, William W. & Joe Keene **Baby Grand** Main listing under Joe Keene.

*Jones, Bruce **Twisted Tales** (Blackthorne 0-932629-73-3, Sep,87 [Aug,87], $9.95, 243pp, tp) Collection of 13 horror stories, mostly originals, illustrated by Richard Corben. There's also supposed to be a mass market edition (not seen).

Jones, Diana Wynne **Archer's Goon** (Berkley 0-425-09888-5, Jun,87 [May,87], $2.95, 241pp, pb) Reprint (Morrow/Greenwillow 1984) young adult fantasy novel, funny and thoroughly entertaining. The Goon is ensconced in the kitchen and won't leave until he gets his 2,000 words. (FCM)

Jones, Diana Wynne **Fire and Hemlock** (Teens 0-416-04022-5, Oct,87, £1.95, 341pp, pb) Reissue (Greenwillow 1984) juvenile fantasy novel.

Jones, Diana Wynne **The Magicians of Caprona** (Beaver 0-09-954280-3, Dec,87, £1.95, 191pp, pb) Reissue (Macmillan 1980) juvenile fantasy novel.

*Jones, Diana Wynne **A Tale of Time City** (Greenwillow 0-688-07315-8, Sep,87 [Oct,87], $11.75, 278pp, hc) Juvenile sf novel of time travel to the future and a city outside of time.

*Jones, Diana Wynne **A Tale of Time City** (Methuen 0-416-02362-2, Oct,87 [1987], £8.95, 160pp, hc) Juvenile sf novel. Simultaneous with US (Greenwillow) edition. [Not seen]

Jones, Diana Wynne **The Time of the Ghost** (Beaver 0-09-935950-2, Dec,87, £1.95, 189pp, pb) Reissue (Macmillan 1981) juvenile fantasy novel.

*Jones, Glyn **The Space Museum** (W.H. Allen 0-491-03295-1, Jan,87, £7.25, 142pp, hc) Juvenile sf novel. Volume 117 in the Doctor Who series.

Jones, Glyn **The Space Museum** (Target 0-426-20289-9, Jun,87, £1.80, 142pp, pb) Reprint (W.H. Allen 1987) juvenile sf novel. Volume 117 in the Doctor Who series.

+Jones, Gwyneth **Divine Endurance** (Arbor House 0-87795-856-4, Mar,87 [Feb,87], $14.95, 233pp, hc) Sf novel of the distant future. First U.S. edition (Allen & Unwin 1984).

*Jones, Lloyd S. **Black Rainbow** (Aeolus 0-918805-34-1, Jul,87 [Jun,87], $16.95, 213pp, hc) Near-future techno-thriller with ESP thrown in.

Jones, Terry **Nicobobinus** (Puffin 0-14-032091-1, May,87, £2.25, 175pp, tp) Reprint (Pavilion 1985) juvenile fantasy novel.

*Jong, Erica **Serenissima** (Houghton Mifflin 0-395-42922-6, Apr,87 [Mar,87], $17.95, 240pp, hc) Fantasy time travel novel of the present and the Venice of Shakespeare's time, with Shakespeare as a lead character.

Jong, Erica **Serenissima** (Bantam UK 0-593-01365-4, Sep,87, £10.95, 225pp, hc) Reprint (Houghton Mifflin 1987) time-travel/romantic novel. [First U.K. edition]

*Jordan, Brenda **The Brentwood Witches** (Ace 0-441-07297-6, Oct,87 [Sep,87], $2.95, 186pp, pb) Contemporary fantasy novel. Probably a first novel.

Jordan, Robert **Conan the Victorious** (Sphere 0-7221-5213-2, Apr,87, £2.50, 229pp, pb) Reprint (Tor 1984) fantasy novel. Volume 26 in the Sphere "Conan" series. [First U.K. edition]

*Joron, Andrew **Force Fields** (Starmont House 0-930261-86-0, Apr,87, $8.95, 55pp, tp) Collection of sf poetry, illustrated by Richard Herman.

Justice, Kenneth L., ed. **Science Fiction Master Index of Names** (McFarland 0-89950-183-4, Jun,87, £29.95, 394pp, hc) Reprint (McFarland 1986) non-fiction bibliography. [First U.K. edition, not seen]

Kahn, James **Poltergeist II: The Other Side** (Firecrest 0-85997-908-3, Jan,87, £8.95, 184pp, hc) Reprint (Ballantine 1986) horror film novelization. [Not seen]

*Kahn, James **Timefall** (St. Martin's 0-312-00195-9, Feb,87 [Jan,87], $16.95, 295pp, hc) Sf novel of time travel, doppelgangers, and approaching doom.

*Kahn, James, Donald F. Glut & George Lucas **The Star Wars Trilogy** Main listing under George Lucas.

*Kahn, Joan, ed. **Ready or Not: Here Come Fourteen Frightening Stories!** (Greenwillow 0-688-07167-8, Aug,87 [Oct,87], $11.75, 159pp, hc) Young adult anthology of 14 horror stories. Most, but not all, are supernatural.

*Kane, Daniel **Power and Magic** (GMP Press 0-85449-078-7, Oct,87 [1987], £4.95, 224pp, pb) Fantasy novel. [Not seen]

Katz, William **Death Dreams** (Warner 0-446-34434-6, Apr,87 [Mar,87], $3.95, 297pp, pb) Reprint (? 1979) horror novel.

*Kaveney, Roz, ed. **Tales from the Forbidden Planet** (Titan 1-85286-004-9, Aug,87, £4.95, 256pp, tp) Original sf anthology. This is supposedly published on 29th October, but was made available for the Worldcon and is now in most specialist shops.

*Kaveney, Roz, ed. **Tales from the Forbidden Planet** (Titan 1-85286-005-7, Aug,87, £9.95, 256pp, hc) Hardback edition of the above.

*Kaveney, Roz, ed. **Tales from the Forbidden Planet** (Titan 1-85286-006-5, Aug,87, £30.00, 256pp, hc) Limited edition of the above.

Kay, Guy Gavriel **The Darkest Road** (SFBC #107011, Apr,87, $4.98, 355pp, hc) Reprint (Arbor House 1986) fantasy novel blending the contemporary with the Tolkien tradition, third in the "Fionavar" trilogy.

Kay, Guy Gavriel **The Darkest Road** (Unwin Hyman 0-04-823361-7, Aug,87, £10.95, 420pp, pb) Reprint (Arbor House 1986) fantasy novel. Volume 3 in the "Fionavar Tapestry" series. [First U.K. edition]

Kay, Guy Gavriel **The Summer Tree** (Unwin 0-04-823339-0, Jun,87, £2.95, 323pp, pb) Reissue (Maclellan & Stewart 1984) fantasy novel. Volume 1 in the "Fionavar Tapestry" series.

Kay, Guy Gavriel **The Wandering Fire** (Unwin 0-04-823362-5, Jun,87, £2.95, 298pp, pb) Reprint (Arbor House 1986) fantasy novel. Volume 2 in the "Fionavar Tapestry" series.

Kay, Guy Gavriel **The Wandering Fire** (Ace 0-441-87046-5, Jul,87 [Jun,87], $3.50, 271pp, pb) Reprint (Arbor House 1986) fantasy novel, second in "The Fionavar Tapestry" trilogy.

Kaye, Marilyn **Max in Love** (Puffin 0-14-032278-7, Jun,87, £1.95, 148pp, pb) Reprint (Pocket 1986) juvenile sf novel.

Kaye, Marilyn **Max on Fire** (Puffin 0-14-032279-5, Oct,87 [Nov,87], £1.95, 147pp, pb) Reprint (Pocket 1986) juvenile sf novel. [First U.K. edition, not seen]

KAYE, MARVIN KING, BERNARD

*Kaye, Marvin **Ghosts of Night and Morning** (Ace Charter 0-441-28612-7, Aug,87 [Jul,87], $3.95, 304pp, pb) Horror novel composed of 5 interlocking episodes; sequel to **A Cold Blue Light**.

Kaye, Marvin & Parke Godwin **Wintermind** For main listing see under Parke Godwin.

*Kaye, Marvin, ed. **Devils and Demons** (SFBC #10336, Sep,87 [Nov,87], $6.98, 587pp, hc) Anthology of 52 horror stories. The book club edition actually pre-dates the Doubleday trade edition listed last month.

*Kaye, Marvin, ed. **Devils and Demons** (Doubleday 0-385-18563-4, Oct,87, $15.95, 587pp, hc) Anthology of 52 stories of devils and demons, divided into various sections. There is a historical introduction plus an afterword, notes, and a bibliography. At least 10 of the stories are new. There is a simultaneous book club edition.

*Keene, Joe & William W. Johnstone **Baby Grand** (Zebra 0-8217-2138-0, Aug,87 [Jul,87], $3.95, 427pp, pb) Horror novel.

*Keeping, Charles, ed. **Charles Keeping's Classic Tales of the Macabre** (Blackie 0-216-92147-3, Sep,87 [Nov,87], £8.95, 172pp, hc) Horror/occult anthology. Illustrated throughout by Charles Keeping.

*Keith, William H., Jr. **Battletech: Decision at Thunder Rift** (FASA 0-931787-69-6, 1986 [May,87], $3.95, 364pp, pb) Sf novel based on a game; part of a series. This has a 1986 copyright, but we had not seen it until now.

*Keith, William H., Jr. **Battletech: Mercenary's Star** (FASA 1-55560-030-1, Aug,87 [Nov,87], $3.95, 367pp, pb) Military sf novel in the "Battletech" series, based on the game.

*Kelleher, Ed & Harriette Vidal **The Breeder** (Leisure 0-8439-2478-0, Aug,87 [Jul,87], $3.95, 383pp, pb) Horror novel.

Kelleher, Victor **The Beast of Heaven** (Univ. of Queensland Press 0-7022-2033-7, Feb,87 [May,87], $8.95, 205pp, tp) Reprint (Univ. of Queensland Press 1984) sf novel, winner of the Ditmar Award. This paperback edition is the 1986 Australian, now available in the U.S.

*Kelleher, Victor **Taronga** (Hamish Hamilton 0-241-12148-5, Sep,87 [Oct,87], £6.95, 208pp, hc) Juvenile novel set in Australia in the 'not too distant' future. [Not seen]

*Kellogg, M. Bradley & William Rossow **Lear's Daughters** (SFBC #107003, Apr,87, $8.98, 725pp, hc) Omnibus edition of **The Wave and the Flame** and **Reign of Fire** (both NAL 1986), a two-part sf novel set on a fascinating planet with a bizarre weather pattern (Rossow provided scientific input). Highly recommended. (FCM)

Kellogg, M. Bradley & William Rossow **The Wave and the Flame** (Gollancz 0-575-04109-9, Sep,87, £10.95, 368pp, hc) Reprint (NAL 1986) sf novel. Volume 1 in the "Lear's Daughters" series. [First U.K. edition, not seen]

Kelly, James Patrick & John Kessel **Freedom Beach** (Unwin 0-04-823385-4, Oct,87, $2.95, 259pp, pb) Reprint (Bluejay 1985) sf novel. [First U.K. edition]

Kelly, Richard **Tread Softly** (W.H. Allen 0-491-03327-3, Jun,87, £11.95, 285pp, hc) Reprint (Tor 1987) horror novel. [First U.K. edition]

Kennealy, Patricia **The Throne of Scone** (NAL/Signet 0-451-14821-5, May,87 [Apr,87], $3.50, 380pp, pb) Reprint (Bluejay 1986) sf novel of Kelts in space; Book One of "The Keltiad".

Kennealy, Patricia **The Throne of Scone** (Grafton 0-586-06832-5, Oct,87, £3.50, 479pp, pb) Reprint (Bluejay 1986) fantasy novel. Volume 3 in the "Keltiad" series. [First U.K. edition]

+Kennedy, Leigh **Faces** (Atlantic Monthly Press 0-87113-140-4, Aug,87 [Jul,87], $15.95, 152pp, hc) Collection of 10 stories, with more literary/associational than sf/fantasy. First U.S. edition (Jonathan Cape 1986).

+Kennedy, Leigh **The Journal of Nicholas the American** (Atlantic Monthly Press 0-87113-108-0, 1986 [Feb,87], $16.95, 204pp, hc) Sf novel, a first novel and Nebula nominee. Sf by courtesy only -- the hero is an empath. First U.S. edition (Cape 1986).

*Kent, Paul **The Crib** (Bantam 0-553-26650-0, Apr,87 [Mar,87], $3.50, 218pp, pb) Horror novel.

Kerr, Katharine **Daggerspell** (Grafton 0-246-13161-6, Apr,87 [Mar,87], £10.95, 414pp, hc) Reprint (Doubleday 1986) fantasy novel. Volume 1 in a new fantasy trilogy. [First U.K. edition]

Kerr, Katharine **Daggerspell** (Grafton 0-246-13168-3, Apr,87, £6.95, 414pp, tp) Paperback edition of the above. [First U.K. edition]

Kerr, Katharine **Daggerspell** (Ballantine/Del Rey 0-345-34430-8, Dec,87 [Nov,87], $3.50, 395pp, pb) Reprint (Doubleday 1986) fantasy novel, first of a trilogy.

*Kerr, Katharine **Darkspell** (Doubleday 0-385-23109-1, Sep,87 [Aug,87], $17.95, 369pp, hc) Fantasy novel, sequel to **Daggerspell**.

Kessel, John & James Patrick Kelly **Freedom Beach** For main entry see under James Patrick Kelly.

*Ketterer, David **Imprisoned in a Tesseract: The Life and Work of James Blish** (Kent State Univ. Press 0-87338-334-6, Sep,87 [Oct,87], $29.50, hc) Non-fiction, critical and biographical study, an exhaustive study of Blish's published, unpublished, and fanzine work, both fiction and non-fiction. Highly recommended. (CNB)

Keyes, Daniel **Flowers For Algernon** (Gollancz 0-575-04061-0, Jun,87 [Jul,87], £3.50, 216pp, tp) Reprint (Harcourt 1966) sf novel. Volume 14 in the Gollancz Classic SF series.

*Kies, Cosette **The Occult in the Western World: An Annotated Bibliography** (Shoestring Press/Library Professional Publications 0-208-02113-2, Aug,86 [Jan,87], $29.50, 233pp, hc) Non-fiction, bibliography -- of associational interest. Published in 1986; missed.

Kilian, Crawford **The Empire of Time** (Ballantine/Del Rey 0-345-34759-5, Sep,87 [Aug,87], $2.95, 183pp, pb) Reissue (Del Rey 1978) sf/time travel novel, first in the "Chronoplane Wars" series; 5th printing.

*Kilian, Crawford **The Fall of the Republic** (Ballantine/Del Rey 0-345-34273-9, Sep,87 [Aug,87], $3.50, 293pp, pb) Sf/time travel novel, second in the "Chronoplane Wars" series.

*Killough, Lee **Blood Hunt** (Tor 0-812-50594-8, Mar,87 [Feb,87], $3.95, 319pp, pb) Horror novel of a homicide detective turned vampire.

*Killough, Lee **The Leopard's Daughter** (Popular Library Questar 0-445-20522-9, Oct,87 [Sep,87], $2.95, 218pp, pb) Fantasy novel set in Africa.

*Kilworth, Garry **Spiral Winds** (Bodley Head 0-370-31112-4, Aug,87, £10.95, 203pp, hc) Mainstream novel by author better known for his sf. Based on the short story of the same title.

Kilworth, Garry **Theatre of Timesmiths** (Unwin 0-04-440082-9, Oct,87, £2.95, 185pp, pb) Reprint (Gollancz 1984) sf novel.

Kilworth, Garry **Witchwater Country** (Grafton 0-586-07271-3, Oct,87, £2.95, 236pp, pb) Reprint (Bodley Head 1986) mainstream novel by author better known for his sf.

*Kilworth, Garry **The Wizard of Woodworld** (Dragon 0-583-31137-7, Nov,87, £1.95, 142pp, pb) Juvenile sf novel.

*King, Bernard **The Destroying Angel** (Sphere 0-7221-4869-0, Jul,87 [Jun,87], £3.50, 272pp, tp) Fantasy novel. Volume 1 in the "Chronicles of the Keeper" series.

+King, Bernard **Starkadder** (St. Martin's 0-312-01095-8, Sep,87 [Aug,87], $16.95, 243pp, hc) Norse mythological fantasy novel. First U.S. edition (NEL 1985).

KING, BERNARD   **KIPLING, RUDYARD**

*King, Bernard **Time-Fighters** (Sphere 0-7221-4868-2, Dec,87 [Nov,87], £3.50, 254pp, tp) Fantasy novel. Volume 2 in the "Chronicles of the Keeper" series.

King, Bernard **Vargr-Moon** (NEL 0-450-40848-5, Apr,87, £2.50, 244pp, pb) Reprint (NEL 1986) fantasy novel. Volume 2 in the "Starkadder" series.

*King, Clive **The Seashore People** (Viking Kestrel 0-670-81723-6, Aug,87 [Dec,87], £7.50, 96pp, hc) Juvenile fantasy novel. [Not seen]

King, Stephen **The Bachman Books** (NEL 0-450-39249-X, Aug,87, £4.95, 865pp, pb) Reprint (NAL/Plume 1985) associational/sf omnibus.

King, Stephen **Christine** (NEL 0-450-05674-0, Oct,87, £3.50, 597pp, pb) Reissue (Viking 1983) horror novel.

King, Stephen **Cujo** (Futura 0-7088-2171-5, Oct,87, £3.50, 345pp, pb) Reissue (Viking 1981) horror novel.

*King, Stephen **The Dark Tower II: The Drawing of the Three** (Donald M. Grant 0-937986-91-7, May,87, $35.00, 400pp, hc) Fantasy novel, volume 2 of the "Dark Tower" series. It takes up just where **The Gunslinger** left off. Illustrated in full color by Phil Hale. There is also a limited, signed deluxe edition (ISBN 0-937986-90-9, $100); not seen.

King, Stephen **The Eyes of the Dragon** (Viking 0-670-81458-X, Feb,87 [Jan,87], $18.95, 326pp, hc) Reprint (Philtrum 1985) juvenile fantasy novel about a young prince who has to defeat a wizard to gain control of his kingdom. The earlier special limited edition is not mentioned in the copyright page. There are some excellent illustrations by David Palladini. (CNB)

King, Stephen **The Eyes of the Dragon** (Macdonald 0-356-14224-8, Apr,87, £10.95, 326pp, hc) Reprint (Viking 1987 revised from an earlier edition, Philtrum 1985) fantasy novel. Interior illustrations by David Palladini. [First U.K. edition]

King, Stephen **The Eyes of the Dragon** (NAL 0-451-15125-9, Jan,88 [Dec,87], $4.50, 380pp, pb) Reprint (Philtrum 1985) young adult fantasy novel. This follows the revised text of the Viking 1987 edition.

King, Stephen **It** (NAL/Signet 0-451-14951-3, Sep,87 [Aug,87], $4.95, 1093pp, pb) Reprint (Viking Penguin 1986) horror novel. It weighs a lot.

King, Stephen **It** (NEL 0-450-41143-5, Oct,87 [Sep,87], £4.50, 1116pp, pb) Reprint (Hodder & Stoughton/Viking 1986) horror novel.

King, Stephen **It** (NEL 0-450-42305-0, Oct,87 [Sep,87], £4.50, 1116pp, pb) This is identical to the above edition except for the ISBN, the colour of the title (yellow instead of white) and a brief note on the cover and inside front page proclaiming it the "Special Collector's Edition".

King, Stephen **Misery** (QPB no ISBN, 1987 [Sep,87], $9.50, 310pp, tp) Reprint (Viking 1987) non-occult horror novel; associational. This is an exact reproduction of the Viking hardcover, minus the ISBN and softbound.

*King, Stephen **Misery** (Viking 0-670-81364-8, Jun,87 [Apr,87], $18.95, 310pp, hc) Non-sf/fantasy, associational. A psychological thriller about a writer held captive by a maniacal fan.

King, Stephen **Misery** (Hodder & Stoughton 0-340-39070-0, Sep,87, £11.95, 320pp, hc) Reprint (Viking 1987) psychological thriller. [First U.K. edition]

King, Stephen **Night Shift** (NEL 0-450-04268-5, Oct,87, £3.50, 409pp, pb) Reissue (Doubleday 1978) horror collection.

King, Stephen **Pet Sematary** (NEL 0-450-05769-0, Oct,87, £3.50, 424pp, pb) Reissue (Doubleday 1983) horror novel.

King, Stephen **Salem's Lot** (NEL 0-450-03106-3, Oct,87, £3.50, 439pp, pb) Reissue (Doubleday 1975) horror novel.

King, Stephen **The Shining** (NEL 0-450-04018-6, Oct,87, £2.95, 416pp, pb) Reissue (Doubleday 1977) horror novel.

King, Stephen **The Stand** (NEL 0-450-04552-8, Oct,87, £3.95, 734pp, pb) Reissue (Doubleday 1978) sf novel.

King, Stephen **Thinner** (NEL 0-450-05883-2, Aug,87, £2.50, 282pp, pb) Reissue (NAL 1984 as by Richard Bachman) horror novel.

*King, Stephen **The Tommyknockers** (Putnam 0-399-13314-3, Nov,87, $19.95, 558pp, hc) Sf/horror novel.

King, Stephen, [ref.] **Kingdom of Fear: The World of Stephen King** Main listing under Tim Underwood.

*King, Stephen, [ref.] **Stephen King Goes to Hollywood** Main listing under Jeff Conner.

*King, Stephen, [ref.] **The Stephen King Phenomenon** Main listing under Michael R. Collings.

King, Tappan & Viido Polikarpus **Down Town** Main listing under Viido Polikarpus.

King, Tappan & Viido Polikarpus **Down Town** (Orbit 0-7088-8213-7, Mar,87, £2.95, 293pp, pb) Reprint (Arbor House 1985) fantasy novel.

*King-Smith, Dick **Tumbleweed** (Gollancz 0-575-03975-2, Apr,87 [Dec,87], £5.95, 119pp, hc) Juvenile fantasy novel.

Kingsbury, Donald A. **The Moon Goddess and the Son** (Baen 0-671-65381-4, Dec,87 [Nov,87], $3.95, 471pp, pb) Reprint (Baen 1986), an excellent near-future hard sf novel. (TM)

Kinsella, W.P. **The Iowa Baseball Confederacy** (Ballantine 0-345-34230-5, Apr,87 [Mar,87], $3.95, 293pp, pb) Reprint (Houghton Mifflin 1986) literary baseball fantasy novel.

Kinsella, W.P. **Shoeless Joe** (Ballantine 0-345-34256-9, Apr,87 [Mar,87], $3.95, 224pp, pb) Reissue (Houghton Mifflin 1982) literary baseball fantasy novel.

*Kipling, Rudyard **The Complete Supernatural Stories of Rudyard Kipling** (W.H. Allen 0-491-03285-4, Jan,87, £12.95, 427pp, hc) Collection of supernatural stories, edited by Peter Haining.

Kipling, Rudyard **The Jungle Book** (Puffin 0-14-031794-5, Jan,87, £2.25, 175pp, pb) Reissue (Macmillan 1894) juvenile fantasy collection, illustrated by Michael Foreman.

Kipling, Rudyard **The Jungle Book** (Puffin 0-14-035074-8, Jan,87, £1.75, 186pp, pb) Reissue (Macmillan 1894) juvenile fantasy collection, illustrated by the author.

Kipling, Rudyard **The Jungle Book** (Viking Kestrel 0-670-80241-7, Jan,87 [Feb,87], £8.95, 175pp, hc) Reissue (Macmillan 1894) juvenile fantasy collection, illustrated by Michael Foreman.

Kipling, Rudyard **The Jungle Book** (Windrush 1-85089-904-5, Feb,87 [Dec,87], £7.65, 232pp, hc) Reprint (Macmillan 1894) juvenile fantasy collection. Large print edition.

Kipling, Rudyard **The Jungle Book** (Purnell 0-361-07468-9, Mar,87 [Dec,87], £2.99, 186pp, hc) Reprint (Macmillan 1894) classic fantasy collection.

Kipling, Rudyard **Jungle Books** (Hamlyn 0-600-55309-4, Nov,87 [Dec,87], £4.95, 416pp, hc) Reprint omnibus of **The Jungle Book** and **The Second Jungle Book**. [Not seen]

Kipling, Rudyard **Just So Stories** (Pavilion 1-85145-105-6, Jan,87, £7.95, 96pp, hc) Reissue (Macmillan 1902) juvenile fantasy collection, illustrated by Safaya Salter.

Kipling, Rudyard **Just So Stories** (Puffin 0-14-031795-3, Jan,87, £1.95, 128pp, pb) Reissue (Macmillan 1902) juvenile fantasy collection, illustrated by Michael Foreman.

Kipling, Rudyard **Just So Stories** (Puffin 0-14-035075-6, Jan,87, £1.75, 172pp, pb) Reissue (Macmillan 1902) juvenile fantasy collection, illustrated by the author.

KIPLING, RUDYARD

KURTZ, KATHERINE

Kipling, Rudyard **Just So Stories** (Viking Kestrel 0-670-80242-5, Jan,87 [Feb,87], £7.95, 128pp, hc) Reissue (Macmillan 1902) juvenile fantasy collection, illustrated by Michael Foreman.

Kipling, Rudyard **Just So Stories** (Purnell 0-361-07469-7, Mar,87, £2.99, 224pp, hc) Reprint (Macmillan 1902) classic fantasy collection. [Not seen]

Kipling, Rudyard **Just So Stories** (Collins 0-00-184425-3, Apr,87 [1987], £4.95, 128pp, hc) Reprint (Macmillan 1902) juvenile fantasy collection. [Not seen]

*Kirchner, Paul **The Bus** (Orbit 0-7088-8244-7, Aug,87, £2.95, 160pp, pb) Hilarious collection of cartoons from *Heavy Metal* about a bus on which strange things happen! Recommended.

+Kirk, Richard **Raven 2: A Time of Ghosts** (Ace 0-441-70561-8, May,87 [Apr,87], $2.95, 199pp, pb) Fantasy novel, second in a series about a woman warrior. First U.S. edition (Corgi 1978).

+Kirk, Richard **Raven 3: The Frozen God** (Ace 0-441-70567-7, Aug,87 [Jul,87], $2.95, 174pp, pb) Third novel in a sword & sorcery series written by Rob Holdstock and Angus Wells. First American edition (Corgi 1978).

+Kirk, Richard **Raven 4: Lords of the Shadows** (Ace 0-441-70573-1, Oct,87 [Sep,87], $2.95, 204pp, pb) Heroic fantasy novel in a series featuring a female warrior. First American edition (Corgi 1979). The authors are Angus Wells and Robert Holdstock.

+Kirk, Richard **Raven 5: A Time of Dying** (Ace 0-441-70575-8, Jan,88 [Dec,87], $2.95, 168pp, pb) Fantasy novel in a series with a female barbarian swordswoman. First American edition (Corgi 1979). The author is Robert Holdstock or Angus Wells or both.

+Kirk, Richard **Raven: Swordsmistress of Chaos** (Ace 0-441-70555-3, Feb,87 [Jan,87], $2.95, 174pp, pb) Sword & Sorcery fantasy novel, first in a pentology. First American edition (Corgi 1978).

*Kittredge, Mary & Kevin O'Donnell, Jr. **The Shelter** (Tor 0-812-52066-1, Aug,87 [Jul,87], $3.95, 376pp, pb) Horror novel.

Klein, Robin **Halfway Across the Galaxy and Turn Left** (Viking Kestrel 0-670-80636-6, Sep,86 [Jan,87], $3.50, 144pp, hc) Reprint (Viking 1985) very juvenile sf humor novella. Published in 1986; missed. It's Australian, and this is an imported worldwide edition from Australia.

Klein, T.E.D. **Dark Gods** (Pan 0-330-29714-7, Jan,87, £2.50, 259pp, pb) Reprint (Viking 1985) collection of 4 horror novellas. [First U.K. edition]

*Klinkowitz, Jerome, Julie Huffman-Klinkowitz & Asa Pieratt, eds. **Kurt Vonnegut: A Comprehensive Bibliography** Main listing under Asa Pieratt.

*Koman, Victor **The Jehovah Contract** (Franklin Watts 0-531-15043-7, Apr,87 [Mar,87], $16.95, 277pp, hc) A professional assassin on the skids in 1999 is hired to assassinate God, with the help of an ancient Hollywood witch and a 12-year-old telepathic hooker. This novel first appeared in Germany as **Der Jehova Vertrag** (Heyne 1985), although written originally in English.

Koontz, Dean R. **Strangers** (Star 0-352-31986-0, Mar,87, £3.95, 710pp, pb) Reprint (W.H. Allen/Putnam 1986) sf/horror novel.

*Koontz, Dean R. **Twilight Eyes** (W.H. Allen 0-491-03475-X, Apr,87, £11.95, 478pp, hc) Fantasy novel expanded and revised from an earlier version (Land of Enchantment 1986).

+Koontz, Dean R. **Twilight Eyes** (Berkley 0-425-10065-0, Sep,87 [Aug,87], $4.95, 451pp, pb) Horror novel. A slightly different version of Part 1 appeared from The Land of Enchantment (under the same title) in 1985. This is the first complete American edition (W.H. Allen 1987).

*Koontz, Dean R. **Watchers** (Putnam 0-399-13263-5, Feb,87 [Jan,87], $17.95, 352pp, hc) Supernatural/sf thriller about genetically manipulated dogs with unusual powers.

Koontz, Dean R. **Watchers** (Headline 0-7472-0041-6, Sep,87, £10.95, 352pp, hc) Reprint (Putnam 1987) plausible, yet terrifying, horror novel about two very different experimental animals escaped from the research labs. Highly recommended. [First U.K. edition]

Koontz, Dean R. **Watchers** (SFBC #10749, Oct,87, $5.98, 406pp, hc) Reprint (Putnam 1987) sf/horror thriller.

*Kornbluth, C.M. & Frederik Pohl **Our Best: The Best of Frederik Pohl and C.M. Kornbluth** Main listing under Frederik Pohl.

Kornbluth, C.M. & Frederik Pohl **The Space Merchants** Main listing under Frederik Pohl.

*Kotani, Eric & John Maddox Roberts **The Island Worlds** (Baen 0-671-65648-1, Jun,87 [May,87], $2.95, 279pp, pb) Sf novel of Earth vs. the asteroid belt in a war of independence.

Kotlan, C.M. & G.C. Edmondson **The Black Magician** Main listing under G.C. Edmondson.

Kotlan, C.M. & G.C. Edmondson **The Cunningham Equations** Main listing under G.C. Edmondson.

*Kotlan, C.M. & G.C. Edmondson **Maximum Effort** Main listing under G.C. Edmondson.

*Kott, Mike & Sue Cornwill **The Official Price Guide to Star Trek and Star Wars Collectibles, Second Edition** Main listing under Sue Cornwill.

*Kress, Nancy **An Alien Light** (Arbor House 0-87795-940-4, Jan,88 [Dec,87], $18.95, 370pp, hc) Sf novel, an intense investigation of the nature of humanity. Highly recommended. (FCM)

*Kube-McDowell, Michael P. **Empery** (Berkley 0-425-09887-7, Jun,87 [May,87], $3.50, 325pp, pb) Sf novel, conclusion of the "Trigon Disunity" trilogy.

*Kube-McDowell, Michael P. **Isaac Asimov's Robot City, Book 1: Odyssey** (Ace 0-441-73122-8, Jul,87 [Jun,87], $2.95, 211pp, pb) Sf novel, first in a shared-world series based on Asimov's Laws of Robotics (and Humanics).

Kunetka, James & Whitley Strieber **Nature's End** Main listing under Whitley Strieber.

Kunetka, James & Whitley Strieber **Nature's End** Main listing under Whitley Strieber.

*Kunstler, James Howard **The Hunt** (Tor 0-812-52093-9, Jan,88 [Dec,87], $3.50, 217pp, pb) Horror novel. Bigfoot hunts the hunters.

*Kurland, Michael **Star Griffin** (Doubleday 0-385-19395-5, Mar,87 [Feb,87], $12.95, 180pp, hc) Sf/fantasy novel of decadence and "futuristic wizardry."

Kurtz, Katherine **The Bishop's Heir** (Ballantine/Del Rey 0-345-34761-7, Sep,87 [Aug,87], $3.95, 363pp, pb) Reissue (Del Rey 1984) fantasy novel in the "Deryni" series, "The Histories of King Kelson" Vol. 1; 4th printing.

Kurtz, Katherine **Camber of Culdi** (Ballantine/Del Rey 0-345-34767-6, Sep,87 [Aug,87], $3.95, 314pp, pb) Reissue (Del Rey 1976) fantasy novel in the "Deryni" series, Vol. 1 of "The Legends of Camber of Culdi"; 16th printing.

Kurtz, Katherine **Camber the Heretic** (Century 0-7126-1585-7, Mar,87 [Aug,87], £11.95, 510pp, hc) Reprint (Del Rey 1981) fantasy novel. Volume 3 in "The Legends of Camber of Culdi".

Kurtz, Katherine **Deryni Checkmate** (Ballantine/Del Rey 0-345-34764-1, Sep,87 [Aug,87], $3.95, 302pp, pb) Reissue (Del Rey 1972) fantasy novel, second in the "Deryni" series; 16th printing.

Kurtz, Katherine **Deryni Rising** (Ballantine/Del Rey 0-345-34763-3, Sep,87 [Aug,87], $3.95, 271pp, pb) Reissue (Del Rey 1970) fantasy novel, first in the "Deryni" series; 15th printing.

KURTZ, KATHERINE

LAUMER, KEITH

Kurtz, Katherine **High Deryni** (Ballantine/Del Rey 0-345-34766-8, Sep,87 [Aug,87], $3.95, 369pp, pb) Reissue (Del Rey 1973) fantasy novel, third in the "Deryni" series; 15th printing.

Kurtz, Katherine **The King's Justice** (Ballantine/Del Rey 0-345-34762-5, Sep,87 [Aug,87], $3.95, 322pp, pb) Reissue (Del Rey 1985) fantasy novel in the "Deryni" series, Vol. 2 of "The Histories of King Kelson"; 3rd printing.

Kurtz, Katherine **The Quest for Saint Camber** (SFBC #106294, Mar,87, $5.98, 401pp, hc) Reprint (Del Rey 1986) fantasy novel in the "Deryni" series.

Kurtz, Katherine **The Quest for Saint Camber** (Arrow 0-09-950360-3, May,87, £3.50, 435pp, tp) Reprint (Del Rey 1986) fantasy novel. Volume 3 in the "Histories of King Kelson". [First U.K. edition]

Kurtz, Katherine **The Quest for Saint Camber** (Century 0-7126-1616-0, Aug,87 [Dec,87], £11.95, 435pp, hc) Reprint (Del Rey 1986) fantasy novel. Volume 3 in the "History of King Kelson" series.

Kurtz, Katherine **The Quest for Saint Camber** (Ballantine/Del Rey 0-345-30099-8, Sep,87 [Aug,87], $3.95, 449pp, pb) Reprint (Del Rey 1986) fantasy novel in the "Deryni" series, Vol. 3 of "The Histories of King Kelson".

Kurtz, Katherine **Saint Camber** (Ballantine/Del Rey 0-345-34768-4, Sep,87 [Aug,87], $3.95, 449pp, pb) Reissue (Del Rey 1978) fantasy novel in the "Deryni" series, "The Legends of Camber of Culdi" Vol. 2; 10th printing.

*Kushner, Ellen **Swordspoint** (Unwin Hyman 0-04-823352-8, Feb,87 [Aug,87], £9.95, 269pp, hc) Fantasy novel. A first novel.

Kushner, Ellen **Swordspoint** (Unwin 0-04-823373-0, Sep,87, £3.95, 269pp, tp) Reprint (Unwin Hyman 1987) fantasy novel.

+Kushner, Ellen **Swordspoint** (Arbor House 0-87795-923-4, Nov,87 [Oct,87], $15.95, 269pp, hc) Fantasy novel set in an imaginary, elegant, decadent civilization. An outstanding first novel. Recommended. (FCM) First U.S. edition (Allen & Unwin 1987).

*Kuttner, Henry **Prince Raynor** (Gryphon 0-936071-06-0, Jul,87, $5.95, 79pp, tp) Small booklet containing 2 Kuttner fantasies from 1939 pulps, plus an introduction by L. Sprague de Camp. Limited to 500 copies.

*L'Amour, Louis **The Haunted Mesa** (Bantam 0-553-05182-2, Jul,87 [Jun,87], $18.95, 357pp, hc) Western novel with an sf element -- a gate between dimensions.

L'Amour, Louis **The Haunted Mesa** (Bantam UK 0-593-01385-9, Nov,87, £10.95, 357pp, hc) Reprint (Bantam 1987) western with sf elements. [First U.K. edition]

L'Engle, Madeleine **Many Waters** (Dell/Laurel Leaf 0-440-95252-2, Sep,87, $3.25, 310pp, pb) Reprint (Farrar, Straus, Giroux 1986) fantasy novel, part of the "Wrinkle in Time" sequence.

*Lackey, Mercedes R. **Arrow's Fall** (DAW 0-88677-255-9, Jan,88 [Dec,87], $3.50, 319pp, pb) Fantasy novel, third in the "Arrows of the Queen" trilogy.

*Lackey, Mercedes R. **Arrow's Flight** (DAW 0-88677-222-2, Sep,87 [Aug,87], $3.50, 318pp, pb) Fantasy novel, second in the "Heralds of Valdemar" trilogy. Despite some signs of "middle book syndrome," this is better written than its predecessor. Recommended. (TM)

*Lackey, Mercedes R. **Arrows of the Queen** (DAW 0-88677-189-7, Mar,87 [Feb,87], $2.95, 320pp, pb) Fantasy novel -- a girl with unusual talents finds a place where she is accepted and trained; a cross between McCaffrey's "Harper Hall" books and Bradley's Free Amazons of Darkover. (CFC) A first novel and the first of an announced trilogy.

*Lafferty, R.A. **My Heart Leaps Up, Chapters 3 & 4** (Drumm 0-936055-30-8, Apr,87, $2.75, 44pp, tp) Two more chapters of a serialized work which is itself the first part of "In a Green Tree". Also available in a signed edition, -31-6, $6.00.

*Lafferty, R.A. **Serpent's Egg** (Morrigan 1-870338-15-4, Aug,87, £27.50, 177pp, hc) Fantasy novel mixing Lafferty's quirky Catholic fundamentalism with clones, robots, and a strange unknown sentient race on a future Earth. 250 copy limited edition, includes an extra story.

*Lafferty, R.A. **Serpent's Egg** (Morrigan 1-870338-10-3, Aug,87, £10.95, 166pp, hc) 750 copy limited edition of the above.

Laidlaw, Marc **Dad's Nuke** (Critic's Choice 1-55547-147-1, Feb,87 [Jan,87], $3.50, 255pp, pb) Reprint (Fine 1985) satirical sf novel.

Langford, David **The Space Eater** (Baen 0-671-65619-8, Feb,87 [Jan,87], $2.95, 281pp, pb) Reprint (Arrow 1982) sf novel.

*Langford, David & John Grant **Earthdoom!** (Grafton 0-586-06739-6, May,87, £2.95, 303pp, pb) Spoof disaster novel featuring villainous aliens, rabid lemmings and cloned Hitlers, among others.

*Lansdale, Joe R. **The Nightrunners** (Dark Harvest 0-913165-17-4, Aug,87, $18.95, 241pp, hc) Horror novel, illustrated by Gregory Manchess, with an introduction by Dean R. Koontz. The blurb warns, "Extreme violence, language and sexual situations may offend some readers." A deluxe limited edition was announced; not seen.

*Lantz, Fran **Eileen Goudge's Swept Away #2: Woodstock Magic** (Avon/Flare 0-380-75129-1, Sep,86 [Feb,87], $2.50, 166pp, pb) Young-adult sf/romance novel in a series about time-traveling teens -- time travel to Woodstock! Issued in 1986; not seen until now.

*Lantz, Fran **Eileen Goudge's Swept Away #8: All Shook Up** (Avon Flare 0-380-75136-4, Sep,87 [Aug,87], $2.50,   , pb) Teenage timetravel romance, set in 1950 with the birth of rock'n'roll.

*Larson, Glen A. & Robert Thurston **Battlestar Galactica #14: Surrender the Galactica!** (Ace 0-441-05104-9, Jan,88 [Dec,87], $2.95, 203pp, pb) Sf novelization based on the long-gone tv series.

Larson, Majliss **Pawns and Symbols** (Firecrest 0-85997-926-1, Jul,87 [1987], £7.95, 288pp, hc) Reprint (Pocket 1985) sf novel. Volume 41 in the Star Trek Novels series. [First U.K. edition, not seen]

*Larson, Randall D. **The Complete Robert Bloch: An Illustrated, Comprehensive Bibliography** (Fandom Unlimited 0-9607178-1-1, Jul,86 [Aug,87], $10.00, 126pp, tp) Non-fiction, bibliography. The copyright is 1986, but we were not sent a copy until 1987.

*Larson, Randall D. **Robert Bloch** (Starmont House 0-930261-58-5, Dec,86 [Jan,87], $8.95, 148pp, tp) Non-fiction, critical study, "Starmont Reader's Guide 37", including primary and secondary bibliographies.

Lasky, Kathryn **Home Free** (Dell/Laurel-Leaf 0-440-20038-5, Jan,88 [Dec,87], $2.95, 245pp, pb) Reprint (Four Winds 1985) young adult novel of naturalists vs. developers, and children with strange powers.

Laumer, Keith **Retief to the Rescue** (Baen 0-671-65376-8, Jan,88 [Dec,87], $2.95, 250pp, pb) Reprint (Simon & Schuster/Timescape 1983) sf novel in an endless humorous series.

Laumer, Keith **Retief: Diplomat at Arms** (Baen 0-671-65358-X, Oct,87 [Sep,87], $2.95, 214pp, pb) Reprint (Timescape 1982) collection of sf stories featuring Retief.

*Laumer, Keith **Retief: Envoy to New Worlds** (Baen 0-671-65635-X, Apr,87 [Mar,87], $2.95, 245pp, pb) Collection of Retief stories which includes the six stories from **Envoy to New Worlds** (Ace 1963) plus "Rank Injustice" (which first appeared in **New Destinies** earlier this year). To add to the confusion, five of the six **Envoy** stories appeared along with a short novel as **Retief Unbound** (Ace 1979).

Laumer, Keith **Time Trap** (Baen 0-671-65340-7, Aug,87 [Jul,87], $2.95, 156pp, pb) Reprint (Putnam 1970) sf time travel novel.

Laumer, Keith **The Ultimax Man** (Baen 0-671-65652-X, Jun,87 [May,87], $2.95, 249pp, pb) Reprint (Putnam 1978) sf adventure novel.

Laumer, Keith & Rosel George Brown **Earthblood** (Baen 0-671-65348-2, Aug,87 [Jul,87], $2.95, 311pp, pb) Reprint (Doubleday 1966) sf novel.

LAW, RICHARD　　　　　　　　　　　　　　　　　　　　　**LEESON, ROBERT**

*Law, Richard, Marleen S. Barr & Ruth Salvaggio **Suzy McKee Charnas, Joan Vinge, Octavia Butler** Main listing under Marleen S. Barr.

Lawhead, Stephen R. **In the Hall of the Dragon King** (Lion 0-85648-859-3, Jan,87, £2.95, 351pp, pb) Reissue (Crossway 1982) fantasy novel. Volume 1 in the "Dragonking Saga".

Lawhead, Stephen R. **The Sword and the Flame** (Lion 0-85648-875-5, Jan,87 [May,87], £2.95, 313pp, pb) Reissue (Crossway 1984) fantasy novel. Volume 3 in the "Dragonking Saga".

*Lawhead, Stephen R. **Taliesin** (Crossway 0-89107-407-4, Aug,87 [Oct,87], $10.95, 452pp, tp) Fantasy novel, first in the "Pendragon Cycle".

Lawhead, Stephen R. **The Warlords of Nin** (Lion 0-85648-874-7, Jan,87, £2.95, 367pp, pb) Reissue (Crossway 1983) fantasy novel. Volume 2 in the "Dragonking Saga" series.

Lawrence, Louise **Moonwind** (Harper & Row/Starwanderer 0-694-05617-0, Sep,87, $2.95, 180pp, pb) Reprint (Harper & Row 1986) young adult sf novel where an Earth boy falls in love with an astral spirit.

Lawrence, Louise **Moonwind** (Lions 0-00-672750-6, Nov,87, £1.95, 154pp, pb) Reprint (Bodley Head 1986) juvenile sf novel.

Lawrence, Louise **Star Lord** (Bodley Head 0-370-31153-1, Oct,87 [Dec,87], £4.50, 154pp, tp) Reprint (US 1978) juvenile sf novel. This edition is 'substantially revised'.

Laws, Stephen **Ghost Train** (Sphere 0-7221-5386-4, Mar,87, £2.95, 343pp, pb) Reprint (Souvenir Press 1985) horror novel.

Laws, Stephen **Spectre** (Tor 0-812-52102-1, Jul,87 [Jun,87], $3.95, 279pp, pb) Reprint (Souvenir Press 1986) horror novel.

*Laws, Stephen **The Wyrm** (Souvenir Press 0-285-62810-0, Oct,87, £9.95, 301pp, hc) Horror novel.

+Laymon, Richard **The Beast House** (Paperjacks 0-7701-0684-6, Sep,87 [Aug,87], $3.95, 294pp, pb) Horror novel. First U.S. edition (NEL 1986).

+Laymon, Richard **Beware!** (Paperjacks 0-7701-0703-6, Oct,87 [Sep,87], $3.95, 268pp, pb) Horror novel of an invisible killer. First American edition (NEL 1985).

*Laymon, Richard **Flesh** (W.H. Allen 0-491-03487-3, Oct,87 [Nov,87], £11.95, 333pp, hc) Horror novel.

+Laymon, Richard **Tread Softly** (Tor 0-812-52108-0, Feb,87 [Jan,87], $3.95, 311pp, pb) Horror novel of evil in the woods. First American edition (Sphere 1986).

Le Fanu, Joseph Sheridan **In a Glass Darkly** (Alan Sutton 0-86299-379-2, Sep,87, £3.50, 192pp, tp) Reprint (Richard Bently 1872) ghost/horror collection. [Not seen]

Le Guin, Ursula K. **The Beginning Place** (Bantam Spectra 0-553-26282-3, Aug,87 [Jul,87], $2.95, 183pp, pb) Reissue (Harper & Row 1980) young-adult fantasy novel; 4th printing.

*Le Guin, Ursula K. **Buffalo Gals and Other Animal Presences** (Capra Press 0-88496-270-9, Sep,87 [Aug,87], $15.95, 196pp, hc) Collection of stories and poetry about animals (and plants and minerals) -- sf, fantasy, and associational. The title story is a fine original. (FCM) *PW* described the book and Le Guin as "a mixture of prodigious talent and stubborn polemic, which has alternately exhilarated and exasperated sf readers since the '60s" -- a perfect summing-up (CNB).

Le Guin, Ursula K. **The Compass Rose** (Bantam Spectra 0-553-23512-5, Nov,87 [Oct,87], $3.50, 271pp, pb) Reissue (Harper & Row 1982) collection of 20 stories. 4th printing.

Le Guin, Ursula K. **Orsinian Tales** (Harper & Row/Perennial Library 0-06-091433-5, Sep,87, $6.95, 179pp, tp) Reprint (Harper & Row 1976) collection of 11 stories -- almost mainstream, but set in an imaginary country.

Le Guin, Ursula K. **The Wind's Twelve Quarters** (Harper & Row/Perennial Library 0-06-091434-3, Sep,87, $6.95, 303pp, tp) Reprint (Harper & Row 1975) collection of 17 stories.

*Leatherdale, Clive, ed. **The Origins of "Dracula": The Background to Bram Stoker's Gothic Masterpiece** (Kimber 0-7183-0657-0, Oct,87 [Dec,87], £12.50, 239pp, hc) Collection of essays about Dracula.

*Ledger, Peter & Christy Marx **The Sisterhood of Steel** Main listing under Christy Marx.

Lee, John **The Unicorn Quest** (Orbit 0-7088-8216-1, Mar,87, £2.95, 381pp, pb) Reprint (Tor 1986) fantasy novel. First of a trilogy. [First U.K. edition]

*Lee, Samantha & Robert Louis Stevenson **Dr. Jekyll and Mr. Hyde** (Beaver 0-09-949740-9, Feb,87, £1.75, 148pp, pb) Juvenile retelling of classic horror story. Volume 3 in the Fleshcreepers series.

*Lee, Samantha & Robert Louis Stevenson **Dr. Jekyll and Mr. Hyde** (Hutchinson 0-09-172573-9, Mar,87 [1987], £5.95, 144pp, hc) Hardcover edition of the above. [Not seen]

Lee, Tanith **Delirium's Mistress** (Arrow 0-09-951580-6, Oct,87, £3.50, 416pp, pb) Reprint (DAW 1986) fantasy novel. Volume 4 in the "Flat Earth" series. [First U.K. edition]

Lee, Tanith **Delusion's Master** (DAW 0-88677-197-8, Apr,87 [Mar,87], $2.95, 206pp, pb) Reissue (DAW 1981) fantasy novel, Book Three of the "Flat Earth" series; fifth printing.

Lee, Tanith **Delusion's Master** (Arrow 0-09-948120-0, Sep,87, £2.50, 206pp, pb) Reprint (DAW 1981) fantasy novel. Volume 3 in the "Flat Earth" series. [First U.K. edition]

Lee, Tanith **Don't Bite the Sun** (Starmont House 1-557-42044-0, Nov,87 [Dec,87], $19.95, 158pp, hc) Reprint (DAW 1976) sf novel. This first trade hardcover edition has a laminated cover and no d/w. It's offset from the original DAW plates and is obviously aimed at libraries.

Lee, Tanith **Night's Master** (Arrow 0-09-951740-X, Sep,87, £2.50, 188pp, pb) Reprint (DAW 1978) fantasy novel. Volume 1 in the "Flat Earth" series.

*Lee, Tanith **Night's Sorceries** (DAW 0-88677-194-3, Apr,87 [Mar,87], $3.50, 287pp, pb) Fantasy collection, part of the "Flat Earth" series. There are 7 stories with no previous printing history (or a contents page). They may all be original.

Lee, Tanith **Sabella** (Unwin 0-04-823353-6, Jul,87, £2.50, 157pp, pb) Reprint (DAW 1980) horror novel. [First U.K. edition]

*Lee, Tanith **Tales from the Flat Earth: Night's Daughter** (SFBC #11345, Oct,87, $14.98, 2 vols, 601pp, hc) Omnibus edition of two books in the "Flat Earth" fantasy series, **Delirium's Mistress** (DAW 1986) and **Night's Sorceries** (DAW 1987). Part of a two-volume set.

*Lee, Tanith **Tales from the Flat Earth: The Lords of Darkness** (SFBC #11360, Oct,87, $14.98, 2 vol.s, 726pp, hc) Omnibus edition of 3 books from the "Flat Earth" fantasy series: **Night's Master** (DAW 1978), **Death's Master** (DAW 1979), and **Delusion's Master** (DAW 1981). Part of a two-volume set.

*Lee, Vernon **Supernatural Tales: Excursions Into Fantasy** (Peter Owen 0-7206-0680-2, Feb,87, £10.95, 222pp, hc) Collection of 6 supernatural stories set in different periods in Italian history. This is a pseudonym for Violet Paget. Available in the US from DuFour Editions for $18.95.

*Lee, Walt & Richard Delap **Shapes** Main listing under Richard Delap.

*Leeson, Robert **Slambash Wangs of a Compo Gormer** (Collins 0-00-184787-2, Nov,87, £6.95, 288pp, hc) Juvenile fantasy novel.

LEESON, ROBERT

Leeson, Robert **Time Rope** (Corgi 0-552-52344-5, Jul,87, £1.95, 124pp, pb) Reprint (Longman 1986) juvenile sf novel. Volume 1 in the "Time Rope" series.

+Lefanu, Sarah & Jen Green, eds. **Despatches From the Frontiers of the Female Mind** Main listing under Jen Green.

LeGuin, Ursula K. **The Earthsea Trilogy** (Puffin 0-14-031766-X, Oct,87, £5.95, 477pp, tp) Reissue (Puffin 1979) juvenile fantasy omnibus.

Leiber, Fritz **The Wanderer** (Penguin 0-14-009201-3, May,87, £3.95, 346pp, tp) Reissue (Ballantine 1964) sf novel. In the Penguin Classic SF series.

Leiber, Fritz **The Wanderer** (SFBC #11385, Nov,87, $4.98, 311pp, hc) Reissue (Ballantine 1964) sf novel, a Hugo winner.

*Leiber, Justin **Beyond Humanity** (Tor 0-812-54433-1, Apr,87 [Mar,87], $2.95, 254pp, pb) Sf novel.

*Leigh, Stephen **The Crystal Memory** (Avon 0-380-89960-4, Sep,87 [Aug,87], $3.50, 245pp, pb) A very good sf adventure; recommended. (TM)

*Lem, Stanislaw **Fiasco** (Harcourt Brace Jovanovich 0-15-130640-0, May,87, $17.95, 322pp, hc) Sf novel of attempted alien contact, translated from the Polish by Michael Kandel.

Lem, Stanislaw **Fiasco** (Andre Deutsch 0-233-98141-1, Aug,87, £11.95, 372pp, hc) Reprint (Harcourt Brace Jovanovich 1987) sf novel. Translated from the Polish by Michael Kandel. [First U.K. edition]

Lem, Stanislaw **Solaris** (HBJ Harvest 0-15-683750-1, May,87, $4.95, 204pp, pb) Reprint (Walker 1970) sf novel, translated from the Polish by Joanna Kilmartin and Steve Cox.

*Leonard, Elmore **Touch** (Arbor House 0-87795-905-6, Sep,87 [Aug,87], $17.95, 245pp, hc) Quasi-fantasy/religious allegory novel about a priest with the power to heal. The Christ-figure in modern times. It reads almost the same as **Godbody** by Theodore Sturgeon, with some striking parallels. Like **Godbody**, it was written many years ago and was considered unpublishable until recently.

*Leragis, Peter **Star Trek IV: The Journey Home** (Simon & Schuster/ Wanderer 0-671-63243-4, Dec,86 [Feb,87], $5.95, 91pp, pb) Movie tie-in (juvenile version) with color stills from the film. A 1986 book, not seen until 1987.

*Leroe, Ellen **Robot Raiders** (Harper & Row 0-06-023835-6, Jul,87, $11.95, 181pp, hc) Juvenile science fiction novel.

Leroux, Gaston **The Phantom of the Opera** (O'Mara 0-948397-17-9, Oct,87 [Dec,87], £12.00, 245pp, hc) Reprint (Bobbs-Merril 1911) horror novel, with new introduction by Richard Dalby. Illustrated by Andre Castaigne.

*Letendre, Serge & Regis Loisel **Roxanna #2: The Temple of Oblivion** (NBM 0-918348-34-X, Sep,87 [Aug,87], $7.95, 48pp, tp) Graphic novel.

*Lewins, Anna **Dream For Danger** (Blackie 0-216-92082-5, May,87, £7.95, 140pp, hc) Juvenile sf/fantasy novel. [Not seen]

Lewis, C.S. **The Horse and His Boy** (Collins 0-00-183182-8, Oct,87 [Nov,87], £6.95, 175pp, hc) Reissue (Geoffrey Bles 1954) juvenile fantasy novel. Volume 5 in the "Narnia" series.

Lewis, C.S. **The Lion, the Witch and the Wardrobe** (Collins 0-00-183180-1, Jun,87 [Jul,87], £6.95, 171pp, hc) Reissue (Geoffrey Bles 1950) juvenile fantasy novel. Volume 1 in the "Narnia" series.

Lewis, C.S. **The Silver Chair** (Collins 0-00-183181-X, Jun,87 [Jul,87], £6.95, 191pp, hc) Reissue (Geoffrey Bles 1953) juvenile fantasy novel. Volume 4 in the "Narnia" series.

*Lewis, C.S. **Tales of Narnia** (Collins 0-00-184294-3, Dec,87, £4.95, 543pp, hc) Juvenile fantasy omnibus. Printed for, and distributed by, W.H. Smith only.

Lewis, C.S. & Glyn Robbins **The Lion, the Witch and the Wardrobe** For main entry see under Glyn Robbins.

*Lewis, C.S., [ref.] **C.S. Lewis** Main listing under Joe R. Christopher.

*Lewis, C.S., [ref.] **C.S. Lewis and His World** Main listing under David Barratt.

*Lewis, C.S., [ref.] **Companion to Narnia** Main listing under Paul F. Ford.

Lewis, Richard **Spiders** (Arrow 0-09-938330-6, Aug,87, £2.25, 153pp, pb) Reprint (Hamlyn 1978) horror novel.

*Lewitt, S.N. **Angel at Apogee** (Berkley 0-425-09637-8, Mar,87 [Feb,87], $2.95, 219pp, pb) Sf novel of a female space pilot.

*Lewitt, S.N. **U.S.S.A. Book 2** (Avon 0-380-75181-X, Feb,87 [Jan,87], $2.95, 172pp, pb) Near-future sf novel of high school teens vs. a military dictatorship, second in a series with different authors.

*Lewitt, S.N. **U.S.S.A. Book 4** (Avon 0-380-75183-6, Jun,87 [May,87], $2.95, 172pp, pb) Book 4 and the last volume in a series: future teenagers against a military dictatorship.

*Lindahn, Ron & Val Lakey Lindahn, eds. **A Southern Fantasy: 13th World Fantasy Convention Program Book** (Nashville World Fantasy Convention no ISBN, Oct,87, free with membership, 88pp, 8.5 x 11 pb) Program book for the 13th World Fantasy Convention held in Nashville.

*Lindahn, Val Lakey & Ron Lindahn, eds. **A Southern Fantasy: 13th World Fantasy Convention Program Book** Main listing under Ron Lindahn.

*Lindbergh, Anne **The Shadow on the Dial** (Harper & Row 0-06-023882-8, Jul,87 [Nov,87], $11.95, 153pp, hc) Young adult time travel novel.

Lindholm, Megan **Wizard of the Pigeons** (Corgi 0-552-13014-1, Feb,87, £2.50, 254pp, pb) Reprint (Ace 1985) modern-day fantasy. [First U.K. edition]

Lindsay, David **The Haunted Woman** (Canongate 0-86241-162-9, Oct,87, £3.95, 256pp, tp) Reprint (Methuen 1922) fantasy novel. [Not seen]

Ling, Peter **The Mind Robber** (Target 0-426-20286-4, Apr,87, £1.75, 144pp, pb) Reprint (W.H. Allen 1986) juvenile sf novel. Volume 115 in the Doctor Who series.

Lively, Penelope **The Ghost of Thomas Kempe** (Puffin 0-14-031496-2, Mar,87, £1.75, 159pp, pb) Reissue (Heinemann 1973) juvenile ghost story.

Lively, Penelope **Uninvited Ghosts and Other Stories** (Puffin 0-14-031966-2, Mar,87, £1.50, 120pp, pb) Reissue (Heinemann 1984) juvenile ghost collection.

Lively, Penelope **The Whispering Knights** (Puffin 0-14-031977-8, Mar,87, £1.75, 155pp, pb) Reprint (Heinemann 1971) juvenile fantasy/ horror novel.

Lively, Penelope **The Wild Hunt of Hagworthy** (Lythway Large Print 0-7451-0491-6, Mar,87 [1987], £6.95, 256pp, hc) Reprint (Heinemann 1971) juvenile fantasy novel. [Not seen]

*Livingstone, Ian **Casket of Souls** (Penguin 0-14-031970-0, Nov,87, £3.95, 32pp, tp) Fantasy short story/puzzle, illustrated by Iain McCaig.

*Livingstone, Ian **Casket of Souls** (Oxford Univ. Press 0-19-279791-3, Nov,87, £5.95, 32pp, hc) Hardcover edition of the above. [Not seen]

Llywelyn, Morgan **Bard: The Odyssey of the Irish** (Tor 0-812-58515-1, Mar,87 [Feb,87], $4.50, 415pp, pb) Reprint (Houghton Mifflin 1984) Celtic historical novel with elements of fantasy.

*Loisel, Regis & Serge Letendre **Roxanna #2: The Temple of Oblivion** Main listing under Serge Letendre.

LONDON, JACK

MACHEN, ARTHUR

London, Jack **Star Rover** (Journeyman Press 0-904526-10-0, Jul,87, £2.95, 320pp, pb) Reprint (Macmillan 1915) sf novel. [Not seen]

Long, John **The Sign of the Guardian** (Tor 0-812-52118-8, Apr,87 [Mar,87], $3.50, 253pp, pb) Reissue (Tor 1981) quasi-occult horror novel.

*Longyear, Barry B. **Sea of Glass** (St. Martin's 0-312-00780-9, Jan,87, $18.95, 375pp, hc) Sf novel of an overpopulated future.

Longyear, Barry B. **Sea of Glass** (Avon 0-380-70055-7, Jan,88 [Dec,87], $3.50, 375pp, pb) Reprint (St. Martin's 1987) sf novel about overpopulation.

*Lord, J. Edward **Elixir** (Ballantine 0-345-34070-1, Jun,87, $3.50, 305pp, pb) Horror novel of an evil potion.

*Lord, J. Edward **Incantation** (Ballantine 0-345-34072-8, Nov,87 [Oct,87], $3.50, 288pp, pb) Contemporary horror novel complete with ancient Egyptian rituals, curses, and magicians -- set in Denver!

Lore, Elana, ed. **Alfred Hitchcock's Choice of Evils** (Severn House 0-7278-1452-4, Jul,87 [Dec,87], £10.95, 348pp, hc) Reprint (Davis 1983) thriller/horror anthology. [First U.K. edition]

Lorrah, Jean **Star Trek #20: The Vulcan Academy Murders** (Pocket 0-671-64744-X, Nov,87 [Oct,87], $3.95, 274pp, pb) Reissue (Pocket 1984) Star Trek novel.

*Lorrah, Jean & Winston A. Howlett **Wulfston's Odyssey** (NAL/Signet 0-451-15056-2, Nov,87 [Oct,87], $2.95, 206pp, pb) Fantasy novel in the "Savage Empire" series.

*Love, G.B. & Walter Irwin, eds. **The Best of Trek #12** Main listing under Walter Irwin.

Lovecraft, H.P. **At the Mountains of Madness** (Grafton 0-586-06322-6, Jun,87 [Sep,87], £3.50, 552pp, pb) Reissue (Panther 1985) horror collection.

Lovecraft, H.P. **Dagon and Other Macabre Tales** (Grafton 0-586-06324-2, Jun,87 [Sep,87], £3.50, 512pp, pb) Reissue (Panther 1985) horror collection.

Lovecraft, H.P. **The Haunter of the Dark** (Grafton 0-586-06323-4, Jun,87 [Sep,87], £3.50, 544pp, pb) Reissue (Panther 1985) horror collection.

*Lucarotti, John **The Massacre** (W.H. Allen 0-491-03423-7, Jun,87 [Jul,87], £7.50, 144pp, hc) Juvenile sf novel. Volume 122 in the Doctor Who series.

Lucarotti, John **The Massacre** (Target 0-426-20297-X, Nov,87, £1.95, 144pp, pb) Reprint (W.H. Allen 1987) juvenile sf novel. Volume 122 in the "Doctor Who" series.

*Lucas, George, Donald F. Glut & James Kahn **The Star Wars Trilogy** (Ballantine/Del Rey 0-345-34806-0, May,87, $8.95, 471pp, tp) Omnibus of the three film novelizations from *Star Wars*, a "special tenth-anniversary edition."

*Lumley, Brian **The Compleat Crow** (Ganley 0-932445-21-7, Jul,87 [Jun,87], $7.50, 191pp, tp) Collection, a gathering of the "Titus Crow" psychic detective horror stories, illustrated by Stephen E. Fabian. Hardcover and deluxe signed editions have been announced, but we have not seen them.

*Lumley, Brian **Demogorgon** (Grafton 0-586-07031-1, Apr,87, £2.95, 333pp, pb) Occult thriller.

+Lundwall, Sam J. & Brian W. Aldiss, eds. **The Penguin World Omnibus of Science Fiction** Main listing under Brian W. Aldiss.

Lupoff, Richard A. **Lovecraft's Book** (Grafton 0-586-07209-8, Sep,87, £2.95, 287pp, pb) Reprint (Arkham House 1985) parallel-history novel. [First U.K. edition]

Lupoff, Richard A. **Sun's End** (Grafton 0-586-07098-2, Feb,87, £2.95, 348pp, pb) Reprint (Berkley 1984) sf novel. [First U.K. edition]

Lustbader, Eric Van **Shallows of the Night** (Berkley 0-425-09964-4, May,87 [Apr,87], $3.50, 288pp, pb) Reissue (Doubleday 1978) fantasy novel, #2 in the "Sunset Warrior" trilogy. 8th Berkley printing.

Lustbader, Eric Van **The Sunset Warrior** (Berkley 0-425-09786-2, Mar,87 [Feb,87], $3.50, 220pp, pb) Reissue (Doubleday 1977) fantasy novel, first in the "Sunset Warrior" trilogy; 8th Berkley printing.

Lynn, Elizabeth A. **The Dancers of Arun** (Arrow 0-09-950210-0, Apr,87, £2.95, 256pp, tp) Reprint (Berkley 1979) fantasy novel. Volume 2 in the "Chronicles of Tornor" series.

Lynn, Elizabeth A. **A Different Light** (Berkley 0-425-10032-4, Apr,87 [Mar,87], $2.95, 183pp, pb) Reissue (Berkley 1978) sf novel. Sixth printing.

Lynn, Elizabeth A. **The Northern Girl** (Arrow 0-09-950410-3, Apr,87, £3.50, 382pp, tp) Reprint (Berkley 1980) fantasy novel. Volume 3 in the "Chronicles of Tornor" series.

Lynn, Elizabeth A. **Watchtower** (Arrow 0-09-942010-4, Apr,87, £2.95, 208pp, tp) Reprint (Berkley 1979) fantasy novel. Volume 1 in the "Chronicles of Tornor" series.

*MacAvoy, R.A. **The Grey Horse** (Bantam Spectra 0-553-26557-1, May,87 [Apr,87], $3.95, 247pp, pb) Fantasy novel of late 19th century Ireland, a magical creature, and romance. Recommended. (FCM)

MacAvoy, R.A. **Tea with the Black Dragon** (Bantam UK 0-553-23205-3, Sep,87, £1.95, 166pp, pb) Reprint (Bantam 1983) refreshingly unusual fantasy novel. Recommended. Volume 1 in the "Black Dragon" series.

MacAvoy, R.A. **Tea with the Black Dragon** (Hypatia Press 0-940841-03-7, Dec,87 [Nov,87], $20.00, 204pp, hc) Reprint (Bantam 1983) fantasy novel, with a new introduction by Anne McCaffrey. There are 4 editions, all signed, with various bindings and boxes. All editions are out of print from the publisher and must be purchased at bookstores.

MacAvoy, R.A. **Twisting the Rope** (Bantam UK 0-553-17385-5, Oct,87, £2.50, 242pp, pb) Reprint (Bantam 1986) fantasy novel. Volume 2 in the "Black Dragon" series. [First U.K. edition]

MacDonald, George **The Light Princess and Other Stories** (Kelpies 0-86241-164-5, Oct,87, £1.95, 288pp, pb) Reprint (Gollancz 1961) juvenile fantasy collection.

MacDonald, George **Lilith** (Schocken/Allison & Busby 0-85031-626-X, Mar,87 [May,87], $6.95, 240pp, tp) Reprint (Chatto & Windus 1895) fantasy novel.

MacDonald, George **The Princess and the Goblin** (Windrush 1-85089-915-0, Oct,87, $12.95, 249pp, hc) Reprint (Routledge 1871) juvenile fantasy novel, large print edition. U.S. distribution of the British edition from Oxford Windrush. Order from ABC-Clio.

MacDonald, George **The Princess and the Goblin** (Eerdman's 0-7208-2384-6, Dec,87, $14.95, 93pp, hc) Juvenile fantasy novella, an abridged version of the 1871 children's classic, with illustrations by Alan Parry.

*MacDonald, George, [ref.] **Fantasy King: A Biography of George MacDonald** Main listing under William Raeper.

*MacDonald, George, [ref.] **George MacDonald** Main listing under Michael R. Phillips.

*MacDonald, George, [ref.] **George MacDonald: A Short Life** Main listing under Elizabeth Saintsbury.

+Mace, David **Nightrider** (Ace 0-441-57613-3, Oct,87 [Sep,87], $2.95, 242pp, pb) Sf novel of "the ultimate war machine." First U.S. edition (Panther 1985).

*MacGregor, Loren **The Net** (Ace 0-441-56941-2, Jun,87 [May,87], $2.95, 225pp, pb) Sf novel, a first novel and an Ace Special.

*Machen, Arthur **The Collected Arthur Machen** (Duckworth 0-7156-2120-3, Oct,87, £14.95, 380pp, hc) Fantasy/horror/occult collection. [Not seen]

MACHEN, ARTHUR   **MARTIN, GRAHAM DUNSTAN**

*Machen, Arthur **Guinevere and Lancelot & Others** (Purple Mouth 0-9603300-2-X, Dec,86 [Feb,87], $10.00, 47pp, tp) Collection of essays and stories, edited by Michael T. Shoemaker and Cuyler W. Brooks, Jr., illustrated by Steve Fabian.

+Mackay, Colin **The Song of the Forest** (Available Press 0-345-34647-5, Aug,87 [Jul,87], $5.95, 233pp, tp) Celtic fantasy novel. First American edition (Canongate 1986).

*Mackie, Mary **The People of the Horse** (W.H. Allen 0-491-03307-9, Sep,87, £12.95, 415pp, hc) Historical novel about Boudicca, with touches of the supernatural.

*Maclay, John **Other Engagements** (Dream House no ISBN, Oct,87, $9.95, 124pp, hc) Collection of horror stories and poems from small press publications, bound to look like an engagement book. Issued without d/w.

MacManus, Yvonne **The Presence** (Critic's Choice/Bart 1-55547-163-3, Mar,87, $3.95, 275pp, pb) Reprint (? 1982) horror novel.

Mahy, Margaret **Aliens in the Family** (Scholastic Apple 0-590-40321-4, Apr,87 [Jun,87], $2.50, 174pp, pb) Reprint (Scholastic 1985) young adult sf novel, an excellent blend of drama, humor, and sf, by one of the best writers in the young adult field. Recommended. (FCM)

Mahy, Margaret **Aliens in the Family** (Hippo 0-590-70557-1, Oct,87 [Nov,87], £1.50, 168pp, pb) Reissue (Ashton Scholastic 1986) juvenile sf novel.

Mahy, Margaret **The Changeover** (Teens 0-416-08822-8, Oct,87 [Nov,87], £1.95, 224pp, pb) Reprint (Dent 1984) juvenile occult novel.

+Mahy, Margaret **The Tricksters** (Macmillan McElderry 0-689-50400-4, Mar,87, $12.95, 266pp, hc) Young-adult fantasy novel about a girl whose obsession with writing a romantic novel uncovers a family secret and calls up the ghosts of three boys. First American edition (Australia 1986).

*Maitland, Sara **The Book of Spells** (Michael Joseph 0-7181-2755-2, Sep,87, £9.95, 174pp, hc) Collection of short stories (mainly original) about magic.

*Maloney, Mack **Wingman** (Zebra 0-8217-2015-5, Mar,87 [Feb,87], $3.95, 460pp, pb) Post-holocaust sf adventure novel.

*Maloney, Mack **Wingman: The Circle War** (Zebra 0-8217-2120-8, Jul,87, $3.95, 413pp, pb) Post-holocaust adventure novel.

*Manguel, Alberto & Gianni Guadalupi **The Dictionary of Imaginary Places, Expanded Edition** (HBJ Harvest 0-15-626054-9, Sep,87, $14.95, 454pp, tp) Non-fiction, reference. Dictionary of places from Atlantis to Middle Earth. This is revised from an earlier edition (Macmillan 1980).

*Manley, Mark **Throwback** (Popular Library 0-445-20277-7, Nov,87 [Oct,87], $3.50, 218pp, pb) Horror novel about a woman regressing to become a vicious beast.

*Mann, Philip **The Fall of the Families** (Gollancz 0-575-03808-X, May,87 [Aug,87], £11.95, 298pp, hc) sf novel. Volume 2 of The Story of the Gardener.

*Manson, Cynthia & Sheila Williams, eds. **Tales From Isaac Asimov's Science Fiction Magazine** Main listing under Sheila Williams.

*Margroff, Robert E. & Piers Anthony **Dragon's Gold** Main listing under Piers Anthony.

Marney, Dean **The Computer That Ate My Brother** (Scholastic 0-590-40267-6, Mar,87 [Feb,87], $2.50, 124pp, pb) Reprint (Houghton Mifflin 1985) young-adult sf novel.

Marsh, Geoffrey **The King of Satan's Eyes** (Tor 0-812-50650-2, Feb,87 [Jan,87], $3.50, 281pp, pb) Reprint (Doubleday 1984) adventure novel with fantasy elements, first in the "Lincoln Blackthorne" series. Marsh is a pseudonym for Charles L. Grant.

*Marsh, Geoffrey **Patch of the Odin Soldier** (Doubleday 0-385-15938-2, Apr,87 [Mar,87], $12.95, 182pp, hc) Fantasy adventure novel. Part of the Lincoln Blackthorne series -- a Doc Savage/Indiana Jones type character. The author is actually Charles L. Grant.

*Marten, Jacqueline **Dream Walker** (Pocket 0-671-63521-2, Feb,87 [Mar,87], $3.95, 440pp, pb) Romance novel with fantasy elements. An artist in New York seeks to recapture the love of a past life that literally haunts her, causing her to relive in flashbacks her life as an early American painter and Revolutionary spy.

*Marter, Ian **The Reign of Terror** (W.H. Allen 0-491-03702-3, Mar,87, £7.50, 160pp, hc) Juvenile sf novel. Volume 119 in the Doctor Who series.

Marter, Ian **The Reign of Terror** (Target 0-426-20264-3, Aug,87, £1.95, 160pp, pb) Reprint (W.H. Allen 1987) juvenile sf novel. Volume 119 in the Doctor Who series.

*Marter, Ian **The Rescue** (W.H. Allen 0-491-03317-6, Aug,87, £7.95, 144pp, hc) Juvenile sf novel. Volume 124 in the Doctor Who series. [Not seen]

Martin, George R.R. **Nightflyers** (Tor 0-812-54562-1, Feb,87 [Jan,87], $2.95, 295pp, pb) Reprint (Bluejay 1985) collection. This edition says "soon to be a major motion picture."

*Martin, George R.R. **Portraits of His Children** (Dark Harvest 0-913165-18-2, Jul,87, $39.95, 263pp, hc) Collection of 11 stories, with an introduction by Roger Zelazny and illustrations by Ron and Val Lakey Lindholm. This is the signed, boxed, limited (400 copy) edition.

*Martin, George R.R. **Portraits of His Children** (Dark Harvest 0-913165-19-0, Jul,87, $18.95, 263pp, hc) Trade edition of the above; collection including several classics.

Martin, George R.R. **Tuf Voyaging** (Baen 0-671-65624-4, Mar,87 [Feb,87], $3.50, 376pp, pb) Reprint (Baen 1986) episodic sf novel.

Martin, George R.R. **Tuf Voyaging** (Gollancz 0-575-04049-1, Aug,87, £10.95, 374pp, hc) Reprint (Baen 1986) sf collection. [First U.K. edition]

*Martin, George R.R., Pat Broderick, Neal McPheeters & Doug Moench **Sandkings** (DC Graphics 0-930289-20-X, Jan,87, $5.95, 48pp, tp) "Graphic novel" adaptation of the 1979 sf story by George R.R. Martin.

Martin, George R.R., ed. **Night Visions** (Century 0-7126-1155-X, Aug,87, £11.95, 298pp, hc) Reprint (Dark Harvest 1986, as **Night Visions III**) original horror anthology. [First U.K. edition]

Martin, George R.R., ed. **Night Visions** (Legend 0-09-952750-2, Dec,87, £2.95, 298pp, pb) Reprint (Dark Harvest 1986, as **Night Visions III**) original horror anthology.

*Martin, George R.R., ed. **Wild Cards II: Aces High** (Bantam Spectra 0-553-26464-8, Apr,87 [Mar,87], $3.95, 390pp, pb) Original anthology/braided sf mega-novel, part of a series. There are 9 or 10 connected stories, but no contents page.

*Martin, George R.R., ed. **Wild Cards III: Jokers Wild** (Bantam Spectra 0-553-26699-3, Nov,87 [Oct,87], $3.95, 376pp, pb) Original shared-world anthology ("mosaic novel") of sf stories with connective material by Martin; third in a series. Authors are Melinda M. Snodgrass, Leanne C. Harper, Walton Simons, Lewis Shiner, John J. Miller, George R.R. Martin, and Edward Bryant.

Martin, George R.R., ed. **Wildcards** (SFBC #10930, Jun,87, $6.98, 408pp, hc) Reprint (Bantam Spectra 1987) shared-world original anthology; first hardcover edition.

*Martin, Graham Dunstan **Dream Wall** (Unwin Hyman 0-04-823337-4, May,87, £8.95, 231pp, hc) Sf novel about England under Soviet rule in the 22nd Century. [Not seen]

*Martin, Graham Dunstan **Dream Wall** (Unwin 0-04-823363-3, May,87, £2.95, 231pp, tp) Paperback edition of the above.

MARTINE-BARNES, ADRIENNE　　　　　　　　　　　　　　　　　　　　　　　　　　**MCCRUMB, SHARYN**

*Martine-Barnes, Adrienne **The Crystal Sword** (Avon 0-380-75454-1, Jan,88 [Dec,87], $3.50, 278pp, pb) Fantasy novel, sequel to **The Fire Sword**.

*Marx, Christy & Peter Ledger **The Sisterhood of Steel: Baronwe: Daughter of Death** (Eclipse/Moonfire 0-913035-23-8, Oct,87, $8.95, 71pp, tp) Graphic novel, a fantasy with swordswomen and some magic.

Masefield, John **The Midnight Folk** (Windrush Large Print 1-85089-927-4, Nov,87 [Dec,87], £8.70, 304pp, hc) Reprint (Heinemann 1927) juvenile fantasy novel. Volume 1 in the "Kay Harker" series.

*Masello, Robert **The Spirit Wood** (Pocket 0-671-63572-7, Jun,87 [May,87], $3.50, 345pp, pb) Horror novel.

Masterton, Graham **Death Trance** (Sphere 0-7221-6124-7, Sep,87, £2.99, 424pp, pb) Reprint (Tor 1986) horror novel. [First U.K. edition]

Masterton, Graham **Death Trance** (Severn House 0-7278-1420-6, Nov,87, £11.95, 432pp, hc) Reprint (Tor 1986) horror novel. [Not seen]

Masterton, Graham **The Manitou** (Tor 0-812-52183-8, May,87 [Apr,87], $3.95, 216pp, pb) Reissue (1975) horror novel; 2nd Tor printing.

Masterton, Graham **Night Warriors** (Severn House 0-7278-1461-3, Jun,87, £10.95, 416pp, hc) Reprint (Sphere 1986) horror novel. [Not seen]

Masterton, Graham **Revenge of the Manitou** (Tor 0-812-52181-1, Oct,87 [Sep,87], $3.95, 261pp, pb) Reissue (? 1979) horror novel, a sequel to **The Manitou**.

*Mastrangelo, Judy, ed. & Jean L. Scrocco, ill. **Antique Fairy Tales** Main listing under Jean L. Scrocco.

Matheson, Richard **I Am Legend** (Robinson 0-948164-33-6, Sep,87 [Aug,87], £2.95, 151pp, tp) Reprint (Gold Medal 1954) horror novel.

*Matheson, Richard Christian **Scars** (Scream/Press 0-910489-15-7, Aug,87 [Oct,87], $20.00, 168pp, hc) Collection of 27 fantasy and horror stories, including 9 originals. Foreword by Stephen King, introduction by Dennis Etchison, and illustrations by Harry O. Morris.

*Mathews, Jack **The Battle of Brazil: The Authorized Story and Annotated Screenplay of Terry Gilliam's Landmark Film** (Crown 0-517-56538-2, May,87 [Jun,87], $19.95, 228pp, hc) Sf screenplay plus background material on the fight to get the finished movie shown over the objections of the studio. It also compares the three edited versions extant. A fascinating book (CNB).

*Matthews, Jack **Ghostly Populations** (Johns Hopkins 0-8018-3391-4, Jan,87 [Aug,87], $14.95, 171pp, hc) Collection of 17 literary stories, some with elements of the supernatural. This appeared in January 1987 but was not seen.

*Matthews, Rodney & Michael Moorcock **Elric at the End of Time** For main entry see under Michael Moorcock.

Maugham, W. Somerset **The Magician** (Society of Metaphysicians 1-85228-527-3, Jan,87, £5.00, 233pp, pb) Reprint (Heinemann 1908) occult novel. [Not seen]

Maxim, John R. **Platforms** (Tor 0-812-52215-X, Nov,87 [Oct,87], $3.95, 336pp, pb) Reprint (St. Martin's 1980) horror novel.

Maxim, John R. **Time Out of Mind** (Tor 0-812-58569-0, Feb,87 [Jan,87], $4.50, 511pp, pb) Reprint (Houghton Mifflin 1986) fantasy novel, a "multigenerational ghost story." Whenever it snows, the lead character returns to 1880.

Maxim, John R. **Time Out of Mind** (Century 0-7126-9539-7, Dec,86 [Aug,87], £10.95, 502pp, hc) Reprint (Houghton Mifflin 1986) time-travel fantasy novel. [First U.K. edition]

Maxwell, Ann **Fire Dancer** (Futura 0-7088-8237-4, Dec,87 [Nov,87], £2.50, 203pp, pb) Reprint (Signet 1983) sf novel. [First U.K. edition]

*May, Julian **Intervention** (Houghton Mifflin 0-395-43782-2, Aug,87, $18.95, 546pp, hc) Sf novel, an engaging "Galactic Milieu" prequel. Recommended. (FCM)

May, Julian **Intervention** (Collins 0-00-223086-0, Nov,87, £10.95, 546pp, hc) Reprint (Houghton Mifflin 1987) sf novel. This novel sets the scene for the forthcoming "Galactic Milieu" trilogy. [First U.K. edition]

Maybury, Ged **Time Twister** (Hippo 0-590-70587-3, Feb,87, £1.50, 135pp, pb) Reprint (Scholastic [New Zealand] 1986) juvenile time-travel novel.

*Mayhar, Ardath **Battletech: The Sword and the Dagger** (FASA 0-931787-77-7, 1987 [May,87], $3.95, 279pp, pb) Sf novel based on a game; part of a series.

*Mayhar, Ardath **Makra Choria** (Atheneum/Argo 0-689-31326-8, Mar,87, $13.95, 193pp, hc) Young adult fantasy novel.

*Mayhar, Ardath **The Wall** (Space & Time 0-917053-06-0, Jul,87 [Jun,87], $6.95, 121pp, tp) Mystery/horror short novel.

*Mayhar, Ardath & Ron Fortier **Trail of the Seahawks** (TSR/Windwalker 0-88038-463-8, Jun,87 [May,87], $2.95, 222pp, pb) Sf adventure novel.

Mayne, William **Kelpie** (Cape 0-224-02427-2, Apr,87, £6.95, 80pp, hc) Juvenile fantasy novel. [Not seen]

McCaffrey, Anne **The Coelura** (Tor 0-312-93042-9, Nov,87 [Oct,87], $13.95, 156pp, hc) Reprint (Underwood-Miller 1983) sf short novel with numerous illustrations by Ned Dameron.

*McCaffrey, Anne **The Lady** (Ballantine 0-345-33675-5, Nov,87 [Oct,87], $17.95, 461pp, hc) Associational. Contemporary Irish novel. Listed for McCaffrey completists.

McCaffrey, Anne **Nerilka's Story** (Ballantine/Del Rey 0-345-33949-5, Feb,87 [Jan,87], $3.95, 182pp, pb) Reprint (Del Rey 1986) sf short novel of Pern.

*McCaffrey, Anne **Nerilka's Story & The Coelura** (Bantam UK 0-593-01043-4, Jan,87, £8.95, 192pp, hc) Omnibus edition of two fantasy novellas.

McCaffrey, Anne **Nerilka's Story & The Coelura** (Corgi 0-552-12817-1, Oct,87 [Sep,87], £1.95, 192pp, pb) Reprint (Bantam UK 1987) fantasy omnibus.

McCaffrey, Anne **The Year of the Lucy** (Corgi 0-552-12818-X, Feb,87, £2.95, 333pp, pb) Reprint (Underwood-Miller 1986) romantic novel, of associational interest.

McCaffrey, Anne **The Year of the Lucy** (Tor 0-812-58565-8, Oct,87 [Sep,87], $3.95, 311pp, pb) Reprint (Underwood-Miller 1986) contemporary mainstream novel; associational.

*McCammon, Robert R. **Swan Song** (Pocket 0-671-31117-4, Jun,87 [May,87], $4.95, 956pp, pb) Pre- and post-holocaust sf/horror novel of America destroyed, with a possibility of redemption. An epic tale in the mode of Stephen King's **The Stand**.

*McCay, Claudia **Promise of the Rose Stone** (New Victoria 0-934678-10-3, Nov,86 [May,87], $7.95, 238pp, tp) Feminist sf novel of a warrior woman and a mystic stone. This appeared late last year, but we had not seen it until now.

McCollum, Michael **Antares Dawn** (Ballantine/Del Rey 0-345-32313-0, Dec,87 [Nov,87], $2.95, 310pp, pb) Reissue (Del Rey 1986) sf novel; 4th printing.

*McCollum, Michael **Antares Passage** (Ballantine/Del Rey 0-345-32314-9, Dec,87 [Nov,87], $3.50, 311pp, pb) Sf novel, sequel to **Antares Dawn**.

*McCrumb, Sharyn **Bimbos of the Death Sun** (TSR/Windwalker 0-88038-455-7, Mar,87, $2.95, 219pp, pb) Associational, a mystery novel centered around the death of a fantasy novelist at Rubicon, a science fiction convention. Incredibly fannish. (CFC)

*McCullough, Colleen **The Ladies of Missalonghi** (Harper & Row 0-06-015739-9, Apr,87 [Mar,87], $12.95, 189pp, hc) Historical fantasy novel. In a small town in Australia just before WWI, a repressed 33-year-old woman seeks romance. A charming story of genteelly poor, male-dominated women who finally turn the tables on their rich relations, this ultimately turns out to be a ghost story. Recommended to readers of historical romance for its detailed depiction of the time. (CFC)

*McCullough, Colleen **The Ladies of Missalonghi** (Hutchinson 0-09-170600-9, Jun,87, £7.95, 132pp, hc) Ghost novel. Simultaneous with US (Harper & Row) edition.

*McCutchan, Philip **A Time For Survival** (Firecrest 0-85997-918-0, May,87 [1987], £8.95, 208pp, hc) Post-nuclear sf novel. [Not seen]

*McDonough, Thomas R. **The Architects of Hyperspace** (Avon 0-380-75144-5, Dec,87 [Nov,87], $2.95, 265pp, pb) Hard science space opera sf novel by a noted scientist; a first novel.

McElroy, Joseph **Plus** (Carroll & Graf 0-88184-289-3, Jan,87, $8.95, 215pp, tp) Reprint (Knopf 1976) literary sf novel of a disembodied consciousness orbiting Earth as part of Project Light Travel. New introduction by Tom LeClair.

McEvoy, Seth **Killer Robot** (Dragon 0-583-31123-7, Jul,87 [Aug,87], £1.95, 146pp, pb) Reprint (Archway 1986) juvenile sf novel. Volume 6 in the "Not Quite Human" series. [First U.K. edition]

McEvoy, Seth **Terror at Play** (Dragon 0-583-31122-9, Jul,87 [Sep,87], £1.95, 149pp, pb) Reprint (Archway 1986) juvenile sf novel. Volume 5 in the "Not Quite Human" series. [First U.K. edition]

*McEwan, Ian **The Child in Time** (Cape 0-224-02499-X, Sep,87 [1987], £10.95, 220pp, hc) Novel with sf touches.

*McGowen, Tom **The Magician's Apprentice** (Dutton/Lodestar 0-525-67189-7, Jan,87, $12.95, 119pp, hc) Young-adult sf/fantasy novel, a quest for lost "magic" from the 20th century, 3000 years later.

McIntyre, Vonda N. **Enterprise: The First Adventure** (Grafton 0-586-07321-3, Apr,87, £2.95, 371pp, pb) Reprint (Pocket 1986) *Star Trek* novel. [First U.K. edition]

McIntyre, Vonda N. **The Entropy Effect** (Pocket 0-671-63930-7, Sep,87 [Oct,87], $3.95, 224pp, pb) Reissue (Timescape 1981) Star Trek novel.

McIntyre, Vonda N. **The Exile Waiting** (Pan 0-330-25295-X, May,87, £2.95, 236pp, pb) Reissue (SFBC 1975) sf novel.

McIntyre, Vonda N. **Fireflood and Other Stories** (Pan 0-330-26537-7, Jan,87, £2.50, 256pp, pb) Reissue (Pocket 1981) collection of 11 sf stories.

McIntyre, Vonda N. **Star Trek IV: The Voyage Home** (SFBC #106302, Mar,87, $4.98, 188pp, hc) Reprint (Pocket 1986) novelization of the 4th "Star Trek" film.

McIntyre, Vonda N. **Star Trek IV: The Voyage Home** (Grafton 0-586-07318-3, Apr,87, £2.50, 274pp, pb) Reprint (Pocket 1986) novelization of a *Star Trek* film. [First U.K. edition]

McIntyre, Vonda N. **Star Trek IV: The Voyage Home** (Severn House 0-7278-1519-9, Jul,87, £9.95, 288pp, hc) Reprint (Pocket 1986) sf novel. [Not seen]

*McKenzie, Ellen Kindt **Kashka** (Holt 0-8050-0327-4, Sep,87 [Oct,87], $14.95, 258pp, hc) Young adult magical kingdom fantasy novel, sequel to **Taash and the Jesters**.

McKiernan, Dennis L. **The Brega Path** (NAL/Signet 0-451-14893-2, Jul,87 [Jun,87], $2.95, 255pp, pb) Reprint (Doubleday 1986) fantasy novel, second and last of a duology.

McKiernan, Dennis L. **Trek to Kraggen-Cor** (NAL/Signet 0-451-14787-1, Apr,87 [Mar,87], $2.95, 251pp, pb) Reprint (Doubleday 1986) fantasy novel, first in the "Silver Call" duology.

*McKillip, Patricia A. **Fool's Run** (Warner 0-446-51278-8, Apr,87 [Feb,87], $15.95, 221pp, hc) Sf novel. Musicians affected by a past mass-murder seek to understand the alien "vision" that drove the murderer. Interesting characters highlight this inconclusive adventure. (CFC)

McKillip, Patricia A. **Fool's Run** (Orbit 0-7088-8219-6, Jun,87, £2.50, 252pp, pb) Reprint (Warner 1987) fantasy novel. [First U.K. edition]

McKillip, Patricia A. **Fool's Run** (Macdonald 0-356-14394-5, Aug,87, £10.95, 256pp, hc) Reprint (Warner 1987) sf novel. [Not seen]

McKillip, Patricia A. **The Forgotten Beasts of Eld** (Orbit 0-7088-8242-0, Jul,87, £2.50, 217pp, pb) Reprint (Atheneum 1974) fantasy novel. [First U.K. edition]

McKillip, Patricia A. **The Throme of the Erril of Sherril** (Ace 0-441-80840-9, Aug,87 [Jul,87], $2.95, 165pp, pb) Reprint (Ace/Tempo 1984) collection of the very juvenile title novella (Atheneum 1973) plus a juvenile novelette plus numerous illustrations by Judith Mitchell.

McKinley, Robin & Anna Sewell **Black Beauty** (Hamish Hamilton 0-241-12102-7, Mar,87, £7.95, 72pp, hc) Associational interest. Famous children's story illustrated by Susan Jeffers and 'adapted' by Robin McKinley. [Not seen]

McKinley, Robin, ed. **Imaginary Lands** (Julia MacRae 0-86203-280-6, Mar,87, £8.95, 256pp, hc) Reprint (Ace 1985) juvenile fantasy anthology. [First U.K. edition, not seen]

McKinley, Robin, ed. **Imaginary Lands** (Orbit 0-7088-8223-4, Jun,87, £3.95, 246pp, tp) Reprint (Ace 1985) original fantasy anthology.

*McKinney, Jack **Robotech # 1: Genesis** (Ballantine/Del Rey 0-345-34133-3, Mar,87 [Feb,87], $2.95, 214pp, pb) Novelization based on the animated tv sf show.

*McKinney, Jack **Robotech # 2: Battle Cry** (Ballantine/Del Rey 0-345-34134-1, Mar,87 [Feb,87], $2.95, 216pp, pb) Sf novelization based on the tv show.

*McKinney, Jack **Robotech # 3: Homecoming** (Ballantine/Del Rey 0-345-34136-8, Mar,87 [Feb,87], $2.95, 214pp, pb) Sf novelization based on the tv show.

*McKinney, Jack **Robotech # 4: Battlehymn** (Ballantine/Del Rey 0-345-34137-6, Mar,87 [Feb,87], $2.95, 212pp, pb) Sf novelization based on the tv show.

*McKinney, Jack **Robotech # 5: Force of Arms** (Ballantine/Del Rey 0-345-34138-4, May,87 [Apr,87], $2.95, 214pp, pb) Sf novel based on the tv show.

*McKinney, Jack **Robotech # 6: Doomsday** (Ballantine/Del Rey 0-345-34139-2, Jun,87 [May,87], $2.95, 216pp, pb) Novelization, based on the tv sf animated series.

*McKinney, Jack **Robotech # 7: Southern Cross** (Ballantine/Del Rey 0-345-34140-6, Jul,87 [Jun,87], $2.95, 215pp, pb) Sf novel based on the tv sf series.

*McKinney, Jack **Robotech # 8: Metal Fire** (Ballantine/Del Rey 0-345-34141-4, Aug,87 [Jul,87], $2.95, 216pp, pb) Sf novel based on the animated tv show.

*McKinney, Jack **Robotech # 9: The Final Nightmare** (Ballantine/Del Rey 0-345-34142-2, Sep,87 [Aug,87], $2.95, 248pp, pb) Sf novel based on a tv show, latest in the series.

*McKinney, Jack **Robotech #10: Invid Invasion** (Ballantine/Del Rey 0-345-34143-0, Oct,87 [Sep,87], $2.95, 212pp, pb) Sf novel based on a tv show.

*McKinney, Jack **Robotech #11: Metamorphosos** (Ballantine/Del Rey 0-345-34144-9, Nov,87 [Oct,87], $2.95, 212pp, pb) Sf novel based on a tv show.

*McKinney, Jack **Robotech #12: Symphony of Light** (Ballantine/Del Rey 0-345-34145-7, Dec,87 [Nov,87], $2.95, 212pp, pb) Sf novelization based on the tv series.

*McLoughlin, John **Tookmaker Koan** (Baen 0-671-65354-7, Oct,87 [Sep,87], $16.95, 344pp, hc) Sf novel.

McNally, Clare **Ghost House Revenge** (Severn House 0-7278-1383-8, Feb,87, £8.95, 240pp, hc) Reprint (Corgi 1981) horror novel. Sequel to **Ghost House**. [Not seen]

*McNally, Clare **Somebody Come and Play** (Corgi 0-552-13033-8, Aug,87, £2.50, 256pp, pb) Horror novel. Simultaneous with U.S. edition from Tor.

*McNally, Clare **Somebody Come and Play** (Tor 0-812-52164-1, Sep,87 [Aug,87], $3.95, 311pp, pb) Horror novel.

*McPheeters, Neal, Pat Broderick, George R.R. Martin & Doug Moench **Sandkings** Main listing under George R.R. Martin.

*McQuay, Mike **Isaac Asimov's Robot City, Book 2: Suspicion** (Ace 0-441-73126-0, Sep,87 [Aug,87], $2.95, 177pp, pb) Sf novelization, second in a round-robin serial based on Asimov's "Laws of Humanics"; each book has a different author. The plot doesn't seem to go anywhere. Art by Paul Rivoche.

*McQuay, Mike **Memories** (Bantam Spectra 0-553-25888-5, Jun,87 [May,87], $3.95, 401pp, pb) Sf novel of time travel and voyages deep into the mysteries of memory and mind. McQuay's best novel, this deserves to be on all the award short-lists. Highly recommended. (FCM)

*McSherry, Frank D., Jr., Martin H. Greenberg & Charles G. Waugh, eds. **Nightmares in Dixie: Thirteen Horror Tales From the American South** (August House 0-87483-034-6, Apr,87, $19.95, 260pp, hc) Anthology of 13 stories, one from each Southern state.

*McSherry, Frank D., Jr., Martin H. Greenberg & Charles G. Waugh, eds. **Nightmares in Dixie: Thirteen Horror Tales From the American South** (August House 0-87483-035-4, Apr,87, $8.95, 260pp, tp) Trade paperback of the above.

*McSherry, Frank D., Jr., Martin H. Greenberg & Charles G. Waugh, eds. **Strange Maine** Main listing under Charles G. Waugh.

Meacham, Beth, Wayne Douglas Barlowe & Ian Summers **Barlowe's Guide to Extraterrestrials** Main listing under Wayne Douglas Barlowe.

*Melamed, Leo **The Tenth Planet** (Bonus Books 0-933893-37-X, Sep,87 [Aug,87], $8.95, 318pp, tp) Sf novel about a 3-million-year-old android and the missing link in human evolution. This is a first novel by a "financial wizard," described as "a sci-fi mystery even humanoids can't solve."

*Melanos, Jack A. **Sindbad and the Evil Genie** (Stacey 0-87602-251-4, Jan,87, £3.50, 90pp, pb) Fantasy play. [Not seen]

+Melling, O.R. **The Singing Stone** (Viking Kestrel 0-670-80817-2, May,87 [Dec,87], $13.95, 206pp, hc) Young adult fantasy novel of mythic Ireland. First American edition (Penguin Canada 1986).

*Meredith, Richard C. **Timeliner Trilogy** (Arrow 0-09-951690-X, Aug,87, £3.95, 712pp, pb) Sf omnibus. Volume 14 in the Venture SF series. [First U.K. edition]

Meredith, Richard C. **We All Died at Breakaway Station** (Arrow 0-09-938880-4, Apr,87, £2.25, 244pp, pb) Reissue (Ballantine 1969) sf novel. Volume 1 in the Venture SF series.

Meredith, Scott **Writing to Sell** (Harper & Row 0-06-015637-6, Apr,87, $15.95, 227pp, hc) Non-fiction, associational; "how-to" book. Third revised edition. The revisions since the 1950 original are minor. The funny new introduction by Arthur C. Clarke is entertaining, but the book is more of historical interest than of practical use today.

Michaels, Barbara **Ammie, Come Home** (Berkley 0-425-09949-0, May,87 [Apr,87], $3.50, 248pp, pb) Reprint (Meredith 1968) novel, a ghost story. By now the Sixties setting of this well-told tale seem almost as historical as the glimpses of Georgetown in the days of the American Revolution. (FCM)

Michaels, Barbara **Be Buried in the Rain** (Berkley 0-425-09634-3, Mar,87 [Feb,87], $3.95, 326pp, pb) Reprint (Atheneum 1985) suspense novel with elements of horror. It's an absorbing, entertaining mystery, though the real horror comes very late. (FCM)

*Michaels, Melisa C. **Pirate Prince** (Tor 0-812-54572-9, Feb,87 [Jan,87], $2.95, 254pp, pb) Sf adventure novel, the fourth volume in the "Skyrider" series featuring a female hotshot space pilot.

Michaels, Melisa C. **Skirmish** (The Women's Press 0-7043-4906-X, Oct,87 [Dec,87], £3.50, 230pp, tp) Reprint (Tor 1985) juvenile sf novel. Volume 1 in the "Skyrider" series. [First U.K. edition]

Michaels, Melisa C. **Skirmish** (Tor 0-812-54574-5, Dec,87 [Nov,87], $3.50, 252pp, pb) Reissue (Tor 1985) sf novel/space opera, first in the "Skyrider" series; 2nd printing.

*Middleton, Haydn **The People in the Picture** (Bantam UK 0-593-01288-7, Aug,87, £10.95, 208pp, hc) Thriller with fantasy elements. A first novel.

*Miklowitz, Gloria D. **After the Bomb: Week One** (Scholastic Point 0-590-40155-6, Feb,87 [Jan,87], $2.50, 137pp, pb) Young-adult sf novel, sequel to **After the Bomb**.

Milan, Victor **The Cybernetic Samurai** (NEL 0-450-41374-8, Sep,87, £2.95, 300pp, pb) Reprint (Arbor House 1985) sf novel. [First U.K. edition]

*Milan, Victor & Melinda M. Snodgrass **Runespear** (Popular Library Questar 0-445-20247-5, Apr,87 [Mar,87], $3.50, 278pp, pb) Fantasy novel of Nordic gods vs. Nazis in 1936 -- a la Indiana Jones.

Miller, Chuck & Tim Underwood, eds. **Kingdom of Fear: The World of Stephen King** Main listing under Tim Underwood.

*Miller, Frank **Ronin** (Warner 0-446-38674-X, Sep,87, $12.95, unpaginated, tp) Graphic novel collecting 6 sf comics.

*Miller, Miranda **Smiles and the Millenium** (Virago 0-86068-915-8, Jul,87, £10.95, 243pp, hc) Novel about London in the year 2000.

*Miller, Miranda **Smiles and the Millenium** (Virago 0-86068-916-6, Jul,87, £3.95, 243pp, tp) Paperback edition of the above.

*Miller, Moira **The Doom of Soulis** (Pied Piper 0-416-02422-X, Nov,87, £7.95, 126pp, hc) Juvenile fantasy novel.

*Miller, Rex **Slob** (NAL/Signet 0-451-15005-8, Nov,87 [Oct,87], $3.95, 301pp, pb) Associational. Horror/slasher novel, a first novel. Not supernatural despite the quotes from King, Ellison, and many other sf/fantasy people.

*Miller, Russell **Bare-Faced Messiah** (Michael Joseph 0-7181-2764-1, Oct,87 [Nov,87], £12.95, 390pp, hc) Biography of L. Ron Hubbard.

Miller, Walter M., Jr. & Martin H. Greenberg, eds. **Beyond Armageddon** (Robinson 0-948164-43-3, May,87, £3.95, 386pp, tp) Reprint (Fine 1985) anthology of post-holocaust stories. [First U.K. edition]

*Milne, Janis **Starship Dunroamin** (Dent 0-460-06263-8, Jun,87 [Jul,87], £8.50, 126pp, hc) Juvenile sf novel.

*Minta, Stephen **Garcia Marquez: Writer of Colombia** (Harper & Row 0-06-435755-4, Apr,87, $17.95, 197pp, hc) Non-fiction, critical study, with biographical and political background on the "magic realist" author. There is a prior or simultaneous British edition, under the title **Gabriel Garcia Marquez: Writer of Colombia**.

*Mitchell, Elizabeth, ed. **Free Lancers** (Baen 0-671-65352-0, Sep,87 [Aug,87], $2.95, 248pp, pb) Original anthology with works by Orson Scott Card, David Drake, and Lois McMaster Bujold; all involve mercenaries of sorts (the Card very loosely). An excellent gathering -- highly recommended (FCM & TM).

*Mitchell, Kirk **Never the Twain** (Ace 0-441-56973-0, Nov,87 [Oct,87], $3.50, 294pp, pb) Sf time travel novel involving literary skullduggery and Mark Twain.

Mitchison, Naomi **The Big House** (Kelpies 0-86241-159-9, Nov,87, £1.95, 169pp, pb) Reprint (Faber 1950) juvenile fantasy novel.

*Mitchison, Naomi **Early in Orcadia** (Richard Drew 0-86267-176-0, Feb,87, £9.95, 176pp, hc) Fantasy novel set in prehistoric Orkney. [Not seen]

*Mitchison, Naomi **Early in Orcadia** (Richard Drew 0-86267-175-2, Feb,87 [Dec,87], £3.95, 176pp, tp) Paperback edition of the above.

Mitchison, Naomi **Travel Light** (Penguin 0-14-016174-0, Oct,87 [Dec,87], $6.95, 147pp, tp) Reissue (Faber & Faber 1952) fantasy novel. This has the 1985 introduction by Elizabeth Longford.

Mixon, Laura J. **Astro Pilots** (Dragon 0-583-31095-8, Jun,87 [Aug,87], £2.25, 220pp, pb) Reprint (Scholastic 1987 as **Omni: Astropilots**) juvenile sf novel. Volume 1 in the "Omni Odysseys" series. [First U.K. edition]

*Mixon, Laura J. **Omni: Astropilots** (Scholastic/Omni 0-590-40277-3, Jul,87 [Jun,87], $2.50, 236pp, pb) Young adult sf novel, first in a series from Scholastic and *Omni* magazine.

*Modesitt, L.E., Jr. **The Silent Warrior** (Tor 0-812-54588-5, Dec,87 [Nov,87], $3.50, 280pp, pb) Sf novel, 2nd in a series that started with **Dawn for a Distant Earth**.

*Moench, Doug, Pat Broderick, George R.R. Martin & Neal McPheeters **Sandkings** Main listing under George R.R. Martin.

*Moffett, Judith **Pennterra** (Congdon & Weed 0-86553-189-7, Sep,87 [Aug,87], $17.95, 382pp, hc) Sf novel, a first novel, in the "Isaac Asimov Presents" series. Quakers have settled an alien planet, and fit in with the strange natives. New high-tech settlers upset the balance, and things begin to happen.

*Mohan, Kim & Pamela O'Neill **Planet in Peril** (Ace/New Infinities 0-441-66883-6, Dec,87 [Nov,87], $3.50, 318pp, pb) Sf novel, first in the "Cyborg Commando" trilogy, featuring human brains in android bodies. The Cyborgs are called by serial numbers so they won't forget they're not human. This book has two editions, one with the Ace logo on the spine, the other without. The second is a non-returnable direct distribution to game stores by New Infinities. The first is distributed by Ace to bookstores. All other New Infinites titles probably have two editions.

*Monaco, Richard **Unto the Beast** (Bantam Spectra 0-553-26144-4, Apr,87 [Mar,87], $3.95, 473pp, pb) Occult Nazi fantasy horror time travel novel.

*Moncuse, Steve **The Fish Police** (Warner 0-446-38739-8, Dec,87 [Oct,87], $8.95, unpaginated, tp) Graphic novel with the first 4 issues of the comic, relettered and colored.

Monette, Paul **Predator** (Star 0-352-32146-6, Sep,87, £2.25, 200pp, pb) Reprint (Jove 1987) novelization of sf thriller. [First U.K. edition]

*Monteleone, Thomas F. **The Magnificent Gallery** (Tor 0-812-52216-8, Jun,87 [May,87], $3.95, 248pp, pb) Bradburyesque dark fantasy novel, a la **Something Wicked This Way Comes**.

Monteleone, Thomas F. **Night Train** (Arrow 0-09-943170-X, Feb,87 [Dec,87], £2.50, 357pp, pb) Reprint (Pocket 1984) horror novel. [First U.K. edition]

*Monteleone, Thomas F. & John DeChancie **Crooked House** (Tor 0-812-52218-4, Dec,87 [Nov,87], $3.95, 346pp, pb) Horror novel.

Moorcock, Michael **An Alien Heat** (Ace 0-441-13660-5, Jul,87 [Jun,87], $2.95, 180pp, pb) Reprint (MacGibbon & Kee 1972) sf novel, first in the "Dancers at the End of Time" trilogy.

Moorcock, Michael **Behold the Man** (Carroll & Graf 0-88184-369-5, Oct,87 [Sep,87], $2.95, 143pp, pb) Reprint (Allison & Busby 1969) sf novel.

Moorcock, Michael **Breakfast in the Ruins** (Avon 0-380-49148-6, Mar,87 [Feb,87], $3.50, 172pp, pb) Reissue (NEL 1972) sf novel.

+Moorcock, Michael **The Brothel in Rosenstrasse** (Carroll & Graf 0-88184-333-4, Jul,87 [Jun,87], $15.95, 191pp, hc) Quasi-historical novel set in Moorcock's imaginary city of Mirenburg at the end of the 19th century. First U.S. edition (NEL 1982). Indirect sequel to **The War Hound and the World's Pain**.

Moorcock, Michael **The Chronicles of Corum** (Grafton 0-586-06745-0, Oct,87 [Sep,87], £3.50, 454pp, pb) Reprint (Berkley 1978) omnibus of the second three books in the "Corum" series.

Moorcock, Michael **The City in the Autumn Stars** (Grafton 0-586-06891-0, Apr,87, £3.50, 405pp, pb) Reprint (Grafton 1986) fantasy novel. Volume 2 in the "Von Bek" series.

+Moorcock, Michael **The City in the Autumn Stars** (Ace 0-441-10629-3, Nov,87 [Oct,87], $16.95, 344pp, hc) Fantasy novel, an indirect sequel to **The Warhound and the World's Pain**. First U.S. edition (Grafton 1986).

*Moorcock, Michael **The Cornelius Chronicles, Vol. III** (Avon 0-380-70255-X, Feb,87 [Jan,87], $3.50, 341pp, pb) Omnibus of two novels in the "Jerry Cornelius" series.

Moorcock, Michael **The Dragon in the Sword** (Grafton 0-246-13129-2, Jul,87 [Jun,87], £10.95, 283pp, hc) Reprint (Ace 1986) fantasy novel. Volume 3 (and last?) in the "Eternal Champion" series. [First U.K. edition]

Moorcock, Michael **The Dragon in the Sword** (Grafton 0-246-13185-3, Nov,87 [Oct,87], £6.95, 283pp, tp) Reprint (Ace 1986) fantasy novel. Volume 3 (and last) in the "Eternal Champion" series.

Moorcock, Michael **The Dragon in the Sword** (Ace 0-441-16610-5, Dec,87 [Nov,87], $3.50, 266pp, pb) Reprint (Ace 1986) fantasy novel in the "Eternal Champion" series. The Eternal Champion confronts Hitler.

Moorcock, Michael **Elric at the End of Time** (DAW 0-88677-228-1, Jul,87 [Jun,87], $3.50, 221pp, pb) Reissue (NEL 1984) fantasy collection, #7 in the "Elric" series, even though only 3 of the stories are about Elric; 5th printing.

Moorcock, Michael **The Entropy Tango** (NEL 0-450-05663-5, May,87 [Apr,87], £2.50, 152pp, tp) Reprint (NEL 1981) sf novel. Volume 5 in the "Jerry Cornelius" series.

Moorcock, Michael **The Eternal Champion** (Berkley 0-425-09562-2, Feb,87 [Jan,87], $2.95, 188pp, pb) Reprint (Dell 1970) fantasy novel. Although it doesn't indicate it, this is actually the 1978 revised text done for the Harper & Row hardcover.

Moorcock, Michael **The Hollow Lands** (Ace 0-441-13661-3, Nov,87 [Oct,87], $2.95, 178pp, pb) Reprint (Harper & Row 1974) sf novel, Book II of "The Dancers at the End of Time".

Moorcock, Michael **The Ice Schooner** (Berkley 0-425-09706-4, May,87 [Apr,87], $2.95, 207pp, pb) Reprint (Sphere 1969) sf novel. This edition follows the revised text (Harper & Row 1977).

Moorcock, Michael **The Lives and Times of Jerry Cornelius** (Harrap 0-245-54374-0, Feb,87, £7.95, 185pp, hc) Reprint (Allison & Busby 1976) sf collection. This 'revised edition' contains a new introduction and epilogue (reprinted from a fanzine) but is otherwise unchanged.

Moorcock, Michael **The Lives and Times of Jerry Cornelius** (Grafton 0-586-06356-0, Feb,87, £2.50, 185pp, pb) Paperback edition of the above.

MOORCOCK, MICHAEL

MOSS, ROGER

Moorcock, Michael **The Swords of Corum** (Grafton 0-586-06746-9, Jun,87, £3.95, 509pp, pb) Reprint (Berkley 1977 as **The Swords Trilogy**) omnibus of the first three books in the "Corum" series.

*Moorcock, Michael **Wizardry and Wild Romance** (Gollancz 0-575-04147-1, Aug,87, £5.95, 160pp, tp) Non-fiction, "a study of epic fantasy."

*Moorcock, Michael **Wizardry and Wild Romance** (Gollancz 0-575-04146-3, Aug,87, £10.95, 160pp, hc) Hardcover edition of the above.

*Moorcock, Michael & Rodney Matthews **Elric at the End of Time** (Paper Tiger 1-85028-032-0, Jun,87 [Jul,87], £7.95, 120pp, tp) Fully illustrated edition of Moorcock's "Elric" novella.

*Moorcock, Michael & Rodney Matthews **Elric at the End of Time** (Paper Tiger 1-85028-033-9, Jun,87 [Jul,87], £12.95, 120pp, hc) Hardback edition of the above. [Not seen]

*Moore, Alan **Saga of the Swamp Thing** (Warner 0-446-38690-1, Oct,87 [Sep,87], $10.95, unpaginated, tp) Graphic novel, an omnibus of 7 horror comics. Foreword by Ramsey Campbell.

*Moore, Alan **Watchmen** (Warner 0-446-38689-8, Nov,87 [Oct,87], $14.95, unpaginated, tp) Graphic novel. Near-simultaneous with the DC edition, which went to the comics trade. This edition is for the book trade.

Moore, C.L. **Doomsday Morning** (Popular Library Questar 0-445-20462-1, Jul,87 [Jun,87], $3.50, 236pp, pb) Reprint (Doubleday 1957) sf novel.

*Moore, Rudin **Ultra-Vue and Selected Peripheral Visions** (self published no ISBN, Aug,87 [Jul,87], price unknown, 389pp, tp) Collection of five original fantasy stories. Order from Gary Smith (Rudin Moore), 715 SW Bay St., Newport OR 97365.

Moore, Ward **Bring the Jubilee** (Gollancz 0-575-04121-8, Dec,87, £3.95, 194pp, tp) Reprint (Farrar, Straus & Young 1953) sf novel. Volume 19 in the "Gollancz Classic SF" series.

Moore, Ward **Greener Than You Think** (QPB no ISBN, Dec,86 [Jan,87], $7.95, 322pp, tp) Reprint (Sloane 1947) sf novel. This is an exact reprint in paperback of the 1985 Crown edition. This appeared in 1986 but was not seen until 1987.

+Moran, Daniel **The Flame Key** (Tor 0-812-54600-8, Apr,87 [Mar,87], $2.95, 222pp, pb) Fantasy novel, Book I of "Keys to Paradise". The author is actually Robert Vardeman, and the entire trilogy appeared in England last year in one volume as **The Keys to Paradise** (NEL).

Moran, Richard **Cold Sea Rising** (Berkley 0-425-09558-4, Feb,87 [Jan,87], $3.95, 344pp, pb) Reprint (Arbor House 1986) near-future thriller.

Moran, Richard **Cold Sea Rising** (Fontana 0-00-617349-7, Apr,87, £2.95, 350pp, pb) Reprint (Arbor House 1986) futuristic disaster novel. [First U.K. edition]

*Morressy, John **The Questing of Kedrigern** (Ace 0-441-69721-6, Aug,87 [Jul,87], $2.95, 201pp, pb) Humorous fantasy novel rewritten from a series of stories in *F&SF*. Sequel to **A Voice for Princess**.

Morris, Janet **Beyond the Veil** (Ace 0-441-05512-5, Feb,87 [Jan,87], $2.95, 245pp, pb) Reprint (Baen 1985) "Thieves' World" fantasy novel, sequel to **Beyond Sanctuary**.

Morris, Janet **Beyond Wizardwall** (Ace 0-441-05722-5, May,87 [Apr,87], $2.95, 250pp, pb) Reprint (Baen 1986) "Thieves' World" novel, conclusion of the "Tempus" trilogy.

*Morris, Janet **Tempus** (Baen 0-671-65631-7, Apr,87 [Mar,87], $3.50, 277pp, pb) Episodic fantasy novel set in Thieves' World. Some sections have appeared before in "Thieves' World" anthologies, but about half the book is original.

*Morris, Janet **Warlord!** (Pocket 0-671-61923-3, Sep,87 [Aug,87], $3.95, 376pp, pb) Near-future thriller taking place on the moon and Earth.

*Morris, Janet & C.J. Cherryh **Kings in Hell** Main listing under C.J. Cherryh.

*Morris, Janet & David Drake **Kill Ratio** Main listing under David Drake.

*Morris, Janet, ed. **Angels in Hell** (Baen 0-671-65360-1, Oct,87 [Sep,87], $3.50, 307pp, pb) Shared-world fantasy original anthology, in the "Heroes in Hell" series. 8 stories.

*Morris, Janet, ed. **Crusaders in Hell** (Baen 0-671-65639-2, May,87 [Apr,87], $3.50, 278pp, pb) Original shared-world fantasy anthology of 9 stories, including works by Benford and Cherryh.

*Morris, Janet, ed. **Masters in Hell** (Baen 0-671-65379-2, Dec,87 [Nov,87], $3.50, 280pp, pb) Original anthology in the "Heroes in Hell" shared world fantasy series, with 9 stories.

Morris, Jean **The Troy Game** (Bodley Head 0-370-30759-3, Feb,87 [May,87], £6.95, 112pp, hc) Juvenile fantasy novel involving the Wild Hunt.

*Morris, Jim **Spurlock: Sheriff of Purgatory** (Tor 0-812-50683-9, Apr,87 [Mar,87], $3.95, 320pp, pb) Near-future adventure novel of Russian-occupied America. This is a revised edition of **The Sheriff of Purgatory** (Doubleday 1979). The earlier version is not listed on the copyright page.

Morris, William **The Dream of John Ball** (Journeyman Press 0-904526-08-9, Jun,87 [1987], £0.75, 76pp, pb) Reprint (Reeves & Turner 1888) fantasy novella. This is the US (Oriole Chapbooks) edition with a UK price sticker. [Not seen]

Morris, William, [ref.] **Romances of William Morris** Main listing under Amanda Hodgson.

*Morrison, Toni **Beloved** (Chatto & Windus 0-7011-3060-1, Oct,87 [Dec,87], £11.95, 285pp, hc) Literary occult novel.

Morrow, James **This Is the Way the World Ends** (Gollancz 0-575-03972-8, Feb,87 [Aug,87], £10.95, 319pp, hc) Reprint (Holt 1986) sf novel. [First U.K. edition]

+Morwood, Peter **The Demon Lord** (DAW 0-88677-204-4, Jun,87 [May,87], $3.50, 285pp, pb) Fantasy novel, #2 in the "Book of Years" tetralogy. First U.S. edition (Century 1984).

Morwood, Peter **The Demon Lord** (Century 0-7126-1754-X, Nov,87, £11.95, 304pp, hc) Reprint (Century 1984) fantasy novel. Volume 2 in the "Drusalan Empire" series. This is a pseudonym for Robert Peter Smyth. [Not seen]

Morwood, Peter **The Dragon Lord** (Century 0-7126-1590-3, Mar,87 [Oct,87], £10.95, 318pp, hc) Reprint (Arrow 1986) fantasy novel. Volume 3 in the "Drusalan Empire" series.

+Morwood, Peter **The Dragon Lord** (DAW 0-88677-252-4, Dec,87 [Nov,87], $3.50, 303pp, pb) Fantasy novel, third in the "Book of Years" series. First U.S. edition (Century 1986).

*Morwood, Peter & Diane E. Duane **The Romulan Way** For main entry see under Diane E. Duane.

*Morwood, Peter & Diane E. Duane **Star Trek #35: The Romulan Way** Main listing under Diane E. Duane.

Mosher, Howard Frank **Disappearances** (Godine Nonpareil 0-87923-524-1, Aug,87, $9.95, 255pp, tp) Reissue (Viking 1977) novel of fantasy, time travel, and a wilderness rite of passage.

Moskowitz, Sam, ed. **A Sense of Wonder** (NEL 0-450-02247-1, Aug,87, £2.25, 175pp, pb) Reissue (Doubleday 1967, as **Three Stories**) sf anthology.

Moss, Roger **The Game of the Pink Pagoda** (Flamingo 0-00-654202-6, Aug,87, £3.95, 269pp, tp) Reprint (Collins 1986). Although billed as a novel and marketed as fantasy, this is actually a collection of vignettes based around a common theme and set of characters, only one of which has any sf aspects (and that is 'hard sf'). Despite that, it is a fascinating book and is strongly recommended.

MOTTER, DEAN

*Motter, Dean, Gilbert Hernandez, Jaime Hernandez & Mario Hernandez **The Return of Mister X** Main listing under Gilbert Hernandez.

Murdock, M.S. **Star Trek #10: Web of the Romulans** (Pocket 0-671-60549-6, Jan,87, $3.50, 220pp, pb) Reissue (Pocket 1983) Star Trek novel. 4th printing.

*Murdock, M.S. **Vendetta** (Popular Library Questar 0-445-20520-2, Aug,87 [Jul,87], $2.95, 292pp, pb) Sf novel. "A young slave must stop a madman from murdering a child -- and whole worlds."

*Murphy, Gloria **Nightmare** (Popular Library 0-445-20404-4, Jun,87 [May,87], $3.50, 232pp, pb) Horror novel of a "high-tech underground village" and children in peril.

Murphy, Pat **The Falling Woman** (Tor 0-812-54620-2, Sep,87 [Aug,87], $3.95, 283pp, pb) Reprint (Tor 1986) fantasy novel.

*Murphy, Shirley Rousseau **The Ivory Lyre** (Harper & Row 0-06-024362-7, Mar,87 [Feb,87], $12.95, 250pp, hc) Young-adult fantasy novel, second in the "Dragonbards Trilogy".

Murphy, Shirley Rousseau **Nightpool** (Harper & Row/Starwanderer 0-694-05605-7, Apr,87, $2.95, 250pp, pb) Reprint (Harper & Row 1985) young-adult fantasy novel.

*Murphy, Warren & Molly Cochran **High Priest** (NAL 0-453-00537-3, Nov,87, $17.95, 355pp, hc) Near-future thriller with sf/fantasy elements.

*Myers, Amy, ed. **The Third Book of After Midnight Stories** (Kimber 0-7183-0667-8, Oct,87, £9.50, 208pp, hc) Original ghost/occult anthology.

Nader, George **Chrome** (Alyson 1-55583-114-1, Aug,87 [Jul,87], $7.95, 369pp, tp) Reprint (Putnam 1978) gay sf novel about a man who loves a robot.

*Naha, Ed **Robocop** (Dell 0-440-17479-1, Jul,87, $3.50, 189pp, pb) Novelization of the movie.

Neiderman, Andrew **Night Howl** (Severn House 0-7278-1435-4, Jan,87, £9.95, 320pp, hc) Reprint (Pocket 1986) horror novel. [First U.K. edition, not seen]

Neiderman, Andrew **Night Howl** (Arrow 0-09-949680-1, Jun,87, £2.50, 277pp, pb) Reprint (Pocket 1986) sf novel.

*Neiderman, Andrew **Reflection** (Worldwide 0-373-50605-8, Dec,87, £2.95, 378pp, pb) Romantic novel with supernatural elements.

*Neiderman, Andrew **Sight Unseen** (Zebra 0-8217-2038-4, Apr,87 [Mar,87], $3.95, 283pp, pb) Horror novel.

Neill, Robert **Mist Over Pendle** (Arrow 0-09-906780-3, Jun,87, £2.95, 384pp, pb) Reissue (Hutchinson 1951) classic witchcraft novel.

Neill, Robert **Witch Bane** (Inner Circle 1-85018-066-0, Aug,87, £9.50, 224pp, hc) Reprint (Hutchinson 1967) occult novel. [Not seen]

Neill, Robert **Witch Bane** (Arrow 0-09-907710-8, Sep,87, £2.50, 224pp, pb) Reissue (Hutchinson 1967) occult novel.

Nelson, Ray & Philip K. Dick **The Ganymede Takeover** Main listing under Philip K. Dick.

Nesbit, Edith **Five Children and It** (Windrush Large Print 1-85089-912-6, Jul,87 [Oct,87], £8.95, 246pp, hc) Reprint (T. Fisher Unwin 1902) juvenile fantasy novel. Volume 1 in the "Psammaed" series. Available in the US from ABC-Clio, $12.95.

Nesbit, Edith **The Phoenix and the Carpet** (Dell/Yearling 0-440-47035-8, Feb,87 [Jan,87], $4.95, 239pp, tp) Reprint (Newnes 1904) classic juvenile fantasy novel, There is a new afterword by Susan Cooper.

Nesbit, Edith **The Story of the Amulet** (Dell/Yearling 0-440-47719-0, Apr,87 [Mar,87], $4.95, 270pp, pb) Reprint (Unwin 1906) classic juvenile fantasy novel.

Nichols, Leigh **The Door To December** (Fontana 0-00-617377-2, Aug,87, £3.50, 432pp, pb) Reprint (NAL 1985, as by Richard Paige) horror novel. This is a pseudonym for Dean R. Koontz. [First U.K. edition]

*Nichols, Leigh **Shadowfires** (Avon 0-380-75216-6, Feb,87 [Jan,87], $3.95, 436pp, pb) Supernatural horror novel. Nichols is a pseudoynm for Dean Koontz.

Nichols, Leigh **Shadowfires** (Fontana 0-00-617444-2, Dec,87, £3.50, 479pp, pb) Reprint (Avon 1987) horror novel. This is a pseudonym for Dean R. Koontz. [First U.K. edition]

Nichols, Leigh **Shadowfires** (Collins 0-00-223164-6, Dec,87, £10.95, 479pp, hc) Hardback edition of the above. [First U.K. edition, not seen]

*Niederman, Andrew **Playmates** (Berkley 0-425-09898-2, May,87 [Apr,87], $3.95, 312pp, pb) Horror novel.

*Niles, Douglas **Forgotten Realms, Book #1: Darkwalker on Moonshae** (TSR 0-88038-451-4, Jun,87 [May,87], $3.95, 380pp, pb) Fantasy novel, first in a series taking place in the "Forgotten Realms" fantasy game setting.

+Nimmo, Jenny **The Snow Spider** (Dutton 0-525-44306-1, Jul,87 [Aug,87], $11.95, 136pp, hc) Contemporary young-adult fantasy in which a young magician helps heal a breach in his family. First U.S. edition (Methuen 1986).

Nimmo, Jenny **The Snow Spider** (Magnet 0-416-06492-2, Nov,87, £1.75, 142pp, pb) Reprint (Methuen 1986) juvenile fantasy novel.

*Niven, Larry **The Smoke Ring** (Ballantine/Del Rey 0-345-30256-7, May,87 [Mar,87], $16.95, 302pp, hc) Sf novel, sequel to **The Integral Trees**.

Niven, Larry **The Smoke Ring** (Macdonald 0-356-10439-7, Aug,87, £11.95, 362pp, hc) Reprint (Del Rey 1987) sf novel. Sequel to **The Integral Trees**. [First U.K. edition]

Niven, Larry **The Smoke Ring** (SFBC #11496, Nov,87, $4.50, 237pp, hc) Reprint (Del Rey 1987) sf novel, sequel to **The Integral Trees**.

Niven, Larry & Jerry E. Pournelle **The Mote in God's Eye** (QPB no ISBN, 1987 [Sep,87], $7.95, 537pp, tp) Reprint (Simon & Schuster 1974) sf novel. This is an exact reprint of the 1974 hardcover, minus the ISBN and in softcover.

*Niven, Larry, Jerry E. Pournelle & Steven Barnes **The Legacy of Heorot** (Gollancz 0-575-04015-7, May,87, £10.95, 352pp, hc) Sf novel. This British edition is the first edition, with the U.S. to follow next month. Listed as a note for collectors.

*Niven, Larry, Jerry E. Pournelle & Steven Barnes **The Legacy of Heorot** (Simon & Schuster 0-671-64094-1, Jul,87 [Jun,87], $17.95, 367pp, hc) Sf novel, published nearly simultaneously in the U.K. by Gollancz. (The British beat it by a month). Fast-paced action sf of colonists facing a hostile planet. The alien menace is very well handled. Recommended. (TM)

Niven, Larry, Jerry E. Pournelle & Steven Barnes **The Legacy of Heorot** (SFBC #111159, Aug,87, $5.98, 348pp, hc) Reprint (Gollancz 1987) sf novel.

*Noel, Atanielle Annyn **Murder on Usher's Planet** (Avon 0-380-75012-0, Apr,87 [Mar,87], $3.95, 183pp, pb) Humorous sf mystery novel.

*Noel, Atanielle Annyn **Speaker to Heaven** (Arbor House 0-87795-859-9, Mar,87 [Feb,87], $16.95, 279pp, hc) Sf novel of rogue psi powers, an academic murder mystery set in post-holocaust Baja.

+Nooteboom, Cees **In the Dutch Mountains** (Louisiana State Univ. Press 0-8071-1425-1, Oct,87 [Nov,87], $14.95, 128pp, hc) Supernatural fantasy novel. English-language edition (Uitgeverij De Arbeiderspes [Netherlands] 1984). There is an earlier or simultaneous British edition from Viking U.K.

NORMAN, JOHN

NUGENT, JAMES

Norman, John **Blood Brothers of Gor** (DAW 0-88677-157-9, Mar,87 [Feb,87], $3.95, 480pp, pb) Reissue (DAW 1982) sf novel, "Gor" #18; 6th printing.

Norman, John **Hunters of Gor** (DAW 0-88677-205-2, Mar,87 [Feb,87], $3.95, 320pp, pb) Reissue (DAW 1974) sf novel, "Gor" #8; 20th printing.

Norman, John **Savages of Gor** (DAW 0-88677-191-9, Mar,87 [Feb,87], $3.95, 335pp, pb) Reissue (DAW 1982) sf novel, "Gor" #17; 4th printing.

*Norman, John **Vagabonds of Gor** (DAW 0-88677-188-9, Mar,87 [Feb,87], $3.95, 495pp, pb) Sf novel, "Gor" #24.

Norman, John **Vagabonds of Gor** (Star 0-352-32092-3, Aug,87, £3.95, 480pp, pb) Reprint (DAW 1987) fantasy novel. Volume 24 in the "Gor" series. [First U.K. edition]

Norton, Andre **Android at Arms** (Ballantine/Del Rey 0-345-34282-8, Aug,87 [Jul,87], $2.95, 233pp, pb) Reprint (Harcourt Brace Jovanovich 1971) sf novel.

Norton, Andre **The Beast Master** (Puffin 0-14-031159-9, Jan,87, £1.95, 185pp, pb) Reissue (Harcourt Brace and World 1959) juvenile sf novel. Volume 1 in the "Hosteen Storm" series.

Norton, Andre **The Book of Andre Norton** (DAW 0-88677-247-8, Sep,87 [Aug,87], $2.95, 221pp, pb) Reissue (Chilton 1974 as **The Many Worlds of Andre Norton**) collection; 6th DAW printing.

Norton, Andre **Catseye** (Puffin 0-14-030315-4, Jan,87, £1.95, 205pp, pb) Reissue (Harcourt, Brace and World 1961) juvenile sf novel.

Norton, Andre **The Crystal Gryphon** (Puffin 0-14-032109-8, Nov,87, £2.50, 248pp, pb) Reissue (Atheneum 1982) juvenile fantasy novel. In the "Witch World" series. Volume 3 in the "Gryphon" trilogy.

Norton, Andre **The Defiant Agents** (Ace 0-441-14249-4, Oct,87 [Sep,87], $2.95, 218pp, pb) Reissue (World 1962) sf novel, #3 in the "Ross Murdock" series; 9th printing.

Norton, Andre **Flight in Yiktor** (Tor 0-812-54721-7, Apr,87 [Mar,87], $2.95, 251pp, pb) Reprint (Tor 1986) sf novel, sequel to **Moon of Three Rings** and **Exile of the Stars**.

Norton, Andre **Galactic Derelict** (Ace 0-441-27234-7, May,87 [Apr,87], $2.95, 246pp, pb) Reissue (World 1959) sf novel, #2 in the "Ross Murdock" series. 9th Ace printing since 1972.

Norton, Andre **Garan the Eternal** (DAW 0-88677-244-3, Sep,87 [Aug,87], $2.95, 206pp, pb) Reissue (FPCI 1972) fantasy quasi-novel of 5 linked stories; 8th DAW printing.

*Norton, Andre **The Gate of the Cat** (Ace 0-441-27376-9, Oct,87 [Sep,87], $16.95, 243pp, hc) Fantasy novel in the "Witch World" series.

Norton, Andre **Huon of the Horn** (Ballantine/Del Rey 0-345-34126-0, Apr,87 [Mar,87], $2.95, 192pp, pb) Reprint (Harcourt Brace 1951) juvenile fantasy novel. A retelling of the legend from the Charlemagne cycle.

Norton, Andre **Iron Cage** (Puffin 0-14-032108-X, Aug,87, £2.50, 288pp, pb) Reprint (Viking 1974) sf novel.

Norton, Andre **Judgement on Janus** (Ballantine/Del Rey 0-345-34365-4, May,87 [Apr,87], $2.95, 255pp, pb) Reprint (Harcourt Brace & World 1963) sf novel.

Norton, Andre **Key Out of Time** (Ace 0-441-43676-5, Dec,87 [Nov,87], $2.95, 188pp, pb) Reissue (World 1963) sf novel, Book 4 in the "Time Traders" series; 8th Ace printing.

Norton, Andre **Lore of the Witch World** (DAW 0-88677-243-5, Jul,87, $3.50, 269pp, pb) Reissue (DAW 1980) collection of 7 stories in the "Witch World" series; 6th printing.

Norton, Andre **Merlin's Mirror** (DAW 0-88677-245-1, Sep,87 [Aug,87], $2.95, 205pp, pb) Reissue (DAW 1975) sf novel about Merlin; 9th printing.

Norton, Andre **Moon of Three Rings** (Ace 0-441-53900-9, Feb,87 [Jan,87], $2.95, 294pp, pb) Reissue (Viking 1966) sf novel; 13th printing.

Norton, Andre **Perilous Dreams** (DAW 0-88677-248-6, Sep,87 [Aug,87], $2.95, 199pp, pb) Reissue (DAW 1976) collection of 4 connected stories. 7th printing; has a typo in the title (it says "Perilous Dream").

Norton, Andre **Quag Keep** (DAW 0-88677-250-8, Sep,87 [Aug,87], $2.95, 192pp, pb) Reissue (Atheneum 1978) fantasy novel; 5th printing.

Norton, Andre **Sea Siege** (Ballantine/Del Rey 0-345-34364-6, Jul,87 [Jun,87], $2.95, 214pp, pb) Reprint (Harcourt Brace 1957) sf novel.

Norton, Andre **Shadow Hawk** (Ballantine/Del Rey 0-345-34366-2, Jun,87 [May,87], $2.95, 253pp, pb) Reprint (Harcourt Brace 1960) Egyptian historical novel. Associational.

Norton, Andre **Spell of the Witch World** (DAW 0-88677-242-7, Jul,87, $3.50, 159pp, pb) Reissue (DAW 1972) fantasy novel, 7th in the "Witch World" series; 14th printing. This was the first DAW book, and it is now reissued with the original Jack Gaughan cover.

Norton, Andre **Star Man's Son** (Gollancz 0-575-04124-2, Dec,87, £2.50, 220pp, pb) Reprint (Harcourt, Brace & Co. 1952, as **Star Man's Son, 2250 A.D.**) sf novel.

Norton, Andre **Stargate** (Gollancz 0-575-04007-6, Jul,87, £2.50, 192pp, pb) Reprint (Harcourt 1958) sf novel.

Norton, Andre **Three Against the Witch World** (Gollancz 0-575-03998-1, Oct,87, £2.50, 191pp, pb) Reprint (Ace 1965) fantasy novel. Volume 4 in the "Witch World" series.

Norton, Andre **The Time Traders** (Ace 0-441-81255-4, Apr,87 [Mar,87], $2.95, 220pp, pb) Reissue (World 1958) sf novel, first of a tetralogy. It's labelled "Seventh Ace printing," which is probably off by a factor of five.

Norton, Andre **Web of the Witch World** (Gollancz 0-575-03996-5, Jun,87, £2.50, 192pp, pb) Reprint (Ace 1964) fantasy novel. Volume 2 in the "Witch World" series.

Norton, Andre **Witch World** (Gollancz 0-575-03995-7, May,87, £2.50, 222pp, pb) Reprint (Ace 1963) fantasy novel. Volume 1 in the "Witch World" series.

Norton, Andre **Year of the Unicorn** (Gollancz 0-575-03999-X, Aug,87 [Jul,87], £2.50, 221pp, pb) Reprint (Ace 1965) fantasy novel. Volume 3 in the "Witch World" series.

Norton, Andre **Yurth Burden** (DAW 0-88677-249-4, Sep,87 [Aug,87], $2.95, 206pp, pb) Reissue (DAW 1978) sf novel; 6th printing.

*Norton, Andre, ed. **Tales of the Witch World** (Tor 0-312-94475-6, Sep,87 [Aug,87], $15.95, 343pp, hc) Original shared-world anthology set in Norton's Witch World.

*Norton, Andre & Robert Adams, eds. **Magic in Ithkar 4** (Tor 0-812-54719-5, Jul,87 [Jun,87], $3.50, 278pp, pb) Original anthology of 15 stories, latest in the "Ithkar" shared world fantasy series.

Norton, Mary **Are All the Giants Dead?** (Magnet 0-416-00742-2, May,87, £1.75, 119pp, pb) Reprint (Dent 1975) juvenile fantasy novel.

*Norwood, Warren G. **Shudderchild** (Bantam Spectra 0-553-26455-9, May,87 [Apr,87], $3.95, 350pp, pb) Near-future sf novel of a devastated Earth.

Nourse, Alan E. **The Universe Between** (Ace 0-441-85456-7, May,87 [Apr,87], $2.95, 169pp, pb) Reprint (McKay 1965) sf novel.

*Nugent, James **The Brass Halo** (Critic's Choice 1-55547-183-8, Aug,87, $3.95, 346pp, pb) Novel of occult horror, "The Talisman" #1.

Nyberg, Bjorn, Lin Carter, L. Sprague de Camp & Robert E. Howard **Conan the Swordsman** Main listing under Robert E. Howard.

O'Brien, Robert C. **Z for Zachariah** (Collier 0-02-044650-0, Oct,87 [Sep,87], $3.95, 249pp, pb) Reissue (Atheneum 1974) sf novel, winner of the Edgar Allan Poe Award.

O'Brien, Tim **The Nuclear Age** (Flamingo 0-00-654188-7, Apr,87, £3.95, 312pp, tp) Reprint (Collins 1986) futuristic literary novel.

*O'Connell, Nicholas **At the Field's End: Interviews with 20 Pacific Northwest Writers** (Madrona 0-88089-026-6, Oct,87, $12.95, 322pp, tp) Associational: non-fiction, book of interviews of authors including Jean M. Auel, Ursula K. Le Guin, and Tom Robbins. Also announced in hardcover.

*O'Day-Flannery, Constance **Timeswept Lovers** (Zebra 0-8217-2057-0, Apr,87, $3.95, 492pp, pb) Time travel/romance/fantasy novel of a lady railroad owner swept into the past, "and into the arms of the original Marlboro man!"

*O'Donnell, Kevin, Jr. & Mary Kittredge **The Shelter** Main listing under Mary Kittredge.

O'Neill, Joseph **Land Under England** (Penguin 0-14-008956-X, Jan,87, £3.95, 296pp, pb) Reprint (Gollancz 1935) sf novel. In the "Penguin Science Fiction Classics" series.

*O'Neill, Pamela & Kim Mohan **Planet in Peril** Main listing under Kim Mohan.

*O'Reilly, Tim, ed. **The Maker of Dune: Insights of a Master of Science Fiction** Main listing under Frank Herbert.

*O'Riordan, Robert **Cadre Lucifer** (Ace 0-441-09019-2, May,87 [Apr,87], $2.95, 202pp, pb) Sf novel, sequel to **Cadre One**.

*O'Shea, Pat **Finn MacCool and the Small Men of Deeds** (Oxford 0-19-274134-9, Oct,87, £5.95, 96pp, hc) Juvenile fantasy novel. [Not seen]

O'Shea, Pat **The Hounds of the Morrigan** (Puffin 0-14-032207-8, Jul,87, £2.95, 469pp, pb) Reprint (Oxford University Press 1985) juvenile fantasy in the world of Irish mythology.

Offutt, Andrew J. **Conan #15: The Sword of Skelos** (Ace 0-441-11480-6, Sep,87 [Aug,87], $2.95, 192pp, pb) Reprint (Bantam 1979) heroic fantasy novel based on the Robert E. Howard character.

*Offutt, Andrew J. **Shadowspawn** (Ace 0-441-76039-2, Sep,87 [Aug,87], $3.50, 278pp, pb) Shared-world fantasy novel; the fourth "Thieves' World" novel.

*Oldfield, Pamela **The Ghosts of Bellering Oast** (Blackie 0-216-92093-0, Jun,87, £6.95, 80pp, hc) Juvenile ghost story. [Not seen]

*Oldfield, Pamela **Pamela Oldfield's Spine Chillers** (Blackie 0-216-92240-2, Oct,87, £6.95, 96pp, hc) Juvenile ghost/horror collection. [Not seen]

*Olsen, Lance **Eclipse of Uncertainty: An Introduction to Postmodern Fantasy** (Greenwood 0-313-25511-3, Mar,87 [May,87], $27.95, xi + 134pp, hc) Non-fiction, critical study examining works by Kafka, Borges, and other literary fantasists. UK price £26.50.

*Oltion, Jerry **Frame of Reference** (Popular Library Questar 0-445-20330-7, Mar,87 [Feb,87], $3.50, 262pp, pb) Sf novel about man's reclaiming Earth from alien invaders. A first novel.

*Ore, Rebecca **Becoming Alien** (Tor 0-812-54794-2, Jan,88 [Dec,87], $3.50, 313pp, pb) Sf novel, a first novel. Recommended. (FCM)

*Orlov, Vladimir **Danilov the Violist** (Morrow 0-688-04655-X, Jul,87 [Aug,87], $18.95, 307pp, hc) Literary fantasy/social satire about a half-demon musician who's not as dedicated to evil as his masters would wish. First English language edition (Novy Mir 1980), translated from the Russian by Antonin W. Bouis.

Orton, Joe **Head to Toe** (St. Martin's 0-312-00718-3, Jul,87 [Aug,87], $13.95, 187pp, hc) Reprint (Anthony Blond 1971) literary fantasy novel. A man unwittingly wanders onto the head of a giant.

Orwell, George **Animal Farm** (Secker & Warburg 0-436-35030-0, Sep,87 [Dec,87], £12.95, 203pp, hc) Reissue (Secker & Warburg 1945) literary fantasy / political satire novel.

Orwell, George **Nineteen Eighty-Four** (Secker & Warburg 0-436-35031-9, Sep,87 [Dec,87], £12.95, 341pp, hc) Reissue (Harcourt 1949) literary sf novel.

Osier, John **Rankin: Enemy of the State** (Penguin 0-14-009818-6, Jul,87, $3.50, 160pp, pb) Reprint (St. Lukes 1986) post-holocaust adventure novel.

Ould, Chris **Road Lines** (Grafton 0-586-07030-3, Feb,87, £2.95, 303pp, pb) Reprint (Andre Deutsch 1985) futuristic thriller "in the great Mad Max tradition".

*Ounsley, Simon, John Clute & David Pringle, eds. **Interzone: The 2nd Anthology** Main listing under John Clute.

*Paget, Clarence, ed. **The 28th Pan Book of Horror Stories** (Pan 0-330-30133-0, Nov,87, £1.95, 156pp, pb) Original horror anthology.

Palmer, David R. **Emergence** (NEL 0-450-41106-0, Jun,87 [May,87], £2.95, 291pp, pb) Reprint (Bantam 1984) sf novel. [First U.K. edition]

Palmer, David R. **Threshold** (NEL 0-450-41204-0, Aug,87 [Jul,87], £2.95, 274pp, pb) Reprint (Bantam 1985) sf novel. [First U.K. edition]

Panshin, Alexei **Rite of Passage** (Methuen 0-413-15720-2, Sep,87, £2.50, 254pp, pb) Reissue (Ace 1978) sf novel.

*Pardoe, Rosemary & Richard Dalby, eds. **Ghosts and Scholars** (Crucible 1-85274-022-1, Oct,87 [Nov,87], £12.95, 272pp, hc) Collection of ghost stories, with at least one story original to this collection.

*Park, Paul **Soldiers of Paradise** (Arbor House 0-87795-861-0, Sep,87 [Aug,87], $17.95, 280pp, hc) Sf novel, a first novel, of an intricate, brutal society, vividly presented. A sequel is planned. Park is a very promising new writer. Recommended. (FCM)

*Park, Ruth **My Sister Sif** (Viking Kestrel 0-670-81524-1, Apr,87, £5.95, 192pp, hc) Juvenile novel with a touch of the supernatural. [Not seen]

*Parker, Chris **Kyoki** (Malvern 0-947993-31-2, Mar,87, £10.95, 222pp, hc) Horror novel.

*Parvin, Brian **The Golden Garden** (Robert Hale 0-7090-2927-6, May,87, £9.95, 176pp, hc) Animal fantasy novel about hedgehogs. [Not seen]

Pattrick, William, ed. **Duel and Other Horror Stories of the Road** (Star 0-352-32164-4, Dec,87 [Nov,87], £2.50, 223pp, pb) Reprint (W.H. Allen 1987, as **Mysterious Motoring Stories**) supernatural anthology.

*Pattrick, William, ed. **Mysterious Motoring Stories** (W.H. Allen 0-491-03643-4, Feb,87, £10.95, 224pp, hc) Anthology of supernatural stories about cars. Reprinted (Star 1987) as **Duel and Other Horror Stories of the Road**.

+Pattrick, William, ed. **Mysterious Sea Stories** (Dell 0-440-16088-X, Sep,87 [Aug,87], $3.50, 247pp, pb) Anthology of strange or supernatural sea stories. First American edition (W.H. Allen 1985).

*Pautz, Peter D. & Kathryn Cramer, eds. **The Architecture of Fear** Main listing under Kathryn Cramer.

*Paxson, Diana L. **The Earthstone** (Tor 0-812-54862-0, Sep,87 [Aug,87], $3.50, 278pp, pb) Fantasy novel, #4 in the "Westria" series.

*Paxson, Diana L. **The Paradise Tree** (Ace 0-441-65134-8, Aug,87 [Jul,87], $2.95, 243pp, pb) Contemporary fantasy novel.

PAYNE, BERNAL C., JR.

POE, EDGAR ALLAN

*Payne, Bernal C., Jr. **Experiment in Terror** (Houghton Mifflin 0-395-44260-5, Oct,87, $13.95, 215pp, hc) Young adult sf/psi novel about a young man with strange powers.

Pearce, Philippa **Tom's Midnight Garden** (Windrush 1-85089-914-2, 1987 [Oct,87], $12.95, 256pp, hc) Reprint (Oxford 1958) juvenile fantasy novel, large print edition. U.S. distribution of British edition from Windrush. Order from ABC-Clio.

+Pearce, Philippa **Who's Afraid? and Other Strange Stories** (Morrow/Greenwillow 0-688-06895-2, Apr 20,87 [Apr,87], $10.25, 152pp, hc) Collection of young-adult "spooky stories." First U.S. edition (Kestrel Penguin 1986).

Peck, Richard **Blossom Culp and the Sleep of Death** (Dell/Yearling 0-440-40676-5, Jul,87 [Jun,87], $2.95, 185pp, tp) Reprint (Delacorte 1986) young adult fantasy novel in the "Blossom Culp" series.

Peck, Richard **The Dreadful Future of Blossom Culp** (Dell/Yearling 0-440-42154-3, Jun,87 [May,87], $2.95, 183pp, tp) Reprint (Delacorte 1983) humorous young-adult fantasy/sf novel of psychic powers and time travel, third in the "Blossom Culp" series.

Peck, Richard **The Ghost Belonged to Me** (Dell/Yearling 0-440-42861-0, Apr,87 [May,87], $2.95, 183pp, pb) Reprint (Viking 1975) young-adult humor/horror novel in the "Blossom Culp" series.

Peck, Richard **Ghosts I Have Been** (Dell/Yearling 0-440-42864-5, May,87, $2.95, 214pp, pb) Reissue (Viking 1977) young-adult fantasy in the "Blossom Culp" series. 2nd Laurel Leaf printing.

*Peeters & Francois Schuiten **The Great Walls of Samaris** Main listing under Francois Schuiten.

*Peirce, Hayford **Napoleon Disentimed** (Tor 0-812-54898-1, Nov,87 [Oct,87], $3.50, 306pp, pb) Alternate world time travel novel where Napoleon conquered England, and France rules the world. A first novel and a "Ben Bova Discovery" book.

*Pendleton, Don **Heart to Heart** (Popular Library 0-445-20258-0, Nov,87 [Oct,87], $2.95, 240pp, pb) "Ashton Ford #5", latest in a men's adventure series about a psychic spy.

*Pendleton, Don **Life to Life** (Popular Library 0-445-20256-4, Aug,87 [Jul,87], $3.95, 256pp, pb) Occult fantasy private eye novel, "Ashton Ford" #4.

*Perry, Steve **Conan the Defiant** (Tor 0-812-54264-9, Oct,87 [Sep,87], $6.95, 245pp, tp) Heroic fantasy novel based on the Robert E. Howard character.

*Perry, Steve & Michael Reaves **Dome** Main listing under Michael Reaves.

*Peters, David **Photon #1: For the Glory** (Berkley 0-425-09811-7, Apr,87 [Mar,87], $2.50, 155pp, pb) Juvenile sf novel; first in an "intergalactic action series."

*Peters, David **Photon #2: High Stakes** (Berkley 0-425-09812-5, Apr,87 [Mar,87], $2.50, 150pp, pb) Juvenile sf novel.

*Peters, David **Photon #3: In Search of Mom** (Berkley Pacer 0-425-10106-1, Jul,87 [Jun,87], $2.50, 155pp, pb) "Photon Adventure Novel #3", latest in a juvenile sf series.

*Peters, David **Photon #4: This is Your Life, Bhodi Li** (Berkley Pacer 0-425-10185-1, Sep,87 [Aug,87], $2.50, 149pp, pb) Young-adult sf novel, "Photon Adventure #4".

*Peters, David **Photon #5: Exile** (Berkley Pacer 0-425-10611-X, Nov,87 [Oct,87], $2.50, 152pp, pb) Young-adult sf novel, latest in a series.

*Petherick, Simon, ed. **Classic Stories of Mystery, Horror and Suspense** (Robert Hale 0-7090-2933-0, Jun,87 [Nov,87], £9.95, 224pp, hc) Horror anthology.

*Pfefferle, Seth **Stickman** (Tor 0-812-52417-9, Jul,87 [Jun,87], $3.95, 279pp, pb) Horror novel of African spirits.

*Phillips, Michael R. **George MacDonald** (Bethany House 0-87123-944-2, Jun,87 [Jul,87], $12.95, 400pp, hc) Non-fiction, biography. His fantasy writing plays only a small part in this primarily Christian-oriented, exhaustive study of his life. The book has no price on it, and the $12.95 was a tentative advance one. For further information, write Bethany House Publishing, 6820 Auto Club Road, Minneapolis MN 55438.

*Pieratt, Asa, Julie Huffman-Klinkowitz & Jerome Klinkowitz, eds. **Kurt Vonnegut: A Comprehensive Bibliography** (Shoestring/Archon 0-208-02071-3, Jun,87, $34.50, 289pp, hc) Non-fiction, reference book.

*Pierce, John J. **Foundations of Science Fiction: A Study in Imagination and Evolution** (Greenwood 0-313-25455-9, Apr,87 [Mar,87], $35.00, 290pp, hc) Non-fiction, critical/historical study. This work traces the sf field via theme rather than chronologically. UK price £33.00.

*Pierce, John J. **Great Themes of Science Fiction** (Greenwood 0-313-25456-7, Oct,87 [Nov,87], $37.95, 250pp, hc) Non-fiction, critical study with a history by theme instead of chronologically. This is the second part of a three-volume history of sf which started with **Foundations of Science Fiction**. It's very clearly written and is recommended. (CNB)

Pierce, Meredith Ann **The Woman Who Loved Reindeer** (Hodder & Stoughton 0-340-40946-0, Mar,87, £7.95, 242pp, hc) Reprint (Atlantic Monthly 1985) juvenile fantasy novel set in a 'Lap-like' culture. [First U.K. edition, not seen]

Piercy, Marge **Woman on the Edge of Time** (The Women's Press 0-7043-3837-8, May,87 [Jun,87], £3.50, 381pp, pb) Reissue (Knopf 1976) sf novel.

Pini, Richard, Lynn Abbey & Robert Lynn Asprin, eds. **Elfquest, Vol.1: The Blood of Ten Chiefs** (Tor 0-812-53043-8, Dec,87 [Nov,87], $3.50, 314pp, pb) Reprint (Tor 1986) original shared world fantasy anthology.

Piserchia, Doris **Star Rider** (The Women's Press 0-7043-4071-2, May,87, £3.95, 219pp, tp) Reprint (Bantam 1974) sf novel. [First U.K. edition]

*Plante, Edmund **Transformation** (Leisure 0-8439-2490-X, May,87 [Aug,87], $3.95, 351pp, pb) Horror novel of a woman pregnant with "inhuman seed."

*Platt, Charles **Dream Makers: SF and Fantasy Writers at Work (Revised)** (Ungar/Crossroad/Continuum 0-8044-2745-3, Mar,87 [Apr,87], $17.95, 280pp, hc) Non-fiction, selection of interviews from **Dream Makers** (Berkley 1980, 15 of the 29 interviews) and **Dream Makers, Volume II** (Berkley 1983, 9 of the 28 interviews). There are no new interviews or revisions except a short introduction and afterword.

+Platt, Charles **How to Be a Happy Cat** (Main Street 1-55562-019-1, May,87, $5.95, 94pp, tp) Non-sf, not quite fantasy; humor book, with cartoons by Gray Jolliffe. It's told from the cat's viewpoint and translated from the feline by Platt. Our promotional copy came with a free bag of catnip. This is the first U.S. edition. The 1986 Gollancz edition was a British best seller.

Platt, Charles **Less Than Human** (Grafton 0-586-07079-6, Sep,87, £2.95, 238pp, pb) Reprint (Avon 1986, as by Robert Clarke) humourous sf novel. [First U.K. edition]

*Platt, Charles **Piers Anthony's Worlds of Chthon: Plasm** (NAL/Signet 0-451-15015-5, Oct,87 [Sep,87], $3.50, 284pp, pb) Sf novel set in a world invented by Anthony; a sequel to his **Chthon** and **Phthor**.

Poe, Edgar Allan **The Fall of the House of Usher** (Star 0-352-32053-2, Feb,87, £1.95, 143pp, pb) Reprint collection of horror stories. This is identical to the Target (1986) edition.

Poe, Edgar Allan **Tales of Mystery and Imagination** (Mystic Press 1-85170-124-9, Aug,87 [Dec,87], £14.95, 412pp, hc) Reprint (Everyman Library 1908) horror collection.

Poe, Edgar Allan **Tales of Mystery and Imagination** (Everyman 0-460-11336-4, Sep,87, £2.95, 572pp, pb) Reissue (Everyman Library 1908) horror collection.

Poe, Edgar Allan **Tales of Mystery and Imagination** (O'Mara 0-948397-46-2, Sep,87 [Dec,87], £12.00, 304pp, hc) Reprint (Everyman Library 1908) horror collection. Facsimile of Harrap (1919) edition with new introduction by Richard Dalby. Illustrated by Harry Clarke.

*Poe, Edgar Allan & Melvin R. White **The Tell-Tale Heart** (Hanbury 1-85205-030-6, May,87 [Jun,87], £1.95, 18pp, pb) Play adaptation of Poe's short story. [Not seen]

*Pohl, Frederik **The Annals of the Heechee** (Ballantine/Del Rey 0-345-32565-6, Mar,87 [Feb,87], $16.95, 338pp, hc) Sf novel, conclusion of the "Heechee Saga". Pohl succeeds in doing what "Doc" Smith never could -- tying up a galaxy-spanning saga satisfactorily. Highly recommended. (CNB)

Pohl, Frederik **The Annals of the Heechee** (SFBC #11278, Sep,87, $4.98, 278pp, hc) Reprint (Del Rey 1987) sf novel, #4 in the "Heechee" series.

Pohl, Frederik **The Annals of the Heechee** (Gollancz 0-575-04149-8, Nov,87, £10.95, 352pp, hc) Reprint (Del Rey 1987) sf novel. Volume 4 in the "Heechee" series. [First U.K. edition, not seen]

Pohl, Frederik **Black Star Rising** (Orbit 0-7088-8218-8, Apr,87, £2.95, 282pp, pb) Reprint (Del Rey 1985) sf novel.

*Pohl, Frederik **Chernobyl** (Bantam Spectra 0-553-05210-1, Sep,87 [Aug,87], $18.95, 355pp, hc) Associational; a novel based on the nuclear disaster at Chernobyl.

*Pohl, Frederik **Chernobyl** (Bantam UK 0-553-17502-5, Sep,87, £4.95, 355pp, tp) Mainstream novel by author better known for his sf. Simultaneous with US (Bantam) edition.

Pohl, Frederik **The Coming of the Quantum Cats** (Gollancz 0-575-04016-5, Mar,87, £9.95, 243pp, hc) Reprint (Bantam 1986) sf novel. [First U.K. edition]

Pohl, Frederik **Man Plus** (Gollancz 0-575-03981-7, Apr,87, £3.50, 215pp, tp) Reprint (Random House 1976) sf novel. Volume 12 of the Gollancz Classic SF series.

Pohl, Frederik **Starburst** (NEL 0-450-05685-6, Aug,87, £2.50, 217pp, pb) Reissue (Del Rey 1982) sf novel.

Pohl, Frederik **Years of the City** (NEL 0-450-40416-1, Feb,87 [Jan,87], £2.95, 375pp, pb) Reprint (Simon & Schuster 1984) collection of linked sf stories.

Pohl, Frederik & C.M. Kornbluth **Gladiator-at-Law** (Gollancz 0-575-04127-7, Oct,87, £3.95, 192pp, tp) Reprint (Ballantine 1953) sf novel. This appears to contain the original text, rather than the revised (Baen 1986) version. Volume 18 in the Gollancz Classic SF series.

*Pohl, Frederik & C.M. Kornbluth **Our Best: The Best of Frederik Pohl and C.M. Kornbluth** (Baen 0-671-65620-1, Feb,87 [Jan,87], $2.95, 286pp, pb) Collection of 12 collaborative stories, with new introductions by Pohl.

Pohl, Frederik & C.M. Kornbluth **The Space Merchants** (St. Martin's 0-312-90655-2, Mar,87 [Feb,87], $3.50, 169pp, pb) Reprint (Ballantine 1953) sf novel. One of the classics of satire done during the early Fifties. Note: although St. Martin's also announced a new edition of the Pohl sequel, **The Merchants War**, they redistributed their 1986 edition instead.

Pohl, Frederik & Elizabeth Anne Hull, eds. **Tales from the Planet Earth** (St. Martin's 0-312-90779-6, Nov,87 [Oct,87], $3.95, 268pp, pb) Reprint (St. Martin's 1986) anthology of 19 stories from all over the world, including many translated originals.

*Pohl, Frederik, [ref.] **Frederik Pohl** Main listing under Thomas D. Clareson.

Polikarpus, Viido & Tappan King **Down Town** (Tor 0-812-54937-6, Mar,87 [Feb,87], $2.95, 294pp, pb) Reprint (Arbor House 1985) fantasy novel, illustrated by Polikarpus.

Polikarpus, Viido & Tappan King **Down Town** For main listing see under Tappan King.

*Pollack, Rachel **Alqua Dreams** (Franklin Watts 0-531-15070-4, Nov,87 [Oct,87], $16.95, 246pp, hc) Sf novel, a first novel.

*Popkes, Steven **Caliban Landing** (Congdon & Weed 0-86553-188-9, Nov,87 [Oct,87], $16.95, 281pp, hc) Sf novel (part of the "Isaac Asimov Presents" line), with an introduction by Asimov. A first novel. Anthropological sf set on an alien planet and told from the alien's viewpoint.

*Pouns, Brauna E. **Amerika** (Pocket 0-671-63345-7, Feb,87, $4.50, 412pp, pb) Novelization of the tv miniseries about a near-future Soviet takeover of the U.S.

Pournelle, Jerry E. **Birth of Fire** (Baen 0-671-65649-X, Jun,87 [May,87], $2.95, 229pp, pb) Reprint (Laser 1976) sf novel.

*Pournelle, Jerry E. **Janissaries III: Storms of Victory** (Ace 0-441-38297-5, May,87 [Apr,87], $16.95, 359pp, hc) Military sf novel, third in the series. The book is a collaboration with Roland Green, but for commercial reasons only Pournelle's name is on the cover and in the advertising.

Pournelle, Jerry E. **King David's Spaceship** (Baen 0-671-65616-3, Feb,87 [Jan,87], $2.95, 366pp, pb) Reprint (Simon & Schuster 1981) of an expansion of A Spaceship for the King (DAW 1978). Sf adventure novel.

Pournelle, Jerry E. **West of Honor** (Baen 0-671-65347-4, Aug,87 [Jul,87], $2.95, 213pp, pb) Reprint (Laser 1976) military sf novel. This edition follows the slightly revised 1978 Pocket text.

*Pournelle, Jerry E., Steven Barnes & Larry Niven **The Legacy of Heorot** Main listing under Larry Niven.

Pournelle, Jerry E. & Larry Niven **The Mote in God's Eye** Main listing under Larry Niven.

*Pournelle, Jerry E., ed. **Imperial Stars, Vol. 2: Republic and Empire** (Baen 0-671-65359-8, Oct,87 [Sep,87], $3.95, 399pp, pb) Anthology of stories and non-fiction.

*Pournelle, Jerry E., ed. **There Will Be War, Vol. VI: Guns of Darkness** (Tor 0-812-54961-9, Jun,87 [May,87], $3.95, 406pp, pb) Anthology of both fiction and non-fiction work on war; 12 of the 24 items are original.

Powell, Anthony **The Fisher King** (Sceptre 0-340-40781-6, May,87, £3.95, 250pp, tp) Reprint (Heinemann 1986) modern novel based on the Arthurian legend.

Powell, Anthony **The Fisher King** (Isis Large Print 1-85089-188-5, Nov,87 [Oct,87], £11.75, 334pp, hc) Reprint (Heinemann 1986) modern novel based on the Arthurian legend. [Not seen]

*Powers, Louise E. **Eileen Goudge's Swept Away #3: Love on the Range** (Avon/Flare 0-380-75130-5, Nov,86 [Feb,87], $2.50, 201pp, pb) Young-adult sf/romance novel in a series about time-traveling teens. This appeared in 1986, but we did not see it until now.

Powers, Tim **Dinner at Deviant's Palace** (Grafton 0-586-07105-9, May,87, £2.95, 300pp, pb) Reprint (Ace 1984) sf novel.

Powers, Tim **The Drawing of the Dark** (Grafton 0-583-13319-3, May,87, £3.50, 383pp, pb) Reissue (Ballantine 1979) fantasy novel.

*Powers, Tim **On Stranger Tides** (Ace 0-441-62683-1, Nov,87 [Oct,87], $16.95, 325pp, hc) Pirate fantasy adventure novel set in 1817.

*Poyer, D.C. **Stepfather Bank** (St. Martin's 0-312-00687-X, Aug,87 [Jul,87], $16.95, 277pp, hc) Sf novel of a freelance poet vs. a monolithic 22nd-century government/bank.

Prantera, Amanda **The Cabalist** (Abacus 0-349-12800-6, Mar,87, £3.50, 184pp, tp) Reprint (Cape 1985) supernatural novel.

PRANTERA, AMANDA

REXNER, ROMULUS

*Prantera, Amanda **Conversations with Lord Byron on Perversion, 163 Years After His Lordship's Death** (Cape 0-224-02423-X, Mar,87 [Aug,87], £9.95, 174pp, hc) Novel about Lord Byron, using an advanced computer with 'artificial intelligence' as framing device.

+Prantera, Amanda **Conversations with Lord Byron on Perversion, 163 Years After His Lordship's Death** (Atheneum 0-689-11882-1, Oct,87 [Sep,87], $16.95, 174pp, hc) Literary sf/ghost story novel; modern researchers communicate with a computer recreation of the Romantic poet, and get more response than they expect. For the most part, the book is a lot of fun, until things just get *too* silly as Byron's "secret" is revealed. (FCM) First U.S. edition (U.K. 1987).

*Pratchett, Terry **Equal Rites** (Gollancz 0-575-03950-7, Jan,87 [Aug,87], £9.95, 200pp, hc) Humourous fantasy novel. Volume 3 in the "Colour of Magic" series. This one features a female wizard.

Pratchett, Terry **Equal Rites** (Corgi 0-552-13105-9, Nov,87 [Oct,87], £2.50, 205pp, pb) Reprint (Gollancz 1987) humourous fantasy novel. While not as hilarious as its predecessors, it still has some marvellous moments and is way ahead of the 'competition'. Strongly recommended. Volume 3 in the "Colour of Magic" series.

+Pratchett, Terry **The Light Fantastic** (SFBC #111154, Aug,87, $4.98, 189pp, hc) Humorous fantasy novel, part of a series. First U.S. edition (Colin Smythe 1986).

*Pratchett, Terry **Mort** (Gollancz 0-575-04171-4, Nov,87, £10.95, 221pp, hc) Fantasy novel. Volume 4 in the "Colour of Magic" series.

*Preiss, Byron, ed. **The Universe** (Bantam Spectra 0-553-05227-6, Nov,87 [Oct,87], $27.95, 333pp, hc) Original anthology of sf stories, science articles, and illustrations by numerous space artists.

Preiss, Byron, ed. **The Universe** (QPB no ISBN, Nov,87, $13.50, 333pp, tp) Reprint (Bantam 1987) original anthology of sf and non-fiction. This is exactly the same as the Bantam hardcover, except for the binding and lack of ISBN.

*Preuss, Paul **Arthur C. Clarke's Venus Prime, Volume 1: Breaking Strain** (Avon 0-380-75344-8, Nov,87 [Oct,87], $3.95, 265pp, pb) Sf novel based on a concept by Clarke, first in a series. It includes 16 pages of "blueprints" by Darrell Anderson, showing the structure of the Venus space station.

*Price, Patrick L. & Martin H. Greenberg, eds. **Fantastic Stories: Tales of the Weird and Wondrous** Main listing under Martin H. Greenberg.

*Price, Susan **The Ghost Drum** (Faber & Faber 0-571-14613-9, Jan,87 [Aug,87], £6.95, 167pp, hc) Fantasy novel.

Priest, Christopher **A Dream of Wessex** (Abacus 0-349-12811-1, Jul,87, £3.95, 199pp, tp) Reprint (Faber 1977) sf novel.

Priest, Christopher **Inverted World** (Gollancz 0-575-03993-0, Jun,87 [Jul,87], £3.50, 251pp, tp) Reprint (Faber 1974) sf novel. Volume 13 in the Gollancz Classic SF series.

*Pringle, David **Imaginary People** (Grafton 0-246-12968-9, Oct,87, £14.95, 518pp, hc) Associational book by well-known fan and *Interzone* editor. A fascinating collection of potted biographies (and bibliographies) of fictional characters ranging from Sherlock Holmes to Arthur Dent. Recommended.

+Pringle, David **Science Fiction: The 100 Best Novels** (Carroll & Graf 0-88184-346-6, Nov,87 [Oct,87], $7.95, 224pp, tp) Non-fiction, critical study choosing 100 sf classics. First U.S. edition (Xanadu 1985).

*Pringle, David, John Clute & Simon Ounsley, eds. **Interzone: The 2nd Anthology** Main listing under John Clute.

*Pulver, Mary Monica **Murder at the War** (St. Martin's 0-312-00622-5, Aug,87 [Jul,87], $16.95, 260pp, hc) Associational; murder mystery set in an SCA war.

Queen, Ellery **A Room to Die In** (Kinnell 1-870532-00-7, Dec,87, £9.95, 150pp, hc) Associational. Reprint (Pocket 1965) mystery novel. First UK (and first hardcover) edition. The author is actually Jack Vance.

*Quinn, Tim & Dicky Howett **The Doctor Who Fun Book** (Target 0-426-20300-3, May,87, £1.95, 64pp, tp) Collection of games and pastimes of associational interest.

*Rabin, Jennifer **Eileen Goudge's Swept Away #5: Spellbound** (Avon/Flare 0-380-75132-1, Mar,87 [Feb,87], $2.50, 188pp, pb) Young adult sf/romance novel in a series about time-traveling teens.

*Rabinowitz, Ann **Knight on Horseback** (Macmillan 0-02-775660-2, Oct,87, $13.95, 197pp, hc) Young adult novel about the ghost of Richard III. A first novel.

*Rabkin, Eric S., Colin Greenland & George E. Slusser, eds. **Storm Warnings: Science Fiction Confronts the Future** Main listing under George E. Slusser.

*Rabkin, Eric S. & George E. Slusser, eds. **Aliens: The Anthropology of Science Fiction** Main listing under George E. Slusser.

*Rabkin, Eric S. & George E. Slusser, eds. **Intersections: Fantasy and Science Fiction** Main listing under George E. Slusser.

*Raeper, William **Fantasy King: A Biography of George MacDonald** (Lion 0-7459-1123-4, Sep,87, £12.95, 416pp, hc) Biographical book. [Not seen]

*Randisi, Robert J. & Kevin D. Randle **Once Upon a Murder** (TSR/Windwalker 0-88038-450-6, Mar,87, $2.95, 219pp, pb) Fantasy/mystery/time travel novel.

*Randle, Kevin D. & Robert J. Randisi **Once Upon a Murder** Main listing under Robert J. Randisi.

*Ransom, Daniel **Night Caller** (Zebra 0-8217-2186-0, Oct,87 [Sep,87], $3.95, 301pp, pb) Horror novel.

Raspe, R.E. **The Adventures of Baron Munchausen** (Methuen 0-413-14000-8, Mar,87, £6.95, 272pp, tp) Reprint collection of fantastic tales, illustrated by Ronald Searle. [Not seen]

Ray, Satyajit **The Unicorn Expedition and Other Fantastic Tales of India** (Dutton 0-525-24544-8, Jul,87, $16.95, 190pp, hc) Collection of 11 tales, originally published in Britain as **Stories**.

*Reaves, Michael & Steve Perry **Dome** (Berkley 0-425-09560-6, Feb,87 [Jan,87], $3.50, 274pp, pb) Sf novel of an undersea laboratory that survives worldwide biological warfare.

*Reed, Dana **The Gatekeeper** (Leisure 0-8439-2500-0, Aug,87 [Jul,87], $3.95, 399pp, pb) Horror novel.

*Reed, Robert **The Leeshore** (Donald I. Fine/Primus 0-917657-98-5, Apr,87 [Mar,87], $9.95, 253pp, tp) Sf novel of Earthmen vs. computer worshippers on a water planet. A first novel. Under the pen name Robert Touzalin, Reed won last year's Writers of the Future Award.

*Reichert, Mickey Zucker **Godslayer** (DAW 0-88677-207-9, Jul,87, $2.95, 222pp, pb) Fantasy novel of elves, dragons, and Norse gods, with the hero, a Vietnam soldier, inhabiting the body of an elvish warrior.

*Relling, William, Jr. **New Moon** (Tor 0-812-52512-4, Oct,87 [Sep,87], $3.95, 280pp, pb) Horror novel.

*Rendell, Ruth, ed. **A Warning to the Curious: The Ghost Stories of M.R. James** Main listing under M.R. James.

*Resnick, Mike **The Dark Lady: A Romance of the Far Future** (Tor 0-812-55116-8, Nov,87 [Oct,87], $3.50, 279pp, pb) Sf novel of a mysterious, eternally young woman. An entertaining adventure with mystical elements. (FCM)

Resnick, Mike **Stalking the Unicorn** (Arrow 0-09-951070-7, Sep,87, £2.95, 314pp, pb) Reprint (Tor 1987) fantasy novel. [First U.K. edition]

*Rexner, Romulus **Planetary Legion for Peace: Story of Their War and Our Peace, 1940 - 2000** (Veritas 0-948202-03-3, Jul,87 [Aug,87], £4.95, 240pp, tp) Sf/occult novel? [Not seen]

*Reynolds, Kay, ed. **Robotech Art 2** (Donning/Starblaze 0-89865-417-3, Oct,87, $12.95, 131pp, tp) Non-fiction, art book based on a tv cartoon show.

Rhinehart, Luke **Adventures of Wim** (Grafton 0-586-06752-3, Nov,87, £3.95, 409pp, pb) Reprint (Grafton 1986) sf novel.

*Rhodes, Daniel **Next, After Lucifer** (St. Martin's/Thomas Dunne 0-312-00567-9, Jul,87, $16.95, 258pp, hc) Horror novel of the spirit of a Templar sorcerer returning to modern France. A first novel.

+ Ribiero, Stella Carr **Sambaqui** (Avon/Bard 0-380-89624-9, Mar,87 [Feb,87], $3.95, 132pp, pb) Prehistoric novel. English translation of **O Homen Do Sambaqui: Una Estoria Na Pre-Historia** (Edicoes Quiron); English translation copyright 1975 by Claudia Van der Heuvel.

Rice, Anne **The Vampire Lestat** (Macdonald 0-356-13032-0, Mar,87, £9.95, 480pp, hc) Reprint (Knopf 1985) horror novel. [Not seen]

*Richards, Tony **The Harvest Bride** (Tor 0-812-52520-5, May,87 [Apr,87], $3.95, 279pp, pb) Horror novel.

*Richardson, Jean, ed. **Beware, Beware - Strange and Sinister Tales** (Hamish Hamilton 0-241-12104-3, Oct,87, £6.95, 128pp, hc) Juvenile ghost/horror anthology. [Not seen]

*Ridgway, Jim & Michele Benjamin, eds. **PsiFi: Psychological Theories and Science Fictions** (The British Psychological Society 0-901715-62-X, Jan,87 [Aug,87], £8.95, 229pp, tp) Anthology of sf stories with psychological commentaries.

*Riding, Julia **Space Traders Unlimited** (Pied Piper 0-416-02212-X, May,87, £5.95, 160pp, hc) Juvenile sf novel. [Not seen]

*Rifbjerg, Klaus **Witness to the Future** (Fjord 0-940242-18-4, Sep,87, $8.95, 214pp, tp) Literary sf novel, translated from Danish (**De Hellige Aber**, Gyldendal 1981) by Steve Murray. Two boys suddenly find themselves in 1988, having entered a cave in 1941. Also announced in a library hardcover (-21-4) at $17.95. Order from Fjord Press, Box 16501, Seattle WA 98116.

Rivkin, J.F. **Silverglass** (Orbit 0-7088-8241-2, May,87, £2.50, 186pp, pb) Reprint (Ace 1986) fantasy novel. [First U.K. edition]

*Rivkin, J.F. **Web of Wind** (Ace 0-441-87883-0, Dec,87 [Nov,87], $2.95, 202pp, pb) Fantasy novel with a female barbarian hero, sequel to **Silverglass**.

*Robbins, David **Endworld #5: Dakota Run** (Leisure 0-8439-2473-X, Apr,87, $2.95, 256pp, pb) Post-holocaust giant ant sf adventure novel.

*Robbins, David **Endworld #6: Citadel Run** (Leisure 0-8439-2507-8, Aug,87 [Jul,87], $2.95, 255pp, pb) Post-holocaust sf adventure novel.

Robbins, Glyn & C.S. Lewis **The Lion, the Witch and the Wardrobe** (French 0-573-05081-3, May,87 [Jul,87], £3.50, 56pp, tp) Play adaptation of classic children's fantasy. [Not seen]

Roberson, Jennifer **Shapechangers** (Corgi 0-552-13118-0, May,87, £2.50, 306pp, pb) Reprint (DAW 1984) fantasy novel. Volume 1 in the "Chronicles of the Cheysuli" series. [First U.K. edition]

Roberson, Jennifer **The Song of Homana** (DAW 0-88677-195-1, Apr,87 [Mar,87], $3.50, 352pp, pb) Reissue (DAW 1985) fantasy novel, "Chronicles of the Cheysuli" #2; 3rd printing.

Roberson, Jennifer **The Song of Homana** (Corgi 0-552-13119-9, Oct,87, £2.95, 348pp, pb) Reprint (DAW 1985) fantasy novel. Volume 2 in the "Chronicles of Cheysuli" series. [First U.K. edition]

*Roberson, Jennifer **Track of the White Wolf** (DAW 0-88677-193-5, Apr,87 [Mar,87], $3.50, 375pp, pb) Fantasy novel, "Chronicles of the Cheysuli" #4.

*Roberts, John Maddox **Conan the Champion** (Tor 0-812-54260-6, Apr,87 [Mar,87], $3.50, 280pp, pb) Fantasy novel based on Howard's mighty-thewed character. This volume also has an up-to-date Conan chronology which includes all the Conan continuations plus a Conan history.

*Roberts, John Maddox **Conan the Marauder** (Tor 0-812-54266-5, Jan,88 [Dec,87], $3.50, 277pp, pb) Fantasy novelization in the "Conan" shared-hero series.

Roberts, John Maddox **Conan the Valorous** (Sphere 0-7221-7396-2, Sep,87, £2.50, 216pp, pb) Reprint (Tor 1985) fantasy novel. Volume 27 in the "Conan" series. [First U.K. edition]

*Roberts, John Maddox & Eric Kotani **The Island Worlds** Main listing under Eric Kotani.

*Roberts, Keith **Grainne** (Kerosina 0-948893-07-9, May,87 [Apr,87], £12.50, 175pp, hc) Quasi-fantasy/alternate world novel. It follows the heroine "from her student days in Oxford, through a meteoric career in television to her self-ordained destiny as high priestess of a radically new social movement." Distributed in the U.S. through specialty dealers only. Limited to 750 copies in this form.

*Roberts, Keith **Grainne** (Kerosina 0-948893-06-0, May,87 [Aug,87], £35.00, 175pp, hc) Limited (250 copies) edition of above, supplied in slipcase with hardback of **A Heron Caught in Weeds**.

*Roberts, Keith **A Heron Caught in Weeds** (Kerosina 0-948893-09-5, Apr,87, £3.95, 46pp, tp) Poetry collection, edited by Jim Goddard. Limited to 350 copies in this form.

*Roberts, Keith **A Heron Caught in Weeds** (Kerosina 0-948893-08-7, Apr,87 [Aug,87], , 46pp, hc) Limited (300 copies) hardback edition of above, distributed with Collector's edition of **Grainne**.

Roberts, Keith **Kiteworld** (SFBC #105239, Jan,87, $6.98, 288pp, hc) Reprint (Gollancz 1985) episodic sf novel.

Roberts, Keith **The Lordly Ones** (David & Charles/Gollancz 0-575-03864-0, Apr,87 [Jan,87], $18.95, 160pp, hc) Collection of 7 stories; first U.S. appearance. This is a false entry, the 1986 British edition with a U.S. price.

*Robeson, Kenneth **Doc Savage Omnibus #2** (Bantam 0-553-26207-6, Jan,87, $3.95, 410pp, pb) Omnibus of 4 Doc Savage short novels from the magazine.

*Robeson, Kenneth **Doc Savage Omnibus #3** (Bantam 0-553-26738-8, Jun,87 [May,87], $3.95, 378pp, pb) Omnibus of 4 Doc Savage short novels from the magazine.

*Robeson, Kenneth **Doc Savage Omnibus #4** (Bantam 0-553-26802-3, Oct,87 [Dec,87], $3.95, 392pp, pb) Omnibus edition of four short "Doc Savage" adventure novels.

*Robinson, Frank M. & Thomas N. Scortia **Blow-Out!** Main listing under Thomas N. Scortia.

Robinson, Kim Stanley **The Memory of Whiteness** (Orbit 0-7088-8211-0, Jan,87, $2.95, 351pp, pb) Reprint (Tor 1985) sf novel.

Robinson, Kim Stanley **The Planet on the Table** (Tor 0-812-55237-7, Jul,87 [Jun,87], $3.50, 241pp, pb) Reprint (Tor 1986) collection of 8 stories.

Robinson, Kim Stanley **The Planet on the Table** (Orbit 0-7088-8232-3, Aug,87, £2.95, 241pp, pb) Reprint (Tor 1986) sf collection. [First U.K. edition]

Robinson, Logan **Evil Star** (Zebra 0-8217-1992-0, Feb,87 [Jan,87], $2.95, 256pp, pb) Reprint (Norton 1986) near-future sf novel of strange astronomic happenings and the threat of global war.

*Robinson, Nigel **The Sensorites** (W.H. Allen 0-491-03455-5, Feb,87, £7.50, 143pp, hc) Juvenile sf novel. Volume 118 in the Doctor Who series.

Robinson, Nigel **The Sensorites** (Target 0-426-20295-3, Jul,87, £1.95, 143pp, pb) Reprint (W.H. Allen 1987) juvenile sf novel. Volume 118 in the Doctor Who series.

*Robinson, Nigel **The Time Meddler** (W.H. Allen 0-491-03337-0, Oct,87 [Dec,87], £7.95, 141pp, hc) Juvenile sf novel. Volume 126 in the Doctor Who series.

ROBINSON, ROGER, COMP.

*Robinson, Roger, comp. **Who's Hugh?: An SF Reader's Guide to Pseudonyms** (Beccon 1-870824-02-4, Aug,87 [Oct,87], £9.50, 173pp, tp) Despite some infuriating misprints, this is the most accurate and comprehensive guide to sf pseudonyms around. Recommended. Order from Beccon Publications, 75 Rosslyn Ave, Harold Wood, ROMFORD, RM3 0RG, England.

*Robinson, Roger, comp. **Who's Hugh?: An SF Reader's Guide to Pseudonyms** (Beccon 1-870824-01-6, Aug,87 [Oct,87], £14.50, 173pp, hc) Hardback edition of the above.

*Robinson, Roger, ed. **The Writings of Henry Kenneth Bulmer** (Beccon 1-870824-00-8, Aug,87 [Oct,87], £1.00, 52pp, pb) Latest edition of the definitive bibliography of Ken Bulmer. [Not seen]

*Robinson, Spider **Time Pressure** (Ace 0-441-80932-4, Oct,87 [Sep,87], $16.95, 217pp, hc) Sf novel. Sequel and prequel to **Mindkiller**.

Robinson, Spider **Time Travelers Strictly Cash** (Berkley 0-425-09722-6, Mar,87 [Feb,87], $2.95, 200pp, pb) Reprint (Ace 1981) collection of 11 items plus even more introductions.

*Rochlin, Doris **Frobisch's Angel** (Taplinger 0-8008-3058-X, Jun,87 [Sep,87], $16.95, 331pp, hc) Seriocomic fantasy novel. Frobisch sees an angel in Rome who tells him to "do good," and gives him clairvoyance. A first novel.

*Roemer, Kenneth, Gorman Beauchamp & Nicholas D. Smith, eds. **Utopian Studies 1** Main listing under Gorman Beauchamp.

*Rogers, Michael **Forbidden Sequence** (Bantam 0-553-27080-X, Jan,88 [Nov,87], $4.50, 329pp, pb) Very-near-future sf novel of gene splicing and high-tech skullduggery.

Rohan, Michael Scott **The Anvil of Ice** (Orbit 0-7088-8210-2, Feb,87, £2.95, 352pp, pb) Reprint (Macdonald 1986) fantasy novel with a superb cover. Volume 1 in the "Winter of the World" trilogy. Highly recommended. (PS-P)

*Rohan, Michael Scott **The Forge in the Forest** (Macdonald 0-356-10750-7, Feb,87, £10.95, 408pp, hc) Fantasy novel. Volume 2 in the "Winter of the World" trilogy. Sustains the promise of Volume 1. Highly recommended. (PS-P)

+Rohan, Michael Scott **The Forge in the Forest** (Morrow 0-688-07367-0, Nov,87 [Oct,87], $15.95, 379pp, hc) Epic fantasy novel, second in the "Winter of the World" saga. First American edition (Macdonald 1987).

*Rohmer, Richard **Starmageddon** (Irwin 0-7725-1560-3, 1986 [May,87], price unknown, 241pp, hc) Near-future star wars thriller. This is a 1986 Canadian edition being distributed in the U.S. We missed it last year.

*Roland, Paul **The Curious Case of Richard Fielding and Other Stories** (Lary Press No ISBN, Nov,87 [1987], £1.80, 95pp, pb) Collection of 10 weird stories and 16 lyrics to songs. Illustrated throughout by Alan Hunter.

Ronson, Mark **Ghoul** (Critic's Choice 1-55547-153-6, Mar,87, $2.95, 202pp, pb) Reprint (? 1980) horror novel.

+Ronson, Mark **Ogre** (Critic's Choice 1-55547-161-7, Apr,87, $2.95, 198pp, pb) Horror novel featuring a prehistoric monster. First U.S. edition (Hamlin UK 1980).

+Ronson, Mark **Plague Pit** (Critic's Choice 1-55547-169-2, Apr,87, $2.95, 191pp, pb) Horror/plague novel. First U.S. edition (Hamlin 1981).

*Rosenberg, Joel **The Heir Apparent** (NAL/Signet 0-451-14820-7, May,87 [Apr,87], $3.50, 319pp, pb) Fantasy novel, Book Four of "Guardians of the Flame".

Rosenberg, Joel **The Silver Crown** (NAL/Signet 0-451-14947-5, May,87 [Apr,87], $3.50, 302pp, pb) Reissue (NAL/Signet 1985) fantasy novel, Book 3 of "Guardians of the Flame".

Rosenberg, Joel **The Sleeping Dragon** (NAL/Signet 0-451-14833-9, May,87 [Apr,87], $3.50, 253pp, pb) Reissue (NAL/Signet 1983) fantasy novel, Book 1 of "Guardians of the Flame".

Rosenberg, Joel **The Sword and the Chain** (NAL/Signet 0-451-14946-7, May,87 [Apr,87], $3.50, 251pp, pb) Reissue (NAL/Signet 1984) fantasy novel, Book 2 of "Guardians of the Flame".

*Rosinski, Grzegorz & Jean Van Hamme **Thorgal: The Archers** Main listing under Jean Van Hamme.

*Rossow, William & M. Bradley Kellogg **Lear's Daughters** Main listing under M. Bradley Kellogg.

Rossow, William & M. Bradley Kellogg **The Wave and the Flame** Main listing under M. Bradley Kellogg.

Rovin, Jeff **The Encyclopedia of Superheroes** (Facts on File 0-8160-1679-8, Apr,87 [Mar,87], $19.95, 443pp, tp) Reissue (Facts on File 1985) reference book on comic superheroes. Second printing. UK price £10.95.

*Rovin, Jeff **The Encyclopedia of Supervillains** (Facts on File 0-8160-1356-X, Nov,87 [Oct,87], $29.95, 416pp, hc) Non-fiction, illustrated reference book, a "Who's Who" of comic book villains. This is a companion volume to Rovin's earlier **Encyclopedia of Superheroes**. The current volume mentions a softcover edition on the copyright page, but we have not seen it. UK price £17.95.

*Rovin, Jeff **Re-Animator** (Pocket 0-671-63723-1, May,87 [Apr,87], $3.50, 223pp, pb) Horror novelization.

Rowley, Christopher B. **The Black Ship** (Arrow 0-09-949260-1, Jan,87, £2.95, 310pp, pb) Reprint (Del Rey 1985) sf novel. Sequel to **The War for Eternity**. [First U.K. edition]

Rowley, Christopher B. **The Black Ship** (Century 0-7126-1589-X, Mar,87 [Aug,87], £10.95, 320pp, hc) Reprint (Del Rey 1985) sf novel.

*Rowley, Christopher B. **Golden Sunlands** (Ballantine/Del Rey 0-345-33174-5, Jul,87 [Jun,87], $3.50, 340pp, pb) Sf novel of "a whole world abducted into a Universe of strange possibilities."

Rowley, Christopher B. **Star Hammer** (Arrow 0-09-949270-9, Jul,87, £2.50, 297pp, pb) Reprint (Del Rey 1986) sf novel. [First U.K. edition]

Rowley, Christopher B. **Star Hammer** (Century 0-7126-1627-6, Sep,87, £10.95, 304pp, hc) Reprint (Del Rey 1986) sf novel. [Not seen]

Roy, Archie **Devil in the Darkness** (Apogee 1-869935-04-7, Apr,87 [Jul,87], £1.95, 184pp, pb) Reprint (John Long 1978) horror novel.

Roy, Archie **Sable Night** (Apogee 1-869935-03-9, Apr,87 [Jul,87], £1.95, 184pp, pb) Reprint (John Long 1973) horror novel.

Rubens, Bernice **Our Father** (Hamish Hamilton 0-241-11979-0, Mar,87 [Aug,87], £9.95, 212pp, hc) Reprint (Delacorte) novel about a woman who keeps meeting God.

*Rubin, Marty **The Boiled Frog Syndrome** (Alyson 1-55583-108-7, Sep,87 [Nov,87], $7.95, 231pp, tp) Sf novel, set in the near future, about the U.S. government repressing gays, and the resistance against it.

*Rucker, Rudy **Mind Tools** (Houghton Mifflin 0-395-38315-3, Apr,87, $17.95, 327pp, hc) Non-fiction, associational. A study subtitled "The Five Levels of Mathematical Reality". Rucker writes non-fiction in much the same way he writes sf.

Rucker, Rudy **Software** (Avon 0-380-70177-4, Oct,87 [Sep,87], $2.95, 167pp, pb) Reprint (Ace 1982) sf novel. Winner of the first Philip K. Dick Award.

*Rucker, Rudy, ed. **Mathenauts: Tales of Mathematical Wonder** (Arbor House 0-87795-891-2, Jun,87 [May,87], $18.95, 300pp, hc) Anthology of sf stories dealing with (or taking off from) mathematical concepts.

RUCKER, RUDY, ED.   **SAGE, ALISON**

*Rucker, Rudy, ed. **Mathenauts: Tales of Mathematical Wonder** (Arbor House 0-87795-890-4, Jun,87 [May,87], $9.95, 300pp, tp) Published simultaneously with the hardback edition.

*Rule, Jane **Memory Board** (Pandora 0-86358-190-0, Oct,87, £10.95, 256pp, hc) Literary fantasy novel. [Not seen]

*Rule, Jane **Memory Board** (Pandora 0-86358-191-9, Oct,87 [Dec,87], £4.95, 256pp, tp) Literary fantasy novel.

*Rundle, Anne **Moonbranches** (Macmillan 0-02-777190-3, Oct,86 [Jan,87], $11.95, 163pp, hc) Young-adult Victorian gothic novel of ghosts and terror. Published in 1986 but not seen until now.

Russ, Joanna **The Female Man** (Beacon Press 0-8070-6313-4, 1986 [Jan,87], $7.95, 214pp, tp) Reprint (Bantam 1975) polemic sf novel. This has a 1986 date, but we did not see it until now.

Russ, Joanna **Magic Mommas, Trembling Sisters, Puritans & Perverts** (Crossing Press 0-89594-164-3, 1987 [Jan,87], $16.95, 119pp, hc) Reprint (Crossing Press 1985); associational, collection of essays -- mostly not sf-oriented. Instant hardcover of last year's paperback, previously unseen.

*Russ, Joanna **On Strike Against God** (Women's Press 0-7043-4074-7, Mar,87 [Jul,87], £2.95, 107pp, pb) Reprint (Out & Out Books 1982) of associational interest. A feminist 'coming-out' story. [First U.K. edition]

Russ, Joanna **We Who Are About To** (Women's Press 0-7043-4085-2, Aug,87, £3.50, 170pp, pb) Reprint (Dell 1977) sf novel. This is billed as "First UK publication", but has previously appeared from Methuen.

Russell, Eric Frank **The Best of Eric Frank Russell** (Del Rey 0-345-33223-7, Mar,87 [Jul,87], £2.95, 366pp, pb) Reissue (Del Rey 1978) sf collection. Distributed in the UK by Futura.

Russell, Eric Frank **Sentinels From Space** (Methuen 0-413-15640-0, Nov,87, £2.95, 227pp, pb) Reprint (Bouregy & Curl 1953) sf novel. This contains the Jack Chalker introduction from the Del Rey edition.

Russell, Eric Frank **Three to Conquer** (Methuen 0-413-15650-8, Nov,87, £2.95, 211pp, pb) Reprint (Avalon 1956) sf novel. This contains the Jack Chalker introduction from the Del Rey edition.

+Russell, Jean, ed. **Supernatural Stories: 13 Tales of the Unexpected** (Franklin Watts Orchard 0-531-05723-2, Sep,87, $11.95, 156pp, hc) Anthology of young adult horror stories. First American edition (Orchard UK 1987).

Russo, John **Inhuman** (Grafton 0-586-07314-0, Dec,87 [Nov,87], £2.50, 223pp, pb) Reprint (Pocket 1986) horror novel. [First U.K. edition]

*Russo, John **Voodoo Dawn** (Imagine 0-911137-12-2, Jul,87 [Jun,87], $9.95, 190pp, tp) Voodoo horror novel.

*Russo, Richard, ed. **Dreams Are Wiser Than Men** (North Atlantic 0-938190-94-6, Aug,87 [Jul,87], $14.95, 374pp, tp) Anthology of articles, poems, and stories about dreams, most surreal or fantastic, including five poems by Ursula K. Le Guin from **Wild Angels**.

Ryan, Alan, ed. **Halloween Horrors** (Ace Charter 0-441-31607-7, Oct,87 [Sep,87], $3.50, 245pp, pb) Reprint (Doubleday 1986) horror original anthology.

Ryan, Alan, ed. **Halloween Horrors** (Sphere 0-7221-7561-2, Nov,87 [Oct,87], £2.75, 215pp, pb) Reprint (Doubleday 1986) original horror anthology. This edition appears to have been 'edited' unofficially and was withdrawn and pulped before distribution. Only a few copies appeared in shops. [First U.K. edition]

*Ryan, Alan, ed. **Vampires** (SFBC #10445, Apr,87 [May,87], $6.98, 621pp, hc) Anthology of two centuries of vampire stories, with 32 stories in all plus a recommended list of vampire novels and films. A regular trade edition has been announced, but is predated by the Book Club one.

Ryan, Alan, ed. **Vampires** (Doubleday 0-385-18562-6, Jul,87 [Jun,87], $15.95, 621pp, hc) Reprint (SFBC 1987) anthology of vampire stories.

+Ryman, Geoff **The Unconquered Country** (Bantam Spectra 0-553-26654-3, Jun,87 [May,87], $2.95, 131pp, pb) Sf, fantasy, and surrealism blend in a moving reworking of the Cambodian tragedy. Recommended. (FCM) First U.S. edition (Allen & Unwin 1986).

Saberhagen, Fred **Berserker: Blue Death** (Tor 0-812-55329-2, Sep,87 [Aug,87], $3.50, 282pp, pb) Reprint (Tor 1985) sf novel in the "Berserker" series.

Saberhagen, Fred **Empire of the East, Book 1: The Broken Lands** (Baen 0-671-65380-6, Dec,87 [Nov,87], $2.95, 192pp, pb) Reprint (Ace 1968) fantasy novel. Although this only has the 1968 copyright, it seems to be a photo reprint of the first part of the revised 1979 Ace one-volume edition **Empire of the East**. It also has the Zelazny introduction from the omnibus volume.

Saberhagen, Fred **The First Book of Lost Swords: Woundhealer's Story** (Tor 0-812-55337-3, Jan,88 [Dec,87], $3.95, 289pp, pb) Reprint (Tor 1986) fantasy novel. First book of the second "Swords" trilogy.

Saberhagen, Fred **The Golden People** (Baen 0-671-65378-4, Oct,87 [Sep,87], $3.50, 270pp, pb) Reissue (Baen 1984) sf novel sf novel, an expansion of a short novel (Ace 1964); 2nd printing.

Saberhagen, Fred **The Mask of the Sun** (Tor 0-812-55309-8, Mar,87 [Feb,87], $2.95, 234pp, pb) Reprint (Ace 1979) sf time travel novel.

Saberhagen, Fred **Octagon** (Baen 0-671-65353-9, Sep,87 [Aug,87], $2.95, 281pp, pb) Reprint (Ace 1981) sf novel of a computer game.

Saberhagen, Fred **An Old Friend of the Family** (Tor 0-812-52550-7, Mar,87 [Feb,87], $3.50, 247pp, pb) Reprint (Ace 1979) quasi-horror novel with Dracula as hero. Sequel to **The Holmes-Dracula File**.

*Saberhagen, Fred **Saberhagen: My Best** (Baen 0-671-65645-7, May,87 [Apr,87], $2.95, 311pp, pb) Collection of 17 stories.

*Saberhagen, Fred **The Second Book of Lost Swords: Sightbinder's Story** (Tor 0-312-93032-1, Nov,87 [Oct,87], $14.95, 248pp, hc) Fantasy novel set in a magic kingdom, #2 in the second "Swords" series and fifth in the overall series.

Saberhagen, Fred **The Veils of Azlaroc** (Tor 0-812-55324-1, Jul,87 [Jun,87], $2.95, 216pp, pb) Reprint (Ace 1978) sf novel.

Saberhagen, Fred, ed. **Berserker Base** (Tor 0-812-55327-6, Jun,87 [May,87], $3.95, 316pp, pb) Original anthology of "Berserker" stories by Saberhagen and 6 others, described as a "collaborative novel."

*Sackett, Jeffrey **Stolen Souls** (Bantam 0-553-26937-2, Dec,87 [Nov,87], $3.95, 341pp, pb) Horror novel of ancient Egyptian cults in Upstate New York; a first novel.

*Sadler, Barry **Casca #17: The Warrior** (Ace Charter 0-441-09353-1, Feb,87 [Jan,87], $2.95, 185pp, pb) Fantasy novel in the "Eternal Mercenary" series. This time, Casca encounters "cannibals and carnage in a savage paradise."

*Sadler, Barry **Casca #18: The Cursed** (Jove 0-515-09109-X, Aug,87 [Jul,87], $2.95, 187pp, pb) Latest in a fantasy adventure series about an eternal mercenary. This one is set in China at the turn of the century.

Sagan, Carl **Contact** (Arrow 0-09-946950-2, Apr,87 [Mar,87], £3.50, 431pp, pb) Reprint (Simon & Schuster 1985) sf novel. This has a 1986 copyright date, but has only just appeared.

*Sage, Alison & Dennis Wheatley **The Devil Rides Out** (Beaver 0-09-949750-6, May,87 [Oct,87], £1.75, 155pp, pb) Juvenile abridged retelling of classic Black Magic novel. Volume 4 in the "Fleshcreepers" series.

*Sage, Alison & Dennis Wheatley **The Devil Rides Out** (Hutchinson 0-09-172578-X, May,87 [Oct,87], £5.95, 160pp, hc) Hardcover edition of the above. [Not seen]

SAHA, ARTHUR W., ED.

*Saha, Arthur W., ed. **The Year's Best Fantasy Stories: 13** (DAW 0-88677-233-8, Nov,87 [Oct,87], $2.95, 238pp, pb) Anthology of 11 stories from 1986 plus an introduction/summation of the year in fantasy.

*Saha, Arthur W. & Donald A. Wollheim, ed. **The 1987 Annual World's Best SF** Main listing under Donald A. Wollheim.

Saha, Arthur W. & Donald A. Wollheim, ed. **The 1987 Annual World's Best SF** Main listing under Donald A. Wollheim.

*Saint, H.F. **Memoirs of an Invisible Man** (Atheneum 0-689-11735-3, Apr,87 [Mar,87], $18.95, 396pp, hc) Sf novel. A modern version of Wells' **Invisible Man**.

Saint, H.F. **Memoirs of an Invisible Man** (Viking UK 0-670-81638-8, May,87, £10.95, 396pp, hc) Reprint (Atheneum 1987) literary sf novel. [First U.K. edition]

Saint, H.F. **Memoirs of an Invisible Man** (QPB no ISBN, Jun,87, $9.95, 396pp, tp) Reprint (Atheneum 1987) sf novel, a modern version of **The Invisible Man**. This book club edition is an exact copy of the hardcover, with the jacket printed as the paperback cover, and no ISBN.

*Saintsbury, Elizabeth **George MacDonald: A Short Life** (Canongate 0-86241-092-4, Nov,87, £9.95, 176pp, hc) Biography of George MacDonald. [Not seen]

*Sale, Tim, Lynn Abbey & Robert Lynn Asprin **Thieves' World Graphics 4** (Donning/Starblaze 0-89865-458-0, Jan,87 [Feb,87], $3.95, 55pp, tp) "Graphic novel" adaptation of stories from the fantasy series edited by Asprin and Abbey, with art by Tim Sale.

*Salvaggio, Ruth, Marleen S. Barr & Richard Law **Suzy McKee Charnas, Joan Vinge, Octavia Butler** Main listing under Marleen S. Barr.

*San Souci, Robert D. **Short & Shivery** (Doubleday 0-385-23886-X, Oct,87, $10.95, 175pp, hc) Young-adult anthology of 30 short horror stories from folklore around the world, retold by San Souci.

*Sapir, Richard Ben **Quest** (Dutton 0-525-24548-0, Aug,87, $18.95, 390pp, hc) Fantasy/adventure novel, a pursuit of the Holy Grail in contemporary Manhattan.

*Sarabande, William **The First Americans: Beyond the Sea of Ice** (Bantam 0-553-26889-0, Dec,87 [Nov,87], $4.50, 373pp, pb) Prehistoric novel, first in a new series by the creators of "Wagons West".

*Sarabande, William **Wolves of the Dawn** (Bantam 0-553-25802-8, Feb,87 [Jan,87], $4.50, 453pp, pb) Fantasy novel of ancient Celtic Britain. A chieftain's son seeks his fortune.

*Saramago, Jose **Baltasar and Blimunda** (Harcourt Brace Jovanovich 0-15-110555-3, Oct,87 [Sep,87], $19.95, 304pp, hc) Literary fantasy novel set in old Portugal. Translated from Portuguese by Giovanni Pontiero.

*Sargent, Craig **Last Ranger #4: The Rabid Brigadier** (Popular Library 0-445-20433-8, Aug,87 [Jul,87], $3.50, 216pp, pb) Post-holocaust adventure novel.

*Sargent, Craig **Last Ranger #5: The War Weapons** (Popular Library 0-445-20434-6, Oct,87 [Sep,87], $2.95, pb) Post-holocaust sf adventure novel.

*Sargent, Craig **Last Ranger #6: The Warlord's Revenge** (Popular Library 0-445-20436-2, Jan,88 [Dec,87], $2.95, 184pp, pb) Post-holocaust adventure novel.

*Sargent, Pamela **The Best of Pamela Sargent** (Academy Chicago 0-89733-242-3, Oct,87, $15.95, 322pp, hc) Collection of 14 sf stories plus a foreword by Michael Bishop and an introduction by Pamela Sargent. Edited by Martin H. Greenberg.

*Sargent, Pamela **The Best of Pamela Sargent** (Academy Chicago 0-89733-241-5, Oct,87, $5.95, 322pp, tp) Edited by Martin H. Greenberg. Trade paperback of the above.

Sargent, Pamela **Earthseed** (Harper & Row/Starwanderer 0-694-05600-6, Apr,87, $2.95, 289pp, pb) Reprint (Harper & Row 1983) young-adult sf novel.

Sargent, Pamela **The Shore of Women** (Chatto 0-7011-3239-6, Apr,87, £10.95, 464pp, hc) Reprint (Crown 1986) post-nuclear fantasy novel. [First U.K. edition]

Sargent, Pamela **The Shore of Women** (Bantam Spectra 0-553-26854-6, Oct,87 [Sep,87], $4.95, 471pp, pb) Reprint (Crown 1986) sf novel.

*Sarrantonio, Al **The Boy With Penny Eyes** (Tor 0-812-52560-4, Apr,87 [Mar,87], $3.50, 278pp, pb) Horror novel.

Sarrantonio, Al **Campbell Wood** (Berkley 0-425-10575-X, Nov,87 [Oct,87], $2.95, 180pp, pb) Reprint (Doubleday 1986) horror novel.

Saul, John **Hellfire** (Century 0-7126-1164-9, Oct,87, £10.95, 352pp, hc) Reprint (Bantam 1986) horror novel. [Not seen]

*Saul, John **The Unwanted** (Bantam 0-553-26657-8, Aug,87 [Jul,87], $4.50, 339pp, pb) Horror novel.

*Saul, John **The Unwanted** (Bantam UK 0-553-17462-2, Oct,87, £2.95, 339pp, pb) Horror novel.

*Saunders, David **Encyclopaedia of the Worlds of Doctor Who: A-D** (Piccadilly 0-946826-54-4, Nov,87 [Dec,87], £5.95, 128pp, hc) Volume 1 of another book about Doctor Who.

Saward, Eric **Slipback** (Target 0-426-20263-5, Jan,87, £1.75, 144pp, pb) Reprint (W.H. Allen 1986) novelization of 1st "Doctor Who" radio serial.

*Saxton, Josephine **Little Tours of Hell** (Methuen/Pandora 0-86358-095-5, Dec,86 [Aug,87], $8.95, 146pp, tp) Collection of 14 stories with elements of horror and humor, "Tall Tales of Food and Holidays". This is the 1986 British edition from Routledge & Kegan Paul/Pandora, now available in the U.S. through Methuen. A hardcover at $19.95 is also listed; not seen.

Scanlon, Noel **Black Ashes** (St. Martin's 0-312-90270-0, Jun,87 [Aug,87], $3.95, 222pp, pb) Reprint (St. Martin's 1985) novel of supernatural horror in modern India.

Scarborough, Elizabeth Ann **Bronwyn's Bane** (Bantam UK 0-553-17284-0, Oct,87, £2.95, 286pp, pb) Reprint (Bantam 1983) fantasy novel. Volume 3 in the "Argonia" series. [First U.K. edition]

*Scarborough, Elizabeth Ann **The Goldcamp Vampire** (Bantam Spectra 0-553-26717-5, Nov,87 [Oct,87], $3.50, 247pp, pb) Humorous fantasy novel about a vampire in the Yukon during the 1897 Gold Rush.

Scarborough, Elizabeth Ann **The Harem of Aman Akbar** (Bantam Spectra 0-553-26718-3, Sep,87 [Aug,87], $3.50, 265pp, pb) Reissue (Bantam Spectra 1984) humorous Arabian Nights fantasy novel; 2nd printing.

Scarborough, Elizabeth Ann **Song of Sorcery** (Bantam UK 0-553-17282-4, Apr,87, £1.95, 216pp, pb) Reprint (Bantam 1982) humourous fantasy novel. Volume 1 in the "Argonia" series. [First U.K. edition]

*Scarborough, Elizabeth Ann **Songs from the Seashell Archives, Vol. 1** (Bantam Spectra 0-553-26957-7, Oct,87 [Sep,87], $4.95, 552pp, pb) Omnibus edition of the first 2 books in the "Argonia" fantasy series, **Song of Sorcery** (Bantam 1982) and **The Unicorn Creed** (Bantam 1983).

Scarborough, Elizabeth Ann **The Unicorn Creed** (Bantam UK 0-553-17283-2, Jul,87 [Jun,87], £2.95, 340pp, pb) Reprint (Bantam 1983) humourous fantasy novel. Volume 2 in the "Argonia" series. [First U.K. edition]

SCHIFF, STUART DAVID, ED.

Schiff, Stuart David, ed. **Whispers** (Jove 0-515-08881-1, Feb,87 [Jan,87], $3.50, 253pp, pb) Reprint (Doubleday 1977) horror original anthology.

Schiff, Stuart David, ed. **Whispers II** (Jove 0-515-09252-5, Nov,87 [Oct,87], $3.95, 256pp, pb) Reprint (Doubleday 1979) horror original anthology.

Schiff, Stuart David, ed. **Whispers III** (Jove 0-515-09363-7, Jan,88 [Dec,87], $3.95, 258pp, pb) Reprint (Doubleday 1981) original anthology of 14 horror stories.

*Schiff, Stuart David, ed. **Whispers VI** (Doubleday 0-385-19927-9, Jul,87, $12.95, 181pp, hc) Original anthology of 15 horror stories.

Schmidt, Dennis **Groa's Other Eye** (Orbit 0-7088-3041-2, Jan,87, £2.50, 295pp, pb) Reprint (Ace 1986) fantasy novel. Volume 2 in the "Twilight of the Gods" series. [First U.K. edition]

*Schmidt, Dennis **Twilight of the Gods, Book III: Three Trumps Sounding** (Ace 0-441-83287-3, Jan,88 [Dec,87], $3.95, 342pp, pb) Nordic fantasy novel.

*Schmidt, Stanley, ed. **6 Decades: The Best of Analog** (Davis no ISBN, 1986, free to subscribers, 128pp, pb) Anthology of 6 science fiction stories sent free to new subscribers of *Analog*.

Schoch, Tim **Creeps: An Alien in our School** (Hippo 0-590-70625-X, Jul,87 [Aug,87], £1.50, 150pp, pb) Reprint (Camelot 1985) juvenile sf novel.

*Schuiten, Francois & Peeters **The Great Walls of Samaris** (NBM Publishing 0-918348-36-6, Sep,87 [Oct,87], $9.95, 48pp, tp) Graphic novel. First English translation of the text (Casterman, France, 1984).

Schulman, J. Neil **Alongside Night** (Avon 0-380-75281-6, Aug,87 [Jul,87], $3.50, 240pp, pb) Reprint (Crown 1980) libertarian sf novel. Contains an essay by Samuel Edward Konkin III about economic libertarianism, which is new to this edition.

Schulman, Paul H. & Gary Gerani **Fantastic Television** For main entry see under Gary Gerani.

*Schweitzer, Darrell, ed. **Discovering H.P. Lovecraft** (Starmont House 0-916732-81-9, Sep,87 [Aug,87], $9.95, 153pp, tp) Non-fiction, essays on and by Lovecraft.

Scliar, Moacyr **The Centaur in the Garden** (Ballantine 0-345-35194-0, Jan,88 [Dec,87], $3.95, 248pp, pb) Reprint (Available Press 1985) magic realism fantasy novel. Originally published in Portugal by Editora Nova Fronteira in 1984.

Scliar, Moacyr **The Gods of Raquel** (Ballantine 0-345-35357-9, Jan,88 [Dec,87], $3.50, 119pp, pb) Reprint (Available Press 1986) religious fantasy novel. Originally published in Portugal by L&PM Editoes Ltda., 1978.

*Scortia, Thomas N. & Frank M. Robinson **Blow-Out!** (Franklin Watts 0-531-15030-5, Apr,87, $16.95, 393pp, hc) Near-future disaster novel of threats to a New York-to-Chicago tunnel.

*Scott, Melissa **The Empress of Earth** (Baen 0-671-65364-4, Nov,87 [Oct,87], $3.50, 346pp, pb) Sf novel, third in the "Silence Leigh" trilogy.

*Scott, Melissa **The Kindly Ones** (Baen 0-671-65351-2, Sep,87 [Aug,87], $3.50, 373pp, pb) Sf novel. Absorbing story of a society with an extremely rigid code of honor. (TM)

Scott, Melissa **The Kindly Ones** (SFBC #11443, Oct,87 [Nov,87], $5.98, 342pp, hc) Reprint (Baen 1987) sf novel, first hardcover edition.

+Scott, Michael **Burial Rites** (Berkley 0-425-10109-6, Aug,87 [Jul,87], $3.50, 248pp, pb) Horror novel -- archeologists dig up a Thing. Previously published in England as **The Ice King** (NEL 1986); first American edition. Scott is a pen name for Michael Scott Rohan and Allan J. Scott.

Scott, Michael **The Ice King** (NEL 0-450-40414-5, Feb,87 [Jan,87], £2.50, 252pp, pb) Reprint (NEL 1986) fantasy/horror novel. This is a pseudonym for Michael Scott Rohan & Allan Scott.

*Scott, Michael **The Last of the Fianna** (Pied Piper 0-416-95920-2, Apr,87 [1987], £5.95, 112pp, hc) Juvenile fantasy novel. [Not seen]

*Scott, Michael **Magician's Law** (Sphere 0-7221-7775-5, May,87, £3.50, 305pp, tp) Fantasy Novel. Volume 1 of "Tales of the Bard".

Scott, Sir Walter **The Supernatural Short Stories of Sir Walter Scott** (Riverrun/Calder 0-7145-4086-2, Oct,86 [Jan,87], $8.95, 217pp, tp) Reprint (Calder 1977) collection of ghost stories edited by Michael Hayes. Published in 1986; missed. This is a universal edition, published in England with names of UK, US, and Canadian publishers; distributed in the US by Kampmann.

*Scrocco, Jean L., ill. & Judy Mastrangelo, ed. **Antique Fairy Tales** (Unicorn 0-88101-070-7, Oct,87, $16.95, 216pp, hc) Anthology of 19 fairytales from around the world, abundantly illustrated in color by Mastrangelo. These seem to be retold versions by the editor, Scrocco, with no earlier copyrights given.

*See, Carolyn **Golden Days** (McGraw-Hill 0-07-056120-6, Oct,86 [Jan,87], $15.95, 196pp, hc) Literary novel, partly mainstream but eventually moving into sf and the depiction of nuclear horrors. Published in 1986; missed.

See, Carolyn **Golden Days** (Ballantine Fawcett 0-449-21437-0, Dec,87 [Nov,87], $3.95, 215pp, pb) Reprint (McGraw-Hill 1987) literary sf/fantasy novel.

*Segrelles, Vincente **The Art of Segrelles** (NBM Publishing 0-918348-39-0, Jan,88 [Nov,87], $13.95, 64pp, tp) 8.5" x 11" book of fantasy art, with comments by the artist.

*Segrelles, Vincente **The Mercenary: The Cult of the Sacred Fire and the Formula** (NBM 0-918348-27-7, Oct,87, $10.95, 96pp, tp) Graphic novel, first in a series. First English language edition (Norma Serveis Grafics, Spain, 1983).

*Selves, David **Life Goes on Forever...** (Ansty 0-9511740-0-2, Mar,87 [1987], £9.95, 545pp, hc) Literary sf novel. [Not seen]

*Senn, Steven **The Sand Witch** (Avon/Camelot 0-380-75298-0, Jun,87 [May,87], $2.50, 88pp, pb) Juvenile sf short novel with witches and aliens.

*Serling, Carol, Martin H. Greenberg & Charles G. Waugh, eds. **Rod Serling's Night Gallery Reader** (Dembner 0-934878-93-5, Dec,87 [Nov,87], $15.95, 326pp, hc) Anthology of 18 stories that were made into *Night Gallery* tv episodes.

*Service, Pamela F. **Tomorrow's Magic** (Atheneum 0-689-31320-9, Sep,87 [Oct,87], $14.95, 191pp, hc) Arthurian post-holocaust fantasy novel, sequel to **The Winter of Magic's Return**.

*Service, Pamela F. **When the Night Wind Howls** (Atheneum 0-689-31306-3, Jul,87 [Jun,87], $12.95, 153pp, hc) Juvenile ghost story.

Sewell, Anna & Robin McKinley **Black Beauty** For main listing see under Robin McKinley.

Seymour, Miranda **The Vampire of Verdonia** (Knight 0-340-41466-9, Sep,87 [Nov,87], £1.95, 100pp, tp) Reprint (Deutsch 1986) juvenile horror novel.

Sharp, Allen W. **Book of Science Fiction** (Cambridge Univ. Press 0-521-34020-9, Sep,87, £4.95, 352pp, tp) Collection of four sf gamebooks.

*Sharpe, John Rufus, III **Hogar Lord of the Asyr** (NAL/Signet 0-451-15112-7, Dec,87 [Nov,87], $2.95, 239pp, pb) Fantasy novel, a first novel. "His kingdom stolen by sorcery, can Hogar fight evil in a dark land?"

Shaw, Bob **Medusa's Children** (Gollancz 0-575-04096-3, Sep,87, £2.50, 184pp, pb) Reprint (Gollancz 1977) sf novel.

Shaw, Bob **Night Walk** (Gollancz 0-575-03987-6, May,87, £2.50, 188pp, pb) Reprint (Banner 1967) sf novel.

Shaw, Bob **The Peace Machine** (Grafton 0-586-06991-7, Jan,87, £2.50, 187pp, pb) Reprint (Gollancz 1985) sf novel. Slightly revised edition of **Ground Zero Man** (Avon 1971).

+Shaw, Bob **The Ragged Astronauts** (Baen 0-671-65644-9, Jun,87 [May,87], $15.95, 310pp, hc) Sf novel, first in a trilogy. First U.S. edition (Gollancz 1986). A Hugo nominee.

Shaw, Bob **The Ragged Astronauts** (Orbit 0-7088-8227-7, Aug,87, £2.95, 310pp, pb) Reprint (Gollancz 1986) sf novel. Volume 1 in the "Land of Overland" trilogy.

Shaw, Bob **A Wreath of Stars** (Gollancz 0-575-03980-9, Feb,87, £2.95, 189pp, tp) Reprint (Gollancz 1976) sf novel. Volume 10 of the Gollancz Classic sf series.

Shaw, Bob **A Wreath of Stars** (Baen 0-671-65365-2, Nov,87 [Oct,87], $2.95, 220pp, pb) Reprint (Gollancz 1976) sf novel.

*Shea, Michael **Fat Face** (Axolotl 0-939879-13-1, May,87, $30.00, 36pp, hc) A Chthulhu Mythos horror novelette, with an introduction by Karl Edward Wagner. Limited edition of 300, signed by Shea and Wagner. There are also 50 leatherbound copies, for $65.00.

*Shea, Michael **Fat Face** (Axolotl 0-939879-14-X, May,87 [May,87], $6.00, 36pp, ph) Trade paperback edition of the above. Limited to 500 copies, also signed.

Shea, Michael **In Yana, The Touch of Undying** (Grafton 0-586-07145-8, Aug,87, £3.50, 332pp, pb) Reprint (DAW 1985) fantasy novel. [First U.K. edition]

*Shea, Michael **Polyphemus** (Arkham House 0-87054-155-2, Nov,87 [Oct,87], $16.95, 245pp, hc) Collection of 7 stories plus an introduction by Algis Budrys. Recommended. (FCM)

Sheckley, Robert **The 10th Victim** (NAL/Signet 0-451-14969-6, Sep,87 [Aug,87], $2.95, 158pp, pb) Reprint (Ballantine 1966) sf novel, first in the "Victim" series and basis of the movie *The Seventh Victim*.

*Sheckley, Robert **Hunter/Victim** (NAL/Signet 0-451-15142-9, Jan,88 [Dec,87], $3.50, 269pp, pb) Sf novel, sequel to **The 10th Victim** and **Victim Prime**.

Sheckley, Robert **Journey Beyond Tomorrow** (Gollancz 0-575-04122-6, Aug,87, £3.50, 189pp, tp) Reprint (Signet 1962) sf novel. Volume 15 in the Gollancz Classic SF series.

Sheckley, Robert **The Tenth Victim** (Methuen 0-413-16560-4, Dec,87 [Nov,87], £2.50, 118pp, pb) Reprint (Ballantine 1966) sf novel. Volume 1 in the "Hunt" series.

*Sheckley, Robert **Victim Prime** (Methuen 0-413-41790-5, Jan,87, £9.95, 203pp, hc) Sf novel, an indirect (and very minor) sequel to **The Seventh Victim** (FCM).

+Sheckley, Robert **Victim Prime** (NAL/Signet 0-451-14864-9, Jun,87 [May,87], $3.50, 221pp, pb) Sf novel, sequel to **The 10th Victim**. First U.S. edition (Methuen 1987).

Sheckley, Robert **Victim Prime** (Methuen 0-413-41800-6, Jul,87, £2.50, 203pp, pb) Reprint (Methuen 1986) sf novel. Volume 2 in the "Hunt" series.

Sheffield, Charles **Between the Strokes of Night** (Headline 0-7472-3077-3, Dec,87, £2.95, 346pp, pb) Reprint (Baen 1985) sf novel. [First U.K. edition]

Sheffield, Charles **The McAndrew Chronicles** (Tor 0-812-55429-9, Jan,88 [Dec,87], $3.50, 243pp, pb) Reissue (Tor 1983) sf novel; 2nd printing.

*Shefner, Evelyn **Common Body, Royal Bones** (Coffee House Press 0-918273-33-1, Dec,87 [Nov,87], $9.95, 119pp, tp) Collection of 3 literary stories, one about a woman who transmits her thoughts and another about a 7-foot-tall princess from a mythical European country.

Shelley, Mary W. **Frankenstein** (Running Press 0-89471-520-8, Dec,87, £3.95, 170pp, tp) Reprint (Lackington, Hughes, Harding, Mavor & Jones 1818) horror novel. [Not seen]

*Shelley, Mary W. & David Campton **Frankenstein** For main entry see under David Campton.

*Shelley, Mary W., [ref.] **The Monster in the Mirror: Gender and the Sentimental/Gothic Myth in Frankenstein** Main listing under Mary K. Patterson Thornburg.

Shepard, Leslie A., ed. **Dracula Book of Great Vampire Stories** (Citadel 0-8065-0704-7, May,87 [Jun,87], £6.95, 270pp, tp) Reissue (Citadel 1977) horror anthology. [First U.K. edition, not seen]

Shepard, Lucius **Green Eyes** (Grafton 0-586-07104-0, Jun,87, £3.50, 332pp, pb) Reprint (Ace 1984) sf/occult novel.

*Shepard, Lucius **The Jaguar Hunter** (Arkham House 0-87054-154-4, May,87 [Mar,87], $21.95, 404pp, hc) Collection of 11 stories by the best of the new writers. Most of these were awards nominees. Highly recommended. (CNB)

*Shepard, Lucius **Life During Wartime** (Bantam 0-553-34381-5, Oct,87 [Sep,87], $7.95, 438pp, tp) Sf novel based on Shepard's stories of near-future war in Guatamala, including the Nebula-winning "R&R".

*Sherrell, Carl **Skraelings** (Ace/New Infinities 0-441-76891-1, Aug,87 [Jul,87], $2.95, pb) Viking fantasy novel. Probably a sequel to **Raver** (1977).

*Shetterly, Will & Emma Bull, eds. **Liavek: Wizard's Row** (Ace 0-441-48190-6, Sep,87 [Aug,87], $2.95, 212pp, pb) Shared-world original anthology, third in the series. 8 stories, plus appendices of songs and background material.

Shinn, Thelma J. **Worlds With Women: Myth and Mythmaking in Fantastic Literature by Women** (Greenwood 0-313-25101-0, Jan,87, £27.00, 240pp, hc) Reprint (Greenwood 1986) critical study of sf written by women. [First U.K. edition]

Shirley, John **Eclipse** (Popular Library Questar 0-445-20506-7, Nov,87 [Oct,87], $3.50, 310pp, pb) Reprint (Bluejay 1985) sf novel, first in trilogy "A Song Called Youth." A post-holocaust "apolyptic, pop-inflected, rock-driven vision!" (or so it says on the cover, which also dubs this "The Ultimate Cyberpunk Saga").

*Shoemaker, Michael T. & Cuyler W. Brooks, Jr., eds. **Guinevere and Lancelot & Others** Main listing under Arthur Machen.

*Shwartz, Susan M. **Byzantium's Crown** (Popular Library Questar 0-445-20356-0, Apr,87 [Mar,87], $3.50, 272pp, pb) Fantasy novel set in an alternate Byzantium where magic works.

Shwartz, Susan M. **Byzantium's Crown** (Pan 0-330-29789-9, Aug,87 [Jul,87], £2.95, 254pp, pb) Reprint (Questar 1987) alternate history novel. Volume 1 in the "Heirs to Byzantium" series. [First U.K. edition]

*Shwartz, Susan M. **The Woman of Flowers** (Popular Library Questar 0-445-20358-7, Nov,87 [Oct,87], $3.50, 308pp, pb) Alternate world historical fantasy novel, where Antony and Cleopatra conquered Rome; "Heirs to Byzantium", Book 2.

*Shwartz, Susan M. **The Woman of Flowers** (Pan 0-330-30065-2, Dec,87 [Nov,87], £2.95, 294pp, pb) Sf novel. Simultaneous with US (Questar) edition. Volume 2 in the "Heirs to Byzantium" series.

*Sibley, Brian **Snow White and the Seven Dwarfs & the Making of the Classic Film** (Simon & Schuster 0-671-64439-4, Aug,87 [Jul,87], $14.95, 88pp, hc) Non-fiction, film history with photos and illustrations.

*Siegel, Barbara & Scott Siegel **Firebrats #1: The Burning Land** (Pocket Archway 0-671-55007-1, Jul,87 [Jun,87], $2.50, 152pp, pb) First in a young-adult post-holocaust sf adventure series(!) A high school jock and an aspiring teenage actress survive WWIII.

*Siegel, Barbara & Scott Siegel **Firebrats #2: Survivors** (Pocket Archway 0-671-55733-5, Jul,87 [Jun,87], $2.50, 150pp, pb) Young adult post-holocaust adventure novel.

*Siegel, Barbara & Scott Siegel **Firebrats #3: Thunder Mountain** (Pocket Archway 0-671-55794-7, Sep,87 [Aug,87], $2.50, 146pp, pb) Latest in a juvenile post-holocaust adventure series.

*Siegel, Scott & Barbara Siegel **Firebrats #1: The Burning Land** Main listing under Barbara Siegel.

*Siegel, Scott & Barbara Siegel **Firebrats #2: Survivors** Main listing under Barbara Siegel.

*Siegel, Scott & Barbara Siegel **Firebrats #3: Thunder Mountain** Main listing under Barbara Siegel.

*Sievert, John **C.A.D.S. #4: Tech Strike Force** (Zebra 0-8217-1993-9, Feb,87 [Jan,87], $2.95, 270pp, pb) Fourth novel in the sf post-holocaust adventure series.

Silverberg, Robert **Beyond the Safe Zone** (Warner 0-446-30174-4, Jun,87 [May,87], $3.95, 565pp, pb) Reprint (Donald I. Fine 1986) collection. These stories, written 1968 to 1974, are most of Silverberg's best. Highly recommended. (CNB)

Silverberg, Robert **The Book of Skulls** (NEL 0-450-42161-9, Aug,87, £2.50, 222pp, pb) Reissue (Scribner's 1971) sf novel.

Silverberg, Robert **Capricorn Games** (Pan 0-330-25631-9, Apr,87 [May,87], £2.50, 191pp, pb) Reissue (Random House 1976) sf collection.

Silverberg, Robert **The Feast of Saint Dionysus** (NEL 0-450-42160-0, Aug,87, £2.95, 255pp, pb) Reprint (Scribner's 1975) sf collection.

Silverberg, Robert **Invaders From Earth** (Tor 0-812-55464-7, Mar,87 [Feb,87], $2.95, 190pp, pb) Reprint (Ace 1958) sf novel.

Silverberg, Robert **The Man in the Maze** (Avon 0-380-00198-5, May,87 [Apr,87], $2.95, 192pp, pb) Reissue (Avon 1969) sf novel; 5th printing.

Silverberg, Robert **The Masks of Time** (Gollancz 0-575-03990-6, May,87, £2.95, 252pp, pb) Reprint (Ballantine 1968) sf novel.

Silverberg, Robert **Nightwings** (Avon 0-380-41467-8, Apr,87 [Mar,87], $3.50, 190pp, pb) Reissue (Avon 1969) sf novel. The first section of this book won a Hugo. Contains some of Silverberg's best writing. Recommended. (CNB)

Silverberg, Robert **Nightwings** (Futura 0-7088-8235-8, Jul,87, £2.50, 192pp, pb) Reprint (Avon 1969) sf novel.

*Silverberg, Robert **Project Pendulum** (Walker 0-8027-6712-5, Sep,87 [Oct,87], $15.95, 200pp, hc) Young adult sf novel with illustrations by Moebius.

Silverberg, Robert **The Second Trip** (Avon 0-380-54874-7, Jun,87 [May,87], $3.50, 192pp, pb) Reissue (SFBC 1972) sf novel.

Silverberg, Robert **Son of Man** (Warner 0-446-34511-3, Sep,87 [Aug,87], $3.95, 213pp, pb) Reprint (Ballantine 1971) sf novel.

Silverberg, Robert **Star of Gypsies** (SFBC #10579, Feb,87, $5.98, 378pp, hc) Reprint (Fine 1986) sf novel.

Silverberg, Robert **Star of Gypsies** (Gollancz 0-575-04014-9, Mar,87 [Aug,87], £11.95, 397pp, hc) Reprint (Fine 1986) sf novel. [First U.K. edition]

Silverberg, Robert **The Stochastic Man** (Warner 0-446-34507-5, Jul,87 [Jun,87], $3.95, 240pp, pb) Reprint (Harper & Row 1975) sf novel.

Silverberg, Robert **Thorns** (Orbit 0-7088-8238-2, Dec,87 [Nov,87], £2.50, 158pp, pb) Reprint (Ballantine 1967) sf novel. This is arguably Silverberg's best novel. Strongly recommended.

Silverberg, Robert **Those Who Watch** (NAL/Signet 0-451-15019-8, Oct,87 [Sep,87], $2.95, 143pp, pb) Reissue (NAL 1967) sf novel.

Silverberg, Robert **To Live Again** (Gollancz 0-575-03989-2, Jul,87, £2.95, 231pp, pb) Reprint (Doubleday 1969) sf novel.

Silverberg, Robert **Tom O'Bedlam** (Orbit 0-7088-3372-1, May,87, £2.95, 320pp, pb) Reprint (Fine 1985) sf novel.

Silverberg, Robert **Tower of Glass** (Warner 0-446-34509-1, Aug,87 [Jul,87], $3.95, 184pp, pb) Reprint (Scribner's 1970) sf novel.

Silverberg, Robert **Tower of Glass** (Orbit 0-7088-8243-9, Oct,87, £2.50, 206pp, pb) Reprint (Scribner's 1970) sf novel.

Silverberg, Robert **Up the Line** (Gollancz 0-575-04038-6, Dec,87, £2.95, 250pp, pb) Reprint (Ballantine 1969) sf novel.

*Silverberg, Robert, ed. **Robert Silverberg's Worlds of Wonder** (Warner 0-446-51369-5, Oct,87 [Sep,87], $17.95, 352pp, hc) Anthology of 13 stories. Introduction and biographical essay by Silverberg.

Silverberg, Robert & Martin H. Greenberg, eds. **Great Science Fiction of the 20th Century** (Crown/Avenel 0-517-64124-0, 1987 [Nov,87], $8.98, 726pp, hc) Anthology. This is an "instant remainder" of **The Arbor House Treasury of Modern Science Fiction**, omitting one story, "The Marching Morons" by C.M. Kornbluth.

*Simak, Clifford D. **Brother and Other Stories** (Severn House 0-7278-1417-6, Apr,87 [Mar,87], £8.95, 165pp, hc) A new collection of Simak's short stories, edited by Francis Lyall. This has a 1986 copyright date, but has only just appeared.

Simak, Clifford D. **Cemetery World** (Methuen 0-413-41990-8, Mar,87, £2.50, 191pp, pb) Reissue (Putnam 1973) sf novel.

Simak, Clifford D. **The Fellowship of the Talisman** (Ballantine/Del Rey 0-345-33957-6, Feb,87 [Jan,87], $3.50, 314pp, pb) Reissue (Del Rey 1978) fantasy novel; 5th printing.

Simak, Clifford D. **The Goblin Reservation** (Methuen 0-413-14530-1, Mar,87, £2.50, 190pp, pb) Reprint (Putnam 1968) sf novel.

Simak, Clifford D. **Highway to Eternity** (Severn House 0-7278-1498-2, Aug,87 [Dec,87], £9.95, 289pp, hc) Reprint (Del Rey 1986, as **Highway of Eternity**) sf novel. Listed as **Highway of Eternity** on title page only. [First U.K. edition]

Simak, Clifford D. **The Marathon Photograph** (Methuen 0-413-59060-7, Jun,87, £2.50, 171pp, pb) Reprint (Severn House 1986) sf collection.

Simak, Clifford D. **Out of Their Minds** (Methuen 0-413-15320-7, Sep,87, £2.50, 175pp, pb) Reprint (Putnam 1970) sf novel.

Simmons, Dan **Song of Kali** (Headline 0-7472-3044-7, Aug,87, £2.95, 311pp, pb) Reprint (Bluejay 1985) horror novel. [First U.K. edition]

Simmons, Dan **Song of Kali** (Headline 0-7472-0033-5, Sep,87, £9.95, 320pp, hc) Reprint (Bluejay 1985) horror novel. [Not seen]

*Simon, Jo **Beloved Captain** (Avon 0-380-89771-7, Jan,88 [Dec,87], $3.95, 320pp, pb) Time travel fantasy romance novel set in Nantucket.

*Singer, Marilyn **Ghost Host** (Harper & Row 0-06-025623-0, Aug,87, $11.95, 182pp, hc) Juvenile ghost story, with a teenage football player and a poltergeist.

Skipp, John M. & Craig Spector **The Clean-up** (Bantam UK 0-553-17381-2, Aug,87, £2.95, 379pp, pb) Reprint (Bantam 1987) humourous horror novel. [First U.K. edition]

*Skipp, John M. & Craig Spector **The Cleanup** (Bantam 0-553-26056-1, Mar,87, $3.95, 379pp, pb) Horror novel.

+Sladek, John **Roderick** (Carroll & Graf 0-88184-325-3, Jul,87 [Jun,87], $3.95, 347pp, pb) Satiric sf novel. First complete American edition (Granada 1980). The first half has appeared in the U.S. as **Roderick** (Pocket Timescape 1982), but the second half appears here for the first time. This hilarious novel of a robot growing up is highly recommended. (CNB)

Sleator, William **Fingers** (Bantam Starfire 0-553-25004-3, Nov,87 [Oct,87], $2.50, 197pp, pb) Reissue (Atheneum 1983) young adult humorous supernatural novel; 2nd Bantam printing.

Sleator, William **Interstellar Pig** (Hodder & Stoughton 0-340-39787-X, Jan,87 [Jun,87], £6.95, 197pp, hc) Reprint (Dutton 1984) juvenile sf novel. [First U.K. edition]

SLONCZEWSKI, JOAN   **SOBCHACK, VIVIAN**

Slonczewski, Joan **A Door Into Ocean** (Avon 0-380-70150-2, Feb,87 [Jan,87], $3.95, 406pp, pb) Reprint (Arbor House 1986) anthropological sf novel set on a watery world of women who share everything.

Slonczewski, Joan **A Door Into Ocean** (The Women's Press 0-7043-4069-0, May,87, £4.95, 403pp, tp) Reprint (Arbor House 1986) sf novel.

Slote, Alfred **My Robot Buddy** (Harper & Row/Trophy 0-06-440165-0, May,86 [Jan,87], $2.50, 70pp, tp) Reissue (Lippincott 1975) juvenile sf novella. Published in 1986; missed.

Slote, Alfred **My Trip to Alpha 1** (Harper & Row/Trophy 0-06-440166-9, May,86 [Jan,87], $2.50, 96pp, tp) Reprint (Lippincott 1978) juvenile sf novella. Published in 1986; missed.

*Slusser, George E. & Eric S. Rabkin, eds. **Aliens: The Anthropology of Science Fiction** (Southern Illinois Univ. Press 0-8093-1375-8, Nov,87 [Dec,87], $27.50, 243pp, hc) Non-fiction, critical studies; essays on aliens in sf. These essays are from the 1986 J. Lloyd Eaton conference.

*Slusser, George E. & Eric S. Rabkin, eds. **Intersections: Fantasy and Science Fiction** (Southern Illinois Univ. Press 0-8093-1374-X, Oct,87, $29.95, 252pp, hc) Non-fiction, 17 essays on fantasy and science fiction from the seventh annual J. Lloyd Eaton Conference. These tend to grapple with the differences and similarities between sf and fantasy. Nobody agrees, but there's lots of food for thought. Recommended. (CNB)

*Slusser, George E., Eric S. Rabkin & Colin Greenland, eds. **Storm Warnings: Science Fiction Confronts the Future** (S. Illinois Univ. Press 0-8093-1376-6, Apr,87, $26.95, xi + 278pp, hc) Non-fiction, 17 essays written for the sixth Eaton Conference on Fantasy and Science Fiction, held in 1984. The most interesting section is about **1984** the novel. (CNB)

Smith, A.C.H. **Labyrinth** (P. Maitland 0-03-062436-3, Oct,87 [1987], £3.25, 186pp, hc) Reprint (Holt 1986) juvenile fantasy novel. [Not seen]

Smith, Cordwainer **Quest of the Three Worlds** (Gollancz 0-575-04125-0, Dec,87, £2.50, 184pp, pb) Reprint (Ace 1966) sf collection. [First U.K. edition]

*Smith, David C. **H.G. Wells, Desperately Mortal** (Yale 0-300-03672-8, Sep,86 [Jan,87], $29.95, 634pp, hc) Non-fiction, biography by "a believer in the possibility of a Wellsian future." Published in 1986 but missed. This is a fascinating story of Wells' life and loves. Wells the fiction writer gets little notice. (CNB)

Smith, E.E. "Doc" **Children of the Lens** (Berkley 0-425-10034-0, Jun,87 [May,87], $2.95, 255pp, pb) Reissue (Fantasy Press 1954) sf novel, "Lensman" #6. The finale of the most famous space opera series of all time. 3rd Berkley printing.

Smith, E.E. "Doc" **Gray Lensman** (Berkley 0-425-09664-5, Feb,87 [Jan,87], $2.95, 253pp, pb) Reissue (Fantasy Press 1951) sf novel, #4 in the "Lensman" series; 3rd Berkley printing.

Smith, E.E. "Doc" **The Imperial Stars** (Grafton 0-586-04334-9, Feb,87 [Jul,87], £1.95, 155pp, pb) Reissue (Pyramid 1976) sf novel. Volume 1 in the "Family D'Alembert" series.

Smith, E.E. "Doc" **Second Stage Lensman** (Berkley 0-425-09787-0, Apr,87 [Mar,87], $2.95, 271pp, pb) Reissue (Fantasy Press 1953) sf novel, Book 5 of the most famous space opera series.

Smith, Gregory Blake **The Devil in the Dooryard** (Ballantine 0-345-34706-4, Sep,87 [Aug,87], $4.95, 308pp, pb) Reprint (Morrow 1980) fantasy novel, a comic ghost story.

*Smith, Gregory J. **Starquest, Vol.2: Operation Master Planet** (Bethany House 0-87123-673-7, Oct,86 [Jan,87], $4.95, 189pp, tp) Sf novel, second in a Christian-oriented series. Issued in 1986 but not seen until now.

*Smith, Guy N. **Alligators** (Arrow 0-09-950150-3, Mar,87, £2.25, 176pp, pb) Horror novel.

Smith, Guy N. **Bats Out of Hell** (NEL 0-450-03873-4, Oct,87 [Sep,87], £1.95, 157pp, pb) Reissue (NEL 1978) horror novel.

*Smith, Guy N. **Bloodshow** (Arrow 0-09-952270-5, Jul,87, £2.50, 207pp, pb) Horror novel.

Smith, Guy N. **Death Bell** (Arrow 0-09-938230-X, Jul,87, £2.25, 200pp, pb) Reissue (Hamlyn 1980) horror novel.

*Smith, Guy N. **Demons** (Arrow 0-09-948470-6, Nov,87, £2.50, 184pp, pb) Horror novel. Sequel to **Death Bell**.

+Smith, Guy N. **Entombed** (Dell 0-440-12280-5, Nov,87 [Oct,87], $3.50, 189pp, pb) Horror novel. First U.S. edition (Arrow 1982).

Smith, Guy N. **Locusts** (Arrow 0-09-950300-X, Sep,87, £2.50, 230pp, pb) Reprint (Hamlyn 1979) horror novel.

*Smith, Guy N. **The Plague** (NEL 0-450-41686-0, Oct,87 [Sep,87], £1.95, 160pp, pb) Horror novel. Sequel to **Thirst**.

+Smith, Guy N. **The Wood** (Dell 0-440-19753-8, Dec,87 [Nov,87], $3.50, 191pp, pb) Horror novel. First U.S. edition (NEL 1985).

*Smith, L.J. **The Night of the Solstice** (Macmillan 0-02-785840-5, Oct,87, $14.95, 231pp, hc) Young adult fantasy novel of magic and an evil sorcerer trying to gain entrance to our world. A first novel.

Smith, Martin Cruz **Nightwing** (Hill & Co. 0-940595-05-2, May,87, $9.95, 224pp, tp) Reprint (Norton 1977) thriller/horror novel with an American Indian mythology background.

*Smith, Nicholas D., Gorman Beauchamp & Kenneth Roemer, eds. **Utopian Studies 1** Main listing under Gorman Beauchamp.

*Smith, Stephanie **The Boy Who Was Thrown Away** (Atheneum 0-689-31343-8, Sep,87 [Oct,87], $14.95, 250pp, hc) Young adult fantasy novel, a sequel to **Snow Eyes**.

*Smith, Susan **Samantha Slade #2: Confessions of a Teenage Frog** (Pocket Archway 0-671-63714-2, Oct,87, $2.50, 133pp, pb) Juvenile fantasy novel.

*Smith, Susan **Samantha Slade #3: Our Friend, Public Nuisance No. 1** (Pocket Archway 0-671-63715-0, Dec,87 [Nov,87], $2.50, 144pp, pb) Juvenile fantasy novel, third in a series about the sitter for an "Addams Family"-like family. Includes magic, pet dinosaurs, etc.

*Smith, Susan **Samantha Slade, Monster-Sitter** (Pocket Archway 0-671-63713-4, Oct,87, $2.50, 130pp, pb) Juvenile fantasy novel, first in a series.

*Smith, Terrence Lore **Yours Truly, From Hell** (St. Martin's 0-312-89828-2, Jul,87, $17.95, 336pp, hc) Horror novel of a psychic and his visions of Jack the Ripper.

Smith, Thomas G. **Industrial Light & Magic: The Art of Special Effects** (Ballantine/Del Rey 0-345-32263-0, Nov,87 [Oct,87], $55.00, 279pp, hc) Reissue (Del Rey 1986) non-fiction/art book. 2nd printing.

*Snodgrass, Melinda M. **Circuit Breaker** (Berkley 0-425-09776-5, May,87 [Apr,87], $2.95, 263pp, pb) Sf novel, sequel to **Circuit**.

*Snodgrass, Melinda M. & Victor Milan **Runespear** Main listing under Victor Milan.

*Snodgrass, Melinda M., ed. **A Very Large Array** (Univ. of New Mexico Press 0-8263-1013-3, Dec,87 [Nov,87], $16.95, 264pp, hc) Anthology of 12 sf stories (3 originals) by writers living in New Mexico.

*Snyder, Midori **Soulstring** (Ace 0-441-77591-8, Nov,87 [Oct,87], $2.95, 182pp, pb) Fantasy novel. A first novel.

*Sobchack, Vivian **Screening Space: The American Science Fiction Film** (Ungar 0-8044-6886-9, Jan,87, $14.95, 345pp, tp) Non-fiction; film reference/critical study. This is partially a reprint of The Limits of Infinity: The American Science Fiction Film 1950-1975 (1980), with a new chapter added to bring it up to date. It's an academic/philosophical look at sf films.

*Sobol, Donald J. **The Amazing Power of Ashur Fine** (Macmillan 0-02-786270-4, Nov,86 [Jan,87], $10.95, 114pp, hc) Juvenile fantasy novel of a boy endowed with extraordinary powers by an ancient African elephant. Published in 1986, but missed.

Sommer-Bodenburg, Angela **The Vampire Takes a Trip** (Pocket 0-671-64822-5, Oct,87, $2.50, 155pp, pb) Reprint (Dial 1984) juvenile fantasy novel. Originally published in German (Rowoht Taschenbuch Verlag 1982).

*Sommers, Beverly **Time and Again** (Worldwide Library 0-373-97042-0, Aug,87, $3.95, 253pp, pb) Yet another time travel romance. A modern woman finds herself in 1906 San Francisco.

Somtow, S.P. **The Aquiliad: Aquila in the New World** (Ballantine/Del Rey 0-345-33867-7, Jan,88 [Dec,87], $3.50, 247pp, pb) Reprint (Timescape 1983) alternate-world novel with the whole world ruled by a more modern Rome.

*Somtow, S.P. **Forgetting Places** (Tor 0-312-93030-5, Oct,87 [Sep,87], $14.95, 216pp, hc) Non-sf, associational. A straight novel by a well-known sf writer (Somtow Sucharitkul).

Somtow, S.P. **The Shattered Horse** (Tor 0-812-55515-5, Dec,87 [Nov,87], $3.95, 464pp, pb) Reprint (Tor 1986) fantasy novel about the Trojan War.

+Sonntag, Linda, ed. **The Ghost Story Treasury** (Putnam 0-399-21477-1, Nov,87 [Oct,87], $12.95, 93pp, hc) Anthology of 15 ghost stories. First U.S. edition (Kingfisher 1987).

*South, Malcolm, ed. **Mythical and Fabulous Creatures: A Sourcebook and Research Guide** (Greenwood 0-313-24338-7, Mar,87 [Apr,87], $49.95, 393pp, hc) Non-fiction, reference book. Of particular interest to would-be fantasy trilogists.

*Spark, Muriel **Mary Shelley: A Biography** (Dutton/William Abrahms 0-525-24535-9, Jul,87 [Aug,87], $18.95, 248pp, hc) Non-fiction, biography; this may be an expansion of an earlier work.

*Spark, Muriel **The Stories of Muriel Spark** (Bodley Head 0-370-31020-9, Apr,87 [Oct,87], £12.95, 314pp, hc) Collection of short stories, some with a supernatural element.

Spearing, Judith **Ghosts Who Went to School** (Hippo 0-590-40452-0, Aug,87, £1.95, 139pp, pb) Reprint (Atheneum 1966) juvenile ghost novel. [First U.K. edition]

Spector, Craig & John M. Skipp **The Clean-up** For main entry see under John Skipp.

*Spector, Craig & John M. Skipp **The Cleanup** Main listing under John M. Skipp.

*Spencer, Kathleen **Charles Williams** (Starmont House 0-916732-79-7, Jan,87, $7.95, 104pp, tp) Nonfiction, critical study.

*Spinrad, Norman **Little Heroes** (Bantam Spectra 0-553-05207-1, Jul,87 [Jun,87], $18.95, 486pp, hc) Sf novel of sex, drugs, and rock'n'roll.

*Spivack, Charlotte **Merlin's Daughters: Contemporary Women Writers of Fantasy** (Greenwood 0-313-24194-5, Jan,87 [Mar,87], $29.95, 185pp, hc) Nonfiction, critical study of 10 women fantasy writers.

Springer, Nancy **Chains of Gold** (Macdonald 0-356-14801-7, Aug,87, £10.95, 230pp, hc) Reprint (Arbor House 1986) fantasy novel. [First U.K. edition]

*Springer, Nancy **Chance & Other Gestures of the Hand of Fate** (Baen 0-671-65337-7, Sep,87 [Aug,87], $3.50, 240pp, pb) Collection of 8 stories and three poems; the second half of the title work is a new continuation. Grim, effective fantasy and horror (FCM).

*Springer, Nancy **A Horse to Love** (Harper & Row 0-06-025824-1, 1987 [Feb,87], $11.50, 181pp, hc) Non-sf/fantasy, associational; juvenile novel by an sf author.

*Springer, Nancy **Madbond** (Tor 0-812-55486-8, Jun,87 [May,87], $2.95, 214pp, pb) Fantasy novel, Book I in the "Sea King" trilogy.

*Springer, Nancy **Mindbond** (Tor 0-812-55492-2, Nov,87 [Oct,87], $2.95, 243pp, pb) Fantasy novel, Vol. II of "The Sea King Trilogy".

*St. Alcorn, Lloyd **Halberd: Dream Warrior** (NAL/Signet 0-451-15016-3, Oct,87 [Sep,87], $2.95, 253pp, pb) Fantasy novel of a Viking warrior/shaman, first in the "Dreamquest" series. The author's real name, according to the copyright page, is David N. Meyer II. Why a pseudonym?

*St. Clair, David **The Devil Rocked Her Cradle** (Corgi 0-552-12705-1, Sep,87, £2.95, 362pp, pb) Horror novel about a possessed child.

St. Clair, David **Mine to Kill** (Critic's Choice 1-55547-165-X, Apr,87, $3.95, 351pp, pb) Reprint (Pinnacle 1985) occult horror novel based on a 19th century case of spiritual possession.

*St. George, Judith **Haunted** (Methuen 0-416-02452-1, Apr,87, £7.95, 160pp, hc) Juvenile supernatural novel. [Not seen]

St. George, Judith **Haunted** (Teens 0-416-06232-6, Oct,87, £1.95, 158pp, pb) Reprint (Methuen 1987) juvenile ghost novel.

*St. George, Judith **Who's Scared? Not Me!** (Putnam 0-399-21481-X, Oct,87, $13.95, 174pp, hc) Juvenile fantasy time travel ghost story novel.

Stacy, Ryder **Doomsday Warrior # 4: Bloody America** (Futura 0-7088-3234-2, Mar,87, £2.50, 271pp, pb) Reprint (Zebra 1985) post-holocaust adventure novel. [First U.K. edition]

Stacy, Ryder **Doomsday Warrior # 5: America's Last Declaration** (Futura 0-7088-3565-1, Oct,87 [Nov,87], £2.50, 256pp, pb) Reprint (Zebra 1985) post-holocaust adventure. [First U.K. edition]

*Stacy, Ryder **Doomsday Warrior #10: American Nightmare** (Zebra 0-8217-2021-X, Mar,87 [Feb,87], $2.50, 256pp, pb) Post-holocaust sf adventure novel.

*Stacy, Ryder **Doomsday Warrior #11: American Eden** (Zebra 0-8217-2098-8, May,87, $2.50, 268pp, pb) Post-holocaust sf novel.

*Stacy, Ryder **Doomsday Warrior #12: Death, American Style** (Zebra 0-8217-2211-5, Nov,87 [Oct,87], $2.50, 272pp, pb) Post-holocaust sf adventure novel.

*Stamey, Sara **Wild Card Run** (Berkley 0-425-09705-6, Apr,87 [Mar,87], $2.95, 232pp, pb) Science fiction novel, a first novel.

*Stamper, J.B. **More Tales for the Midnight Hour** (Scholastic Apple 0-590-41184-5, Oct,87, $2.50, 117pp, pb) Original collection of 13 juvenile horror stories.

Standring, Lesley **The Doctor Who Illustrated A-Z** (Target 0-426-20299-6, Mar,87, £3.50, 121pp, tp) Reprint (W.H. Allen 1985) associational book about Doctor Who.

Stapledon, Olaf **Last and First Men** (Penguin 0-14-008088-0, Mar,87, £3.95, 327pp, tp) Reissue (Methuen 1930) philosophical sf novel. In the Penguin sf Classics series.

Stapledon, Olaf **Star Maker** (St. Martin's/Jeremy P. Tarcher 0-87477-435-7, Apr,87, $8.95, 272pp, tp) Reprint (Methuen 1937) classic sf novel, with a new foreword by Brian Aldiss. This contains "the original, unpublished **Star Maker** glossary." This is the "50th anniversary edition" of a cross between a novel and a philosophical exploration of the future. It retains all its awesome power and has not dated at all. (CNB)

*Stapledon, Olaf, [ref.] **Talking Across the World** Main listing under Robert Crossley.

Stasheff, Christopher **Her Majesty's Wizard** (SFBC #10906, Jun,87, $5.98, 343pp, hc) Reprint (Del Rey 1986) fantasy novel; first hc edition.

STASHEFF, CHRISTOPHER　　　　　　　　　　　　　　　　　　　　　　**STRIEBER, WHITLEY**

*Stasheff, Christopher **The Warlock Heretical** (Ace 0-441-87286-7, Aug,87 [Jul,87], $2.95, 233pp, pb) Quasi-science fiction novel, part of the seemingly endless "Warlock" series. Stasheff's interest in the role of religion in a medieval society manifests in this tale of an ambitious abbot opposing the rulers of the planet Gramarye. Once again, Rod Gallowglass steps in to promote democracy, but exposition outweighs both puns and action. (CFC)

*Stchur, John **Down on the Farm** (St. Martin's 0-312-01021-4, Dec,87 [Nov,87], $15.95, 216pp, hc) Horror novel.

Steakley, John **Armor** (DAW 0-87997-979-8, Jul,87 [Jun,87], $3.95, 426pp, pb) Reissue (DAW 1984) military sf novel; 5th printing.

Steele, Mary Q. **The First of the Penguins** (NAL/Signet 0-451-14792-8, Sep,87 [Nov,87], $2.50, 158pp, pb) Reprint (Greenwillow 1973) young adult fantasy time travel novel.

*Steiner, Merrilee **Eileen Goudge's Swept Away #7: Pirate Moon** (Avon Flare 0-380-75134-8, Aug,87 [Jul,87], $2.50, 168pp, pb) Juvenile time travel romance novel. A computer sends Ramona back to pirate times to meet the perfect boy.

Stephens, Reed **The Man Who Killed His Brother** (Fontana 0-00-616355-6, Jun,87 [Dec,87], £2.50, 192pp, pb) Reissue (Ballantine 1981) detective novel of associational interest. This is a pseudonym for Stephen R Donaldson

Stephens, Reed **Man Who Risked His Partner** (Fontana 0-00-617492-2, Jun,87 [Dec,87], £2.95, 283pp, pb) Reissue (Ballantine 1984) detective novel of associational interest - the author is a pseudonym of Stephen R. Donaldson.

Sterling, Bruce **The Artificial Kid** (Ace 0-441-03095-5, May,87 [Apr,87], $2.95, 233pp, pb) Reprint (Harper & Row 1980) sf novel.

*Sterman, Betsy & Samuel Sterman **Too Much Magic** (Lippincott 0-397-32186-4, Apr,87 [Mar,87], $11.95, 154pp, hc) Juvenile science fiction novel (with magic).

*Sterman, Samuel & Betsy Sterman **Too Much Magic** Main listing under Betsy Sterman.

*Steussy, Marti **Forest of the Night** (Ballantine/Del Rey 0-345-33815-4, Jun,87 [May,87], $2.95, 265pp, pb) Sf novel of alien, possibly sentient, tigers. This may be a first novel.

*Stevenson, Drew **The Case of the Visiting Vampire** (Dodd, Mead 0-396-08856-2, Nov,86 [Jan,87], $10.95, 124pp, hc) Associational; juvenile humorous "horror" novel, latest in the "Raymond Almond" series. The "vampire" turns out to be non-supernatural. Published in 1986; missed.

Stevenson, Robert Louis **Dr. Jekyll and Mr. Hyde** (Star 0-352-32054-0, Apr,87, £1.95, 192pp, pb) Reprint (George Munro 1886) horror collection. Identical to Target (1986) edition.

Stevenson, Robert Louis **Dr. Jekyll and Mr. Hyde** (NAL/Signet Classic 0-451-52138-2, Oct,87, $2.25, 124pp, pb) Reprint (Longmans 1886) classic horror novel, with the 1980 introduction by Vladimir Nabokov.

Stevenson, Robert Louis **Dr. Jekyll and Mr. Hyde and Weir of Herminston** (The World's Classics 0-19-281740-X, Apr,87, £2.95, 229pp, pb) Reprint omnibus of classic horror novel (Longmans, Green 1886) and historical novel (Cassell 1896).

*Stevenson, Robert Louis & Samantha Lee **Dr. Jekyll and Mr. Hyde** Main listing under Samantha Lee.

*Stewart, Michael & Peter Jay **Apocalypse 2000: Economic Breakdown and the Suicide of Democracy** Main listing under Peter Jay.

*Stewart, Ramona **The Nightmare Candidate** (Arlington 0-85140-707-2, Sep,87, £9.95, 224pp, hc) Thriller with an element of the supernatural. [Not seen]

*Stiegler, Marc **David's Sling** (Baen 0-671-65369-5, Jan,88 [Dec,87], $3.50, 346pp, pb) Near-future high-tech political sf novel.

*Stine, Jovian Bob **Spaceballs: The Book** (Scholastic Point 0-590-41226-4, Jun,87 [May,87], $2.50, 122pp, pb) Novelization of Mel Brooks' parody sf movie, based on a screenplay by Brooks, Thomas Meehan, and Ronny Graham. No stills are included.

Stine, Jovian Bob **Spaceballs: The Book** (Hippo 0-590-70841-4, Oct,87, £1.50, 122pp, pb) Reprint (Scholastic 1987) juvenile sf novel. Based on the screenplay by Mel Brooks, Thomas Meehan and Ronny Graham. [First U.K. edition]

*Stith, John E. **Death Tolls** (Ace 0-441-14214-1, Sep,87 [Aug,87], $2.95, 230pp, pb) Sf/murder mystery novel.

*Stoker, Bram **Dracula** (Armada 0-00-692673-8, Jan,87, £1.75, 125pp, pb) Classic (Constable 1897) horror novel, abridged by Doris Dickens.

Stoker, Bram **Dracula** (Longman 0-582-52282-X, Jun,87, £1.25, 80pp, pb) Reprint (Constable 1897) classic horror novel. Abridged by J. Turvey. [Not seen]

*Stoker, Bram, [ref.] **Origins of "Dracula": Background to Bram Stoker's Gothic Masterpiece** Main listing under Clive Leatherdale.

*Stolbov, Bruce **Last Fall** (Doubleday 0-385-23028-1, May,87 [Apr,87], $12.95, 175pp, hc) Anthropological sf novel.

*Stout, Tim **The Raging** (Grafton 0-586-06854-6, Feb,87, £2.50, 256pp, pb) Horror novel. A first novel.

Stover, Marjorie Filley **When the Dolls Woke** (Scholastic Apple 0-590-40419-9, Dec,87, $2.50, 250pp, pb) Reprint (Albert Whitman & Co. 1985) juvenile fantasy novel about dolls coming to life.

*Stover, Professor Leon **The Prophetic Soul: A Reading of H.G. Wells' Things to Come** (McFarland 0-89950-289-X, Dec,87, $39.95, 301pp, hc) Non-fiction, critical study of the film *Things to Come*, including the film treatment by Wells and the complete production script.

*Stover, Professor Leon **Robert A. Heinlein** (G.K. Hall/Twayne 0-8057-7509-9, Dec,87, $17.95, 147pp, hc) Non-fiction, very sympathetic essay on Heinlein and his work.

Stow, Randolph **Visitants** (Taplinger 0-8008-8017-X, Mar,87 [Jan,87], $7.95, 189pp, tp) Reprint (Australia 1979) literary novel set in Australia, with elements of sf.

*Strasser, Todd **The Mall From Outer Space** (Scholastic Apple 0-590-40319-2, Oct,87, $2.50, 116pp, pb) Juvenile sf novel about the takeover of shopping malls on Earth.

Straub, Peter **Full Circle** (Corgi 0-552-10471-X, Jan,87, £2.50, 254pp, pb) Reissue (US 1975 as Julia) horror novel.

Strauss, Victoria **Worldstone** (NAL/Signet 0-451-14756-1, Mar,87 [Feb,87], $3.50, 301pp, pb) Reprint (Macmillan/Four Winds 1985) young adult fantasy novel of parallel worlds.

Strieber, Whitley **Black Magic** (Severn House 0-7278-1460-5, Aug,87, £9.95, 304pp, hc) Reprint (Morrow 1982) horror novel. [First U.K. edition, not seen]

Strieber, Whitley **Cat Magic** (Tor 0-812-51550-1, Jul,87, $4.95, 441pp, pb) Reprint (Tor 1986) horror novel. This was originally published as by Jonathan Barry and Whitley Strieber.

Strieber, Whitley **Cat Magic** (Grafton 0-246-13211-6, Sep,87 [Aug,87], £10.95, 414pp, hc) Reprint (Tor 1986) horror novel. [First U.K. edition]

Strieber, Whitley & Jonathan Barry **Catmagic** Main listing under Jonathan Barry.

Strieber, Whitley & James Kunetka **Nature's End** (SFBC #06472, Oct,86 [Jan,87], $4.98, 404pp, hc) Reprint (Warner 1986) near-future sf novel. This appeared in 1986 but wasn't seen until 1987.

Strieber, Whitley & James Kunetka **Nature's End** (Warner 0-446-34355-2, May,87 [Apr,87], $4.95, 418pp, pb) Reprint (Warner 1986) near-future disaster novel.

Strieber, Whitley & James Kunetka **Nature's End** (Grafton 0-586-07069-9, Sep,87, £3.50, 479pp, pb) Reprint (Warner 1986) near-future thriller.

*Strugatsky, Arkady & Boris Strugatsky **The Time Wanderers** (Richardson & Steirman 0-931933-31-5, Mar,87 [Feb,87], $16.95, 213pp, hc) Sf novel, translated from the Russian by Antonina W. Bouis.

*Strugatsky, Boris & Arkady Strugatsky **The Time Wanderers** Main listing under Arkady Strugatsky.

Sturgeon, Theodore **The Dreaming Jewels** (Carroll & Graf 0-88184-351-2, Jan,88 [Dec,87], $3.95, 180pp, pb) Reprint (Greenberg 1950) sf novel.

Sturgeon, Theodore **Godbody** (NAL/Signet 0-451-14702-2, Feb,87 [Jan,87], $3.50, 205pp, pb) Reprint (Fine 1986) fantasy novel. This was Sturgeon's final novel.

*Sturgeon, Theodore **Pruzy's Pot** (Hypatia Press no ISBN, Oct,86 [Jan,87], $17.95, 32pp, hc) Short story by Sturgeon, with an introduction by Spider Robinson and an afterword by Jane Tannehill Sturgeon. There are 333 copies of this regular edition and 133 special leather slipcase with a cassette of Sturgeon reading the story. This came out in late 1986, but we did not see it until now.

*Sturgeon, Theodore **To Marry Medusa** (Baen 0-671-65370-9, Dec,87 [Nov,87], $2.95, 251pp, pb) Collection of two stories, "To Marry Medusa" (1958) and "Killdozer" (1944). The former is actually a reprint of **The Cosmic Rape** (Dell 1958) instead of "To Marry Medusa" (*Galaxy* 1958). The magazine version was much shorter.

*Sturgeon, Theodore **A Touch of Sturgeon** (Simon & Schuster UK 0-671-65526-4, Aug,87 [Jul,87], £10.95, 235pp, hc) Collection of 8 stories. Published in Britain only, by the British arm of Simon & Schuster. Available in U.S. as an import. Selected and introduced by David Pringle.

Sucharitkul, Somtow **The Alien Swordmaster** (NEL 0-450-39251-1, Jan,87, £1.95, 185pp, pb) Reprint (Pinnacle 1985) sf novel. Volume 7 in the "V" series based on the tv show. [First U.K. edition]

*Suckling, Nigel **Heroic Dreams** (Paper Tiger 1-85028-035-5, Jul,87, £14.95, 159pp, hc) Collection of fantasy art with linking text by Suckling.

Sullivan, Eleanor, ed. **Alfred Hitchcock's Book of Horror Stories: Book 6** Main listing under Alfred Hitchcock.

Sullivan, Timothy **V: The New England Resistance** (NEL 0-450-40229-0, May,87, £1.95, 180pp, pb) Reprint (Warner 1985) novelization of TV sf series. Volume 8 in the "V" series. [First U.K. edition]

*Sullivan, Timothy **V: To Conquer the Throne** (Tor 0-812-55728-X, Nov,87 [Oct,87], $2.95, 216pp, pb) Sf novelization, latest in a series based on the tv show.

Summers, Ian, Wayne Douglas Barlowe & Beth Meacham **Barlowe's Guide to Extraterrestrials** Main listing under Wayne Douglas Barlowe.

Suskind, Patrick **Perfume** (QPB no ISBN, May,87, $8.95, 255pp, tp) Reprint (Knopf 1986) horror novel. This is an exact reproduction of the Knopf edition, in trade paperback and without the ISBN number.

Suskind, Patrick **Perfume** (Pocket 0-671-64370-3, Jun,87 [May,87], $4.50, 310pp, pb) "Special export edition." Reprint (Knopf 1986) horror novel of a murderer with a hypersensitivity to odor; a fascinating, if gruesome, exploration of a neglected sense. (FCM) Translated from the German by John E. Woods.

Suskind, Patrick **Perfume** (Pocket 0-671-64370-3, Sep,87 [Aug,87], $4.50, 310pp, pb) Reprint (Knopf 1986) literary horror novel; first U.S. paperback, with the same ISBN as the June 1987 "special export edition."

Sutcliff, Rosemary **Song For a Dark Queen** (Knight 0-340-24864-5, Jan,87, £1.95, 176pp, pb) Reissue (Knight 1980) juvenile historical novel about Boadicea, with fantasy elements.

Sutcliff, Rosemary **Sword at Sunset** (Tor 0-812-58852-5, Mar,87 [Feb,87], $4.50, 498pp, pb) Reprint (Hodder & Stoughton 1963) Arthurian historical/fantasy novel. The fantasy is minor. This is the best attempt to put Arthur into historical perspective. Highly recommended. (CNB)

Swanwick, Michael **In the Drift** (Ace 0-441-37072-1, Feb,87 [Jan,87], $2.95, 195pp, pb) Reissue (Ace 1985) sf novel; 2nd printing.

*Swanwick, Michael **Vacuum Flowers** (Arbor House 0-87795-870-X, Feb,87 [Jan,87], $15.95, 248pp, hc) Sf "cyberpunk" novel set in the far future.

Swanwick, Michael **Vacuum Flowers** (SFBC #10905, Jun,87, $4.98, 248pp, hc) Reprint (Arbor House 1987) cyberpunk sf novel.

Swanwick, Michael **Vacuum Flowers** (Ace 0-441-85876-7, Jan,88 [Dec,87], $2.95, 248pp, pb) Reprint (Arbor House 1987) sf cyberpunk novel.

Swift, Jonathan **Gulliver's Travels** (Longman 0-582-52285-4, Jun,87, £1.25, 64pp, pb) Reprint (Benjamin Motte 1726) classic satirical sf novel. Abridged by D.K. Swan and M. West. [Not seen]

Swift, Jonathan **Gulliver's Travels: A Voyage to Lilliput** (Armada 0-00-692899-4, Dec,87, £1.75, 94pp, tp) Reprint (Benjamin Motte 1726) first book of the classic satirical sf novel.

Swigart, Rob **Vector** (St. Martin's 0-312-90453-3, Jan,88 [Dec,87], $3.95, 288pp, pb) Reprint (Bluejay 1986) near-future sf thriller.

*Sykes, S.C. **U.S.S.A. Book 3** (Avon 0-380-75182-8, Apr,87 [Mar,87], $2.95, 170pp, pb) High school students battle a military dictatorship in 1996.

*Syvertsen, Ryder & Adrian Fletcher **Psychic Spawn** (Popular Library 0-445-20420-6, Oct,87 [Sep,87], $3.95, pb) Horror novel.

Talbot, Michael **The Bog** (Jove 0-515-09049-2, Jul,87 [Jun,87], $3.95, 314pp, pb) Reprint (Morrow 1986) horror novel.

*Tannehill, Jayne **V: The Oregon Invasion** (Tor 0-812-55729-8, Jan,88 [Dec,87], $3.50, 215pp, pb) Sf novelization in the "V" series; failed tv programs live again.

*Tapp, Kathy Kennedy **Flight of the Moth-Kin** (Macmillan McElderry 0-689-50401-2, Sep,87 [Oct,87], $11.95, 118pp, hc) Juvenile fantasy novel about 1" tall flying people, a sequel to **Moth-Kin Magic**. Illustrated by Michele Chessare.

*Tapp, Kathy Kennedy **The Scorpio Ghosts and the Black Hole Gang** (Harper & Row 0-06-026171-4, Apr,87 [Mar,87], $11.95, 151pp, hc) Juvenile fantasy novel.

Tarr, Judith **The Golden Horn** (Corgi 0-552-12853-8, Sep,87, £2.75, 272pp, pb) Reprint (Bluejay 1985) fantasy novel. Volume 2 in the "Hound and the Falcon" trilogy.

Tarr, Judith **The Hounds of God** (Tor 0-812-55605-4, May,87 [Apr,87], $3.50, 344pp, pb) Reprint (Bluejay 1986) fantasy novel, third in "The Hound and the Falcon" trilogy.

Tarr, Judith **The Hounds of God** (Bantam UK 0-593-01018-3, May,87, £9.95, 334pp, hc) Reprint (Bluejay 1986) fantasy novel. Volume 3 in the "Hound and the Falcon" trilogy. [First U.K. edition]

Tarr, Judith **The Isle of Glass** (Corgi 0-552-12852-X, Apr,87, £2.50, 288pp, pb) Reprint (Bluejay 1985) fantasy novel. Volume 1 in the "Hound and the Falcon" trilogy.

*Tarr, Judith **The Lady of Han-Gilen** (Tor 0-312-94271-0, Jun,87 [May,87], $16.95, 310pp, hc) Fantasy novel, Volume Two of "Avaryan Rising". This one seems less original than the first, with a wayward heroine whose dilemmas are diverse and well described, but too familiar.

*Taylor, Keith **Bard IV: Raven's Gathering** (Ace 0-441-04924-9, Nov,87 [Oct,87], $2.95, 235pp, pb) Fantasy novel, fourth in a series.

TEPPER, SHERI S.

TOLKIEN, J.R.R.

*Tepper, Sheri S. **After Long Silence** (Bantam Spectra 0-553-26944-5, Dec,87 [Nov,87], $3.95, 344pp, pb) Sf novel of musicians on a planet of dangerous -- and magnificent -- crystal monoliths. Recommended. (FCM)

*Tepper, Sheri S. **The Awakeners** (SFBC #11277, Sep,87, $6.98, hc) Omnibus edition of sf duology **Northshore** (Tor 1987) and **Southshore** (Tor 1987). They really form one novel, so this could be considered the first complete edition.

*Tepper, Sheri S. **The Awakeners: Northshore** (Tor 0-312-93006-2, Mar,87 [Feb,87], $14.95, 248pp, hc) "Science-fantasy" novel (first of a duology) set on a river-girdled world where human lives are controlled by alien and human religious intrigues -- a dark and complexly rich narrative. (CFC)

Tepper, Sheri S. **Blood Heritage** (Corgi 0-552-13193-8, Dec,87 [Nov,87], £2.95, 240pp, pb) Reprint (Tor 1986) horror novel. Volume 1 in a new series. [First U.K. edition]

*Tepper, Sheri S. **The End of the Game** (SFBC #105205, Jan,87, $7.98, 529pp, hc) Omnibus edition of the "Jinian" fantasy trilogy and the third trilogy in the "True Game" deklogy sans uno.

*Tepper, Sheri S. **Southshore** (Tor 0-312-93016-X, Jun,87 [May,87], $15.95, 250pp, hc) Science-fantasy novel, sequel to **Northshore** and conclusion of "The Awakeners" duology. A grim and weird but satisfying finale forces various characters to face the myths on which their hopes have been built, and to see new myths arise from the harsh realities discovered in the process. Don't try to read only one piece. **The Awakeners** is actually a single novel published in two volumes for commercial reasons. (CFC)

Tessier, Thomas **Finishing Touches** (Pocket 0-671-63093-8, Feb,87 [Jan,87], $3.50, 276pp, pb) Reprint (Atheneum 1986) horror novel.

Tessier, Thomas **Finishing Touches** (Grafton 0-586-06741-8, Jul,87, £2.95, 253pp, pb) Reprint (Atheneum 1986) horror novel. [First U.K. edition]

Theroux, Paul **O-Zone** (Penguin 0-14-009989-1, Sep,87, £3.95, 547pp, pb) Reprint (Putnam 1986) near-future thriller.

Theroux, Paul **O-Zone** (Ballantine Ivy 0-8041-0151-5, Oct,87 [Sep,87], $4.95, 535pp, pb) Reprint (Putnam 1986) near-future sf novel.

*Thomas, Elizabeth Marshall **Reindeer Moon** (Houghton Mifflin 0-395-42112-8, Feb,87 [Jan,87], $17.95, 338pp, hc) Prehistoric novel -- speculative anthropology.

Thomas, Elizabeth Marshall **Reindeer Moon** (SFBC #10895, Aug,87, $5.98, 336pp, hc) Reprint (Houghton Mifflin 1987) prehistoric/fantasy novel, a first novel.

*Thomas, Thomas T. **First Citizen** (Baen 0-671-65368-7, Dec,87 [Nov,87], $3.50, 373pp, pb) Near-future political/economic sf novel. His first novel was published under the pen name Thomas Wren.

Thompson, Joyce **Bigfoot and the Hendersons** (Puffin 0-14-032463-1, Dec,87, £1.95, 189pp, pb) Reprint (Berkley 1987 as **Harry and the Hendersons**) juvenile sf novel. Based on the screenplay by William Dear, William E. Martin & Ezra D. Rappaport. [First U.K. edition]

*Thompson, Joyce **Harry and the Hendersons** (Berkley 0-425-10155-X, Jun,87 [May,87], $3.50, 233pp, pb) Novelization based on a screenplay by William Dear, William E. Martin, and Ezra D. Rappaport. "Harry" is apparently a Bigfoot.

*Thompson, Paul B. **Sundipper** (St. Martin's 0-312-90706-0, Aug,87 [Jul,87], $3.50, 215pp, pb) Sf novel.

*Thompson, W.R. **Sideshow** (Baen 0-671-65375-X, Jan,88 [Dec,87], $3.50, 346pp, pb) Sf novel about telepaths, set in a near-future Los Angeles. Probably a first novel.

Thompson, William Irwin **Islands Out of Time** (Grafton 0-586-07108-3, Apr,87, £2.95, 270pp, pb) Reprint (Doubleday 1985) fantasy novel about the last days of Atlantis. [First U.K. edition]

*Thornburg, Mary K. Patterson **The Monster in the Mirror: Gender and the Sentimental/Gothic Myth in Frankenstein** (UMI 0-8357-1798-4, Jul,87 [Jun,87], $39.95, 154pp, hc) Non-fiction, critical study; a revision of a 1984 thesis.

*Thornton, Lawrence **Imagining Argentina** (Bloomsbury 0-7475-0085-1, Nov,87, £11.95, 214pp, hc) Political thriller whose protagonist is clairvoyant. A first novel.

*Thurston, Robert & Glen A. Larson **Battlestar Galactica #14: Surrender the Galactica!** Main listing under Glen A. Larson.

*Tigges, John **Hands of Lucifer** (Leisure 0-8439-2443-8, Aug,87 [Jul,87], $3.95, 384pp, pb) Horror novel.

Tilley, Patrick **Cloud Warrior** (Sphere 0-7221-8516-2, May,87, £2.95, 311pp, pb) Reissue (Sphere 1983) sf novel. Volume 1 in the "Amtrak Wars" series.

Tilley, Patrick **Fade-Out** (Grafton 0-586-07442-2, Jun,87, £3.50, 541pp, pb) Reprint (Hodder & Stoughton 1975) sf novel. This edition is supposed to be revised, although the changes are not immediately obvious.

Tilley, Patrick **First Family** (Sphere 0-7221-8517-0, May,87, £2.95, 344pp, pb) Reissue (Sphere 1985) sf novel. Volume 2 in the "Amtrak Wars" series.

*Tilley, Patrick **Iron Master** (Sphere 0-7221-8518-9, May,87, £3.50, 405pp, pb) Sf novel. Volume 3 in the "Amtrak Wars" series.

*Tilley, Patrick **Iron Master** (Baen 0-671-65338-5, Jul,87 [Jun,87], $3.95, 433pp, pb) Post-holocaust sf novel, Book III of "The Amtrak Wars". Published simultaneously in the U.K. by Sphere.

Timlett, Peter Valentine **The Power of the Serpent** (Orbit 0-7088-3105-2, Jan,87, £2.50, 246pp, pb) Reprint (Corgi 1976) occult fantasy novel. Volume 2 in the "Seedbearers" trilogy.

Timlett, Peter Valentine **The Twilight of the Serpent** (Orbit 0-7088-3106-0, Apr,87, £2.50, 210pp, pb) Reprint (Corgi 1977) occult fantasy novel. Volume 3 in the "Seedbearers" series.

*Tine, Robert **Midnight City** (NAL/Signet 0-451-15036-8, Dec,87, $3.95, 284pp, pb) 21st-century cop novel.

Tolkien, J.R.R. **The Book of Lost Tales I** (Unwin 0-04-823281-5, Jun,87, £3.95, 297pp, tp) Reissue (Allen & Unwin 1983) collection of stories related to Middle Earth.

Tolkien, J.R.R. **The Fellowship of the Ring** (Houghton Mifflin 0-395-08254-4, Mar,87, $14.95, 423pp, hc) Reissue (Ballantine 1965) fantasy novel, Volume 1 of "The Lord of the Rings." This is the first American printing to include all the corrections made piecemeal in the British editions. It also has a fascinating new note on the publishing history of the various corrected editions. The books are available separately with dust jackets or in a box without jackets as "The Lord of the Rings" ($43.35).

Tolkien, J.R.R. **The Fellowship of the Ring** (Unwin Hyman 0-04-823045-6, Mar,87, £9.95, 423pp, hc) Reissue (Allen & Unwin 1954) fantasy novel. Volume 1 of "The Lord of the Rings".

Tolkien, J.R.R. **The Hobbit** (Unwin 0-04-823188-6, Mar,87, £2.50, 287pp, tp) Reprint (Allen & Unwin 1937) fantasy novel. 50th Anniversary edition.

Tolkien, J.R.R. **The Hobbit** (Unwin Hyman 0-04-823386-2, Mar,87, £7.95, 256pp, hc) Reprint (Allen & Unwin 1937) fantasy novel. 50th Anniversary edition, including new introduction by Christopher Tolkien, new illustrations by the author and "the sole surviving page of the original draft of the first chapter".

Tolkien, J.R.R. **The Hobbit** (Unwin 0-04-823380-3, Sep,87, £8.95, 290pp, tp) Reprint (Allen & Unwin 1937 for text, 1984 for illustrations) fantasy novel. Fully illustrated by Michael Hague.

Tolkien, J.R.R. **The Hobbit** (Houghton Mifflin 0-395-45402-6, Nov,87 [Dec,87], $29.95, 317pp, hc) Reprint (George Allen & Unwin 1937) classic fantasy novel, "50th anniversary edition," with a new introduction by Christopher Tolkien. Boxed edition in a fine binding with nine illustrations by the author. It appeared slightly earlier in England from Unwin.

Tolkien, J.R.R. **The Lays of Beleriand** (Unwin 0-04-440018-7, Sep,87, £3.95, 393pp, tp) Reprint (Allen & Unwin 1985) associational/fantasy collection. Volume 3 in the "History of Middle-Earth" series.

Tolkien, J.R.R. **The Lord of the Rings** (Unwin 0-04-823229-7, Aug,87, £8.95, 1193pp, tp) Reissue (Allen & Unwin 1955) fantasy novel.

Tolkien, J.R.R. **Lord of the Rings and Hobbit Boxed Set** (Unwin 0-04-823216-5, Sep,87, £13.75, , tp) Classic fantasy series.

Tolkien, J.R.R. **Lord of the Rings Boxed Set** (Unwin Hyman 0-04-440010-1, Sep,87, £32.50, , hc) Classic fantasy series.

*Tolkien, J.R.R. **The Lost Road and Other Writings** (Unwin Hyman 0-04-823349-8, Aug,87, £16.95, 455pp, hc) Fantasy collection. Volume 5 in the "History of Middle-Earth" series.

+Tolkien, J.R.R. **The Lost Road and Other Writings** (Houghton Mifflin 0-395-45519-7, Dec,87 [Nov,87], $18.95, 455pp, hc) Collection of fantasy, etc., Vol. 5 of "The History of Middle Earth", edited by Christopher Tolkien. Various fragments about Middle Earth. First U.S. edition (Allen & Unwin 1987).

Tolkien, J.R.R. **The Return of the King** (Houghton Mifflin 0-395-08256-0, Mar,87, $14.95, 440pp, hc) Reissue (Ballantine 1965) fantasy novel, Volume 3 of "The Lord of the Rings". Eighteenth printing. The first American printing to include all corrections and changes. Available separately in d/w or as three volumes boxed without d/w.

Tolkien, J.R.R. **The Return of the King** (Unwin Hyman 0-04-823047-2, Mar,87, £9.95, 440pp, hc) Reissue (Allen & Unwin 1955) fantasy novel. Volume 3 of "The Lord of the Rings".

Tolkien, J.R.R. **The Two Towers** (Houghton Mifflin 0-395-08255-2, Mar,87, $14.95, 352pp, hc) Reissue (Ballantine 1965) fantasy novel. Volume 2 of "Lord of the Rings". Eighteenth printing. The first American printing to include all corrections and changes. Available separately in d/w or as three volumes boxed without d/w.

Tolkien, J.R.R. **The Two Towers** (Unwin Hyman 0-04-823046-4, Mar,87, £9.95, 352pp, hc) Reissue (Allen & Unwin 1954) fantasy novel. Volume 2 of "The Lord of the Rings".

Topol, Dr. B.H. **A Fistful of Ego** (Critic's Choice 1-55547-167-6, Apr,87, $3.75, 260pp, pb) Reprint (self-published 1985) near-future political thriller.

+Townsend, John Rowe **The Persuading Stick** (Morrow/Lothrop, Lee & Shepard 0-688-07260-7, Nov,87 [Oct,87], $10.25, 103pp, hc) Juvenile fantasy short novel about a girl with a magic stick. First American edition (Viking Kestrel 1986).

*Tremayne, Peter **Nicor!** (Sphere 0-7221-8609-6, Jun,87 [May,87], £2.50, 211pp, pb) Horror novel.

*Tremayne, Peter **Trollnight** (Sphere 0-7221-8608-8, Dec,87 [Nov,87], £2.75, 248pp, pb) Horror novel.

Tremayne, Peter **Zombie!** (St. Martin's 0-312-90923-3, Dec,87 [Nov,87], $2.95, 183pp, pb) Reprint (UK 1981) horror novel.

Trevor, Elleston **Deathwatch** (Star 0-352-31574-1, Jun,87, £3.50, 277pp, pb) Reissue (W.H. Allen 1985) thriller about a super-virus.

Tully, John **Natfact 7** (Magnet 0-416-00542-X, Jan,87, £1.75, 208pp, pb) Reprint (Methuen 1984) juvenile sf novel.

*Turek, Leslie, ed. **If I Ran The Zoo [cross out Zoo]...Con: The Smofcon 3 Game** (MCFI 0-9603146-4-4, Dec,86 [Jan,87], $5.00 + $1 postage/handling, 109pp, tp) 8.5" x 11" stapled. Non-fiction, humorous "game"/comments on running sf conventions. If you want to be involved in running conventions, you need this.

*Turk, H.C. **Ether Ore** (Tor 0-812-55635-6, Nov,87 [Oct,87], $3.50, 282pp, pb) Humorous sf novel, a first novel in the "Ben Bova Discovery" series.

*Turner, George **The Sea and Summer** (Faber & Faber 0-571-14846-8, Aug,87 [Sep,87], £10.95, 352pp, hc) Sf novel.

*Turtledove, Harry **Agent of Byzantium** (Congdon & Weed/Contemporary 0-86553-183-8, Apr,87, $15.95, 246pp, hc) Historical alternate-world (14th century) quasi-novel. The stories originally appeared in *Amazing* and *Isaac Asimov's SF Magazine*. They feature Basil Argyros, agent of the Empire. All are good by themselves, but they need bridging material to make them work as a novel. Although 15 years are said to elapse in the book, one gets little feeling of this; they could have taken place within months of each other. Still, the book is enjoyable and worth reading. (TM)

Turtledove, Harry **Agent of Byzantium** (SFBC #11117, Jul,87 [Aug,87], $4.98, 210pp, hc) Reprint (Congdon & Weed 1987) alternate-history novel.

*Turtledove, Harry **An Emperor For the Legion** (Ballantine/Del Rey 0-345-33068-4, May,87 [Apr,87], $3.50, 322pp, pb) Fantasy novel, Book Two of "The Videssos Cycle".

*Turtledove, Harry **The Legion of Videssos** (Ballantine/Del Rey 0-345-33069-2, Aug,87 [Jul,87], $3.95, 413pp, pb) Alternate world historical fantasy novel, third book in "The Videssos Cycle".

*Turtledove, Harry **The Misplaced Legion** (Ballantine/Del Rey 0-345-33067-6, Feb,87 [Jan,87], $2.95, 323pp, pb) Fantasy novel of Roman soldiers transported to a magic kingdom; first of a new series, "The Videssos Cycle".

*Turtledove, Harry **Noninterference** (Ballantine/Del Rey 0-345-34338-7, Jan,88 [Dec,87], $3.95, 213pp, pb) Sf novel about alien contact and political intrigue in a galactic survey. It originally appeared as two short stories and a serial in *Analog*.

*Turtledove, Harry **Swords of the Legion** (Ballantine/Del Rey 0-345-33070-6, Oct,87 [Sep,87], $3.95, 394pp, pb) Alternate world historical fantasy novel, Book 4 in "The Videssos Cycle".

Tuttle, Lisa **Encyclopedia of Feminism** (Arrow 0-09-944900-5, Feb,87, £6.95, 399pp, tp) Reprint (Longman 1986) associational item listed for Tuttle fans.

*Tuttle, Lisa **Gabriel** (Severn House 0-7278-1468-0, May,87, £8.95, 216pp, hc) Horror novel.

Tuttle, Lisa **Gabriel** (Sphere 0-7221-8648-7, Nov,87, £2.99, 216pp, pb) Reprint (Severn House 1987) horror novel.

*Tuttle, Lisa **A Spaceship Built of Stone and Other Stories** (Women's Press 0-7043-4084-4, Aug,87, £4.50, 192pp, tp) Sf collection.

*Twitchell, James B. **Dreadful Pleasures** (Oxford 0-19-505067-3, Sep,87, £7.95, 368pp, tp) Study of horror fiction. [Not seen]

*Tyers, Kathy **Firebird** (Bantam Spectra 0-553-26716-7, Jun,87 [May,87], $3.50, 265pp, pb) Sf adventure novel with a female protagonist; a first novel.

Underwood, Tim & Chuck Miller, eds. **Kingdom of Fear: The World of Stephen King** (NEL 0-450-41021-8, Aug,87, $2.50, 283pp, pb) Reprint (Underwood-Miller 1986) associational book about Stephen King. [First U.K. edition]

Underwood, Tim & Chuck Miller, eds. **Kingdom of Fear: The World of Stephen King** (NAL/Signet 0-451-14962-9, Oct,87 [Sep,87], $3.95, 316pp, pb) Reprint (Underwood-Miller 1986) non-fiction, essays by writers, critics, and filmmakers about King.

Updike, John **The Witches of Eastwick** (Penguin 0-14-010218-3, Aug,87 [Sep,87], £2.95, 316pp, pb) Reissue (Knopf 1984) literary fantasy novel.

VALENTINE, MARK

VOLLMANN, WILLIAM T.

*Valentine, Mark **14 Bellchamber Tower** (Crimson Altar Press No ISBN, Nov,87 [1987], £1.30, 35pp, pb) Three stories about psychic investigator Ralph Tyler. Illustrated by Stella Hender.

*Van Ash, Cay **The Fires of Fu Manchu** (Harper & Row 0-06-015819-0, Oct,87, $15.95, 277pp, hc) Fantasy/adventure novel set in 1917. A continuation of Sax Rohmer's "Fu Manchu" series, by Rohmer's biographer.

*Van Hamme, Jean & Grzegorz Rosinski **Thorgal: The Archers** (Donning 0-9617885-0-X, 1987 [Nov,87], $6.95, 48pp, hc) Fantasy graphic novel. First English language edition (France 1985).

Van Hise, Della **Killing Time** (Firecrest 0-85997-925-3, Jul,87 [1987], £7.95, 320pp, hc) Reprint (Pocket 1985) sf novel. Volume 39 in the Star Trek Novels series. [First U.K. edition, not seen]

*Van Lustbader, Eric **Shan** (Grafton 0-246-13101-2, Jan,87, £10.95, 543pp, hc) Thriller with fantasy elements. Volume 2 in the "China Maroc" series.

*Van Scyoc, Sydney J. **Drowntide** (Berkley 0-425-09775-7, May,87 [Apr,87], $2.95, 220pp, pb) Sf novel of a planet dominated by ocean, and a young man's quest for his sea-going kin far from his own shoreline kingdom.

Van Scyoc, Sydney J. **Drowntide** (Orbit 0-7088-8228-5, Aug,87, £2.50, 220pp, pb) Reprint (Berkley 1987) sf novel. [First U.K. edition]

Van Vogt, A.E. **Tyranopolis** (Sphere 0-7221-8723-8, Dec,87, £2.50, 170pp, pb) Reissue (Ace 1973, as **Future Glitter**) sf novel.

*Vance, Jack **Araminta Station** (Underwood-Miller 0-88733-059-2, Sep,87 [Oct,87], $60.00, 458pp, hc) Sf novel of adventure and intrigue, set on a distant planet in a distant future. First in the "Cadwal Chronicles" trilogy. Signed, boxed edition of 500 copies.

Vance, Jack **The Asutra** (Gollancz 0-575-04052-1, Dec,87, £2.50, 187pp, pb) Reprint (Dell 1974) sf novel. Volume 3 in the "Durdane" trilogy.

Vance, Jack **The Asutra** (Ace 0-441-03297-4, Jan,88 [Dec,87], $2.95, 204pp, pb) Reissue (Dell 1973) sf novel, third in the "Durdane" trilogy; 3rd Ace printing.

Vance, Jack **The Blue World** (Grafton 0-583-12497-6, Mar,87, £2.50, 204pp, pb) Reprint (Ballantine 1966) fantasy novel.

Vance, Jack **The Brave Free Men** (Gollancz 0-575-04053-X, Aug,87 [Jul,87], £2.50, 224pp, pb) Reprint (Dell 1973) sf novel. Volume 2 in the "Durdane" trilogy.

Vance, Jack **The Brave Free Men** (Ace 0-441-07204-6, Oct,87 [Sep,87], $2.95, 251pp, pb) Reissue (Dell 1973) sf novel, #2 in the "Durdane Trilogy".

Vance, Jack **The Faceless Man** (Ace 0-441-22555-1, May,87 [Apr,87], $2.95, 224pp, pb) Reissue (Dell 1973 as **The Anome**) sf novel, first in the "Durdane" trilogy. Second Ace printing.

Vance, Jack **The Faceless Man** (Gollancz 0-575-04032-7, May,87, £2.50, 206pp, pb) Reprint (Dell 1973 as **The Anome**) sf novel. Volume 1 in the "Durdane" series.

Vance, Jack **Fantasms and Magics** (Grafton 0-583-12498-4, Dec,87 [Nov,87], £2.50, 192pp, pb) Reissue (Mayflower 1978) fantasy collection, containing six stories from **Eight Fantasms and Magics** (Macmillan 1969).

Vance, Jack **The Green Pearl** (Berkley 0-425-09636-X, Mar,87 [Feb,87], $3.95, 407pp, pb) Reprint (Underwood-Miller 1985 as **Lyonesse: The Green Pearl**) fantasy novel, second in the "Lyonesse" saga.

Vance, Jack **Rhialto the Marvellous** (Severn House 0-7278-1375-7, Feb,87, £8.95, 240pp, hc) Reprint (Underwood-Miller 1984) fantasy collection. Volume 4 in the "Dying Earth" series. [Not seen]

Vance, Jack **To Live Forever** (Grafton 0-586-07275-6, Nov,87 [Oct,87], £2.50, 253pp, pb) Reprint (Ballantine 1956) sf novel.

Vance, Jack **Trullion: Alastor 2262** (Grafton 0-583-12496-8, Jul,87 [Jun,87], £2.50, 229pp, pb) Reissue (Ballantine 1973) sf novel. Volume 1 in the "Alastor" series.

*Vardeman, Robert E. **The Jade Demons Quartet** (NEL 0-450-41351-9, Nov,87 [Oct,87], £4.95, 829pp, tp) Fantasy omnibus.

*Vardeman, Robert E. **The Keys to Paradise** (NEL 0-450-39001-2, Aug,87, £3.95, 540pp, tp) Reissue (NEL 1986) fantasy omnibus.

*Vardeman, Robert E. **Masters of Space #2: The Alien Web** (Avon 0-380-75005-8, May,87 [Apr,87], $2.95, 166pp, pb) Sf space adventure novel, second in a series.

*Vardeman, Robert E. **Masters of Space #3: A Plague in Paradise** (Avon 0-380-75006-6, Sep,87 [Aug,87], $2.95, 169pp, pb) Sf novel, third in a series. Barton Kinsolving vs. an interstellar assassin/robot master.

*Vardeman, Robert E. **The Weapons of Chaos, Book 2: Equations of Chaos** (Ace 0-441-87631-5, Jul,87 [Jun,87], $2.95, 201pp, pb) Sf novel, second in a series.

+Vardeman, Robert E., writing as Daniel Moran **The Skeleton Lord's Key** (Tor 0-812-54602-4, Aug,87 [Jul,87], $2.95, 186pp, pb) This fantasy novel originally appeared in England as part of **The Keys to Paradise** (NEL 1986), an omnibus volume with the other two books in the "Keys" trilogy.

*Versluis, Arthur **Telos** (Arkana 1-85063-053-4, Sep,87, £3.95, 156pp, tp) Sf novel. Distributed in the U.S. by Methuen, $8.95.

+Versluis, Arthur **Telos** (Methuen/Arkana 1-85063-053-4, Nov,87 [Dec,87], $8.95, 156pp, tp) Sf novel. This is the British Arkana edition,

*Vidal, Harriette & Ed Kelleher **The Breeder** Main listing under Ed Kelleher.

Vinge, Joan D. **Ladyhawke** (Swift 0-85997-694-7, Jul,87, £5.95, 176pp, hc) Reprint (Signet 1985) fantasy film novelization. [Not seen]

*Vinge, Joan D., [ref.] **Suzy McKee Charnas, Joan Vinge, Octavia Butler** Main listing under Marleen S. Barr.

Vinge, Vernor **Marooned in Real Time** (Pan 0-330-29960-3, Oct,87, £2.95, 270pp, pb) Reprint (Bluejay 1986) sf novel. Volume 2 in the "Real Time" series. [First U.K. edition]

Vinge, Vernor **Marooned in Realtime** (Baen 0-671-65647-3, Jun,87 [May,87], $3.50, 313pp, pb) Reprint (Bluejay 1986) sf novel, sequel to **The Peace War**. A Hugo nominee and one of the best hard science books in years. Highly recommended. (CNB)

Vinge, Vernor **The Peace War** (Pan 0-330-29959-X, Oct,87, £2.95, 317pp, pb) Reprint (Bluejay 1984) sf novel. Volume 1 in the "Real Time" series. [First U.K. edition]

*Vinge, Vernor **Tatja Grimm's World** (Baen 0-671-65336-9, Jul,87 [Jun,87], $3.50, 277pp, pb) Collects 3 Tatja stories. The last 2 were previously published together as **Grimm's World** (Berkley 1969).

*Vinge, Vernor **True Names and Other Dangers** (Baen 0-671-65363-6, Nov,87 [Oct,87], $2.95, 275pp, pb) Collection of 5 stories (one a collaboration with Joan D. Vinge), plus author's notes.

Vinge, Vernor **The Witling** (Baen 0-671-65634-1, Apr,87 [Mar,87], $2.95, 220pp, pb) Reprint (DAW 1976) sf novel.

*Vivelo, Jackie **A Trick of the Light** (Putnam 0-399-21468-2, Oct,87, $13.95, 124pp, hc) Collection of 9 juvenile mystery/horror stories, subtitled "Stories to Read at Dusk".

*Volk, Stephen **Gothic** (Grafton 0-586-07335-3, Feb,87, £2.95, 223pp, pb) Novelization of Ken Russell's film.

*Vollmann, William T. **You Bright and Risen Angels** (Atheneum 0-689-11852-X, May,87, $22.95, 635pp, hc) Pynchonesque comic/surreal novel of magic and technology; a first novel.

*Volsky, Paula **The Luck of Relian Kru** (Ace 0-441-83816-2, Jun,87 [May,87], $2.95, 294pp, pb) Humorous fantasy novel. Plagued by strange bad luck since infancy, young Relian is forced to learn to use his "supranormal" powers by a gross, egotistical master, in a land of poisonous mystery and rampant eccentricity.

*Vomovich, Vladimir **Moscow 2042** (Harcourt Brace Jovanovich 0-15-162444-5, Jun,87 [May,87], $16.95, 424pp, hc) Sf time travel novel. First English language edition. Orginally published in Russian, 1986.

*Vonnegut, Kurt, Jr. **Bluebeard** (Delacorte 0-385-29590-1, Oct,87 [Sep,87], $17.95, 300pp, hc) Novel, non-sf/fantasy -- of associational interest. The "autobiography" of a minor character in **Breakfast of Champions**.

Vonnegut, Kurt, Jr. **Galapagos** (Grafton 0-586-06482-6, Mar,87, £2.95, 269pp, pb) Reprint (Delacorte 1985) sf novel.

*Vonnegut, Kurt, Jr., [ref.] **Kurt Vonnegut: A Comprehensive Bibliography** Main listing under Asa Pieratt.

Wagner, Karl Edward **Conan #16: The Road of Kings** (Ace 0-441-11618-3, Dec,87 [Nov,87], $2.95, 211pp, pb) Reprint (Bantam 1979). Another fantasy novel in the interminable series.

*Wagner, Karl Edward **Why Not You and I?** (Tor 0-812-52708-9, Sep,87 [Aug,87], $3.95, 306pp, pb) Collection of 9 horror stories, one as by "Curtiss Stryker".

*Wagner, Karl Edward **Why Not You and I?** (Dark Harvest 0-913165-25-5, Nov,87 [Oct,87], $34.95, 240pp, hc) Collection of 11 horror stories. It contains all of the stories from the September '87 Tor book of the same title, plus two additional stories, "Lacunae" and "Lost Exits". Full page illustrations by Ron & Val Lakey Lindahn. Limited to 300 signed numbered boxed copies.

*Wagner, Karl Edward **Why Not You and I?** (Dark Harvest 0-913165-26-3, Nov,87 [Oct,87], $18.95, 240pp, hc) Trade edition of the above.

*Wagner, Karl Edward, ed. **Echoes of Valor** (Tor 0-812-55750-6, Feb,87 [Jan,87], $2.95, 286pp, pb) Anthology of 3 novelettes by Robert E. Howard, Fritz Leiber, and Henry Kuttner. The Howard Conan story, "The Black Stranger", appears here complete for the first time. The Leiber, "Adept's Gambit", a Grey Mouser/Fafhrd tale, appears here in its original 1947 form, which is different from its later book versions.

*Wagner, Karl Edward, ed. **The Valley So Low: Southern Mountain Stories** Main listing under Manly Wade Wellman.

*Wagner, Karl Edward, ed. **The Year's Best Horror Stories: XV** (DAW 0-88677-226-5, Oct,87 [Sep,87], $3.50, 300pp, pb) Anthology of 18 horror stories from 1986.

*Wagner, Matt **Mage, Volume One: The Hero Discovered** (Donning/ Starblaze 0-89865-465-3, May,87, $12.95, 144pp, tp) Graphic novel. Omnibus of the first 5 issues of the Arthurian/ contemporary fantasy comic "Mage".

*Waldrop, Howard **All About Strange Monsters of the Recent Past** (Ursus Imprints 0-942681-00-2, Jun,87, $35.00, 125pp, hc) Collection by one of the wildest talents in short fiction; includes one original story. Introduction by Gardner Dozois. Numbered, signed (by Waldrop, Dozois, and the artists), slipcased, limited edition of 600 copies; illustrations in b&w and color by various artists. An elegantly designed book -- highly recommended. (FCM)

*Walker, Robert **Aftershock** (St. Martin's 0-312-90906-3, Nov,87 [Oct,87], $3.95, 248pp, pb) Horror novel. Headless mutant escapes laboratory during earthquake, and eats Hollywood.

*Wallace, David Foster **The Broom of the System** (Viking 0-670-81230-7, Jan,87, $18.95, 467pp, hc) Pynchonesque literary sf novel of the near future.

*Wallace, David Foster **The Broom of the System** (Penguin 0-14-009868-2, Jan,87, $7.95, 467pp, tp) Paperback edition of the above.

Wallace, Edgar **Planetoid 127** (Greenhill 0-947898-47-6, Jan,87 [1987], £8.95, 144pp, hc) Reprint (Reader's Library 1929) sf novel. Earliest example of the "twin world" theme in sf. [Not seen]

*Wallace, Patricia **Water Baby** (Zebra 0-8217-2188-7, Oct,87 [Sep,87], $3.95, 301pp, pb) Horror novel. "She was caught between the devil and the deep blue sea...."

*Waller, Gregory A., ed. **American Horrors** (Univ. of Illinois Press 0-252-01448-0, Jan,88 [Dec,87], $14.50, 228pp, tp) Non-fiction, essays on modern American horror films. A hardcover was announced (0-292-01447-2, $34.95), but not seen.

*Walsh, Jill Paton **Torch** (Viking Kestrel 0-670-81554-3, Oct,87, £6.95, 176pp, hc) Juvenile sf novel. [Not seen]

*Wardman, Gordon **Reparations** (Secker & Warburg 0-436-56171-9, Jan,87 [Feb,87], £9.95, 196pp, hc) Near-future thriller.

Warren, Bill **Keep Watching the Skies! American Science Fiction Movies of the Fifties: Vol. 2** (McFarland 0-89950-170-2, Jan,87, $39.95, 839pp, hc) Reprint (McFarland 1986). Volume 2 of a bibliography of sf movies. [Not seen]

*Warrick, Patricia S. **Mind in Motion: The Fiction of Philip K. Dick** (Southern Illinois Univ. Press 0-8093-1326-X, Jul,87, $18.95, 222pp, tp) Non-fiction, critical discussion of the major fiction of Philip K. Dick. An excellent study written in a clear narrative style, with reference only to the primary literature. Recommended. (CNB)

Warrington, Freda **A Blackbird in Silver** (NEL 0-450-05849-2, Aug,87, £2.95, 302pp, tp) Reissue (NEL 1986) fantasy novel.

Watson, Ian **Deathhunter** (St. Martin's 0-312-90033-3, Jul,87 [Aug,87], $2.95, 173pp, pb) Reprint (Gollancz 1981) metaphysical sf novel.

*Watson, Ian **Evil Water** (Gollancz 0-575-03953-1, Mar,87 [Aug,87], £10.95, 200pp, hc) Sf collection.

*Watson, Ian **The Power** (Headline 0-7472-3041-2, Sep,87, £2.50, 232pp, pb) Uneasy mixture of political manifesto about courageous anti-nuclear protestors and horror novel about re-animated, but rotting, corpses.

Watson, Ian **The Power** (Headline 0-7472-0031-9, Oct,87, £8.95, 240pp, hc) Reprint (Headline 1987) horror novel. [Not seen]

Watson, Ian **Slow Birds** (Grafton 0-586-07143-1, Jul,87, £2.50, 224pp, pb) Reprint (Gollancz 1985) sf collection.

Watt-Evans, Lawrence **The Book of Silence** (Ballantine/Del Rey 0-345-33963-0, Apr,87 [Mar,87], $3.50, 326pp, pb) Reissue (Del Rey 1984) fantasy novel, Book Four of "The Lords of Dus"; fourth printing.

Watt-Evans, Lawrence **The Book of Silence** (Grafton 0-586-07152-0, Sep,87, £3.50, 399pp, pb) Reprint (Del Rey 1984) fantasy novel. Volume 4 in the "Lords of Dus" series. [First U.K. edition]

Watt-Evans, Lawrence **The Cyborg and the Sorcerers** (Ballantine/Del Rey 0-345-34439-1, Aug,87, $2.95, 248pp, pb) Reissue (Del Rey 1982) science fantasy novel, first in a series; 6th printing.

Watt-Evans, Lawrence **The Lure of the Basilisk** (Ballantine/Del Rey 0-345-33960-6, Mar,87 [Feb,87], $3.50, 227pp, pb) Reissue (Del Rey 1980) fantasy novel, Book One of "The Lords of Dus". Third printing.

Watt-Evans, Lawrence **The Lure of the Basilisk** (Grafton 0-586-07149-0, Mar,87, £2.50, 224pp, pb) Reprint (Del Rey 1980) fantasy novel. Volume 1 in the "Lords of Dus" series. [First U.K. edition]

Watt-Evans, Lawrence **The Seven Altars of Dusarra** (Grafton 0-586-07150-4, May,87, £2.95, 270pp, pb) Reprint (Ballantine 1981) fantasy novel. Volume 2 in the "Lords of Dus" series. [First U.K. edition]

Watt-Evans, Lawrence **The Sword of Bheleu** (Ballantine/Del Rey 0-345-33962-2, Apr,87 [Mar,87], $3.50, 272pp, pb) Reissue (Del Rey 1982) fantasy novel, Book Three of "The Lords of Dus"; fifth printing.

WATT-EVANS, LAWRENCE

WEIS, MARGARET

Watt-Evans, Lawrence **The Sword of Bheleu** (Grafton 0-586-07151-2, Jul,87 [Jun,87], £2.95, 301pp, pb) Reprint (Del Rey 1982) fantasy novel. Volume 3 in the "Lords of Dus" series. [First U.K. edition]

*Watt-Evans, Lawrence **With a Single Spell** (Ballantine/Del Rey 0-345-32616-4, Mar,87 [Feb,87], $3.50, 263pp, pb) Fantasy novel set in the world of **The Misenchanted Sword**.

*Watt-Evans, Lawrence **The Wizard and the War Machine** (Ballantine/Del Rey 0-345-33459-0, Sep,87 [Aug,87], $3.50, 291pp, pb) Science fantasy novel, sequel to **The Cyborg and the Sorcerers**.

Waugh, Charles G., Isaac Asimov & Martin H. Greenberg, eds. **Cosmic Knights** For main entry see under Isaac Asimov.

*Waugh, Charles G., Isaac Asimov & Martin H. Greenberg, eds. **Flying Saucers** Main listing under Isaac Asimov.

Waugh, Charles G., Isaac Asimov & Martin H. Greenberg, eds. **Giants** For main entry see under Isaac Asimov.

*Waugh, Charles G., Isaac Asimov & Martin H. Greenberg, eds. **Isaac Asimov's Magical Worlds of Fantasy #8: Devils** Main listing under Isaac Asimov.

*Waugh, Charles G., Isaac Asimov & Martin H. Greenberg, eds. **Isaac Asimov's Magical Worlds of Fantasy #9: Atlantis** Main listing under Isaac Asimov.

*Waugh, Charles G., Isaac Asimov & Martin H. Greenberg, eds. **Isaac Asimov's Wonderful Worlds of Science Fiction #6: Neanderthals** Main listing under Isaac Asimov.

*Waugh, Charles G., Isaac Asimov & Martin H. Greenberg, eds. **Isaac Asimov's Wonderful Worlds of Science Fiction #7: Space Shuttles** Main listing under Isaac Asimov.

*Waugh, Charles G., Isaac Asimov & Martin H. Greenberg, eds. **Young Witches & Warlocks** Main listing under Isaac Asimov.

*Waugh, Charles G. & Martin H. Greenberg, eds. **Battlefields Beyond Tomorrow: Science Fiction War Stories** (Crown/Bonanza 0-517-64105-4, Dec,87, $8.98, 650pp, hc) Anthology of 25 sf stories with an introduction by Robert Silverberg. An "instant remainder" book.

*Waugh, Charles G. & Martin H. Greenberg, eds. **House Shudders** Main listing under Martin H. Greenberg.

*Waugh, Charles G. & Martin H. Greenberg, eds. **Vamps** Main listing under Martin H. Greenberg.

*Waugh, Charles G., Martin H. Greenberg & Joe W. Haldeman, eds. **Supertanks** Main listing under Joe W. Haldeman.

*Waugh, Charles G., Martin H. Greenberg & Frank D. McSherry, Jr., eds. **Strange Maine** (Tapley 0-912769-10-6, Oct,86 [Jan,87], $9.95, 295pp, tp) Anthology of sf, fantasy, and horror stories set in Maine, with works by King, Leiber, Pangborn, etc.

*Waugh, Charles G., Martin H. Greenberg & Carol Serling, eds. **Rod Serling's Night Gallery Reader** Main listing under Carol Serling.

*Waugh, Charles G., Martin H. Greenberg & Jane Yolen, eds. **Spaceships and Spells** Main listing under Jane Yolen.

*Waugh, Charles G., Frank D. McSherry, Jr. & Martin H. Greenberg, eds. **Nightmares in Dixie: Thirteen Horror Tales From the American South** Main listing under Frank D. McSherry, Jr.

Waugh, Harriet **Kate's House** (St. Martin's 0-312-90142-9, May,87 [Apr,87], $3.50, 216pp, pb) Reprint (St. Martin's 1983) horror novel.

*Weathers, Brenda **The House at Pelham Falls** (Naiad 0-930044-79-7, Jul,87 [Jun,87], $7.95, 226pp, tp) Lesbian romance/ghost story.

*Weaver, Michael D. **Mercedes Nights** (St. Martin's 0-312-01066-4, Dec,87 [Nov,87], $16.95, 240pp, hc) Sf novel, hardboiled but not cyberpunk, involving cloning.

*Weaver, Michael D. **Wolf-Dreams** (Avon 0-380-75198-4, May,87 [Apr,87], $2.95, 186pp, pb) Fantasy novel featuring a werewolf/swordswoman, first in the announced "Bloodfang" series. A first novel.

Webb, Jackie **Wilkes the Wizard and the S.P.A.M.** (Dragon 0-583-30935-6, Apr,87, £1.95, 143pp, pb) Reprint (Grafton 1986) juvenile fantasy novel.

*Webb, Sharon **Pestis 18** (Tor 0-312-93003-8, Mar,87 [Feb,87], $17.95, 400pp, hc) Medical suspense novel of terrorists and plague; non-sf: associational.

*Webster, Lyn **The Illumination of Alice J. Cunningham** (Dedalus 0-946626-15-4, May,87, £9.95/$19.95, 306pp, hc) Modern, feminist updating of the "through the looking glass" tale, a first novel. This single edition for British and American markets is distributed in the U.S. by Hippocrene, Inc., 171 Madison Ave., New York NY 10016.

*Weinberg, George **Numberland: A Fable** (St. Martin's 0-312-00170-3, Feb,87 [Jan,87], $9.99, 119pp, hc) Numerical fantasy whose hero is the number Six. A first novel.

Weinberg, Robert E., ed. **Far Below and Other Horrors** (Starmont House 0-930261-56-9, Feb,87 [Jan,87], $9.95, 151pp, tp) Anthology of horror stories.

*Weiner, Andrew **Station Gehenna** (Congdon & Weed 0-86553-191-9, Sep,87 [Aug,87], $15.95, 216pp, hc) Sf/mystery novel set on a planetary station, a first novel in the series "Isaac Asimov Presents".

Weinstein, Howard **Deep Domain** (Titan 0-907610-86-2, Jun,87, £2.95, 275pp, pb) Reprint (Pocket 1987) sf novel. Volume 33 in the Star Trek Novels series. [First U.K. edition]

*Weinstein, Howard **Star Trek #33: Deep Domain** (Pocket 0-671-63329-5, Apr,87 [Mar,87], $3.50, 275pp, pb) Star Trek novel.

*Weinstein, Howard **V: Path to Conquest** (Tor 0-812-55725-5, Sep,87 [Aug,87], $2.95, 209pp, pb) Sf novel, latest in the series based on the cancelled tv show.

*Weis, Margaret & Tracy Hickman **The Darksword Trilogy, Volume 1: Forging the Darksword** (Bantam Spectra 0-553-26894-5, Jan,88 [Dec,87], $3.95, 391pp, pb) Fantasy novel.

Weis, Margaret & Tracy Hickman **DragonLance Legends, Vol. 1: Time of the Twins** (Penguin 0-14-010109-8, Mar,87, £2.95, 398pp, pb) Reprint (TSR 1986) fantasy novel. [First U.K. edition]

Weis, Margaret & Tracy Hickman **DragonLance Legends, Vol. 2: War of the Twins** (Penguin 0-14-010110-1, May,87, £2.95, 387pp, pb) Reprint (TSR 1986) fantasy novel. [First U.K. edition]

Weis, Margaret & Tracy Hickman **DragonLance Legends, Vol. 3: Test of the Twins** (Penguin 0-14-010111-X, Jul,87, £2.95, 344pp, pb) Reprint (TSR 1986) fantasy novel. [First U.K. edition]

*Weis, Margaret, ed. **The Art of the DragonLance Saga** (TSR 0-88038-447-6, May,87, $16.95, 126pp, tp) Art book. Drawings of scenes from the "DragonLance" books. UK price £12.95.

*Weis, Margaret & Tracy Hickman, eds. **DragonLance Tales Vol. 1: The Magic of Krynn** (TSR 0-88038-454-9, Apr,87 [Mar,87], $3.95, 352pp, pb) Original shared-world fantasy anthology set in the "DragonLance" universe.

*Weis, Margaret & Tracy Hickman, eds. **DragonLance Tales Vol. 2: Kender, Gully Dwarves, and Gnomes** (TSR 0-88038-382-8, Aug,87, $3.95, 307pp, pb) Original anthology, second volume of stories set in a shared fantasy world.

*Weis, Margaret & Tracy Hickman, eds. **DragonLance Tales Vol. 3: Love and War** (TSR 0-88038-519-7, Nov,87, $3.95, 386pp, pb) Original shared world anthology of 10 fantasy stories set in the "DragonLance" universe.

WEIS, MARGARET   **WILHELM, KATE**

*Weis, Margaret & Tracy Hickman, eds. **Leaves from the Inn of the Last Home** (TSR 0-88038-465-4, Mar,87, $12.95, 255pp, tp) Reference book on the "DragonLance" series, subtitled "the complete Krynn source book."

*Welfare, Mary **Yeti of the Glen** (Pied Piper 0-416-00652-3, Apr,87, £5.95, 96pp, hc) Juvenile fantasy novel. [Not seen]

*Welfare, Simon & John Fairley **Arthur C. Clarke's Chronicles of the Strange and Mysterious** For main entry see under John Fairley.

*Weller, Tom **Cvltvre Made Stvpid** (Houghton Mifflin 0-395-40461-4, Oct,87 [Sep,87], $7.95, 73pp, tp) Associational, part-pictorial humor -- a look at Cvltvre vs. Culture.

Welles, Patricia **Sara's Ghost** (Paperjacks 0-7701-0663-3, Aug,87, $3.50, 286pp, pb) Reprint (Donald I. Fine 1986 as **The Ghost of S.W.1**) ghostly love story.

*Wellman, Manly Wade **The Valley So Low: Southern Mountain Stories** (Doubleday 0-385-23675-1, Dec,87 [Nov,87], $12.95, 212pp, hc) Collection of 23 stories, edited and with an introduction by Karl Edward Wagner.

Wells, H.G. **The Dream** (The Hogarth Press 0-7012-0705-1, Aug,87, £5.95, 336pp, tp) Reprint (Macmillan 1923) scientific romance with a new introduction by Brian Aldiss.

Wells, H.G. **The First Men in the Moon** (Penguin 0-14-007999-8, Jan,87, £3.50, 191pp, pb) Reprint (Newnes 1901) sf novel. In the "Penguin Science Fiction Classics" series.

Wells, H.G. **The Invisible Man** (Bantam Classics 0-553-21253-2, Jun,87 [May,87], $2.50, 138pp, pb) Reprint (Pearson 1897) classic novel. New introduction by Anthony West, Wells' grandson and biographer.

Wells, H.G. **The Invisible Man** (Pan 0-330-29785-6, Oct,87, £2.50, 102pp, pb) Reissue (C. Arthur Pearson 1897) sf novel.

Wells, H.G. **Men Like Gods** (Penguin 0-14-007998-X, May,87, £3.95, 232pp, tp) Reprint (Cassell 1923) sf novel. In the Penguin Classic SF series.

Wells, H.G. **The Time Machine** (Pan 0-330-01697-0, Jan,87, £2.50, 123pp, pb) Reissue (Pan 1953) sf collection.

*Wells, H.G., [ref.] **The Definitive Time Machine: A Critical Edition of H.G. Wells' Scientific Romance** Main Listing under Harry M. Geduld.

*Wells, H.G., [ref.] **H.G. Wells, Desperately Mortal** Main listing under David C. Smith.

*Wells, H.G., [ref.] **The Prophetic Soul: A Reading of H.G. Wells' Things to Come** Main listing under Professor Leon Stover.

*Wendorf, Patricia **Blanche** (Futura 0-7088-2861-2, Apr,87, £2.95, 504pp, pb) Reprint (Hamish Hamilton 1986) historical novel with a touch of fantasy in the form of a magic coral necklace. Volume 2 in the "Patteran" trilogy.

*Wendorf, Patricia **Bye Bye Blackbird** (Hamish Hamilton 0-241-12387-9, Oct,87 [Nov,87], £10.95, 388pp, hc) Historical romance with fantasy touches. Volume 3 in the "Patteran" trilogy.

Westall, Robert **Rachel and the Angel and Other Stories** (Morrow/Greenwillow 0-688-07370-0, 1987 [Oct,87], $10.25, 187pp, hc) Collection of 7 young adult fantasy and horror stories. First U.S. edition (Macmillan UK 1986).

*Westall, Robert **Urn Burial** (Viking Kestrel 0-670-81537-3, Jun,87 [Jul,87], £6.95, 157pp, hc) Juvenile supernatural novel.

*Westerly, Daniel **Devotion** (Pocket 0-671-63175-6, Mar,87 [Aug,87], $3.50, 279pp, pb) Horror novel.

Weston, Carolyn **Children of the Light** (St. Martin's 0-312-90305-7, May,87 [Apr,87], $3.50, 262pp, pb) Reprint (St. Martin's 1985) post-holocaust sf novel. A fine first novel; recommended. (FCM)

Westwood, Jennifer **Albion: A Guide to Legendary Britain** (Paladin 0-586-08416-9, Feb,87, £6.95, 567pp, tp) Reprint (Granada 1985) gazetteer of British legends and folklore.

*Wheatley, Dennis & Alison Sage **The Devil Rides Out** For main listing see under Alison Sage.

*Wheeler, Scott **Matters of Form** (DAW 0-88677-225-7, Oct,87 [Sep,87], $2.95, 240pp, pb) Sf novel of aliens shipwrecked on Earth.

*Whelan, Michael **Michael Whelan's Works of Wonder** (Ballantine/Del Rey 0-345-32679-2, Nov,87 [Oct,87], $25.00, 109pp, hc) Non-fiction, art book with sf and fantasy illustrations by multiple Hugo winner Whelan. This book is limited to Del Rey covers.

Whelan, Michael **Works of Wonder** (Columbus 0-86287-391-6, Oct,87 [Nov,87], £16.95, 128pp, hc) Reprint art book. [First U.K. edition]

White, James **All Judgement Fled** (Orbit 0-7088-8222-6, May,87, £2.50, 215pp, pb) Reprint (Rapp & Whiting 1968) sf novel.

White, James **All Judgement Fled** (Macdonald 0-356-14397-X, Aug,87, £10.95, 224pp, hc) Reprint (Rapp & Whiting 1968) sf novel. [Not seen]

White, James **Ambulance Ship** (Macdonald 0-356-14003-2, May,87 [Aug,87], £10.95, 184pp, hc) Reprint (Ballantine 1979) sf collection.

*White, James **Code Blue--Emergency!** (Ballantine/Del Rey 0-345-34172-4, Jul,87 [Jun,87], $2.95, 280pp, pb) Sf novel in the "Sector General" series.

White, James **Major Operation** (Orbit 0-7088-8185-8, Feb,87, £1.95, 183pp, pb) Reprint (Ballantine 1971) collection of 5 linked short stories. Volume 3 in the "Sector General" series. [First U.K. edition]

White, James **Sector General** (Ballantine/Del Rey 0-345-34627-0, Jul,87 [Jun,87], $2.95, 196pp, pb) Reissue (Del Rey 1983) collection of 4 novelettes in the "Sector General" series; 5th printing.

White, James **Sector General** (Orbit 0-7088-8186-6, Sep,87, £2.50, 196pp, pb) Reprint (Del Rey 1983) original sf collection. Volume 5 in the "Sector General" series. [First U.K. edition]

White, James **Star Healer** (Orbit 0-7088-8187-4, Nov,87, £2.50, 217pp, pb) Reprint (Del Rey 1985) sf novel. Volume 6 in the "Sector General" series. [First U.K. edition]

White, James **Star Surgeon** (Macdonald 0-356-14794-0, Nov,87, £10.95, 160pp, hc) Reprint (Ballantine 1963) sf novel. Volume 2 in the "Sector General" series. [Not seen]

*White, Mel & Robert Lynn Asprin **Duncan and Mallory: The Bar-None Ranch** Main listing under Robert Lynn Asprin.

*White, Melvin R. & Edgar Allan Poe **The Tell-Tale Heart** Main listing under Edgar Allan Poe.

White, T.H. **The Book of Merlyn** (Fontana 0-00-615725-4, Dec,87, £2.95, 176pp, tp) Reissue (University of Texas Press 1977) fantasy novel.

White, T.H. **The Once and Future King** (Fontana 0-00-615310-0, Dec,87, £4.95, 638pp, tp) Reissue (Collins 1958) fantasy omnibus.

*Whiteford, Wynne **The Hyades Contact** (Ace 0-441-35446-7, Sep,87 [Aug,87], $2.95, 249pp, pb) Sf novel of Earthlings kidnapped by aliens. Parts of the book previously appeared in Australian anthologies.

Wilder, Cherry **The Summer's King** (Unicorn 0-04-823311-0, Jan,87, £3.50, 244pp, pb) Reprint (Atheneum 1986) fantasy novel. Volume 3 in the "Rulers of Hylor" series. [First U.K. edition]

Wilder, Cherry **The Summer's King** (Baen 0-671-65617-1, Feb,87 [Jan,87], $2.95, 281pp, pb) Reprint (Atheneum 1986) fantasy novel conclusion of the "Rulers of Hylor" trilogy.

*Wilhelm, Kate **The Hamlet Trap** (St. Martin's 0-312-94000-9, Sep,8? [Aug,87], $15.95, 234pp, hc) Mystery novel; associational.

WILHELM, KATE

Wilhelm, Kate **Welcome Chaos** (Arrow 0-09-950080-9, Sep,87, £2.95, 297pp, pb) Reprint (Houghton Mifflin 1983) sf novel.

Wilkins, Cary **The Mammoth Book of Classic Fantasy** (Robinson 0-948164-40-9, May,87, £4.95, 472pp, tp) Reprint (Crown 1984 as **A Treasury of Fantasy**) fantasy anthology. [First U.K. edition]

Wilkins, Cary **The Mammoth Book of Classic Fantasy** (Firecrest 0-85997-934-2, Jul,87 [1987], £9.95, 472pp, hc) Reprint (Crown 1984, as **A Treasury of Fantasy**) fantasy anthology. [Not seen]

*Williams, Charles, [ref.] **Charles Williams** Main listing under Kathleen Spencer.

*Williams, Mary **Haunted Waters** (Kimber 0-7183-0650-3, Oct,87, £9.50, 190pp, hc) Original ghost collection.

*Williams, Michael Lindsay **FTL: Further Than Life** (Avon 0-380-89632-X, Mar,87 [Feb,87], $3.50, 327pp, pb) Sf novel, sequel to **Martian Spring**.

*Williams, Sheila & Cynthia Manson, eds. **Tales From Isaac Asimov's Science Fiction Magazine** (Harcourt Brace Jovanovich 0-15-284209-8, Oct,86 [Mar,87], $15.95, 298pp, hc) Young-adult anthology of 17 stories from *Asimov's*; introduction by Isaac Asimov. This has a 1986 copyright, but we did not see it until 1987.

Williams, Walter Jon **Ambassador of Progress** (Orbit 0-7088-8221-8, Mar,87, £3.50, 432pp, pb) Reprint (Tor 1984) sf novel. [First U.K. edition]

Williams, Walter Jon **Ambassador of Progress** (Tor 0-812-55791-3, May,87 [Apr,87], $3.50, 432pp, pb) Reissue (Tor 1984) sf novel; 2nd printing.

*Williams, Walter Jon **The Crown Jewels** (Tor 0-812-55798-0, Oct,87 [Sep,87], $3.50, 247pp, pb) Sf novel of manners.

Williams, Walter Jon **Hardwired** (Tor 0-812-55796-4, Apr,87 [Mar,87], $3.50, 343pp, pb) Reprint (Tor 1986) sf cyberpunk novel.

Williams, Walter Jon **Hardwired** (Macdonald 0-356-14872-6, Aug,87, £11.95, 343pp, hc) Reprint (Tor 1986) sf novel. [First U.K. edition]

Williams, Walter Jon **Knight Moves** (Orbit 0-7088-8233-1, Aug,87, £2.95, 317pp, pb) Reprint (Tor 1985) sf novel. [First U.K. edition]

*Williams, Walter Jon **Voice of the Whirlwind** (Tor 0-312-93013-5, May,87 [Apr,87], $16.95, 278pp, hc) Sf novel, an indirect sequel to **Hardwired**, set 200 years in the future. This futuristic novel of murder and conspiracy belongs less obviously to the cyberpunk subgenre than its predecessor. It's good, taut adventure. (FCM)

*Williamson, Chet **Ash Wednesday** (Tor 0-312-93002-X, Feb,87 [Jan,87], $16.95, 372pp, hc) Horror novel. All the dead in a small town rise as ghosts in the form they had at the moment of their deaths.

Williamson, Chet **Soulstorm** (Headline 0-7472-3072-2, Dec,87, £2.95, 311pp, pb) Reprint (Tor 1986) horror novel. [First U.K. edition]

+Williamson, Duncan **The Broonie, Silkies & Fairies: Travellers' Tales of the Other World** (Crown Harmony 0-517-56525-0, Mar,87 [Aug,87], $15.95, 153pp, hc) Collection of retold tales from Scotland's West Country, illustrated by Alan B. Herriot. First U.S. edition (Canongate 1985).

Williamson, J.N. **Brotherkind** (Leisure 0-8439-2436-5, Oct,86 [Jan,87], $3.50, 286pp, pb) Reissue (Leisure 1982) sf horror novel about aliens who impregnate a human.

*Williamson, J.N. **Evil Offspring** (Leisure 0-8439-2468-3, Apr,87 [Jul,87], $3.95, 394pp, pb) Horror novel.

Williamson, J.N. **The Evil One** (Zebra 0-8217-2144-5, Aug,87 [Jul,87], $3.95, 333pp, pb) Reissue (Zebra 1982) horror novel, 2nd printing.

Williamson, J.N. **Horror House** (Leisure 0-8439-2492-6, May,87 [Aug,87], $3.95, 382pp, pb) Reissue (Leisure 1981) horror novel.

*Williamson, J.N., ed. **How to Write Tales of Horror, Fantasy & Science Fiction** (Writer's Digest Books 0-89879-270-3, Apr,87, $15.95, 242pp, hc) Non-fiction, writer's guide, an anthology of new articles by Bloch, Bradbury, Bradley, etc.

*Williamson, J.N., ed. **Masques II** (Maclay & Assoc. 0-940776-24-3, Jun,87 [Jul,87], $19.95, 221pp, hc) Original anthology of 27 horror stories, including work by Stephen King, Ramsey Campbell, and Richard Matheson. Issued in silver boards without dust wrapper.

Williamson, Jack **Firechild** (SFBC #10581, Feb,87, $7.98, 281pp, hc) Reprint (Bluejay 1986) sf novel.

Williamson, Jack **Firechild** (Tor 0-812-55800-6, Aug,87 [Jul,87], $3.95, 377pp, pb) Reprint (Bluejay 1986) sf novel.

Williamson, Jack **Lifeburst** (Sphere 0-7221-9117-0, Mar,87, £2.95, 271pp, pb) Reprint (Del Rey 1984) sf novel.

*Willis, Connie **Lincoln's Dreams** (Bantam Spectra 0-553-05197-0, May,87 [Mar,87], $15.95, 212pp, hc) Contemporary fantasy novel featuring dreams of the Civil War.

*Wilson, Colin **The Delta** (Grafton 0-246-13150-0, Oct,87, £10.95, 304pp, hc) Sf novel. Volume 2 in the "Spider World" series.

*Wilson, Colin **The Delta** (Grafton 0-246-13222-1, Oct,87, £6.95, 304pp, tp) Trade paperback edition of the above.

Wilson, Colin **The Essential Colin Wilson** (Grafton 0-586-06865-1, Feb,87, £4.95, 336pp, tp) Reprint (Harrap 1985) collection of non-fiction and fiction including some occult and sf.

*Wilson, Colin **The Tower** (Grafton 0-246-12510-1, Feb,87 [Jan,87], £10.95, 398pp, hc) sf/fantasy novel about giant spiders in 25th Century Earth. Volume 1 in the "Spider World" series.

*Wilson, Colin **The Tower** (Grafton 0-246-13146-2, Feb,87, £6.95, 398pp, tp) Trade paperback of the above.

*Wilson, Gahan **Eddy Deco's Last Caper: An Illustrated Mystery** (Times Books 0-8129-1671-9, Nov,87, $14.95, 213pp, hc) Fantasy/detective farce novel illustrated by the author -- the illustrations are part of the story.

*Wilson, Richard **The Kid From Ozone Park & Other Stories** (Drumm 0-936055-32-4, Aug,87 [Jul,87], $3.50, 62pp, pb) Small pamphlet collection of 8 original stories, put together by the author before his death in March 1987. Drumm Booklet #27.

*Wilson, Robert Charles **Memory Wire** (Bantam 0-553-26853-8, Jan,88 [Dec,87], $3.50, 219pp, pb) Sf novel.

*Wilson, Rudy **The Red Truck** (Knopf 0-394-55846-4, May,87, $15.95, 178pp, hc) Literary first novel of hallucinatory fantasy -- or maybe just madness. The hero envisions Christ as a red truck.

Wilson, Steve **The Lost Traveler** (Ballantine 0-345-34113-9, Jul,87 [Jun,87], $2.95, 228pp, pb) Reprint (U.K. 1976) post-holocaust sf novel.

Windsor, Patricia **Killing Time** (Pan 0-330-30111-X, Sep,87, £1.95, 188pp, pb) Reprint (Harper & Row 1980) horror novel. [First U.K. edition]

Winslow, Pauline Glen **Judgement Day** (Baen 0-671-65646-5, Jun,87 [May,87], $3.50, 308pp, pb) Reprint (St. Martin's 1984) horror/dark fantasy novel.

*Wiseman, David **Adam's Common** (Blackie 0-216-92098-1, Feb,87, £7.95, 156pp, hc) Juvenile supernatural novel. [Not seen]

*Wismer, Don **Warrior Planet** (Baen 0-671-65642-2, May,87 [Apr,87], $2.95, 275pp, pb) Sf novel with fantasy elements -- "thieves vs. wizards -- and the galaxy is the prize!"

+Wittig, Monique **Across the Acheron** (Dufour Editions/Peter Owen 0-7206-0664-0, Dec,87, $17.95, 119pp, hc) Surreal fantasy novel, translated from French. This is the 1987 British edition from Peter Owen, with a Dufour paste-in.

Wolfe, Bernard **Limbo** (Carroll & Graf 0-88184-327-X, Aug,87 [Jul,87], $4.95, 413pp, pb) Reprint (Random House 1952) black-humor sf novel where war is prevented by voluntary amputation. A science fiction classic. Highly recommended (CNB). Also published as **Limbo 90**.

Wolfe, Gene **Soldier of the Mist** (Orbit 0-7088-8225-0, Aug,87, £2.95, 335pp, pb) Reprint (Gollancz/Tor 1986) fantasy novel. Dreary start to yet another fantasy series.

Wolfe, Gene **Soldier of the Mist** (Tor 0-812-55815-4, Oct,87 [Sep,87], $3.95, 335pp, pb) Reprint (Tor 1986) historical fantasy novel.

*Wolfe, Gene **The Urth of the New Sun** (Gollancz 0-575-04116-1, Aug,87, £11.95, 372pp, hc) Fantasy novel. Volume 5 in the "Book of the New Sun" series.

*Wolfe, Gene **The Urth of the New Sun** (Tor 0-312-93033-X, Nov,87 [Oct,87], $17.95, 372pp, hc) Sf novel, a coda to the "Book of the New Sun" series.

*Wolfe, Joyce **The White Spider** (Leisure 0-8439-2513-2, Aug,87 [Jul,87], $3.95, 400pp, pb) Horror novel.

*Wollheim, Donald A. & Arthur W. Saha, ed. **The 1987 Annual World's Best SF** (DAW 0-88677-203-6, Jun,87 [May,87], $3.95, 303pp, pb) Anthology of "bests" from 1986 with 10 stories, including several Hugo and Nebula nominees. Has the Nebula-winning novella, "R&R" by Lucius Shepard. Recommended. (CNB)

Wollheim, Donald A. & Arthur W. Saha, ed. **The 1987 Annual World's Best SF** (SFBC #11115, Jul,87 [Aug,87], $4.98, 271pp, hc) Reprint (DAW 1987) anthology with 10 sf stories.

*Womack, Jack **Ambient** (Weidenfeld & Nicolson 1-55584-082-5, Apr,87, $15.95, 259pp, hc) Dystopian sf novel of 21st-century Manhattan in the style of **A Clockwork Orange**.

*Wongar, B. **Gabo Djara** (Dodd, Mead 0-396-08861-9, Jul,87 [Aug,87], $16.95, 242pp, hc) Allegorical literary fantasy novel (third in a trilogy) about the destruction of aboriginal Australia, told from the point of view of a giant green ant (part of aboriginal mythology).

*Wood, Bari **Amy Girl** (NAL 0-453-00534-9, Apr,87 [Mar,87], $17.95, 346pp, hc) Horror novel about a 9-year-old psychic who can dominate other people's minds.

Wood, Bari **The Killing Gift** (NAL/Signet 0-451-14003-6, Apr,87 [Jun,87], $3.95, 313pp, pb) Reissue (Putnam 1975) horror novel; 13th printing.

Wood, Bari **The Tribe** (NAL/Signet 0-451-14004-4, Apr,87 [Jun,87], $3.95, 339pp, pb) Reissue (NAL 1981) horror novel; 6th printing.

Wood, Bari & Jack Geasland **Twins** (NAL/Signet 0-451-13654-3, Apr,87 [Jul,87], $3.95, 343pp, pb) Reissue (Putnam 1977) horror novel; 10th printing.

*Wood, Bridget **The Minstrel's Lute** (Robert Hale 0-7090-2880-6, Jan,87, £9.95, 208pp, hc) Supernatural thriller. [Not seen]

*Wood, Bridget **Satanic Lute** (Robert Hale 0-7090-2881-4, May,87, £10.25, 208pp, hc) Supernatural thriller. Sequel to **The Minstrel's Lute**. [Not seen]

*Wood, Robert **The Avatar** (Poplar 0-907657-14-1, May,87 [Jul,87], £9.95, 290pp, hc) Mainstream novel with fantasy touches.

+Woodroffe, Patrick **A Closer Look: The Art Techniques of Patrick Woodroffe** (Crown Harmony 0-517-56506-4, Apr,87 [Mar,87], $14.95, 127pp, tp) Fantasy art including work in progress and discussions on technique. First U.S. edition (Paper Tiger 1986).

*Woodroffe, Patrick **The Second Earth** (Paper Tiger 1-85028-042-8, Dec,87 [Jan,88], £12.95, 143pp, hc) Heavily revised version of **The Pentateuch**.

*Woodroffe, Patrick **The Second Earth** (Paper Tiger 1-85028-043-6, Dec,87 [Jan,88], £7.95, 143pp, tp) Trade paperback edition of the above.

Woods, Stuart **Under the Lake** (Heinemann 0-434-87811-1, Aug,87, £10.95, 301pp, hc) Reprint (Simon & Schuster 1987) ghost/horror novel. [First U.K. edition]

*Wooley, Persia **Child of the Northern Spring** (Simon & Schuster Poseidon 0-671-62200-5, May,87 [Apr,87], $17.95, 428pp, hc) Arthurian fantasy novel, seen through the eyes of Guinevere.

Woolverton, Linda **Star Wind** (Corgi 0-552-52459-X, Jul,87, £1.95, 177pp, pb) Reprint (Houghton Mifflin 1986) sf novel. [First U.K. edition]

*Wrede, Patricia C. **Caught in Crystal** (Ace 0-441-76006-6, Mar,87 [Feb,87], $2.95, 293pp, pb) Fantasy novel set in the world of **Shadow Magic** and **Daughter of Witches**. Now settled as a mother and innkeeper, Kayl is forced to retrace her adventurer's steps as dark forces resurface.

Wright, Betty Ren **Christina's Ghost** (Scholastic Apple 0-590-40284-6, Oct,87, $2.50, 105pp, pb) Reprint (Holiday House 1985) juvenile short novel of ghosts.

Wright, Gene **Horror Shows** (David & Charles 0-7153-9012-0, Mar,87 [Jun,87], £15.00, 296pp, hc) Reprint (Facts on File 1986) book on horror films, TV and radio shows. [First U.K. edition]

Wright, T.M. **Strange Seed** (Tor 0-812-52762-3, Dec,87 [Nov,87], $3.95, 309pp, pb) Reprint (Everest House 1978) horror novel.

Wrightson, Patricia **A Little Fear** (Penguin Puffin 0-14-031847-X, Mar,87, £1.50, 111pp, pb) Reprint (Hutchinson 1983) young-adult fantasy novel. Inported to US at $3.95.

*Wrightson, Patricia **Moon-dark** (Hutchinson 0-09-172559-3, Oct,87 [Dec,87], £6.50, 147pp, hc) Juvenile fantasy novel.

*Wu, William F. **Isaac Asimov's Robot City, Book 3: Cyborg** (Ace 0-441-37383-6, Nov,87 [Oct,87], $2.95, 169pp, pb) Sf novelization based on Isaac Asimov's robots.

*Wu, William F. **Masterplay** (Popular Library Questar 0-445-20504-0, Aug,87 [Jul,87], $3.50, 215pp, pb) Sf wargaming novel, a first novel. Parts have appeared in magazines in slightly different form.

*Wurts, Janny & Raymond E. Feist **Daughter of the Empire** Main listing under Raymond E. Feist.

*Wylie, Jonathan **The Centre of the Circle** (Corgi 0-552-13134-2, Jul,87 [Jun,87], £2.95, 351pp, pb) Fantasy novel. Volume 2 in the Servants of Ark trilogy. This is a pseudonym for Mark J.A. Smith & Julia Smith.

*Wylie, Jonathan **The First Named** (Corgi 0-552-13101-6, Mar,87, £2.50, 349pp, pb) Fantasy novel. Volume 1 of the "Servants of Ark" trilogy. This is a pseudonym for Mark J.A. Smith & Julia Smith. This is their first novel.

+Wylie, Jonathan **The First Named** (Bantam Spectra 0-553-26953-4, Nov,87 [Oct,87], $3.95, 281pp, pb) Fantasy novel, first in a trilogy, "Servants of Ark". First U.S. edition (Corgi 1987). "Wylie" is a pen name for Mark and Julia Smith.

Wylie, Laura **The Night Visitor** (Critic's Choice 1-55547-174-9, Jun,87 [May,87], $3.50, 288pp, pb) Reprint (Pinnacle 1979) horror novel.

Wyndham, John **Chocky** (Penguin 0-14-003121-9, Aug,87, £2.25, 153pp, pb) Reissue (Ballantine 1968) sf novel.

Wyndham, John **The Chrysalids** (Penguin 0-14-001308-3, Aug,87, £2.50, 200pp, pb) Reissue (Ballantine 1955) sf novel.

WYNDHAM, JOHN

ZELAZNY, ROGER

Wyndham, John **The Kraken Wakes** (Penguin 0-14-001075-0, Aug,87, £2.50, 240pp, pb) Reissue (Michael Joseph 1953) sf novel.

Wyndham, John **The Midwich Cuckoos** (Penguin 0-14-001440-3, Aug,87, £2.50, 220pp, pb) Reissue (Michael Joseph 1957) sf novel.

Wyndham, John **The Secret People** (NEL 0-450-42014-0, Aug,87, £2.50, 192pp, pb) Reprint (George Newnes 1935) sf novel.

Wyndham, John **Sleepers of Mars** (NEL 0-450-42023-X, Aug,87, £2.25, 155pp, pb) Reprint (Coronet 1973) sf collection.

Wyndham, John **Stowaway to Mars** (NEL 0-450-42024-8, Aug,87, £2.50, 189pp, pb) Reprint (George Newnes 1936, as **Planet Plane**) sf novel.

Wyndham, John **Wanderers of Time** (NEL 0-450-42015-9, Aug,87, £2.25, 158pp, pb) Reprint (Coronet 1973) sf collection.

Wyndham, John **Web** (Penguin 0-14-005338-7, Jun,87, £1.95, 141pp, pb) Reissue (Michael Joseph 1979) sf novel.

Yarbro, Chelsea Quinn **Ariosto** (Tor 0-812-55852-9, Jan,88 [Dec,87], $3.95, 361pp, pb) Reprint (Pocket 1980) alternate world historical fantasy novel.

*Yarbro, Chelsea Quinn **Firecode** (Popular Library 0-445-20229-7, Apr,87 [Mar,87], $3.95, 453pp, pb) Horror novel.

*Yarbro, Chelsea Quinn **A Flame in Byzantium** (Tor 0-312-93026-7, Oct,87 [Sep,87], $17.95, 470pp, hc) First in a new historical/vampire trilogy, featuring Olivia. A spinoff from her "Saint Germain" series.

Yarbro, Chelsea Quinn **Signs and Portents** (Jove 0-515-09345-9, Oct,87 [Sep,87], $2.95, 188pp, pb) Reprint (Dream Press 1984) collection of 10 stories, with an introduction by Charles L. Grant and an afterword by the author.

Yep, Laurence **Monster Makers, Inc.** (NAL/Signet 0-451-15055-4, Nov,87 [Oct,87], $2.95, 235pp, pb) Reprint (Arbor House 1986) young adult sf novel about a family that genetically engineers monsters for fun and profit.

Yep, Laurence **Shadow Lord** (Firecrest 0-85997-927-X, Jul,87 [1987], £7.95, 288pp, hc) Reprint (Pocket 1985) sf novel. Volume 37 in the Star Trek Novels series. [First U.K. edition, not seen]

*Yolen, Jane **A Sending of Dragons** (Julia MacRae 0-86203-322-5, Sep,87, £7.95, 256pp, hc) Juvenile fantasy novel. Volume 3 in the "Dragon's Blood" trilogy. [First U.K. edition, not seen]

*Yolen, Jane **A Sending of Dragons** (Delacorte 0-385-29587-1, Oct,87, $14.95, 189pp, hc) Young adult sf novel, conclusion of the "Dragons" trilogy; illustrated by Tom McKeveny.

Yolen, Jane **Tales of Wonder** (Orbit 0-7088-8226-9, Apr,87, £2.95, 275pp, pb) Reprint (Schocken 1983) fantasy collection. [First U.K. edition]

*Yolen, Jane, Martin H. Greenberg & Charles G. Waugh, eds. **Spaceships and Spells** (Harper & Row 0-06-026796-8, Nov,87, $12.95, 182pp, hc) Original anthology of 13 juvenile sf and fantasy stories.

*York, Carol Beach **Nights in Ghostland** (Pocket Archway 0-671-63792-4, Nov,87 [Oct,87], $2.50, 121pp, pb) Juvenile novel of ghosts.

*York, Rebecca **The Peregrine Connection #3: In Search of the Dove** (Dell 0-440-11038-6, Nov,86 [Feb,87], $2.95, 220pp, pb) Recruited by agents of the ultra-secret Peregrine Connection, Jessica Duval uses her special psychic gifts to help her trace a deadly drug and her missing brother, encountering a deadly voodoo cult. Adventure with fantasy elements.

*Zahava, Irene, ed. **Hear the Silence: Stories of Myth, Magic and Renewal** (Crossing Press 0-89594-212-7, Sep,86 [Jan,87], $22.95, 194pp, hc) Original anthology of feminist sf and fantasy stories of spirituality and self-renewal; 11 of the stories are original, 4 are reprints. Several are pieces of novels in progress. Published in 1986 but not seen until 1987.

*Zahava, Irene, ed. **Hear the Silence: Stories of Myth, Magic and Renewal** (Crossing Press 0-89594-211-9, Sep,86 [Jan,87], $8.95, 194pp, tp) Paperback edition of the above.

Zahn, Timothy **Cascade Point** (Baen 0-671-65633-3, Apr,87 [Mar,87], $3.95, 405pp, pb) Reprint (Bluejay 1986) collection of 13 stories.

Zahn, Timothy **Cobra** (Arrow 0-09-951410-9, Oct,87, £2.95, 346pp, pb) Reprint (Baen 1985) sf novel. Volume 15 in the Venture SF series. [First U.K. edition]

Zahn, Timothy **Spinneret** (Arrow 0-09-949690-9, Jul,87, £2.95, 339pp, pb) Reprint (Bluejay 1985) sf novel. [First U.K. edition]

*Zahn, Timothy **Triplet** (Baen 0-671-65341-5, Aug,87 [Jul,87], $3.50, 369pp, pb) A novel of magic and high technology, a la Zelazny's **Jack of Shadows**.

Zamyatin, Yevgeny **We** (Avon 0-380-63313-2, Jul,87 [Jun,87], $3.95, 232pp, pb) Reissue (Viking 1972) classic Russian sf novel, translated by Mira Ginsburg; 5th printing. The first English edition appeared in 1924, but this follows the 1972 retranslation. The book was first published in Russian in 1921.

Zebrowski, George, ed. **Nebula Awards 21: SFWA's Choices for the Best in Science Fiction & Fantasy 1985** (Harcourt Brace Jovanovich 0-15-164928-6, Jan,87, $19.95, 333pp, hc) Reprint (HBJ 1986) anthology. The paperback, listed last year, apparently came out several months before the hardcover.

*Zebrowski, George, ed. **Synergy; New Science Fiction: Vol. 1** (Harcourt Brace Jovanovich 0-15-687700-7, Nov,87, $5.95, 234pp, tp) Original anthology of 6 stories, a poem, and an article on sf. The centerpiece is a novella by Frederik Pohl, "My Life as a Born-Again Pig".

Zelazny, Roger **Blood of Amber** (SFBC #105197, Jan,87, $4.98, 182pp, hc) Reprint (Arbor House 1986) fantasy novel, seventh in the "Amber" series.

Zelazny, Roger **Blood of Amber** (Avon 0-380-89636-2, Jul,87 [Jun,87], $3.50, 215pp, pb) Reprint (Arbor House 1986) fantasy novel, seventh in the "Amber" series.

Zelazny, Roger **Blood of Amber** (Sphere 0-7221-9412-9, Oct,87, £2.75, 215pp, pb) Reprint (Arbor House 1986) fantasy novel. Volume 7 in the "Amber" series. [First U.K. edition]

*Zelazny, Roger **A Dark Traveling** (Walker Millennium 0-8027-6686-2, Apr,87 [May,87], $15.95, 143pp, hc) Parallel-world juvenile sf novel.

Zelazny, Roger **The Doors of His Face, the Lamps of His Mouth** (Methuen 0-413-40970-8, Jan,87, £2.50, 271pp, pb) Reprint (Doubleday 1971) collection of sf/fantasy stories.

Zelazny, Roger **The Doors of His Face, the Lamps of His Mouth** (Avon 0-380-01146-8, Oct,87 [Sep,87], $3.50, 252pp, pb) Reissue (Doubleday 1971) collection; 5th Avon printing.

Zelazny, Roger **The Dream Master** (Ace 0-441-16706-3, Mar,87 [Feb,87], $2.95, 182pp, pb) Reissue (Ace 1966) sf novel. Despite the cover blurb, this novel didn't win the Nebula. A shorter version did. It's still excellent and doesn't need any extra hype. The copyright page lists it as a "third printing" -- probably off by a factor of 10. Ace has had it continually in print for 20 years. (CNB)

Zelazny, Roger **Lord of Light** (Avon 0-380-44834-3, Feb,87 [Jan,87], $2.95, 319pp, pb) Reissue (Doubleday 1967) sf novel, a Hugo Award winner; 21st printing!

Zelazny, Roger **My Name is Legion** (Sphere 0-7221-9421-8, Oct,87 [Dec,87], £2.75, 204pp, pb) Reissue (Ballantine 1976) SF/fantasy collection.

*Zelazny, Roger **Sign of Chaos** (Arbor House 0-87795-926-9, Sep,87 [Aug,87], $15.95, 214pp, hc) Fantasy novel, 8th in the "Amber" series. It was supposed to be the final volume in the second series, but didn't make it. There will be two further books (or maybe more), making it a dekalogy.

ZELAZNY, ROGER

Zelazny, Roger **Sign of Chaos** (SFBC #11625, Dec,87, $4.98, 184pp, hc) Reprint (Arbor House 1987) fantasy novel, 8th in the "Amber" series.

Zelazny, Roger **Unicorn Variations** (Avon 0-380-70287-8, Apr,87 [Mar,87], $3.50, 249pp, pb) Reprint (Simon & Schuster/Timescape 1983) collection of 20 stories.

*Zimmer, Paul Edwin **A Gathering of Heroes** (Ace 0-441-27421-8, Sep,87 [Aug,87], $3.50, 368pp, pb) Fantasy novel, third in the "Dark Border" series.

*Zipes, Jack, ed. **The Complete Fairy Tales of the Brothers Grimm** (Bantam Classics 0-553-05184-9, Feb,87 [Jan,87], $21.95, 733pp, hc) Collection of fairy tales based on the Grimm Brothers' original volumes, including 32 stories previously unpublished in English; translated by Zipes, with illustrations by John Gruelle.

Zipes, Jack, ed. **The Complete Fairy Tales of the Brothers Grimm** (QPB 21-2155, Mar,87 [Feb,87], $11.50, 733pp, tp) Reprint (Bantam 1987) collection. This is an exact copy in paperback of the Bantam hardcover edition, less the ISBN and price.

+Zipes, Jack, ed. **Don't Bet on the Prince: Contemporary Feminist Fairy Tales in North America and Europe** (Methuen 0-416-01381-3, Feb,87 [Apr,87], $11.95, 270pp, tp) Anthology of modern fairy stories, "a fresh look at the fairy tale, with contributors Angela Carter, Tanith Lee and other notables offering an alternative view of the world." It's an excellent selection; recommended (FCM). A 1986 British book, now reprinted in America by Methuen U.S. There may or may not be a hardcover.

*Zipes, Jack, ed. **Don't Bet on the Prince: Contemporary Feminist Fairy Tales in North America and Europe** (Gower 0-566-05460-4, Mar,87 [1987], £6.95, 270pp, tp) Anthology of fairy stories. Simultaneous with US (Methuen) edition.

*Zipes, Jack, ed. **Victorian Fairy Tales: The Revolt of the Fairies and Elves** (Methuen 0-416-42080-X, Feb,87, £18.95, 381pp, hc) Compilation of fairytales by noted Victorian authors. Published simultaneously in Great Britain and America by Methuen. US price $25.00.

Title List: Books

THE 10TH VICTIM

The 10th Victim, Robert Sheckley, n.
* 14 Bellchamber Tower, Mark Valentine, oc
* The 1987 Annual World's Best SF, ed. Donald A. Wollheim & Arthur W. Saha, an
* 1987 Fiction Writer's Market, Laurie Henry, nf
+ 2001: A Space Odyssey/The City and the Stars/The Deep Range/A Fall of Moondust/Rendezvous With Rama, Arthur C. Clarke, om
* 2020: Vision of the Future, Andrew Hale, n.
* 2061: Odyssey Three, Arthur C. Clarke, n.
* The 28th Pan Book of Horror Stories, ed. Clarence Paget, oa
* 3 By Finney, Jack Finney, om
334, Thomas M. Disch, n.
* 6 Decades: The Best of Analog, ed. Stanley Schmidt, an
The Abandoned, Paul Gallico, n.
* Abyssos, Raymond Hardie, n.
+ Across the Acheron, Monique Wittig, n.
* Across the Sea of Suns, Gregory Benford, n.
* Adam's Common, David Wiseman, n.
+ The Adding Machine: Collected Essays, William S. Burroughs, nf
The Adventures of Baron Munchausen, R.E. Raspe, co
Adventures of Wim, Luke Rhinehart, n.
* AEgypt, John Crowley, n.
* After Long Silence, Sheri S. Tepper, n.
* After the Bomb: Week One, Gloria D. Miklowitz, n.
* After the Zap, Michael Armstrong, n.
* Aftershock, Robert Walker, n.
Against Infinity, Gregory Benford, n.
* Against the Night, the Stars: The Science Fiction of Arthur C. Clarke, John Hollow, nf
* Agent of Byzantium, Harry Turtledove, n.
* Agnes Day, Lionel Fenn, n.
* The AI War, Stephen Ames Berry, n.
Aiki, John Gilbert, n.
Albion: A Guide to Legendary Britain, Jennifer Westwood, nf
* Alchemical Texts, Bruce Boston, co
* The Alexandrian Ring, William R. Forstchen, n.
Alfred Hitchcock's Book of Horror Stories: Book 6, ed. Alfred Hitchcock, an
Alfred Hitchcock's Choice of Evils, ed. Elana Lore, an
Alfred Hitchcock's Murderers' Row, ed. Alfred Hitchcock, an
Alice in Wonderland, Lewis Carroll, n.
Alice's Adventures in Wonderland, Lewis Carroll, n.
An Alien Heat, Michael Moorcock, n.
* An Alien Light, Nancy Kress, n.
The Alien Swordmaster, Somtow Sucharitkul, n.
* Alien to Femininity, Marleen S. Barr, nf
Aliens, Alan Dean Foster, n.
Aliens in the Family, Margaret Mahy, n.
* Aliens in the Home: The Child in Horror Fiction, Sabine Bussing, nf
* Aliens: The Anthropology of Science Fiction, ed. George E. Slusser & Eric S. Rabkin, nf
* All About Strange Monsters of the Recent Past, Howard Waldrop, co
All Judgement Fled, James White, n.
* All the Clocks Are Melting, Bruce Boston, co
* Alligators, Guy N. Smith, n.
Alongside Night, J. Neil Schulman, n.
* Alqua Dreams, Rachel Pollack, n.
Alternate Asimovs, Isaac Asimov, oc
* Alternative Third World War, 1985 - 2035: A Personal History, Sir William Jackson, nf
The Amazing Power of Ashur Fine, Donald J. Sobol, n.
Amazing Science Fiction Stories: The War Years 1936-1945, ed. Martin H. Greenberg, an
Amazing Science Fiction Stories: The Wild Years 1946-1955, ed. Martin H. Greenberg, an
Amazing Science Fiction Stories: The Wonder Years 1926-1935, ed. Martin H. Greenberg, an
Ambassador of Progress, Walter Jon Williams, n.
The Ambassadors of Death, Terrance Dicks, n.
Ambient, Jack Womack, n.
Ambulance Ship, James White, co
America 2040 #3: The City in the Mist, Evan Innes, n.
The American Book of the Dead, Stephen Billias, n.
American Gothic, Robert Bloch, n.
American Horrors, ed. Gregory A. Waller, nf
Amerika, Brauna E. Pouns, n.
Ammie, Come Home, Barbara Michaels, n.

BATTLEFIELDS BEYOND TOMORROW: SCIENCE FICTION WAR...

* Amy Girl, Bari Wood, n.
Anasazi, Dean Ing, co
* Anatomy of Wonder, Third Edition, Neil Barron, nf
* Ancient Light, Mary Gentle, n.
Ancient of Days, Michael Bishop, n.
* And the Gods Laughed, Fredric Brown, co
Andersen's Fairy Tales, Hans Christian Andersen, co
Android at Arms, Andre Norton, n.
* Angel at Apogee, S.N. Lewitt, n.
Angel With the Sword, C.J. Cherryh, n.
* Angels in Hell, ed. Janet Morris, oa
Animal Farm, George Orwell, n.
* Annabelle, Ruby Jean Jensen, n.
* The Annals of the Heechee, Frederik Pohl, n.
Annerton Pit, Peter Dickinson, n.
Antares Dawn, Michael McCollum, n.
* Antares Passage, Michael McCollum, n.
* The Antelope Company at Large, Willis Hall, n.
* Antique Fairy Tales, ed. Jean L. Scrocco, ill. & Judy Mastrangelo, an
The Anvil of Ice, Michael Scott Rohan, n.
* Apocalypse 2000: Economic Breakdown and the Suicide of Democracy, Peter Jay & Michael Stewart, n.
The Aquiliad: Aquila in the New World, S.P. Somtow, n.
* Araminta Station, Jack Vance, n.
Archer's Goon, Diana Wynne Jones, n.
* The Architects of Hyperspace, Thomas R. McDonough, n.
* The Architecture of Fear, ed. Kathryn Cramer & Peter D. Pautz, oa
* Archon!, Stuart Gordon, n.
Are All the Giants Dead?, Mary Norton, n.
Ariosto, Chelsea Quinn Yarbro, n.
The Ark, Paul Erickson, n.
Armor, John Steakley, n.
* Arrow's Fall, Mercedes R. Lackey, n.
* Arrow's Flight, Mercedes R. Lackey, n.
* Arrows of the Queen, Mercedes R. Lackey, n.
Arslan, M.J. Engh, n.
The Art of Horror Stories, Peter Haining, nf
* The Art of Segrelles, Vincente Segrelles, pi
* The Art of the DragonLance Saga, ed. Margaret Weis, pi
* Arthur C. Clarke's Chronicles of the Strange and Mysterious, John Fairley & Simon Welfare, nf
Arthur C. Clarke's July 20, 2019, ed. Arthur C. Clarke, nf
* Arthur C. Clarke's Venus Prime, Volume 1: Breaking Strain, Paul Preuss, n.
The Artificial Kid, Bruce Sterling, n.
* Arzach and Other Fantasy Stories, Jean "Moebius" Giraud, pi
* Ascian in Rose, Charles de Lint, na
* Ash Wednesday, Chet Williamson, n.
Assault on the Gods, Stephen Goldin, n.
Assignment in Eternity, Robert A. Heinlein, co
Astro Pilots, Laura J. Mixon, n.
The Asutra, Jack Vance, n.
* At the Field's End: Interviews with 20 Pacific Northwest Writers, Nicholas O'Connell, nf
At the Mountains of Madness, H.P. Lovecraft, co
* Atlas of the Dragonlance World, Karen Wynn Fonstad, pi
* The Avatar, Robert Wood, n.
* The Awakeners, Sheri S. Tepper, om
* The Awakeners: Northshore, Sheri S. Tepper, n.
Babel 17, Samuel R. Delany, n.
* Baby Grand, Joe Keene & William W. Johnstone, n.
The Bachman Books, Stephen King, om
Bagdad, Ian Dennis, n.
* Ballantine Books: The First Decade, David Aronovitz, nf
* Baltasar and Blimunda, Jose Saramago, n.
* Bard IV: Raven's Gathering, Keith Taylor, n.
Bard: The Odyssey of the Irish, Morgan Llywelyn, n.
* Bare-Faced Messiah, Russell Miller, nf
Barlowe's Guide to Extraterrestrials, Wayne Douglas Barlowe, Beth Meacham & Ian Summers, pi
Bats Out of Hell, Guy N. Smith, n.
* Batteries Not Included, Wayland Drew, n.
* The Battle of Brazil: The Authorized Story and Annotated Screenplay of Terry Gilliam's Landmark Film, Jack Mathews, co
* Battle Station, Ben Bova, co
Battlefield Earth, L. Ron Hubbard, n.
* Battlefields Beyond Tomorrow: Science Fiction War Stories, ed. Charles G. Waugh & Martin H. Greenberg, an

BATTLESTAR GALACTICA #14: SURRENDER THE GALACTICA!   **CAPTIVE UNIVERSE**

* Battlestar Galactica #14: Surrender the Galactica!, Glen A. Larson
  & Robert Thurston, n.
* Battletech: Decision at Thunder Rift, William H. Keith, Jr., n.
* Battletech: Mercenary's Star, William H. Keith, Jr., n.
* Battletech: The Sword and the Dagger, Ardath Mayhar, n.
  Be Buried in the Rain, Barbara Michaels, n.
  Bearing an Hourglass, Piers Anthony, n.
+ The Beast House, Richard Laymon, n.
  The Beast Master, Andre Norton, n.
  The Beast of Heaven, Victor Kelleher, n.
* Beast Rising, Gregg Almquist, n.
  Beasts, John Crowley, n.
  The Beasts of Valhalla, George C. Chesbro, n.
* Becoming Alien, Rebecca Ore, n.
  The Beggar's Curse, Ann Cheetham, n.
  The Beginning Place, Ursula K. Le Guin, n.
  Behold the Man, Michael Moorcock, n.
* Being a Green Mother, Piers Anthony, n.
* Being Invisible, Thomas Berger, n.
  Bella Arabella, Liza Fosburgh, n.
* Beloved, Toni Morrison, n.
* Beloved Captain, Jo Simon, n.
* Beowulf, Julian Glover, pm
  Berserker Base, ed. Fred Saberhagen, oa
  Berserker: Blue Death, Fred Saberhagen, n.
  The Best Mysteries of Isaac Asimov, Isaac Asimov, co
  The Best of Eric Frank Russell, Eric Frank Russell, co
* The Best of Pamela Sargent, Pamela Sargent, co
* The Best of Trek #12, ed. Walter Irwin & G.B. Love, nf
  The Best Science Fiction of Isaac Asimov, Isaac Asimov, co
  Best SF of the Year 16, ed. Terry Carr, an
  Bestiary Mountain, John Forrester, n.
  Between Planets, Robert A. Heinlein, n.
  Between the Strokes of Night, Charles Sheffield, n.
+ Beware!, Richard Laymon, n.
* Beware, Beware - Strange and Sinister Tales, ed. Jean Richardson,
  an
* Bewitching of Alison Allbright, Alan Davidson, n.
  Beyond Armageddon, ed. Walter M. Miller, Jr. & Martin H. Greenberg,
  an
* Beyond Humanity, Justin Leiber, n.
* Beyond that River, Paul Christopher, oc
  Beyond the Safe Zone, Robert Silverberg, co
  Beyond the Stars, ed. Isaac Asimov, an
  Beyond the Veil, Janet Morris, n.
  Beyond Wizardwall, Janet Morris, n.
  The Big House, Naomi Mitchison, n.
  The Big Jump, Leigh Brackett, n.
  Bigfoot and the Hendersons, Joyce Thompson, n.
* Bimbos of the Death Sun, Sharyn McCrumb, n.
  Birth of Fire, Jerry E. Pournelle, n.
  The Bishop's Heir, Katherine Kurtz, n.
  Black Ashes, Noel Scanlon, n.
  Black Beauty, Robin McKinley & Anna Sewell, nv
  Black Harvest, Ann Cheetham, n.
  Black Hearts in Battersea, Joan Aiken, n.
  Black Magic, Whitley Strieber, n.
  The Black Magician, G.C. Edmondson & C.M. Kotlan, n.
  Black Orchid, Terence Dudley, n.
* Black Rainbow, Lloyd S. Jones, n.
  The Black Ship, Christopher B. Rowley, n.
  Black Star Rising, Frederik Pohl, n.
* The Black Unicorn, Terry Brooks, n.
  Black Vulmea's Vengeance, Robert E. Howard, co
  A Blackbird in Silver, Freda Warrington, n.
  Blade of the Poisoner, Douglas Hill, n.
* Blanche, Patricia Wendorf, n.
  The Blind Spot, Austin Hall & Homer Eon Flint, n.
  Blood Brothers of Gor, John Norman, n.
  Blood Heritage, Sheri S. Tepper, n.
* Blood Hunt, Lee Killough, n.
* Blood Mist, Robert James, n.
* Blood Moon, Leslie Horvitz, n.
  Blood of Amber, Roger Zelazny, n.
* Blood of Eagles, Dean Ing, n.
  Bloodhype, Alan Dean Foster, n.
* Bloodshow, Guy N. Smith, n.
* Bloodthirst, J.M. Dillard, n.

* Bloodworm, John Halkin, n.
  The Bloody Chamber, Angela Carter, co
  The Bloody Sun, Marion Zimmer Bradley, n.
  Blossom Culp and the Sleep of Death, Richard Peck, n.
* Blow-Out!, Thomas N. Scortia & Frank M. Robinson, n.
  Blue Adept, Piers Anthony, n.
  The Blue World, Jack Vance, n.
* Bluebeard, Kurt Vonnegut, Jr., n.
* Bluebeard's Egg, Margaret Atwood, co
  The Bog, Michael Talbot, n.
* The Boiled Frog Syndrome, Marty Rubin, n.
* Bones of the Moon, Jonathan Carroll, n.
* Bonny Starr and the Riddles of Time, Gwen Grant, n.
  The Book of Andre Norton, Andre Norton, co
  The Book of Lost Tales I, J.R.R. Tolkien, co
  The Book of Merlyn, T.H. White, n.
* The Book of Mordred, Peter Hanratty, n.
  Book of Science Fiction, Allen W. Sharp, nf
  The Book of Silence, Lawrence Watt-Evans, n.
  The Book of Skulls, Robert Silverberg, n.
* The Book of Spells, Sara Maitland, oc
  Books of Blood, Clive Barker, om
  Born of the Sun, Gillian Cross, n.
* Born to Howl, Mel Gilden, n.
  A Box of Nothing, Peter Dickinson, n.
* The Boy Who Was Thrown Away, Stephanie Smith, n.
* The Boy With Penny Eyes, Al Sarrantonio, n.
  Brak the Barbarian, John Jakes, n.
* The Brass Halo, James Nugent, n.
  The Brave Free Men, Jack Vance, n.
  Breakfast in the Ruins, Michael Moorcock, n.
* The Breeder, Ed Kelleher & Harriette Vidal, n.
+ Breeding Ground, Shaun Hutson, n.
  The Brega Path, Dennis L. McKiernan, n.
* The Brentwood Witches, Brenda Jordan, n.
  The Bridge, Iain Banks, n.
* The Bridge of Lost Desire, Samuel R. Delany, co
* Bright and Shining Tiger, Claudia J. Edwards, n.
  Bring the Jubilee, Ward Moore, n.
  The Broken Sword, Poul Anderson, n.
  Bronwyn's Bane, Elizabeth Ann Scarborough, n.
  The Bronze King, Suzy McKee Charnas, n.
* The Broom of the System, David Foster Wallace, n.
+ The Broonie, Silkies & Fairies: Travellers' Tales of the Other
  World, Duncan Williamson, co
+ The Brothel in Rosenstrasse, Michael Moorcock, n.
* Brother and Other Stories, Clifford D. Simak, co
  Brotherkind, J.N. Williamson, n.
* Brothers, William Goldman, n.
* The Bruce Boston Omnibus, Bruce Boston, om
* Buckskin Brigades, L. Ron Hubbard, n.
* Budspy, David Dvorkin, n.
* Buffalo Gals and Other Animal Presences, Ursula K. Le Guin, co
+ Burial Rites, Michael Scott, n.
  Burning Chrome, William Gibson, co
* The Bus, Paul Kirchner, pi
* Bye Bye Blackbird, Patricia Wendorf, n.
* Byzantium's Crown, Susan M. Shwartz, n.
* C.A.D.S. #4: Tech Strike Force, John Sievert, n.
* C.S. Lewis, Joe R. Christopher, nf
* C.S. Lewis and His World, David Barratt, nf
  The Cabalist, Amanda Prantera, n.
  Cachalot, Alan Dean Foster, n.
* Cadre Lucifer, Robert O'Riordan, n.
* Caliban Landing, Steven Popkes, n.
  The California Iceberg, Harry Harrison, n.
* The Calvin Nullifier, Gene DeWeese, n.
  Caly, Sharon Combes, n.
  Camber of Culdi, Katherine Kurtz, n.
  Camber the Heretic, Katherine Kurtz, n.
* Cameron's Closet, Gary Brandner, n.
  Campbell Wood, Al Sarrantonio, n.
* Candlelight Ecstasy Romance #462: Out of This World, Lori
  Copeland, n.
* Candlelight Ecstasy Supreme #125: Moonlight & Magic, Melanie
  Catley, n.
  Capricorn Games, Robert Silverberg, co
  Captive Universe, Harry Harrison, n.

CARDOGRAPHY

* **Cardography**, Orson Scott Card, co
  Carrion, Gary Brandner, n.
* **Casca #17: The Warrior**, Barry Sadler, n.
* **Casca #18: The Cursed**, Barry Sadler, n.
  Cascade Point, Timothy Zahn, co
  A Case of Conscience, James Blish, n.
* **The Case of the Visiting Vampire**, Drew Stevenson, n.
  Casket of Souls, Ian Livingstone, ss
* **Casting the Runes and Other Ghost Stories**, M.R. James, co
  Castle of Crossed Destinies, Italo Calvino, co
  Cat Karina, Michael G. Coney, n.
  Cat Magic, Whitley Strieber, n.
* **Cat's Pawn**, Leslie Gadallah, n.
  Catmagic, Jonathan Barry & Whitley Strieber, n.
  Catseye, Andre Norton, n.
* **Caught in Crystal**, Patricia C. Wrede, n.
  The Celery Stalks at Midnight, James Howe, nv
  Cemetery World, Clifford D. Simak, n.
  The Centaur in the Garden, Moacyr Scliar, n.
* **The Centre of the Circle**, Jonathan Wylie, n.
* **Chain Letter**, Ruby Jean Jensen, n.
  Chain of Attack, Gene DeWeese, n.
  Chains of Gold, Nancy Springer, n.
  Challenge of the Clans, Kenneth C. Flint, n.
  Champions of the Sidhe, Kenneth C. Flint, n.
* **Chance & Other Gestures of the Hand of Fate**, Nancy Springer, co
  The Changeover, Margaret Mahy, n.
  Chanur's Homecoming, C.J. Cherryh, n.
  Chapterhouse: Dune, Frank Herbert, n.
* **Charles Keeping's Classic Tales of the Macabre**, ed. Charles
    Keeping, an
* **Charles Williams**, Kathleen Spencer, nf
  Charlie and the Chocolate Factory, Roald Dahl, n.
  Charlie and the Great Glass Elevator, Roald Dahl, n.
  Charlotte Sometimes, Penelope Farmer, n.
* **Charon's Ark**, Rick Gauger, n.
* **Chernobyl**, Frederik Pohl, n.
  Cherron, Sharon Combes, n.
* **The Child in Time**, Ian McEwan, n.
* **Child of the Northern Spring**, Persia Wooley, n.
  Childhood's End, Arthur C. Clarke, n.
  Children of Morrow, H.M. Hoover, n.
  Children of the Lens, E.E. "Doc" Smith, n.
  Children of the Light, Carolyn Weston, n.
  Chocky, John Wyndham, n.
  Christina's Ghost, Betty Ren Wright, n.
  Christine, Stephen King, n.
* **Christmas 1993**, Leslie Bricusse, pm
* **Christmas Ghosts**, ed. Kathryn Cramer & David G. Hartwell, an
  Chrome, George Nader, n.
  The Chronicles of Corum, Michael Moorcock, om
  The Chrysalids, John Wyndham, n.
  Chthon, Piers Anthony, n.
* **Cinemonsters**, ed. Martin H. Greenberg, an
* **Circuit Breaker**, Melinda M. Snodgrass, n.
  A Circus of Hells, Poul Anderson, n.
  Cirque, Terry Carr, n.
  Citizen of the Galaxy, Robert A. Heinlein, n.
  The City and the Stars, Arthur C. Clarke, n.
  The City in the Autumn Stars, Michael Moorcock, n.
  City of Gold and Lead, John Christopher, n.
* **City of Hawks**, Gary Gygax, n.
  City of Sorcery, Marion Zimmer Bradley, n.
  Clan Ground, Clare Bell, n.
  The Clan of the Cave Bear, Jean M. Auel, n.
  Classic Book of Fairy Stories, ed. Dinah Maria Craik, an
  Classic Stories of Mystery, Horror and Suspense, ed. Simon
    Petherick, an
  The Classical Wizard/Magus Mirabilis in Oz, L. Frank Baum, n.
  Classics of the Macabre, Daphne du Maurier, co
  The Clean-up, John M. Skipp & Craig Spector, n.
  The Cleanup, John M. Skipp & Craig Spector, n.
  A Clockwork Orange, Anthony Burgess, pl
  Closed System, Zach Hughes, n.
  A Closer Look: The Art Techniques of Patrick Woodroffe, Patrick
    Woodroffe, nf
  Cloud Warrior, Patrick Tilley, n.
  Cobra, Timothy Zahn, n.

+ **Cobwebwalking**, Sara Banerji, n.
* **Code Blue--Emergency!**, James White, n.
  The Coelura, Anne McCaffrey, n.
* **Cold Print**, Ramsey Campbell, co
  Cold Sea Rising, Richard Moran, n.
* **The Collected Arthur Machen**, Arthur Machen, co
* **Collected Short Stories**, Kingsley Amis, co
* **The Collected Stories of Philip K. Dick, Vol. Five: The Little Black
    Box**, Philip K. Dick, co
* **The Collected Stories of Philip K. Dick, Vol. Four: The Days of
    Perky Pat**, Philip K. Dick, co
* **The Collected Stories of Philip K. Dick, Vol. One: Beyond Lies the
    Wub**, Philip K. Dick, co
* **The Collected Stories of Philip K. Dick, Vol. Three: The Father
    Thing**, Philip K. Dick, co
* **The Collected Stories of Philip K. Dick, Vol. Two: Second Variety**,
    Philip K. Dick, co
  Come Hunt an Earthman, Philip E. High, n.
  The Coming of the Quantum Cats, Frederik Pohl, n.
* **Common Body, Royal Bones**, Evelyn Shefner, co
* **Companion to Narnia**, Paul F. Ford, nf
  The Compass Rose, Ursula K. Le Guin, co
* **The Compleat Crow**, Brian Lumley, co
  The Compleat Traveller in Black, John Brunner, co
* **The Complete Adventures of Charlie and Mr. Willy Wonka**, Roald
    Dahl, om
* **The Complete Alice and The Hunting of the Snark**, Lewis Carroll, om
* **The Complete Fairy Tales of the Brothers Grimm**, ed. Jack Zipes, co
  Complete Illustrated Works, Lewis Carroll, co
* **The Complete Robert Bloch: An Illustrated, Comprehensive
    Bibliography**, Randall D. Larson, nf
+ **The Complete Short Stories of L.P. Hartley**, L.P. Hartley, om
* **The Complete Supernatural Stories of Rudyard Kipling**, Rudyard
    Kipling, co
  Comprador, David R. Cudlip, n.
  The Computer That Ate My Brother, Dean Marney, n.
  Conan #15: The Sword of Skelos, Andrew J. Offutt, n.
  Conan #16: The Road of Kings, Karl Edward Wagner, n.
  Conan of Cimmeria, Robert E. Howard, L. Sprague de Camp & Lin
    Carter, co
* **Conan the Champion**, John Maddox Roberts, n.
* **Conan the Defiant**, Steve Perry, n.
  Conan the Liberator, L. Sprague de Camp & Lin Carter, n.
* **Conan the Marauder**, John Maddox Roberts, n.
  Conan the Raider, Leonard Carpenter, n.
  Conan the Swordsman, Robert E. Howard, Lin Carter, L. Sprague de
    Camp & Bjorn Nyberg, co
  Conan the Valorous, John Maddox Roberts, n.
  Conan the Victorious, Robert Jordan, n.
* **Consider Phlebas**, Iain Banks, n.
  Contact, Carl Sagan, n.
  Continent, Jim Crace, oc
* **Conversations with Lord Byron on Perversion, 163 Years After His
    Lordship's Death**, Amanda Prantera, n.
* **Copernick's Rebellion**, Leo A. Frankowski, n.
* **The Cornelius Chronicles, Vol. III**, Michael Moorcock, om
  Cosmic Knights, ed. Isaac Asimov, Martin H. Greenberg & Charles G.
    Waugh, an
  The Cosmic Puppets, Philip K. Dick, n.
  Cosmicomics, Italo Calvino, co
* **Cosmogony and Cosmology**, Philip K. Dick, nf
* **Count Dracula, Me and Norma D.**, Jessica Hatchigan, n.
  Count Zero, William Gibson, n.
* **Counting the Cost**, David Drake, n.
  Cracken at Critical, Brian W. Aldiss, n.
  Cracken at Critical/The Magic of the Past, Brian W. Aldiss, om
  The Cradle will Fall, Mary Higgins Clark, n.
  Creeps: An Alien in our School, Tim Schoch, n.
* **The Crib**, Paul Kent, n.
* **A Crock of Clear Water**, Barbara Harrington, n.
+ **The Crone**, Bill Garnett, n.
* **Crooked House**, Thomas F. Monteleone & John DeChancie, n.
* **The Crown Jewels**, Walter Jon Williams, n.
* **Crows' Parliament**, Jack Curtis, n.
* **Crusaders in Hell**, ed. Janet Morris, oa
  A Cry in the Night, Mary Higgins Clark, n.
* **Cry Wolf**, Alan B. Chronister, n.
  Cryptozoic!, Brian W. Aldiss, n.

The Crystal Gryphon, Andre Norton, n.
* The Crystal Memory, Stephen Leigh, n.
* The Crystal Sword, Adrienne Martine-Barnes, n.
* Cthulhu: The Mythos and Kindred Horrors, Robert E. Howard, co
Cuckoo's Egg, C.J. Cherryh, n.
Cujo, Stephen King, n.
The Cunningham Equations, G.C. Edmondson & C.M. Kotlan, n.
* The Curious Case of Richard Fielding and Other Stories, Paul Roland, oc
* The Curse of the Obelisk, Ron Goulart, n.
Cutting Edge, ed. Dennis Etchison, an
* Cvltvre Made Stvpid, Tom Weller, pi
The Cybernetic Samurai, Victor Milan, n.
The Cyborg and the Sorcerers, Lawrence Watt-Evans, n.
Cyclops, Clive Cussler, n.
Dad's Nuke, Marc Laidlaw, n.
Daggerspell, Katharine Kerr, n.
Dagon and Other Macabre Tales, H.P. Lovecraft, co
+The Damnation Game, Clive Barker, n.
The Dancer from Atlantis, Poul Anderson, n.
The Dancers of Arun, Elizabeth A. Lynn, n.
* The Dandelion Caper, Gene DeWeese, n.
The Danger Quotient, Annabel Johnson & Edgar Johnson, n.
Danger! Space Pirates, Maggie Freeman, n.
Dangerous Visions, ed. Harlan Ellison, oa
* Danilov the Violist, Vladimir Orlov, n.
* Danni's Desperate Journey, Ann Grocott, n.
* Daphne Du Maurier's Classics of the Macabre, Daphne du Maurier, co
* Daredevils, Ltd., Ron Goulart, n.
Dark Angel, Virginia Andrews, n.
The Dark Cry of the Moon, Charles L. Grant, n.
* The Dark Descent, ed. David G. Hartwell, an
The Dark Design, Philip Jose Farmer, n.
* The Dark Druid, Kenneth C. Flint, n.
* Dark Feasts, Ramsey Campbell, co
Dark Gods, T.E.D. Klein, co
The Dark Is Rising Sequence, Susan Cooper, om
* The Dark Lady: A Romance of the Far Future, Mike Resnick, n.
Dark Messiah, David Alexander, n.
Dark of the Moon, P.C. Hodgell, n.
Dark Romance: Sexuality in the Horror Film, David J. Hogan, nf
* Dark Seeker, K.W. Jeter, n.
* The Dark Side, Zach Hughes, n.
* The Dark Tower II: The Drawing of the Three, Stephen King, n.
* A Dark Traveling, Roger Zelazny, n.
The Dark Void, ed. Isaac Asimov, an
* A Darker Magic, Michael Bedard, n.
The Darkest Road, Guy Gavriel Kay, n.
A Darkness at Sethanon, Raymond E. Feist, n.
Darkover Landfall, Marion Zimmer Bradley, n.
Darkside, Dennis Etchison, n.
* Darkspell, Katharine Kerr, n.
* The Darksword Trilogy, Volume 1: Forging the Darksword, Margaret Weis & Tracy Hickman, n.
Daughter of Regals, Stephen R. Donaldson, co
* Daughter of the Bear King, Eleanor Arnason, n.
* Daughter of the Empire, Raymond E. Feist & Janny Wurts, n.
Daughters of a Coral Dawn, Katherine V. Forrest, n.
* The Daughters of Megwyn, Antoinette Kelsall Bird, n.
* David's Sling, Marc Stiegler, n.
* Dawn, Octavia E. Butler, n.
The Day It Rained Forever, Ray Bradbury, co
* The Day of Creation, J.G. Ballard, n.
Day of the Starwind, Douglas Hill, n.
* The Daymaker, Ann Halam, n.
* Dayworld Rebel, Philip Jose Farmer, n.
Deadly Friend, Diana Henstell, n.
Death Bell, Guy N. Smith, n.
Death Dreams, William Katz, n.
Death Is a Lonely Business, Ray Bradbury, n.
* A Death of Honor, Joe Clifford Faust, n.
* Death Tolls, John E. Stith, n.
Death Trance, Graham Masterton, n.
* Death's Arms, K.W. Jeter, n.
* Deathday, Shaun Hutson, n.
Deathhunter, Ian Watson, n.
* Deathlands #3: Neutron Solstice, James Axler, n.

* Deathlands #4: Crater Lake, James Axler, n.
Deathwatch, Elleston Trevor, n.
Deathwing Over Veynaa, Douglas Hill, n.
Deathworld, Harry Harrison, n.
Deathworld 1, Harry Harrison, n.
Deathworld 2, Harry Harrison, n.
Deathworld 3, Harry Harrison, n.
The Deceivers, Alfred Bester, n.
The Deep, John Crowley, n.
Deep Domain, Howard Weinstein, n.
The Deep Range, Arthur C. Clarke, n.
The Defiant Agents, Andre Norton, n.
* The Definitive Time Machine: A Critical Edition of H.G. Wells' Scientific Romance, Harry M. Geduld, n.
* The Delights of Terror: An Aesthetics of the Tale of Terror, Terry Heller, nf
The Delikon, H.M. Hoover, n.
Delirium's Mistress, Tanith Lee, n.
* The Delta, Colin Wilson, n.
* The Deluge Drivers, Alan Dean Foster, n.
Delusion's Master, Tanith Lee, n.
* Demogorgon, Brian Lumley, n.
The Demolished Man, Alfred Bester, n.
* A Demon Close Behind, Leslie Halliwell, oc
+The Demon Lord, Peter Morwood, n.
* Demons, Guy N. Smith, n.
* Demons!, ed. Jack M. Dann & Gardner R. Dozois, an
The Demu Trilogy, F.M. Busby, om
Deryni Checkmate, Katherine Kurtz, n.
Deryni Rising, Katherine Kurtz, n.
+Despatches from the Frontiers of the Female Mind, ed. Jen Green & Sarah Lefanu, an
* The Destroying Angel, Bernard King, n.
Devil in the Darkness, Archie Roy, n.
The Devil in the Dooryard, Gregory Blake Smith, n.
The Devil in Velvet, John Dickson Carr, n.
Devil on My Back, Monica Hughes, n.
* The Devil Rides Out, Alison Sage & Dennis Wheatley, n.
* The Devil Rocked Her Cradle, David St. Clair, n.
* The Devil's Advocate: An Ambrose Bierce Reader, Ambrose Bierce, co
* The Devil's Cat, William W. Johnstone, n.
+Devil's Child, Margaret Bingley, n.
* The Devil's Mistress, Virginia Coffman, n.
Devil's Race, Avi, n.
The Devil's Virgin, Virginia Coffman, n.
* Devils and Demons, ed. Marvin Kaye, an
* Devotion, Daniel Westerly, n.
* The Devouring, F.W. Armstrong, n.
* The Dictionary of Imaginary Places, Expanded Edition, Alberto Manguel & Gianni Guadalupi, nf
A Different Light, Elizabeth A. Lynn, n.
* A Difficulty With Dwarves, Craig Shaw Gardner, n.
Dinner at Deviant's Palace, Tim Powers, n.
* Dirk Gently's Holistic Detective Agency, Douglas Adams, n.
Disappearances, Howard Frank Mosher, n.
* Discovering H.P. Lovecraft, ed. Darrell Schweitzer, nf
The Discovery of King Arthur, Geoffrey Ashe & Debrett's Peerage, nf
* A Distant Soil, Colleen Doran, gn
+Divine Endurance, Gwyneth Jones, n.
* Doc Savage Omnibus #2, Kenneth Robeson, om
* Doc Savage Omnibus #3, Kenneth Robeson, om
* Doc Savage Omnibus #4, Kenneth Robeson, om
* The Doctor Who Fun Book, Tim Quinn & Dicky Howett, nf
The Doctor Who Illustrated A-Z, Lesley Standring, nf
Doctor Who: The Key to Time, Peter Haining, nf
* Doctor Who: The Time-Travellers' Guide, Peter Haining, nf
The Doll Who Ate His Mother, Ramsey Campbell, n.
Dolphin Island, Arthur C. Clarke, n.
* Dome, Michael Reaves & Steve Perry, n.
* Don't Bet on the Prince: Contemporary Feminist Fairy Tales in North America and Europe, ed. Jack Zipes, an
Don't Bite the Sun, Tanith Lee, n.
* Don't Panic: The Official Hitch Hiker's Guide to the Galaxy Companion, Neil Gaiman, nf
* Doom City, ed. Charles L. Grant, oa
* The Doom of Soulis, Moira Miller, n.
Doom Wind, Max Gunther, n.

DOOMSDAY MORNING

THE EVIL ONE

Doomsday Morning, C.L. Moore, n.
Doomsday Warrior # 4: Bloody America, Ryder Stacy, n.
Doomsday Warrior # 5: America's Last Declaration, Ryder Stacy, n.
* Doomsday Warrior #10: American Nightmare, Ryder Stacy, n.
* Doomsday Warrior #11: American Eden, Ryder Stacy, n.
* Doomsday Warrior #12: Death, American Style, Ryder Stacy, n.
* The Door Between, Nancy Garden, n.
A Door Into Ocean, Joan Slonczewski, n.
The Door To December, Leigh Nichols, n.
The Doors of His Face, the Lamps of His Mouth, Roger Zelazny, co
* Doppelganger, Eric C. Higgs, n.
Dorothy and the Wizard in Oz, L. Frank Baum, n.
Double Nocturne, Cynthia Felice, n.
* Double Trouble, Barthe DeClements & Christopher Greimes, n.
* Dover Beach, Richard Bowker, n.
* Down on the Farm, John Stchur, n.
Down Town, Tappan King & Viido Polikarpus, n.
Down Town, Viido Polikarpus & Tappan King, n.
Downbelow Station, C.J. Cherryh, n.
Downtime, Peter Fox, n.
Dr. Adder, K.W. Jeter, n.
Dr. Bloodmoney, Philip K. Dick, n.
* Dr. Chill's Project, Thomas Hoobler, n.
* Dr. Dredd's Wagon of Wonders, Bill Brittain, n.
* Dr. Jekyll and Mr. Hyde, Samantha Lee & Robert Louis Stevenson, n.
Dr. Jekyll and Mr. Hyde, Robert Louis Stevenson, co
Dr. Jekyll and Mr. Hyde and Weir of Herminston, Robert Louis
　Stevenson, om
* Dracula, Bram Stoker, n.
Dracula Book of Great Vampire Stories, ed. Leslie A. Shepard, an
* The Dracula Centenary Book, Peter Haining, nf
* Dracula's Brood, ed. Richard Dalby, an
* Dracula's Children, R. Chetwynd-Hayes, oc
* Dragon, Nigel Frith, n.
The Dragon in the Sword, Michael Moorcock, n.
+ The Dragon Lord, Peter Morwood, n.
* Dragon's Gold, Piers Anthony & Robert E. Margroff, n.
DragonLance Legends, Vol. 1: Time of the Twins, Margaret Weis &
　Tracy Hickman, n.
DragonLance Legends, Vol. 2: War of the Twins, Margaret Weis &
　Tracy Hickman, n.
DragonLance Legends, Vol. 3: Test of the Twins, Margaret Weis &
　Tracy Hickman, n.
* DragonLance Tales Vol. 1: The Magic of Krynn, ed. Margaret Weis &
　Tracy Hickman, oa
* DragonLance Tales Vol. 2: Kender, Gully Dwarves, and Gnomes,
　ed. Margaret Weis & Tracy Hickman, oa
* DragonLance Tales Vol. 3: Love and War, ed. Margaret Weis & Tracy
　Hickman, oa
The Drawing of the Dark, Tim Powers, n.
The Dreadful Future of Blossom Culp, Richard Peck, n.
* Dreadful Pleasures, James B. Twitchell, nf
The Dream, H.G. Wells, n.
* The Dream Auditor, Lesley Choyce, oc
+ The Dream Catcher, Monica Hughes, n.
* Dream For Danger, Anna Lewins, n.
* Dream Makers: SF and Fantasy Writers at Work (Revised), Charles
　Platt, nf
The Dream Master, Roger Zelazny, n.
The Dream of John Ball, William Morris, na
A Dream of Wessex, Christopher Priest, n.
* Dream Walker, Jacqueline Marten, n.
* Dream Wall, Graham Dunstan Martin, n.
The Dreaming Jewels, Theodore Sturgeon, n.
* Dreams and Swords, Katherine V. Forrest, oc
* Dreams Are Wiser Than Men, ed. Richard Russo, an
Dreams of the Raven, Carmen Carter, n.
The Dreamstone, C.J. Cherryh, n.
* Drink the Fire From the Flames, Scott Baker, n.
The Drowned World, J.G. Ballard, n.
* Drowntide, Sydney J. Van Scyoc, n.
* Dualists, Stephen Bowkett, n.
Duel and Other Horror Stories of the Road, ed. William Pattrick, an
* Duncan and Mallory: The Bar-None Ranch, Robert Lynn Asprin &
　Mel White, gn
Dune, Frank Herbert, n.
Dwellers in the Crucible, Margaret Wander Bonanno, n.
* Early in Orcadia, Naomi Mitchison, n.

The Earth Book of Stormgate - 1, Poul Anderson, co
The Earth Book of Stormgate - 2, Poul Anderson, co
The Earth Book of Stormgate - 3, Poul Anderson, co
The Earth Goddess, Richard Herley, n.
* Earth's Children, Jean M. Auel, om
Earthblood, Keith Laumer & Rosel George Brown, n.
* Earthclan, David Brin, om
* Earthdoom!, David Langford & John Grant, n.
The Earthsea Trilogy, Ursula K. LeGuin, om
Earthseed, Pamela Sargent, n.
* The Earthstone, Diana L. Paxson, n.
Earthwind, Robert P. Holdstock, n.
* Echoes of Valor, ed. Karl Edward Wagner, an
Eclipse, John Shirley, n.
* Eclipse of Uncertainty: An Introduction to Postmodern Fantasy,
　Lance Olsen, nf
* Eddy Deco's Last Caper: An Illustrated Mystery, Gahan Wilson, n.
+ Eden, W.A. Harbinson, n.
An Edge in My Voice, Harlan Ellison, nf
* Eileen Goudge's Swept Away #1: Gone With the Wish, Eileen
　Goudge, n.
* Eileen Goudge's Swept Away #2: Woodstock Magic, Fran Lantz, n.
* Eileen Goudge's Swept Away #3: Love on the Range, Louise E.
　Powers, n.
* Eileen Goudge's Swept Away #4: Star Struck, Eileen Goudge, n.
* Eileen Goudge's Swept Away #5: Spellbound, Jennifer Rabin, n.
* Eileen Goudge's Swept Away #6: Once Upon a Kiss, Mar Garrido, n.
* Eileen Goudge's Swept Away #7: Pirate Moon, Merrilee Steiner, n.
* Eileen Goudge's Swept Away #8: All Shook Up, Fran Lantz, n.
* The Einstein Legacy, Richard Elliott, n.
* Einstein's Monsters, Martin Amis, co
* The El Dorado Adventure, Lloyd Alexander, n.
Elfquest, Vol.1: The Blood of Ten Chiefs, ed. Richard Pini, Lynn
　Abbey & Robert Lynn Asprin, oa
* Eli's Ghost, Betsy Bearne, n.
* Elixir, J. Edward Lord, n.
Elric at the End of Time, Michael Moorcock, co
* Elric at the End of Time, Michael Moorcock & Rodney Matthews, pi
Emergence, David R. Palmer, n.
+ Emma in Winter, Penelope Farmer, n.
* An Emperor For the Legion, Harry Turtledove, n.
* Empery, Michael P. Kube-McDowell, n.
Empire of the East, Book 1: The Broken Lands, Fred Saberhagen, n.
Empire of the Sun, J.G. Ballard, n.
The Empire of Time, Crawford Kilian, n.
* The Empress of Earth, Melissa Scott, n.
Enchanters' End Game, David Eddings, n.
* The Enchantments of Flesh and Spirit, Storm Constantine, n.
Encyclopaedia of Horror, ed. Richard Davis, n.
* Encyclopaedia of the Worlds of Doctor Who: A-D, David Saunders, nf
Encyclopaedia of Feminism, Lisa Tuttle, nf
The Encyclopedia of Ghosts, Daniel Cohen, nf
+ The Encyclopedia of Horror Movies, Phil Hardy, nf
The Encyclopedia of Monsters, Daniel Cohen, nf
The Encyclopedia of Superheroes, Jeff Rovin, nf
* The Encyclopedia of Supervillains, Jeff Rovin, nf
* The End of the Game, Sheri S. Tepper, om
Ender's Game, Orson Scott Card, n.
* Endgame Enigma, James P. Hogan, n.
* Endworld #5: Dakota Run, David Robbins, n.
* Endworld #6: Citadel Run, David Robbins, n.
* The Enemy Stars, Poul Anderson, co
Enterprise: The First Adventure, Vonda N. McIntyre, n.
+ Entombed, Guy N. Smith, n.
The Entropy Effect, Vonda N. McIntyre, n.
The Entropy Tango, Michael Moorcock, n.
Eon, Greg Bear, n.
* Equal Rites, Terry Pratchett, n.
* Espedair Street, Iain Banks, n.
The Essential Colin Wilson, Colin Wilson, co
* The Essential Ellison, Harlan Ellison, co
The Essential G.K. Chesterton, G.K. Chesterton, co
The Eternal Champion, Michael Moorcock, n.
* Etheldreda, Moyra Caldecott, n.
* Ether Ore, H.C. Turk, n.
The Eve of Saint Venus, Anthony Burgess, n.
* Evil Offspring, J.N. Williamson, n.
The Evil One, J.N. Williamson, n.

EVIL STAR

Evil Star, Logan Robinson, n.
* Evil Water, Ian Watson, co
The Exile Waiting, Vonda N. McIntyre, n.
* Exile's Gate, C.J. Cherryh, n.
Exiles of Colsec, Douglas Hill, n.
* Exit Earth, Martin Caidin, n.
The Exorcist, William Peter Blatty, n.
Expedition to Earth, Arthur C. Clarke, co
* Experiment in Terror, Bernal C. Payne, Jr., n.
* The Exploits of Ebenezvm, Craig Shaw Gardner, om
Eye, Frank Herbert, co
Eye Among the Blind, Robert P. Holdstock, n.
Eye in the Sky, Philip K. Dick, n.
The Eyes of the Dragon, Stephen King, n.
The Eyes of the Killer Robot, John Bellairs, n.
* F-Cubed, Daniel da Cruz, n.
The Faceless Man, Jack Vance, n.
The Faceless Ones, Terrance Dicks, n.
+ Faces, Leigh Kennedy, co
Facial Justice, L.P. Hartley, n.
Fade-Out, Patrick Tilley, n.
* The Faded Sun Trilogy, C.J. Cherryh, om
Fahrenheit 451, Ray Bradbury, n.
+ Fahrenheit 451/The Illustrated Man/Dandelion Wine/The Golden
    Apples of the Sun/The Martian Chronicles, Ray Bradbury, om
+ The Fall of Atlantis, Marion Zimmer Bradley, om
A Fall of Moondust, Arthur C. Clarke, n.
* The Fall of the Families, Philip Mann, n.
The Fall of the House of Usher, Edgar Allan Poe, co
* The Fall of the Republic, Crawford Kilian, n.
Falling Angel, William Hjortsberg, n.
The Falling Woman, Pat Murphy, n.
* Fandom Directory No. 9 (1987-1988), Mariane S. Hopkins, nf
* Fangs of the Werewolf, John Halkin, n.
Fantasms and Magics, Jack Vance, co
* Fantastic Mr. Fox: A Play, Roald Dahl, pl
* Fantastic Stories: Tales of the Weird and Wondrous, ed. Martin H.
    Greenberg & Patrick L. Price, an
Fantastic Television, Gary Gerani & Paul H. Schulman, nf
* Fantastic Voyage II: Destination Brain, Isaac Asimov, n.
* Fantasy King: A Biography of George MacDonald, William Raeper,
    nf
Far Below and Other Horrors, ed. Robert E. Weinberg, an
* The Far Side of Forever, Sharon Green, n.
* Fat Face, Michael Shea, nv
The Feast of Saint Dionysus, Robert Silverberg, co
The Fellowship of the Ring, J.R.R. Tolkien, n.
The Fellowship of the Talisman, Clifford D. Simak, n.
The Female Man, Joanna Russ, n.
* Feral Cell, Richard Bowes, n.
* Fever Dream, Ray Bradbury, ss
* Fever Season: Merovingen Nights #2, ed. C.J. Cherryh, oa
* Fiasco, Stanislaw Lem, n.
* Fictions of Nuclear Disaster, David Dowling, nf
* The Fifth Omni Book of Science Fiction, ed. Ellen Datlow, an
* The Final Planet, Andrew M. Greeley, n.
A Fine and Private Place, Peter S. Beagle, n.
Fingers, William Sleator, n.
Finishing Touches, Thomas Tessier, n.
* Finn MacCool and the Small Men of Deeds, Pat O'Shea, n.
Fire and Hemlock, Diana Wynne Jones, n.
Fire Dancer, Ann Maxwell, n.
* Fire Get, Cheryl J. Franklin, n.
Fire, Burn!, John Dickson Carr, n.
* Fireball, Paul Davies, n.
* Firebird, Kathy Tyers, n.
* The Firebrand, Marion Zimmer Bradley, n.
* Firebrats #1: The Burning Land, Barbara Siegel & Scott Siegel, n.
* Firebrats #2: Survivors, Barbara Siegel & Scott Siegel, n.
* Firebrats #3: Thunder Mountain, Barbara Siegel & Scott Siegel, n.
Firechild, Jack Williamson, n.
* Firecode, Chelsea Quinn Yarbro, n.
* Firefight 2000, Dean Ing, co
Fireflood and Other Stories, Vonda N. McIntyre, co
Fires of Azeroth, C.J. Cherryh, n.
* The Fires of Fu Manchu, Cay Van Ash, n.
* The Fires of Pele, Hollace Davids & Paul Davids, pi
The Fires of Windameir, Niel Hancock, n.

* Fireshaper's Doom, Tom Deitz, n.
Fireworks, Angela Carter, co
Fireworks: Nine Profane Pieces, Angela Carter, co
* The First Americans: Beyond the Sea of Ice, William Sarabande, n.
The First Book of Lost Swords: Woundhealer's Story, Fred
    Saberhagen, n.
* First Citizen, Thomas T. Thomas, n.
First Family, Patrick Tilley, n.
* First Love From Silhouette #174: Adrienne and the Blob, Judith
    Enderle, n.
* First Love From Silhouette #176: Daughter of the Moon, Lynn
    Carlock, n.
* First Love From Silhouette #198: A Touch of Genius, Jeffie Ross
    Gordon, n.
The First Men in the Moon, H.G. Wells, n.
* The First Named, Jonathan Wylie, n.
The First of the Penguins, Mary Q. Steele, n.
* FirstFlight, Chris Claremont, n.
* The Fish Police, Steve Moncuse, gn
The Fisher King, Anthony Powell, n.
* The Fisherman's Curse, M. Coleman Easton, n.
A Fistful of Ego, Dr. B.H. Topol, n.
Five Children and It, Edith Nesbit, n.
* A Flame in Byzantium, Chelsea Quinn Yarbro, n.
+ The Flame Key, Daniel Moran, n.
Flatland, Edwin A. Abbott, n.
* Flesh, Richard Laymon, n.
Flight in Yiktor, Andre Norton, n.
The Flight of the Dragonfly, Robert L. Forward, n.
* Flight of the Moth-Kin, Kathy Kennedy Tapp, n.
The Flint Lord, Richard Herley, n.
Flowers For Algernon, Daniel Keyes, n.
Flowers in the Attic, V.C. Andrews, n.
Fluke, James Herbert, n.
Flying Saucers, ed. Isaac Asimov, Martin H. Greenberg & Charles G.
    Waugh, an
The Fog, James Herbert, n.
Fog Hounds, Wind Cat, Sea Mice, Joan Aiken, co
The Folk of the Air, Peter S. Beagle, n.
* Folk Tales and Fables of the World, Barbara Hayes & Robert Ingpen,
    co
* Fool's Run, Patricia A. McKillip, n.
* Forbidden Sequence, Michael Rogers, n.
The Forbidden Tower, Marion Zimmer Bradley, n.
* The Force, Ames J. Edward, n.
* Force Fields, Andrew Joron, co
* Forest of the Night, Marti Steussy, n.
The Forever Man, Gordon R. Dickson, n.
* The Forge in the Forest, Michael Scott Rohan, n.
* The Forge of God, Greg Bear, n.
* Forgetting Places, S.P. Somtow, n.
The Forgotten Beasts of Eld, Patricia A. McKillip, n.
* Forgotten Realms, Book #1: Darkwalker on Moonshae, Douglas
    Niles, n.
Foundation, Isaac Asimov, n.
Foundation and Earth, Isaac Asimov, n.
Foundation and Empire, Isaac Asimov, n.
Foundation's Edge, Isaac Asimov, n.
* Foundations of Science Fiction: A Study in Imagination and
    Evolution, John J. Pierce, nf
The Fourth Plane at the Flypast, Dennis Hamley, n.
* Frame of Reference, Jerry Oltion, n.
* Frankenstein, David Campton & Mary W. Shelley, n.
Frankenstein, Mary W. Shelley, n.
* Frederik Pohl, Thomas D. Clareson, nf
* Free Lancers, ed. Elizabeth Mitchell, oa
Freedom Beach, James Patrick Kelly & John Kessel, n.
* Freehold, William C. Dietz, n.
* Friday the 13th, Part I, Simon Hawke, n.
* Friends of the Horseclans, ed. Robert Adams & Pamela Crippen
    Adams, oa
* Frobisch's Angel, Doris Rochlin, n.
Frost, Robin Wayne Bailey, n.
* FTL: Further Than Life, Michael Lindsay Williams, n.
Full Circle, Peter Straub, n.
* Gabo Djara, B. Wongar, n.
* Gabriel, Lisa Tuttle, n.
* Galactic Chronicles, Paul Christopher, n.

*Galactic Convoy, Bill Baldwin, n.
Galactic Derelict, Andre Norton, n.
Galactic Pot-Healer, Philip K. Dick, n.
Galactic Warlord, Douglas Hill, n.
Galapagos, Kurt Vonnegut, Jr., n.
*Galaxy High School, Ann Hodgman, n.
*Galloping Galaxies, Bob Block, n.
The Game of the Pink Pagoda, Roger Moss, n.
The Ganymede Takeover, Philip K. Dick & Ray Nelson, n.
Garan the Eternal, Andre Norton, n.
*Garcia Marquez: Writer of Colombia, Stephen Minta, nf
*Garden of Shadows, V.C. Andrews, n.
*The Garden of the Shaped, Sheila Finch, n.
Gate of Ivrel, C.J. Cherryh, n.
*Gate of Ivrel: Claiming Rites, Jane Fancher, gn
*The Gate of the Cat, Andre Norton, n.
*The Gatekeeper, Dana Reed, n.
*A Gathering of Heroes, Paul Edwin Zimmer, n.
*The Gauntlet of Malice, Deborah Turner Harris, n.
*The Gemini Factor, Thea Bennett, n.
*George MacDonald, Michael R. Phillips, nf
*George MacDonald: A Short Life, Elizabeth Saintsbury, nf
*Getting Home, F.M. Busby, co
The Ghastly Glasses, Beatrice Gormley, n.
Ghost, Piers Anthony, n.
Ghost After Ghost, ed. Aidan Chambers, oa
*The Ghost and the Gory Story, Duncan Ball, n.
The Ghost Belonged to Me, Richard Peck, n.
*The Ghost Dance, Robert Faulcon, om
*The Ghost Drum, Susan Price, n.
*Ghost Host, Marilyn Singer, n.
Ghost House Revenge, Clare McNally, n.
Ghost in the Sunlight, Kathleen Herbert, n.
The Ghost of 29 Megacycles, John G. Fuller, nf
The Ghost of Thomas Kempe, Penelope Lively, n.
*The Ghost Squad and the Prowling Hermits, E.W. Hildick, n.
Ghost Stories, M.R. James, n.
+The Ghost Stories of M.R. James, M.R. James, co
+The Ghost Story Treasury, ed. Linda Sonntag, an
Ghost Train, Stephen Laws, n.
*Ghost's Playground, Harry Gilbert, na
Ghosthunt, Jo Clayton, n.
+Ghostly Companions, Vivian Alcock, co
*Ghostly Populations, Jack Matthews, co
*Ghosts and Scholars, ed. Rosemary Pardoe & Richard Dalby, oa
Ghosts I Have Been, Richard Peck, n.
*The Ghosts of Bellering Oast, Pamela Oldfield, nv
*Ghosts of Night and Morning, Marvin Kaye, n.
Ghosts Who Went to School, Judith Spearing, n.
Ghoul, Mark Ronson, n.
Giants, ed. Isaac Asimov, Martin H. Greenberg & Charles G. Waugh, an
A Gift From Another Galaxy, Philip Curtis, n.
Giles Goat Boy, John Barth, n.
Gladiator-at-Law, Frederik Pohl & C.M. Kornbluth, n.
*Glass and Amber, C.J. Cherryh, co
The Glass Hammer, K.W. Jeter, n.
Glide Path, Arthur C. Clarke, n.
*Glory Lane, Alan Dean Foster, n.
*The Glove of Maiden's Hair, Michael Jan Friedman, n.
The Goblin Reservation, Clifford D. Simak, n.
The Goblin Tower, L. Sprague de Camp, n.
God Game, Andrew M. Greeley, n.
*God Help the Queen, Geoffrey Cush, n.
*God of a Thousand Faces, Michael Falconer Anderson, n.
Godbody, Theodore Sturgeon, n.
The Gods of Raquel, Moacyr Scliar, n.
*Godslayer, Mickey Zucker Reichert, n.
Gold Star, Zach Hughes, n.
*The Goldcamp Vampire, Elizabeth Ann Scarborough, n.
The Golden Child, George C. Chesbro, n.
*Golden Days, Carolyn See, n.
*The Golden Garden, Brian Parvin, n.
The Golden Horn, Judith Tarr, n.
The Golden People, Fred Saberhagen, n.
*Golden Sunlands, Christopher B. Rowley, n.
Golgotha, John Gardner, n.
*Goliath, John Denis, n.
*Gollancz/Sunday Times SF Competition Stories, ed. Anonymous, oc

*A Goose on Your Grave, Joan Aiken, oc
*Gothic, Stephen Volk, n.
*Grainne, Keith Roberts, n.
*Graven Image, D.G. Finlay, n.
*Graveyard, Mason Burgess, n.
Gray Lensman, E.E. "Doc" Smith, n.
Great Science Fiction of the 20th Century, ed. Robert Silverberg & Martin H. Greenberg, an
*Great Sky River, Gregory Benford, n.
*Great Themes of Science Fiction, John J. Pierce, nf
*The Great Walls of Samaris, Francois Schuiten & Peeters, gn
*The Great Wheel, Joyce Ballou Gregorian, n.
Green Eyes, Lucius Shepard, n.
The Green Pearl, Jack Vance, n.
*Greenbriar Queen, Sheila Gilluly, n.
Greener Than You Think, Ward Moore, n.
*The Grey Horse, R.A. MacAvoy, n.
*Greyhawk Adventures #3: Master Wolf, Rose Estes, n.
*Greyhawk Adventures #4: The Price of Power, Rose Estes, n.
Groa's Other Eye, Dennis Schmidt, n.
The Grotto of the Formigans, Daniel da Cruz, n.
*The Guardians #8: Desolation Road, Richard Austin, n.
*The Guardians #9: Vengeance Day, Richard Austin, n.
Guardians of the Tall Stones, Moyra Caldecott, om
*Guardians of the West, David Eddings, n.
*Guinevere and Lancelot & Others, Arthur Machen, co
Gulliver's Travels, Jonathan Swift, n.
Gulliver's Travels: A Voyage to Lilliput, Jonathan Swift, n.
*H.G. Wells, Desperately Mortal, David C. Smith, nf
*Halberd: Dream Warrior, Lloyd St. Alcorn, n.
Halfway Across the Galaxy and Turn Left, Robin Klein, na
Halloween Horrors, ed. Alan Ryan, oa
*Halo, Chet Day, n.
*The Hamlet Trap, Kate Wilhelm, n.
*Hammer's Slammers, David Drake, co
The Handmaid's Tale, Margaret Atwood, n.
*Hands of Lucifer, John Tigges, n.
Hardwired, Walter Jon Williams, n.
The Harem of Aman Akbar, Elizabeth Ann Scarborough, n.
*Harry and the Hendersons, Joyce Thompson, n.
*The Harvest Bride, Tony Richards, n.
*Haunted, Judith St. George, n.
The Haunted House, Rebecca Brown, n.
*The Haunted Mesa, Louis L'Amour, n.
*Haunted Waters, Mary Williams, oc
The Haunted Woman, David Lindsay, n.
Haunted Women: The Best Supernatural Tales by American Women Writers, ed. Alfred Bendixen, an
The Haunter of the Dark, H.P. Lovecraft, co
The Haunting of Hill House, Shirley Jackson, n.
A Hawk in Silver, Mary Gentle, n.
The Hawkline Monster, Richard Brautigan, n.
Hawksmoor, Peter Ackroyd, n.
Head to Toe, Joe Orton, n.
Healer, Peter Dickinson, n.
*Hear the Silence: Stories of Myth, Magic and Renewal, ed. Irene Zahava, oa
Heart of the Comet, Gregory Benford & David Brin, n.
*Heart to Heart, Don Pendleton, n.
The Heaven Makers, Frank Herbert, n.
*Hegira, Greg Bear, n.
*The Heir Apparent, Joel Rosenberg, n.
Hellborn, Gary Brandner, n.
Hellfire, John Saul, n.
Helliconia Winter, Brian W. Aldiss, n.
Her Majesty's Wizard, Christopher Stasheff, n.
*Her Story, Dan Jacobson, n.
The Heritage of Hastur, Marion Zimmer Bradley, n.
*Heroic Dreams, Nigel Suckling, pi
*Heroing, Dafydd ab Hugh, n.
*A Heron Caught in Weeds, Keith Roberts, co
Hestia, C.J. Cherryh, n.
High Deryni, Katherine Kurtz, n.
The High Kings, Joy Chant, nf
*High Priest, Warren Murphy & Molly Cochran, n.
*The Highly Flavoured Ladies, Patricia Angadi, n.
Highway to Eternity, Clifford D. Simak, n.
Hitler Victorious, ed. Gregory Benford & Martin H. Greenberg, an

The Hobbit, J.R.R. Tolkien, n.
* Hogar Lord of the Asyr, John Rufus Sharpe, III, n.
The Hollow Lands, Michael Moorcock, n.
Home Free, Kathryn Lasky, n.
Horror House, J.N. Williamson, n.
Horror Shows, Gene Wright, nf
* Horror Wears Blue, Lin Carter, n.
The Horse and His Boy, C.S. Lewis, n.
* A Horse to Love, Nancy Springer, n.
* Horseclans #16: Trumpets of War, Robert Adams, n.
* Horseclans #17: Madman's Army, Robert Adams, n.
* A Horsewoman in Godsland, Claudia J. Edwards, n.
The Hounds of God, Judith Tarr, n.
The Hounds of the Morrigan, Pat O'Shea, n.
The Hour of the Oxrun Dead, Charles L. Grant, n.
* The Hour of the Thin Ox, Colin Greenland, n.
* The Hourglass Crisis, Lonn Hoklin, n.
* The House at Pelham Falls, Brenda Weathers, n.
* The House in the Snow, M.J. Engh, n.
* The House of Dracula, R. Chetwynd-Hayes, oc
* House Shudders, ed. Martin H. Greenberg & Charles G. Waugh, an
* How Dear the Dawn, Marc Eliot, n.
* How Much for Just the Planet?, John M. Ford, n.
+ How to Be a Happy Cat, Charles Platt, ms
* How to Enjoy Writing: A Book of Aid and Comfort, Janet Asimov & Isaac Asimov, nf
* How to Write Tales of Horror, Fantasy & Science Fiction, ed. J.N. Williamson, nf
Howliday Inn, James Howe, n.
The Howling III: Echoes, Gary Brandner, n.
* The Hub, Chris Beebee, n.
The Hungry Moon, Ramsey Campbell, n.
* The Hunt, James Howard Kunstler, n.
Hunter of Worlds, C.J. Cherryh, n.
* Hunter/Victim, Robert Sheckley, n.
Hunters of Gor, John Norman, n.
* The Hunting Season, John Coyne, n.
Huon of the Horn, Andre Norton, n.
* The Hyades Contact, Wynne Whiteford, n.
I Am Legend, Richard Matheson, n.
I Hope I Shall Arrive Soon, Philip K. Dick, co
The Ice King, Michael Scott, n.
The Ice Schooner, Michael Moorcock, n.
Icerigger, Alan Dean Foster, n.
* If I Ran The Zoo [cross out Zoo]...Con: The Smofcon 3 Game, ed. Leslie Turek, nf
* An Ill Fate Marshalling, Glen Cook, n.
The Illearth War, Stephen R. Donaldson, n.
* The Illumination of Alice J. Cunningham, Lyn Webster, n.
The Illyrian Adventure, Lloyd Alexander, n.
Imaginary Lands, ed. Robin McKinley, an
* Imaginary People, David Pringle, nf
* Imagining Argentina, Lawrence Thornton, n.
The Imperial Stars, E.E. "Doc" Smith, n.
* Imperial Stars, Vol. 2: Republic and Empire, ed. Jerry E. Pournelle, an
* Imprisoned in a Tesseract: The Life and Work of James Blish, David Ketterer, nf
In a Glass Darkly, Joseph Sheridan Le Fanu, co
In Alien Flesh, Gregory Benford, co
* In Conquest Born, C.S. Friedman, n.
In Milton Lumky Territory, Philip K. Dick, n.
* In the Bone: The Best Science Fiction of Gordon R. Dickson, Gordon R. Dickson, co
* In the Caves of Exile, Ru Emerson, n.
* In the Country of the Last Things, Paul Auster, n.
In the Drift, Michael Swanwick, n.
+ In the Dutch Mountains, Cees Nooteboom, n.
* In the Field of Fire, ed. Jeanne Van Buren Dann & Jack M. Dann, oa
In the Flesh, Clive Barker, oc
In the Hall of the Dragon King, Stephen R. Lawhead, n.
In the Ocean of Night, Gregory Benford, n.
In Yana, The Touch of Undying, Michael Shea, n.
* Incantation, J. Edward Lord, n.
* The Incomer, Margaret Elphinstone, n.
* The Incorporated Knight, L. Sprague de Camp & Catherine Crook de Camp, n.
The Indian in the Cupboard, Lynne Reid Banks, n.

Industrial Light & Magic: The Art of Special Effects, Thomas G. Smith, nf
* Infernal Devices, K.W. Jeter, n.
Inhuman, John Russo, n.
The Inhuman Condition, Clive Barker, oc
* Innerspace, Nathan Elliott, n.
* Interface for Murder, Lloyd Biggle, Jr., n.
* Intersections: Fantasy and Science Fiction, ed. George E. Slusser & Eric S. Rabkin, nf
Interstellar Empire, John Brunner, co
Interstellar Pig, William Sleator, n.
* Intervention, Julian May, n.
* Interzone: The 2nd Anthology, ed. John Clute, David Pringle & Simon Ounsley, an
Into the Out Of, Alan Dean Foster, n.
Into the Sea of Stars, William R. Forstchen, n.
* Intuit, Hal Clement, co
Invaders From Earth, Robert Silverberg, n.
Invasion of the Body Snatchers, Jack Finney, n.
Invasion: Earth, Harry Harrison, n.
Inverted World, Christopher Priest, n.
The Invisible Man, H.G. Wells, n.
The Iowa Baseball Confederacy, W.P. Kinsella, n.
Iron Cage, Andre Norton, n.
* Iron Master, Patrick Tilley, n.
* Isaac Asimov Presents the Great SF Stories: 16 (1954), ed. Isaac Asimov & Martin H. Greenberg, an
* Isaac Asimov Presents the Great SF Stories: 17 (1955), ed. Isaac Asimov & Martin H. Greenberg, an
* Isaac Asimov's Magical Worlds of Fantasy #8: Devils, ed. Isaac Asimov, Martin H. Greenberg & Charles G. Waugh, an
* Isaac Asimov's Magical Worlds of Fantasy #9: Atlantis, ed. Isaac Asimov, Martin H. Greenberg & Charles G. Waugh, an
* Isaac Asimov's Robot City, Book 1: Odyssey, Michael P. Kube-McDowell, n.
* Isaac Asimov's Robot City, Book 2: Suspicion, Mike McQuay, n.
* Isaac Asimov's Robot City, Book 3: Cyborg, William F. Wu, n.
* Isaac Asimov's Robot City, Book 4: Prodigy, Arthur Byron Cover, n.
* Isaac Asimov's Wonderful Worlds of Science Fiction #6: Neanderthals, ed. Isaac Asimov, Martin H. Greenberg & Charles G. Waugh, an
* Isaac Asimov's Wonderful Worlds of Science Fiction #7: Space Shuttles, ed. Isaac Asimov, Martin H. Greenberg & Charles G. Waugh, an
Ishmael, Barbara Hambly, n.
* The Island Worlds, Eric Kotani & John Maddox Roberts, n.
Islands in the Sky, Arthur C. Clarke, n.
Islands Out of Time, William Irwin Thompson, n.
The Isle of Glass, Judith Tarr, n.
It, Stephen King, n.
The Ivanhoe Gambit, Simon Hawke, n.
* The Ivory Lyre, Shirley Rousseau Murphy, n.
* Jack the Giant Killer, Charles de Lint, n.
* Jackbird: Tales of Illusion & Identity, Bruce Boston, co
* The Jade Demons Quartet, Robert E. Vardeman, om
* The Jaguar Hunter, Lucius Shepard, co
* Janissaries III: Storms of Victory, Jerry E. Pournelle, n.
* The Jehovah Contract, Victor Koman, n.
+ The Journal of Nicholas the American, Leigh Kennedy, n.
Journey Beyond Tomorrow, Robert Sheckley, n.
* Journey to Membliar, Sharon Baker, n.
Judgement Day, Pauline Glen Winslow, n.
Judgement on Janus, Andre Norton, n.
The Jungle Book, Rudyard Kipling, co
Jungle Books, Rudyard Kipling, om
A Jungle of Stars, Jack L. Chalker, n.
Junior Doctor Who and the Brain of Morbius, Terrance Dicks, n.
The Jupiter Plague, Harry Harrison, n.
Just So Stories, Rudyard Kipling, co
* K.I.D.S., Trevor Hoyle, n.
* K9 and Company, Terence Dudley, n.
* Kashka, Ellen Kindt McKenzie, n.
Kate's House, Harriet Waugh, n.
Keep Watching the Skies! American Science Fiction Movies of the Fifties: Vol. 2, Bill Warren, nf
The Keeper's Price, Marion Zimmer Bradley & The Friends of Darkover, oa
* Keepers of Edanvant, Carole Nelson Douglas, n.

KELPIE　　　　　　　　　　　　　　　　　**THE MAMMOTH HUNTERS**

Kelpie, William Mayne, n.
Key Out of Time, Andre Norton, n.
The Keys to Paradise, Robert E. Vardeman, om
* The Kid From Ozone Park & Other Stories, Richard Wilson, oc
* Kidnap in Space, Nathan Elliott, n.
* Kill Ratio, David Drake & Janet Morris, n.
Killer Robot, Seth McEvoy, n.
The Killing Gift, Bari Wood, n.
Killing Time, Della Van Hise, n.
Killing Time, Patricia Windsor, n.
* The Kindly Ones, Melissa Scott, n.
* The King Awakes, Janice Elliott, n.
King David's Spaceship, Jerry E. Pournelle, n.
King Death's Garden, Ann Halam, n.
The King of Satan's Eyes, Geoffrey Marsh, n.
* The King of Ys 2: Gallicenae, Poul Anderson & Karen Anderson, n.
* The King of Ys: Dahut, Poul Anderson & Karen Anderson, n.
The King's Justice, Katherine Kurtz, n.
Kingdom of Fear: The World of Stephen King, ed. Tim Underwood & Chuck Miller, nf
* Kings in Hell, C.J. Cherryh & Janet Morris, n.
* The Kinsman Saga, Ben Bova, n.
Kiss Me Again, Stranger, Daphne du Maurier, co
Kiteworld, Keith Roberts, n.
* Knave & the Game, Laurence M. Janifer, co
* Knight Life, Peter David, n.
Knight Moves, Walter Jon Williams, n.
A Knight of Ghosts and Shadows, Poul Anderson, n.
* Knight on Horseback, Ann Rabinowitz, n.
* Knights of God, Richard Cooper, n.
The Kraken Wakes, John Wyndham, n.
* Kurt Vonnegut: A Comprehensive Bibliography, ed. Asa Pieratt, Julie Huffman-Klinkowitz & Jerome Klinkowitz, nf
* Kyoki, Chris Parker, n.
* L. Ron Hubbard Presents Writers of the Future, Vol. III, ed. Algis Budrys, oa
* L. Ron Hubbard: Messiah or Madman?, Bent Corydon & L. Ron Hubbard, Jr., nf
* The Labyrinth, Robert Faulcon, n.
Labyrinth, A.C.H. Smith, n.
* The Labyrinth of Dreams, Jack L. Chalker, n.
The Ladies of Mandrigyn, Barbara Hambly, n.
The Ladies of Missalonghi, Colleen McCullough, n.
* The Lady, Anne McCaffrey, n.
* Lady Blade, Lord Fighter, Sharon Green, n.
* The Lady of Han-Gilen, Judith Tarr, n.
+ Lady of Hay, Barbara Erskine, n.
Ladyhawke, Joan D. Vinge, n.
Lanark, Alasdair Gray, n.
* Land of Dreams, James P. Blaylock, n.
The Land of Laughs, Jonathan Carroll, n.
Land Under England, Joseph O'Neill, n.
Last and First Men, Olaf Stapledon, n.
Last Come the Children, David Hagberg, n.
The Last Election, Pete Davies, n.
* Last Fall, Bruce Stolbov, n.
The Last Knight of Albion, Peter Hanratty, n.
* The Last Museum, Brion Gysin, n.
* The Last of the Fianna, Michael Scott, n.
* Last Ranger #4: The Rabid Brigadier, Craig Sargent, n.
* Last Ranger #5: The War Weapons, Craig Sargent, n.
* Last Ranger #6: The Warlord's Revenge, Craig Sargent, n.
The Last Unicorn, Peter S. Beagle, n.
* The Laying of the Noone Walker, Rosalind Ashe, n.
The Lays of Beleriand, J.R.R. Tolkien, n.
* Lear's Daughters, M. Bradley Kellogg & William Rossow, om
* Leaves from the Inn of the Last Home, ed. Margaret Weis & Tracy Hickman, nf
* The Leeshore, Robert Reed, n.
The Legacy, John Coyne, n.
* The Legacy of Heorot, Larry Niven, Jerry E. Pournelle & Steven Barnes, n.
* The Legion of Videssos, Harry Turtledove, n.
* Legions of Hell, C.J. Cherryh, n.
* The Leipzig Vampire, Mary Anderson, n.
* The Leopard's Daughter, Lee Killough, n.
Less Than Human, Charles Platt, n.
Letters from the Dead, Campbell Black, n.

* Liavek: Wizard's Row, ed. Will Shetterly & Emma Bull, oa
* Liege-Killer, Christopher Hinz, n.
* Life During Wartime, Lucius Shepard, n.
* Life Goes on Forever..., David Selves, n.
* Life to Life, Don Pendleton, n.
Lifeburst, Jack Williamson, n.
+ The Light Fantastic, Terry Pratchett, n.
* The Light of Eden, W.A. Harbinson, n.
The Light Princess and Other Stories, George MacDonald, co
Lilith, George MacDonald, n.
Limbo, Bernard Wolfe, n.
* Lincoln's Dreams, Connie Willis, n.
The Lion of Comarre & Against the Fall of Night, Arthur C. Clarke, om
* A Lion on Tharthee, Grant D. Callin, n.
The Lion, the Witch and the Wardrobe, C.S. Lewis, n.
The Lion, the Witch and the Wardrobe, Glyn Robbins & C.S. Lewis, pl
* Liquid Sky, Anne Carlisle, n.
A Little Fear, Patricia Wrightson, n.
* Little Heroes, Norman Spinrad, n.
Little Myth Marker, Robert Lynn Asprin, n.
* Little Tours of Hell, Josephine Saxton, oc
Little, Big, John Crowley, n.
Live Girls, Ray Garton, n.
The Lives and Times of Jerry Cornelius, Michael Moorcock, co
* The Living Dead, Jeffrey Goddin, n.
* Living Fire and Other S.F. Stories, Nicholas Fisk, oc
Living in Ether, Patricia Geary, n.
Locusts, Guy N. Smith, n.
* The Long Tomorrow and Other Science Fiction Stories, Jean "Moebius" Giraud, pi
* Looking for Hamlet, Hope Campbell, n.
Lord Foul's Bane, Stephen R. Donaldson, n.
Lord of Light, Roger Zelazny, n.
* Lord of the Crooked Paths, Patrick H. Adkins, n.
The Lord of the Rings, J.R.R. Tolkien, n.
Lord of the Rings and Hobbit Boxed Set, J.R.R. Tolkien, om
Lord of the Rings Boxed Set, J.R.R. Tolkien, om
The Lordly Ones, Keith Roberts, co
Lords of the Levels, Michael Bentine, n.
Lore of the Witch World, Andre Norton, co
* The Lost Boys, Craig Shaw Gardner, n.
* Lost in Time and Space with Lefty Feep, Robert Bloch, co
* The Lost Road and Other Writings, J.R.R. Tolkien, co
The Lost Star, H.M. Hoover, n.
The Lost Traveler, Steve Wilson, n.
Lovecraft's Book, Richard A. Lupoff, n.
* The Luck of Relian Kru, Paula Volsky, n.
The Luck of the Vails, E.F. Benson, n.
The Lure of the Basilisk, Lawrence Watt-Evans, n.
* M. Is for Monster, Mel Gilden, nv
* M.Y.T.H. Inc. Link, Robert Lynn Asprin, n.
* The Macra Terror, Ian Stuart Black, n.
* Mad and Bad Fairies, ed. Anonymous, oa
* Madbond, Nancy Springer, n.
* Mage, Volume One: The Hero Discovered, Matt Wagner, gn
+ The Magic Cottage, James Herbert, n.
* Magic in Ithkar 4, ed. Andre Norton & Robert Adams, oa
Magic Kingdom for Sale--Sold!, Terry Brooks, n.
* The Magic Kiss and Other Tales of Princes and Princesses, ed. Tony Bradman, an
Magic Mommas, Trembling Sisters, Puritans & Perverts, Joanna Russ, nf
* The Magic of the Past, Brian W. Aldiss, oc
The Magician, W. Somerset Maugham, n.
* The Magician's Apprentice, Tom McGowen, n.
* Magician's Law, Michael Scott, n.
The Magicians of Caprona, Diana Wynne Jones, n.
* The Magnificent Gallery, Thomas F. Monteleone, n.
Mail-Order Wings, Beatrice Gormley, n.
Major Operation, James White, co
* The Maker of Dune: Insights of a Master of Science Fiction, Frank Herbert, nf
* Makra Choria, Ardath Mayhar, n.
* The Mall From Outer Space, Todd Strasser, n.
The Mammoth Book of Best New Science Fiction, ed. Gardner R. Dozois, an
The Mammoth Book of Classic Fantasy, Cary Wilkins, an
The Mammoth Hunters, Jean M. Auel, n.

The Man from Earth, Gordon R. Dickson, co
The Man in the High Castle, Philip K. Dick, n.
The Man in the Maze, Robert Silverberg, n.
Man of Two Worlds, Frank Herbert & Brian Herbert, n.
Man Plus, Frederik Pohl, n.
* A Man Rides Through, Stephen R. Donaldson, n.
The Man Who Killed His Brother, Reed Stephens, n.
* The Man Who Pulled Down the Sky, John Barnes, n.
Man Who Risked His Partner, Reed Stephens, n.
The Man Who Sold the Moon, Robert A. Heinlein, co
The Man Who Used the Universe, Alan Dean Foster, n.
The Man Who Was Thursday, G.K. Chesterton, n.
The Manitou, Graham Masterton, n.
The Manna Enzyme, Richard Hoyt, n.
* The Manse, Lisa W. Cantrell, n.
* Mantis, K.W. Jeter, n.
Many Waters, Madeleine L'Engle, n.
The Marathon Photograph, Clifford D. Simak, co
* Marlborough Street, Richard Bowker, n.
Marooned in Real Time, Vernor Vinge, n.
Marooned in Realtime, Vernor Vinge, n.
The Martian Chronicles, Ray Bradbury, n.
Martians Go Home, Fredric Brown, n.
The Marvellous Land Of Oz, L. Frank Baum, n.
* Mary and the Giant, Philip K. Dick, n.
* Mary Shelley: A Biography, Muriel Spark, nf
* A Mask for the General, Lisa Goldstein, n.
The Mask of the Sun, Fred Saberhagen, n.
The Masks of Time, Robert Silverberg, n.
* Masques II, ed. J.N. Williamson, oa
* The Massacre, John Lucarotti, n.
* The Master, Louise Cooper, n.
The Master and Margarita, Mikhail Bulgakov, n.
* Master of Fiends, Douglas Hill, n.
Master of His Fate, J. MacLaren Cobban, n.
Master of the Sidhe, Kenneth C. Flint, n.
* Masterplay, William F. Wu, n.
* Masters in Hell, ed. Janet Morris, oa
* Masters of Darkness II, ed. Dennis Etchison, an
* Masters of Fantasy 3: M.R. James, M.R. James, co
* Masters of Space #2: The Alien Web, Robert E. Vardeman, n.
* Masters of Space #3: A Plague in Paradise, Robert E. Vardeman, n.
* Mathenauts: Tales of Mathematical Wonder, ed. Rudy Rucker, an
* Matters of Form, Scott Wheeler, n.
Max in Love, Marilyn Kaye, n.
Max on Fire, Marilyn Kaye, n.
* Maximum Effort, G.C. Edmondson & C.M. Kotlan, n.
A Maze of Death, Philip K. Dick, pb
The McAndrew Chronicles, Charles Sheffield, n.
+ The Medusa Frequency, Russell Hoban, n.
Medusa's Children, Bob Shaw, n.
* Meet Mr. Majimpsey, John Hosken, n.
* Meggie's Journeys, Margaret D'Ambrosio, n.
Melvaig's Vision, Richard Ford, n.
* Memoirs of an Invisible Man, H.F. Saint, n.
* Memories, Mike McQuay, n.
* Memory Board, Jane Rule, n.
The Memory of Whiteness, Kim Stanley Robinson, n.
* Memory Wire, Robert Charles Wilson, n.
Men Like Gods, H.G. Wells, n.
The Menace From Earth, Robert A. Heinlein, co
* Mercedes Nights, Michael D. Weaver, n.
* The Mercenary: The Cult of the Sacred Fire and the Formula, Vincente Segrelles, pi
* Merlin's Daughters: Contemporary Women Writers of Fantasy, Charlotte Spivack, nf
Merlin's Mirror, Andre Norton, n.
* Merovingen Nights: Festival Moon, ed. C.J. Cherryh, oa
* Miamigrad, Jerry Ahern & Sharon Ahern, n.
* Michael Hague's World of Unicorns, Michael Hague, pi
* Michael Whelan's Works of Wonder, Michael Whelan, nf
* Midnight Boy, Stephen Gresham, n.
* Midnight City, Robert Tine, n.
The Midnight Folk, John Masefield, n.
* Midnight Pleasures, Robert Bloch, co
The Midwich Cuckoos, John Wyndham, n.
* Mind in Motion: The Fiction of Philip K. Dick, Patricia S. Warrick, nf
The Mind Robber, Peter Ling, n.

* Mind Tools, Rudy Rucker, nf
* Mind-Hold, Wilanne Schneider Belden, n.
* Mindbenders, Nicholas Fisk, n.
* Mindbond, Nancy Springer, n.
* Mindplayers, Pat Cadigan, n.
Mindshadow, J.M. Dillard, n.
Mine to Kill, David St. Clair, n.
* The Minstrel's Lute, Bridget Wood, n.
* Mirage, Louise Cooper, n.
* Miranty and the Alchemist, Vera Chapman, n.
The Mirror of Her Dreams, Stephen R. Donaldson, n.
* Misery, Stephen King, n.
* The Misplaced Legion, Harry Turtledove, n.
Mission Earth, Vol. 3: The Enemy Within, L. Ron Hubbard, n.
Mission Earth, Vol. 4: An Alien Affair, L. Ron Hubbard, n.
Mission Earth, Vol. 5: Fortune of Fear, L. Ron Hubbard, n.
* Mission Earth, Vol. 6: Death Quest, L. Ron Hubbard, n.
* Mission Earth, Vol. 7: Voyage of Vengeance, L. Ron Hubbard, n.
* Mission Earth, Vol. 8: Disaster, L. Ron Hubbard, n.
* Mission Earth, Vol. 9: Villainy Victorious, L. Ron Hubbard, n.
* Mission Earth, Vol.10: The Doomed Planet, L. Ron Hubbard, n.
Mission of Gravity, Hal Clement, n.
Mission to Moulokin, Alan Dean Foster, n.
Mist Over Pendle, Robert Neill, n.
* The Model, Robert Aickman, n.
* Moebius 1: Upon a Star, Jean "Moebius" Giraud, gn
* The Monster in the Mirror: Gender and the Sentimental/Gothic Myth in Frankenstein, Mary K. Patterson Thornburg, nf
Monster Makers, Inc., Laurence Yep, n.
Montezuma's Revenge, Harry Harrison, n.
Moon, James Herbert, n.
The Moon Goddess and the Son, Donald A. Kingsbury, n.
The Moon is a Harsh Mistress, Robert A. Heinlein, n.
Moon of Three Rings, Andre Norton, n.
* The Moon's Revenge, Joan Aiken, nv
* Moon-dark, Patricia Wrightson, n.
* Moonbranches, Anne Rundle, n.
* Moondial, Helen Cresswell, n.
* Moonslasher, Douglas D. Hawke, n.
Moonwind, Louise Lawrence, n.
* More Tales for the Midnight Hour, J.B. Stamper, oc
More Things in Heaven, John Brunner, n.
* Mort, Terry Pratchett, n.
* Moscow 2042, Vladimir Vomovich, n.
The Mote in God's Eye, Larry Niven & Jerry E. Pournelle, n.
* Motherland, Martin DiCarlantonio, n.
The Mountains of Channadran, Susan Dexter, n.
Mouth Open, Story Jump Out, Grace Hallworth, oc
* The Movement of Mountains, Michael Blumlein, n.
* Mr. Scott's Guide to the Enterprise, Shane Johnson, pi
Ms. Faust, Chris Dubbs, n.
The Multiple Man, Ben Bova, n.
* Murder at the War, Mary Monica Pulver, n.
* Murder in Orbit, Bruce Coville, n.
* Murder on Usher's Planet, Atanielle Annyn Noel, n.
Mute, Piers Anthony, n.
* My Heart Leaps Up, Chapters 3 & 4, R.A. Lafferty, ph
My Name is Legion, Roger Zelazny, co
My Robot Buddy, Alfred Slote, nv
* My Sister Sif, Ruth Park, n.
My Trip to Alpha 1, Alfred Slote, nv
A Mysterious House, Algernon Blackwood, ss
* Mysterious Motoring Stories, ed. William Pattrick, an
* The Mysterious Planet, Terrance Dicks, n.
+ Mysterious Sea Stories, ed. William Pattrick, an
* Mystery of the Night Raiders, Nancy Garden, n.
* Myth Adventures Two, Phil Foglio & Robert Lynn Asprin, gn
* Myth Alliances, Robert Lynn Asprin, om
* Myth-Nomers and Im-pervections, Robert Lynn Asprin, n.
* Mythical and Fabulous Creatures: A Sourcebook and Research Guide, ed. Malcolm South, nf
* The Nanny, Dan Greenburg, n.
* Napoleon Disentimed, Hayford Peirce, n.
Natfact 7, John Tully, n.
Native Tongue, Suzette Haden Elgin, n.
* Native Tongue II: The Judas Rose, Suzette Haden Elgin, n.
Nature's End, Whitley Strieber & James Kunetka, n.

Nebula Awards 21: SFWA's Choices for the Best in Science Fiction
  & Fantasy 1985, ed. George Zebrowski, an
Nerilka's Story, Anne McCaffrey, n.
* Nerilka's Story & The Coelura, Anne McCaffrey, om
  The Nest, Gregory A. Douglas, n.
* The Net, Loren MacGregor, n.
* Never the Twain, Kirk Mitchell, n.
  The Neverending Story, Michael Ende, n.
* New Destinies, Vol. 1/Spring 1987, ed. Jim Baen, oa
* New Destinies, Vol. 2/Fall 1987, ed. Jim Baen, oa
  New Guide To Science, Isaac Asimov, nf
* New Moon, William Relling, Jr., n.
* New Morning Dragon, Diana Henstell, n.
  New York by Knight, Esther M. Friesner, n.
* Next, After Lucifer, Daniel Rhodes, n.
  The Nick of Time, George Alec Effinger, n.
  Nicobobinus, Terry Jones, n.
* Nicor!, Peter Tremayne, n.
* Night Arrant, Gary Gygax, oc
  Night Birds on Nantucket, Joan Aiken, n.
* Night Caller, Daniel Ransom, n.
* Night Games, Marilyn Harris, n.
  Night Howl, Andrew Neiderman, n.
+ Night Hunter, Robert Faulcon, n.
+ Night Hunter 2: The Talisman, Robert Faulcon, n.
+ Night Hunter 3: The Ghost Dance, Robert Faulcon, n.
* A Night in the Netherhells, Craig Shaw Gardner, n.
* The Night of the Solstice, L.J. Smith, n.
  Night Shift, Stephen King, co
  Night Train, Thomas F. Monteleone, n.
  Night Visions, ed. George R.R. Martin, oa
* Night Visions 4, ed. Anonymous, oa
  Night Visions: Dead Image, ed. Charles L. Grant, oa
  The Night Visitor, Laura Wylie, n.
  Night Walk, Bob Shaw, n.
  Night Warriors, Graham Masterton, n.
  Night's Master, Tanith Lee, n.
* Night's Sorceries, Tanith Lee, oc
  Nightbirds on Nantucket, Joan Aiken, n.
* Nightfall, John Farris, n.
  Nightflyers, George R.R. Martin, co
* Nightmare, Gloria Murphy, n.
* The Nightmare Candidate, Ramona Stewart, n.
  Nightmares 2, ed. Mary Danby, an
* Nightmares in Dixie: Thirteen Horror Tales From the American
    South, ed. Frank D. McSherry, Jr., Martin H. Greenberg & Charles
    G. Waugh, an
  The Nightmares on Elm Street, Jeffrey Cooper, n.
* The Nightmares on Elm Street, Parts 1, 2, 3: The Continuing Story,
    Jeffrey Cooper, n.
  Nightpool, Shirley Rousseau Murphy, n.
+ Nightrider, David Mace, n.
* The Nightrunners, Joe R. Lansdale, n.
* Nights in Ghostland, Carol Beach York, n.
  Nightwing, Martin Cruz Smith, n.
  Nightwings, Robert Silverberg, n.
* Nightworld, Bruce Carter, n.
* Nighty-Nightmare, James Howe, n.
  The Nine Billion Names of God, Arthur C. Clarke, co
  Nineteen Eighty-Four, George Orwell, n.
* The No-Sided Professor, Martin Gardner, co
  Non-Stop, Brian W. Aldiss, n.
* Noninterference, Harry Turtledove, n.
  Nor Crystal Tears, Alan Dean Foster, n.
* Norby and the Queen's Necklace, Janet Asimov & Isaac Asimov, n.
* Norby Finds a Villain, Janet Asimov & Isaac Asimov, n.
* Norby: Robot for Hire, Janet Asimov & Isaac Asimov, om
  The Northern Girl, Elizabeth A. Lynn, n.
  Not Wanted on the Voyage, Timothy Findley, n.
  Nowhere, Thomas Berger, n.
  The Nuclear Age, Tim O'Brien, n.
* Nuclear Futures, Bruce Boston, co
* Nuclear Holocausts: Atomic War in Fiction, 1895-1984, Paul Brians,
    nf
  The Number of the Beast, Robert A. Heinlein, n.
* Numberland: A Fable, George Weinberg, n.
  O-Zone, Paul Theroux, n.

* The Occult in the Western World: An Annotated Bibliography,
    Cosette Kies, nf
  Octagon, Fred Saberhagen, n.
* Of Chiefs and Champions, Robert Adams, n.
  The Official Batman Batbook, Joel Eisner, nf
* The Official Price Guide to Star Trek and Star Wars Collectibles,
    Second Edition, Sue Cornwill & Mike Kott, nf
+ Ogre, Mark Ronson, n.
  An Old Friend of the Family, Fred Saberhagen, n.
* Ollie and the Bogle, Julia Jarman, n.
* The Omcri Matrix, Jay D. Blakeney, n.
* Omni: Astropilots, Laura J. Mixon, n.
  On a Pale Horse, Piers Anthony, n.
* On Stranger Tides, Tim Powers, n.
* On Strike Against God, Joanna Russ, n.
  On the Flip Side, Nicholas Fisk, n.
* On the Rim of the Mandala, Paul Cook, n.
  The Once and Future King, T.H. White, om
* Once Upon a Murder, Robert J. Randisi & Kevin D. Randle, n.
  The One Tree, Stephen R. Donaldson, n.
* The Orbit Poster Book, ed. Anonymous, pi
* The Origins of "Dracula": The Background to Bram Stoker's Gothic
    Masterpiece, ed. Clive Leatherdale, nf
* Origins of Futuristic Fiction, Paul K. Alkon, nf
  Orphans of the Sky, Robert A. Heinlein, co
  Orsinian Tales, Ursula K. Le Guin, co
* Orvis, H.M. Hoover, n.
* Other Edens, ed. Christopher Evans & Robert Holdstock, oa
* Other Engagements, John Maclay, co
* The Other Side of the Mirror, Marion Zimmer Bradley & The Friends
    of Darkover, oa
  The Other Side of the Sky, Arthur C. Clarke, co
* Our Best: The Best of Frederik Pohl and C.M. Kornbluth, Frederik
    Pohl & C.M. Kornbluth, co
  Our Father, Bernice Rubens, n.
* Out of Phaze, Piers Anthony, n.
  Out of the Dark World, Grace Chetwin, n.
  Out of Their Minds, Clifford D. Simak, n.
* Outbreak, Robin Cook, n.
  The Owl Service, Alan Garner, n.
  The Oxford Book of English Ghost Stories, ed. Michael Cox & R.A.
    Gilbert, an
  Palace of Kings, Mike Jefferies, n.
  Pale Rider, Alan Dean Foster, n.
* Pamela Oldfield's Spine Chillers, Pamela Oldfield, co
* The Paradise Tree, Diana L. Paxson, n.
  Pardon My Ghoulish Laughter, Fredric Brown, co
* The Particolored Unicorn, Jon DeCles, n.
  The Past Through Tomorrow Vol. 1, Robert A. Heinlein, co
  The Past Through Tomorrow Vol. 2, Robert A. Heinlein, co
  Past Times, Poul Anderson, co
  The Pastel City, M. John Harrison, n.
* Patch of the Odin Soldier, Geoffrey Marsh, n.
  Pawns and Symbols, Majliss Larson, n.
  The Peace Machine, Bob Shaw, n.
  The Peace War, Vernor Vinge, n.
  Pebble in the Sky, Isaac Asimov, n.
  The Penguin Book of Ghost Stories, ed. J Cuddon, an
  The Penguin Book of Horror Stories, ed. J Cuddon, an
  The Penguin Complete Ghost Stories of M.R. James, M.R. James, co
+ The Penguin World Omnibus of Science Fiction, ed. Brian W. Aldiss
    & Sam J. Lundwall, an
* Pennterra, Judith Moffett, n.
+ Pentecost and the Chosen One, W.J. Corbett, n.
* The People in the Picture, Haydn Middleton, n.
* The People of the Horse, Mary Mackie, n.
  The People: No Different Flesh, Zenna Henderson, co
* Perception Barriers, Robert Frazier, co
* The Peregrine Connection #3: In Search of the Dove, Rebecca
    York, n.
  Perfume, Patrick Suskind, n.
  Perilous Dreams, Andre Norton, co
+ The Persuading Stick, John Rowe Townsend, n.
* Pestis 18, Sharon Webb, n.
  The Pet, Charles L. Grant, n.
  Pet Sematary, Stephen King, n.
  Peter Pan, J.M. Barrie, n.
  The Phantom of the Opera, Gaston Leroux, n.

* **Philip K. Dick: The Dream Connection**, ed. D. Scott Apel, nf
* **Phoenix #1: Dark Messiah**, David Alexander, n.
* **Phoenix #2: Ground Zero**, David Alexander, n.
  The Phoenix and the Carpet, Edith Nesbit, n.
* **The Phoenix Bells**, Kathryn Grant, n.
* **Photon #1: For the Glory**, David Peters, n.
* **Photon #2: High Stakes**, David Peters, n.
* **Photon #3: In Search of Mom**, David Peters, n.
* **Photon #4: This is Your Life, Bhodi Li**, David Peters, n.
* **Photon #5: Exile**, David Peters, n.
* **Photon: Thieves of Light**, Michael Hudson, n.
  Phthor, Piers Anthony, n.
* **Piers Anthony's Worlds of Chthon: Plasm**, Charles Platt, n.
* **The Pig, the Prince & the Unicorn**, Karen A. Brush, n.
  Pilgrimage, Zenna Henderson, n.
  Pillar of the Sky, Cecilia Holland, n.
* **Pirate Prince**, Melisa C. Michaels, n.
* **Pirates of the Thunder**, Jack L. Chalker, n.
* **The Pit**, Ann Cheetham, n.
+ **A Place Among the Fallen**, Adrian Cole, n.
  The Place of Dead Roads, William S. Burroughs, n.
* **The Plague**, Guy N. Smith, n.
  Plague From Space, Harry Harrison, n.
* **Plague Moon**, Nathan Elliott, n.
+ **Plague Pit**, Mark Ronson, n.
* **Planet in Peril**, Kim Mohan & Pamela O'Neill, n.
  Planet of No Return, Harry Harrison, n.
  Planet of the Damned, Harry Harrison, n.
  Planet of the Warlord, Douglas Hill, n.
  The Planet on the Table, Kim Stanley Robinson, co
* **Planetary Legion for Peace: Story of Their War and Our Peace, 1940 - 2000**, Romulus Rexner, n.
  Planetoid 127, Edgar Wallace, n.
  Platforms, John R. Maxim, n.
* **Playmates**, Andrew Niederman, n.
  Plus, Joseph McElroy, n.
  Poltergeist II: The Other Side, James Kahn, n.
* **Poltergeist: Tales of Deadly Ghosts**, ed. Peter Haining, an
* **Polyphemus**, Michael Shea, co
  Port Eternity, C.J. Cherryh, n.
* **Portraits of His Children**, George R.R. Martin, co
  The Postman, David Brin, n.
* **The Power**, Ian Watson, n.
* **Power and Magic**, Daniel Kane, n.
  The Power and the Prophet, Robert Don Hughes, n.
  The Power of the Serpent, Peter Valentine Timlett, n.
  The Power That Preserves, Stephen R. Donaldson, n.
  The Practice Effect, David Brin, n.
  Predator, Paul Monette, n.
  The Presence, Yvonne MacManus, n.
  The Preserving Machine, Philip K. Dick, co
  The Pride of Chanur, C.J. Cherryh, n.
  Priestess of the Damned, Virginia Coffman, n.
  The Priests of Ferris, Morris Gee, n.
  Prime Number, Harry Harrison, oc
* **The Prince of Stars**, Ian Dennis, n.
  The Prince of Whales, R.L. Fisher, n.
* **Prince Raynor**, Henry Kuttner, co
  The Princess and the Goblin, George MacDonald, n.
  The Princess Bride, William Goldman, n.
  The Princess of Flames, Ru Emerson, n.
  Prisoner of Vampires, Nancy Garden, n.
* **Prisoners of Arionn**, Brian Herbert, n.
* **Private School #6: The Last Alien**, Steven Charles, n.
* **Project Pendulum**, Robert Silverberg, n.
* **Project: Millennium**, Curtis H. Hoffman, n.
* **Promise of the Rose Stone**, Claudia McCay, n.
  The Prophet of Lamath, Robert Don Hughes, n.
* **The Prophetic Soul: A Reading of H.G. Wells' Things to Come**, Professor Leon Stover, nf
  Protectorate, Mick Farren, n.
  The Proteus Operation, James P. Hogan, n.
* **Pruzy's Pot**, Theodore Sturgeon, ss
* **PsiFi: Psychological Theories and Science Fictions**, ed. Jim Ridgway & Michele Benjamin, an
* **Psychic Spawn**, Ryder Syvertsen & Adrian Fletcher, n.
  Psycho 2, Robert Bloch, n.
* **Puppet Master: A Novel**, Liz Greene, n.

  The Puppet Masters, Robert A. Heinlein, n.
  Puttering About in a Small Land, Philip K. Dick, n.
  Quag Keep, Andre Norton, n.
  The Quallsford Inheritance, Lloyd Biggle, Jr., n.
  Queen of the Lightning, Kathleen Herbert, n.
  Queen Victorica's Revenge, Harry Harrison, n.
* **Quest**, Richard Ben Sapir, n.
  Quest for a Kelpie, Frances Hendry, n.
  The Quest for Saint Camber, Katherine Kurtz, n.
  Quest of the Three Worlds, Cordwainer Smith, co
* **The Questing of Kedrigern**, John Morressy, n.
* **A Quiver Of Ghosts**, ed. Aidan Chambers, oa
  Rachel and the Angel and Other Stories, Robert Westall, co
  Racso and the Rats of NIMH, Jane Leslie Conly, n.
  Radio Free Albemuth, Philip K. Dick, n.
+ **The Ragged Astronauts**, Bob Shaw, n.
* **The Raging**, Tim Stout, n.
* **The Raging Tide**, Edward Gorey, pi
* **Raider's Sky**, Mary Haynes, n.
  The Ram of Sweetriver, Colin Dann, n.
  Rankin: Enemy of the State, John Osier, n.
* **The Rapture Effect**, Jeffrey A. Carver, n.
* **The Rat**, Gunter Grass, n.
  Ratha's Creature, Clare Bell, n.
+ **Raven 2: A Time of Ghosts**, Richard Kirk, n.
+ **Raven 3: The Frozen God**, Richard Kirk, n.
+ **Raven 4: Lords of the Shadows**, Richard Kirk, n.
+ **Raven 5: A Time of Dying**, Richard Kirk, n.
* **The Raven in the Glass**, Jill Downie, n.
+ **Raven: Swordsmistress of Chaos**, Richard Kirk, n.
* **Re-Animator**, Jeff Rovin, n.
* **Ready or Not: Here Come Fourteen Frightening Stories!**, ed. Joan Kahn, an
* **Reap the East Wind**, Glen Cook, n.
* **The Rebel Dynasty, Volume I**, F.M. Busby, om
* **The Rebel Dynasty, Volume II**, F.M. Busby, om
* **The Rebel Prince**, Sharon Green, n.
  Rebel's Quest, F.M. Busby, n.
  Red Dreams, Dennis Etchison, co
  Red Flame Burning, Ward Hawkins, n.
* **The Red Magician**, Lisa Goldstein, n.
  Red Planet, Robert A. Heinlein, n.
* **Red Prophet**, Orson Scott Card, n.
  Red Storm Rising, Tom Clancy, n.
* **Red Sun of Darkover**, Marion Zimmer Bradley & The Friends of Darkover, oa
* **The Red Truck**, Rudy Wilson, n.
+ **Redwall**, Brian Jacques, n.
* **Reflection**, Andrew Neiderman, n.
* **Reflections on the Fantastic: Selected Essays from the Fourth International Conference on the Fantastic in the Arts**, ed. Michael R. Collings, nf
* **The Regiment**, John Dalmas, n.
* **The Reign of Terror**, Ian Marter, n.
* **Reindeer Moon**, Elizabeth Marshall Thomas, n.
  Relics, Shaun Hutson, n.
  Rendezvous With Rama, Arthur C. Clarke, n.
* **Reparations**, Gordon Wardman, n.
  Replay, Ken Grimwood, n.
* **The Rescue**, Ian Marter, n.
  Restless Nights: Selected Stories of Dino Buzzati, Dino Buzzati, co
  Retief to the Rescue, Keith Laumer, n.
  Retief: Diplomat at Arms, Keith Laumer, co
* **Retief: Envoy to New Worlds**, Keith Laumer, co
* **The Return of Mister X**, Gilbert Hernandez, Jaime Hernandez, Mario Hernandez & Dean Motter, gn
  Return of the Howling, Gary Brandner, n.
  The Return of the Indian, Lynne Reid Banks, n.
  The Return of the King, J.R.R. Tolkien, n.
* **Return of the Seventh Carrier**, Peter Albano, n.
  The Return of the Time Machine, Egon Friedell, n.
* **Return to Fanglith**, John Dalmas, n.
* **Return to Shangri-La**, Leslie Halliwell, n.
  Revenge of the Manitou, Graham Masterton, n.
  Rhialto the Marvellous, Jack Vance, co
* **Rhysling Anthology 1987**, ed. Anonymous, an
* **Richard and the Vratch**, Beatrice Gormley, n.
* **The Riddle and the Rune**, Grace Chetwin, n.

The Ring of Allaire, Susan Dexter, n.
Rings of Ice, Piers Anthony, n.
Rip Van Winkle, Washington Irving, nv
The Rishi, Leo Giroux, Jr., n.
Rite of Passage, Alexei Panshin, n.
The River of Time, David Brin, co
Road Lines, Chris Ould, n.
The Road to Underfall, Mike Jefferies, n.
Roald Dahl's Book of Ghost Stories, ed. Roald Dahl, an
* **Robert A. Heinlein**, Professor Leon Stover, nf
* **Robert Adams' Book of Alternate Worlds**, ed. Robert Adams, Pamela
　　Crippen Adams & Martin H. Greenberg, an
* **Robert Bloch**, Randall D. Larson, nf
* **Robert E. Howard**, Marc A. Cerasini & Charles Hoffman, nf
* **Robert Silverberg's Worlds of Wonder**, ed. Robert Silverberg, an
* **Robocop**, Ed Naha, n.
* **Robot**, Peter Grimwade, n.
　Robot Dreams, Isaac Asimov, oc
* **Robot Raiders**, Ellen Leroe, hc
* **Robotech # 1: Genesis**, Jack McKinney, n.
* **Robotech # 2: Battle Cry**, Jack McKinney, n.
* **Robotech # 3: Homecoming**, Jack McKinney, n.
* **Robotech # 4: Battlehymn**, Jack McKinney, n.
* **Robotech # 5: Force of Arms**, Jack McKinney, n.
* **Robotech # 6: Doomsday**, Jack McKinney, n.
* **Robotech # 7: Southern Cross**, Jack McKinney, n.
* **Robotech # 8: Metal Fire**, Jack McKinney, n.
* **Robotech # 9: The Final Nightmare**, Jack McKinney, n.
* **Robotech #10: Invid Invasion**, Jack McKinney, n.
* **Robotech #11: Metamorphosos**, Jack McKinney, n.
* **Robotech #12: Symphony of Light**, Jack McKinney, n.
* **Robotech Art 2**, ed. Kay Reynolds, pi
　Robotech: The Graphic Novel, Mike Baron, gn
　Rocketship Galileo, Robert A. Heinlein, n.
+ **The Rod of Light**, Barrington J. Bayley, n.
* **Rod Serling's Night Gallery Reader**, ed. Carol Serling, Martin H.
　　Greenberg & Charles G. Waugh, an
+ **Roderick**, John Sladek, n.
* **Roger Zelazny's Alien Speedway 1: Clypsis**, Jeffrey A. Carver, n.
　Rogue Moon, Algis Budrys, n.
* **Rogue Pirate**, John Gregory Betancourt, n.
　Romance of Two Worlds, Marie Corelli, n.
* **Romances of William Morris**, Amanda Hodgson, nf
* **The Romans**, Donald Cotton, n.
* **The Romulan Way**, Diane E. Duane & Peter Morwood, n.
* **Ronin**, Frank Miller, gn
　A Room to Die In, Ellery Queen, n.
* **A Rose-Red City**, Dave Duncan, n.
　The Roving Mind, Isaac Asimov, nf
* **Roxanna #2: The Temple of Oblivion**, Serge Letendre & Regis Loisel,
　　gn
* **Ruins**, Brian W. Aldiss, nv
　The Ruins of Isis, Marion Zimmer Bradley, n.
* **Rumors of Spring**, Richard Grant, n.
* **Runespear**, Victor Milan & Melinda M. Snodgrass, n.
　Russian Hide-and-Seek, Kingsley Amis, n.
　Sabella, Tanith Lee, n.
* **Saberhagen: My Best**, Fred Saberhagen, co
　Sable Night, Archie Roy, n.
* **Saga of the Lost Lands, Volume 1: Blood of the Tiger**, Rose Estes, n.
* **Saga of the Swamp Thing**, Alan Moore, gn
　Saint Camber, Katherine Kurtz, n.
　Saints and Strangers, Angela Carter, co
　Salem's Lot, Stephen King, n.
* **Samantha Slade #2: Confessions of a Teenage Frog**, Susan Smith,
　　n.
* **Samantha Slade #3: Our Friend, Public Nuisance No. 1**, Susan
　　Smith, n.
* **Samantha Slade, Monster-Sitter**, Susan Smith, n.
+ **Sambaqui**, Stella Carr Ribiero, n.
* **The Sand Witch**, Steven Senn, n.
* **Sandkings**, George R.R. Martin, Pat Broderick, Neal McPheeters &
　　Doug Moench, gn
　The Sands of Mars, Arthur C. Clarke, n.
　The Santaroga Barrier, Frank Herbert, n.
　Sara's Ghost, Patricia Welles, n.
　Saraband of Lost Time, Richard Grant, n.
* **Satanic Lute**, Bridget Wood, n.

　Savages of Gor, John Norman, n.
* **Scared Stiff: Tales of Sex and Death**, Ramsey Campbell, co
* **Scars**, Richard Christian Matheson, co
　The Scars of Dracula, Angus Hall, n.
* **Science Fiction and Fantasy Reference Index, 1878-1985**, Hal W.
　　Hall, nf
　Science Fiction Hall of Fame, Vol. 4, ed. Terry Carr, an
　Science Fiction Master Index of Names, ed. Kenneth L. Justice, nf
* **Science Fiction, Fantasy, & Horror: 1986**, Charles N. Brown &
　　William G. Contento, nf
+ **Science Fiction: The 100 Best Novels**, David Pringle, nf
* **The Scorpio Ghosts and the Black Hole Gang**, Kathy Kennedy Tapp,
　　n.
* **Screening Space: The American Science Fiction Film**, Vivian
　　Sobchack, nf
* **Scryer**, Linda Crockett Gray, n.
* **The Sea and Summer**, George Turner, n.
* **Sea of Death**, Gary Gygax, n.
* **Sea of Glass**, Barry B. Longyear, n.
* **The Sea of Silence**, Niel Hancock, n.
　Sea Siege, Andre Norton, n.
　Search the Seven Hills, Barbara Hambly, n.
* **The Seashore People**, Clive King, n.
　Seaward, Susan Cooper, n.
* **The Second Book of Lost Swords: Sightbinder's Story**, Fred
　　Saberhagen, n.
* **The Second Earth**, Patrick Woodroffe, n.
　Second Foundation, Isaac Asimov, n.
* **The Second Great Dune Trilogy**, Frank Herbert, om
　Second Stage Lensman, E.E. "Doc" Smith, n.
　The Second Trip, Robert Silverberg, n.
* **The Secret Ascension**, Michael Bishop, n.
　The Secret Garden, Frances Hodgson Burnett, n.
* **The Secret of the Round Beast**, John Forrester, n.
　The Secret People, John Wyndham, n.
* **Secrets of the Deep**, Gordon R. Dickson, om
　Sector General, James White, oc
* **Selected Tales of Grim and Grue from the Horror Pulps**, ed.
　　Sheldon R. Jaffery, an
* **A Sending of Dragons**, Jane Yolen, n.
　A Sense of Wonder, ed. Sam Moskowitz, an
* **The Sensitives**, Herbert Burkholz, n.
* **The Sensorites**, Nigel Robinson, n.
　Sentinels From Space, Eric Frank Russell, n.
* **Sepulchre**, James Herbert, n.
* **Serenissima**, Erica Jong, n.
* **Serpent's Egg**, R.A. Lafferty, n.
* **The Settlement on Planet B**, Clare Cooper, n.
　The Seven Altars of Dusarra, Lawrence Watt-Evans, n.
　Seven Citadels: Prince of the Godborn, Geraldine Harris, n.
　Seven Citadels: The Children of the Wind, Geraldine Harris, n.
　Seven Citadels: The Dead Kingdom, Geraldine Harris, n.
　Seven Citadels: The Seventh Gate, Geraldine Harris, n.
* **Seventh Son**, Orson Scott Card, n.
　Shade of the Tree, Piers Anthony, n.
* **Shadow**, Dave Duncan, n.
* **Shadow Child**, Joseph Citro, n.
* **Shadow Dancers**, Lillian Stewart Carl, n.
* **The Shadow Dancers**, Jack L. Chalker, n.
　The Shadow Guests, Joan Aiken, n.
　Shadow Hawk, Andre Norton, n.
　Shadow Lord, Laurence Yep, n.
　Shadow of a Broken Man, George C. Chesbro, n.
* **The Shadow of His Wings**, Bruce Fergusson, n.
* **The Shadow on the Dial**, Anne Lindbergh, n.
* **The Shadow on the Doorstep/Trilobyte**, James P. Blaylock &
　　Edward Bryant, oa
* **Shadowfires**, Leigh Nichols, n.
　Shadows, ed. Charles L. Grant, oa
　Shadows, Shaun Hutson, n.
　Shadows 7, ed. Charles L. Grant, oa
　Shadows 8, ed. Charles L. Grant, oa
* **Shadows 10**, ed. Charles L. Grant, oa
　Shadows II, ed. Charles L. Grant, an
* **Shadowspawn**, Andrew J. Offutt, n.
　Shallows of the Night, Eric Van Lustbader, n.
* **Shan**, Eric Van Lustbader, n.
　Shapechangers, Jennifer Roberson, n.

* **Shapes**, Richard Delap & Walt Lee, n.
  The Shattered Chain, Marion Zimmer Bradley, n.
  The Shattered Horse, S.P. Somtow, n.
* **She Comes When You're Leaving & Other Stories**, Bruce Boston, co
  Shelter, Marty Asher, nv
* **The Shelter**, Mary Kittredge & Kevin O'Donnell, Jr., n.
* **The Shift**, Hugh Cook, n.
* **The Shift Key**, John Brunner, n.
  The Shining, Stephen King, n.
  Shoeless Joe, W.P. Kinsella, n.
  The Shore of Women, Pamela Sargent, n.
* **The Shores of the Near Past**, Michael Chester, n.
* **Short & Shivery**, Robert D. San Souci, an
  The Shroud, John Coyne, n.
* **Shudderchild**, Warren G. Norwood, n.
* **Sideshow**, W.R. Thompson, n.
* **Sight Unseen**, Andrew Neiderman, n.
* **Sign of Chaos**, Roger Zelazny, n.
  The Sign of the Guardian, John Long, n.
  Signs and Portents, Chelsea Quinn Yarbro, co
  The Silent Tower, Barbara Hambly, n.
* **The Silent Warrior**, L.E. Modesitt, Jr., n.
  The Silver Chair, C.S. Lewis, n.
  The Silver Citadel, Anthony Horowitz, n.
  The Silver Crown, Joel Rosenberg, n.
* **The Silver Vortex**, Moyra Caldecott, n.
  Silverglass, J.F. Rivkin, n.
* **Sindbad and the Evil Genie**, Jack A. Melanos, pl
+ **The Singing Stone**, O.R. Melling, n.
* **The Sinister Ray**, Lester Dent, co
  Sister Wolf, Ann Arensberg, n.
* **The Sisterhood of Steel: Baronwe: Daughter of Death**, Christy Marx & Peter Ledger, gn
  Sixth Column, Robert A. Heinlein, n.
* **Skallagrigg**, William Horwood, n.
  Skeen's Leap, Jo Clayton, n.
* **Skeen's Return**, Jo Clayton, n.
* **Skeen's Search**, Jo Clayton, n.
+ **The Skeleton Lord's Key**, Robert E. Vardeman, writing as Daniel Moran, n.
  Skirmish, Melisa C. Michaels, n.
* **Skraelings**, Carl Sherrell, n.
* **Slambash Wangs of a Compo Gormer**, Robert Leeson, n.
* **Sleep Tight**, Matthew Costello, n.
  Sleepers of Mars, John Wyndham, co
  The Sleeping Dragon, Joel Rosenberg, n.
  Slipback, Eric Saward, n.
* **Slob**, Rex Miller, n.
  Slow Birds, Ian Watson, co
+ **Slugs**, Shaun Hutson, n.
* **Smiles and the Millenium**, Miranda Miller, n.
* **Smoke**, Ruby Jean Jensen, n.
* **Smoke from the Ashes**, William W. Johnstone, n.
* **The Smoke Ring**, Larry Niven, n.
+ **The Snow Spider**, Jenny Nimmo, n.
* **Snow White and the Seven Dwarfs & the Making of the Classic Film**, Brian Sibley, nf
  The Soft Whisper of the Dead, Charles L. Grant, n.
  Software, Rudy Rucker, n.
* **Solar Kill**, Charles Ingrid, n.
  Solar Lottery, Philip K. Dick, n.
  Solaris, Stanislaw Lem, n.
  Soldier of the Mist, Gene Wolfe, n.
* **Soldiers of Paradise**, Paul Park, n.
* **Somebody Come and Play**, Clare McNally, n.
  Son of Man, Robert Silverberg, n.
  Son of the Endless Night, John Farris, n.
  Song For a Dark Queen, Rosemary Sutcliff, n.
  The Song of Homana, Jennifer Roberson, n.
  Song of Kali, Dan Simmons, n.
  The Song of Phaid the Gambler, Mick Farren, n.
  Song of Sorcery, Elizabeth Ann Scarborough, n.
+ **The Song of the Forest**, Colin Mackay, n.
  Songmaster, Orson Scott Card, n.
* **Songs from the Seashell Archives, Vol. 1**, Elizabeth Ann Scarborough, om
  The Songs of Distant Earth, Arthur C. Clarke, n.
* **The Sorcerer's Apprentices**, Nicholas Stuart Gray, ss

  Soul Eater, K.W. Jeter, n.
  Soul-Eater, Dana Brookins, n.
  Soulstorm, Chet Williamson, n.
* **Soulstring**, Midori Snyder, n.
  The Sound of Midnight, Charles L. Grant, n.
  The Sound of Wings, Spencer Dunmore, n.
* **A Southern Fantasy: 13th World Fantasy Convention Program Book**, ed. Ron Lindahn & Val Lakey Lindahn, oa
* **Southshore**, Sheri S. Tepper, n.
  The Space Eater, David Langford, n.
  Space Family Stone, Robert A. Heinlein, n.
  The Space Merchants, Frederik Pohl & C.M. Kornbluth, n.
* **The Space Museum**, Glyn Jones, n.
  Space Skimmer, David Gerrold, n.
  The Space Swimmers, Gordon R. Dickson, n.
* **Space Traders Unlimited**, Julia Riding, n.
* **Spaceballs: The Book**, Jovian Bob Stine, n.
* **A Spaceship Built of Stone and Other Stories**, Lisa Tuttle, co
* **Spaceships and Spells**, ed. Jane Yolen, Martin H. Greenberg & Charles G. Waugh, oa
+ **Spaceways**, ed. John Foster, an
  Spacial Delivery, Gordon R. Dickson, n.
  Speaker for the Dead, Orson Scott Card, n.
* **Speaker to Heaven**, Atanielle Annyn Noel, n.
  Speaking of Dinosaurs, Philip E. High, n.
* **Specter or Delusion? The Supernatural in Gothic Fiction**, Margaret L. Carter, nf
  Spectre, Stephen Laws, n.
  Spell of the Sorcerer's Skull, John Bellairs, n.
  Spell of the Witch World, Andre Norton, n.
  The Spell Sword, Marion Zimmer Bradley, n.
* **The Spellkey**, Ann Downer, n.
* **Spellsinger's Scherzo**, Alan Dean Foster, om
* **Sphere**, Michael Crichton, n.
  Spiders, Richard Lewis, n.
  Spinneret, Timothy Zahn, n.
* **Spiral Winds**, Garry Kilworth, n.
* **The Spirit Wood**, Robert Masello, n.
* **Spurlock: Sheriff of Purgatory**, Jim Morris, n.
* **Spychodrome**, Simon Hawke, n.
  SS-GB, Len Deighton, n.
* **The Stainless Steel Rat Gets Drafted**, Harry Harrison, n.
* **The Stalking**, Robert Faulcon, om
  Stalking the Unicorn, Mike Resnick, n.
  The Stand, Stephen King, n.
  Stand on Zanzibar, John Brunner, n.
  Star Beast, Robert A. Heinlein, n.
* **Star Commandos: Colony in Peril**, P.M. Griffin, n.
* **Star Griffin**, Michael Kurland, n.
  Star Hammer, Christopher B. Rowley, n.
  Star Healer, James White, n.
  Star Hunters, Jo Clayton, n.
  Star Lord, Louise Lawrence, n.
  Star Maker, Olaf Stapledon, n.
  Star Man's Son, Andre Norton, n.
  Star of Gypsies, Robert Silverberg, n.
  Star Rebel, F.M. Busby, n.
  Star Rider, Doris Piserchia, n.
  Star Rover, Jack London, n.
  Star Surgeon, James White, n.
  Star Trek #10: Web of the Romulans, M.S. Murdock, n.
  Star Trek #11: Yesterday's Son, A.C. Crispin, n.
  Star Trek #13: The Wounded Sky, Diane E. Duane, n.
  Star Trek #20: The Vulcan Academy Murders, Jean Lorrah, n.
* **Star Trek #32: Chain of Attack**, Gene DeWeese, n.
* **Star Trek #33: Deep Domain**, Howard Weinstein, n.
* **Star Trek #34: Dreams of the Raven**, Carmen Carter, n.
* **Star Trek #35: The Romulan Way**, Diane E. Duane & Peter Morwood, n.
* **Star Trek #36: How Much for Just the Planet?**, John M. Ford, n.
* **Star Trek #37: Bloodthirst**, J.M. Dillard, n.
  The Star Trek Compendium, Allan Asherman, nf
* **Star Trek IV: The Journey Home**, Peter Leragis, pi
  Star Trek IV: The Voyage Home, Vonda N. McIntyre, n.
* **Star Trek, The Next Generation: Encounter at Farpoint**, David Gerrold, n.
* **Star Trek: Final Frontier**, Diane Carey, n.
* **Star Trek: Strangers From the Sky**, Margaret Wander Bonanno, n.

*The Star Wars Trilogy, George Lucas, Donald F. Glut & James Kahn, om
Star Wind, Linda Woolverton, n.
Starburst, Frederik Pohl, n.
*Starclipper and the Galactic Final, Brian Earnshaw, n.
Stargate, Andre Norton, n.
Starhunt, David Gerrold, n.
Staring at the Sun, Julian Barnes, n.
*Starjacked!, William Greenleaf, n.
+Starkadder, Bernard King, n.
*Starlight, Scott Ely, n.
*Starmageddon, Richard Rohmer, n.
Starman Jones, Robert A. Heinlein, n.
*Starpirate's Brain, Ron Goulart, n.
*Starquest, Vol.2: Operation Master Planet, Gregory J. Smith, n.
The Stars My Destination, Alfred Bester, n.
The Stars, Like Dust, Isaac Asimov, n.
*Starship Dunroamin, Janis Milne, n.
Starship Troopers, Robert A. Heinlein, n.
*The Starwolves, Thorarinn Gunnarsson, n.
Statesman, Piers Anthony, n.
*Station Gehenna, Andrew Weiner, n.
*Stepfather Bank, D.C. Poyer, n.
*Stephen King Goes to Hollywood, Jeff Conner, nf
*The Stephen King Phenomenon, Michael R. Collings, nf
Steven Spielberg's Amazing Stories, Steven Bauer, oc
*Stickman, Seth Pfefferle, n.
*Stigma, Bill Clendenen, n.
*Still River, Hal Clement, n.
The Stochastic Man, Robert Silverberg, n.
*Stolen Souls, Jeffrey Sackett, n.
Stone 588, Gerald A. Browne, n.
+The Stone and the Flute, Hans Bemmann, n.
The Stone Arrow, Richard Herley, n.
*The Stories of Muriel Spark, Muriel Spark, co
A Storm of Wings, M. John Harrison, n.
*Storm Warnings: Science Fiction Confronts the Future, ed. George
    E. Slusser, Eric S. Rabkin & Colin Greenland, nf
The Story of the Amulet, Edith Nesbit, n.
Stowaway to Mars, John Wyndham, n.
*Strange Maine, ed. Charles G. Waugh, Martin H. Greenberg & Frank
    D. McSherry, Jr., an
Strange Seed, T.M. Wright, n.
*Strange Toys, Patricia Geary, n.
Strange Visitation, Marie Corelli, n.
*The Stranger, Gordon R. Dickson, co
Stranger in a Strange Land, Robert A. Heinlein, n.
A Stranger is Watching, Mary Higgins Clark, n.
Strangers, Dean R. Koontz, n.
Strangers From Earth, Poul Anderson, co
Strangers From the Sky, Margaret Wander Bonanno, n.
A String in the Harp, Nancy Bond, n.
The Subatomic Monster, Isaac Asimov, nf
*Sugar and Other Stories, Antonia Byatt, co
The Summer Birds, Penelope Farmer, n.
The Summer Tree, Guy Gavriel Kay, n.
The Summer's King, Cherry Wilder, n.
Sun's End, Richard A. Lupoff, n.
*The Sun, the Moon, and the Stars, Steven Brust, n.
*Sundipper, Paul B. Thompson, n.
Sundiver, David Brin, n.
*Sundrinker, Zach Hughes, n.
The Sunset Warrior, Eric Van Lustbader, n.
*Superman at Fifty: The Persistence of a Legend, Dennis Dooley &
    Gary Engle, nf
*Superman IV, B.B. Hiller, n.
The Supernatural Short Stories of Sir Walter Scott, Sir Walter Scott,
    co
+Supernatural Stories: 13 Tales of the Unexpected, ed. Jean
    Russell, an
*Supernatural Tales: Excursions Into Fantasy, Vernon Lee, co
*Supertanks, ed. Joe W. Haldeman, Martin H. Greenberg & Charles G.
    Waugh, an
The Survivalist #13: Pursuit, Jerry Ahern, n.
The Survivalist #14: Terror, Jerry Ahern, n.
*The Survivalist #15: Overlord, Jerry Ahern, n.
*Suzy McKee Charnas, Joan Vinge, Octavia Butler, Marleen S. Barr,
    Richard Law & Ruth Salvaggio, nf

*Swan Song, Robert R. McCammon, n.
*Sweet Silver Blues, Glen Cook, n.
*Swimmers Beneath the Bright, M. Coleman Easton, n.
*Sword and Sorceress IV, ed. Marion Zimmer Bradley, oa
The Sword and the Chain, Joel Rosenberg, n.
The Sword and the Flame, Stephen R. Lawhead, n.
Sword at Sunset, Rosemary Sutcliff, n.
The Sword of Bheleu, Lawrence Watt-Evans, n.
The Sword of Calandra, Susan Dexter, n.
Sword of Chaos, Marion Zimmer Bradley & The Friends of Darkover,
    oa
Sword of Fire, Ward Hawkins, n.
The Swords of Corum, Michael Moorcock, om
Swords of Shahrazar, Robert E. Howard, co
*Swords of the Legion, Harry Turtledove, n.
*Swordspoint, Ellen Kushner, n.
*Synergy; New Science Fiction: Vol. 1, ed. George Zebrowski, oa
*Takeoff Too!, Randall Garrett, co
*A Tale of Time City, Diana Wynne Jones, n.
*The Tale That Wags the God, James Blish, nf
*Tales From Isaac Asimov's Science Fiction Magazine, ed. Sheila
    Williams & Cynthia Manson, an
*Tales from the Flat Earth: Night's Daughter, Tanith Lee, om
*Tales from the Flat Earth: The Lords of Darkness, Tanith Lee, om
*Tales from the Forbidden Planet, ed. Roz Kaveney, oa
Tales from the Planet Earth, ed. Frederik Pohl & Elizabeth Anne Hull,
    an
+Tales of Dungeons and Dragons, ed. Peter Haining, an
Tales of Mystery and Imagination, Edgar Allan Poe, co
*Tales of Narnia, C.S. Lewis, om
*Tales of Natural and Unnatural Catastrophes, Patricia Highsmith, oc
Tales of Ten Worlds, Arthur C. Clarke, co
*Tales of the Dark, ed. Lincoln Child, an
*Tales of the Dark 2, ed. Lincoln Child, an
*Tales of the Witch World, ed. Andre Norton, oa
Tales of Wonder, Jane Yolen, co
*Taliesin, Stephen R. Lawhead, n.
*Talking Across the World, ed. Robert Crossley, nf
Talking Man, Terry Bisson, n.
Taming the Forest King, Claudia J. Edwards, n.
*Taronga, Victor Kelleher, n.
*Tarot, Piers Anthony, om
*Tatja Grimm's World, Vernor Vinge, co
Tea with the Black Dragon, R.A. MacAvoy, n.
*Team Yankee, H.W. Coyle, n.
*The Tell-Tale Heart, Edgar Allan Poe & Melvin R. White, pl
*Telos, Arthur Versluis, n.
*Tempus, Janet Morris, n.
*The Tenth Planet, Leo Melamed, n.
The Tenth Victim, Robert Sheckley, n.
*Teot's War, Heather Gladney, n.
The Terminal Beach, J.G. Ballard, co
The Terminator, Shaun Hutson, n.
Terror at Play, Seth McEvoy, n.
*Terror of the Vervoids, Pip Baker & Jane Baker, n.
*Terror Under the Tent, Mary Anderson, n.
*Terry Carr's Best Science Fiction and Fantasy of the Year #16, ed.
    Terry Carr, an
*Tesseracts 2, ed. Phyllis Gotlieb & Douglas Barbour, an
*Test of Honor, Lois McMaster Bujold, om
*Texas Triumphant, Daniel da Cruz, n.
Theatre of Timesmiths, Garry Kilworth, n.
*Their Master's War, Mick Farren, n.
Thendara House, Marion Zimmer Bradley, n.
There Will Be Time, Poul Anderson, n.
*There Will Be War, Vol. VI: Guns of Darkness, ed. Jerry E. Pournelle,
    an
*These Green Foreign Hills, Roland J. Green, n.
The Thief of Bagdad, Achmed Abdullah, n.
*Thieves' World 10: Aftermath, ed. Robert Lynn Asprin & Lynn Abbey,
    oa
*Thieves' World Graphics 4, Tim Sale, Lynn Abbey & Robert Lynn
    Asprin, gn
Thinner, Stephen King, n.
*The Third Book of After Midnight Stories, ed. Amy Myers, oa
This Is the Way the World Ends, James Morrow, n.
*This Place Has No Atmosphere, Paula Danziger, n.
This Time of Darkness, H.M. Hoover, n.

THORGAL: THE ARCHERS　　　　　　　　　　　　　　　　　　　　　　　VALIS

* **Thorgal: The Archers**, Jean Van Hamme & Grzegorz Rosinski, gn
  Thorns, Robert Silverberg, n.
  Those Who Watch, Robert Silverberg, n.
  Three Against the Witch World, Andre Norton, n.
  Three to Conquer, Eric Frank Russell, n.
  Three-Bladed Doom, Robert E. Howard, n.
  Threshold, David R. Palmer, n.
  The Throme of the Erril of Sherril, Patricia A. McKillip, co
* **Throne of Fools**, Adrian Cole, n.
  The Throne of Scone, Patricia Kennealy, n.
* **Through Darkest America**, Neal Barrett, Jr., n.
+ **Through the Dolls' House Door**, Jane Gardam, n.
* **Throwback**, Mark Manley, n.
  The Ticket That Exploded, William S. Burroughs, n.
  Tiger! Tiger!, Alfred Bester, n.
  Time After Time, Allen Appel, n.
* **Time and Again**, Beverly Sommers, n.
  Time and the Hunter, Italo Calvino, co
  Time and the Rani, Pip Baker & Jane Baker, n.
* **Time Capsule**, Mitch Berman, n.
* **A Time For Survival**, Philip McCutchan, n.
  Time for the Stars, Robert A. Heinlein, n.
  The Time Machine, H.G. Wells, co
* **The Time Meddler**, Nigel Robinson, n.
  The Time of the Ghost, Diana Wynne Jones, n.
  The Time of the Transference, Alan Dean Foster, n.
  Time Out, Helen Cresswell, na
  Time Out of Joint, Philip K. Dick, n.
  Time Out of Mind, John R. Maxim, n.
* **Time Pressure**, Spider Robinson, n.
  Time Rope, Robert Leeson, n.
  The Time Traders, Andre Norton, n.
  Time Trap, Nicholas Fisk, n.
  Time Trap, Keith Laumer, n.
  Time Travelers Strictly Cash, Spider Robinson, co
  Time Twister, Ged Maybury, n.
* **The Time Wanderers**, Arkady Strugatsky & Boris Strugatsky, n.
* **Time Wars #7: The Arbonaut Affair**, Simon Hawke, n.
* **Time-Fighters**, Bernard King, n.
* **Timefall**, James Kahn, n.
  The Timekeeper Conspiracy, Simon Hawke, n.
* **Timeliner Trilogy**, Richard C. Meredith, om
  Timescape, Gregory Benford, n.
* **Timeswept Lovers**, Constance O'Day-Flannery, n.
  Tin Toys, Ursula Holden, n.
  To Live Again, Robert Silverberg, n.
  To Live Forever, Jack Vance, n.
* **To Make Death Love Us**, Sovereign Falconer, n.
* **To Marry Medusa**, Theodore Sturgeon, co
* **To Sail Beyond the Sunset**, Robert A. Heinlein, n.
* **To the Haunted Mountains**, Ru Emerson, n.
  To the Stars, Harry Harrison, om
  Tom O'Bedlam, Robert Silverberg, n.
  Tom's Midnight Garden, Philippa Pearce, n.
* **The Tommyknockers**, Stephen King, n.
* **Tomorrow's Magic**, Pamela F. Service, n.
* **Too Much Magic**, Betsy Sterman & Samuel Sterman, n.
* **Tookmaker Koan**, John McLoughlin, n.
* **Tool of the Trade**, Joe W. Haldeman, n.
* **Torch**, Jill Paton Walsh, n.
* **Torch of Fear**, Ward Hawkins, n.
* **Torture Tomb**, C. Dean Anderson, n.
* **Touch**, Elmore Leonard, n.
* **A Touch of Sturgeon**, Theodore Sturgeon, co
  Tourmalin's Time Cheques, F. Anstey, n.
* **The Tower**, Colin Wilson, n.
  Tower of Glass, Robert Silverberg, n.
* **Track of the White Wolf**, Jennifer Roberson, n.
* **Trail of the Seahawks**, Ardath Mayhar & Ron Fortier, n.
* **Transformation**, Edmund Plante, n.
  The Transmigration of Timothy Archer, Philip K. Dick, n.
  Travel Light, Naomi Mitchison, n.
* **Traveler # 9: The Stalking Time**, D.B. Drumm, n.
* **Traveler #10: Hell on Earth**, D.B. Drumm, n.
* **Traveler #11: The Children's Crusade**, D.B. Drumm, n.
* **Traveler #12: The Prey**, D.B. Drumm, n.
* **Traveler #13: Ghost Dancers**, D.B. Drumm, n.
  Tread Softly, Richard Kelly, n.

+ **Tread Softly**, Richard Laymon, n.
* **Treasure Planet**, Nathan Elliott, n.
  The Tree of Swords and Jewels, C.J. Cherryh, n.
  Trek to Kraggen-Cor, Dennis L. McKiernan, n.
* **Trekmaster**, James B. Johnson, n.
  The Tribe, Bari Wood, n.
* **The Tribe of Gum**, Anthony Coburn, pl
* **A Trick of the Light**, Jackie Vivelo, oc
+ **The Tricksters**, Margaret Mahy, n.
* **Triplet**, Timothy Zahn, n.
  The Troll's Grindstone, Elizabeth H. Boyer, n.
* **Trollnight**, Peter Tremayne, n.
  The Troy Game, Jean Morris, n.
* **True Names and Other Dangers**, Vernor Vinge, co
  Trullion: Alastor 2262, Jack Vance, n.
  Tuf Voyaging, George R.R. Martin, co
* **Tumbleweed**, Dick King-Smith, n.
  The Turn of the Screw & Other Stories, Henry James, co
* **Twilight Eyes**, Dean R. Koontz, n.
* **Twilight of the Gods, Book III: Three Trumps Sounding**, Dennis Schmidt, n.
  The Twilight of the Serpent, Peter Valentine Timlett, n.
  The Twilight Realm, Christopher Carpenter, n.
  Twilight World, Poul Anderson, n.
* **Twilight's Kingdoms**, Nancy Asire, n.
  Twins, Bari Wood & Jack Geasland, n.
* **Twisted Circuits**, ed. Mick Gowar, oa
* **Twisted Tales**, Bruce Jones, oc
  Twisting the Rope, R.A. MacAvoy, n.
  Two Tales and Eight Tomorrows, Harry Harrison, co
  Two to Conquer, Marion Zimmer Bradley, n.
  The Two Towers, J.R.R. Tolkien, n.
  Tyranopolis, A.E. Van Vogt, n.
* **U.S.S.A. Book 1**, Tom DeHaven, n.
* **U.S.S.A. Book 2**, S.N. Lewitt, n.
* **U.S.S.A. Book 3**, S.C. Sykes, n.
* **U.S.S.A. Book 4**, S.N. Lewitt, n.
  The Ultimax Man, Keith Laumer, n.
* **Ultra-Vue and Selected Peripheral Visions**, Rudin Moore, oc
* **The Uncanny X-Men**, Chris Claremont, et al, gn
+ **The Unconquered Country**, Geoff Ryman, n.
  Under the Lake, Stuart Woods, n.
  Undersea, Paul E. Hazel, n.
  Undertow, Drake Douglas, n.
* **The Unholy**, Michael Falconer Anderson, n.
* **Unicorn & Dragon**, Lynn Abbey, n.
  The Unicorn Creed, Elizabeth Ann Scarborough, n.
  The Unicorn Expedition and Other Fantastic Tales of India, Satyajit Ray, co
  The Unicorn Quest, John Lee, n.
  Unicorn Variations, Roger Zelazny, co
  The Uninvited, John Farris, n.
  The Uninvited, William W. Johnstone, n.
  Uninvited Ghosts and Other Stories, Penelope Lively, co
* **The Universe**, ed. Byron Preiss, oa
  Universe 15, ed. Terry Carr, oa
* **Universe 17**, ed. Terry Carr, oa
  The Universe Between, Alan E. Nourse, n.
  The Unlikely Ones, Mary Brown, n.
  The Unpleasant Profession of Jonathan Hoag, Robert A. Heinlein, co
* **The Unquiet Dead**, Margaret Bingley, n.
* **The Unschooled Wizard**, Barbara Hambly, om
* **Unto the Beast**, Richard Monaco, n.
* **The Unwanted**, John Saul, n.
  Up the Line, Robert Silverberg, n.
* **The Uplift War**, David Brin, n.
* **Urn Burial**, Robert Westall, n.
* **The Urth of the New Sun**, Gene Wolfe, n.
* **Utopian Studies 1**, ed. Gorman Beauchamp, Kenneth Roemer & Nicholas D. Smith, nf
* **V: Path to Conquest**, Howard Weinstein, n.
  V: The New England Resistance, Timothy Sullivan, n.
* **V: The Oregon Invasion**, Jayne Tannehill, n.
* **V: To Conquer the Throne**, Timothy Sullivan, n.
* **Vacuum Flowers**, Michael Swanwick, n.
* **Vagabonds of Gor**, John Norman, n.
* **Vale of the Vole**, Piers Anthony, n.
  Valis, Philip K. Dick, n.

THE VALLEY OF HORSES

THE WOMAN IN BLACK

The Valley of Horses, Jean M. Auel, n.
*Valley of Lights, Stephen Gallagher, n.
*The Valley So Low: Southern Mountain Stories, Manly Wade Wellman, co
The Vampire Lestat, Anne Rice, n.
*Vampire Master, Virginia Ironside, n.
The Vampire of Verdonia, Miranda Seymour, n.
The Vampire Takes a Trip, Angela Sommer-Bodenburg, n.
*Vampires, ed. Alan Ryan, an
*Vamps, ed. Martin H. Greenberg & Charles G. Waugh, an
Vargr-Moon, Bernard King, n.
The Varkaus Conspiracy, John Dalmas, n.
Vector, Rob Swigart, n.
Veil, George C. Chesbro, n.
The Veils of Azlaroc, Fred Saberhagen, n.
*Vendetta, M.S. Murdock, n.
*A Very Large Array, ed. Melinda M. Snodgrass, an
*Victim Prime, Robert Sheckley, n.
*Victims, Shaun Hutson, n.
*Victorian Fairy Tales: The Revolt of the Fairies and Elves, ed. Jack Zipes, an
*The Virago Book of Ghost Stories, ed. Richard Dalby, oa
Visitants, Randolph Stow, n.
*Voice of the Whirlwind, Walter Jon Williams, n.
Volume II of Steven Spielberg's Amazing Stories, Steven Bauer, co
*Voodoo Dawn, John Russo, n.
Votan, John James, n.
*The Voyage of the Poppykettle, Robert Ingpen, nv
*A Voyage to Inishneefa, John Paul Brady, n.
Voyage to the City of the Dead, Alan Dean Foster, n.
Voyagers, Ben Bova, n.
Voyagers II: The Alien Within, Ben Bova, n.
Wait Till Helen Comes, Mary Dowing Hahn, n.
*The Wall, Ardath Mayhar, n.
The Wanderer, Fritz Leiber, n.
Wanderers of Time, John Wyndham, co
The Wandering Fire, Guy Gavriel Kay, n.
The Wanting, Campbell Black, n.
*War for the Oaks, Emma Bull, n.
*War*Moon, Tom Cooper, n.
*Warhaven, M. Elayn Harvey, n.
*The Warlock Heretical, Christopher Stasheff, n.
*Warlord!, Janet Morris, n.
The Warlords of Nin, Stephen R. Lawhead, n.
A Warning to the Curious, M.R. James, co
*A Warning to the Curious: The Ghost Stories of M.R. James, M.R. James, co
*Warrior Planet, Don Wismer, n.
Warrior Woman, Marion Zimmer Bradley, n.
*Warriors of the Storm, Jack L. Chalker, n.
*Watchers, Dean R. Koontz, n.
*Watchmen, Alan Moore, gn
Watchtower, Elizabeth A. Lynn, n.
*Water Baby, Patricia Wallace, n.
*Water Song, Mary Caraker, n.
The Wave and the Flame, M. Bradley Kellogg & William Rossow, n.
*Way of the Pilgrim, Gordon R. Dickson, n.
We, Yevgeny Zamyatin, n.
We All Died at Breakaway Station, Richard C. Meredith, n.
We Have Always Lived in the Castle, Shirley Jackson, n.
We Who Are About To, Joanna Russ, n.
*The Weapons of Chaos, Book 2: Equations of Chaos, Robert E. Vardeman, n.
*Weaveworld, Clive Barker, n.
Web, John Wyndham, n.
*Web of Defeat, Lionel Fenn, n.
The Web of the Chozen, Jack L. Chalker, n.
Web of the Witch World, Andre Norton, n.
*Web of Wind, J.F. Rivkin, n.
*The Weird Disappearance of Jordan Hall, Judie Angell, n.
*The Weirds, ed. Sheldon R. Jaffery, an
Welcome Chaos, Kate Wilhelm, n.
Welcome to Moonbase, Ben Bova, nf
Well of Shiuan, C.J. Cherryh, n.
*Werewolf: Horror Stories of the Man Beast, ed. Peter Haining, an
West of Honor, Jerry E. Pournelle, n.
What Mad Universe, Fredric Brown, n.
When Flesh Begins to Creep, Judith Gorog, oc

When Gravity Fails, George Alec Effinger, n.
*When the Changewinds Blow, Jack L. Chalker, n.
When the Dolls Woke, Marjorie Filley Stover, n.
*When the Night Wind Howls, Pamela F. Service, n.
Where are the Children?, Mary Higgins Clark, n.
A Whiff of Death, Isaac Asimov, n.
The Whispering Knights, Penelope Lively, n.
Whispers, ed. Stuart David Schiff, oa
Whispers II, ed. Stuart David Schiff, oa
Whispers III, ed. Stuart David Schiff, oa
*Whispers VI, ed. Stuart David Schiff, oa
White Gold Wielder, Stephen R. Donaldson, n.
The White Mountains, John Christopher, n.
*The White Spider, Joyce Wolfe, n.
Who Made Stevie Crye?, Michael Bishop, n.
+Who's Afraid? and Other Strange Stories, Philippa Pearce, co
*Who's Hugh?: An SF Reader's Guide to Pseudonyms, Roger Robinson, comp., nf
*Who's Scared? Not Me!, Judith St. George, n.
*Who's Who in Space: The First 25 Years, Michael Cassutt, nf
Who?, Algis Budrys, n.
*Whom the Gods Destroy, Robert Bosshardt, n.
*Why Not You and I?, Karl Edward Wagner, co
Wielding a Red Sword, Piers Anthony, n.
*Wild Card Run, Sara Stamey, n.
*Wild Cards II: Aces High, ed. George R.R. Martin, oa
*Wild Cards III: Jokers Wild, ed. George R.R. Martin, oa
The Wild Hunt of Hagworthy, Penelope Lively, n.
+Wild Man of the Woods, Joan Clark, n.
Wildcards, ed. George R.R. Martin, oa
Wildwood, John Farris, n.
Wilkes the Wizard and the S.P.A.M., Jackie Webb, n.
*The Wind From the Sun, Arthur C. Clarke, co
The Wind in the Rosebush and Other Tales of the Supernatural, Mary E. Wilkins Freeman, co
The Wind's Twelve Quarters, Ursula K. Le Guin, co
Windmaster's Bane, Tom Deitz, n.
The Winds of Altair, Ben Bova, n.
The Winds of Darkover, Marion Zimmer Bradley, n.
*The Winged Assassin, Catherine Cooke, n.
*Wingman, Mack Maloney, n.
*Wingman: The Circle War, Mack Maloney, n.
*Wingwomen of Hera, Sandi Hall, n.
*Winston Three Three Three, Dennis Barker, n.
Winter in Eden, Harry Harrison, n.
Winterking, Paul E. Hazel, n.
Wintermind, Parke Godwin & Marvin Kaye, n.
*Wise Child, Monica Furlong, n.
The Wish Giver, Bill Brittain, oc
Witch Bane, Robert Neill, n.
*The Witch King, Maeve Henry, n.
The Witch of Lagg, Ann Cheetham, n.
Witch World, Andre Norton, n.
The Witches of Eastwick, John Updike, n.
*The Witches of Wenshar, Barbara Hambly, n.
Witchwater Country, Garry Kilworth, n.
*The Witchwood Cradle, Esther M. Friesner, n.
*With a Single Spell, Lawrence Watt-Evans, n.
With a Tangled Skein, Piers Anthony, n.
The Witling, Vernor Vinge, n.
*Witness to the Future, Klaus Rifbjerg, n.
*The Wizard and the War Machine, Lawrence Watt-Evans, n.
The Wizard and the Warlord, Elizabeth H. Boyer, n.
The Wizard in Waiting, Robert Don Hughes, n.
*The Wizard of 4th Street, Simon Hawke, n.
Wizard of Oz, L. Frank Baum, n.
The Wizard of Oz, L. Frank Baum, n.
Wizard of the Pigeons, Megan Lindholm, n.
*The Wizard of Woodworld, Garry Kilworth, n.
+Wizard War, Hugh Cook, n.
*Wizardry and Wild Romance, Michael Moorcock, nf
The Wizards & the Warriors, Hugh Cook, n.
*Wolf in Shadow, David Gemmell, n.
*Wolf-Dreams, Michael D. Weaver, n.
Wolfsbane, William W. Johnstone, n.
*Wolves of the Dawn, William Sarabande, n.
The Wolves of Willoughby Chase, Joan Aiken, n.
The Woman in Black, Susan Hill, n.

THE WOMAN OF FLOWERS

* **The Woman of Flowers**, Susan M. Shwartz, n.
  Woman on the Edge of Time, Marge Piercy, n.
* **The Woman Who Is the Midnight Wind**, Terence M. Green, co
  The Woman Who Loved Reindeer, Meredith Ann Pierce, n.
* **The Women and the Warlords**, Hugh Cook, n.
  The Wonderful Wizard of Oz, L. Frank Baum, n.
+ **The Wood**, Guy N. Smith, n.
* **The Wordsmiths and the Warguild**, Hugh Cook, n.
  Works of Wonder, Michael Whelan, pi
  The World Wreckers, Marion Zimmer Bradley, n.
  **Worlds With Women: Myth and Mythmaking in Fantastic Literature
    by Women**, Thelma J. Shinn, nf
  Worldstone, Victoria Strauss, n.
* **Worm**, Simon Ian Childer, n.
  Worms of the Earth, Robert E. Howard, co
  The Wounded Land, Stephen R. Donaldson, n.
  Wrack and Roll, Bradley Denton, n.
  A Wreath of Stars, Bob Shaw, n.
  Writing to Sell, Scott Meredith, nf
* **The Writings of Henry Kenneth Bulmer**, ed. Roger Robinson, nf
* **Wulfston's Odyssey**, Jean Lorrah & Winston A. Howlett, n.
* **The Wyrm**, Stephen Laws, n.
* **Wyrms**, Orson Scott Card, n.
  Xorander, Christine Brooke-Rose, n.
* **The Year Before Yesterday**, Brian W. Aldiss, n.
  The Year of the Lucy, Anne McCaffrey, n.
  Year of the Unicorn, Andre Norton, n.
* **The Year's Best Fantasy Stories: 13**, ed. Arthur W. Saha, an
* **The Year's Best Horror Stories: XV**, ed. Karl Edward Wagner, an
* **The Year's Best Science Fiction, Fourth Annual Collection**, ed.
    Gardner R. Dozois, an
  Years of the City, Frederik Pohl, co
  Yearwood, Paul E. Hazel, n.
* **Yeti of the Glen**, Mary Welfare, n.
  The Yngling, John Dalmas, n.
* **You Bright and Risen Angels**, William T. Vollmann, n.
  Young Legionary, Douglas Hill, n.
* **Young Witches & Warlocks**, ed. Isaac Asimov, Martin H. Greenberg &
    Charles G. Waugh, an
* **Yours Truly, From Hell**, Terrence Lore Smith, n.
  Yurth Burden, Andre Norton, n.
  Z for Zachariah, Robert C. O'Brien, n.
  Zombie!, Peter Tremayne, n.

1987 Original Publications

AANDAHL, VANCE

Aandahl, Vance
Deathmarch in Disneyland, nv *F&SF* Jul,1987

ab Hugh, Dafydd
Heroing, n. Baen Oct,1987

Abbey, Lynn
First-Bath, nv **Festival Moon**, ed. C.J.
Cherryh, DAW,1987
Life Assurance, nv **Fever Season**, ed. C.J.
Cherryh, DAW,1987
Seeing Is Believing (But Love Is Blind), nv
Aftermath, ed. Robert Lynn Asprin & Lynn
Abbey, Ace,1987
Spitting in the Wind, nv **Masters of Hell**,
ed. Janet Morris et al, Baen,1987
Unicorn & Dragon, n. Avon Feb,1987

Abbey, Lynn & Robert Lynn Asprin, eds.
Thieves' World 10: Aftermath, oa Ace
Nov,1987

Abbey, Lynn, Robert Lynn Asprin & Tim Sale
Thieves' World Graphics 4, gn
Donning/Starblaze Jan,1987

Abrams, Bernard & Jeffrey Jones
The Twilight Zone Gallery: The Art of Jeffrey
Jones, pi *Twilight Zone* Aug,1987

Adams, Douglas
Dirk Gently's Holistic Detective Agency, n.
Simon & Schuster May,1987

Adams, Pamela Crippen & Robert Adams, eds.
Friends of the Horseclans, oa NAL/Signet
Apr,1987

Adams, Pamela Crippen, Robert Adams &
Martin H. Greenberg, eds.
Robert Adams' Book of Alternate Worlds,
an NAL/Signet Jul,1987

Adams, Robert
Horseclans #16: Trumpets of War, n.
NAL/Signet Feb,1987
Horseclans #17: Madman's Army, n.
NAL/Signet Sep,1987
Of Chiefs and Champions, n. NAL/Signet
Dec,1987

Adams, Robert & Pamela Crippen Adams, eds.
Friends of the Horseclans, oa NAL/Signet
Apr,1987

Adams, Robert, Pamela Crippen Adams &
Martin H. Greenberg, eds.
Robert Adams' Book of Alternate Worlds,
an NAL/Signet Jul,1987

Adams, Robert & Andre Norton, eds.
Magic in Ithkar 4, oa Tor Jul,1987

Adder, Dr.
Florida Frolics, fa *New Pathways* Nov,1987

Adkins, Patrick H.
Lord of the Crooked Paths, n. Ace Oct,1987

Adkisson, Michael G.
Apocalypse Now: The Final Climax, ed *New
Pathways* Nov,1987
Book Reviews, br *New Pathways* Apr,1987
Book Reviews, br *New Pathways* Nov,1987
Entropy Comix, cs *New Pathways* Apr,1987
Entropy Comix, cs *New Pathways* Aug,1987
The Interdisciplinary Viewpoint of Science
Fiction, ar *New Pathways* Apr,1987

Adkisson, Michael G. (continued)
Winter in America: Fact or Fiction?, ar *New
Pathways* Aug,1987

Adkisson, Michael G., ed.
*New Pathways Into Science Fiction And
Fantasy* [v.1 #6, Jan/Feb 1987]
*New Pathways Into Science Fiction And
Fantasy* [v.1 #7, April/May 1987]
*New Pathways Into Science Fiction And
Fantasy* [v.1 #8, August 1987]
*New Pathways Into Science Fiction And
Fantasy* [v.1 #9, November 1987]

Ahern, Jerry
The Survivalist #15: Overlord, n. Zebra
May,1987

Ahern, Jerry & Sharon Ahern
Miamigrad, n. Pocket May,1987

Ahern, Sharon & Jerry Ahern
Miamigrad, n. Pocket May,1987

Aickman, Robert
The Model, n. Arbor House Apr,1987

Aiken, Joan
Aunt Susan, ss **A Goose on Your Grave**,
Gollancz,1987
The End of Silence, ss **A Quiver of Ghosts**,
ed. Aiden Chambers, Bodley Head,1987
A Goose on Your Grave, oc Gollancz
May,1987
The Lame King, ss **A Goose on Your
Grave**, Gollancz,1987
The Moon's Revenge, nv Cape Oct,1987
The Moon's Revenge, nv Knopf Oct,1987
The Old Poet, ss **A Goose on Your Grave**,
Gollancz,1987
Your Mind is a Mirror, ss **A Goose on Your
Grave**, Gollancz,1987

Albano, Peter
Return of the Seventh Carrier, n. Zebra
Jun,1987

Alberhasky, Peggy Sue
Stiffened in a Banquet Dish, pm *Grue*
#5,1987

Alcock, Vivian
Ghostly Companions, co Delacorte
May,1987

Aldiss, Brian W.
The Magic of the Past, nv **The Magic of the
Past**, Kerosina,1987
The Magic of the Past, oc Kerosina
Aug,1987
My Country 'Tis Not Only of Thee, nv **In the
Field of Fire**, ed. Jeanne Van Buren Dann
& Jack M. Dann, Tor,1987
The Price of Cabbages, nv **Other Edens**,
ed. Christopher Evans & Robert
Holdstock, Unwin: London,1987
Ruins, nv Hutchinson Sep,1987
SF: From Secret Movement to Big Business,
ar *Aboriginal SF* May,1987
Tourney, ss **Tales from the Forbidden
Planet**, ed. Roz Kaveney, Titan,1987
The Year Before Yesterday, n. Franklin
Watts Apr,1987

Aldiss, Brian W. & Sam J. Lundwall, eds.
**The Penguin World Omnibus of Science
Fiction**, an Penguin Oct,1987

ANDERSON, MICHAEL FALCONER

Aldridge, Ray
The Flesh Tinker and the Loneliest Man, ss
Amazing Jul,1987

Alexander, David
Phoenix #1: Dark Messiah, n. Leisure
May,1987
Phoenix #2: Ground Zero, n. Leisure
Aug,1987

Alexander, Lloyd
The El Dorado Adventure, n. Dutton
Apr,1987

Alkon, Paul K.
Origins of Futuristic Fiction, nf Univ. of
Georgia Press Dec,1987

Allen, J.B.
Multiple Origami, ss *Amazing* Jul,1987

Allen, Lori
Time Windows, ss *F&SF* Jun,1987

Allen, Roger MacBride
A Hole in the Sun, nv *Analog* Apr,1987

Almquist, Gregg
Beast Rising, n. Pocket Sep,1987

Amis, Kingsley
Collected Short Stories, co Hutchinson
Apr,1987

Amis, Martin
Einstein's Monsters, co Cape Apr,1987

Anderson, C. Dean
Torture Tomb, n. Popular Library May,1987

Anderson, Gretta M.
Preface, pr *2AM* Spr,1987
Preface, pr *2AM* Sum,1987
Preface, pr *2AM* Fll,1987
Preface, pr *2AM* Win,1987

Anderson, Gretta M., ed.
2AM [v.1 #3, Spring 1987]
2AM [v.1 #4, Summer 1987]
2AM [v.2 #1, Fall 1987]
2AM [v.2 #2, Winter 1987]

Anderson, James
Deathstroke, ss *Eldritch Tales* #14,1987
Thatcher's Bluff, ss *Haunts* #9,1987

Anderson, Karen & Poul Anderson
The King of Ys 2: Gallicenae, n. Baen
Sep,1987
The King of Ys: Dahut, n. Baen Jan,1988

Anderson, Kevin J.
A Glimpse of the Ankou, ss *The Horror Show*
Win,1987

Anderson, Mary
The Leipzig Vampire, n. Dell/Yearling
Oct,1987
Terror Under the Tent, n. Dell/Yearling
Nov,1987

Anderson, Michael Falconer
God of a Thousand Faces, n. Robert Hale
Oct,1987
The Unholy, n. Robert Hale Feb,1987
The Unholy, n. St. Martin's Jun,1987

ANDERSON, POUL

Anderson, Poul
  The Enemy Stars, co Baen Jul,1987
  Iron [Part 2], sl **New Destinies** v1, ed. Jim
    Baen, Baen,1987
  Letter from Tomorrow, ss *Analog* Aug,1987
  Requiem For a Universe, ss **Universe**, ed.
    Byron Preiss, Bantam Spectra,1987

Anderson, Poul & Karen Anderson
  The King of Ys 2: Gallicenae, n. Baen
    Sep,1987
  The King of Ys: Dahut, n. Baen Jan,1988

Andreski, Luke
  Skiophanes' Proof, ss **Gollancz - Sunday
    Times Best SF Stories**, Gollancz,1987

Andrews, Arlan
  Ancient Ages, pm *Fantasy Book* Mar,1987
  Epiphany, ss *Analog* Sep,1987
  Occidental Injury, vi *Analog* Oct,1987
  QTL, vi *Analog* Feb,1987

Andrews, Elton
  Elegy to a Dead Satellite: Luna, pm
    Amazing Nov,1987

Andrews, V.C.
  Garden of Shadows, n. Pocket Nov,1987

Angadi, Patricia
  The Highly Flavoured Ladies, n. Gollancz
    Jul,1987

Angell, Judie
  The Weird Disappearance of Jordan Hall,
    n. Franklin Watts Orchard Sep,1987

Anonymous
  Hollywood Grapevine, ar *Twilight Zone*
    Apr,1987
  Illuminations: The Return of Lefty Feep, br
    Twilight Zone Aug,1987
  The Leading Edge, br **New Destinies** v1,
    ed. Jim Baen, Baen,1987
  Monster Squad, mr *American Fantasy*
    Sum,1987
  Nightmares, ar *The Horror Show* Jan,1987
  Nightmares, ar *The Horror Show* Spr,1987
  Nightmares, ar *The Horror Show* Sum,1987
  Nightmares, ar *The Horror Show* Fll,1987
  Nightmares, ar *The Horror Show* Win,1987
  Syndicated Television: What Is It, Anyway?,
    ar *Twilight Zone* Dec,1987
  The Twilight Zone Movie Trial: An Opinion,
    ms *Twilight Zone* Aug,1987

Anonymous, ed.
  **Gollancz/Sunday Times SF Competition
    Stories**, oa David &
    Charles/Gollancz,1987
  **Gollancz/Sunday Times SF Competition
    Stories**, oc Gollancz Aug,1987
  Mad and Bad Fairies, oa Attic Press
    Jul,1987
  Night Visions 4, oa Dark Harvest Oct,1987
  The Orbit Poster Book, pi Orbit Aug,1987
  Rhysling Anthology 1987, an SF Poetry
    Assc. Sep,1987

Anthony, Patricia
  Blood Brothers, ss *Aboriginal SF* Feb,1987
  What Brothers Are For, ss *Aboriginal SF*
    Nov,1987

Anthony, Piers
  Being a Green Mother, n. Ballantine/Del
    Rey Dec,1987

Anthony, Piers (continued)
  Imp to Nymph, ss **World Fantasy
    Convention Program Book** #13,1987
  Life, ss *Twilight Zone* Dec,1987
  Out of Phaze, n. Ace/Putnam Jun,1987
  Tarot, om Ace Nov,1987
  Vale of the Vole, n. Avon Oct,1987

Anthony, Piers & Robert E. Margroff
  Dragon's Gold, n. Tor Jul,1987

Anthony, Piers & Stanley Wiater
  A Conversation with Piers Anthony, iv
    Twilight Zone Dec,1987

Antieau, Kim
  Occupant, ss **Doom City**, ed. Charles L.
    Grant, Tor,1987

Anvil, Christopher
  Interesting Times, ss *Analog* Dec,1987
  Rags from Riches, ss *Amazing* Nov,1987

Apel, D. Scott
  Philip K. Dick: The Dream Connection, ar
    Philip K. Dick: The Dream Connection,
    D. Scott Apel, Permanent Press,1987

Apel, D. Scott, ed.
  Philip K. Dick: The Dream Connection, nf
    Permanent Press Mar,1987

Apel, D. Scott, Kevin C. Briggs & Philip K. Dick
  Philip K. Dick in Interview, iv **Philip K. Dick:
    The Dream Connection**, D. Scott Apel,
    Permanent Press,1987

Ardai, Charles
  Wordware, gr *Twilight Zone* Dec,1987

Arguelles, Ivan
  Baudelaire's Brain, pm *Ice River* Sum,1987

Arkee, Sister M. Anne, O.S.F.
  O Civile, pm *Amazing* Mar,1987

Armstrong, F.W.
  The Devouring, n. Tor Apr,1987

Armstrong, Michael
  After the Zap, n. Popular Library Questar
    Jun,1987
  Between the Devil and the Deep Blue Sea,
    nv **Crusaders in Hell**, ed. Janet Morris,
    New York: Baen,1987
  God's Eyes, nv **Masters of Hell**, ed. Janet
    Morris et al, Baen,1987
  The Verts Get a Nuke, ss *F&SF* Aug,1987

Arnason, Eleanor
  Daughter of the Bear King, n. Avon
    Aug,1987
  Glam's Story, ss *Tales of the Unanticipated*
    #2,1987
  There Was an Old Lady..., pm *Tales of the
    Unanticipated* #2,1987

Arno, Ed
  Cartoon, ct *F&SF* Apr,1987
  Cartoon, ct *F&SF* Sep,1987
  Cartoon, ct *F&SF* Oct,1987
  Cartoon, ct *F&SF* Nov,1987

Arnold, Mark
  Illuminations: Bad Feng-Shui Killed Bruce
    Lee, ar *Twilight Zone* Jun,1987
  Illuminations: Expeditions to the Unknown,
    ar *Twilight Zone* Jun,1987

Arnold, Mark (continued)
  Illuminations: First Pooch Sees Ghost, ar
    Twilight Zone Aug,1987
  Illuminations: I Sing the Body Eclectic, ar
    Twilight Zone Oct,1987
  The Other Side: Gore-Gonzola, ar *Twilight
    Zone* Jun,1987
  The Other Side: Horrible Twisted Things
    Crawling, ar *Twilight Zone* Jun,1987
  The Other Side: In God We Rust, ar *Twilight
    Zone* Apr,1987
  Ultimate Getaways, ar *Twilight Zone*
    Oct,1987

Aronovitz, David
  Ballantine Books: The First Decade, nf
    Bailiwick Books Sep,1987

Arroyo, Rane
  Loved Ones, pm *Ice River* Sum,1987
  The Red House, pm *Ice River* Sum,1987

Arthurs, Bruce D.
  Death and the Ugly Woman, ss **Sword and
    Sorceress #4**, ed. Marion Zimmer
    Bradley,1987

Ashe, Rosalind
  The Laying of the Noone Walker, n.
    Bantam UK Feb,1987

Ashworth, Malcolm
  A Senoi Dream, ss **Gollancz - Sunday
    Times Best SF Stories**, Gollancz,1987

Asimov, Isaac
  Academe, ed *IASFM* mid-Dec,1987
  The Fable of the Three Princes, nv
    Spaceships & Spells, ed. Jane Yolen,
    Martin H. Greenberg & Charles G. Waugh,
    Harper & Row,1987
  Fantastic Voyage II: Destination Brain, n.
    Doubleday Sep,1987
  The Fights of Spring, ss *IASFM* Feb,1987
  Forgetfullness, ed *IASFM* Jun,1987
  Galatea, ss *IASFM* mid-Dec,1987
  Harlan Ellison's I, Robot, ar *IASFM* Nov,1987
  Intellectual Cliches, ed *IASFM* Feb,1987
  Intimations of Mortality, ed *IASFM* Mar,1987
  Left to Right, vi *Analog* Jan,1987
  Memory, ed *IASFM* Dec,1987
  New Writers, ed *IASFM* Jan,1987
  Plausibility, ed *IASFM* Sep,1987
  Romance, ed *IASFM* Jul,1987
  Science: A Sacred Poet, ar *F&SF* Sep,1987
  Science: Asking the Right Question, ar *F&SF*
    Nov,1987
  Science: Beginning With Bone, ar *F&SF*
    May,1987
  Science: Brightening Stars, ar *F&SF* Jul,1987
  Science: New Stars, ar *F&SF* Jun,1987
  Science: Opposite!, ar *F&SF* Jan,1987
  Science: Sail On! Sail On!, ar *F&SF* Feb,1987
  Science: Super-Exploding Stars, ar *F&SF*
    Aug,1987
  Science: The Incredible Shrinking Planet, ar
    F&SF Mar,1987
  Science: The Light-Bringer, ar *F&SF*
    Apr,1987
  Science: The Road to Humanity, ar *F&SF*
    Dec,1987
  Science: The Very Error of the Moon, ar
    F&SF Oct,1987
  Space Flight, ed *IASFM* May,1987
  Survivors, ed *IASFM* Nov,1987
  Truth and Fiction, ed *IASFM* Apr,1987
  Unification, ed *IASFM* Aug,1987
  Unknown, ed *IASFM* Oct,1987

ASIMOV, ISAAC

Asimov, Isaac (continued)
What Is the Universe?, ar **Universe**, ed. Byron Preiss, Bantam Spectra,1987

Asimov, Isaac & Janet Asimov
How to Enjoy Writing: A Book of Aid and Comfort, nf Walker Jul,1987
Norby Finds a Villain, n. Walker Sep,1987
Norby: Robot for Hire, om Ace Feb,1987

Asimov, Isaac & Martin H. Greenberg, eds.
Isaac Asimov Presents the Great SF Stories: 16 (1954), an DAW May,1987
Isaac Asimov Presents the Great SF Stories: 17 (1955), an DAW Jan,1988

Asimov, Isaac, Martin H. Greenberg & Charles G. Waugh, eds.
Isaac Asimov's Magical Worlds of Fantasy #8: Devils, an NAL/Signet Jun,1987
Isaac Asimov's Magical Worlds of Fantasy #9: Atlantis, an NAL/Signet Jan,1988
Isaac Asimov's Wonderful Worlds of Science Fiction #6: Neanderthals, an NAL/Signet Feb,1987
Isaac Asimov's Wonderful Worlds of Science Fiction #7: Space Shuttles, an NAL/Signet Oct,1987
Young Witches & Warlocks, an Harper & Row Jul,1987

Asimov, Isaac & Harrison Roth
Left to Right, and Beyond, vi *Analog* Jul,1987

Asimov, Janet & Isaac Asimov
How to Enjoy Writing: A Book of Aid and Comfort, nf Walker Jul,1987
Norby Finds a Villain, n. Walker Sep,1987
Norby: Robot for Hire, om Ace Feb,1987

Asire, Nancy
By Invitation Only, nv **Crusaders in Hell**, ed. Janet Morris, New York: Baen,1987
Cat's Tale, nv **Festival Moon**, ed. C.J. Cherryh, DAW,1987
Houseguests, nv **Masters of Hell**, ed. Janet Morris et al, Baen,1987
Night Ride, nv **Fever Season**, ed. C.J. Cherryh, DAW,1987
Twilight's Kingdoms, n. Baen Nov,1987

Asire, Nancy & C.J. Cherryh
The Conscience of the King, na **Angels in Hell**, ed. Janet Morris, Baen,1987

Asprin, Robert Lynn
The Ex-Khan, ss **Angels in Hell**, ed. Janet Morris, Baen,1987
Myth Alliances, om SFBC Jul,1987
Myth-Nomers and Im-pervections, n. Donning/Starblaze Oct,1987
Two Gentlemen of the Trade, ss **Festival Moon**, ed. C.J. Cherryh, DAW,1987

Asprin, Robert Lynn & Lynn Abbey, eds.
Thieves' World 10: Aftermath, oa Ace Nov,1987

Asprin, Robert Lynn, Lynn Abbey & Tim Sale
Thieves' World Graphics 4, gn Donning/Starblaze Jan,1987

Asprin, Robert Lynn & Phil Foglio
Myth Adventures Two, gn Donning/Starblaze Jan,1987

Asprin, Robert Lynn & Mel White
Duncan and Mallory: The Bar-None Ranch, gn Donning/Starblaze Sep,1987

Atwood, Margaret
Bluebeard's Egg, co Cape Jun,1987

Auel, Jean M.
Earth's Children, om Hodder & Stoughton Oct,1987

Auer, Rev. Benedict, O.S.B.
The Photofinish: On Attending a Lecture at Fermi Lab, pm *Amazing* Jul,1987

Aulisio, Janet
On Exhibit, il *Amazing* Jan,1987

Auster, Paul
In the Country of the Last Things, n. Viking Apr,1987

Austin, Richard
The Guardians #8: Desolation Road, n. Jove Jun,1987
The Guardians #9: Vengeance Day, n. Jove Nov,1987

Axler, James
Deathlands #3: Neutron Solstice, n. Worldwide Library Mar,1987
Deathlands #4: Crater Lake, n. Gold Eagle Aug,1987

Babinski, Edward T.
The Griffon, pm *Apex!* #1,1987

Baen, Jim, ed.
New Destinies, Vol. 1/Spring 1987, oa Baen Mar,1987
New Destinies, Vol. 2/Fall 1987, oa Baen Aug,1987

Baichtal, H.W.
The Handbug, ss *Tales of the Unanticipated* #2,1987

Bailey, Robin Wayne
The Woodland of Zarad-Thra, nv **Sword and Sorceress #4**, ed. Marion Zimmer Bradley,1987

Bailey, Robin Wayne & Robert Chilson
Primatives, nv *Amazing* Jul,1987

Bailly, Sharon
An Application to Succeed, ss *Space & Time* #73,1987

Baker, Charles L.
Eldritch Lair - Dungeon Level, ed *Eldritch Tales* #13,1987
Shadow of the Immortal (Part 2 of 3), sl *Eldritch Tales* #13,1987
Shadow of the Immortal (Part 3 of 3), sl *Eldritch Tales* #14,1987

Baker, Herbert Jerry
The Halls of Doom, ss *Eldritch Tales* #14,1987

Baker, Jane & Pip Baker
Terror of the Vervoids, n. W.H. Allen Sep,1987
Time and the Rani, n. W.H. Allen Dec,1987

Baker, Pip & Jane Baker
Terror of the Vervoids, n. W.H. Allen Sep,1987
Time and the Rani, n. W.H. Allen Dec,1987

Baker, Scott
Drink the Fire From the Flames, n. Tor Aug,1987
Nesting Instinct, nv **The Architecture of Fear**, ed. Kathryn Cramer & Peter D. Pautz, Arbor House,1987

Baker, Sharon
Journey to Membliar, n. Avon Jul,1987

Bakst, Harold
A Good Knight's Tale, nv **DragonLance Tales** v3, Margaret Weis & Tracy Hickman, TSR,1987
Lord Toede's Disastrous Hunt, nv **DragonLance Tales** v2, Margaret Weis & Tracy Hickman, TSR,1987

Baldwin, Bill
Galactic Convoy, n. Popular Library Questar Dec,1987

Ball, Duncan
The Ghost and the Gory Story, n. Angus & Robertson Nov,1987

Ballard, J.G.
The Day of Creation, n. Gollancz Sep,1987

Ballard, J.G. & David Pringle
J.G. Ballard, iv *Interzone* #22,1987

Ballard, William
Retrograde Analysis, ss *Analog* Dec,1987

Banerji, Sara
Cobwebwalking, n. Adler & Adler Oct,1987

Banks, Iain
Consider Phlebas, n. Macmillan Apr,1987
Descendant, nv **Tales from the Forbidden Planet**, ed. Roz Kaveney, Titan,1987
Espedair Street, n. Macmillan Sep,1987
A Gift from the Culture, ss *Interzone* #20,1987

Barbour, Douglas & Phyllis Gotlieb, eds.
Tesseracts 2, an Porcepic Nov,1987

Baricevic, Mark
Wallflower, ss *2AM* Fll,1987

Bark, John
Big Cats, ss **Gollancz - Sunday Times Best SF Stories**, Gollancz,1987

Barker, A.L.
Element of Doubt, ss **After Midnight Stories #3**,1987

Barker, Clive
The Damnation Game, n. Ace/Putnam May,1987
Weaveworld, n. Collins Oct,1987
Weaveworld, n. Simon & Schuster Poseidon Oct,1987

Barker, Clive, Nancy Garcia & Robert T. Garcia
Clive Barker Interview, iv *American Fantasy* Win,1987

BARKER, CLIVE

Barker, Clive & Douglas E. Winter
  Talking Terror With Clive Barker, iv *Twilight Zone* Jun,1987

Barker, David
  Red Paint, ss *The Horror Show* Sum,1987

Barker, Dennis
  Winston Three Three Three, n. Grafton Aug,1987

Barnes, John
  Digressions from the Second Person Future, ss *IASFM* Jan,1987
  The Man Who Pulled Down the Sky, n. Congdon & Weed/Contemporary Apr,1987

Barnes, Steve
  Yelloweye, nv **Friends of the Horseclans**, ed. Robert Adams & Pamela Crippen Adams, Signet,1987

Barnes, Steven, Larry Niven & Jerry E. Pournelle
  The Legacy of Heorot, n. Gollancz May,1987
  The Legacy of Heorot, n. Simon & Schuster Jul,1987

Barr, Marleen S.
  Alien to Femininity, nf Greenwood Jul,1987

Barratt, David
  C.S. Lewis and His World, nf Eerdman's Aug,1987

Barrett, Neal, Jr.
  Class of '61, ss *IASFM* Oct,1987
  Diner, ss *Omni* Nov,1987
  Highbrow, ss *IASFM* Jul,1987
  Perpetuity Blues, nv *IASFM* May,1987
  Through Darkest America, n. Congdon & Weed/Contemporary Apr,1987

Barron, Neil
  Anatomy of Wonder, Third Edition, nf R.R. Bowker Aug,1987

Barwood, Lee
  Victim, pm *Weirdbook* #22,1987

Baxter, S.M.
  The Xeelee Flower, ss *Interzone* #19,1987

Bayley, Barrington J.
  The Rod of Light, n. Arbor House Dec,1987

Bear, Greg
  The Forge of God, ex Tor: New York Sep,1987
  The Forge of God, n. Gollancz Aug,1987
  The Forge of God, n. Tor Sep,1987
  Galactic Checks and Balances: An Introduction to **The Forge of God**, is *Twilight Zone* Oct,1987
  Hegira, n. Gollancz May,1987
  The Visitation, vi *Omni* Jun,1987

Bearne, Betsy
  Eli's Ghost, n. Macmillan McElderry Mar,1987

Beasley, Conger, Jr.
  A Rider on a Blue Horse Waits Outside the Hospital Wall, vi *Ice River* Sum,1987
  Woman with a Hole in the Center of Her Chest, vi *New Pathways* Aug,1987

Beason, Doug
  Final Exam, vi *2AM* Win,1987
  Lifeguard, nv **New Destinies** v1, ed. Jim Baen, Baen,1987
  The Man I'll Never Be, ss *Amazing* May,1987

Beauchamp, Gorman, Kenneth Roemer & Nicholas D. Smith, eds.
  Utopian Studies 1, nf Univ. Press of America May,1987

Bedard, Michael
  A Darker Magic, n. Atheneum Oct,1987

Beebee, Chris
  The Hub, n. Macdonald Aug,1987

Beer, Gaye & Ben Daily
  Puzzle Pages, pz *Salarius* v1#4,1987

Behrendt, Fred
  Cauldron of Rain, pm *Space & Time* #73,1987

Behunin, Judith R.
  Community Service, vi *Footsteps* Nov,1987

Belden, Wilanne Schneider
  Fenneca, nv **Tales of the Witch World**, ed. Andre Norton, St. Martin's,1987
  Mind-Hold, n. HBJ/Gulliver Mar,1987

Bellomi, Antonio
  The Mercenary, ss *SF International* #2,1987

Bemmann, Hans
  The Stone and the Flute, n. Viking May,1987

Benford, Gregory
  Across the Sea of Suns, n. Bantam Spectra Aug,1987
  Bleak Velocities, pm **Synergy** v1, ed. George Zebrowski,1987
  The Gods of the Gaps, na **Crusaders in Hell**, ed. Janet Morris, New York: Baen,1987
  Great Sky River, n. Bantam Spectra Dec,1987
  Hard? Science? Fiction?, br *Amazing* Jul,1987
  How to Sound Like an Expert, ar **L. Ron Hubbard Presents Writers of the Future** v3, ed. Algis Budrys, Bridge,1987
  Mandikini, ss **Universe**, ed. Byron Preiss, Bantam Spectra,1987
  Was Frankenstein Simply Einstein Being Frank? or Scientists in Science Fiction, ar **New Destinies** v2, ed. Jim Baen, Baen,1987
  What Are You Going to Be When You Grow Up?, nv **Spaceships & Spells**, ed. Jane Yolen, Martin H. Greenberg & Charles G. Waugh, Harper & Row,1987

Benjamin, Michele & Jim Ridgway, eds.
  PsiFi: Psychological Theories and Science Fictions, an The British Psychological Society Jan,1987

Bennett, Thea
  The Gemini Factor, n. Magnet Nov,1987

Bensink, John Robert
  Lake George in High August, ss **Masques** #2, ed. J.N. Williamson,1987

Berberick, Nancy Varian
  Harvests, nv **DragonLance Tales** v1, Margaret Weis & Tracy Hickman, TSR,1987
  Hearth Cat and Winter Wren, nv **DragonLance Tales** v2, Margaret Weis & Tracy Hickman, TSR,1987
  Hide and Go Seek, nv **DragonLance Tales** v3, Margaret Weis & Tracy Hickman, TSR,1987
  Snowsong, nv **DragonLance Tales** v2, Margaret Weis & Tracy Hickman, TSR,1987
  A Tale at Rilling's Inn, ss *Amazing* Mar,1987

Berger, Thomas
  Being Invisible, n. Little, Brown Apr,1987

Berman, Mitch
  Time Capsule, n. Putnam Jan,1987

Berman, Ruth
  Magic Trick, pm *Minnesota Fantasy Review* #1,1987
  Professor and Colonel, ss **Mathenauts**, ed. Rudy Rucker, Arbor House,1987

Bernard, Sidney
  The Liberty Watchers, ar *Pulpsmith* Win,1987

Berry, Stephen Ames
  The AI War, n. Tor May,1987

Betancourt, John Gregory
  The Darkfishers, ss *Aboriginal SF* Jul,1987
  Fantasy Book Reviews, br *Fantasy Book* Mar,1987
  Messiah, ss *Amazing* May,1987
  Rogue Pirate, n. TSR/Windwalker Jun,1987
  Well Bottled at Slab's, ss *The Dragon* Oct,1987

Betancourt, John Gregory & Darrell Schweitzer
  The Children of Lommos, ss *Night Cry* v2#4,1987

Bethke, Bruce
  It Came from the Slushpile, ss *Aboriginal SF* Jul,1987

Betts, Michael Arthur
  Tattler, mr *The Horror Show* Jan,1987
  Tattler, mr *The Horror Show* Sum,1987
  Tattler, mr *The Horror Show* Fll,1987
  Tattler, mr *The Horror Show* Win,1987

Betts, Michael Arthur & Wes Craven
  Tattler, mr *The Horror Show* Spr,1987

Bierce, Ambrose
  The Devil's Advocate: An Ambrose Bierce Reader, co Chronicle Dec,1987
  John Mortonson's Funeral, vi *Night Cry* v2#4,1987

Biggle, Lloyd, Jr.
  Interface for Murder, n. Doubleday Crime Club Nov,1987

Bigley, Leo
  Elysium Horizon, ss *Mage* Spr,1987

Billias, Stephen
  The American Book of the Dead, n. Popular Library Questar May,1987

Bingley, Margaret
  Devil's Child, n. Popular Library Dec,1987

Bingley, Margaret (continued)
The Unquiet Dead, n. Piatkus Jan,1987

Binns, Mervyn R.
The Science Fiction World, ar *Aphelion* #5,1987

Bird, Antoinette Kelsall
The Daughters of Megwyn, n. Headline Aug,1987

Bishop, Michael
The Egret, ss *Playboy* Jun,1987
An Episode in the Death of Philip K. Dick, vi *New Pathways* Aug,1987
For Thus Do I Remember Carthage, ss **Universe**, ed. Byron Preiss, Bantam Spectra,1987
God's Hour, vi *Omni* Jun,1987
In the Memory Room, ss **The Architecture of Fear**, ed. Kathryn Cramer & Peter D. Pautz, Arbor House,1987
The Secret Ascension, n. Tor Nov,1987

Bishop, Michael & Misha Chocholak
Close Encounters with Michael Bishop, iv *New Pathways* Jan,1987

Black, Ian Stuart
The Macra Terror, n. W.H. Allen Jul,1987

Blake, E. Michael
A Glorious Triumph for the People, ss **There Will Be War** v6, ed. Jerry E. Pournelle,1987

Blakeney, Jay D.
The Omcri Matrix, n. Ace Mar,1987

Blaylock, James P.
Land of Dreams, n. Arbor House Aug,1987
Myron Chester and the Toads, ss *IASFM* Feb,1987

Blaylock, James P. & Edward Bryant
The Shadow on the Doorstep/Trilobyte, oa Axolotl Aug,1987

Bleiler, Everett F.
Books, br *Twilight Zone* Feb,1987
Books, br *Twilight Zone* Apr,1987

Blish, James
The Tale That Wags the God, nf Advent Jul,1987

Bloch, Robert
Die--Nasty, ss **Midnight Pleasures**, Doubleday,1987
Heir Apparent, ss **Tales of the Witch World**, ed. Andre Norton, St. Martin's,1987
Lost in Time and Space with Lefty Feep, co Creatures at Large Apr,1987
Midnight Pleasures, co Doubleday Apr 17,1987
The New Season, ss **Masques #2**, ed. J.N. Williamson,1987
A Snitch in Time, ss **Lost in Time and Space with Lefty Feep**, Creatures at Large,1987

Block, Bob
Galloping Galaxies, n. Target Jun,1987

Blockley, Bartholomew
A Sort of Sun Spot, ss **Gollancz - Sunday Times Best SF Stories**, Gollancz,1987

Blue, Tyson
Illuminations: An Audience with the King, ar *Twilight Zone* Aug,1987
Illuminations: Many Happy Returns, ar *Twilight Zone* Aug,1987
The Other Side: Vanishing Hitchikers and Dead Cats, ar *Twilight Zone* Oct,1987

Blumlein, Michael
The Movement of Mountains, n. St. Martin's Aug,1987

Boal, Nina
Flight, ss **Red Sun of Darkover**, ed. Marion Zimmer Bradley & The Friends of Darkover, DAW,1987

Bonanno, Margaret Wander
Star Trek: Strangers From the Sky, n. Pocket Jul,1987

Bonansinga, Jay
Poltergeist III, mr *American Fantasy* Sum,1987

Booth, Bob
Play's the Thing, nv **Doom City**, ed. Charles L. Grant, Tor,1987

Borden, William
Clove's Essence, ss *Pulpsmith* Win,1987

Boren, Terry
Sliding Rock, ss **A Very Large Array**, ed. Melinda M. Snodgrass, University of New Mexico Press,1987

Bosshardt, Robert
Whom the Gods Destroy, n. Maverick,1987

Boston, Bruce
The Bruce Boston Omnibus, om Ocean View Dec,1987
Celestian Grapevine, pm *Space & Time* #73,1987
The Changeling Uncovered, pm *IASFM* Jan,1987
Clear to Eternity, pm *Amazing* Jul,1987
Curse of the Demon's Wife, pm *IASFM* Aug,1987
Dream Webs, pm *Night Cry* v2#3,1987
Forecast for a Burning Planet, pm **Nuclear Futures**, Velocities Chapbook Series,1987
A Hero of the Spican Conflict, pm *Aboriginal SF* Nov,1987
In the Eyes of the Pilot, pm *Amazing* Mar,1987
In the Garden of the State, pm *Amazing* May,1987
Interstellar Tract, pm **Nuclear Futures**, Velocities Chapbook Series,1987
Night Ride, pm *Night Cry* v2#3,1987
Night Rides, gp *Night Cry* v2#3,1987
Nightmare Collector, pm *Night Cry* v2#3,1987
No Longer the Stars, pm **Nuclear Futures**, Velocities Chapbook Series,1987
Nuclear Futures, co Velocities Chapbook Series,1987
One-Trick Dog, vi *IASFM* May,1987
Some Concrete Notions About Demons, ss *The Magazine of Speculative Poetry* #5,1987
The Widow Renounced, pm *Night Cry* v2#3,1987

Botsis, Peter
On Exhibit, il *Amazing* Nov,1987

Bova, Ben
Battle Station, co Tor Oct,1987
Battle Station, na **Battle Station**, Tor,1987
Brothers, ss **In the Field of Fire**, ed. Jeanne Van Buren Dann & Jack M. Dann, Tor,1987
For Mars, Vote NO, ed *Analog* Sep,1987
The Kinsman Saga, n. Tor Oct,1987
MHD, ar **Battle Station**, Tor,1987
Moonbase Orientation Manual I: Transport and Manufacturing, ar *Analog* Jun,1987
Moonbase Orientation Manual II: Research and Recreation, ar *Analog* Jul,1987
Silent Night, ss *IASFM* Dec,1987
To Touch a Star, ss **Universe**, ed. Byron Preiss, Bantam Spectra,1987
Welcome to Moonbase, nf Ballantine Nov,1987

Bowerman, Tony
Gardens and Fountains, ss **Gollancz - Sunday Times Best SF Stories**, Gollancz,1987

Bowes, Richard
Feral Cell, n. Popular Library Questar May,1987

Bowker, Richard
Dover Beach, n. Bantam Spectra Oct,1987
Marlborough Street, n. Doubleday Feb,1987

Bowkett, Stephen
Dualists, n. Gollancz Sep,1987

Bowles, Paul
An Inopportune Visit, ss *Threepenny Review* Spr,1987

Boyd, J.P.
The Anger of Time, ss *F&SF* Feb,1987

Boyett, Steven R.
Minutes of the Last Meeting at Olduvai, vi *Aboriginal SF* Nov,1987

Bradbury, Ray
Art and Science Fiction: Unbuilt Cities/Unrealized Dreams, ar **Universe**, ed. Byron Preiss, Bantam Spectra,1987
Fahrenheit 451/The Illustrated Man/Dandelion Wine/The Golden Apples of the Sun/The Martian Chronicles, om Octopus/Heinemann,1987
Fever Dream, ss St. Martin's Nov,1987

Bradley, Marion Zimmer
The Ballad of Hastur and Cassilda, sg **Red Sun of Darkover**, ed. Marion Zimmer Bradley & The Friends of Darkover, DAW,1987
Bitch, ss *F&SF* Feb,1987
Bride Price, ss **The Other Side of the Mirror**, ed. Marion Zimmer Bradley & The Friends of Darkover, DAW,1987
Dance at the Gym, ss *The San Francisco Chronicle* Sep 17,1987
Everything but Freedom, na **The Other Side of the Mirror**, ed. Marion Zimmer Bradley & The Friends of Darkover, DAW,1987
The Fall of Atlantis, om Baen Feb,1987
The Firebrand, n. Simon & Schuster Oct,1987
Oathbreaker, nv **The Other Side of the Mirror**, ed. Marion Zimmer Bradley & The Friends of Darkover, DAW,1987

Bradley, Marion Zimmer (continued)
 The Shadow, nv **Red Sun of Darkover**, ed.
 Marion Zimmer Bradley & The Friends of
 Darkover, DAW,1987
 The Walker Behind, ss *F&SF* Jul,1987

Bradley, Marion Zimmer, ed.
 Sword and Sorceress IV, oa DAW Jul,1987

**Bradley, Marion Zimmer & The Friends of
 Darkover**
 The Other Side of the Mirror, oa DAW
 Feb,1987
 Red Sun of Darkover, oa DAW Nov,1987

Bradley, Rebecca
 Allsouls, ss **The Pan Book of Horror
 Stories** #28, Pan,1987
 Tea Leaves, ss **The Pan Book of Horror
 Stories** #28, Pan,1987

Bradman, Tony
 Cinderella, ss **The Magic Kiss and Other
 Tales of Princes and Princesses**, Tony
 Bradman, Blackie,1987
 The Magic Kiss, ss **The Magic Kiss and
 Other Tales of Princes and Princesses**,
 Tony Bradman, Blackie,1987

Bradman, Tony, ed.
 **The Magic Kiss and Other Tales of
 Princes and Princesses**, an Blackie
 Aug,1987

Brady, John Paul
 A Voyage to Inishneefa, n. John Daniel
 Jul,1987

Brandner, Gary
 Cameron's Closet, n. Ballantine Fawcett
 Feb,1987

Branham, R.V.
 In the Sickbay, nv **L. Ron Hubbard
 Presents Writers of the Future** v3, ed.
 Algis Budrys, Bridge,1987

Brantingham, Juleen
 Toad, Singular, ss **Whispers** #6, ed. Stuart
 David Schiff,1987

Braunbeck, Gary A.
 A Death in the Day of, ss *The Horror Show*
 Win,1987
 The Eldritch Eye, ss *Eldritch Tales* #14,1987

Brennan, Joseph Payne
 Cornstalk Riddles, pm *Grue* #4,1987
 Jendick's Swamp, ss **Doom City**, ed.
 Charles L. Grant, Tor,1987

Brennert, Alan
 Other Voices, is *Twilight Zone* Oct,1987
 Voices in the Earth, ss *Twilight Zone*
 Oct,1987

Bretnor, Reginald
 Decisive Warfare: Retrospect and Prospect,
 ar **There Will Be War** v6, ed. Jerry E.
 Pournelle,1987
 Nobelist Schimmelhorn, nv *F&SF* May,1987
 There's Magic in Shakespeare, nv *Night Cry*
 v2#4,1987

Brians, Paul
 **Nuclear Holocausts: Atomic War in
 Fiction, 1895-1984**, nf Kent State Univ.
 Press Aug,1987

Briarton, Grendel
 Through Time & Space with Ferdinand
 Feghoot I, vi *Amazing* Jul,1987
 Through Time & Space with Ferdinand
 Feghoot i, vi *Amazing* Mar,1987

Bricusse, Leslie
 Christmas 1993, pm Faber & Faber
 Sep,1987

Briggs, Kevin C., D. Scott Apel & Philip K. Dick
 Philip K. Dick in Interview, iv **Philip K. Dick:
 The Dream Connection**, D. Scott Apel,
 Permanent Press,1987

Brin, David
 Bubbles, ss **Universe**, ed. Byron Preiss,
 Bantam Spectra,1987
 Earthclan, om SFBC Dec,1987
 The Uplift War, n. Phantasia Press Apr,1987
 The Uplift War, n. Phantasia: West
 Bloomfield, MI hc Apr,1987

Brite, Poppy Z.
 Angels (Goldengrove Unleaving), ss *The
 Horror Show* Fll,1987
 The Elder, ss *The Horror Show* Jan,1987
 Love (Ash I), ss *The Horror Show* Fll,1987

Brite, Poppy Z. & William J. Grabowski
 Poppy Z. Brite, iv *The Horror Show* Fll,1987

Brittain, Bill
 Dr. Dredd's Wagon of Wonders, n. Harper
 & Row Jul,1987

Briyles, Donald
 The Eye of Klagg, vi *Eldritch Tales* #13,1987

Brizzolara, John
 Nightskin, ss *Twilight Zone* Feb,1987

Broaddus, John C.
 First Plane I See Tonight, ss *Grue* #4,1987

Broderick, Damien
 Thy Sting, vi *Omni* Jun,1987

**Broderick, Pat, George R.R. Martin, Neal
 McPheeters & Doug Moench**
 Sandkings, gn DC Graphics Jan,1987

Bromley, Darwin
 The Legal Problems of a Thieves' World, ar
 American Fantasy Spr,1987

Bromley, Robin
 Television, ar *Twilight Zone* Jun,1987

Brooks, Stan
 Book Reviews, br *Footsteps* Nov,1987

Brooks, Terry
 The Black Unicorn, n. Ballantine/Del Rey
 Oct,1987

Brower, John
 Harmony of Fear, mr *Minnesota Fantasy
 Review* #1,1987

Brown, Ann R.
 The Clockwork Woman, ss **Magic in Ithkar**
 #4, ed. Andre Norton & Robert
 Adams,1987

Brown, Charles N.
 1986, The SF Year in Review, ar,1987

Brown, Charles N. & William G. Contento
 Science Fiction, Fantasy, & Horror: 1986,
 nf Locus Press Sep,1987

Brown, Eric
 The Girl Who Died for Art, and Lived, ss
 Interzone #22,1987
 Krash-Bangg Joe and the Pineal-Zen
 Equation, ss *Interzone* #21,1987

Brown, Fredric
 And the Gods Laughed, co Phantasia
 Press Oct,1987

Brown, George Mackay
 The Tree and the Harp, ss **A Quiver of
 Ghosts**, ed. Aiden Chambers, Bodley
 Head,1987

Brown, Ray
 Cobwebs, nv *Analog* Aug,1987

Broxon, Mildred Downey
 First Do No Harm, ss **Magic in Ithkar** #4,
 ed. Andre Norton & Robert Adams,1987

Brumbaugh, J.D.
 Afternoon Sail, ss *American Fantasy*
 Spr,1987

Brunelle, Beverly
 Sweet Dreams, ss *Haunts* #9,1987

Brunet, James
 Symphony in Ursa Major, ss *Aboriginal SF*
 Jul,1987

Brunner, John
 A Case of Painter's Ear, ss **Tales from the
 Forbidden Planet**, ed. Roz Kaveney,
 Titan,1987
 The Fable of the Farmer and the Fox, vi
 Omni Jun,1987
 Mercy Worse Than None, nv **Aftermath**, ed.
 Robert Lynn Asprin & Lynn Abbey,
 Ace,1987
 The Shift Key, n. Methuen May,1987

Brush, Karen A.
 The Pig, the Prince & the Unicorn, n. Avon
 Jun,1987

Brust, Steven
 The Sun, the Moon, and the Stars, n. Ace
 May,1987

Brust, Steven & Megan Lindholm
 An Act of Mercy, ss **Liavek: Wizard's Row**,
 ed. Will Shetterly & Emma Bull, Ace,1987

Brutvan, Michael J.
 Subatomic Particles, ss *Mage* Win,1987

Bryant, Edward
 The Baku, nv **Night Visions** #4,1987
 Books, br *Twilight Zone* Jun,1987
 Books, br *Twilight Zone* Aug,1987
 Books, br *Twilight Zone* Oct,1987
 Books, br *Twilight Zone* Dec,1987
 Buggage, ss **Night Visions** #4,1987
 Coon Dawgs, ss **Trilobyte/The Shadow on
 the Doorstep**, ed. Edward Bryant/James
 P. Blaylock, Seattle: Axolotl,1987
 Doing Colfax, ss **Night Visions** #4,1987
 Drummer's Star, ss **Trilobyte/The Shadow
 on the Doorstep**, ed. Edward
 Bryant/James P. Blaylock, Seattle:
 Axolotl,1987

BRYANT, EDWARD   CANTRELL, LISA W.

Bryant, Edward (continued)
An Easter Treasure, ss **Trilobyte/The
    Shadow on the Doorstep**, ed. Edward
    Bryant/James P. Blaylock, Seattle:
    Axolotl,1987
Frat Rat Bash, ss **Night Visions** #4,1987
Haunted, ss **Night Visions** #4,1987
Predators, ss **Night Visions** #4,1987
The Twilight Zone Review: 1986 - Fiction, br
    Twilight Zone Feb,1987

Bryant, Edward & James P. Blaylock
The Shadow on the Doorstep/Trilobyte,
    oa Axolotl Aug,1987

Buard, Patricia Anne
Devil's Advocate, ss **Red Sun of Darkover**,
    ed. Marion Zimmer Bradley & The Friends
    of Darkover, DAW,1987

Buchanan, P.J.
Different Path, nv **Red Sun of Darkover**, ed.
    Marion Zimmer Bradley & The Friends of
    Darkover, DAW,1987

Bucklin, Nathan A.
Imperfect Catch, ss *Tales of the
    Unanticipated* #2,1987

Budrys, Algis
Books, br *F&SF* Jan,1987
Books, br *F&SF* Feb,1987
Books, br *F&SF* Mar,1987
Books, br *F&SF* Apr,1987
Books, br *F&SF* May,1987
Books, br *F&SF* Jun,1987
Books, br *F&SF* Jul,1987
Books, br *F&SF* Aug,1987
Books, br *F&SF* Oct,1987
Books, br *F&SF* Nov,1987
That Fearful Symmetry, vi *Twilight Zone*
    Apr,1987

Budrys, Algis, ed.
**L. Ron Hubbard Presents Writers of the
    Future, Vol. III**, oa Bridge Apr,1987

Buettner, John
Stay Out of Innsmouth, pm *Eldritch Tales*
    #14,1987

uffington, mel
perverse love, pm *Ice River* Sum,1987
placebo, pm *Ice River* Sum,1987
prophylaxis, pm *Ice River* Sum,1987

Bujold, Lois McMaster
The Borders of Infinity, na **Free Lancers**,
    ed. Elizabeth Mitchell, Baen,1987
Falling Free [Part 1 of 4], sl *Analog*
    Dec,1987
Falling Free [Part 2 of 4], sl *Analog* mid-
    Dec,1987
Garage Sale, vi *American Fantasy* Spr,1987
Test of Honor, om SFBC May,1987

Bull, Emma
War for the Oaks, n. Ace Jul,1987

Bull, Emma & Will Shetterly, eds.
Liavek: Wizard's Row, oa Ace Sep,1987

Bunch, David R.
Miracle of the Flowers, ss *Pulpsmith*
    Win,1987

Burgess, Anthony
A Clockwork Orange, pl Hutchinson
    Feb,1987

Burgess, Mason
Graveyard, n. Leisure Oct,1987

Burkholz, Herbert
The Sensitives, n. Atheneum Jul,1987

Burkunk, Wim
Leakage, ss *SF International* #1,1987

Burleson, Donald R.
Classified Ads, ss *The Horror Show* Spr,1987
Family Dentistry, ss *F&SF* Aug,1987

Burleson, Mollie L.
Home for Dinner, ss *Eldritch Tales* #13,1987

Burnett, Arthur B.
University Field Observation Guide for the
    Planet Earth or U.F.O. Handbook, ss
    Salarius #3,1987

Burnham, Crispin
Book Review, br *Eldritch Tales* #14,1987
Eldritch Lair, ed *Eldritch Tales* #13,1987
Eldritch Lair, ed *Eldritch Tales* #14,1987
In Memoriam: Manly Wade Wellman, bg
    Eldritch Tales #13,1987

Burnham, Crispin, ed.
Eldritch Tales No. 13 [v.4 #1]
Eldritch Tales No. 14 [v.4 #2]

Burns, Christopher
Among the Wounded, ss *Interzone* #22,1987

Burns, Stephen L.
In the Kingdom at Morning, nv *Analog*
    Feb,1987
Redeemer's Riddle, nv **Sword and
    Sorceress** #4, ed. Marion Zimmer
    Bradley,1987
The Weather With Morgana, ss *2AM*
    Sum,1987

Burroughs, William S.
The Ghost Lemurs of Madagascar, ss *Omni*
    Apr,1987

Burt, John Wayne
Mr. Valdoom's Backyard, ss *Space & Time*
    #73,1987

Busby, David
The Gallery of Masks, nv *F&SF* Aug,1987

Busby, F.M.
Getting Home, co Ace Aug,1987
The Rebel Dynasty, Volume I, om Bantam
    Spectra Dec,1987
The Rebel Dynasty, Volume II, om Bantam
    Spectra Jan,1988

Bussing, Sabine
**Aliens in the Home: The Child in Horror
    Fiction**, nf Greenwood Mar,1987

Butler, Octavia E.
Dawn, n. Warner May,1987
The Evening and the Morning and the
    Night, nv *Omni* May,1987

Buxton, Meg
The Neighbours, ss **After Midnight Stories**
    #3,1987

Byatt, Antonia
Sugar and Other Stories, co Scribner's
    Jul,1987

Cabot, Laurie & James Verniere
The Witch of Salem, iv *Twilight Zone*
    Jun,1987

Cadigan, Pat
Angel, ss *IASFM* May,1987
The Boy in the Rain, ss *Twilight Zone*
    Jun,1987
By Lost Ways, nv **Wild Cards** v2, ed.
    George R.R. Martin, Bantam,1987
Lunatic Bridge, nv **The Omni Book of
    Science Fiction** #5, ed. Ellen Datlow,1987
Mindplayers, n. Bantam Spectra Aug,1987
Patterns, ss *Omni* Aug,1987

Caidin, Martin
Exit Earth, n. Baen Apr,1987

Calcamuggio, Mark
The Driftwood in the Fox's Den, ss *Space &
    Time* #72,1987

Caldecott, Moyra
Etheldreda, n. Arkana Sep,1987
The Silver Vortex, n. Arrow May,1987

Callin, Grant D.
A Lion on Tharthee, n. Baen Oct,1987

Campbell, Hope
Looking for Hamlet, n. Macmillan Oct,1987

Campbell, Ramsey
Another World, ss **Tales from the
    Forbidden Planet**, ed. Roz Kaveney,
    Titan,1987
Cold Print, co Tor Nov,1987
Dark Feasts, co Robinson Sep,1987
Merry May, nv **Scared Stiff**, Los Angeles:
    Scream/Press,1987
The Other Side, ss *Twilight Zone* Apr,1987
Rising Generation, ss *Night Cry* v2#5,1987
Scared Stiff: Tales of Sex and Death, co
    Scream/Press Jul,1987
Second Sight, ss **Masques** #2, ed. J.N.
    Williamson,1987
Stages, nv **Scared Stiff**, Los Angeles:
    Scream/Press,1987
Where the Heart Is, ss **The Architecture of
    Fear**, ed. Kathryn Cramer & Peter D.
    Pautz, Arbor House,1987

Campbell, Ramsey, Nancy Garcia & Robert T.
    Garcia
Ramsey Campbell Interview, iv *American
    Fantasy* Win,1987

Campbell, Ramsey & Stanley Wiater
A Conversation With Ramsey Campbell, iv
    Twilight Zone Apr,1987

Campton, David
Repossession, ss **Whispers** #6, ed. Stuart
    David Schiff,1987

Campton, David & Mary W. Shelley
Frankenstein, n. Beaver Oct,1987

Cannon, Peter
H.P. Lovecraft: Problems in Critical
    Recognition, ar *Mage* Win,1987

Cantrell, Lisa W.
The Manse, n. Tor Nov,1987

CANTRY, THOMAS

Cantry, Thomas & Greg Ketter
Thomas Canty, pi *American Fantasy*
Spr,1987

Caraker, Mary
Lumisland, ss *F&SF* Sep,1987
Out of the Cradle, nv *F&SF* Jul,1987
Water Song, n. Popular Library Questar
Sep,1987

Carbonaro, John & Ann Cathey
Saga of the Crimson Knight [Part 2], sl
Salarius #3,1987

Card, Orson Scott
Adolescence and Adulthood in Science
Fiction, ar *Amazing* Nov,1987
America, nv *IASFM* Jan,1987
Books to Look For, br *F&SF* May,1987
Books to Look For, br *F&SF* Jun,1987
Books to Look For, br *F&SF* Jul,1987
Books to Look For, br *F&SF* Aug,1987
Books to Look For, br *F&SF* Sep,1987
Books to Look For, br *F&SF* Oct,1987
Books to Look For, br *F&SF* Nov,1987
Books to Look For, br *F&SF* Dec,1987
Cardography, co Hypatia Press Mar,1987
Carthage City, na *IASFM* Sep,1987
A Christian in Wonderland, ar *Apex!* #1,1987
Eye for Eye, na *IASFM* Mar,1987
Red Prophet, n. Tor Jan,1988
Runaway, nv *IASFM* Jun,1987
Saving Grace, ss *Night Cry* v2#5,1987
Seventh Son, n. Tor Jul,1987
West, na **Free Lancers**, ed. Elizabeth
Mitchell, Baen,1987
Wyrms, n. Arbor House Jul,1987

Carey, Diane
Star Trek: Final Frontier, n. Pocket
Jan,1988

Carl, Lillian Stewart
Out of Darkness, ss *IASFM* Apr,1987
Shadow Dancers, n. Ace Nov,1987

Carletti, Eduardo Julio
Susi's Lovely World, ss *SF International*
#2,1987

Carlisle, Anne
Liquid Sky, n. Doubleday Nov,1987

Carpenter, Leonard
The Devourer, pm *2AM* Spr,1987
The Egg, pm *Eldritch Tales* #13,1987
Fearing's Fall, ss *Amazing* Sep,1987
The Fungoid Intruder, pm *2AM* Win,1987
The Priests, pm *Eldritch Tales* #14,1987

Carr, Jayge
Inky, ss *Whispers* #23,1987

Carr, John F. & Roland J. Green
Nightfriend, nv **Friends of the Horseclans**,
ed. Robert Adams & Pamela Crippen
Adams, Signet,1987

Carr, Terry
You Got It, ss *F&SF* May,1987

Carr, Terry, ed.
**Terry Carr's Best Science Fiction and
Fantasy of the Year #16**, an Tor Sep,1987
Universe 17, oa Doubleday Jun,1987

Carroll, Jonathan
Bones of the Moon, n. Arbor
House/Morrow Jan,1988
Bones of the Moon, n. Century May,1987
Friend's Best Man, ss *F&SF* Jan,1987

Carroll, L.E.
The Very Last Party at #13 Mallory Way, nv
**L. Ron Hubbard Presents Writers of the
Future** v3, ed. Algis Budrys, Bridge,1987

Carroll, Lewis
**The Complete Alice and The Hunting of
the Snark**, om Salem House Apr,1987

Carter, Angela
Ashputtle, vi **The Virago Book of Ghost
Stories**, ed. Richard Dalby, Virago,1987

Carter, Bruce
Nightworld, n. Century Jul,1987

Carter, Carmen
Star Trek #34: Dreams of the Raven, n.
Pocket Jun,1987

Carter, Lin
Horror Wears Blue, n. Doubleday Nov,1987

Carter, Margaret L.
**Specter or Delusion? The Supernatural in
Gothic Fiction**, nf UMI Aug,1987

Carter, Tonya R. & Paul B. Thompson
The Exiles, nv **DragonLance Tales** v3,
Margaret Weis & Tracy Hickman,
TSR,1987

Cartwright, Phil
The Computer Game, ss **Twisted Circuits**,
ed. Mick Gowar, Beaver,1987

Carver, Jeffrey A.
The Rapture Effect, n. Tor Feb,1987
**Roger Zelazny's Alien Speedway 1:
Clypsis**, n. Bantam Spectra Oct,1987

Case, George
The Preacher Behind the Wall, ss *Space &
Time* #72,1987

Casper, Susan
Covenant With a Dragon, ss **In the Field of
Fire**, ed. Jeanne Van Buren Dann & Jack
M. Dann, Tor,1987
Under Her Skin, ss *Amazing* Mar,1987

Casper, Susan & Gardner R. Dozois
The Stray, ss *Twilight Zone* Dec,1987

Cassutt, Michael
Who's Who in Space: The First 25 Years,
nf G.K. Hall Apr,1987

Castle, Mort
De-Programming Rose Ellen, vi *2AM*
Sum,1987
If You Take My Hand, My Son, ss **Masques**
#2, ed. J.N. Williamson,1987
Sharing, vi *Grue* #4,1987

Cather, J.B.
Pulsebeat, nv *Analog* Dec,1987

Cathey, Ann
Dragon, pm *Salarius* v1#4,1987
Haiku, pm *Salarius* v1#4,1987
Mother Moon, pm *Salarius* v1#4,1987

Cathey, Ann (continued)
Pipe Dream, pm *Salarius* #3,1987
True Sight, pm *Salarius* #3,1987

Cathey, Ann & John Carbonaro
Saga of the Crimson Knight [Part 2], sl
Salarius #3,1987

Cave, Hugh B.
The Back of the Mirror, ss *Border Land*
Oct,1987
No Flowers for Henry, ss *Whispers* #23,1987

Cerasini, Marc A. & Charles Hoffman
Robert E. Howard, nf Starmont House
Apr,1987

Chaddock, Kathleen
Finders Keepers, vi *2AM* Fll,1987

Chaisson, Eric J.
Our Galaxy, ar **Universe**, ed. Byron Preiss,
Bantam Spectra,1987

Chalker, Jack L.
The Labyrinth of Dreams, n. Tor Mar,1987
Pirates of the Thunder, n. Ballantine/Del
Rey Mar,1987
The Shadow Dancers, n. Tor Jul,1987
Warriors of the Storm, n. Ballantine/Del
Rey Aug,1987
When the Changewinds Blow, n. Ace
Sep,1987

Chambers, Aidan
The Tower, ss **A Quiver of Ghosts**, ed.
Aiden Chambers, Bodley Head,1987

Chambers, Aidan, ed.
A Quiver Of Ghosts, oa Bodley Head
Mar,1987

Chapman, Irwin M.
John Borkowski: An Appreciation, bg *2AM*
Fll,1987
Small Press Reviews, br *2AM* Spr,1987
Small Press Reviews, br *2AM* Sum,1987
Small Press Reviews, br *2AM* Fll,1987
Small Press Reviews, br *2AM* Win,1987

Chapman, Vera
Miranty and the Alchemist, n. Marilyn
Malin Jun,1987

Charles, David M.
Are You Receiving Me?, ss *Amazing*
Nov,1987

Charles, Steven
Private School #6: The Last Alien, n.
Pocket Feb,1987

Charnock, Graham
Fullwood's Web, ss **Other Edens**, ed.
Christopher Evans & Robert Holdstock,
Unwin: London,1987

Chase, Robert R.
The Changeling Hunt, nv *Analog* Jul,1987

Cheetham, Ann
The Pit, n. Armada Jun,1987

Cheney, Thomas
Cartoon, ct *Twilight Zone* Feb,1987
Cartoon, ct *Twilight Zone* Apr,1987
Cartoon, ct *Twilight Zone* Jun,1987
Cartoon, ct *Twilight Zone* Aug,1987

Cheney, Thomas (continued)
Cartoon, ct *Twilight Zone* Oct,1987
Cartoon, ct *Twilight Zone* Dec,1987

Cherkes, Joseph K.
Final Words: A Letter From the Editor, aw
Haunts #9,1987

Cherkes, Joseph K., ed.
Haunts [# 9/10, Fall 1987]

Cherryh, C.J.
The Avoidance Factor, ar **Glass and Amber**,
NESFA,1987
Black Water (Suicide) [music], sg **Festival
Moon**, ed. C.J. Cherryh, DAW,1987
Exile's Gate, n. DAW Jan,1988
The Faded Sun Trilogy, om Methuen
Apr,1987
Festival Moon, ss **Festival Moon**, ed. C.J.
Cherryh, DAW,1987
Festival Moon (final reprise), vi **Festival
Moon**, ed. C.J. Cherryh, DAW,1987
Festival Moon (reprised), vi **Festival Moon**,
ed. C.J. Cherryh, DAW,1987
Fever Season, ss **Fever Season**, ed. C.J.
Cherryh, DAW,1987
Fever Season (final reprise), ms **Fever
Season**, ed. C.J. Cherryh, DAW,1987
Fever Season (Music), sg **Fever Season**,
ed. C.J. Cherryh, DAW,1987
Fever Season (reprised), ms **Fever Season**,
ed. C.J. Cherryh, DAW,1987
A Gift of Prophecy, ss **Glass and Amber**,
NESFA,1987
Glass and Amber, co NESFA Feb,1987
Legions of Hell, n. Baen Jul,1987
Mist-Thoughts (Music), sg **Fever Season**,
ed. C.J. Cherryh, DAW,1987
Partners (Music), sg **Fever Season**, ed. C.J.
Cherryh, DAW,1987
Pawn in Play, nv **Masters of Hell**, ed. Janet
Morris et al, Baen,1987
Perspectives in SF, sp **Glass and Amber**,
NESFA,1987
Private Conversation [music], sg **Festival
Moon**, ed. C.J. Cherryh, DAW,1987
Sharper than a Serpent's Tooth, nv
Crusaders in Hell, ed. Janet Morris, New
York: Baen,1987

Cherryh, C.J., ed.
Fever Season: Merovingen Nights #2, oa
DAW Oct,1987
Merovingen Nights: Festival Moon, oa
DAW Apr,1987

Cherryh, C.J. & Nancy Asire
The Conscience of the King, na **Angels in
Hell**, ed. Janet Morris, Baen,1987

Cherryh, C.J. & Janet Morris
Kings in Hell, n. Baen Feb,1987

Chetwin, Grace
The Riddle and the Rune, n. Macmillan
Bradbury Sep,1987

Chetwynd-Hayes, R.
Benjamin, nv **Dracula's Children**,
Kimber,1987
Caroline, na **The House of Dracula**,
Kimber,1987
Cuthbert, nv **Dracula's Children**,
Kimber,1987
Dracula's Children, oc Kimber May,1987
Gilbert, nv **The House of Dracula**,
Kimber,1987

Chetwynd-Hayes, R. (continued)
The House of Dracula, oc Kimber Oct,1987
Irma, nv **Dracula's Children**, Kimber,1987
Karl, nv **The House of Dracula**, Kimber,1987
Louis, nv **The House of Dracula**,
Kimber,1987
Marcus, nv **Dracula's Children**,
Kimber,1987
Marikova, nv **The House of Dracula**,
Kimber,1987
Moving Day, ss **After Midnight Stories**
#3,1987
Rudolph, nv **Dracula's Children**,
Kimber,1987
Zena, nv **Dracula's Children**, Kimber,1987

Chevalier, J. John
The Master of Time, ss *Space & Time*
#73,1987

Child, Lincoln, ed.
Tales of the Dark, an St. Martin's Jul,1987
Tales of the Dark 2, an St. Martin's
Sep,1987

Childer, Simon Ian
Worm, n. Grafton May,1987

Chilson, Robert
Brain Jag, ss *Analog* Jun,1987
The Bureaucratic Brain, ss *Analog* Mar,1987

Chilson, Robert & Robin Wayne Bailey
Primatives, nv *Amazing* Jul,1987

Chilson, Robert & William F. Wu
High Power, ss *Analog* Sep,1987
A Hog on Ice, ss *Analog* Dec,1987
No Damn Atoms, nv *Analog* Oct,1987

Chin, M. Lucie
Catmagic, ss **Devils & Demons**, ed. Marvin
Kaye, SFBC/Doubleday,1987

Chocholak, Misha
Book Reviews, br *New Pathways* Apr,1987
Book Reviews, br *New Pathways* Aug,1987
Book Reviews, br *New Pathways* Nov,1987
Prayers of Steel, vi *Ice River* Sum,1987

Chocholak, Misha & Michael Bishop
Close Encounters with Michael Bishop, iv
New Pathways Jan,1987

Chocholak, Misha & Paul Williams
Paul Williams talks to New Pathways, iv *New
Pathways* Jan,1987

Chocholak, Misha & Mark Ziesing
Interview with Mark Ziesing: Bookseller &
Publisher, iv *New Pathways* Jan,1987

Christopher, Joe R.
C.S. Lewis, nf G.K. Hall/Twayne Apr,1987

Christopher, Paul
Beyond that River, oc Pal Books Nov,1987
Beyond That River, ss **Beyond That River**,
Pal Books,1987
Bobbie, nv **Beyond That River**, Pal
Books,1987
A Bottle on the Beach, ss **Beyond That
River**, Pal Books,1987
Dora, ss **Beyond That River**, Pal Books,1987
For the Love of Mother, ss **Beyond That
River**, Pal Books,1987
Galactic Chronicles, n. Pal Books Nov,1987

Christopher, Paul (continued)
Hermione Gould, nv **Beyond That River**,
Pal Books,1987
In the Tube, vi **Beyond That River**, Pal
Books,1987
Little White Mongrel, ss **Beyond That River**,
Pal Books,1987
Masters of the Void, ss **Beyond That River**,
Pal Books,1987
Mushrooms, nv **Beyond That River**, Pal
Books,1987
Once Upon a Chair, nv **Beyond That River**,
Pal Books,1987
The Purple Hour, ss **Beyond That River**, Pal
Books,1987
Pyramids, ss **Beyond That River**, Pal
Books,1987
Sunday Special, ss **Beyond That River**, Pal
Books,1987
To Be Blind, ss **Beyond That River**, Pal
Books,1987
Waiting for Sunlight, ss **Beyond That River**,
Pal Books,1987

Chronister, Alan B.
Cry Wolf, n. Zebra Jun,1987

Cipriani, D.J., III
Jonathon, vi *Mage* Spr,1987

Citro, Joseph
Shadow Child, n. Zebra Jul,1987

Claremont, Chris
FirstFlight, n. Ace Dec,1987

Claremont, Chris, et al
The Uncanny X-Men, gn Marvel
Comics,1987

Clareson, Thomas D.
Frederik Pohl, nf Starmont House Nov,1987

Clarke, Arthur C.
**2001: A Space Odyssey/The City and the
Stars/The Deep Range/A Fall of
Moondust/Rendezvous With Rama**, om
Octopus/Heinemann,1987
2061: Odyssey Three, n. Ballantine/Del
Rey Jan,1988
On Golden Seas, ss *Omni* May,1987
On Weaponry, ar *Analog* mid-Dec,1987
The Wind From the Sun, co NAL/Signet
Mar,1987

Clarke, J. Brian
The Testament of Geoffrey, ss *Analog*
May,1987

Clayton, Jo
Skeen's Return, n. DAW Jun,1987
Skeen's Search, n. DAW Dec,1987

Clee, Mona A.
Iron Butterflies, ss *Twilight Zone* Dec,1987
Just Like Their Masters, ss **Shadows** #10,
ed. Charles L. Grant,1987

Clement, Hal
Intuit, co NESFA Sep,1987
Status Symbol, nv **Intuit**, NESFA,1987
Still River, n. Ballantine/Del Rey Jun,1987

Clemons, Jack
Will Little Note, Nor Long Remember, nv
Amazing Nov,1987

Clendenen, Bill
Stigma, n. Bantam Jan,1988

Clute, John
Book Reviews, br *Interzone* #19,1987
Book Reviews, br *Interzone* #20,1987
Book Reviews, br *Interzone* #21,1987
Book Reviews, br *Interzone* #22,1987

Clute, John, Simon Ounsley & David Pringle, eds.
Interzone: The 2nd Anthology, an Simon & Schuster UK Aug,1987

Coats, Tim
The Buildings Are Falling, ss *Grue* #4,1987

Coburn, Anthony
The Tribe of Gum, pl Titan Dec,1987

Cochran, Molly & Warren Murphy
High Priest, n. NAL Nov,1987

Coffman, Virginia
The Devil's Mistress, n. Piatkus Feb,1987

Cohen, Jon
Preserves, ss *Twilight Zone* Feb,1987

Cohen, Martin
Starbirth and Maturity, ar **Universe**, ed. Byron Preiss, Bantam Spectra,1987

Cole, Adrian
A Place Among the Fallen, n. Arbor House May,1987
Throne of Fools, n. Unwin Nov,1987

Colley, Jon & Mary Sikes
Salarius Recommends, br *Salarius* #3,1987

Colley, Ruth, ed.
Salarius [v.1 #4]

Collings, Michael R.
The Stephen King Phenomenon, nf Starmont House Apr,1987
Succubi, pm *Footsteps* Nov,1987

Collins, Paul
Kool Running, ss *SF International* #1,1987

Collins, Paul & Trevor Donohue
Waltz of the Flowers, ss *Aphelion* #5,1987

Comeau, J.L.
Stinkers, ss *Grue* #6,1987

Commander USA & Kathleen E. Jurgens
Kathleen Jurgens interviews Commander USA, iv *2AM* Fll,1987

Congreve, Bill
Collector, ss *Aphelion* #5,1987

Conner, Jeff
Stephen King Goes to Hollywood, nf NAL Plume Aug,1987
Stephen King Goes to Hollywood, nf NAL Jul,1987

Connolly, Lawrence C.
Moon and the Devil, ss *The Horror Show* Spr,1987

Constantine, Storm
The Enchantments of Flesh and Spirit, n. Macdonald Aug,1987

Contento, William G. & Charles N. Brown
Science Fiction, Fantasy, & Horror: 1986, nf Locus Press Sep,1987

Cook, Glen
An Ill Fate Marshalling, n. Tor Jan,1988
Reap the East Wind, n. Tor Jun,1987
Sweet Silver Blues, n. NAL/Signet Aug,1987

Cook, Hugh
The Shift, n. Cape Jan,1987
The Shift, n. Random Vintage Jun,1987
Wizard War, n. Popular Library Questar Jun,1987
The Women and the Warlords, n. Corgi Dec,1987
The Wordsmiths and the Warguild, n. Colin Smythe Nov,1987
The Wordsmiths and the Warguild, n. Corgi Jun,1987

Cook, Paul
On the Rim of the Mandala, n. Bantam Spectra Jun,1987

Cook, Rick
Catalyst, ss *Analog* Oct,1987
Mortality, ss *Analog* Jan,1987

Cook, Robin
Outbreak, n. Putnam Jan,1987

Cooke, Catherine
The Winged Assassin, n. Ace Jun,1987

Cooke, Catherine & John P. Cooke
Sweet Chariot, ss *Space & Time* #72,1987

Cooke, John P. & Catherine Cooke
Sweet Chariot, ss *Space & Time* #72,1987

Cooper, Anne
The Frog Prince, ss **Mad and Bad Fairies**, ed. Anonymous, Attic Press,1987

Cooper, Clare
The Settlement on Planet B, n. Hodder & Stoughton Jun,1987

Cooper, Jeffrey
The Nightmares on Elm Street, Parts 1, 2, 3: The Continuing Story, n. St. Martin's Feb,1987

Cooper, Louise
The Master, n. Tor May,1987
The Master, n. Unicorn Apr,1987
Mirage, n. Unwin Sep,1987
Tithing Night, ss **Tales from the Forbidden Planet**, ed. Roz Kaveney, Titan,1987

Cooper, Richard
Knights of God, n. Lions Sep,1987

Cooper, Tom
War*Moon, n. Worldwide Library Feb,1987

Coover, Robert
Intermission, ss *Playboy* Feb,1987

Corbett, W.J.
Pentecost and the Chosen One, n. Delacorte Jun,1987

Cording, H.J.
Character Assassination, ss *Haunts* #9,1987

Cornell, Richard
Spell of Binding, ss **Sword and Sorceress** #4, ed. Marion Zimmer Bradley,1987

Cornwill, Sue & Mike Kott
The Official Price Guide to Star Trek and Star Wars Collectibles, Second Edition, nf Ballantine/House of Collectibles Jan,1988

Cortesi, David E.
A Bomb in the Head, ss *Amazing* May,1987

Corwin, Matt
Backwater Time, ss *F&SF* Feb,1987

Corwin, Richard
The Eyes of the Gods, ss **Sword and Sorceress** #4, ed. Marion Zimmer Bradley,1987

Corydon, Bent & L. Ron Hubbard, Jr.
L. Ron Hubbard: Messiah or Madman?, nf Lyle Stuart Aug,1987

Costello, Matthew
Sleep Tight, n. Zebra Jul,1987

Costello, Matthew J.
Gaming, gr *IASFM* Jan,1987
Gaming, gr *IASFM* Feb,1987
Gaming, gr *IASFM* Mar,1987
Gaming, gr *IASFM* Apr,1987
Gaming, gr *IASFM* May,1987
Gaming, gr *IASFM* Jun,1987
Gaming, gr *IASFM* Jul,1987
Gaming, gr *IASFM* Aug,1987
Gaming, gr *IASFM* Sep,1987
Gaming, gr *IASFM* Oct,1987
Gaming, gr *IASFM* Nov,1987
Gaming, gr *IASFM* Dec,1987
Gaming, gr *IASFM* mid-Dec,1987
On Gaming, gr *Analog* Jan,1987
On Gaming, gr *Analog* Feb,1987
On Gaming, gr *Analog* Mar,1987
On Gaming, gr *Analog* Apr,1987
On Gaming, gr *Analog* May,1987
On Gaming, gr *Analog* Jun,1987
On Gaming, gr *Analog* Jul,1987
On Gaming, gr *Analog* Aug,1987
On Gaming, gr *Analog* Sep,1987
On Gaming, gr *Analog* Oct,1987
On Gaming, gr *Analog* Nov,1987
On Gaming, gr *Analog* Dec,1987
On Gaming, gr *Analog* mid-Dec,1987
The Second Wave, ar *Amazing* Mar,1987

Costley, Bill
Legitimate Lady, or I Stash My Cash Behind My Golden Door, vi *Pulpsmith* Win,1987

Cotton, Donald
The Romans, n. W.H. Allen Apr,1987

Cottrell, William D.
Watch Doll, ss *Whispers* #23,1987

Coulson, Robert
Humorists in a Strange Land, br *Amazing* May,1987

Cover, Arthur Byron
Isaac Asimov's Robot City, Book 4: Prodigy, n. Ace Jan,1988

Coville, Bruce
Murder in Orbit, n. Dragon Aug,1987

Coville, Bruce (continued)
Watch Out!, ss **Spaceships & Spells**, ed.
Jane Yolen, Martin H. Greenberg &
Charles G. Waugh, Harper & Row,1987

Cowles, Frederick
Princess of Darkness, ss **Dracula's Brood**,
ed. Richard Dalby, Crucible,1987
The Strange Affair at Upton Strangewold, ss
Ghosts & Scholars, ed. Rosemary
Pardoe,1987

Cox, Greg
The Homework Horror, ss *Amazing*
May,1987

Coyle, H.W.
Team Yankee, n. Presidio Press Sep,1987

Coyne, John
The Hunting Season, n. Macmillan
Sep,1987

Cramer, John G.
The Alternate View: Artificial Gravity: Which
Way Is Up?, ar *Analog* Feb,1987
The Alternate View: Laser Propulsion and
the Four P's, ar *Analog* Aug,1987
The Alternate View: Recent Results, ar
Analog Jun,1987
The Alternate View: SN1987A--Supernova
Astrophysics Grows Up, ar *Analog*
Dec,1987
The Alternate View: Strings and Things, ar
Analog Apr,1987
The Alternate View: Warm Superconductors,
ar *Analog* Oct,1987

Cramer, Kathryn
Forbidden Knowledge, ss **Mathenauts**, ed.
Rudy Rucker, Arbor House,1987

Cramer, Kathryn & David G. Hartwell, eds.
Christmas Ghosts, an Arbor House
Sep,1987

Cramer, Kathryn & Peter D. Pautz, eds.
The Architecture of Fear, oa Arbor House
Oct,1987

Craven, Wes & Michael Arthur Betts
Tattler, mr *The Horror Show* Spr,1987

Craven, Wes, Robert Englund & Heather
Langencamp
Nightmare on Elm Street 3, iv *The Horror
Show* Spr,1987

Crawford, Gary William
Craving, pm *Grue* #5,1987
A Dream of Theobold, pm *Eldritch Tales*
#13,1987

Crazy Alien, A
The Clean Up Your Own Mess, ms
Aboriginal SF Sep,1987
The Drones are Willing..., ms *Aboriginal SF*
Jul,1987
A Matter of Trust, ms *Aboriginal SF* Nov,1987
Narrow Escape from a Sauna, ms *Aboriginal
SF* Feb,1987
A Statistical Proposition, ms *Aboriginal SF*
May,1987

Creek, Jack
Showdown, ss *2AM* Win,1987

Cresswell, Helen
Moondial, n. Faber & Faber Oct,1987
Moondial, n. Macmillan Oct,1987

Crichton, Michael
Sphere, n. Knopf Jun,1987

Crispin, A.C.
Bloodspell, nv **Tales of the Witch World**,
ed. Andre Norton, St. Martin's,1987

Croft, Fred
Mermaids, pm *Eldritch Tales* #13,1987

Crompton, Anne Eliot
Truce, ss **Spaceships & Spells**, ed. Jane
Yolen, Martin H. Greenberg & Charles G.
Waugh, Harper & Row,1987

Crone, Joni
The Story of Emer, ss **Mad and Bad
Fairies**, ed. Anonymous, Attic Press,1987
Thumbelina the Left Wing Fairy, ss **Mad
and Bad Fairies**, ed. Anonymous, Attic
Press,1987

Cronwall, Brian
She Told Me, Honor, pm *Tales of the
Unanticipated* #2,1987

Cross, Ronald Anthony
The Heavenly Blue Answer, ss **In the Field
of Fire**, ed. Jeanne Van Buren Dann &
Jack M. Dann, Tor,1987
Shiva Shiva, nv *F&SF* Sep,1987

Crossley, Robert, ed.
Talking Across the World, nf Univ. Press of
New England Dec,1987

Crouch, Annette S.
Inheritance, ss *Grue* #6,1987

Crowley, John
AEgypt, n. Bantam Spectra Apr,1987

Crowley, John & Gregory Feeley
John Crowley Interview, iv *Interzone*
#21,1987

Crunk, Paula & Linda Frankel
Blood Hunt, na **The Other Side of the
Mirror**, ed. Marion Zimmer Bradley & The
Friends of Darkover, DAW,1987

Cumberland, Sharon
Arithmetic of Mourning, pm *Pulpsmith*
Win,1987

Cunningham, P.E.
Satisfaction Guaranteed, ss *F&SF* Jun,1987

Cunningham, William P.
Blessed Are Those..., ss *Mage* FII,1987

Curry, Mike
An Extraterrestrial, Ish, pm *Amazing*
May,1987
A Starship Commander, McPheeter, pm
Amazing Sep,1987

Curtis, Jack
Crows' Parliament, n. Bantam UK Mar,1987

Curtis, Paul
Working Stiff, ss *Fantasy Book* Mar,1987

Cush, Geoffrey
God Help the Queen, n. Abacus Apr,1987

D'Ambrosio, Margaret
Meggie's Journeys, n. Polygon Dec,1987

da Cruz, Daniel
F-Cubed, n. Ballantine/Del Rey Jun,1987
Texas Triumphant, n. Ballantine/Del Rey
Dec,1987

Dahl, Roald
**The Complete Adventures of Charlie and
Mr. Willy Wonka**, om Unwin Hyman
Oct,1987
Fantastic Mr. Fox: A Play, pl Puffin May,1987

Daily, Ben
Puzzle Pages, pz *Salarius* #3,1987

Daily, Ben & Gaye Beer
Puzzle Pages, pz *Salarius* v1#4,1987

Dalby, Richard, ed.
Dracula's Brood, an Crucible May,1987
The Virago Book of Ghost Stories, oa
Virago Nov,1987

Dalby, Richard & Rosemary Pardoe, eds.
Ghosts and Scholars, oa Crucible Oct,1987

Dalkey, Kara
The World in the Rock, ss **Liavek: Wizard's
Row**, ed. Will Shetterly & Emma Bull,
Ace,1987

Dalmas, John
The Regiment, n. Baen Mar,1987
Return to Fanglith, n. Baen Aug,1987

Daniel, David
Leave Them Raving, vi *The Horror Show*
Jan,1987
Roomie, ss *2AM* Win,1987
Static, ss *The Horror Show* Jan,1987

Daniels, Keith Allen
The Passing of the Elves, pm *2AM* Win,1987
prognostication, pm *Grue* #4,1987

Dann, Jack M.
Eight Poems from **Songs from a White
Heart**, ar *Twilight Zone* Aug,1987
"It is a circle.", pm *Twilight Zone* Aug,1987
"It was a good day to die...", pm *Twilight
Zone* Aug,1987
Nerve, pm *Twilight Zone* Aug,1987
"Oh, Wakan Tanka...", pm *Twilight Zone*
Aug,1987
"The medicine man tells me...", pm *Twilight
Zone* Aug,1987
Visitors, ss *IASFM* Oct,1987

Dann, Jack M. & Jeanne Van Buren Dann
The Apotheosis of Isaac Rosen, vi *Omni*
Jun,1987

Dann, Jack M. & Jeanne Van Buren Dann, eds.
In the Field of Fire, oa Tor Feb,1987

Dann, Jack M. & Gardner R. Dozois, eds.
Demons!, an Ace Jul,1987

Dann, Jack M. & Barry N. Malzberg
Bringing It Home, ss *Twilight Zone* Feb,1987

DANN, JEANNE VAN BUREN

Dann, Jeanne Van Buren & Jack M. Dann
The Apotheosis of Isaac Rosen, vi *Omni*
Jun,1987

Dann, Jeanne Van Buren & Jack M. Dann, eds.
In the Field of Fire, oa Tor Feb,1987

Darke, Marjorie
Rent-a-Joke, ss **Twisted Circuits**, ed. Mick
Gowar, Beaver,1987

Darling, Jean
The Perfect Gift, ss *Night Cry* v2#4,1987

Darlington, Andrew
The Great Counterfeit Memory Sin-Drome,
ss *Back Brain Recluse* #7,1987

Datlow, Ellen, ed.
The Fifth Omni Book of Science Fiction,
an Zebra Apr,1987

Daves, J. Hunter
Ten Times Black, ss *Grue* #5,1987

David, Peter
Knight Life, n. Ace Apr,1987

Davidson, Alan
Bewitching of Alison Allbright, n.
Hutchinson May,1987

Davidson, Avram
The Engine of Samoset Erastus Hale and
One Other, Unknown, ss *Amazing* Jul,1987
Mountaineers Are Always Free, ss *F&SF*
Oct,1987
Vergil and the Caged Bird, ss *Amazing*
Jan,1987

Davidson, Avram & Grania Davis
Addict, ss *F&SF* Jan,1987

Davies, Dick
Cold Christmas, cs *The Horror Show*
Jan,1987
Double Gross-Out at the Uh-Oh Saloon, cs
The Horror Show Sum,1987
Me Pal Jonesy, cs *The Horror Show* Spr,1987

Davies, Dorothy
A Little Piece of Home, ss *SF International*
#1,1987

Davies, Paul
Fireball, n. Heinemann Aug,1987

Davis, Dorothy
F&SF Crossword, pz *F&SF* Feb,1987

Davis, Grania & Avram Davidson
Addict, ss *F&SF* Jan,1987

Davis, R.D.
Hackers in the Dewey, vi *Mage* Win,1987
Mr. Wizard, ss *Mage* Spr,1987

Davison, Gary
Cartoon, ct *Twilight Zone* Dec,1987

Dawes, Joseph
Cartoon, ct *F&SF* May,1987
Cartoon, ct *F&SF* Sep,1987
Cartoon, ct *F&SF* Oct,1987

Day, Chet
Halo, n. Pocket Oct,1987

de Avalle-Arce, Diane
Cordoba to Die, ss *Apex!* #1,1987

de Camp, Catherine Crook & L. Sprague de
Camp
The Incorporated Knight, n. Phantasia
Press Aug,1987

de Camp, L. Sprague
Rubber Dinosaurs and Wooden Elephants,
ar *Analog* mid-Dec,1987

de Camp, L. Sprague & Catherine Crook de
Camp
The Incorporated Knight, n. Phantasia
Press Aug,1987

de Lint, Charles
Ascian in Rose, na Axolotl Press: Seattle WA
hc Apr,1987
Jack the Giant Killer, n. Ace Nov,1987
Uncle Dobbin's Parrot Fair, nv *IASFM*
Nov,1987
The Weeping Oak, ss **Sword and
Sorceress** #4, ed. Marion Zimmer
Bradley,1987
The White Road, nv **Tales of the Witch
World**, ed. Andre Norton, St. Martin's,1987
A Wish Named Arnold, ss **Spaceships &
Spells**, ed. Jane Yolen, Martin H.
Greenberg & Charles G. Waugh, Harper &
Row,1987

de Teran, Lisa St. Aubin
Diamond Jim, ss **The Virago Book of
Ghost Stories**, ed. Richard Dalby,
Virago,1987

Dean, Pamela
Paint the Meadows with Delight, nv **Liavek:
Wizard's Row**, ed. Will Shetterly & Emma
Bull, Ace,1987

Dean, Sandy
Cartoon, ct *Aboriginal SF* Feb,1987

DeChancie, John & Thomas F. Monteleone
Crooked House, n. Tor Dec,1987

Decker, A.M.
So Beautiful She Was, pm *Minnesota
Fantasy Review* #1,1987

DeClements, Barthe & Christopher Greimes
Double Trouble, n. Viking Apr,1987

DeCles, Jon
The Particolored Unicorn, n. Ace Dec,1987

DeHaven, Tom
U.S.S.A. Book 1, n. Avon Feb,1987

Deitz, Tom
Fireshaper's Doom, n. Avon Dec,1987

Delany, Samuel R.
The Bridge of Lost Desire, co Arbor House
Nov,1987
Films, mr *Night Cry* v2#3,1987
The Game of Time and Pain, na **The Bridge
of Lost Desire**, Arbor House,1987
The Tale of Rumor and Desire, na *Callaloo*
Spr,1987

Delap, Richard & Walt Lee
Shapes, n. Ace Charter Feb,1987

DeLong, Dan & Tom Pace
Cheap But Not Dirty: Proposal for a
Spaceplane, ar *Analog* Mar,1987

Dembicer, Peggy
Punk Funeral, pm *Grue* #6,1987

Denis, John
Goliath, n. Fontana Mar,1987

Dennis, Ian
The Prince of Stars, n. Unwin Nov,1987

Dent, Lester
The Sinister Ray, co Gryphon Oct,1987

Denton, Bradley
Baker's Dozen, nv **Liavek: Wizard's Row**,
ed. Will Shetterly & Emma Bull, Ace,1987

Despain, Dezra & Margaret Weis
Raistlin's Daughter, nv **DragonLance Tales**
v3, Margaret Weis & Tracy Hickman,
TSR,1987

Devenport, Emily
Shade and the Elephant Man, ss *Aboriginal
SF* May,1987
Skin Deep, ss *Aboriginal SF* Sep,1987

Devin, John
Daemon, pm *Amazing* Jul,1987
A Detached Interpretation of Voyager's
Greeting to Extraterrestrials, pm *Amazing*
Mar,1987
Light Reading, pm *Amazing* Jan,1987
This Too Is Science:, pm *Amazing* May,1987

DeWeese, Gene
The Calvin Nullifier, n. Putnam Philomel
Nov,1987
Star Trek #32: Chain of Attack, n. Pocket
Feb,1987

Di Filippo, Paul
Agents, ss *F&SF* Apr,1987
Conspiracy of Noise, nv *F&SF* Nov,1987
Kid Charlemagne, ss *Amazing* Sep,1987
Little Doors, nv *Night Cry* v2#5,1987
Winter in America, ss *New Pathways*
Aug,1987

DiCarlantonio, Martin
Motherland, n. Ansunda Publications
Apr,1987

Dick, Philip K.
Cadbury, the Beaver Who Lacked, ss **The
Little Black Box**, Underwood/Miller,1987
**The Collected Stories of Philip K. Dick,
Vol. Five: The Little Black Box**, co
Underwood-Miller May,1987
**The Collected Stories of Philip K. Dick,
Vol. Four: The Days of Perky Pat**, co
Underwood-Miller May,1987
**The Collected Stories of Philip K. Dick,
Vol. One: Beyond Lies the Wub**, co
Underwood-Miller May,1987
**The Collected Stories of Philip K. Dick,
Vol. Three: The Father Thing**, co
Underwood-Miller May,1987
**The Collected Stories of Philip K. Dick,
Vol. Two: Second Variety**, co Underwood-
Miller May,1987
Cosmogony and Cosmology, nf Kerosina
Nov,1987

DICK, PHILIP K.

Dick, Philip K. (continued)
The Day Mr. Computer Fell out of its Tree, ss **The Little Black Box**, Underwood/Miller,1987
The Eye of the Sibyl, ss **Philip K. Dick: The Dream Connection**, D. Scott Apel, Permanent Press,1987
Mary and the Giant, n. Arbor House Mar,1987
Stability, ss **Beyond Lies the Wub**, Underwood/Miller,1987
A Terran Odyssey, nv **The Little Black Box**, Underwood/Miller,1987

Dick, Philip K., D. Scott Apel & Kevin C. Briggs
Philip K. Dick in Interview, iv **Philip K. Dick: The Dream Connection**, D. Scott Apel, Permanent Press,1987

Dicks, Terrance
The Ambassadors of Death, n. W.H. Allen May,1987
The Mysterious Planet, n. W.H. Allen Nov,1987

Dickson, Gordon R.
In the Bone: The Best Science Fiction of Gordon R. Dickson, co Ace Mar,1987
The Stranger, co Tor Mar,1987
Way of the Pilgrim, n. Ace May,1987

Dickson, Ray Clark
Landmarks of the Laboratory, pm *Pulpsmith* Win,1987

Dieckman, S.B.
Cousin Jo, ss *Haunts* #9,1987

Dietz, William C.
Freehold, n. Ace Mar,1987

Dillard, J.M.
Bloodthirst, n. Titan Dec,1987
Star Trek #37: Bloodthirst, n. Pocket Dec,1987

Dillard, Janice
Clawing at the Moon, pm *Footsteps* Nov,1987

Dillingham, Peter
Psi-Rec: Priest of Roses, Paladin of Swords, the War Within, pm **There Will Be War** v6, ed. Jerry E. Pournelle,1987

Dillon, William P.
One April Day, ss *Grue* #4,1987

Disch, Thomas M.
Fool's Mate, pm *Amazing* May,1987
In the News, pm *Night Cry* v2#5,1987
The Pair of Them, pm *Night Cry* v2#5,1987
Palindrome, ss *Omni* Sep,1987
Rude Awakening, vi *Omni* May,1987
Three Sprites, pm *Night Cry* v2#4,1987

Dodds, Bill
Crime of Passion, ss *Aphelion* #5,1987

Doggett, Ken
The Villain, ss *Space & Time* #72,1987

Dolan, Harry
The Dwarf Who Knew Too Much, ss *Mage* Win,1987

Dolan, Harry & Virgil Finlay
A Virgil Finlay Portfolio, pi *Mage* Spr,1987

Donaldson, Stephen R.
A Man Rides Through, n. Ballantine/Del Rey Nov,1987

Donohue, Trevor & Paul Collins
Waltz of the Flowers, ss *Aphelion* #5,1987

Dooley, Dennis & Gary Engle
Superman at Fifty: The Persistence of a Legend, nf Octavia Oct,1987

Doran, Colleen
A Distant Soil, gn Donning/Starblaze Sep,1987

Dorcey, Mary
The Fate of Aoife and the Children of Aobh, ss **Mad and Bad Fairies**, ed. Anonymous, Attic Press,1987

Dorsey, Candas Jane
Willows, ss **Tesseracts 2**, ed. Phyllis Gotlieb & Douglas Barbour, Press Porcepic: Victoria,1987

Douglas, Carole Nelson
Keepers of Edanvant, n. Tor May,1987

Dowling, David
Fictions of Nuclear Disaster, nf Univ. of Iowa Press Feb,1987

Dowling, Terry
For as Long as You Burn, nv *Aphelion* #5,1987

Downer, Ann
The Spellkey, n. Atheneum Oct,1987

Downie, Jill
The Raven in the Glass, n. Paperjacks Oct,1987

Dozois, Gardner R.
Alice Sheldon (1915-1987), bg *IASFM* Oct,1987

Dozois, Gardner R., ed.
Isaac Asimov's Science Fiction Magazine [v.11 # 1, January 1987]
Isaac Asimov's Science Fiction Magazine [v.11 # 2, February 1987]
Isaac Asimov's Science Fiction Magazine [v.11 # 3, March 1987]
Isaac Asimov's Science Fiction Magazine [v.11 # 4, April 1987]
Isaac Asimov's Science Fiction Magazine [v.11 # 5, May 1987]
Isaac Asimov's Science Fiction Magazine [v.11 # 6, June 1987]
Isaac Asimov's Science Fiction Magazine [v.11 # 7, July 1987]
Isaac Asimov's Science Fiction Magazine [v.11 # 8, August 1987]
Isaac Asimov's Science Fiction Magazine [v.11 # 9, September 1987]
Isaac Asimov's Science Fiction Magazine [v.11 #10, October 1987]
Isaac Asimov's Science Fiction Magazine [v.11 #11, November 1987]
Isaac Asimov's Science Fiction Magazine [v.11 #12, December 1987]
Isaac Asimov's Science Fiction Magazine [v.11 #13, Mid-December 1987]
The Year's Best Science Fiction, Fourth Annual Collection, an St. Martin's May,1987

Dozois, Gardner R. & Susan Casper
The Stray, ss *Twilight Zone* Dec,1987

Dozois, Gardner R. & Jack M. Dann, eds.
Demons!, an Ace Jul,1987

Drake, David
Bargain, nv **Masters of Hell**, ed. Janet Morris et al, Baen,1987
The Bull, nv *Whispers* #23,1987
Counting the Cost, n. Baen Nov,1987
The Fool, nv *Whispers* #6, ed. Stuart David Schiff,1987
Hammer's Slammers, co Baen Apr,1987
Hog, ss **World Fantasy Convention Program Book** #13,1987
Inheritor, na **Aftermath**, ed. Robert Lynn Asprin & Lynn Abbey, Ace,1987
Learning Curve, nv **Angels in Hell**, ed. Janet Morris, Baen,1987
Liberty Port, na **Free Lancers**, ed. Elizabeth Mitchell, Baen,1987
Springs Eternal, nv **Crusaders in Hell**, ed. Janet Morris, New York: Baen,1987

Drake, David & Janet Morris
Kill Ratio, n. Ace Oct,1987

Drew, Wayland
Batteries Not Included, n. Berkley Dec,1987

Drexler, Eric & Chris Peterson
Nanotechnology, ar *Analog* mid-Dec,1987

Drippe', Colleen
Little People, ss *Apex!* #1,1987
Standard Procedure, ss *2AM* Spr,1987
Viewpoint: A Few Small Press Magazines, br *Apex!* #1,1987
The Yard, ss *Grue* #6,1987

Drumm, D.B.
Traveler #11: The Children's Crusade, n. Dell Feb,1987
Traveler #12: The Prey, n. Dell Sep,1987
Traveler #13: Ghost Dancers, n. Dell Dec,1987

du Maurier, Daphne
Classics of the Macabre, co Gollancz Sep,1987
Daphne Du Maurier's Classics of the Macabre, co Doubleday Nov,1987

Duane, Diane E. & Peter Morwood
The Romulan Way, n. Titan Aug,1987
Star Trek #35: The Romulan Way, n. Pocket Aug,1987

Dudley, Terence
K9 and Company, n. Target Oct,1987

Dumars, Denise
I am myself, pm *Grue* #4,1987
I Bid You Welcome, pm *Weirdbook* #22,1987
Soliloquy, pm *Grue* #6,1987

Duncan, Dan
Harmonica Song, pm **There Will Be War** v6, ed. Jerry E. Pournelle,1987

Duncan, Dave
A Rose-Red City, n. Ballantine/Del Rey Apr,1987
Shadow, n. Ballantine/Del Rey Nov,1987

Dunn, J.R.
Long Knives, nv **L. Ron Hubbard Presents Writers of the Future** v3, ed. Algis Budrys, Bridge,1987

Dunn, Marylois
Cat and the Other, nv **Tales of the Witch World**, ed. Andre Norton, St. Martin's,1987

Durkin, Barbara W.
Irene, Good Night, ss *Whispers* #23,1987

Dutcher, Roger L.
Gravity Has Always Been Our Enemy, pm *IASFM* Oct,1987
Losing Souls to California Dreaming, pm *IASFM* Sep,1987

Dutcher, Roger L. & Robert Frazier
Nazca Lines, pm *IASFM* May,1987

Dvorkin, David
Budspy, n. Franklin Watts Oct,1987

Earl, Stephen
Hanuman, ss **Gollancz - Sunday Times Best SF Stories**, Gollancz,1987

Earnshaw, Brian
Starclipper and the Galactic Final, n. Pied Piper Mar,1987

Easton, M. Coleman
The Fisherman's Curse, n. Popular Library Questar Feb,1987
Swimmers Beneath the Bright, n. Popular Library Questar Sep,1987

Easton, Richard
The Rivalry, ss *The Virginia Quarterly Review* Win,1987

Easton, Thomas A.
The Reference Library, br *Analog* Jan,1987
The Reference Library, br *Analog* Feb,1987
The Reference Library, br *Analog* Mar,1987
The Reference Library, br *Analog* Apr,1987
The Reference Library, br *Analog* May,1987
The Reference Library, br *Analog* Jun,1987
The Reference Library, br *Analog* Jul,1987
The Reference Library, br *Analog* Aug,1987
The Reference Library, br *Analog* Sep,1987
The Reference Library, br *Analog* Oct,1987
The Reference Library, br *Analog* Nov,1987
The Reference Library, br *Analog* Dec,1987
The Reference Library, br *Analog* mid-Dec,1987

Eddings, David
Guardians of the West, n. Ballantine/Del Rey Apr,1987
Guardians of the West, n. Bantam UK Apr,1987

Edler, Peter
Dan'l Boone Kilt a Saucer Here, ss *Pulpsmith* Win,1987

Edmondson, G.C. & C.M. Kotlan
Maximum Effort, n. Ballantine/Del Rey Nov,1987

Edward, Ames J.
The Force, n. Leisure Apr,1987

Edwards, Claudia J.
Bright and Shining Tiger, n. Popular Library Questar Jan,1988

Edwards, Claudia J. (continued)
A Horsewoman in Godsland, n. Popular Library Questar Jul,1987

Edwards, Paul
The Courage of Friends, ss **Friends of the Horseclans**, ed. Robert Adams & Pamela Crippen Adams, Signet,1987

Effinger, George Alec
Another Dead Grandfather, ss *F&SF* Dec,1987
Glimmer, Glimmer, ss *Playboy* Nov,1987
King of the Cyber Rifles, ss *IASFM* mid-Dec,1987
The Man Who Devoured Literature, ss *Twilight Zone* Apr,1987
Maureen Birnbaum on the Art of War, nv **Friends of the Horseclans**, ed. Robert Adams & Pamela Crippen Adams, Signet,1987
Skylab Done It, nv *F&SF* Mar,1987
So Shall Ye Reap, ss *Analog* Aug,1987

Egan, Greg
Neighbourhood Watch, ss *Aphelion* #5,1987

Egan, Thomas M.
Shelob's Dreme, pm *Eldritch Tales* #13,1987

Eggleton, Bob
On Exhibit, il *Amazing* Sep,1987

Eisenstein, Phyllis
Weasling Out, ss *Whispers* #23,1987

Elflandsson, Galad
A Overruling Passion, nv **Doom City**, ed. Charles L. Grant, Tor,1987

Elgin, Suzette Haden
Native Tongue II: The Judas Rose, n. DAW Feb,1987

Eliot, Marc
How Dear the Dawn, n. Ballantine Aug,1987

Elliott, Janice
The King Awakes, n. Walker Aug,1987

Elliott, Nathan
Innerspace, n. Dragon Dec,1987
Kidnap in Space, n. Dragon Oct,1987
Plague Moon, n. Dragon Oct,1987
Treasure Planet, n. Dragon Oct,1987

Elliott, Richard
The Einstein Legacy, n. Ballantine Fawcett Dec,1987

Ellison, Harlan
The Deadly "Nackles" Affair, ar *Twilight Zone* Feb,1987
Dept. of "What Was the Question?" Dept., ms **The Essential Ellison**, Nemo Press,1987
The Essential Ellison, co Nemo Press Aug,1987
Flintlock: An Unproduced Teleplay (1972), pl **The Essential Ellison**, Nemo Press,1987
Harlan Ellison's Watching, mr *F&SF* Feb,1987
Harlan Ellison's Watching, mr *F&SF* Apr,1987
Harlan Ellison's Watching, mr *F&SF* May,1987
Harlan Ellison's Watching, mr *F&SF* Jul,1987

Ellison, Harlan (continued)
Harlan Ellison's Watching, mr *F&SF* Sep,1987
Harlan Ellison's Watching, mr *F&SF* Oct,1987
I, Robot: The Movie [Part 1 of 3], sl *IASFM* Nov,1987
I, Robot: The Movie [Part 2 of 3], sl *IASFM* Dec,1987
I, Robot: The Movie [Part 3 of 3], sl *IASFM* mid-Dec,1987
Me 'n' Isaac at the Movies, ar *IASFM* Nov,1987
Nackles, pl *Twilight Zone* Feb,1987

Elphinstone, Margaret
The Incomer, n. The Women's Press May,1987

Ely, Scott
Starlight, n. Weidenfeld & Nicolson Apr,1987

Emerson, Ru
In the Caves of Exile, n. Ace Jan,1988
To the Haunted Mountains, n. Ace Feb,1987

Emshwiller, Carol
The Circular Library of Stones, ss *Omni* Feb,1987
Vilcabamba, ss *Twilight Zone* Aug,1987

Emshwiller, Peter R.
Illuminations: Prophet of the "Damned", ar *Twilight Zone* Oct,1987
Illuminations: Red SF, ar *Twilight Zone* Feb,1987
The Other Side: King Kong Lived, ar *Twilight Zone* Apr,1987

Eng, Steve
Forays into Derleth Country, ar *Eldritch Tales* #13,1987
The Isle of the Torturers, pm *Eldritch Tales* #14,1987
Profile: John Gawsworth, bg *Night Cry* v2#3,1987
To Not Return, pm *Space & Time* #73,1987

Engh, M.J.
Aurin Tree, nv *IASFM* Feb,1987
The House in the Snow, n. Franklin Watts Orchard Aug,1987

Engle, Gary & Dennis Dooley
Superman at Fifty: The Persistence of a Legend, nf Octavia Oct,1987

Englund, Robert, Wes Craven & Heather Langencamp
Nightmare on Elm Street 3, iv *The Horror Show* Spr,1987

Engstrom, Elizabeth
The Final Tale, ss *Eldritch Tales* #13,1987
The Old Woman Upstairs, ss *2AM* Win,1987

Erskine, Barbara
Lady of Hay, n. Delacorte Jun,1987

Escott, Les & K.W. Jeter
K.W. Jeter, iv *Interzone* #22,1987

Estes, Rose
Greyhawk Adventures #3: Master Wolf, n. TSR Apr,1987
Greyhawk Adventures #4: The Price of Power, n. TSR Aug,1987

Estes, Rose (continued)
Saga of the Lost Lands, Volume 1: Blood of the Tiger, n. Bantam Spectra Dec,1987

Etchemendy, Nancy
The Flat-Brimmed Hat, ss *Twilight Zone* Apr,1987
Lunch at Etienne's, ss *F&SF* Nov,1987

Etchison, Dennis
Fragments of Horror, ms *The Horror Show* Win,1987
The Scar, ss *The Horror Show* Win,1987

Etchison, Dennis, ed.
Masters of Darkness II, an Tor Jan,1988

Etchison, Dennis & William J. Grabowski
Dennis Etchison, iv *The Horror Show* Win,1987

Evans, Christopher
The Facts of Life, ss **Other Edens**, ed. Christopher Evans & Robert Holdstock, Unwin: London,1987

Evans, Christopher & Robert Holdstock, eds.
Other Edens, oa Unwin Jul,1987

Everman, Welch D.
Video, ar *Twilight Zone* Feb,1987
Video, ar *Twilight Zone* Jun,1987

Ewart, Christopher
A Day in the Life, ss **L. Ron Hubbard Presents Writers of the Future** v3, ed. Algis Budrys, Bridge,1987

Ewing, George M.
A Little Further Up the Fox..., nv *IASFM* Apr,1987

Fabian, Stephen E.
On Exhibit, il *Amazing* Mar,1987

Fairley, John & Simon Welfare
Arthur C. Clarke's Chronicles of the Strange and Mysterious, nf Collins Dec,1987

Falconer, Sovereign
To Make Death Love Us, n. Doubleday Jul,1987

Fancher, Jane
Gate of Ivrel: Claiming Rites, gn Donning/Starblaze Sep,1987

Farber, Sharon N.
Billy Jean at Sea, ss *Amazing* Jul,1987
Ice Dreams, ss *IASFM* Mar,1987

Farmer, Penelope
Emma in Winter, n. Dell/Yearling Nov,1987

Farmer, Philip Jose
Dayworld Rebel, n. Ace/Putnam Jun,1987

Farren, Mick
Their Master's War, n. Ballantine/Del Rey Jan,1988

Farris, John
Nightfall, n. Tor Apr,1987

Farris, Joseph
Cartoon, ct *F&SF* Feb,1987
Cartoon, ct *F&SF* Mar,1987

Farris, Joseph (continued)
Cartoon, ct *F&SF* Apr,1987
Cartoon, ct *F&SF* May,1987
Cartoon, ct *F&SF* Oct,1987
Cartoon, ct *F&SF* Dec,1987

Faulcon, Robert
The Ghost Dance, om Arrow Jul,1987
The Labyrinth, n. Arrow Jun,1987
Night Hunter, n. Ace Charter Jul,1987
Night Hunter 2: The Talisman, n. Ace Charter Sep,1987
Night Hunter 3: The Ghost Dance, n. Ace Charter Nov,1987
The Stalking, om Arrow Jul,1987

Faust, Joe Clifford
A Death of Honor, n. Ballantine/Del Rey Feb,1987
The Helium Farewell, ss *Haunts* #9,1987

Feeley, Gregory & John Crowley
John Crowley Interview, iv *Interzone* #21,1987

Feggo
Cartoon, ct *Twilight Zone* Jun,1987
Cartoon, ct *Twilight Zone* Aug,1987
Cartoon, ct *Twilight Zone* Oct,1987

Feist, Raymond E.
Faerie Tale: The Thing Beneath the Bridge, ex *Twilight Zone* Dec,1987

Feist, Raymond E. & Janny Wurts
Daughter of the Empire, n. Doubleday Jun,1987

Felgenhauer, H.R.
Reach Out and Scorch Someone, pm *Mage* Win,1987

Fenn, Lionel
Agnes Day, n. Tor Aug,1987
Getting Down with Lionel Fenn, iv *American Fantasy* Sum,1987
Web of Defeat, n. Tor Feb,1987

Fenoglio, Mary
The Promise, nv **Red Sun of Darkover**, ed. Marion Zimmer Bradley & The Friends of Darkover, DAW,1987

Ferguson, Brad
The World Next Door, ss *IASFM* Sep,1987

Ferguson, Neil
The Second Third of C, ss *Interzone* #19,1987

Ferguson, Syn
The Tree-Wife of Arketh, ss **Sword and Sorceress** #4, ed. Marion Zimmer Bradley,1987

Fergusson, Bruce
The Shadow of His Wings, n. Arbor House Feb,1987

Fergusson, Bruce Chandler
The Bloodsnare, ss *Space & Time* #72,1987

Ferman, Edward L., ed.
The Magazine of Fantasy & Science Fiction [v.72 #1, January 1987]
The Magazine of Fantasy & Science Fiction [v.72 #2, February 1987]

Ferman, Edward L., ed. (continued)
The Magazine of Fantasy & Science Fiction [v.72 #3, March 1987]
The Magazine of Fantasy & Science Fiction [v.72 #4, April 1987]
The Magazine of Fantasy & Science Fiction [v.72 #5, May 1987]
The Magazine of Fantasy & Science Fiction [v.72 #6, June 1987]
The Magazine of Fantasy & Science Fiction [v.73 #1, July 1987]
The Magazine of Fantasy & Science Fiction [v.73 #2, August 1987]
The Magazine of Fantasy & Science Fiction [v.73 #3, September 1987]
The Magazine of Fantasy & Science Fiction [v.73 #4, October 1987]
The Magazine of Fantasy & Science Fiction [v.73 #5, November 1987]
The Magazine of Fantasy & Science Fiction [v.73 #6, December 1987]

Ferrara, Patricia
Rising Waters, ss *F&SF* Jul,1987

Ferret
Xax Xox, cs *New Pathways* Nov,1987

Ferret, K.W. Jeter & J.B. Reynolds
K.W. Jeter [Part 1], iv *New Pathways* Apr,1987
K.W. Jeter [Part 2], iv *New Pathways* Aug,1987

Ferret & Mink Mole
Grow Your Own Baby, cs *New Pathways* Nov,1987
I Was a Teenage Reptile, cs *New Pathways* Aug,1987
Nuclear FX, cs *New Pathways* Jan,1987
Nuclear FX, cs *New Pathways* Aug,1987
Nuclear FX, cs *New Pathways* Nov,1987

Fialkowski, Konrad R.
Through the Fifth Dimension, ss *SF International* #1,1987

Figueirido, E. Veronica
Paradise, ss *SF International* #2,1987

Filipovic, Dragan R.
Jailhouse Blues, ss *SF International* #2,1987
A Ribbon for Margaret's Doll, ss *SF International* #1,1987

Finch, Sheila
The Garden of the Shaped, n. Bantam Spectra Sep,1987
Hitchhiker, ss *Amazing* Sep,1987

Finlay, D.G.
Graven Image, n. Century Jun,1987

Finlay, Virgil & Harry Dolan
A Virgil Finlay Portfolio, pi *Mage* Spr,1987

Finney, Jack
3 By Finney, om Simon & Schuster Fireside Jul,1987

Fischetti, Joe
The I of the Beholder, ss *Analog* Oct,1987

Fish, Leslie
Amateurs, ss *Night Cry* v2#3,1987
First Night Cruise, nv **Festival Moon**, ed. C.J. Cherryh, DAW,1987

FISH, LESLIE

Fish, Leslie (continued)
Guardian, sg **Festival Moon**, ed. C.J. Cherryh, DAW,1987
War of the Unseen Worlds, nv **Fever Season**, ed. C.J. Cherryh, DAW,1987

Fisk, Nicholas
Brain Blaster, ss **Living Fire and Other S.F. Stories**, Corgi: London,1987
The Golden Lump, nv **Living Fire and Other S.F. Stories**, Corgi: London,1987
The Gun That Didn't Go Bang, nv **Living Fire and Other S.F. Stories**, Corgi: London,1987
Living Fire, ss **Living Fire and Other S.F. Stories**, Corgi: London,1987
Living Fire and Other S.F. Stories, oc Corgi Aug,1987
Love Bytes, ss **Twisted Circuits**, ed. Mick Gowar, Beaver,1987
Mindbenders, n. Viking Kestrel Apr,1987
One is One and All Alone, ss **Living Fire and Other S.F. Stories**, Corgi: London,1987
Susan's Plant, nv **Living Fire and Other S.F. Stories**, Corgi: London,1987

FitzGerald, Gillian
Ties of Faith, nv **Friends of the Horseclans**, ed. Robert Adams & Pamela Crippen Adams, Signet,1987

Fletcher, Adrian & Ryder Syvertsen
Psychic Spawn, n. Popular Library Oct,1987

Fletcher, Hollis
A Letter from Bubba: Extraterrestrials, ss *Amazing* Jul,1987

Flint, Kenneth C.
The Dark Druid, n. Bantam Spectra Aug,1987

Florance-Guthridge, George
Ishbar, The Trueborn, ss *Pulpsmith* Win,1987

Floss, Patricia
The Other Side of the Mirror, na **The Other Side of the Mirror**, ed. Marion Zimmer Bradley & The Friends of Darkover, DAW,1987

Flynn, Michael F.
The Forest of Time, na *Analog* Jun,1987
In the Country of the Blind (Part 1 of 2), sl *Analog* Oct,1987
In the Country of the Blind (Part 2 of 2), sl *Analog* Nov,1987

Foglio, Phil & Robert Lynn Asprin
Myth Adventures Two, gn Donning/Starblaze Jan,1987

Fonstad, Karen Wynn
Atlas of the Dragonlance World, pi TSR Nov,1987

Forbes, Gregory
Auguries, ar *Mage* Win,1987

Ford, John M.
Eel Island Shoals, sg **Liavek: Wizard's Row**, ed. Will Shetterly & Emma Bull, Ace,1987
Green Is the Color, na **Liavek: Wizard's Row**, ed. Will Shetterly & Emma Bull, Ace,1987

Ford, John M. (continued)
How Much for Just the Planet?, n. Titan Oct,1987
Pot-Boil Blues, sg **Liavek: Wizard's Row**, ed. Will Shetterly & Emma Bull, Ace,1987
Star Trek #36: How Much for Just the Planet?, n. Pocket Oct,1987
Tales from the Original Gothic, ss **The Architecture of Fear**, ed. Kathryn Cramer & Peter D. Pautz, Arbor House,1987

Forde, Pat
The Gift, nv *Analog* Dec,1987

Forrest, Katherine V.
Benny's Place, ss **Dreams and Swords**, Naiad,1987
Dreams and Swords, oc Naiad Sep,1987
Force Majeur, ss **Dreams and Swords**, Naiad,1987
The Gift, ss **Dreams and Swords**, Naiad,1987
Jessie, nv **Dreams and Swords**, Naiad,1987
Mandy Larkin, ss **Dreams and Swords**, Naiad,1987
Mother Was an Alien, ss **Dreams and Swords**, Naiad,1987
O Captain, My Captain, na **Dreams and Swords**, Naiad,1987
Survivor, ss **Dreams and Swords**, Naiad,1987
The Test, ss **Dreams and Swords**, Naiad,1987

Forrester, John
Beneath Their Blue, Blue Skins, nv **Spaceships & Spells**, ed. Jane Yolen, Martin H. Greenberg & Charles G. Waugh, Harper & Row,1987

Forstchen, William R.
The Alexandrian Ring, n. Ballantine/Del Rey Oct,1987

Forsyth, Jeremy
Nestled, ss *New Blood* #1,1987

Fortier, Ron & Ardath Mayhar
Trail of the Seahawks, n. TSR/Windwalker Jun,1987

Fortschen, William R.
By Thought Alone, ss **There Will Be War** v6, ed. Jerry E. Pournelle,1987

Forward, Robert L.
Magic Matter, ar **New Destinies** v1, ed. Jim Baen, Baen,1987

Foster, Alan Dean
The Deluge Drivers, n. Ballantine/Del Rey Jun,1987
Glory Lane, n. Ace Aug,1987
Norg Gleeble Gop, ss *F&SF* Aug,1987
The Right Shuttle, ar *Amazing* May,1987
Spellsinger's Scherzo, om SFBC May,1987
The Thunderer, ss *F&SF* Apr,1987

Foster, John, ed.
Spaceways, an Salem House/Oxford Apr,1987

Fowler, Christopher
Final Call for Passenger Paul, ss **The Pan Book of Horror Stories** #28, Pan,1987

FRAZIER, ROBERT

Fowler, Karen Joy
The Faithful Companion at Forty, ss *IASFM* Jul,1987
Letters From Home, ss **In the Field of Fire**, ed. Jeanne Van Buren Dann & Jack M. Dann, Tor,1987

Fox, Janet
Mirror Trick, ss *Tales of the Unanticipated* #2,1987
Strands, ss *Grue* #6,1987
When Jaquerel Walked With Shadows, ss *Weirdbook* #22,1987

Foy, George
Hellbike, ss **Masters of Hell**, ed. Janet Morris et al, Baen,1987

Frahm, Leanne
The Supramarket, ss **Doom City**, ed. Charles L. Grant, Tor,1987

Frame, Ronald
Some Common Misunderstandings about Ghosts, ss **A Quiver of Ghosts**, ed. Aiden Chambers, Bodley Head,1987

Frankel, Linda & Paula Crunk
Blood Hunt, na **The Other Side of the Mirror**, ed. Marion Zimmer Bradley & The Friends of Darkover, DAW,1987

Franklin, Cheryl J.
Fire Get, n. DAW Nov,1987

Frankowski, Leo A.
Copernick's Rebellion, n. Ballantine/Del Rey Apr,1987

Franson, Donald
Call Me Fearful, ss *Eldritch Tales* #14,1987

Frazier, Robert
Across Those Endless Skies, ss **In the Field of Fire**, ed. Jeanne Van Buren Dann & Jack M. Dann, Tor,1987
Birds of the Mutant Rain Forest, pm *IASFM* Mar,1987
The Chrononaut Visits the Famous Pair During Their First Experiment, pm *IASFM* Jul,1987
Cyclopean Hours August 27, 1883, pm *IASFM* Aug,1987
Dreamtigers, ss *Amazing* Mar,1987
Encased in the Amber of Probabilities, pm *IASFM* Mar,1987
Erasure, pm *Amazing* Nov,1987
Hollywood Revisited: The Body Snatchers, pm *IASFM* Feb,1987
Letter to a Grandchild, pm *IASFM* Apr,1987
"A mathematical formula is a hymn of the universe.", pm **Perception Barriers**, BPW&P: Berkeley CA,1987
The Original 11 Observations of Methuselah, pm *IASFM* Aug,1987
Overseas Call, pm *IASFM* Oct,1987
Perception Barriers, co BPW&P Aug,1987
Relative Distances, pm *Amazing* Mar,1987
Tracking Through the Mutant Rain Forest, pm *IASFM* May,1987
Twinned Stars: Newton & Halley, pm **Perception Barriers**, BPW&P: Berkeley CA,1987
Upon Hearing New Evidence That Meteors Caused the Great Extinctions, pm *Amazing* Jan,1987

FRAZIER, ROBERT

Frazier, Robert & Roger L. Dutcher
Nazca Lines, pm *IASFM* May,1987

Frazier, Robert & Andrew Joron
Exiled of Worlds, pm *Amazing* Sep,1987

Freas, Frank Kelly
Portfolio, pi **World Fantasy Convention Program Book** #13,1987

Frezza, Robert A.
Max Weber's War, ss *Amazing* Jan,1987

Friedman, C.S.
In Conquest Born, n. DAW May,1987

Friedman, Michael Jan
The Glove of Maiden's Hair, n. Popular Library Questar Mar,1987

Friends of Darkover, The & Marion Zimmer Bradley
The Other Side of the Mirror, oa DAW Feb,1987
Red Sun of Darkover, oa DAW Nov,1987

Friesner, Esther M.
Honeycomb, nv **Magic in Ithkar** #4, ed. Andre Norton & Robert Adams,1987
The Other Side: Now Revealed: Money-Making Secrets of the Shockmeisters, ar *Twilight Zone* Dec,1987
The Witchwood Cradle, n. Avon Mar,1987

Frith, Nigel
Dragon, n. Unwin Jul,1987

Froehlich, Bill & Cory Glaberson
Interview with Bill Froehlich, iv *American Fantasy* Win,1987

Froehlich, Joey
Ethics and the Work Place, pm *Apex!* #1,1987
Haunted City of the Moon, pm *Eldritch Tales* #13,1987
Moon Boats Taken from the Earth, pm *Space & Time* #72,1987
Singing Nightmares, pm *Grue* #5,1987

Frost, Polly
Fast Forward to the Past, ss *New Yorker* Jul 6,1987
Plan 10 from Zone R-3, ss *New Yorker* Apr 13,1987

Funnell, Augustine
Cat at Play, ss *Night Cry* v2#3,1987
Maxie Silas, ss *F&SF* Jun,1987

Furlong, Monica
Wise Child, n. Knopf Oct,1987

Gabbard, G.N.
Der Golem, pm *2AM* Win,1987

Gadallah, Leslie
Cat's Pawn, n. Ballantine/Del Rey Mar,1987

Gafford, Sam
The Horseman, vi *Eldritch Tales* #14,1987

Gaiman, Neil
Don't Panic: The Official Hitch Hiker's Guide to the Galaxy Companion, nf Titan Jan,1988

Gaiman, Neil & Alan Moore
Alan Moore Interview, iv *American Fantasy* Win,1987

Gallagher, Stephen
Like Clockwork, ss *F&SF* Mar,1987
Like Shadows in the Dark, ss **Shadows** #10, ed. Charles L. Grant,1987
Valley of Lights, n. NEL Jun,1987

Ganley, W. Paul
Editorial, ed *Weirdbook* #22,1987

Ganley, W. Paul, ed.
Weirdbook 22 [Summer 1987]

Garcia y Robertson, R.
The Flying Mountain, nv *Amazing* May,1987
Moon of Popping Trees, nv *Amazing* Sep,1987

Garcia, Nancy
Date with an Angel, mr *American Fantasy* Spr,1987
Shared Secrets: Inside the World of Shared Worlds, ar *American Fantasy* Spr,1987
Thieves' World, ar *American Fantasy* Spr,1987

Garcia, Nancy, Clive Barker & Robert T. Garcia
Clive Barker Interview, iv *American Fantasy* Win,1987

Garcia, Nancy, Ramsey Campbell & Robert T. Garcia
Ramsey Campbell Interview, iv *American Fantasy* Win,1987

Garcia, Nancy & Robert T. Garcia
Editorial, ed *American Fantasy* Spr,1987
Editorial, ed *American Fantasy* Sum,1987
Editorial, ed *American Fantasy* Win,1987

Garcia, Nancy & Robert T. Garcia, eds.
American Fantasy [v.2 #2, Winter 1987]
American Fantasy [v.2 #3, Spring 1987]
American Fantasy [v.2 #4, Summer 1987]

Garcia, Nancy, Andre Norton & Mary Frances Zambreno
Andre Norton Interview and Bibliography, iv *American Fantasy* Win,1987

Garcia, Robert T.
Esoteric References, br *American Fantasy* Sum,1987

Garcia, Robert T., Clive Barker & Nancy Garcia
Clive Barker Interview, iv *American Fantasy* Win,1987

Garcia, Robert T., Ramsey Campbell & Nancy Garcia
Ramsey Campbell Interview, iv *American Fantasy* Win,1987

Garcia, Robert T. & Nancy Garcia
Editorial, ed *American Fantasy* Spr,1987
Editorial, ed *American Fantasy* Sum,1987
Editorial, ed *American Fantasy* Win,1987

Garcia, Robert T. & Nancy Garcia, eds.
American Fantasy [v.2 #2, Winter 1987]
American Fantasy [v.2 #3, Spring 1987]
American Fantasy [v.2 #4, Summer 1987]

Gardam, Jane
Through the Dolls' House Door, n. Morrow/Greenwillow Oct,1987

Garden, Nancy
The Door Between, n. Farrar, Straus & Giroux Aug,1987
Mystery of the Night Raiders, n. Farrar, Straus & Giroux Oct,1987

Gardner, Craig Shaw
Demon Luck, ss **Magic in Ithkar** #4, ed. Andre Norton & Robert Adams,1987
A Difficulty With Dwarves, n. Ace Dec,1987
The Exploits of Ebenezvm, om SFBC Nov,1987
The Lost Boys, n. Berkley Jul,1987
A Night in the Netherhells, n. Ace: New York pb Jun,1987
A Night in the Netherhells, n. Ace Jun,1987
She Closed Her Eyes, nv **Doom City**, ed. Charles L. Grant, Tor,1987

Gardner, Martin
Mysterious Smith, ss **The No-Sided Professor**, Prometheus,1987
The No-Sided Professor, co Prometheus Apr 15,1987
Ranklin Felano Doosevelt, ss **The No-Sided Professor**, Prometheus,1987
The Stranger, vi **The No-Sided Professor**, Prometheus,1987

Garey, Terry A.
The Beach Poet, ed *Tales of the Unanticipated* #2,1987

Garey, Terry A., Eric M. Heideman, Damon Knight & Kate Wilhelm
An Interview with Kate Wilhelm and Damon Knight, iv *Tales of the Unanticipated* #2,1987

Garfield, Frances
A Dream of Castles, ss **World Fantasy Convention Program Book** #13,1987

Garnett, Bill
The Crone, n. St. Martin's Aug,1987

Garnett, David S.
Moonlighter, ss **Other Edens**, ed. Christopher Evans & Robert Holdstock, Unwin: London,1987
The Only One, ss *Interzone* #22,1987

Garrett, Randall
Into My Parlor, vi **Takeoff Too!**, Norfolk, VA: Donning/Starblaze,1987
Takeoff Too!, co Donning/Starblaze Apr,1987

Garrido, Mar
Eileen Goudge's Swept Away #6: Once Upon a Kiss, n. Avon/Flare May,1987

Garton, Ray
Fragments of Horror, ms *The Horror Show* Fll,1987

Gauger, Rick
Charon's Ark, n. Ballantine/Del Rey Aug,1987

Gay, Anne
Wishbone, ss **Gollancz - Sunday Times Best SF Stories**, Gollancz,1987

GEARY, PATRICIA

GRANT, CHARLES L.

Geary, Patricia
Strange Toys, n. Bantam Spectra Jul,1987

Geduld, Harry M.
The Definitive Time Machine: A Critical Edition of H.G. Wells' Scientific Romance, n. Indiana Univ. Press Sep,1987

Gemmell, David
Wolf in Shadow, n. Century Aug,1987

Gentle, Mary
Ancient Light, n. Gollancz Aug,1987

Geras, Adele
Wordfinder, ss **Twisted Circuits**, ed. Mick Gowar, Beaver,1987

Gerberding, Rodger
Frank Utpatel: Wood Engraver, bg *Mage* Win,1987

Gerrold, David
Star Trek, The Next Generation: Encounter at Farpoint, n. Pocket Oct,1987

Gibbins, James
Who's a Clever Boy?, ss **Gollancz - Sunday Times Best SF Stories**, Gollancz,1987

Gibson, William
The Silver Walks, ss *High Times* Nov,1987

Giesler, Andrew
Proallognostication, vi *Analog* Nov,1987

Gilbert, Christopher
Love at the 99th Percentile, ss *F&SF* Nov,1987
Witch Mother, ss *Night Cry* v2#3,1987

Gilbert, Harry
Ghost's Playground, na Piccadilly Jun,1987

Gilden, Mel
Born to Howl, n. Avon/Camelot Dec,1987
M. Is for Monster, nv Avon/Camelot Nov,1987

Gillett, Stephen L., Ph.D.
Weird LAWKI, ar *Amazing* Jul,1987

Gilluly, Sheila
Greenbriar Queen, n. NAL/Signet Jan,1988

Gilman, Carolyn Ives
The Language of the Sea, nv **L. Ron Hubbard Presents Writers of the Future** v3, ed. Algis Budrys, Bridge,1987

Gilster, Paul A.
Merchant Dying, ss *Aboriginal SF* Jul,1987

Giraud, Jean "Moebius"
Arzach and Other Fantasy Stories, pi Marvel/Epic Aug,1987
The Long Tomorrow and Other Science Fiction Stories, pi Marvel/Epic Dec,1987
Moebius 1: Upon a Star, gn Marvel/Epic Jun,1987

Glaberson, Cory
Magic Lantern Show, mr *American Fantasy* Spr,1987
Magic Lantern Show, mr *American Fantasy* Sum,1987

Glaberson, Cory (continued)
Magic Lantern Show, mr *American Fantasy* Win,1987

Glaberson, Cory & Bill Froehlich
Interview with Bill Froehlich, iv *American Fantasy* Win,1987

Glaberson, Cory & Stephen Jones
Hellraiser, mr *American Fantasy* Win,1987

Gladney, Heather
Teot's War, n. Ace May,1987

Gladwin, Philip
Indian Summer, ss **Gollancz - Sunday Times Best SF Stories**, Gollancz,1987

Glave, Thomas, Jr.
Landscape in Black, pm *Pulpsmith* Win,1987

Glover, Julian
Beowulf, pm Alan Sutton Nov,1987

Glut, Donald F., James Kahn & George Lucas
The Star Wars Trilogy, om Ballantine/Del Rey May,1987

Goddin, Jeffrey
The Living Dead, n. Leisure Apr,1987

Goldman, William
Brothers, n. Warner Feb,1987

Goldsmith, Donald
Who Will Speak for Earth? An Essay on Extraterrestrial Intelligence and Contact, ar **Universe**, ed. Byron Preiss, Bantam Spectra,1987

Goldstein, Lisa
Cassandra's Photographs, ss *IASFM* Aug,1987
A Mask for the General, n. Bantam Spectra Nov,1987
The Red Magician, n. Unicorn Feb,1987

Gooding, Paul
The Machine Age, ss **Gollancz - Sunday Times Best SF Stories**, Gollancz,1987

Goodman, Dan
Writing With Percission: Cooking Salmon in the Dishwasher: Nontraditional Computer Use for Science Fiction and Fantasy Writers, Part 1, ar *Tales of the Unanticipated #2*,1987

Gordon, Greg
Buy the Rules?, gr *American Fantasy* Spr,1987
Buy the Rules?, gr *American Fantasy* Win,1987

Gordon, John
The Black Prince, ss **A Quiver of Ghosts**, ed. Aiden Chambers, Bodley Head,1987
User-Friendly, ss **Twisted Circuits**, ed. Mick Gowar, Beaver,1987

Gordon, Stuart
Archon!, n. Macdonald Aug,1987

Gorey, Edward
The Raging Tide, pi Beaufort Nov,1987

Gormley, Beatrice
Richard and the Vratch, n. Avon/Camelot Oct,1987

Gorton, Mark
The Fall, ss **Gollancz - Sunday Times Best SF Stories**, Gollancz,1987

Gotlieb, Phyllis & Douglas Barbour, eds.
Tesseracts 2, an Porcepic Nov,1987

Gotschalk, Felix C.
Menage a Super-Trois, ss *F&SF* May,1987

Goudge, Eileen
Eileen Goudge's Swept Away #4: Star Struck, n. Avon Flare Jan,1987

Goulart, Ron
Business as Usual, ss *F&SF* Jul,1987
The Curse of the Obelisk, n. Avon Nov,1987
Daredevils, Ltd., n. St. Martin's Jun,1987
The Goulart Archipelago, ar *Twilight Zone* Feb,1987
Starpirate's Brain, n. St. Martin's Oct,1987

Gould, Steven
Poppa Was a Catcher, na **New Destinies** v2, ed. Jim Baen, Baen,1987

Gowar, Mick, ed.
Twisted Circuits, oa Beaver Jan,1987

Grabowski, William J.
The Country Wife, vi *Haunts #9*,1987
Swan Song, br *The Horror Show* Spr,1987
Tattler, br *The Horror Show* Jan,1987
Tattler, br *The Horror Show* Spr,1987
Tattler, br *The Horror Show* Sum,1987
Tattler, br *The Horror Show* Fll,1987
Tattler, br *The Horror Show* Win,1987

Grabowski, William J. & Poppy Z. Brite
Poppy Z. Brite, iv *The Horror Show* Fll,1987

Grabowski, William J. & Dennis Etchison
Dennis Etchison, iv *The Horror Show* Win,1987

Grabowski, William J. & Joe R. Lansdale
Interview with Joe R. Lansdale, iv *The Horror Show* Jan,1987

Grabowski, William J. & Bentley Little
Bentley Little, iv *The Horror Show* Fll,1987

Grabowski, William J. & John Maclay
Genre-Love and the Magic of Words: John Maclay, iv *2AM* Fll,1987

Grabowski, William J. & Robert R. McCammon
Interview with Robert R. McCammon, iv *The Horror Show* Spr,1987

Grant, Charles L.
Constant Father, ss **World Fantasy Convention Program Book #13**,1987
Ellen, in Her Time, ss **The Architecture of Fear**, ed. Kathryn Cramer & Peter D. Pautz, Arbor House,1987
Everything to Live For, ss **Whispers #6**, ed. Stuart David Schiff,1987
An Image in Twisted Silver, ss *Twilight Zone* Apr,1987
It Wasn't a Half-Bad Year, br *Amazing* Sep,1987
Listen to the Music in My Hands, ss *Twilight Zone* Feb,1987

GRANT, CHARLES L.

GROVE, VICKI

Grant, Charles L. (continued)
Midnights, br *American Fantasy* Spr,1987
Midnights, br *American Fantasy* Sum,1987
Midnights, br *American Fantasy* Win,1987
One Spring in Wyoming, ss *Aboriginal SF*
Feb,1987
The Sheeted Dead, ss **In the Field of Fire**,
ed. Jeanne Van Buren Dann & Jack M.
Dann, Tor,1987
This Old Man, ss *Night Cry* v2#3,1987

Grant, Charles L., ed.
Doom City, oa Tor Dec,1987
Shadows 10, oa Doubleday Oct,1987

Grant, Charles L. & Douglas E. Winter
A Conversation With Charles L. Grant, iv
Twilight Zone Apr,1987

Grant, Gwen
Bonny Starr and the Riddles of Time, n.
Heinemann Jun,1987

Grant, John & David Langford
Earthdoom!, n. Grafton May,1987

Grant, Kathryn
The Phoenix Bells, n. Ace Mar,1987

Grant, Richard
Rumors of Spring, n. Bantam Spectra
Mar,1987

Grant, Roberta
Catscape, nv *Amazing* Jul,1987

Grass, Gunter
The Rat, n. Harcourt Brace Jovanovich
May,1987

Gray, Linda Crockett
Scryer, n. Tor Mar,1987

Gray, Nicholas Stuart
The Sorcerer's Apprentices, ss St. Martin's
Nov,1987

Greeley, Andrew M.
The Dutchman's Ghost Town, nv *F&SF*
Feb,1987
The Final Planet, n. Warner Jun,1987
Xorinda the Witch, ss *American Fantasy*
Sum,1987

Green, Jen & Sarah Lefanu, eds.
**Despatches from the Frontiers of the
Female Mind**, an Salem House/Women's
Press Mar,1987

Green, Roland J.
The Fantastic Battlefield, ar *Amazing*
Jan,1987
The Leading Edge, br **New Destinies** v2,
ed. Jim Baen, Baen,1987
These Green Foreign Hills, n. Ace
Dec,1987

Green, Roland J. & John F. Carr
Nightfriend, nv **Friends of the Horseclans**,
ed. Robert Adams & Pamela Crippen
Adams, Signet,1987

Green, Scott E.
Roses of Ashes, pm *Eldritch Tales* #14,1987
Slow Roll In Neutral, pm *Eldritch Tales*
#13,1987

Green, Sharon
The Far Side of Forever, n. DAW Jul,1987
Lady Blade, Lord Fighter, n. DAW Dec,1987
A Quiet Day at the Fair, nv **Magic in Ithkar**
#4, ed. Andre Norton & Robert
Adams,1987
The Rebel Prince, n. DAW May,1987
A Vision of Honor, nv **Friends of the
Horseclans**, ed. Robert Adams & Pamela
Crippen Adams, Signet,1987

Green, Terence M.
The Woman Who Is the Midnight Wind, co
Pottersfield Press Apr,1987

Greenberg, Martin H., ed.
**Amazing Science Fiction Stories: The War
Years 1936-1945**, an TSR May,1987
**Amazing Science Fiction Stories: The
Wild Years 1946-1955**, an TSR Aug,1987
**Amazing Science Fiction Stories: The
Wonder Years 1926-1935**, an TSR
Mar,1987
Cinemonsters, an TSR Nov,1987

Greenberg, Martin H., Pamela Crippen Adams
& Robert Adams, eds.
Robert Adams' Book of Alternate Worlds,
an NAL/Signet Jul,1987

Greenberg, Martin H. & Isaac Asimov, eds.
**Isaac Asimov Presents the Great SF
Stories: 16 (1954)**, an DAW May,1987
**Isaac Asimov Presents the Great SF
Stories: 17 (1955)**, an DAW Jan,1988

Greenberg, Martin H., Isaac Asimov & Charles
G. Waugh, eds.
**Isaac Asimov's Magical Worlds of
Fantasy #8: Devils**, an NAL/Signet
Jun,1987
**Isaac Asimov's Magical Worlds of
Fantasy #9: Atlantis**, an NAL/Signet
Jan,1988
**Isaac Asimov's Wonderful Worlds of
Science Fiction #6: Neanderthals**, an
NAL/Signet Feb,1987
**Isaac Asimov's Wonderful Worlds of
Science Fiction #7: Space Shuttles**, an
NAL/Signet Oct,1987
Young Witches & Warlocks, an Harper &
Row Jul,1987

Greenberg, Martin H., Joe W. Haldeman &
Charles G. Waugh, eds.
Supertanks, an Ace Apr,1987

Greenberg, Martin H., Frank D. McSherry, Jr.
& Charles G. Waugh, eds.
**Nightmares in Dixie: Thirteen Horror
Tales From the American South**, an
August House Apr,1987

Greenberg, Martin H. & Patrick L. Price, eds.
**Fantastic Stories: Tales of the Weird and
Wondrous**, an TSR May,1987

Greenberg, Martin H., Carol Serling & Charles
G. Waugh, eds.
Rod Serling's Night Gallery Reader, an
Dembner Dec,1987

Greenberg, Martin H. & Charles G. Waugh,
eds.
**Battlefields Beyond Tomorrow: Science
Fiction War Stories**, an Crown/Bonanza
Dec,1987
House Shudders, an DAW Sep,1987

Greenberg, Martin H. & Charles G. Waugh,
eds. (continued)
Vamps, an DAW Mar,1987

Greenberg, Martin H., Charles G. Waugh &
Jane Yolen, eds.
Spaceships and Spells, oa Harper & Row
Nov,1987

Greenburg, Dan
The Nanny, n. Macmillan Nov,1987

Greene, Liz
Puppet Master: A Novel, n. Arkana
Mar,1987

Greenland, Colin
The Hour of the Thin Ox, n. Allen & Unwin
Mar,1987

Greenland, Colin, Eric S. Rabkin & George E.
Slusser, eds.
**Storm Warnings: Science Fiction
Confronts the Future**, nf S. Illinois Univ.
Press Apr,1987

Greenleaf, William
Starjacked!, n. Ace Apr,1987

Gregorian, Joyce Ballou
The Great Wheel, n. Ace Apr,1987

Greimes, Christopher & Barthe DeClements
Double Trouble, n. Viking Apr,1987

Gresham, Stephen
Midnight Boy, n. Zebra May,1987

Gribbin, Dr. John
The Lost Years of Cosmology, ar *Analog*
Dec,1987

Gribbin, Dr. John & Mary Gribbin
In Praise of Sociobiology, ar **New Destinies**
v1, ed. Jim Baen, Baen,1987

Gribbin, Mary & Dr. John Gribbin
In Praise of Sociobiology, ar **New Destinies**
v1, ed. Jim Baen, Baen,1987

Griffin, A. Arthur
In the Old Places, pm *Weirdbook* #22,1987

Griffin, P.M.
Star Commandos: Colony in Peril, n. Ace
Jun,1987

Griffin, Pauline
Oath-Bound, nv **Tales of the Witch World**,
ed. Andre Norton, St. Martin's,1987

Griffin, Russell M.
Saving Time, na *F&SF* Feb,1987

Grimwade, Peter
Robot, n. Star Jul,1987

Grocott, Ann
Danni's Desperate Journey, n. Angus &
Robertson Oct,1987

Gross, Henry R.
Cubeworld, nv **Mathenauts**, ed. Rudy
Rucker, Arbor House,1987

Grove, Vicki
At the Rummage Sale, ss *Twilight Zone*
Apr,1987

GUADALUPI, GIANNI

HARRISON, HARRY

Guadalupi, Gianni & Alberto Manguel
The Dictionary of Imaginary Places, Expanded Edition, nf HBJ Harvest Sep,1987

Gunnarsson, Thorarinn
The Starwolves, n. Popular Library Questar Jan,1988

Guttenberg, Elyse
Selena's Song, ss **Spaceships & Spells**, ed. Jane Yolen, Martin H. Greenberg & Charles G. Waugh, Harper & Row,1987

Gygax, Gary
Cat or Pigeon?, na **Night Arrant**, Ace/New Infinities,1987
Cats Versus Rats, nv **Night Arrant**, Ace/New Infinities,1987
City of Hawks, n. Ace/New Infinities Nov,1987
The Five Dragon Bowl, nv **Night Arrant**, Ace/New Infinities,1987
The Heart of Darkness, nv **Night Arrant**, Ace/New Infinities,1987
The House in the Tree, nv **Night Arrant**, Ace/New Infinities,1987
Love Laughs at Locks, nv **Night Arrant**, Ace/New Infinities,1987
Night Arrant, oc Ace/New Infinities Sep,1987
A Revel in Rel Mord, na **Night Arrant**, Ace/New Infinities,1987
Sea of Death, n. Ace/New Infinities Jun,1987
Twistbuck's Game, nv **Night Arrant**, Ace/New Infinities,1987
The Weird Occurrence in Odd Alley, na **Night Arrant**, Ace/New Infinities,1987

Haberman, Paul
Ouija, vi *Grue* #4,1987

Hadji, R.S.
Who's Who in the British Horror Scene, ar *American Fantasy* Win,1987

Hadji, R.S., ed.
Border Land [Special World Fantasy Convention Issue, Oct. 1987]

Haining, Peter
Doctor Who: The Time-Travellers' Guide, nf W.H. Allen Sep,1987
The Dracula Centenary Book, nf Souvenir Press Oct,1987

Haining, Peter, ed.
Poltergeist: Tales of Deadly Ghosts, an Severn House Dec,1987
Werewolf: Horror Stories of the Man Beast, an Severn House Sep,1987

Halam, Ann
The Daymaker, n. Orchard May,1987

Haldeman, Jack C., II
Dead Man's Tie, ss *Twilight Zone* Feb,1987

Haldeman, Joe W.
cold rust grit: end of dreams, pm *IASFM* mid-Dec,1987
DX, ss **In the Field of Fire**, ed. Jeanne Van Buren Dann & Jack M. Dann, Tor,1987
Tool of the Trade, n. Morrow Apr,1987

Haldeman, Joe W., Martin H. Greenberg & Charles G. Waugh, eds.
Supertanks, an Ace Apr,1987

Hale, Andrew
2020: Vision of the Future, n. Ada Press Oct,1987

Halkin, John
Bloodworm, n. Arrow Aug,1987
Fangs of the Werewolf, n. Beaver Dec,1987
Fangs of the Werewolf, n. Century Nov,1987

Hall, Hal W.
Science Fiction and Fantasy Reference Index, 1878-1985, nf Gale Apr,1987

Hall, Melissa Mia
Confession of Innocence, ss **Doom City**, ed. Charles L. Grant, Tor,1987
Moonflower, ss **Shadows #10**, ed. Charles L. Grant,1987

Hall, Sandi
Wingwomen of Hera, n. Spinsters/Aunt Lute May,1987

Hall, Willis
The Antelope Company at Large, n. Bodley Head Oct,1987

Halliwell, Leslie
Come Into the Garden, Mawdsley, nv **A Demon Close Behind**, Robert Hale,1987
The Day of the Jester, ss **A Demon Close Behind**, Robert Hale,1987
A Demon Close Behind, oc Robert Hale Apr,1987
Escape to Akureyri, nv **A Demon Close Behind**, Robert Hale,1987
The Haunting of Joshua Tree, ss **A Demon Close Behind**, Robert Hale,1987
The Horror at Hops Cottage, ss **A Demon Close Behind**, Robert Hale,1987
Lover, pm **A Demon Close Behind**, Robert Hale,1987
The Man with the Dundreary Weepers, ss **A Demon Close Behind**, Robert Hale,1987
Memorial Service, ss **A Demon Close Behind**, Robert Hale,1987
La Nuit des Chiens, ss **A Demon Close Behind**, Robert Hale,1987
The Past of Mrs Pickering, nv **A Demon Close Behind**, Robert Hale,1987
Return to Shangri-La, n. Grafton Dec,1987
The Smile on the Face of the Kite, nv **A Demon Close Behind**, Robert Hale,1987
Smoking-Room Story, ss **A Demon Close Behind**, Robert Hale,1987
Take Off Your Cap When a Funeral Passes, ss **A Demon Close Behind**, Robert Hale,1987
Where not to buy Cufflinks in Stockholm, ss **A Demon Close Behind**, Robert Hale,1987

Hambly, Barbara
The Unschooled Wizard, om SFBC Jun,1987
The Witches of Wenshar, n. Ballantine/Del Rey Jul,1987
The Witches of Wenshar, n. Ballantine: New York pb Jul,1987
The Witches of Wenshar, n. Unwin Sep,1987

Hamilton, Dennis
Fish Story, ss **Masques** #2, ed. J.N. Williamson,1987

Hamley, Dennis
Krarg Enters, ss **Twisted Circuits**, ed. Mick Gowar, Beaver,1987

Hammond, Charlotte Brown
Uncle Sherm (A Fantasy), ss *Grue* #4,1987

Hancock, Niel
The Sea of Silence, n. Popular Library Questar Dec,1987

Hannes, Genine
What the Large Night Left, pm *Ice River* Sum,1987

Hanratty, Peter
The Book of Mordred, n. Ace/New Infinities Jan,1988

Hansen, Tom
Winterscape, pm *Pulpsmith* Win,1987

Harbinson, W.A.
Eden, n. Dell May,1987
The Light of Eden, n. Corgi Mar,1987

Hardie, Raymond
Abyssos, n. Tor Sep,1987

Harding, Lawrence
Black Jewels of the Toad, pm *Eldritch Tales* #14,1987
Lost Eons, pm *Space & Time* #72,1987
The Wings of a Bat, pm *Grue* #5,1987

Hardy, Phil
The Encyclopedia of Horror Movies, nf Harper & Row/Perennial Library Mar,1987

Harness, Charles L.
Signals, na **Synergy** v1, ed. George Zebrowski,1987

Harper, Rory
Snorkeling in the River Lethe, ss *Amazing* Jan,1987

Harrington, Barbara
A Crock of Clear Water, n. Robert Hale Apr,1987

Harris, Deborah Turner
The Gauntlet of Malice, n. Tor Jan,1988

Harris, Marilyn
Night Games, n. Doubleday Sep,1987

Harris, Sidney
Cartoon, ct *F&SF* Jan,1987
Cartoon, ct *F&SF* Jul,1987
Cartoon, ct *F&SF* Nov,1987
Cartoon, ct *F&SF* Dec,1987

Harrison, Harry
Ni Venos, Doktoro Zamenof, Ni Venos!, ss **Tales from the Forbidden Planet**, ed. Roz Kaveney, Titan,1987
The Stainless Steel Rat Gets Drafted, n. Bantam Spectra Oct,1987
The Stainless Steel Rat Gets Drafted, n. Bantam UK Aug,1987

Harrison, M. John
Small Heirlooms, ss **Other Edens**, ed.
Christopher Evans & Robert Holdstock,
Unwin: London,1987

Hartman, Sergio Gaut vel
Contaminated People, ss *SF International*
#2,1987

Hartwell, David G., ed.
The Dark Descent, an Tor Oct,1987

Hartwell, David G. & Kathryn Cramer, eds.
Christmas Ghosts, an Arbor House
Sep,1987

Harvey, M. Elayn
Warhaven, n. Franklin Watts Oct,1987

Hatchigan, Jessica
Count Dracula, Me and Norma D., n.
Avon/Camelot Nov,1987

Hautala, Rick
Colt .24, ss **Devils**, ed. Isaac Asimov, Martin
H. Greenberg & Charles G. Waugh,
Signet,1987

Haviland, Keith
Soap, ss **Gollancz - Sunday Times Best SF
Stories**, Gollancz,1987

Hawke, Douglas D.
Moonslasher, n. Critic's Choice Jun,1987

Hawke, Simon
Friday the 13th, Part I, n. NAL/Signet
Sep,1987
Spychodrome, n. Ace Jul,1987
Time Wars #7: The Arbonaut Affair, n. Ace
Aug,1987
The Wizard of 4th Street, n. Popular
Library Questar Oct,1987

Hawkins, Ward
Torch of Fear, n. Ballantine/Del Rey
May,1987

Hay, Daniel J.
Fractured Dimensions, ss *Salarius* #3,1987

Hayes, Barbara & Robert Ingpen
Folk Tales and Fables of the World, co
Paper Tiger Jun,1987

Haynes, Mary
Raider's Sky, n. Morrow/Lothrop, Lee &
Shepard May,1987

Hays, Robert
Thermo, pm *Amazing* Nov,1987

Heapy, Paul
Moral Technology, ss **Gollancz - Sunday
Times Best SF Stories**, Gollancz,1987

Heath, Karen B.
The Last Gays of Parpheii, vi *Salarius*
v1#4,1987

Heath, Phillip C.
The Man Who Collected Bloch, ss *Eldritch
Tales* #13,1987

Heckler, Mary
Cosmos, pm *Weirdbook* #22,1987

Heidbrink, James R.
Of Ancient Swords and Evil Mist, ss **Tales of
the Witch World**, ed. Andre Norton, St.
Martin's,1987

Heideman, Eric M.
Little Magazine That Could, ed *Tales of the
Unanticipated* #2,1987
Time and Chance, nv **L. Ron Hubbard
Presents Writers of the Future** v3, ed.
Algis Budrys, Bridge,1987

Heideman, Eric M., ed.
Tales of the Unanticipated [#2, Spring 1987]

Heideman, Eric M., Terry A. Garey, Damon
Knight & Kate Wilhelm
An Interview with Kate Wilhelm and Damon
Knight, iv *Tales of the Unanticipated*
#2,1987

Heinlein, Robert A.
To Sail Beyond the Sunset, n. Ace/Putnam
Jul,1987

Heinrich, Kurt Hyatt
The Darkworld Contract, ss *Space & Time*
#72,1987

Heiser
Cartoon, ct *IASFM* Oct,1987

Helfand, David J.
Supernovae: Creative Cataclysms in the
Galaxy, ar **Universe**, ed. Byron Preiss,
Bantam Spectra,1987

Helfman, Elizabeth S.
Voices in the Wind, ss **Spaceships &
Spells**, ed. Jane Yolen, Martin H.
Greenberg & Charles G. Waugh, Harper &
Row,1987

Heller, Terry
**The Delights of Terror: An Aesthetics of
the Tale of Terror**, nf Univ. of Illinois
Press Sep,1987

Hellinga, Gerben, Jr.
Narcissus Flower, ss *SF International*
#2,1987

Henderson, C.J.
You Can't Take It With You, ss *Eldritch Tales*
#14,1987

Hendrix, Howard V.
Doctor Doom Conducting, vi *Aboriginal SF*
Sep,1987

Henighan, Tom
Bonsai Man, pm **Tesseracts 2**, ed. Phyllis
Gotlieb & Douglas Barbour, Press
Porcepic: Victoria,1987
Visitation, pm **Tesseracts 2**, ed. Phyllis
Gotlieb & Douglas Barbour, Press
Porcepic: Victoria,1987

Henry, Laurie
1987 Fiction Writer's Market, nf Writer's
Digest Books Apr,1987

Henry, Maeve
The Witch King, n. Orchard Jun,1987

Henson, H. Keith
Memetics and the Modular Mind--Modeling
the Development of Social Movements, ar
Analog Aug,1987

Henstell, Diana
New Morning Dragon, n. Bantam Oct,1987

Herbert, Brian
Prisoners of Arionn, n. Arbor House
Jun,1987

Herbert, Frank
**The Maker of Dune: Insights of a Master
of Science Fiction**, nf Berkley May,1987
The Second Great Dune Trilogy, om
Gollancz Apr,1987

Herbert, James
The Magic Cottage, n. NAL Sep,1987
Maurice and Mog, ss **Masques** #2, ed. J.N.
Williamson,1987
Sepulchre, n. Hodder & Stoughton Jul,1987

Herman, Ira
Promised Star, ss *Amazing* Nov,1987

Hernandez, Gilbert, Jaime Hernandez, Mario
Hernandez & Dean Motter
The Return of Mister X, gn Warner Dec,1987

Hernandez, Jaime, Gilbert Hernandez, Mario
Hernandez & Dean Motter
The Return of Mister X, gn Warner Dec,1987

Hernandez, Mario, Gilbert Hernandez, Jaime
Hernandez & Dean Motter
The Return of Mister X, gn Warner Dec,1987

Herron, Don
Curiosity, pm *Eldritch Tales* #13,1987

Heydt, Dorothy J.
The Noonday Witch, nv **Sword and
Sorceress #4**, ed. Marion Zimmer
Bradley,1987
The Sum of the Parts, nv **Red Sun of
Darkover**, ed. Marion Zimmer Bradley &
The Friends of Darkover, DAW,1987

Heyrman, Peter
Carnivores, ss *The Horror Show* Jan,1987
An Eye for an Eye, ss *Night Cry* v2#5,1987
Heart of Stone, ss *The Horror Show*
Sum,1987
Pick-Up, vi *Twilight Zone* Dec,1987

Hickman, Laura & Kate Novak
Heart of Goldmoon, na **DragonLance Tales**
v3, Margaret Weis & Tracy Hickman,
TSR,1987

Hickman, Tracy & Margaret Weis
**The Darksword Trilogy, Volume 1:
Forging the Darksword**, n. Bantam
Spectra Jan,1988
The Legacy, na **DragonLance Tales** v1,
Margaret Weis & Tracy Hickman,
TSR,1987
"Wanna Bet?", na **DragonLance Tales** v2,
Margaret Weis & Tracy Hickman,
TSR,1987

Hickman, Tracy & Margaret Weis, eds.
**DragonLance Tales Vol. 1: The Magic of
Krynn**, oa TSR Apr,1987
**DragonLance Tales Vol. 2: Kender, Gully
Dwarves, and Gnomes**, oa TSR Aug,1987

Hickman, Tracy & Margaret Weis, eds.
(continued)
DragonLance Tales Vol. 3: Love and War,
oa TSR Nov,1987
Leaves from the Inn of the Last Home, nf
TSR Mar,1987

Higgins, Nina Downey
Apples, ss **Shadows #10**, ed. Charles L.
Grant,1987

Higgs, Eric C.
Doppelganger, n. St. Martin's Mar,1987

Highsmith, Patricia
Moby Dick II; or The Missile Whale, ss **Tales
of Natural and Unnatural Catastrophes**,
Bloomsbury,1987
The Mysterious Cemetery, ss **Tales of
Natural and Unnatural Catastrophes**,
Bloomsbury,1987
Nabuti: Warm Welcome to a UN
Committee, ss **Tales of Natural and
Unnatural Catastrophes**,
Bloomsbury,1987
No End in Sight, ss **Tales of Natural and
Unnatural Catastrophes**,
Bloomsbury,1987
Operation Balsam; or Touch-Me-Not, ss
**Tales of Natural and Unnatural
Catastrophes**, Bloomsbury,1987
President Buck Jones Rallies and Waves the
Flag, nv **Tales of Natural and Unnatural
Catastrophes**, Bloomsbury,1987
Rent-a-Womb vs. The Mighty Right, ss
**Tales of Natural and Unnatural
Catastrophes**, Bloomsbury,1987
Sixtus VI, Pope of the Red Slipper, nv **Tales
of Natural and Unnatural Catastrophes**,
Bloomsbury,1987
Sweet Freedom! and a Picnic on the White
House Lawn, ss **Tales of Natural and
Unnatural Catastrophes**,
Bloomsbury,1987
**Tales of Natural and Unnatural
Catastrophes**, oc Bloomsbury Dec,1987
Trouble at the Jade Towers, nv **Tales of
Natural and Unnatural Catastrophes**,
Bloomsbury,1987

Hildick, E.W.
**The Ghost Squad and the Prowling
Hermits**, n. Dutton Nov,1987

Hill, Douglas
Blade of the Poisoner, n. Gollancz
Jun,1987
Blade of the Poisoner, n. Macmillan
McElderry Oct,1987
Master of Fiends, n. Gollancz Nov,1987

Hill, Jack R.
Epitaph by an Alien in Yellow Moonlight,
pm *Amazing* Sep,1987

Hiller, B.B.
Superman IV, n. Scholastic Point Jul,1987

Hiller, Neil W.
The Orphan, ss *F&SF* May,1987

Hinz, Christopher
Liege-Killer, n. St. Martin's Mar,1987

Hoban, Russell
The Medusa Frequency, n. Atlantic
Monthly Press Oct,1987
What It Said, ss *Sanity* Jan,1987

Hodge, Brian
Red Zone, ss *The Horror Show* Win,1987

Hodgman, Ann
Galaxy High School, n. Bantam Skylark
Sep,1987

Hodgson, Amanda
Romances of William Morris, nf
Cambridge Univ. Press Feb,1987

Hoffman, Charles & Marc A. Cerasini
Robert E. Howard, nf Starmont House
Apr,1987

Hoffman, Curtis H.
Project: Millennium, n. Ace Feb,1987

Hoffman, Nina Kiriki
Waiting for the Hunger, ss **Doom City**, ed.
Charles L. Grant, Tor,1987

Hogan, James P.
Endgame Enigma, n. Bantam Spectra
Aug,1987

Hogan, Wayne
Cartoon, ct *Twilight Zone* Dec,1987

Hohing, Frederick
Down by the Sea Wreck, ss *Ice River*
Sum,1987

Hoklin, Lonn
The Hourglass Crisis, n. Warner Nov,1987

Holder, Nancy
Shift, nv **Doom City**, ed. Charles L. Grant,
Tor,1987
We Have Always Lived in the Forest, ss
Shadows #10, ed. Charles L. Grant,1987

Holdstock, Robert P.
Scarrowfell, nv **Other Edens**, ed.
Christopher Evans & Robert Holdstock,
Unwin: London,1987

Holdstock, Robert & Christopher Evans, eds.
Other Edens, oa Unwin Jul,1987

Hollow, John
**Against the Night, the Stars: The Science
Fiction of Arthur C. Clarke**, nf Ohio Univ.
Press Apr,1987

Holmberg, Dennis
A Little Elevator Music, ss *2AM* Spr,1987

Holsinger, Jon
Film Reviews, mr *2AM* Spr,1987
Film Reviews, mr *2AM* Sum,1987
Film Reviews, mr *2AM* Fll,1987
Film Reviews, mr *2AM* Win,1987

Holzer, James William
Doughfoot Sanctum, ss **There Will Be War**
v6, ed. Jerry E. Pournelle,1987

Honeycutt, Andy
October 31, ss *Haunts #9*,1987

Hoobler, Thomas
Dr. Chill's Project, n. Putnam Oct,1987

Hoover, Dale
Proctor Valley, ss *Grue #6*,1987

Hoover, H.M.
Orvis, n. Viking Kestrel Aug,1987

Hopkins, Mariane S.
Fandom Directory No. 9 (1987-1988), nf
Fandata Mar,1987

Hopp, Jeff
A Day at the Beach With Picasso, cs *Space
& Time #72*,1987

Hopper, Jeannette M.
Under a Hungry Moon, ss *Footsteps*
Nov,1987

Hornig, Doug
The Game of Magical Death, ss *F&SF*
Mar,1987

Horsting, Jessie
The Reel Stuff: A Witchin' Summer, mr
Aboriginal SF May,1987
The Reel Stuff: Dog Days, mr *Aboriginal SF*
Jul,1987
The Reel Stuff: The Good, the Bad and the
Maybes, mr *Aboriginal SF* Feb,1987

Horvitz, Leslie
Blood Moon, n. Pocket Feb,1987

Horwood, William
Skallagrigg, n. Viking UK Oct,1987

Hosken, John
Meet Mr. Majimpsey, n. Pavilion Nov,1987

Houchin, Ron
An Auto Mechanic Considers the Earth, pm
Pulpsmith Win,1987

Houston, Opie R.
aborted dream, pm *Grue #5*,1987

Howard, Robert E.
Black Seas, pm *Fantasy Book* Mar,1987
**Cthulhu: The Mythos and Kindred
Horrors**, co Baen May,1987
I Praise My Nativity, pm *Fantasy Book*
Mar,1987
Silence Falls on Mecca's Walls, pm
**Cthulhu: The Mythos and Kindred
Horrors**, New York: Baen,1987

Howarth, Matt
Sonic Curiosity, cs *New Pathways* Jan,1987
Sonic Curiosity, cs *New Pathways* Apr,1987
Sonic Curiosity, cs *New Pathways* Aug,1987
Sonic Curiosity, cs *New Pathways* Nov,1987

Howe, James
Nighty-Nightmare, n. Atheneum Mar,1987

Howett, Dicky & Tim Quinn
The Doctor Who Fun Book, nf Target
May,1987

Howlett, Winston A. & Jean Lorrah
Wulfston's Odyssey, n. NAL/Signet
Nov,1987

Hoyle, Trevor
K.I.D.S., n. Sphere Jan,1987

Hubbard, L. Ron
Mission Earth, Vol. 6: Death Quest, n.
Bridge Jan,1987
**Mission Earth, Vol. 7: Voyage of
Vengeance**, n. Bridge May,1987

Hubbard, L. Ron (continued)
Mission Earth, Vol. 8: Disaster, n. Bridge Jul,1987
Mission Earth, Vol. 9: Villainy Victorious, n. Bridge Oct,1987
Mission Earth, Vol.10: The Doomed Planet, n. Bridge Nov,1987

Hubbard, L. Ron, Jr. & Bent Corydon
L. Ron Hubbard: Messiah or Madman?, nf Lyle Stuart Aug,1987

Hudson, Michael
Photon: Thieves of Light, n. Berkley Apr,1987

Huff, T.S.
And Who Is Joah?, ss *Amazing* Nov,1987

Huffman-Klinkowitz, Julie, Jerome Klinkowitz & Asa Pieratt, eds.
Kurt Vonnegut: A Comprehensive Bibliography, nf Shoestring/Archon Jun,1987

Hughes, Edward P.
Crown of Thorns, ss **There Will Be War** v6, ed. Jerry E. Pournelle,1987
Test for Tyrants, ss **New Destinies** v2, ed. Jim Baen, Baen,1987

Hughes, Helen
City of Sleep, ss *Pulpsmith* Win,1987

Hughes, Monica
The Dream Catcher, n. Atheneum/Argo Mar,1987

Hughes, Robert Don
Dragon Meat, ss *The Dragon* Apr,1987

Hughes, Zach
The Dark Side, n. NAL/Signet Dec,1987
Sundrinker, n. DAW Jul,1987

Hunt, J.J.
The Famous Hospitality of Dao'i, pm *IASFM* Sep,1987

Hunter, C. Bruce
Eric and the Red Blotches, vi *Eldritch Tales* #14,1987

Hurley, Mike
Witchwood, ss *Haunts* #9,1987

Hussey, Leigh Ann
The Spirit Way, ss *The Dragon* Dec,1987
A Sword in Hand, nv *Fantasy Book* Mar,1987

Huston, Ned
Pliny's Commentaries, nv **Universe** #17, ed. Terry Carr,1987

Hutchinson, Don
Hugh Cave: An Appreciation, bg *Border Land* Oct,1987

Hutson, Shaun
Breeding Ground, n. Leisure Nov,1987
Deathday, n. Star Apr,1987
Slugs, n. Leisure Aug,1987
Victims, n. W.H. Allen Jul,1987

ill., Judy Mastrangelo & Jean L. Scrocco, ed.
Antique Fairy Tales, an Unicorn Oct,1987

Ing, Dean
Blood of Eagles, n. Tor Apr,1987
Firefight 2000, ar **Firefight 2000**, Baen,1987
Firefight 2000, co Baen Jun,1987

Ingpen, Robert
The Voyage of the Poppykettle, nv Paper Tiger Sep,1987

Ingpen, Robert & Barbara Hayes
Folk Tales and Fables of the World, co Paper Tiger Jun,1987

Ingrid, Charles
Solar Kill, n. DAW Jul,1987

Inks, Caralyn
Mandrake, nv **Magic in Ithkar** #4, ed. Andre Norton & Robert Adams,1987
Nine Words in Winter, ss **Tales of the Witch World**, ed. Andre Norton, St. Martin's,1987

Innes, Evan
America 2040 #3: The City in the Mist, n. Bantam Apr,1987

Ironside, Virginia
Vampire Master, n. Walker Aug,1987

Irwin, Walter & G.B. Love, eds.
The Best of Trek #12, nf NAL/Signet Aug,1987

Jablokov, Alexander
At the Cross-Time Jaunter's Ball, nv *IASFM* Aug,1987

Jackson, Sir William
Alternative Third World War, 1985 - 2035: A Personal History, nf Pergamon Sep,1987

Jacobi, Carl
A Quire of Foolscap, ss *Whispers* #23,1987

Jacobs, Harvey
Kitten Kaboodle and Sidney Australia, ss *F&SF* Jun,1987
Stardust, ss *Omni* Aug,1987

Jacobson, Dan
Her Story, n. Andre Deutsch Aug,1987

Jacques, Brian
Redwall, n. Putnam Philomel Jun,1987

Jafek, Bev
There's a Phantom in My Word-Processor, ss *Pulpsmith* Win,1987

Jaffery, Sheldon R., ed.
Selected Tales of Grim and Grue from the Horror Pulps, an Bowling Green Popular Press Aug,1987
The Weirds, an Starmont House Apr,1987

James, M.R.
Casting the Runes and Other Ghost Stories, co World's Classics Apr,1987
Masters of Fantasy 3: M.R. James, co British Fantasy Society May,1987
A Warning to the Curious: The Ghost Stories of M.R. James, co Hutchinson Feb,1987

James, Robert
Blood Mist, n. Leisure Sep,1987

Janifer, Laurence M.
Knave & the Game, co Doubleday Aug,1987
The Swagger Stick, nv **Knave & the Game**, Doubleday,1987
Telephone, vi *Analog* Jun,1987
Worldwreckers, ss *Analog* Oct,1987

Jankus, Hank
On Exhibit, il *Amazing* May,1987

Jarik, J.C.
Three Were Chosen [Chapters 5&6], sl *Salarius* #3,1987
Three Were Chosen [Chapters 7&8], sl *Salarius* v1#4,1987

Jarman, Julia
Ollie and the Bogle, n. Andersen Press Apr,1987

Jay, Peter & Michael Stewart
Apocalypse 2000: Economic Breakdown and the Suicide of Democracy, n. Sidgwick & Jackson Jun,1987

Jefferies, Mike
Palace of Kings, n. Fontana Nov,1987

Jenkins, Scott
Heroes of Audio: Jane Schonberger, bg *American Fantasy* Sum,1987
Heroes of Audio: Mike McDonough, bg *American Fantasy* Win,1987
The Sound and the Fury, ar *American Fantasy* Sum,1987
The Sound and the Fury, ar *American Fantasy* Win,1987

Jennings, Phillip C.
The Castaway, ss *Amazing* Mar,1987
Moondo Bizarro, nv **New Destinies** v2, ed. Jim Baen, Baen,1987

Jensen, Ruby Jean
Annabelle, n. Zebra Mar,1987
Chain Letter, n. Zebra Sep,1987
Smoke, n. Zebra Jan,1988

Jeres, Patricia
Tiny Devils, pm *New Pathways* Jan,1987

Jeter, K.W.
Dark Seeker, n. Tor Feb,1987
Death's Arms, n. Morrigan May,1987
Infernal Devices, n. St. Martin's Apr,1987
Mantis, n. Tor Oct,1987

Jeter, K.W. & Les Escott
K.W. Jeter, iv *Interzone* #22,1987

Jeter, K.W., Ferret & J.B. Reynolds
K.W. Jeter [Part 1], iv *New Pathways* Apr,1987
K.W. Jeter [Part 2], iv *New Pathways* Aug,1987

Johnson, Dale & Michael Whelan
Michael Whelan, iv *American Fantasy* Sum,1987

Johnson, James B.
Conestoga History, ss *Analog* May,1987
Trekmaster, n. DAW Sep,1987

Johnson, Shane
Mr. Scott's Guide to the Enterprise, pi Pocket Jul,1987

JOHNSON, SHELTON ARNEL

Johnson, Shelton Arnel
The Eels, pm *Amazing* Mar,1987
Elegy for Cygnus X-1, pm *Amazing* Nov,1987

Johnson, Susan
Running It Back, mr *American Fantasy*
Spr,1987
Running It Back, mr *American Fantasy*
Win,1987

Johnson, Will
Spider King, pm *Space & Time* #72,1987

Johnston, Jeff
Masks, ss *2AM* Spr,1987

Johnston, Mairin
The Witch-Hunt, ss **Mad and Bad Fairies**,
ed. Anonymous, Attic Press,1987

Johnstone, William W.
The Devil's Cat, n. Zebra May,1987
Smoke from the Ashes, n. Zebra Oct,1987

Johnstone, William W. & Joe Keene
Baby Grand, n. Zebra Aug,1987

Jones, Bruce
The Apartment, ss **Twisted Tales**, San
Diego: Blackthorne,1987
Black Death, ss **Twisted Tales**, San Diego:
Blackthorne,1987
Children of the Stars, nv **Twisted Tales**,
San Diego: Blackthorne,1987
Cycle, ss **Twisted Tales**, San Diego:
Blackthorne,1987
Good Neighbor, ss **Twisted Tales**, San
Diego: Blackthorne,1987
The Hollow, ss **Twisted Tales**, San Diego:
Blackthorne,1987
Jessie's Friend, ss **Twisted Tales**, San
Diego: Blackthorne,1987
Members Only, nv **Twisted Tales**, San
Diego: Blackthorne,1987
Over His Head, ss **Twisted Tales**, San
Diego: Blackthorne,1987
Rendezvous, nv **Twisted Tales**, San Diego:
Blackthorne,1987
Roomers, ss **Twisted Tales**, San Diego:
Blackthorne,1987
Twisted Tales, oc Blackthorne Sep,1987
The Waiting Game, ss **Twisted Tales**, San
Diego: Blackthorne,1987

Jones, Diana Wynne
A Tale of Time City, n. Greenwillow
Sep,1987
A Tale of Time City, n. Methuen Oct,1987

Jones, Glyn
The Space Museum, n. W.H. Allen Jan,1987

Jones, Gwyneth
Divine Endurance, n. Arbor House Mar,1987
The Snow Apples, ss **Tales from the
Forbidden Planet**, ed. Roz Kaveney,
Titan,1987

Jones, Gwyneth & Paul Kincaid
Gwyneth Jones Interview, iv *Interzone*
#19,1987

Jones, Jeffrey & Bernard Abrams
The Twilight Zone Gallery: The Art of Jeffrey
Jones, pi *Twilight Zone* Aug,1987

Jones, Jeffrey & Tappan King
The Twilight Zone Gallery: The Art of Jim
Burns, pi *Twilight Zone* Oct,1987

Jones, Kelvin I.
Mandrake, ss **After Midnight Stories**
#3,1987

Jones, Lanyon
The Nine Lessons and Carols, ss **After
Midnight Stories** #3,1987

Jones, Lloyd S.
Black Rainbow, n. Aeolus Jul,1987

Jones, Stephen & Cory Glaberson
Hellraiser, mr *American Fantasy* Win,1987

Jong, Erica
Serenissima, n. Houghton Mifflin Apr,1987

Jonik, John
Cartoon, ct *New Yorker*,1987

Jordan, Brenda
The Brentwood Witches, n. Ace Oct,1987

Jordan, Dennis
Radionda, ss *Grue* #5,1987

Joron, Andrew
Force Fields, co Starmont House Apr,1987

Joron, Andrew & Robert Frazier
Exiled of Worlds, pm *Amazing* Sep,1987

Jurgens, Kathleen E. & Commander USA
Kathleen Jurgens interviews Commander
USA, iv *2AM* Fll,1987

Jurgens, Kathleen E. & Crematia Mortum
Interview with Crematia Mortum (Roberta
Solomon), iv *2AM* Spr,1987

Kadrey, Richard
Goodbye Houston Street, Goodbye, ss
Interzone #19,1987
The Other Side: Chaos, Inc., ar *Twilight
Zone* Feb,1987

Kadrey, Richard & Rudy Rucker
Rudy Rucker Interview, iv *Interzone*
#20,1987

Kahn, James
Timefall, n. St. Martin's Feb,1987

Kahn, James, Donald F. Glut & George Lucas
The Star Wars Trilogy, om Ballantine/Del
Rey May,1987

Kahn, Joan, ed.
**Ready or Not: Here Come Fourteen
Frightening Stories!**, an Greenwillow
Aug,1987

Kane, Daniel
Power and Magic, n. GMP Press Oct,1987

Kane, Francis X., Stefan T. Possony & Jerry E.
Pournelle
Surprise [substantially revised, first
appeared in **The Strategy of
Technology**, 1970], ar **There Will Be War**
v6, ed. Jerry E. Pournelle,1987

Karlin, Nurit
Cartoon, ct *F&SF* Oct,1987

Karwowski, Christopher
Illuminations: Crystal Revelations, ar
Twilight Zone Jun,1987
Illuminations: Painting the Town Red, ar
Twilight Zone Feb,1987
Illuminations: Radio Sci-Fi, ar *Twilight Zone*
Apr,1987
Illuminations: Starmagic, ar *Twilight Zone*
Apr,1987
Illuminations: Strange Hangups, ar *Twilight
Zone* Jun,1987
Illuminations: TZ Meets the '80s, ar *Twilight
Zone* Feb,1987
Music, ar *Twilight Zone* Jun,1987

Katz, Menke
The Reincarnated Queens of England, pm
Pulpsmith Win,1987

Kaufmann, William J.
The Black Hole, ar **Universe**, ed. Byron
Preiss, Bantam Spectra,1987

Kaveney, Roz, ed.
Tales from the Forbidden Planet, oa Titan
Aug,1987

Kaye, Marvin
Ghosts of Night and Morning, n. Ace
Charter Aug,1987
Ghosts of Night and Morning, ss *Night Cry*
v2#5,1987

Kaye, Marvin, ed.
Devils and Demons, an Doubleday
Oct,1987
Devils and Demons, an SFBC Sep,1987

Keene, Joe & William W. Johnstone
Baby Grand, n. Zebra Aug,1987

Keeping, Charles, ed.
**Charles Keeping's Classic Tales of the
Macabre**, an Blackie Sep,1987

Keith, William H., Jr.
Battletech: Mercenary's Star, n. FASA
Aug,1987

Kelleher, Ed & Harriette Vidal
The Breeder, n. Leisure Aug,1987

Kelleher, Victor
Taronga, n. Hamish Hamilton Sep,1987

Kellogg, M. Bradley & William Rossow
Lear's Daughters, om SFBC Apr,1987

Kelly, James Patrick
Daemon, ss *F&SF* Nov,1987
Glass Cloud, na *IASFM* Jun,1987
Heroics, ss *IASFM* Nov,1987

Kelly, Maeve
Alice in Thunderland, ss **Mad and Bad
Fairies**, ed. Anonymous, Attic Press,1987

Kelly, S.A.
Sound and the Electric Ear Drum, pm
Amazing Nov,1987

Kenin, Millea
Fate and the Dreamer, ss **Sword and
Sorceress** #4, ed. Marion Zimmer
Bradley,1987

Kennedy, Leigh
Faces, co Atlantic Monthly Press Aug,1987

KENNETT, RICK

Kennett, Rick
The Adventure of the Unearthly Spy, vi
Aphelion #5,1987

Kent, Paul
The Crib, n. Bantam Apr,1987

Kerby, Bill
Crusaders in Love, nv **Crusaders in Hell**,
ed. Janet Morris, New York: Baen,1987
Take Two, nv **Masters of Hell**, ed. Janet
Morris et al, Baen,1987

Kerr, Katharine
Darkspell, n. Doubleday Sep,1987

Kerr, Peg
Free Day, ss *Tales of the Unanticipated*
#2,1987

Kessel, John
Credibility, nv **In the Field of Fire**, ed.
Jeanne Van Buren Dann & Jack M. Dann,
Tor,1987
Judgment Call, nv *F&SF* Oct,1987

Ketter, Greg & Thomas Cantry
Thomas Canty, pi *American Fantasy*
Spr,1987

Ketterer, David
**Imprisoned in a Tesseract: The Life and
Work of James Blish**, nf Kent State Univ.
Press Sep,1987

Kilgore, John
Closing the Loop, ss *Space & Time*
#72,1987

Kilian, Crawford
The Fall of the Republic, n. Ballantine/Del
Rey Sep,1987

Killean, Anne
Dick Whittington and Her Cat, ss **Mad and
Bad Fairies**, ed. Anonymous, Attic
Press,1987

Killough, Lee
Blood Hunt, n. Tor Mar,1987
The Leopard's Daughter, n. Popular
Library Questar Oct,1987

Kilworth, Garry
The Black Wedding, ss **Other Edens**, ed.
Christopher Evans & Robert Holdstock,
Unwin: London,1987
Dop*elgan*er, ss *Interzone* #21,1987
The Earth is Flat and We're All Like to
Drown, ss **Tales from the Forbidden
Planet**, ed. Roz Kaveney, Titan,1987
Hogfoot Right and Bird-Hands, ss **Other
Edens**, ed. Christopher Evans & Robert
Holdstock, Unwin: London,1987
Murderers Walk, ss **Other Edens**, ed.
Christopher Evans & Robert Holdstock,
Unwin: London,1987
Paper Moon, ss *Omni* Jan,1987
Spiral Winds, n. Bodley Head Aug,1987
Triptych, gp **Other Edens**, ed. Christopher
Evans & Robert Holdstock, Unwin:
London,1987
The Wizard of Woodworld, n. Dragon
Nov,1987

Kincaid, Paul & Gwyneth Jones
Gwyneth Jones Interview, iv *Interzone*
#19,1987

King, Bernard
The Destroying Angel, n. Sphere Jul,1987
Starkadder, n. St. Martin's Sep,1987
Time-Fighters, n. Sphere Dec,1987

King, Clive
The Seashore People, n. Viking Kestrel
Aug,1987

King, Stephen
**The Dark Tower II: The Drawing of the
Three**, n. Donald M. Grant May,1987
Misery, n. Viking Jun,1987
Popsy, ss **Masques** #2, ed. J.N.
Williamson,1987
The Tommyknockers, n. Putnam Nov,1987

King, Tappan
Boogie Man, ss **Devils & Demons**, ed.
Marvin Kaye, SFBC/Doubleday,1987
Illuminations: A Little Night Music, ar
Twilight Zone Feb,1987
Illuminations: Dreamland, ar *Twilight Zone*
Dec,1987
Illuminations: Eternal Evil, ar *Twilight Zone*
Oct,1987
Illuminations: Latin Lama, ar *Twilight Zone*
Oct,1987
Illuminations: Leaps of Faith, ar *Twilight
Zone* Jun,1987
Illuminations: Magic Underfoot, ar *Twilight
Zone* Aug,1987
Illuminations: The Creature from the Silt in
the Black Lagoon, ar *Twilight Zone*
Oct,1987
In the Twilight Zone, ed *Twilight Zone*
Feb,1987
In the Twilight Zone, ed *Twilight Zone*
Apr,1987
In the Twilight Zone, ed *Twilight Zone*
Jun,1987
In the Twilight Zone, ed *Twilight Zone*
Aug,1987
In the Twilight Zone, ed *Twilight Zone*
Oct,1987
In the Twilight Zone, ed *Twilight Zone*
Dec,1987
Introduction: The Keeper of the Night, in
Night Cry v2#4,1987
The Other Side: Elephant Parts, ar *Twilight
Zone* Oct,1987

King, Tappan, ed.
Rod Serling's The Twilight Zone Magazine
[v.6 #6, February 1987]
Rod Serling's The Twilight Zone Magazine
[v.7 #1, April 1987]
Rod Serling's The Twilight Zone Magazine
[v.7 #2, June 1987]
Rod Serling's The Twilight Zone Magazine
[v.7 #3, August 1987]
Rod Serling's The Twilight Zone Magazine
[v.7 #4, October 1987]
Rod Serling's The Twilight Zone Magazine
[v.7 #5, December 1987]

King, Tappan & Jeffrey Jones
The Twilight Zone Gallery: The Art of Jim
Burns, pi *Twilight Zone* Oct,1987

King-Smith, Dick
Tumbleweed, n. Gollancz Apr,1987

Kipling, Rudyard
**The Complete Supernatural Stories of
Rudyard Kipling**, co W.H. Allen Jan,1987

KNIGHT, DAMON

Kirchner, Paul
The Bus, pi Orbit Aug,1987

Kirchoff, Mary
Finding the Faith, nv **DragonLance Tales**
v1, Margaret Weis & Tracy Hickman,
TSR,1987

Kirk, Richard
Raven 2: A Time of Ghosts, n. Ace
May,1987
Raven 3: The Frozen God, n. Ace Aug,1987
Raven 4: Lords of the Shadows, n. Ace
Oct,1987
Raven 5: A Time of Dying, n. Ace Jan,1988
Raven: Swordsmistress of Chaos, n. Ace
Feb,1987

Kisner, James
The Litter, ss **Masques** #2, ed. J.N.
Williamson,1987
Small Talk, ss *Grue* #4,1987

Kittredge, Mary
IMAGO, ss *Aboriginal SF* May,1987

Kittredge, Mary & Kevin O'Donnell, Jr.
The Shelter, n. Tor Aug,1987

Klein, Arthur L.
Kleinism, ms *Amazing* Jan,1987
Kleinism, ms *Amazing* Mar,1987
Kleinisms, ms *Amazing* Jul,1987

Klein, Jay Kay
Biolog: Arlan Andrews, bg *Analog* Sep,1987
Biolog: David A. Hardy, bg *Analog* Apr,1987
Biolog: George Zebrowski, bg *Analog*
Feb,1987
Biolog: Robert R. Chase, bg *Analog* Jul,1987

Klein, R.E.
The Smoking Mirror, ss *Space & Time*
#73,1987

Klein, T.E.D.
Film, mr *Night Cry* v2#4,1987
Film, mr *Night Cry* v2#5,1987

Klinkowitz, Jerome, Julie Huffman-Klinkowitz
& Asa Pieratt, eds.
**Kurt Vonnegut: A Comprehensive
Bibliography**, nf Shoestring/Archon
Jun,1987

Knaak, Richard A.
By the Measure, nv **DragonLance Tales** v3,
Margaret Weis & Tracy Hickman,
TSR,1987
Definitions of Honor, nv **DragonLance
Tales** v2, Margaret Weis & Tracy Hickman,
TSR,1987
Wayward Children, nv **DragonLance Tales**
v1, Margaret Weis & Tracy Hickman,
TSR,1987

Knight, Arthur
The Invisible Empire, ar *Pulpsmith* Win,1987

Knight, Arthur Winfield
Up in Smoke, pm *2AM* Fll,1987

Knight, Damon, Terry A. Garey, Eric M.
Heideman & Kate Wilhelm
An Interview with Kate Wilhelm and Damon
Knight, iv *Tales of the Unanticipated*
#2,1987

Koja, Kathe
Happy Birthday, Kim White, ss *SF International* #1,1987

Koman, Victor
The Jehovah Contract, n. Franklin Watts Apr,1987

Komatsu, Sakyo
Take Your Choice, ss *SF International* #1,1987

Koontz, Dean R.
Hardshell, nv **Night Visions** #4,1987
The Interrogation, ss *The Horror Show* Sum,1987
Miss Attila the Hun, nv **Night Visions** #4,1987
Twilight Eyes, n. Berkley Sep,1987
Twilight Eyes, n. W.H. Allen Apr,1987
Twilight of the Dawn, nv **Night Visions** #4,1987
Watchers, n. Putnam Feb,1987

Koontz, Dean R. & Leigh Nichols
Dean R. Koontz, iv *The Horror Show* Sum,1987

Kopaska-Merkel, David C.
Goldfish in My Head, pm *Night Cry* v2#4,1987
Pearls of Rain, pm *Night Cry* v2#4,1987

Kopf, L.J.
Cartoon, ct *F&SF* Aug,1987

Kornbluth, C.M. & Frederik Pohl
Our Best: The Best of Frederik Pohl and C.M. Kornbluth, co Baen Feb,1987

Kosiewska, Joseph
Memento Mori, ss *Pulpsmith* Win,1987

Kostelanetz, Richard
Weigh Station, br *Pulpsmith* Win,1987

Koster
Cartoon, ct *Twilight Zone* Aug,1987

Koszowski, Allen
Allen Koszowski, iv *The Horror Show* FII,1987
Illustrations, il *The Horror Show* FII,1987

Kotani, Eric & John Maddox Roberts
The Island Worlds, n. Baen Jun,1987

Kotlan, C.M. & G.C. Edmondson
Maximum Effort, n. Ballantine/Del Rey Nov,1987

Kotowicz, Ann K.
Winter Gathering, ss *Twilight Zone* Apr,1987

Kott, Mike & Sue Cornwill
The Official Price Guide to Star Trek and Star Wars Collectibles, Second Edition, nf Ballantine/House of Collectibles Jan,1988

Kremberg, Rudy
Twenty-One Minutes, ss *Haunts* #9,1987

Kremp, Irmtraud
Fun and Games, ss *SF International* #2,1987

Kress, Nancy
An Alien Light, n. Arbor House Jan,1988
Cannibals, nv *IASFM* May,1987

Kress, Nancy (continued)
Glass, ss *IASFM* Sep,1987
Training Ground, nv **Liavek: Wizard's Row**, ed. Will Shetterly & Emma Bull, Ace,1987

Kriske, Anke M.
Moon Rise, pm *Grue* #6,1987

Krolczyk, Gregory N.
No Matter What They Say, Sometimes It Is Too Late, vi *2AM* Win,1987

Kube-McDowell, Michael P.
Empery, n. Berkley Jun,1987
Isaac Asimov's Robot City, Book 1: Odyssey, n. Ace Jul,1987
Nanny, nv *Analog* Nov,1987

Kubicek, David
A Friend of the Family, ss *Space & Time* #72,1987

Kucharski, Lisa
When the Air Gets Thick and Sweet, pm *Ice River* Sum,1987

Kunstler, James Howard
The Hunt, n. Tor Jan,1988

Kurland, Michael
Star Griffin, n. Doubleday Mar,1987

Kushner, Ellen
Swordspoint, n. Arbor House Nov,1987
Swordspoint, n. Unwin Hyman Feb,1987

Kusnick, Gregory
Chrysalis, ss *Analog* mid-Dec,1987
The Lesser Magic, nv *Analog* Apr,1987

Kuttner, Henry
Prince Raynor, co Gryphon Jul,1987

L'Amour, Louis
The Haunted Mesa, n. Bantam Jul,1987

Labbe, Rodney A. & Robert R. McCammon
An Interview with Robert McCammon, iv *Footsteps* Nov,1987

Lacher, Chris
The Technique, ss *Eldritch Tales* #14,1987

Lackey, Mercedes R.
Arrow's Fall, n. DAW Jan,1988
Arrow's Flight, n. DAW Sep,1987
Arrows of the Queen, n. DAW Mar,1987
Black Water (Suicide) [lyrics], sg **Festival Moon**, ed. C.J. Cherryh, DAW,1987
Deathangel, nv **Festival Moon**, ed. C.J. Cherryh, DAW,1987
Fever Season (Lyrics), sg **Fever Season**, ed. C.J. Cherryh, DAW,1987
The Last One of the Season, ss *American Fantasy* Win,1987
Merovingen Ecology, ms **Festival Moon**, ed. C.J. Cherryh, DAW,1987
Mist-Thoughts (Lyrics), sg **Fever Season**, ed. C.J. Cherryh, DAW,1987
Partners (Lyrics), sg **Fever Season**, ed. C.J. Cherryh, DAW,1987
A Plague on Your Houses, nv **Fever Season**, ed. C.J. Cherryh, DAW,1987
Private Conversation [lyrics], sg **Festival Moon**, ed. C.J. Cherryh, DAW,1987
Should Old Acquaintance... [Part 2], sl *Fantasy Book* Mar,1987

Lackey, Mercedes R. (continued)
Should Old Acquaintance... [Part 3], sl *Fantasy Book* Mar,1987
A Tale of Heroes, nv **Sword and Sorceress** #4, ed. Marion Zimmer Bradley,1987
Were-Hunter, nv **Tales of the Witch World**, ed. Andre Norton, St. Martin's,1987

Lacoe, Addie
Bayou Exterminator, ss *Grue* #6,1987

Lafferty, R.A.
Gray Ghost: A Reminiscence, ss,1987
My Heart Leaps Up, Chapters 3 & 4, ph Drumm Apr,1987
Serpent's Egg, n.,1987
Serpent's Egg, n. Morrigan Aug,1987

Lafferty, R.A. & Ron Wolfe
Counting Grandmothers: R.A. Lafferty, iv *American Fantasy* Sum,1987

Laidlaw, Marc
Faust Forward, ss *F&SF* Mar,1987
The Liquor Cabinet of Dr. Malikudzu, ss *Night Cry* v2#4,1987
Love Comes to the Middleman, ss **Mathenauts**, ed. Rudy Rucker, Arbor House,1987
Nutrimancer, ss *IASFM* Aug,1987
Shalamari, ss *IASFM* Dec,1987
Snowblind, ss *Twilight Zone* Feb,1987

Lake, Christina
Assyria, ss *Interzone* #19,1987

Lake, Paul
Rat Boy, ss *F&SF* May,1987

Lakey, John
On Exhibit, il *Amazing* Jul,1987

Lamming, R.M.
Sanctity, ss **Other Edens**, ed. Christopher Evans & Robert Holdstock, Unwin: London,1987

Lane, M. Travis
Venus, Our Very Favourite Star, pm **Tesseracts 2**, ed. Phyllis Gotlieb & Douglas Barbour, Press Porcepic: Victoria,1987

Langencamp, Heather, Wes Craven & Robert Englund
Nightmare on Elm Street 3, iv *The Horror Show* Spr,1987

Langford, David
In a Land of Sand and Ruin and Gold, ss **Other Edens**, ed. Christopher Evans & Robert Holdstock, Unwin: London,1987

Langford, David & John Grant
Earthdoom!, n. Grafton May,1987

Lannoy, Kathinka
S.O.S., ss *SF International* #2,1987

Lansdale, Joe R.
Boo, Yourself, ss *Whispers* #23,1987
Dead in the West (Part 4 of 4), sl *Eldritch Tales* #13,1987
Dog, Cat, and Baby, vi **Masques** #2, ed. J.N. Williamson,1987
The Fat Man, ss *The Horror Show* Jan,1987
The God of the Razor, ss *Grue* #5,1987

LANSDALE, JOE R.

Lansdale, Joe R. (continued)
The Lansdale House of Horror, mr *The Horror Show* Jan,1987
My Dead Dog, Bobby, vi *The Horror Show* Sum,1987
The Nightrunners, ex Dark Harvest: Niles, IL hc Sep,1987
The Nightrunners, n. Dark Harvest Aug,1987

Lansdale, Joe R. & William J. Grabowski
Interview with Joe R. Lansdale, iv *The Horror Show* Jan,1987

Lansdale, Joe R. & J.K. Potter
Art of Darkness, iv *Twilight Zone* Feb,1987

Lantz, Fran
Eileen Goudge's Swept Away #8: All Shook Up, n. Avon Flare Sep,1987

Larson, Glen A. & Robert Thurston
Battlestar Galactica #14: Surrender the Galactica!, n. Ace Jan,1988

Larson, Randall D.
From Out of the Past, ss *Eldritch Tales* #13,1987

Lash, Batton
Jury Duty, cs *American Fantasy* Spr,1987
A Song of a Pitiful Poor Gawdawful Thing, cs *American Fantasy* Win,1987
Stakeout, cs *American Fantasy* Sum,1987

Laumer, Keith
Rank Injustice, nv **New Destinies** v1, ed. Jim Baen, Baen,1987
Retief: Envoy to New Worlds, co Baen Apr,1987

Lawhead, Stephen R.
Taliesin, n. Crossway Aug,1987

Lawrence, Louise
The Silver Box, nv **A Quiver of Ghosts**, ed. Aiden Chambers, Bodley Head,1987

Laws, Stephen
The Wyrm, n. Souvenir Press Oct,1987

Lawson, Robert
The Silver Leopard, ss **Spaceships & Spells**, ed. Jane Yolen, Martin H. Greenberg & Charles G. Waugh, Harper & Row,1987

Laymon, Richard
The Beast House, n. Paperjacks Sep,1987
Beware!, n. Paperjacks Oct,1987
Flesh, n. W.H. Allen Oct,1987
Tread Softly, n. Tor Feb,1987

Le Guin, Ursula K.
Buffalo Gals and Other Animal Presences, co Capra Press Sep,1987
Buffalo Gals, Won't You Come Out Tonight, nv **Buffalo Gals and Other Animal Presences**, Capra Press,1987
The Crown of Laurel, pm,1987
Daddy's Big Girl, ss *Omni* Jan,1987
Lewis and Clark and After, pm *The Seattle Review* Sum,1987

Learn, Paul
The Other Side: Queen Tut, ar *Twilight Zone* Feb,1987

Leatherdale, Clive, ed.
The Origins of "Dracula": The Background to Bram Stoker's Gothic Masterpiece, nf Kimber Oct,1987

Ledbetter, Kenneth W.
The Canyons of Ariel, nv *F&SF* Dec,1987

Ledger, Peter & Christy Marx
The Sisterhood of Steel: Baronwe: Daughter of Death, gn Eclipse/Moonfire Oct,1987

Lee, James A.
Reflections on Yarbro's **False Dawn**, br *2AM* Win,1987

Lee, Rebecca
Evert Sparrow That Falls, ss *Aboriginal SF* Nov,1987

Lee, Samantha & Robert Louis Stevenson
Dr. Jekyll and Mr. Hyde, n. Beaver Feb,1987
Dr. Jekyll and Mr. Hyde, n. Hutchinson Mar,1987

Lee, Tanith
Black as a Rose, nv **Night's Sorceries**, DAW,1987
By Crystal Light Beneath One Star, nv **Tales from the Forbidden Planet**, ed. Roz Kaveney, Titan,1987
Children of the Night, na **Night's Sorceries**, DAW,1987
Crying in the Rain, ss **Other Edens**, ed. Christopher Evans & Robert Holdstock, Unwin: London,1987
The Daughter of the Magician, na **Night's Sorceries**, DAW,1987
Dooniveh, the Moon, na **Night's Sorceries**, DAW,1987
Game Players, ss **Night's Sorceries**, DAW,1987
Night's Daughter, Day's Desire, nv **Night's Sorceries**, DAW,1987
Night's Sorceries, n. DAW: New York,1987
Night's Sorceries, oc DAW Apr,1987
The Prodigal, nv **Night's Sorceries**, DAW,1987
Tales from the Flat Earth: Night's Daughter, om SFBC Oct,1987
Tales from the Flat Earth: The Lords of Darkness, om SFBC Oct,1987

Lee, Vernon
Supernatural Tales: Excursions Into Fantasy, co Peter Owen Feb,1987

Lee, Walt & Richard Delap
Shapes, n. Ace Charter Feb,1987

Leeson, Robert
Slambash Wangs of a Compo Gormer, n. Collins Nov,1987

Lefanu, Sarah & Jen Green, eds.
Despatches from the Frontiers of the Female Mind, an Salem House/Women's Press Mar,1987

Leiber, Fritz
The Mouser Goes Below, ss *Whispers* #23,1987

Leiber, Justin
Beyond Humanity, n. Tor Apr,1987
Tit for Tat, ss *Amazing* Jul,1987

Leigh, Stephen
The Crystal Memory, n. Avon Sep,1987

Lem, Stanislaw
Fiasco, n. Harcourt Brace Jovanovich May,1987

Leman, Bob
Come Where My Love Lies Dreaming, ss **Shadows #10**, ed. Charles L. Grant,1987
Olida, nv *F&SF* Apr,1987

Lenihan, Kevin
Lovers, ss *The Horror Show* Win,1987

Leonard, Elmore
Touch, n. Arbor House Sep,1987

Lepovetsky, Lisa
Autumn Memories, pm *Grue* #6,1987
Axe, pm *Grue* #4,1987
The Mad Poet's Magic Fails, pm *2AM* Spr,1987

Leroe, Ellen
Robot Raiders, hc Harper & Row Jul,1987

Letendre, Serge & Regis Loisel
Roxanna #2: The Temple of Oblivion, gn NBM Sep,1987

Lewins, Anna
Dream For Danger, n. Blackie May,1987

Lewis, Anthony R.
The Analog Calendar of Upcoming Events, ms *Analog* Jan,1987
The Analog Calendar of Upcoming Events, ms *Analog* Feb,1987
The Analog Calendar of Upcoming Events, ms *Analog* Mar,1987
The Analog Calendar of Upcoming Events, ms *Analog* Apr,1987
The Analog Calendar of Upcoming Events, ms *Analog* May,1987
The Analog Calendar of Upcoming Events, ms *Analog* Jun,1987
The Analog Calendar of Upcoming Events, ms *Analog* Jul,1987
The Analog Calendar of Upcoming Events, ms *Analog* Aug,1987
The Analog Calendar of Upcoming Events, ms *Analog* Sep,1987
The Analog Calendar of Upcoming Events, ms *Analog* Oct,1987
The Analog Calendar of Upcoming Events, ms *Analog* Nov,1987
The Analog Calendar of Upcoming Events, ms *Analog* Dec,1987
The Analog Calendar of Upcoming Events, ms *Analog* mid-Dec,1987

Lewis, C.S.
Tales of Narnia, om Collins Dec,1987

Lewitt, S.N.
Angel at Apogee, n. Berkley Mar,1987
U.S.S.A. Book 2, n. Avon Feb,1987
U.S.S.A. Book 4, n. Avon Jun,1987

Lewitt, Shariann
Sister of Midnight, ss **Friends of the Horseclans**, ed. Robert Adams & Pamela Crippen Adams, Signet,1987

Libertus, Peg
A Lunar Cycle, pm *Aboriginal SF* Feb,1987

LIEBSON, MORRIS

MACPHERSON, JAIME

Liebson, Morris
Obsidian Sphinx, pm *Amazing* Sep,1987

Ligotti, Thomas
Dr. Locrian's Asylum, ss *Grue* #5,1987

Linaweaver, Brad
High Road of Lost Men, nv **Friends of the Horseclans**, ed. Robert Adams & Pamela Crippen Adams, Signet,1987

Lindahn, Ron & Val Lakey Lindahn
Portfolio, pi **World Fantasy Convention Program Book** #13,1987

Lindahn, Ron & Val Lakey Lindahn, eds.
A Southern Fantasy: 13th World Fantasy Convention Program Book, oa Nashville World Fantasy Convention Oct,1987

Lindahn, Val Lakey & Ron Lindahn
Portfolio, pi **World Fantasy Convention Program Book** #13,1987

Lindahn, Val Lakey & Ron Lindahn, eds.
A Southern Fantasy: 13th World Fantasy Convention Program Book, oa Nashville World Fantasy Convention Oct,1987

Lindbergh, Anne
The Shadow on the Dial, n. Harper & Row Jul,1987

Lindholm, Megan & Steven Brust
An Act of Mercy, ss **Liavek: Wizard's Row**, ed. Will Shetterly & Emma Bull, Ace,1987

Linzner, Gordon
The Editor's Page, ed *Space & Time* #72,1987
The Editor's Page, ed *Space & Time* #73,1987

Linzner, Gordon, ed.
Space & Time [#72, Summer 1987]
Space & Time [#73, Winter 1988]

Lipinski, Miroslaw, ed.
The Grabinski Reader [#2, Spring 1987]

Little, Bentley
Comes the Bad Time, ss *The Horror Show* Win,1987
Garage Sale, ss *Space & Time* #72,1987
Lethe Dreams, ss *Night Cry* v2#3,1987
Loony Toon, vi *The Horror Show* Fll,1987
Projections, ss *The Horror Show* Jan,1987
Runt, ss *The Horror Show* Spr,1987
The Show, ss *The Horror Show* Fll,1987
Snow, ss *Grue* #4,1987

Little, Bentley & William J. Grabowski
Bentley Little, iv *The Horror Show* Fll,1987

Livingstone, Ian
Casket of Souls, ss Penguin Nov,1987

Llywelyn, Morgan
Me, Tree, ss **Devils & Demons**, ed. Marvin Kaye, SFBC/Doubleday,1987

Lodi, Edward
On a Clear Day, vi *2AM* Fll,1987

Loisel, Regis & Serge Letendre
Roxanna #2: The Temple of Oblivion, gn NBM Sep,1987

Longyear, Barry B.
Little Green Men, ss **Spaceships & Spells**, ed. Jane Yolen, Martin H. Greenberg & Charles G. Waugh, Harper & Row,1987
Sea of Glass, n. St. Martin's Jan,1987

LoProto, Frank
The Magic, vi *2AM* Fll,1987

Lord, J. Edward
Elixir, n. Ballantine Jun,1987
Incantation, n. Ballantine Nov,1987

Lorimer, Janet
The Natural Way, ss *2AM* Spr,1987

Lorimer, Philip
Under the Carpet, ss **The Pan Book of Horror Stories** #28, Pan,1987

Loring, E. Bertrand
The Man Who Wrote Shakespeare, ss *F&SF* Jan,1987

Lorrah, Jean & Winston A. Howlett
Wulfston's Odyssey, n. NAL/Signet Nov,1987

Lorrey, Rayson
An Arrow of Tempered Silver, ss *Fantasy Book* Mar,1987

Love, G.B. & Walter Irwin, eds.
The Best of Trek #12, nf NAL/Signet Aug,1987

Love, Rosaleen
Alexia and Graham Bell, ss *Aphelion* #5,1987

Lovin, Roger Robert
The Cobbler, ss *F&SF* Dec,1987

Lowe, Jonathan
Sole Survivor, pm *Eldritch Tales* #13,1987

Lowe, Nick
Mutant Popcorn, mr *Interzone* #19,1987
Mutant Popcorn, mr *Interzone* #21,1987

Lowe, W.T.
All in Favor, vi *American Fantasy* Win,1987

Lubow, Michael
The Little Blue Pill, ss *Playboy* Apr,1987

Lucarotti, John
The Massacre, n. W.H. Allen Jun,1987

Lucas, George, Donald F. Glut & James Kahn
The Star Wars Trilogy, om Ballantine/Del Rey May,1987

Lucas, Laurel
Aborigines: A NATO Alliance?, bg *Aboriginal SF* May,1987
Aborigines: Devolution and Disappearances, bg *Aboriginal SF* Feb,1987
Aborigines: NASA Experiments With SF, bg *Aboriginal SF* Sep,1987
Aborigines: Nature Versus Nurture, bg *Aboriginal SF* Nov,1987
Aborigines: Plan 9 From Roslindale, bg *Aboriginal SF* Jul,1987

Lumley, Brian
The Compleat Crow, co Ganley Jul,1987
Demogorgon, n. Grafton Apr,1987

Lumley, Brian (continued)
In the Temple of Terror, nv *Weirdbook* #22,1987
Inception, ss **The Compleat Crow**, Ganley,1987
The Thin People, ss *Whispers* #23,1987

Lundwall, Sam J. & Brian W. Aldiss, eds.
The Penguin World Omnibus of Science Fiction, an Penguin Oct,1987

Lupoff, Richard A.
Etchings of Her Memories, ss *Amazing* Mar,1987

Luserke, Uwe
The End of the Hunt, ss *SF International* #1,1987

Lyons, Joseph
Trust Me, ss **The Architecture of Fear**, ed. Kathryn Cramer & Peter D. Pautz, Arbor House,1987

MacAvoy, R.A.
The Grey Horse, n. Bantam Spectra May,1987

Mace, David
Nightrider, n. Ace Oct,1987

MacGregor, Loren
The Net, n. Ace Jun,1987

Machen, Arthur
The Collected Arthur Machen, co Duckworth Oct,1987

MacIntyre, F. Gwynplaine
Improbable Bestiary: The Bandersnatch (Frumius carrollii), pm *Amazing* Nov,1987

Mackay, Colin
The Song of the Forest, n. Available Press Aug,1987

Mackie, Mary
The People of the Horse, n. W.H. Allen Sep,1987

Maclay, John
Bird Food, pm **Other Engagements**, Madison, WI: Dream House,1987
The Bookman's God, ss **Other Engagements**, Madison, WI: Dream House,1987
Death Flight, vi *Night Cry* v2#4,1987
New York Night, ss **Other Engagements**, Madison, WI: Dream House,1987
Nostalgia, pm *Footsteps* Nov,1987
On the Boardwalk, ss **Other Engagements**, Madison, WI: Dream House,1987
Other Engagements, co Dream House Oct,1987
The Reckoning, vi **Other Engagements**, Madison, WI: Dream House,1987
The Sisters, ss **Other Engagements**, Madison, WI: Dream House,1987
Turning Forty, pm **Other Engagements**, Madison, WI: Dream House,1987

Maclay, John & William J. Grabowski
Genre-Love and the Magic of Words: John Maclay, iv *2AM* Fll,1987

MacPherson, Jaime
Covenant, ss *Apex!* #1,1987

Maddox, Tom
  Spirit of the Night, nv *IASFM* Sep,1987

Mage Staff
  Mage Reviews, br *Mage* Spr,1987
  Mage Reviews, br *Mage* Win,1987

Mahy, Margaret
  The Tricksters, n. Macmillan McElderry
  Mar,1987

Maitland, Sara
  The Book of Spells, oc Michael Joseph
  Sep,1987
  Lady with Unicorn, ss **The Virago Book of
  Ghost Stories**, ed. Richard Dalby,
  Virago,1987
  The Wicked Stepmother's Lament, ss **More
  Tales I Tell My Mother**, Journeyman,1987

Mallonee, Dennis
  Editorial, ed *Fantasy Book* Mar,1987

Mallonee, Dennis & Nick Smith, eds.
  Fantasy Book [v.5 #5, March 1987]

Maloney, Mack
  Wingman, n. Zebra Mar,1987
  Wingman: The Circle War, n. Zebra
  Jul,1987

Malzberg, Barry N.
  Ambition, vi *Twilight Zone* Oct,1987
  Celebrating, ss *F&SF* Aug,1987
  The Queen of Lower Saigon, ss **In the Field
  of Fire**, ed. Jeanne Van Buren Dann &
  Jack M. Dann, Tor,1987

Malzberg, Barry N. & Jack M. Dann
  Bringing It Home, ss *Twilight Zone* Feb,1987

Manguel, Alberto & Gianni Guadalupi
  **The Dictionary of Imaginary Places,
  Expanded Edition**, nf HBJ Harvest
  Sep,1987

Manley, Mark
  Throwback, n. Popular Library Nov,1987

Mann, Philip
  The Fall of the Families, n. Gollancz
  May,1987

Manzione, Joseph
  Candle in a Cosmic Wind, nv *Analog*
  Aug,1987

Margroff, Robert E. & Piers Anthony
  Dragon's Gold, n. Tor Jul,1987

Mark, Jan
  Buzz-Words, ss **A Quiver of Ghosts**, ed.
  Aiden Chambers, Bodley Head,1987
  Closer than a Brother, ss **Twisted Circuits**,
  ed. Mick Gowar, Beaver,1987

Marra, Sue
  Blood Junkie, pm *2AM* Win,1987
  The Music Box, pm *2AM* Spr,1987

Marsh, Geoffrey
  Patch of the Odin Soldier, n. Doubleday
  Apr,1987

Marsh, John
  The Whisperer, ss **After Midnight Stories**
  #3,1987

Marten, Jacqueline
  Dream Walker, n. Pocket Feb,1987

Marter, Ian
  The Reign of Terror, n. W.H. Allen Mar,1987
  The Rescue, n. W.H. Allen Aug,1987

Martin, David
  Hunger, ss *New Pathways* Jan,1987

Martin, George R.R.
  Jube: Five, sl **Wild Cards** v2, ed. George
  R.R. Martin, Bantam,1987
  Jube: Four, sl **Wild Cards** v2, ed. George
  R.R. Martin, Bantam,1987
  Jube: One, sl **Wild Cards** v2, ed. George
  R.R. Martin, Bantam,1987
  Jube: Seven, sl **Wild Cards** v2, ed. George
  R.R. Martin, Bantam,1987
  Jube: Six, sl **Wild Cards** v2, ed. George
  R.R. Martin, Bantam,1987
  Jube: Three, sl **Wild Cards** v2, ed. George
  R.R. Martin, Bantam,1987
  Jube: Two, sl **Wild Cards** v2, ed. George
  R.R. Martin, Bantam,1987
  The Pear-Shaped Man, ss *Omni* Oct,1987
  Portraits of His Children, co Dark Harvest
  Jul,1987
  Winter's Chill, nv **Wild Cards** v2, ed. George
  R.R. Martin, Bantam,1987

Martin, George R.R., ed.
  Wild Cards II: Aces High, oa Bantam
  Spectra Apr,1987
  Wild Cards III: Jokers Wild, oa Bantam
  Spectra Nov,1987

Martin, George R.R., Pat Broderick, Neal
  McPheeters & Doug Moench
  Sandkings, gn DC Graphics Jan,1987

Martin, Graham Dunstan
  Dream Wall, n. Unwin Hyman May,1987

Martin, Henry
  Cartoon, ct *F&SF* Jan,1987
  Cartoon, ct *F&SF* Feb,1987
  Cartoon, ct *F&SF* Mar,1987
  Cartoon, ct *F&SF* Apr,1987
  Cartoon, ct *F&SF* May,1987
  Cartoon, ct *F&SF* Jun,1987
  Cartoon, ct *F&SF* Jul,1987
  Cartoon, ct *F&SF* Aug,1987
  Cartoon, ct *F&SF* Sep,1987
  Cartoon, ct *F&SF* Nov,1987
  Cartoon, ct *F&SF* Dec,1987

Martine-Barnes, Adrienne
  The Crystal Sword, n. Avon Jan,1988

Martinez, B.J.
  Uncle Green-Eye, ss *F&SF* Mar,1987

Marx, Christy & Peter Ledger
  The Sisterhood of Steel: Baronwe: Daughter
  of Death, gn Eclipse/Moonfire Oct,1987

Masear, Arthur
  Cartoon, ct *Twilight Zone* Jun,1987

Masello, Robert
  The Spirit Wood, n. Pocket Jun,1987

Mason, Lisa
  Arachne, ss *Omni* Dec,1987

Mason, Tom
  Cartoon, ct *Aboriginal SF* May,1987

Mason, Tom (continued)
  Cartoon, ct *Twilight Zone* Aug,1987

Massie, Elizabeth
  Bargains at Binsley's, ss *The Horror Show*
  Jan,1987
  Blessed Sleep, vi *2AM* Fll,1987
  Dance of the Spirit Untouched, ss *Footsteps*
  Nov,1987
  Elizabeth Massie, iv *The Horror Show*
  Fll,1987
  To Sooth the Savage Beast, ss *The Horror
  Show* Fll,1987
  Willy Wonka and the L. Walker Biofair, ss
  The Horror Show Fll,1987

Massin, Jim
  Game Review, gr *Salarius* v1#4,1987

Mastrangelo, Judy, ill. & Jean L. Scrocco, ed.
  Antique Fairy Tales, an Unicorn Oct,1987

Matchette, Katharine E.
  The Return, ss *Apex!* #1,1987

Matheson, Richard
  Buried Talents, ss **Masques** #2, ed. J.N.
  Williamson,1987
  The Near Departed, vi **Masques** #2, ed.
  J.N. Williamson,1987

Matheson, Richard Christian
  Break-Up, ss **Scars**, Scream/Press,1987
  Commuters, ss **Scars**, Scream/Press,1987
  Deathbed, vi **Masques** #2, ed. J.N.
  Williamson,1987
  Dust, ss **Scars**, Scream/Press,1987
  Goosebumps, ss **Scars**, Scream/Press,1987
  Hell, ss **Scars**, Scream/Press,1987
  Incorporation, ss **Scars**, Scream/Press,1987
  Mobius, ss **Scars**, Scream/Press,1987
  Mugger, ss **Scars**, Scream/Press,1987
  Obsolete, ss **Scars**, Scream/Press,1987
  Scars, co Scream/Press Aug,1987
  Timed Exposure, ss **Scars**,
  Scream/Press,1987

Matheson, Richard Christian & William
  Relling, Jr.
  Wonderland, ss *Night Cry* v2#5,1987

Mathews, Jack
  **The Battle of Brazil: The Authorized Story
  and Annotated Screenplay of Terry
  Gilliam's Landmark Film**, co Crown
  May,1987

Matic, Rudy
  Ask Not, ss *Night Cry* v2#5,1987

Matthews, Jack
  The Betrayal of the Fives, ss **Ghostly
  Populations**, Johns Hopkins,1987
  Ghostly Populations, co Johns Hopkins
  Jan,1987
  Ghostly Populations, ss **Ghostly
  Populations**, Johns Hopkins,1987
  If Not Us, Then Who?, ss **Ghostly
  Populations**, Johns Hopkins,1987
  Taking Stock, ss **Ghostly Populations**,
  Johns Hopkins,1987

Matthews, Patricia
  The Children of the Sea, ss *F&SF* Feb,1987

Matthews, Rodney & Michael Moorcock
  Elric at the End of Time, pi Paper Tiger
  Jun,1987

Maurer, Allan
Illuminations: Building a Better Egg, ar *Twilight Zone* Dec,1987
Illuminations: Computer Rosetta Stone, ar *Twilight Zone* Dec,1987
Illuminations: You May Be Typecast, ar *Twilight Zone* Dec,1987
The Other Side: Baffling Seneca Guns, ar *Twilight Zone* Dec,1987
The Other Side: Watch Horror Movies and Get Rich, ar *Twilight Zone* Dec,1987

Maximovic, Gerd
The Black Ship, ss *SF International* #2,1987

May, Julian
Intervention, n. Houghton Mifflin Aug,1987

May, Paula
Resonance Ritual, ss **L. Ron Hubbard Presents Writers of the Future** v3, ed. Algis Budrys, Bridge,1987

May, Rex
Cartoon, ct *F&SF* Jan,1987
Cartoon, ct *F&SF* Jun,1987

Mayer, Frederick J.
Grinning Moon, pm *Eldritch Tales* #14,1987

Mayhar, Ardath
Battletech: The Sword and the Dagger, n. FASA,1987
Down in the Dark, ss *The Horror Show* Sum,1987
In the Tank, ss **Masques** #2, ed. J.N. Williamson,1987
The Left Eye of God, vi *Salarius* v1#4,1987
Makra Choria, n. Atheneum/Argo Mar,1987
Neither Rest nor Refuge, ss **Tales of the Witch World**, ed. Andre Norton, St. Martin's,1987
Speaking Wolf, ss *Pulpsmith* Win,1987
That Thing in There, ss *Eldritch Tales* #13,1987
To Trap a Demon, ss **Magic in Ithkar** #4, ed. Andre Norton & Robert Adams,1987
The Wall, n. Space & Time Jul,1987

Mayhar, Ardath & Ron Fortier
Trail of the Seahawks, n. TSR/Windwalker Jun,1987

McAllister, Bruce
Dream Baby, nv **In the Field of Fire**, ed. Jeanne Van Buren Dann & Jack M. Dann, Tor,1987
Kingdom Come, ss *Omni* Feb,1987

McAuley, Paul J.
Among the Stones, nv *Amazing* Jan,1987
A Dragon for Seyour Chan, ss *Interzone* #19,1987
The Heirs of Earth, nv *Amazing* May,1987
The Temporary King, nv *F&SF* Jan,1987

McCaffrey, Anne
The Lady, n. Ballantine Nov,1987
Nerilka's Story & The Coelura, om Bantam UK Jan,1987

McCammon, Robert R.
Best Friends, nv **Night Visions** #4,1987
The Deep End, ss **Night Visions** #4,1987
Doom City, ss **Doom City**, ed. Charles L. Grant, Tor,1987
Fragments of Horror, ms *The Horror Show* Spr,1987

McCammon, Robert R. (continued)
A Life in the Day of, ss **Night Visions** #4,1987
Lights Out [from **Swan Song**], ex Pocket: New York Jun,1987
Swan Song, ex Pocket: New York Jun,1987
Swan Song, n. Pocket Jun,1987
Yellachile's Cage, ss **World Fantasy Convention Program Book** #13,1987

McCammon, Robert R. & William J. Grabowski
Interview with Robert R. McCammon, iv *The Horror Show* Spr,1987

McCammon, Robert R. & Rodney A. Labbe
An Interview with Robert McCammon, iv *Footsteps* Nov,1987

McCarthy, Gerry
Entropanto, ss **Gollancz - Sunday Times Best SF Stories**, Gollancz,1987

McCollum, Michael
Antares Passage, n. Ballantine/Del Rey Dec,1987

McCrumb, Sharyn
Bimbos of the Death Sun, n. TSR/Windwalker Mar,1987

McCullough, Colleen
The Ladies of Missalonghi, n. Harper & Row Apr,1987
The Ladies of Missalonghi, n. Hutchinson Jun,1987

McCutchan, Philip
A Time For Survival, n. Firecrest May,1987

McDaniel, Mary Catherine
A Little of What You Fancy, ss **L. Ron Hubbard Presents Writers of the Future** v3, ed. Algis Budrys, Bridge,1987

McDevitt, Jack
Dutchman, nv *IASFM* Feb,1987
In the Tower, nv **Universe** #17, ed. Terry Carr,1987
To Hell with the Stars, ss *IASFM* Dec,1987

McDonough, Thomas R.
The Architects of Hyperspace, n. Avon Dec,1987

McDowell, Michael
Halley's Passing, ss *Twilight Zone* Jun,1987

McEwan, Ian
The Child in Time, n. Cape Sep,1987

McGowen, Tom
The Magician's Apprentice, n. Dutton/Lodestar Jan,1987

McGregor, Matt
To Sleep Perchance To Dream, ss *Minnesota Fantasy Review* #1,1987

McKay, Ross
The Indian's Grave, ss **After Midnight Stories** #3,1987

McKenzie, Ellen Kindt
Kashka, n. Holt Sep,1987

McKillip, Patricia A.
Fool's Run, n. Warner Apr,1987

McKinney, Jack
Robotech # 1: Genesis, n. Ballantine/Del Rey Mar,1987
Robotech # 2: Battle Cry, n. Ballantine/Del Rey Mar,1987
Robotech # 3: Homecoming, n. Ballantine/Del Rey Mar,1987
Robotech # 4: Battlehymn, n. Ballantine/Del Rey Mar,1987
Robotech # 5: Force of Arms, n. Ballantine/Del Rey May,1987
Robotech # 6: Doomsday, n. Ballantine/Del Rey Jun,1987
Robotech # 7: Southern Cross, n. Ballantine/Del Rey Jul,1987
Robotech # 8: Metal Fire, n. Ballantine/Del Rey Aug,1987
Robotech # 9: The Final Nightmare, n. Ballantine/Del Rey Sep,1987
Robotech #10: Invid Invasion, n. Ballantine/Del Rey Oct,1987
Robotech #11: Metamorphosos, n. Ballantine/Del Rey Nov,1987
Robotech #12: Symphony of Light, n. Ballantine/Del Rey Dec,1987

McLaughlin, Cooper
The Order of the Peacock Angel, nv *F&SF* Jan,1987

McLoughlin, John
Tookmaker Koan, n. Baen Oct,1987

McNally, Clare
Somebody Come and Play, n. Corgi Aug,1987
Somebody Come and Play, n. Tor Sep,1987

McNamara, Peter
Editorial, ed *Aphelion* #5,1987

McNamara, Peter, ed.
Aphelion [# 5, Summer 86/87]

McPheeters, Neal, Pat Broderick, George R.R. Martin & Doug Moench
Sandkings, gn DC Graphics Jan,1987

McPherson, Michael C.
Every Garbage Dump Has One, vi *Haunts* #9,1987
Expert Witness, vi *2AM* Win,1987

McQuay, Mike
Isaac Asimov's Robot City, Book 2: Suspicion, n. Ace Sep,1987
Memories, n. Bantam Spectra Jun,1987

McSherry, Frank D., Jr., Martin H. Greenberg & Charles G. Waugh, eds.
Nightmares in Dixie: Thirteen Horror Tales From the American South, an August House Apr,1987

Meade, Stephen
The Mirror Monster, ss *Night Cry* v2#3,1987

Medcalf, Robert Randolph, Jr.
Mindsword, pm *Space & Time* #72,1987
Werewolfgirl, pm *Eldritch Tales* #13,1987
Zombie Bride, pm *Eldritch Tales* #14,1987

Meier, Shirley
Trave, ss **Magic in Ithkar** #4, ed. Andre Norton & Robert Adams,1987

MEISNER, RICHARD D.

Meisner, Richard D.
Universe--The Ultimate Artifact?, ar *Analog*
Apr,1987

Melamed, Leo
The Tenth Planet, n. Bonus Books
Sep,1987

Melanos, Jack A.
Sindbad and the Evil Genie, pl Stacey
Jan,1987

Melling, O.R.
The Singing Stone, n. Viking Kestrel
May,1987

Melton, Henry
Partly Murphy, ss *Analog* May,1987

Memmott, David
The Aka Fragments [Part 1], sl *New Pathways* Apr,1987
The Aka Fragments [Part 2], sl *New Pathways* Aug,1987
The Aka Fragments [Part 3], sl *New Pathways* Nov,1987

Memmott, David, ed.
Ice River [v1 #1, Summer 1987]

Mercadel, Walter F.
Porcinity's Palace, ss *Space & Time* #73,1987

Merchant, Paul
from A Life of Copernicus, pm *Ice River* Sum,1987

Meredith, Richard C.
Timeliner Trilogy, om Arrow Aug,1987

Merwin, W.S.
Kanaloa, pm *New Yorker* Apr 13,1987

Metzger, Robert A.
True Magic, ss *Aboriginal SF* Nov,1987
A Unfiltered Man, ss *Aboriginal SF* Sep,1987

Meyer, William
The Real, pm *Pulpsmith* Win,1987

Michaels, Melisa C.
Pirate Prince, n. Tor Feb,1987

Middleton, Haydn
The People in the Picture, n. Bantam UK Aug,1987

Miesel, Sandra
The Book-Healer, ss **Magic in Ithkar** #4, ed. Andre Norton & Robert Adams,1987
The Sword That Wept, ss *Amazing* Sep,1987

Miklowitz, Gloria D.
After the Bomb: Week One, n. Scholastic Point Feb,1987

Milan, Victor
With a Little Help From His Friends, nv **Wild Cards** v2, ed. George R.R. Martin, Bantam,1987

Milan, Victor & Melinda M. Snodgrass
Runespear, n. Popular Library Questar Apr,1987

Miller, Frank
Ronin, gn Warner Sep,1987

Miller, G. Wayne
G. Wayne Miller, iv *The Horror Show* Fll,1987
Gnawing, ss *The Horror Show* Spr,1987
God of Self, ss *The Horror Show* Fll,1987
Not Just Traces of Me, vi *The Horror Show* Sum,1987
Nothing There, ss *The Horror Show* Fll,1987
We Who Are His Followers, ss *The Horror Show* Win,1987
Windham's Folly, ss *Space & Time* #73,1987
Wiping the Slate Clean, ss **Masques** #2, ed. J.N. Williamson,1987

Miller, Holmes
Solo, ss *Grue* #5,1987

Miller, Ian
The Angle of Consciousness, pi *Interzone* #21,1987

Miller, John J.
Half Past Dead, nv **Wild Cards** v2, ed. George R.R. Martin, Bantam,1987
Ouroboros, nv **A Very Large Array**, ed. Melinda M. Snodgrass, University of New Mexico Press,1987

Miller, Miranda
Smiles and the Millenium, n. Virago Jul,1987

Miller, Moira
The Doom of Soulis, n. Pied Piper Nov,1987

Miller, Rex
Slob, n. NAL/Signet Nov,1987

Miller, Rob Hollis
Farewells on the Melon Bridge, pm *New Pathways* Jan,1987

Miller, Russell
Bare-Faced Messiah, nf Michael Joseph Oct,1987

Miller, Sasha
Jamie Burke and the Queen of England, ss *F&SF* Jun,1987
To Rebuild the Eyrie, nv **Tales of the Witch World**, ed. Andre Norton, St. Martin's,1987

Miller, Steph
The Sponge, pm *Space & Time* #72,1987

Milne, Janis
Starship Dunroamin, n. Dent Jun,1987

Miner, Brad
Reaching for Paradise, nv **Angels in Hell**, ed. Janet Morris, Baen,1987

Mink Mole
Traveler's Report on Florida's World Famous 'Alligator Alley', fa *New Pathways* Nov,1987

Mink Mole & Ferret
Grow Your Own Baby, cs *New Pathways* Nov,1987
I Was a Teenage Reptile, cs *New Pathways* Aug,1987
Nuclear FX, cs *New Pathways* Jan,1987
Nuclear FX, cs *New Pathways* Aug,1987
Nuclear FX, cs *New Pathways* Nov,1987

Minnion, Keith
The Prince's Birthday, ss *The Dragon* Jun,1987

Minta, Stephen
Garcia Marquez: Writer of Colombia, nf Harper & Row Apr,1987

Mirolla, Michael
Rules of Conduct, ss **Tesseracts 2**, ed. Phyllis Gotlieb & Douglas Barbour, Press Porcepic: Victoria,1987

Mitchell, Elizabeth, ed.
Free Lancers, oa Baen Sep,1987

Mitchell, Joanne
Scout's Honor, ss *Aboriginal SF* Nov,1987

Mitchell, Kirk
Never the Twain, n. Ace Nov,1987

Mitchison, Naomi
Early in Orcadia, n. Richard Drew Feb,1987

Mixon, Laura J.
Omni: Astropilots, n. Scholastic/Omni Jul,1987

Modesitt, L.E., Jr.
The Silent Warrior, n. Tor Dec,1987

Moench, Doug, Pat Broderick, George R.R. Martin & Neal McPheeters
Sandkings, gn DC Graphics Jan,1987

Moffett, Judith
Pennterra, n. Congdon & Weed Sep,1987

Mohan, Kim & Pamela O'Neill
Planet in Peril, n. Ace/New Infinities Dec,1987

Monaco, Richard
Unto the Beast, n. Bantam Spectra Apr,1987

Moncuse, Steve
The Fish Police, gn Warner Dec,1987

Monteleone, Thomas F.
The Magnificent Gallery, n. Tor Jun,1987
The Night Is Freezing Fast, ss **Masques** #2, ed. J.N. Williamson,1987
Yesterday's Child, ss *Grue* #5,1987

Monteleone, Thomas F. & John DeChancie
Crooked House, n. Tor Dec,1987

Montgomerie, Lee
Book Reviews, br *Interzone* #19,1987
Book Reviews, br *Interzone* #20,1987
Book Reviews, br *Interzone* #21,1987
Book Reviews, br *Interzone* #22,1987

Moon, Elizabeth N.
A Delicate Adjustment, na *Analog* Feb,1987
Just Another Day at the Weather Service, vi *Analog* Nov,1987

Moorcock, Michael
The Brothel in Rosenstrasse, n. Carroll & Graf Jul,1987
The City in the Autumn Stars, n. Ace Nov,1987
The Cornelius Chronicles, Vol. III, om Avon Feb,1987
The Frozen Cardinal, ss **Other Edens**, ed. Christopher Evans & Robert Holdstock, Unwin: London,1987
John Dee's Song, pm *Back Brain Recluse* #7,1987

MOORCOCK, MICHAEL

Moorcock, Michael (continued)
The Murderer's Song, nv **Tales from the Forbidden Planet**, ed. Roz Kaveney, Titan,1987
Pierrot on the Moon, pm *Back Brain Recluse* #7,1987
Wizardry and Wild Romance, nf Gollancz Aug,1987

Moorcock, Michael & Rodney Matthews
Elric at the End of Time, pi Paper Tiger Jun,1987

Moorcock, Michael & Chris Reed
Michael Moorcock, iv *Back Brain Recluse* #7,1987

Moore, Alan
A Hypothetical Lizard, nv **Liavek: Wizard's Row**, ed. Will Shetterly & Emma Bull, Ace,1987

Moore, Alan & Neil Gaiman
Alan Moore Interview, iv *American Fantasy* Win,1987

Moore, John F.
Lineage, vi *Salarius* v1#4,1987
Trackdown, ss *Aboriginal SF* Feb,1987

Moore, Roger E.
A Stone's Throw Away, ss **DragonLance Tales** v1, Margaret Weis & Tracy Hickman, TSR,1987

Moore, Rudin
A Ceres Situation, ss **Ultra-Vue and Selected Peripheral Visions**, self published,1987
Hit Me, nv **Ultra-Vue and Selected Peripheral Visions**, self published,1987
The Hoodoo, na **Ultra-Vue and Selected Peripheral Visions**, self published,1987
Ultra-Vue, n. **Ultra-Vue and Selected Peripheral Visions**, self published,1987
Ultra-Vue and Selected Peripheral Visions, oc self published Aug,1987
Wait a Minute!, ss **Ultra-Vue and Selected Peripheral Visions**, self published,1987

Moorhouse, Sue
Rika's World, ss **Gollancz - Sunday Times Best SF Stories**, Gollancz,1987

Moran, Daniel
The Flame Key, n. Tor Apr,1987

Morlan, A.R.
A.R. Morlan, iv *The Horror Show* Fll,1987
Bub and the Zomb Boys, ss *The Horror Show* Fll,1987
The Children of the Kingdom Quiz, qz *The Horror Show* Jan,1987
The Cuttlefish, ss *Twilight Zone* Oct,1987
Dear D.B. ..., ss *Night Cry* v2#5,1987
It's Alive Again! The Return of the Nit-Picky, Utterly Trivial, Totally Picayune Horror-Fantasy (and What the Heck, a Little Sci-Fi) Movie Quiz Part III, qz *The Horror Show* Fll,1987
Just Another Bedtime Story, ss *Night Cry* v2#4,1987
The Last Bedtime Story, ss *Grue* #6,1987
The "Monster Mash" Quiz, qz *The Horror Show* Win,1987
Night Skirt, ss *The Horror Show* Win,1987
The On'ner, ss *Grue* #4,1987

Morlan, A.R. (continued)
The Second Nit-Picky, Utterly Trivial, Totally Picayune Horror-Fantasy Movie Quiz -- or -- Trivial Lives, II, qz *The Horror Show* Sum,1987
The "There Was an Old Woman" Quiz, qz *The Horror Show* Spr,1987
Tomb of Nine Hundred Days, ss *The Horror Show* Fll,1987
What the Janitor Found, pm *Night Cry* v2#3,1987
The Wi'ching Well, ss *The Horror Show* Jan,1987

Morressy, John
A Legend of Fair Women, nv *F&SF* Sep,1987
The Quality of Murphy, nv *F&SF* Mar,1987
The Questing of Kedrigern, n. Ace Aug,1987

Morris, Chris
Handmaids In Hell, ss **Angels in Hell**, ed. Janet Morris, Baen,1987
Hearts and Minds, nv **Fever Season**, ed. C.J. Cherryh, DAW,1987
Night Action, ss **Festival Moon**, ed. C.J. Cherryh, DAW,1987
The Ransom of Hellcat, nv **Masters of Hell**, ed. Janet Morris et al, Baen,1987
Snowballs in Hell, nv **Crusaders in Hell**, ed. Janet Morris, New York: Baen,1987

Morris, Chris & Janet Morris
The Nature of Hell, ss **Crusaders in Hell**, ed. Janet Morris, New York: Baen,1987
Sword Play, na **Festival Moon**, ed. C.J. Cherryh, DAW,1987

Morris, Janet
Gilgamesh Redux, nv **Crusaders in Hell**, ed. Janet Morris, New York: Baen,1987
Instant Karma, nv **Fever Season**, ed. C.J. Cherryh, DAW,1987
Sea Change, nv **Masters of Hell**, ed. Janet Morris et al, Baen,1987
Sea of Stiffs, nv **Angels in Hell**, ed. Janet Morris, Baen,1987
Tempus, n. Baen Apr,1987
Wake of the Riddler, nv **Aftermath**, ed. Robert Lynn Asprin & Lynn Abbey, Ace,1987
Warlord!, n. Pocket Sep,1987

Morris, Janet, ed.
Angels in Hell, oa Baen Oct,1987
Crusaders in Hell, oa Baen May,1987
Masters in Hell, oa Baen Dec,1987

Morris, Janet & C.J. Cherryh
Kings in Hell, n. Baen Feb,1987

Morris, Janet & David Drake
Kill Ratio, n. Ace Oct,1987

Morris, Janet & Chris Morris
The Nature of Hell, ss **Crusaders in Hell**, ed. Janet Morris, New York: Baen,1987
Sword Play, na **Festival Moon**, ed. C.J. Cherryh, DAW,1987

Morris, Jim
Spurlock: Sheriff of Purgatory, n. Tor Apr,1987

Morrison, Michael A.
The American Nightmare: The Fiction of Dennis Etchison, ar *The Horror Show* Win,1987

Morrison, Toni
Beloved, n. Chatto & Windus Oct,1987

Morrow, James
Spelling God with the Wrong Blocks, ss *F&SF* May,1987
Veritas, nv **Synergy** v1, ed. George Zebrowski,1987

Mortensen, Nancy
The Well, ss *SF International* #2,1987

Mortum, Crematia & Kathleen E. Jurgens
Interview with Crematia Mortum (Roberta Solomon), iv *2AM* Spr,1987

Morwood, Peter
The Demon Lord, n. DAW Jun,1987
The Dragon Lord, n. DAW Dec,1987

Morwood, Peter & Diane E. Duane
The Romulan Way, n. Titan Aug,1987
Star Trek #35: The Romulan Way, n. Pocket Aug,1987

Mosiman, Billie Sue
Final Dreams, ss *Mage* Win,1987
Morbid Descent, ss *2AM* Sum,1987

Motter, Dean, Gilbert Hernandez, Jaime Hernandez & Mario Hernandez
The Return of Mister X, gn Warner Dec,1987

Mueller, Richard
Bless This Ship, ss *F&SF* Sep,1987

Munster, Bill
From the Editor, ed *Footsteps* Nov,1987

Munster, Bill, ed.
Footsteps [#8, November 1987]

Munster, Bill & F. Paul Wilson
An Interview with F. Paul Wilson, iv *Footsteps* Nov,1987

Munster, Bill & Gahan Wilson
An Interview with Gahan Wilson, in *Footsteps* Nov,1987

Murdock, M.S.
Vendetta, n. Popular Library Questar Aug,1987

Murphy, Gloria
Nightmare, n. Popular Library Jun,1987

Murphy, Pat
Clay Devils, ss *Twilight Zone* Apr,1987
Rachel in Love, nv *IASFM* Apr,1987

Murphy, Shirley Rousseau
The Ivory Lyre, n. Harper & Row Mar,1987

Murphy, Warren & Molly Cochran
High Priest, n. NAL Nov,1987

Murray, Paula Helm
Kayli's Fire, ss **Sword and Sorceress #4**, ed. Marion Zimmer Bradley,1987

Myers, Amy, ed.
The Third Book of After Midnight Stories, oa Kimber Oct,1987

Nadramia, Peggy
conGRUEities, ed *Grue* #4,1987
conGRUEities, ed *Grue* #5,1987

Nadramia, Peggy (continued)
conGRUEities, ed *Grue* #6,1987

Nadramia, Peggy, ed.
Grue [#4, 1987]
Grue [#5, 1987]
Grue [#6, 1987]

Nagata, Linda
Spectral Expectations, ss *Analog* Apr,1987

Naha, Ed
Robocop, n. Dell Jul,1987

Nazarian, Vera
Kihar, nv **Red Sun of Darkover**, ed. Marion Zimmer Bradley & The Friends of Darkover, DAW,1987

Neiderman, Andrew
Reflection, n. Worldwide Dec,1987
Sight Unseen, n. Zebra Apr,1987

Nelms, Cheryl L.
Don't Fuck With My Brain, pm *2AM* Fll,1987

Nelson, Cheryl Fuller
Just a Little Souvenir, ss **Shadows** #10, ed. Charles L. Grant,1987

Nelson, K.H.
Your Soul to Keep, ss *Space & Time* #73,1987

Nelson, Ray Faraday
A Dream of Amerasia, ar **Philip K. Dick: The Dream Connection**, D. Scott Apel, Permanent Press,1987

Neville, Gail
The Resurrection, ss *Aphelion* #5,1987

Newman, Kim
Mutant Popcorn, mr *Interzone* #20,1987
The Next-But-One Man, ss *Interzone* #19,1987

Newman, R.L. & C. Taylor
Eight Legs Hath the Spider, vi *Haunts* #9,1987

Nichols, Leigh
Shadowfires, n. Avon Feb,1987

Nichols, Leigh & Dean R. Koontz
Dean R. Koontz, iv *The Horror Show* Sum,1987

Nicholson, Geoff
Time Travel for Fun and Profit, ss **Gollancz - Sunday Times Best SF Stories**, Gollancz,1987

Niditch, B.Z.
Holography, pm *Ice River* Sum,1987

Niederman, Andrew
Playmates, n. Berkley May,1987

Niles, Douglas
Forgotten Realms, Book #1: Darkwalker on Moonshae, n. TSR Jun,1987

Nimmo, Jenny
The Snow Spider, n. Dutton Jul,1987

Niven, Larry
The Smoke Ring, n. Ballantine/Del Rey May,1987
The Smoke Ring [Part 1 of 4], sl *Analog* Jan,1987
The Smoke Ring [Part 2 of 4], sl *Analog* Feb,1987
The Smoke Ring [Part 3 of 4], sl *Analog* Mar,1987
The Smoke Ring [Part 4 of 4], sl *Analog* Apr,1987

Niven, Larry, Steven Barnes & Jerry E. Pournelle
The Legacy of Heorot, n. Gollancz May,1987
The Legacy of Heorot, n. Simon & Schuster Jul,1987

Noel, Atanielle Annyn
Murder on Usher's Planet, n. Avon Apr,1987
Speaker to Heaven, n. Arbor House Mar,1987

Nolan, William F.
My Name Is Dolly, ss **Whispers** #6, ed. Stuart David Schiff,1987
The Return, ms *The Horror Show* Jan,1987
The Yard, ss **Masques** #2, ed. J.N. Williamson,1987

Nooteboom, Cees
In the Dutch Mountains, n. Louisiana State Univ. Press Oct,1987

Norman, John
Vagabonds of Gor, n. DAW Mar,1987

Norton, Andre
The Gate of the Cat, n. Ace Oct,1987
Of the Shaping of Ulm's Heir, nv **Tales of the Witch World**, ed. Andre Norton, St. Martin's,1987
Rider on a Mountain, ss **Friends of the Horseclans**, ed. Robert Adams & Pamela Crippen Adams, Signet,1987

Norton, Andre, ed.
Tales of the Witch World, oa Tor Sep,1987

Norton, Andre & Robert Adams, eds.
Magic in Ithkar 4, oa Tor Jul,1987

Norton, Andre, Nancy Garcia & Mary Frances Zambreno
Andre Norton Interview and Bibliography, iv *American Fantasy* Win,1987

Norwood, Warren G.
Shudderchild, n. Bantam Spectra May,1987

Novak, Kate & Laura Hickman
Heart of Goldmoon, na **DragonLance Tales** v3, Margaret Weis & Tracy Hickman, TSR,1987

Nower, Joyce
Ephesus, pm *Ice River* Sum,1987
On the Path to Athene Proneia, Delphi, 1984, pm *Ice River* Sum,1987

Nugent, James
The Brass Halo, n. Critic's Choice Aug,1987

O'Connell, Nicholas
At the Field's End: Interviews with 20 Pacific Northwest Writers, nf Madrona Oct,1987

O'Connor, Clairr
Ophelia's Tale, ss **Mad and Bad Fairies**, ed. Anonymous, Attic Press,1987

O'Day-Flannery, Constance
Timeswept Lovers, n. Zebra Apr,1987

O'Donnell, Kevin, Jr.
The Million Dollar Day, nv *Analog* Oct,1987

O'Donnell, Kevin, Jr. & Mary Kittredge
The Shelter, n. Tor Aug,1987

O'Donohoe, Nick
Dagger-Flight, ss **DragonLance Tales** v2, Margaret Weis & Tracy Hickman, TSR,1987
Hunting Destiny, nv **DragonLance Tales** v3, Margaret Weis & Tracy Hickman, TSR,1987
Love and Ale, nv **DragonLance Tales** v1, Margaret Weis & Tracy Hickman, TSR,1987

O'Malley, Kathleen
The Demon's Gift, nv **Magic in Ithkar** #4, ed. Andre Norton & Robert Adams,1987

O'Neill, Gene
The Armless Conductor, ss *F&SF* Sep,1987

O'Neill, Pamela & Kim Mohan
Planet in Peril, n. Ace/New Infinities Dec,1987

O'Riordan, Robert
Cadre Lucifer, n. Ace May,1987

O'Shea, Pat
Finn MacCool and the Small Men of Deeds, n. Oxford Oct,1987

Oates, Joyce Carol
Haunted, nv **The Architecture of Fear**, ed. Kathryn Cramer & Peter D. Pautz, Arbor House,1987
The Others, ss *Twilight Zone* Aug,1987

Odden, Mike
It Speaks, ed *Minnesota Fantasy Review* #1,1987

Odden, Mike & Ed Shannon, eds.
Minnesota Fantasy Review [v.1 #1, October 1987]

Offutt, Andrew J.
Homecoming, nv **Aftermath**, ed. Robert Lynn Asprin & Lynn Abbey, Ace,1987
Shadowspawn, n. Ace Sep,1987

Oldfield, Pamela
The Ghosts of Bellering Oast, nv Blackie Jun,1987
Pamela Oldfield's Spine Chillers, co Blackie Oct,1987

Oliver, Steven G.
The Waters from Time, vi *Amazing* Sep,1987

Olsen, Lance
Eclipse of Uncertainty: An Introduction to Postmodern Fantasy, nf Greenwood Mar,1987

Olson, Paul F.
Homecoming, ss *The Horror Show* Jan,1987
Iocus: A Retrospective, ar *The Horror Show* Spr,1987

Olson, Paul F. & J.K. Potter
Interview with J.K. Potter, iv *The Horror Show* Jan,1987

Oltion, Jerry
Frame of Reference, n. Popular Library Questar Mar,1987
In the Creation Science Laboratory, ss *Analog* Sep,1987
The Love Song of Laura Morrison, ss *Analog* Aug,1987
Neither Rain Nor Weirdness, ss *Analog* Nov,1987
What's a Nice Girl Like You..., vi *Analog* Oct,1987

Onio
Cartoon, ct *Twilight Zone* Oct,1987
Cartoon, ct *Twilight Zone* Dec,1987

Ordish, Jenny
Bundles of Joy, ss **Gollancz - Sunday Times Best SF Stories**, Gollancz,1987

Ore, Rebecca
Becoming Alien, n. Tor Jan,1988

Orlov, Vladimir
Danilov the Violist, n. Morrow Jul,1987

Ounsley, Simon
Editorial, ed *Interzone* #19,1987

Ounsley, Simon, John Clute & David Pringle, eds.
Interzone: The 2nd Anthology, an Simon & Schuster UK Aug,1987

Ounsley, Simon & David Pringle, eds.
Interzone [#19, Spring 1987]
Interzone [#20, Summer 1987]
Interzone [#21, Autumn 1987]
Interzone [#22, Winter 1987]

Owens, Barbara
Chain, ss *F&SF* Jul,1987
The Greenhill Gang, ss *F&SF* Feb,1987

Pace, Tom & Dan DeLong
Cheap But Not Dirty: Proposal for a Spaceplane, ar *Analog* Mar,1987

Page, Dave
Hawthorne and Mailer, ar *Minnesota Fantasy Review* #1,1987

Page, Gerald W.
The Vampire in the Mirror, nv *Weirdbook* #22,1987

Paget, Clarence, ed.
The 28th Pan Book of Horror Stories, oa Pan Nov,1987

Pahule, Edward J.
Reason Enough, vi *The Horror Show* Spr,1987

Palmer, John Phillips
The Invitation, pm *Weirdbook* #22,1987

Palwick, Susan
Ever After, nv *IASFM* Nov,1987
The Visitation, ss *Amazing* Sep,1987

Pardoe, Rosemary & Richard Dalby, eds.
Ghosts and Scholars, oa Crucible Oct,1987

Parente, Audrey
A Step Back in Time, pm *Minnesota Fantasy Review* #1,1987

Park, John
Retrieval, ss **Tesseracts 2**, ed. Phyllis Gotlieb & Douglas Barbour, Press Porcepic: Victoria,1987

Park, Paul
Soldiers of Paradise, n. Arbor House Sep,1987

Park, Ruth
My Sister Sif, n. Viking Kestrel Apr,1987

Parker, Chris
Kyoki, n. Malvern Mar,1987

Parsonson, Manny
Blood and Tears, nv *Space & Time* #73,1987

Partridge, Diann
Salt, ss **Red Sun of Darkover**, ed. Marion Zimmer Bradley & The Friends of Darkover, DAW,1987

Parvin, Brian
The Golden Garden, n. Robert Hale May,1987

Patterson, Teresa
Star Mistress, pm *Salarius* v1#4,1987

Pattrick, William, ed.
Mysterious Motoring Stories, an W.H. Allen Feb,1987
Mysterious Sea Stories, an Dell Sep,1987

Paulsen, Stephen
Errand Run, vi *Aphelion* #5,1987
Logic Loop, vi *Aphelion* #5,1987

Pautz, Peter D. & Kathryn Cramer, eds.
The Architecture of Fear, oa Arbor House Oct,1987

Paxson, Diana L.
Blood Dancer, ss **Sword and Sorceress** #4, ed. Marion Zimmer Bradley,1987
A Different Kind of Victory, nv **Red Sun of Darkover**, ed. Marion Zimmer Bradley & The Friends of Darkover, DAW,1987
The Earthstone, n. Tor Sep,1987
The Paradise Tree, n. Ace Aug,1987

Payne, Bernal C., Jr.
Experiment in Terror, n. Houghton Mifflin Oct,1987

Pearce, Philippa
Who's Afraid? and Other Strange Stories, co Morrow/Greenwillow Apr 20,1987

Pearson, Wendy G.
The Green Man of Knowledge, ss **Tesseracts 2**, ed. Phyllis Gotlieb & Douglas Barbour, Press Porcepic: Victoria,1987

Peary, Danny
A Shaggy Dog's Tail, nv **DragonLance Tales** v2, Margaret Weis & Tracy Hickman, TSR,1987

Peck, Claudia
The Gentle Art of Making Enemies, nv **Magic in Ithkar** #4, ed. Andre Norton & Robert Adams,1987

Peeples, Mark E., Ph.D.
Huntington's Handle, ar *Analog* Oct,1987

Peeters & Francois Schuiten
The Great Walls of Samaris, gn NBM Publishing Sep,1987

Peirce, Hayford
Napoleon Disentimed, n. Tor Nov,1987

Pelegrimas, Marthayn
Heavy Breathing, pm *2AM* Spr,1987
Living Donor, ss *SPWAO Showcase* #6,1987

Pendleton, Don
Heart to Heart, n. Popular Library Nov,1987
Life to Life, n. Popular Library Aug,1987

Penn-Freeman, Margie
Tooley's Curse, pm *2AM* Fll,1987

Perry, Mark C.
Cade, nv **Aftermath**, ed. Robert Lynn Asprin & Lynn Abbey, Ace,1987

Perry, Steve
Conan the Defiant, n. Tor Oct,1987

Perry, Steve & Michael Reaves
Dome, n. Berkley Feb,1987

Peters, David
Photon #1: For the Glory, n. Berkley Apr,1987
Photon #2: High Stakes, n. Berkley Apr,1987
Photon #3: In Search of Mom, n. Berkley Pacer Jul,1987
Photon #4: This is Your Life, Bhodi Li, n. Berkley Pacer Sep,1987
Photon #5: Exile, n. Berkley Pacer Nov,1987

Peterson, Chris & Eric Drexler
Nanotechnology, ar *Analog* mid-Dec,1987

Petherick, Simon, ed.
Classic Stories of Mystery, Horror and Suspense, an Robert Hale Jun,1987

Pfefferle, Seth
Stickman, n. Tor Jul,1987

Phelps, Donald
Passionate Precision: The Fiction of Robert M. Coates, ar *Pulpsmith* Win,1987

Phillips, Michael R.
George MacDonald, nf Bethany House Jun,1987

PICKLES, J.M.

PRINGLE, DAVID

Pickles, J.M.
More Birds, ss **The Pan Book of Horror
Stories** #28, Pan,1987

Pieratt, Asa, Julie Huffman-Klinkowitz &
Jerome Klinkowitz, eds.
**Kurt Vonnegut: A Comprehensive
Bibliography**, nf Shoestring/Archon
Jun,1987

Pierce, John J.
**Foundations of Science Fiction: A Study
in Imagination and Evolution**, nf
Greenwood Apr,1987
Great Themes of Science Fiction, nf
Greenwood Oct,1987

Pilkington, Ace G.
Cassandra in Wonderland, pm *Amazing*
May,1987
Darwin's Oracle, pm *Amazing* Nov,1987
Jason's Answer, pm *Amazing* Jul,1987

Plante, Edmund
Transformation, n. Leisure May,1987

Platt, Charles
**Dream Makers: SF and Fantasy Writers at
Work (Revised)**, nf
Ungar/Crossroad/Continuum Mar,1987
How to Be a Happy Cat, ms Main Street
May,1987
Piers Anthony's Worlds of Chthon: Plasm,
n. NAL/Signet Oct,1987

Poe, Edgar Allan & Melvin R. White
The Tell-Tale Heart, pl Hanbury May,1987

Pohl, Frederik
Adeste Fideles, ss *Omni* Dec,1987
The Annals of the Heechee, n.
Ballantine/Del Rey Mar,1987
Biofutures: The Next Turn of the Corkscrew,
ar *Twilight Zone* Oct,1987
Chernobyl, n. Bantam Spectra Sep,1987
Chernobyl, n. Bantam UK Sep,1987
Chernobyl and Challenger: That Was the
Year That Was, ar *Aboriginal SF* Sep,1987
The Dark Shadow, ss **Universe**, ed. Byron
Preiss, Bantam Spectra,1987
Fifty Years of Cons, ar *Amazing* Jan,1987
How to Impress an Editor, ar **L. Ron
Hubbard Presents Writers of the Future**
v3, ed. Algis Budrys, Bridge,1987
My Life as a Born-Again Pig, na **Synergy** v1,
ed. George Zebrowski,1987
Search and Destroy, ss *Aboriginal SF*
May,1987
Too Much Loosestrife, ss *Amazing* Nov,1987
The View from Mars Hill, nv *IASFM* May,1987

Pohl, Frederik & C.M. Kornbluth
**Our Best: The Best of Frederik Pohl and
C.M. Kornbluth**, co Baen Feb,1987

Pollack, Rachel
Alqua Dreams, n. Franklin Watts Nov,1987

Pollard, J.A.
Gone Fishing, ss **Atlantis**, ed. Isaac Asimov,
Martin H. Greenberg & Charles G. Waugh,
Signet,1988

Ponder, Michael
Metal, Like Rain, ss *Space & Time* #73,1987

Popkes, Steven
Caliban Landing, n. Congdon & Weed
Nov,1987
The Rose Garden, ss *IASFM* Aug,1987
Stovelighter, nv *IASFM* mid-Dec,1987

Porges, Arthur
The Oddmedod, ss *F&SF* Jun,1987

Possony, Stefan T., Francis X. Kane & Jerry E.
Pournelle
Surprise [substantially revised, first
appeared in **The Strategy of
Technology**, 1970], ar **There Will Be War**
v6, ed. Jerry E. Pournelle,1987

Poster, Carol
Sibyl, pm *Grue* #5,1987

Potter, J.K.
Twilight Zone Gallery, il *Twilight Zone*
Feb,1987

Potter, J.K. & Joe R. Lansdale
Art of Darkness, iv *Twilight Zone* Feb,1987

Potter, J.K. & Paul F. Olson
Interview with J.K. Potter, iv *The Horror
Show* Jan,1987

Pouns, Brauna E.
Amerika, n. Pocket Feb,1987

Pournelle, Jerry E.
Building Plausible Futures, ar **L. Ron
Hubbard Presents Writers of the Future**
v3, ed. Algis Budrys, Bridge,1987
Empire and Republic: Crisis and Future, ar
Imperial Stars v2, ed. Jerry E.
Pournelle,1987
Introduction: The Fog of War, in **There Will
Be War** v6, ed. Jerry E. Pournelle,1987
Janissaries III: Storms of Victory, n. Ace
May,1987
Republic and Empire, ar **Imperial Stars** v2,
ed. Jerry E. Pournelle,1987
Uncertainty and Defense, ar **There Will Be
War** v6, ed. Jerry E. Pournelle,1987

Pournelle, Jerry E., ed.
**Imperial Stars, Vol. 2: Republic and
Empire**, an Baen Oct,1987
**There Will Be War, Vol. VI: Guns of
Darkness**, an Tor Jun,1987

Pournelle, Jerry E., Steven Barnes & Larry
Niven
The Legacy of Heorot, n. Gollancz
May,1987
The Legacy of Heorot, n. Simon &
Schuster Jul,1987

Pournelle, Jerry E., Francis X. Kane & Stefan
T. Possony
Surprise [substantially revised, first
appeared in **The Strategy of
Technology**, 1970], ar **There Will Be War**
v6, ed. Jerry E. Pournelle,1987

Powell, James
The Talking Donkey, ss *Ellery Queen's
Mystery Magazine* mid-Dec,1987

Powell, R. Brent
Reflections of the Past, ss *Salarius*
v1#4,1987
War Game Players, ss *Salarius* #3,1987

Powers, Tim
On Stranger Tides, n. Ace Nov,1987

Poyer, D.C.
Nonlethal, nv **There Will Be War** v6, ed.
Jerry E. Pournelle,1987
The Report on the All-Union Committee on
Recent Rumors Concerning the
Moldavian SSR, ss *Analog* mid-Dec,1987
Stepfather Bank, n. St. Martin's Aug,1987
Turing Test, ss *Analog* Aug,1987

Prantera, Amanda
**Conversations with Lord Byron on
Perversion, 163 Years After His
Lordship's Death**, n. Atheneum Oct,1987
**Conversations with Lord Byron on
Perversion, 163 Years After His
Lordship's Death**, n. Cape Mar,1987

Pratchett, Terry
Equal Rites, n. Gollancz Jan,1987
The Light Fantastic, n. SFBC Aug,1987
Mort, n. Gollancz Nov,1987

Preiss, Byron, ed.
The Universe, oa Bantam Spectra Nov,1987

Preuss, Paul
**Arthur C. Clarke's Venus Prime, Volume
1: Breaking Strain**, n. Avon Nov,1987

Price, Patrick L. & Martin H. Greenberg, eds.
**Fantastic Stories: Tales of the Weird and
Wondrous**, an TSR May,1987

Price, Patrick Lucien, ed.
Amazing Science Fiction Stories [v.61 #5,
January 1987]
Amazing Science Fiction Stories [v.61 #6,
March 1987]
Amazing Science Fiction Stories [v.62 #1,
May 1987]
Amazing Science Fiction Stories [v.62 #2,
July 1987]
Amazing Science Fiction Stories [v.62 #3,
September 1987]
Amazing Science Fiction Stories [v.62 #4,
November 1987]

Price, Susan
The Ghost Drum, n. Faber & Faber
Jan,1987

Priestley, Alma
The Neapolitan Bedroom, ss **After Midnight
Stories** #3,1987

Pringle, David
Editorial, ed *Interzone* #20,1987
Editorial, ed *Interzone* #21,1987
Editorial, ed *Interzone* #22,1987
Imaginary People, nf Grafton Oct,1987
Science Fiction: The 100 Best Novels, nf
Carroll & Graf Nov,1987

Pringle, David & J.G. Ballard
J.G. Ballard, iv *Interzone* #22,1987

Pringle, David, John Clute & Simon Ounsley,
eds.
Interzone: The 2nd Anthology, an Simon &
Schuster UK Aug,1987

Pringle, David & Simon Ounsley, eds.
Interzone [#19, Spring 1987]
Interzone [#20, Summer 1987]
Interzone [#21, Autumn 1987]

PRINGLE, DAVID

Pringle, David & Simon Ounsley, eds.
(continued)
Interzone [#22, Winter 1987]

Pronzini, Bill
The Storm Tunnel, ss *Whispers* #23,1987

Ptacek, Kathryn
Dead Possums, ss **Doom City**, ed. Charles
L. Grant, Tor,1987

Pugmire, W.H.
Swamp Rising, ss *Grue* #4,1987

Pulver, Mary Monica
Murder at the War, n. St. Martin's Aug,1987

Purdy, Andrew James
Master of the Courts, nv *Pulpsmith* Win,1987

Quagmire, Joshua
The Nasty Naughty Nazi Ninja Nudnik
Elves, cs *Fantasy Book* Mar,1987

Quick, W.T.
All the People, All the Time, ss *Analog*
Jul,1987
Cowboys and Engines, ss *Aboriginal SF*
May,1987
Cyberserker, ss *Analog* Feb,1987
Flashbattles, ss *Analog* Sep,1987
Safe to the Liberties of the People, ss
Analog Jun,1987

Quilter, Deborah
Illuminations: Crystal Update, ar *Twilight
Zone* Oct,1987

Quinn, Tim & Dicky Howett
The Doctor Who Fun Book, nf Target
May,1987

Rabin, Jennifer
**Eileen Goudge's Swept Away #5:
Spellbound**, n. Avon/Flare Mar,1987

Rabinowitz, Ann
Knight on Horseback, n. Macmillan
Oct,1987

Rabkin, Eric S., Colin Greenland & George E.
Slusser, eds.
**Storm Warnings: Science Fiction
Confronts the Future**, nf S. Illinois Univ.
Press Apr,1987

Rabkin, Eric S. & George E. Slusser, eds.
**Aliens: The Anthropology of Science
Fiction**, nf Southern Illinois Univ. Press
Nov,1987
**Intersections: Fantasy and Science
Fiction**, nf Southern Illinois Univ. Press
Oct,1987

Radford, Elaine
Another Crow's Eyes, ss *Amazing* Nov,1987
Passing, ss *Aboriginal SF* May,1987

Raeper, William
**Fantasy King: A Biography of George
MacDonald**, nf Lion Sep,1987

Rahman, Glenn
The Butler, vi *Minnesota Fantasy Review*
#1,1987

Rainbird, Phillip
True Love Grue, pm *Minnesota Fantasy
Review* #1,1987

Rainey, Mark
Nightshade Crossing, ss *Minnesota Fantasy
Review* #1,1987

Raisor, G.L.
The Accounting, ss *Night Cry* v2#5,1987
Cheapskate, vi *Night Cry* v2#4,1987
Identity Crisis, ss *Night Cry* v2#3,1987

Ramsland, Katherine
Nothing from Nothing Comes, ss **Masques**
#2, ed. J.N. Williamson,1987

Randall, Marta
Haunted, ss *Twilight Zone* Dec,1987
Lapidary Nights, ss **Universe** #17, ed. Terry
Carr,1987

Randisi, Robert J. & Kevin D. Randle
Once Upon a Murder, n. TSR/Windwalker
Mar,1987

Randle, Kevin
Silver and Steel, nv **DragonLance Tales** v3,
Margaret Weis & Tracy Hickman,
TSR,1987

Randle, Kevin D. & Robert J. Randisi
Once Upon a Murder, n. TSR/Windwalker
Mar,1987

Ransom, Daniel
Night Caller, n. Zebra Oct,1987

raphael, dan
all the comforts of, pm *Ice River* Sum,1987

Rasmussen, William C.
Just Compensation, vi *2AM* Fll,1987

Rathbone, Wendy
Flashing the Black Long Streets, pm
Aboriginal SF Sep,1987

Readers, The
Boomerangs, lt *Aboriginal SF* Feb,1987
Boomerangs, lt *Aboriginal SF* May,1987
Boomerangs, lt *Aboriginal SF* Jul,1987
Boomerangs, lt *Aboriginal SF* Sep,1987
Boomerangs, lt *Aboriginal SF* Nov,1987
Brass Tacks, lt *Analog* Jan,1987
Brass Tacks, lt *Analog* Feb,1987
Brass Tacks, lt *Analog* Mar,1987
Brass Tacks, lt *Analog* Apr,1987
Brass Tacks, lt *Analog* May,1987
Brass Tacks, lt *Analog* Jun,1987
Brass Tacks, lt *Analog* Jul,1987
Brass Tacks, lt *Analog* Aug,1987
Brass Tacks, lt *Analog* Sep,1987
Brass Tacks, lt *Analog* Oct,1987
Brass Tacks, lt *Analog* Nov,1987
Brass Tacks, lt *Analog* Dec,1987
Brass Tacks, lt *Analog* mid-Dec,1987
Forum, lt *New Pathways* Jan,1987
Forum, lt *New Pathways* Apr,1987
Forum, lt *New Pathways* Aug,1987
Inflections, lt *Amazing* Jan,1987
Inflections, lt *Amazing* Mar,1987
Inflections, lt *Amazing* May,1987
Inflections, lt *Amazing* Jul,1987
Inflections, lt *Amazing* Sep,1987
Inflections, lt *Amazing* Nov,1987
Letters, lt *American Fantasy* Sum,1987
Letters, lt *IASFM* Jan,1987

RELLING, WILLIAM, JR.

Readers, The (continued)
Letters, lt *IASFM* Feb,1987
Letters, lt *IASFM* Mar,1987
Letters, lt *IASFM* Apr,1987
Letters, lt *IASFM* May,1987
Letters, lt *IASFM* Jun,1987
Letters, lt *IASFM* Jul,1987
Letters, lt *IASFM* Aug,1987
Letters, lt *IASFM* Sep,1987
Letters, lt *IASFM* Oct,1987
Letters, lt *IASFM* Nov,1987
Letters, lt *IASFM* Dec,1987
Letters, lt *IASFM* mid-Dec,1987
Letters, lt *Interzone* #22,1987
Letters, lt *Twilight Zone* Apr,1987
Letters, lt *Twilight Zone* Dec,1987
Open Orbit, lt *Space & Time* #72,1987
Open Orbit, lt *Space & Time* #73,1987
Readers' Forum, lt *Tales of the
Unanticipated* #2,1987
Readers' Responses, lt *Mage* Spr,1987
Real Time, lt *2AM* Spr,1987
Real Time, lt *2AM* Sum,1987
Real Time, lt *2AM* Fll,1987
Real Time, lt *2AM* Win,1987

Reaves, Michael & Steve Perry
Dome, n. Berkley Feb,1987

Reed, Chris
Second Gibraltar, ss *Back Brain Recluse*
#7,1987

Reed, Chris, ed.
Back Brain Recluse [# 7]

Reed, Chris & Michael Moorcock
Michael Moorcock, iv *Back Brain Recluse*
#7,1987

Reed, Dana
The Gatekeeper, n. Leisure Aug,1987

Reed, Robert
Aeries, ss *Aboriginal SF* Sep,1987
The Leeshore, n. Donald I. Fine/Primus
Apr,1987

Reich, David
Black Dreams, ss *Pulpsmith* Win,1987

Reichert, Mickey Zucker
Godslayer, n. DAW Jul,1987

Reid, Carol
Wondergirls, ss *The Horror Show* Spr,1987

Reitmeyer, David F.
Fog, pm *IASFM* Apr,1987

Reitz, Jean
Monsters, ss **L. Ron Hubbard Presents
Writers of the Future** v3, ed. Algis
Budrys, Bridge,1987

Relling, William, Jr.
Blood, ss *Night Cry* v2#3,1987
Burton's Word, ss *Whispers* #23,1987
Infinite Man, ss *New Blood* #1,1987
New Moon, n. Tor Oct,1987
Profile: Rudyard Kipling, bg *Night Cry*
v2#5,1987
Sharper Than a Serpent's Tooth, ss *The
Horror Show* Spr,1987
Where Does Watson Road Go?, ss *Eldritch
Tales* #14,1987

RELLING, WILLIAM, JR.

Relling, William, Jr. & Richard Christian
   Matheson
   Wonderland, ss *Night Cry* v2#5,1987

Remler, Ariel
   Illuminations: Fantasies for Sale, ar *Twilight Zone* Feb,1987
   The Sky Is a Circle: Exploring the Native American Spirit World, ar *Twilight Zone* Aug,1987
   Spirits of Shadow, ar *Twilight Zone* Aug,1987

Renton, Neil
   In Search of Yuk-Yuk, ss *The Ecphorizer* Mar,1987

Rentz, Tom
   Dreams in Stasis, pm *Mage* Win,1987

Resnick, Mike
   The Dark Lady: A Romance of the Far Future, n. Tor Nov,1987

Rexner, Romulus
   Planetary Legion for Peace: Story of Their War and Our Peace, 1940 - 2000, n. Veritas Jul,1987

Reynolds, J.B., Ferret & K.W. Jeter
   K.W. Jeter [Part 1], iv *New Pathways* Apr,1987
   K.W. Jeter [Part 2], iv *New Pathways* Aug,1987

Reynolds, Kay, ed.
   Robotech Art 2, pi Donning/Starblaze Oct,1987

Rezmerski, John Calvin
   Challengers, pm *Tales of the Unanticipated* #2,1987

Rhodes, Daniel
   Next, After Lucifer, n. St. Martin's/Thomas Dunne Jul,1987

Ribiero, Stella Carr
   Sambaqui, n. Avon/Bard Mar,1987

Rice, Anne
   Interview with Anne Rice, iv *American Fantasy* Spr,1987

Rich, Mark
   The Alien Reads a Romance, pm *Mage* Win,1987
   Fortuneteller, pm *Mage* Spr,1987
   Forward from What Vanishes, pm *Amazing* Jan,1987
   The Trace of Old Fingers, pm *2AM* Sum,1987

Richard, Stephen
   Meteors, ss **Gollancz - Sunday Times Best SF Stories**, Gollancz,1987

Richards, Joel
   Mencken Stuff, ss **Universe** #17, ed. Terry Carr,1987

Richards, Ramona Pope
   The Editorial Privilege, ed *Apex!* #1,1987
   In the Image of Our Fathers, ar *Apex!* #1,1987

Richards, Ramona Pope, ed.
   Apex! [#1]

Richards, Tony
   The Harvest Bride, n. Tor May,1987

Richardson, Jean, ed.
   Beware, Beware - Strange and Sinister Tales, an Hamish Hamilton Oct,1987

Ridgway, Jim & Michele Benjamin, eds.
   PsiFi: Psychological Theories and Science Fictions, an The British Psychological Society Jan,1987

Riding, Julia
   Space Traders Unlimited, n. Pied Piper May,1987

Rifbjerg, Klaus
   Witness to the Future, n. Fjord Sep,1987

Rivkin, J.F.
   Web of Wind, n. Ace Dec,1987

Robbins, David
   Endworld #5: Dakota Run, n. Leisure Apr,1987
   Endworld #6: Citadel Run, n. Leisure Aug,1987

Roberson, Jennifer
   Rite of Passage, nv **Sword and Sorceress #4**, ed. Marion Zimmer Bradley,1987
   Track of the White Wolf, n. DAW Apr,1987

Roberts, John Maddox
   Conan the Champion, n. Tor Apr,1987
   Conan the Marauder, n. Tor Jan,1988

Roberts, John Maddox & Eric Kotani
   The Island Worlds, n. Baen Jun,1987

Roberts, Keith
   Equivalent for Giles, ss **Tales from the Forbidden Planet**, ed. Roz Kaveney, Titan,1987
   Grainne, n. Kerosina May,1987
   A Heron Caught in Weeds, co Kerosina Apr,1987
   Piper's Wait, ss **Other Edens**, ed. Christopher Evans & Robert Holdstock, Unwin: London,1987
   The Tiger Sweater, na *F&SF* Oct,1987

Robertson, Donald Fredrick
   The Phobos Race, ar **New Destinies** v2, ed. Jim Baen, Baen,1987

Robeson, Kenneth
   Doc Savage Omnibus #2, om Bantam Jan,1987
   Doc Savage Omnibus #3, om Bantam Jun,1987
   Doc Savage Omnibus #4, om Bantam Oct,1987

Robinson, Frank M. & Thomas N. Scortia
   Blow-Out!, n. Franklin Watts Apr,1987

Robinson, Kim Stanley
   The Blind Geometer, na *IASFM* Aug,1987
   The Memorial, ss **In the Field of Fire**, ed. Jeanne Van Buren Dann & Jack M. Dann, Tor,1987
   Mother Goddess of the World, na *IASFM* Oct,1987
   The Return from Rainbow Bridge, nv *F&SF* Aug,1987

ROLAND, PAUL

Robinson, Nigel
   The Sensorites, n. W.H. Allen Feb,1987
   The Time Meddler, n. W.H. Allen Oct,1987

Robinson, Peni
   Nereid, ss *Twilight Zone* Apr,1987

Robinson, Roger, comp.
   Who's Hugh?: An SF Reader's Guide to Pseudonyms, nf Beccon Aug,1987

Robinson, Roger, ed.
   The Writings of Henry Kenneth Bulmer, nf Beccon Aug,1987

Robinson, Spider
   Time Pressure, n. Ace Oct,1987

Rochlin, Doris
   Frobisch's Angel, n. Taplinger Jun,1987

Rochon, Esther
   Xils ["Xils", **Aurores Boreales 2** 1985], ss **Tesseracts 2**, ed. Phyllis Gotlieb & Douglas Barbour, Press Porcepic: Victoria,1987

Rodgers, Alan
   The Boy Who Came Back from the Dead, nv **Masques #2**, ed. J.N. Williamson,1987

Rodgers, Alan, ed.
   Night Cry [v.2 #4, Summer 1987]
   Night Cry [v.2 #5, Fall 1987]

Roemer, Kenneth, Gorman Beauchamp & Nicholas D. Smith, eds.
   Utopian Studies 1, nf Univ. Press of America May,1987

Rogal, Stan
   A Little Thing, ss **Tesseracts 2**, ed. Phyllis Gotlieb & Douglas Barbour, Press Porcepic: Victoria,1987

Rogers, Alan
   Down-Home Horrors, in *Night Cry* v2#3,1987
   Introduction: Where the Dead Do Not Die, in *Night Cry* v2#5,1987

Rogers, Michael
   Forbidden Sequence, n. Bantam Jan,1988

Rohan, Michael Scott
   The Forge in the Forest, n. Macdonald Feb,1987
   The Forge in the Forest, n. Morrow Nov,1987

Roland, Paul
   Beau Brummel, sg **The Curious Case of Richard Fielding and Other Stories**, Lary Press,1987
   Cairo, sg **The Curious Case of Richard Fielding and Other Stories**, Lary Press,1987
   The Curious Case of Richard Fielding, ss **The Curious Case of Richard Fielding and Other Stories**, Lary Press,1987
   The Curious Case of Richard Fielding and Other Stories, oc Lary Press Nov,1987
   Death or Glory, sg **The Curious Case of Richard Fielding and Other Stories**, Lary Press,1987
   Demon in a Glass Case, sg **The Curious Case of Richard Fielding and Other Stories**, Lary Press,1987

Roland, Paul (continued)
  Ghost Ships, sg **The Curious Case of Richard Fielding and Other Stories**, Lary Press,1987
  The Great Edwardian Airaid, sg **The Curious Case of Richard Fielding and Other Stories**, Lary Press,1987
  Green Glass Violins, sg **The Curious Case of Richard Fielding and Other Stories**, Lary Press,1987
  The Hanging Judge, sg **The Curious Case of Richard Fielding and Other Stories**, Lary Press,1987
  A Hangman Waits, ss **The Curious Case of Richard Fielding and Other Stories**, Lary Press,1987
  The Hired Executioner, ss **The Curious Case of Richard Fielding and Other Stories**, Lary Press,1987
  In the Opium Den, sg **The Curious Case of Richard Fielding and Other Stories**, Lary Press,1987
  Jumbee, sg **The Curious Case of Richard Fielding and Other Stories**, Lary Press,1987
  Madame Guillotine, sg **The Curious Case of Richard Fielding and Other Stories**, Lary Press,1987
  Madelaine, sg **The Curious Case of Richard Fielding and Other Stories**, Lary Press,1987
  The Miracle Man, ss **The Curious Case of Richard Fielding and Other Stories**, Lary Press,1987
  A Most Singular Specimen, ss **The Curious Case of Richard Fielding and Other Stories**, Lary Press,1987
  Mr. Mephisto, ss **The Curious Case of Richard Fielding and Other Stories**, Lary Press,1987
  Nocturne, ss **The Curious Case of Richard Fielding and Other Stories**, Lary Press,1987
  Pulp, ss **The Curious Case of Richard Fielding and Other Stories**, Lary Press,1987
  The Puppet Master, sg **The Curious Case of Richard Fielding and Other Stories**, Lary Press,1987
  Requiem, sg **The Curious Case of Richard Fielding and Other Stories**, Lary Press,1987
  Return to Raebourne, ss **The Curious Case of Richard Fielding and Other Stories**, Lary Press,1987
  Stowaway, ss **The Curious Case of Richard Fielding and Other Stories**, Lary Press,1987
  Stranger Than Strange, sg **The Curious Case of Richard Fielding and Other Stories**, Lary Press,1987
  Twilight of the Gods, sg **The Curious Case of Richard Fielding and Other Stories**, Lary Press,1987

Ronson, Mark
  Ogre, n. Critic's Choice Apr,1987
  Plague Pit, n. Critic's Choice Apr,1987

Rooke, Leon
  Bats, ss **Tesseracts 2**, ed. Phyllis Gotlieb & Douglas Barbour, Press Porcepic: Victoria,1987

Rose, Rhea
  Squirrels in Frankfurter Highlight, ss **Tesseracts 2**, ed. Phyllis Gotlieb & Douglas Barbour, Press Porcepic: Victoria,1987

Rose, S., (?)
  Cartoon, ct *Twilight Zone* Jun,1987

Rosenbaum, Bob & Carol Serling
  Life with Rod, iv *Twilight Zone* Apr,1987

Rosenberg, Joel
  The Heir Apparent, n. NAL/Signet May,1987
  The Last Time, ss **Friends of the Horseclans**, ed. Robert Adams & Pamela Crippen Adams, Signet,1987
  Not for Country, Not for King, nv **New Destinies** v1, ed. Jim Baen, Baen,1987

Rosenman, John B.
  When a Rose Sings, ss *2AM* Sum,1987

Rosinski, Grzegorz & Jean Van Hamme
  Thorgal: The Archers, gn Donning,1987

Rossow, William & M. Bradley Kellogg
  Lear's Daughters, om SFBC Apr,1987

Roth, Harrison & Isaac Asimov
  Left to Right, and Beyond, vi *Analog* Jul,1987

Rothbell, Jay
  Connie Nova, ss *Pulpsmith* Win,1987

Rothman, Tony
  A Memoir of Nuclear Winter, ar *Analog* Nov,1987

Rovin, Jeff
  The Encyclopedia of Supervillains, nf Facts on File Nov,1987
  Re-Animator, n. Pocket May,1987

Rowley, Christopher B.
  Golden Sunlands, n. Ballantine/Del Rey Jul,1987

Rubin, Marty
  The Boiled Frog Syndrome, n. Alyson Sep,1987

Rucker, Rudy
  Bringing in the Sheaves, ss *IASFM* Jan,1987
  Enlightenment Rabies, vi *New Pathways* Nov,1987
  Inside Out, nv **Synergy** v1, ed. George Zebrowski,1987
  The Man Who Was a Cosmic String, ss **Universe**, ed. Byron Preiss, Bantam Spectra,1987
  Mind Tools, nf Houghton Mifflin Apr,1987
  Viewpoint: Cellular Automata, ar *IASFM* Apr,1987

Rucker, Rudy, ed.
  Mathenauts: Tales of Mathematical Wonder, an Arbor House Jun,1987

Rucker, Rudy & Richard Kadrey
  Rudy Rucker Interview, iv *Interzone* #20,1987

Rule, Jane
  Memory Board, n. Pandora Oct,1987

Rusch, Kristine Kathryn
  Clarion and Speculative Fiction, ar *Amazing* Nov,1987
  Sing, ss *Aboriginal SF* Feb,1987

Russ, Joanna
  On Strike Against God, n. Women's Press Mar,1987

Russell, Jean, ed.
  Supernatural Stories: 13 Tales of the Unexpected, an Franklin Watts Orchard Sep,1987

Russell, Ray
  American Gothic, ss **Masques** #2, ed. J.N. Williamson,1987
  The Kolorized King Kong Kaper, ss *Whispers* #23,1987

Russo, John
  Voodoo Dawn, n. Imagine Jul,1987

Russo, Richard Paul
  Dead Man on the Beach, ss *Twilight Zone* Jun,1987
  In the Season of the Rains, ss **In the Field of Fire**, ed. Jeanne Van Buren Dann & Jack M. Dann, Tor,1987
  Mad City Beneath the Sands, ss *Twilight Zone* Oct,1987
  Prayers of a Rain God, ss *F&SF* May,1987

Russo, Richard, ed.
  Dreams Are Wiser Than Men, an North Atlantic Aug,1987

Rutherford, Brett
  Remembering Medea, pm *Haunts* #9,1987

Ryan, Alan
  The Haunted House of My Childhood, pm *Weirdbook* #22,1987

Ryan, Alan, ed.
  Vampires, an SFBC Apr,1987

Ryan, Charles C.
  Achieving Orbit, ed *Aboriginal SF* Sep,1987
  On Becoming a Writer, ed *Aboriginal SF* Nov,1987
  Our New Format, ed *Aboriginal SF* May,1987
  Sifting for Golden Nuggets, ed *Aboriginal SF* Feb,1987

Ryan, Charles C., ed.
  Aboriginal SF [v.1 #3, Feb.-March 1987]
  Aboriginal SF [v.1 #4, May-June 1987]
  Aboriginal SF [v.1 #5, July-Aug. 1987]
  Aboriginal SF [v.1 #6, Sept.-Oct. 1987]
  Aboriginal SF [v.2 #1, Nov.-Dec. 1987]

Ryman, Geoff
  Love Sickness, Part 1, sl *Interzone* #20,1987
  Love Sickness, Part 2, sl *Interzone* #21,1987
  The Unconquered Country, n. Bantam Spectra Jun,1987

Saberhagen, Fred
  The Graphic of Dorian Gray, nv **New Destinies** v1, ed. Jim Baen, Baen,1987
  Saberhagen: My Best, co Baen May,1987
  The Second Book of Lost Swords: Sightbinder's Story, n. Tor Nov,1987

Sackett, Jeffrey
  Stolen Souls, n. Bantam Dec,1987

Sadler, Barry
  Casca #17: The Warrior, n. Ace Charter
    Feb,1987
  Casca #18: The Cursed, n. Jove Aug,1987

Sage, Alison & Dennis Wheatley
  The Devil Rides Out, n. Beaver May,1987

Saha, Arthur W., ed.
  The Year's Best Fantasy Stories: 13, an
    DAW Nov,1987

Saha, Arthur W. & Donald A. Wollheim, ed.
  The 1987 Annual World's Best SF, an
    DAW Jun,1987

Saint, H.F.
  Memoirs of an Invisible Man, n. Atheneum
    Apr,1987

Saintsbury, Elizabeth
  George MacDonald: A Short Life, nf
    Canongate Nov,1987

Sakers, Don
  All Fall Down, nv *Analog* May,1987
  The Hand of Guilt, ss *Fantasy Book* Mar,1987

Sale, Tim, Lynn Abbey & Robert Lynn Asprin
  Thieves' World Graphics 4, gn
    Donning/Starblaze Jan,1987

Sallee, Wayne Allen
  Joe Lansdale Speaks, pm *Grue* #5,1987
  A Matter of Semantics, vi *Grue* #5,1987
  second thoughts, pm *Grue* #5,1987
  The Touch, ss *Grue* #4,1987

Salmonson, Jessica Amanda
  Bear at the Gate, ss **Spaceships & Spells**,
    ed. Jane Yolen, Martin H. Greenberg &
    Charles G. Waugh, Harper & Row,1987
  Beyond the Reef, pm *Grue* #6,1987
  For E.D., pm *2AM* Win,1987
  The House that Knew No Hate, nv **The
    Architecture of Fear**, ed. Kathryn Cramer
    & Peter D. Pautz, Arbor House,1987
  Strange Doings in Viktor's Village, vi *New
    Pathways* Jan,1987
  The Trilling Princess, ss **Devils & Demons**,
    ed. Marvin Kaye, SFBC/Doubleday,1987

Salonia, John & Traci Salonia
  The Butterflies of Betelgeuse, pm *Space &
    Time* #72,1987
  The Imp in the Bottle, ss *Space & Time*
    #73,1987

Salonia, Traci & John Salonia
  The Butterflies of Betelgeuse, pm *Space &
    Time* #72,1987
  The Imp in the Bottle, ss *Space & Time*
    #73,1987

Salts, Katherine
  Popcorn: A Matter of Survival, vi *Haunts*
    #9,1987

Sampson, Robert
  The Scent of Roses, ss *Space & Time*
    #73,1987

San Souci, Robert D.
  The Adventure of the German Student, ss
    Short & Shivery, Doubleday,1987
  Billy Mosby's Night Ride, ss **Short &
    Shivery**, Doubleday,1987

San Souci, Robert D. (continued)
  Boneless, ss **Short & Shivery**,
    Doubleday,1987
  Brother and Sister, ss **Short & Shivery**,
    Doubleday,1987
  The Cegua, ss **Short & Shivery**,
    Doubleday,1987
  The Deacon's Ghost, ss **Short & Shivery**,
    Doubleday,1987
  The Death Waltz, ss **Short & Shivery**,
    Doubleday,1987
  The Ghost of Misery Hill, ss **Short &
    Shivery**, Doubleday,1987
  The Ghost's Cap, ss **Short & Shivery**,
    Doubleday,1987
  The Ghostly Little Girl, ss **Short & Shivery**,
    Doubleday,1987
  The Goblin Spider, ss **Short & Shivery**,
    Doubleday,1987
  The Golem, ss **Short & Shivery**,
    Doubleday,1987
  The Green Mist, ss **Short & Shivery**,
    Doubleday,1987
  The Halloween Pony, ss **Short & Shivery**,
    Doubleday,1987
  The Hunter in the Haunted Forest, ss **Short
    & Shivery**, Doubleday,1987
  Jack Frost, ss **Short & Shivery**,
    Doubleday,1987
  Lady Eleanor's Mantle, ss **Short & Shivery**,
    Doubleday,1987
  Lavender, ss **Short & Shivery**,
    Doubleday,1987
  The Loup-Garou, ss **Short & Shivery**,
    Doubleday,1987
  The Lovers of Dismal Swamp, ss **Short &
    Shivery**, Doubleday,1987
  The Midnight Mass of the Dead, ss **Short &
    Shivery**, Doubleday,1987
  Nuckelavee, ss **Short & Shivery**,
    Doubleday,1987
  The Robber Bridegroom, ss **Short &
    Shivery**, Doubleday,1987
  Scared To Death, ss **Short & Shivery**,
    Doubleday,1987
  Short & Shivery, an Doubleday Oct,1987
  The Skeleton's Dance, ss **Short & Shivery**,
    Doubleday,1987
  The Soldier and the Vampire, ss **Short &
    Shivery**, Doubleday,1987
  Swallowed Alive, ss **Short & Shivery**,
    Doubleday,1987
  Tailypo, ss **Short & Shivery**,
    Doubleday,1987
  The Waterfall of Ghosts, ss **Short &
    Shivery**, Doubleday,1987
  The Witch Cat, ss **Short & Shivery**,
    Doubleday,1987

Sandage, Allan
  Cosmology: The Quest to Understand the
    Creation and Expansion of the Universe,
    ar **Universe**, ed. Byron Preiss, Bantam
    Spectra,1987

Sandercombe, W. Fraser
  Just a legend, pm *Weirdbook* #22,1987

Sanders (Nippawanock), Thomas E.
  The Great Holy Mystery, ar *Twilight Zone*
    Aug,1987
  Profile: Ambrose Bierce, bg *Night Cry*
    v2#4,1987
  The Rock Bearers, ar *Twilight Zone* Aug,1987

Sapir, Richard Ben
  Quest, n. Dutton Aug,1987

Sarabande, William
  **The First Americans: Beyond the Sea of
    Ice**, n. Bantam Dec,1987
  Wolves of the Dawn, n. Bantam Feb,1987

Saramago, Jose
  Baltasar and Blimunda, n. Harcourt Brace
    Jovanovich Oct,1987

Sargent, Craig
  Last Ranger #4: The Rabid Brigadier, n.
    Popular Library Aug,1987
  Last Ranger #5: The War Weapons, n.
    Popular Library Oct,1987
  Last Ranger #6: The Warlord's Revenge,
    n. Popular Library Jan,1988

Sargent, Pamela
  The Best of Pamela Sargent, co Academy
    Chicago Oct,1987
  The Leash, ss *Twilight Zone* Apr,1987

Sarrantonio, Al
  Bogy, ss **Whispers** #6, ed. Stuart David
    Schiff,1987
  Books, br *Night Cry* v2#3,1987
  Books, br *Night Cry* v2#4,1987
  Books, br *Night Cry* v2#5,1987
  The Boy With Penny Eyes, n. Tor Apr,1987
  Fragments of Horror, ms *The Horror Show*
    Sum,1987
  Pigs, ss **Shadows** #10, ed. Charles L.
    Grant,1987

Sass, Mary
  Brain Blasters, ss *Mage* Spr,1987

Sass, R.A.
  Love is a Circle, vi *2AM* Sum,1987

Saul, John
  The Unwanted, n. Bantam UK Oct,1987
  The Unwanted, n. Bantam Aug,1987

Saunders, Charles R.
  Death's Friend, nv *Weirdbook* #22,1987
  Outsteppin' Fetchit, ss **Masques** #2, ed.
    J.N. Williamson,1987

Saunders, David
  **Encyclopaedia of the Worlds of Doctor
    Who: A-D**, nf Piccadilly Nov,1987

Savage, Adrian
  The Other Side: Welcome, Chaos, ar
    Twilight Zone Oct,1987

Sawyer, Robert J.
  Uphill Climb, vi *Amazing* Mar,1987

Saxby, Anna Lieff
  Prisoners, ss **Gollancz - Sunday Times
    Best SF Stories**, Gollancz,1987

Saxton, Josephine
  The Interferences, ss **Tales from the
    Forbidden Planet**, ed. Roz Kaveney,
    Titan,1987

Saylor, Steven
  The Pawns of Crux, ss *The Dragon* Mar,1987

Sayre, Cheryl Curry
  The Lady Who Lost Her Head, ss *Grue*
    #6,1987

SCARBOROUGH, ELIZABETH ANN

Scarborough, Elizabeth Ann
  The Goldcamp Vampire, n. Bantam
    Spectra Nov,1987
  Milk from a Maiden's Breast, ss **Tales of the
    Witch World**, ed. Andre Norton, St.
    Martin's,1987
  Songs from the Seashell Archives, Vol. 1,
    om Bantam Spectra Oct,1987

Scarlett, Patricia
  Deity, vi *Eldritch Tales* #13,1987

Schaub, Mary H.
  Night Hound's Moon, ss **Tales of the Witch
    World**, ed. Andre Norton, St. Martin's,1987

Schiff, Stuart David
  Editorial, ed *Whispers* #23,1987
  The End, aw *Whispers* #23,1987
  News, ar *Whispers* #23,1987

Schiff, Stuart David, ed.
  Whispers [#23/24, v.6 #3-4, October 1987]
  Whispers VI, oa Doubleday Jul,1987

Schmidt, Dennis
  **Twilight of the Gods, Book III: Three
    Trumps Sounding**, n. Ace Jan,1988

Schmidt, Stanley
  An Alien Viewpoint, ed *Analog* Apr,1987
  Brain Language, ed *Analog* Mar,1987
  Butterfly Futures, ed *Analog* May,1987
  Child Abuse, ed *Analog* Jun,1987
  Final Frontiers, ed *Analog* Oct,1987
  Fundamental Dilemma, ed *Analog* Jan,1987
  Great Oaks from Little Atoms, ed *Analog*
    Nov,1987
  The Gypsy and the Procrastinator, ed
    Analog Feb,1987
  Matters of Opinion, ed *Analog* mid-Dec,1987
  The Memetic Menace, ed *Analog* Aug,1987
  Political Standard Time, ed *Analog* Dec,1987
  The Reactionary Revolution, ed *Analog*
    Jul,1987

Schmidt, Stanley, ed.
  Analog Science Fiction/Science Fact [v.107
    # 1, January 1987]
  Analog Science Fiction/Science Fact [v.107
    # 2, February 1987]
  Analog Science Fiction/Science Fact [v.107
    # 3, March 1987]
  Analog Science Fiction/Science Fact [v.107
    # 4, April 1987]
  Analog Science Fiction/Science Fact [v.107
    # 5, May 1987]
  Analog Science Fiction/Science Fact [v.107
    # 6, June 1987]
  Analog Science Fiction/Science Fact [v.107
    # 7, July 1987]
  Analog Science Fiction/Science Fact [v.107
    # 8, August 1987]
  Analog Science Fiction/Science Fact [v.107
    # 9, September 1987]
  Analog Science Fiction/Science Fact [v.107
    #10, October 1987]
  Analog Science Fiction/Science Fact [v.107
    #11, November 1987]
  Analog Science Fiction/Science Fact [v.107
    #12, December 1987]
  Analog Science Fiction/Science Fact [v.107
    #13, Mid-December 1987]

Schneider, Roy
  The Seed, ss *Eldritch Tales* #14,1987

Schochet
  Cartoon, ct *Twilight Zone* Oct,1987

Schow, David J.
  Pamela's Get, ss *Twilight Zone* Aug,1987

Schreck, Dean
  Semblance, pm *Eldritch Tales* #13,1987

Schuiten, Francois & Peeters
  The Great Walls of Samaris, gn NBM
    Publishing Sep,1987

Schwadron
  Cartoon, ct *Twilight Zone* Dec,1987

Schwartz, Hillel
  Sleeping Beauty, ss *The Short Story Review*
    Win,1987

Schweitzer, Darrell
  Books: A Historical Perspective, br
    Aboriginal SF May,1987
  Books: Books Versus Careers, br *Aboriginal
    SF* Sep,1987
  Books: New Works from Old Masters, br
    Aboriginal SF Feb,1987
  Books: Objectivity, br *Aboriginal SF*
    Nov,1987
  Books: The Whole Spectrum of Fantastic
    Literature, br *Aboriginal SF* Jul,1987
  The Chivalry of Sir Aldingar, ss *Weirdbook*
    #22,1987
  H.P. Lovecraft: Still Eldritch After All These
    Years, ar *Amazing* Mar,1987
  Introduction to The Haunted Ships, ar
    Fantasy Book Mar,1987
  The Other Side: Pennies from Hell, ar
    Twilight Zone Feb,1987
  Pennies from Hell, ss *Night Cry* v2#3,1987
  The Shaper of Animals, ss *Amazing* Jul,1987
  She Just Wanted to Get out of the House,
    pm *Amazing* Sep,1987
  Transients, ss *Amazing* Jan,1987

Schweitzer, Darrell, ed.
  Discovering H.P. Lovecraft, nf Starmont
    House Sep,1987

Schweitzer, Darrell & John Gregory Betancourt
  The Children of Lommos, ss *Night Cry*
    v2#4,1987

Scortia, Thomas N. & Frank M. Robinson
  Blow-Out!, n. Franklin Watts Apr,1987

Scott, Jody
  Mushroom Roulette, ss **Tales from the
    Forbidden Planet**, ed. Roz Kaveney,
    Titan,1987

Scott, Melissa
  The Empress of Earth, n. Baen Nov,1987
  The Kindly Ones, n. Baen Sep,1987

Scott, Michael
  Burial Rites, n. Berkley Aug,1987
  The Last of the Fianna, n. Pied Piper
    Apr,1987
  Magician's Law, n. Sphere May,1987

Scotten, W.C.
  A Matter of Condensation, ss *Analog*
    Jan,1987

Scrocco, Jean L., ill. & Judy Mastrangelo, ed.
  Antique Fairy Tales, an Unicorn Oct,1987

Searles, Baird
  On Books, br *IASFM* Jan,1987
  On Books, br *IASFM* Feb,1987
  On Books, br *IASFM* Mar,1987
  On Books, br *IASFM* May,1987
  On Books, br *IASFM* Jun,1987
  On Books, br *IASFM* Aug,1987
  On Books, br *IASFM* Sep,1987
  On Books, br *IASFM* Nov,1987
  On Books, br *IASFM* mid-Dec,1987

Secula, S.M.
  The Missing Dumbell, ss *Haunts* #9,1987

Segrelles, Vincente
  The Art of Segrelles, pi NBM Publishing
    Jan,1988
  The Mercenary: The Cult of the Sacred Fire
    and the Formula, pi NBM Oct,1987

Seidenstein, B.J.
  Road, ss *Haunts* #9,1987

Seidman, Michael
  The Dream That Follows Darkness, ss
    Twilight Zone Aug,1987

Selinsky, Deloris
  It, pm *2AM* Fll,1987

Selves, David
  Life Goes on Forever..., n. Ansty Mar,1987

Senn, Steven
  The Sand Witch, n. Avon/Camelot Jun,1987

Serling, Carol
  Illuminations: Freedom to Imagine, ar
    Twilight Zone Apr,1987

Serling, Carol, Martin H. Greenberg & Charles
  G. Waugh, eds.
  Rod Serling's Night Gallery Reader, an
    Dembner Dec,1987

Serling, Carol & Bob Rosenbaum
  Life with Rod, iv *Twilight Zone* Apr,1987

Service, Pamela F.
  Tomorrow's Magic, n. Atheneum Sep,1987
  When the Night Wind Howls, n. Atheneum
    Jul,1987

Severance, Carol
  Day of Strange Fortune, ss **Magic in Ithkar**
    #4, ed. Andre Norton & Robert
    Adams,1987
  Isle of Illusion, nv **Tales of the Witch World**,
    ed. Andre Norton, St. Martin's,1987

Shahar, Eluki bes
  Light Fantastic, ss *Amazing* Mar,1987

Shanklin, Rickey L.
  Blood of the Lamb, ss *Eldritch Tales*
    #13,1987

Shannon, Ed
  By the Way, ed *Minnesota Fantasy Review*
    #1,1987
  Internal Shadows, br *Minnesota Fantasy
    Review* #1,1987
  Now Appearing, vi *Minnesota Fantasy
    Review* #1,1987

Shannon, Ed & Mike Odden, eds.
  Minnesota Fantasy Review [v.1 #1, October
    1987]

SHARPE, JOHN RUFUS, III

Sharpe, John Rufus, III
Hogar Lord of the Asyr, n. NAL/Signet
Dec,1987

Shaver, Edward F.
Fear the Light, ss *Amazing* May,1987
The Gods Arrive, nv *F&SF* Sep,1987

Shaw, Bob
The Ragged Astronauts, n. Baen Jun,1987

Shaw-Mathews, Patricia
Coils, ss **Red Sun of Darkover**, ed. Marion
Zimmer Bradley & The Friends of
Darkover, DAW,1987

Shea, Michael
Delivery, ss *F&SF* Dec,1987
The Extra, nv *F&SF* May,1987
Fat Face, nv Axolotl Press: Seattle WA,1987
Polyphemus, co Arkham House Nov,1987

Sheckley, Jay
Alien Mail to the White House, Exclusive:
The Plook Letters, vi *Twilight Zone*
Oct,1987
Lost Soul, ss **Devils & Demons**, ed. Marvin
Kaye, SFBC/Doubleday,1987
Megamouse, ss *Night Cry* v2#5,1987
The Other Side: The Zone of Silence, ar
Twilight Zone Oct,1987
The Other Side: Zoned Again?, ar *Twilight
Zone* Aug,1987

Sheckley, Jay & Robert Sheckley
Spectator Playoffs, ss *Night Cry* v2#3,1987

Sheckley, Robert
Hunter/Victim, n. NAL/Signet Jan,1988
Victim Prime, n. Methuen Jan,1987
Victim Prime, n. NAL/Signet Jun,1987

Sheckley, Robert & Jay Sheckley
Spectator Playoffs, ss *Night Cry* v2#3,1987

Sheerin, Roisin
Some Day My Prince Will Come, vi **Mad
and Bad Fairies**, ed. Anonymous, Attic
Press,1987

Sheffield, Charles
Do You Really Want a Bigger U.S. Space
Program?, ar **New Destinies** v2, ed. Jim
Baen, Baen,1987
The Dreaming Spires of Houston, ss **New
Destinies** v2, ed. Jim Baen, Baen,1987
The Grand Tour, ss *Analog* May,1987
Guilt Trip, ss *Analog* Aug,1987
Obsolete Skill, ss *F&SF* Dec,1987
Running Out, ar **New Destinies** v2, ed. Jim
Baen, Baen,1987
Trader's Cross, nv *Analog* Mar,1987
Trader's Partner, nv *Analog* Jul,1987
Trapalanda, nv *IASFM* Jun,1987

Shefner, Evelyn
The Common Body, na **Common Body,
Royal Bones**, Coffee House Press:
Minneapolis,1987
Common Body, Royal Bones, co Coffee
House Press Dec,1987

Sheldon, Glenn
Accentuated Man in a Gradient Light, pm
Ice River Sum,1987

Shelley, Mary W. & David Campton
Frankenstein, n. Beaver Oct,1987

Shelley, Rick
The Lizard, the Dragon, and the Eater of
Souls, nv *Analog* Sep,1987

Shepard, Lucius
The Black Clay Boy, ss **Whispers** #6, ed.
Stuart David Schiff,1987
Delta Sly Honey, ss **In the Field of Fire**, ed.
Jeanne Van Buren Dann & Jack M. Dann,
Tor,1987
The Exercise of Faith, ss *Twilight Zone*
Jun,1987
The Glassblower's Dragon, ss *F&SF* Apr,1987
The Jaguar Hunter, co Arkham House
May,1987
Life During Wartime, n. Bantam Oct,1987
On the Border, nv *IASFM* Aug,1987
Pictures Made of Stone, ss *Omni* Sep,1987
Shades, nv **In the Field of Fire**, ed. Jeanne
Van Buren Dann & Jack M. Dann, Tor,1987
The Sun Spider, nv *IASFM* Apr,1987
White Trains, pm *Night Cry* v2#3,1987

Sherman, C.H.
Tapestry, ss **Devils & Demons**, ed. Marvin
Kaye, SFBC/Doubleday,1987

Sherman, Delia
The Maid on the Shore, ss *F&SF* Oct,1987

Sherman, Josepha
Danar's Hawk, ss *Fantasy Book* Mar,1987
The Ring of Lifari, ss **Sword and Sorceress**
#4, ed. Marion Zimmer Bradley,1987

Sherrell, Carl
Skraelings, n. Ace/New Infinities Aug,1987

Shetterly, Will & Emma Bull, eds.
Liavek: Wizard's Row, oa Ace Sep,1987

Shiner, Edith & Lewis Shiner
Six Flags Over Jesus, vi *IASFM* Nov,1987

Shiner, Lewis
Dancers, ss *Night Cry* v2#4,1987
The Left-Handed Muse, bg **All About
Strange Monsters of the Recent Past**,
Kansas City, MO: Ursus Imprints,1987
Pennies from Hell, nv **Wild Cards** v2, ed.
George R.R. Martin, Bantam,1987
Rebels, ss *Omni* Nov,1987

Shiner, Lewis & Edith Shiner
Six Flags Over Jesus, vi *IASFM* Nov,1987

Shirley, John
Parakeet, ss *New Pathways* Apr,1987
Ticket to Heaven, ss *F&SF* Dec,1987

Shwartz, Susan M.
Byzantium's Crown, n. Popular Library
Questar Apr,1987
Temple to a Minor Goddess, ss *Amazing*
Jan,1987
The Woman of Flowers, n. Pan Dec,1987
The Woman of Flowers, n. Popular Library
Questar Nov,1987

Sibley, Brian
**Snow White and the Seven Dwarfs & the
Making of the Classic Film**, nf Simon &
Schuster Aug,1987

Siegel, Barbara & Scott Siegel
The Blood Sea Monster, nv **DragonLance
Tales** v1, Margaret Weis & Tracy
Hickman, TSR,1987

SILVERBERG, ROBERT

Siegel, Barbara & Scott Siegel (continued)
Firebrats #1: The Burning Land, n. Pocket
Archway Jul,1987
Firebrats #2: Survivors, n. Pocket Archway
Jul,1987
Firebrats #3: Thunder Mountain, n.
Pocket Archway Sep,1987
A Painter's Vision, nv **DragonLance Tales**
v3, Margaret Weis & Tracy Hickman,
TSR,1987
The Storyteller, nv **DragonLance Tales** v2,
Margaret Weis & Tracy Hickman,
TSR,1987

Siegel, Scott & Barbara Siegel
The Blood Sea Monster, nv **DragonLance
Tales** v1, Margaret Weis & Tracy
Hickman, TSR,1987
Firebrats #1: The Burning Land, n. Pocket
Archway Jul,1987
Firebrats #2: Survivors, n. Pocket Archway
Jul,1987
Firebrats #3: Thunder Mountain, n.
Pocket Archway Sep,1987
A Painter's Vision, nv **DragonLance Tales**
v3, Margaret Weis & Tracy Hickman,
TSR,1987
The Storyteller, nv **DragonLance Tales** v2,
Margaret Weis & Tracy Hickman,
TSR,1987

Sievert, John
C.A.D.S. #4: Tech Strike Force, n. Zebra
Feb,1987

Sikes, Mary
Salarius Recommends, br *Salarius*
v1#4,1987

Sikes, Mary, ed.
Salarius [No. 3, March 1987]

Sikes, Mary & Jon Colley
Salarius Recommends, br *Salarius* #3,1987

Silbar, Margaret L.
Cellular Automata, ar *Analog* Sep,1987

Silva, David B.
Hellnotes, ed *The Horror Show* Jan,1987
Hellnotes, ed *The Horror Show* Spr,1987
Hellnotes, ed *The Horror Show* Sum,1987
Hellnotes, ed *The Horror Show* Fll,1987
Hellnotes, ed *The Horror Show* Win,1987
Ice Sculptures, ss **Masques** #2, ed. J.N.
Williamson,1987
Matchsticks, vi *Eldritch Tales* #13,1987
Metanoia, ss *New Blood* #1,1987
Shifting Passions, vi *Footsteps* Nov,1987
Watershead, vi *Grue* #5,1987

Silva, David B., ed.
The Horror Show [v.5 #1, January 1987]
The Horror Show [v.5 #2, Spring 1987]
The Horror Show [v.5 #3, Summer 1987]
The Horror Show [v.5 #4, Fall 1987]
The Horror Show [v.5 #5, Winter 1987]

Silverberg, Robert
"Colony": I Trusted the Rug Completely,
ar,1987
"Common Time": With All of Love, ar,1987
"Day Million": A Boy, a Girl, a Love Story,
ar,1987
The Fascination of the Abomination, na
IASFM Jul,1987
"Fondly Fahrenheit": Who Am I, Which Are
You?, ar,1987

Silverberg, Robert (continued)
"Four in One": Complications With Elegance, ar,1987
Hardware, ss *Omni* Oct,1987
"Home Is the Hunter": The Triumph of Honest Roger Bellamy, ar,1987
"Hothouse": The Fuzzypuzzle Odyssey, ar,1987
The Iron Star, ss **Universe**, ed. Byron Preiss, Bantam Spectra,1987
"Light of Other Days": Beyond the Radius of Capture, ar,1987
"The Little Black Bag": Press Button for Triple Bypass, ar,1987
"The Monsters": Don't Forget to Kill Your Wife, ar,1987
"The New Prime": Six Plots for the Price of One, ar,1987
"No Woman Born": Flowing From Ring to Ring, ar,1987
The Pardoner's Tale, ss *Playboy* Jun,1987
Project Pendulum, n. Walker Sep,1987
Reflections, ar *Amazing* Jan,1987
Reflections, ar *Amazing* Mar,1987
Reflections, ar *Amazing* May,1987
Reflections, ar *Amazing* Jul,1987
Reflections, ar *Amazing* Sep,1987
Reflections, ar *Amazing* Nov,1987
"Scanners Live in Vain": Under the Wire With the Habermans, ar,1987
The Secret Sharer, na *IASFM* Sep,1987

Silverberg, Robert, ed.
Robert Silverberg's Worlds of Wonder, an Warner Oct,1987

Simak, Clifford D.
Brother and Other Stories, co Severn House Apr,1987

Simmons, Dan
E-Ticket to Namland, ss *Omni* Nov,1987

Simon, Jo
Beloved Captain, n. Avon Jan,1988

Simon, Margaret B.
Beyond Suawanee, pm *Minnesota Fantasy Review* #1,1987
Sense of Wonder, ar *Minnesota Fantasy Review* #1,1987
Spacer Trivia, pm *Amazing* Jul,1987

Simon, Morris
The Wizard's Spectacles, nv **DragonLance Tales** v2, Margaret Weis & Tracy Hickman, TSR,1987

Simons, Walton
If Looks Could Kill, ss **Wild Cards** v2, ed. George R.R. Martin, Bantam,1987

Simpson, Robert
Children of the Night, ar *Twilight Zone* Dec,1987
Games, gr *Twilight Zone* Aug,1987
Illuminations: Really Weird Tales, ar *Twilight Zone* Apr,1987
Magic in the Streets, ar *Twilight Zone* Apr,1987
The Other Side: Children of the Night, ar *Twilight Zone* Jun,1987
The Other Side: Dial "T" for Terror, ar *Twilight Zone* Apr,1987
The Other Side: It Came from Across the Pond, ar *Twilight Zone* Aug,1987
The Other Side: Surrealistic Wonkiness, ar *Twilight Zone* Jun,1987

Simpson, Robert (continued)
The Real Children of the Night, ar *Twilight Zone* Dec,1987

Sims, Mike
Warm as Snow, ss **After Midnight Stories** #3,1987

Sinclair, Kathryn A.
Raindance, ss **Tesseracts 2**, ed. Phyllis Gotlieb & Douglas Barbour, Press Porcepic: Victoria,1987

Singer, Marilyn
Ghost Host, n. Harper & Row Aug,1987

Singer, Richard
Pop Stars, vi *Grue* #4,1987

Sjolie, Dennis John
A Thing or Two About Razzle-Dazzle, ss *Mage* Spr,1987

Skeet, Michael
Rain, ss **Tesseracts 2**, ed. Phyllis Gotlieb & Douglas Barbour, Press Porcepic: Victoria,1987

Skipp, John M. & Craig Spector
The Cleanup, n. Bantam Mar,1987
The Cleanup, ss *Night Cry* v2#4,1987
Gentlemen, nv **The Architecture of Fear**, ed. Kathryn Cramer & Peter D. Pautz, Arbor House,1987

Sladek, John
Roderick, n. Carroll & Graf Jul,1987

Slaughter, Rick
Delicate Immortal Meanings, ss **Gollancz - Sunday Times Best SF Stories**, Gollancz,1987

Slusser, George E., Colin Greenland & Eric S. Rabkin, eds.
Storm Warnings: Science Fiction Confronts the Future, nf S. Illinois Univ. Press Apr,1987

Slusser, George E. & Eric S. Rabkin, eds.
Aliens: The Anthropology of Science Fiction, nf Southern Illinois Univ. Press Nov,1987
Intersections: Fantasy and Science Fiction, nf Southern Illinois Univ. Press Oct,1987

Smeds, Dave
Goats, nv **In the Field of Fire**, ed. Jeanne Van Buren Dann & Jack M. Dann, Tor,1987
Gullrider, ss **Sword and Sorceress** #4, ed. Marion Zimmer Bradley,1987
A Hard Ride Home, ss *Mayfair* Sep,1987
Something in the Wind, ss *Tales of the Unanticipated* #2,1987
Termites, ss *IASFM* May,1987

Smirl, D.E.
A Question of Belief, ss *Apex!* #1,1987

Smith, Brent R.
Falling in Love Again, ss **The Pan Book of Horror Stories** #28, Pan,1987

Smith, Dean Wesley
The Jukebox Man, ss *Night Cry* v2#5,1987

Smith, Guy N.
Alligators, n. Arrow Mar,1987
Bloodshow, n. Arrow Jul,1987
Demons, n. Arrow Nov,1987
Entombed, n. Dell Nov,1987
The Plague, n. NEL Oct,1987
The Wood, n. Dell Dec,1987

Smith, Harding E.
Quasars and Active Galaxies, ar **Universe**, ed. Byron Preiss, Bantam Spectra,1987

Smith, Harry
The Ballad of Devil's Pasture, ss *Pulpsmith* Win,1987
The Queen of the Night, pm *Pulpsmith* Win,1987

Smith, Harry, ed.
Pulpsmith [v.6 #4, Winter '87]

Smith, James Robert
Things Not Seen, vi *2AM* Spr,1987

Smith, L.J.
The Night of the Solstice, n. Macmillan Oct,1987

Smith, Nicholas D., Gorman Beauchamp & Kenneth Roemer, eds.
Utopian Studies 1, nf Univ. Press of America May,1987

Smith, Nick
The Life and Times of Nick Smith, pi *Salarius* v1#4,1987

Smith, Nick & Dennis Mallonee, eds.
Fantasy Book [v.5 #5, March 1987]

Smith, Stephanie
The Boy Who Was Thrown Away, n. Atheneum Sep,1987

Smith, Susan
Samantha Slade #2: Confessions of a Teenage Frog, n. Pocket Archway Oct,1987
Samantha Slade #3: Our Friend, Public Nuisance No. 1, n. Pocket Archway Dec,1987
Samantha Slade, Monster-Sitter, n. Pocket Archway Oct,1987

Smith, Terrence Lore
Yours Truly, From Hell, n. St. Martin's Jul,1987

Smith, Warren B.
Dreams of Darkness, Dreams of Light, nv **DragonLance Tales** v1, Margaret Weis & Tracy Hickman, TSR,1987

SMS
The Good Robot, cs *Interzone* #22,1987

Snellings, John H.
First Come, First Served, ss **The Pan Book of Horror Stories** #28, Pan,1987

Sneyd, Steve
The Package Tourist, ss *Back Brain Recluse* #7,1987

Snodgrass, Melinda M.
Circuit Breaker, n. Berkley May,1987
Relative Difficulties, nv **Wild Cards** v2, ed. George R.R. Martin, Bantam,1987

SNODGRASS, MELINDA M.

Snodgrass, Melinda M. (continued)
Requiem, ss **A Very Large Array**, ed.
Melinda M. Snodgrass, University of New
Mexico Press,1987

Snodgrass, Melinda M., ed.
A Very Large Array, an Univ. of New
Mexico Press Dec,1987

Snodgrass, Melinda M. & Victor Milan
Runespear, n. Popular Library Questar
Apr,1987

Snyder, Maryanne K.
Eleanor Meets God, pm *Grue #6*,1987

Snyder, Midori
Soulstring, n. Ace Nov,1987

Sobchack, Vivian
**Screening Space: The American Science
Fiction Film**, nf Ungar Jan,1987

Sokolov, Alexandra
The Price of an Egg, nv **Angels in Hell**, ed.
Janet Morris, Baen,1987

Solomon, Theodore
A Hot Prospect, ss *Mage* Spr,1987

Sommers, Beverly
Time and Again, n. Worldwide Library
Aug,1987

Somtow, S.P.
Forgetting Places, n. Tor Oct,1987
ResurrecTech, nv *Night Cry* v2#3,1987

Sonntag, Linda, ed.
The Ghost Story Treasury, an Putnam
Nov,1987

Sontheimer, Lee Ann
Presences, pm *2AM* Sum,1987

Soukup, Martha
Frenchmen and Plumbers, ss *Aboriginal SF*
Sep,1987
Living in the Jungle, ss **L. Ron Hubbard
Presents Writers of the Future** v3, ed.
Algis Budrys, Bridge,1987
Master of the Game, ss *F&SF* Nov,1987

Sourbut, Elizabeth
The African Quota, ss **Gollancz - Sunday
Times Best SF Stories**, Gollancz,1987

South, Malcolm, ed.
**Mythical and Fabulous Creatures: A
Sourcebook and Research Guide**, nf
Greenwood Mar,1987

Spark, Muriel
Mary Shelley: A Biography, nf
Dutton/William Abrahms Jul,1987
The Stories of Muriel Spark, co Bodley
Head Apr,1987

Spears, Heather
One, nv **Tesseracts 2**, ed. Phyllis Gotlieb &
Douglas Barbour, Press Porcepic:
Victoria,1987

Spector, Craig & John M. Skipp
The Cleanup, n. Bantam Mar,1987
The Cleanup, ss *Night Cry* v2#4,1987

Spector, Craig & John M. Skipp (continued)
Gentlemen, nv **The Architecture of Fear**,
ed. Kathryn Cramer & Peter D. Pautz,
Arbor House,1987

Speirs, Kevin
Down Under, ss *Haunts #9*,1987

Spencer, Kathleen
Charles Williams, nf Starmont House
Jan,1987

Spinrad, Hyron
Galaxies and Clusters, ar **Universe**, ed.
Byron Preiss, Bantam Spectra,1987

Spinrad, Norman
Little Heroes, n. Bantam Spectra Jul,1987
On Books: Dreamers of Space, br *IASFM*
Oct,1987
On Books: Sturgeon, Vonnegut, and Trout,
br *IASFM* Apr,1987
On Books: The Edge of the Envelope, br
IASFM Jul,1987

Spivack, Charlotte
**Merlin's Daughters: Contemporary
Women Writers of Fantasy**, nf
Greenwood Jan,1987

Spivack, Richard
My Best Ever Holiday, ss **Gollancz -
Sunday Times Best SF Stories**,
Gollancz,1987

Springer, Nancy
The Bard, ss **Chance & Other Gestures of
the Hand of Fate**, Baen,1987
Chance, na **Under the Wheel: Alien Stars
Vol. III**, ed. Elizabeth Mitchell, Baen,1987
**Chance & Other Gestures of the Hand of
Fate**, co Baen Sep,1987
The Golden Face of Fate, na **Chance &
Other Gestures of the Hand of Fate**,
Baen,1987
A Horse to Love, n. Harper & Row,1987
Madbond, n. Tor Jun,1987
Mindbond, n. Tor Nov,1987
Primal Cry, nv **Chance & Other Gestures
of the Hand of Fate**, Baen,1987
We Build a Shrine, pm **Chance & Other
Gestures of the Hand of Fate**, Baen,1987

St. Alcorn, Lloyd
Halberd: Dream Warrior, n. NAL/Signet
Oct,1987

St. Clair, David
The Devil Rocked Her Cradle, n. Corgi
Sep,1987

St. George, Judith
Haunted, n. Methuen Apr,1987
Who's Scared? Not Me!, n. Putnam
Oct,1987

St. Leger, Philip
Modern History, ss **Gollancz - Sunday
Times Best SF Stories**, Gollancz,1987

Stableford, Brian M.
Layers of Meaning, ss *Interzone #21*,1987
Sexual Chemistry, ss *Interzone #20*,1987

Stacy, Ryder
**Doomsday Warrior #10: American
Nightmare**, n. Zebra Mar,1987

Stacy, Ryder (continued)
Doomsday Warrior #11: American Eden,
n. Zebra May,1987
**Doomsday Warrior #12: Death, American
Style**, n. Zebra Nov,1987

Staff
Book Reviews, br *New Pathways* Jan,1987

Staig, Laurence
Hello, Hugo, ss **Twisted Circuits**, ed. Mick
Gowar, Beaver,1987

Stall, Dave
Winged Death, ss *Minnesota Fantasy
Review #1*,1987

Stamey, Sara
Wild Card Run, n. Berkley Apr,1987

Stamper, J.B.
At Midnight, ss **More Tales for the
Midnight Hour**, Apple/Scholastic,1987
The Black Mare, ss **More Tales for the
Midnight Hour**, Apple/Scholastic,1987
The Collector, ss **More Tales for the
Midnight Hour**, Apple/Scholastic,1987
Footsteps, ss **More Tales for the Midnight
Hour**, Apple/Scholastic,1987
A Ghost Story, ss **More Tales for the
Midnight Hour**, Apple/Scholastic,1987
The Hearse, ss **More Tales for the
Midnight Hour**, Apple/Scholastic,1987
In the Lantern's Light, ss **More Tales for
the Midnight Hour**, Apple/Scholastic,1987
The Love Charm, ss **More Tales for the
Midnight Hour**, Apple/Scholastic,1987
The Mask, ss **More Tales for the Midnight
Hour**, Apple/Scholastic,1987
More Tales for the Midnight Hour, oc
Scholastic Apple Oct,1987
A Night in the Woods, ss **More Tales for
the Midnight Hour**, Apple/Scholastic,1987
Right Inn, ss **More Tales for the Midnight
Hour**, Apple/Scholastic,1987
The Shortcut, ss **More Tales for the
Midnight Hour**, Apple/Scholastic,1987
Trick-or-Treat, ss **More Tales for the
Midnight Hour**, Apple/Scholastic,1987

Stanford, Derek
Meeting Mr. Singleton, ss **After Midnight
Stories #3**,1987

Stanley, John
Shock Supplement, mr *American Fantasy*
Spr,1987
Shock Supplement, mr *American Fantasy*
Sum,1987
Shock Supplement, mr *American Fantasy*
Win,1987

Stanley, Stephen
2087, ct *Aphelion #5*,1987

Starkey, David
Confession, vi *Grue #4*,1987
The Hand of God, ss *2AM* Sum,1987
Trimmings, ss *Grue #5*,1987

Stasheff, Christopher
The Warlock Heretical, n. Ace Aug,1987

Stathis, Lou
Illuminations: Comic Relief, ar *Twilight Zone*
Apr,1987
The Other Side: Apocalyptic Voivod, ar
Twilight Zone Dec,1987

STATHIS, LOU

Stathis, Lou (continued)
The Other Side: Dark Knight, ar *Twilight Zone* Jun,1987
The Other Side: Giger Counting, ar *Twilight Zone* Dec,1987
The Other Side: Opera of the Red Death, ar *Twilight Zone* Feb,1987
The Other Side: Things Without Faces, ar *Twilight Zone* Jun,1987

Stchur, John
Down on the Farm, n. St. Martin's Dec,1987

Steakley, John
The Swordsman Smada, nv **Friends of the Horseclans**, ed. Robert Adams & Pamela Crippen Adams, Signet,1987

Steiner, Merrilee
Eileen Goudge's Swept Away #7: Pirate Moon, n. Avon Flare Aug,1987

Stephenson, Bryan G.
Dubious Pleasures, ss *Amazing* Sep,1987

Sterling, Bruce
Flowers for Edo, nv *IASFM* May,1987
The Little Magic Shop, ss *IASFM* Oct,1987

Sterling, Bruce & Don Webb
Bruce Sterling, iv *New Pathways* Aug,1987

Sterman, Betsy & Samuel Sterman
Too Much Magic, n. Lippincott Apr,1987

Sterman, Samuel & Betsy Sterman
Too Much Magic, n. Lippincott Apr,1987

Steussy, Marti
Forest of the Night, n. Ballantine/Del Rey Jun,1987

Stevens, James A.
Borboleta, ss *Aboriginal SF* Jul,1987

Stevens, Julie
Century Farm, ss *Whispers* #23,1987

Stevenson, Robert Louis & Samantha Lee
Dr. Jekyll and Mr. Hyde, n. Beaver Feb,1987
Dr. Jekyll and Mr. Hyde, n. Hutchinson Mar,1987

Stevermer, Caroline
Cenedwine Brocade, ss **Liavek: Wizard's Row**, ed. Will Shetterly & Emma Bull, Ace,1987

Stewart, Ian
Billy the Kid, ss *Analog* Jan,1987
Captives of the Slavestone, nv *Analog* mid-Dec,1987
Displaced Person, na *Analog* May,1987
The Electronic Mathematician, ar *Analog* Jan,1987

Stewart, Michael & Peter Jay
Apocalypse 2000: Economic Breakdown and the Suicide of Democracy, n. Sidgwick & Jackson Jun,1987

Stewart, Ramona
The Nightmare Candidate, n. Arlington Sep,1987

Stiegler, Marc
David's Sling, n. Baen Jan,1988

Stiegler, Marc (continued)
The Third Alternative, nv *Analog* Nov,1987

Stine, G. Harry
The Alternate View: Cultural Differences, ar *Analog* Sep,1987
The Alternate View: Frontiers and Wars, ar *Analog* Jan,1987
The Alternate View: Hardening Humans, ar *Analog* mid-Dec,1987
The Alternate View: Overreaction, ar *Analog* Jul,1987
The Alternate View: Stealth, ar *Analog* May,1987
The Alternate View: The Fits and Flops of Fuzzy Logic, ar *Analog* Mar,1987
The Alternate View: The Selling of Proton, ar *Analog* Nov,1987
The Dream Is Down, ar *Analog* Feb,1987
The Space Beat: How to Stop a Space Program, ar **New Destinies** v1, ed. Jim Baen, Baen,1987

Stine, Jovian Bob
Spaceballs: The Book, n. Scholastic Point Jun,1987

Stith, John E.
Death Tolls, n. Ace Sep,1987
Doing Time, ss *Aboriginal SF* Jul,1987

Stoker, Bram
Dracula, n. Armada Jan,1987

Stokes, Tawn
No Pets, ss **L. Ron Hubbard Presents Writers of the Future** v3, ed. Algis Budrys, Bridge,1987

Stolbov, Bruce
Last Fall, n. Doubleday May,1987

Stout, Tim
The Raging, n. Grafton Feb,1987

Stover, Professor Leon
The Prophetic Soul: A Reading of H.G. Wells' Things to Come, nf McFarland Dec,1987
Robert A. Heinlein, nf G.K. Hall/Twayne Dec,1987

Strasser, Todd
The Mall From Outer Space, n. Scholastic Apple Oct,1987

Strauss, Erwin S.
SF Conventional Calendar, ms *IASFM* Jan,1987
SF Conventional Calendar, ms *IASFM* Feb,1987
SF Conventional Calendar, ms *IASFM* Mar,1987
SF Conventional Calendar, ms *IASFM* Apr,1987
SF Conventional Calendar, ms *IASFM* May,1987
SF Conventional Calendar, ms *IASFM* Jun,1987
SF Conventional Calendar, ms *IASFM* Jul,1987
SF Conventional Calendar, ms *IASFM* Aug,1987
SF Conventional Calendar, ms *IASFM* Sep,1987
SF Conventional Calendar, ms *IASFM* Oct,1987

Strauss, Erwin S. (continued)
SF Conventional Calendar, ms *IASFM* Nov,1987
SF Conventional Calendar, ms *IASFM* Dec,1987
SF Conventional Calendar, ms *IASFM* mid-Dec,1987

Strete, Craig Kee
As If Bloodied on a Hunt Before Sleep, ss *Twilight Zone* Aug,1987
The Game of Cat and Eagle, nv **In the Field of Fire**, ed. Jeanne Van Buren Dann & Jack M. Dann, Tor,1987

Strickland, Brad
Oh Tin Man, Tin Man, There's No Place Like Home, ss *F&SF* May,1987

Strickland, John
Terrorstorm, ss *The Horror Show* Win,1987

Stricklin, Robert
Autograph, ss *2AM* Spr,1987

Stross, Charles
The Boys, ss *Interzone* #22,1987

Strugatsky, Arkady & Boris Strugatsky
The Time Wanderers, n. Richardson & Steirman Mar,1987

Strugatsky, Boris & Arkady Strugatsky
The Time Wanderers, n. Richardson & Steirman Mar,1987

Stuart, Kiel
Cutting Up, ss *Muscle Training Illustrated* Sep,1987
Death Spiral, ss *Muscle Training Illustrated* Aug,1987
Green in High Hallack, ss **Tales of the Witch World**, ed. Andre Norton, St. Martin's,1987

Studach, Stephen
The Black Things, pm *Eldritch Tales* #14,1987
Tomb Mate, pm *Eldritch Tales* #13,1987

Sturgeon, Theodore
To Marry Medusa, co Baen Dec,1987
A Touch of Sturgeon, co Simon & Schuster UK Aug,1987

Suckling, Nigel
Heroic Dreams, pi Paper Tiger Jul,1987

Sullivan, Jean
Bloody Waters, ss *Eldritch Tales* #13,1987

Sullivan, Thomas
The Fence, ss **Shadows** #10, ed. Charles L. Grant,1987
The Man Who Drowned Puppies, ss **Masques** #2, ed. J.N. Williamson,1987
Prayerwings, nv **Doom City**, ed. Charles L. Grant, Tor,1987

Sullivan, Tim
Dinosaur on a Bicycle, nv *IASFM* Mar,1987

Sullivan, Timothy
V: To Conquer the Throne, n. Tor Nov,1987

Summa, Alan Jude
Alan Jude Summa, bg *2AM* Win,1987
Dreams of Imagination, pm *2AM* Win,1987

Sutton, David
Waking, ss *2AM* Win,1987

Svedbeck, Heather
After a Brief Commercial Message, ss
Twilight Zone Apr,1987
One Special, Perfect Way, ss *2AM* Fll,1987

Swanwick, Michael
Foresight, ss *Interzone* #20,1987
Vacuum Flowers, n. Arbor House Feb,1987
Vacuum Flowers [Part 2 of 3], sl *IASFM*
Jan,1987
Vacuum Flowers [Part 3 of 3], sl *IASFM*
Feb,1987

Sykes, S.C.
U.S.S.A. Book 3, n. Avon Apr,1987

Syvertsen, Ryder & Adrian Fletcher
Psychic Spawn, n. Popular Library Oct,1987

Tagrin, Lawrence
Art in Space, ar *Salarius* v1#4,1987
Ice, ss *Salarius* v1#4,1987

Tannehill, Jayne
V: The Oregon Invasion, n. Tor Jan,1988

Tapp, Kathy Kennedy
Flight of the Moth-Kin, n. Macmillan
McElderry Sep,1987
**The Scorpio Ghosts and the Black Hole
Gang**, n. Harper & Row Apr,1987

Tarr, Judith
The Lady of Han-Gilen, n. Tor Jun,1987

Tarzia, Wade
Alandriar Goes To Earth, ss *Mage* Spr,1987
Decay in the Hero's Way, ar *Mage* Spr,1987
Message Intercepted On Hyperspatial
Frequency, vi *Mage* Win,1987
A Trace of Inbetween, ar *Mage* Win,1987

Tatro, Edgar F.
"War on Imagination" Feedback, lt *2AM*
Spr,1987

Taylor, C. & R.L. Newman
Eight Legs Hath the Spider, vi *Haunts*
#9,1987

Taylor, D.W.
Dog Meat, ss *Footsteps* Nov,1987

Taylor, Keith
Bard IV: Raven's Gathering, n. Ace
Nov,1987

Taylor, Richard
Shards, pm *Ice River* Sum,1987
The Visitor, ss *2AM* Fll,1987

Taylor, Stephanie
Third Generation, ss *SF International*
#2,1987

Tem, Melanie & Steve Rasnic Tem
The Sing, ss *SF International* #1,1987

Tem, Steve Rasnic
Dinosaur, ss *IASFM* May,1987
Fogwell, ss **Doom City**, ed. Charles L.
Grant, Tor,1987
Ghost Signs, pm *Eldritch Tales* #14,1987
Hidey Hole, ss **Masques** #2, ed. J.N.
Williamson,1987

Tem, Steve Rasnic (continued)
L Is for Love, vi *Footsteps* Nov,1987
Last Dragon, ss *Amazing* Sep,1987
Leaks, ss **Whispers** #6, ed. Stuart David
Schiff,1987
Mother Hag, ss *Grue* #5,1987
Off the Subject I: On Genre, Magical
Realism, and Writing Seriously, ar *The
Horror Show* Sum,1987
Off the Subject II: Background and
Foreground, ar *The Horror Show* Fll,1987
Wake, ss *Eldritch Tales* #13,1987
The Woman on the Corner, ss *Whispers*
#23,1987

Tem, Steve Rasnic & Melanie Tem
The Sing, ss *SF International* #1,1987

Temperley, Alan
The Abandoned Dam, nv **The Pan Book of
Horror Stories** #28, Pan,1987

Teng, Tais
What Avails a Psalm in the Cinders of
Gehenna?, ss *SF International* #2,1987

Tepper, Sheri S.
After Long Silence, n. Bantam Spectra
Dec,1987
The Awakeners, om SFBC Sep,1987
The Awakeners: Northshore, n. Tor
Mar,1987
The End of the Game, om SFBC Jan,1987
Northshore, n. Tor: New York,1987
Southshore, n. Tor: New York,1987
Southshore, n. Tor Jun,1987

Thomas, Elizabeth Marshall
Reindeer Moon, n. Houghton Mifflin
Feb,1987

Thomas, Thomas T.
First Citizen, n. Baen Dec,1987

Thompson, Joyce
Harry and the Hendersons, n. Berkley
Jun,1987

Thompson, Paul B.
Sundipper, n. St. Martin's Aug,1987

Thompson, Paul B. & Tonya R. Carter
The Exiles, nv **DragonLance Tales** v3,
Margaret Weis & Tracy Hickman,
TSR,1987

Thompson, W.R.
The Extremists, na *Analog* Jan,1987
Health Food, ss *Analog* May,1987
Lightning Rod, nv *Analog* Aug,1987
Oracle, ss *Analog* Jun,1987
Sideshow, n. Baen Jan,1988

Thornburg, Mary K. Patterson
**The Monster in the Mirror: Gender and
the Sentimental/Gothic Myth in
Frankenstein**, nf UMI Jul,1987

Thornton, Lawrence
Imagining Argentina, n. Bloomsbury
Nov,1987

Thurston, Robert & Glen A. Larson
**Battlestar Galactica #14: Surrender the
Galactica!**, n. Ace Jan,1988

Tigges, John
Hands of Lucifer, n. Leisure Aug,1987

Tilley, Patrick
Iron Master, n. Baen Jul,1987
Iron Master, n. Sphere May,1987

Tilton, Lois
Across the Fog-Gray Sea, ss *The Dragon*
Feb,1987
The Passing of Kings, ss *The Dragon*
Sep,1987

Tine, Robert
Midnight City, n. NAL/Signet Dec,1987

Tiptree, James, Jr.
In Midst of Life, ss *F&SF* Nov,1987
Second Going, nv **Universe** #17, ed. Terry
Carr,1987
Yanqui Doodle, nv *IASFM* Jul,1987

Tobin, Pat
Merovingian City Maps and Merovin
Hemispheric Maps, il **Festival Moon**, ed.
C.J. Cherryh, DAW,1987
Sea Floor Maps, il **Festival Moon**, ed. C.J.
Cherryh, DAW,1987

Toelly, Richard
Unborn, pm *Space & Time* #73,1987

Tolkien, J.R.R.
The Lost Road and Other Writings, co
Houghton Mifflin Dec,1987
The Lost Road and Other Writings, co
Unwin Hyman Aug,1987

Tolley, Michael
Tesseractuality, br *Aphelion* #5,1987

Torren, Asher
The African Woman, pm *Mage* Spr,1987
Huayno, pm *Mage* Win,1987

Townsend, John Rowe
The Persuading Stick, n. Morrow/Lothrop,
Lee & Shepard Nov,1987

Travis, J.J.
Halloween in Arkham, ss *Eldritch Tales*
#13,1987

Trefil, James
The New Physics and the Universe, ar
Universe, ed. Byron Preiss, Bantam
Spectra,1987

Tremayne, Peter
Nicor!, n. Sphere Jun,1987
Trollnight, n. Sphere Dec,1987

Trewin, J.C.
The Manse, ss **After Midnight Stories**
#3,1987

Trexler, Roger Dale
Dead Beat, ss *Minnesota Fantasy Review*
#1,1987
In Time, pm **The Dark Road and Other
Poems of Darkness**,1987

Tritten, Larry
The Dead Woods, ss *F&SF* Jul,1987
Hooray for Hollywood, vi *The Horror Show*
Win,1987
In Video Veritas, ss *F&SF* Dec,1987

Tucker, Wallace
The Intergalactic Medium, ar **Universe**, ed.
Byron Preiss, Bantam Spectra,1987

TUMLIN, JOHN S.

Tumlin, John S.
Tiger's Hunt, ss *Aboriginal SF* May,1987

Turk, H.C.
Ether Ore, n. Tor Nov,1987

Turner, George
Not in Front of the Children, ss *Aphelion*
#5,1987
The Sea and Summer, n. Faber & Faber
Aug,1987

Turney, C. Dell
Portraits of a Young Artist, ss *Space & Time*
#72,1987

Turtledove, Harry
6+, na *Analog* Sep,1987
Agent of Byzantium, n. Congdon &
Weed/Contemporary Apr,1987
Crybaby, ss *Twilight Zone* Dec,1987
An Emperor For the Legion, n.
Ballantine/Del Rey May,1987
Images, nv *IASFM* Mar,1987
The Irvhank Effect, ss **New Destinies** v2, ed.
Jim Baen, Baen,1987
Last Favor, nv *Analog* mid-Dec,1987
The Legion of Videssos, n. Ballantine/Del
Rey Aug,1987
The Misplaced Legion, n. Ballantine/Del
Rey Feb,1987
Noninterference, n. Ballantine/Del Rey
Jan,1988
The Report on Bilbeis IV, na *Analog* May
+2,1987
The Report on Bilbeis IV [Part 1 of 3], sl
Analog May,1987
The Report on Bilbeis IV [Part 2 of 3], sl
Analog Jun,1987
The Report on Bilbeis IV [Part 3 of 3], sl
Analog Jul,1987
Superwine, na *IASFM* Apr,1987
Swords of the Legion, n. Ballantine/Del
Rey Oct,1987
The Weather's Fine, ss *Playboy* Jul,1987

Tuttle, Lisa
A Birthday, ss **Tales from the Forbidden
Planet**, ed. Roz Kaveney, Titan,1987
The Colinization of Edward Beal, ss *F&SF*
Oct,1987
Gabriel, n. Severn House May,1987
Jamie's Grave, ss **Shadows** #10, ed.
Charles L. Grant,1987
Memories of the Body, ss *Interzone*
#22,1987
**A Spaceship Built of Stone and Other
Stories**, co Women's Press Aug,1987
The Wound, ss **Other Edens**, ed.
Christopher Evans & Robert Holdstock,
Unwin: London,1987

Twitchell, James B.
Dreadful Pleasures, nf Oxford Sep,1987

Tyers, Kathy
Firebird, n. Bantam Spectra Jun,1987

unknown
Cartoon, ct *IASFM* Sep,1987
Cartoon, ct *Twilight Zone* Feb,1987
Cartoon, ct *Twilight Zone* Aug,1987
Cartoon, ct *Twilight Zone* Oct,1987

Urquhart, Fred
Swing High, Willie Brodie, ss **After Midnight
Stories** #3,1987

Valentine, Mark
14 Bellchamber Tower, oc Crimson Altar
Press Nov,1987
The Folly, ss **14 Bellchamber Tower**,
Crimson Altar Press,1987
Madberry Hill, ss **14 Bellchamber Tower**,
Crimson Altar Press,1987
St. Michael & All Angels, ss **14 Bellchamber
Tower**, Crimson Altar Press,1987

Van Ash, Cay
The Fires of Fu Manchu, n. Harper & Row
Oct,1987

van Ewyck, Annemarie
Camels for Calvin, ss *SF International*
#1,1987

Van Hamme, Jean & Grzegorz Rosinski
Thorgal: The Archers, gn Donning,1987

van Loggem, Manuel
Touchvision, ss *SF International* #1,1987

Van Lustbader, Eric
Shan, n. Grafton Jan,1987

Van Scyoc, Sydney J.
Drowntide, n. Berkley May,1987

van Zandt, Kit
Photographs, ss *Whispers* #23,1987

Vance, Jack
Araminta Station, n. Underwood-Miller
Sep,1987

Vander Putten, Joan
Hooked On Love, pm *Grue* #6,1987
Just a Little Thing, ss **Devils & Demons**, ed.
Marvin Kaye, SFBC/Doubleday,1987
When You Wish Upon a Corpse, ss *2AM*
Win,1987

Vardeman, Robert E.
At the Bentnail Inn, ss **Doom City**, ed.
Charles L. Grant, Tor,1987
The Jade Demons Quartet, om NEL
Nov,1987
Masters of Space #2: The Alien Web, n.
Avon May,1987
**Masters of Space #3: A Plague in
Paradise**, n. Avon Sep,1987
The Road of Dreams and Death, nv **Tales of
the Witch World**, ed. Andre Norton, St.
Martin's,1987
**The Weapons of Chaos, Book 2:
Equations of Chaos**, n. Ace Jul,1987

Vardeman, Robert E., writing as Daniel Moran
The Skeleton Lord's Key, n. Tor Aug,1987

Vaughan, Bill
Here There Be Dragons, ss *Analog* Mar,1987

Vaughan, Ralph E.
Fluxed in Nova Byzantium, ss *Aboriginal SF*
Nov,1987

Verniere, James
Angel Heart, mr *Twilight Zone* Apr,1987
Illuminations: Mother Was an Alien, ar
Twilight Zone Feb,1987
Illuminations: The Man Who Would Be
Spock, ar *Twilight Zone* Jun,1987
On Film, mr *Twilight Zone* Aug,1987
On Film, mr *Twilight Zone* Oct,1987

Verniere, James (continued)
The Other Mel Brooks, ar *Twilight Zone*
Aug,1987
The Other Side: Over the Edge, ar *Twilight
Zone* Feb,1987
The Other Side: Weirder than Fiction, ar
Twilight Zone Apr,1987
The Spielberg Touch, ar *Twilight Zone*
Oct,1987
The Twilight Zone Review: 1986 - Film, mr
Twilight Zone Feb,1987
The Witches of Eastwick, mr *Twilight Zone*
Jun,1987

Verniere, James & Laurie Cabot
The Witch of Salem, iv *Twilight Zone*
Jun,1987

Vernon, William J.
A Good Day in March, a Bearded Man, pm
Ice River Sum,1987

Versandi, Bob
The Grandpa Urn, ss **Doom City**, ed.
Charles L. Grant, Tor,1987

Versluis, Arthur
Telos, n. Arkana Sep,1987
Telos, n. Methuen/Arkana Nov,1987

Vidal, Harriette & Ed Kelleher
The Breeder, n. Leisure Aug,1987

Vinge, Vernor
Tatja Grimm's World, co Baen Jul,1987
True Names and Other Dangers, co Baen
Nov,1987

Vinicoff, Eric
Displaced, nv *Analog* Mar,1987
Independents, ss *Analog* Apr,1987

Vivelo, Jackie
The Children of Winter, ss **A Trick of the
Light**, Putnam,1987
A Dog Names Ransom, ss **A Trick of the
Light**, Putnam,1987
The Fireside Book of Ghost Stories, ss **A
Trick of the Light**, Putnam,1987
A Game of Statues, ss **A Trick of the Light**,
Putnam,1987
The Girl Who Painted Raindrops, ss **A Trick
of the Light**, Putnam,1987
Night Vision, ss **A Trick of the Light**,
Putnam,1987
A Plague of Crowders, Or, Birds of a
Feather, ss **A Trick of the Light**,
Putnam,1987
Reading to Matthew, ss **A Trick of the
Light**, Putnam,1987
Take Your Best Shot, ss **A Trick of the
Light**, Putnam,1987
A Trick of the Light, oc Putnam Oct,1987

Vogel, Deborah M.
Bloodstones, vi **Sword and Sorceress #4**,
ed. Marion Zimmer Bradley,1987

Volk, Stephen
Gothic, n. Grafton Feb,1987

Vollmann, William T.
You Bright and Risen Angels, n. Atheneum
May,1987

Volsky, Paula
The Luck of Relian Kru, n. Ace Jun,1987

VOLSKY, PAULA

Volsky, Paula (continued)
The Tenancy of Mr. Eex, nv **Devils & Demons**, ed. Marvin Kaye, SFBC/Doubleday,1987

Vomovich, Vladimir
Moscow 2042, n. Harcourt Brace Jovanovich Jun,1987

Vonnegut, Kurt, Jr.
Bluebeard, n. Delacorte Oct,1987

Wagar, W. Warren
Madonna of the Red Sun, ss **Synergy** v1, ed. George Zebrowski,1987
The Night of No Joy, nv *F&SF* Jun,1987

Wagner, Karl Edward
Endless Night, ss **The Architecture of Fear**, ed. Kathryn Cramer & Peter D. Pautz, Arbor House,1987
Lost Exits, ss **Why Not You and I?**, Dark Harvest,1987
Manly Wade Wellman: A Biography, bg *The Horror Show* Spr,1987
Satan's Gun, ex **World Fantasy Convention Program Book** #13,1987
Silted In, ss **Why Not You and I?**, Tor,1987
Why Not You and I?, co Dark Harvest Nov,1987
Why Not You and I?, co Tor Sep,1987

Wagner, Karl Edward, ed.
Echoes of Valor, an Tor Feb,1987
The Year's Best Horror Stories: XV, an DAW Oct,1987

Wagner, Matt
Mage, Volume One: The Hero Discovered, gn Donning/Starblaze May,1987

Waldrop, Howard
All About Strange Monsters of the Recent Past, co Ursus Imprints Jun,1987
He-We-Await, nv **All About Strange Monsters of the Recent Past**, Kansas City, MO: Ursus Imprints,1987
Night of the Cooters, ss *Omni* Apr,1987

Walker, Larry
Harbard, ss *Amazing* Jan,1987

Walker, Robert
Aftershock, n. St. Martin's Nov,1987

Wallace, David Foster
The Broom of the System, n. Viking Jan,1987

Wallace, Patricia
Water Baby, n. Zebra Oct,1987

Waller, Gregory A., ed.
American Horrors, nf Univ. of Illinois Press Jan,1988

Walsh, Jill Paton
Green Gravel, ss **A Quiver of Ghosts**, ed. Aiden Chambers, Bodley Head,1987
Torch, n. Viking Kestrel Oct,1987

Walton, Paul
Grass Shark, ss *Twilight Zone* Jun,1987

Ward, Frank
Smile!, ss *Amazing* Nov,1987

Wardman, Gordon
Reparations, n. Secker & Warburg Jan,1987

Warner, Bob
Marta's Cat, vi *2AM* Spr,1987
Supreme Being, pm *Apex!* #1,1987

Warren, Bill
The Twilight Zone Review: 1986 - TV, mr *Twilight Zone* Feb,1987

Warren, Rosalind
The Messenger, ss *F&SF* Jun,1987

Warrick, Patricia S.
Mind in Motion: The Fiction of Philip K. Dick, nf Southern Illinois Univ. Press Jul,1987

Waters, Elisabeth
Playfellow, ss **Red Sun of Darkover**, ed. Marion Zimmer Bradley & The Friends of Darkover, DAW,1987

Watkins, William Jon
When the Vikings Owned the Mythology, pm *Amazing* Jul,1987

Watkinson, B.F.
Jennifer's Island, ss *Eldritch Tales* #13,1987

Watson, Ian
The Emir's Clock, ss **Other Edens**, ed. Christopher Evans & Robert Holdstock, Unwin: London,1987
Evil Water, co Gollancz Mar,1987
Evil Water, nv *F&SF* Mar,1987
Hyperzoo, ss *IASFM* mid-Dec,1987
Jewels in an Angel's Wing, nv **Synergy** v1, ed. George Zebrowski,1987
The Milk of Knowledge, ss *Aboriginal SF* Sep,1987
The Moon and Michelangelo, nv *IASFM* Oct,1987
The Power, n. Headline Sep,1987
Salvage Rites, ss *F&SF* Jan,1987

Watt-Evans, Lawrence
Why I Left Harry's All-Night Hamburgers, ss *IASFM* Jul,1987
With a Single Spell, n. Ballantine/Del Rey Mar,1987
The Wizard and the War Machine, n. Ballantine/Del Rey Sep,1987

Waugh, Charles G., Isaac Asimov & Martin H. Greenberg, eds.
Isaac Asimov's Magical Worlds of Fantasy #8: Devils, an NAL/Signet Jun,1987
Isaac Asimov's Magical Worlds of Fantasy #9: Atlantis, an NAL/Signet Jan,1988
Isaac Asimov's Wonderful Worlds of Science Fiction #6: Neanderthals, an NAL/Signet Feb,1987
Isaac Asimov's Wonderful Worlds of Science Fiction #7: Space Shuttles, an NAL/Signet Oct,1987
Young Witches & Warlocks, an Harper & Row Jul,1987

Waugh, Charles G. & Martin H. Greenberg, eds.
Battlefields Beyond Tomorrow: Science Fiction War Stories, an Crown/Bonanza Dec,1987
House Shudders, an DAW Sep,1987

Waugh, Charles G. & Martin H. Greenberg, eds. (continued)
Vamps, an DAW Mar,1987

Waugh, Charles G., Martin H. Greenberg & Joe W. Haldeman, eds.
Supertanks, an Ace Apr,1987

Waugh, Charles G., Martin H. Greenberg & Frank D. McSherry, Jr., eds.
Nightmares in Dixie: Thirteen Horror Tales From the American South, an August House Apr,1987

Waugh, Charles G., Martin H. Greenberg & Carol Serling, eds.
Rod Serling's Night Gallery Reader, an Dembner Dec,1987

Waugh, Charles G., Martin H. Greenberg & Jane Yolen, eds.
Spaceships and Spells, oa Harper & Row Nov,1987

Weathers, Brenda
The House at Pelham Falls, n. Naiad Jul,1987

Weaver, Michael D.
Mercedes Nights, n. St. Martin's Dec,1987
Wolf-Dreams, n. Avon May,1987

Webb, Don
The Hag of Carmel Towers, vi *New Pathways* Jan,1987
Kaj, vi *Grue* #5,1987
Lesser Myths of Milwaukee, vi *New Pathways* Apr,1987
One Hundred, ss *Ice River* Sum,1987

Webb, Don & Bruce Sterling
Bruce Sterling, iv *New Pathways* Aug,1987

Webb, Don & Rosemary Webb
Book Reviews, br *New Pathways* Aug,1987
Book Reviews, br *New Pathways* Nov,1987

Webb, Rosemary & Don Webb
Book Reviews, br *New Pathways* Aug,1987
Book Reviews, br *New Pathways* Nov,1987

Webb, Sharon
Pestis 18, n. Tor Mar,1987

Webb, Wendy
Law of Averages, ss **Shadows** #10, ed. Charles L. Grant,1987

Webster, Lyn
The Illumination of Alice J. Cunningham, n. Dedalus May,1987

Weinberg, George
Numberland: A Fable, n. St. Martin's Feb,1987

Weiner, Andrew
The Alien in the Lake, ss *IASFM* Sep,1987
Fake-out, ss *Amazing* Nov,1987
Going to Meet the Alien, nv *F&SF* Aug,1987
Rider, nv *IASFM* Jul,1987
Station Gehenna, n. Congdon & Weed Sep,1987
Waves, nv *IASFM* Mar,1987

WEINLAND, SHIRLEY

Weinland, Shirley
When the Haloperidol Runs Out and the Blue Fairy Never Comes, ss *Amazing* Mar,1987

Weinstein, Howard
Star Trek #33: Deep Domain, n. Pocket Apr,1987
V: Path to Conquest, n. Tor Sep,1987

Weis, Margaret
The Test of the Twins, ss **DragonLance Tales** v1, Margaret Weis & Tracy Hickman, TSR,1987

Weis, Margaret, ed.
The Art of the DragonLance Saga, pi TSR May,1987

Weis, Margaret & Dezra Despain
Raistlin's Daughter, nv **DragonLance Tales** v3, Margaret Weis & Tracy Hickman, TSR,1987

Weis, Margaret & Tracy Hickman
The Darksword Trilogy, Volume 1: Forging the Darksword, n. Bantam Spectra Jan,1988
The Legacy, na **DragonLance Tales** v1, Margaret Weis & Tracy Hickman, TSR,1987
"Wanna Bet?", na **DragonLance Tales** v2, Margaret Weis & Tracy Hickman, TSR,1987

Weis, Margaret & Tracy Hickman, eds.
DragonLance Tales Vol. 1: The Magic of Krynn, oa TSR Apr,1987
DragonLance Tales Vol. 2: Kender, Gully Dwarves, and Gnomes, oa TSR Aug,1987
DragonLance Tales Vol. 3: Love and War, oa TSR Nov,1987
Leaves from the Inn of the Last Home, nf TSR Mar,1987

Welfare, Mary
Yeti of the Glen, n. Pied Piper Apr,1987

Welfare, Simon & John Fairley
Arthur C. Clarke's Chronicles of the Strange and Mysterious, nf Collins Dec,1987

Wellen, Edward
Dead Ringer, na **Space Shuttles**, ed. Isaac Asimov, Martin H. Greenberg & Charles G. Waugh, Signet,1987
Waswolf, ss *F&SF* Sep,1987

Weller, Tom
Cvltvre Made Stvpid, pi Houghton Mifflin Oct,1987

Wellman, Manly Wade
The Valley So Low: Southern Mountain Stories, co Doubleday Dec,1987
Where Did She Wander?, ss *Whispers* #23,1987

Welsh, F.R.
First Blood, ss **The Pan Book of Horror Stories** #28, Pan,1987

Wendorf, Patricia
Blanche, n. Futura Apr,1987
Bye Bye Blackbird, n. Hamish Hamilton Oct,1987

Westall, Robert
Urn Burial, n. Viking Kestrel Jun,1987

Westerly, Daniel
Devotion, n. Pocket Mar,1987

Wheatley, Dennis & Alison Sage
The Devil Rides Out, n. Beaver May,1987

Wheeler, Deborah
Storm God, ss **Sword and Sorceress #4**, ed. Marion Zimmer Bradley,1987
The Wasteland, ss **Red Sun of Darkover**, ed. Marion Zimmer Bradley & The Friends of Darkover, DAW,1987

Wheeler, Scott
Matters of Form, n. DAW Oct,1987

Wheeler, William H.
Editor's Note, ed *SF International* #1,1987

Wheeler, William H., ed.
SF International [No. 1, January/February 1987]
SF International [No. 2, March/April 1987]

Whelan, Michael
Michael Whelan's Works of Wonder, nf Ballantine/Del Rey Nov,1987

Whelan, Michael & Dale Johnson
Michael Whelan, iv *American Fantasy* Sum,1987

Whitbourn, John
Waiting for a Bus, ss **After Midnight Stories** #3,1987

White, D.T.
Short Are My Days of Light and Shade, ss *Aphelion* #5,1987

White, James
Code Blue--Emergency!, n. Ballantine/Del Rey Jul,1987
The Interpreters, ss *F&SF* Mar,1987

White, Jonathan
Book Notes, br *Twilight Zone* Feb,1987
The Other Side: American Pie in the Face, ar *Twilight Zone* Apr,1987
The Other Side: Of Maus and Men, ar *Twilight Zone* Feb,1987

White, Lori Ann
Old Mickey Flip Had a Marvelous Ship, nv **L. Ron Hubbard Presents Writers of the Future** v3, ed. Algis Budrys, Bridge,1987

White, Mel & Robert Lynn Asprin
Duncan and Mallory: The Bar-None Ranch, gn Donning/Starblaze Sep,1987

White, Melvin R. & Edgar Allan Poe
The Tell-Tale Heart, pl Hanbury May,1987

Whiteaker, Marny
The Dare, ss **Red Sun of Darkover**, ed. Marion Zimmer Bradley & The Friends of Darkover, DAW,1987

Whiteford, Wynne
The Hyades Contact, n. Ace Sep,1987

Whitehorn, Ingrid
The Jerra-Mee, ss *Aphelion* #5,1987

Whitlock, Dean
Containment, ss *Aboriginal SF* Feb,1987
The Million-Dollar Wound, ss *F&SF* Jan,1987
Roadkill, nv *IASFM* Nov,1987

Wiater, Stanley
Moist Dreams, ss **Masques** #2, ed. J.N. Williamson,1987

Wiater, Stanley & Piers Anthony
A Conversation with Piers Anthony, iv *Twilight Zone* Dec,1987

Wiater, Stanley & Ramsey Campbell
A Conversation With Ramsey Campbell, iv *Twilight Zone* Apr,1987

Wiggs, Susan Lilas
Sliders, ss *Grue* #6,1987

Wightman, Wayne
Cage 37, nv *F&SF* Apr,1987

Wilcox, Joe
A Cell Opens, nv **Red Sun of Darkover**, ed. Marion Zimmer Bradley & The Friends of Darkover, DAW,1987

Wilde, Jay
Death from Autophilia, ss **The Pan Book of Horror Stories** #28, Pan,1987

Wilder, Cherry
The Decline of Sunshine, ss *Interzone* #22,1987

Wilhelm, Kate
The Disassembler, ss *F&SF* Oct,1987
Forever Yours, Anna, ss *Omni* Jul,1987
The Hamlet Trap, n. St. Martin's Sep,1987

Wilhelm, Kate, Terry A. Garey, Eric M. Heideman & Damon Knight
An Interview with Kate Wilhelm and Damon Knight, iv *Tales of the Unanticipated* #2,1987

Wilhelmsen, George
The Other Side: Land of the Rising Moon, ar *Twilight Zone* Aug,1987

Wilkerson, Cherie
The Man Who Watched the Glaciers Run, nv **Universe** #17, ed. Terry Carr,1987
The Moment of the Rose, ss *IASFM* Feb,1987

Wilkins, Mark
Wartours, ss **Gollancz - Sunday Times Best SF Stories**, Gollancz,1987

Willett, F.J.
Scare Tactics, vi *Aphelion* #5,1987
Splitting Hares, vi *Aphelion* #5,1987

Williams, Mary
Coppard's End, ss **Haunted Waters**, Kimber,1987
Dorothea, nv **Haunted Waters**, Kimber,1987
Haunted Waters, n. **Haunted Waters**, Kimber,1987
Haunted Waters, oc Kimber Oct,1987

Williams, Michael
From the Yearning for War and the War's Ending, nv **DragonLance Tales** v3, Margaret Weis & Tracy Hickman, TSR,1987

WILLIAMS, MICHAEL

WOELTJEN, L.D.

Williams, Michael (continued)
Into the Heart of the Story, nv **DragonLance Tales** v2, Margaret Weis & Tracy Hickman, TSR,1987
Riverwind and The Crystal Staff, pm **DragonLance Tales** v1, Margaret Weis & Tracy Hickman, TSR,1987

Williams, Michael Lindsay
FTL: Further Than Life, n. Avon Mar,1987

Williams, Paul & Misha Chocholak
Paul Williams talks to New Pathways, iv *New Pathways* Jan,1987

Williams, Randy
Intersections, vi *2AM* Fll,1987

Williams, Walter Jon
The Crown Jewels, n. Tor Oct,1987
Dinosaurs, nv *IASFM* Jun,1987
Ligdan and the Young Pretender, nv **There Will Be War** v6, ed. Jerry E. Pournelle,1987
Mr. Koyama's Comet, ss **Wild Cards** v2, ed. George R.R. Martin, Bantam,1987
Unto the Sixth Generation: Epilogue, sl **Wild Cards** v2, ed. George R.R. Martin, Bantam,1987
Unto the Sixth Generation: Part One, sl **Wild Cards** v2, ed. George R.R. Martin, Bantam,1987
Unto the Sixth Generation: Part Two, sl **Wild Cards** v2, ed. George R.R. Martin, Bantam,1987
Unto the Sixth Generation: Prologue, sl **Wild Cards** v2, ed. George R.R. Martin, Bantam,1987
Voice of the Whirlwind, n. Tor May,1987
Wolf Time, nv *IASFM* Jan,1987

Williamson, Chet
Ants, vi *Twilight Zone* Jun,1987
Ash Wednesday, n. Tor Feb,1987
Letters to Mother, ss *F&SF* Apr,1987
Play Dead, ss *F&SF* Aug,1987
Sen Yet Babbo & the Heavenly Host, ss *Playboy* Aug,1987

Williamson, David
The Sandman, ss **The Pan Book of Horror Stories #28**, Pan,1987

Williamson, Duncan
The Broonie, Silkies & Fairies: Travellers' Tales of the Other World, co Crown Harmony Mar,1987

Williamson, J.N.
Dark Corner, br *2AM* Spr,1987
Dark Corner, br *2AM* Sum,1987
Dark Corner, br *2AM* Fll,1987
Dark Corner, br *2AM* Win,1987
Evil Offspring, n. Leisure Apr,1987
Fragments of Horror, ms *The Horror Show* Jan,1987
Happy Hour, ss *Twilight Zone* Feb,1987
The Night Seasons [Part 2], sl *Night Cry* v2#3,1987
The Night Seasons [Part 3], sl *Night Cry* v2#4,1987
The Night Seasons [Part 4], sl *Night Cry* v2#5,1987
Privacy Rights, ss **Whispers #6**, ed. Stuart David Schiff,1987
Starry Coping, ss *Eldritch Tales* #14,1987
Townkiller, ss *Grue* #4,1987
Watchwolf, ss *Footsteps* Nov,1987

Williamson, J.N. (continued)
Wordsong, ss **Masques #2**, ed. J.N. Williamson,1987

Williamson, J.N., ed.
How to Write Tales of Horror, Fantasy & Science Fiction, nf Writer's Digest Books Apr,1987
Masques II, oa Maclay & Assoc. Jun,1987

Willis, Connie
Circus Story, ss *Aboriginal SF* Feb,1987
Lincoln's Dreams, n. Bantam Spectra May,1987
Lord of Hosts, vi *Omni* Jun,1987
Schwarzschild Radius, ss **Universe**, ed. Byron Preiss, Bantam Spectra,1987
Winter's Tale, nv *IASFM* Dec,1987

Wilson, Colin
The Delta, n. Grafton Oct,1987
The Tower, n. Grafton Feb,1987

Wilson, F. Paul
Dat-Tay-Vao, ss *Amazing* Mar,1987
Doc Johnson, nv **Doom City**, ed. Charles L. Grant, Tor,1987
A Novel Preview: **Black Wind**, ex *Footsteps* Nov,1987
Traps, ss *Night Cry* v2#4,1987
The Years the Music Died, ss **Whispers #6**, ed. Stuart David Schiff,1987

Wilson, F. Paul & Bill Munster
An Interview with F. Paul Wilson, iv *Footsteps* Nov,1987

Wilson, Gahan
Eddy Deco's Last Caper: An Illustrated Mystery, n. Times Books Nov,1987
Screen, mr *Twilight Zone* Feb,1987
Screen, mr *Twilight Zone* Apr,1987
Screen, mr *Twilight Zone* Jun,1987
Screen, mr *Twilight Zone* Aug,1987
Screen, mr *Twilight Zone* Oct,1987
Screen, mr *Twilight Zone* Dec,1987

Wilson, Gahan & Bill Munster
An Interview with Gahan Wilson, in *Footsteps* Nov,1987

Wilson, Richard
Able Baker Camel, nv *Amazing* Jan,1987
The Blue Lady, ss **The Kid from Ozone Park and Other Stories**, Drumm,1987
Fair Morsel, vi **The Kid from Ozone Park and Other Stories**, Drumm,1987
The Greater Powers, ss **The Kid from Ozone Park and Other Stories**, Drumm,1987
Green Is the Color, ss **The Kid from Ozone Park and Other Stories**, Drumm,1987
Harry Protagonist, Inseminator General, ss **The Kid from Ozone Park and Other Stories**, Drumm,1987
IBM, My Shipmate; or, the Difference Between Orbit and Obit, pm *Amazing* Sep,1987
The Kid from Ozone Park, ss **The Kid from Ozone Park and Other Stories**, Drumm,1987
The Kid From Ozone Park & Other Stories, oc Drumm Aug,1987
A Letter from a Lady, ss **The Kid from Ozone Park and Other Stories**, Drumm,1987
Sleeping Booty, ss **Whispers #6**, ed. Stuart David Schiff,1987

Wilson, Richard (continued)
That's All, Folks, pm *Amazing* May,1987
Waiting for the Buyer, ss **The Kid from Ozone Park and Other Stories**, Drumm,1987

Wilson, Robert Anton
"Afterwards", aw **Philip K. Dick: The Dream Connection**, D. Scott Apel, Permanent Press,1987

Wilson, Robert Charles
Ballads in 3/4 Time, ss *F&SF* Apr,1987
Extras, nv *F&SF* Dec,1987
Memory Wire, n. Bantam Jan,1988

Wilson, Robin Scott
The Greening of Mrs. Edmiston, ss *F&SF* Jan,1987

Wilson, Robley, Jr.
Flaggers, ss *IASFM* Jun,1987

Wilson, Rudy
The Red Truck, n. Knopf May,1987

Winkle, Michael D.
Typo, ss *Fantasy Book* Mar,1987

Winter, Douglas E.
Movie Preview: Raising Hell with Clive Barker, mr *Twilight Zone* Dec,1987
Office Hours, ss **Shadows #10**, ed. Charles L. Grant,1987
Splatter, ss **Masques #2**, ed. J.N. Williamson,1987

Winter, Douglas E. & Clive Barker
Talking Terror With Clive Barker, iv *Twilight Zone* Jun,1987

Winter, Douglas E. & Charles L. Grant
A Conversation With Charles L. Grant, iv *Twilight Zone* Apr,1987

Winter-Damon, t.
if only icarus had climbed the night, pm *Fantasy Book* Mar,1987
Martyr Without Canon, pm *Grue* #4,1987

Wiseman, David
Adam's Common, n. Blackie Feb,1987

Wisman, Ken
The Finder-Keeper, ss **Shadows #10**, ed. Charles L. Grant,1987
The Philosophical Stone, ss *Interzone* #21,1987

Wismer, Don
Warrior Planet, n. Baen May,1987

Witcover, Paul
The Cats of Thermidor, ss *Night Cry* v2#4,1987

Wittig, Monique
Across the Acheron, n. Dufour Editions/Peter Owen Dec,1987

Wnorowska, Diane
Seven Come Heaven?, ss **Devils & Demons**, ed. Marvin Kaye, SFBC/Doubleday,1987

Woeltjen, L.D.
Die Like a Man, ss **Sword and Sorceress #4**, ed. Marion Zimmer Bradley,1987

WOLF, ROSE

Wolf, Rose
Cat and Muse, ss **Magic in Ithkar #4**, ed. Andre Norton & Robert Adams,1987

Wolfe, Gene
All the Hues of Hell, ss **Universe**, ed. Byron Preiss, Bantam Spectra,1987
The Ethos of Elfland, ar *Twilight Zone* Dec,1987
In the House of Gingerbread, ss **The Architecture of Fear**, ed. Kathryn Cramer & Peter D. Pautz, Arbor House,1987
The Peace Spy, ss *IASFM* Jan,1987
The Urth of the New Sun, n. Gollancz Aug,1987
The Urth of the New Sun, n. Tor Nov,1987

Wolfe, Joyce
The White Spider, n. Leisure Aug,1987

Wolfe, Ron
Illuminations: A Dark and Stormy Plight, ar *Twilight Zone* Dec,1987
Illuminations: Awright, Larson! --Up Against the Wall, ar *Twilight Zone* Dec,1987
Illuminations: Forstchen in Maine's Eyes, ar *Twilight Zone* Aug,1987
Illuminations: Frog Heaven, ar *Twilight Zone* Apr,1987
Illuminations: Radio- Vision, ar *Twilight Zone* Aug,1987
Illuminations: TV or Not TV?, ar *Twilight Zone* Oct,1987
The Other Side: Bad-Dream Girl, ar *Twilight Zone* Aug,1987
The Other Side: Coming Soon to a Theater Somewhere, Mayby, ar *Twilight Zone* Dec,1987
The Other Side: Faces of Fear, ar *Twilight Zone* Aug,1987
The Other Side: Flies on the Screen, ar *Twilight Zone* Aug,1987
The Other Side: Grass-Roots Gore, ar *Twilight Zone* Feb,1987
The Other Side: Guilt by Association, ar *Twilight Zone* Apr,1987
The Other Side: Have Yourself a Merry Little Xenophobe Understanding Day, ar *Twilight Zone* Aug,1987
The Other Side: Mary & Percy & Byron & Claire, ar *Twilight Zone* Oct,1987
The Other Side: More Hokey Holidays, ar *Twilight Zone* Oct,1987
The Other Side: Rats in the Malls, ar *Twilight Zone* Oct,1987

Wolfe, Ron & R.A. Lafferty
Counting Grandmothers: R.A. Lafferty, iv *American Fantasy* Sum,1987

Wolfenbarger, Billy
Final Dreams, pm *Grue #5*,1987
Reunion, pm *Eldritch Tales #13*,1987

Wollheim, Donald A. & Arthur W. Saha, ed.
The 1987 Annual World's Best SF, an DAW Jun,1987

Wolverton, Dave
On My Way to Paradise, na **L. Ron Hubbard Presents Writers of the Future** v3, ed. Algis Budrys, Bridge,1987

Womack, Jack
Ambient, n. Weidenfeld & Nicolson Apr,1987

Wongar, B.
Gabo Djara, n. Dodd, Mead Jul,1987

Wood, Bari
Amy Girl, n. NAL Apr,1987

Wood, Bridget
The Minstrel's Lute, n. Robert Hale Jan,1987
Satanic Lute, n. Robert Hale May,1987

Wood, Robert
The Avatar, n. Poplar May,1987

Woodroffe, Patrick
A Closer Look: The Art Techniques of Patrick Woodroffe, nf Crown Harmony Apr,1987
The Second Earth, n. Paper Tiger Dec,1987

Wooley, Persia
Child of the Northern Spring, n. Simon & Schuster Poseidon May,1987

Wrede, Patricia C.
Caught in Crystal, n. Ace Mar,1987
The Improper Princess, ss **Spaceships & Spells**, ed. Jane Yolen, Martin H. Greenberg & Charles G. Waugh, Harper & Row,1987

Wright, T.M.
Stuff of Horror, or Gray Matter All Over the Inside of Your Skull, ar *American Fantasy* Sum,1987
A World Without Toys, ss **Shadows #10**, ed. Charles L. Grant,1987

Wrightson, Patricia
Moon-dark, n. Hutchinson Oct,1987

Wu, William F.
Davi Leiko Till Midnight, ss *Twilight Zone* Oct,1987
Isaac Asimov's Robot City, Book 3: Cyborg, n. Ace Nov,1987
Masterplay, n. Popular Library Questar Aug,1987

Wu, William F. & Robert Chilson
High Power, ss *Analog* Sep,1987
A Hog on Ice, ss *Analog* Dec,1987
No Damn Atoms, nv *Analog* Oct,1987

Wurts, Janny & Raymond E. Feist
Daughter of the Empire, n. Doubleday Jun,1987

Wyatt, Scott
Teach the Children, pm *Minnesota Fantasy Review #1*,1987

Wylde, Thomas
The Prize, ss *Night Cry* v2#5,1987

Wylie, Jonathan
The Centre of the Circle, n. Corgi Jul,1987
The First Named, n. Bantam Spectra Nov,1987
The First Named, n. Corgi Mar,1987

Yarbro, Chelsea Quinn
Firecode, n. Popular Library Apr,1987
A Flame in Byzantium, n. Tor Oct,1987

Yen, Johnny
Upstarts, ss **The Pan Book of Horror Stories #28**, Pan,1987

Yolen, Jane
The Ballad of the Quick Levars, sg **Liavek: Wizard's Row**, ed. Will Shetterly & Emma Bull, Ace,1987
City of Luck, sg **Liavek: Wizard's Row**, ed. Will Shetterly & Emma Bull, Ace,1987
Frog Prince, pm *F&SF* Oct,1987
The King's Dragon, ss **Spaceships & Spells**, ed. Jane Yolen, Martin H. Greenberg & Charles G. Waugh, Harper & Row,1987
Regenesis, pm *Fantasy Book* Mar,1987
Science Fiction, pm *IASFM* Jul,1987
A Sending of Dragons, n. Delacorte Oct,1987
A Sending of Dragons, n. Julia MacRae Sep,1987
The White Babe, nv *IASFM* Jun,1987
Wolf/Child, ss *Twilight Zone* Jun,1987

Yolen, Jane, Martin H. Greenberg & Charles G. Waugh, eds.
Spaceships and Spells, oa Harper & Row Nov,1987

York, Carol Beach
Nights in Ghostland, n. Pocket Archway Nov,1987

Young, Robert F.
The Giant, the Colleen, and the Twenty-one Cows, nv *F&SF* Jun,1987
What Bleak Land, ss *F&SF* Jan,1987

Yule, Jeffrey V.
At Night, pm *Mage* Spr,1987
A Consideration of Negative-Future Fiction, ed *Mage* Win,1987
Four Years Later..., ed *Mage* Fll,1987
The Mage: A Retrospective, pi *Mage* Fll,1987
Science Fiction--Judging the Genre, ed *Mage* Spr,1987
William Gibson: A Cyberpunk Examined, ar *Mage* Spr,1987

Yule, Jeffrey V., ed.
The Best of the Mage [# 8, Fall 1987]
The Mage [# 6, Winter 1987]
The Mage [# 7, Spring 1987]

Zahn, Timothy
Banshee, na *Analog* Sep,1987
Point Man, nv **New Destinies** v1, ed. Jim Baen, Baen,1987
The President's Doll, ss *Analog* Jul,1987
The Talisman, nv **Magic in Ithkar #4**, ed. Andre Norton & Robert Adams,1987
Triplet, n. Baen Aug,1987

Zambreno, Mary Frances
Roaming Fancy, br *American Fantasy* Spr,1987
Roaming Fancy, br *American Fantasy* Sum,1987
Roaming Fancy, br *American Fantasy* Win,1987

Zambreno, Mary Frances, Nancy Garcia & Andre Norton
Andre Norton Interview and Bibliography, iv *American Fantasy* Win,1987

Zebrowski, George
Behind the Night, ss *F&SF* Apr,1987
General Jaruzelski at the Zoo, ss *Twilight Zone* Apr,1987
Introduction: Synergists, in **Synergy** v1, ed. George Zebrowski,1987

ZEBROWSKI, GEORGE

Zebrowski, George (continued)
This Life and Later Ones, ss *Analog* Feb,1987

Zebrowski, George, ed.
Synergy; New Science Fiction: Vol. 1, oa Harcourt Brace Jovanovich Nov,1987

Zelazny, Roger
Ashes to Ashes, nv **Wild Cards** v2, ed. George R.R. Martin, Bantam,1987
A Dark Traveling, n. Walker Millennium Apr,1987
Quest's End, vi *Omni* Jun,1987
Sign of Chaos, n. Arbor House Sep,1987

Zeller, J.M.
The Hand of the Survivor, ss *Amazing* Jul,1987

Zicree, Marc Scott
Science Fiction in the Twilight Zone, ar *Twilight Zone* Oct,1987

Ziesing, Mark & Misha Chocholak
Interview with Mark Ziesing: Bookseller & Publisher, iv *New Pathways* Jan,1987

Zimmer, Paul Edwin
A Gathering of Heroes, n. Ace Sep,1987

Zipes, Jack, ed.
The Complete Fairy Tales of the Brothers Grimm, co Bantam Classics Feb,1987
Don't Bet on the Prince: Contemporary Feminist Fairy Tales in North America and Europe, an Gower Mar,1987
Don't Bet on the Prince: Contemporary Feminist Fairy Tales in North America and Europe, an Methuen Feb,1987
Victorian Fairy Tales: The Revolt of the Fairies and Elves, an Methuen Feb,1987

[Misc. Material]
1987 World Fantasy Award Nominees, bi **World Fantasy Convention Program Book** #13,1987
1st Annual Readers' Award Results, bi *IASFM* Oct,1987
About the Editor, bg **Synergy** v1, ed. George Zebrowski,1987
The Analytical Laboratory, ms *Analog* Jun,1987
Art Sampler, pi *Salarius* v1#4,1987
Art Section, pi *Salarius* #3,1987
The Complete Bibliography of F. Paul Wilson, bi *Footsteps* Nov,1987
Con-Notations, ms *Space & Time* #73,1987
F&SF Competition: Report on Competition 42, ms *F&SF* May,1987
F&SF Competition: Report on Competition 43, ms *F&SF* Sep,1987
Film Preview: Spaceballs, pi *Twilight Zone* Aug,1987
First Annual Readers' Award Ballot, ms *IASFM* Jan,1987
A Handbook for the Apprentice Magician, ms **Liavek: Wizard's Row**, ed. Will Shetterly & Emma Bull, Ace,1987
Hollywood Grapevine, ar *Twilight Zone* Jun,1987
Hollywood Grapevine, ar *Twilight Zone* Aug,1987
Hollywood Grapevine, ar *Twilight Zone* Oct,1987
Hollywood Grapevine, ar *Twilight Zone* Dec,1987
Index, ix *Analog* Jan,1987

[Misc. Material] (continued)
Index, ix *IASFM* Jan,1987
Index to Volume 72, ix *F&SF* Jun,1987
Index to Volume 73, ix *F&SF* Dec,1987
An Index to *Fantasy Book*, Volume 5, ix *Fantasy Book* Mar,1987
Merovan Ecology, ms **Fever Season**, ed. C.J. Cherryh, DAW,1987
Music to Read 2AM by -- Contest Winner, ms *2AM* Sum,1987
Oddities & Entities, ms *American Fantasy* Spr,1987
Oddities & Entities, ms *American Fantasy* Sum,1987
Oddities & Entities, ms *American Fantasy* Win,1987
A Selected Damon Knight Bibliography, bi *Tales of the Unanticipated* #2,1987
A Selected Kate Wilhelm Bibliography, bi *Tales of the Unanticipated* #2,1987

Subject List

SCIENCE FICTION NOVELS

Science Fiction Novels . . . .

Adams, Douglas
Dirk Gently's Holistic Detective Agency

Adams, Robert
Horseclans #16: Trumpets of War
Horseclans #17: Madman's Army
Of Chiefs and Champions

Ahern, Jerry
The Survivalist #15: Overlord

Ahern, Jerry & Sharon Ahern
Miamigrad

Albano, Peter
Return of the Seventh Carrier

Aldiss, Brian W.
The Year Before Yesterday

Alexander, David
Phoenix #1: Dark Messiah
Phoenix #2: Ground Zero

Armstrong, Michael
After the Zap

Asimov, Isaac
Fantastic Voyage II: Destination Brain

Asimov, Janet & Isaac Asimov
Norby and the Queen's Necklace
Norby Finds a Villain

Auster, Paul
In the Country of the Last Things

Austin, Richard
The Guardians #8: Desolation Road
The Guardians #9: Vengeance Day

Axler, James
Deathlands #3: Neutron Solstice
Deathlands #4: Crater Lake

Baker, Pip & Jane Baker
Terror of the Vervoids
Time and the Rani

Baker, Sharon
Journey to Membliar

Baldwin, Bill
Galactic Convoy

Banerji, Sara
Cobwebwalking

Banks, Iain
Consider Phlebas

Barker, Dennis
Winston Three Three Three

Barnes, John
The Man Who Pulled Down the Sky

Barrett, Neal, Jr.
Through Darkest America

Bayley, Barrington J.
The Rod of Light

Bear, Greg
The Forge of God
Hegira

Beebee, Chris
The Hub

Belden, Wilanne Schneider
Mind-Hold

Benford, Gregory
Across the Sea of Suns
Great Sky River

Bennett, Thea
The Gemini Factor

Berman, Mitch
Time Capsule

Berry, Stephen Ames
The AI War

Billias, Stephen
The American Book of the Dead

Bishop, Michael
The Secret Ascension

Black, Ian Stuart
The Macra Terror

Blakeney, Jay D.
The Omcri Matrix

Block, Bob
Galloping Galaxies

Blumlein, Michael
The Movement of Mountains

Bonanno, Margaret Wander
Star Trek: Strangers From the Sky

Bosshardt, Robert
Whom the Gods Destroy

Bova, Ben
The Kinsman Saga

Bowker, Richard
Dover Beach

Bowkett, Stephen
Dualists

Brin, David
The Uplift War

Brunner, John
The Shift Key

Burkholz, Herbert
The Sensitives

Butler, Octavia E.
Dawn

Cadigan, Pat
Mindplayers

Caidin, Martin
Exit Earth

Callin, Grant D.
A Lion on Tharthee

Caraker, Mary
Water Song

Card, Orson Scott
Wyrms

Carey, Diane
Star Trek: Final Frontier

Carlisle, Anne
Liquid Sky

Carroll, Jonathan
Bones of the Moon

Carter, Carmen
Star Trek #34: Dreams of the Raven

Carter, Lin
Horror Wears Blue

Carver, Jeffrey A.
The Rapture Effect
Roger Zelazny's Alien Speedway 1:
Clypsis

Chalker, Jack L.
The Labyrinth of Dreams
Pirates of the Thunder
The Shadow Dancers
Warriors of the Storm

Charles, Steven
Private School #6: The Last Alien

Cherryh, C.J.
Exile's Gate

Chester, Michael
The Shores of the Near Past

Christopher, Paul
Galactic Chronicles

Claremont, Chris
FirstFlight

Clarke, Arthur C.
2061: Odyssey Three

Clayton, Jo
Skeen's Return
Skeen's Search

Clement, Hal
Still River

Constantine, Storm
The Enchantments of Flesh and Spirit

Cook, Hugh
The Shift

Cook, Paul
On the Rim of the Mandala

Cook, Robin
Outbreak

Cooper, Clare
The Settlement on Planet B

Cooper, Richard
Knights of God

Cooper, Tom
War*Moon

Copeland, Lori
Candlelight Ecstasy Romance #462: Out
of This World

Cotton, Donald
The Romans

SCIENCE FICTION NOVELS

Cover, Arthur Byron
Isaac Asimov's Robot City, Book 4: Prodigy

Coville, Bruce
Murder in Orbit

Coyle, H.W.
Team Yankee

Crichton, Michael
Sphere

Cush, Geoffrey
God Help the Queen

da Cruz, Daniel
F-Cubed
Texas Triumphant

Dalmas, John
The Regiment
Return to Fanglith

Danziger, Paula
This Place Has No Atmosphere

Davies, Paul
Fireball

DeHaven, Tom
U.S.S.A. Book 1

Delap, Richard & Walt Lee
Shapes

Denis, John
Goliath

DeWeese, Gene
The Calvin Nullifier
The Dandelion Caper
Star Trek #32: Chain of Attack

Dicks, Terrance
The Ambassadors of Death
The Mysterious Planet

Dickson, Gordon R.
Way of the Pilgrim

Dietz, William C.
Freehold

Dillard, J.M.
Bloodthirst
Star Trek #37: Bloodthirst

Drake, David
Counting the Cost

Drake, David & Janet Morris
Kill Ratio

Drew, Wayland
Batteries Not Included

Drumm, D.B.
Traveler # 9: The Stalking Time
Traveler #10: Hell on Earth
Traveler #11: The Children's Crusade
Traveler #12: The Prey
Traveler #13: Ghost Dancers

Duane, Diane E. & Peter Morwood
The Romulan Way
Star Trek #35: The Romulan Way

Dudley, Terence
K9 and Company

Duncan, Dave
Shadow

Dvorkin, David
Budspy

Earnshaw, Brian
Starclipper and the Galactic Final

Easton, M. Coleman
Swimmers Beneath the Bright

Edmondson, G.C. & C.M. Kotlan
Maximum Effort

Elgin, Suzette Haden
Native Tongue II: The Judas Rose

Elliott, Nathan
Innerspace
Kidnap in Space
Plague Moon
Treasure Planet

Elliott, Richard
The Einstein Legacy

Elphinstone, Margaret
The Incomer

Ely, Scott
Starlight

Enderle, Judith
First Love From Silhouette #174: Adrienne and the Blob

Farmer, Philip Jose
Dayworld Rebel

Farren, Mick
Their Master's War

Faust, Joe Clifford
A Death of Honor

Finch, Sheila
The Garden of the Shaped

Fisk, Nicholas
Mindbenders

Ford, John M.
How Much for Just the Planet?
Star Trek #36: How Much for Just the Planet?

Forrester, John
The Secret of the Round Beast

Forstchen, William R.
The Alexandrian Ring

Foster, Alan Dean
The Deluge Drivers
Glory Lane

Frankowski, Leo A.
Copernick's Rebellion

Friedman, C.S.
In Conquest Born

Gadallah, Leslie
Cat's Pawn

Garrido, Mar
Eileen Goudge's Swept Away #6: Once Upon a Kiss

Gauger, Rick
Charon's Ark

Geduld, Harry M.
The Definitive Time Machine: A Critical Edition of H.G. Wells' Scientific Romance

Gerrold, David
Star Trek, The Next Generation: Encounter at Farpoint

Goldman, William
Brothers

Goldstein, Lisa
A Mask for the General

Gormley, Beatrice
Richard and the Vratch

Goudge, Eileen
Eileen Goudge's Swept Away #1: Gone With the Wish
Eileen Goudge's Swept Away #4: Star Struck

Goulart, Ron
Daredevils, Ltd.
Starpirate's Brain

Grant, Richard
Rumors of Spring

Greeley, Andrew M.
The Final Planet

Green, Roland J.
These Green Foreign Hills

Green, Sharon
The Rebel Prince

Greenleaf, William
Starjacked!

Griffin, P.M.
Star Commandos: Colony in Peril

Grimwade, Peter
Robot

Grocott, Ann
Danni's Desperate Journey

Gunnarsson, Thorarinn
The Starwolves

Haldeman, Joe W.
Tool of the Trade

Hale, Andrew
2020: Vision of the Future

Hall, Sandi
Wingwomen of Hera

Harrison, Harry
The Stainless Steel Rat Gets Drafted

Harvey, M. Elayn
Warhaven

SCIENCE FICTION NOVELS

Hawke, Simon
Spychodrome
Time Wars #7: The Arbonaut Affair

Hawkins, Ward
Torch of Fear

Haynes, Mary
Raider's Sky

Heinlein, Robert A.
To Sail Beyond the Sunset

Herbert, Brian
Prisoners of Arionn

Hiller, B.B.
Superman IV

Hinz, Christopher
Liege-Killer

Hodgman, Ann
Galaxy High School

Hoffman, Curtis H.
Project: Millennium

Hogan, James P.
Endgame Enigma

Hoklin, Lonn
The Hourglass Crisis

Hoobler, Thomas
Dr. Chill's Project

Hoover, H.M.
Orvis

Horwood, William
Skallagrigg

Hubbard, L. Ron
Mission Earth, Vol. 6: Death Quest
Mission Earth, Vol. 7: Voyage of
Vengeance
Mission Earth, Vol. 8: Disaster
Mission Earth, Vol. 9: Villainy Victorious
Mission Earth, Vol.10: The Doomed Planet

Hudson, Michael
Photon: Thieves of Light

Hughes, Monica
The Dream Catcher

Hughes, Zach
The Dark Side
Sundrinker

Ingrid, Charles
Solar Kill

Innes, Evan
America 2040 #3: The City in the Mist

Jacobson, Dan
Her Story

Jay, Peter & Michael Stewart
Apocalypse 2000: Economic Breakdown
and the Suicide of Democracy

Jeter, K.W.
Dark Seeker
Death's Arms
Infernal Devices

Johnson, James B.
Trekmaster

Johnstone, William W.
Smoke from the Ashes

Jones, Diana Wynne
A Tale of Time City

Jones, Glyn
The Space Museum

Jones, Gwyneth
Divine Endurance

Jones, Lloyd S.
Black Rainbow

Kahn, James
Timefall

Keith, William H., Jr.
Battletech: Decision at Thunder Rift
Battletech: Mercenary's Star

Kelleher, Victor
Taronga

Kennedy, Leigh
The Journal of Nicholas the American

Kilian, Crawford
The Fall of the Republic

Kilworth, Garry
The Wizard of Woodworld

King, Stephen
The Tommyknockers

Koman, Victor
The Jehovah Contract

Koontz, Dean R.
Watchers

Kotani, Eric & John Maddox Roberts
The Island Worlds

Kress, Nancy
An Alien Light

Kube-McDowell, Michael P.
Empery
Isaac Asimov's Robot City, Book 1:
Odyssey

Kurland, Michael
Star Griffin

L'Amour, Louis
The Haunted Mesa

Lafferty, R.A.
Serpent's Egg

Langford, David & John Grant
Earthdoom!

Lantz, Fran
Eileen Goudge's Swept Away #2:
Woodstock Magic
Eileen Goudge's Swept Away #8: All
Shook Up

Larson, Glen A. & Robert Thurston
Battlestar Galactica #14: Surrender the
Galactica!

Leiber, Justin
Beyond Humanity

Leigh, Stephen
The Crystal Memory

Lem, Stanislaw
Fiasco

Lewins, Anna
Dream For Danger

Lewitt, S.N.
Angel at Apogee
U.S.S.A. Book 2
U.S.S.A. Book 4

Lindbergh, Anne
The Shadow on the Dial

Longyear, Barry B.
Sea of Glass

Lucarotti, John
The Massacre

Mace, David
Nightrider

MacGregor, Loren
The Net

Maloney, Mack
Wingman
Wingman: The Circle War

Mann, Philip
The Fall of the Families

Marter, Ian
The Reign of Terror
The Rescue

Martin, Graham Dunstan
Dream Wall

May, Julian
Intervention

Mayhar, Ardath
Battletech: The Sword and the Dagger

Mayhar, Ardath & Ron Fortier
Trail of the Seahawks

McCammon, Robert R.
Swan Song

McCay, Claudia
Promise of the Rose Stone

McCollum, Michael
Antares Passage

McCutchan, Philip
A Time For Survival

McDonough, Thomas R.
The Architects of Hyperspace

McEwan, Ian
The Child in Time

McGowen, Tom
The Magician's Apprentice

McKillip, Patricia A.
Fool's Run

SCIENCE FICTION NOVELS

McKinney, Jack
Robotech # 1: Genesis
Robotech # 2: Battle Cry
Robotech # 3: Homecoming
Robotech # 4: Battlehymn
Robotech # 5: Force of Arms
Robotech # 6: Doomsday
Robotech # 7: Southern Cross
Robotech # 8: Metal Fire
Robotech # 9: The Final Nightmare
Robotech #10: Invid Invasion
Robotech #11: Metamorphosos
Robotech #12: Symphony of Light

McLoughlin, John
Tookmaker Koan

McQuay, Mike
Isaac Asimov's Robot City, Book 2:
Suspicion
Memories

Melamed, Leo
The Tenth Planet

Michaels, Melisa C.
Pirate Prince

Miklowitz, Gloria D.
After the Bomb: Week One

Miller, Miranda
Smiles and the Millenium

Milne, Janis
Starship Dunroamin

Mitchell, Kirk
Never the Twain

Mixon, Laura J.
Omni: Astropilots

Modesitt, L.E., Jr.
The Silent Warrior

Moffett, Judith
Pennterra

Mohan, Kim & Pamela O'Neill
Planet in Peril

Monaco, Richard
Unto the Beast

Morris, Janet
Warlord!

Morris, Jim
Spurlock: Sheriff of Purgatory

Murdock, M.S.
Vendetta

Murphy, Gloria
Nightmare

Murphy, Warren & Molly Cochran
High Priest

Naha, Ed
Robocop

Niven, Larry
The Smoke Ring

Niven, Larry, Jerry E. Pournelle & Steven
Barnes
The Legacy of Heorot

Noel, Atanielle Annyn
Murder on Usher's Planet
Speaker to Heaven

Norman, John
Vagabonds of Gor

Norwood, Warren G.
Shudderchild

O'Riordan, Robert
Cadre Lucifer

Oltion, Jerry
Frame of Reference

Ore, Rebecca
Becoming Alien

Park, Paul
Soldiers of Paradise

Payne, Bernal C., Jr.
Experiment in Terror

Peirce, Hayford
Napoleon Disentimed

Peters, David
Photon #1: For the Glory
Photon #2: High Stakes
Photon #3: In Search of Mom
Photon #4: This is Your Life, Bhodi Li
Photon #5: Exile

Platt, Charles
Piers Anthony's Worlds of Chthon: Plasm

Pohl, Frederik
The Annals of the Heechee

Pollack, Rachel
Alqua Dreams

Popkes, Steven
Caliban Landing

Pouns, Brauna E.
Amerika

Pournelle, Jerry E.
Janissaries III: Storms of Victory

Powers, Louise E.
Eileen Goudge's Swept Away #3: Love on
the Range

Poyer, D.C.
Stepfather Bank

Prantera, Amanda
Conversations with Lord Byron on
Perversion, 163 Years After His
Lordship's Death

Preuss, Paul
Arthur C. Clarke's Venus Prime, Volume
1: Breaking Strain

Rabin, Jennifer
Eileen Goudge's Swept Away #5:
Spellbound

Reaves, Michael & Steve Perry
Dome

Reed, Robert
The Leeshore

Resnick, Mike
The Dark Lady: A Romance of the Far
Future

Rexner, Romulus
Planetary Legion for Peace: Story of Their
War and Our Peace, 1940 - 2000

Ribiero, Stella Carr
Sambaqui

Riding, Julia
Space Traders Unlimited

Rifbjerg, Klaus
Witness to the Future

Robbins, David
Endworld #5: Dakota Run
Endworld #6: Citadel Run

Robinson, Nigel
The Sensorites
The Time Meddler

Robinson, Spider
Time Pressure

Rogers, Michael
Forbidden Sequence

Rohmer, Richard
Starmageddon

Rowley, Christopher B.
Golden Sunlands

Rubin, Marty
The Boiled Frog Syndrome

Ryman, Geoff
The Unconquered Country

Saint, H.F.
Memoirs of an Invisible Man

Sarabande, William
The First Americans: Beyond the Sea of
Ice

Sargent, Craig
Last Ranger #4: The Rabid Brigadier
Last Ranger #5: The War Weapons
Last Ranger #6: The Warlord's Revenge

Scortia, Thomas N. & Frank M. Robinson
Blow-Out!

Scott, Melissa
The Empress of Earth
The Kindly Ones

See, Carolyn
Golden Days

Selves, David
Life Goes on Forever...

Senn, Steven
The Sand Witch

SCIENCE FICTION NOVELS

Service, Pamela F.
Tomorrow's Magic

Shaw, Bob
The Ragged Astronauts

Sheckley, Robert
Hunter/Victim
Victim Prime

Shepard, Lucius
Life During Wartime

Shwartz, Susan M.
The Woman of Flowers

Siegel, Barbara & Scott Siegel
Firebrats #1: The Burning Land
Firebrats #2: Survivors
Firebrats #3: Thunder Mountain

Sievert, John
C.A.D.S. #4: Tech Strike Force

Silverberg, Robert
Project Pendulum

Sladek, John
Roderick

Smith, Gregory J.
Starquest, Vol.2: Operation Master Planet

Snodgrass, Melinda M.
Circuit Breaker

Sommers, Beverly
Time and Again

Spinrad, Norman
Little Heroes

Stacy, Ryder
Doomsday Warrior #10: American Nightmare
Doomsday Warrior #11: American Eden
Doomsday Warrior #12: Death, American Style

Stamey, Sara
Wild Card Run

Stasheff, Christopher
The Warlock Heretical

Steiner, Merrilee
Eileen Goudge's Swept Away #7: Pirate Moon

Sterman, Betsy & Samuel Sterman
Too Much Magic

Steussy, Marti
Forest of the Night

Stiegler, Marc
David's Sling

Stine, Jovian Bob
Spaceballs: The Book

Stith, John E.
Death Tolls

Stolbov, Bruce
Last Fall

Strasser, Todd
The Mall From Outer Space

Strugatsky, Arkady & Boris Strugatsky
The Time Wanderers

Sullivan, Timothy
V: To Conquer the Throne

Swanwick, Michael
Vacuum Flowers

Sykes, S.C.
U.S.S.A. Book 3

Syvertsen, Ryder & Adrian Fletcher
Psychic Spawn

Tannehill, Jayne
V: The Oregon Invasion

Tepper, Sheri S.
After Long Silence
The Awakeners: Northshore Southshore

Thomas, Elizabeth Marshall
Reindeer Moon

Thomas, Thomas T.
First Citizen

Thompson, Paul B.
Sundipper

Thompson, W.R.
Sideshow

Tilley, Patrick
Iron Master

Tine, Robert
Midnight City

Turk, H.C.
Ether Ore

Turner, George
The Sea and Summer

Turtledove, Harry
Agent of Byzantium
Noninterference

Tyers, Kathy
Firebird

Van Scyoc, Sydney J.
Drowntide

Vance, Jack
Araminta Station

Vardeman, Robert E.
Masters of Space #2: The Alien Web
Masters of Space #3: A Plague in Paradise
The Weapons of Chaos, Book 2: Equations of Chaos

Versluis, Arthur
Telos

Vollmann, William T.
You Bright and Risen Angels

Vomovich, Vladimir
Moscow 2042

FANTASY NOVELS

Wallace, David Foster
The Broom of the System

Walsh, Jill Paton
Torch

Wardman, Gordon
Reparations

Watt-Evans, Lawrence
The Wizard and the War Machine

Weaver, Michael D.
Mercedes Nights

Weiner, Andrew
Station Gehenna

Weinstein, Howard
Star Trek #33: Deep Domain
V: Path to Conquest

Wheeler, Scott
Matters of Form

White, James
Code Blue--Emergency!

Whiteford, Wynne
The Hyades Contact

Williams, Michael Lindsay
FTL: Further Than Life

Williams, Walter Jon
The Crown Jewels
Voice of the Whirlwind

Wilson, Colin
The Delta
The Tower

Wilson, Robert Charles
Memory Wire

Wismer, Don
Warrior Planet

Wolfe, Gene
The Urth of the New Sun

Womack, Jack
Ambient

Wu, William F.
Isaac Asimov's Robot City, Book 3: Cyborg
Masterplay

Yolen, Jane
A Sending of Dragons

Zahn, Timothy
Triplet

Zelazny, Roger
A Dark Traveling

Fantasy Novels . . . .

ab Hugh, Dafydd
Heroing

Abbey, Lynn
Unicorn & Dragon

FANTASY NOVELS

Adams, Douglas
Dirk Gently's Holistic Detective Agency

Adkins, Patrick H.
Lord of the Crooked Paths

Aickman, Robert
The Model

Alexander, Lloyd
The El Dorado Adventure

Anderson, Mary
Terror Under the Tent

Anderson, Michael Falconer
The Unholy

Anderson, Poul & Karen Anderson
The King of Ys 2: Gallicenae
The King of Ys: Dahut

Angadi, Patricia
The Highly Flavoured Ladies

Angell, Judie
The Weird Disappearance of Jordan Hall

Anthony, Piers
Being a Green Mother
Out of Phaze
Vale of the Vole

Anthony, Piers & Robert E. Margroff
Dragon's Gold

Arnason, Eleanor
Daughter of the Bear King

Ashe, Rosalind
The Laying of the Noone Walker

Asire, Nancy
Twilight's Kingdoms

Asprin, Robert Lynn
M.Y.T.H. Inc. Link
Myth-Nomers and Im-pervections

Baker, Scott
Drink the Fire From the Flames

Ball, Duncan
The Ghost and the Gory Story

Banerji, Sara
Cobwebwalking

Barker, Clive
Weaveworld

Bearne, Betsy
Eli's Ghost

Bedard, Michael
A Darker Magic

Bemmann, Hans
The Stone and the Flute

Berger, Thomas
Being Invisible

Betancourt, John Gregory
Rogue Pirate

Bingley, Margaret
The Unquiet Dead

Bird, Antoinette Kelsall
The Daughters of Megwyn

Blaylock, James P.
Land of Dreams

Bowes, Richard
Feral Cell

Bowker, Richard
Marlborough Street

Bradley, Marion Zimmer
The Firebrand

Brady, John Paul
A Voyage to Inishneefa

Brittain, Bill
Dr. Dredd's Wagon of Wonders

Brooks, Terry
The Black Unicorn

Brush, Karen A.
The Pig, the Prince & the Unicorn

Brust, Steven
The Sun, the Moon, and the Stars

Bull, Emma
War for the Oaks

Caldecott, Moyra
Etheldreda
The Silver Vortex

Campbell, Hope
Looking for Hamlet

Card, Orson Scott
Red Prophet
Seventh Son

Carl, Lillian Stewart
Shadow Dancers

Carlock, Lynn
First Love From Silhouette #176:
Daughter of the Moon

Carroll, Jonathan
Bones of the Moon

Carter, Bruce
Nightworld

Catley, Melanie
Candlelight Ecstasy Supreme #125:
Moonlight & Magic

Chalker, Jack L.
When the Changewinds Blow

Chapman, Vera
Miranty and the Alchemist

Cherryh, C.J.
Exile's Gate
Legions of Hell

Cherryh, C.J. & Janet Morris
Kings in Hell

Chetwin, Grace
The Riddle and the Rune

Clark, Joan
Wild Man of the Woods

Clendenen, Bill
Stigma

Coffman, Virginia
The Devil's Mistress

Cole, Adrian
A Place Among the Fallen
Throne of Fools

Cook, Glen
An Ill Fate Marshalling
Reap the East Wind
Sweet Silver Blues

Cook, Hugh
Wizard War
The Women and the Warlords
The Wordsmiths and the Warguild

Cooke, Catherine
The Winged Assassin

Cooper, Jeffrey
The Nightmares on Elm Street, Parts 1, 2,
3: The Continuing Story

Cooper, Louise
The Master
Mirage

Corbett, W.J.
Pentecost and the Chosen One

Cresswell, Helen
Moondial

Crowley, John
AEgypt

Curtis, Jack
Crows' Parliament

D'Ambrosio, Margaret
Meggie's Journeys

David, Peter
Knight Life

de Camp, L. Sprague & Catherine Crook de Camp
The Incorporated Knight

de Lint, Charles
Jack the Giant Killer

DeClements, Barthe & Christopher Greimes
Double Trouble

DeCles, Jon
The Particolored Unicorn

Deitz, Tom
Fireshaper's Doom

Dennis, Ian
The Prince of Stars

DiCarlantonio, Martin
Motherland

Donaldson, Stephen R.
A Man Rides Through

FANTASY NOVELS

Douglas, Carole Nelson
Keepers of Edanvant

Downer, Ann
The Spellkey

Duncan, Dave
A Rose-Red City

Easton, M. Coleman
The Fisherman's Curse

Eddings, David
Guardians of the West

Edwards, Claudia J.
Bright and Shining Tiger
A Horsewoman in Godsland

Elliott, Janice
The King Awakes

Ely, Scott
Starlight

Emerson, Ru
In the Caves of Exile
To the Haunted Mountains

Engh, M.J.
The House in the Snow

Erskine, Barbara
Lady of Hay

Estes, Rose
Greyhawk Adventures #3: Master Wolf
Greyhawk Adventures #4: The Price of Power
Saga of the Lost Lands, Volume 1: Blood of the Tiger

Falconer, Sovereign
To Make Death Love Us

Farmer, Penelope
Emma in Winter

Faulcon, Robert
Night Hunter 2: The Talisman

Feist, Raymond E. & Janny Wurts
Daughter of the Empire

Fenn, Lionel
Agnes Day
Web of Defeat

Fergusson, Bruce
The Shadow of His Wings

Finlay, D.G.
Graven Image

Flint, Kenneth C.
The Dark Druid

Franklin, Cheryl J.
Fire Get

Friedman, Michael Jan
The Glove of Maiden's Hair

Friesner, Esther M.
The Witchwood Cradle

Frith, Nigel
Dragon

Furlong, Monica
Wise Child

Gardam, Jane
Through the Dolls' House Door

Garden, Nancy
The Door Between

Gardner, Craig Shaw
A Difficulty With Dwarves
A Night in the Netherhells

Geary, Patricia
Strange Toys

Gemmell, David
Wolf in Shadow

Gentle, Mary
Ancient Light

Gilden, Mel
Born to Howl

Gilluly, Sheila
Greenbriar Queen

Gladney, Heather
Teot's War

Goldstein, Lisa
The Red Magician

Gordon, Jeffie Ross
First Love From Silhouette #198: A Touch of Genius

Gordon, Stuart
Archon!

Goulart, Ron
The Curse of the Obelisk

Grant, Gwen
Bonny Starr and the Riddles of Time

Grant, Kathryn
The Phoenix Bells

Grant, Richard
Rumors of Spring

Grass, Gunter
The Rat

Green, Sharon
The Far Side of Forever
Lady Blade, Lord Fighter

Greene, Liz
Puppet Master: A Novel

Greenland, Colin
The Hour of the Thin Ox

Gregorian, Joyce Ballou
The Great Wheel

Gygax, Gary
City of Hawks
Sea of Death

Gysin, Brion
The Last Museum

Halam, Ann
The Daymaker

Hall, Willis
The Antelope Company at Large

Halliwell, Leslie
Return to Shangri-La

Hambly, Barbara
The Witches of Wenshar

Hancock, Niel
The Sea of Silence

Hanratty, Peter
The Book of Mordred

Harbinson, W.A.
Eden
The Light of Eden

Harrington, Barbara
A Crock of Clear Water

Harris, Deborah Turner
The Gauntlet of Malice

Harris, Marilyn
Night Games

Harvey, M. Elayn
Warhaven

Hatchigan, Jessica
Count Dracula, Me and Norma D.

Hawke, Simon
The Wizard of 4th Street

Henry, Maeve
The Witch King

Henstell, Diana
New Morning Dragon

Hildick, E.W.
The Ghost Squad and the Prowling Hermits

Hill, Douglas
Blade of the Poisoner
Master of Fiends

Hoban, Russell
The Medusa Frequency

Horwood, William
Skallagrigg

Hosken, John
Meet Mr. Majimpsey

Howe, James
Nighty-Nightmare

Jacques, Brian
Redwall

Jarman, Julia
Ollie and the Bogle

Jefferies, Mike
Palace of Kings

Jeter, K.W.
Infernal Devices

Jones, Diana Wynne
A Tale of Time City

FANTASY NOVELS

Jong, Erica
Serenissima

Jordan, Brenda
The Brentwood Witches

Kane, Daniel
Power and Magic

Kaye, Marvin
Ghosts of Night and Morning

Kerr, Katharine
Darkspell

Killough, Lee
The Leopard's Daughter

King, Bernard
The Destroying Angel
Starkadder
Time-Fighters

King, Clive
The Seashore People

King, Stephen
The Dark Tower II: The Drawing of the Three

King-Smith, Dick
Tumbleweed

Kirk, Richard
Raven 2: A Time of Ghosts
Raven 3: The Frozen God
Raven 4: Lords of the Shadows
Raven 5: A Time of Dying
Raven: Swordsmistress of Chaos

Koman, Victor
The Jehovah Contract

Koontz, Dean R.
Twilight Eyes
Watchers

Kurland, Michael
Star Griffin

Kushner, Ellen
Swordspoint

Lackey, Mercedes R.
Arrow's Fall
Arrow's Flight
Arrows of the Queen

Lafferty, R.A.
Serpent's Egg

Lawhead, Stephen R.
Taliesin

Leeson, Robert
Slambash Wangs of a Compo Gormer

Leonard, Elmore
Touch

Lewins, Anna
Dream For Danger

Lorrah, Jean & Winston A. Howlett
Wulfston's Odyssey

Lumley, Brian
Demogorgon

MacAvoy, R.A.
The Grey Horse

Mackay, Colin
The Song of the Forest

Mackie, Mary
The People of the Horse

Mahy, Margaret
The Tricksters

Marsh, Geoffrey
Patch of the Odin Soldier

Marten, Jacqueline
Dream Walker

Martine-Barnes, Adrienne
The Crystal Sword

Mayhar, Ardath
Makra Choria

McCay, Claudia
Promise of the Rose Stone

McCullough, Colleen
The Ladies of Missalonghi

McGowen, Tom
The Magician's Apprentice

McKenzie, Ellen Kindt
Kashka

Melling, O.R.
The Singing Stone

Middleton, Haydn
The People in the Picture

Milan, Victor & Melinda M. Snodgrass
Runespear

Miller, Moira
The Doom of Soulis

Mitchison, Naomi
Early in Orcadia

Monaco, Richard
Unto the Beast

Monteleone, Thomas F.
The Magnificent Gallery

Moorcock, Michael
The Brothel in Rosenstrasse
The City in the Autumn Stars

Moran, Daniel
The Flame Key

Morressy, John
The Questing of Kedrigern

Morris, Janet
Tempus

Morrison, Toni
Beloved

Morwood, Peter
The Demon Lord
The Dragon Lord

Murphy, Shirley Rousseau
The Ivory Lyre

Murphy, Warren & Molly Cochran
High Priest

Neiderman, Andrew
Reflection

Nichols, Leigh
Shadowfires

Niles, Douglas
Forgotten Realms, Book #1: Darkwalker on Moonshae

Nimmo, Jenny
The Snow Spider

Nooteboom, Cees
In the Dutch Mountains

Norton, Andre
The Gate of the Cat

Nugent, James
The Brass Halo

O'Day-Flannery, Constance
Timeswept Lovers

O'Shea, Pat
Finn MacCool and the Small Men of Deeds

Offutt, Andrew J.
Shadowspawn

Orlov, Vladimir
Danilov the Violist

Park, Ruth
My Sister Sif

Parvin, Brian
The Golden Garden

Paxson, Diana L.
The Earthstone
The Paradise Tree

Pendleton, Don
Heart to Heart
Life to Life

Perry, Steve
Conan the Defiant

Powers, Tim
On Stranger Tides

Prantera, Amanda
Conversations with Lord Byron on Perversion, 163 Years After His Lordship's Death

Pratchett, Terry
Equal Rites
The Light Fantastic
Mort

Price, Susan
The Ghost Drum

Rabinowitz, Ann
Knight on Horseback

FANTASY NOVELS

Randisi, Robert J. & Kevin D. Randle
Once Upon a Murder

Reichert, Mickey Zucker
Godslayer

Rexner, Romulus
Planetary Legion for Peace: Story of Their War and Our Peace, 1940 - 2000

Rivkin, J.F.
Web of Wind

Roberson, Jennifer
Track of the White Wolf

Roberts, John Maddox
Conan the Champion
Conan the Marauder

Roberts, Keith
Grainne

Rochlin, Doris
Frobisch's Angel

Rohan, Michael Scott
The Forge in the Forest

Rosenberg, Joel
The Heir Apparent

Rule, Jane
Memory Board

Rundle, Anne
Moonbranches

Ryman, Geoff
The Unconquered Country

Saberhagen, Fred
The Second Book of Lost Swords: Sightbinder's Story

Sadler, Barry
Casca #17: The Warrior
Casca #18: The Cursed

Sage, Alison & Dennis Wheatley
The Devil Rides Out

Sapir, Richard Ben
Quest

Sarabande, William
Wolves of the Dawn

Saramago, Jose
Baltasar and Blimunda

Scarborough, Elizabeth Ann
The Goldcamp Vampire

Schmidt, Dennis
Twilight of the Gods, Book III: Three Trumps Sounding

Scott, Michael
The Last of the Fianna
Magician's Law

Senn, Steven
The Sand Witch

Service, Pamela F.
Tomorrow's Magic
When the Night Wind Howls

Sharpe, John Rufus, III
Hogar Lord of the Asyr

Sherrell, Carl
Skraelings

Shwartz, Susan M.
Byzantium's Crown
The Woman of Flowers

Simon, Jo
Beloved Captain

Singer, Marilyn
Ghost Host

Smith, L.J.
The Night of the Solstice

Smith, Stephanie
The Boy Who Was Thrown Away

Smith, Susan
Samantha Slade #2: Confessions of a Teenage Frog
Samantha Slade #3: Our Friend, Public Nuisance No. 1
Samantha Slade, Monster-Sitter

Snyder, Midori
Soulstring

Sobol, Donald J.
The Amazing Power of Ashur Fine

Springer, Nancy
Madbond
Mindbond

St. Alcorn, Lloyd
Halberd: Dream Warrior

St. George, Judith
Haunted
Who's Scared? Not Me!

Stasheff, Christopher
The Warlock Heretical

Stevenson, Drew
The Case of the Visiting Vampire

Stewart, Ramona
The Nightmare Candidate

Tapp, Kathy Kennedy
Flight of the Moth-Kin
The Scorpio Ghosts and the Black Hole Gang

Tarr, Judith
The Lady of Han-Gilen

Taylor, Keith
Bard IV: Raven's Gathering

Tepper, Sheri S.
The Awakeners: Northshore
Southshore

Thompson, Joyce
Harry and the Hendersons

Thornton, Lawrence
Imagining Argentina

Townsend, John Rowe
The Persuading Stick

Turtledove, Harry
An Emperor For the Legion
The Legion of Videssos
The Misplaced Legion
Swords of the Legion

Van Ash, Cay
The Fires of Fu Manchu

Van Lustbader, Eric
Shan

Vardeman, Robert E., writing as Daniel Moran
The Skeleton Lord's Key

Volk, Stephen
Gothic

Vollmann, William T.
You Bright and Risen Angels

Volsky, Paula
The Luck of Relian Kru

Watt-Evans, Lawrence
With a Single Spell
The Wizard and the War Machine

Weathers, Brenda
The House at Pelham Falls

Weaver, Michael D.
Wolf-Dreams

Webster, Lyn
The Illumination of Alice J. Cunningham

Weinberg, George
Numberland: A Fable

Weis, Margaret & Tracy Hickman
The Darksword Trilogy, Volume 1: Forging the Darksword

Welfare, Mary
Yeti of the Glen

Wendorf, Patricia
Blanche
Bye Bye Blackbird

Westall, Robert
Urn Burial

Willis, Connie
Lincoln's Dreams

Wilson, Colin
The Tower

Wilson, Gahan
Eddy Deco's Last Caper: An Illustrated Mystery

Wilson, Rudy
The Red Truck

Wiseman, David
Adam's Common

Wismer, Don
Warrior Planet

Wittig, Monique
Across the Acheron

Wolfe, Gene
The Urth of the New Sun

FANTASY NOVELS

Wongar, B.
Gabo Djara

Wood, Bridget
The Minstrel's Lute
Satanic Lute

Wood, Robert
The Avatar

Woodroffe, Patrick
The Second Earth

Wooley, Persia
Child of the Northern Spring

Wrede, Patricia C.
Caught in Crystal

Wrightson, Patricia
Moon-dark

Wylie, Jonathan
The Centre of the Circle
The First Named

Yarbro, Chelsea Quinn
A Flame in Byzantium

Yolen, Jane
A Sending of Dragons

York, Carol Beach
Nights in Ghostland

York, Rebecca
The Peregrine Connection #3: In Search of the Dove

Zahn, Timothy
Triplet

Zelazny, Roger
Sign of Chaos

Zimmer, Paul Edwin
A Gathering of Heroes

Horror Novels . . . .

Adams, Douglas
Dirk Gently's Holistic Detective Agency

Almquist, Gregg
Beast Rising

Anderson, C. Dean
Torture Tomb

Anderson, Mary
The Leipzig Vampire

Anderson, Michael Falconer
God of a Thousand Faces
The Unholy

Andrews, V.C.
Garden of Shadows

Armstrong, F.W.
The Devouring

Barker, Clive
The Damnation Game
Weaveworld

Bedard, Michael
A Darker Magic

Bingley, Margaret
Devil's Child

Brandner, Gary
Cameron's Closet

Burgess, Mason
Graveyard

Campton, David & Mary W. Shelley
Frankenstein

Cantrell, Lisa W.
The Manse

Cheetham, Ann
The Pit

Childer, Simon Ian
Worm

Chronister, Alan B.
Cry Wolf

Citro, Joseph
Shadow Child

Clendenen, Bill
Stigma

Cook, Robin
Outbreak

Cooper, Jeffrey
The Nightmares on Elm Street, Parts 1, 2, 3: The Continuing Story

Costello, Matthew
Sleep Tight

Coyne, John
The Hunting Season

Davidson, Alan
Bewitching of Alison Allbright

Day, Chet
Halo

Delap, Richard & Walt Lee
Shapes

Downie, Jill
The Raven in the Glass

Edward, Ames J.
The Force

Eliot, Marc
How Dear the Dawn

Falconer, Sovereign
To Make Death Love Us

Farris, John
Nightfall

Faulcon, Robert
The Labyrinth
Night Hunter
Night Hunter 2: The Talisman
Night Hunter 3: The Ghost Dance

Gallagher, Stephen
Valley of Lights

HORROR NOVELS

Garden, Nancy
Mystery of the Night Raiders

Gardner, Craig Shaw
The Lost Boys

Garnett, Bill
The Crone

Gilden, Mel
Born to Howl

Goddin, Jeffrey
The Living Dead

Gray, Linda Crockett
Scryer

Greenburg, Dan
The Nanny

Gresham, Stephen
Midnight Boy

Halkin, John
Bloodworm
Fangs of the Werewolf

Hardie, Raymond
Abyssos

Harris, Marilyn
Night Games

Hawke, Douglas D.
Moonslasher

Hawke, Simon
Friday the 13th, Part I

Henstell, Diana
New Morning Dragon

Herbert, James
The Magic Cottage
Sepulchre

Higgs, Eric C.
Doppelganger

Horvitz, Leslie
Blood Moon

Hoyle, Trevor
K.I.D.S.

Hutson, Shaun
Breeding Ground
Deathday
Slugs
Victims

Ironside, Virginia
Vampire Master

James, Robert
Blood Mist

Jensen, Ruby Jean
Annabelle
Chain Letter
Smoke

Jeter, K.W.
Dark Seeker
Mantis

HORROR NOVELS

Johnstone, William W.
The Devil's Cat

Kaye, Marvin
Ghosts of Night and Morning

Keene, Joe & William W. Johnstone
Baby Grand

Kelleher, Ed & Harriette Vidal
The Breeder

Kent, Paul
The Crib

Killough, Lee
Blood Hunt

King, Stephen
The Dark Tower II: The Drawing of the Three
The Tommyknockers

Kittredge, Mary & Kevin O'Donnell, Jr.
The Shelter

Koontz, Dean R.
Twilight Eyes

Kunstler, James Howard
The Hunt

Lansdale, Joe R.
The Nightrunners

Laws, Stephen
The Wyrm

Laymon, Richard
The Beast House
Beware!
Flesh
Tread Softly

Lee, Samantha & Robert Louis Stevenson
Dr. Jekyll and Mr. Hyde

Lord, J. Edward
Elixir
Incantation

Manley, Mark
Throwback

Masello, Robert
The Spirit Wood

Mayhar, Ardath
The Wall

McCammon, Robert R.
Swan Song

McNally, Clare
Somebody Come and Play

Miller, Rex
Slob

Monaco, Richard
Unto the Beast

Monteleone, Thomas F.
The Magnificent Gallery

Monteleone, Thomas F. & John DeChancie
Crooked House

Murphy, Gloria
Nightmare

Neiderman, Andrew
Sight Unseen

Nichols, Leigh
Shadowfires

Niederman, Andrew
Playmates

Nugent, James
The Brass Halo

Parker, Chris
Kyoki

Pfefferle, Seth
Stickman

Plante, Edmund
Transformation

Ransom, Daniel
Night Caller

Reed, Dana
The Gatekeeper

Relling, William, Jr.
New Moon

Rhodes, Daniel
Next, After Lucifer

Richards, Tony
The Harvest Bride

Ronson, Mark
Ogre
Plague Pit

Rovin, Jeff
Re-Animator

Rundle, Anne
Moonbranches

Russo, John
Voodoo Dawn

Sackett, Jeffrey
Stolen Souls

Sarrantonio, Al
The Boy With Penny Eyes

Saul, John
The Unwanted

Scott, Michael
Burial Rites

Skipp, John M. & Craig Spector
The Cleanup

Smith, Guy N.
Alligators
Bloodshow
Demons
Entombed
The Plague
The Wood

Smith, Terrence Lore
Yours Truly, From Hell

St. Clair, David
The Devil Rocked Her Cradle

Stchur, John
Down on the Farm

Stoker, Bram
Dracula

Stout, Tim
The Raging

Tigges, John
Hands of Lucifer

Tremayne, Peter
Nicor!
Trollnight

Tuttle, Lisa
Gabriel

Walker, Robert
Aftershock

Wallace, Patricia
Water Baby

Watson, Ian
The Power

Westerly, Daniel
Devotion

Williamson, Chet
Ash Wednesday

Williamson, J.N.
Evil Offspring

Wolfe, Joyce
The White Spider

Wood, Bari
Amy Girl

Yarbro, Chelsea Quinn
Firecode
A Flame in Byzantium

Novelizations . . . .

Baker, Pip & Jane Baker
Terror of the Vervoids
Time and the Rani

Bennett, Thea
The Gemini Factor

Black, Ian Stuart
The Macra Terror

Block, Bob
Galloping Galaxies

Bonanno, Margaret Wander
Star Trek: Strangers From the Sky

Carey, Diane
Star Trek: Final Frontier

Carlisle, Anne
Liquid Sky

Carter, Carmen
Star Trek #34: Dreams of the Raven

NOVELIZATIONS

Carver, Jeffrey A.
Roger Zelazny's Alien Speedway 1: Clypsis

Cherryh, C.J.
Legions of Hell

Cherryh, C.J. & Janet Morris
Kings in Hell

Coburn, Anthony
The Tribe of Gum, pl

Cooper, Jeffrey
The Nightmares on Elm Street, Parts 1, 2, 3: The Continuing Story

Cooper, Richard
Knights of God

Cotton, Donald
The Romans

Cover, Arthur Byron
Isaac Asimov's Robot City, Book 4: Prodigy

DeHaven, Tom
U.S.S.A. Book 1

DeWeese, Gene
Star Trek #32: Chain of Attack

Dicks, Terrance
The Ambassadors of Death
The Mysterious Planet

Dillard, J.M.
Star Trek #37: Bloodthirst

Drew, Wayland
Batteries Not Included

Duane, Diane E. & Peter Morwood
Star Trek #35: The Romulan Way

Elliott, Nathan
Innerspace

Estes, Rose
Greyhawk Adventures #3: Master Wolf
Greyhawk Adventures #4: The Price of Power

Ford, John M.
Star Trek #36: How Much for Just the Planet?

Gardner, Craig Shaw
The Lost Boys

Garrido, Mar
Eileen Goudge's Swept Away #6: Once Upon a Kiss

Gerrold, David
Star Trek, The Next Generation: Encounter at Farpoint

Goudge, Eileen
Eileen Goudge's Swept Away #1: Gone With the Wish
Eileen Goudge's Swept Away #4: Star Struck

Gygax, Gary
City of Hawks
Night Arrant, oc

Gygax, Gary (continued)
Sea of Death

Hawke, Simon
Friday the 13th, Part I

Hiller, B.B.
Superman IV

Hodgman, Ann
Galaxy High School

Jones, Glyn
The Space Museum

Keith, William H., Jr.
Battletech: Decision at Thunder Rift
Battletech: Mercenary's Star

Kube-McDowell, Michael P.
Isaac Asimov's Robot City, Book 1: Odyssey

Lantz, Fran
Eileen Goudge's Swept Away #2: Woodstock Magic
Eileen Goudge's Swept Away #8: All Shook Up

Larson, Glen A. & Robert Thurston
Battlestar Galactica #14: Surrender the Galactica!

Leragis, Peter
Star Trek IV: The Journey Home, pi

Lewitt, S.N.
U.S.S.A. Book 2
U.S.S.A. Book 4

Lucarotti, John
The Massacre

Lucas, George, Donald F. Glut & James Kahn
The Star Wars Trilogy, om

Marter, Ian
The Reign of Terror
The Rescue

Mayhar, Ardath
Battletech: The Sword and the Dagger

McKinney, Jack
Robotech # 1: Genesis
Robotech # 2: Battle Cry
Robotech # 3: Homecoming
Robotech # 4: Battlehymn
Robotech # 5: Force of Arms
Robotech # 6: Doomsday
Robotech # 7: Southern Cross
Robotech # 8: Metal Fire
Robotech # 9: The Final Nightmare
Robotech #10: Invid Invasion
Robotech #11: Metamorphosos
Robotech #12: Symphony of Light

McQuay, Mike
Isaac Asimov's Robot City, Book 2: Suspicion

Morris, Janet
Tempus

Naha, Ed
Robocop

Offutt, Andrew J.
Shadowspawn

Perry, Steve
Conan the Defiant

Platt, Charles
Piers Anthony's Worlds of Chthon: Plasm

Pouns, Brauna E.
Amerika

Powers, Louise E.
Eileen Goudge's Swept Away #3: Love on the Range

Preuss, Paul
Arthur C. Clarke's Venus Prime, Volume 1: Breaking Strain

Rabin, Jennifer
Eileen Goudge's Swept Away #5: Spellbound

Roberts, John Maddox
Conan the Champion
Conan the Marauder

Robinson, Nigel
The Sensorites
The Time Meddler

Rovin, Jeff
Re-Animator

Steiner, Merrilee
Eileen Goudge's Swept Away #7: Pirate Moon

Stine, Jovian Bob
Spaceballs: The Book

Sullivan, Timothy
V: To Conquer the Throne

Sykes, S.C.
U.S.S.A. Book 3

Tannehill, Jayne
V: The Oregon Invasion

Thompson, Joyce
Harry and the Hendersons

Van Ash, Cay
The Fires of Fu Manchu

Volk, Stephen
Gothic

Weinstein, Howard
Star Trek #33: Deep Domain
V: Path to Conquest

Wu, William F.
Isaac Asimov's Robot City, Book 3: Cyborg

Juvenile/Young Adult . . . .

Aiken, Joan
The Moon's Revenge, nv

Alcock, Vivian
Ghostly Companions, co

JUVENILE/YOUNG ADULT

Alexander, Lloyd
The El Dorado Adventure

Anderson, Mary
The Leipzig Vampire
Terror Under the Tent

Angell, Judie
The Weird Disappearance of Jordan Hall

Asimov, Isaac, Martin H. Greenberg & Charles G. Waugh, eds.
Young Witches & Warlocks, an

Asimov, Janet & Isaac Asimov
Norby and the Queen's Necklace
Norby Finds a Villain

Baker, Pip & Jane Baker
Terror of the Vervoids
Time and the Rani

Ball, Duncan
The Ghost and the Gory Story

Bearne, Betsy
Eli's Ghost

Bedard, Michael
A Darker Magic

Bennett, Thea
The Gemini Factor

Black, Ian Stuart
The Macra Terror

Block, Bob
Galloping Galaxies

Bowkett, Stephen
Dualists

Bradman, Tony, ed.
The Magic Kiss and Other Tales of Princes and Princesses, an

Brittain, Bill
Dr. Dredd's Wagon of Wonders

Campbell, Hope
Looking for Hamlet

Campton, David & Mary W. Shelley
Frankenstein

Carroll, Lewis
The Complete Alice and The Hunting of the Snark, om

Chambers, Aidan, ed.
A Quiver Of Ghosts, oa

Cheetham, Ann
The Pit

Chetwin, Grace
The Riddle and the Rune

Cooper, Clare
The Settlement on Planet B

Cooper, Richard
Knights of God

Corbett, W.J.
Pentecost and the Chosen One

Cotton, Donald
The Romans

Coville, Bruce
Murder in Orbit

Cresswell, Helen
Moondial

Dahl, Roald
The Complete Adventures of Charlie and Mr. Willy Wonka, om
Fantastic Mr. Fox: A Play, pl

Davidson, Alan
Bewitching of Alison Allbright

DeClements, Barthe & Christopher Greimes
Double Trouble

DeWeese, Gene
The Calvin Nullifier

Dicks, Terrance
The Ambassadors of Death
The Mysterious Planet

Dickson, Gordon R.
Secrets of the Deep, om

Downer, Ann
The Spellkey

Dudley, Terence
K9 and Company

Earnshaw, Brian
Starclipper and the Galactic Final

Elliott, Janice
The King Awakes

Elliott, Nathan
Kidnap in Space
Plague Moon
Treasure Planet

Engh, M.J.
The House in the Snow

Farmer, Penelope
Emma in Winter

Fisk, Nicholas
Mindbenders

Foster, John, ed.
Spaceways, an

Furlong, Monica
Wise Child

Gardam, Jane
Through the Dolls' House Door

Garden, Nancy
The Door Between
Mystery of the Night Raiders

Garrido, Mar
Eileen Goudge's Swept Away #6: Once Upon a Kiss

Gilbert, Harry
Ghost's Playground, na

Gilden, Mel
Born to Howl

Gilden, Mel (continued)
M. Is for Monster, nv

Gormley, Beatrice
Richard and the Vratch

Goudge, Eileen
Eileen Goudge's Swept Away #1: Gone With the Wish
Eileen Goudge's Swept Away #4: Star Struck

Gowar, Mick, ed.
Twisted Circuits, oa

Grant, Gwen
Bonny Starr and the Riddles of Time

Grocott, Ann
Danni's Desperate Journey

Halam, Ann
The Daymaker

Halkin, John
Fangs of the Werewolf

Hall, Willis
The Antelope Company at Large

Hatchigan, Jessica
Count Dracula, Me and Norma D.

Haynes, Mary
Raider's Sky

Henry, Maeve
The Witch King

Hildick, E.W.
The Ghost Squad and the Prowling Hermits

Hill, Douglas
Blade of the Poisoner
Master of Fiends

Hodgman, Ann
Galaxy High School

Hoobler, Thomas
Dr. Chill's Project

Hoover, H.M.
Orvis

Hosken, John
Meet Mr. Majimpsey

Howe, James
Nighty-Nightmare

Hudson, Michael
Photon: Thieves of Light

Hughes, Monica
The Dream Catcher

Ingpen, Robert
The Voyage of the Poppykettle, nv

Ironside, Virginia
Vampire Master

Jacques, Brian
Redwall

Science Fiction, Fantasy, & Horror: 1987

JUVENILE/YOUNG ADULT

Jarman, Julia
Ollie and the Bogle

Jones, Diana Wynne
A Tale of Time City

Kahn, Joan, ed.
Ready or Not: Here Come Fourteen Frightening Stories!, an

Kelleher, Victor
Taronga

Kilworth, Garry
The Wizard of Woodworld

King, Clive
The Seashore People

King-Smith, Dick
Tumbleweed

Lantz, Fran
Eileen Goudge's Swept Away #2: Woodstock Magic
Eileen Goudge's Swept Away #8: All Shook Up

Lee, Samantha & Robert Louis Stevenson
Dr. Jekyll and Mr. Hyde

Leeson, Robert
Slambash Wangs of a Compo Gormer

Leroe, Ellen
Robot Raiders, hc

Lewins, Anna
Dream For Danger

Lewis, C.S.
Tales of Narnia, om

Lindbergh, Anne
The Shadow on the Dial

Lucarotti, John
The Massacre

Marter, Ian
The Reign of Terror
The Rescue

McKenzie, Ellen Kindt
Kashka

Melling, O.R.
The Singing Stone

Miller, Moira
The Doom of Soulis

Milne, Janis
Starship Dunroamin

Mixon, Laura J.
Omni: Astropilots

Nimmo, Jenny
The Snow Spider

O'Shea, Pat
Finn MacCool and the Small Men of Deeds

Oldfield, Pamela
The Ghosts of Bellering Oast, nv
Pamela Oldfield's Spine Chillers, co

Park, Ruth
My Sister Sif

Payne, Bernal C., Jr.
Experiment in Terror

Pearce, Philippa
Who's Afraid? and Other Strange Stories, co

Peters, David
Photon #1: For the Glory
Photon #2: High Stakes
Photon #3: In Search of Mom
Photon #4: This is Your Life, Bhodi Li
Photon #5: Exile

Powers, Louise E.
Eileen Goudge's Swept Away #3: Love on the Range

Rabin, Jennifer
Eileen Goudge's Swept Away #5: Spellbound

Rabinowitz, Ann
Knight on Horseback

Richardson, Jean, ed.
Beware, Beware - Strange and Sinister Tales, an

Riding, Julia
Space Traders Unlimited

Robinson, Nigel
The Sensorites
The Time Meddler

Russell, Jean, ed.
Supernatural Stories: 13 Tales of the Unexpected, an

Sage, Alison & Dennis Wheatley
The Devil Rides Out

San Souci, Robert D., ed.
Short & Shivery, an

Scott, Michael
The Last of the Fianna

Scrocco, Jean L., ill. & Judy Mastrangelo, ed.
Antique Fairy Tales, an

Senn, Steven
The Sand Witch

Service, Pamela F.
When the Night Wind Howls

Siegel, Barbara & Scott Siegel
Firebrats #1: The Burning Land
Firebrats #2: Survivors
Firebrats #3: Thunder Mountain

Silverberg, Robert
Project Pendulum

Singer, Marilyn
Ghost Host

Smith, L.J.
The Night of the Solstice

Smith, Stephanie
The Boy Who Was Thrown Away

Smith, Susan
Samantha Slade #2: Confessions of a Teenage Frog
Samantha Slade #3: Our Friend, Public Nuisance No. 1
Samantha Slade, Monster-Sitter

Sobol, Donald J.
The Amazing Power of Ashur Fine

St. George, Judith
Haunted
Who's Scared? Not Me!

Steiner, Merrilee
Eileen Goudge's Swept Away #7: Pirate Moon

Strasser, Todd
The Mall From Outer Space

Tapp, Kathy Kennedy
Flight of the Moth-Kin
The Scorpio Ghosts and the Black Hole Gang

Townsend, John Rowe
The Persuading Stick

Vivelo, Jackie
A Trick of the Light, oc

Walsh, Jill Paton
Torch

Welfare, Mary
Yeti of the Glen

Westall, Robert
Urn Burial

Williams, Sheila & Cynthia Manson, eds.
Tales From Isaac Asimov's Science Fiction Magazine, an

Wiseman, David
Adam's Common

Wrightson, Patricia
Moon-dark

Yolen, Jane
A Sending of Dragons

Yolen, Jane, Martin H. Greenberg & Charles G. Waugh, eds.
Spaceships and Spells, oa

York, Carol Beach
Nights in Ghostland

Zelazny, Roger
A Dark Traveling

Omnibus Volumes . . . .

Anthony, Piers
Tarot

Asimov, Janet & Isaac Asimov
Norby: Robot for Hire

Asprin, Robert Lynn
Myth Alliances

Auel, Jean M.
Earth's Children

OMNIBUS VOLUMES

Boston, Bruce
  The Bruce Boston Omnibus

Bradbury, Ray
  **Fahrenheit 451/The Illustrated
  Man/Dandelion Wine/The Golden
  Apples of the Sun/The Martian
  Chronicles**

Bradley, Marion Zimmer
  The Fall of Atlantis

Brin, David
  Earthclan

Bujold, Lois McMaster
  Test of Honor

Busby, F.M.
  **The Rebel Dynasty, Volume I
  The Rebel Dynasty, Volume II**

Carroll, Lewis
  **The Complete Alice and The Hunting of
  the Snark**

Cherryh, C.J.
  The Faded Sun Trilogy

Clarke, Arthur C.
  **2001: A Space Odyssey/The City and the
  Stars/The Deep Range/A Fall of
  Moondust/Rendezvous With Rama**

Dahl, Roald
  **The Complete Adventures of Charlie and
  Mr. Willy Wonka**

Dickson, Gordon R.
  Secrets of the Deep

Faulcon, Robert
  **The Ghost Dance
  The Stalking**

Finney, Jack
  3 By Finney

Foster, Alan Dean
  Spellsinger's Scherzo

Gardner, Craig Shaw
  The Exploits of Ebenezvm

Hambly, Barbara
  The Unschooled Wizard

Hartley, L.P.
  The Complete Short Stories of L.P. Hartley

Herbert, Frank
  The Second Great Dune Trilogy

Kellogg, M. Bradley & William Rossow
  Lear's Daughters

Lee, Tanith
  **Tales from the Flat Earth: Night's
  Daughter
  Tales from the Flat Earth: The Lords of
  Darkness**

Lewis, C.S.
  Tales of Narnia

Lucas, George, Donald F. Glut & James Kahn
  The Star Wars Trilogy

McCaffrey, Anne
  Nerilka's Story & The Coelura

Meredith, Richard C.
  Timeliner Trilogy

Moorcock, Michael
  The Cornelius Chronicles, Vol. III

Robeson, Kenneth
  **Doc Savage Omnibus #2
  Doc Savage Omnibus #3
  Doc Savage Omnibus #4**

Scarborough, Elizabeth Ann
  Songs from the Seashell Archives, Vol. 1

Tepper, Sheri S.
  **The Awakeners
  The End of the Game**

Vardeman, Robert E.
  The Jade Demons Quartet

Collections . . . .

Aiken, Joan
  A Goose on Your Grave, oc

Alcock, Vivian
  Ghostly Companions

Aldiss, Brian W.
  The Magic of the Past, oc

Amis, Kingsley
  Collected Short Stories

Amis, Martin
  Einstein's Monsters

Anderson, Poul
  The Enemy Stars

Anonymous, ed.
  **Gollancz/Sunday Times SF Competition
  Stories**, oc

Atwood, Margaret
  Bluebeard's Egg

Bierce, Ambrose
  **The Devil's Advocate: An Ambrose Bierce
  Reader**

Blaylock, James P. & Edward Bryant
  The Shadow on the Doorstep/Trilobyte, oc

Bloch, Robert
  **Lost in Time and Space with Lefty Feep
  Midnight Pleasures**

Boston, Bruce
  **Alchemical Texts
  All the Clocks Are Melting
  Jackbird: Tales of Illusion & Identity
  Nuclear Futures
  She Comes When You're Leaving & Other
  Stories**

Bova, Ben
  Battle Station

Brown, Fredric
  And the Gods Laughed

Busby, F.M.
  Getting Home

Byatt, Antonia
  Sugar and Other Stories

Campbell, Ramsey
  **Cold Print
  Dark Feasts
  Scared Stiff: Tales of Sex and Death**

Card, Orson Scott
  Cardography

Cherryh, C.J.
  Glass and Amber

Chetwynd-Hayes, R.
  Dracula's Children, oc
  The House of Dracula, oc

Choyce, Lesley
  The Dream Auditor, oc

Christopher, Paul
  Beyond that River, oc

Clarke, Arthur C.
  The Wind From the Sun

Clement, Hal
  Intuit

Delany, Samuel R.
  The Bridge of Lost Desire

Dent, Lester
  The Sinister Ray

Dick, Philip K.
  **The Collected Stories of Philip K. Dick,
  Vol. Five: The Little Black Box
  The Collected Stories of Philip K. Dick,
  Vol. Four: The Days of Perky Pat
  The Collected Stories of Philip K. Dick,
  Vol. One: Beyond Lies the Wub
  The Collected Stories of Philip K. Dick,
  Vol. Three: The Father Thing
  The Collected Stories of Philip K. Dick,
  Vol. Two: Second Variety**

Dickson, Gordon R.
  **In the Bone: The Best Science Fiction of
  Gordon R. Dickson
  The Stranger**

Drake, David
  Hammer's Slammers

du Maurier, Daphne
  **Classics of the Macabre
  Daphne Du Maurier's Classics of the
  Macabre**

Ellison, Harlan
  The Essential Ellison

Fisk, Nicholas
  Living Fire and Other S.F. Stories, oc

Forrest, Katherine V.
  Dreams and Swords, oc

Frazier, Robert
  Perception Barriers

Gardner, Martin
  The No-Sided Professor

COLLECTIONS

Garrett, Randall
Takeoff Too!

Green, Terence M.
The Woman Who Is the Midnight Wind

Gygax, Gary
Night Arrant, oc

Halliwell, Leslie
A Demon Close Behind, oc

Hayes, Barbara & Robert Ingpen
Folk Tales and Fables of the World

Highsmith, Patricia
Tales of Natural and Unnatural Catastrophes, oc

Howard, Robert E.
Cthulhu: The Mythos and Kindred Horrors

Ing, Dean
Firefight 2000

James, M.R.
Casting the Runes and Other Ghost Stories
The Ghost Stories of M.R. James
Masters of Fantasy 3: M.R. James
A Warning to the Curious: The Ghost Stories of M.R. James

Janifer, Laurence M.
Knave & the Game

Jones, Bruce
Twisted Tales, oc

Joron, Andrew
Force Fields

Kennedy, Leigh
Faces

Kipling, Rudyard
The Complete Supernatural Stories of Rudyard Kipling

Kuttner, Henry
Prince Raynor

Laumer, Keith
Retief: Envoy to New Worlds

Le Guin, Ursula K.
Buffalo Gals and Other Animal Presences

Lee, Tanith
Night's Sorceries, oc

Lee, Vernon
Supernatural Tales: Excursions Into Fantasy

Lumley, Brian
The Compleat Crow

Machen, Arthur
The Collected Arthur Machen
Guinevere and Lancelot & Others

Maclay, John
Other Engagements

Maitland, Sara
The Book of Spells, oc

Martin, George R.R.
Portraits of His Children

Matheson, Richard Christian
Scars

Mathews, Jack
The Battle of Brazil: The Authorized Story and Annotated Screenplay of Terry Gilliam's Landmark Film

Matthews, Jack
Ghostly Populations

Moore, Rudin
Ultra-Vue and Selected Peripheral Visions, oc

Oldfield, Pamela
Pamela Oldfield's Spine Chillers

Pearce, Philippa
Who's Afraid? and Other Strange Stories

Pohl, Frederik & C.M. Kornbluth
Our Best: The Best of Frederik Pohl and C.M. Kornbluth

Roberts, Keith
A Heron Caught in Weeds

Roland, Paul
The Curious Case of Richard Fielding and Other Stories, oc

Saberhagen, Fred
Saberhagen: My Best

Sargent, Pamela
The Best of Pamela Sargent

Saxton, Josephine
Little Tours of Hell, oc

Shea, Michael
Polyphemus

Shefner, Evelyn
Common Body, Royal Bones

Shepard, Lucius
The Jaguar Hunter

Simak, Clifford D.
Brother and Other Stories

Spark, Muriel
The Stories of Muriel Spark

Springer, Nancy
Chance & Other Gestures of the Hand of Fate

Stamper, J.B.
More Tales for the Midnight Hour, oc

Sturgeon, Theodore
To Marry Medusa
A Touch of Sturgeon

Tolkien, J.R.R.
The Lost Road and Other Writings

Tuttle, Lisa
A Spaceship Built of Stone and Other Stories

Valentine, Mark
14 Bellchamber Tower, oc

Vinge, Vernor
Tatja Grimm's World
True Names and Other Dangers

Vivelo, Jackie
A Trick of the Light, oc

Wagner, Karl Edward
Why Not You and I?

Waldrop, Howard
All About Strange Monsters of the Recent Past

Watson, Ian
Evil Water

Wellman, Manly Wade
The Valley So Low: Southern Mountain Stories

Williams, Mary
Haunted Waters, oc

Williamson, Duncan
The Broonie, Silkies & Fairies: Travellers' Tales of the Other World

Wilson, Richard
The Kid From Ozone Park & Other Stories, oc

Zipes, Jack, ed.
The Complete Fairy Tales of the Brothers Grimm

Anthologies . . . .

Adams, Robert & Pamela Crippen Adams, eds.
Friends of the Horseclans, oa

Adams, Robert, Pamela Crippen Adams & Martin H. Greenberg, eds.
Robert Adams' Book of Alternate Worlds

Aldiss, Brian W. & Sam J. Lundwall, eds.
The Penguin World Omnibus of Science Fiction

Anonymous, ed.
Gollancz/Sunday Times SF Competition Stories, oa
Mad and Bad Fairies, oa
Night Visions 4, oa
Rhysling Anthology 1987

Asimov, Isaac & Martin H. Greenberg, eds.
Isaac Asimov Presents the Great SF Stories: 16 (1954)
Isaac Asimov Presents the Great SF Stories: 17 (1955)

Asimov, Isaac, Martin H. Greenberg & Charles G. Waugh, eds.
Isaac Asimov's Magical Worlds of Fantasy #8: Devils
Isaac Asimov's Magical Worlds of Fantasy #9: Atlantis
Isaac Asimov's Wonderful Worlds of Science Fiction #6: Neanderthals
Isaac Asimov's Wonderful Worlds of Science Fiction #7: Space Shuttles
Young Witches & Warlocks

ANTHOLOGIES

Asprin, Robert Lynn & Lynn Abbey, eds.
Thieves' World 10: Aftermath, oa

Baen, Jim, ed.
New Destinies, Vol. 1/Spring 1987, oa
New Destinies, Vol. 2/Fall 1987, oa

Bradley, Marion Zimmer, ed.
Sword and Sorceress IV, oa

Bradley, Marion Zimmer & The Friends of Darkover
The Other Side of the Mirror, oa
Red Sun of Darkover, oa

Bradman, Tony, ed.
The Magic Kiss and Other Tales of Princes and Princesses

Budrys, Algis, ed.
L. Ron Hubbard Presents Writers of the Future, Vol. III, oa

Carr, Terry, ed.
Terry Carr's Best Science Fiction and Fantasy of the Year #16
Universe 17, oa

Chambers, Aidan, ed.
A Quiver Of Ghosts, oa

Cherryh, C.J., ed.
Fever Season: Merovingen Nights #2, oa
Merovingen Nights: Festival Moon, oa

Child, Lincoln, ed.
Tales of the Dark
Tales of the Dark 2

Clute, John, David Pringle & Simon Ounsley, eds.
Interzone: The 2nd Anthology

Cramer, Kathryn & David G. Hartwell, eds.
Christmas Ghosts

Cramer, Kathryn & Peter D. Pautz, eds.
The Architecture of Fear, oa

Dalby, Richard, ed.
Dracula's Brood
The Virago Book of Ghost Stories, oa

Dann, Jack M. & Gardner R. Dozois, eds.
Demons!

Dann, Jeanne Van Buren & Jack M. Dann, eds.
In the Field of Fire, oa

Datlow, Ellen, ed.
The Fifth Omni Book of Science Fiction

Dozois, Gardner R., ed.
The Year's Best Science Fiction, Fourth Annual Collection

Etchison, Dennis, ed.
Masters of Darkness II

Evans, Christopher & Robert Holdstock, eds.
Other Edens, oa

Foster, John, ed.
Spaceways

Gotlieb, Phyllis & Douglas Barbour, eds.
Tesseracts 2

Gowar, Mick, ed.
Twisted Circuits, oa

Grant, Charles L., ed.
Doom City, oa
Shadows 10, oa

Green, Jen & Sarah Lefanu, eds.
Despatches from the Frontiers of the Female Mind

Greenberg, Martin H., ed.
Amazing Science Fiction Stories: The War Years 1936-1945
Amazing Science Fiction Stories: The Wild Years 1946-1955
Amazing Science Fiction Stories: The Wonder Years 1926-1935
Cinemonsters

Greenberg, Martin H. & Patrick L. Price, eds.
Fantastic Stories: Tales of the Weird and Wondrous

Greenberg, Martin H. & Charles G. Waugh, eds.
House Shudders
Vamps

Haining, Peter, ed.
Poltergeist: Tales of Deadly Ghosts
Tales of Dungeons and Dragons
Werewolf: Horror Stories of the Man Beast

Haldeman, Joe W., Martin H. Greenberg & Charles G. Waugh, eds.
Supertanks

Hartwell, David G., ed.
The Dark Descent

Jaffery, Sheldon R., ed.
Selected Tales of Grim and Grue from the Horror Pulps
The Weirds

Kahn, Joan, ed.
Ready or Not: Here Come Fourteen Frightening Stories!

Kaveney, Roz, ed.
Tales from the Forbidden Planet, oa

Kaye, Marvin, ed.
Devils and Demons

Keeping, Charles, ed.
Charles Keeping's Classic Tales of the Macabre

Lindahn, Ron & Val Lakey Lindahn, eds.
A Southern Fantasy: 13th World Fantasy Convention Program Book, oa

Martin, George R.R., ed.
Wild Cards II: Aces High, oa
Wild Cards III: Jokers Wild, oa

McSherry, Frank D., Jr., Martin H. Greenberg & Charles G. Waugh, eds.
Nightmares in Dixie: Thirteen Horror Tales From the American South

Mitchell, Elizabeth, ed.
Free Lancers, oa

Morris, Janet, ed.
Angels in Hell, oa

Morris, Janet, ed. (continued)
Crusaders in Hell, oa
Masters in Hell, oa

Myers, Amy, ed.
The Third Book of After Midnight Stories, oa

Norton, Andre, ed.
Tales of the Witch World, oa

Norton, Andre & Robert Adams, eds.
Magic in Ithkar 4, oa

Paget, Clarence, ed.
The 28th Pan Book of Horror Stories, oa

Pardoe, Rosemary & Richard Dalby, eds.
Ghosts and Scholars, oa

Pattrick, William, ed.
Mysterious Motoring Stories
Mysterious Sea Stories

Petherick, Simon, ed.
Classic Stories of Mystery, Horror and Suspense

Pournelle, Jerry E., ed.
Imperial Stars, Vol. 2: Republic and Empire
There Will Be War, Vol. VI: Guns of Darkness

Preiss, Byron, ed.
The Universe, oa

Richardson, Jean, ed.
Beware, Beware - Strange and Sinister Tales

Ridgway, Jim & Michele Benjamin, eds.
PsiFi: Psychological Theories and Science Fictions

Rucker, Rudy, ed.
Mathenauts: Tales of Mathematical Wonder

Russell, Jean, ed.
Supernatural Stories: 13 Tales of the Unexpected

Russo, Richard, ed.
Dreams Are Wiser Than Men

Ryan, Alan, ed.
Vampires

Saha, Arthur W., ed.
The Year's Best Fantasy Stories: 13

San Souci, Robert D., ed.
Short & Shivery

Schiff, Stuart David, ed.
Whispers VI, oa

Schmidt, Stanley, ed.
6 Decades: The Best of Analog

Scrocco, Jean L., ill. & Judy Mastrangelo, ed.
Antique Fairy Tales

Serling, Carol, Martin H. Greenberg & Charles G. Waugh, eds.
Rod Serling's Night Gallery Reader

ANTHOLOGIES

Shetterly, Will & Emma Bull, eds.
Liavek: Wizard's Row, oa

Silverberg, Robert, ed.
Robert Silverberg's Worlds of Wonder

Snodgrass, Melinda M., ed.
A Very Large Array

Sonntag, Linda, ed.
The Ghost Story Treasury

Wagner, Karl Edward, ed.
Echoes of Valor
The Year's Best Horror Stories: XV

Waugh, Charles G. & Martin H. Greenberg, eds.
Battlefields Beyond Tomorrow: Science Fiction War Stories

Waugh, Charles G., Martin H. Greenberg & Frank D. McSherry, Jr., eds.
Strange Maine

Weis, Margaret & Tracy Hickman, eds.
DragonLance Tales Vol. 1: The Magic of Krynn, oa
DragonLance Tales Vol. 2: Kender, Gully Dwarves, and Gnomes, oa
DragonLance Tales Vol. 3: Love and War, oa

Williams, Sheila & Cynthia Manson, eds.
Tales From Isaac Asimov's Science Fiction Magazine

Williamson, J.N., ed.
Masques II, oa

Wollheim, Donald A. & Arthur W. Saha, ed.
The 1987 Annual World's Best SF

Yolen, Jane, Martin H. Greenberg & Charles G. Waugh, eds.
Spaceships and Spells, oa

Zahava, Irene, ed.
Hear the Silence: Stories of Myth, Magic and Renewal, oa

Zebrowski, George, ed.
Synergy; New Science Fiction: Vol. 1, oa

Zipes, Jack, ed.
Don't Bet on the Prince: Contemporary Feminist Fairy Tales in North America and Europe
Victorian Fairy Tales: The Revolt of the Fairies and Elves

Magazines . . . .

2AM
v.1 #3, Spring 1987, Gretta M. Anderson, ed.
v.1 #4, Summer 1987, Gretta M. Anderson, ed.
v.2 #1, Fall 1987, Gretta M. Anderson, ed.
v.2 #2, Winter 1987, Gretta M. Anderson, ed.

Aboriginal SF
v.1 #3, Feb.-March 1987, Charles C. Ryan, ed.
v.1 #4, May-June 1987, Charles C. Ryan, ed.
v.1 #5, July-Aug. 1987, Charles C. Ryan, ed.
v.1 #6, Sept.-Oct. 1987, Charles C. Ryan, ed.
v.2 #1, Nov.-Dec. 1987, Charles C. Ryan, ed.

Amazing Science Fiction Stories
v.61 #5, January 1987, Patrick Lucien Price, ed.
v.61 #6, March 1987, Patrick Lucien Price, ed.
v.62 #1, May 1987, Patrick Lucien Price, ed.
v.62 #2, July 1987, Patrick Lucien Price, ed.
v.62 #3, September 1987, Patrick Lucien Price, ed.
v.62 #4, November 1987, Patrick Lucien Price, ed.

American Fantasy
v.2 #2, Winter 1987, Robert T. Garcia & Nancy Garcia, eds.
v.2 #3, Spring 1987, Robert T. Garcia & Nancy Garcia, eds.
v.2 #4, Summer 1987, Robert T. Garcia & Nancy Garcia, eds.

Analog Science Fiction/Science Fact
v.107 # 1, January 1987, Stanley Schmidt, ed.
v.107 # 2, February 1987, Stanley Schmidt, ed.
v.107 # 3, March 1987, Stanley Schmidt, ed.
v.107 # 4, April 1987, Stanley Schmidt, ed.
v.107 # 5, May 1987, Stanley Schmidt, ed.
v.107 # 6, June 1987, Stanley Schmidt, ed.
v.107 # 7, July 1987, Stanley Schmidt, ed.
v.107 # 8, August 1987, Stanley Schmidt, ed.
v.107 # 9, September 1987, Stanley Schmidt, ed.
v.107 #10, October 1987, Stanley Schmidt, ed.
v.107 #11, November 1987, Stanley Schmidt, ed.
v.107 #12, December 1987, Stanley Schmidt, ed.
v.107 #13, Mid-December 1987, Stanley Schmidt, ed.

Apex!
#1, Ramona Pope Richards, ed.

Aphelion
5, Summer 86/87, Peter McNamara, ed.

Back Brain Recluse
7, Chris Reed, ed.

The Best of the Mage
8, Fall 1987, Jeffrey V. Yule, ed.

Border Land
Special World Fantasy Convention Issue, Oct. 1987, R.S. Hadji, ed.

Eldritch Tales No. 13
v.4 #1, Crispin Burnham, ed.

Eldritch Tales No. 14
v.4 #2, Crispin Burnham, ed.

Fantasy Book
v.5 #5, March 1987, Dennis Mallonee & Nick Smith, eds.

Fantasy Tales
v.8 #16, Winter 1986, Stephen Jones, ed.

Footsteps
#8, November 1987, Bill Munster, ed.

The Grabinski Reader
#2, Spring 1987, Miroslaw Lipinski, ed.

Grue
#4, 1987, Peggy Nadramia, ed.
#5, 1987, Peggy Nadramia, ed.
#6, 1987, Peggy Nadramia, ed.

Haunts
9/10, Fall 1987, Joseph K. Cherkes, ed.

The Horror Show
v.5 #1, January 1987, David B. Silva, ed.
v.5 #2, Spring 1987, David B. Silva, ed.
v.5 #3, Summer 1987, David B. Silva, ed.
v.5 #4, Fall 1987, David B. Silva, ed.
v.5 #5, Winter 1987, David B. Silva, ed.

Ice River
v1 #1, Summer 1987, David Memmott, ed.

Interzone
#19, Spring 1987, Simon Ounsley & David Pringle, eds.
#20, Summer 1987, Simon Ounsley & David Pringle, eds.
#21, Autumn 1987, Simon Ounsley & David Pringle, eds.
#22, Winter 1987, Simon Ounsley & David Pringle, eds.

Isaac Asimov's Science Fiction Magazine
v.11 # 1, January 1987, Gardner R. Dozois, ed.
v.11 # 2, February 1987, Gardner R. Dozois, ed.
v.11 # 3, March 1987, Gardner R. Dozois, ed.
v.11 # 4, April 1987, Gardner R. Dozois, ed.
v.11 # 5, May 1987, Gardner R. Dozois, ed.
v.11 # 6, June 1987, Gardner R. Dozois, ed.
v.11 # 7, July 1987, Gardner R. Dozois, ed.
v.11 # 8, August 1987, Gardner R. Dozois, ed.
v.11 # 9, September 1987, Gardner R. Dozois, ed.
v.11 #10, October 1987, Gardner R. Dozois, ed.
v.11 #11, November 1987, Gardner R. Dozois, ed.
v.11 #12, December 1987, Gardner R. Dozois, ed.
v.11 #13, Mid-December 1987, Gardner R. Dozois, ed.

The Magazine of Fantasy & Science Fiction
v.72 #1, January 1987, Edward L. Ferman, ed.
v.72 #2, February 1987, Edward L. Ferman, ed.
v.72 #3, March 1987, Edward L. Ferman, ed.
v.72 #4, April 1987, Edward L. Ferman, ed.
v.72 #5, May 1987, Edward L. Ferman, ed.
v.72 #6, June 1987, Edward L. Ferman, ed.
v.73 #1, July 1987, Edward L. Ferman, ed.
v.73 #2, August 1987, Edward L. Ferman, ed.
v.73 #3, September 1987, Edward L. Ferman, ed.
v.73 #4, October 1987, Edward L. Ferman, ed.
v.73 #5, November 1987, Edward L. Ferman, ed.
v.73 #6, December 1987, Edward L. Ferman, ed.

The Mage
6, Winter 1987, Jeffrey V. Yule, ed.
7, Spring 1987, Jeffrey V. Yule, ed.

MAGAZINES

Minnesota Fantasy Review
v.1 #1, October 1987, Ed Shannon & Mike Odden, eds.

New Pathways Into Science Fiction And Fantasy
v.1 #6, Jan/Feb 1987, Michael G. Adkisson, ed.
v.1 #7, April/May 1987, Michael G. Adkisson, ed.
v.1 #8, August 1987, Michael G. Adkisson, ed.
v.1 #9, November 1987, Michael G. Adkisson, ed.

Night Cry
v.2 #3, Spring 1987, Alan Rodgers, ed.
v.2 #4, Summer 1987, Alan Rodgers, ed.
v.2 #5, Fall 1987, Alan Rodgers, ed.

Pulpsmith
v.6 #4, Winter '87, Harry Smith, ed.

Rod Serling's The Twilight Zone Magazine
v.6 #6, February 1987, Tappan King, ed.
v.7 #1, April 1987, Tappan King, ed.
v.7 #2, June 1987, Tappan King, ed.
v.7 #3, August 1987, Tappan King, ed.
v.7 #4, October 1987, Tappan King, ed.
v.7 #5, December 1987, Tappan King, ed.

Salarius
No. 3, March 1987, Mary Sikes, ed.
v.1 #4, Ruth Colley, ed.

SF International
No. 1, January/February 1987, William H. Wheeler, ed.
No. 2, March/April 1987, William H. Wheeler, ed.

Space & Time
#72, Summer 1987, Gordon Linzner, ed.
#73, Winter 1988, Gordon Linzner, ed.

Tales of the Unanticipated
#2, Spring 1987, Eric M. Heideman, ed.

Weirdbook 22
Summer 1987, W. Paul Ganley, ed.

Whispers
#23/24, v.6 #3-4, October 1987, Stuart David Schiff, ed.

Reference . . . .

Alkon, Paul K.
Origins of Futuristic Fiction

Apel, D. Scott, ed.
Philip K. Dick: The Dream Connection

Aronovitz, David
Ballantine Books: The First Decade

Barr, Marleen S.
Alien to Femininity

Barr, Marleen S., Richard Law & Ruth Salvaggio
Suzy McKee Charnas, Joan Vinge, Octavia Butler

Barratt, David
C.S. Lewis and His World

Barron, Neil
Anatomy of Wonder, Third Edition

Beauchamp, Gorman, Kenneth Roemer & Nicholas D. Smith, eds.
Utopian Studies 1

Blish, James
The Tale That Wags the God

Brians, Paul
Nuclear Holocausts: Atomic War in Fiction, 1895-1984

Brown, Charles N. & William G. Contento
Science Fiction, Fantasy, & Horror: 1986

Burroughs, William S.
The Adding Machine: Collected Essays

Bussing, Sabine
Aliens in the Home: The Child in Horror Fiction

Carter, Margaret L.
Specter or Delusion? The Supernatural in Gothic Fiction

Cassutt, Michael
Who's Who in Space: The First 25 Years

Cerasini, Marc A. & Charles Hoffman
Robert E. Howard

Christopher, Joe R.
C.S. Lewis

Clareson, Thomas D.
Frederik Pohl

Collings, Michael R.
The Stephen King Phenomenon

Collings, Michael R., ed.
Reflections on the Fantastic: Selected Essays from the Fourth International Conference on the Fantastic in the Arts

Conner, Jeff
Stephen King Goes to Hollywood

Cornwill, Sue & Mike Kott
The Official Price Guide to Star Trek and Star Wars Collectibles, Second Edition

Corydon, Bent & L. Ron Hubbard, Jr.
L. Ron Hubbard: Messiah or Madman?

Crossley, Robert, ed.
Talking Across the World

Dooley, Dennis & Gary Engle
Superman at Fifty: The Persistence of a Legend

Dowling, David
Fictions of Nuclear Disaster

Fonstad, Karen Wynn
Atlas of the Dragonlance World, pi

Ford, Paul F.
Companion to Narnia

Geduld, Harry M.
The Definitive Time Machine: A Critical Edition of H.G. Wells' Scientific Romance, n.

Hall, Hal W.
Science Fiction and Fantasy Reference Index, 1878-1985

Hardy, Phil
The Encyclopedia of Horror Movies

Heller, Terry
The Delights of Terror: An Aesthetics of the Tale of Terror

Henry, Laurie
1987 Fiction Writer's Market

Herbert, Frank
The Maker of Dune: Insights of a Master of Science Fiction

Hodgson, Amanda
Romances of William Morris

Hollow, John
Against the Night, the Stars: The Science Fiction of Arthur C. Clarke

Hopkins, Mariane S.
Fandom Directory No. 9 (1987-1988)

Ketterer, David
Imprisoned in a Tesseract: The Life and Work of James Blish

Kies, Cosette
The Occult in the Western World: An Annotated Bibliography

Larson, Randall D.
The Complete Robert Bloch: An Illustrated, Comprehensive Bibliography Robert Bloch

Manguel, Alberto & Gianni Guadalupi
The Dictionary of Imaginary Places, Expanded Edition

Mathews, Jack
The Battle of Brazil: The Authorized Story and Annotated Screenplay of Terry Gilliam's Landmark Film, co

Minta, Stephen
Garcia Marquez: Writer of Colombia

Moorcock, Michael
Wizardry and Wild Romance

Olsen, Lance
Eclipse of Uncertainty: An Introduction to Postmodern Fantasy

Phillips, Michael R.
George MacDonald

Pieratt, Asa, Julie Huffman-Klinkowitz & Jerome Klinkowitz, eds.
Kurt Vonnegut: A Comprehensive Bibliography

Pierce, John J.
Foundations of Science Fiction: A Study in Imagination and Evolution
Great Themes of Science Fiction

Platt, Charles
Dream Makers: SF and Fantasy Writers at Work (Revised)

REFERENCE

Pringle, David
Science Fiction: The 100 Best Novels

Raeper, William
Fantasy King: A Biography of George MacDonald

Ridgway, Jim & Michele Benjamin, eds.
PsiFi: Psychological Theories and Science Fictions, an

Robinson, Roger, comp.
Who's Hugh?: An SF Reader's Guide to Pseudonyms

Robinson, Roger, ed.
The Writings of Henry Kenneth Bulmer

Rovin, Jeff
The Encyclopedia of Supervillains

Saintsbury, Elizabeth
George MacDonald: A Short Life

Schweitzer, Darrell, ed.
Discovering H.P. Lovecraft

Slusser, George E. & Eric S. Rabkin, eds.
Aliens: The Anthropology of Science Fiction
Intersections: Fantasy and Science Fiction

Slusser, George E., Eric S. Rabkin & Colin Greenland, eds.
Storm Warnings: Science Fiction Confronts the Future

Smith, David C.
H.G. Wells, Desperately Mortal

Sobchack, Vivian
Screening Space: The American Science Fiction Film

South, Malcolm, ed.
Mythical and Fabulous Creatures: A Sourcebook and Research Guide

Spark, Muriel
Mary Shelley: A Biography

Spencer, Kathleen
Charles Williams

Spivack, Charlotte
Merlin's Daughters: Contemporary Women Writers of Fantasy

Stover, Professor Leon
The Prophetic Soul: A Reading of H.G. Wells' Things to Come
Robert A. Heinlein

Thornburg, Mary K. Patterson
The Monster in the Mirror: Gender and the Sentimental/Gothic Myth in Frankenstein

Twitchell, James B.
Dreadful Pleasures

Waller, Gregory A., ed.
American Horrors

Warrick, Patricia S.
Mind in Motion: The Fiction of Philip K. Dick

Weis, Margaret & Tracy Hickman, eds.
Leaves from the Inn of the Last Home

Williamson, J.N., ed.
How to Write Tales of Horror, Fantasy & Science Fiction

Art Books . . . .

Aiken, Joan
The Moon's Revenge, nv

Anonymous, ed.
The Orbit Poster Book

Asprin, Robert Lynn & Mel White
Duncan and Mallory: The Bar-None Ranch, gn

Bradbury, Ray
Fever Dream, ss

Carroll, Lewis
The Complete Alice and The Hunting of the Snark, om

Claremont, Chris, et al
The Uncanny X-Men, gn

Davids, Hollace & Paul Davids
The Fires of Pele

Doran, Colleen
A Distant Soil, gn

Fancher, Jane
Gate of Ivrel: Claiming Rites, gn

Foglio, Phil & Robert Lynn Asprin
Myth Adventures Two, gn

Fonstad, Karen Wynn
Atlas of the Dragonlance World

Giraud, Jean "Moebius"
Arzach and Other Fantasy Stories
The Long Tomorrow and Other Science Fiction Stories
Moebius 1: Upon a Star, gn

Gorey, Edward
The Raging Tide

Gray, Nicholas Stuart
The Sorcerer's Apprentices, ss

Hague, Michael
Michael Hague's World of Unicorns

Hernandez, Gilbert, Jaime Hernandez, Mario Hernandez & Dean Motter
The Return of Mister X, gn

Johnson, Shane
Mr. Scott's Guide to the Enterprise

Kirchner, Paul
The Bus

Letendre, Serge & Regis Loisel
Roxanna #2: The Temple of Oblivion, gn

Martin, George R.R., Pat Broderick, Neal McPheeters & Doug Moench
Sandkings, gn

Marx, Christy & Peter Ledger
The Sisterhood of Steel: Baronwe: Daughter of Death, gn

Miller, Frank
Ronin, gn

Moncuse, Steve
The Fish Police, gn

Moorcock, Michael & Rodney Matthews
Elric at the End of Time

Moore, Alan
Saga of the Swamp Thing, gn
Watchmen, gn

Preiss, Byron, ed.
The Universe, oa

Reynolds, Kay, ed.
Robotech Art 2

Sale, Tim, Lynn Abbey & Robert Lynn Asprin
Thieves' World Graphics 4, gn

Schuiten, Francois & Peeters
The Great Walls of Samaris, gn

Segrelles, Vincente
The Art of Segrelles
The Mercenary: The Cult of the Sacred Fire and the Formula

Sibley, Brian
Snow White and the Seven Dwarfs & the Making of the Classic Film, nf

Suckling, Nigel
Heroic Dreams

Van Hamme, Jean & Grzegorz Rosinski
Thorgal: The Archers, gn

Wagner, Matt
Mage, Volume One: The Hero Discovered, gn

Weis, Margaret, ed.
The Art of the DragonLance Saga

Weller, Tom
Cvltvre Made Stvpid

Whelan, Michael
Michael Whelan's Works of Wonder, nf

Wilson, Gahan
Eddy Deco's Last Caper: An Illustrated Mystery, n.

Woodroffe, Patrick
A Closer Look: The Art Techniques of Patrick Woodroffe, nf

Associational . . . .

Aldiss, Brian W.
Ruins, nv

Amis, Kingsley
Collected Short Stories, co

Amis, Martin
Einstein's Monsters, co

ASSOCIATIONAL

Asimov, Janet & Isaac Asimov
How to Enjoy Writing: A Book of Aid and Comfort, nf

Atwood, Margaret
Bluebeard's Egg, co

Ballard, J.G.
The Day of Creation, n.

Banks, Iain
Espedair Street, n.

Biggle, Lloyd, Jr.
Interface for Murder, n.

Bova, Ben
Welcome to Moonbase, nf

Burroughs, William S.
The Adding Machine: Collected Essays, nf

Byatt, Antonia
Sugar and Other Stories, co

Cassutt, Michael
Who's Who in Space: The First 25 Years, nf

Dick, Philip K.
Cosmogony and Cosmology, nf
Mary and the Giant, n.

Ely, Scott
Starlight, n.

Fairley, John & Simon Welfare
Arthur C. Clarke's Chronicles of the Strange and Mysterious, nf

Forrest, Katherine V.
Dreams and Swords, oc

Gaiman, Neil
Don't Panic: The Official Hitch Hiker's Guide to the Galaxy Companion, nf

Gardner, Martin
The No-Sided Professor, co

Goldman, William
Brothers, n.

Haining, Peter
Doctor Who: The Time-Travellers' Guide, nf
The Dracula Centenary Book, nf

Hartley, L.P.
The Complete Short Stories of L.P. Hartley, om

Hubbard, L. Ron
Buckskin Brigades, n.

Ing, Dean
Blood of Eagles, n.

Irwin, Walter & G.B. Love, eds.
The Best of Trek #12, nf

Jackson, Sir William
Alternative Third World War, 1985 - 2035: A Personal History, nf

Kennedy, Leigh
Faces, co

Kilworth, Garry
Spiral Winds, n.

King, Stephen
Misery, n.

Lafferty, R.A.
My Heart Leaps Up, Chapters 3 & 4, ph

Le Guin, Ursula K.
Buffalo Gals and Other Animal Presences, co

Leatherdale, Clive, ed.
The Origins of "Dracula": The Background to Bram Stoker's Gothic Masterpiece, nf

Marten, Jacqueline
Dream Walker, n.

McCaffrey, Anne
The Lady, n.

McCrumb, Sharyn
Bimbos of the Death Sun, n.

Miller, Rex
Slob, n.

Miller, Russell
Bare-Faced Messiah, nf

Moorcock, Michael
The Brothel in Rosenstrasse, n.

O'Connell, Nicholas
At the Field's End: Interviews with 20 Pacific Northwest Writers, nf

Platt, Charles
How to Be a Happy Cat, ms

Pohl, Frederik
Chernobyl, n.

Pringle, David
Imaginary People, nf

Pulver, Mary Monica
Murder at the War, n.

Quinn, Tim & Dicky Howett
The Doctor Who Fun Book, nf

Roberts, Keith
A Heron Caught in Weeds, co

Rucker, Rudy
Mind Tools, nf

Russ, Joanna
On Strike Against God, n.

Russo, Richard, ed.
Dreams Are Wiser Than Men, an

Saunders, David
Encyclopaedia of the Worlds of Doctor Who: A-D, nf

See, Carolyn
Golden Days, n.

Somtow, S.P.
Forgetting Places, n.

Spark, Muriel
The Stories of Muriel Spark, co

Springer, Nancy
A Horse to Love, n.

Stevenson, Drew
The Case of the Visiting Vampire, n.

Turek, Leslie, ed.
If I Ran The Zoo [cross out Zoo]...Con: The Smofcon 3 Game, nf

Van Ash, Cay
The Fires of Fu Manchu, n.

Vonnegut, Kurt, Jr.
Bluebeard, n.

Webb, Sharon
Pestis 18, n.

Weller, Tom
Cvltvre Made Stvpid, pi

Wilhelm, Kate
The Hamlet Trap, n.

Wilson, Gahan
Eddy Deco's Last Caper: An Illustrated Mystery, n.

Wilson, Rudy
The Red Truck, n.

MISCELLANEOUS

Miscellaneous . . . .

Bricusse, Leslie
Christmas 1993, pm

Burgess, Anthony
A Clockwork Orange, pl

de Lint, Charles
Ascian in Rose, na

Glover, Julian
Beowulf, pm

Livingstone, Ian
Casket of Souls, ss

Melanos, Jack A.
Sindbad and the Evil Genie, pl

Poe, Edgar Allan & Melvin R. White
The Tell-Tale Heart, pl

Shea, Michael
Fat Face, nv

Sturgeon, Theodore
Pruzy's Pot, ss

Author List: Stories

ALDISS, BRIAN W.

Aldiss, Brian W. (continued)
Poor Little Warrior!, ss *F&SF* Apr,1958
  Great Science Fiction of the 20th Century, ed. Robert
    Silverberg+, Crown/Avenel, 1987
The Price of Cabbages, nv **Other Edens**, ed. Christopher Evans &
  Robert Holdstock, Unwin: London,1987
SF: From Secret Movement to Big Business, ar *Aboriginal SF*
  May,1987
Three Coins in Clockwork Fountains [Three Coins in Enigmatic
  Fountains], gp **New Writings in SF** #26,1975
    Carefully Observed Women; ss
    The Daffodil Returns the Smile; ss
    The Year of the Quiet Computer; ss
  New Pathways Nov,1987
Tourney, ss **Tales from the Forbidden Planet**, ed. Roz Kaveney,
  Titan,1987
Waiting for the Universe to Begin, ss **Epoch**, ed. Roger Elwood &
  Robert Silverberg, Berkley,1975
    The Aperture Moment; gp
  New Pathways Apr,1987
What Should an SF Novel Be About?, ar *Fantasy Review* Apr,1986
  Synergy; New Science Fiction: Vol. 1, ed. George Zebrowski,
    Harcourt Brace Jovanovich, 1987
The Year of the Quiet Computer, ss **New Writings in SF** #26,1975
    Three Coins in Clockwork Fountains; gp
  New Pathways Nov,1987

Aldridge, Ray
The Flesh Tinker and the Loneliest Man, ss *Amazing* Jul,1987

Alecsandrai, Vasile
The Vampyre, pm *English Illustrated Magazine* Nov,1886
  Dracula's Brood, ed. Richard Dalby, Crucible, 1987

Allen, J.B.
Multiple Origami, ss *Amazing* Jul,1987

Allen, Lori
Time Windows, ss *F&SF* Jun,1987

Allen, Roger MacBride
A Hole in the Sun, nv *Analog* Apr,1987

Amis, Kingsley
The 2003 Claret, ss **The Compleat Imbiber** #2, ed. Cyril Ray,1958
  Collected Short Stories, Hutchinson, 1987
Affairs of Death, ss **Shakespeare's Stories**,1982
  Collected Short Stories, Hutchinson, 1987
All the Blood Within Me, ss *The Spectator*,1962
  Collected Short Stories, Hutchinson, 1987
Court of Enquiry, ss *The Spectator*,1956
  Collected Short Stories, Hutchinson, 1987
The Darkwater Hall Mystery, ss *Playboy*,1978
  Collected Short Stories, Hutchinson, 1987
Dear Illusion, ss **Covent Garden Stories** #1,1972
  Collected Short Stories, Hutchinson, 1987
The Friends of Plonk, ss *Town*,1964
  Collected Short Stories, Hutchinson, 1987
Hemingway in Space, ss *Punch* Dec,1960
  Collected Short Stories, Hutchinson, 1987
The House on the Headland, ss *The Times*,1979
  Collected Short Stories, Hutchinson, 1987
I Spy Strangers, ss **My Enemy's Enemy**, London: Gollancz,1962
  Collected Short Stories, Hutchinson, 1987
Introduction, in
  Collected Short Stories, Hutchinson, 1987
Investing in Futures, ss **The Compleat Imbiber**, ed. Cyril Ray,1986
  Collected Short Stories, Hutchinson, 1987
Mason's Life, ss *The Sunday Times*,1972
  Collected Short Stories, Hutchinson, 1987
Moral Fibre, ss *Esquire*,1958
  Collected Short Stories, Hutchinson, 1987
My Enemy's Enemy, ss *Encounter*,1955
  Collected Short Stories, Hutchinson, 1987
Something Strange, nv *The Spectator*,1960; *F&SF* Jul,1961
  Collected Short Stories, Hutchinson, 1987
To See the Sun, ss
  Collected Short Stories, Hutchinson, 1987

Amis, Kingsley (continued)
Too Much Trouble, ss **Penguin Modern Stories** #11,1972
  Collected Short Stories, Hutchinson, 1987
Who or What was It?, ss *Playboy*,1972
  Collected Short Stories, Hutchinson, 1987

Amis, Martin
Bujak and the Strong Force, or God's Love, nv *The London Review of
  Books*
  Einstein's Monsters, Cape, 1987
The Immortals, ss
  Einstein's Monsters, Cape, 1987
Insight at Flame Lake, ss *Vanity Fair*
  Einstein's Monsters, Cape, 1987
The Little Puppy That Could, nv *The Literary Review*
  Einstein's Monsters, Cape, 1987
Thinkability, ms
  Einstein's Monsters, Cape, 1987
The Time Disease, ss *Granta*
  Einstein's Monsters, Cape, 1987

Andersen, Hans Christian
The Barnyard Cock and the Weathercock, vi
  Andersen's Fairy Tales, NAL/Signet Classic, 1987
The Butterfly, vi
  Andersen's Fairy Tales, NAL/Signet Classic, 1987
The Candles, vi
  Andersen's Fairy Tales, NAL/Signet Classic, 1987
Cloddy Hans, ss
  Andersen's Fairy Tales, NAL/Signet Classic, 1987
The Collar, vi
  Andersen's Fairy Tales, NAL/Signet Classic, 1987
The Darning Needle, ss
  Andersen's Fairy Tales, NAL/Signet Classic, 1987
The Drop of Water, vi
  Andersen's Fairy Tales, NAL/Signet Classic, 1987
The Dung Beetle, ss
  Andersen's Fairy Tales, NAL/Signet Classic, 1987
The Emperor's New Cloths, ss
  Andersen's Fairy Tales, NAL/Signet Classic, 1987
The Evil Prince, vi
  Andersen's Fairy Tales, NAL/Signet Classic, 1987
The Fable Alludes to You, vi
  Andersen's Fairy Tales, NAL/Signet Classic, 1987
The Flea and the Professor, ss
  Andersen's Fairy Tales, NAL/Signet Classic, 1987
The Flying Trunk, ss
  Andersen's Fairy Tales, NAL/Signet Classic, 1987
The Garden of Paradise, ss
  Andersen's Fairy Tales, NAL/Signet Classic, 1987
The Gardener and the Lord and Lady, ss
  Andersen's Fairy Tales, NAL/Signet Classic, 1987
The Gate Key, ss
  Andersen's Fairy Tales, NAL/Signet Classic, 1987
The Girl Who Trod on the Loaf, ss
  Andersen's Fairy Tales, NAL/Signet Classic, 1987
The Happy Family, vi
  Andersen's Fairy Tales, NAL/Signet Classic, 1987
In a Thousand Years, vi
  Andersen's Fairy Tales, NAL/Signet Classic, 1987
In the Duck Yard, ss
  Andersen's Fairy Tales, NAL/Signet Classic, 1987
It's Quite True, vi
  Andersen's Fairy Tales, NAL/Signet Classic, 1987
The Jumpers, vi
  Andersen's Fairy Tales, NAL/Signet Classic, 1987
Little Claus and Big Claus, ss
  Andersen's Fairy Tales, NAL/Signet Classic, 1987
The Little Match Girl, vi
  Andersen's Fairy Tales, NAL/Signet Classic, 1987
The Little Mermaid, nv
  Andersen's Fairy Tales, NAL/Signet Classic, 1987
The Most Incredible Thing, ss
  Andersen's Fairy Tales, NAL/Signet Classic, 1987
The Nightingale, ss
  Andersen's Fairy Tales, NAL/Signet Classic, 1987
The Nisse at the Sausagemonger's, ss
  Andersen's Fairy Tales, NAL/Signet Classic, 1987

ANDERSEN, HANS CHRISTIAN

Andersen, Hans Christian (continued)
Pen and Inkwell, vi
  Andersen's Fairy Tales, NAL/Signet Classic, 1987
The Piggy Bank, vi
  Andersen's Fairy Tales, NAL/Signet Classic, 1987
The Princess and the Pea, vi
  Andersen's Fairy Tales, NAL/Signet Classic, 1987
The Red Shoes, ss
  Andersen's Fairy Tales, NAL/Signet Classic, 1987
The Rose Elf, ss
  Andersen's Fairy Tales, NAL/Signet Classic, 1987
The Shepherdess and the Chimney Sweep, ss
  Andersen's Fairy Tales, NAL/Signet Classic, 1987
The Snail and the Rosebush, vi
  Andersen's Fairy Tales, NAL/Signet Classic, 1987
The Snow Queen, nv,1844
  Andersen's Fairy Tales, NAL/Signet Classic, 1987
The Snowman, ss
  Andersen's Fairy Tales, NAL/Signet Classic, 1987
Soup from a Sausage Stick, ss
  Andersen's Fairy Tales, NAL/Signet Classic, 1987
The Steadfast Tin Soldier, ss
  Andersen's Fairy Tales, NAL/Signet Classic, 1987
The Sweethearts (The Top of the Ball), vi
  Andersen's Fairy Tales, NAL/Signet Classic, 1987
The Swineherd, ss
  Andersen's Fairy Tales, NAL/Signet Classic, 1987
The Talisman, vi
  Andersen's Fairy Tales, NAL/Signet Classic, 1987
The Teapot, vi
  Andersen's Fairy Tales, NAL/Signet Classic, 1987
The Tinderbox, ss,1835
  Andersen's Fairy Tales, NAL/Signet Classic, 1987
Two Virgins, vi
  Andersen's Fairy Tales, NAL/Signet Classic, 1987
The Ugly Duckling, ss
  Andersen's Fairy Tales, NAL/Signet Classic, 1987
What Papa Does Is Always Right, ss
  Andersen's Fairy Tales, NAL/Signet Classic, 1987

Anderson, Gretta M.
Preface, pr *2AM* Spr,1987
Preface, pr *2AM* Sum,1987
Preface, pr *2AM* Fll,1987
Preface, pr *2AM* Win,1987

Anderson, James
Deathstroke, ss *Eldritch Tales* #14,1987
Thatcher's Bluff, ss *Haunts* #9,1987

Anderson, Karen
Treaty in Tartessos, ss *F&SF* May,1963
  Isaac Asimov's Magical Worlds of Fantasy #9: Atlantis, ed. Isaac
    Asimov+, NAL/Signet, 1988

Anderson, Kevin J.
A Glimpse of the Ankou, ss *The Horror Show* Win,1987
The Old Man and the Cherry Tree, ss *Grue* #3,1986
  The Year's Best Fantasy Stories: 13, ed. Arthur W. Saha, DAW,
    1987

Anderson, Poul
Delenda Est, nv *F&SF* Dec,1955
  Isaac Asimov Presents the Great SF Stories: 17 (1955), ed. Isaac
    Asimov+, DAW, 1988
The Enemy Stars, n. J.B. Lippincott,1959
  The Enemy Stars, Baen, 1987
Eve Times Four, nv *Fantastic* Apr,1960
  Fantastic Stories: Tales of the Weird and Wondrous, ed. Martin
    H. Greenberg+, TSR, 1987
Foreword, fw
  The Enemy Stars, Baen, 1987
Hunter's Moon, nv *Analog* Nov,1978
  The Dark Void, ed. Isaac Asimov, Severn House, 1987
Introduction, in
  Intuit, Hal Clement, NESFA, 1987
Iron [Part 2], sl **New Destinies** v1, ed. Jim Baen, Baen,1987
Letter from Tomorrow, ss *Analog* Aug,1987

Anderson, Poul (continued)
The Long Remembering, ss *F&SF* Nov,1957
  **Isaac Asimov's Wonderful Worlds of Science Fiction #6:
    Neanderthals**, ed. Isaac Asimov+, NAL/Signet, 1987
The Queen of Air and Darkness, na *F&SF* Apr,1971
  Great Science Fiction of the 20th Century, ed. Robert
    Silverberg+, Crown/Avenel, 1987
Rachaela, nv *Fantasy Fiction* Jun,1953
  Devils and Demons, ed. Marvin Kaye, Doubleday, 1987
Requiem For a Universe, ss **Universe**, ed. Byron Preiss, Bantam
  Spectra,1987
The Ways of Love, nv *Destinies* v1#2, ed. James Baen,1979
  The Enemy Stars, Baen, 1987

Andreski, Luke
Skiophanes' Proof, ss **Gollancz - Sunday Times Best SF Stories**,
  Gollancz,1987

Andrews, Arlan
Ancient Ages, pm *Fantasy Book* Mar,1987
Epiphany, ss *Analog* Sep,1987
Glossanalia [Glossolalia], ss *Analog* Jul,1982;
  Computer Shopper Nov,1987
Occidental Injury, vi *Analog* Oct,1987
QTL, vi *Analog* Feb,1987

Andrews, Elton
Elegy to a Dead Satellite: Luna, pm *Amazing* Nov,1987

Andreyev, Leonid
Silence, ss **Silence**, Leonid Andreyev,1910
  Classic Stories of Mystery, Horror and Suspense, ed. Simon
    Petherick, Robert Hale, 1987

Anonymous
The Demon Lover, pm
  Devils and Demons, ed. Marvin Kaye, Doubleday, 1987
Ghost and the Skeleton, pm
  The Ghost Story Treasury, ed. Linda Sonntag, Putnam, 1987
Hollywood Grapevine, ar *Twilight Zone* Apr,1987
Illuminations: The Return of Lefty Feep, br *Twilight Zone* Aug,1987
The Leading Edge, br **New Destinies** v1, ed. Jim Baen, Baen,1987
The Man Who Wasn't There, pm
  The Ghost Story Treasury, ed. Linda Sonntag, Putnam, 1987
Monster Squad, mr *American Fantasy* Sum,1987
Mr. Nobody, pm
  The Ghost Story Treasury, ed. Linda Sonntag, Putnam, 1987
The Mysterious Stranger, nv *Odds and Ends*,1860
  Vampires, ed. Alan Ryan, SFBC, 1987
Nightmares, ar *The Horror Show* Jan,1987
Nightmares, ar *The Horror Show* Spr,1987
Nightmares, ar *The Horror Show* Sum,1987
Nightmares, ar *The Horror Show* Fll,1987
Nightmares, ar *The Horror Show* Win,1987
Scottish Prayer, pm
  The Ghost Story Treasury, ed. Linda Sonntag, Putnam, 1987
Syndicated Television: What Is It, Anyway?, ar *Twilight Zone* Dec,1987
The Twilight Zone Movie Trial: An Opinion, ms *Twilight Zone* Aug,1987

Anstey, F.
The Curse of the Catafalques, nv
  Christmas Ghosts, ed. Kathryn Cramer+, Arbor House, 1987

Anthony, Patricia
Blood Brothers, ss *Aboriginal SF* Feb,1987
What Brothers Are For, ss *Aboriginal SF* Nov,1987

Anthony, Piers
Faith of Tarot, n. Berkley: New York,1980
  Tarot, Ace, 1987
God of Tarot, n. Berkley: New York,1979
  Tarot, Ace, 1987
Imp to Nymph, ss **World Fantasy Convention Program Book**
  #13,1987
    First English publication, originally published as "Vom Kobold zur
    Nymphe" in **Goldmann Fantasy Foliant**.
Life, ss *Twilight Zone* Dec,1987

Anthony, Piers (continued)
  Vision of Tarot, n. Berkley: New York,1980
    Tarot, Ace, 1987

Anthony, Piers & Stanley Wiater
  A Conversation with Piers Anthony, iv *Twilight Zone* Dec,1987

Antieau, Kim
  Occupant, ss **Doom City**, ed. Charles L. Grant, Tor,1987
  Sanctuary, ss **Shadows #9**, ed. Charles L. Grant,1986
    The Year's Best Fantasy Stories: 13, ed. Arthur W. Saha, DAW,
    1987

Anvil, Christopher
  Ideological Defeat, nv *Analog* Sep,1972
    There Will Be War, Vol. VI: Guns of Darkness, ed. Jerry E.
    Pournelle, Tor, 1987
  Interesting Times, ss *Analog* Dec,1987
  Rags from Riches, ss *Amazing* Nov,1987

Apel, D. Scott
  Phil as I Knew Him, in
    Philip K. Dick: The Dream Connection, D. Scott Apel, Permanent
    Press, 1987
  Philip K. Dick: The Dream Connection, ar **Philip K. Dick: The Dream
    Connection**, D. Scott Apel, Permanent Press,1987
  Preface, pr
    Philip K. Dick: The Dream Connection, D. Scott Apel, Permanent
    Press, 1987

Apel, D. Scott, Kevin C. Briggs & Philip K. Dick
  Philip K. Dick in Interview, iv **Philip K. Dick: The Dream Connection**,
    D. Scott Apel, Permanent Press,1987

Ardai, Charles
  Wordware, gr *Twilight Zone* Dec,1987

Arguelles, Ivan
  Autoincineration of the Right Stuff, pm *Exquisite Corpse* May,1986
    Rhysling Anthology 1987, ed. Anonymous, SF Poetry Assc., 1987
  Baudelaire's Brain, pm *Ice River* Sum,1987

Arkee, Sister M. Anne, O.S.F.
  O Civile, pm *Amazing* Mar,1987

Armstrong, Charlotte
  Three Day Magic, na *F&SF* Sep,1952
    A shorter version was first printed in 1948.
    Strange Maine, ed. Charles G. Waugh +, Tapley, 1986

Armstrong, Michael
  Between the Devil and the Deep Blue Sea, nv **Crusaders in Hell**, ed.
    Janet Morris, New York: Baen,1987
  God's Eyes, nv **Masters of Hell**, ed. Janet Morris et al, Baen,1987
  The Verts Get a Nuke, ss *F&SF* Aug,1987

Arnason, Eleanor
  Glam's Story, ss *Tales of the Unanticipated #2*,1987
  There Was an Old Lady..., pm *Tales of the Unanticipated #2*,1987

Arno, Ed
  Cartoon, ct *F&SF* Apr,1987
  Cartoon, ct *F&SF* Sep,1987
  Cartoon, ct *F&SF* Oct,1987
  Cartoon, ct *F&SF* Nov,1987

Arnold, Margot
  The Girl in the Mirror, ss,1976
    Ready or Not, ed. Joan Kahn, Greenwillow, 1987

Arnold, Mark
  Illuminations: Bad Feng-Shui Killed Bruce Lee, ar *Twilight Zone*
    Jun,1987
  Illuminations: Expeditions to the Unknown, ar *Twilight Zone* Jun,1987
  Illuminations: First Pooch Sees Ghost, ar *Twilight Zone* Aug,1987
  Illuminations: I Sing the Body Eclectic, ar *Twilight Zone* Oct,1987
  The Other Side: Gore-Gonzola, ar *Twilight Zone* Jun,1987

Arnold, Mark (continued)
  The Other Side: Horrible Twisted Things Crawling, ar *Twilight Zone*
    Jun,1987
  The Other Side: In God We Rust, ar *Twilight Zone* Apr,1987
  Ultimate Getaways, ar *Twilight Zone* Oct,1987

Arroyo, Rane
  Loved Ones, pm *Ice River* Sum,1987
  The Red House, pm *Ice River* Sum,1987

Arthur, Robert
  The Wonderful Day [Miracle on Main Street], nv *Argosy Weekly* Jul
    6,1940
    Young Witches & Warlocks, ed. Isaac Asimov +, Harper & Row,
    1987

Arthurs, Bruce D.
  Death and the Ugly Woman, ss **Sword and Sorceress #4**, ed. Marion
    Zimmer Bradley,1987

Ashworth, Malcolm
  A Senoi Dream, ss **Gollancz - Sunday Times Best SF Stories**,
    Gollancz,1987

Asimov, Isaac
  1 to 999 [One in a Thousand], ss *Gallery* Sep,1981
    Mathenauts, ed. Rudy Rucker, Arbor House, 1987
  Academe, ed *IASFM* mid-Dec,1987
  The Bicentennial Man, nv **Stellar #2**, ed. Judy-Lynn del Rey,1976
    Great Science Fiction of the 20th Century, ed. Robert
    Silverberg +, Crown/Avenel, 1987
  Beyond the Stars, ed. Isaac Asimov, Severn House, 1987
  The Brazen Locked Room [also as "Gimmicks Three"], ss *F&SF*
    Nov,1956
    Devils and Demons, ed. Marvin Kaye, Doubleday, 1987
  The Dead Past, nv *Astounding* Apr,1956
    6 Decades: The Best of Analog, ed. Stanley Schmidt, Davis, 1986
  The Devil, in
    Isaac Asimov's Magical Worlds of Fantasy #8: Devils, ed. Isaac
    Asimov +, NAL/Signet, 1987
  Dreaming Is a Private Thing, ss *F&SF* Dec,1955
    Isaac Asimov Presents the Great SF Stories: 17 (1955), ed. Isaac
    Asimov +, DAW, 1988
  The Fable of the Three Princes, nv **Spaceships & Spells**, ed. Jane
    Yolen, Martin H. Greenberg & Charles G. Waugh, Harper &
    Row,1987
  The Feeling of Power, ss *If* Feb,1958
    Mathenauts, ed. Rudy Rucker, Arbor House, 1987
  The Fights of Spring, ss *IASFM* Feb,1987
  Forgetfullness, ed *IASFM* Jun,1987
  Galatea, ss *IASFM* mid-Dec,1987
  Harlan Ellison's I, Robot, ar *IASFM* Nov,1987
  How Exciting!, in
    Young Witches & Warlocks, ed. Isaac Asimov +, Harper & Row,
    1987
  The Ifs of History, in
    Agent of Byzantium, Harry Turtledove, Congdon &
    Weed/Contemporary, 1987
  Intellectual Cliches, ed *IASFM* Feb,1987
  Intimations of Mortality, ed *IASFM* Mar,1987
  Introduction, in
    Tales From Isaac Asimov's Science Fiction Magazine, ed. Sheila
    Williams +, Harcourt Brace Jovanovich, 1986
    Amazing Science Fiction Stories: The War Years 1936-1945, ed.
    Martin H. Greenberg, TSR, 1987
  Introduction: Neanderthal Man, in
    **Isaac Asimov's Wonderful Worlds of Science Fiction #6:
    Neanderthals**, ed. Isaac Asimov +, NAL/Signet, 1987
  Introduction: Shuttles, in
    **Isaac Asimov's Wonderful Worlds of Science Fiction #7: Space
    Shuttles**, ed. Isaac Asimov +, NAL/Signet, 1987
  Introduction: The Lost City, in
    Isaac Asimov's Magical Worlds of Fantasy #9: Atlantis, ed. Isaac
    Asimov +, NAL/Signet, 1988
  Introduction: What Again?, in
    Beyond the Stars, ed. Isaac Asimov, Severn House, 1987

ASIMOV, ISAAC

BAGNOLD, ENID

Asimov, Isaac (continued)
　The Last Shuttle, ss,1981
　　Isaac Asimov's Wonderful Worlds of Science Fiction #7: Space Shuttles, ed. Isaac Asimov+, NAL/Signet, 1987
　Left to Right, vi *Analog* Jan,1987
　The Machine That Won the War, ss *F&SF* Oct,1961
　　Battlefields Beyond Tomorrow, ed. Charles G. Waugh+, Crown/Bonanza, 1987
　Memory, ed *IASFM* Dec,1987
　New Writers, ed *IASFM* Jan,1987
　Plausibility, ed *IASFM* Sep,1987
　Potential, ss *IASFM* Feb,1983
　　Tales From Isaac Asimov's Science Fiction Magazine, ed. Sheila Williams+, Harcourt Brace Jovanovich, 1986
　Robot AL-76 Goes Astray, ss *Amazing* Feb,1942
　　Amazing Science Fiction Stories: The War Years 1936-1945, ed. Martin H. Greenberg, TSR, 1987
　Romance, ed *IASFM* Jul,1987
　Satisfaction Guaranteed, ss *Amazing* Apr,1951
　　Amazing Science Fiction Stories: The Wild Years 1946-1955, ed. Martin H. Greenberg, TSR, 1987
　Science: A Sacred Poet, ar *F&SF* Sep,1987
　Science: Asking the Right Question, ar *F&SF* Nov,1987
　Science: Beginning With Bone, ar *F&SF* May,1987
　Science: Brightening Stars, ar *F&SF* Jul,1987
　Science: New Stars, ar *F&SF* Jun,1987
　Science: Opposite!, ar *F&SF* Jan,1987
　Science: Sail On! Sail On!, ar *F&SF* Feb,1987
　Science: Super-Exploding Stars, ar *F&SF* Aug,1987
　Science: The Incredible Shrinking Planet, ar *F&SF* Mar,1987
　Science: The Light-Bringer, ar *F&SF* Apr,1987
　Science: The Road to Humanity, ar *F&SF* Dec,1987
　Science: The Very Error of the Moon, ar *F&SF* Oct,1987
　Space Flight, ed *IASFM* May,1987
　Survivors, ed *IASFM* Nov,1987
　Truth and Fiction, ed *IASFM* Apr,1987
　The Ugly Little Boy [Lastborn], na *Galaxy* Sep,1958
　　Isaac Asimov's Wonderful Worlds of Science Fiction #6: Neanderthals, ed. Isaac Asimov+, NAL/Signet, 1987
　Unification, ed *IASFM* Aug,1987
　Unknown, ed *IASFM* Oct,1987
　What If..., ss *Fantastic* Sum,1952
　　Fantastic Stories: Tales of the Weird and Wondrous, ed. Martin H. Greenberg+, TSR, 1987
　What Is the Universe?, ar **Universe**, ed. Byron Preiss, Bantam Spectra,1987

Asimov, Isaac & Janet Asimov
　Norby and the Invaders, n. Walker: New York,1985
　　Norby: Robot for Hire, Janet Asimov+, Ace, 1987
　Norby and the Lost Princess, n. Walker: New York,1985
　　Norby: Robot for Hire, Janet Asimov+, Ace, 1987

Asimov, Isaac & Harrison Roth
　Left to Right, and Beyond, vi *Analog* Jul,1987

Asimov, Janet & Isaac Asimov
　Norby and the Invaders, n. Walker: New York,1985
　　Norby: Robot for Hire, Janet Asimov+, Ace, 1987
　Norby and the Lost Princess, n. Walker: New York,1985
　　Norby: Robot for Hire, Janet Asimov+, Ace, 1987

Asire, Nancy
　By Invitation Only, nv **Crusaders in Hell**, ed. Janet Morris, New York: Baen,1987
　Cat's Tale, nv **Festival Moon**, ed. C.J. Cherryh, DAW,1987
　Houseguests, nv **Masters of Hell**, ed. Janet Morris et al, Baen,1987
　Night Ride, nv **Fever Season**, ed. C.J. Cherryh, DAW,1987

Asire, Nancy & C.J. Cherryh
　The Conscience of the King, na **Angels in Hell**, ed. Janet Morris, Baen,1987

Askew, Alice & Claude Askew
　Aylmer Vance and the Vampire, ss *The Weekly Tale-Teller*,1914
　　Dracula's Brood, ed. Richard Dalby, Crucible, 1987

Askew, Claude & Alice Askew
　Aylmer Vance and the Vampire, ss *The Weekly Tale-Teller*,1914
　　Dracula's Brood, ed. Richard Dalby, Crucible, 1987

Asprin, Robert Lynn
　The Ex-Khan, ss **Angels in Hell**, ed. Janet Morris, Baen,1987
　Introduction, in
　　Thieves' World 10: Aftermath, ed. Robert Lynn Asprin+, Ace, 1987
　Little Myth Marker, n. The Donning Company/Publishers: Norfolk & Virginia Beach, VA,1985
　　Myth Alliances, SFBC, 1987
　M.Y.T.H. Inc. Link, n. The Donning Company/Publishers: Norfolk & Virginia Beach, VA,1986
　　Myth Alliances, SFBC, 1987
　Myth-ing Persons, n. The Donning Company/Publishers: Norfolk & Virginia Beach, VA,1984
　　Myth Alliances, SFBC, 1987
　Two Gentlemen of the Trade, ss **Festival Moon**, ed. C.J. Cherryh, DAW,1987

Asquith, Cynthia
　The Follower, ss **My Grimmest Nightmare**, George Allen: London,1935
　　The Virago Book of Ghost Stories, ed. Richard Dalby, Virago, 1987

Atwood, Margaret
　Bluebeard's Egg, nv McLelland & Stewart: Toronto,1983
　　Don't Bet on the Prince, ed. Jack Zipes, Methuen, 1987
　　Bluebeard's Egg, Cape, 1987
　Freeforall, ss *The Toronto Star Weekly* Sep 20,1986
　　Tesseracts 2, ed. Phyllis Gotlieb+, Porcepic, 1987
　Hurricane Haze, nv
　　Bluebeard's Egg, Cape, 1987
　In Search of the Rattlesnake Plantain, ss *Harper's* Aug,1986
　　Bluebeard's Egg, Cape, 1987
　Loulou; or The Domestic Life of the Language, nv *Science Fiction Story-Reader*
　　Bluebeard's Egg, Cape, 1987
　The Salt Garden, nv *Ms.* Sep,1984
　　Bluebeard's Egg, Cape, 1987
　Scarlet Ibis, nv
　　Bluebeard's Egg, Cape, 1987
　Significant Moments in the Life of My Mother, ss *Queen's Quarterly*
　　Bluebeard's Egg, Cape, 1987
　Spring Song of the Frogs, ss
　　From Company
　　Bluebeard's Egg, Cape, 1987
　The Sunrise, nv
　　Bluebeard's Egg, Cape, 1987
　Uglypuss, nv
　　Bluebeard's Egg, Cape, 1987
　Unearthing Suite, ss
　　Bluebeard's Egg, Cape, 1987
　Walking on Water, ss
　　From Chateleine
　　Bluebeard's Egg, Cape, 1987
　The Whirlpool Rapids, ss *Toronto Globe and Mail*; *Red Book Magazine* Nov,1986
　　Bluebeard's Egg, Cape, 1987

Auer, Rev. Benedict, O.S.B.
　The Photofinish: On Attending a Lecture at Fermi Lab, pm *Amazing* Jul,1987

Aulisio, Janet
　On Exhibit, il *Amazing* Jan,1987

B
　The Stone Coffin, ss *Magdalene Collage Magazine* Dec,1913
　　Ghosts and Scholars, ed. Rosemary Pardoe+, Crucible, 1987

Babinski, Edward T.
　The Griffon, pm *Apex! #1*,1987

Bagnold, Enid
　The Amorous Ghost, ss **The Ghost-Book**, ed. Cynthia Asquith, Hutchinson,1926
　　The Virago Book of Ghost Stories, ed. Richard Dalby, Virago, 1987

Baichtal, H.W.
   The Handbug, ss *Tales of the Unanticipated* #2,1987

Bailey, Robin Wayne
   The Woodland of Zarad-Thra, nv **Sword and Sorceress** #4, ed.
      Marion Zimmer Bradley,1987

Bailey, Robin Wayne & Robert Chilson
   Primatives, nv *Amazing* Jul,1987

Bailly, Sharon
   An Application to Succeed, ss *Space & Time* #73,1987

Baker, Carlos
   The Prevaricator, ss **The Talismans and Other Stories**,1976
      Strange Maine, ed. Charles G. Waugh +, Tapley, 1986

Baker, Charles L.
   Eldritch Lair - Dungeon Level, ed *Eldritch Tales* #13,1987
   Shadow of the Immortal (Part 2 of 3), sl *Eldritch Tales* #13,1987
   Shadow of the Immortal (Part 3 of 3), sl *Eldritch Tales* #14,1987

Baker, Herbert Jerry
   The Halls of Doom, ss *Eldritch Tales* #14,1987

Baker, Russell
   High-Tech Insolence, vi *New York Times* May 18,1986
      Devils and Demons, ed. Marvin Kaye, Doubleday, 1987

Baker, Scott
   Nesting Instinct, nv **The Architecture of Fear**, ed. Kathryn Cramer &
      Peter D. Pautz, Arbor House,1987
   Sea Change, ss *F&SF* Mar,1986
      The Year's Best Science Fiction, Fourth Annual Collection, ed.
      Gardner R. Dozois, St. Martin's, 1987

Bakst, Harold
   A Good Knight's Tale, nv **DragonLance Tales** v3, Margaret Weis &
      Tracy Hickman, TSR,1987
   Lord Toede's Disastrous Hunt, nv **DragonLance Tales** v2, Margaret
      Weis & Tracy Hickman, TSR,1987

Baldwin, Dick
   The Shadow Watchers, ss **Fiends and Creatures**, ed. Marvin Kaye,
      Popular Library,1975
      Devils and Demons, ed. Marvin Kaye, Doubleday, 1987

Ballard, J.G.
   The Man Who Walked on the Moon, ss *Interzone* #13,1985
      Interzone: The 2nd Anthology, ed. John Clute +, Simon &
      Schuster UK, 1987
   A Question of Re-Entry, nv *Fantastic* Mar,1963
      Fantastic Stories: Tales of the Weird and Wondrous, ed. Martin
      H. Greenberg +, TSR, 1987

Ballard, J.G. & David Pringle
   J.G. Ballard, iv *Interzone* #22,1987

Ballard, William
   Retrograde Analysis, ss *Analog* Dec,1987

Balzac, Honore de
   The Mysterious Mansion, ss
      Classic Stories of Mystery, Horror and Suspense, ed. Simon
      Petherick, Robert Hale, 1987

Bangs, John Kendrick
   A Midnight Visitor, ss *Harper's Weekly* Dec 10,1892
      Devils and Demons, ed. Marvin Kaye, Doubleday, 1987
   The Water Ghost of Harrowby Hall, ss *Harper's Weekly* Jun 27,1891
      Christmas Ghosts, ed. Kathryn Cramer +, Arbor House, 1987

Banks, Iain
   Descendant, nv **Tales from the Forbidden Planet**, ed. Roz Kaveney,
      Titan,1987
   A Gift from the Culture, ss *Interzone* #20,1987

Banks, Raymond E.
   The Short Ones, nv *F&SF* Mar,1955
      Isaac Asimov Presents the Great SF Stories: 17 (1955), ed. Isaac
      Asimov +, DAW, 1988

Barbour, Douglas
   Afterword, aw
      Tesseracts 2, ed. Phyllis Gotlieb +, Porcepic, 1987

Baricevic, Mark
   Wallflower, ss *2AM* FII,1987

Baring-Gould, Sabine
   A Dead Finger, ss **A Book of Ghosts**, Methuen: London,1904
      Dracula's Brood, ed. Richard Dalby, Crucible, 1987
   On the Leads, ss **A Book of Ghosts**, Methuen: London,1904
      Ghosts and Scholars, ed. Rosemary Pardoe +, Crucible, 1987

Bark, John
   Big Cats, ss **Gollancz - Sunday Times Best SF Stories**,
      Gollancz,1987

Barker, A.L.
   Element of Doubt, ss **After Midnight Stories** #3,1987

Barker, Clive
   Babel's Children, nv **Clive Barker's Books of Blood** v5,1985;
      Omni Mar,1987
   The Bare Bones: An Introduction, in
      Scared Stiff: Tales of Sex and Death, Ramsey Campbell,
      Scream/Press, 1987
   Down, Satan!, ss **Clive Barker's Books of Blood** v4,1985
      Twilight Zone Jun,1987
   Dread, nv **Clive Barker's Books of Blood** v2,1984
      The Dark Descent, ed. David G. Hartwell, Tor, 1987
   Introduction, in
      Night Visions 4, ed. Anonymous, Dark Harvest, 1987

Barker, Clive, Nancy Garcia & Robert T. Garcia
   Clive Barker Interview, iv *American Fantasy* Win,1987

Barker, Clive & Douglas E. Winter
   Talking Terror With Clive Barker, iv *Twilight Zone* Jun,1987

Barker, David
   Red Paint, ss *The Horror Show* Sum,1987

Barnes, John
   Digressions from the Second Person Future, ss *IASFM* Jan,1987

Barnes, Steve
   Yelloweye, nv **Friends of the Horseclans**, ed. Robert Adams &
      Pamela Crippen Adams, Signet,1987

Barrett, Neal, Jr.
   Class of '61, ss *IASFM* Oct,1987
   Diner, ss *Omni* Nov,1987
   Highbrow, ss *IASFM* Jul,1987
   Perpetuity Blues, nv *IASFM* May,1987
   Sallie C., ss **Best of the West**, ed. Western Writers of America,
      Garden City, NY: Doubleday,1986
      The Year's Best Science Fiction, Fourth Annual Collection, ed.
      Gardner R. Dozois, St. Martin's, 1987

Barwood, Lee
   Victim, pm *Weirdbook* #22,1987

Batten, Ken
   The Ghost Car, ss *Ghost Stories* Oct,1928
      Mysterious Motoring Stories, ed. William Pattrick, W.H. Allen, 1987

Baudelaire, Charles Pierre
   The Generous Gambler, vi
      Devils and Demons, ed. Marvin Kaye, Doubleday, 1987

Baxter, S.M.
   The Xeelee Flower, ss *Interzone* #19,1987

BEAR, GREG   **BENSON, ROBERT HUGH**

Bear, Greg
  The Forge of God, ex Tor: New York Sep,1987
    Twilight Zone Oct,1987
  Galactic Checks and Balances: An Introduction to **The Forge of God**,
    is *Twilight Zone* Oct,1987
  Tangents, ss *Omni* Jan,1986
    The Year's Best Science Fiction, Fourth Annual Collection, ed.
      Gardner R. Dozois, St. Martin's, 1987
    Mathenauts, ed. Rudy Rucker, Arbor House, 1987
  The Visitation, vi *Omni* Jun,1987

Beasley, Conger, Jr.
  A Rider on a Blue Horse Waits Outside the Hospital Wall, vi *Ice River*
    Sum,1987
  Woman with a Hole in the Center of Her Chest, vi *New Pathways*
    Aug,1987

Beason, Doug
  Final Exam, vi *2AM* Win,1987
  Lifeguard, nv **New Destinies** v1, ed. Jim Baen, Baen,1987
  The Man I'll Never Be, ss *Amazing* May,1987

Beaugrand, Henry
  The Werwolves, ss *The Century* Aug,1898
    Werewolf: Horror Stories of the Man Beast, ed. Peter Haining,
      Severn House, 1987

Beaumont, Charles
  Auto Suggestion, ss *Gamma* Sep,1965
    Mysterious Motoring Stories, ed. William Pattrick, W.H. Allen, 1987
  The Howling Man [as by C.B. Lovehill], ss *Rogue* Nov,1959
    Isaac Asimov's Magical Worlds of Fantasy #8: Devils, ed. Isaac
      Asimov+, NAL/Signet, 1987
  Place of Meeting, ss *Orbit #2*,1954
    Vampires, ed. Alan Ryan, SFBC, 1987
  The Vanishing American, ss *F&SF* Aug,1955
    Isaac Asimov Presents the Great SF Stories: 17 (1955), ed. Isaac
      Asimov+, DAW, 1988

Beer, Gaye & Ben Daily
  Puzzle Pages, pz *Salarius* v1#4,1987

Behrendt, Fred
  Cauldron of Rain, pm *Space & Time* #73,1987

Behunin, Judith R.
  Community Service, vi *Footsteps* Nov,1987

Belden, Wilanne Schneider
  Fenneca, nv **Tales of the Witch World**, ed. Andre Norton, St.
    Martin's,1987

Bell, M. Shayne
  Jacob's Ladder, nv *The Leading Edge* #10,1985
    L. Ron Hubbard Presents Writers of the Future, Vol. III, ed. Algis
      Budrys, Bridge, 1987

Bellomi, Antonio
  The Mercenary, ss *SF International* #2,1987

Benet, Stephen Vincent
  The Devil and Daniel Webster [also as "All That Money Can Buy"], ss
    The Saturday Evening Post Oct 24,1936
    Isaac Asimov's Magical Worlds of Fantasy #8: Devils, ed. Isaac
      Asimov+, NAL/Signet, 1987
  Litany for Dictatorships, pm
    Imperial Stars, Vol. 2: Republic and Empire, ed. Jerry E.
      Pournelle, Baen, 1987

Benford, Gregory
  Bleak Velocities, pm **Synergy** v1, ed. George Zebrowski,1987
  Freezeframe, ss *Interzone* #17,1986
    Amazing May,1987
    Interzone: The 2nd Anthology, ed. John Clute+, Simon &
      Schuster UK, 1987
  The Future of the Jovian System, ss **The Planets**, ed. Byron Preiss,
    Bantam,1985
    IASFM Aug,1987

Benford, Gregory (continued)
  The Gods of the Gaps, na **Crusaders in Hell**, ed. Janet Morris, New
    York: Baen,1987
  Hard? Science? Fiction?, br *Amazing* Jul,1987
  How to Sound Like an Expert, ar **L. Ron Hubbard Presents Writers
    of the Future** v3, ed. Algis Budrys, Bridge,1987
  Mandikini, ss **Universe**, ed. Byron Preiss, Bantam Spectra,1987
  Reactionary Utopias, ar **Far Frontiers** v4, ed. Jerry Pournelle & Jim
    Baen,1986
    Imperial Stars, Vol. 2: Republic and Empire, ed. Jerry E.
      Pournelle, Baen, 1987
  Time's Rub, ss Cheap Street: New Castle, VA,1984
    Mathenauts, ed. Rudy Rucker, Arbor House, 1987
  Was Frankenstein Simply Einstein Being Frank? or Scientists in
    Science Fiction, ar **New Destinies** v2, ed. Jim Baen, Baen,1987
  What Are You Going to Be When You Grow Up?, nv **Spaceships &
    Spells**, ed. Jane Yolen, Martin H. Greenberg & Charles G.
    Waugh, Harper & Row,1987

Benford, Gregory & James Benford
  Battleground, ss *If* Jun,1971
    There Will Be War, Vol. VI: Guns of Darkness, ed. Jerry E.
      Pournelle, Tor, 1987

Benford, James & Gregory Benford
  Battleground, ss *If* Jun,1971
    There Will Be War, Vol. VI: Guns of Darkness, ed. Jerry E.
      Pournelle, Tor, 1987

Benjamin, Michele & Jim Ridgway
  Commentary on Burden of Proof, ar
    PsiFi: Psychological Theories and Science Fictions, ed. Jim
      Ridgway+, The British Psychological Society, 1987
  Commentary on Come to Venus Melancholy, ar
    PsiFi: Psychological Theories and Science Fictions, ed. Jim
      Ridgway+, The British Psychological Society, 1987
  Commentary on Field Test, ar
    PsiFi: Psychological Theories and Science Fictions, ed. Jim
      Ridgway+, The British Psychological Society, 1987
  Commentary on Orr's Dreams, ar
    PsiFi: Psychological Theories and Science Fictions, ed. Jim
      Ridgway+, The British Psychological Society, 1987
  Commentary on The Question of Sex, ar
    PsiFi: Psychological Theories and Science Fictions, ed. Jim
      Ridgway+, The British Psychological Society, 1987
  Commentary on They, ar
    PsiFi: Psychological Theories and Science Fictions, ed. Jim
      Ridgway+, The British Psychological Society, 1987
  Commentary on What to Do Until the Analyst Comes, ar
    PsiFi: Psychological Theories and Science Fictions, ed. Jim
      Ridgway+, The British Psychological Society, 1987

Bensink, John Robert
  Lake George in High August, ss **Masques** #2, ed. J.N.
    Williamson,1987

Benson, A.C.
  The Slype House, ss **The Isles of Sunset**, Isbister: London,1904
    Ghosts and Scholars, ed. Rosemary Pardoe+, Crucible, 1987

Benson, E.F.
  The Dust-Cloud, ss **The Room in the Tower and Other Stories**,
    London: Mills Boon,1912
    Mysterious Motoring Stories, ed. William Pattrick, W.H. Allen, 1987
  The Room in the Tower, ss **The Room in the Tower and Other
    Stories**, London: Mills Boon,1912
    Vampires, ed. Alan Ryan, SFBC, 1987
  Thursday Evenings, ss
    Poltergeist: Tales of Deadly Ghosts, ed. Peter Haining, Severn
      House, 1987

Benson, Robert Hugh
  Father Macclesfield's Tale, ss **A Mirror of Shalott**, Pitman:
    London,1907
    Ghosts and Scholars, ed. Rosemary Pardoe+, Crucible, 1987
  Father Meuron's Tale, ss **A Mirror of Shalott**, Pitman: London,1907
    Devils and Demons, ed. Marvin Kaye, Doubleday, 1987

Benson, Steve
An Empty Gift, ss *Analog* Dec,1983
   Supertanks, ed. Joe W. Haldeman +, Ace, 1987

Berberick, Nancy Varian
Harvests, nv **DragonLance Tales** v1, Margaret Weis & Tracy
   Hickman, TSR,1987
Hearth Cat and Winter Wren, nv **DragonLance Tales** v2, Margaret
   Weis & Tracy Hickman, TSR,1987
Hide and Go Seek, nv **DragonLance Tales** v3, Margaret Weis & Tracy
   Hickman, TSR,1987
Snowsong, nv **DragonLance Tales** v2, Margaret Weis & Tracy
   Hickman, TSR,1987
A Tale at Rilling's Inn, ss *Amazing* Mar,1987

Bergeron, Alain
Happy Birthday Universe! [Bonne Fete Univers!], nv *Solaris* #65,1986
   Translated by Mary Shelton.
   Tesseracts 2, ed. Phyllis Gotlieb +, Porcepic, 1987

Berman, Ruth
Magic Trick, pm *Minnesota Fantasy Review* #1,1987
Open-Ended Universe, pm *Amazing* Jul,1986
   Rhysling Anthology 1987, ed. Anonymous, SF Poetry Assc., 1987
Professor and Colonel, ss **Mathenauts**, ed. Rudy Rucker, Arbor
   House,1987

Bernard, Sidney
The Liberty Watchers, ar *Pulpsmith* Win,1987

Bester, Alfred
Fondly Fahrenheit, nv *F&SF* Aug,1954
   Isaac Asimov Presents the Great SF Stories: 16 (1954), ed. Isaac
   Asimov +, DAW, 1987
   Robert Silverberg's Worlds of Wonder, ed. Robert Silverberg,
   Warner, 1987
Hobson's Choice, ss *F&SF* Aug,1952
   Great Science Fiction of the 20th Century, ed. Robert
   Silverberg +, Crown/Avenel, 1987

Betancourt, John Gregory
The Darkfishers, ss *Aboriginal SF* Jul,1987
Fantasy Book Reviews, br *Fantasy Book* Mar,1987
Messiah, ss *Amazing* May,1987
Well Bottled at Slab's, ss *The Dragon* Oct,1987

Betancourt, John Gregory & Darrell Schweitzer
The Children of Lommos, ss *Night Cry* v2#4,1987

Bethke, Bruce
It Came from the Slushpile, ss *Aboriginal SF* Jul,1987

Betts, Michael Arthur
Tattler, mr *The Horror Show* Jan,1987
Tattler, mr *The Horror Show* Sum,1987
Tattler, mr *The Horror Show* Fll,1987
Tattler, mr *The Horror Show* Win,1987

Betts, Michael Arthur & Wes Craven
Tattler, mr *The Horror Show* Spr,1987

Bierce, Ambrose
The Boarded Window, ss **In the Midst of Life**, E.L.G. Steele: San
   Francisco CA,1891
   Night Cry v2#5,1987
The Damned Thing, ss **Can Such Things Be?**, Cassell: New
   York,1893; *Weird Tales* Sep,1923
   Tales of the Dark 2, ed. Lincoln Child, St. Martin's, 1987
   The Dark Descent, ed. David G. Hartwell, Tor, 1987
   The Devil's Advocate, Chronicle, 1987
The Death of Halpin Frayser, ss **Can Such Things Be?**, Cassell: New
   York,1893
   The Devil's Advocate, Chronicle, 1987
A Fruitless Assignment, ss
   Poltergeist: Tales of Deadly Ghosts, ed. Peter Haining, Severn
   House, 1987

Bierce, Ambrose (continued)
Haiti the Shepherd, ss **In the Midst of Life**, E.L.G. Steele: San
   Francisco CA,1891
   The Devil's Advocate, Chronicle, 1987
John Mortonson's Funeral, vi *Night Cry* v2#4,1987
The Man and the Snake, ss **In the Midst of Life**, E.L.G. Steele: San
   Francisco CA,1891
   Classic Stories of Mystery, Horror and Suspense, ed. Simon
   Petherick, Robert Hale, 1987
   The Devil's Advocate, Chronicle, 1987
The Middle Toe of the Right Foot, ss **In the Midst of Life**, E.L.G.
   Steele: San Francisco CA,1891
   Night Cry v2#4,1987
The Moonlit Road, ss **Can Such Things Be?**, Cassell: New York,1893
   The Devil's Advocate, Chronicle, 1987
Moxon's Master, ss **Can Such Things Be?**, Cassell: New York,1893
   The Devil's Advocate, Chronicle, 1987
My Favorite Murder, ss
   The Devil's Advocate, Chronicle, 1987
Oil of Dog, ss
   The Devil's Advocate, Chronicle, 1987
One Summer Night, vi **Can Such Things Be?**, Cassell: New
   York,1893
   The Devil's Advocate, Chronicle, 1987
A Watcher by the Dead, ss **In the Midst of Life**, E.L.G. Steele: San
   Francisco CA,1891
   The Devil's Advocate, Chronicle, 1987

Bigley, Leo
Elysium Horizon, ss *Mage* Spr,1987
The Panama Mechanism, ss *Mage* Spr,1986
   Mage Fll,1987

Binder, Eando
Adam Link's Vengeance, nv *Amazing* Feb,1940
   Amazing Science Fiction Stories: The War Years 1936-1945, ed.
   Martin H. Greenberg, TSR, 1987

Binney, Cecil
The Saint and the Vicar, ss **50 Years of Ghost Stories**, ed.
   Anonymous, Hutchinson: London,1935
   Ghosts and Scholars, ed. Rosemary Pardoe +, Crucible, 1987

Binns, Archie
The Last Trip, ss *Weird Tales* Aug,1925
   Mysterious Motoring Stories, ed. William Pattrick, W.H. Allen, 1987

Binns, Mervyn R.
The Science Fiction World, ar *Aphelion* #5,1987

Birtha, Becky
Baby Town, ss **Hear the Silence**, ed. Irene Zahava, Crossing
   Press,1986
The Saints and Sinners Run, ss **Hear the Silence**, ed. Irene Zahava,
   Crossing Press,1986

Bishop, Michael
The Egret, ss *Playboy* Jun,1987
An Episode in the Death of Philip K. Dick, vi *New Pathways* Aug,1987
For Thus Do I Remember Carthage, ss **Universe**, ed. Byron Preiss,
   Bantam Spectra,1987
Foreword, fw
   The Jaguar Hunter, Lucius Shepard, Arkham House, 1987
   The Best of Pamela Sargent, Pamela Sargent, Academy Chicago,
   1987
God's Hour, vi *Omni* Jun,1987
In the Memory Room, ss **The Architecture of Fear**, ed. Kathryn
   Cramer & Peter D. Pautz, Arbor House,1987
Within the Walls of Tyre, nv *Weirdbook* #13,1978
   The Dark Descent, ed. David G. Hartwell, Tor, 1987

Bishop, Michael & Misha Chocholak
Close Encounters with Michael Bishop, iv *New Pathways* Jan,1987

Bixby, Jerome
The Draw, ss *Amazing* Mar,1954
   Amazing Science Fiction Stories: The Wild Years 1946-1955, ed.
   Martin H. Greenberg, TSR, 1987

BIXBY, JEROME

Bixby, Jerome (continued)
One Way Street, ss *Amazing* Jan,1954
  Robert Adams' Book of Alternate Worlds, ed. Robert Adams +, NAL/Signet, 1987
Trace, ss,1961
  Isaac Asimov's Magical Worlds of Fantasy #8: Devils, ed. Isaac Asimov +, NAL/Signet, 1987

Blackwood, Algernon
The Empty House, ss **The Empty House**, Eveleigh Nash,1906
  Tales of the Dark 2, ed. Lincoln Child, St. Martin's, 1987
A Mysterious House, ss *Belgravia* Jul,1889
  A Mysterious House, Algernon Blackwood, Tragara Press, 1987
Secret Worship, nv **John Silence**,1908
  Devils and Demons, ed. Marvin Kaye, Doubleday, 1987
The Singular Death of Morton, ss *The Tramp* Dec,1910
  Dracula's Brood, ed. Richard Dalby, Crucible, 1987
The Transfer, ss *Country Life* Dec 9,1911
  Vampires, ed. Alan Ryan, SFBC, 1987
The Willows, nv **The Listener and Other Stories**,1907
  The Dark Descent, ed. David G. Hartwell, Tor, 1987
The Wolves of God, ss **The Wolves of God**, Cassell,1921
  Werewolf: Horror Stories of the Man Beast, ed. Peter Haining, Severn House, 1987

Blake, E. Michael
A Glorious Triumph for the People, ss **There Will Be War** v6, ed. Jerry E. Pournelle,1987

Blassingame, Wyatt
The Horror at His Heels, ss *Horror Stories* Aug,1936
  The Weirds, ed. Sheldon R. Jaffery, Starmont House, 1987
The Tongueless Horror, nv *Dime Mystery Magazine* Apr,1934
  Selected Tales of Grim and Grue from the Horror Pulps, ed. Sheldon R. Jaffery, Bowling Green Popular Press, 1987

Blaylock, James P.
Myron Chester and the Toads, ss *IASFM* Feb,1987
The Shadow on the Doorstep, ss *IASFM* May,1986
  The Shadow on the Doorstep/Trilobyte, James P. Blaylock +, Axolotl, 1987

Bleiler, Everett F.
Books, br *Twilight Zone* Feb,1987
Books, br *Twilight Zone* Apr,1987

Blish, James
Common Time, ss *Science Fiction Quarterly* Aug,1953
  Great Science Fiction of the 20th Century, ed. Robert Silverberg +, Crown/Avenel, 1987
  Robert Silverberg's Worlds of Wonder, ed. Robert Silverberg, Warner, 1987
There Shall Be No Darkness, nv *Thrilling Wonder Stories* Apr,1950
  Cinemonsters, ed. Martin H. Greenberg, TSR, 1987

Bloch, Robert
But First These Words--, ss *F&SF* May,1977
  Midnight Pleasures, Doubleday, 1987
The Cloak, ss *Unknown* May,1939
  Vamps, ed. Martin H. Greenberg +, DAW, 1987
Comeback, ss *Previews* Oct,1984
  Midnight Pleasures, Doubleday, 1987
Die--Nasty, ss **Midnight Pleasures**, Doubleday,1987
Double Whammy, ss *Fantastic* Feb,1970
  Fantastic Stories: Tales of the Weird and Wondrous, ed. Martin H. Greenberg +, TSR, 1987
Enoch, ss *Weird Tales* Sep,1946
  Devils and Demons, ed. Marvin Kaye, Doubleday, 1987
Everybody Needs a Little Love, ss **Masques #1**, ed. J.N. Williamson,1984
  Midnight Pleasures, Doubleday, 1987
Gather Round the Flowing Bowler, ss *Fantastic Adventures* May,1942
  Lost in Time and Space with Lefty Feep, Creatures at Large, 1987
The Golden Opportunity of Lefty Feep, nv *Fantastic Adventures* Nov,1942
  Lost in Time and Space with Lefty Feep, Creatures at Large, 1987
Heir Apparent, ss **Tales of the Witch World**, ed. Andre Norton, St. Martin's,1987

Bloch, Robert (continued)
Introduction, in
  Amazing Science Fiction Stories: The Wild Years 1946-1955, ed. Martin H. Greenberg, TSR, 1987
Jerk the Giant Killer, nv *Fantastic Adventures* Oct,1942
  Lost in Time and Space with Lefty Feep, Creatures at Large, 1987
The Little Man Who Wasn't All There, ss *Fantastic Adventures* Aug,1942
  Lost in Time and Space with Lefty Feep, Creatures at Large, 1987
The Living Dead [also as "Underground"], ss *Ellery Queen's Mystery Magazine* Apr,1967
  Vampires, ed. Alan Ryan, SFBC, 1987
Lizzie Borden Took an Axe, ss *Weird Tales* Nov,1946
  House Shudders, ed. Martin H. Greenberg +, DAW, 1987
The Man Who Cried "Wolf!", ss *Weird Tales* May,1945
  Werewolf: Horror Stories of the Man Beast, ed. Peter Haining, Severn House, 1987
The New Season, ss **Masques #2**, ed. J.N. Williamson,1987
The Night Before Christmas, nv **Dark Forces**, ed. Kirby McCauley, Viking,1980
  Midnight Pleasures, Doubleday, 1987
Nocturne, ss **Greystone Bay**, ed. Charles L. Grant, Tor,1985
  Midnight Pleasures, Doubleday, 1987
Oh Say Can You See--, ss **Analog Yearbook #1**,1978
  Midnight Pleasures, Doubleday, 1987
Picture, ss **Shadows #1**, ed. Charles L. Grant,1978
  Midnight Pleasures, Doubleday, 1987
The Pied Piper Fights the Gestapo, ss *Fantastic Adventures* Jun,1942
  Lost in Time and Space with Lefty Feep, Creatures at Large, 1987
Pranks, ss **Halloween Horrors**, ed. Alan Ryan, Doubleday,1986
  Midnight Pleasures, Doubleday, 1987
Pumpkin, nv *Twilight Zone* Dec,1984
  Midnight Pleasures, Doubleday, 1987
The Rubber Room, ss **New Terrors #2**, ed. Ramsey Campbell, Pan,1980
  Midnight Pleasures, Doubleday, 1987
The Skull of the Marquis de Sade, nv *Weird Tales* Sep,1945
  Cinemonsters, ed. Martin H. Greenberg, TSR, 1987
A Snitch in Time, ss **Lost in Time and Space with Lefty Feep**, Creatures at Large,1987
Son of a Witch, nv *Fantastic Adventures* Sep,1942
  Lost in Time and Space with Lefty Feep, Creatures at Large, 1987
The Spoiled Wife, ss **Chrysalis #3**, ed. Roy Torgeson,1978
  Midnight Pleasures, Doubleday, 1987
That Hell-Bound Train, ss *F&SF* Sep,1958
  Isaac Asimov's Magical Worlds of Fantasy #8: Devils, ed. Isaac Asimov +, NAL/Signet, 1987
Time Wounds All Heels, ss *Fantastic Adventures* Apr,1942
  Lost in Time and Space with Lefty Feep, Creatures at Large, 1987
The Totem Pole, ss *Weird Tales* Aug,1939
  Midnight Pleasures, Doubleday, 1987
The Undead, ss **The Book Sail 16th Anniversary Catalog**,1984
  Midnight Pleasures, Doubleday, 1987
The Weird Doom of Floyd Scrilch, ss *Fantastic Adventures* Jul,1942
  Lost in Time and Space with Lefty Feep, Creatures at Large, 1987
You Could Be Wrong, ss *Amazing* Mar,1955
  Amazing Science Fiction Stories: The Wild Years 1946-1955, ed. Martin H. Greenberg, TSR, 1987
The Yougoslaves, nv *Night Cry* v1#5,1986
  The Year's Best Horror Stories: XV, ed. Karl Edward Wagner, DAW, 1987
Yours Truly, Jack the Ripper, ss *Weird Tales* Jul,1943
  The Dark Descent, ed. David G. Hartwell, Tor, 1987

Blockley, Bartholomew
A Sort of Sun Spot, ss **Gollancz - Sunday Times Best SF Stories**, Gollancz,1987

Blue, Tyson
Illuminations: An Audience with the King, ar *Twilight Zone* Aug,1987
Illuminations: Many Happy Returns, ar *Twilight Zone* Aug,1987
The Other Side: Vanishing Hitchikers and Dead Cats, ar *Twilight Zone* Oct,1987

Blumlein, Michael
The Brains of Rats, ss *Interzone* #16,1986
  Interzone: The 2nd Anthology, ed. John Clute +, Simon & Schuster UK, 1987

Boal, Nina
Flight, ss **Red Sun of Darkover**, ed. Marion Zimmer Bradley & The Friends of Darkover, DAW,1987

Bonansinga, Jay
Poltergeist III, mr *American Fantasy* Sum,1987

Bond, Ruskin
The Wind on Haunted Hill, ss **The Ghost Story Treasury**, ed. Linda Sonntag, Putnam, 1987

Booth, Bob
Play's the Thing, nv **Doom City**, ed. Charles L. Grant, Tor,1987

Borden, William
Clove's Essence, ss *Pulpsmith* Win,1987

Boren, Terry
Sliding Rock, ss **A Very Large Array**, ed. Melinda M. Snodgrass, University of New Mexico Press,1987

Boston, Bruce
The Alchemist Among Us, pm
  Alchemical Texts, Ocean View, 1985
The Alchemist Discovers a Universal Solvent, pm *IASFM* Dec,1984
  Alchemical Texts, Ocean View, 1985
The Alchemist in Place, pm
  Alchemical Texts, Ocean View, 1985
The Alchemist in Transit, pm
  Alchemical Texts, Ocean View, 1985
The Alchemist Is Born in a Sudden Changing of Seasons, pm
  Alchemical Texts, Ocean View, 1985
The Alchemist Takes a Lover in the Infinite Variety of Fire, pm
  Alchemical Texts, Ocean View, 1985
America, America, America, pm *Last Wave* #5,1986
  Nuclear Futures, Velocities Chapbook Series, 1987
Ancient Catch, pm
  All the Clocks Are Melting, Velocities Chapbook Series, 1984
The Berserker Enters a Plea on the Death of Greater Los Angeles, pm *IASFM* May,1985
  Nuclear Futures, Velocities Chapbook Series, 1987
Break, ss **New Worlds Quarterly** #7, Moorcock/Platt/Bailey,1974
  Jackbird: Tales of Illusion & Identity, Berkeley Poets' Workshop & Press, 1976
Broken Portraiture, ss *Gallimaufry* #5,1975
  She Comes When You're Leaving & Other Stories, Berkeley Poets' Workshop & Press, 1982
Celestian Grapevine, pm *Space & Time* #73,1987
The Changeling Uncovered, pm *IASFM* Jan,1987
Clear to Eternity, pm *Amazing* Jul,1987
Curse of the Demon's Wife, pm *IASFM* Aug,1987
Defeat at the Hands of Alien Scholars, pm *Star*Line*,1979
  All the Clocks Are Melting, Velocities Chapbook Series, 1984
Denizens, pm
  All the Clocks Are Melting, Velocities Chapbook Series, 1984
Depression Seance, nv *Fiction Magazine* #9,1976
  Jackbird: Tales of Illusion & Identity, Berkeley Poets' Workshop & Press, 1976
Doctor's Dozen, ss *The Portland Review*,1981
  She Comes When You're Leaving & Other Stories, Berkeley Poets' Workshop & Press, 1982
Don't Drink the Sky at Myrmidon, pm *IASFM* Jan,1984
  All the Clocks Are Melting, Velocities Chapbook Series, 1984
Dream Webs, pm *Night Cry* v2#3,1987
  Night Rides; gp
The Evolution of the Death Murals, pm *IASFM* Sep,1985
  Nuclear Futures, Velocities Chapbook Series, 1987
Faith of the Progeny, pm *Bifrost*
  Nuclear Futures, Velocities Chapbook Series, 1987
The Faithless, pm
  All the Clocks Are Melting, Velocities Chapbook Series, 1984
A Feast for the Vanquished, pm
  All the Clocks Are Melting, Velocities Chapbook Series, 1984
For Spacers Snarled in the Hair of Comets, pm *IASFM* Apr,1984
  All the Clocks Are Melting, Velocities Chapbook Series, 1984
Forecast for a Burning Planet, pm **Nuclear Futures**, Velocities Chapbook Series,1987

Boston, Bruce (continued)
From the Mouths of Lizards, pm
  All the Clocks Are Melting, Velocities Chapbook Series, 1984
The FTL Addict Fixes, pm *Velocities*,1983
  All the Clocks Are Melting, Velocities Chapbook Series, 1984
A Hero of the Spican Conflict, pm *Aboriginal SF* Nov,1987
Horses of Light, pm
  All the Clocks Are Melting, Velocities Chapbook Series, 1984
Human Remains, pm *Star*Line* v5#4,1982
  All the Clocks Are Melting, Velocities Chapbook Series, 1984
If Gravity Were Like Weather, pm *Star*Line*,1982
  All the Clocks Are Melting, Velocities Chapbook Series, 1984
In Days of Cataclysm, pm
  All the Clocks Are Melting, Velocities Chapbook Series, 1984
In the Eyes of the Pilot, pm *Amazing* Mar,1987
In the Garden of the State, pm *Amazing* May,1987
Interstellar Tract, pm **Nuclear Futures**, Velocities Chapbook Series,1987
Interview with a Gentleman Farmer, ss *City Miner* #1,1976
  She Comes When You're Leaving & Other Stories, Berkeley Poets' Workshop & Press, 1982
Jackbird, ss *Gallimaufry* #3,1974
  Jackbird: Tales of Illusion & Identity, Berkeley Poets' Workshop & Press, 1976
Limb Still Kicking from a Stillborn Novel, ss *Gallimaufry* #7,1976
  She Comes When You're Leaving & Other Stories, Berkeley Poets' Workshop & Press, 1982
Luminaries, pm **Aliens & Lovers**, ed. Millea Kenin, Unique Graphics,1983
  All the Clocks Are Melting, Velocities Chapbook Series, 1984
Mathematician, pm *Star*Line*,1978
  All the Clocks Are Melting, Velocities Chapbook Series, 1984
The Mating of the Storm Birds, pm **Aliens & Lovers**, ed. Millea Kenin, Unique Graphics,1983
  All the Clocks Are Melting, Velocities Chapbook Series, 1984
The Monster and the Moon, ss *Fiction Magazine* #4,1973
  She Comes When You're Leaving & Other Stories, Berkeley Poets' Workshop & Press, 1982
Mulligan [from **Stained Glass Rain**], ex *Berkeley Poets' Co-op* #2,1971
  Jackbird: Tales of Illusion & Identity, Berkeley Poets' Workshop & Press, 1976
Nativity of Thought, pm
  All the Clocks Are Melting, Velocities Chapbook Series, 1984
Night Flight, pm *Star*Line*,1978
  All the Clocks Are Melting, Velocities Chapbook Series, 1984
Night Ride, pm *Night Cry* v2#3,1987
  Night Rides; gp
Nightmare Collector, pm *Night Cry* v2#3,1987
  Night Rides; gp
No Longer the Stars, pm **Nuclear Futures**, Velocities Chapbook Series,1987
One-Trick Dog, vi *IASFM* May,1987
The Poets' War, ss *City Miner* #7,1977
  She Comes When You're Leaving & Other Stories, Berkeley Poets' Workshop & Press, 1982
She Comes When You're Leaving, ss *Berkeley Poets' Co-op* #9,1975
  She Comes When You're Leaving & Other Stories, Berkeley Poets' Workshop & Press, 1982
Soldier, Sailor, nv *Fiction Magazine* #7,1974
  Jackbird: Tales of Illusion & Identity, Berkeley Poets' Workshop & Press, 1976
Some Concrete Notions About Demons, ss *The Magazine of Speculative Poetry* #5,1987
The Star Drifter Grounded, pm *Star*Line*,1979
  All the Clocks Are Melting, Velocities Chapbook Series, 1984
Sunday Review, vi *City Miner* #3,1976
  She Comes When You're Leaving & Other Stories, Berkeley Poets' Workshop & Press, 1982
Tarfu's Last Show, ss **Future Pastimes**, ed. Scott Edelstein, Aurora,1977
  Jackbird: Tales of Illusion & Identity, Berkeley Poets' Workshop & Press, 1976
A Thousand Faces, pm
  Alchemical Texts, Ocean View, 1985
Time's House, pm *IASFM* Sep,1983
  All the Clocks Are Melting, Velocities Chapbook Series, 1984

BOSTON, BRUCE

Boston, Bruce (continued)
Tongues, pm
Alchemical Texts, Ocean View, 1985
Uroboros, pm *Fungi* #11,1986
Rhysling Anthology 1987, ed. Anonymous, SF Poetry Assc., 1987
View from the Abscissa, pm
All the Clocks Are Melting, Velocities Chapbook Series, 1984
Want Ad, pm *Star*Line*,1981
All the Clocks Are Melting, Velocities Chapbook Series, 1984
The Wave We Ride, pm
All the Clocks Are Melting, Velocities Chapbook Series, 1984
The Widow Renounced, pm *Night Cry* v2#3,1987
Night Rides; gp
A Wrecker's Tale, pm *The Magazine of Speculative Poetry* Sum,1985
Nuclear Futures, Velocities Chapbook Series, 1987

Botsis, Peter
On Exhibit, il *Amazing* Nov,1987

Bottome, Phyllis
The Waiting-Room, ss **Strange Fruit**,1928
The Virago Book of Ghost Stories, ed. Richard Dalby, Virago, 1987

Boucher, Anthony
Balaam, ss **9 Tales of Space and Time**, ed. Raymond J. Healey, Holt,1954
Isaac Asimov Presents the Great SF Stories: 16 (1954), ed. Isaac Asimov+, DAW, 1987
Nellthu, vi *F&SF* Aug,1955
Demons!, ed. Jack M. Dann+, Ace, 1987
Snulbug, ss *Unknown* Dec,1941; *F&SF* May,1953
Demons!, ed. Jack M. Dann+, Ace, 1987

Boucher, Sandy
The Healing, nv **Hear the Silence**, ed. Irene Zahava, Crossing Press,1986

Bounds, Sydney J.
The Ghost Train, ss
The Ghost Story Treasury, ed. Linda Sonntag, Putnam, 1987

Bova, Ben
Battle Station, na **Battle Station**, Tor,1987
Beisbol, ss *Analog* Nov,1985
Battle Station, Tor, 1987
Born Again, ss *Analog* May,1984
Battle Station, Tor, 1987
Brothers, ss **In the Field of Fire**, ed. Jeanne Van Buren Dann & Jack M. Dann, Tor,1987
Build Me a Mountain, ss **2020 Vision**, ed. Jerry Pournelle,1974
The Kinsman Saga, Ben Bova, Tor, 1987
Fifteen Miles, ss *F&SF* May,1967
The Kinsman Saga, Ben Bova, Tor, 1987
Foeman [Foeman, Where Do You Flee?], na *Galaxy* Jan,1969
Battle Station, Tor, 1987
For Mars, Vote NO, ed *Analog* Sep,1987
Foreword, fw
Battle Station, Tor, 1987
Freedom From Fear, ed *Analog* Nov,1984
Battle Station, Tor, 1987
Isolation Area, nv *F&SF* Oct,1984
Battle Station, Tor, 1987
The Jefferson Orbit, ar **Far Frontiers** v1, ed. Jerry Pournelle & Jim Baen,1985
Battle Station, Tor, 1987
Kinsman, ex *Omni* Sep,1979
The Kinsman Saga, Ben Bova, Tor, 1987
Kinsman, n. Quantum Science Fiction, The Dial Press: New York,1979
The Kinsman Saga, Ben Bova, Tor, 1987
Laser Propulsion, ar,1984
Battle Station, Tor, 1987
The Lieutenant and the Folksinger, ss **Maxwell's Demons**,1978
The Kinsman Saga, Ben Bova, Tor, 1987
MHD, ar **Battle Station**, Tor,1987
Millennium, n. Random House: New York,1976
The Kinsman Saga, Ben Bova, Tor, 1987
Moonbase Orientation Manual I: Transport and Manufacturing, ar *Analog* Jun,1987

Bova, Ben (continued)
Moonbase Orientation Manual II: Research and Recreation, ar *Analog* Jul,1987
Nuclear Autumn, ss **Far Frontiers** v2, ed. Jerry Pournelle & Jim Baen,1985
Battle Station, Tor, 1987
Primary, ss *IASFM* Feb,1985
Battle Station, Tor, 1987
The Sightseers, vi **Future City**, ed. Roger Elwood, Trident,1973
Battle Station, Tor, 1987
Silent Night, ss *IASFM* Dec,1987
Space Station, ar,1985
Battle Station, Tor, 1987
Space Weapons, ar *Amazing* Jul,1985
Battle Station, Tor, 1987
Symbolism in Science Fiction, ar *The Writer* Jun,1984
Battle Station, Tor, 1987
Telefuture, ar *Omni* Feb,1985
Battle Station, Tor, 1987
Test in Orbit, ss *Analog* Sep,1965
The Kinsman Saga, Ben Bova, Tor, 1987
To Touch a Star, ss **Universe**, ed. Byron Preiss, Bantam Spectra,1987
Zero Gee, nv **Again, Dangerous Visions**, ed. Harlan Ellison, Doubleday,1972
The Kinsman Saga, Ben Bova, Tor, 1987

Bowen, Elizabeth
The Cat Jumps, ss **The Cat Jumps and Other Stories**,1934
House Shudders, ed. Martin H. Greenberg+, DAW, 1987
The Demon Lover, ss **The Demon Lover**, J. Cape,1945
Mysterious Motoring Stories, ed. William Pattrick, W.H. Allen, 1987
The Happy Autumn Fields, ss **The Demon Lover**, J. Cape,1945
The Virago Book of Ghost Stories, ed. Richard Dalby, Virago, 1987

Bowen, Marjorie
The Accident, vi **Dark Ann, and Other Stories**, John Lane: London,1927
The Virago Book of Ghost Stories, ed. Richard Dalby, Virago, 1987
The Crown Derby Plate, ss,1952
Christmas Ghosts, ed. Kathryn Cramer+, Arbor House, 1987
A Persistent Woman, vi **Dark Ann, and Other Stories**, John Lane: London,1927
The Virago Book of Ghost Stories, ed. Richard Dalby, Virago, 1987

Bowerman, Tony
Gardens and Fountains, ss **Gollancz - Sunday Times Best SF Stories**, Gollancz,1987

Bowkett, Steve
Moonwatcher, pm *Star*Line* Sep,1986
Rhysling Anthology 1987, ed. Anonymous, SF Poetry Assc., 1987

Bowles, Paul
An Inopportune Visit, ss *Threepenny Review* Spr,1987

Boyd, J.P.
The Anger of Time, ss *F&SF* Feb,1987

Boyett, Steven R.
Minutes of the Last Meeting at Olduvai, vi *Aboriginal SF* Nov,1987

Bradbury, Ray
And the Moon Be Still as Bright, ss *Thrilling Wonder Stories* Jun,1948
Fahrenheit 451/The Illustrated Man/Dandelion Wine/The Golden Apples of the Sun/The Martian Chronicles, Octopus/Heinemann, 1987
The April Witch, ss *The Saturday Evening Post* Apr 5,1952
Fahrenheit 451/The Illustrated Man/Dandelion Wine/The Golden Apples of the Sun/The Martian Chronicles, Octopus/Heinemann, 1987
Young Witches & Warlocks, ed. Isaac Asimov+, Harper & Row, 1987
Art and Science Fiction: Unbuilt Cities/Unrealized Dreams, ar **Universe**, ed. Byron Preiss, Bantam Spectra,1987
The Big Black and White Game, ss *The American Mercury* Aug,1945
Fahrenheit 451/The Illustrated Man/Dandelion Wine/The Golden Apples of the Sun/The Martian Chronicles, Octopus/Heinemann, 1987

BRADBURY, RAY

Bradbury, Ray (continued)
Chrysalis, ss *Amazing* Jul,1946
Amazing Science Fiction Stories: The Wild Years 1946-1955, ed. Martin H. Greenberg, TSR, 1987
The City [Purpose], ss *Startling Stories* Jul,1950
Fahrenheit 451/The Illustrated Man/Dandelion Wine/The Golden Apples of the Sun/The Martian Chronicles, Octopus/Heinemann, 1987
The Concrete Mixer, ss *Thrilling Wonder Stories* Apr,1949
Fahrenheit 451/The Illustrated Man/Dandelion Wine/The Golden Apples of the Sun/The Martian Chronicles, Octopus/Heinemann, 1987
The Crowd, ss *Weird Tales* May,1943
The Dark Descent, ed. David G. Hartwell, Tor, 1987
Dandelion Wine, co Doubleday: Garden City, NY,1957
Fahrenheit 451/The Illustrated Man/Dandelion Wine/The Golden Apples of the Sun/The Martian Chronicles, Octopus/Heinemann, 1987
Dandelion Wine, ss *Gourmet* Jun,1953
Fahrenheit 451/The Illustrated Man/Dandelion Wine/The Golden Apples of the Sun/The Martian Chronicles, Octopus/Heinemann, 1987
Dinner at Dawn, ss *Everywoman's Magazine* Feb,1954
Fahrenheit 451/The Illustrated Man/Dandelion Wine/The Golden Apples of the Sun/The Martian Chronicles, Octopus/Heinemann, 1987
The Earth Men, ss *Thrilling Wonder Stories* Aug,1948
Fahrenheit 451/The Illustrated Man/Dandelion Wine/The Golden Apples of the Sun/The Martian Chronicles, Octopus/Heinemann, 1987
Embroidery, ss *Marvel* Nov,1951
Fahrenheit 451/The Illustrated Man/Dandelion Wine/The Golden Apples of the Sun/The Martian Chronicles, Octopus/Heinemann, 1987
En La Noche [Torrid Sacrifice], ss *Cavalier* Nov,1952
Fahrenheit 451/The Illustrated Man/Dandelion Wine/The Golden Apples of the Sun/The Martian Chronicles, Octopus/Heinemann, 1987
Epilogue, aw **The Illustrated Man**,1951
Fahrenheit 451/The Illustrated Man/Dandelion Wine/The Golden Apples of the Sun/The Martian Chronicles, Octopus/Heinemann, 1987
The Exiles [The Mad Wizards of Mars], ss *Maclean's* Sep 15,1949; *F&SF* WiS,1950
Fahrenheit 451/The Illustrated Man/Dandelion Wine/The Golden Apples of the Sun/The Martian Chronicles, Octopus/Heinemann, 1987
Fahrenheit 451, n. Ballantine: New York,1953
Expanded from "The Fireman", *Galaxy* Feb,51.
Fahrenheit 451/The Illustrated Man/Dandelion Wine/The Golden Apples of the Sun/The Martian Chronicles, Octopus/Heinemann, 1987
Fever Dream, ss *Weird Tales* Sep,1948
Fever Dream, Ray Bradbury, St. Martin's, 1987
The Fire Balloons [In This Sign], ss *Imagination* Apr,1951
Fahrenheit 451/The Illustrated Man/Dandelion Wine/The Golden Apples of the Sun/The Martian Chronicles, Octopus/Heinemann, 1987
The Flying Machine, ss **The Golden Apples of the Sun**, Doubleday,1953
Fahrenheit 451/The Illustrated Man/Dandelion Wine/The Golden Apples of the Sun/The Martian Chronicles, Octopus/Heinemann, 1987
The Fog Horn [The Beast from 20,000 Fathoms], ss *The Saturday Evening Post* Jun 23,1951
Fahrenheit 451/The Illustrated Man/Dandelion Wine/The Golden Apples of the Sun/The Martian Chronicles, Octopus/Heinemann, 1987
Cinemonsters, ed. Martin H. Greenberg, TSR, 1987
The Fox and the Forest [To the Future], ss *Colliers* May 13,1950
Fahrenheit 451/The Illustrated Man/Dandelion Wine/The Golden Apples of the Sun/The Martian Chronicles, Octopus/Heinemann, 1987
The Fruit at the Bottom of the Bowl [Touch and Go], ss *Detective Book* Nov,1948; *Ellery Queen's Mystery Magazine* Jan,1953
Fahrenheit 451/The Illustrated Man/Dandelion Wine/The Golden Apples of the Sun/The Martian Chronicles, Octopus/Heinemann, 1987

Bradbury, Ray (continued)
The Garbage Collector, ss *The Nation* Oct,1953
Fahrenheit 451/The Illustrated Man/Dandelion Wine/The Golden Apples of the Sun/The Martian Chronicles, Octopus/Heinemann, 1987
The Golden Apples of the Sun, co Doubleday: Garden City, NY,1953
Fahrenheit 451/The Illustrated Man/Dandelion Wine/The Golden Apples of the Sun/The Martian Chronicles, Octopus/Heinemann, 1987
The Golden Apples of the Sun, ss *Planet Stories* Nov,1953
Fahrenheit 451/The Illustrated Man/Dandelion Wine/The Golden Apples of the Sun/The Martian Chronicles, Octopus/Heinemann, 1987
The Golden Kite, the Silver Wind, ss *Epoch* Win,1953
Fahrenheit 451/The Illustrated Man/Dandelion Wine/The Golden Apples of the Sun/The Martian Chronicles, Octopus/Heinemann, 1987
Good-By, Grandma, ss *The Saturday Evening Post* May 25,1957
Fahrenheit 451/The Illustrated Man/Dandelion Wine/The Golden Apples of the Sun/The Martian Chronicles, Octopus/Heinemann, 1987
The Great Fire, ss *Seventeen* Mar,1949
Fahrenheit 451/The Illustrated Man/Dandelion Wine/The Golden Apples of the Sun/The Martian Chronicles, Octopus/Heinemann, 1987
The Great Wide World Over There [Cora and the Great Wide World Over There], ss *Maclean's* Aug 15,1952
Fahrenheit 451/The Illustrated Man/Dandelion Wine/The Golden Apples of the Sun/The Martian Chronicles, Octopus/Heinemann, 1987
The Green Machine, ss *Argosy (UK)* Mar,1951
Fahrenheit 451/The Illustrated Man/Dandelion Wine/The Golden Apples of the Sun/The Martian Chronicles, Octopus/Heinemann, 1987
The Green Morning, ss **The Martian Chronicles**,1950
Fahrenheit 451/The Illustrated Man/Dandelion Wine/The Golden Apples of the Sun/The Martian Chronicles, Octopus/Heinemann, 1987
Green Wine for Dreaming, ss **Dandelion Wine**, Ray Bradbury, Doubleday,1957
Fahrenheit 451/The Illustrated Man/Dandelion Wine/The Golden Apples of the Sun/The Martian Chronicles, Octopus/Heinemann, 1987
Hail and Farewell, ss *Today* Mar 29,1953
Fahrenheit 451/The Illustrated Man/Dandelion Wine/The Golden Apples of the Sun/The Martian Chronicles, Octopus/Heinemann, 1987
The Happiness Machine [also as "The Time Machine"], ss *The Saturday Evening Post* Sep 14,1957
Fahrenheit 451/The Illustrated Man/Dandelion Wine/The Golden Apples of the Sun/The Martian Chronicles, Octopus/Heinemann, 1987
The Highway [as by Leonard Spalding], ss *Copy* Spr,1950
Fahrenheit 451/The Illustrated Man/Dandelion Wine/The Golden Apples of the Sun/The Martian Chronicles, Octopus/Heinemann, 1987
I See You Never, vi *New Yorker* Nov 8,1947
Fahrenheit 451/The Illustrated Man/Dandelion Wine/The Golden Apples of the Sun/The Martian Chronicles, Octopus/Heinemann, 1987
I, Rocket, ss *Amazing* May,1944
Amazing Science Fiction Stories: The War Years 1936-1945, ed. Martin H. Greenberg, TSR, 1987
Illumination, ss *Reporter* May 16,1957
Fahrenheit 451/The Illustrated Man/Dandelion Wine/The Golden Apples of the Sun/The Martian Chronicles, Octopus/Heinemann, 1987
The Illustrated Man, co Doubleday: Garden City, NY,1951
Fahrenheit 451/The Illustrated Man/Dandelion Wine/The Golden Apples of the Sun/The Martian Chronicles, Octopus/Heinemann, 1987
Interim, vi **The Martian Chronicles**,1950
Fahrenheit 451/The Illustrated Man/Dandelion Wine/The Golden Apples of the Sun/The Martian Chronicles, Octopus/Heinemann, 1987

BRADBURY, RAY

Bradbury, Ray (continued)
  Invisible Boy, ss *Mademoiselle* Nov,1945
    Fahrenheit 451/The Illustrated Man/Dandelion Wine/The Golden Apples of the Sun/The Martian Chronicles, Octopus/Heinemann, 1987
  Kaleidoscope, ss *Thrilling Wonder Stories* Oct,1949
    Great Science Fiction of the 20th Century, ed. Robert Silverberg +, Crown/Avenel, 1987
    Fahrenheit 451/The Illustrated Man/Dandelion Wine/The Golden Apples of the Sun/The Martian Chronicles, Octopus/Heinemann, 1987
  The Last Night of the World, ss *Esquire* Feb,1951
    Fahrenheit 451/The Illustrated Man/Dandelion Wine/The Golden Apples of the Sun/The Martian Chronicles, Octopus/Heinemann, 1987
  The Last, the Very Last [also as "The Time Machine"], ss *Reporter* Jun 2,1955
    Fahrenheit 451/The Illustrated Man/Dandelion Wine/The Golden Apples of the Sun/The Martian Chronicles, Octopus/Heinemann, 1987
  The Lawns of Summer, ss *Nation's Business* Feb,1952
    Fahrenheit 451/The Illustrated Man/Dandelion Wine/The Golden Apples of the Sun/The Martian Chronicles, Octopus/Heinemann, 1987
  The Locusts, vi **The Martian Chronicles**,1950
    Fahrenheit 451/The Illustrated Man/Dandelion Wine/The Golden Apples of the Sun/The Martian Chronicles, Octopus/Heinemann, 1987
  The Long Rain [Death-by-Rain], ss *Planet Stories* Sum,1950
    Fahrenheit 451/The Illustrated Man/Dandelion Wine/The Golden Apples of the Sun/The Martian Chronicles, Octopus/Heinemann, 1987
  The Long Years [also as "Dwellers in Silence"], ss *Maclean's* Sep 15,1948
    Fahrenheit 451/The Illustrated Man/Dandelion Wine/The Golden Apples of the Sun/The Martian Chronicles, Octopus/Heinemann, 1987
  The Luggage Store, vi **The Martian Chronicles**,1950
    Fahrenheit 451/The Illustrated Man/Dandelion Wine/The Golden Apples of the Sun/The Martian Chronicles, Octopus/Heinemann, 1987
  The Man, ss *Thrilling Wonder Stories* Feb,1949
    Fahrenheit 451/The Illustrated Man/Dandelion Wine/The Golden Apples of the Sun/The Martian Chronicles, Octopus/Heinemann, 1987
  Marionettes, Inc., ss *Startling Stories* Mar,1949
    Fahrenheit 451/The Illustrated Man/Dandelion Wine/The Golden Apples of the Sun/The Martian Chronicles, Octopus/Heinemann, 1987
  The Martian [Impossible], ss *Super Science Stories* Nov,1949
    Fahrenheit 451/The Illustrated Man/Dandelion Wine/The Golden Apples of the Sun/The Martian Chronicles, Octopus/Heinemann, 1987
  The Martian Chronicles, co Doubleday: Garden City, NY,1950
    Fahrenheit 451/The Illustrated Man/Dandelion Wine/The Golden Apples of the Sun/The Martian Chronicles, Octopus/Heinemann, 1987
  The Meadow, ss **Best One Act Plays**,1948
    Fahrenheit 451/The Illustrated Man/Dandelion Wine/The Golden Apples of the Sun/The Martian Chronicles, Octopus/Heinemann, 1987
  The Million-Year Picnic, ss *Planet Stories* Sum,1946
    Fahrenheit 451/The Illustrated Man/Dandelion Wine/The Golden Apples of the Sun/The Martian Chronicles, Octopus/Heinemann, 1987
  The Murderer, ss *Argosy (UK)* Jun,1953
    Fahrenheit 451/The Illustrated Man/Dandelion Wine/The Golden Apples of the Sun/The Martian Chronicles, Octopus/Heinemann, 1987
  The Musicians, vi **The Martian Chronicles**,1950
    Fahrenheit 451/The Illustrated Man/Dandelion Wine/The Golden Apples of the Sun/The Martian Chronicles, Octopus/Heinemann, 1987
  The Naming of Names, vi **The Martian Chronicles**,1950
    Fahrenheit 451/The Illustrated Man/Dandelion Wine/The Golden Apples of the Sun/The Martian Chronicles, Octopus/Heinemann, 1987

Bradbury, Ray (continued)
  The Night, ss *Weird Tales* Jul,1946
    Fahrenheit 451/The Illustrated Man/Dandelion Wine/The Golden Apples of the Sun/The Martian Chronicles, Octopus/Heinemann, 1987
  Night Meeting, ss **The Martian Chronicles**,1950
    Fahrenheit 451/The Illustrated Man/Dandelion Wine/The Golden Apples of the Sun/The Martian Chronicles, Octopus/Heinemann, 1987
  No Particular Night or Morning, ss **The Illustrated Man**,1951
    Fahrenheit 451/The Illustrated Man/Dandelion Wine/The Golden Apples of the Sun/The Martian Chronicles, Octopus/Heinemann, 1987
  The Off Season, ss *Thrilling Wonder Stories* Dec,1948
    Fahrenheit 451/The Illustrated Man/Dandelion Wine/The Golden Apples of the Sun/The Martian Chronicles, Octopus/Heinemann, 1987
  The Old Ones, vi **The Martian Chronicles**,1950
    Fahrenheit 451/The Illustrated Man/Dandelion Wine/The Golden Apples of the Sun/The Martian Chronicles, Octopus/Heinemann, 1987
  The Other Foot, ss *New Story* Mar,1951
    Fahrenheit 451/The Illustrated Man/Dandelion Wine/The Golden Apples of the Sun/The Martian Chronicles, Octopus/Heinemann, 1987
  The Pedestrian, ss *Reporter* Aug 7,1951; *F&SF* Feb,1952
    Fahrenheit 451/The Illustrated Man/Dandelion Wine/The Golden Apples of the Sun/The Martian Chronicles, Octopus/Heinemann, 1987
  The Playground, ss *Esquire* Oct,1953
    Ready or Not, ed. Joan Kahn, Greenwillow, 1987
  Powerhouse, ss *Charm* Mar,1948
    Fahrenheit 451/The Illustrated Man/Dandelion Wine/The Golden Apples of the Sun/The Martian Chronicles, Octopus/Heinemann, 1987
  Prologue: The Illustrated Man, ss **The Illustrated Man**,1951
    Fahrenheit 451/The Illustrated Man/Dandelion Wine/The Golden Apples of the Sun/The Martian Chronicles, Octopus/Heinemann, 1987
  The Rocket [Outcast of the Stars], ss *Super Science Stories* Mar,1950
    Fahrenheit 451/The Illustrated Man/Dandelion Wine/The Golden Apples of the Sun/The Martian Chronicles, Octopus/Heinemann, 1987
  The Rocket Man, ss *Maclean's* Mar 1,1951
    Fahrenheit 451/The Illustrated Man/Dandelion Wine/The Golden Apples of the Sun/The Martian Chronicles, Octopus/Heinemann, 1987
  Rocket Summer, vi **The Martian Chronicles**,1950
    Fahrenheit 451/The Illustrated Man/Dandelion Wine/The Golden Apples of the Sun/The Martian Chronicles, Octopus/Heinemann, 1987
  Season of Disbelief, ss *Colliers* Nov 25,1950
    Fahrenheit 451/The Illustrated Man/Dandelion Wine/The Golden Apples of the Sun/The Martian Chronicles, Octopus/Heinemann, 1987
  The Season of Sitting, ar *Charm* Aug,1951
    Fahrenheit 451/The Illustrated Man/Dandelion Wine/The Golden Apples of the Sun/The Martian Chronicles, Octopus/Heinemann, 1987
  The Settlers, vi **The Martian Chronicles**,1950
    Fahrenheit 451/The Illustrated Man/Dandelion Wine/The Golden Apples of the Sun/The Martian Chronicles, Octopus/Heinemann, 1987
  The Shore, vi **The Martian Chronicles**,1950
    Fahrenheit 451/The Illustrated Man/Dandelion Wine/The Golden Apples of the Sun/The Martian Chronicles, Octopus/Heinemann, 1987
  The Silent Towns, ss *Charm* Mar,1949
    Fahrenheit 451/The Illustrated Man/Dandelion Wine/The Golden Apples of the Sun/The Martian Chronicles, Octopus/Heinemann, 1987
  A Sound of Thunder, ss *Colliers* Jun 28,1952
    Fahrenheit 451/The Illustrated Man/Dandelion Wine/The Golden Apples of the Sun/The Martian Chronicles, Octopus/Heinemann, 1987

Bradbury, Ray (continued)
  Statues, ss **Dandelion Wine**, Ray Bradbury, Doubleday,1957
    **Fahrenheit 451/The Illustrated Man/Dandelion Wine/The
    Golden Apples of the Sun/The Martian Chronicles**,
    Octopus/Heinemann, 1987
  Summer in the Air [also as "The Sound of Summer Running"], ss *The
    Saturday Evening Post* Feb 18,1956
    **Fahrenheit 451/The Illustrated Man/Dandelion Wine/The
    Golden Apples of the Sun/The Martian Chronicles**,
    Octopus/Heinemann, 1987
  The Summer Night [The Spring Night], vi *Arkham Sampler* Win,1948
    **Fahrenheit 451/The Illustrated Man/Dandelion Wine/The
    Golden Apples of the Sun/The Martian Chronicles**,
    Octopus/Heinemann, 1987
  Sun and Shadow, ss *Reporter* Mar 17,1953
    **Fahrenheit 451/The Illustrated Man/Dandelion Wine/The
    Golden Apples of the Sun/The Martian Chronicles**,
    Octopus/Heinemann, 1987
  The Swan, ss *Cosmopolitan* Sep,1954
    **Fahrenheit 451/The Illustrated Man/Dandelion Wine/The
    Golden Apples of the Sun/The Martian Chronicles**,
    Octopus/Heinemann, 1987
  The Taxpayer, vi **The Martian Chronicles**,1950
    **Fahrenheit 451/The Illustrated Man/Dandelion Wine/The
    Golden Apples of the Sun/The Martian Chronicles**,
    Octopus/Heinemann, 1987
  There Will Come Soft Rains, ss *Colliers* May 6,1950
    **Fahrenheit 451/The Illustrated Man/Dandelion Wine/The
    Golden Apples of the Sun/The Martian Chronicles**,
    Octopus/Heinemann, 1987
  The Third Expedition, ss *Planet Stories* Fll,1948
    **Fahrenheit 451/The Illustrated Man/Dandelion Wine/The
    Golden Apples of the Sun/The Martian Chronicles**,
    Octopus/Heinemann, 1987
  The Trolley, ss *Good Housekeeping* Jul,1955
    **Fahrenheit 451/The Illustrated Man/Dandelion Wine/The
    Golden Apples of the Sun/The Martian Chronicles**,
    Octopus/Heinemann, 1987
  Usher II [Carnival of Madness], ss *Thrilling Wonder Stories* Apr,1950
    **Fahrenheit 451/The Illustrated Man/Dandelion Wine/The
    Golden Apples of the Sun/The Martian Chronicles**,
    Octopus/Heinemann, 1987
  The Veldt [The World the Children Made], ss *The Saturday Evening
    Post* Sep 23,1950
    **Fahrenheit 451/The Illustrated Man/Dandelion Wine/The
    Golden Apples of the Sun/The Martian Chronicles**,
    Octopus/Heinemann, 1987
  The Visitor, ss *Startling Stories* Nov,1948
    **Fahrenheit 451/The Illustrated Man/Dandelion Wine/The
    Golden Apples of the Sun/The Martian Chronicles**,
    Octopus/Heinemann, 1987
  The Watchers, vi **The Martian Chronicles**,1950
    **Fahrenheit 451/The Illustrated Man/Dandelion Wine/The
    Golden Apples of the Sun/The Martian Chronicles**,
    Octopus/Heinemann, 1987
  Way in the Middle of the Air, ss *Other Worlds* Jul,1950
    **Fahrenheit 451/The Illustrated Man/Dandelion Wine/The
    Golden Apples of the Sun/The Martian Chronicles**,
    Octopus/Heinemann, 1987
  The Whole Town's Sleeping, ss *McCalls* Sep,1950
    **Fahrenheit 451/The Illustrated Man/Dandelion Wine/The
    Golden Apples of the Sun/The Martian Chronicles**,
    Octopus/Heinemann, 1987
  The Wilderness, ss *F&SF* Nov,1952
    **Fahrenheit 451/The Illustrated Man/Dandelion Wine/The
    Golden Apples of the Sun/The Martian Chronicles**,
    Octopus/Heinemann, 1987
  The Window, ss *Colliers* Aug 5,1950
    **Fahrenheit 451/The Illustrated Man/Dandelion Wine/The
    Golden Apples of the Sun/The Martian Chronicles**,
    Octopus/Heinemann, 1987
  Ylla [I'll Not Look for Wine], ss *Maclean's* Jan 1,1950
    **Fahrenheit 451/The Illustrated Man/Dandelion Wine/The
    Golden Apples of the Sun/The Martian Chronicles**,
    Octopus/Heinemann, 1987

Bradbury, Ray (continued)
  Zero Hour, ss *Planet Stories* Fll,1947
    **Fahrenheit 451/The Illustrated Man/Dandelion Wine/The
    Golden Apples of the Sun/The Martian Chronicles**,
    Octopus/Heinemann, 1987

Braddon, Mary Elizabeth
  Good Lady Ducayne, nv *The Strand* Feb,1896
    Vampires, ed. Alan Ryan, SFBC, 1987
    Dracula's Brood, ed. Richard Dalby, Crucible, 1987

Bradfield, Scott
  Unmistakably the Finest, nv *Interzone* #8,1984
    Interzone: The 2nd Anthology, ed. John Clute+, Simon &
    Schuster UK, 1987

Bradley, Marion Zimmer
  The Ballad of Hastur and Cassilda, sg **Red Sun of Darkover**, ed.
    Marion Zimmer Bradley & The Friends of Darkover, DAW,1987
  Bitch, ss *F&SF* Feb,1987
  Bride Price, ss **The Other Side of the Mirror**, ed. Marion Zimmer
    Bradley & The Friends of Darkover, DAW,1987
  Dance at the Gym, ss *The San Francisco Chronicle* Sep 17,1987
  Everything but Freedom, na **The Other Side of the Mirror**, ed.
    Marion Zimmer Bradley & The Friends of Darkover, DAW,1987
  Introduction, in
    The Other Side of the Mirror, ed. Marion Zimmer Bradley+, DAW,
    1987
    Sword and Sorceress IV, ed. Marion Zimmer Bradley, DAW, 1987
    Red Sun of Darkover, ed. Marion Zimmer Bradley+, DAW, 1987
  Oathbreaker, nv **The Other Side of the Mirror**, ed. Marion Zimmer
    Bradley & The Friends of Darkover, DAW,1987
  The Shadow, nv **Red Sun of Darkover**, ed. Marion Zimmer Bradley &
    The Friends of Darkover, DAW,1987
  The Walker Behind, ss *F&SF* Jul,1987

Bradley, Rebecca
  Allsouls, ss **The Pan Book of Horror Stories** #28, Pan,1987
  Tea Leaves, ss **The Pan Book of Horror Stories** #28, Pan,1987

Bradman, Tony
  Cinderella, ss **The Magic Kiss and Other Tales of Princes and
    Princesses**, Tony Bradman, Blackie,1987
  The Magic Kiss, ss **The Magic Kiss and Other Tales of Princes and
    Princesses**, Tony Bradman, Blackie,1987

Brandner, Gary
  Bad Actor, ss *Alfred Hitchcock's Mystery Magazine* May,1973
    Alfred Hitchcock's Book of Horror Stories: Book 6, ed. Alfred
    Hitchcock, Coronet, 1987

Branham, R.V.
  In the Sickbay, nv **L. Ron Hubbard Presents Writers of the Future
    v3**, ed. Algis Budrys, Bridge,1987

Brantingham, Juleen
  Toad, Singular, ss **Whispers** #6, ed. Stuart David Schiff,1987

Braunbeck, Gary A.
  A Death in the Day of, ss *The Horror Show* Win,1987
  The Eldritch Eye, ss *Eldritch Tales* #14,1987

Brennan, Joseph Payne
  Cornstalk Riddles, pm *Grue* #4,1987
  Jendick's Swamp, ss **Doom City**, ed. Charles L. Grant, Tor,1987
  The Willow Platform, ss *Whispers* #1,1973
    Demons!, ed. Jack M. Dann+, Ace, 1987
  Zombique, ss *Alfred Hitchcock's Mystery Magazine* Oct,1972
    Masters of Darkness II, ed. Dennis Etchison, Tor, 1988

Brennert, Alan
  Other Voices, is *Twilight Zone* Oct,1987
  Voices in the Earth, ss *Twilight Zone* Oct,1987

Bretnor, Reginald
  Decisive Warfare: Retrospect and Prospect, ar **There Will Be War** v6,
    ed. Jerry E. Pournelle,1987

BRETNOR, REGINALD   **BROWN, FREDRIC**

Bretnor, Reginald (continued)
  Dr. Birdmouse, ss *Fantastic* Apr,1962
    Fantastic Stories: Tales of the Weird and Wondrous, ed. Martin
      H. Greenberg+, TSR, 1987
  Nobelist Schimmelhorn, nv *F&SF* May,1987
  There's Magic in Shakespeare, nv *Night Cry* v2#4,1987

Breuer, Miles J., M.D.
  The Man with the Strange Head, ss *Amazing* Jan,1927
    Amazing Science Fiction Stories: The Wonder Years 1926-1935,
      ed. Martin H. Greenberg, TSR, 1987

Briarton, Grendel
  Through Time & Space with Ferdinand Feghoot I, vi *Amazing* Jul,1987
  Through Time & Space with Ferdinand Feghoot i, vi *Amazing*
    Mar,1987

Briggs, Kevin C., D. Scott Apel & Philip K. Dick
  Philip K. Dick in Interview, iv **Philip K. Dick: The Dream Connection**,
    D. Scott Apel, Permanent Press,1987

Brin, David
  Bubbles, ss **Universe**, ed. Byron Preiss, Bantam Spectra,1987
  Startide Rising, n. Bantam: New York pb Sep,1983
    Earthclan, SFBC, 1987
  The Uplift War, n. Phantasia: West Bloomfield, MI hc Apr,1987
    Earthclan, SFBC, 1987

Brite, Poppy Z.
  Angels (Goldengrove Unleaving), ss *The Horror Show* Fll,1987
  The Elder, ss *The Horror Show* Jan,1987
  Love (Ash I), ss *The Horror Show* Fll,1987

Brite, Poppy Z. & William J. Grabowski
  Poppy Z. Brite, iv *The Horror Show* Fll,1987

Briyles, Donald
  The Eye of Klagg, vi *Eldritch Tales* #13,1987

Brizzolara, John
  Nightskin, ss *Twilight Zone* Feb,1987

Broaddus, John C.
  First Plane I See Tonight, ss *Grue* #4,1987

Broderick, Damien
  Thy Sting, vi *Omni* Jun,1987

Bromley, Darwin
  The Legal Problems of a Thieves' World, ar *American Fantasy*
    Spr,1987

Bromley, Robin
  Television, ar *Twilight Zone* Jun,1987

Brooks, Stan
  Book Reviews, br *Footsteps* Nov,1987

Broster, Dorothy K.
  Juggernaut, ss **Couching at the Door**, Heinemann: London,1942
    The Virago Book of Ghost Stories, ed. Richard Dalby, Virago, 1987

Broumas, Olga
  Little Red Riding Hood, pm **Beginning With O**, New Haven, CT: Yale
    Univ. Press,1977
    Don't Bet on the Prince, ed. Jack Zipes, Methuen, 1987

Brower, John
  Harmony of Fear, mr *Minnesota Fantasy Review* #1,1987

Brown, Ann R.
  The Clockwork Woman, ss **Magic in Ithkar** #4, ed. Andre Norton &
    Robert Adams,1987

Brown, Charles N.
  1986, The SF Year in Review, ar,1987
    Terry Carr's Best Science Fiction and Fantasy of the Year #16,
      ed. Terry Carr, Tor, 1987

Brown, Eric
  The Girl Who Died for Art, and Lived, ss *Interzone* #22,1987
  Krash-Bangg Joe and the Pineal-Zen Equation, ss *Interzone* #21,1987

Brown, Fredric
  Abominable, vi *Dude* Mar,1960
    Portfolio; gp
    And the Gods Laughed, Phantasia Press, 1987
  And the Gods Laughed, ss *Tops In Science Fiction* Fll,1953
    And the Gods Laughed, Phantasia Press, 1987
  Answer, vi **Angels and Spaceships**, Dutton,1954
    Isaac Asimov Presents the Great SF Stories: 16 (1954), ed. Isaac
      Asimov+, DAW, 1987
  Arena, nv *Astounding* Jun,1944
    And the Gods Laughed, Phantasia Press, 1987
  Armageddon, ss *Unknown* Aug,1941
    Devils and Demons, ed. Marvin Kaye, Doubleday, 1987
  Bear Possibility, vi *Dude* Mar,1960
    Portfolio; gp
    And the Gods Laughed, Phantasia Press, 1987
  Blood, vi *F&SF* Feb,1955
    And the Gods Laughed, Phantasia Press, 1987
  Bright Beard, vi **Nightmares and Geezenstacks**, Bantam,1961
    And the Gods Laughed, Phantasia Press, 1987
  Cat Burglar, vi **Nightmares and Geezenstacks**, Bantam,1961
    And the Gods Laughed, Phantasia Press, 1987
  Contact [Earthmen Bearing Gifts], vi *Galaxy* Jun,1960
    And the Gods Laughed, Phantasia Press, 1987
  Dead Letter, vi **Nightmares and Geezenstacks**, Bantam,1961
    And the Gods Laughed, Phantasia Press, 1987
  Death Is a White Rabbit, nv *Strange Detective Mysteries* Jan,1942
    Strange Maine, ed. Charles G. Waugh+, Tapley, 1986
    Pardon My Ghoulish Laughter, Dennis McMillan, 1987
  Death of a Vampire, nv *Strange Detective Mysteries* May,1943
    Pardon My Ghoulish Laughter, Dennis McMillan, 1987
  Death on the Mountain, vi **Nightmares and Geezenstacks**,
    Bantam,1961
    And the Gods Laughed, Phantasia Press, 1987
  The Dome, ss *Thrilling Wonder Stories* Aug,1951
    And the Gods Laughed, Phantasia Press, 1987
  The End [Nightmare in Time], vi *Dude* May,1961
    Five Nightmares; gp
    And the Gods Laughed, Phantasia Press, 1987
  Entity Trap [From These Ashes], ss *Amazing* Aug,1950
    And the Gods Laughed, Phantasia Press, 1987
  Expedition, vi *F&SF* Feb,1957
    And the Gods Laughed, Phantasia Press, 1987
  Experiment, vi *Galaxy* Feb,1954
    Two Timer; gp
    And the Gods Laughed, Phantasia Press, 1987
  Fatal Error, vi **Nightmares and Geezenstacks**, Bantam,1961
    And the Gods Laughed, Phantasia Press, 1987
  First Time Machine, vi *Ellery Queen's Mystery Magazine* Sep,1955
    And the Gods Laughed, Phantasia Press, 1987
  Fish Story, vi **Nightmares and Geezenstacks**, Bantam,1961
    And the Gods Laughed, Phantasia Press, 1987
  The Geezenstacks, ss *Weird Tales* Sep,1943
    And the Gods Laughed, Phantasia Press, 1987
  Ghost Breakers, nv *Thrilling Detective* Jul,1944
    Pardon My Ghoulish Laughter, Dennis McMillan, 1987
  Granny's Birthday, vi *Alfred Hitchcock's Mystery Magazine* Jun,1960
    And the Gods Laughed, Phantasia Press, 1987
  Great Lost Discoveries I - Invisibility, vi *Gent* Feb,1961
    And the Gods Laughed, Phantasia Press, 1987
  Great Lost Discoveries II - Invulnerability, vi *Gent* Feb,1961
    And the Gods Laughed, Phantasia Press, 1987
  Great Lost Discoveries III - Immortality, vi *Gent* Feb,1961
    And the Gods Laughed, Phantasia Press, 1987
  Hall of Mirrors, ss *Galaxy* Dec,1953
    And the Gods Laughed, Phantasia Press, 1987
  Hobbyist, vi *Playboy* May,1961
    And the Gods Laughed, Phantasia Press, 1987
  Honeymoon in Hell, nv *Galaxy* Nov,1950
    And the Gods Laughed, Phantasia Press, 1987
  Horse Race, vi **Nightmares and Geezenstacks**, Bantam,1961
    And the Gods Laughed, Phantasia Press, 1987
  The House, vi *Fantastic* Aug,1960
    And the Gods Laughed, Phantasia Press, 1987

Brown, Fredric (continued)
  Imagine, a Proem, pm *F&SF* May,1955
    And the Gods Laughed, Phantasia Press, 1987
  The Incredible Bomber, nv *G-Man Detective* Mar,1942
    Pardon My Ghoulish Laughter, Dennis McMillan, 1987
  Jaycee, vi *F&SF*,1955
    And the Gods Laughed, Phantasia Press, 1987
  The Joke, ss **Nightmares and Geezenstacks**, Bantam,1961
    And the Gods Laughed, Phantasia Press, 1987
  Keep Out, ss *Amazing* Mar,1954
    And the Gods Laughed, Phantasia Press, 1987
  The Last Martian, ss *Galaxy* Oct,1950
    And the Gods Laughed, Phantasia Press, 1987
  The Little Lamb, ss *Manhunt* Aug,1953
    And the Gods Laughed, Phantasia Press, 1987
  A Lock of Satan's Hair, nv *Dime Mystery Magazine* Jan,1943
    Pardon My Ghoulish Laughter, Dennis McMillan, 1987
  Man of Distinction, ss *Thrilling Wonder Stories* Feb,1951
    And the Gods Laughed, Phantasia Press, 1987
  Millennium, vi *F&SF* Mar,1955
    And the Gods Laughed, Phantasia Press, 1987
  Mitkey Rides Again, nv *Planet Stories* Nov,1950
    And the Gods Laughed, Phantasia Press, 1987
  Mouse, ss *Thrilling Wonder Stories* Jun,1949
    And the Gods Laughed, Phantasia Press, 1987
  Murder in Ten Easy Lessons, ss *Ten Detective Aces* May,1945
    And the Gods Laughed, Phantasia Press, 1987
  Nasty, vi *Playboy* Apr,1959
    And the Gods Laughed, Phantasia Press, 1987
  Naturally, vi *Beyond Fantasy Fiction* Sep,1954
    Double Whammy; gp
    And the Gods Laughed, Phantasia Press, 1987
  Nightmare in Blue, vi *Dude* May,1961
    Five Nightmares; gp
    And the Gods Laughed, Phantasia Press, 1987
  Nightmare in Gray, vi *Dude* May,1961
    Five Nightmares; gp
    And the Gods Laughed, Phantasia Press, 1987
  Nightmare in Green, vi **Nightmares and Geezenstacks**, Bantam,1961
    And the Gods Laughed, Phantasia Press, 1987
  Nightmare in Red, vi *Dude* May,1961
    Five Nightmares; gp
    And the Gods Laughed, Phantasia Press, 1987
  Nightmare in White, vi **Nightmares and Geezenstacks**, Bantam,1961
    And the Gods Laughed, Phantasia Press, 1987
  Nightmare in Yellow, vi *Dude* May,1961
    Five Nightmares; gp
    And the Gods Laughed, Phantasia Press, 1987
  Not Yet the End, vi *Captain Future* Win,1941
    And the Gods Laughed, Phantasia Press, 1987
  Pardon My Ghoulish Laughter, ss *Strange Detective Mysteries* Feb,1942
    Pardon My Ghoulish Laughter, Dennis McMillan, 1987
  Rebound [The Power], vi *Galaxy* Apr,1960
    And the Gods Laughed, Phantasia Press, 1987
  Recessional, vi *Dude* Mar,1960
    Portfolio; gp
    And the Gods Laughed, Phantasia Press, 1987
  The Ring of Hans Carvel, vi **Nightmares and Geezenstacks**, Bantam,1961
    And the Gods Laughed, Phantasia Press, 1987
  Rope Trick, vi *Adam* May,1959
    And the Gods Laughed, Phantasia Press, 1987
  Runaround [Starvation], ss *Astounding* Sep,1942
    And the Gods Laughed, Phantasia Press, 1987
  Rustle of Wings, ss *F&SF* Aug,1953
    Isaac Asimov's Magical Worlds of Fantasy #8: Devils, ed. Isaac Asimov+, NAL/Signet, 1987
    And the Gods Laughed, Phantasia Press, 1987
  Second Chance, vi **Nightmares and Geezenstacks**, Bantam,1961
    And the Gods Laughed, Phantasia Press, 1987
  Sentry, vi *Galaxy* Feb,1954
    Two Timer; gp
    And the Gods Laughed, Phantasia Press, 1987
  The Short Happy Lives of Eustace Weaver I, vi *Ellery Queen's Mystery Magazine* Jun,1961
    And the Gods Laughed, Phantasia Press, 1987

Brown, Fredric (continued)
  The Short Happy Lives of Eustace Weaver II, vi *Ellery Queen's Mystery Magazine* Jun,1961
    And the Gods Laughed, Phantasia Press, 1987
  The Short Happy Lives of Eustace Weaver III, vi *Ellery Queen's Mystery Magazine* Jun,1961
    And the Gods Laughed, Phantasia Press, 1987
  The Star Mouse, ss *Planet Stories* Spr,1942
    And the Gods Laughed, Phantasia Press, 1987
  Three Little Owls, vi **Nightmares and Geezenstacks**, Bantam,1961
    And the Gods Laughed, Phantasia Press, 1987
  Too Far, vi *F&SF* Sep,1955
    And the Gods Laughed, Phantasia Press, 1987
  Twice-Killed Corpse, nv *Ten Detective Aces* Mar,1942
    Pardon My Ghoulish Laughter, Dennis McMillan, 1987
  Unfortunately, vi *F&SF* Oct,1958
    And the Gods Laughed, Phantasia Press, 1987
  Vengeance Fleet [Vengeance, Unlimited], vi *Super Science Stories* Jul,1950
    And the Gods Laughed, Phantasia Press, 1987
  Voodoo, vi *Beyond Fantasy Fiction* Sep,1954
    Double Whammy; gp
    And the Gods Laughed, Phantasia Press, 1987
  The Weapon, ss *Astounding* Apr,1951
    And the Gods Laughed, Phantasia Press, 1987
  A Word from Our Sponsor, ss *Other Worlds* Sep,1951
    And the Gods Laughed, Phantasia Press, 1987

Brown, Fredric & Mack Reynolds
  Cartoonist [Garrigan's Bems], ss *Planet Stories* May,1951
    And the Gods Laughed, Phantasia Press, 1987
  Dark Interlude, ss *Galaxy* Jan,1951
    And the Gods Laughed, Phantasia Press, 1987
  The Gamblers, nv *Startling Stories* Nov,1951
    And the Gods Laughed, Phantasia Press, 1987
  Me and Flapjack and the Martians, ss *Astounding* Dec,1952
    And the Gods Laughed, Phantasia Press, 1987
  Six-Legged Svengali, ss *Worlds Beyond* Dec,1950
    And the Gods Laughed, Phantasia Press, 1987
  The Switcheroo, ss *Other Worlds* Mar,1951
    And the Gods Laughed, Phantasia Press, 1987

Brown, George Mackay
  The Tree and the Harp, ss **A Quiver of Ghosts**, ed. Aiden Chambers, Bodley Head,1987

Brown, Ray
  Cobwebs, nv *Analog* Aug,1987

Broxon, Mildred Downey
  First Do No Harm, ss **Magic in Ithkar #4**, ed. Andre Norton & Robert Adams,1987

Brumbaugh, J.D.
  Afternoon Sail, ss *American Fantasy* Spr,1987

Brunelle, Beverly
  Sweet Dreams, ss *Haunts* #9,1987

Brunet, James
  Symphony in Ursa Major, ss *Aboriginal SF* Jul,1987

Brunner, John
  A Case of Painter's Ear, ss **Tales from the Forbidden Planet**, ed. Roz Kaveney, Titan,1987
  Elixir for the Emperor, ss *Fantastic* Nov,1964
    Fantastic Stories: Tales of the Weird and Wondrous, ed. Martin H. Greenberg+, TSR, 1987
  The Fable of the Farmer and the Fox, vi *Omni* Jun,1987
  Introduction, in
    The Collected Stories of Philip K. Dick, Vol. Three: The Father Thing, Philip K. Dick, Underwood-Miller, 1987
  Mercy Worse Than None, nv **Aftermath**, ed. Robert Lynn Asprin & Lynn Abbey, Ace,1987

Brust, Steven & Megan Lindholm
  An Act of Mercy, ss **Liavek: Wizard's Row**, ed. Will Shetterly & Emma Bull, Ace,1987

Brutvan, Michael J.
  Subatomic Particles, ss *Mage* Win,1987

Bryant, Edward
  The Baku, nv **Night Visions** #4,1987
  Books, br *Twilight Zone* Jun,1987
  Books, br *Twilight Zone* Aug,1987
  Books, br *Twilight Zone* Oct,1987
  Books, br *Twilight Zone* Dec,1987
  Buggage, ss **Night Visions** #4,1987
  Coon Dawgs, ss **Trilobyte/The Shadow on the Doorstep**, Edward
    Bryant & James P. Blaylock, Seattle: Axolotl,1987
    The Shadow on the Doorstep/Trilobyte, James P. Blaylock +,
    Axolotl, 1987
  Doing Colfax, ss **Night Visions** #4,1987
  Drummer's Star, ss **Trilobyte/The Shadow on the Doorstep**, Edward
    Bryant & James P. Blaylock, Seattle: Axolotl,1987
    The Shadow on the Doorstep/Trilobyte, James P. Blaylock +,
    Axolotl, 1987
  Drummer's Star, ss **Trilobyte/The Shadow on the Doorstep**, Seattle:
    Axolotl,1987
    F&SF Oct,1987
  An Easter Treasure, ss **Trilobyte/The Shadow on the Doorstep**,
    Edward Bryant & James P. Blaylock, Seattle: Axolotl,1987
    The Shadow on the Doorstep/Trilobyte, James P. Blaylock +,
    Axolotl, 1987
  Frat Rat Bash, ss **Night Visions** #4,1987
  Haunted, ss **Night Visions** #4,1987
  Predators, ss **Night Visions** #4,1987
  Shark, nv **Orbit** #12, ed. Damon Knight,1973
    Battlefields Beyond Tomorrow, ed. Charles G. Waugh +,
    Crown/Bonanza, 1987
  Teeth Marks, ss *F&SF* Jun,1979
    House Shudders, ed. Martin H. Greenberg +, DAW, 1987
  The Twilight Zone Review: 1986 - Fiction, br *Twilight Zone* Feb,1987

Buard, Patricia Anne
  Devil's Advocate, ss **Red Sun of Darkover**, ed. Marion Zimmer
    Bradley & The Friends of Darkover, DAW,1987

Buchanan, P.J.
  Different Path, nv **Red Sun of Darkover**, ed. Marion Zimmer Bradley
    & The Friends of Darkover, DAW,1987

Bucklin, Nathan A.
  Imperfect Catch, ss *Tales of the Unanticipated* #2,1987

Budrys, Algis
  Books, br *F&SF* Jan,1987
  Books, br *F&SF* Feb,1987
  Books, br *F&SF* Mar,1987
  Books, br *F&SF* Apr,1987
  Books, br *F&SF* May,1987
  Books, br *F&SF* Jun,1987
  Books, br *F&SF* Jul,1987
  Books, br *F&SF* Aug,1987
  Books, br *F&SF* Oct,1987
  Books, br *F&SF* Nov,1987
  The End of Summer, nv *Astounding* Nov,1954
    Isaac Asimov Presents the Great SF Stories: 16 (1954), ed. Isaac
    Asimov +, DAW, 1987
  Foreword, fw
    Polyphemus, Michael Shea, Arkham House, 1987
  Introduction, in
    L. Ron Hubbard Presents Writers of the Future, Vol. III, ed. Algis
    Budrys, Bridge, 1987
  Nobody Bothers Gus [as by Paul Janvier], ss *Astounding* Nov,1955
    Isaac Asimov Presents the Great SF Stories: 17 (1955), ed. Isaac
    Asimov +, DAW, 1988
  The Nuptial Flight of Warbirds, nv *Analog* May,1978
    Battlefields Beyond Tomorrow, ed. Charles G. Waugh +,
    Crown/Bonanza, 1987
  That Fearful Symmetry, vi *Twilight Zone* Apr,1987
  Wall of Crystal, Eye of Night, nv *Galaxy* Dec,1961
    Great Science Fiction of the 20th Century, ed. Robert
    Silverberg +, Crown/Avenel, 1987

Buettner, John
  Stay Out of Innsmouth, pm *Eldritch Tales* #14,1987

buffington, mel
  perverse love, pm *Ice River* Sum,1987
  placebo, pm *Ice River* Sum,1987
  prophylaxis, pm *Ice River* Sum,1987

Bujold, Lois McMaster
  The Borders of Infinity, na **Free Lancers**, ed. Elizabeth Mitchell,
    Baen,1987
  Falling Free [Part 1 of 4], sl *Analog* Dec,1987
  Falling Free [Part 2 of 4], sl *Analog* mid-Dec,1987
  Garage Sale, vi *American Fantasy* Spr,1987
  Shards of Honor, n. Baen: New York,1986
  Test of Honor, SFBC, 1987
  The Warrior's Apprentice, n. Baen: New York,1986
  Test of Honor, SFBC, 1987

Bulwer-Lytton, Sir Edward George, Lord Lytton
  The Haunted and the Haunters, nv *Blackwood's* Aug,1859
    This version restores the full original text.
    Poltergeist: Tales of Deadly Ghosts, ed. Peter Haining, Severn
    House, 1987
  The House and the Brain, nv *Blackwood's* Aug,1859;
    Weird Tales May,1923
    House Shudders, ed. Martin H. Greenberg +, DAW, 1987

Bunch, David R.
  Miracle of the Flowers, ss *Pulpsmith* Win,1987
  A Small Miracle of Fishhooks and Straight Pins, ss *Fantastic* Jun,1961
    Fantastic Stories: Tales of the Weird and Wondrous, ed. Martin
    H. Greenberg +, TSR, 1987

Burks, Arthur J.
  Dance of the Damned, nv *Horror Stories* Aug,1936
    Selected Tales of Grim and Grue from the Horror Pulps, ed.
    Sheldon R. Jaffery, Bowling Green Popular Press, 1987

Burkunk, Wim
  Leakage, ss *SF International* #1,1987
    Translated by Annemarie van Ewyck.

Burleson, Donald R.
  Classified Ads, ss *The Horror Show* Spr,1987
  Family Dentistry, ss *F&SF* Aug,1987
  The Fictive World View of H.P. Lovecraft, ar *Mage* Spr,1986
    Mage Fll,1987

Burleson, Mollie L.
  Home for Dinner, ss *Eldritch Tales* #13,1987

Burnett, Arthur B.
  University Field Observation Guide for the Planet Earth or U.F.O.
    Handbook, ss *Salarius* #3,1987

Burnham, Crispin
  Book Review, br *Eldritch Tales* #14,1987
  Eldritch Lair, ed *Eldritch Tales* #13,1987
  Eldritch Lair, ed *Eldritch Tales* #14,1987
  In Memoriam: Manly Wade Wellman, bg *Eldritch Tales* #13,1987

Burns, Christopher
  Among the Wounded, ss *Interzone* #22,1987

Burns, Stephen L.
  In the Kingdom at Morning, nv *Analog* Feb,1987
  Redeemer's Riddle, nv **Sword and Sorceress** #4, ed. Marion Zimmer
    Bradley,1987
  The Weather With Morgana, ss *2AM* Sum,1987

Burrage, A.M.
  Between the Minute and the Hour, ss **Some Ghost Stories**,1927
    Charles Keeping's Classic Tales of the Macabre, ed. Charles
    Keeping, Blackie, 1987

Burroughs, William S.
  The Ghost Lemurs of Madagascar, ss *Omni* Apr,1987

BURT, JOHN WAYNE

Burt, John Wayne
  Mr. Valdoom's Backyard, ss *Space & Time* #73,1987

Busby, David
  The Gallery of Masks, nv *F&SF* Aug,1987

Busby, F.M.
  2000 1/2: A Spaced Oddity, ss *Vertex* Aug,1973
    Getting Home, Ace, 1987
  The Absence of Tom Leone [Here, There and Everywhere], ss
    Clarion #2, ed. Robert Scott Wilson,1972
    Getting Home, Ace, 1987
  Advantage, vi *Vertex* Aug,1975
    Getting Home, Ace, 1987
  The Alien Debt, n. Bantam: New York,1984
    The Rebel Dynasty, Volume II, Bantam Spectra, 1988
  Getting Home, nv *F&SF* Apr,1974
    Getting Home, Ace, 1987
  A Gun for Grandfather, ss *Future* FII,1957
    Getting Home, Ace, 1987
  I'm Going to Get You, ss *Fantastic* Mar,1974
    Getting Home, Ace, 1987
  If This Is Winnetka, You Must Be Judy, nv **Universe** #5, ed. Terry
    Carr,1974
    Getting Home, Ace, 1987
  Introduction, in
    Getting Home, Ace, 1987
  The Learning of Eeshta, ss *If* Oct,1973
    Getting Home, Ace, 1987
  Misconception, ss *Vertex* Apr,1975
    Getting Home, Ace, 1987
  Of Mice and Otis, ss *Amazing* Mar,1972
    Getting Home, Ace, 1987
  Once Upon a Unicorn, ss *Fantastic* Apr,1973
    Getting Home, Ace, 1987
  Proof, ss *Amazing* Sep,1972
    Getting Home, Ace, 1987
  The Puiss of Krrlik, ss *Fantastic* Apr,1972
    Getting Home, Ace, 1987
  The Real World, ss *Fantastic* Dec,1972
    Getting Home, Ace, 1987
  Rebel's Quest, n. Bantam: New York,1984
    The Rebel Dynasty, Volume I, Bantam Spectra, 1987
  Rebel's Seed, n. Bantam: New York,1986
    The Rebel Dynasty, Volume II, Bantam Spectra, 1988
  Retroflex, vi *Vertex* Oct,1974
    Getting Home, Ace, 1987
  Road Map, ss *Clarion* #3, ed. Robert Scott Wilson,1973
    Getting Home, Ace, 1987
  The Signing of Tulip, ss *Vertex* Jun,1975
    Getting Home, Ace, 1987
  Star Rebel, n. Bantam: New York,1984
    The Rebel Dynasty, Volume I, Bantam Spectra, 1987
  Tell Me All About Yourself, ss **New Dimensions** #3, ed. Robert
    Silverberg/Marta Randall,1973
    Getting Home, Ace, 1987
  Three Tinks on the House, ss *Vertex* Jun,1973
    Getting Home, Ace, 1987
  Time of Need, ss *Vertex* Aug,1974
    Getting Home, Ace, 1987

Butler, Octavia E.
  The Evening and the Morning and the Night, nv *Omni* May,1987
  Speech Sounds, ss *IASFM* mid-Dec,1983
    Tales From Isaac Asimov's Science Fiction Magazine, ed. Sheila
      Williams+, Harcourt Brace Jovanovich, 1986

Buxton, Meg
  The Neighbours, ss **After Midnight Stories** #3,1987

Byrne, Leon
  Guest-Room in Hell, ss *Horror Stories* Oct,1936
    The Weirds, ed. Sheldon R. Jaffery, Starmont House, 1987

Cabot, Laurie & James Verniere
  The Witch of Salem, iv *Twilight Zone* Jun,1987

Cadigan, Pat
  Angel, ss *IASFM* May,1987
  The Boy in the Rain, ss *Twilight Zone* Jun,1987
  By Lost Ways, nv **Wild Cards** v2, ed. George R.R. Martin,
    Bantam,1987
  Lunatic Bridge, nv **The Omni Book of Science Fiction** #5, ed. Ellen
    Datlow,1987
  Patterns, ss *Omni* Aug,1987
  Pretty Boy Crossover, ss *IASFM* Jan,1986
    The Year's Best Science Fiction, Fourth Annual Collection, ed.
      Gardner R. Dozois, St. Martin's, 1987
    The 1987 Annual World's Best SF, ed. Donald A. Wollheim+,
      DAW, 1987

Calcamuggio, Mark
  The Driftwood in the Fox's Den, ss *Space & Time* #72,1987

Caldecott, Sir Andrew
  Christmas Reunion, ss **Not Exactly Ghosts**, E. Arnold: London,1946
    Christmas Ghosts, ed. Kathryn Cramer+, Arbor House, 1987
    Ghosts and Scholars, ed. Rosemary Pardoe+, Crucible, 1987

Callin, Grant D.
  Deborah's Children, ss *Analog* Sep,1983
    **Isaac Asimov's Wonderful Worlds of Science Fiction #7: Space
      Shuttles**, ed. Isaac Asimov+, NAL/Signet, 1987

Cameron, Anne
  Magic in a World of Magic, nv **Hear the Silence**, ed. Irene Zahava,
    Crossing Press,1986

Campbell, John W., Jr.
  Constitution for Utopia [Constitution], ed *Analog* Mar,1961
    Imperial Stars, Vol. 2: Republic and Empire, ed. Jerry E.
      Pournelle, Baen, 1987
  The Last Evolution, ss *Amazing* Aug,1932
    Amazing Science Fiction Stories: The Wonder Years 1926-1935,
      ed. Martin H. Greenberg, TSR, 1987
  Who Goes There? [as by Don A. Stuart], na *Astounding* Aug,1938
    Cinemonsters, ed. Martin H. Greenberg, TSR, 1987

Campbell, Ramsey
  Above the World, ss *Whispers* #2, ed. Stuart David Schiff,1979
    Dark Feasts, Robinson, 1987
  Again, ss *Twilight Zone* Nov,1981
    Dark Feasts, Robinson, 1987
  Another World, ss **Tales from the Forbidden Planet**, ed. Roz
    Kaveney, Titan,1987
  Apples, ss **Halloween Horrors**, ed. Alan Ryan, Doubleday,1986
    Dark Feasts, Robinson, 1987
    The Year's Best Horror Stories: XV, ed. Karl Edward Wagner,
      DAW, 1987
  Boiled Alive, ss *Interzone* #18,1986
    Dark Feasts, Robinson, 1987
  The Brood, ss **Dark Forces**, ed. Kirby McCauley, Viking,1980
    Dark Feasts, Robinson, 1987
  Call First, ss **Night Chills**, ed. Kirby McCauley, Avon,1975
    Dark Feasts, Robinson, 1987
  Calling Card, ss,1981
    Christmas Ghosts, ed. Kathryn Cramer+, Arbor House, 1987
  The Chimney, ss *Whispers* #1, ed. Stuart David Schiff,1977
    Dark Feasts, Robinson, 1987
  Cold Print, ss **Tales of the Cthulhu Mythos**, ed. August Derleth,
    Arkham,1969
    Dark Feasts, Robinson, 1987
  The Companion, ss **Frights**, ed. Kirby McCauley, St. Martins,1976
    Dark Feasts, Robinson, 1987
  The Depths, nv **Dark Companions**, Macmillan,1982
    Dark Feasts, Robinson, 1987
  Dolls, nv **The Mayflower Book of Black Magic Stories** #4, ed.
    Michael Parry,1976
    Scared Stiff: Tales of Sex and Death, Scream/Press, 1987
  The End of a Summer's Day, ss **Demons By Daylight**,1973
    Dark Feasts, Robinson, 1987
  The Ferries, ss **Fontana Book of Great Ghost Stories** #18,
    Fontana,1982
    Dark Feasts, Robinson, 1987

CAMPBELL, RAMSEY

Campbell, Ramsey (continued)
The Fit, ss **New Terrors** #1, ed. Ramsey Campbell, Pan,1980
   Dark Feasts, Robinson, 1987
The Guy, ss **Demons By Daylight**,1973
   Dark Feasts, Robinson, 1987
The Hands, ss **Cutting Edge**, ed. Dennis Etchison, Doubleday,1986
   Dark Feasts, Robinson, 1987
Hearing Is Believing, ss **Shadows** #4, ed. Charles L. Grant,1981
   Dark Feasts, Robinson, 1987
Horror House of Blood, ss **The Height of the Scream**,1976
   Dark Feasts, Robinson, 1987
In the Bag, ss **Cold Fear**, ed. Hugh Lamb, W.H. Allen,1977
   Dark Feasts, Robinson, 1987
The Interloper, ss **Demons By Daylight**,1973
   Dark Feasts, Robinson, 1987
Introduction, in
   Dark Feasts, Robinson, 1987
Just Waiting, ss *Twilight Zone* Dec,1983
   Dark Feasts, Robinson, 1987
Lilith's, ss **The Mayflower Book of Black Magic Stories** #5, ed.
   Michael Parry,1976
   Scared Stiff: Tales of Sex and Death, Scream/Press, 1987
Loveman's Comeback, nv **More Devil's Kisses**, ed. Linda Lovecraft,
   Corgi,1977
   Scared Stiff: Tales of Sex and Death, Scream/Press, 1987
Mackintosh Willy, ss **Shadows** #2, ed. Charles L. Grant,1979
   Dark Feasts, Robinson, 1987
   The Dark Descent, ed. David G. Hartwell, Tor, 1987
The Man in the Underpass, ss **The Year's Best Horror Stories**
   #3,1975
   Dark Feasts, Robinson, 1987
Merry May, nv **Scared Stiff**, Los Angeles: Scream/Press,1987
Midnight Hobo, ss **Nightmares**, ed. Charles L. Grant, Playboy,1979
   Dark Feasts, Robinson, 1987
The Other Side, ss *Twilight Zone* Apr,1987
   Story based on a J.K. Potter illustration.
The Other Woman, nv **The Devil's Kisses**, ed. Linda Lovecraft,
   Corgi,1976
   Scared Stiff: Tales of Sex and Death, Scream/Press, 1987
Out of Copyright, ss *Whispers* #15,1982
   Dark Feasts, Robinson, 1987
Rising Generation, ss *Night Cry* v2#5,1987
The Room in the Castle, ss **The Inhabitant of the Lake**, Arkham,1964
   Dark Feasts, Robinson, 1987
The Scar, ss *Startling Mystery Stories* Sum,1969
   Dark Feasts, Robinson, 1987
Second Sight, ss **Masques** #2, ed. J.N. Williamson,1987
The Seductress, nv **The Mayflower Book of Black Magic Stories** #6,
   ed. Michael Parry,1976
   Scared Stiff: Tales of Sex and Death, Scream/Press, 1987
Seeing the World, ss **Shadows** #7, ed. Charles L. Grant,1984
   Dark Feasts, Robinson, 1987
Stages, nv **Scared Stiff**, Los Angeles: Scream/Press,1987
The Sunshine Club, ss **The Dodd, Mead Gallery of Horror**, ed.
   Charles L. Grant, Dodd Mead,1983
   Vampires, ed. Alan Ryan, SFBC, 1987
This Time, ss **Night Visions** #3,1986
   Ghosts and Scholars, ed. Rosemary Pardoe +, Crucible, 1987
The Voice of the Beach, nv *Fantasy Tales* Sum,1982
   Dark Feasts, Robinson, 1987
Where the Heart Is, ss **The Architecture of Fear**, ed. Kathryn Cramer
   & Peter D. Pautz, Arbor House,1987
The Whining, ss **The Hounds of Hell**, ed. Michel Parry, Gollancz,1974
   Dark Feasts, Robinson, 1987
The Words That Count, ss **The Height of the Scream**,1976
   Dark Feasts, Robinson, 1987

Campbell, Ramsey, Nancy Garcia & Robert T. Garcia
Ramsey Campbell Interview, iv *American Fantasy* Win,1987

Campbell, Ramsey & Stanley Wiater
A Conversation With Ramsey Campbell, iv *Twilight Zone* Apr,1987

Campton, David
Repossession, ss **Whispers** #6, ed. Stuart David Schiff,1987

Cannon, Peter
H.P. Lovecraft: Problems in Critical Recognition, ar *Mage* Win,1987

Cantry, Thomas & Greg Ketter
Thomas Canty, pi *American Fantasy* Spr,1987

Caraker, Mary
Lumisland, ss *F&SF* Sep,1987
Out of the Cradle, nv *F&SF* Jul,1987

Carbonaro, John & Ann Cathey
Saga of the Crimson Knight [Part 2], sl *Salarius* #3,1987

Card, Orson Scott
Adolescence and Adulthood in Science Fiction, ar *Amazing* Nov,1987
America, nv *IASFM* Jan,1987
Books to Look For, br *F&SF* May,1987
Books to Look For, br *F&SF* Jun,1987
Books to Look For, br *F&SF* Jul,1987
Books to Look For, br *F&SF* Aug,1987
Books to Look For, br *F&SF* Sep,1987
Books to Look For, br *F&SF* Oct,1987
Books to Look For, br *F&SF* Nov,1987
Books to Look For, br *F&SF* Dec,1987
The Bully and the Beast, na **Other Worlds** #1, ed. Roy
   Torgesson,1979
   Cardography, Hypatia Press, 1987
Carthage City, na *IASFM* Sep,1987
The Changed Man and the King of Words, nv *Omni* Dec,1982
   The Fifth Omni Book of Science Fiction, ed. Ellen Datlow, Zebra,
   1987
A Christian in Wonderland, ar *Apex!* #1,1987
Ender's Game, na *Analog* Aug,1977
   Battlefields Beyond Tomorrow, ed. Charles G. Waugh +,
   Crown/Bonanza, 1987
Eye for Eye, na *IASFM* Mar,1987
Hatrack River, nv *IASFM* Aug,1986
   The Year's Best Science Fiction, Fourth Annual Collection, ed.
   Gardner R. Dozois, St. Martin's, 1987
   Terry Carr's Best Science Fiction and Fantasy of the Year #16,
   ed. Terry Carr, Tor, 1987
Living in a World of Maps, aw
   Cardography, Hypatia Press, 1987
Middle Woman, ss
   Cardography, Hypatia Press, 1987
The Porcelain Salamander, ss **Unaccompanied Sonata**,1981
   Cardography, Hypatia Press, 1987
The Princess and the Bear, nv **The Berkley Showcase** v1, ed. Victoria
   Schochet & John W. Silbersack,1980
   Cardography, Hypatia Press, 1987
Runaway, nv *IASFM* Jun,1987
Sandmagic, nv **Swords Against Darkness** #4, ed. Andrew J.
   Offutt,1979
   Cardography, Hypatia Press, 1987
Saving Grace, ss *Night Cry* v2#5,1987
West, na **Free Lancers**, ed. Elizabeth Mitchell, Baen,1987

Carey, Mary
The Entrance Exam, ss **The Witch Book**, ed. Anonymous, Rand
   McNally,1976
   Young Witches & Warlocks, ed. Isaac Asimov +, Harper & Row,
   1987

Carl, Lillian Stewart
Out of Darkness, ss *IASFM* Apr,1987

Carleton, Patrick
Dr Horder's Room, ss **Thrills**, Anon (Charles Birkin), Philip Allan,1935
   Ghosts and Scholars, ed. Rosemary Pardoe +, Crucible, 1987

Carletti, Eduardo Julio
Susi's Lovely World, ss *SF International* #2,1987

Carpenter, Leonard
The Devourer, pm *2AM* Spr,1987
The Egg, pm *Eldritch Tales* #13,1987
Fearing's Fall, ss *Amazing* Sep,1987
The Fungoid Intruder, pm *2AM* Win,1987
The Priests, pm *Eldritch Tales* #14,1987

Carr, Jayge
Inky, ss *Whispers* #23,1987

Carr, John Dickson
Blind Man's Hood [as by Carter Dickson], ss **The Department of Queer Complaints**, Morrow,1940
Ghosts and Scholars, ed. Rosemary Pardoe + , Crucible, 1987

Carr, John F. & Roland J. Green
Nightfriend, nv **Friends of the Horseclans**, ed. Robert Adams & Pamela Crippen Adams, Signet,1987

Carr, Robert S.
Phantom Fingers, ss *Weird Tales* May,1927
Poltergeist: Tales of Deadly Ghosts, ed. Peter Haining, Severn House, 1987

Carr, Terry
Introduction, in
Terry Carr's Best Science Fiction and Fantasy of the Year #16, ed. Terry Carr, Tor, 1987
Recommended Reading, bi
Terry Carr's Best Science Fiction and Fantasy of the Year #16, ed. Terry Carr, Tor, 1987
You Got It, ss *F&SF* May,1987

Carroll, Jonathan
Friend's Best Man, ss *F&SF* Jan,1987

Carroll, L.E.
The Very Last Party at #13 Mallory Way, nv **L. Ron Hubbard Presents Writers of the Future** v3, ed. Algis Budrys, Bridge,1987

Carroll, Lewis
Alice in Wonderland, n.,1967
The Complete Alice and The Hunting of the Snark, Salem House, 1987
Bruno's Revenge, ss *Aunt Judy's Magazine*,1867
Victorian Fairy Tales, ed. Jack Zipes, Methuen, 1987
The Hunting of the Snark, n.,1978
The Complete Alice and The Hunting of the Snark, Salem House, 1987
Through the Looking Glass, n.,1972
The Complete Alice and The Hunting of the Snark, Salem House, 1987

Carter, Angela
Ashputtle, vi **The Virago Book of Ghost Stories**, ed. Richard Dalby, Virago,1987
The Donkey Prince, ss,1970
Don't Bet on the Prince, ed. Jack Zipes, Methuen, 1987

Carter, Paul A.
The Last Objective, nv *Astounding* Aug,1946
Battlefields Beyond Tomorrow, ed. Charles G. Waugh + , Crown/Bonanza, 1987

Carter, Tonya R. & Paul B. Thompson
The Exiles, nv **DragonLance Tales** v3, Margaret Weis & Tracy Hickman, TSR,1987

Cartwright, Phil
The Computer Game, ss **Twisted Circuits**, ed. Mick Gowar, Beaver,1987

Cary, Joyce
A Private Ghost, ss **Spring Song and Other Stories**, Michael Joseph,1960
Ready or Not, ed. Joan Kahn, Greenwillow, 1987

Case, David
Twins, ss *Fantasy Tales* #16,1986

Case, George
The Preacher Behind the Wall, ss *Space & Time* #72,1987

Casper, Susan
Covenant With a Dragon, ss **In the Field of Fire**, ed. Jeanne Van Buren Dann & Jack M. Dann, Tor,1987
Under Her Skin, ss *Amazing* Mar,1987

Casper, Susan & Gardner R. Dozois
The Stray, ss *Twilight Zone* Dec,1987

Castle, Mort
De-Programming Rose Ellen, vi *2AM* Sum,1987
If You Take My Hand, My Son, ss **Masques #2**, ed. J.N. Williamson,1987
Sharing, vi *Grue* #4,1987

Cather, J.B.
Pulsebeat, nv *Analog* Dec,1987

Cathey, Ann
Dragon, pm *Salarius* v1#4,1987
Haiku, pm *Salarius* v1#4,1987
Mother Moon, pm *Salarius* v1#4,1987
Pipe Dream, pm *Salarius* #3,1987
True Sight, pm *Salarius* #3,1987

Cathey, Ann & John Carbonaro
Saga of the Crimson Knight [Part 2], sl *Salarius* #3,1987

Cave, Hugh B.
After the Funeral, ss *Fantasy Tales* #16,1986
The Back of the Mirror, ss *Border Land* Oct,1987
Death Tolls the Bell, nv *Terror Tales* Jul,1935
Selected Tales of Grim and Grue from the Horror Pulps, ed. Sheldon R. Jaffery, Bowling Green Popular Press, 1987
No Flowers for Henry, ss *Whispers* #23,1987
Take Me, For Instance, ss *Whispers* #5,1974
Border Land Oct,1987

Cecil, Lord David
Introduction, in
The Complete Short Stories of L.P. Hartley, L.P. Hartley, Beaufort, 1986

Chaddock, Kathleen
Finders Keepers, vi *2AM* Fll,1987

Chaisson, Eric J.
Our Galaxy, ar **Universe**, ed. Byron Preiss, Bantam Spectra,1987

Chalker, Jack L.
No Hiding Place, nv **Stellar** #3, ed. Judy-Lynn del Rey,1977
House Shudders, ed. Martin H. Greenberg + , DAW, 1987

Chambers, Aidan
The Tower, ss **A Quiver of Ghosts**, ed. Aiden Chambers, Bodley Head,1987

Chambers, Robert W.
The Repairer of Reputations, nv **The King in Yellow**, New York & Chicago: F. Tennyson Neely,1895
The Dark Descent, ed. David G. Hartwell, Tor, 1987
The Yellow Sign, nv **The King in Yellow**, New York & Chicago: F. Tennyson Neely,1895
Tales of the Dark, ed. Lincoln Child, St. Martin's, 1987

Champetier, Joel
Soluble-Fish ["Poisson-Soluble", **Aurores Boreales 2** 1985], vi *Solaris* #59,1985
Translated by Louise Samson.
Tesseracts 2, ed. Phyllis Gotlieb + , Porcepic, 1987

Chandler, A. Bertram
The Hairy Parents, ss *Void* #2,1975
Isaac Asimov's Wonderful Worlds of Science Fiction #6: Neanderthals, ed. Isaac Asimov + , NAL/Signet, 1987

CHANOFF, DAVID

Chanoff, David & Doan Van Toai
  Learning from Viet Nam, ar *Encounter* Sep,1982
    There Will Be War, Vol. VI: Guns of Darkness, ed. Jerry E.
      Pournelle, Tor, 1987

Chapman, Irwin M.
  John Borkowski: An Appreciation, bg *2AM* Fll,1987
  Small Press Reviews, br *2AM* Spr,1987
  Small Press Reviews, br *2AM* Sum,1987
  Small Press Reviews, br *2AM* Fll,1987
  Small Press Reviews, br *2AM* Win,1987

Charles, David M.
  Are You Receiving Me?, ss *Amazing* Nov,1987

Charnas, Suzy McKee
  A Musical Interlude [chapter 4 of **The Vampire Tapestry**], ex Simon
    & Schuster: New York,1980
    A Very Large Array, ed. Melinda M. Snodgrass, Univ. of New
      Mexico Press, 1987
  Unicorn Tapestry, na **New Dimensions** #11, ed. Robert
    Silverberg/Marta Randall,1980
    Vampires, ed. Alan Ryan, SFBC, 1987

Charnock, Graham
  Fullwood's Web, ss **Other Edens**, ed. Christopher Evans & Robert
    Holdstock, Unwin: London,1987

Charteris, Leslie
  The Well-Meaning Mayor, ss,1935
    Devils and Demons, ed. Marvin Kaye, Doubleday, 1987

Chase, Robert R.
  The Changeling Hunt, nv *Analog* Jul,1987

Cheney, Thomas
  Cartoon, ct *Twilight Zone* Feb,1987
    Twilight Zone Jun,1987
  Cartoon, ct *Twilight Zone* Apr,1987
  Cartoon, ct *Twilight Zone* Jun,1987
  Cartoon, ct *Twilight Zone* Aug,1987
  Cartoon, ct *Twilight Zone* Oct,1987
  Cartoon, ct *Twilight Zone* Dec,1987

Cherkes, Joseph K.
  Final Words: A Letter From the Editor, aw *Haunts* #9,1987

Cherryh, C.J.
  The Avoidance Factor, ar **Glass and Amber**, NESFA,1987
  Black Water (Suicide) [music], sg **Festival Moon**, ed. C.J. Cherryh,
    DAW,1987
  Cassandra, ss *F&SF* Oct,1978
    The Dark Void, ed. Isaac Asimov, Severn House, 1987
  The Dark King, ss **The Year's Best Fantasy Stories #3**,1977
    Glass and Amber, NESFA, 1987
  The Faded Sun: Kesrith, n. DAW: New York,1978
    The Faded Sun Trilogy, Methuen, 1987
  The Faded Sun: Kutath, n. DAW: New York,1980
    The Faded Sun Trilogy, Methuen, 1987
  The Faded Sun: Shon'Jir, n. DAW: New York,1979
    The Faded Sun Trilogy, Methuen, 1987
  Festival Moon, ss **Festival Moon**, ed. C.J. Cherryh, DAW,1987
  Festival Moon (final reprise), vi **Festival Moon**, ed. C.J. Cherryh,
    DAW,1987
  Festival Moon (reprised), vi **Festival Moon**, ed. C.J. Cherryh,
    DAW,1987
  Fever Season, ss **Fever Season**, ed. C.J. Cherryh, DAW,1987
  Fever Season (final reprise), ms **Fever Season**, ed. C.J. Cherryh,
    DAW,1987
  Fever Season (Music), sg **Fever Season**, ed. C.J. Cherryh, DAW,1987
  Fever Season (reprised), ms **Fever Season**, ed. C.J. Cherryh,
    DAW,1987
  A Gift of Prophecy, ss **Glass and Amber**, NESFA,1987
  Homecoming, ss *Shayol* Dec,1979
    Glass and Amber, NESFA, 1987
  In Alien Tongues, ar *Sorcerer's Apprentice* WiS,1981
    Glass and Amber, NESFA, 1987
  Mist-Thoughts (Music), sg **Fever Season**, ed. C.J. Cherryh, DAW,1987

Cherryh, C.J. (continued)
  Of Law and Magic, nv **Moonsinger's Friends**, ed. Susan Shwartz,
    Bluejay,1985
    Glass and Amber, NESFA, 1987
  Partners (Music), sg **Fever Season**, ed. C.J. Cherryh, DAW,1987
  Pawn in Play, nv **Masters of Hell**, ed. Janet Morris et al, Baen,1987
  Perspectives in SF, sp **Glass and Amber**, NESFA,1987
  Pots, nv **Afterwar**, ed. Janet Morris, Baen,1985
    Glass and Amber, NESFA, 1987
  Private Conversation [music], sg **Festival Moon**, ed. C.J. Cherryh,
    DAW,1987
  Romantic/Science Fiction, sp Archon 2 (convention),1978;
    Lan's Lantern Jun,1980
    Glass and Amber, NESFA, 1987
  Sea Change, ss **Elsewhere** v1, ed. Terri Winding & Mark Allan
    Arnold,1981
    Glass and Amber, NESFA, 1987
  Sharper than a Serpent's Tooth, nv **Crusaders in Hell**, ed. Janet
    Morris, New York: Baen,1987
  The Use of Archaeology in Worldbuilding, ar *SFWA Bulletin*,1978
    Glass and Amber, NESFA, 1987
  Willow, nv **Hecate's Cauldron**, ed. Susan M. Shwartz, DAW,1982
    Glass and Amber, NESFA, 1987

Cherryh, C.J. & Nancy Asire
  The Conscience of the King, na **Angels in Hell**, ed. Janet Morris,
    Baen,1987

Chesterton, G.K.
  The Blast of the Book [The Five Fugitives], ss *The Storyteller* Oct,1933;
    Ellery Queen's Mystery Magazine Jul,1943
    Classic Stories of Mystery, Horror and Suspense, ed. Simon
      Petherick, Robert Hale, 1987

Chetwynd-Hayes, R.
  Acquiring a Family, nv **Tales from the Shadows**, Kimber,1986
    The Year's Best Horror Stories: XV, ed. Karl Edward Wagner,
      DAW, 1987
  Benjamin, nv **Dracula's Children**, Kimber,1987
  Caroline, na **The House of Dracula**, Kimber,1987
  Cuthbert, nv **Dracula's Children**, Kimber,1987
  Draculain Genealogical Table, ms
    The House of Dracula, Kimber, 1987
  Gilbert, nv **The House of Dracula**, Kimber,1987
  Introduction, in
    The House of Dracula, Kimber, 1987
  Irma, nv **Dracula's Children**, Kimber,1987
  Karl, nv **The House of Dracula**, Kimber,1987
  Long, Long Ago, nv **Tales from the Shadows**, Kimber,1986
    The Year's Best Fantasy Stories: 13, ed. Arthur W. Saha, DAW,
      1987
  Louis, nv **The House of Dracula**, Kimber,1987
  Marcus, nv **Dracula's Children**, Kimber,1987
  Marikova, nv **The House of Dracula**, Kimber,1987
  Moving Day, ss **After Midnight Stories** #3,1987
  Rudolph, nv **Dracula's Children**, Kimber,1987
  The Werewolf and the Vampire, nv **The Monster Club**,1975
    Vampires, ed. Alan Ryan, SFBC, 1987
  Zena, nv **Dracula's Children**, Kimber,1987

Chevalier, J. John
  The Master of Time, ss *Space & Time* #73,1987

Child, Lincoln
  Introduction, in
    Tales of the Dark, ed. Lincoln Child, St. Martin's, 1987
    Tales of the Dark 2, ed. Lincoln Child, St. Martin's, 1987

Childe-Pemberton, Harriet Louisa
  All my Doing; or Red Riding-Hood Over Again, nv **Fairy Tales of
    Every Day**, London: Christian Knowledge Society,1882
    Victorian Fairy Tales, ed. Jack Zipes, Methuen, 1987

Chilson, Robert
  Brain Jag, ss *Analog* Jun,1987
  The Bureaucratic Brain, ss *Analog* Mar,1987

CHILSON, ROBERT

Chilson, Robert (continued)
Truck Driver, ss *Analog* Jan,1972
  Isaac Asimov's Wonderful Worlds of Science Fiction #7: Space Shuttles, ed. Isaac Asimov+, NAL/Signet, 1987

Chilson, Robert & Robin Wayne Bailey
Primatives, nv *Amazing* Jul,1987

Chilson, Robert & William F. Wu
High Power, ss *Analog* Sep,1987
A Hog on Ice, ss *Analog* Dec,1987
No Damn Atoms, nv *Analog* Oct,1987

Chin, M. Lucie
Catmagic, ss **Devils & Demons**, ed. Marvin Kaye, SFBC/Doubleday,1987

Chisholm, Lee
Someone Else's House, nv *IASFM* Mar,1979
  Tales From Isaac Asimov's Science Fiction Magazine, ed. Sheila Williams+, Harcourt Brace Jovanovich, 1986

Chocholak, Misha
Book Reviews, br *New Pathways* Apr,1987
Book Reviews, br *New Pathways* Aug,1987
Book Reviews, br *New Pathways* Nov,1987
Prayers of Steel, vi *Ice River* Sum,1987

Chocholak, Misha & Michael Bishop
Close Encounters with Michael Bishop, iv *New Pathways* Jan,1987

Chocholak, Misha & Paul Williams
Paul Williams talks to New Pathways, iv *New Pathways* Jan,1987

Chocholak, Misha & Mark Ziesing
Interview with Mark Ziesing: Bookseller & Publisher, iv *New Pathways* Jan,1987

Cholmondeley, Mary
Let Loose, ss,1898
  Dracula's Brood, ed. Richard Dalby, Crucible, 1987

Choyce, Lesley
Beaverbrook in Love, ss *Potboiler* Spr,1983
  The Dream Auditor, Ragweed Press/Indivisible Books, 1986
Boylan Briggs Salutes the New Cause, ss *The Lunatic Gazette* Dec,1982
  The Dream Auditor, Ragweed Press/Indivisible Books, 1986
Buddha at the Laundromat, ss *New Quarterly* Sum,1982
  The Dream Auditor, Ragweed Press/Indivisible Books, 1986
The Day the Nurk Field Collapsed, ss **The Dream Auditor**, Indivisible Books,1986
The Dream Auditor, ss **The Dream Auditor**, Indivisible Books,1986
The Loneliness of the Long-Distance Writer, ss *Orion* v1#2,1982
  The Dream Auditor, Ragweed Press/Indivisible Books, 1986
Princess Thirty Moonbeams and the Hard Luck Bargaining Kit, ss **The Dream Auditor**, Indivisible Books,1986
Privileged Information, ss **The Dream Auditor**, Indivisible Books,1986
Renaissance Man, ss **The Dream Auditor**, Indivisible Books,1986
Thanotopolis Revisited, ss **The Dream Auditor**, Indivisible Books,1986

Christopher, Paul
Beyond That River, ss **Beyond That River**, Pal Books,1987
Bobbie, nv **Beyond That River**, Pal Books,1987
A Bottle on the Beach, ss **Beyond That River**, Pal Books,1987
Dora, ss **Beyond That River**, Pal Books,1987
For the Love of Mother, ss **Beyond That River**, Pal Books,1987
Hermione Gould, nv **Beyond That River**, Pal Books,1987
In the Tube, vi **Beyond That River**, Pal Books,1987
Little White Mongrel, ss **Beyond That River**, Pal Books,1987
Masters of the Void, ss **Beyond That River**, Pal Books,1987
Mushrooms, nv **Beyond That River**, Pal Books,1987
Once Upon a Chair, nv **Beyond That River**, Pal Books,1987
The Purple Hour, ss **Beyond That River**, Pal Books,1987
Pyramids, ss **Beyond That River**, Pal Books,1987
Sunday Special, ss **Beyond That River**, Pal Books,1987
To Be Blind, ss **Beyond That River**, Pal Books,1987
Waiting for Sunlight, ss **Beyond That River**, Pal Books,1987

Cipriani, D.J., III
Jonathon, vi *Mage* Spr,1987

Clarke, Arthur C.
2001: A Space Odyssey, n. New American Library: New York,1968
  2001: A Space Odyssey/The City and the Stars/The Deep Range/A Fall of Moondust/Rendezvous With Rama, Octopus/Heinemann, 1987
The City and the Stars, n. Harcourt Brace: New York,1956
  Revised and expanded from **Against the Fall of Night** (Gnome 1953).
  2001: A Space Odyssey/The City and the Stars/The Deep Range/A Fall of Moondust/Rendezvous With Rama, Octopus/Heinemann, 1987
The Cruel Sky, ss *Boy's Life* Jul+1,1967
  The Wind From the Sun, NAL/Signet, 1987
Crusade, ss **The Farthest Reaches**, ed. Joseph Elder, Trident,1968
  The Wind From the Sun, NAL/Signet, 1987
The Deep Range, n. Harcourt Brace: New York,1957
  Expanded from "The Deep Range", **Star Science Fiction Stories #3**, Frederik Pohl ed., Ballantine 1954.
  2001: A Space Odyssey/The City and the Stars/The Deep Range/A Fall of Moondust/Rendezvous With Rama, Octopus/Heinemann, 1987
The Deep Range, ss **Star Science Fiction Stories #3**, ed. Frederik Pohl, Ballantine,1954; *Argosy (UK)* Apr,1954
  Isaac Asimov Presents the Great SF Stories: 16 (1954), ed. Isaac Asimov+, DAW, 1987
Dial "F" for Frankenstein, ss *Playboy* Jan,1965
  The Wind From the Sun, NAL/Signet, 1987
A Fall of Moondust, n. Harcourt Brace & World: New York,1961
  2001: A Space Odyssey/The City and the Stars/The Deep Range/A Fall of Moondust/Rendezvous With Rama, Octopus/Heinemann, 1987
The Food of the Gods, ss *Playboy* May,1964
  The Wind From the Sun, NAL/Signet, 1987
Guardian Angel, nv *New Worlds* Win,1950
  Isaac Asimov's Magical Worlds of Fantasy #8: Devils, ed. Isaac Asimov+, NAL/Signet, 1987
Herbert George Morley Roberts Wells, Esq., ed *If* Dec,1967
  The Wind From the Sun, NAL/Signet, 1987
Introduction to the 1987 Edition, in
  The Wind From the Sun, NAL/Signet, 1987
The Last Command, ss *Bizarre Mystery* Nov,1965
  The Wind From the Sun, NAL/Signet, 1987
The Light of Darkness, ss *Playboy* Jun,1966
  The Wind From the Sun, NAL/Signet, 1987
The Longest Science-Fiction Story Ever Told, ss **The Wind from the Sun**, HBJ,1972
  The Wind From the Sun, NAL/Signet, 1987
Love That Universe, ss *Escapade*,1961
  The Wind From the Sun, NAL/Signet, 1987
Maelstrom II, ss *Playboy* Apr,1965
  The Wind From the Sun, NAL/Signet, 1987
A Meeting with Medusa, na *Playboy* Dec,1971
  The Wind From the Sun, NAL/Signet, 1987
The Neutron Tide, ss *Galaxy* May,1970
  The Wind From the Sun, NAL/Signet, 1987
On Golden Seas, ss *Omni* May,1987
On Weaponry, ar *Analog* mid-Dec,1987
Playback, ss *Playboy* Dec,1966
  The Wind From the Sun, NAL/Signet, 1987
Preface, pr
  The Wind From the Sun, NAL/Signet, 1987
Quarantine, vi *IASFM* Spr,1977
  The Wind From the Sun, NAL/Signet, 1987
Rendezvous with Rama, n. Gollancz: London,1973
  2001: A Space Odyssey/The City and the Stars/The Deep Range/A Fall of Moondust/Rendezvous With Rama, Octopus/Heinemann, 1987
Rescue Party, nv *Astounding* May,1946
  Great Science Fiction of the 20th Century, ed. Robert Silverberg+, Crown/Avenel, 1987
Reunion, ss *Infinity #2*, ed. Robert Hoskins,1971
  The Wind From the Sun, NAL/Signet, 1987
The Secret [The Secret of the Men in the Moon], ss *This Week* Aug 11,1963
  The Wind From the Sun, NAL/Signet, 1987

Clarke, Arthur C. (continued)
The Shining Ones, ss *Playboy* Aug,1964
The Wind From the Sun, NAL/Signet, 1987
siseneG, vi *Analog* May,1984
The Wind From the Sun, NAL/Signet, 1987
The Star, ss *Infinity* Nov,1955
Isaac Asimov Presents the Great SF Stories: 17 (1955), ed. Isaac Asimov+, DAW, 1988
Superiority, ss *F&SF* Aug,1951
Battlefields Beyond Tomorrow, ed. Charles G. Waugh+, Crown/Bonanza, 1987
Transit of Earth, ss *Playboy* Jan,1971
The Wind From the Sun, NAL/Signet, 1987
When the Twerms Came, vi *Playboy* May,1972
The Wind From the Sun, NAL/Signet, 1987
The Wind from the Sun [Sunjammer], nv *Boy's Life* Mar,1964
The Wind From the Sun, NAL/Signet, 1987

Clarke, J. Brian
The Testament of Geoffrey, ss *Analog* May,1987

Clausewitz, Karl von
Friction in War [from **On War**], ar
There Will Be War, Vol. VI: Guns of Darkness, ed. Jerry E. Pournelle, Tor, 1987
Information in War [from **On War**], ar
There Will Be War, Vol. VI: Guns of Darkness, ed. Jerry E. Pournelle, Tor, 1987

Clee, Mona A.
Iron Butterflies, ss *Twilight Zone* Dec,1987
Just Like Their Masters, ss **Shadows** #10, ed. Charles L. Grant,1987

Cleeve, Brian
The Devil in Exile, ss,1968
Isaac Asimov's Magical Worlds of Fantasy #8: Devils, ed. Isaac Asimov+, NAL/Signet, 1987

Clement, Hal
Author's Foreword, Intuition: The Guide Who Needs Steering, fw
Intuit, NESFA, 1987
The Logical Life, ss **Stellar** #1, ed. Judy-Lynn del Rey,1974
Intuit, NESFA, 1987
Status Symbol, nv **Intuit**, NESFA,1987
Stuck With It, nv **Stellar** #2, ed. Judy-Lynn del Rey,1976
Intuit, NESFA, 1987
Uncommon Sense, ss *Astounding* Sep,1945
Intuit, NESFA, 1987

Clemons, Jack
Will Little Note, Nor Long Remember, nv *Amazing* Nov,1987

Clifford, Lucy Lane
The New Mother, ss,1882
The Dark Descent, ed. David G. Hartwell, Tor, 1987
Wooden Tony, ss **The Last Touches and Other Stories**, London: Adam & Charles Black,1892
Victorian Fairy Tales, ed. Jack Zipes, Methuen, 1987

Clingerman, Mildred
Letters from Laura, ss *F&SF* Oct,1954
Isaac Asimov Presents the Great SF Stories: 16 (1954), ed. Isaac Asimov+, DAW, 1987

Clute, John
Book Reviews, br *Interzone* #19,1987
Book Reviews, br *Interzone* #20,1987
Book Reviews, br *Interzone* #21,1987
Book Reviews, br *Interzone* #22,1987

Clute, John, Simon Ounsley & David Pringle
Introduction, in
Interzone: The 2nd Anthology, ed. John Clute+, Simon & Schuster UK, 1987

Coats, Tim
The Buildings Are Falling, ss *Grue* #4,1987

Coatsworth, Elizabeth
Witch Girl, ss
Young Witches & Warlocks, ed. Isaac Asimov+, Harper & Row, 1987

Cogswell, Theodore R.
Deal with the D.E.V.I.L., vi *Fantasy Book* Dec,1981
Isaac Asimov's Magical Worlds of Fantasy #8: Devils, ed. Isaac Asimov+, NAL/Signet, 1987
The Specter General, na *Astounding* Jun,1952
Battlefields Beyond Tomorrow, ed. Charles G. Waugh+, Crown/Bonanza, 1987

Cohen, Jon
Preserves, ss *Twilight Zone* Feb,1987

Cohen, Martin
Starbirth and Maturity, ar **Universe**, ed. Byron Preiss, Bantam Spectra,1987

Cole, Everett B.
These Shall Not Be Lost, nv *Astounding* Jan,1953
Imperial Stars, Vol. 2: Republic and Empire, ed. Jerry E. Pournelle, Baen, 1987

Colley, Jon & Mary Sikes
Salarius Recommends, br *Salarius* #3,1987

Collier, John
Evening Primrose, ss,1940
The Dark Descent, ed. David G. Hartwell, Tor, 1987

Collings, Michael R.
Succubi, pm *Footsteps* Nov,1987

Collins, Meghan B.
The Green Woman, ss *Ms.*,1982
Don't Bet on the Prince, ed. Jack Zipes, Methuen, 1987

Collins, Paul
Kool Running, ss *SF International* #1,1987

Collins, Paul & Trevor Donohue
Waltz of the Flowers, ss *Aphelion* #5,1987

Collins, William Wilkie
The Dead Hand, nv
Tales of the Dark 2, ed. Lincoln Child, St. Martin's, 1987
The Dream-Woman [The Ostler], nv *Household Words* Chr,1855
Classic Stories of Mystery, Horror and Suspense, ed. Simon Petherick, Robert Hale, 1987

Comeau, J.L.
Stinkers, ss *Grue* #6,1987

Commander USA & Kathleen E. Jurgens
Kathleen Jurgens interviews Commander USA, iv *2AM* Fll,1987

Compton, S.R.
Retreat, pm *Star*Line* Sep,1986
Rhysling Anthology 1987, ed. Anonymous, SF Poetry Assc., 1987

Congreve, Bill
Collector, ss *Aphelion* #5,1987

Connolly, Lawrence C.
Moon and the Devil, ss *The Horror Show* Spr,1987

Cook, Rick
Catalyst, ss *Analog* Oct,1987
Mortality, ss *Analog* Jan,1987

Cooke, Catherine & John P. Cooke
Sweet Chariot, ss *Space & Time* #72,1987

Cooke, John P. & Catherine Cooke
Sweet Chariot, ss *Space & Time* #72,1987

COOPER, ANNE

Cooper, Anne
    The Frog Prince, ss **Mad and Bad Fairies**, ed. Anonymous, Attic
        Press,1987

Cooper, Louise
    Tithing Night, ss **Tales from the Forbidden Planet**, ed. Roz Kaveney,
        Titan,1987

Coover, Robert
    Intermission, ss *Playboy* Feb,1987

Copper, Basil
    Cry Wolf, ss **Vampires, Werewolves and Other Monsters**, ed. Roger
        Elwood,1974
    Werewolf: Horror Stories of the Man Beast, ed. Peter Haining,
        Severn House, 1987

Cording, H.J.
    Character Assassination, ss *Haunts* #9,1987

Cornell, Richard
    Spell of Binding, ss **Sword and Sorceress #4**, ed. Marion Zimmer
        Bradley,1987

Cortesi, David E.
    A Bomb in the Head, ss *Amazing* May,1987

Corwin, Matt
    Backwater Time, ss *F&SF* Feb,1987

Corwin, Richard
    The Eyes of the Gods, ss **Sword and Sorceress #4**, ed. Marion
        Zimmer Bradley,1987

Costello, Matthew J.
    Gaming, gr *IASFM* Jan,1987
    Gaming, gr *IASFM* Feb,1987
    Gaming, gr *IASFM* Mar,1987
    Gaming, gr *IASFM* Apr,1987
    Gaming, gr *IASFM* May,1987
    Gaming, gr *IASFM* Jun,1987
    Gaming, gr *IASFM* Jul,1987
    Gaming, gr *IASFM* Aug,1987
    Gaming, gr *IASFM* Sep,1987
    Gaming, gr *IASFM* Oct,1987
    Gaming, gr *IASFM* Nov,1987
    Gaming, gr *IASFM* Dec,1987
    Gaming, gr *IASFM* mid-Dec,1987
    On Gaming, gr *Analog* Jan,1987
    On Gaming, gr *Analog* Feb,1987
    On Gaming, gr *Analog* Mar,1987
    On Gaming, gr *Analog* Apr,1987
    On Gaming, gr *Analog* May,1987
    On Gaming, gr *Analog* Jun,1987
    On Gaming, gr *Analog* Jul,1987
    On Gaming, gr *Analog* Aug,1987
    On Gaming, gr *Analog* Sep,1987
    On Gaming, gr *Analog* Oct,1987
    On Gaming, gr *Analog* Nov,1987
    On Gaming, gr *Analog* Dec,1987
    On Gaming, gr *Analog* mid-Dec,1987
    The Second Wave, ar *Amazing* Mar,1987

Costley, Bill
    Legitimate Lady, or I Stash My Cash Behind My Golden Door, vi
        Pulpsmith Win,1987

Cottrell, William D.
    Watch Doll, ss *Whispers* #23,1987

Coulson, Robert
    Humorists in a Strange Land, br *Amazing* May,1987

Counselman, Mary Elizabeth
    Korowaar, ss
        Minnesota Fantasy Review #1,1987

Counselman, Mary Elizabeth (continued)
    Parasite Mansion, nv *Weird Tales* Jan,1942
        Poltergeist: Tales of Deadly Ghosts, ed. Peter Haining, Severn
            House, 1987

Coville, Bruce
    Watch Out!, ss **Spaceships & Spells**, ed. Jane Yolen, Martin H.
        Greenberg & Charles G. Waugh, Harper & Row,1987

Cowles, Frederick
    Princess of Darkness, ss **Dracula's Brood**, ed. Richard Dalby,
        Crucible,1987
    The Strange Affair at Upton Strangewold, ss **Ghosts & Scholars**, ed.
        Rosemary Pardoe,1987

Cox, Greg
    The Homework Horror, ss *Amazing* May,1987

Cox, Michael
    Explanatory Notes, ms
        Casting the Runes and Other Ghost Stories, M.R. James, World's
            Classics, 1987
    Foreword, in
        Ghosts and Scholars, ed. Rosemary Pardoe+, Crucible, 1987
    Introduction, in
        Casting the Runes and Other Ghost Stories, M.R. James, World's
            Classics, 1987

Cramer, John G.
    The Alternate View: Artificial Gravity: Which Way Is Up?, ar *Analog*
        Feb,1987
    The Alternate View: Laser Propulsion and the Four P's, ar *Analog*
        Aug,1987
    The Alternate View: Recent Results, ar *Analog* Jun,1987
    The Alternate View: SN1987A--Supernova Astrophysics Grows Up, ar
        Analog Dec,1987
    The Alternate View: Strings and Things, ar *Analog* Apr,1987
    The Alternate View: Warm Superconductors, ar *Analog* Oct,1987

Cramer, Kathryn
    Afterword: Houses of the Mind, aw
        The Architecture of Fear, ed. Kathryn Cramer+, Arbor House, 1987
    Forbidden Knowledge, ss **Mathenauts**, ed. Rudy Rucker, Arbor
        House,1987

Craven, Wes & Michael Arthur Betts
    Tattler, mr *The Horror Show* Spr,1987

Craven, Wes, Robert Englund & Heather Langencamp
    Nightmare on Elm Street 3, iv *The Horror Show* Spr,1987

Crawford, Anne
    A Mystery of the Campagna, nv *Unwins's Annual*,1887
        Dracula's Brood, ed. Richard Dalby, Crucible, 1987

Crawford, F. Marion
    The Doll's Ghost, ss **Wandering Ghosts**, Macmillan,1911;
        F&SF Apr,1952
        Ready or Not, ed. Joan Kahn, Greenwillow, 1987
    For the Blood Is the Life, ss **Wandering Ghosts**, Macmillan,1911
        Vamps, ed. Martin H. Greenberg+, DAW, 1987
        Vampires, ed. Alan Ryan, SFBC, 1987
    The Upper Berth, nv *The Broken Shaft, Unwin's Annual*,1886
        Tales of the Dark, ed. Lincoln Child, St. Martin's, 1987

Crawford, Gary William
    Craving, pm *Grue* #5,1987
    A Dream of Theobold, pm *Eldritch Tales* #13,1987

Crazy Alien, A
    The Clean Up Your Own Mess, ms *Aboriginal SF* Sep,1987
    The Drones are Willing..., ms *Aboriginal SF* Jul,1987
    A Matter of Trust, ms *Aboriginal SF* Nov,1987
    Narrow Escape from a Sauna, ms *Aboriginal SF* Feb,1987
    A Statistical Proposition, ms *Aboriginal SF* May,1987

Creek, Jack
    Showdown, ss *2AM* Win,1987

Crispin, A.C.
  Bloodspell, nv **Tales of the Witch World**, ed. Andre Norton, St. Martin's,1987

Croft, Fred
  Mermaids, pm *Eldritch Tales* #13,1987

Crompton, Anne Eliot
  Truce, ss **Spaceships & Spells**, ed. Jane Yolen, Martin H. Greenberg & Charles G. Waugh, Harper & Row,1987

Crone, Joni
  The Story of Emer, ss **Mad and Bad Fairies**, ed. Anonymous, Attic Press,1987
  Thumbelina the Left Wing Fairy, ss **Mad and Bad Fairies**, ed. Anonymous, Attic Press,1987

Cronwall, Brian
  She Told Me, Honor, pm *Tales of the Unanticipated* #2,1987

Cross, Ronald Anthony
  The Forever Summer, nv *IASFM* Mar,1983
    Tales From Isaac Asimov's Science Fiction Magazine, ed. Sheila Williams+, Harcourt Brace Jovanovich, 1986
  The Heavenly Blue Answer, ss **In the Field of Fire**, ed. Jeanne Van Buren Dann & Jack M. Dann, Tor,1987
  Shiva Shiva, nv *F&SF* Sep,1987

Crouch, Annette S.
  Inheritance, ss *Grue* #6,1987

Crowe, Catherine
  The Lycanthropist, ss,1850
    Werewolf: Horror Stories of the Man Beast, ed. Peter Haining, Severn House, 1987

Crowley, John & Gregory Feeley
  John Crowley Interview, iv *Interzone* #21,1987

Crowquill, Alfred
  Heinrich; or, The Love of Gold, ss **Fairy Footsteps; or, Lessons from Legends**, London: H. Lea,1860
    Victorian Fairy Tales, ed. Jack Zipes, Methuen, 1987

Cruikshank, George
  Cinderella and the Glass Slipper, ss,1854
    Victorian Fairy Tales, ed. Jack Zipes, Methuen, 1987

Crunk, Paula & Linda Frankel
  Blood Hunt, na **The Other Side of the Mirror**, ed. Marion Zimmer Bradley & The Friends of Darkover, DAW,1987

Cumberland, Sharon
  Arithmetic of Mourning, pm *Pulpsmith* Win,1987

Cunningham, Allan
  The Haunted Ships, nv **Traditional Tales of the English and Scottish Peasantry**, London: Taylor & Hessey,1822
    Fantasy Book Mar,1987

Cunningham, P.E.
  Satisfaction Guaranteed, ss *F&SF* Jun,1987

Cunningham, William P.
  Blessed Are Those..., ss *Mage* FII,1987
  Gray Nights, vi *Mage* Win,1985
    Mage FII,1987

Curry, Mike
  An Extraterrestrial, Ish, pm *Amazing* May,1987
  A Starship Commander, McPheeter, pm *Amazing* Sep,1987

Curtis, Paul
  Working Stiff, ss *Fantasy Book* Mar,1987

Dahl, Roald
  Charlie and the Chocolate Factory, n. Knopf: New York,1964
    The Complete Adventures of Charlie and Mr. Willy Wonka, Unwin Hyman, 1987
  Charlie and the Great Glass Elevator, n. Knopf: New York,1972
    The Complete Adventures of Charlie and Mr. Willy Wonka, Unwin Hyman, 1987
  The Hitch-Hiker, ss **Henry Sugar and Other Stories**, 1977,1977
    Mysterious Motoring Stories, ed. William Pattrick, W.H. Allen, 1987
  The Wish, ss,1948
    Ready or Not, ed. Joan Kahn, Greenwillow, 1987

Daily, Ben
  Puzzle Pages, pz *Salarius* #3,1987

Daily, Ben & Gaye Beer
  Puzzle Pages, pz *Salarius* v1#4,1987

Dalby, Richard
  The Ghost Stories of M.R. James, ar
    Masters of Fantasy 3: M.R. James, M.R. James, British Fantasy Society, 1987
  Introduction, in
    Masters of Fantasy 3: M.R. James, M.R. James, British Fantasy Society, 1987
    Dracula's Brood, ed. Richard Dalby, Crucible, 1987
  Preface, pr
    The Virago Book of Ghost Stories, ed. Richard Dalby, Virago, 1987
  Selected Bibliography, bi
    Masters of Fantasy 3: M.R. James, M.R. James, British Fantasy Society, 1987

Dalby, Richard & Rosemary Pardoe
  Introduction, in
    Ghosts and Scholars, ed. Rosemary Pardoe+, Crucible, 1987

Dalkey, Kara
  The World in the Rock, ss **Liavek: Wizard's Row**, ed. Will Shetterly & Emma Bull, Ace,1987

Daniel, David
  Leave Them Raving, vi *The Horror Show* Jan,1987
  Roomie, ss *2AM* Win,1987
  Static, ss *The Horror Show* Jan,1987

Daniels, Keith Allen
  My Eyes, My Eyes Are Melting, pm *Star*Line* Jan,1986
    Rhysling Anthology 1987, ed. Anonymous, SF Poetry Assc., 1987
  The Passing of the Elves, pm *2AM* Win,1987
  prognostication, pm *Grue* #4,1987

Dann, Jack M.
  Ceremony, pm **The Anthology of Speculative Poetry**, ed. Robert Frazier,1980
    Twilight Zone Aug,1987
  Eight Poems from **Songs from a White Heart**, ar *Twilight Zone* Aug,1987
  "I died for a while...", pm **The Anthology of Speculative Poetry**, ed. Robert Frazier,1980
    Twilight Zone Aug,1987
  "It is a circle.", pm *Twilight Zone* Aug,1987
  "It was a good day to die...", pm *Twilight Zone* Aug,1987
  Nerve, pm *Twilight Zone* Aug,1987
  "Oh, Wakan Tanka...", pm *Twilight Zone* Aug,1987
  Tattoos, nv *Omni* Nov,1986
    The Year's Best Science Fiction, Fourth Annual Collection, ed. Gardner R. Dozois, St. Martin's, 1987
    The Year's Best Horror Stories: XV, ed. Karl Edward Wagner, DAW, 1987
  "The ground has a face...", pm **The Anthology of Speculative Poetry**, ed. Robert Frazier,1980
    Twilight Zone Aug,1987
  "The medicine man tells me...", pm *Twilight Zone* Aug,1987
  Visitors, ss *IASFM* Oct,1987
    The Architecture of Fear, ed. Kathryn Cramer+, Arbor House, 1987

Dann, Jack M. & Jeanne Van Buren Dann
  The Apotheosis of Isaac Rosen, vi *Omni* Jun,1987

DANN, JACK M.

Dann, Jack M. & Jeanne Van Buren Dann (continued)
Introduction, in
In the Field of Fire, ed. Jeanne Van Buren Dann +, Tor, 1987

Dann, Jack M. & Barry N. Malzberg
Bringing It Home, ss *Twilight Zone* Feb,1987

Dann, Jeanne Van Buren & Jack M. Dann
The Apotheosis of Isaac Rosen, vi *Omni* Jun,1987
Introduction, in
In the Field of Fire, ed. Jeanne Van Buren Dann +, Tor, 1987

Dare, Peter
The Beam, ss
Poltergeist: Tales of Deadly Ghosts, ed. Peter Haining, Severn
House, 1987

Darke, Marjorie
Rent-a-Joke, ss **Twisted Circuits**, ed. Mick Gowar, Beaver,1987

Darling, Jean
The Perfect Gift, ss *Night Cry* v2#4,1987

Darlington, Andrew
Euroshima Mon Amour/Radical Kisses, pm *The Mentor* Jan,1986
Rhysling Anthology 1987, ed. Anonymous, SF Poetry Assc., 1987
The Great Counterfeit Memory Sin-Drome, ss *Back Brain Recluse*
#7,1987

Darnay, Arsen
The Tank and Its Wife, ss *Analog* Jan,1978
Supertanks, ed. Joe W. Haldeman +, Ace, 1987

Datlow, Ellen
Introduction, in
The Fifth Omni Book of Science Fiction, ed. Ellen Datlow, Zebra,
1987

Daubeny, Ulric
The Sumach, ss **The Elemental**, Routledge: London,1919
Dracula's Brood, ed. Richard Dalby, Crucible, 1987

Daves, J. Hunter
Ten Times Black, ss *Grue* #5,1987

Davidov, Harry
The Wizard of the Wood, pm *Fantasy Book* Jun,1986
Rhysling Anthology 1987, ed. Anonymous, SF Poetry Assc., 1987

Davidson, Avram
The Engine of Samoset Erastus Hale and One Other, Unknown, ss
Amazing Jul,1987
Goslin Day, ss **Orbit #6**, ed. Damon Knight,1970
Demons!, ed. Jack M. Dann +, Ace, 1987
Mountaineers Are Always Free, ss *F&SF* Oct,1987
The Ogre, ss *If* Jul,1959
**Isaac Asimov's Wonderful Worlds of Science Fiction #6:
Neanderthals**, ed. Isaac Asimov +, NAL/Signet, 1987
Or All the Seas with Oysters, ss *Galaxy* May,1958
Great Science Fiction of the 20th Century, ed. Robert
Silverberg +, Crown/Avenel, 1987
Vergil and the Caged Bird, ss *Amazing* Jan,1987

Davidson, Avram & Grania Davis
Addrict, ss *F&SF* Jan,1987

Davidson, John
A Ballad of Hell, pm
Devils and Demons, ed. Marvin Kaye, Doubleday, 1987

Davies, Dick
Cold Christmas, cs *The Horror Show* Jan,1987
Double Gross-Out at the Uh-Oh Saloon, cs *The Horror Show* Sum,1987
Me Pal Jonesy, cs *The Horror Show* Spr,1987

Davies, Dorothy
A Little Piece of Home, ss *SF International* #1,1987

Davis, Dorothy
F&SF Crossword, pz *F&SF* Feb,1987

Davis, Frederick C.
The Mole Men Want Your Eyes, na *Horror Stories* Apr,1938
The Weirds, ed. Sheldon R. Jaffery, Starmont House, 1987

Davis, Grania & Avram Davidson
Addrict, ss *F&SF* Jan,1987

Davis, R.D.
Hackers in the Dewey, vi *Mage* Win,1987
Mage Fll,1987
Mr. Wizard, ss *Mage* Spr,1987

Davison, Gary
Cartoon, ct *Twilight Zone* Dec,1987

Dawes, Joseph
Cartoon, ct *F&SF* May,1987
Cartoon, ct *F&SF* Sep,1987
Cartoon, ct *F&SF* Oct,1987

de Avalle-Arce, Diane
Cordoba to Die, ss *Apex!* #1,1987

de Camp, L. Sprague
Aristotle and the Gun, nv *Astounding* Feb,1958
Robert Adams' Book of Alternate Worlds, ed. Robert Adams +,
NAL/Signet, 1987
The Coronet, ss *F&SF* Nov,1976
The Incorporated Knight, L. Sprague de Camp +, Phantasia Press,
1987
Eudoric's Unicorn, ss **The Year's Best Fantasy Stories #3**,1977
The Incorporated Knight, L. Sprague de Camp +, Phantasia Press,
1987
The Gnarly Man, nv *Unknown* Jun,1939
**Isaac Asimov's Wonderful Worlds of Science Fiction #6:
Neanderthals**, ed. Isaac Asimov +, NAL/Signet, 1987
Henry Kuttner: An Introduction, in
Prince Raynor, Henry Kuttner, Gryphon, 1987
The Lamp [also as "The Lamp from Atlantis"], nv *F&SF* Mar,1975
Isaac Asimov's Magical Worlds of Fantasy #9: Atlantis, ed. Isaac
Asimov +, NAL/Signet, 1988
The Purple Pterodactyls, ss *F&SF* Aug,1976
Demons!, ed. Jack M. Dann +, Ace, 1987
Rubber Dinosaurs and Wooden Elephants, ar *Analog* mid-Dec,1987
Spider Love, ss *F&SF* Nov,1977
The Incorporated Knight, L. Sprague de Camp +, Phantasia Press,
1987
Two Yards of Dragon, nv **Flashing Swords! #3**, ed. Lin Carter,1976
The Incorporated Knight, L. Sprague de Camp +, Phantasia Press,
1987

de la Mare, Walter
Seaton's Aunt, nv **The Riddle and Other Stories**, London: Selwyn
and Blount,1923
The Dark Descent, ed. David G. Hartwell, Tor, 1987

de Larrabeiti, Michael
Malagan and the Lady of Rascas, ss **Elsewhere** v3, ed. Terri Winding
& Mark Allan Arnold,1984
Don't Bet on the Prince, ed. Jack Zipes, Methuen, 1987

de Lint, Charles
Ascian in Rose, na Axolotl Press: Seattle WA hc Apr,1987
Uncle Dobbin's Parrot Fair, nv *IASFM* Nov,1987
The Weeping Oak, ss **Sword and Sorceress #4**, ed. Marion Zimmer
Bradley,1987
The White Road, nv **Tales of the Witch World**, ed. Andre Norton, St.
Martin's,1987
A Wish Named Arnold, ss **Spaceships & Spells**, ed. Jane Yolen,
Martin H. Greenberg & Charles G. Waugh, Harper & Row,1987

De Morgan, Mary
A Toy Princess, ss **On a Pincushion**, London: Seeley, Jackson &
Halliday,1877
Victorian Fairy Tales, ed. Jack Zipes, Methuen, 1987

DE TERAN, LISA ST. AUBIN

de Teran, Lisa St. Aubin
Diamond Jim, ss **The Virago Book of Ghost Stories**, ed. Richard Dalby, Virago, 1987

Dean, Pamela
Paint the Meadows with Delight, nv **Liavek: Wizard's Row**, ed. Will Shetterly & Emma Bull, Ace, 1987

Dean, Sandy
Cartoon, ct *Aboriginal SF* Feb, 1987

Decker, A.M.
So Beautiful She Was, pm *Minnesota Fantasy Review* #1, 1987

Defoe, Daniel
True Revelation of the Apparition of One Mrs. Veal, ar, 1706
Classic Stories of Mystery, Horror and Suspense, ed. Simon Petherick, Robert Hale, 1987

deFord, Miriam Allen
The Apotheosis of Ki, ss *F&SF* Dec, 1956
Isaac Asimov's Wonderful Worlds of Science Fiction #6: Neanderthals, ed. Isaac Asimov +, NAL/Signet, 1987

del Rey, Lester
The Still Waters, ss *Fantastic* Apr, 1955
Fantastic Stories: Tales of the Weird and Wondrous, ed. Martin H. Greenberg +, TSR, 1987

Delafield, E.M.
Sophy Mason Comes Back, ss *Time & Tide*, 1930
The Virago Book of Ghost Stories, ed. Richard Dalby, Virago, 1987

Delany, Samuel R.
Films, mr *Night Cry* v2#3, 1987
The Game of Time and Pain, na **The Bridge of Lost Desire**, Arbor House, 1987
The Tale of Gorgik [long version], na *IASFM* Sum, 1979
The Bridge of Lost Desire, Arbor House, 1987
The Tale of Rumor and Desire, na *Callaloo* Spr, 1987
The Bridge of Lost Desire, Arbor House, 1987

DeLong, Dan & Tom Pace
Cheap But Not Dirty: Proposal for a Spaceplane, ar *Analog* Mar, 1987

Dembicer, Peggy
Punk Funeral, pm *Grue* #6, 1987

Dent, Lester
Flame Horror, na *Chapters*, 1980
The Sinister Ray, Gryphon, 1987
The Mummy Murders, na *Detective Dragnet* Dec, 1932
The Sinister Ray, Gryphon, 1987
The Sinister Ray, nv *Detective Dragnet* Mar, 1932
The Sinister Ray, Gryphon, 1987

Denton, Bradley
Baker's Dozen, nv **Liavek: Wizard's Row**, ed. Will Shetterly & Emma Bull, Ace, 1987

Derleth, August
The Dark Boy, ss *F&SF* Feb, 1957
Rod Serling's Night Gallery Reader, ed. Carol Serling +, Dembner, 1987
The Drifting Snow [as by Stephen Grendon], ss *Weird Tales* Feb, 1939
Vamps, ed. Martin H. Greenberg +, DAW, 1987
Vampires, ed. Alan Ryan, SFBC, 1987
House--with Ghost, ss **Lonesome Places**, Arkham: Sauk City, WI, 1962
Rod Serling's Night Gallery Reader, ed. Carol Serling +, Dembner, 1987
A Knocking in the Wall, ss *Weird Tales* Jul, 1951
Poltergeist: Tales of Deadly Ghosts, ed. Peter Haining, Severn House, 1987

Despain, Dezra & Margaret Weis
Raistlin's Daughter, nv **DragonLance Tales** v3, Margaret Weis & Tracy Hickman, TSR, 1987

Desy, Jeanne
The Princess Who Stood On Her Own Two Feet, ss **Stories for Free Children**, ed. Letty Pogrebin, New York: McGraw Hill, 1982
Don't Bet on the Prince, ed. Jack Zipes, Methuen, 1987

Devenport, Emily
Shade and the Elephant Man, ss *Aboriginal SF* May, 1987
Skin Deep, ss *Aboriginal SF* Sep, 1987

Devin, John
Daemon, pm *Amazing* Jul, 1987
A Detached Interpretation of Voyager's Greeting to Extraterrestrials, pm *Amazing* Mar, 1987
Light Reading, pm *Amazing* Jan, 1987
This Too Is Science:, pm *Amazing* May, 1987

Di Filippo, Paul
Agents, ss *F&SF* Apr, 1987
Conspiracy of Noise, nv *F&SF* Nov, 1987
Kid Charlemagne, ss *Amazing* Sep, 1987
Little Doors, nv *Night Cry* v2#5, 1987
Winter in America, ss *New Pathways* Aug, 1987

Dick, Philip K.
Adjustment Team, nv *Orbit* #4, 1954
The Collected Stories of Philip K. Dick, Vol. Two: Second Variety, Underwood-Miller, 1987
The Alien Mind, ss *The Yuba City High Times* Feb 20, 1981; *F&SF* Oct, 1981
The Collected Stories of Philip K. Dick, Vol. Five: The Little Black Box, Underwood-Miller, 1987
Autofac, nv *Galaxy* Nov, 1955
The Collected Stories of Philip K. Dick, Vol. Four: The Days of Perky Pat, Underwood-Miller, 1987
Beyond Lies the Wub, ss *Planet Stories* Jul, 1952
The Collected Stories of Philip K. Dick, Vol. One: Beyond Lies the Wub, Underwood-Miller, 1987
Beyond the Door, ss *Fantastic Universe* Jan, 1954
The Collected Stories of Philip K. Dick, Vol. Two: Second Variety, Underwood-Miller, 1987
Breakfast at Twilight, ss *Amazing* Jul, 1954
The Collected Stories of Philip K. Dick, Vol. Two: Second Variety, Underwood-Miller, 1987
Amazing Science Fiction Stories: The Wild Years 1946-1955, ed. Martin H. Greenberg, TSR, 1987
The Builder, ss *Amazing* Jan, 1954
The Collected Stories of Philip K. Dick, Vol. One: Beyond Lies the Wub, Underwood-Miller, 1987
Cadbury, the Beaver Who Lacked, ss **The Little Black Box**, Underwood/Miller, 1987
Captive Market, ss *If* Apr, 1955
The Collected Stories of Philip K. Dick, Vol. Four: The Days of Perky Pat, Underwood-Miller, 1987
Isaac Asimov Presents the Great SF Stories: 17 (1955), ed. Isaac Asimov +, DAW, 1988
Chains of Air, Web of Aether, nv **Stellar** #5, ed. Judy-Lynn del Rey, 1980
The Collected Stories of Philip K. Dick, Vol. Five: The Little Black Box, Underwood-Miller, 1987
The Chromium Fence, ss *Imagination* Jul, 1955
The Collected Stories of Philip K. Dick, Vol. Three: The Father Thing, Underwood-Miller, 1987
Colony, ss *Galaxy* Jun, 1953
The Collected Stories of Philip K. Dick, Vol. One: Beyond Lies the Wub, Underwood-Miller, 1987
Robert Silverberg's Worlds of Wonder, ed. Robert Silverberg, Warner, 1987
The Commuter, ss *Amazing* Sep, 1953
The Collected Stories of Philip K. Dick, Vol. Two: Second Variety, Underwood-Miller, 1987
The Cookie Lady, ss *Fantasy Fiction* Jun, 1953
The Collected Stories of Philip K. Dick, Vol. Two: Second Variety, Underwood-Miller, 1987
The Cosmic Poachers, ss *Imagination* Jul, 1953
The Collected Stories of Philip K. Dick, Vol. Two: Second Variety, Underwood-Miller, 1987

DICK, PHILIP K.

Dick, Philip K. (continued)
  The Crawlers, ss *Imagination* Jul,1954
    The Collected Stories of Philip K. Dick, Vol. Three: The Father Thing, Underwood-Miller, 1987
  The Crystal Crypt, ss *Planet Stories* Jan,1954
    The Collected Stories of Philip K. Dick, Vol. One: Beyond Lies the Wub, Underwood-Miller, 1987
  The Day Mr. Computer Fell out of its Tree, ss **The Little Black Box**, Underwood/Miller,1987
  The Days of Perky Pat, nv *Amazing* Dec,1963
    expanded to **The Three Stigmata of Palmer Eldrich**; Doubleday: Garden City, NY,1964
    The Collected Stories of Philip K. Dick, Vol. Four: The Days of Perky Pat, Underwood-Miller, 1987
  The Defenders, nv *Galaxy* Jan,1953
    The Collected Stories of Philip K. Dick, Vol. One: Beyond Lies the Wub, Underwood-Miller, 1987
    Battlefields Beyond Tomorrow, ed. Charles G. Waugh +, Crown/Bonanza, 1987
  The Electric Ant, nv *F&SF* Oct,1969
    The Collected Stories of Philip K. Dick, Vol. Five: The Little Black Box, Underwood-Miller, 1987
  Exhibit Piece, ss *If* Aug,1954
    The Collected Stories of Philip K. Dick, Vol. Three: The Father Thing, Underwood-Miller, 1987
  The Exit Door Leads In, ss *Rolling Stone College Papers* #1,1979
    The Collected Stories of Philip K. Dick, Vol. Five: The Little Black Box, Underwood-Miller, 1987
  Expendable, ss *F&SF* Jul,1953
    The Collected Stories of Philip K. Dick, Vol. One: Beyond Lies the Wub, Underwood-Miller, 1987
  Explorers We, ss *F&SF* Jan,1959
    The Collected Stories of Philip K. Dick, Vol. Four: The Days of Perky Pat, Underwood-Miller, 1987
  The Eye of the Sibyl, ss **Philip K. Dick: The Dream Connection**, D. Scott Apel, Permanent Press,1987
    The Collected Stories of Philip K. Dick, Vol. Five: The Little Black Box, Underwood-Miller, 1987
  The Eyes Have It, ss *(The Original) Science Fiction Stories* #1,1953
    The Collected Stories of Philip K. Dick, Vol. Three: The Father Thing, Underwood-Miller, 1987
  Fair Game, ss *If* Sep,1959
    The Collected Stories of Philip K. Dick, Vol. Three: The Father Thing, Underwood-Miller, 1987
  Faith of Our Fathers, nv **Dangerous Visions**, ed. Harlan Ellison, Doubleday,1967
    The Collected Stories of Philip K. Dick, Vol. Five: The Little Black Box, Underwood-Miller, 1987
  The Father-Thing, ss *F&SF* Dec,1954
    Isaac Asimov Presents the Great SF Stories: 16 (1954), ed. Isaac Asimov +, DAW, 1987
    The Collected Stories of Philip K. Dick, Vol. Three: The Father Thing, Underwood-Miller, 1987
  Foster, You're Dead, nv **Star Science Fiction Stories** #3, ed. Frederik Pohl, Ballantine,1954
    The Collected Stories of Philip K. Dick, Vol. Three: The Father Thing, Underwood-Miller, 1987
  A Game of Unchance, ss *Amazing* Jul,1964
    The Collected Stories of Philip K. Dick, Vol. Five: The Little Black Box, Underwood-Miller, 1987
  The Golden Man, nv *If* Apr,1954
    The Collected Stories of Philip K. Dick, Vol. Three: The Father Thing, Underwood-Miller, 1987
  The Great C, ss *Cosmos SF&F* Sep,1953
    The Collected Stories of Philip K. Dick, Vol. One: Beyond Lies the Wub, Underwood-Miller, 1987
  The Gun, ss *Planet Stories* Sep,1952
    The Collected Stories of Philip K. Dick, Vol. One: Beyond Lies the Wub, Underwood-Miller, 1987
  The Hanging Stranger, ss *Science Fiction Adventures* Dec,1954
    The Collected Stories of Philip K. Dick, Vol. Three: The Father Thing, Underwood-Miller, 1987
  Holy Quarrel, nv *Worlds of Tomorrow* May,1966
    The Collected Stories of Philip K. Dick, Vol. Five: The Little Black Box, Underwood-Miller, 1987
  The Hood Maker, ss *Imagination* Jun,1955
    The Collected Stories of Philip K. Dick, Vol. Two: Second Variety, Underwood-Miller, 1987

Dick, Philip K. (continued)
  Human Is, ss *Startling Stories* Win,1955
    The Collected Stories of Philip K. Dick, Vol. Two: Second Variety, Underwood-Miller, 1987
  I Hope I Shall Arrive Soon [Frozen Journey], ss *Playboy* Dec,1980
    The Collected Stories of Philip K. Dick, Vol. Five: The Little Black Box, Underwood-Miller, 1987
  If There Were No Benny Cemoli, ss *Galaxy* Dec,1963
    The Collected Stories of Philip K. Dick, Vol. Four: The Days of Perky Pat, Underwood-Miller, 1987
  The Impossible Planet, ss *If* Oct,1953
    The Collected Stories of Philip K. Dick, Vol. Two: Second Variety, Underwood-Miller, 1987
  Impostor, ss *Astounding* Jun,1953
    Great Science Fiction of the 20th Century, ed. Robert Silverberg +, Crown/Avenel, 1987
    The Collected Stories of Philip K. Dick, Vol. Two: Second Variety, Underwood-Miller, 1987
  The Indefatigable Frog, ss *Fantastic Story* Jul,1953
    The Collected Stories of Philip K. Dick, Vol. One: Beyond Lies the Wub, Underwood-Miller, 1987
  The Infinites, ss *Planet Stories* May,1953
    The Collected Stories of Philip K. Dick, Vol. One: Beyond Lies the Wub, Underwood-Miller, 1987
  James P. Crow, ss *Planet Stories* May,1954
    The Collected Stories of Philip K. Dick, Vol. Two: Second Variety, Underwood-Miller, 1987
  Jon's World, nv **Time to Come**, ed. August Derleth, Farrar,1954
    The Collected Stories of Philip K. Dick, Vol. Two: Second Variety, Underwood-Miller, 1987
  The King of the Elves, nv *Beyond Fantasy Fiction* Sep,1953
    The Collected Stories of Philip K. Dick, Vol. One: Beyond Lies the Wub, Underwood-Miller, 1987
  The Last of the Masters, nv *Orbit* #5,1954
    The Collected Stories of Philip K. Dick, Vol. Three: The Father Thing, Underwood-Miller, 1987
  A Letter to Patricia Warrick from Philip Dick, lt Sep 11,1978
    Philip K. Dick: The Dream Connection, D. Scott Apel, Permanent Press, 1987
  A Letter to Scott Apel from Philip Dick, lt Aug 8,1980
    Philip K. Dick: The Dream Connection, D. Scott Apel, Permanent Press, 1987
  The Little Black Box, nv *Worlds of Tomorrow* Aug,1964
    The Collected Stories of Philip K. Dick, Vol. Five: The Little Black Box, Underwood-Miller, 1987
  The Little Movement, ss *F&SF* Nov,1952
    The Collected Stories of Philip K. Dick, Vol. One: Beyond Lies the Wub, Underwood-Miller, 1987
  A Little Something for Us Tempunauts, nv **Final Stage**, ed. Edward L. Ferman & Barry N. Malzberg, Charterhouse,1974
    The Collected Stories of Philip K. Dick, Vol. Five: The Little Black Box, Underwood-Miller, 1987
    The Dark Descent, ed. David G. Hartwell, Tor, 1987
  Martians Come in Clouds, ss *Fantastic Universe* Jun,1954
    The Collected Stories of Philip K. Dick, Vol. Two: Second Variety, Underwood-Miller, 1987
  Meddler, ss *Future* Oct,1954
    The Collected Stories of Philip K. Dick, Vol. One: Beyond Lies the Wub, Underwood-Miller, 1987
  The Minority Report, ss *Fantastic Universe* Jan,1956
    The Collected Stories of Philip K. Dick, Vol. Four: The Days of Perky Pat, Underwood-Miller, 1987
  Misadjustment, ss *Science Fiction Quarterly* Feb,1957
    The Collected Stories of Philip K. Dick, Vol. Three: The Father Thing, Underwood-Miller, 1987
  The Mold of Yancy, nv *If* Aug,1955
    The Collected Stories of Philip K. Dick, Vol. Four: The Days of Perky Pat, Underwood-Miller, 1987
  Mr. Spaceship, nv *Imagination* Jan,1953
    The Collected Stories of Philip K. Dick, Vol. One: Beyond Lies the Wub, Underwood-Miller, 1987
  Nanny, ss *Startling Stories* Spr,1955
    The Collected Stories of Philip K. Dick, Vol. One: Beyond Lies the Wub, Underwood-Miller, 1987
  Not By Its Cover, ss *Famous Science Fiction* Sum,1968
    The Collected Stories of Philip K. Dick, Vol. Five: The Little Black Box, Underwood-Miller, 1987

Dick, Philip K. (continued)
  Novelty Act, nv *Fantastic* Feb,1964
    Fantastic Stories: Tales of the Weird and Wondrous, ed. Martin
      H. Greenberg +, TSR, 1987
    **The Collected Stories of Philip K. Dick, Vol. Four: The Days of
      Perky Pat**, Underwood-Miller, 1987
  Null-O, ss *If* Dec,1958
    **The Collected Stories of Philip K. Dick, Vol. Three: The Father
      Thing**, Underwood-Miller, 1987
  Of Withered Apples, ss *Cosmos SF&F* Jul,1954
    **The Collected Stories of Philip K. Dick, Vol. Two: Second
      Variety**, Underwood-Miller, 1987
  Oh, to Be a Blobel!, ss *Galaxy* Feb,1964
    **The Collected Stories of Philip K. Dick, Vol. Four: The Days of
      Perky Pat**, Underwood-Miller, 1987
  Orpheus with Clay Feet [as by Jack Dowland], ss *Escapade*,1964
    **The Collected Stories of Philip K. Dick, Vol. Four: The Days of
      Perky Pat**, Underwood-Miller, 1987
  Out in the Garden, ss *Fantasy Fiction* Aug,1953
    **The Collected Stories of Philip K. Dick, Vol. One: Beyond Lies
      the Wub**, Underwood-Miller, 1987
  Pay for the Printer, ss *Satellite* Oct,1956
    **The Collected Stories of Philip K. Dick, Vol. Three: The Father
      Thing**, Underwood-Miller, 1987
  Paycheck, nv *Imagination* Jun,1953
    **The Collected Stories of Philip K. Dick, Vol. One: Beyond Lies
      the Wub**, Underwood-Miller, 1987
  Piper in the Woods, ss *Imagination* Feb,1953
    **The Collected Stories of Philip K. Dick, Vol. One: Beyond Lies
      the Wub**, Underwood-Miller, 1987
  Planet for Transients, ss *Fantastic Universe* Oct,1953
    **The Collected Stories of Philip K. Dick, Vol. Two: Second
      Variety**, Underwood-Miller, 1987
  The Pre-Persons, nv *F&SF* Oct,1974
    **The Collected Stories of Philip K. Dick, Vol. Five: The Little
      Black Box**, Underwood-Miller, 1987
  Precious Artifact, ss *Galaxy* Oct,1964
    **The Collected Stories of Philip K. Dick, Vol. Five: The Little
      Black Box**, Underwood-Miller, 1987
  Preface, pr
    From a letter to John Betancourt.
    **The Collected Stories of Philip K. Dick, Vol. One: Beyond Lies
      the Wub**, Underwood-Miller, 1987
  A Present for Pat, ss *Startling Stories* Jan,1954
    **The Collected Stories of Philip K. Dick, Vol. Two: Second
      Variety**, Underwood-Miller, 1987
  The Preserving Machine, ss *F&SF* Jun,1953
    **The Collected Stories of Philip K. Dick, Vol. One: Beyond Lies
      the Wub**, Underwood-Miller, 1987
  Prize Ship, ss *Thrilling Wonder Stories* Win,1954
    **The Collected Stories of Philip K. Dick, Vol. One: Beyond Lies
      the Wub**, Underwood-Miller, 1987
  Progeny, ss *If* Nov,1954
    **The Collected Stories of Philip K. Dick, Vol. Two: Second
      Variety**, Underwood-Miller, 1987
  Project: Earth, ss *Imagination* Dec,1953
    **The Collected Stories of Philip K. Dick, Vol. Two: Second
      Variety**, Underwood-Miller, 1987
  Prominant Author, ss *If* May,1954
    **The Collected Stories of Philip K. Dick, Vol. Two: Second
      Variety**, Underwood-Miller, 1987
  Psi-Man Heal My Child! [also as "Psi-Man"], nv *Imaginative Tales*
    Nov,1955
    **The Collected Stories of Philip K. Dick, Vol. Three: The Father
      Thing**, Underwood-Miller, 1987
  Rautavaara's Case, ss *Omni* Oct,1980
    **The Collected Stories of Philip K. Dick, Vol. Five: The Little
      Black Box**, Underwood-Miller, 1987
  Recall Mechanism, ss *If* Jul,1959
    **The Collected Stories of Philip K. Dick, Vol. Four: The Days of
      Perky Pat**, Underwood-Miller, 1987
  Retreat Syndrome, ss *Worlds of Tomorrow* Jan,1965
    **The Collected Stories of Philip K. Dick, Vol. Five: The Little
      Black Box**, Underwood-Miller, 1987
  Return Match, ss *Galaxy* Feb,1967
    **The Collected Stories of Philip K. Dick, Vol. Five: The Little
      Black Box**, Underwood-Miller, 1987

Dick, Philip K. (continued)
  Roog, ss *F&SF* Feb,1953
    **The Collected Stories of Philip K. Dick, Vol. One: Beyond Lies
      the Wub**, Underwood-Miller, 1987
  Sales Pitch, ss *Future* Jun,1954
    **The Collected Stories of Philip K. Dick, Vol. Three: The Father
      Thing**, Underwood-Miller, 1987
  Second Variety, nv *Space Science Fiction* May,1953
    **The Collected Stories of Philip K. Dick, Vol. Two: Second
      Variety**, Underwood-Miller, 1987
  Service Call, ss *(The Original) Science Fiction Stories* Jul,1955
    **The Collected Stories of Philip K. Dick, Vol. Four: The Days of
      Perky Pat**, Underwood-Miller, 1987
  Shell Game, ss *Galaxy* Sep,1954
    **The Collected Stories of Philip K. Dick, Vol. Three: The Father
      Thing**, Underwood-Miller, 1987
  The Short Happy Life of the Brown Oxford, ss *F&SF* Jan,1954
    **The Collected Stories of Philip K. Dick, Vol. One: Beyond Lies
      the Wub**, Underwood-Miller, 1987
  The Skull, ss *If* Sep,1952
    **The Collected Stories of Philip K. Dick, Vol. One: Beyond Lies
      the Wub**, Underwood-Miller, 1987
  Small Town, ss *Amazing* May,1954
    **The Collected Stories of Philip K. Dick, Vol. Two: Second
      Variety**, Underwood-Miller, 1987
  Some Kinds of Life [as by Richard Phillips], ss *Fantastic Universe*
    Oct,1953
    **The Collected Stories of Philip K. Dick, Vol. Two: Second
      Variety**, Underwood-Miller, 1987
  Souvenir, ss *Fantastic Universe* Oct,1954
    **The Collected Stories of Philip K. Dick, Vol. Two: Second
      Variety**, Underwood-Miller, 1987
  Stability, ss **Beyond Lies the Wub**, Underwood/Miller,1987
  Stand-By [also as "Top Standby Job"], ss *Amazing* Oct,1963
    **The Collected Stories of Philip K. Dick, Vol. Four: The Days of
      Perky Pat**, Underwood-Miller, 1987
  The Story to End All Stories for Harlan Ellison's Anthology **Dangerous
    Visions**, vi *Niekas* Fll,1968
    **The Collected Stories of Philip K. Dick, Vol. Five: The Little
      Black Box**, Underwood-Miller, 1987
  Strange Eden, ss *Imagination* Dec,1954
    **The Collected Stories of Philip K. Dick, Vol. Three: The Father
      Thing**, Underwood-Miller, 1987
  Strange Memories of Death, ss *Interzone* #8,1984
    **The Collected Stories of Philip K. Dick, Vol. Five: The Little
      Black Box**, Underwood-Miller, 1987
  A Surface Raid, ss *Fantastic Universe* Jul,1955
    **The Collected Stories of Philip K. Dick, Vol. Two: Second
      Variety**, Underwood-Miller, 1987
  Survey Team, ss *Fantastic Universe* May,1954
    **The Collected Stories of Philip K. Dick, Vol. Two: Second
      Variety**, Underwood-Miller, 1987
  The "Tagore" Letter, lt Sep 23,1981
    Philip K. Dick: The Dream Connection, D. Scott Apel, Permanent
      Press, 1987
  A Terran Odyssey, nv **The Little Black Box**, Underwood/Miller,1987
    Put together by Dick from sections of **Dr. Bloodmoney**.
  Thoughts on **VALIS**, lt Mar 5,1979
    Excerpted from a letter to John B. Ross.
    New Pathways Apr,1987
  To Serve the Master, ss *Imagination* Feb,1956
    **The Collected Stories of Philip K. Dick, Vol. Three: The Father
      Thing**, Underwood-Miller, 1987
  Tony and the Beetles [also as "Retreat from Rigel"], ss *Orbit* #2,1953
    **The Collected Stories of Philip K. Dick, Vol. Three: The Father
      Thing**, Underwood-Miller, 1987
  The Trouble with Bubbles, ss *If* Sep,1953
    **The Collected Stories of Philip K. Dick, Vol. Two: Second
      Variety**, Underwood-Miller, 1987
  The Turning Wheel, nv *(The Original) Science Fiction Stories* #2,1954
    **The Collected Stories of Philip K. Dick, Vol. Three: The Father
      Thing**, Underwood-Miller, 1987
    Imperial Stars, Vol. 2: Republic and Empire, ed. Jerry E.
      Pournelle, Baen, 1987
  The Unreconstructed M, nv *(The Original) Science Fiction Stories*
    Jan,1957
    **The Collected Stories of Philip K. Dick, Vol. Four: The Days of
      Perky Pat**, Underwood-Miller, 1987

DICK, PHILIP K.   **DISCH, THOMAS M.**

Dick, Philip K. (continued)
  Upon the Dull Earth, nv *Beyond Fantasy Fiction* Sep,1954
    **The Collected Stories of Philip K. Dick, Vol. Three: The Father
      Thing**, Underwood-Miller, 1987
  The Variable Man, na *Space Science Fiction* Sep,1953
    **The Collected Stories of Philip K. Dick, Vol. One: Beyond Lies
      the Wub**, Underwood-Miller, 1987
  War Game, ss *Galaxy* Dec,1959
    **The Collected Stories of Philip K. Dick, Vol. Four: The Days of
      Perky Pat**, Underwood-Miller, 1987
  War Veteran, nv *If* Mar,1955
    **The Collected Stories of Philip K. Dick, Vol. Three: The Father
      Thing**, Underwood-Miller, 1987
  The War with the Fnools, ss *Galaxy* Feb,1969
    **The Collected Stories of Philip K. Dick, Vol. Five: The Little
      Black Box**, Underwood-Miller, 1987
  Waterspider, nv *If* Jan,1964
    **The Collected Stories of Philip K. Dick, Vol. Four: The Days of
      Perky Pat**, Underwood-Miller, 1987
  We Can Remember It for You Wholesale, nv *F&SF* Apr,1966
    **The Collected Stories of Philip K. Dick, Vol. Five: The Little
      Black Box**, Underwood-Miller, 1987
  What the Dead Men Say, na *Worlds of Tomorrow* Jun,1964
    **The Collected Stories of Philip K. Dick, Vol. Four: The Days of
      Perky Pat**, Underwood-Miller, 1987
  What'll We Do with Ragland Park?, nv *Amazing* Nov,1963
    **The Collected Stories of Philip K. Dick, Vol. Four: The Days of
      Perky Pat**, Underwood-Miller, 1987
  A World of Talent, nv *Galaxy* Oct,1954
    **The Collected Stories of Philip K. Dick, Vol. Three: The Father
      Thing**, Underwood-Miller, 1987
  The World She Wanted, ss *Science Fiction Quarterly* May,1953
    **The Collected Stories of Philip K. Dick, Vol. Two: Second
      Variety**, Underwood-Miller, 1987
  Your Appointment Will Be Yesterday, ss *Amazing* Aug,1966
    **The Collected Stories of Philip K. Dick, Vol. Five: The Little
      Black Box**, Underwood-Miller, 1987

Dick, Philip K., D. Scott Apel & Kevin C. Briggs
  Philip K. Dick in Interview, iv **Philip K. Dick: The Dream Connection**,
    D. Scott Apel, Permanent Press,1987

Dickens, Charles
  A Christmas Tree, ss
    Christmas Ghosts, ed. Kathryn Cramer +, Arbor House, 1987
  A Confession Found in a Prison in the Time of Charles the Second, ss
    Classic Stories of Mystery, Horror and Suspense, ed. Simon
      Petherick, Robert Hale, 1987
  The Magic Fishbone, ss *Our Young Folks*,1868
    Victorian Fairy Tales, ed. Jack Zipes, Methuen, 1987
  The Signalman [from "Mugby Junction"], ss *All the Year Round*
    Chr,1866
    Tales of the Dark, ed. Lincoln Child, St. Martin's, 1987
    The Dark Descent, ed. David G. Hartwell, Tor, 1987
  The Story of the Goblins Who Stole a Sexton, ss
    Christmas Ghosts, ed. Kathryn Cramer +, Arbor House, 1987

Dickson, Gordon R.
  Act of Creation, ss *Satellite* Apr,1957
    In the Bone, Ace, 1987
  And Then There Was Peace, ss *If* Sep,1962
    The Stranger, Tor, 1987
  Black Charlie, ss *Galaxy* Apr,1954
    Isaac Asimov Presents the Great SF Stories: 16 (1954), ed. Isaac
      Asimov +, DAW, 1987
  Brother Charlie, nv *F&SF* Jul,1958
    In the Bone, Ace, 1987
  Call Him Lord, ss *Analog* May,1966
    In the Bone, Ace, 1987
  The Catch, ss *Astounding* Apr,1959
    The Stranger, Tor, 1987
  Cloak and Stagger, nv *Future* FII,1957
    The Stranger, Tor, 1987
  The Cloak and the Staff, nv *Analog* Aug,1980
    Way of the Pilgrim, Gordon R. Dickson, Ace, 1987
  Dolphin's Way, ss *Analog* Jun,1964
    In the Bone, Ace, 1987

Dickson, Gordon R. (continued)
  E Gubling Dow, ss *Satellite* May,1959
    The Stranger, Tor, 1987
  Enter a Pilgrim, ss *Analog* Aug,1974
    Way of the Pilgrim, Gordon R. Dickson, Ace, 1987
  The Friendly Man, ss *Astounding* Feb,1951
    The Stranger, Tor, 1987
  God Bless Them, nv **The Best of Omni #3**,1982
    In the Bone, Ace, 1987
    The Stranger, Tor, 1987
  The Green Building, ss *Satellite* Dec,1956
    The Stranger, Tor, 1987
  Hilifter, ss *Analog* Feb,1963
    In the Bone, Ace, 1987
  House of Weapons, na **Far Frontiers** v2, ed. Jerry Pournelle & Jim
    Baen,1985
    Way of the Pilgrim, Gordon R. Dickson, Ace, 1987
  Idiot Solvant, ss *Analog* Jan,1962
    In the Bone, Ace, 1987
  In the Bone, nv *If* Oct,1966
    In the Bone, Ace, 1987
  IT, Out of Darkest Jungle, ss *Fantastic* Dec,1964
    The Stranger, Tor, 1987
  James, ss *F&SF* May,1955
    The Stranger, Tor, 1987
  MX Knows Best, nv *Saturn* Jul,1957
    The Stranger, Tor, 1987
  Of the People, ss *F&SF* Dec,1955
    In the Bone, Ace, 1987
  The Quarry, ss *Astounding* Sep,1958
    The Stranger, Tor, 1987
  Secret Under Antarctica, n. Holt, Rinehart & Winston: New York,1963
    Secrets of the Deep, Critic's Choice, 1985
  Secret Under the Caribbean, n. Holt, Rinehart & Winston: New
    York,1964
    Secrets of the Deep, Critic's Choice, 1985
  Secret Under the Sea, n. Henry Holt,1960
    Secrets of the Deep, Critic's Choice, 1985
  See Now, a Pilgrim, na *Analog* Sep,1985
    Way of the Pilgrim, Gordon R. Dickson, Ace, 1987
    There Will Be War, Vol. VI: Guns of Darkness, ed. Jerry E.
      Pournelle, Tor, 1987
  The Stranger, ss *Imagination* May,1952
    The Stranger, Tor, 1987
  Tempus Non Fugit, nv *(The Original) Science Fiction Stories* Mar,1957
    The Stranger, Tor, 1987
  Three-Part Puzzle, ss *Analog* Jun,1962
    The Stranger, Tor, 1987
  Tiger Green, nv *If* Nov,1965
    In the Bone, Ace, 1987
  Twig, nv **Stellar #1**, ed. Judy-Lynn del Rey,1974
    In the Bone, Ace, 1987

Dickson, Ray Clark
  Landmarks of the Laboratory, pm *Pulpsmith* Win,1987

Dieckman, S.B.
  Cousin Jo, ss *Haunts* #9,1987

Dillard, Janice
  Clawing at the Moon, pm *Footsteps* Nov,1987

Dillingham, Peter
  Psi-Rec: Priest of Roses, Paladin of Swords, the War Within, pm
    There Will Be War v6, ed. Jerry E. Pournelle,1987

Dillon, William P.
  One April Day, ss *Grue* #4,1987

Disch, Thomas M.
  The Asian Shore, nv *Orbit* #6, ed. Damon Knight,1970
    The Dark Descent, ed. David G. Hartwell, Tor, 1987
  Canned Goods, ss *Interzone* #9,1984
    Interzone: The 2nd Anthology, ed. John Clute +, Simon &
      Schuster UK, 1987
  Come to Venus Melancholy, ss *F&SF* Nov,1965
    PsiFi: Psychological Theories and Science Fictions, ed. Jim
      Ridgway +, The British Psychological Society, 1987

DISCH, THOMAS M.

Disch, Thomas M. (continued)
 Fool's Mate, pm *Amazing* May,1987
 In the News, pm *Night Cry* v2#5,1987
 Introduction, in
  **The Collected Stories of Philip K. Dick, Vol. Five: The Little
  Black Box**, Philip K. Dick, Underwood-Miller, 1987
 The Pair of Them, pm *Night Cry* v2#5,1987
 Palindrome, ss *Omni* Sep,1987
 The Roaches, ss *Escapade* Oct,1965
  The Dark Descent, ed. David G. Hartwell, Tor, 1987
 Rude Awakening, vi *Omni* May,1987
 Three Sprites, pm *Night Cry* v2#4,1987

Dnieprov, Anatoly
 The Maxwell Equations, ss **Destination: Amaltheia**, ed. Richard
  Dixon, Moscow: Foreign Languages Publishing House,1963
  Mathenauts, ed. Rudy Rucker, Arbor House, 1987

Dodds, Bill
 Crime of Passion, ss *Aphelion* #5,1987

Doggett, Ken
 The Villain, ss *Space & Time* #72,1987

Dolan, Harry
 The Dwarf Who Knew Too Much, ss *Mage* Win,1987
  Mage Fll,1987

Dolan, Harry & Virgil Finlay
 A Virgil Finlay Portfolio, pi *Mage* Spr,1987

Donaldson, Stephen R.
 Unworthy of the Angel, nv **Nine Visions**, Seabury Press,1983
  A Very Large Array, ed. Melinda M. Snodgrass, Univ. of New
  Mexico Press, 1987

Donohue, Trevor & Paul Collins
 Waltz of the Flowers, ss *Aphelion* #5,1987

Dorcey, Mary
 The Fate of Aoife and the Children of Aobh, ss **Mad and Bad Fairies**,
  ed. Anonymous, Attic Press,1987

Dorr, James S.
 A Neo-Canterbury Tale: The Hog Driver's Tale, pm *Fantasy Book*
  Jun,1986
  Rhysling Anthology 1987, ed. Anonymous, SF Poetry Assc., 1987

Dorsey, Candas Jane
 Willows, ss **Tesseracts 2**, ed. Phyllis Gotlieb & Douglas Barbour,
  Press Porcepic: Victoria,1987

Dowling, Terry
 For as Long as You Burn, nv *Aphelion* #5,1987
 Introduction: Sublime Rebel, in
  The Essential Ellison, Harlan Ellison, Nemo Press, 1987

Doyle, Arthur Conan
 How It Happened, ss *The Strand* Sep,1913
  Mysterious Motoring Stories, ed. William Pattrick, W.H. Allen, 1987
 The Leather Funnel, ss *The Strand* Jun,1903
  Tales of the Dark 2, ed. Lincoln Child, St. Martin's, 1987
 Lot No. 249, nv *Harper's* Sep,1892
  Charles Keeping's Classic Tales of the Macabre, ed. Charles
  Keeping, Blackie, 1987
 The Parasite, nv *Harper's Weekly* Nov 10,1894
  Dracula's Brood, ed. Richard Dalby, Crucible, 1987

Dozois, Gardner R.
 Alice Sheldon (1915-1987), bg *IASFM* Oct,1987
 A Dream at Noonday, ss *Orbit* #7, ed. Damon Knight,1970
  In the Field of Fire, ed. Jeanne Van Buren Dann+, Tor, 1987
 Introduction, in
  All About Strange Monsters of the Recent Past, Howard
  Waldrop, Ursus Imprints, 1987
 Summation: 1986, in
  The Year's Best Science Fiction, Fourth Annual Collection, ed.
  Gardner R. Dozois, St. Martin's, 1987

DU MAURIER, DAPHNE

Dozois, Gardner R. & Susan Casper
 The Stray, ss *Twilight Zone* Dec,1987

Drake, David
 Backdrop to Chaos, ms **Hammer's Slammers**, Ace,1979
  Hammer's Slammers, Baen, 1987
 Bargain, nv **Masters of Hell**, ed. Janet Morris et al, Baen,1987
 The Bonding Authority, ms **Hammer's Slammers**, Ace,1979
  Hammer's Slammers, Baen, 1987
 The Bull, nv *Whispers* #23,1987
 But Loyal to His Own, nv *Galaxy* Oct,1975
  Hammer's Slammers, Baen, 1987
 The Butcher's Bill, nv *Galaxy* Nov,1974
  Hammer's Slammers, Baen, 1987
 Caught in the Crossfire, nv **Chrysalis** #2, ed. Roy Torgeson,1978
  Hammer's Slammers, Baen, 1987
 The Church of the Lord's Universe, ms **Hammer's Slammers**,
  Ace,1979
  Hammer's Slammers, Baen, 1987
 Cultural Conflict, nv **Destinies** v1#2, ed. James Baen,1979
  Hammer's Slammers, Baen, 1987
 The Fool, nv **Whispers** #6, ed. Stuart David Schiff,1987
 Hammer's Slammers, co Ace: New York pb Apr,1979
  Hammer's Slammers, Baen, 1987
 Hangman, na **Hammer's Slammers**, Ace,1979
  Supertanks, ed. Joe W. Haldeman+, Ace, 1987
  Hammer's Slammers, Baen, 1987
  Battlefields Beyond Tomorrow, ed. Charles G. Waugh+,
  Crown/Bonanza, 1987
 Hog, ss **World Fantasy Convention Program Book** #13,1987
 Inheritor, na **Aftermath**, ed. Robert Lynn Asprin & Lynn Abbey,
  Ace,1987
 Introduction, in
  Cthulhu: The Mythos and Kindred Horrors, Robert E. Howard,
  Baen, 1987
 Learning Curve, nv **Angels in Hell**, ed. Janet Morris, Baen,1987
 Liberty Port, na **Free Lancers**, ed. Elizabeth Mitchell, Baen,1987
 Powerguns, ms **Hammer's Slammers**, Ace,1979
  Hammer's Slammers, Baen, 1987
 Springs Eternal, nv **Crusaders in Hell**, ed. Janet Morris, New York:
  Baen,1987
 Standing Down, nv **Hammer's Slammers**, Ace,1979
  Hammer's Slammers, Baen, 1987
 Supertanks, ms **Hammer's Slammers**, Ace,1979
  Hammer's Slammers, Baen, 1987
 Table of Orginization and Equipment, Hammer's Regiment, ms
  Hammer's Slammers, Ace,1979
  Hammer's Slammers, Baen, 1987
 The Tank Lords, na **Far Frontiers** v6, ed. Jerry Pournelle & Jim
  Baen,1986
  Hammer's Slammers, Baen, 1987
 Under the Hammer, nv *Galaxy* Oct,1974
  Hammer's Slammers, Baen, 1987

Drexler, Eric & Chris Peterson
 Nanotechnology, ar *Analog* mid-Dec,1987

Drippe', Colleen
 Little People, ss *Apex!* #1,1987
 Standard Procedure, ss *2AM* Spr,1987
 Viewpoint: A Few Small Press Magazines, br *Apex!* #1,1987
 The Yard, ss *Grue* #6,1987

du Maurier, Daphne
 The Alibi, nv
  Classics of the Macabre, Gollancz, 1987
 The Apple Tree, nv **The Apple Tree**, Gollancz,1952
  Classics of the Macabre, Gollancz, 1987
 The Birds, nv *Good Housekeeping* Oct,1952
  Classics of the Macabre, Gollancz, 1987
 The Blue Lenses, nv **Breaking Point**, Gollancz,1959
  Classics of the Macabre, Gollancz, 1987
 Don't Look Now, na,1970
  Classics of the Macabre, Gollancz, 1987
 Not After Midnight, na
  Classics of the Macabre, Gollancz, 1987
 Note to the Reader, pr
  Classics of the Macabre, Gollancz, 1987

DUFF, CHARLES

Duff, Charles
The Haunted Bungalow, ss
Poltergeist: Tales of Deadly Ghosts, ed. Peter Haining, Severn House, 1987

Duffin, Emma S.
The House-Party, vi *The Spectator* Chr,1930
Ghosts and Scholars, ed. Rosemary Pardoe +, Crucible, 1987

Dumars, Denise
I am myself, pm *Grue* #4,1987
I Bid You Welcome, pm *Weirdbook* #22,1987
Soliloquy, pm *Grue* #6,1987

Duncan, Dan
Harmonica Song, pm **There Will Be War** v6, ed. Jerry E. Pournelle,1987

Dunn, J.R.
Long Knives, nv **L. Ron Hubbard Presents Writers of the Future** v3, ed. Algis Budrys, Bridge,1987

Dunn, Marylois
Cat and the Other, nv **Tales of the Witch World**, ed. Andre Norton, St. Martin's,1987

Durkin, Barbara W.
Irene, Good Night, ss *Whispers* #23,1987

Dutcher, Roger L.
Gravity Has Always Been Our Enemy, pm *IASFM* Oct,1987
Losing Souls to California Dreaming, pm *IASFM* Sep,1987

Dutcher, Roger L. & Robert Frazier
Nazca Lines, pm *IASFM* May,1987

Earl, Stephen
Hanuman, ss **Gollancz - Sunday Times Best SF Stories**, Gollancz,1987

Easton, Richard
The Rivalry, ss *The Virginia Quarterly Review* Win,1987

Easton, Thomas A.
Alas, Poor Yorick, ss *F&SF* Aug,1981
Isaac Asimov's Wonderful Worlds of Science Fiction #6: Neanderthals, ed. Isaac Asimov +, NAL/Signet, 1987
Mood Wendigo, ss *Analog* May,1980
Strange Maine, ed. Charles G. Waugh +, Tapley, 1986
The Reference Library, br *Analog* Jan,1987
The Reference Library, br *Analog* Feb,1987
The Reference Library, br *Analog* Mar,1987
The Reference Library, br *Analog* Apr,1987
The Reference Library, br *Analog* May,1987
The Reference Library, br *Analog* Jun,1987
The Reference Library, br *Analog* Jul,1987
The Reference Library, br *Analog* Aug,1987
The Reference Library, br *Analog* Sep,1987
The Reference Library, br *Analog* Oct,1987
The Reference Library, br *Analog* Nov,1987
The Reference Library, br *Analog* Dec,1987
The Reference Library, br *Analog* mid-Dec,1987

Edler, Peter
Dan'l Boone Kilt a Saucer Here, ss *Pulpsmith* Win,1987

Edwards, Paul
The Courage of Friends, ss **Friends of the Horseclans**, ed. Robert Adams & Pamela Crippen Adams, Signet,1987

Effinger, George Alec
Another Dead Grandfather, ss *F&SF* Dec,1987
Glimmer, Glimmer, ss *Playboy* Nov,1987
Masters of Darkness II, ed. Dennis Etchison, Tor, 1988
King of the Cyber Rifles, ss *IASFM* mid-Dec,1987
The Man Who Devoured Literature, ss *Twilight Zone* Apr,1987
Maureen Birnbaum on the Art of War, nv **Friends of the Horseclans**, ed. Robert Adams & Pamela Crippen Adams, Signet,1987

Effinger, George Alec (continued)
Skylab Done It, nv *F&SF* Mar,1987
So Shall Ye Reap, ss *Analog* Aug,1987
Target: Berlin!, nv **New Dimensions** #6, ed. Robert Silverberg/Marta Randall,1976
Robert Adams' Book of Alternate Worlds, ed. Robert Adams +, NAL/Signet, 1987

Egan, Doris
Timerider, nv *Amazing* Mar,1986
The 1987 Annual World's Best SF, ed. Donald A. Wollheim +, DAW, 1987

Egan, Greg
Neighbourhood Watch, ss *Aphelion* #5,1987

Egan, Thomas M.
Shelob's Dreme, pm *Eldritch Tales* #13,1987

Eggleton, Bob
On Exhibit, il *Amazing* Sep,1987

Eisenberg, Larry
The Time of His Life, ss *F&SF* Apr,1968
Great Science Fiction of the 20th Century, ed. Robert Silverberg +, Crown/Avenel, 1987

Eisenstein, Phyllis
Weasling Out, ss *Whispers* #23,1987

Elflandsson, Galad
A Overruling Passion, nv **Doom City**, ed. Charles L. Grant, Tor,1987

Elgin, Suzette Haden
Lo, How an Oak E'er Blooming, ss *F&SF* Feb,1986
The 1987 Annual World's Best SF, ed. Donald A. Wollheim +, DAW, 1987

Ellin, Stanley
Robert, ss *Sluth Mystery Magazine* Oct,1958
Ready or Not, ed. Joan Kahn, Greenwillow, 1987

Elliott, Bruce
The Devil Was Sick, ss *F&SF* Apr,1951
Isaac Asimov's Magical Worlds of Fantasy #8: Devils, ed. Isaac Asimov +, NAL/Signet, 1987

Ellis, Elijah
Death by Misadventure, ss *Alfred Hitchcock's Mystery Magazine* Jan,1964
Alfred Hitchcock's Book of Horror Stories: Book 6, ed. Alfred Hitchcock, Coronet, 1987

Ellison, Harlan
Adrift Just Off the Islets of Langerhans: Latitude 38° 54' N, Longitude 77° 00' 13" W, nv *F&SF* Oct,1974
The Essential Ellison, Nemo Press, 1987
Afterword, aw
The Essential Ellison, Nemo Press, 1987
Alive and Well on a Friendless Voyage, ss *F&SF* Jul,1977
The Essential Ellison, Nemo Press, 1987
All the Birds Come Home to Roost, ss *Playboy* Mar,1979
The Essential Ellison, Nemo Press, 1987
Along the Scenic Route [Dogfight on 101], ss *Adam* Aug,1969; *Amazing* Sep,1969
The Essential Ellison, Nemo Press, 1987
At the Mouse Circus, ss **New Dimensions** #1, ed. Robert Silverberg/Marta Randall,1971
The Essential Ellison, Nemo Press, 1987
Basilisk, ss *F&SF* Aug,1972
In the Field of Fire, ed. Jeanne Van Buren Dann +, Tor, 1987
A Boy and His Dog [revised], nv *New Worlds* Apr,1969
The Essential Ellison, Nemo Press, 1987
Corpse, ss *F&SF* Jan,1972
The Essential Ellison, Nemo Press, 1987
Daniel White for the Greater Good, ss *Rogue* Mar,1961
The Essential Ellison, Nemo Press, 1987
The Deadly "Nackles" Affair, ar *Twilight Zone* Feb,1987

ELLISON, HARLAN

Ellison, Harlan (continued)
The Deathbird, nv *F&SF* Mar,1973
　The Essential Ellison, Nemo Press, 1987
Dept. of "What Was the Question?" Dept., ms **The Essential Ellison**, Nemo Press,1987
Driving the Spikes, ar *Los Angeles*,1983
　The Essential Ellison, Nemo Press, 1987
Ecowareness, ss *Sideshow* Sep,1974
　The Essential Ellison, Nemo Press, 1987
Erotophobia, ss *Penthouse* Aug,1971
　The Essential Ellison, Nemo Press, 1987
Face Down in Gloria Swanson's Swimming Pool, ar *Los Angeles*,1978
　The Essential Ellison, Nemo Press, 1987
Final Shtick, ss *Rogue* Aug,1960
　The Essential Ellison, Nemo Press, 1987
Flintlock: An Unproduced Teleplay (1972), pl **The Essential Ellison**, Nemo Press,1987
Free With This Box!, ss *The Saint* Mar,1958
　The Essential Ellison, Nemo Press, 1987
From Alabamy, with Hate [March to Montgomery], ar *Knight* Sep,1965
　The Essential Ellison, Nemo Press, 1987
From Competition 4: Story Leads from the Year's Worst Fantasy and SF, ms *F&SF* Apr,1973
　The Essential Ellison, Nemo Press, 1987
From Competition 8: Near-Miss SF Titles, ms *F&SF* Sep,1974
　The Essential Ellison, Nemo Press, 1987
From Competition 23: Unwieldy SF Titles, ms *F&SF* Feb,1980
　The Essential Ellison, Nemo Press, 1987
From Competition 26: Imaginary Collaborations, ms *F&SF* Mar,1981
　The Essential Ellison, Nemo Press, 1987
From Competition 39: Complete the Following Sentence..., ms *F&SF* Mar,1986
　The Essential Ellison, Nemo Press, 1987
The Gloconda, ss *The Cleveland News*,1949
　The Essential Ellison, Nemo Press, 1987
Glowworm, ss *Infinity* Feb,1956
　The Essential Ellison, Nemo Press, 1987
Gopher in the Gilly, ss **Stalking the Nightmare**,1982
　The Essential Ellison, Nemo Press, 1987
Grail, nv *Twilight Zone* Apr,1981
　Demons!, ed. Jack M. Dann+, Ace, 1987
　The Essential Ellison, Nemo Press, 1987
Harlan Ellison's Watching, mr *F&SF* Feb,1987
Harlan Ellison's Watching, mr *F&SF* Apr,1987
Harlan Ellison's Watching, mr *F&SF* May,1987
Harlan Ellison's Watching, mr *F&SF* Jul,1987
Harlan Ellison's Watching, mr *F&SF* Sep,1987
Harlan Ellison's Watching, mr *F&SF* Oct,1987
I Have No Mouth, and I Must Scream, ss *If* Mar,1967
　The Essential Ellison, Nemo Press, 1987
I, Robot: The Movie [Part 1 of 3], sl *IASFM* Nov,1987
I, Robot: The Movie [Part 2 of 3], sl *IASFM* Dec,1987
I, Robot: The Movie [Part 3 of 3], sl *IASFM* mid-Dec,1987
In Lonely Lands, ss *Fantastic Universe* Jan,1959
　The Essential Ellison, Nemo Press, 1987
Introdiction to Glowworm, is *Unearth* Win,1977
　The Essential Ellison, Nemo Press, 1987
Jeffty Is Five, ss *F&SF* Jul,1977
　The Dark Void, ed. Isaac Asimov, Severn House, 1987
　The Essential Ellison, Nemo Press, 1987
Knox, ss *Crawdaddy* Mar,1974
　The Essential Ellison, Nemo Press, 1987
Life Hutch, ss *If* Apr,1956
　The Essential Ellison, Nemo Press, 1987
Lonelyache, ss *Knight* Jul,1964
　The Essential Ellison, Nemo Press, 1987
A Love Song for Jerry Falwell, ar,1984
　The Essential Ellison, Nemo Press, 1987
The Man on the Mushroom, in **Ellison Wonderland**, Paperback Library,1974
　The Essential Ellison, Nemo Press, 1987
The Man Who Was Heavily into Revenge, ss *Analog* Aug,1978
　The Essential Ellison, Nemo Press, 1987
Me 'n' Isaac at the Movies, ar *IASFM* Nov,1987
Mom, nv *Silver Foxes* Aug,1976
　The Essential Ellison, Nemo Press, 1987

Ellison, Harlan (continued)
My Father, ar *Los Angeles Free Press*,1972
　The Essential Ellison, Nemo Press, 1987
My Mother, ar *Saint Louis Literary Supplement*,1976
　The Essential Ellison, Nemo Press, 1987
Nackles, pl *Twilight Zone* Feb,1987
Neither Your Jenny Nor Mine, ss *Knight* Apr,1964
　The Essential Ellison, Nemo Press, 1987
The Night of Delicate Terrors, ss *The Paper: A Chicago Weekly* Apr 8,1961
　The Essential Ellison, Nemo Press, 1987
One Life, Furnished in Early Poverty, ss **Orbit** #8, ed. Damon Knight,1970
　The Essential Ellison, Nemo Press, 1987
The Other Eye of Polyphemus, ss *Cosmos* Nov,1977
　The Essential Ellison, Nemo Press, 1987
"Our Little Miss", ar *Los Angeles Free Press*,1970
　The Essential Ellison, Nemo Press, 1987
The Outpost Undiscovered By Tourists, ss *F&SF* Jan,1982
　The Essential Ellison, Nemo Press, 1987
A Prayer for One's Enemy, nv *Cad* Mar,1966
　The Essential Ellison, Nemo Press, 1987
Pretty Maggie Moneyeyes, nv *Knight* May,1967
　The Essential Ellison, Nemo Press, 1987
The Prowler in the City at the Edge of the World, nv **Dangerous Visions**, ed. Harlan Ellison, Doubleday,1967
　The Essential Ellison, Nemo Press, 1987
Punky and the Yale Man, nv *Knight* Jan,1966
　The Essential Ellison, Nemo Press, 1987
"Repent, Harlequin!" Said the Ticktockman, ss *Galaxy* Dec,1965
　The Essential Ellison, Nemo Press, 1987
The Resurgence of Miss Ankle-Strap Wedgie, ss **Love Ain't Nothing But Sex Misspelled**, Trident,1968
　The Essential Ellison, Nemo Press, 1987
S.R.O. [as by Ellis Hart], ss *Amazing* Mar,1957
　The Essential Ellison, Nemo Press, 1987
The Saga of Machine Gun Joe, vi *Sundial* Jan,1955
　The Essential Ellison, Nemo Press, 1987
Shattered Like a Glass Goblin, ss **Orbit** #4, ed. Damon Knight,1968
　The Essential Ellison, Nemo Press, 1987
The Sky Is Burning, ss *If* Aug,1958
　The Essential Ellison, Nemo Press, 1987
Soldier [Soldier from Tomorrow], ss *Fantastic Universe* Oct,1957
　The Essential Ellison, Nemo Press, 1987
Somehow, I Don't Think We're In Kansas, Toto [revised], ar *Genesis*,1974
　The Essential Ellison, Nemo Press, 1987
Strange Wine, ss *Amazing* Jun,1976
　The Essential Ellison, Nemo Press, 1987
The Sword of Parmagon, ss *The Cleveland News*,1949
　The Essential Ellison, Nemo Press, 1987
Telltale Tics and Tremors, ar *Unearth* FII,1977
　The Essential Ellison, Nemo Press, 1987
The Thick Red Moment, ar *The Los Angeles Weekly News*,1981
　The Essential Ellison, Nemo Press, 1987
The Time of the Eye, ss *The Saint* May,1959
　The Essential Ellison, Nemo Press, 1987
Tired Old Man, ss *Mike Shane Mystery Magazine* Jan,1976
　The Essential Ellison, Nemo Press, 1987
The Tombs: An Excerpt from **Memos from Purgatory**, ar **Memos from Purgatory**, Harlan Ellison, Regency,1961
　The Essential Ellison, Nemo Press, 1987
True Love: Groping for the Holy Grail [How I Survived the Great Videotape Matchmaker], ar *Los Angeles*,1978
　The Essential Ellison, Nemo Press, 1987
Valerie, ss *Los Angeles Free Press* Nov 3,1972
　The Essential Ellison, Nemo Press, 1987
The Very Last Day of a Good Woman [The Last Day], ss *Rogue* Nov,1958
　The Essential Ellison, Nemo Press, 1987
The Voice in the Garden, vi *Lighthouse* Jun,1967
　The Essential Ellison, Nemo Press, 1987
The Whimper of Whipped Dogs, nv **Bad Moon Rising**, ed. Thomas M. Disch,1973
　The Essential Ellison, Nemo Press, 1987
　The Dark Descent, ed. David G. Hartwell, Tor, 1987
The Wilder One, vi *Sundial* Jan,1955
　The Essential Ellison, Nemo Press, 1987

ELLISON, HARLAN   **FARRIS, JOSEPH**

Ellison, Harlan & Robert Silverberg
  The Song the Zombie Sang, ss *Cosmopolitan* Dec,1970
    The Essential Ellison, Nemo Press, 1987

Ellison, Harlan & A.E. van Vogt
  The Human Operators, nv *F&SF* Jan,1971
    Great Science Fiction of the 20th Century, ed. Robert
      Silverberg +, Crown/Avenel, 1987

Ely, David
  The Academy, ss *Playboy* Jun,1965
    Rod Serling's Night Gallery Reader, ed. Carol Serling +,
      Dembner, 1987

Emmons, Betsy
  The Ghost of the Model T, ss *Weird Tales* Nov,1942
    Mysterious Motoring Stories, ed. William Pattrick, W.H. Allen, 1987

Emshwiller, Carol
  The Circular Library of Stones, ss *Omni* Feb,1987
  Hunting Machine, ss *(The Original) Science Fiction Stories* May,1957
    Great Science Fiction of the 20th Century, ed. Robert
      Silverberg +, Crown/Avenel, 1987
  Vilcabamba, ss *Twilight Zone* Aug,1987

Emshwiller, Peter R.
  Illuminations: Prophet of the "Damned", ar *Twilight Zone* Oct,1987
  Illuminations: Red SF, ar *Twilight Zone* Feb,1987
  The Other Side: King Kong Lived, ar *Twilight Zone* Apr,1987

Endore, Guy
  The Wolf Girl, ss *Argosy* Dec,1920
    Werewolf: Horror Stories of the Man Beast, ed. Peter Haining,
      Severn House, 1987

Eng, Steve
  Forays into Derleth Country, ar *Eldritch Tales* #13,1987
  The Isle of the Torturers, pm *Eldritch Tales* #14,1987
  Profile: John Gawsworth, bg *Night Cry* v2#3,1987
  To Not Return, pm *Space & Time* #73,1987

Engh, M.J.
  Aurin Tree, nv *IASFM* Feb,1987

Englund, Robert, Wes Craven & Heather Langencamp
  Nightmare on Elm Street 3, iv *The Horror Show* Spr,1987

Engstrom, Elizabeth
  The Final Tale, ss *Eldritch Tales* #13,1987
  The Old Woman Upstairs, ss *2AM* Win,1987

Escott, Les & K.W. Jeter
  K.W. Jeter, iv *Interzone* #22,1987

Eshbach, Lloyd Arthur
  The Voice from the Ether, nv *Amazing* May,1931
    Amazing Science Fiction Stories: The Wonder Years 1926-1935,
      ed. Martin H. Greenberg, TSR, 1987

Etchemendy, Nancy
  The Flat-Brimmed Hat, ss *Twilight Zone* Apr,1987
  Lunch at Etienne's, ss *F&SF* Nov,1987

Etchison, Dennis
  Deathtracks, ss **Death**, ed. Stuart David Schiff, Playboy,1982
    In the Field of Fire, ed. Jeanne Van Buren Dann +, Tor, 1987
  Fragments of Horror, ms *The Horror Show* Win,1987
  Introduction, in
    Scars, Richard Christian Matheson, Scream/Press, 1987
  The Olympic Runner, nv *Fantasy Tales* #16,1986
    The Year's Best Horror Stories: XV, ed. Karl Edward Wagner,
      DAW, 1987
  Preface, pr
    Masters of Darkness II, ed. Dennis Etchison, Tor, 1988
  The Scar, ss *The Horror Show* Win,1987
  The Woman in Black, ss *Whispers* #21,1984
    Whispers VI, ed. Stuart David Schiff, Doubleday, 1987

Etchison, Dennis (continued)
  You Can Go Now, ss *Mike Shane Mystery Magazine* Sep,1980
    The Dark Descent, ed. David G. Hartwell, Tor, 1987

Etchison, Dennis & William J. Grabowski
  Dennis Etchison, iv *The Horror Show* Win,1987

Evans, Christopher
  The Facts of Life, ss **Other Edens**, ed. Christopher Evans & Robert
    Holdstock, Unwin: London,1987

Evans, Christopher & Robert P. Holdstock
  Introduction, in
    Other Edens, ed. Christopher Evans +, Unwin, 1987

Everett, Henrietta D.
  The Crimson Blind, ss **The Death-Mask, and Other Ghosts**, Philip
    Allan: London,1920
    The Virago Book of Ghost Stories, ed. Richard Dalby, Virago, 1987

Everman, Welch D.
  Video, ar *Twilight Zone* Feb,1987
  Video, ar *Twilight Zone* Jun,1987

Ewart, Christopher
  A Day in the Life, ss **L. Ron Hubbard Presents Writers of the Future**
    v3, ed. Algis Budrys, Bridge,1987

Ewing, George M.
  A Little Further Up the Fox..., nv *IASFM* Apr,1987

Ewing, Juliana Horatia
  The Ogre Courting, ss *Aunt Judy's Magazine*,1871
    Victorian Fairy Tales, ed. Jack Zipes, Methuen, 1987

Fabian, Stephen E.
  On Exhibit, il *Amazing* Mar,1987

Farber, Sharon N.
  Billy Jean at Sea, ss *Amazing* Jul,1987
  Ice Dreams, ss *IASFM* Mar,1987

Farjeon, Eleanor
  The Blue Lotus, ss
    The Magic Kiss and Other Tales of Princes and Princesses, ed.
      Tony Bradman, Blackie, 1987

Farley, Ralph Milne
  The Living Mist [also as "We, the Mist"], nv *Amazing* Aug,1940
    Amazing Science Fiction Stories: The War Years 1936-1945, ed.
      Martin H. Greenberg, TSR, 1987

Farlow, James
  The Demythologised Lycanthrope, ss
    Werewolf: Horror Stories of the Man Beast, ed. Peter Haining,
      Severn House, 1987

Farmer, Philip Jose
  The Alley Man, na *F&SF* Jun,1959
    **Isaac Asimov's Wonderful Worlds of Science Fiction #6:
      Neanderthals**, ed. Isaac Asimov +, NAL/Signet, 1987
  The Making of Revelation, Part I, nv **After the Fall**, ed. Robert
    Sheckley, Ace,1980
    Isaac Asimov's Magical Worlds of Fantasy #8: Devils, ed. Isaac
      Asimov +, NAL/Signet, 1987
  The Shadow of Space, nv *If* Nov,1967
    Great Science Fiction of the 20th Century, ed. Robert
      Silverberg +, Crown/Avenel, 1987

Farris, Joseph
  Cartoon, ct *F&SF* Feb,1987
  Cartoon, ct *F&SF* Mar,1987
  Cartoon, ct *F&SF* Apr,1987
  Cartoon, ct *F&SF* May,1987
  Cartoon, ct *F&SF* Oct,1987
  Cartoon, ct *F&SF* Dec,1987

FAULCON, ROBERT

Faulcon, Robert
  The Ghost Dance, n. Arrow Books: London,1983
    The Ghost Dance, Arrow, 1987
  The Shrine, n. Arrow Books: London,1984
    The Ghost Dance, Arrow, 1987
  The Stalking, n. Arrow Books: London,1983
    The Stalking, Arrow, 1987
  The Talisman, n. Arrow Books: London,1983
    The Stalking, Arrow, 1987

Faulkner, William
  A Rose for Emily, ss *The Forum* Apr,1930
    The Dark Descent, ed. David G. Hartwell, Tor, 1987

Faust, Joe Clifford
  The Helium Farewell, ss *Haunts* #9,1987

Feeley, Gregory & John Crowley
  John Crowley Interview, iv *Interzone* #21,1987

Feggo
  Cartoon, ct *Twilight Zone* Jun,1987
  Cartoon, ct *Twilight Zone* Aug,1987
  Cartoon, ct *Twilight Zone* Oct,1987

Fehrenbach, T.R.
  Remember the Alamo!, ss *Analog* Dec,1961
    Robert Adams' Book of Alternate Worlds, ed. Robert Adams+,
      NAL/Signet, 1987

Feist, Raymond E.
  Faerie Tale: The Thing Beneath the Bridge, ex *Twilight Zone* Dec,1987

Felgenhauer, H.R.
  Reach Out and Scorch Someone, pm *Mage* Win,1987

Felice, Cynthia
  Track of a Legend, ss *Omni* Dec,1982
    The Fifth Omni Book of Science Fiction, ed. Ellen Datlow, Zebra,
      1987

Fenn, Lionel
  Getting Down with Lionel Fenn, iv *American Fantasy* Sum,1987

Fenoglio, Mary
  The Promise, nv **Red Sun of Darkover**, ed. Marion Zimmer Bradley &
    The Friends of Darkover, DAW,1987

Ferguson, Brad
  The World Next Door, ss *IASFM* Sep,1987

Ferguson, Neil
  The Second Third of C, ss *Interzone* #19,1987
    Interzone: The 2nd Anthology, ed. John Clute+, Simon &
      Schuster UK, 1987

Ferguson, Syn
  The Tree-Wife of Arketh, ss **Sword and Sorceress** #4, ed. Marion
    Zimmer Bradley,1987

Fergusson, Bruce Chandler
  The Bloodsnare, ss *Space & Time* #72,1987

Ferrara, Patricia
  Rising Waters, ss *F&SF* Jul,1987

Ferret
  Xax Xox, cs *New Pathways* Nov,1987

Ferret, K.W. Jeter & J.B. Reynolds
  K.W. Jeter [Part 1], iv *New Pathways* Apr,1987
  K.W. Jeter [Part 2], iv *New Pathways* Aug,1987

Ferret & Mink Mole
  Grow Your Own Baby, cs *New Pathways* Nov,1987
  I Was a Teenage Reptile, cs *New Pathways* Aug,1987
  Nuclear FX, cs *New Pathways* Jan,1987
  Nuclear FX, cs *New Pathways* Aug,1987

Ferret & Mink Mole (continued)
  Nuclear FX, cs *New Pathways* Nov,1987

Fialkowski, Konrad R.
  Through the Fifth Dimension, ss *SF International* #1,1987
    Translated by Stanley G. Rud.

Figueirido, E. Veronica
  Paradise, ss *SF International* #2,1987

Filipovic, Dragan R.
  Jailhouse Blues, ss *SF International* #2,1987
  A Ribbon for Margaret's Doll, ss *SF International* #1,1987
    Translated by Mire Adzic.

Finch, Sheila
  Hitchhiker, ss *Amazing* Sep,1987
    **Isaac Asimov's Wonderful Worlds of Science Fiction #7: Space
      Shuttles**, ed. Isaac Asimov+, NAL/Signet, 1987

Finlay, Virgil & Harry Dolan
  A Virgil Finlay Portfolio, pi *Mage* Spr,1987

Finney, Jack
  I'm Scared, ss *Colliers* Sep 15,1951
    Great Science Fiction of the 20th Century, ed. Robert
      Silverberg+, Crown/Avenel, 1987
  Marion's Wall, n. Simon & Schuster: New York,1973
    3 By Finney, Simon & Schuster Fireside, 1987
  The Night People, n. Doubleday: Garden City, NY,1977
    3 By Finney, Simon & Schuster Fireside, 1987
  Second Chance, ss **The Third Level**, New York: Rinehart & Co.,1957
    Mysterious Motoring Stories, ed. William Pattrick, W.H. Allen, 1987
  The Woodrow Wilson Dime, n. Simon & Schuster: New York,1968
    3 By Finney, Simon & Schuster Fireside, 1987

Fischetti, Joe
  The I of the Beholder, ss *Analog* Oct,1987

Fish, Leslie
  Amateurs, ss *Night Cry* v2#3,1987
  First Night Cruise, nv **Festival Moon**, ed. C.J. Cherryh, DAW,1987
  Guardian, sg **Festival Moon**, ed. C.J. Cherryh, DAW,1987
  War of the Unseen Worlds, nv **Fever Season**, ed. C.J. Cherryh,
    DAW,1987

Fisk, Nicholas
  The Boy, the Dog and the Spaceship, ss,1974
    Living Fire and Other S.F. Stories, Corgi, 1987
  Brain Blaster, ss **Living Fire and Other S.F. Stories**, Corgi:
    London,1987
  Ghost Alarm, ss,1986
    Living Fire and Other S.F. Stories, Corgi, 1987
  The Golden Lump, nv **Living Fire and Other S.F. Stories**, Corgi:
    London,1987
  The Gun That Didn't Go Bang, nv **Living Fire and Other S.F. Stories**,
    Corgi: London,1987
  Living Fire, ss **Living Fire and Other S.F. Stories**, Corgi: London,1987
  Love Bytes, ss **Twisted Circuits**, ed. Mick Gowar, Beaver,1987
  Monster, ss,1984
    Living Fire and Other S.F. Stories, Corgi, 1987
  One is One and All Alone, ss **Living Fire and Other S.F. Stories**,
    Corgi: London,1987
  Susan's Plant, nv **Living Fire and Other S.F. Stories**, Corgi:
    London,1987
  Whooo-ooo Flupper!, ss,1986
    Living Fire and Other S.F. Stories, Corgi, 1987

FitzGerald, Gillian
  Ties of Faith, nv **Friends of the Horseclans**, ed. Robert Adams &
    Pamela Crippen Adams, Signet,1987

Flagg, Francis
  The Machine Man of Ardathia, ss *Amazing* Nov,1927
    Amazing Science Fiction Stories: The Wonder Years 1926-1935,
      ed. Martin H. Greenberg, TSR, 1987

FLEMING-ROBERTS, G.T.

Fleming-Roberts, G.T.
  Moulder of Monsters, ss *Terror Tales* Jul,1937
    Selected Tales of Grim and Grue from the Horror Pulps, ed.
      Sheldon R. Jaffery, Bowling Green Popular Press, 1987

Fletcher, Hollis
  A Letter from Bubba: Extraterrestrials, ss *Amazing* Jul,1987

Florance-Guthridge, George
  Ishbar, The Trueborn, ss *Pulpsmith* Win,1987

Floss, Patricia
  The Other Side of the Mirror, na **The Other Side of the Mirror**, ed.
    Marion Zimmer Bradley & The Friends of Darkover, DAW,1987

Flynn, Michael F.
  The Forest of Time, na *Analog* Jun,1987
  In the Country of the Blind (Part 1 of 2), sl *Analog* Oct,1987
  In the Country of the Blind (Part 2 of 2), sl *Analog* Nov,1987

Forbes, Gregory
  Auguries, ar *Mage* Win,1987
  Children's Books, br *Mage* Sum,1985
    Mage Fll,1987
  The Roots of Fantasy, ar *Mage* Spr,1985
    Mage Fll,1987
  Science Fiction & Fantasy Cover Art, ar *Mage* Win,1985
    Mage Fll,1987

Ford, John M.
  Eel Island Shoals, sg **Liavek: Wizard's Row**, ed. Will Shetterly &
    Emma Bull, Ace,1987
  Green Is the Color, na **Liavek: Wizard's Row**, ed. Will Shetterly &
    Emma Bull, Ace,1987
  Pot-Boil Blues, sg **Liavek: Wizard's Row**, ed. Will Shetterly & Emma
    Bull, Ace,1987
  Tales from the Original Gothic, ss **The Architecture of Fear**, ed.
    Kathryn Cramer & Peter D. Pautz, Arbor House,1987

Forde, Pat
  The Gift, nv *Analog* Dec,1987

Forrest, Katherine V.
  Benny's Place, ss **Dreams and Swords**, Naiad,1987
  Force Majeur, ss **Dreams and Swords**, Naiad,1987
  The Gift, ss **Dreams and Swords**, Naiad,1987
  Jessie, nv **Dreams and Swords**, Naiad,1987
  Mandy Larkin, ss **Dreams and Swords**, Naiad,1987
  Mother Was an Alien, ss **Dreams and Swords**, Naiad,1987
  O Captain, My Captain, na **Dreams and Swords**, Naiad,1987
  Survivor, ss **Dreams and Swords**, Naiad,1987
  The Test, ss **Dreams and Swords**, Naiad,1987
  Xessex, ss *F&SF* Feb,1983
    Dreams and Swords, Naiad, 1987

Forrester, John
  Beneath Their Blue, Blue Skins, nv **Spaceships & Spells**, ed. Jane
    Yolen, Martin H. Greenberg & Charles G. Waugh, Harper &
    Row,1987

Forsyth, Jeremy
  Nestled, ss *New Blood* #1,1987

Fortschen, William R.
  By Thought Alone, ss **There Will Be War** v6, ed. Jerry E.
    Pournelle,1987

Forward, Robert L.
  Magic Matter, ar **New Destinies** v1, ed. Jim Baen, Baen,1987

Foster, Alan Dean
  The Moment of the Magician, n. Phantasia: West Bloomfield, MI hc
    Sep,1984
    Spellsinger's Scherzo, SFBC, 1987
  Norg Gleeble Gop, ss *F&SF* Aug,1987
  The Paths of the Perambulator, n. Phantasia: West Bloomfield, MI
    hc Nov,1985
    Spellsinger's Scherzo, SFBC, 1987

Foster, Alan Dean (continued)
  The Right Shuttle, ar *Amazing* May,1987
  The Thunderer, ss *F&SF* Apr,1987
  The Time of the Transference, n. Phantasia: West Bloomfield, MI hc
    Aug,1986
    Spellsinger's Scherzo, SFBC, 1987

Fowler, Christopher
  Final Call for Passenger Paul, ss **The Pan Book of Horror Stories**
    #28, Pan,1987

Fowler, Karen Joy
  Contention, ss **Artificial Things**, New York: Bantam,1986
    Twilight Zone Feb,1987
  The Faithful Companion at Forty, ss *IASFM* Jul,1987
  The Gate of Ghosts, nv **Artificial Things**, New York: Bantam,1986
    The Year's Best Science Fiction, Fourth Annual Collection, ed.
      Gardner R. Dozois, St. Martin's, 1987
  Letters From Home, ss **In the Field of Fire**, ed. Jeanne Van Buren
    Dann & Jack M. Dann, Tor,1987

Fox, Janet
  Mirror Trick, ss *Tales of the Unanticipated* #2,1987
  Strands, ss *Grue* #6,1987
  When Jaquerel Walked With Shadows, ss *Weirdbook* #22,1987

Foy, George
  Hellbike, ss **Masters of Hell**, ed. Janet Morris et al, Baen,1987

Frahm, Leanne
  The Supramarket, ss **Doom City**, ed. Charles L. Grant, Tor,1987

Fraknoi, Andrew
  Selected Readings, bi
    The Universe, ed. Byron Preiss, Bantam Spectra, 1987
  The Universe: An Introduction, in
    The Universe, ed. Byron Preiss, Bantam Spectra, 1987

Frame, Ronald
  Some Common Misunderstandings about Ghosts, ss **A Quiver of
    Ghosts**, ed. Aiden Chambers, Bodley Head,1987

Frankel, Linda & Paula Crunk
  Blood Hunt, na **The Other Side of the Mirror**, ed. Marion Zimmer
    Bradley & The Friends of Darkover, DAW,1987

Franson, Donald
  Call Me Fearful, ss *Eldritch Tales* #14,1987

Frazier, Robert
  Across Those Endless Skies, ss **In the Field of Fire**, ed. Jeanne Van
    Buren Dann & Jack M. Dann, Tor,1987
  The Anorexic, pm
    Perception Barriers, BPW&P, 1987
  The Anorexic Poses for Giacometti, pm
    Perception Barriers, BPW&P, 1987
  The Anorexic Speaks Out On May Day, pm
    Perception Barriers, BPW&P, 1987
  Arbitrating Neptune's Complaint, pm *Analog* mid-Dec,1985
    Perception Barriers, BPW&P, 1987
  Birds of the Mutant Rain Forest, pm *IASFM* Mar,1987
  Black Ice, pm
    Perception Barriers, BPW&P, 1987
  Cetacean Dreams, pm **Light Years and Dark**, ed. Michael Bishop,
    Berkley,1984
    Perception Barriers, BPW&P, 1987
  Children's Lesson at Loines Observatory, pm *IASFM* Dec,1984
    Perception Barriers, BPW&P, 1987
  The Chrononaut Visits the Famous Pair During Their First Experiment,
    pm *IASFM* Jul,1987
  "Complete disorder is impossible.", pm
    Perception Barriers, BPW&P, 1987
  Cyclopean Hours August 27, 1883, pm *IASFM* Aug,1987
  Doppler Effects, pm *IASFM* Feb,1985
    Perception Barriers, BPW&P, 1987
  Dream Tables, pm
    Perception Barriers, BPW&P, 1987
  Dreamtigers, ss *Amazing* Mar,1987

FRAZIER, ROBERT

Frazier, Robert (continued)
Ed White, Spacewalking, June 3, 1965, pm *IASFM* May,1985
　Perception Barriers, BPW&P, 1987
Encased in the Amber of Probabilities, pm *IASFM* Mar,1987
　There Will Be War, Vol. VI: Guns of Darkness, ed. Jerry E.
　　Pournelle, Tor, 1987
Erasure, pm *Amazing* Nov,1987
"The eternal form eludes us.", pm
　Perception Barriers, BPW&P, 1987
The First Spacewoman: An Inquiry, pm *IASFM* mid-Dec,1984
　Perception Barriers, BPW&P, 1987
Flash Sleep, pm **Night Visions**,1981
　Perception Barriers, BPW&P, 1987
Hollywood Revisited: The Body Snatchers, pm *IASFM* Feb,1987
A Human Nerve Cell, pm
　Perception Barriers, BPW&P, 1987
Johannes Kepler and His Cosmic Mystery, pm *IASFM* Mar,1983
　Perception Barriers, BPW&P, 1987
July 16, 1945, 5:29:45 AM, Mountain War Time, pm *IASFM* Oct,1986
　Perception Barriers, BPW&P, 1987
Letter to a Grandchild, pm *IASFM* Apr,1987
Loren Eiseley's Time Passages, pm *IASFM* mid-Dec,1982
　Perception Barriers, BPW&P, 1987
Marie Curie Contemplating the Role of Women Scientists in the Glow
　of a Beaker, pm *IASFM* mid-Dec,1983
　Perception Barriers, BPW&P, 1987
"A mathematical formula is a hymn of the universe.", pm **Perception
　Barriers**, BPW&P: Berkeley CA,1987
The Original 11 Observations of Methuselah, pm *IASFM* Aug,1987
Overseas Call, pm *IASFM* Oct,1987
Past Light, pm *IASFM* Jun,1986
　Perception Barriers, BPW&P, 1987
Perception Barriers, pm *IASFM* Dec,1985
　Perception Barriers, BPW&P, 1987
Postmarked: the Crab Nebula, pm
　Perception Barriers, BPW&P, 1987
Quasars, Black Holes, and Maarten Schmidt's Bad Day at the Office,
　pm *Arc* Spr,1985
　Perception Barriers, BPW&P, 1987
A Quotella for Ted Sturgeon, pm *IASFM* Jan,1986
　Perception Barriers, BPW&P, 1987
Relative Distances, pm *Amazing* Mar,1987
　Perception Barriers, BPW&P, 1987
Rest Stops in the Sawing of a Log, pm
　Perception Barriers, BPW&P, 1987
A Starpilot Muses on the Universal Tidal Pool, pm *IASFM* Aug,1986
　Perception Barriers, BPW&P, 1987
A Still from the Mead Collection, pm *IASFM* Jan,1984
　Perception Barriers, BPW&P, 1987
The Supremacy of Bacteria [revised from *IASFM* Aug,83], pm **Light
　Years and Dark**, ed. Michael Bishop, Berkley,1984
　Perception Barriers, BPW&P, 1987
Telephone Ghosts, pm *Pig Iron* #10,1982
　Perception Barriers, BPW&P, 1987
Tourist Spots for Time Travelers, pm *IASFM* Dec,1986
　Rhysling Anthology 1987, ed. Anonymous, SF Poetry Assc., 1987
Tracking Through the Mutant Rain Forest, pm *IASFM* May,1987
Twinned Stars: Newton & Halley, pm **Perception Barriers**, BPW&P:
　Berkeley CA,1987
Upon Hearing New Evidence That Meteors Caused the Great
　Extinctions, pm *Amazing* Jan,1987
Veneers of Sleep, pm **Alternate Lives**,1986
　Rhysling Anthology 1987, ed. Anonymous, SF Poetry Assc., 1987
The Vexation of Percival Lowell's Sight, pm *IASFM* Jul,1984
　Perception Barriers, BPW&P, 1987
"We cannot escape humility.", pm *F&SF* Nov,1983
　Perception Barriers, BPW&P, 1987
The William Carlos Williams Variations, pm *Arc* Spr,1985
　Perception Barriers, BPW&P, 1987

Frazier, Robert & Roger L. Dutcher
Nazca Lines, pm *IASFM* May,1987

Frazier, Robert & Andrew Joron
Exiled of Worlds, pm *Amazing* Sep,1987

Freas, Frank Kelly
Portfolio, pi **World Fantasy Convention Program Book** #13,1987

Freeman, Mary E. Wilkins
Luella Miller, ss **The Wind in the Rose-Bush and Other Stories of
　the Supernatural**, Doubleday,1903
　Vamps, ed. Martin H. Greenberg +, DAW, 1987
　Vampires, ed. Alan Ryan, SFBC, 1987

Frezza, Robert A.
Max Weber's War, ss *Amazing* Jan,1987

Friesner, Esther M.
Honeycomb, nv **Magic in Ithkar** #4, ed. Andre Norton & Robert
　Adams,1987
The Other Side: Now Revealed: Money-Making Secrets of the
　Shockmeisters, ar *Twilight Zone* Dec,1987

Froehlich, Bill & Cory Glaberson
Interview with Bill Froehlich, iv *American Fantasy* Win,1987

Froehlich, Joey
Ethics and the Work Place, pm *Apex!* #1,1987
Haunted City of the Moon, pm *Eldritch Tales* #13,1987
Moon Boats Taken from the Earth, pm *Space & Time* #72,1987
Singing Nightmares, pm *Grue* #5,1987

Frost, Polly
Fast Forward to the Past, ss *New Yorker* Jul 6,1987
Plan 10 from Zone R-3, ss *New Yorker* Apr 13,1987

Funnell, Augustine
Cat at Play, ss *Night Cry* v2#3,1987
Maxie Silas, ss *F&SF* Jun,1987

Gabbard, G.N.
Der Golem, pm *2AM* Win,1987

Gafford, Sam
The Horseman, vi *Eldritch Tales* #14,1987

Gaiman, Neil & Alan Moore
Alan Moore Interview, iv *American Fantasy* Win,1987

Galbraith, Winifred
'Here He Lies Where He Longed to Be', vi *The Spectator* Chr,1930
　Ghosts and Scholars, ed. Rosemary Pardoe +, Crucible, 1987

Gallagher, Stephen
Like Clockwork, ss *F&SF* Mar,1987
Like Shadows in the Dark, ss **Shadows** #10, ed. Charles L. Grant,1987

Ganley, W. Paul
Editorial, ed *Weirdbook* #22,1987

Garcia y Robertson, R.
The Flying Mountain, nv *Amazing* May,1987
Moon of Popping Trees, nv *Amazing* Sep,1987

Garcia, Nancy
Date with an Angel, mr *American Fantasy* Spr,1987
Shared Secrets: Inside the World of Shared Worlds, ar *American
　Fantasy* Spr,1987
Thieves' World, ar *American Fantasy* Spr,1987

Garcia, Nancy, Clive Barker & Robert T. Garcia
Clive Barker Interview, iv *American Fantasy* Win,1987

Garcia, Nancy, Ramsey Campbell & Robert T. Garcia
Ramsey Campbell Interview, iv *American Fantasy* Win,1987

Garcia, Nancy & Robert T. Garcia
Editorial, ed *American Fantasy* Spr,1987
Editorial, ed *American Fantasy* Sum,1987
Editorial, ed *American Fantasy* Win,1987

Garcia, Nancy, Andre Norton & Mary Frances Zambreno
Andre Norton Interview and Bibliography, iv *American Fantasy*
　Win,1987

GARCIA, ROBERT T.   **GARRETT, RANDALL**

Garcia, Robert T.
  Esoteric References, br *American Fantasy* Sum,1987

Garcia, Robert T., Clive Barker & Nancy Garcia
  Clive Barker Interview, iv *American Fantasy* Win,1987

Garcia, Robert T., Ramsey Campbell & Nancy Garcia
  Ramsey Campbell Interview, iv *American Fantasy* Win,1987

Garcia, Robert T. & Nancy Garcia
  Editorial, ed *American Fantasy* Spr,1987
  Editorial, ed *American Fantasy* Sum,1987
  Editorial, ed *American Fantasy* Win,1987

Gardner, Craig Shaw
  Demon Luck, ss **Magic in Ithkar** #4, ed. Andre Norton & Robert
      Adams,1987
  A Malady of Magicks, n. Ace: New York pb Feb,1986
    The Exploits of Ebenezvm, SFBC, 1987
  A Multitude of Monsters, n. Ace: New York pb Sep,1986
    The Exploits of Ebenezvm, SFBC, 1987
  A Night in the Netherhells, n. Ace: New York pb Jun,1987
    The Exploits of Ebenezvm, SFBC, 1987
  She Closed Her Eyes, nv **Doom City**, ed. Charles L. Grant, Tor,1987

Gardner, Martin
  At the Feet of Karl Klodhopper, ss *Esquire* May,1948
    The No-Sided Professor, Prometheus, 1987
  The Blue Birthmark, vi *Hence* Jul,1948
    The No-Sided Professor, Prometheus, 1987
  The Conspicuous Turtle, ss *Esquire* Apr,1947
    The No-Sided Professor, Prometheus, 1987
  The Devil and the Trombone, ss *The Record Changer* May,1948
    The No-Sided Professor, Prometheus, 1987
  The Dome of Many Colors, ss *The University of Kansas City Review*
      Win,1944
    The No-Sided Professor, Prometheus, 1987
  The Fall of Flatbush Smith, vi *Esquire* Sep,1947
    The No-Sided Professor, Prometheus, 1987
  Good Dancing, Sailor!, ss *The University of Kansas City Review*
      Spr,1946
    The No-Sided Professor, Prometheus, 1987
  The Horrible Horns, ss *London Mystery Magazine* Dec,1950
    The No-Sided Professor, Prometheus, 1987
  The Horse on the Escalator, ss *Esquire* Oct,1946
    The No-Sided Professor, Prometheus, 1987
  Left or Right?, ss *Esquire*,1951
    Mathenauts, ed. Rudy Rucker, Arbor House, 1987
  Love and the Tiddlywinks, vi *Esquire* Sep,1949
    The No-Sided Professor, Prometheus, 1987
  The Loves of Lady Coldpence, ss *Esquire* Mar,1948
    The No-Sided Professor, Prometheus, 1987
  Merlina and the Colored Ice, ss *A.D.* Fll,1951
    The No-Sided Professor, Prometheus, 1987
  Mysterious Smith, ss **The No-Sided Professor**, Prometheus,1987
  No-Sided Professor, ss *Esquire* Jan,1947; *F&SF* Feb,1951
    The No-Sided Professor, Prometheus, 1987
    Mathenauts, ed. Rudy Rucker, Arbor House, 1987
  Nora Says "Check.", ss *Esquire* Jan,1948
    The No-Sided Professor, Prometheus, 1987
  Old Man Gloom, ss *Esquire* Nov,1950
    The No-Sided Professor, Prometheus, 1987
  One More Martini, ss *Esquire* Feb,1950
    The No-Sided Professor, Prometheus, 1987
  Oom, vi *The Journal of Science-Fiction* Fll,1951
    The No-Sided Professor, Prometheus, 1987
  Preface, pr
    The No-Sided Professor, Prometheus, 1987
  Private Eye Oglesby [as "Crunchy Wunchy's First Case"], ss *London
      Mystery Magazine* Feb,1951;
      Ellery Queen's Mystery Magazine Dec,1964
    The No-Sided Professor, Prometheus, 1987
  Ranklin Felano Doosevelt, ss **The No-Sided Professor**,
      Prometheus,1987
  Sibyl Sits In, vi *The Record Changer* Oct,1948
    The No-Sided Professor, Prometheus, 1987
  The Sixth Ship, ss *Our Navy* Sep,1951
    The No-Sided Professor, Prometheus, 1987

Gardner, Martin (continued)
  So Long Old Girl, pm,1945
    The No-Sided Professor, Prometheus, 1987
  The Son of the Mighty Casey [as by Nitram Rendrag], pm **The
      Annotated Casey at the Bat**, ed. Martin Gardner, Clarkson
      Potter,1967
    The No-Sided Professor, Prometheus, 1987
  The Stranger, vi **The No-Sided Professor**, Prometheus,1987
  Thang, vi *Comment* Fll,1948
    The No-Sided Professor, Prometheus, 1987
  The Three Cowboys, vi *Humpty Dumpty's Magazine* Jan,1959
    The No-Sided Professor, Prometheus, 1987
  The Virgin from Kalamazoo, vi *Men Only* Jun,1951
    The No-Sided Professor, Prometheus, 1987

Garey, Terry A.
  The Beach Poet, ed *Tales of the Unanticipated* #2,1987

Garey, Terry A., Eric M. Heideman, Damon Knight & Kate Wilhelm
  An Interview with Kate Wilhelm and Damon Knight, iv *Tales of the
      Unanticipated* #2,1987

Garfield, Frances
  A Dream of Castles, ss **World Fantasy Convention Program Book**
      #13,1987

Garnett, David S.
  Moonlighter, ss **Other Edens**, ed. Christopher Evans & Robert
      Holdstock, Unwin: London,1987
  The Only One, ss *Interzone* #22,1987

Garratt, Peter T.
  If the Driver Vanishes..., ss *Interzone* #13,1985
    Interzone: The 2nd Anthology, ed. John Clute +, Simon &
      Schuster UK, 1987

Garrett, Randall
  ...After a Few Words... [as by Seaton McKettrig], ss *Analog* Oct,1962
    Takeoff Too!, Donning/Starblaze, 1987
  Ballade for Convention Lovers, pm,1963
    Takeoff Too!, Donning/Starblaze, 1987
  Blank?, ss *Infinity* Jun,1957
    Takeoff Too!, Donning/Starblaze, 1987
  The Breakfast Party [League of the Living Dead], ss *Mystic* Nov,1953
    Takeoff Too!, Donning/Starblaze, 1987
  The Briefing, vi *Fantastic* Aug,1969
    Takeoff Too!, Donning/Starblaze, 1987
  Code in the Head, ss *Future* #29,1956
    Takeoff Too!, Donning/Starblaze, 1987
  Cum Grano Salis [as by David Gordon], nv *Astounding* May,1959
    Takeoff Too!, Donning/Starblaze, 1987
  The Egyptian Diamond, pm,1961
      Parts of this poem were quoted in the story "The Foreign Hand-
      Tie".
    Takeoff Too!, Donning/Starblaze, 1987
  The Foreign Hand-Tie [as by David Gordon], nv *Analog* Dec,1961
    Takeoff Too!, Donning/Starblaze, 1987
  Hell to Pay, nv *Beyond Fantasy Fiction* Mar,1954
    Takeoff Too!, Donning/Starblaze, 1987
  The Highest Treason, nv *Analog* Jan,1961
    There Will Be War, Vol. VI: Guns of Darkness, ed. Jerry E.
      Pournelle, Tor, 1987
  The Hunting Lodge, nv *Astounding* Jul,1954
    Isaac Asimov Presents the Great SF Stories: 16 (1954), ed. Isaac
      Asimov +, DAW, 1987
  I've Got a Little List, pm *F&SF* Nov,1953
    Takeoff Too!, Donning/Starblaze, 1987
  Infinite Resources, ss *F&SF* Jul,1954
    Takeoff Too!, Donning/Starblaze, 1987
  Into My Parlor, vi **Takeoff Too!**, Norfolk, VA: Donning/Starblaze,1987
  James Blish and Michael Sherman's "**The Duplicated Man**", pm
      Future #29,1956
    Takeoff Too!, Donning/Starblaze, 1987
  A Memory of John W. Campbell, bg,1968
    Takeoff Too!, Donning/Starblaze, 1987
  ...Or Your Money Back [as by David Gordon], ss *Astounding*
      Sep,1959
    Takeoff Too!, Donning/Starblaze, 1987

Garrett, Randall (continued)
  Our Patrol, sg,1978
    Takeoff Too!, Donning/Starblaze, 1987
  Overproof [as by Jonathan Blake Mackenzie], nv *Analog* Oct,1965
    Takeoff Too!, Donning/Starblaze, 1987
  The Pocket Song, ss,1977
    Takeoff Too!, Donning/Starblaze, 1987
  Pride and Primacy, ss *If* Apr,1974
    Takeoff Too!, Donning/Starblaze, 1987
  Psicopath [as by Darrell T. Langart], ss *Analog* Oct,1960
    Takeoff Too!, Donning/Starblaze, 1987
  Small Miracle, ss *Amazing* Jun,1959
    Takeoff Too!, Donning/Starblaze, 1987
  A Spaceship Named McGuire, nv *Analog* Jul,1961
    Takeoff Too!, Donning/Starblaze, 1987
  There's No Fool... [as by David Gordon], ss *Astounding* Aug,1956
    Takeoff Too!, Donning/Starblaze, 1987
  The World of E.E. "Doc" Smith, ar *The Comics Journal*,1978
    Takeoff Too!, Donning/Starblaze, 1987

Garton, Ray
  Fragments of Horror, ms *The Horror Show* Fll,1987

Gautier, Theophile
  Clarimonda, nv **One of Cleopatra's Nights and Other Fantastic
    Romances**, B. Worthington: New York,1882
    translated by Lafcadio Hearn
  Vamps, ed. Martin H. Greenberg +, DAW, 1987

Gawsworth, John
  Cafe Royal, pm
    Night Cry v2#3,1987
  Naiads, pm
    Night Cry v2#3,1987
  Roman Headstone, pm
    Night Cry v2#3,1987
  Scylla and Charybdis, vi **New Tales of Horror By Eminent Authors**,
    ed. Anonymous, Hutchinson,1934
    Night Cry v2#3,1987
  World's End, pm
    Night Cry v2#3,1987

Gay, Anne
  Wishbone, ss **Gollancz - Sunday Times Best SF Stories**,
    Gollancz,1987

Geras, Adele
  Wordfinder, ss **Twisted Circuits**, ed. Mick Gowar, Beaver,1987

Gerberding, Rodger
  Frank Utpatel: Wood Engraver, bg *Mage* Win,1987

Gibbins, James
  Who's a Clever Boy?, ss **Gollancz - Sunday Times Best SF Stories**,
    Gollancz,1987

Gibbons, Stella
  Roaring Tower, ss **Roaring Tower**,1937
  The Virago Book of Ghost Stories, ed. Richard Dalby, Virago, 1987

Gibson, William
  New Rose Hotel, ss *Omni* Jul,1984
    The Fifth Omni Book of Science Fiction, ed. Ellen Datlow, Zebra,
    1987
  The Silver Walks, ss *High Times* Nov,1987
  The Winter Market, nv *Vancouver* Nov,1985
    The Year's Best Science Fiction, Fourth Annual Collection, ed.
    Gardner R. Dozois, St. Martin's, 1987
  Tesseracts 2, ed. Phyllis Gotlieb +, Porcepic, 1987

Giesler, Andrew
  Proallognostication, vi *Analog* Nov,1987

Gilbert, Christopher
  Love at the 99th Percentile, ss *F&SF* Nov,1987
  Witch Mother, ss *Night Cry* v2#3,1987

Gilbert, Sandra M. & Susan Gubar
  The Queen's Looking Glass, cr **The Mad Woman in the Attic**, New
    Haven, CT: Yale Univ. Press,1979
  Don't Bet on the Prince, ed. Jack Zipes, Methuen, 1987

Gilbert, William
  The Last Lords of Gardonal, ss *Argosy* Jul +3,1867
  Dracula's Brood, ed. Richard Dalby, Crucible, 1987

Gilford, C.B.
  Hush, Dear Conscience, ss *Alfred Hitchcock's Mystery Magazine*
    May,1974
  Alfred Hitchcock's Book of Horror Stories: Book 6, ed. Alfred
    Hitchcock, Coronet, 1987

Gillett, Stephen L., Ph.D.
  Weird LAWKI, ar *Amazing* Jul,1987

Gilman, Carolyn Ives
  The Language of the Sea, nv **L. Ron Hubbard Presents Writers of
    the Future** v3, ed. Algis Budrys, Bridge,1987

Gilman, Charlotte Perkins
  The Yellow Wallpaper, ss *New England Magazine* Jan,1892
  Tales of the Dark, ed. Lincoln Child, St. Martin's, 1987
  House Shudders, ed. Martin H. Greenberg +, DAW, 1987
  The Dark Descent, ed. David G. Hartwell, Tor, 1987

Gilster, Paul A.
  Merchant Dying, ss *Aboriginal SF* Jul,1987

Glaberson, Cory
  Magic Lantern Show, mr *American Fantasy* Spr,1987
  Magic Lantern Show, mr *American Fantasy* Sum,1987
  Magic Lantern Show, mr *American Fantasy* Win,1987

Glaberson, Cory & Bill Froehlich
  Interview with Bill Froehlich, iv *American Fantasy* Win,1987

Glaberson, Cory & Stephen Jones
  Hellraiser, mr *American Fantasy* Win,1987

Gladwin, Philip
  Indian Summer, ss **Gollancz - Sunday Times Best SF Stories**,
    Gollancz,1987

Glasgow, Ellen
  The Shadowy Third, ss *Scribner's* Dec,1916
  The Virago Book of Ghost Stories, ed. Richard Dalby, Virago, 1987

Glave, Thomas, Jr.
  Landscape in Black, pm *Pulpsmith* Win,1987

Glut, Donald F.
  The Empire Strikes Back, n. Ballantine: New York,1980
  The Star Wars Trilogy, George Lucas +, Ballantine/Del Rey, 1987

Godersky, Steven Owen
  Foreword, fw
    **The Collected Stories of Philip K. Dick, Vol. One: Beyond Lies
    the Wub**, Philip K. Dick, Underwood-Miller, 1987

Godfrey, David
  4179, ss *Rampike* v4#2,1985
  Tesseracts 2, ed. Phyllis Gotlieb +, Porcepic, 1987

Godwin, Earl
  Daddy, ss **Shadows #7**, ed. Charles L. Grant,1984
  Devils and Demons, ed. Marvin Kaye, Doubleday, 1987

Godwin, Parke
  Influencing the Hell Out of Time and Teresa Golowitz, ss *Twilight
    Zone* Jan,1982
  Devils and Demons, ed. Marvin Kaye, Doubleday, 1987

GODWIN, TOM

Godwin, Tom
The Cold Equations, nv *Astounding* Aug,1954
Isaac Asimov Presents the Great SF Stories: 16 (1954), ed. Isaac Asimov+, DAW, 1987

Gold, Horace L.
Man of Parts, ss **9 Tales of Space and Time**, ed. Raymond J. Healey, Holt,1954
Isaac Asimov Presents the Great SF Stories: 16 (1954), ed. Isaac Asimov+, DAW, 1987

Goldsmith, Donald
Who Will Speak for Earth? An Essay on Extraterrestrial Intelligence and Contact, ar **Universe**, ed. Byron Preiss, Bantam Spectra,1987

Goldstein, Lisa
Cassandra's Photographs, ss *IASFM* Aug,1987

Gooding, Paul
The Machine Age, ss **Gollancz - Sunday Times Best SF Stories**, Gollancz,1987

Goodman, Dan
Writing With Percission: Cooking Salmon in the Dishwasher: Nontraditional Computer Use for Science Fiction and Fantasy Writers, Part 1, ar *Tales of the Unanticipated* #2,1987

Gordon, George, Lord Byron
A Fragment of a Novel, uw,1816
Vampires, ed. Alan Ryan, SFBC, 1987

Gordon, Greg
Buy the Rules?, gr *American Fantasy* Spr,1987
Buy the Rules?, gr *American Fantasy* Win,1987

Gordon, John
The Black Prince, ss **A Quiver of Ghosts**, ed. Aiden Chambers, Bodley Head,1987
User-Friendly, ss **Twisted Circuits**, ed. Mick Gowar, Beaver,1987

Gorog, Judith
A Story About Death, ss **A Taste for Quiet**, Putnam,1982
The Ghost Story Treasury, ed. Linda Sonntag, Putnam, 1987

Gorst, Hester
The Doll's House, ss **Horrors**, ed. Anonymous, Philip Allan: London,1933
The Virago Book of Ghost Stories, ed. Richard Dalby, Virago, 1987

Gorton, Mark
The Fall, ss **Gollancz - Sunday Times Best SF Stories**, Gollancz,1987

Gotlieb, Phyllis
Foreword: You Are Here, fw
Tesseracts 2, ed. Phyllis Gotlieb+, Porcepic, 1987

Gotschalk, Felix C.
Menage a Super-Trois, ss *F&SF* May,1987

Gottfried, Frederick D.
Hermes to the Ages, nv *Analog* Jan,1980
Isaac Asimov's Wonderful Worlds of Science Fiction #7: Space Shuttles, ed. Isaac Asimov+, NAL/Signet, 1987

Goulart, Ron
Business as Usual, ss *F&SF* Jul,1987
The Goulart Archipelago, ar *Twilight Zone* Feb,1987
Junior Partner, ss *Fantastic* Sep,1962
Fantastic Stories: Tales of the Weird and Wondrous, ed. Martin H. Greenberg+, TSR, 1987

Gould, Steven
Poppa Was a Catcher, na **New Destinies** v2, ed. Jim Baen, Baen,1987

Gowar, Mick
Editor's Foreword, in
Twisted Circuits, ed. Mick Gowar, Beaver, 1987

Grabinski, Stefan
Before the Long Journey, ss,1921
The Grabinski Reader [#2, Spring 1987]
Saturnin Sektor, ss,1920
The Grabinski Reader [#2, Spring 1987]

Grabowski, William J.
The Country Wife, vi *Haunts* #9,1987
Swan Song, br *The Horror Show* Spr,1987
Tattler, br *The Horror Show* Jan,1987
Tattler, br *The Horror Show* Spr,1987
Tattler, br *The Horror Show* Sum,1987
Tattler, br *The Horror Show* Fll,1987
Tattler, br *The Horror Show* Win,1987

Grabowski, William J. & Poppy Z. Brite
Poppy Z. Brite, iv *The Horror Show* Fll,1987

Grabowski, William J. & Dennis Etchison
Dennis Etchison, iv *The Horror Show* Win,1987

Grabowski, William J. & Joe R. Lansdale
Interview with Joe R. Lansdale, iv *The Horror Show* Jan,1987

Grabowski, William J. & Bentley Little
Bentley Little, iv *The Horror Show* Fll,1987

Grabowski, William J. & John Maclay
Genre-Love and the Magic of Words: John Maclay, iv *2AM* Fll,1987

Grabowski, William J. & Robert R. McCammon
Interview with Robert R. McCammon, iv *The Horror Show* Spr,1987

Grahame, Kenneth
The Reluctant Dragon, ss **Dream Days**, London: John Lane,1898
Victorian Fairy Tales, ed. Jack Zipes, Methuen, 1987

Grahn, Judy
Ernesta [from "Mundane's World"], ex **Hear the Silence**, ed. Irene Zahava, Crossing Press,1986

Grant, Charles L.
The Children, They Laugh So Sweetly, ss *F&SF* Oct,1985
House Shudders, ed. Martin H. Greenberg+, DAW, 1987
Constant Father, ss **World Fantasy Convention Program Book** #13,1987
Crystal, ss *F&SF* Aug,1986
The Year's Best Horror Stories: XV, ed. Karl Edward Wagner, DAW, 1987
Ellen, in Her Time, ss **The Architecture of Fear**, ed. Kathryn Cramer & Peter D. Pautz, Arbor House,1987
Everything to Live For, ss **Whispers** #6, ed. Stuart David Schiff,1987
A Garden of Blackred Roses, nv **Dark Forces**, ed. Kirby McCauley, Viking,1980
Masters of Darkness II, ed. Dennis Etchison, Tor, 1988
If Damon Comes, ss **The Year's Best Horror Stories** #6,1978
The Dark Descent, ed. David G. Hartwell, Tor, 1987
An Image in Twisted Silver, ss *Twilight Zone* Apr,1987
Story based on a J.K. Potter illustration.
Introduction, in
Shadows 10, ed. Charles L. Grant, Doubleday, 1987
Doom City, ed. Charles L. Grant, Tor, 1987
It Wasn't a Half-Bad Year, br *Amazing* Sep,1987
Listen to the Music in My Hands, ss *Twilight Zone* Feb,1987
Love-Starved, ss *F&SF* Aug,1979
Vampires, ed. Alan Ryan, SFBC, 1987
Midnights, br *American Fantasy* Spr,1987
Midnights, br *American Fantasy* Sum,1987
Midnights, br *American Fantasy* Win,1987
One Spring in Wyoming, ss *Aboriginal SF* Feb,1987
The Sheeted Dead, ss **In the Field of Fire**, ed. Jeanne Van Buren Dann & Jack M. Dann, Tor,1987
This Old Man, ss *Night Cry* v2#3,1987

Grant, Charles L. & Douglas E. Winter
A Conversation With Charles L. Grant, iv *Twilight Zone* Apr,1987

GRANT, ROBERTA

Grant, Roberta
  Catscape, nv *Amazing* Jul,1987

Gray, Arthur
  Brother John's Bequest, ss **Tedious Brief Tales of Granta and Gramarye**, Cambridge: Heffer,1919
    Ghosts and Scholars, ed. Rosemary Pardoe+, Crucible, 1987

Greeley, Andrew M.
  The Dutchman's Ghost Town, nv *F&SF* Feb,1987
  Xorinda the Witch, ss *American Fantasy* Sum,1987

Green, J.C. & George W. Proctor
  The Night of the Piasa, nv **Nightmares**, ed. Charles L. Grant, Playboy,1979
    Nightmares in Dixie, ed. Frank D. McSherry, Jr.+, August House, 1987

Green, Joseph
  Single Combat, ss *New Worlds* Aug,1964
    Battlefields Beyond Tomorrow, ed. Charles G. Waugh+, Crown/Bonanza, 1987

Green, Joseph & Patrice Milton
  The Speckled Gantry, ss **Destinies** v1#2, ed. James Baen,1979
    Isaac Asimov's Wonderful Worlds of Science Fiction #7: Space Shuttles, ed. Isaac Asimov+, NAL/Signet, 1987

Green, Roger Lancelyn
  Introduction, in
    The Light Princess and Other Stories, George MacDonald, Kelpies, 1987

Green, Roland J.
  The Fantastic Battlefield, ar *Amazing* Jan,1987
  The Leading Edge, br **New Destinies** v2, ed. Jim Baen, Baen,1987

Green, Roland J. & John F. Carr
  Nightfriend, nv **Friends of the Horseclans**, ed. Robert Adams & Pamela Crippen Adams, Signet,1987

Green, Scott E.
  Roses of Ashes, pm *Eldritch Tales* #14,1987
  Slow Roll In Neutral, pm *Eldritch Tales* #13,1987

Green, Sharon
  A Quiet Day at the Fair, nv **Magic in Ithkar #4**, ed. Andre Norton & Robert Adams,1987
  A Vision of Honor, nv **Friends of the Horseclans**, ed. Robert Adams & Pamela Crippen Adams, Signet,1987

Green, Terence M.
  Ashland, Kentucky, nv *IASFM* Nov,1985
    The Woman Who Is the Midnight Wind, Pottersfield Press, 1987
    Tesseracts 2, ed. Phyllis Gotlieb+, Porcepic, 1987
  Barking Dogs, ss *F&SF* May,1984
    The Woman Who Is the Midnight Wind, Pottersfield Press, 1987
  Japanese Tea, ss **Alien Worlds**, ed. Paul Collins, Void,1979
    The Woman Who Is the Midnight Wind, Pottersfield Press, 1987
  Legacy, ss *F&SF* Mar,1985
    The Woman Who Is the Midnight Wind, Pottersfield Press, 1987
  Of Children in the Foliage, ss **Aurora: New Canadian Writing 1979**, ed. Morris Wolfe, Doubleday Canada,1979
    The Woman Who Is the Midnight Wind, Pottersfield Press, 1987
  Point Zero, ss *F&SF* May,1986
    The Woman Who Is the Midnight Wind, Pottersfield Press, 1987
  Room 1786, ss *Leisure Ways* Nov,1982
    The Woman Who Is the Midnight Wind, Pottersfield Press, 1987
  Susie Q2, ss *IASFM* Aug,1983
    The Woman Who Is the Midnight Wind, Pottersfield Press, 1987
  Till Death Do Us Part, ss *F&SF* Dec,1981
    The Woman Who Is the Midnight Wind, Pottersfield Press, 1987
  The Woman Who Is the Midnight Wind, ss **Tesseracts**, ed. Judith Merril, Press Porcepic: Victoria,1985
    The Woman Who Is the Midnight Wind, Pottersfield Press, 1987

Greenberg, Martin H.
  1954 Introduction, in
    Isaac Asimov Presents the Great SF Stories: 16 (1954), ed. Isaac Asimov+, DAW, 1987
  1955 Introduction, in
    Isaac Asimov Presents the Great SF Stories: 17 (1955), ed. Isaac Asimov+, DAW, 1988
  Introduction: "Horror and the Hearth of Darkness", in
    House Shudders, ed. Martin H. Greenberg+, DAW, 1987

Greenberg, Martin H. & Robert Silverberg
  Introduction, in
    Great Science Fiction of the 20th Century, ed. Robert Silverberg+, Crown/Avenel, 1987

Gribbin, Dr. John
  The Lost Years of Cosmology, ar *Analog* Dec,1987

Gribbin, Dr. John & Mary Gribbin
  In Praise of Sociobiology, ar **New Destinies** v1, ed. Jim Baen, Baen,1987

Gribbin, Mary & Dr. John Gribbin
  In Praise of Sociobiology, ar **New Destinies** v1, ed. Jim Baen, Baen,1987

Griffin, A. Arthur
  In the Old Places, pm *Weirdbook* #22,1987

Griffin, Pauline
  Oath-Bound, nv **Tales of the Witch World**, ed. Andre Norton, St. Martin's,1987

Griffin, Russell M.
  Saving Time, na *F&SF* Feb,1987

Gross, Henry R.
  Cubeworld, nv **Mathenauts**, ed. Rudy Rucker, Arbor House,1987

Grove, Vicki
  At the Rummage Sale, ss *Twilight Zone* Apr,1987

Grubb, Davis
  Cry Havoc, ss *Ellery Queen's Mystery Magazine* Aug,1976
    Nightmares in Dixie, ed. Frank D. McSherry, Jr.+, August House, 1987
  The Horsehair Trunk [The Secret Darkness], ss *Ellery Queen's Mystery Magazine* Oct,1956
    Rod Serling's Night Gallery Reader, ed. Carol Serling+, Dembner, 1987

Gubar, Susan & Sandra M. Gilbert
  The Queen's Looking Glass, cr **The Mad Woman in the Attic**, New Haven, CT: Yale Univ. Press,1979
    Don't Bet on the Prince, ed. Jack Zipes, Methuen, 1987

Gunn, James E.
  The Cave of Night, ss *Galaxy* Feb,1955
    Isaac Asimov Presents the Great SF Stories: 17 (1955), ed. Isaac Asimov+, DAW, 1988
  Donor, nv *Fantastic* Nov,1960
    Fantastic Stories: Tales of the Weird and Wondrous, ed. Martin H. Greenberg+, TSR, 1987
  Introduction, in
    Fantastic Stories: Tales of the Weird and Wondrous, ed. Martin H. Greenberg+, TSR, 1987

Guttenberg, Elyse
  Selena's Song, ss **Spaceships & Spells**, ed. Jane Yolen, Martin H. Greenberg & Charles G. Waugh, Harper & Row,1987

Gygax, Gary
  Cat or Pigeon?, na **Night Arrant**, Ace/New Infinities,1987
  Cats Versus Rats, nv **Night Arrant**, Ace/New Infinities,1987
  The Five Dragon Bowl, nv **Night Arrant**, Ace/New Infinities,1987
  The Heart of Darkness, nv **Night Arrant**, Ace/New Infinities,1987
  The House in the Tree, nv **Night Arrant**, Ace/New Infinities,1987
  Love Laughs at Locks, nv **Night Arrant**, Ace/New Infinities,1987

GYGAX, GARY

Gygax, Gary (continued)
A Revel in Rel Mord, na **Night Arrant**, Ace/New Infinities,1987
Twistbuck's Game, nv **Night Arrant**, Ace/New Infinities,1987
The Weird Occurrence in Odd Alley, na **Night Arrant**, Ace/New Infinities,1987

Haberman, Paul
Ouija, vi *Grue* #4,1987

Hadji, R.S.
Who's Who in the British Horror Scene, ar *American Fantasy* Win,1987

Haining, Peter
Introduction, in
The Complete Supernatural Stories of Rudyard Kipling, Rudyard Kipling, W.H. Allen, 1987
Werewolf: Horror Stories of the Man Beast, ed. Peter Haining, Severn House, 1987
Poltergeist: Tales of Deadly Ghosts, ed. Peter Haining, Severn House, 1987

Haisty, Robert
Seventh Sense, ss *Omni* Sep,1983
The Fifth Omni Book of Science Fiction, ed. Ellen Datlow, Zebra, 1987

Haldeman, Jack C., II
Dead Man's Tie, ss *Twilight Zone* Feb,1987
Playing for Keeps, ss *IASFM* May,1982
Tales From Isaac Asimov's Science Fiction Magazine, ed. Sheila Williams+, Harcourt Brace Jovanovich, 1986
Wet Behind the Ears, ss *IASFM* Oct,1982
Tales From Isaac Asimov's Science Fiction Magazine, ed. Sheila Williams+, Harcourt Brace Jovanovich, 1986

Haldeman, Joe W.
cold rust grit: end of dreams, pm *IASFM* mid-Dec,1987
DX, ss **In the Field of Fire**, ed. Jeanne Van Buren Dann & Jack M. Dann, Tor,1987
The Gift, pm **Dealing in Futures**, Viking,1985
IASFM Feb,1987
Hero, na *Analog* Jun,1972
Battlefields Beyond Tomorrow, ed. Charles G. Waugh+, Crown/Bonanza, 1987
Introduction, in
Supertanks, ed. Joe W. Haldeman+, Ace, 1987
Tricentennial, ss *Analog* Jul,1976
Beyond the Stars, ed. Isaac Asimov, Severn House, 1987

Hall, Melissa Mia
Confession of Innocence, ss **Doom City**, ed. Charles L. Grant, Tor,1987
Moonflower, ss **Shadows** #10, ed. Charles L. Grant,1987

Halliwell, Leslie
Author's Note, in
A Demon Close Behind, Robert Hale, 1987
Come Into the Garden, Mawdsley, nv **A Demon Close Behind**, Robert Hale,1987
The Day of the Jester, ss **A Demon Close Behind**, Robert Hale,1987
Escape to Akureyri, nv **A Demon Close Behind**, Robert Hale,1987
The Haunting of Joshua Tree, ss **A Demon Close Behind**, Robert Hale,1987
The Horror at Hops Cottage, ss **A Demon Close Behind**, Robert Hale,1987
Lover, pm **A Demon Close Behind**, Robert Hale,1987
The Man with the Dundreary Weepers, ss **A Demon Close Behind**, Robert Hale,1987
Memorial Service, ss **A Demon Close Behind**, Robert Hale,1987
La Nuit des Chiens, ss **A Demon Close Behind**, Robert Hale,1987
The Past of Mrs Pickering, nv **A Demon Close Behind**, Robert Hale,1987
The Smile on the Face of the Kite, nv **A Demon Close Behind**, Robert Hale,1987
Smoking-Room Story, ss **A Demon Close Behind**, Robert Hale,1987
Take Off Your Cap When a Funeral Passes, ss **A Demon Close Behind**, Robert Hale,1987

Halliwell, Leslie (continued)
Where not to buy Cufflinks in Stockholm, ss **A Demon Close Behind**, Robert Hale,1987

Hallworth, Grace
The Guitarist, ss **Mouth Open Story Jump Out**, Methuen,1984
The Ghost Story Treasury, ed. Linda Sonntag, Putnam, 1987

Hambly, Barbara
The Ladies of Mandrigyn, n. Ballantine: New York pb Mar,1984
The Unschooled Wizard, SFBC, 1987
The Witches of Wenshar, n. Ballantine: New York pb Jul,1987
The Unschooled Wizard, SFBC, 1987

Hamilton, Dale Colleen
Blood, Sweat and Fears, ss **Hear the Silence**, ed. Irene Zahava, Crossing Press,1986

Hamilton, Dennis
Fish Story, ss **Masques** #2, ed. J.N. Williamson,1987

Hamilton, Edmond
Devolution, ss *Amazing* Dec,1936
Amazing Science Fiction Stories: The War Years 1936-1945, ed. Martin H. Greenberg, TSR, 1987
The Man Who Saw the Future, ss *Amazing* Oct,1930
Amazing Science Fiction Stories: The Wonder Years 1926-1935, ed. Martin H. Greenberg, TSR, 1987
The Vengeance of Ulios [The Avenger from Atlantis], nv *Weird Tales* Jul,1935
Isaac Asimov's Magical Worlds of Fantasy #9: Atlantis, ed. Isaac Asimov+, NAL/Signet, 1988

Hamilton, Virginia
The Peculiar Such Thing, ss **The People Could Fly: American Black Folktales**, Knopf,1985
The Ghost Story Treasury, ed. Linda Sonntag, Putnam, 1987

Hamley, Dennis
Krarg Enters, ss **Twisted Circuits**, ed. Mick Gowar, Beaver,1987

Hammond, Charlotte Brown
Uncle Sherm (A Fantasy), ss *Grue* #4,1987

Hannes, Genine
What the Large Night Left, pm *Ice River* Sum,1987

Hansen, Tom
Winterscape, pm *Pulpsmith* Win,1987

Harding, Lawrence
Black Jewels of the Toad, pm *Eldritch Tales* #14,1987
Lost Eons, pm *Space & Time* #72,1987
The Wings of a Bat, pm *Grue* #5,1987

Hardy, Thomas
The Withered Arm, nv *Blackwood's* Jan,1888
Classic Stories of Mystery, Horror and Suspense, ed. Simon Petherick, Robert Hale, 1987
Charles Keeping's Classic Tales of the Macabre, ed. Charles Keeping, Blackie, 1987

Harness, Charles L.
An Ornament to His Profession, nv *Analog* Feb,1966
Demons!, ed. Jack M. Dann+, Ace, 1987
Signals, na **Synergy** v1, ed. George Zebrowski,1987

Harper, Rory
Snorkeling in the River Lethe, ss *Amazing* Jan,1987

Harris, Clare Winger
The Miracle of the Lily, nv *Amazing* Apr,1928
Amazing Science Fiction Stories: The Wonder Years 1926-1935, ed. Martin H. Greenberg, TSR, 1987

Harris, Sidney
Cartoon, ct *F&SF* Jan,1987
Cartoon, ct *F&SF* Jul,1987

HARRIS, SIDNEY

HARVEY, W.F.

Harris, Sidney (continued)
  Cartoon, ct *F&SF* Nov,1987
  Cartoon, ct *F&SF* Dec,1987

Harrison, Harry
  Ni Venos, Doktoro Zamenof, Ni Venos!, ss **Tales from the Forbidden Planet**, ed. Roz Kaveney, Titan,1987
  No War, or Battle's Sound [Or Battle's Sound], nv *If* Oct,1968
    Battlefields Beyond Tomorrow, ed. Charles G. Waugh +, Crown/Bonanza, 1987

Harrison, M. John
  Small Heirlooms, ss **Other Edens**, ed. Christopher Evans & Robert Holdstock, Unwin: London,1987

Hartley, L.P.
  Apples, ss **The White Wand and Other Stories**, Hamilton,1954
    The Complete Short Stories of L.P. Hartley, Beaufort, 1986
  A Change of Ownership, ss
    The Complete Short Stories of L.P. Hartley, Beaufort, 1986
  A Condition of Release, ss **The White Wand and Other Stories**, Hamilton,1954
    The Complete Short Stories of L.P. Hartley, Beaufort, 1986
  Conrad and the Dragon, nv
    The Complete Short Stories of L.P. Hartley, Beaufort, 1986
  The Corner Cupboard, ss
    The Complete Short Stories of L.P. Hartley, Beaufort, 1986
  The Cotillon, ss
    The Complete Short Stories of L.P. Hartley, Beaufort, 1986
  The Crossways, ss
    The Complete Short Stories of L.P. Hartley, Beaufort, 1986
  The Face, nv
    The Complete Short Stories of L.P. Hartley, Beaufort, 1986
  Fall In at the Double, ss
    The Complete Short Stories of L.P. Hartley, Beaufort, 1986
  Feet Foremost, nv
    The Complete Short Stories of L.P. Hartley, Beaufort, 1986
  A High Dive, ss
    The Complete Short Stories of L.P. Hartley, Beaufort, 1986
  Hilda's Letter, nv **The White Wand and Other Stories**, Hamilton,1954
    The Complete Short Stories of L.P. Hartley, Beaufort, 1986
  Home, Sweet Home, ss
    The Complete Short Stories of L.P. Hartley, Beaufort, 1986
  Interference, ss
    The Complete Short Stories of L.P. Hartley, Beaufort, 1986
  The Island, ss **The Travelling Grave and Other Stories**, Arkham,1948
    The Complete Short Stories of L.P. Hartley, Beaufort, 1986
  The Killing Bottle, nv
    The Complete Short Stories of L.P. Hartley, Beaufort, 1986
  Monkshood Manor, ss **The White Wand and Other Stories**, Hamilton,1954
    The Complete Short Stories of L.P. Hartley, Beaufort, 1986
  Mr. Blandfoot's Picture, nv **The White Wand and Other Stories**, Hamilton,1954
    The Complete Short Stories of L.P. Hartley, Beaufort, 1986
  Mrs. Carteret Receives, co,1971
    The Complete Short Stories of L.P. Hartley, Beaufort, 1986
  Mrs. Carteret Receives, nv
    The Complete Short Stories of L.P. Hartley, Beaufort, 1986
  Night Fears, ss
    The Complete Short Stories of L.P. Hartley, Beaufort, 1986
  Noughts and Crosses, ss
    The Complete Short Stories of L.P. Hartley, Beaufort, 1986
  Pains and Pleasures, ss
    The Complete Short Stories of L.P. Hartley, Beaufort, 1986
  The Pampas Clump, ss
    The Complete Short Stories of L.P. Hartley, Beaufort, 1986
  Paradise Paddock, ss
    The Complete Short Stories of L.P. Hartley, Beaufort, 1986
  Per Far L'Amore, ss
    The Complete Short Stories of L.P. Hartley, Beaufort, 1986
  Please Do Not Touch, ss
    The Complete Short Stories of L.P. Hartley, Beaufort, 1986
  Podolo, ss **The Travelling Grave and Other Stories**, Arkham,1948
    The Complete Short Stories of L.P. Hartley, Beaufort, 1986
  The Prayer, ss
    The Complete Short Stories of L.P. Hartley, Beaufort, 1986

Hartley, L.P. (continued)
  The Price of the Absolute, ss **The White Wand and Other Stories**, Hamilton,1954
    The Complete Short Stories of L.P. Hartley, Beaufort, 1986
  The Pylon, ss
    The Complete Short Stories of L.P. Hartley, Beaufort, 1986
  A Rewarding Experience, ss **The White Wand and Other Stories**, Hamilton,1954
    The Complete Short Stories of L.P. Hartley, Beaufort, 1986
  Roman Charity, nv
    The Complete Short Stories of L.P. Hartley, Beaufort, 1986
  The Shadow on the Wall, ss
    The Complete Short Stories of L.P. Hartley, Beaufort, 1986
  The Silver Clock, ss
    The Complete Short Stories of L.P. Hartley, Beaufort, 1986
  Simonetta Perkins, na,1925
    The Complete Short Stories of L.P. Hartley, Beaufort, 1986
  Someone in the Lift, ss
    The Complete Short Stories of L.P. Hartley, Beaufort, 1986
  A Summons, ss **The White Wand and Other Stories**, Hamilton,1954
    The Complete Short Stories of L.P. Hartley, Beaufort, 1986
  The Thought, ss **The Travelling Grave and Other Stories**, Arkham,1948
    The Complete Short Stories of L.P. Hartley, Beaufort, 1986
  Three, or Four, for Dinner, ss
    The Complete Short Stories of L.P. Hartley, Beaufort, 1986
  A Tonic, ss **The White Wand and Other Stories**, Hamilton,1954
    The Complete Short Stories of L.P. Hartley, Beaufort, 1986
  Travelling Grave, co Arkham House: Sauk City, WI,1948
    The Complete Short Stories of L.P. Hartley, Beaufort, 1986
  The Travelling Grave, ss
    The Complete Short Stories of L.P. Hartley, Beaufort, 1986
  Two for the River, co,1961
    The Complete Short Stories of L.P. Hartley, Beaufort, 1986
  Two for the River, ss
    The Complete Short Stories of L.P. Hartley, Beaufort, 1986
  The Two Vaynes, ss **The White Wand and Other Stories**, Hamilton,1954
    The Complete Short Stories of L.P. Hartley, Beaufort, 1986
  Up the Garden Path, ss **The White Wand and Other Stories**, Hamilton,1954
    The Complete Short Stories of L.P. Hartley, Beaufort, 1986
  A Very Present Help, nv
    The Complete Short Stories of L.P. Hartley, Beaufort, 1986
  A Visitor from Down Under, ss **The Ghost-Book**, ed. Cynthia Asquith, Hutchinson,1926
    The Complete Short Stories of L.P. Hartley, Beaufort, 1986
  W.S., ss **Ghost Book #2**, ed. Aidan Chambers/James Turner,1952
    The Complete Short Stories of L.P. Hartley, Beaufort, 1986
  The Waits, ss
    The Complete Short Stories of L.P. Hartley, Beaufort, 1986
  The White Wand, co,1954
    The Complete Short Stories of L.P. Hartley, Beaufort, 1986
  The White Wand, nv **The White Wand and Other Stories**, Hamilton,1954
    The Complete Short Stories of L.P. Hartley, Beaufort, 1986
  Witheling End, ss **The White Wand and Other Stories**, Hamilton,1954
    The Complete Short Stories of L.P. Hartley, Beaufort, 1986
  Won By a Fall, ss
    The Complete Short Stories of L.P. Hartley, Beaufort, 1986

Hartman, Sergio Gaut vel
  Contaminated People, ss *SF International* #2,1987

Hartwell, David G.
  Introduction, in
    Cardography, Orson Scott Card, Hypatia Press, 1987
    The Dark Descent, ed. David G. Hartwell, Tor, 1987
  Introduction: The Spirit of Christmas, in
    Christmas Ghosts, ed. Kathryn Cramer +, Arbor House, 1987

Harvey, W.F.
  Miss Cornelius, ss **The Beast With Five Fingers**, J.M. Dent,1928
    Poltergeist: Tales of Deadly Ghosts, ed. Peter Haining, Severn House, 1987

Hautala, Rick
  Colt .24, ss **Devils**, ed. Isaac Asimov, Martin H. Greenberg & Charles
      G. Waugh, Signet,1987

Haviland, Keith
  Soap, ss **Gollancz - Sunday Times Best SF Stories**, Gollancz,1987

Hawthorne, Julian
  Ken's Mystery, nv **David Poindexter's Disappearance**, Appleton,1888
      Vamps, ed. Martin H. Greenberg +, DAW, 1987
      Dracula's Brood, ed. Richard Dalby, Crucible, 1987

Hawthorne, Nathaniel
  The Christmas Banquet, nv *Democratic Review* Dec,1843
      Christmas Ghosts, ed. Kathryn Cramer +, Arbor House, 1987
  Young Goodman Brown, ss *New England Magazine* Apr,1835
      The Dark Descent, ed. David G. Hartwell, Tor, 1987

Hay, Daniel J.
  Fractured Dimensions, ss *Salarius #3*,1987

Hay, Sara Henderson
  Rapunzel, pm **Story Hour**, Fayetteville: Univ. of Arkansas Press,1982
      Don't Bet on the Prince, ed. Jack Zipes, Methuen, 1987

Hayes, Michael
  Introduction, in
      The Supernatural Short Stories of Sir Walter Scott, Sir Walter
          Scott, Riverrun/Calder, 1986

Hays, Robert
  Thermo, pm *Amazing* Nov,1987

Heapy, Paul
  Moral Technology, ss **Gollancz - Sunday Times Best SF Stories**,
      Gollancz,1987

Hearn, Lafcadio
  The Boy Who Drew Cats, ss,1898
      Young Witches & Warlocks, ed. Isaac Asimov +, Harper & Row,
          1987
  Rokuro-Kubi, ss **Kwaidan**,1904
      Devils and Demons, ed. Marvin Kaye, Doubleday, 1987

Heath, Karen B.
  The Last Gays of Parpheii, vi *Salarius v1#4*,1987

Heath, Phillip C.
  The Man Who Collected Bloch, ss *Eldritch Tales #13*,1987

Heckler, Mary
  Cosmos, pm *Weirdbook #22*,1987

Heidbrink, James R.
  Of Ancient Swords and Evil Mist, ss **Tales of the Witch World**, ed.
      Andre Norton, St. Martin's,1987

Heideman, Eric M.
  Little Magazine That Could, ed *Tales of the Unanticipated #2*,1987
  Time and Chance, nv **L. Ron Hubbard Presents Writers of the
      Future** v3, ed. Algis Budrys, Bridge,1987

Heideman, Eric M., Terry A. Garey, Damon Knight & Kate Wilhelm
  An Interview with Kate Wilhelm and Damon Knight, iv *Tales of the
      Unanticipated #2*,1987

Heinlein, Robert A.
  "All You Zombies-", ss *F&SF* Mar,1959
      Great Science Fiction of the 20th Century, ed. Robert
          Silverberg +, Crown/Avenel, 1987
  The Black Pits of Luna, ss *The Saturday Evening Post* Jan 10,1948
      The Past Through Tomorrow Vol. 1, NEL, 1987
  Blowups Happen, nv *Astounding* Sep,1940
      The Past Through Tomorrow Vol. 1, NEL, 1987
  Coventry, na *Astounding* Jul,1940
      The Past Through Tomorrow Vol. 2, NEL, 1987
  Delilah and the Space-Rigger, ss *Blue Book* Dec,1949
      The Past Through Tomorrow Vol. 1, NEL, 1987

Heinlein, Robert A. (continued)
  Gentlemen, Be Seated!, ss *Argosy* May,1948
      The Past Through Tomorrow Vol. 1, NEL, 1987
  The Green Hills of Earth, ss *The Saturday Evening Post* Feb 8,1947
      The Past Through Tomorrow Vol. 2, NEL, 1987
  If This Goes On-, na *Astounding* Feb,1940
      The Past Through Tomorrow Vol. 2, NEL, 1987
  It's Great to be Back!, ss *The Saturday Evening Post* Jul 26,1947
      The Past Through Tomorrow Vol. 1, NEL, 1987
  Life-Line, ss *Astounding* Aug,1939
      The Past Through Tomorrow Vol. 1, NEL, 1987
  Logic of Empire, nv *Astounding* Mar,1941
      The Past Through Tomorrow Vol. 2, NEL, 1987
  The Long Watch, ss *American Legion Magazine* Dec,1949
      The Past Through Tomorrow Vol. 1, NEL, 1987
      Battlefields Beyond Tomorrow, ed. Charles G. Waugh +,
          Crown/Bonanza, 1987
  The Man Who Sold the Moon, nv **The Man Who Sold the Moon**,
      Shasta,1950
      The Past Through Tomorrow Vol. 1, NEL, 1987
  The Menace from Earth, ss *F&SF* Aug,1957
      The Past Through Tomorrow Vol. 2, NEL, 1987
  Misfit, ss *Astounding* Nov,1939
      The Past Through Tomorrow Vol. 2, NEL, 1987
  Ordeal in Space, ss *Town & Country* May,1948
      The Past Through Tomorrow Vol. 2, NEL, 1987
  Requiem, ss *Astounding* Jan,1940
      The Past Through Tomorrow Vol. 1, NEL, 1987
  The Roads Must Roll, nv *Astounding* Jun,1940
      The Past Through Tomorrow Vol. 1, NEL, 1987
  Searchlight, vi *Scientific American* Aug,1962
      The Past Through Tomorrow Vol. 2, NEL, 1987
  Space Jockey, ss *The Saturday Evening Post* Apr 26,1947
      The Past Through Tomorrow Vol. 1, NEL, 1987
  They, ss *Unknown* Apr,1941
      PsiFi: Psychological Theories and Science Fictions, ed. Jim
          Ridgway +, The British Psychological Society, 1987
  We Also Walk Dogs, ss *Astounding* Jul,1941
      The Past Through Tomorrow Vol. 2, NEL, 1987

Heinrich, Kurt Hyatt
  The Darkworld Contract, ss *Space & Time #72*,1987

Heiser
  Cartoon, ct *IASFM* Oct,1987

Helfand, David J.
  Supernovae: Creative Cataclysms in the Galaxy, ar **Universe**, ed.
      Byron Preiss, Bantam Spectra,1987

Helfman, Elizabeth S.
  Voices in the Wind, ss **Spaceships & Spells**, ed. Jane Yolen, Martin
      H. Greenberg & Charles G. Waugh, Harper & Row,1987

Hellinga, Gerben, Jr.
  Narcissus Flower, ss *SF International #2*,1987

Henderson, C.J.
  You Can't Take It With You, ss *Eldritch Tales #14*,1987

Henderson, Zenna
  Stevie and the Dark [The Dark Came Out to Play], ss *Imagination*
      May,1952
      Young Witches & Warlocks, ed. Isaac Asimov +, Harper & Row,
          1987

Hendrix, Howard V.
  Doctor Doom Conducting, vi *Aboriginal SF* Sep,1987

Henighan, Tom
  Bonsai Man, pm **Tesseracts 2**, ed. Phyllis Gotlieb & Douglas
      Barbour, Press Porcepic: Victoria,1987
  Visitation, pm **Tesseracts 2**, ed. Phyllis Gotlieb & Douglas Barbour,
      Press Porcepic: Victoria,1987

Henry, O.
  The Enchanted Kiss, ss
      Cinemonsters, ed. Martin H. Greenberg, TSR, 1987

Henson, H. Keith
Memetics and the Modular Mind--Modeling the Development of
Social Movements, ar *Analog* Aug,1987

Herbert, Frank
Chapterhouse Dune, n. Gollancz: London,1985
The Second Great Dune Trilogy, Gollancz, 1987
Committee of the Whole, nv *Galaxy* Apr,1965
Battlefields Beyond Tomorrow, ed. Charles G. Waugh+,
Crown/Bonanza, 1987
God Emperor of Dune, n. Gollancz: London,1981
The Second Great Dune Trilogy, Gollancz, 1987
Heretics of Dune, n. Gollancz: London,1984
The Second Great Dune Trilogy, Gollancz, 1987

Herbert, James
Maurice and Mog, ss **Masques #2**, ed. J.N. Williamson,1987

Herman, Ira
Promised Star, ss *Amazing* Nov,1987

Heron-Allen, E.
Another Squaw?, ss **Some Women of the University**, Stockwell:
London,1934
Dracula's Brood, ed. Richard Dalby, Crucible, 1987

Herron, Don
Curiosity, pm *Eldritch Tales* #13,1987

Hertzog, Norris D.
The Hyperbolic Super-Blitz, vi *Heart of Texas Commodore Home User
Group Newsletter* Jan,1986
2AM Fll,1987

Heydron, Vicki Ann
An Evening In, ar **Moments of Love**, New York: Bantam,1979
Takeoff Too!, Randall Garrett, Donning/Starblaze, 1987
Introduction, in
Takeoff Too!, Randall Garrett, Donning/Starblaze, 1987

Heydt, Dorothy J.
The Noonday Witch, nv **Sword and Sorceress #4**, ed. Marion
Zimmer Bradley,1987
The Sum of the Parts, nv **Red Sun of Darkover**, ed. Marion Zimmer
Bradley & The Friends of Darkover, DAW,1987

Heyrman, Peter
Carnivores, ss *The Horror Show* Jan,1987
An Eye for an Eye, ss *Night Cry* v2#5,1987
Heart of Stone, ss *The Horror Show* Sum,1987
Pick-Up, vi *Twilight Zone* Dec,1987

Hichens, Robert S.
How Love Came to Professor Guildea, nv **Tongues of Conscience**,
Methuen,1900; *Fear!* Jul,1960
The Dark Descent, ed. David G. Hartwell, Tor, 1987

Hickman, Laura & Kate Novak
Heart of Goldmoon, na **DragonLance Tales** v3, Margaret Weis &
Tracy Hickman, TSR,1987

Hickman, Tracy & Margaret Weis
Foreword, fw
DragonLance Tales Vol. 2: Kender, Gully Dwarves, and Gnomes,
ed. Margaret Weis+, TSR, 1987
DragonLance Tales Vol. 3: Love and War, ed. Margaret Weis+,
TSR, 1987
The Legacy, na **DragonLance Tales** v1, Margaret Weis & Tracy
Hickman, TSR,1987
"Wanna Bet?", na **DragonLance Tales** v2, Margaret Weis & Tracy
Hickman, TSR,1987

Higgins, Nina Downey
Apples, ss **Shadows #10**, ed. Charles L. Grant,1987

Highsmith, Patricia
Moby Dick II; or The Missile Whale, ss **Tales of Natural and
Unnatural Catastrophes**, Bloomsbury,1987

Highsmith, Patricia (continued)
The Mysterious Cemetery, ss **Tales of Natural and Unnatural
Catastrophes**, Bloomsbury,1987
Nabuti: Warm Welcome to a UN Committee, ss **Tales of Natural and
Unnatural Catastrophes**, Bloomsbury,1987
No End in Sight, ss **Tales of Natural and Unnatural Catastrophes**,
Bloomsbury,1987
Operation Balsam; or Touch-Me-Not, ss **Tales of Natural and
Unnatural Catastrophes**, Bloomsbury,1987
President Buck Jones Rallies and Waves the Flag, nv **Tales of
Natural and Unnatural Catastrophes**, Bloomsbury,1987
Rent-a-Womb vs. The Mighty Right, ss **Tales of Natural and
Unnatural Catastrophes**, Bloomsbury,1987
Sixtus VI, Pope of the Red Slipper, nv **Tales of Natural and
Unnatural Catastrophes**, Bloomsbury,1987
Sweet Freedom! and a Picnic on the White House Lawn, ss **Tales of
Natural and Unnatural Catastrophes**, Bloomsbury,1987
Trouble at the Jade Towers, nv **Tales of Natural and Unnatural
Catastrophes**, Bloomsbury,1987

Hill, Jack R.
Epitaph by an Alien in Yellow Moonlight, pm *Amazing* Sep,1987

Hiller, Neil W.
The Orphan, ss *F&SF* May,1987

Hoban, Russell
What It Said, ss *Sanity* Jan,1987

Hoch, Edward D.
The Man Who Came Back, nv *Alfred Hitchcock's Mystery Magazine*
May,1973
Alfred Hitchcock's Book of Horror Stories: Book 6, ed. Alfred
Hitchcock, Coronet, 1987
The Maze and the Monster, ss *The Magazine of Horror* Aug,1963
Devils and Demons, ed. Marvin Kaye, Doubleday, 1987
The Ring with the Velvet Ropes, ss **With Malice Toward All**, ed.
Robert L. Fish,1968
Rod Serling's Night Gallery Reader, ed. Carol Serling+,
Dembner, 1987

Hodge, Brian
Red Zone, ss *The Horror Show* Win,1987

Hodgson, Sheila
'Come Follow!', ss **Ghosts & Scholars #4**, ed. Rosemary Pardoe,1982
Ghosts and Scholars, ed. Rosemary Pardoe+, Crucible, 1987

Hodgson, William Hope
The Voice in the Night, ss *Blue Book* Nov,1907
Tales of the Dark, ed. Lincoln Child, St. Martin's, 1987

Hoffman, Nina Kiriki
Waiting for the Hunger, ss **Doom City**, ed. Charles L. Grant, Tor,1987

Hoffman, Roald
Napkin Engineering, pm *The Manhattan Review* Fll,1986
Rhysling Anthology 1987, ed. Anonymous, SF Poetry Assc., 1987

Hofstadter, Douglas
The Tale of Happiton, ss **Metamagical Themas**, Basic Books,1985
Mathenauts, ed. Rudy Rucker, Arbor House, 1987

Hogan, Wayne
Cartoon, ct *Twilight Zone* Dec,1987

Hogg, James
Some Terrible Letters from Scotland, ss
Classic Stories of Mystery, Horror and Suspense, ed. Simon
Petherick, Robert Hale, 1987

Hohing, Frederick
Down by the Sea Wreck, ss *Ice River* Sum,1987

Holder, Nancy
Shift, nv **Doom City**, ed. Charles L. Grant, Tor,1987
We Have Always Lived in the Forest, ss **Shadows #10**, ed. Charles L.
Grant,1987

Holdstock, Robert P.
  Scarrowfell, nv **Other Edens**, ed. Christopher Evans & Robert
    Holdstock, Unwin: London,1987

Holdstock, Robert P. & Christopher Evans
  Introduction, in
    Other Edens, ed. Christopher Evans+, Unwin, 1987

Hollowood, Jane
  In a Dark, Dark Box, ss **Spooky**, ed. Pamela Lonsdale,1985
    The Ghost Story Treasury, ed. Linda Sonntag, Putnam, 1987

Holmberg, Dennis
  A Little Elevator Music, ss *2AM* Spr,1987

Holsinger, Jon
  Film Reviews, mr *2AM* Spr,1987
  Film Reviews, mr *2AM* Sum,1987
  Film Reviews, mr *2AM* Fll,1987
  Film Reviews, mr *2AM* Win,1987

Holtby, Winifred
  The Voice of God, ss **Truth Is Not Sober**,1934
    The Virago Book of Ghost Stories, ed. Richard Dalby, Virago, 1987

Holzer, James William
  Doughfoot Sanctum, ss **There Will Be War** v6, ed. Jerry E.
    Pournelle,1987

Honeycutt, Andy
  October 31, ss *Haunts* #9,1987

Hoover, Dale
  Proctor Valley, ss *Grue* #6,1987

Hopp, Jeff
  A Day at the Beach With Picasso, cs *Space & Time* #72,1987

Hopper, Jeannette M.
  Under a Hungry Moon, ss *Footsteps* Nov,1987

Hornig, Doug
  The Game of Magical Death, ss *F&SF* Mar,1987

Horowitz, David
  Nicaragua: A Speech to My Former Comrades on the Left, ar
    Commentary Jun,1986
    Imperial Stars, Vol. 2: Republic and Empire, ed. Jerry E.
    Pournelle, Baen, 1987

Horsting, Jessie
  The Reel Stuff: A Witchin' Summer, mr *Aboriginal SF* May,1987
  The Reel Stuff: Dog Days, mr *Aboriginal SF* Jul,1987
  The Reel Stuff: The Good, the Bad and the Maybes, mr *Aboriginal SF*
    Feb,1987

Houchin, Ron
  An Auto Mechanic Considers the Earth, pm *Pulpsmith* Win,1987

Housman, Laurence
  Maggie's Bite, ss,1947
    Poltergeist: Tales of Deadly Ghosts, ed. Peter Haining, Severn
    House, 1987
  The Rooted Lover, ss **A Farm in Fairyland**, London: Kegan Paul,1894
    Victorian Fairy Tales, ed. Jack Zipes, Methuen, 1987

Houston, Opie R.
  aborted dream, pm *Grue* #5,1987

Howard, Elizabeth Jane
  Three Miles Up, ss **We Are for the Dark**, Cape: London,1951
    The Virago Book of Ghost Stories, ed. Richard Dalby, Virago, 1987

Howard, Hayden
  To Grab Power, ss *If* Jan,1971
    **Isaac Asimov's Wonderful Worlds of Science Fiction #7: Space
    Shuttles**, ed. Isaac Asimov+, NAL/Signet, 1987

Howard, Robert E.
  Arkham, pm *Weird Tales* Aug,1932
    Cthulhu: The Mythos and Kindred Horrors, Baen, 1987
  The Black Bear Bites, ss *From Beyond the Dark Gateway* Apr,1974
    Swords of Shahrazar, Ace, 1987
  Black Seas, pm *Fantasy Book* Mar,1987
  The Black Stone, ss *Weird Tales* Nov,1931
    Cthulhu: The Mythos and Kindred Horrors, Baen, 1987
  The Black Stranger [complete version], na *Fantasy* Mar,1953
    Echoes of Valor, ed. Karl Edward Wagner, Tor, 1987
  The Brazen Peacock, nv *REH: Lone Star Fictioneer* Fll,1975
    Swords of Shahrazar, Ace, 1987
  The Curse of the Crimson God, nv **Swords of Shahrazar**,
    Futura/Orbit,1976
    Swords of Shahrazar, Ace, 1987
  Dig Me No Grave, ss *Weird Tales* Feb,1937
    Cthulhu: The Mythos and Kindred Horrors, Baen, 1987
  The Fire of Asshurbanipal, ss *Weird Tales* Dec,1936
    Cthulhu: The Mythos and Kindred Horrors, Baen, 1987
  I Praise My Nativity, pm *Fantasy Book* Mar,1987
  Old Garfield's Heart, ss *Weird Tales* Dec,1933
    Cthulhu: The Mythos and Kindred Horrors, Baen, 1987
  An Open Window, pm *Weird Tales* Sep,1932
    Cthulhu: The Mythos and Kindred Horrors, Baen, 1987
  People of the Dark, nv *Strange Tales of Mystery and Terror* Jun,1932
    Cthulhu: The Mythos and Kindred Horrors, Baen, 1987
  Pigeons from Hell, nv *Weird Tales* May,1938
    Cthulhu: The Mythos and Kindred Horrors, Baen, 1987
  The Shadow Kingdom, nv *Weird Tales* Aug,1929
    Isaac Asimov's Magical Worlds of Fantasy #9: Atlantis, ed. Isaac
    Asimov+, NAL/Signet, 1988
  The Shadow of the Beast, ss **The Shadow of the Beast**, Glenn
    Lord,1977
    Cthulhu: The Mythos and Kindred Horrors, Baen, 1987
  Silence Falls on Mecca's Walls, pm **Cthulhu: The Mythos and
    Kindred Horrors**, New York: Baen,1987
  Swords of Shahrazar [also as "The Treasure of Shaibar Kahn"], na
    Top-Notch Oct,1934
    Swords of Shahrazar, Ace, 1987
  The Thing on the Roof, ss *Weird Tales* Feb,1932
    Cthulhu: The Mythos and Kindred Horrors, Baen, 1987
  The Treasures of Tartary, nv *Thrilling Adventures* Jan,1935
    Swords of Shahrazar, Ace, 1987
  The Valley of the Worm, ss *Weird Tales* Feb,1934
    Cthulhu: The Mythos and Kindred Horrors, Baen, 1987
  Wolfshead, nv *Weird Tales* Apr,1926
    Werewolf: Horror Stories of the Man Beast, ed. Peter Haining,
    Severn House, 1987
  Worms of the Earth, nv *Weird Tales* Nov,1932
    Cthulhu: The Mythos and Kindred Horrors, Baen, 1987

Howarth, Matt
  Sonic Curiosity, cs *New Pathways* Jan,1987
  Sonic Curiosity, cs *New Pathways* Apr,1987
  Sonic Curiosity, cs *New Pathways* Aug,1987
  Sonic Curiosity, cs *New Pathways* Nov,1987

Hubbard, L. Ron
  Art and Communication, ar,1977
    L. Ron Hubbard Presents Writers of the Future, Vol. III, ed. Algis
    Budrys, Bridge, 1987

Huff, T.S.
  And Who Is Joah?, ss *Amazing* Nov,1987

Hughes, Edward P.
  Crown of Thorns, ss **There Will Be War** v6, ed. Jerry E. Pournelle,1987
  In the Name of the Father, nv *F&SF* Sep,1980
    Battlefields Beyond Tomorrow, ed. Charles G. Waugh+,
    Crown/Bonanza, 1987
  Test for Tyrants, ss **New Destinies** v2, ed. Jim Baen, Baen,1987

Hughes, Helen
  City of Sleep, ss *Pulpsmith* Win,1987

Hughes, Robert Don
  Dragon Meat, ss *The Dragon* Apr,1987

HUNT, J.J.

JAMES, M.R.

Hunt, J.J.
    The Famous Hospitality of Dao'i, pm *IASFM* Sep,1987

Hunter, C. Bruce
    Eric and the Red Blotches, vi *Eldritch Tales* #14,1987

Hurley, Mike
    Witchwood, ss *Haunts* #9,1987

Hurwood, Bernhardt J.
    The Vampire Cat of Nabeshima, ss **Monsters Galore**, ed. Bernhardt
        J. Hurwood, Fawcett,1965
        Devils and Demons, ed. Marvin Kaye, Doubleday, 1987

Hussey, Leigh Ann
    The Spirit Way, ss *The Dragon* Dec,1987
    A Sword in Hand, nv *Fantasy Book* Mar,1987

Huston, Ned
    Pliny's Commentaries, nv **Universe** #17, ed. Terry Carr,1987

Hutchinson, Don
    Hugh Cave: An Appreciation, bg *Border Land* Oct,1987

Huxley, Julian
    The Tissue-Culture King, ss *Yale Review*,1926; *Amazing* Aug,1927
        Amazing Science Fiction Stories: The Wonder Years 1926-1935,
        ed. Martin H. Greenberg, TSR, 1987

Ing, Dean
    Comes the Revolution [from **The Future of Flight**], ar,1985
        Firefight 2000, Baen, 1987
    Evileye, ss **Far Frontiers** v2, ed. Jerry Pournelle & Jim Baen,1985
        Firefight 2000, Baen, 1987
    Firefight 2000, ar **Firefight 2000**, Baen,1987
    Fleas, ss **Destinies** v1#3, ed. James Baen,1979
        Firefight 2000, Baen, 1987
    Liquid Assets, ss **Destinies** v1#4, ed. James Baen,1979
        Firefight 2000, Baen, 1987
    Lost in Translation, ss **Far Frontiers** v1, ed. Jerry Pournelle & Jim
        Baen,1985
        Firefight 2000, Baen, 1987
    Malf, nv **Analog Annual**, ed. Ben Bova, Pyramid,1976
        Firefight 2000, Baen, 1987
    Manaspill, na **The Magic May Return**, ed. Larry Niven,1981
        Firefight 2000, Baen, 1987
    Preface, pr
        Firefight 2000, Baen, 1987
    Vehicles for Future Wars [also as "Military Vehicles: Into the Third
        Millennium"], ar **Destinies** v1#4, ed. James Baen,1979
        Firefight 2000, Baen, 1987
    Vital Signs, na **Destinies** v2#3, ed. James Baen,1980
        Firefight 2000, Baen, 1987

Ingelow, Jean
    The Prince's Dream, ss **The Little Wonder-Horn**, London: Henry S.
        King,1872
        Victorian Fairy Tales, ed. Jack Zipes, Methuen, 1987

Inks, Caralyn
    Mandrake, nv **Magic in Ithkar** #4, ed. Andre Norton & Robert
        Adams,1987
    Nine Words in Winter, ss **Tales of the Witch World**, ed. Andre Norton,
        St. Martin's,1987

Iverson, Pat Shaw
    Afterword, bg,1965
        Andersen's Fairy Tales, Hans Christian Andersen, NAL/Signet
        Classic, 1987

Izzo, Francis E.
    Tank, ss *IASFM* Mar,1979
        Tales From Isaac Asimov's Science Fiction Magazine, ed. Sheila
        Williams+, Harcourt Brace Jovanovich, 1986
        Supertanks, ed. Joe W. Haldeman+, Ace, 1987

Jablokov, Alexander
    At the Cross-Time Jaunter's Ball, nv *IASFM* Aug,1987

Jackson, Shirley
    The Beautiful Stranger, ss **Come Along With Me**, Viking,1968
        The Dark Descent, ed. David G. Hartwell, Tor, 1987
    The Summer People, ss *Charm*,1950
        The Dark Descent, ed. David G. Hartwell, Tor, 1987

Jacobi, Carl
    The Cravin', pm *Ski-U-Mah* May,1930
        Minnesota Fantasy Review #1,1987
    Head in His Hands, ss *Thrilling Mystery Stories* Nov,1937
        Minnesota Fantasy Review #1,1987
    A Quire of Foolscap, ss *Whispers* #23,1987
    Revelations in Black, ss *Weird Tales* Apr,1933
        Vampires, ed. Alan Ryan, SFBC, 1987

Jacobs, Harvey
    Kitten Kaboodle and Sidney Australia, ss *F&SF* Jun,1987
    Stardust, ss *Omni* Aug,1987

Jacobson, Edith & Ejler Jacobson
    Corpses on Parade, nv *Dime Mystery Magazine* Apr,1938
        Selected Tales of Grim and Grue from the Horror Pulps, ed.
        Sheldon R. Jaffery, Bowling Green Popular Press, 1987

Jacobson, Ejler & Edith Jacobson
    Corpses on Parade, nv *Dime Mystery Magazine* Apr,1938
        Selected Tales of Grim and Grue from the Horror Pulps, ed.
        Sheldon R. Jaffery, Bowling Green Popular Press, 1987

Jafek, Bev
    There's a Phantom in My Word-Processor, ss *Pulpsmith* Win,1987

Jaffery, Sheldon R.
    Preface, pr
        Selected Tales of Grim and Grue from the Horror Pulps, ed.
        Sheldon R. Jaffery, Bowling Green Popular Press, 1987
    The Weirds, in
        The Weirds, ed. Sheldon R. Jaffery, Starmont House, 1987

Jaffrey, Madhur
    Savitri and Satyavan, ss **Seasons of Splendour**, Pavilion,1985
        The Magic Kiss and Other Tales of Princes and Princesses, ed.
        Tony Bradman, Blackie, 1987

James, Francis
    Arms of the Flame Goddess, nv *Dime Mystery Magazine* Apr,1938
        Selected Tales of Grim and Grue from the Horror Pulps, ed.
        Sheldon R. Jaffery, Bowling Green Popular Press, 1987
    Dance of the Bloodless Ones, nv *Terror Tales* Jul,1937
        The Weirds, ed. Sheldon R. Jaffery, Starmont House, 1987

James, Henry
    The Ghostly Rental, nv *Scribner's* Sep,1876
        Classic Stories of Mystery, Horror and Suspense, ed. Simon
        Petherick, Robert Hale, 1987
    The Jolly Corner, nv
        The Dark Descent, ed. David G. Hartwell, Tor, 1987

James, M.R.
    The Ash-Tree, ss **Ghost Stories of an Antiquary**,1904
        A Warning to the Curious: The Ghost Stories of M.R. James,
        Hutchinson, 1987
        The Dark Descent, ed. David G. Hartwell, Tor, 1987
    Canon Alberic's Scrap-Book, ss *National Review* Mar,1895
        A Warning to the Curious: The Ghost Stories of M.R. James,
        Hutchinson, 1987
        Casting the Runes and Other Ghost Stories, World's Classics,
        1987
    Casting the Runes, nv **More Ghost Stories of an Antiquary**,
        Arnold,1911
        A Warning to the Curious: The Ghost Stories of M.R. James,
        Hutchinson, 1987
        Casting the Runes and Other Ghost Stories, World's Classics,
        1987
        Cinemonsters, ed. Martin H. Greenberg, TSR, 1987
    Count Magnus, ss **Ghost Stories of an Antiquary**,1904
        A Warning to the Curious: The Ghost Stories of M.R. James,
        Hutchinson, 1987

JAMES, M.R.

James, M.R. (continued)
    Casting the Runes and Other Ghost Stories, World's Classics, 1987
The Diary of Mr. Poynter, nv **A Thin Ghost**, Longmans, Green,1919
    Casting the Runes and Other Ghost Stories, World's Classics, 1987
An Episode of Cathedral History, ss **A Thin Ghost**, Longmans, Green,1919
    Vampires, ed. Alan Ryan, SFBC, 1987
    Casting the Runes and Other Ghost Stories, World's Classics, 1987
The Experiment, ss
    Casting the Runes and Other Ghost Stories, World's Classics, 1987
Ghost Story Competition, ms *The Spectator* Chr,1930
    Ghosts and Scholars, ed. Rosemary Pardoe+, Crucible, 1987
Ghosts - Treat Them Gently, ar *London Evening News* Apr 17,1931
    Masters of Fantasy 3: M.R. James, British Fantasy Society, 1987
    Ghosts and Scholars, ed. Rosemary Pardoe+, Crucible, 1987
M.R. James on Ghost Stories, ar
    Casting the Runes and Other Ghost Stories, World's Classics, 1987
The Malice of Inanimate Objects, ss *The Masquerade* Jun,1933
    Casting the Runes and Other Ghost Stories, World's Classics, 1987
The Mezzotint, ss **Ghost Stories of an Antiquary**,1904
    A Warning to the Curious: The Ghost Stories of M.R. James, Hutchinson, 1987
    Casting the Runes and Other Ghost Stories, World's Classics, 1987
Mr. Humphreys and His Inheritance, nv **More Ghost Stories of an Antiquary**, Arnold,1911
    A Warning to the Curious: The Ghost Stories of M.R. James, Hutchinson, 1987
    Casting the Runes and Other Ghost Stories, World's Classics, 1987
    Tales of the Dark 2, ed. Lincoln Child, St. Martin's, 1987
A Neighbour's Landmark, ss *The Eton Chronic* Mar 17,1924
    Casting the Runes and Other Ghost Stories, World's Classics, 1987
Number 13, ss **Ghost Stories of an Antiquary**,1904
    A Warning to the Curious: The Ghost Stories of M.R. James, Hutchinson, 1987
    Casting the Runes and Other Ghost Stories, World's Classics, 1987
"Oh, Whistle, and I'll Come to You, My Lad", nv **Ghost Stories of an Antiquary**,1904
    A Warning to the Curious: The Ghost Stories of M.R. James, Hutchinson, 1987
    Casting the Runes and Other Ghost Stories, World's Classics, 1987
    Charles Keeping's Classic Tales of the Macabre, ed. Charles Keeping, Blackie, 1987
Rats, ss
    Casting the Runes and Other Ghost Stories, World's Classics, 1987
The Rose Garden, ss **More Ghost Stories of an Antiquary**, Arnold,1911
    Casting the Runes and Other Ghost Stories, World's Classics, 1987
A School Story, ss **More Ghost Stories of an Antiquary**, Arnold,1911
    Casting the Runes and Other Ghost Stories, World's Classics, 1987
    Masters of Fantasy 3: M.R. James, British Fantasy Society, 1987
The Stalls of Barchester Cathedral, ss *Contemporary Review* v97#35,1910
    A Warning to the Curious: The Ghost Stories of M.R. James, Hutchinson, 1987
    Casting the Runes and Other Ghost Stories, World's Classics, 1987
The Tractate Middoth, ss **More Ghost Stories of an Antiquary**, Arnold,1911
    A Warning to the Curious: The Ghost Stories of M.R. James, Hutchinson, 1987
    Casting the Runes and Other Ghost Stories, World's Classics, 1987

James, M.R. (continued)
    The Treasure of Abbot Thomas, ss **Ghost Stories of an Antiquary**,1904
    A Warning to the Curious: The Ghost Stories of M.R. James, Hutchinson, 1987
    Casting the Runes and Other Ghost Stories, World's Classics, 1987
The Uncommon Prayer Book, ss **A Warning to the Curious**,1925
    A Warning to the Curious: The Ghost Stories of M.R. James, Hutchinson, 1987
    Casting the Runes and Other Ghost Stories, World's Classics, 1987
A Vignette, ss *The London Mercury* v35,1936
    Casting the Runes and Other Ghost Stories, World's Classics, 1987
Wailing Well, ss,1927
    Dracula's Brood, ed. Richard Dalby, Crucible, 1987
A Warning to the Curious, ss *The London Mercury* Aug,1925
    A Warning to the Curious: The Ghost Stories of M.R. James, Hutchinson, 1987
    Casting the Runes and Other Ghost Stories, World's Classics, 1987

Janifer, Laurence M.
    About the Author, bg
        Knave & the Game, Doubleday, 1987
    Expiration Policy, ss *Analog* Nov,1983
        Knave & the Game, Doubleday, 1987
    Introduction: Knave's World, in
        Knave & the Game, Doubleday, 1987
    The Lost Secret, nv **The Best of Omni** #5,1983
        Knave & the Game, Doubleday, 1987
    Love in Bloom, ss *Analog* mid-Dec,1984
        Knave & the Game, Doubleday, 1987
    The Samaritan Rule, ss *Analog* Mar,1984
        Knave & the Game, Doubleday, 1987
    The Swagger Stick, nv **Knave & the Game**, Doubleday,1987
    Telephone, vi *Analog* Jun,1987
    Testing..., ss *Analog* Nov,1980
        Knave & the Game, Doubleday, 1987
    Toadstool Sinfonia, nv *Analog* Jul,1980
        Knave & the Game, Doubleday, 1987
    The Very Best Defense, nv *ROM*
        Knave & the Game, Doubleday, 1987
    The Wheelbarrow Thief, nv *ROM*
        Knave & the Game, Doubleday, 1987
    Worldwreckers, ss *Analog* Oct,1987

Jankus, Hank
    On Exhibit, il *Amazing* May,1987

Jarik, J.C.
    Three Were Chosen [Chapters 5&6], sl *Salarius* #3,1987
    Three Were Chosen [Chapters 7&8], sl *Salarius* v1#4,1987

Jenkins, Elizabeth
    On No Account, My Love, ss **Ghost Book #3**, ed. Aidan Chambers/James Turner,1955
    The Virago Book of Ghost Stories, ed. Richard Dalby, Virago, 1987

Jenkins, Scott
    Heroes of Audio: Jane Schonberger, bg *American Fantasy* Sum,1987
    Heroes of Audio: Mike McDonough, bg *American Fantasy* Win,1987
    The Sound and the Fury, ar *American Fantasy* Sum,1987
    The Sound and the Fury, ar *American Fantasy* Win,1987

Jennings, Phillip C.
    The Castaway, ss *Amazing* Mar,1987
    Moondo Bizarro, nv **New Destinies** v2, ed. Jim Baen, Baen,1987

Jeres, Patricia
    Tiny Devils, pm *New Pathways* Jan,1987

Jeter, K.W. & Les Escott
    K.W. Jeter, iv *Interzone* #22,1987

Jeter, K.W., Ferret & J.B. Reynolds
    K.W. Jeter [Part 1], iv *New Pathways* Apr,1987

JETER, K.W.

Jeter, K.W., Ferret & J.B. Reynolds (continued)
   K.W. Jeter [Part 2], iv *New Pathways* Aug,1987

Johnson, Dale & Michael Whelan
   Michael Whelan, iv *American Fantasy* Sum,1987

Johnson, James B.
   Conestoga History, ss *Analog* May,1987

Johnson, Pamela Hansford
   The Empty Schoolroom, ss **The Uncertain Element**, ed. Kay Dick,
     Jarrolds: London,1950
   The Virago Book of Ghost Stories, ed. Richard Dalby, Virago, 1987

Johnson, Shelton Arnel
   The Eels, pm *Amazing* Mar,1987
   Elegy for Cygnus X-1, pm *Amazing* Nov,1987

Johnson, Susan
   Running It Back, mr *American Fantasy* Spr,1987
   Running It Back, mr *American Fantasy* Win,1987

Johnson, Will
   Spider King, pm *Space & Time* #72,1987

Johnston, Jeff
   Masks, ss *2AM* Spr,1987

Johnston, Mairin
   The Witch-Hunt, ss **Mad and Bad Fairies**, ed. Anonymous, Attic
     Press,1987

Jones, Bruce
   The Apartment, ss **Twisted Tales**, San Diego: Blackthorne,1987
   Black Death, ss **Twisted Tales**, San Diego: Blackthorne,1987
   Children of the Stars, nv **Twisted Tales**, San Diego: Blackthorne,1987
   Cycle, ss **Twisted Tales**, San Diego: Blackthorne,1987
   Good Neighbor, ss **Twisted Tales**, San Diego: Blackthorne,1987
   The Hollow, ss **Twisted Tales**, San Diego: Blackthorne,1987
   Jessie's Friend, ss **Twisted Tales**, San Diego: Blackthorne,1987
   Members Only, nv **Twisted Tales**, San Diego: Blackthorne,1987
   Over His Head, ss **Twisted Tales**, San Diego: Blackthorne,1987
   Pride of the Fleet, ss **Swords Against Darkness** #1, ed. Andrew J.
     Offutt,1977
   Twisted Tales, Blackthorne, 1987
   Rendezvous, nv **Twisted Tales**, San Diego: Blackthorne,1987
   Roomers, ss **Twisted Tales**, San Diego: Blackthorne,1987
   The Waiting Game, ss **Twisted Tales**, San Diego: Blackthorne,1987

Jones, Eva
   The Wanderer, vi *Mage* Win,1985
   Mage Fll,1987

Jones, Gwyneth
   The Snow Apples, ss **Tales from the Forbidden Planet**, ed. Roz
     Kaveney, Titan,1987

Jones, Gwyneth & Paul Kincaid
   Gwyneth Jones Interview, iv *Interzone* #19,1987

Jones, Jeffrey & Bernard Abrams
   The Twilight Zone Gallery: The Art of Jeffrey Jones, pi *Twilight Zone*
     Aug,1987

Jones, Jeffrey & Tappan King
   The Twilight Zone Gallery: The Art of Jim Burns, pi *Twilight Zone*
     Oct,1987

Jones, Kelvin I.
   Mandrake, ss **After Midnight Stories** #3,1987

Jones, Lanyon
   The Nine Lessons and Carols, ss **After Midnight Stories** #3,1987

Jones, Neil R.
   The Jameson Satellite, nv *Amazing* Jul,1931
   Amazing Science Fiction Stories: The Wonder Years 1926-1935,
     ed. Martin H. Greenberg, TSR, 1987

Jones, Robert Kenneth
   Index to Weird Menace Pulps, ix **The Weird Menace**, Opar Press,1972
   Selected Tales of Grim and Grue from the Horror Pulps, ed.
     Sheldon R. Jaffery, Bowling Green Popular Press, 1987
   Popular's Weird Menace Pulps, ar **The Weird Menace**, Opar
     Press,1972
   Selected Tales of Grim and Grue from the Horror Pulps, ed.
     Sheldon R. Jaffery, Bowling Green Popular Press, 1987

Jones, Stephen & Cory Glaberson
   Hellraiser, mr *American Fantasy* Win,1987

Jones, Terry
   The Snuff-Box, ss **Fairy Tales**, Terry Jones, Pavilion,1981
   The Magic Kiss and Other Tales of Princes and Princesses, ed.
     Tony Bradman, Blackie, 1987

Jonik, John
   Cartoon, ct *New Yorker*,1987
   F&SF Oct,1987

Jordan, Dennis
   Radionda, ss *Grue* #5,1987

Joron, Andrew
   Agency, pm
     Force Fields, Starmont House, 1987
   All Equations are Lesion's Equal, pm
     Force Fields, Starmont House, 1987
   Asleep in the Arms of Mother Night, pm
     Force Fields, Starmont House, 1987
   Beacon, pm
     Force Fields, Starmont House, 1987
   A Beautiful Disease, pm *Pig Iron* #10,1982
     Force Fields, Starmont House, 1987
   Breaking into the Crystal Text, pm
     Force Fields, Starmont House, 1987
   Bulletin from the Galactic Center, pm
     Force Fields, Starmont House, 1987
   Event Horizon, pm
     Force Fields, Starmont House, 1987
   Hegemony, pm
     Force Fields, Starmont House, 1987
   His Master's Voice, pm
     Force Fields, Starmont House, 1987
   The Hunter: A.D. 20,000, pm *Amazing* Nov,1982
     Force Fields, Starmont House, 1987
   An Illuminated Manuscript, pm
     Force Fields, Starmont House, 1987
   Kaleidoscope of Dust, pm
     Force Fields, Starmont House, 1987
   Mirror of Prometheus, pm
     Force Fields, Starmont House, 1987
   The Navigator, pm
     Force Fields, Starmont House, 1987
   The Old Ones, pm
     Force Fields, Starmont House, 1987
   Palaces on Pluto?, pm *Amazing* Nov,1986
     Force Fields, Starmont House, 1987
   Panspermia, pm
     Force Fields, Starmont House, 1987
   Post-Historic Pastorale, pm
     Force Fields, Starmont House, 1987
   Shipwrecked on Destiny Five, pm *IASFM* May,1985
     Force Fields, Starmont House, 1987
   The Sonic Flowerfall of Primes, pm *New Worlds* #216,1982
     Force Fields, Starmont House, 1987
   Stormtower, pm
     Force Fields, Starmont House, 1987
   Telecommunion, pm
     Force Fields, Starmont House, 1987
   Tetrahedron Letters, pm *The Portland Review*,1979
     Force Fields, Starmont House, 1987
   Thought Experiment, pm
     Force Fields, Starmont House, 1987
   Two Walkers Across the Time Flats, pm
     Force Fields, Starmont House, 1987

JORON, ANDREW

Joron, Andrew (continued)
  Vehicular Man, pm
    Force Fields, Starmont House, 1987
  Vox Sanguinis, pm
    Force Fields, Starmont House, 1987
  The Webbed Axis, pm
    Force Fields, Starmont House, 1987

Joron, Andrew & Robert Frazier
  Exiled of Worlds, pm *Amazing* Sep,1987

Jurgens, Kathleen E. & Commander USA
  Kathleen Jurgens interviews Commander USA, iv *2AM* Fll,1987

Jurgens, Kathleen E. & Crematia Mortum
  Interview with Crematia Mortum (Roberta Solomon), iv *2AM* Spr,1987

Kadrey, Richard
  Goodbye Houston Street, Goodbye, ss *Interzone* #19,1987
  The Other Side: Chaos, Inc., ar *Twilight Zone* Feb,1987

Kadrey, Richard & Rudy Rucker
  Rudy Rucker Interview, iv *Interzone* #20,1987

Kagan, Norman
  Four Brands of Impossible, nv *F&SF* Sep,1964
    Mathenauts, ed. Rudy Rucker, Arbor House, 1987
  The Mathenauts, nv *If* Jul,1964
    Mathenauts, ed. Rudy Rucker, Arbor House, 1987

Kahn, James
  Return of the Jedi, n. Ballantine: New York,1983
    The Star Wars Trilogy, George Lucas+, Ballantine/Del Rey, 1987

Kahn, Joan
  Introduction, in
    Ready or Not, ed. Joan Kahn, Greenwillow, 1987

Kane, Francis X., Stefan T. Possony & Jerry E. Pournelle
  Surprise [substantially revised, first appeared in **The Strategy of Technology**, 1970], ar **There Will Be War** v6, ed. Jerry E. Pournelle,1987

Karlin, Nurit
  Cartoon, ct *F&SF* Oct,1987

Karwowski, Christopher
  Illuminations: Crystal Revelations, ar *Twilight Zone* Jun,1987
  Illuminations: Painting the Town Red, ar *Twilight Zone* Feb,1987
  Illuminations: Radio Sci-Fi, ar *Twilight Zone* Apr,1987
  Illuminations: Starmagic, ar *Twilight Zone* Apr,1987
  Illuminations: Strange Hangups, ar *Twilight Zone* Jun,1987
  Illuminations: TZ Meets the '80s, ar *Twilight Zone* Feb,1987
  Music, ar *Twilight Zone* Jun,1987

Katz, Menke
  The Reincarnated Queens of England, pm *Pulpsmith* Win,1987

Kaufmann, William J.
  The Black Hole, ar **Universe**, ed. Byron Preiss, Bantam Spectra,1987

Kaveney, Roz
  Introduction, in
    Tales from the Forbidden Planet, ed. Roz Kaveney, Titan, 1987

Kaye, Marvin
  Appendix I: Miscellaneous Notes, ms
    Devils and Demons, ed. Marvin Kaye, Doubleday, 1987
  Appendix II: Who in Hell Are All These Devils? (An Infernal "Lowerarchy"), ms
    Devils and Demons, ed. Marvin Kaye, Doubleday, 1987
  Appendix III: Selected Bibliography and Filmography, bi
    Devils and Demons, ed. Marvin Kaye, Doubleday, 1987
  Damned Funny [as by Eugene D. Goodwin], ss **Fiends and Creatures**, ed. Marvin Kaye, Popular Library,1975
    Devils and Demons, ed. Marvin Kaye, Doubleday, 1987
  Ghosts of Night and Morning, ss *Night Cry* v2#5,1987

Kaye, Marvin (continued)
  Introduction, in
    Devils and Demons, ed. Marvin Kaye, Doubleday, 1987

Kearns, Richard
  Grave Angels, nv *F&SF* Apr,1986
    The Year's Best Science Fiction, Fourth Annual Collection, ed. Gardner R. Dozois, St. Martin's, 1987
    Terry Carr's Best Science Fiction and Fantasy of the Year #16, ed. Terry Carr, Tor, 1987

Keating, H.R.F.
  A Hell of a Story, ss *Ellery Queen's Mystery Magazine* Jun,1982
    Ready or Not, ed. Joan Kahn, Greenwillow, 1987

Keeping, Charles
  Introduction, in
    Charles Keeping's Classic Tales of the Macabre, ed. Charles Keeping, Blackie, 1987

Keizer, Gregg
  Edges, ss *Omni* Jun,1983
    The Fifth Omni Book of Science Fiction, ed. Ellen Datlow, Zebra, 1987

Keller, David H., M.D.
  Heredity, ss *The Vortex* #2,1947
    Vamps, ed. Martin H. Greenberg+, DAW, 1987
  The Thing in the Cellar, ss *Weird Tales* Mar,1932
    House Shudders, ed. Martin H. Greenberg+, DAW, 1987

Kellogg, M. Bradley & William Rossow
  Reign of Fire, n. New American Library: New York,1986
    Lear's Daughters, M. Bradley Kellogg+, SFBC, 1987
  The Wave and the Flame, n. New American Library: New York,1986
    Lear's Daughters, M. Bradley Kellogg+, SFBC, 1987

Kelly, James Patrick
  Daemon, ss *F&SF* Nov,1987
  Glass Cloud, na *IASFM* Jun,1987
  Heroics, ss *IASFM* Nov,1987
  The Prisoner of Chillon, nv *IASFM* Jun,1986
    The Year's Best Science Fiction, Fourth Annual Collection, ed. Gardner R. Dozois, St. Martin's, 1987
    Terry Carr's Best Science Fiction and Fantasy of the Year #16, ed. Terry Carr, Tor, 1987

Kelly, Maeve
  Alice in Thunderland, ss **Mad and Bad Fairies**, ed. Anonymous, Attic Press,1987

Kelly, S.A.
  Sound and the Electric Ear Drum, pm *Amazing* Nov,1987

Kenin, Millea
  Fate and the Dreamer, ss **Sword and Sorceress** #4, ed. Marion Zimmer Bradley,1987

Kennett, Rick
  The Adventure of the Unearthly Spy, vi *Aphelion* #5,1987

Kerby, Bill
  Crusaders in Love, nv **Crusaders in Hell**, ed. Janet Morris, New York: Baen,1987
  Take Two, nv **Masters of Hell**, ed. Janet Morris et al, Baen,1987

Kerr, Peg
  Free Day, ss *Tales of the Unanticipated* #2,1987

Kessel, John
  Credibility, nv **In the Field of Fire**, ed. Jeanne Van Buren Dann & Jack M. Dann, Tor,1987
  Judgment Call, nv *F&SF* Oct,1987
  The Pure Product, nv *IASFM* Mar,1986
    The Year's Best Science Fiction, Fourth Annual Collection, ed. Gardner R. Dozois, St. Martin's, 1987

KETTER, GREG

Ketter, Greg & Thomas Cantry
Thomas Canty, pi *American Fantasy* Spr,1987

Kidd, A.F.
An Incident in the City, ss **Ghosts & Scholars #1**, ed. Rosemary
Pardoe,1979
Ghosts and Scholars, ed. Rosemary Pardoe+, Crucible, 1987

Kilgore, John
Closing the Loop, ss *Space & Time* #72,1987

Killean, Anne
Dick Whittington and Her Cat, ss **Mad and Bad Fairies**, ed.
Anonymous, Attic Press,1987

Kilworth, Garry
The Black Wedding, ss **Other Edens**, ed. Christopher Evans & Robert
Holdstock, Unwin: London,1987
Triptych; gp
Dop*elgan*er, ss *Interzone* #21,1987
The Earth is Flat and We're All Like to Drown, ss **Tales from the
Forbidden Planet**, ed. Roz Kaveney, Titan,1987
Hogfoot Right and Bird-Hands, ss **Other Edens**, ed. Christopher
Evans & Robert Holdstock, Unwin: London,1987
Triptych; gp
Murderers Walk, ss **Other Edens**, ed. Christopher Evans & Robert
Holdstock, Unwin: London,1987
Triptych; gp
Paper Moon, ss *Omni* Jan,1987
The Songbirds of Pain, ss **The Songbirds of Pain**, Gollancz,1984;
Omni Aug,1985
The Fifth Omni Book of Science Fiction, ed. Ellen Datlow, Zebra,
1987
Spiral Sands [Spiral Winds], ss *Interzone* #9,1984
Interzone: The 2nd Anthology, ed. John Clute+, Simon &
Schuster UK, 1987
Triptych, gp **Other Edens**, ed. Christopher Evans & Robert
Holdstock, Unwin: London,1987
The Black Wedding; ss
Murderers Walk; ss
Hogfoot Right and Bird-Hands; ss

Kincaid, Paul & Gwyneth Jones
Gwyneth Jones Interview, iv *Interzone* #19,1987

King, Stephen
The Boogeyman, ss *Cavalier* Mar,1973
House Shudders, ed. Martin H. Greenberg+, DAW, 1987
Crouch End, nv **New Tales of the Cthulhu Mythos**, Arkham,1980
The Dark Descent, ed. David G. Hartwell, Tor, 1987
Foreword, fw
Scars, Richard Christian Matheson, Scream/Press, 1987
Gray Matter, ss *Cavalier* Oct,1973
The 28th Pan Book of Horror Stories, ed. Clarence Paget, Pan,
1987
The Mangler, nv *Cavalier* Dec,1972
Demons!, ed. Jack M. Dann+, Ace, 1987
The Monkey, nv *Gallery* Nov,1980
The Dark Descent, ed. David G. Hartwell, Tor, 1987
One for the Road, ss *Maine* Mar,1977
Strange Maine, ed. Charles G. Waugh+, Tapley, 1986
Vamps, ed. Martin H. Greenberg+, DAW, 1987
Popsy, ss **Masques #2**, ed. J.N. Williamson,1987
The Reach [Do the Dead Sing?], ss *Yankee* Nov,1981
The Dark Descent, ed. David G. Hartwell, Tor, 1987
Trucks, ss *Cavalier* Jun,1973
Mysterious Motoring Stories, ed. William Pattrick, W.H. Allen, 1987

King, Tappan
Boogie Man, ss **Devils & Demons**, ed. Marvin Kaye,
SFBC/Doubleday,1987
Illuminations: A Little Night Music, ar *Twilight Zone* Feb,1987
Illuminations: Dreamland, ar *Twilight Zone* Dec,1987
Illuminations: Eternal Evil, ar *Twilight Zone* Oct,1987
Illuminations: Latin Lama, ar *Twilight Zone* Oct,1987
Illuminations: Leaps of Faith, ar *Twilight Zone* Jun,1987
Illuminations: Magic Underfoot, ar *Twilight Zone* Aug,1987

KIPLING, RUDYARD

King, Tappan (continued)
Illuminations: The Creature from the Silt in the Black Lagoon, ar
Twilight Zone Oct,1987
In the Twilight Zone, ed *Twilight Zone* Feb,1987
In the Twilight Zone, ed *Twilight Zone* Apr,1987
In the Twilight Zone, ed *Twilight Zone* Jun,1987
In the Twilight Zone, ed *Twilight Zone* Aug,1987
In the Twilight Zone, ed *Twilight Zone* Oct,1987
In the Twilight Zone, ed *Twilight Zone* Dec,1987
Introduction: The Keeper of the Night, in *Night Cry* v2#4,1987
The Other Side: Elephant Parts, ar *Twilight Zone* Oct,1987

King, Tappan & Jeffrey Jones
The Twilight Zone Gallery: The Art of Jim Burns, pi *Twilight Zone*
Oct,1987

Kingsbury, Donald
Shipwright, na *Analog* Apr,1978
Imperial Stars, Vol. 2: Republic and Empire, ed. Jerry E.
Pournelle, Baen, 1987

Kip, Leonard
The Ghosts at Grantley, nv
Christmas Ghosts, ed. Kathryn Cramer+, Arbor House, 1987

Kipling, Rudyard
At the End of the Passage, ss *Boston Herald* Jul 20,1890
The Complete Supernatural Stories of Rudyard Kipling, W.H.
Allen, 1987
Baboo Mookerji's Undertaking [as by The Witness], vi *The Civil and
Military Gazette* Sep 1,1888
The Complete Supernatural Stories of Rudyard Kipling, W.H.
Allen, 1987
The Bisara of Pooree, ss *The Civil and Military Gazette* Mar 4,1887
The Complete Supernatural Stories of Rudyard Kipling, W.H.
Allen, 1987
The Brushwood Boy, nv *The Century* Dec,1895
The Complete Supernatural Stories of Rudyard Kipling, W.H.
Allen, 1987
Bubbling Well Road [as by The Traveler], vi *The Civil and Military
Gazette* Jan 18,1888
The Complete Supernatural Stories of Rudyard Kipling, W.H.
Allen, 1987
By Word of Mouth, vi *The Civil and Military Gazette* Jun 10,1887
The Complete Supernatural Stories of Rudyard Kipling, W.H.
Allen, 1987
The Courting of Dinah Shadd, nv *Macmillan's* Mar,1890
The Complete Supernatural Stories of Rudyard Kipling, W.H.
Allen, 1987
The Dream of Duncan Parrenness, ss *The Civil and Military Gazette*
Dec 25,1884
The Complete Supernatural Stories of Rudyard Kipling, W.H.
Allen, 1987
The Dreitarbund, vi *The Civil and Military Gazette* Oct 22,1887
The Complete Supernatural Stories of Rudyard Kipling, W.H.
Allen, 1987
The Finest Story in the World, nv *Contemporary Review* Jul,1891
The Complete Supernatural Stories of Rudyard Kipling, W.H.
Allen, 1987
The Gardener, ss **Debits and Credits**, London: Macmillan,1926
The Complete Supernatural Stories of Rudyard Kipling, W.H.
Allen, 1987
The Gods of the Copybook Headings, pm
Imperial Stars, Vol. 2: Republic and Empire, ed. Jerry E.
Pournelle, Baen, 1987
Haunted Subalterns, ss *The Civil and Military Gazette* May 27,1887
The Complete Supernatural Stories of Rudyard Kipling, W.H.
Allen, 1987
Poltergeist: Tales of Deadly Ghosts, ed. Peter Haining, Severn
House, 1987
The House Surgeon, nv *Harper's* Sep +1,1909
The Complete Supernatural Stories of Rudyard Kipling, W.H.
Allen, 1987
In the House of Suddhoo, ss *The Civil and Military Gazette* Apr 30,1886
The Complete Supernatural Stories of Rudyard Kipling, W.H.
Allen, 1987

KIPLING, RUDYARD

Kipling, Rudyard (continued)
  An Indian Ghost in England, ss *The Pioneer* Dec 10,1885
    The Complete Supernatural Stories of Rudyard Kipling, W.H.
      Allen, 1987
  The Joker [as by anonymous], ss *The Pioneer* Jan 1,1889
    The Complete Supernatural Stories of Rudyard Kipling, W.H.
      Allen, 1987
  The Last Department, pm
    Imperial Stars, Vol. 2: Republic and Empire, ed. Jerry E.
      Pournelle, Baen, 1987
  The Lost Legion, ss *The Strand* May,1892
    The Complete Supernatural Stories of Rudyard Kipling, W.H.
      Allen, 1987
  A Madonna of the Trenches, ss *London Pall Mall Magazine* Sep,1924
    The Complete Supernatural Stories of Rudyard Kipling, W.H.
      Allen, 1987
  The Mark of the Beast, ss *The Pioneer* Jul 12,1890
    The Complete Supernatural Stories of Rudyard Kipling, W.H.
      Allen, 1987
  My Own True Ghost Story, ss *The Week's News* Feb 25,1888
    The Complete Supernatural Stories of Rudyard Kipling, W.H.
      Allen, 1987
  The Phantom Rickshaw, ss *Quartette* Chr,1885
    The Complete Supernatural Stories of Rudyard Kipling, W.H.
      Allen, 1987
  The Potted Princess, ss *St. Nicholas Magazine*,1893
    Victorian Fairy Tales, ed. Jack Zipes, Methuen, 1987
  The Recurring Smash [as by S.T.], vi *The Civil and Military Gazette*
      Oct 13,1887
    The Complete Supernatural Stories of Rudyard Kipling, W.H.
      Allen, 1987
  The Return of Imray [The Recrudescence of Imray], ss **Mine Own
      People**, New York: Hurst & Co.,1891;
    Ellery Queen's Mystery Magazine Sep,1958
    The Complete Supernatural Stories of Rudyard Kipling, W.H.
      Allen, 1987
  The Sending of Dana Da, ss *The Week's News* Feb 11,1888
    The Complete Supernatural Stories of Rudyard Kipling, W.H.
      Allen, 1987
  Sleipner, Late Thurinda, ss *The Week's News* May 12,1888
    The Complete Supernatural Stories of Rudyard Kipling, W.H.
      Allen, 1987
  The Solid Muldoon, ss *The Week's News* Jun 2,1888
    The Complete Supernatural Stories of Rudyard Kipling, W.H.
      Allen, 1987
  The Strange Ride of Morrowbie Jukes, nv *Quartette* Chr,1885
    The Complete Supernatural Stories of Rudyard Kipling, W.H.
      Allen, 1987
    Night Cry v2#5,1987
  Swept and Garnished, ss *London Pall Mall Magazine* Jan,1915
    The Complete Supernatural Stories of Rudyard Kipling, W.H.
      Allen, 1987
  "They", nv *Scribner's* Aug,1904
    The Complete Supernatural Stories of Rudyard Kipling, W.H.
      Allen, 1987
    Tales of the Dark, ed. Lincoln Child, St. Martin's, 1987
  The Tomb of His Ancestors, nv *McClure's* Dec,1897
    The Complete Supernatural Stories of Rudyard Kipling, W.H.
      Allen, 1987
  The Unlimited Draw of Tick Boileau, ss *Quartette* Chr,1885
    The Complete Supernatural Stories of Rudyard Kipling, W.H.
      Allen, 1987
  Wireless, ss *Scribner's* Aug,1902
    The Complete Supernatural Stories of Rudyard Kipling, W.H.
      Allen, 1987
  The Wish House, ss *McClure's* Oct 15,1924
    The Complete Supernatural Stories of Rudyard Kipling, W.H.
      Allen, 1987

Kiplinger, Christina
  Eradication's Rise, pm *Fantasy Tales* #16,1986

Kirchoff, Mary
  Finding the Faith, nv **DragonLance Tales** v1, Margaret Weis & Tracy
    Hickman, TSR,1987

Kirk, Russell
  Sorworth Place, nv *F&SF* Nov,1962
    Rod Serling's Night Gallery Reader, ed. Carol Serling +,
      Dembner, 1987
  There's a Long, Long Trail A-Winding, nv **Frights**, ed. Kirby
    McCauley, St. Martins,1976
    The Dark Descent, ed. David G. Hartwell, Tor, 1987

Kisner, James
  The Litter, ss **Masques #2**, ed. J.N. Williamson,1987
  Small Talk, ss *Grue #4*,1987

Kittredge, Mary
  IMAGO, ss *Aboriginal SF* May,1987

Klein, Arthur L.
  Kleinism, ms *Amazing* Jan,1987
  Kleinism, ms *Amazing* Mar,1987
  Kleinisms, ms *Amazing* Jul,1987

Klein, Gerard
  Hide and Seek, vi,1973
    Translated by John Brunner; *Omni* Jun,1987

Klein, Jay Kay
  Biolog: Arlan Andrews, bg *Analog* Sep,1987
  Biolog: David A. Hardy, bg *Analog* Apr,1987
  Biolog: George Zebrowski, bg *Analog* Feb,1987
  Biolog: Robert R. Chase, bg *Analog* Jul,1987

Klein, R.E.
  The Smoking Mirror, ss *Space & Time* #73,1987

Klein, T.E.D.
  Film, mr *Night Cry* v2#4,1987
  Film, mr *Night Cry* v2#5,1987

Knaak, Richard A.
  By the Measure, nv **DragonLance Tales** v3, Margaret Weis & Tracy
    Hickman, TSR,1987
  Definitions of Honor, nv **DragonLance Tales** v2, Margaret Weis &
    Tracy Hickman, TSR,1987
  Wayward Children, nv **DragonLance Tales** v1, Margaret Weis &
    Tracy Hickman, TSR,1987

Knatchbull-Hugessen, Edward H.
  Charlie Among the Elves, ss **Moonshine**, London: Macmillan,1871
    Victorian Fairy Tales, ed. Jack Zipes, Methuen, 1987

Kneale, Nigel
  Minuke, ss *Harper's* Sep,1950
    Poltergeist: Tales of Deadly Ghosts, ed. Peter Haining, Severn
      House, 1987

Knight, Arthur
  The Invisible Empire, ar *Pulpsmith* Win,1987

Knight, Arthur Winfield
  Up in Smoke, pm *2AM* Fll,1987

Knight, Damon
  Anachron, ss *If* Jan,1954
    Isaac Asimov Presents the Great SF Stories: 16 (1954), ed. Isaac
      Asimov +, DAW, 1987
  Four in One, nv *Galaxy* Feb,1953
    Robert Silverberg's Worlds of Wonder, ed. Robert Silverberg,
      Warner, 1987
  Introduction, in
    The Past Through Tomorrow Vol. 1, Robert A. Heinlein, NEL, 1987
    The Past Through Tomorrow Vol. 2, Robert A. Heinlein, NEL, 1987
  Stranger Station, nv *F&SF* Dec,1956
    Great Science Fiction of the 20th Century, ed. Robert
      Silverberg +, Crown/Avenel, 1987
  Strangers on Paradise [Strangers in Paradise], ss *F&SF* Apr,1986
    The Year's Best Science Fiction, Fourth Annual Collection, ed.
      Gardner R. Dozois, St. Martin's, 1987
    The 1987 Annual World's Best SF, ed. Donald A. Wollheim +,
      DAW, 1987

KNIGHT, DAMON

KUTTNER, HENRY

Knight, Damon (continued)
Masters of Darkness II, ed. Dennis Etchison, Tor, 1988

Knight, Damon, Terry A. Garey, Eric M. Heideman & Kate Wilhelm
An Interview with Kate Wilhelm and Damon Knight, iv *Tales of the Unanticipated* #2,1987

Knox, John H.
The Buyer of Souls, nv *Horror Stories* Aug,1936
Selected Tales of Grim and Grue from the Horror Pulps, ed. Sheldon R. Jaffery, Bowling Green Popular Press, 1987

Koja, Kathe
Happy Birthday, Kim White, ss *SF International* #1,1987

Komatsu, Sakyo
Take Your Choice, ss *SF International* #1,1987
Translated by Shiro Tamura & Grania Davis.

Koontz, Dean R.
Down in the Darkness, nv *The Horror Show* Sum,1986
The Architecture of Fear, ed. Kathryn Cramer+, Arbor House, 1987
Hardshell, nv **Night Visions** #4,1987
The Interrogation, ss *The Horror Show* Sum,1987
Miss Attila the Hun, nv **Night Visions** #4,1987
Ollie's Hands, ss *Infinity* #4, ed. Robert Hoskins,1972
The Horror Show Sum,1987
Twilight of the Dawn, nv **Night Visions** #4,1987

Koontz, Dean R. & Leigh Nichols
Dean R. Koontz, iv *The Horror Show* Sum,1987

Kopaska-Merkel, David C.
Goldfish in My Head, pm *Night Cry* v2#4,1987
Pearls of Rain, pm *Night Cry* v2#4,1987

Kopf, L.J.
Cartoon, ct *F&SF* Aug,1987

Kornbluth, C.M.
The Little Black Bag, nv *Astounding* Jul,1950
Robert Silverberg's Worlds of Wonder, ed. Robert Silverberg, Warner, 1987
Rod Serling's Night Gallery Reader, ed. Carol Serling+, Dembner, 1987
The Mindworm, ss *Worlds Beyond* Dec,1950
Vampires, ed. Alan Ryan, SFBC, 1987

Kornbluth, C.M. & Frederik Pohl
Critical Mass, na *Galaxy* Feb,1962
Our Best: The Best of Frederik Pohl and C.M. Kornbluth, Frederik Pohl+, Baen, 1987
The Engineer, ss *Infinity* Feb,1956
Our Best: The Best of Frederik Pohl and C.M. Kornbluth, Frederik Pohl+, Baen, 1987
A Gentle Dying, ss *Galaxy* Jun,1961
Our Best: The Best of Frederik Pohl and C.M. Kornbluth, Frederik Pohl+, Baen, 1987
The Gift of Garigolli, nv *Galaxy* Aug,1974
Our Best: The Best of Frederik Pohl and C.M. Kornbluth, Frederik Pohl+, Baen, 1987
Gravy Planet, ex *Galaxy* Aug,1952
Our Best: The Best of Frederik Pohl and C.M. Kornbluth, Frederik Pohl+, Baen, 1987
Mars-Tube [as by S.D. Gottesman], ss *Astonishing Stories* Sep,1941
Our Best: The Best of Frederik Pohl and C.M. Kornbluth, Frederik Pohl+, Baen, 1987
The Meeting, ss *F&SF* Nov,1972
Our Best: The Best of Frederik Pohl and C.M. Kornbluth, Frederik Pohl+, Baen, 1987
Mute Inglorious Tam, ss *F&SF* Oct,1974
Our Best: The Best of Frederik Pohl and C.M. Kornbluth, Frederik Pohl+, Baen, 1987
Nightmare with Zeppelins, nv *Galaxy* Dec,1958
Our Best: The Best of Frederik Pohl and C.M. Kornbluth, Frederik Pohl+, Baen, 1987

Kornbluth, C.M. & Frederik Pohl (continued)
The Quaker Cannon, nv *Analog* Aug,1961
Our Best: The Best of Frederik Pohl and C.M. Kornbluth, Frederik Pohl+, Baen, 1987
Trouble in Time [as by S.D. Gottesman], ss *Astonishing Stories* Dec,1940
Our Best: The Best of Frederik Pohl and C.M. Kornbluth, Frederik Pohl+, Baen, 1987
The World of Myrion Flowers, ss *F&SF* Oct,1961
Our Best: The Best of Frederik Pohl and C.M. Kornbluth, Frederik Pohl+, Baen, 1987

Kosiewska, Joseph
Memento Mori, ss *Pulpsmith* Win,1987

Kostelanetz, Richard
Weigh Station, br *Pulpsmith* Win,1987

Koster
Cartoon, ct *Twilight Zone* Aug,1987

Koszowski, Allen
Allen Koszowski, iv *The Horror Show* Fll,1987
Illustrations, il *The Horror Show* Fll,1987

Kotowicz, Ann K.
Winter Gathering, ss *Twilight Zone* Apr,1987
First place winner, TZ short story contest.

Kotzwinkle, William E. & Robert Shiarella
The Philosophy of Sebastian Trump or The Art of Outrage, ss **Brother Theodore's Chamber of Horrors**, ed. Marvin Kaye, Pinnacle,1975
Devils and Demons, ed. Marvin Kaye, Doubleday, 1987

Kremberg, Rudy
Twenty-One Minutes, ss *Haunts* #9,1987

Kremp, Irmtraud
Fun and Games, ss *SF International* #2,1987

Kress, Nancy
Cannibals, nv *IASFM* May,1987
Glass, ss *IASFM* Sep,1987
Phone Repairs, ss *IASFM* Dec,1986
The Year's Best Fantasy Stories: 13, ed. Arthur W. Saha, DAW, 1987
Training Ground, nv **Liavek: Wizard's Row**, ed. Will Shetterly & Emma Bull, Ace,1987

Kriske, Anke M.
Moon Rise, pm *Grue* #6,1987

Krolczyk, Gregory N.
No Matter What They Say, Sometimes It Is Too Late, vi *2AM* Win,1987

Kube-McDowell, Michael P.
Nanny, nv *Analog* Nov,1987

Kubicek, David
A Friend of the Family, ss *Space & Time* #72,1987

Kucharski, Lisa
When the Air Gets Thick and Sweet, pm *Ice River* Sum,1987

Kusnick, Gregory
Chrysalis, ss *Analog* mid-Dec,1987
The Lesser Magic, nv *Analog* Apr,1987

Kuttner, Henry
The Citadel of Darkness, nv *Strange Stories* Aug,1939
Prince Raynor, Gryphon, 1987
Cursed Be the City, nv *Strange Stories* Apr,1939
Prince Raynor, Gryphon, 1987
Dragon Moon, na *Weird Tales* Jan,1941
Isaac Asimov's Magical Worlds of Fantasy #9: Atlantis, ed. Isaac Asimov+, NAL/Signet, 1988
The Graveyard Rats, ss *Weird Tales* Mar,1936
Devils and Demons, ed. Marvin Kaye, Doubleday, 1987

KUTTNER, HENRY   **LAUMER, KEITH**

Kuttner, Henry (continued)
  Home Is the Hunter, ss *Galaxy* Jul,1953
    Robert Silverberg's Worlds of Wonder, ed. Robert Silverberg, Warner, 1987
  Private Eye, nv *Astounding* Jan,1949
    Great Science Fiction of the 20th Century, ed. Robert Silverberg +, Crown/Avenel, 1987
  Wet Magic, na *Unknown* Feb,1943
    Echoes of Valor, ed. Karl Edward Wagner, Tor, 1987

Kuttner, Robert
  The Imitation Demon, ss *Weird Tales* Sep,1954
    Devils and Demons, ed. Marvin Kaye, Doubleday, 1987

Labbe, Rodney A. & Robert R. McCammon
  An Interview with Robert McCammon, iv *Footsteps* Nov,1987

Lacher, Chris
  The Technique, ss *Eldritch Tales* #14,1987

Lackey, Mercedes R.
  Black Water (Suicide) [lyrics], sg **Festival Moon**, ed. C.J. Cherryh, DAW,1987
  Deathangel, nv **Festival Moon**, ed. C.J. Cherryh, DAW,1987
  Fever Season (Lyrics), sg **Fever Season**, ed. C.J. Cherryh, DAW,1987
  The Last One of the Season, ss *American Fantasy* Win,1987
  Merovingen Ecology, ms **Festival Moon**, ed. C.J. Cherryh, DAW,1987
  Mist-Thoughts (Lyrics), sg **Fever Season**, ed. C.J. Cherryh, DAW,1987
  Partners (Lyrics), sg **Fever Season**, ed. C.J. Cherryh, DAW,1987
  A Plague on Your Houses, nv **Fever Season**, ed. C.J. Cherryh, DAW,1987
  Private Conversation [lyrics], sg **Festival Moon**, ed. C.J. Cherryh, DAW,1987
  Should Old Acquaintance... [Part 2], sl *Fantasy Book* Mar,1987
  Should Old Acquaintance... [Part 3], sl *Fantasy Book* Mar,1987
  A Tale of Heroes, nv **Sword and Sorceress** #4, ed. Marion Zimmer Bradley,1987
  Were-Hunter, nv **Tales of the Witch World**, ed. Andre Norton, St. Martin's,1987

Lacoe, Addie
  Bayou Exterminator, ss *Grue* #6,1987

Lafferty, R.A.
  Gray Ghost: A Reminiscence, ss,1987
    Serpent's Egg, R.A. Lafferty, Morrigan, 1987
  Serpent's Egg, n.,1987
    Serpent's Egg, R.A. Lafferty, Morrigan, 1987

Lafferty, R.A. & Ron Wolfe
  Counting Grandmothers: R.A. Lafferty, iv *American Fantasy* Sum,1987

Laidlaw, Marc
  400 Boys, ss *Omni* Nov,1982
    The Fifth Omni Book of Science Fiction, ed. Ellen Datlow, Zebra, 1987
  Faust Forward, ss *F&SF* Mar,1987
  The Liquor Cabinet of Dr. Malikudzu, ss *Night Cry* v2#4,1987
  Love Comes to the Middleman, ss **Mathenauts**, ed. Rudy Rucker, Arbor House,1987
  Nutrimancer, ss *IASFM* Aug,1987
  The Random Man, vi *IASFM* Jul,1984
    Tales From Isaac Asimov's Science Fiction Magazine, ed. Sheila Williams +, Harcourt Brace Jovanovich, 1986
  Shalamari, ss *IASFM* Dec,1987
  Snowblind, ss *Twilight Zone* Feb,1987

Lake, Christina
  Assyria, ss *Interzone* #19,1987

Lake, Paul
  Rat Boy, ss *F&SF* May,1987

Lakey, John
  On Exhibit, il *Amazing* Jul,1987

Lambe, Marjory E.
  The Return, ss *Hutchinson's Mystery Story Magazine* Mar,1924
    The Virago Book of Ghost Stories, ed. Richard Dalby, Virago, 1987

Lamming, R.M.
  Sanctity, ss **Other Edens**, ed. Christopher Evans & Robert Holdstock, Unwin: London,1987

Lane, Joel
  The Foggy, Foggy Dew, ss **Foggy, Foggy Dew**, Joel Lane,1986
    The Year's Best Horror Stories: XV, ed. Karl Edward Wagner, DAW, 1987

Lane, M. Travis
  Venus, Our Very Favourite Star, pm **Tesseracts 2**, ed. Phyllis Gotlieb & Douglas Barbour, Press Porcepic: Victoria,1987

Lang, Andrew
  The Princess Nobody, ss,1884
    Victorian Fairy Tales, ed. Jack Zipes, Methuen, 1987

Langencamp, Heather, Wes Craven & Robert Englund
  Nightmare on Elm Street 3, iv *The Horror Show* Spr,1987

Langford, David
  In a Land of Sand and Ruin and Gold, ss **Other Edens**, ed. Christopher Evans & Robert Holdstock, Unwin: London,1987

Lanier, Sterling E.
  The Brigadier in Check -- and Mate, na **The Curious Quest of Brigadier Ffellowes**, Donald M. Grant,1986
    Isaac Asimov's Magical Worlds of Fantasy #9: Atlantis, ed. Isaac Asimov +, NAL/Signet, 1988

Lannoy, Kathinka
  S.O.S., ss *SF International* #2,1987

Lansdale, Joe R.
  Boo, Yourself, ss *Whispers* #23,1987
  Dead in the West (Part 4 of 4), sl *Eldritch Tales* #13,1987
  Dog, Cat, and Baby, vi **Masques** #2, ed. J.N. Williamson,1987
  The Fat Man, ss *The Horror Show* Jan,1987
  The God of the Razor, ss *Grue* #5,1987
  The Lansdale House of Horror, mr *The Horror Show* Jan,1987
  My Dead Dog, Bobby, vi *The Horror Show* Sum,1987
  The Nightrunners, ex Dark Harvest: Niles, IL hc Sep,1987
    The Horror Show Sum,1987
  Tight Little Stitches in a Dead Man's Back, nv **Nukes**, ed. John Maclay, Maclay,1986
    The Year's Best Horror Stories: XV, ed. Karl Edward Wagner, DAW, 1987

Lansdale, Joe R. & William J. Grabowski
  Interview with Joe R. Lansdale, iv *The Horror Show* Jan,1987

Lansdale, Joe R. & J.K. Potter
  Art of Darkness, iv *Twilight Zone* Feb,1987

Larson, Randall D.
  From Out of the Past, ss *Eldritch Tales* #13,1987

Lash, Batton
  Jury Duty, cs *American Fantasy* Spr,1987
  A Song of a Pitiful Poor Gawdawful Thing, cs *American Fantasy* Win,1987
  Stakeout, cs *American Fantasy* Sum,1987

Laumer, Keith
  Aide Memoire, nv *If* Jul,1962
    Retief: Envoy to New Worlds, Baen, 1987
  Cultural Exchange, nv *If* Sep,1962
    Retief: Envoy to New Worlds, Baen, 1987
  Field Test, ss *Analog* Mar,1976
    PsiFi: Psychological Theories and Science Fictions, ed. Jim Ridgway +, The British Psychological Society, 1987
    Supertanks, ed. Joe W. Haldeman +, Ace, 1987

LAUMER, KEITH   **LEDBETTER, KENNETH W.**

Laumer, Keith (continued)
  The Night of the Trolls, na *Worlds of Tomorrow* Oct,1963
    Battlefields Beyond Tomorrow, ed. Charles G. Waugh +,
      Crown/Bonanza, 1987
  Palace Revolution [Gambler's World], nv *If* Nov,1961
    Retief: Envoy to New Worlds, Baen, 1987
  Policy [The Madman from Earth], nv *If* Mar,1962
    Retief: Envoy to New Worlds, Baen, 1987
  Protocol [The Yllian Way], nv *If* Jan,1962
    Retief: Envoy to New Worlds, Baen, 1987
  Rank Injustice, nv *New Destinies* v1, ed. Jim Baen, Baen,1987
    Retief: Envoy to New Worlds, Baen, 1987
  Sealed Orders [Retief of the Red-Tape Mountain], nv *If* May,1962
    Retief: Envoy to New Worlds, Baen, 1987

Lawrence, D.H.
  The Rocking-Horse Winner, ss **The Ghost-Book**, ed. Cynthia Asquith,
      Hutchinson,1926
    The Dark Descent, ed. David G. Hartwell, Tor, 1987

Lawrence, Louise
  The Silver Box, nv **A Quiver of Ghosts**, ed. Aiden Chambers, Bodley
      Head,1987

Lawrence, Margery
  The Haunted Saucepan, ss **Nights of the Round Table**, Hutchinson:
      London,1926
    The Virago Book of Ghost Stories, ed. Richard Dalby, Virago, 1987

Lawson, Robert
  The Silver Leopard, ss **Spaceships & Spells**, ed. Jane Yolen, Martin
      H. Greenberg & Charles G. Waugh, Harper & Row,1987

Le Fanu, Joseph Sheridan
  Carmilla, na *The Dark Blue*,1871
    Vamps, ed. Martin H. Greenberg +, DAW, 1987
    Vampires, ed. Alan Ryan, SFBC, 1987
  Green Tea, nv *All the Year Round* Oct 23,1869
    Tales of the Dark, ed. Lincoln Child, St. Martin's, 1987
  Mr. Justice Harbottle, nv *Belgravia* Jan,1872
    The Dark Descent, ed. David G. Hartwell, Tor, 1987
  Schalken the Painter, ss *Dublin University Magazine* May,1839
    The Dark Descent, ed. David G. Hartwell, Tor, 1987
  Sir Dominick's Bargain [revised from "The Fortunes of Sir Robert
      Ardagh" *Dublin University Magazine* Mar,1838], ss *All the Year
      Round*,1872
    Devils and Demons, ed. Marvin Kaye, Doubleday, 1987

Le Guin, Ursula K.
  "The Author of the Acacia Seeds" and Other Extracts from the Journal
      of the Association of Therolinguistics, ss **Fellowship of the Stars**,
      ed. Terry Carr, Simon & Schuster,1974
    Buffalo Gals and Other Animal Presences, Capra Press, 1987
  The Basalt, pm *Open Places* Spr,1982
    Buffalo Gals and Other Animal Presences, Capra Press, 1987
  Black Leonard in Negative Space, pm,1978
    Buffalo Gals and Other Animal Presences, Capra Press, 1987
  Buffalo Gals, Won't You Come Out Tonight, nv **Buffalo Gals and
      Other Animal Presences**, Capra Press,1987
    F&SF Nov,1987
  A Conversation with a Silence, pm,1986
    Buffalo Gals and Other Animal Presences, Capra Press, 1987
  The Crown of Laurel, pm,1987
    Buffalo Gals and Other Animal Presences, Capra Press, 1987
  Daddy's Big Girl, ss *Omni* Jan,1987
  The Direction of the Road, ss *Orbit* #12, ed. Damon Knight,1973
    Buffalo Gals and Other Animal Presences, Capra Press, 1987
  Five Vegetable Poems, si
    Buffalo Gals and Other Animal Presences, Capra Press, 1987
  Flints, pm,1986
    Buffalo Gals and Other Animal Presences, Capra Press, 1987
  For Leonard, Darko, and Burton Watson, pm,1982
    Buffalo Gals and Other Animal Presences, Capra Press, 1987
  For Ted, pm **Wild Angels**, Capra Press,1975
    Buffalo Gals and Other Animal Presences, Capra Press, 1987
  Found Poem, pm,1986
    Buffalo Gals and Other Animal Presences, Capra Press, 1987

Le Guin, Ursula K. (continued)
  Four Cat Poems, si
    Buffalo Gals and Other Animal Presences, Capra Press, 1987
  Horse Camp, ss *New Yorker* Aug 25,1986
    Buffalo Gals and Other Animal Presences, Capra Press, 1987
  Introduction, in
    Buffalo Gals and Other Animal Presences, Capra Press, 1987
  Lewis and Clark and After, pm *The Seattle Review* Sum,1987
    Buffalo Gals and Other Animal Presences, Capra Press, 1987
  The Man Eater, pm,1986
    Buffalo Gals and Other Animal Presences, Capra Press, 1987
  May's Lion, ss *The Little Magazine* v14#1,1983
    Buffalo Gals and Other Animal Presences, Capra Press, 1987
  Mazes, ss *Epoch*, ed. Roger Elwood & Robert Silverberg, Berkley,1975
    Buffalo Gals and Other Animal Presences, Capra Press, 1987
  Mount St. Helens/Omphalos, pm **Wild Angels**, Capra Press,1975
    Buffalo Gals and Other Animal Presences, Capra Press, 1987
  The New Atlantis, na **The New Atlantis**, ed. Robert Silverberg,1975
    Isaac Asimov's Magical Worlds of Fantasy #9: Atlantis, ed. Isaac
      Asimov +, NAL/Signet, 1988
  Orr's Dreams [from **The Lathe of Heaven**], ex Scribners: New
      York,1971
    PsiFi: Psychological Theories and Science Fictions, ed. Jim
      Ridgway +, The British Psychological Society, 1987
  The Question of Sex [from **The Left Hand of Darkness**], ex Ace:
      New York,1969
    PsiFi: Psychological Theories and Science Fictions, ed. Jim
      Ridgway +, The British Psychological Society, 1987
  The Rule of Names, ss *Fantastic* Apr,1964
    Fantastic Stories: Tales of the Weird and Wondrous, ed. Martin
      H. Greenberg +, TSR, 1987
  Schrodinger's Cat, ss **Universe** #5, ed. Terry Carr,1974
    Buffalo Gals and Other Animal Presences, Capra Press, 1987
  Seven Bird and Beast Poems, si
    Buffalo Gals and Other Animal Presences, Capra Press, 1987
  She Unnames Them, vi *New Yorker* Jan 21,1985
    Hear the Silence, ed. Irene Zahava, Crossing Press, 1986
    Buffalo Gals and Other Animal Presences, Capra Press, 1987
  Sleeping Out, pm,1985
    Buffalo Gals and Other Animal Presences, Capra Press, 1987
  Tabby Lorenzo, pm,1984
    Buffalo Gals and Other Animal Presences, Capra Press, 1987
  Three Rock Poems, si
    Buffalo Gals and Other Animal Presences, Capra Press, 1987
  Torrey Pines Reserve, pm **Hard Words & Other Poems**, Harper &
      Row,1981
    Buffalo Gals and Other Animal Presences, Capra Press, 1987
  Totem, pm **Hard Words & Other Poems**, Harper & Row,1981
    Buffalo Gals and Other Animal Presences, Capra Press, 1987
  Vaster Than Empires and More Slow, nv **New Dimensions** #1, ed.
      Robert Silverberg/Marta Randall,1971
    Buffalo Gals and Other Animal Presences, Capra Press, 1987
  West Texas, pm,1980
    Buffalo Gals and Other Animal Presences, Capra Press, 1987
  What is Going on in The Oaks Around the Barn, pm,1986
    Buffalo Gals and Other Animal Presences, Capra Press, 1987
  The White Donkey, ss *TriQuarterly* #49,1980
    Buffalo Gals and Other Animal Presences, Capra Press, 1987
  The Wife's Story, ss **The Compass Rose**, Harper & Row,1982
    Buffalo Gals and Other Animal Presences, Capra Press, 1987
  Winter Downs, pm **Hard Words & Other Poems**, Harper & Row,1981
    Buffalo Gals and Other Animal Presences, Capra Press, 1987
  Winter's King, nv **Orbit** #5, ed. Damon Knight,1969
    Great Science Fiction of the 20th Century, ed. Robert
      Silverberg +, Crown/Avenel, 1987
  Xmas Over, pm *Clinton Street Quarterly*,1984
    Buffalo Gals and Other Animal Presences, Capra Press, 1987

Le Queux, William
  The Car with the Green Lights, ss *The Premier Magazine* Feb,1916
    Mysterious Motoring Stories, ed. William Pattrick, W.H. Allen, 1987

Learn, Paul
  The Other Side: Queen Tut, ar *Twilight Zone* Feb,1987

Ledbetter, Kenneth W.
  The Canyons of Ariel, nv *F&SF* Dec,1987

LEE, JAMES A.

Lee, James A.
　Reflections on Yarbro's **False Dawn**, br *2AM* Win,1987

Lee, Rebecca
　Evert Sparrow That Falls, ss *Aboriginal SF* Nov,1987

Lee, Samantha
　Bon Appetit, vi *Fantasy Tales* #16,1986

Lee, Tanith
　Beauty Is the Beast, ss *American Fantasy* Fll,1986
　　The Year's Best Fantasy Stories: 13, ed. Arthur W. Saha, DAW,
　　　1987
　Bite-Me-Not or, Fleur de Feu, nv *IASFM* Oct,1984
　　Vampires, ed. Alan Ryan, SFBC, 1987
　Black as a Rose, nv **Night's Sorceries**, DAW,1987
　By Crystal Light Beneath One Star, nv **Tales from the Forbidden
　　Planet**, ed. Roz Kaveney, Titan,1987
　Children of the Night, na **Night's Sorceries**, DAW,1987
　Crying in the Rain, ss **Other Edens**, ed. Christopher Evans & Robert
　　Holdstock, Unwin: London,1987
　The Daughter of the Magician, na **Night's Sorceries**, DAW,1987
　Death's Master, n. DAW: New York,1979
　　Tales from the Flat Earth: The Lords of Darkness, SFBC, 1987
　Delirium's Mistress, n. DAW: New York,1986
　　Tales from the Flat Earth: Night's Daughter, SFBC, 1987
　Delusion's Master, n. DAW: New York,1981
　　Tales from the Flat Earth: The Lords of Darkness, SFBC, 1987
　Dooniveh, the Moon, na **Night's Sorceries**, DAW,1987
　Game Players, ss **Night's Sorceries**, DAW,1987
　Gemini, nv **Chrysalis #9**, ed. Roy Torgeson,1981
　　Masters of Darkness II, ed. Dennis Etchison, Tor, 1988
　The Golden Rope, nv **Red As Blood**, DAW,1983
　　Demons!, ed. Jack M. Dann +, Ace, 1987
　Into Gold, nv *IASFM* Mar,1986
　　The Year's Best Science Fiction, Fourth Annual Collection, ed.
　　　Gardner R. Dozois, St. Martin's, 1987
　　The 1987 Annual World's Best SF, ed. Donald A. Wollheim +,
　　　DAW, 1987
　Night's Daughter, Day's Desire, nv **Night's Sorceries**, DAW,1987
　Night's Master, n. DAW: New York,1978
　　Tales from the Flat Earth: The Lords of Darkness, SFBC, 1987
　Night's Sorceries, n. DAW: New York,1987
　　Tales from the Flat Earth: Night's Daughter, SFBC, 1987
　Prince Amilec, ss **Princess Hynchatti and Some Other Surprises**,
　　London: Macmillan,1972
　　Don't Bet on the Prince, ed. Jack Zipes, Methuen, 1987
　The Princess and Her Future, ss **Red As Blood**, DAW,1983
　　Devils and Demons, ed. Marvin Kaye, Doubleday, 1987
　The Prodigal, nv **Night's Sorceries**, DAW,1987
　Red as Blood, ss *F&SF* Jul,1979
　　Vamps, ed. Martin H. Greenberg +, DAW, 1987
　Three Days, nv **Shadows #7**, ed. Charles L. Grant,1984
　　The Dark Descent, ed. David G. Hartwell, Tor, 1987
　Wolfland, nv *F&SF* Oct,1980
　　Don't Bet on the Prince, ed. Jack Zipes, Methuen, 1987

Lee, Vernon
　Amour Dure, nv **Hauntings, Fantastic Stories**, Heinemann:
　　London,1890
　　Supernatural Tales: Excursions Into Fantasy, Peter Owen, 1987
　The Legend of Madame Krasinska, nv **Vanitas**, Heinemann:
　　London,1892
　　Supernatural Tales: Excursions Into Fantasy, Peter Owen, 1987
　Marsyas in Flanders, ss,1900
　　Dracula's Brood, ed. Richard Dalby, Crucible, 1987
　Prince Alberic and the Snake Lady, na **Pope Jacynth and Other
　　Fantastic Tales**, Grant Richards: London,1904
　　Supernatural Tales: Excursions Into Fantasy, Peter Owen, 1987
　The Virgin of the Seven Daggers, nv **For Maurice, Five Unlikely
　　Stories**, John Lane: London,1927
　　Supernatural Tales: Excursions Into Fantasy, Peter Owen, 1987
　A Wedding Chest, ss **Pope Jacynth and Other Fantastic Tales**,
　　Grant Richards: London,1904
　　Supernatural Tales: Excursions Into Fantasy, Peter Owen, 1987
　A Wicked Voice, nv **Hauntings, Fantastic Stories**, Heinemann:
　　London,1890
　　Supernatural Tales: Excursions Into Fantasy, Peter Owen, 1987

Lee, William M.
　A Message from Charity, ss *F&SF* Nov,1967
　　Young Witches & Warlocks, ed. Isaac Asimov +, Harper & Row,
　　　1987

Leiber, Fritz
　Adept's Gambit, na **Night's Black Agents**, Arkham,1947
　　Echoes of Valor, ed. Karl Edward Wagner, Tor, 1987
　　Robert Adams' Book of Alternate Worlds, ed. Robert Adams +,
　　　NAL/Signet, 1987
　Belsen Express, ss **The Second Book of Fritz Leiber**, DAW,1975
　　The Dark Descent, ed. David G. Hartwell, Tor, 1987
　Black Corridor, ss *Galaxy* Dec,1967
　　Masters of Darkness II, ed. Dennis Etchison, Tor, 1988
　Catch That Zeppelin!, ss *F&SF* Mar,1975
　　Beyond the Stars, ed. Isaac Asimov, Severn House, 1987
　The Dead Man, nv *Weird Tales* Nov,1950
　　Rod Serling's Night Gallery Reader, ed. Carol Serling +,
　　　Dembner, 1987
　The Girl with the Hungry Eyes, ss **The Girl With the Hungry Eyes**,
　　ed. Donald A. Wollheim, Avon,1949
　　Vamps, ed. Martin H. Greenberg +, DAW, 1987
　　Vampires, ed. Alan Ryan, SFBC, 1987
　　Rod Serling's Night Gallery Reader, ed. Carol Serling +,
　　　Dembner, 1987
　The Man Who Never Grew Young, ss **Night's Black Agents**,
　　Arkham,1947
　　Great Science Fiction of the 20th Century, ed. Robert
　　　Silverberg +, Crown/Avenel, 1987
　The Mouser Goes Below, ss *Whispers* #23,1987
　Smoke Ghost, ss *Unknown* Oct,1941
　　The Dark Descent, ed. David G. Hartwell, Tor, 1987
　Yesterday House, nv *Galaxy* Aug,1952
　　Strange Maine, ed. Charles G. Waugh +, Tapley, 1986

Leiber, Justin
　Tit for Tat, ss *Amazing* Jul,1987

Leigh, Stephen
　Encounter, nv **Destinies** v1#3, ed. James Baen,1979
　　Supertanks, ed. Joe W. Haldeman +, Ace, 1987

Leinster, Murray
　The Other World, na *Startling Stories* Nov,1949
　　Robert Adams' Book of Alternate Worlds, ed. Robert Adams +,
　　　NAL/Signet, 1987

Leman, Bob
　Come Where My Love Lies Dreaming, ss **Shadows #10**, ed. Charles
　　L. Grant,1987
　Olida, nv *F&SF* Apr,1987

Leming, Ron
　Retirement [Even Death Gets Tired], ss *Outlaw Biker* Mar,1986
　　The Year's Best Horror Stories: XV, ed. Karl Edward Wagner,
　　　DAW, 1987

Lenihan, Kevin
　Lovers, ss *The Horror Show* Win,1987

Leodhas, Sorche Nic
　The House That Lacked a Bogle, ss,1981
　　The Ghost Story Treasury, ed. Linda Sonntag, Putnam, 1987

Lepovetsky, Lisa
　Autumn Memories, pm *Grue* #6,1987
　Axe, pm *Grue* #4,1987
　The Mad Poet's Magic Fails, pm *2AM* Spr,1987

Leslie, Shane
　As in a Glass Dimly, ss
　　Ghosts and Scholars, ed. Rosemary Pardoe +, Crucible, 1987

Level, Maurice
　A Madman, vi
　　　English adaptation by Marvin Kaye.
　　Devils and Demons, ed. Marvin Kaye, Doubleday, 1987

LEVERTOV, DENISE

LOVECRAFT, H.P.

Levertov, Denise
  Come Into Animal Presence, pm,1961
    Buffalo Gals and Other Animal Presences, Ursula K. Le Guin,
    Capra Press, 1987

Lewis, Anthony R.
  The Analog Calendar of Upcoming Events, ms *Analog* Jan,1987
  The Analog Calendar of Upcoming Events, ms *Analog* Feb,1987
  The Analog Calendar of Upcoming Events, ms *Analog* Mar,1987
  The Analog Calendar of Upcoming Events, ms *Analog* Apr,1987
  The Analog Calendar of Upcoming Events, ms *Analog* May,1987
  The Analog Calendar of Upcoming Events, ms *Analog* Jun,1987
  The Analog Calendar of Upcoming Events, ms *Analog* Jul,1987
  The Analog Calendar of Upcoming Events, ms *Analog* Aug,1987
  The Analog Calendar of Upcoming Events, ms *Analog* Sep,1987
  The Analog Calendar of Upcoming Events, ms *Analog* Oct,1987
  The Analog Calendar of Upcoming Events, ms *Analog* Nov,1987
  The Analog Calendar of Upcoming Events, ms *Analog* Dec,1987
  The Analog Calendar of Upcoming Events, ms *Analog* mid-Dec,1987

Lewis, C.S.
  The Lion, the Witch and the Wardrobe, n. The Blakiston Co.:
    Philadelphia,1950
    Tales of Narnia, Collins, 1987
  Prince Caspian, n. The Blakiston Co.: Philadelphia,1951
    Tales of Narnia, Collins, 1987
  The Voyage of the Dawn Treader, n. The Blakiston Co.:
    Philadelphia,1952
    Tales of Narnia, Collins, 1987

Lewitt, Shariann
  Sister of Midnight, ss **Friends of the Horseclans**, ed. Robert Adams
    & Pamela Crippen Adams, Signet,1987

Libertus, Peg
  A Lunar Cycle, pm *Aboriginal SF* Feb,1987

Lieberman, Marcia K.
  'Some Day My Prince Will Come': Female Acculturation through the
    Fairy Tale, cr *College English* #34,1972
    Don't Bet on the Prince, ed. Jack Zipes, Methuen, 1987

Liebson, Morris
  Obsidian Sphinx, pm *Amazing* Sep,1987

Ligotti, Thomas
  Dr. Locrian's Asylum, ss *Grue* #5,1987

Linaweaver, Brad
  High Road of Lost Men, nv **Friends of the Horseclans**, ed. Robert
    Adams & Pamela Crippen Adams, Signet,1987

Lindahl, Ron & Val Lakey Lindahn
  Portfolio, pi **World Fantasy Convention Program Book** #13,1987

Lindahn, Val Lakey & Ron Lindahn
  Portfolio, pi **World Fantasy Convention Program Book** #13,1987

Lindholm, Megan & Steven Brust
  An Act of Mercy, ss **Liavek: Wizard's Row**, ed. Will Shetterly & Emma
    Bull, Ace,1987

Linton, Eliza Lynn
  The Fate of Madame Cabanel, ss **With a Silken Thread**, Chatto &
    Windus: London,1880
    Dracula's Brood, ed. Richard Dalby, Crucible, 1987

Linzner, Gordon
  The Editor's Page, ed *Space & Time* #72,1987
  The Editor's Page, ed *Space & Time* #73,1987

Lipinski, Miroslaw
  Introduction, in
    The Grabinski Reader [#2, Spring 1987]

Little, Bentley
  Comes the Bad Time, ss *The Horror Show* Win,1987
  Garage Sale, ss *Space & Time* #72,1987

Little, Bentley (continued)
  Lethe Dreams, ss *Night Cry* v2#3,1987
  Loony Toon, vi *The Horror Show* Fll,1987
  Projections, ss *The Horror Show* Jan,1987
  Runt, ss *The Horror Show* Spr,1987
  The Show, ss *The Horror Show* Fll,1987
  Snow, ss *Grue* #4,1987

Little, Bentley & William J. Grabowski
  Bentley Little, iv *The Horror Show* Fll,1987

Livingstone, James B.
  Mindrace, pm *Mage* Spr,1986
  Mage Fll,1987

Llywelyn, Morgan
  Me, Tree, ss **Devils & Demons**, ed. Marvin Kaye,
    SFBC/Doubleday,1987

Lodi, Edward
  On a Clear Day, vi *2AM* Fll,1987

Lofts, Norah
  A Curious Experience, ss *Woman's Journal*,1971
    The Virago Book of Ghost Stories, ed. Richard Dalby, Virago, 1987

London, Jack
  Lost Face, ss *New York Herald* Dec 13,1908
    Classic Stories of Mystery, Horror and Suspense, ed. Simon
    Petherick, Robert Hale, 1987

Long, Amelia Reynolds
  Omega, ss *Amazing* Jul,1932
    Amazing Science Fiction Stories: The Wonder Years 1926-1935,
    ed. Martin H. Greenberg, TSR, 1987

Long, Frank Belknap
  Cottage Tenant, nv *Fantastic* Apr,1975
    Masters of Darkness II, ed. Dennis Etchison, Tor, 1988
  The Eye Above the Mantel, ss *The United Amateur*,1921
    Pulpsmith Win,1987

Longyear, Barry B.
  Adagio, nv *Omni* Sep,1984
    The Fifth Omni Book of Science Fiction, ed. Ellen Datlow, Zebra,
    1987
  The Book of Baraboo, na *IASFM* Mar,1980
    **Isaac Asimov's Wonderful Worlds of Science Fiction #7: Space
    Shuttles**, ed. Isaac Asimov+, NAL/Signet, 1987
  Little Green Men, ss **Spaceships & Spells**, ed. Jane Yolen, Martin H.
    Greenberg & Charles G. Waugh, Harper & Row,1987

LoProto, Frank
  The Magic, vi *2AM* Fll,1987

Lorimer, Janet
  The Natural Way, ss *2AM* Spr,1987

Lorimer, Philip
  Under the Carpet, ss **The Pan Book of Horror Stories** #28, Pan,1987

Loring, E. Bertrand
  The Man Who Wrote Shakespeare, ss *F&SF* Jan,1987

Lorrey, Rayson
  An Arrow of Tempered Silver, ss *Fantasy Book* Mar,1987

Love, Rosaleen
  Alexia and Graham Bell, ss *Aphelion* #5,1987

Lovecraft, H.P.
  The Call of Cthulhu, nv *Weird Tales* Feb,1928
    The Dark Descent, ed. David G. Hartwell, Tor, 1987
  The Colour out of Space [also as "Monster of Terror"], nv *Amazing*
    Sep,1927
    Amazing Science Fiction Stories: The Wonder Years 1926-1935,
    ed. Martin H. Greenberg, TSR, 1987

LOVECRAFT, H.P.

Lovecraft, H.P. (continued)
Cool Air, ss *Tales Of Magic and Mystery* Mar,1928;
    Weird Tales Sep,1939
    Rod Serling's Night Gallery Reader, ed. Carol Serling +,
        Dembner, 1987
Herbert West--Reanimator ["Grewsome Tales", *Home Brew*: Feb-Jul
    1922], gp *Weird Tales* Mar,1942
    From the Dark; *Weird Tales* Mar,1942
    The Plague Demon; *Weird Tales* Jul,1942
    Six Shots by Moonlight; *Weird Tales* Sep,1942
    The Scream of the Dead; *Weird Tales* Nov,1942
    The Horror from the Shadows; *Weird Tales* Sep,1943
    The Tomb-Legions; *Weird Tales* Nov,1943
    Cinemonsters, ed. Martin H. Greenberg, TSR, 1987
The Hound, ss *Weird Tales* Feb,1924
    Devils and Demons, ed. Marvin Kaye, Doubleday, 1987
Pickman's Model, ss *Weird Tales* Oct,1927
    Rod Serling's Night Gallery Reader, ed. Carol Serling +,
        Dembner, 1987
The Rats in the Walls, ss *Weird Tales* Mar,1924
    House Shudders, ed. Martin H. Greenberg +, DAW, 1987
    The Dark Descent, ed. David G. Hartwell, Tor, 1987
The Statement of Randolph Carter, ss *The Vagrant* May,1920
    Charles Keeping's Classic Tales of the Macabre, ed. Charles
        Keeping, Blackie, 1987

Lovin, Roger Robert
The Cobbler, ss *F&SF* Dec,1987

Lowe, Jonathan
Sole Survivor, pm *Eldritch Tales* #13,1987

Lowe, Nick
Mutant Popcorn, mr *Interzone* #19,1987
Mutant Popcorn, mr *Interzone* #21,1987

Lowe, W.T.
All in Favor, vi *American Fantasy* Win,1987

Lubow, Michael
The Little Blue Pill, ss *Playboy* Apr,1987

Lucas, George
Star Wars, n. Ballantine: New York,1976
    The Star Wars Trilogy, George Lucas +, Ballantine/Del Rey, 1987

Lucas, Laurel
Aborigines: A NATO Alliance?, bg *Aboriginal SF* May,1987
Aborigines: Devolution and Disappearances, bg *Aboriginal SF*
    Feb,1987
Aborigines: NASA Experiments With SF, bg *Aboriginal SF* Sep,1987
Aborigines: Nature Versus Nurture, bg *Aboriginal SF* Nov,1987
Aborigines: Plan 9 From Roslindale, bg *Aboriginal SF* Jul,1987

Lumley, Brian
Billy's Oak, ss *The Arkham Collector* Win,1970
    The Compleat Crow, Ganley, 1987
The Black Recalled, ss **World Fantasy Convention Program
    Book**,1983
    The Compleat Crow, Ganley, 1987
The Caller of the Black, nv **The Caller of the Black**, Arkham,1971
    The Compleat Crow, Ganley, 1987
Concerning Titus Crow, in
    The Compleat Crow, Ganley, 1987
Darghud's Doll, ss **The Horror at Oakdene and Others**, Arkham,1977
    The Compleat Crow, Ganley, 1987
De Marigny's Clock, ss **The Caller of the Black**, Arkham,1971
    The Compleat Crow, Ganley, 1987
In the Temple of Terror, nv *Weirdbook* #22,1987
Inception, ss **The Compleat Crow**, Ganley,1987
An Item of Supporting Evidence, ss *The Arkham Collector* Win,1970
    The Compleat Crow, Ganley, 1987
Lord of the Worms, na *Weirdbook* #17,1983
    The Compleat Crow, Ganley, 1987
The Mirror of Nitocris, ss **The Caller of the Black**, Arkham,1971
    The Compleat Crow, Ganley, 1987
Name and Number, nv *Kadath* Jul,1982
    The Compleat Crow, Ganley, 1987

Lumley, Brian (continued)
Necros, ss **After Midnight Stories** #2,1986
    The Year's Best Horror Stories: XV, ed. Karl Edward Wagner,
        DAW, 1987
The Thin People, ss *Whispers* #23,1987
    The Third Book of After Midnight Stories, ed. Amy Myers, Kimber,
        1987
The Viking's Stone, ss **The Horror at Oakdene and Others**,
    Arkham,1977
    The Compleat Crow, Ganley, 1987

Lunde, David
Limits, pm *IASFM* Feb,1986
    Rhysling Anthology 1987, ed. Anonymous, SF Poetry Assc., 1987

Lupoff, Richard A.
Etchings of Her Memories, ss *Amazing* Mar,1987
Introduction: Honeymoons and Geezenstacks and Fredric William
    Brown, in
    And the Gods Laughed, Fredric Brown, Phantasia Press, 1987

Luserke, Uwe
The End of the Hunt, ss *SF International* #1,1987

Lyall, Francis
Introduction, in
    Brother and Other Stories, Clifford D. Simak, Severn House, 1987

Lyons, Joseph
Trust Me, ss **The Architecture of Fear**, ed. Kathryn Cramer & Peter
    D. Pautz, Arbor House,1987

Macaulay, Rose
Whitewash, ss **Ghost Book #2**, ed. Aidan Chambers/James
    Turner,1952
    The Virago Book of Ghost Stories, ed. Richard Dalby, Virago, 1987

MacDonald, George
The Carasoyn, nv **Works of Fancy and Imagination**,1871
    The Light Princess and Other Stories, Kelpies, 1987
Cross Purposes, nv **Dealing With Fairies**,1867
    The Light Princess and Other Stories, Kelpies, 1987
The Day Boy and the Night Girl, nv,1879
    Victorian Fairy Tales, ed. Jack Zipes, Methuen, 1987
    The Light Princess and Other Stories, Kelpies, 1987
The Giant's Heart, nv
    The Light Princess and Other Stories, Kelpies, 1987
The Golden Key, nv **Dealing With Fairies**,1867
    The Light Princess and Other Stories, Kelpies, 1987
The Light Princess, nv
    The Light Princess and Other Stories, Kelpies, 1987
Little Daylight, ss **Works of Fancy and Imagination**,1871
    The Light Princess and Other Stories, Kelpies, 1987
The Shadows, nv
    The Light Princess and Other Stories, Kelpies, 1987

MacDonald, John D.
The Legend of Joe Lee, ss *Cosmopolitan* Oct,1964
    Nightmares in Dixie, ed. Frank D. McSherry, Jr. +, August House,
        1987

Machen, Arthur
Art and Luck, ar *The Independent* Nov 25,1933
    Guinevere and Lancelot & Others, Purple Mouth, 1986
Bridles and Spurs, ar,1951
    Guinevere and Lancelot & Others, Purple Mouth, 1986
Gipsies, ar *The Academy and Literature* Dec 9,1911
    Guinevere and Lancelot & Others, Purple Mouth, 1986
The Grande Trouvaille, ar,1923
    Guinevere and Lancelot & Others, Purple Mouth, 1986
Guinevere and Lancelot, ss,1926
    Guinevere and Lancelot & Others, Purple Mouth, 1986
Introduction (from Notes and Queries), in,1926
    Guinevere and Lancelot & Others, Purple Mouth, 1986
Introduction (from The Dragon of the Alchemists), in,1926
    Guinevere and Lancelot & Others, Purple Mouth, 1986
Local Colour, ar *Literature* Apr 23,1898
    Guinevere and Lancelot & Others, Purple Mouth, 1986

Machen, Arthur (continued)
  A New Christmas Carol, vi,1924
    Christmas Ghosts, ed. Kathryn Cramer+, Arbor House, 1987
  The Novel of the White Powder [also as "The White Powder"], nv **The Three Impostors**, John Lane,1895
    Tales of the Dark 2, ed. Lincoln Child, St. Martin's, 1987
    Devils and Demons, ed. Marvin Kaye, Doubleday, 1987
  Preface (from Afterglow), pr,1924
    Guinevere and Lancelot & Others, Purple Mouth, 1986
  Ritual, ss,1937
    Guinevere and Lancelot & Others, Purple Mouth, 1986
  Savages [from "Concealed Savages of Tudor England"], ar *The American Mercury* Feb,1936
    Guinevere and Lancelot & Others, Purple Mouth, 1986

MacIntyre, F. Gwynplaine
  Improbable Bestiary: The Bandersnatch (Frumius carrollii), pm *Amazing* Nov,1987

Maclay, John
  After the Last War, pm **Anti-War Poems**,1985
    Other Engagements, Dream House, 1987
  At the Last, pm *Footsteps* Spr,1985
    Other Engagements, Dream House, 1987
  Bird Food, pm **Other Engagements**, Madison, WI: Dream House,1987
  The Bookman's God, ss **Other Engagements**, Madison, WI: Dream House,1987
  Cedars, pm *The Poet* Fll,1984
    Other Engagements, Dream House, 1987
  Dark Stretch of Road, ss *Grue* #3,1986
    Other Engagements, Dream House, 1987
  Death Flight, vi *Night Cry* v2#4,1987
  The Flood, ss *The Horror Show* Fll,1986
    Other Engagements, Dream House, 1987
  Glass, pm *Footsteps* Spr,1985
    Other Engagements, Dream House, 1987
  Harvest, vi *Dementia* #1,1986
    Other Engagements, Dream House, 1987
  Heir to the Kingdom, ss *Australian Horror & Fantasy Magazine*
    Other Engagements, Dream House, 1987
  In The Wilderness, ss *Etchings & Odysseys* #7,1985
    Other Engagements, Dream House, 1987
  The Knife, ss *Crosscurrents* Fll,1984
    Other Engagements, Dream House, 1987
  Locking Up, ss *Night Cry* v2#1,1986
    Other Engagements, Dream House, 1987
  Marriages, pm *Scavenger's Newsletter*
    Other Engagements, Dream House, 1987
  New York Night, ss **Other Engagements**, Madison, WI: Dream House,1987
  Night Firing--1967, pm *Fungi* #9,1986
    Other Engagements, Dream House, 1987
  Nostalgia, pm *Footsteps* Nov,1987
  On the Boardwalk, ss **Other Engagements**, Madison, WI: Dream House,1987
  The One Thing to Fear, ss *Footsteps* Fll,1986
    Other Engagements, Dream House, 1987
  The Reckoning, vi **Other Engagements**, Madison, WI: Dream House,1987
  Recycle, pm *SPWAO Showcase* #5,1985
    Other Engagements, Dream House, 1987
  Refill, pm *Twisted* #1,1985
    Other Engagements, Dream House, 1987
  The Sisters, ss **Other Engagements**, Madison, WI: Dream House,1987
  The Step Beyond, ss **Darkness on the Edge of Town**, an,1985
    Other Engagements, Dream House, 1987
  Sunset, pm *Twisted* #2,1985
    Other Engagements, Dream House, 1987
  Tanning, ss *Etchings & Odysseys* #5,1984
    Other Engagements, Dream House, 1987
  To a Cockroach, pm *Scavenger's Newsletter* Apr,1985
    Other Engagements, Dream House, 1987
  The Tower, ss *Etchings & Odysseys* #9,1986
    Other Engagements, Dream House, 1987
  Turning Forty, pm **Other Engagements**, Madison, WI: Dream House,1987
  The Undertaker Reflects, pm *Fungi* #12,1986
    Other Engagements, Dream House, 1987

Maclay, John (continued)
  The Unforgiven, pm *Weirdbook* #20,1985
    Other Engagements, Dream House, 1987
  Who Walks at Night, ss *The Horror Show* Sum,1986
    Other Engagements, Dream House, 1987

Maclay, John & William J. Grabowski
  Genre-Love and the Magic of Words: John Maclay, iv *2AM* Fll,1987

MacPherson, Jaime
  Covenant, ss *Apex!* #1,1987

Maddox, Tom
  Snake-Eyes, nv *Omni* Apr,1986
    The Year's Best Science Fiction, Fourth Annual Collection, ed. Gardner R. Dozois, St. Martin's, 1987
  Spirit of the Night, nv *IASFM* Sep,1987

Mage Staff
  Mage Reviews, br *Mage* Spr,1987
  Mage Reviews, br *Mage* Win,1987

Mahy, Margaret
  The Haunting, ex J.M. Dent: London,1982
    The Ghost Story Treasury, ed. Linda Sonntag, Putnam, 1987
  The Princess and the Clown, ss **Mahy Magic**, Dent,1986
    The Magic Kiss and Other Tales of Princes and Princesses, ed. Tony Bradman, Blackie, 1987

Maitland, Sara
  Angel Maker, ss
    The Book of Spells, Michael Joseph, 1987
  The Eighth Planet, ss
    The Book of Spells, Michael Joseph, 1987
  A Fall from Grace, ss **Weddings and Funerals**, Latourette/Maitland, Brilliance,1984
    The Book of Spells, Michael Joseph, 1987
  Flower Garden, ss
    The Book of Spells, Michael Joseph, 1987
  Heart Throb, ss **Passion Fruit**, Winterson, Pandora,1986
    The Book of Spells, Michael Joseph, 1987
  Lady with Unicorn, ss **The Virago Book of Ghost Stories**, ed. Richard Dalby, Virago,1987
  'Let us Now Praise Unknown Women and Our Mothers who Begat Us', ss **Stepping Out**, Oosthuizen,1986
    The Book of Spells, Michael Joseph, 1987
  Lullaby for My Dyke and Her Cat, ss
    The Book of Spells, Michael Joseph, 1987
  Maybe a Love Poem for my Friend, pm
    The Book of Spells, Michael Joseph, 1987
  Miss Manning's Angelic Moment, ss
    The Book of Spells, Michael Joseph, 1987
  Particles of a Wave. An Afterword, aw
    The Book of Spells, Michael Joseph, 1987
  Promises, ss
    The Book of Spells, Michael Joseph, 1987
  Seal-Self, ss
    The Book of Spells, Michael Joseph, 1987
  The Tale of the Valiant Demoiselle, nv
    The Book of Spells, Michael Joseph, 1987
  Triptych, ss
    The Book of Spells, Michael Joseph, 1987
  The Wicked Stepmother's Lament, ss **More Tales I Tell My Mother**, Journeyman,1987
    The Book of Spells, Michael Joseph, 1987

Malden, R.H.
  Between Sunset and Moonrise, ss **Nine Ghosts**, E. Arnold: London,1943
    Ghosts and Scholars, ed. Rosemary Pardoe+, Crucible, 1987

Mallonee, Dennis
  Editorial, ed *Fantasy Book* Mar,1987

Malzberg, Barry N.
  Ambition, vi *Twilight Zone* Oct,1987
  Celebrating, ss *F&SF* Aug,1987

MALZBERG, BARRY N.

Malzberg, Barry N. (continued)
A Galaxy Called Rome, nv *F&SF* Jul,1975
Great Science Fiction of the 20th Century, ed. Robert
Silverberg+, Crown/Avenel, 1987
On Ice, ss *Amazing* Jan,1973
Masters of Darkness II, ed. Dennis Etchison, Tor, 1988
The Queen of Lower Saigon, ss **In the Field of Fire**, ed. Jeanne Van
Buren Dann & Jack M. Dann, Tor,1987

Malzberg, Barry N. & Jack M. Dann
Bringing It Home, ss *Twilight Zone* Feb,1987

Manzione, Joseph
Candle in a Cosmic Wind, nv *Analog* Aug,1987

Mark, Jan
Buzz-Words, ss **A Quiver of Ghosts**, ed. Aiden Chambers, Bodley
Head,1987
Closer than a Brother, ss **Twisted Circuits**, ed. Mick Gowar,
Beaver,1987
They Wait, ss **They Wait and Other Spine Chillers**, ed. Lance
Salway, Pepper Press,1983
The Ghost Story Treasury, ed. Linda Sonntag, Putnam, 1987

Marks, Winston K.
He Stepped on the Devil's Tail, ss *Fantastic Universe* Feb,1955
Isaac Asimov's Magical Worlds of Fantasy #8: Devils, ed. Isaac
Asimov+, NAL/Signet, 1987

Marra, Sue
Blood Junkie, pm *2AM* Win,1987
The Music Box, pm *2AM* Spr,1987

Marsh, John
The Whisperer, ss **After Midnight Stories #3**,1987

Martin, David
Hunger, ss *New Pathways* Jan,1987

Martin, George R.R.
Closing Time, ss *IASFM* Nov,1982
Portraits of His Children, Dark Harvest, 1987
The Computer Cried Charge!, ss *Amazing* Jan,1976
Supertanks, ed. Joe W. Haldeman+, Ace, 1987
The Exit to San Breta, ss *Fantastic* Feb,1972
Fantastic Stories: Tales of the Weird and Wondrous, ed. Martin
H. Greenberg+, TSR, 1987
The Glass Flower, nv *IASFM* Sep,1986
Portraits of His Children, Dark Harvest, 1987
The Ice Dragon, nv **Dragons of Light**, ed. Orson Scott Card, Ace,1980
Portraits of His Children, Dark Harvest, 1987
In the Lost Lands, ss **Amazons #2**, ed. Jessica Amanda
Salmonson,1982
Portraits of His Children, Dark Harvest, 1987
A Very Large Array, ed. Melinda M. Snodgrass, Univ. of New
Mexico Press, 1987
Jube: Five, sl **Wild Cards** v2, ed. George R.R. Martin, Bantam,1987
Jube: Four, sl **Wild Cards** v2, ed. George R.R. Martin, Bantam,1987
Jube: One, sl **Wild Cards** v2, ed. George R.R. Martin, Bantam,1987
Jube: Seven, sl **Wild Cards** v2, ed. George R.R. Martin, Bantam,1987
Jube: Six, sl **Wild Cards** v2, ed. George R.R. Martin, Bantam,1987
Jube: Three, sl **Wild Cards** v2, ed. George R.R. Martin, Bantam,1987
Jube: Two, sl **Wild Cards** v2, ed. George R.R. Martin, Bantam,1987
The Last Super Bowl, nv *Gallery* Feb,1975
Portraits of His Children, Dark Harvest, 1987
The Lonely Songs of Laren Dorr, nv *Fantastic* May,1976
Portraits of His Children, Dark Harvest, 1987
The Monkey Treatment, nv *F&SF* Jul,1983
Masters of Darkness II, ed. Dennis Etchison, Tor, 1988
The Pear-Shaped Man, ss *Omni* Oct,1987
Portraits of His Children, nv *IASFM* Nov,1985
Portraits of His Children, Dark Harvest, 1987
The Second Kind of Loneliness, ss *Analog* Dec,1972
Portraits of His Children, Dark Harvest, 1987
Under Siege, nv *Omni* Oct,1985
Portraits of His Children, Dark Harvest, 1987
Unsound Variations, na *Amazing* Jan,1982
Portraits of His Children, Dark Harvest, 1987

Martin, George R.R. (continued)
Winter's Chill, nv **Wild Cards** v2, ed. George R.R. Martin, Bantam,1987
With Morning Comes Mistfall, ss *Analog* May,1973
Portraits of His Children, Dark Harvest, 1987

Martin, Henry
Cartoon, ct *F&SF* Jan,1987
Cartoon, ct *F&SF* Feb,1987
Cartoon, ct *F&SF* Mar,1987
Cartoon, ct *F&SF* Apr,1987
Cartoon, ct *F&SF* May,1987
Cartoon, ct *F&SF* Jun,1987
Cartoon, ct *F&SF* Jul,1987
Cartoon, ct *F&SF* Aug,1987
Cartoon, ct *F&SF* Sep,1987
Cartoon, ct *F&SF* Nov,1987
Cartoon, ct *F&SF* Dec,1987

Martin, Marcia & Eric Vinicoff
Render Unto Caesar, ss *Analog* Aug,1976
There Will Be War, Vol. VI: Guns of Darkness, ed. Jerry E.
Pournelle, Tor, 1987

Martinez, B.J.
Uncle Green-Eye, ss *F&SF* Mar,1987

Martino, Joseph P.
...Not a Prison Make, nv *Analog* Sep,1966
Battlefields Beyond Tomorrow, ed. Charles G. Waugh+,
Crown/Bonanza, 1987
Pushbutton War, ss *Analog* Aug,1960
**Isaac Asimov's Wonderful Worlds of Science Fiction #7: Space
Shuttles**, ed. Isaac Asimov+, NAL/Signet, 1987

Masear, Arthur
Cartoon, ct *Twilight Zone* Jun,1987

Mason, Lisa
Arachne, ss *Omni* Dec,1987

Mason, Tom
Cartoon, ct *Aboriginal SF* May,1987
Cartoon, ct *Twilight Zone* Aug,1987

Massie, Elizabeth
Bargains at Binsley's, ss *The Horror Show* Jan,1987
Blessed Sleep, vi *2AM* Fll,1987
Dance of the Spirit Untouched, ss *Footsteps* Nov,1987
Elizabeth Massie, iv *The Horror Show* Fll,1987
To Sooth the Savage Beast, ss *The Horror Show* Fll,1987
Willy Wonka and the L. Walker Biofair, ss *The Horror Show* Fll,1987

Massin, Jim
Game Review, gr *Salarius* v1#4,1987

Matchette, Katharine E.
The Return, ss *Apex!* #1,1987

Matheson, Richard
Big Surprise [What Was in the Box], ss *Ellery Queen's Mystery
Magazine* Apr,1959
Rod Serling's Night Gallery Reader, ed. Carol Serling+,
Dembner, 1987
Born of Man and Woman, ss *F&SF* Sum,1950
The Dark Descent, ed. David G. Hartwell, Tor, 1987
Buried Talents, ss **Masques #2**, ed. J.N. Williamson,1987
The Children of Noah, ss *Alfred Hitchcock's Mystery Magazine*
Mar,1957
Strange Maine, ed. Charles G. Waugh+, Tapley, 1986
Dress of White Silk, ss *F&SF* Oct,1951
Vamps, ed. Martin H. Greenberg+, DAW, 1987
Drink My Blood ["Drink My Red Blood", also as "Blood Son"], ss
Imagination Apr,1951
Vampires, ed. Alan Ryan, SFBC, 1987
Duel, nv *Playboy* Apr,1971
Mysterious Motoring Stories, ed. William Pattrick, W.H. Allen, 1987
Mother by Protest [also as "Trespass"], nv *Fantastic* Oct,1953
Cinemonsters, ed. Martin H. Greenberg, TSR, 1987

MATHESON, RICHARD

Matheson, Richard (continued)
  The Near Departed, vi **Masques #2**, ed. J.N. Williamson,1987
  The Test, ss *F&SF* Nov,1954
    Isaac Asimov Presents the Great SF Stories: 16 (1954), ed. Isaac Asimov+, DAW, 1987

Matheson, Richard Christian
  Beholder, ss **Whispers #4**, ed. Stuart David Schiff,1983
    Scars, Scream/Press, 1987
  Break-Up, ss **Scars**, Scream/Press,1987
  Cancelled, vi *Twilight Zone* Jun,1986
    Scars, Scream/Press, 1987
  Commuters, ss **Scars**, Scream/Press,1987
  Conversation Piece, ss **Whispers #2**, ed. Stuart David Schiff,1979
    Scars, Scream/Press, 1987
  The Dark Ones, vi *Twilight Zone* Jun,1982
    Scars, Scream/Press, 1987
  Dead End, ss **Shadows #2**, ed. Charles L. Grant,1979
    Scars, Scream/Press, 1987
  Deathbed, vi **Masques #2**, ed. J.N. Williamson,1987
  Dust, ss **Scars**, Scream/Press,1987
  Echoes, ss *The Horror Show* Win,1986
    Scars, Scream/Press, 1987
  The Good Always Come Back, ss *Twilight Zone* Apr,1986
    Scars, Scream/Press, 1987
  Goosebumps, ss **Scars**, Scream/Press,1987
  Graduation, ss *Whispers* #10,1977
    Scars, Scream/Press, 1987
  Hell, ss **Scars**, Scream/Press,1987
  Holiday, ss *Twilight Zone* Feb,1982
    Scars, Scream/Press, 1987
  Incorporation, ss **Scars**, Scream/Press,1987
  Intruder, ss *Gallery* Sep,1986
    Scars, Scream/Press, 1987
  Mobius, ss **Scars**, Scream/Press,1987
  Mr. Right, vi *Whispers* #21,1984
    Scars, Scream/Press, 1987
  Mugger, ss **Scars**, Scream/Press,1987
  Obsolete, ss **Scars**, Scream/Press,1987
  Red, vi *Night Cry* v1#6,1986
    Fantasy Tales #16,1986
    Scars, Scream/Press, 1987
  Sentences, ss **Death**, ed. Stuart David Schiff, Playboy,1982
    Scars, Scream/Press, 1987
  Third Wind, ss **Masques #1**, ed. J.N. Williamson,1984
    Scars, Scream/Press, 1987
  Timed Exposure, ss **Scars**, Scream/Press,1987
  Unknown Drives, ss **Nightmares**, ed. Charles L. Grant, Playboy,1979
    Scars, Scream/Press, 1987
  Vampire, ss **Cutting Edge**, ed. Dennis Etchison, Doubleday,1986
    Scars, Scream/Press, 1987

Matheson, Richard Christian & Richard Matheson
  Where There's a Will, ss **Dark Forces**, ed. Kirby McCauley, Viking,1980
    Scars, Scream/Press, 1987

Matheson, Richard Christian & William Relling, Jr.
  Wonderland, ss *Night Cry* v2#5,1987

Matheson, Richard & Richard Christian Matheson
  Where There's a Will, ss **Dark Forces**, ed. Kirby McCauley, Viking,1980
    Scars, Richard Christian Matheson, Scream/Press, 1987

Mathieson, Theodore
  Second Spring, nv *The Saint* Jun,1959
    Alfred Hitchcock's Book of Horror Stories: Book 6, ed. Alfred Hitchcock, Coronet, 1987

Matic, Rudy
  Ask Not, ss *Night Cry* v2#5,1987

Matthews, Jack
  The Amnesia Ballet, ss *Mundus Artium* Sum,1971
    Ghostly Populations, Johns Hopkins, 1987
  Amos Bond, the Gunsmith, ss *Michigan Quarterly Review*
    Ghostly Populations, Johns Hopkins, 1987

Matthews, Jack (continued)
  The Betrayal of the Fives, ss **Ghostly Populations**, Johns Hopkins,1987
  Dark, Dark, ss *The Antioch Review* Spr,1984
    Ghostly Populations, Johns Hopkins, 1987
  The Ghost of First Crow, ss *Niobe*
    Ghostly Populations, Johns Hopkins, 1987
  Ghostly Populations, ss **Ghostly Populations**, Johns Hopkins,1987
  If Not Us, Then Who?, ss **Ghostly Populations**, Johns Hopkins,1987
  The Immortal Dog, ss *Jeopardy*
    Ghostly Populations, Johns Hopkins, 1987
  Quest for an Unnamed Place, ss *Kansas Quarterly*
    Ghostly Populations, Johns Hopkins, 1987
  Return to an Unknown City, ss *Mississippi Valley Review*
    Ghostly Populations, Johns Hopkins, 1987
  The Secret Hour, ss *Premiere*
    Ghostly Populations, Johns Hopkins, 1987
  The Story Mac Told, ss *Western Humanities Review*
    Ghostly Populations, Johns Hopkins, 1987
  Tableau with Three Ghostly Women, ss *Chariton Review*,1979
    Ghostly Populations, Johns Hopkins, 1987
  Taking Stock, ss **Ghostly Populations**, Johns Hopkins,1987
  The Tour of the Sleeping Steamboat, ss *The Carleton Miscellany*
    Ghostly Populations, Johns Hopkins, 1987
  Toward a Distant Train, ss *Southwest Review*
    Ghostly Populations, Johns Hopkins, 1987
  The Visionary Land, ss *Michigan Quarterly Review*
    Ghostly Populations, Johns Hopkins, 1987

Matthews, Patricia
  The Children of the Sea, ss *F&SF* Feb,1987

Matuszewicz, J. Michael
  Power Times One, ss *IASFM* Feb,1983
    Tales From Isaac Asimov's Science Fiction Magazine, ed. Sheila Williams+, Harcourt Brace Jovanovich, 1986

Maugham, W. Somerset
  A Friend in Need, ss,1925
    Devils and Demons, ed. Marvin Kaye, Doubleday, 1987

Maupassant, Guy de
  The Horla, nv *Gil Blas* Oct 26,1886; *Weird Tales* Aug,1926
    Classic Stories of Mystery, Horror and Suspense, ed. Simon Petherick, Robert Hale, 1987

Maurer, Allan
  Illuminations: Building a Better Egg, ar *Twilight Zone* Dec,1987
  Illuminations: Computer Rosetta Stone, ar *Twilight Zone* Dec,1987
  Illuminations: You May Be Typecast, ar *Twilight Zone* Dec,1987
  The Other Side: Baffling Seneca Guns, ar *Twilight Zone* Dec,1987
  The Other Side: Watch Horror Movies and Get Rich, ar *Twilight Zone* Dec,1987

Maurois, Andre
  The House, vi,1931
    Rod Serling's Night Gallery Reader, ed. Carol Serling+, Dembner, 1987

Maximovic, Gerd
  The Black Ship, ss *SF International* #2,1987

May, Paula
  Resonance Ritual, ss **L. Ron Hubbard Presents Writers of the Future** v3, ed. Algis Budrys, Bridge,1987

May, Rex
  Cartoon, ct *F&SF* Jan,1987
  Cartoon, ct *F&SF* Jun,1987

Mayer, Frederick J.
  Grinning Moon, pm *Eldritch Tales* #14,1987

Mayhar, Ardath
  Down in the Dark, ss *The Horror Show* Sum,1987
  In the Tank, ss **Masques #2**, ed. J.N. Williamson,1987
  The Left Eye of God, vi *Salarius* v1#4,1987

MAYHAR, ARDATH

Mayhar, Ardath (continued)
  Neither Rest nor Refuge, ss **Tales of the Witch World**, ed. Andre
    Norton, St. Martin's,1987
  Speaking Wolf, ss *Pulpsmith* Win,1987
  That Thing in There, ss *Eldritch Tales* #13,1987
  To Trap a Demon, ss **Magic in Ithkar** #4, ed. Andre Norton & Robert
    Adams,1987

Mayor, F.M.
  Miss de Mannering of Asham, ss **The Room Opposite**, Longmans,
    Green: London,1935
  The Virago Book of Ghost Stories, ed. Richard Dalby, Virago, 1987

McAllister, Bruce
  Dream Baby, nv **In the Field of Fire**, ed. Jeanne Van Buren Dann &
    Jack M. Dann, Tor,1987
  IASFM Oct,1987
  Kingdom Come, ss *Omni* Feb,1987

McAuley, Paul J.
  Among the Stones, nv *Amazing* Jan,1987
  A Dragon for Seyour Chan, ss *Interzone* #19,1987
  The Heirs of Earth, nv *Amazing* May,1987
  The King of the Hill, ss *Interzone* #14,1985
  Interzone: The 2nd Anthology, ed. John Clute+, Simon &
    Schuster UK, 1987
  The Temporary King, nv *F&SF* Jan,1987

McCaffrey, Anne
  The Coelura, na Underwood-Miller: Columbia, PA,1983
  Nerilka's Story & The Coelura, Bantam UK, 1987
  Nerilka's Story, n. Bantam: New York hc Mar,1986
  Nerilka's Story & The Coelura, Bantam UK, 1987

McCammon, Robert R.
  Best Friends, nv **Night Visions** #4,1987
  The Deep End, ss **Night Visions** #4,1987
  Doom City, ss **Doom City**, ed. Charles L. Grant, Tor,1987
  Fragments of Horror, ms *The Horror Show* Spr,1987
  A Life in the Day of, ss **Night Visions** #4,1987
  Lights Out [from **Swan Song**], ex Pocket: New York Jun,1987
  Twilight Zone Aug,1987
  Swan Song, ex Pocket: New York Jun,1987
  The Horror Show Spr,1987
  Yellachile's Cage, ss **World Fantasy Convention Program Book**
    #13,1987

McCammon, Robert R. & William J. Grabowski
  Interview with Robert R. McCammon, iv *The Horror Show* Spr,1987

McCammon, Robert R. & Rodney A. Labbe
  An Interview with Robert McCammon, iv *Footsteps* Nov,1987

McCarthy, Gerry
  Entropanto, ss **Gollancz - Sunday Times Best SF Stories**,
    Gollancz,1987

McCormack, Ford
  Hell-Bent [contest story], ss *F&SF* Jun,1951
  Devils and Demons, ed. Marvin Kaye, Doubleday, 1987

McDaniel, Mary Catherine
  A Little of What You Fancy, ss **L. Ron Hubbard Presents Writers of
    the Future** v3, ed. Algis Budrys, Bridge,1987

McDevitt, Jack
  Dutchman, nv *IASFM* Feb,1987
  In the Tower, nv **Universe** #17, ed. Terry Carr,1987
  To Hell with the Stars, ss *IASFM* Dec,1987

McDowell, Michael
  Halley's Passing, ss *Twilight Zone* Jun,1987

McGregor, Matt
  To Sleep Perchance To Dream, ss *Minnesota Fantasy Review* #1,1987

McIntyre, George A.
  Our Christmas Spirit, ss *Fantasy Tales* #16,1986

McIntyre, Vonda N.
  Of Mist, and Grass, and Sand, nv *Analog* Oct,1973
  6 Decades: The Best of Analog, ed. Stanley Schmidt, Davis, 1986
  Great Science Fiction of the 20th Century, ed. Robert
    Silverberg+, Crown/Avenel, 1987

McKay, Ross
  The Indian's Grave, ss **After Midnight Stories** #3,1987

McKenna, Richard
  Casey Agonistes, ss *F&SF* Sep,1958
  Masters of Darkness II, ed. Dennis Etchison, Tor, 1988

McLaughlin, Cooper
  The Order of the Peacock Angel, nv *F&SF* Jan,1987

McLaughlin, Dean
  Hawk Among the Sparrows, na *Analog* Jul,1968
  Battlefields Beyond Tomorrow, ed. Charles G. Waugh+,
    Crown/Bonanza, 1987

McMorrow, Will F.
  Man o' Dreams, ss *Argosy All-Story Weekly* Jan 5,1929
  **Isaac Asimov's Wonderful Worlds of Science Fiction #6:
    Neanderthals**, ed. Isaac Asimov+, NAL/Signet, 1987

McNamara, Peter
  Editorial, ed *Aphelion* #5,1987

McPherson, Michael C.
  Every Garbage Dump Has One, vi *Haunts* #9,1987
  Expert Witness, vi *2AM* Win,1987

McSherry, Frank D., Jr.
  Introduction, in
    Nightmares in Dixie, ed. Frank D. McSherry, Jr.+, August House,
    1987

Meade, Stephen
  The Mirror Monster, ss *Night Cry* v2#3,1987

Medcalf, Robert Randolph, Jr.
  Mindsword, pm *Space & Time* #72,1987
  Werewolfgirl, pm *Eldritch Tales* #13,1987
  Zombie Bride, pm *Eldritch Tales* #14,1987

Meier, Shirley
  Trave, ss **Magic in Ithkar** #4, ed. Andre Norton & Robert Adams,1987

Meisner, Richard D.
  Universe--The Ultimate Artifact?, ar *Analog* Apr,1987

Melton, Henry
  Partly Murphy, ss *Analog* May,1987

Memmott, David
  The Aka Fragments [Part 1], sl *New Pathways* Apr,1987
  The Aka Fragments [Part 2], sl *New Pathways* Aug,1987
  The Aka Fragments [Part 3], sl *New Pathways* Nov,1987

Mercadel, Walter F.
  Porcinity's Palace, ss *Space & Time* #73,1987

Merchant, Paul
  from A Life of Copernicus, pm *Ice River* Sum,1987

Meredith, Jerry & D.E. Smirl
  Dream in a Bottle, ss **L. Ron Hubbard Presents Writers of the
    Future** v2, ed. Algis Budrys, Bridge,1986
  The 1987 Annual World's Best SF, ed. Donald A. Wollheim+,
    DAW, 1987

Meredith, Richard C.
  At the Narrow Passage, n. Putnam: New York,1973
  Timeliner Trilogy, Arrow, 1987
  No Brother, No Friend, n. Doubleday: Garden City, NY,1976
  Timeliner Trilogy, Arrow, 1987

MEREDITH, RICHARD C.   **MOON, ELIZABETH N.**

Meredith, Richard C. (continued)
  Vestiges of Time, n. Doubleday: Garden City, NY,1978
  Timeliner Trilogy, Arrow, 1987

Merril, Judith
  The Shrine of Temptation, ss *Fantastic* Apr,1962
    Fantastic Stories: Tales of the Weird and Wondrous, ed. Martin
      H. Greenberg+, TSR, 1987

Merseyside Fairy Story Collective, The
  Snow White, ss *Spare Rib* #51,1972
    Don't Bet on the Prince, ed. Jack Zipes, Methuen, 1987

Merwin, W.S.
  Kanaloa, pm *New Yorker* Apr 13,1987

Metzger, Deena
  In the Beginning There Was Humming [from "What Dinah Thought"],
    ex **Hear the Silence**, ed. Irene Zahava, Crossing Press,1986
  The Tree on the Mountain [from "What Dinah Thought"], ex **Hear the
    Silence**, ed. Irene Zahava, Crossing Press,1986

Metzger, Robert A.
  True Magic, ss *Aboriginal SF* Nov,1987
  A Unfiltered Man, ss *Aboriginal SF* Sep,1987

Meyer, William
  The Real, pm *Pulpsmith* Win,1987

Miesel, Sandra
  The Book-Healer, ss **Magic in Ithkar** #4, ed. Andre Norton & Robert
    Adams,1987
  The Sword That Wept, ss *Amazing* Sep,1987

Milan, Victor
  Feast of John the Baptist, ss,1982
    A Very Large Array, ed. Melinda M. Snodgrass, Univ. of New
      Mexico Press, 1987
  With a Little Help From His Friends, nv **Wild Cards** v2, ed. George
    R.R. Martin, Bantam,1987

Miller, G. Wayne
  G. Wayne Miller, iv *The Horror Show* Fll,1987
  Gnawing, ss *The Horror Show* Spr,1987
  God of Self, ss *The Horror Show* Fll,1987
  Not Just Traces of Me, vi *The Horror Show* Sum,1987
  Nothing There, ss *The Horror Show* Fll,1987
  We Who Are His Followers, ss *The Horror Show* Win,1987
  Windham's Folly, ss *Space & Time* #73,1987
  Wiping the Slate Clean, ss **Masques** #2, ed. J.N. Williamson,1987

Miller, Holmes
  Solo, ss *Grue* #5,1987

Miller, Ian
  The Angle of Consciousness, pi *Interzone* #21,1987

Miller, John J.
  Half Past Dead, nv **Wild Cards** v2, ed. George R.R. Martin,
    Bantam,1987
  Ouroboros, nv **A Very Large Array**, ed. Melinda M. Snodgrass,
    University of New Mexico Press,1987

Miller, P. Schuyler
  Over the River, ss *Unknown* Apr,1941
    Vampires, ed. Alan Ryan, SFBC, 1987

Miller, Rob Hollis
  Farewells on the Melon Bridge, pm *New Pathways* Jan,1987

Miller, Sasha
  Jamie Burke and the Queen of England, ss *F&SF* Jun,1987
  To Rebuild the Eyrie, nv **Tales of the Witch World**, ed. Andre Norton,
    St. Martin's,1987

Miller, Steph
  The Sponge, pm *Space & Time* #72,1987

Miller, Walter M., Jr.
  The Darfsteller, na *Astounding* Jan,1955
    Isaac Asimov Presents the Great SF Stories: 17 (1955), ed. Isaac
      Asimov+, DAW, 1988
  I Made You, ss *Astounding* Mar,1954
    Supertanks, ed. Joe W. Haldeman+, Ace, 1987
  The Little Creeps, nv *Amazing* Dec,1951
    Amazing Science Fiction Stories: The Wild Years 1946-1955, ed.
      Martin H. Greenberg, TSR, 1987

Milton, Patrice & Joseph Green
  The Speckled Gantry, ss **Destinies** v1#2, ed. James Baen,1979
    **Isaac Asimov's Wonderful Worlds of Science Fiction #7: Space
      Shuttles**, ed. Isaac Asimov+, NAL/Signet, 1987

Miner, Brad
  Reaching for Paradise, nv **Angels in Hell**, ed. Janet Morris, Baen,1987

Mink Mole
  Traveler's Report on Florida's World Famous 'Alligator Alley', fa *New
    Pathways* Nov,1987

Mink Mole & Ferret
  Grow Your Own Baby, cs *New Pathways* Nov,1987
  I Was a Teenage Reptile, cs *New Pathways* Aug,1987
  Nuclear FX, cs *New Pathways* Jan,1987
  Nuclear FX, cs *New Pathways* Aug,1987
  Nuclear FX, cs *New Pathways* Nov,1987

Minnion, Keith
  The Prince's Birthday, ss *The Dragon* Jun,1987

Mirolla, Michael
  Rules of Conduct, ss **Tesseracts 2**, ed. Phyllis Gotlieb & Douglas
    Barbour, Press Porcepic: Victoria,1987

Mitchell, Edward Page
  The Devilish Rat, ss *The Sun* Jan 27,1878
    Devils and Demons, ed. Marvin Kaye, Doubleday, 1987
  The Last Cruise of the Judas Iscariot, ss *The Sun* Apr 16,1882
    Strange Maine, ed. Charles G. Waugh+, Tapley, 1986

Mitchell, Joanne
  Scout's Honor, ss *Aboriginal SF* Nov,1987

Moffett, Judith
  Surviving, nv *F&SF* Jun,1986
    The Year's Best Science Fiction, Fourth Annual Collection, ed.
      Gardner R. Dozois, St. Martin's, 1987
    Terry Carr's Best Science Fiction and Fantasy of the Year #16,
      ed. Terry Carr, Tor, 1987

Molesworth, Mary Louisa
  The Story of a King's Daughter, ss **Christmas-Tree Land**, London:
    Macmillan,1884
    Victorian Fairy Tales, ed. Jack Zipes, Methuen, 1987

Molloy, Frances
  The Irish Fairy Tale, vi **The Female Line: Northern Irish Writers**
    Mad and Bad Fairies, ed. Anonymous, Attic Press, 1987

Monteleone, Thomas F.
  The Night Is Freezing Fast, ss **Masques** #2, ed. J.N. Williamson,1987
  Taking the Night Train, nv *Night Voyages* Spr,1981
    Masters of Darkness II, ed. Dennis Etchison, Tor, 1988
  Yesterday's Child, ss *Grue* #5,1987

Montgomerie, Lee
  Book Reviews, br *Interzone* #19,1987
  Book Reviews, br *Interzone* #20,1987
  Book Reviews, br *Interzone* #21,1987
  Book Reviews, br *Interzone* #22,1987
  War and/or Peace, ss *Interzone* #11,1985
    Interzone: The 2nd Anthology, ed. John Clute+, Simon &
      Schuster UK, 1987

Moon, Elizabeth N.
  A Delicate Adjustment, na *Analog* Feb,1987

MOON, ELIZABETH N.   **MUNSTER, BILL**

Moon, Elizabeth N. (continued)
  Just Another Day at the Weather Service, vi *Analog* Nov,1987

Moorcock, Michael
  **The Adventures of Una Persson and Catherine Cornelius in the
    Twentieth Century**, n. Quartet: London,1976
    The Cornelius Chronicles, Vol. III, Avon, 1987
  The Alchemist's Question, n. **The Opium General**, Harper &
    Row,1984
    The Cornelius Chronicles, Vol. III, Avon, 1987
  The Frozen Cardinal, ss **Other Edens**, ed. Christopher Evans &
    Robert Holdstock, Unwin: London,1987
  John Dee's Song, pm *Back Brain Recluse* #7,1987
  The Murderer's Song, nv **Tales from the Forbidden Planet**, ed. Roz
    Kaveney, Titan,1987
  Pierrot on the Moon, pm *Back Brain Recluse* #7,1987

Moorcock, Michael & Chris Reed
  Michael Moorcock, iv *Back Brain Recluse* #7,1987

Moore, Alan
  A Hypothetical Lizard, nv **Liavek: Wizard's Row**, ed. Will Shetterly &
    Emma Bull, Ace,1987

Moore, Alan & Neil Gaiman
  Alan Moore Interview, iv *American Fantasy* Win,1987

Moore, C.L.
  No Woman Born, nv *Astounding* Dec,1944
    Robert Silverberg's Worlds of Wonder, ed. Robert Silverberg,
    Warner, 1987
  Shambleau, nv *Weird Tales* Nov,1933
    Vampires, ed. Alan Ryan, SFBC, 1987

Moore, John F.
  Lineage, vi *Salarius* v1#4,1987
  Trackdown, ss *Aboriginal SF* Feb,1987

Moore, Roger E.
  A Stone's Throw Away, ss **DragonLance Tales** v1, Margaret Weis &
    Tracy Hickman, TSR,1987

Moore, Rudin
  A Ceres Situation, ss **Ultra-Vue and Selected Peripheral Visions**,
    self published,1987
  Hit Me, nv **Ultra-Vue and Selected Peripheral Visions**, self
    published,1987
  The Hoodoo, na **Ultra-Vue and Selected Peripheral Visions**, self
    published,1987
  Ultra-Vue, n. **Ultra-Vue and Selected Peripheral Visions**, self
    published,1987
  Wait a Minute!, ss **Ultra-Vue and Selected Peripheral Visions**, self
    published,1987

Moore, Ward
  Peacebringer [Sword of Peace], nv *Amazing* Mar,1950
    Amazing Science Fiction Stories: The Wild Years 1946-1955, ed.
    Martin H. Greenberg, TSR, 1987

Moorhouse, Sue
  Rika's World, ss **Gollancz - Sunday Times Best SF Stories**,
    Gollancz,1987

Moran, Daniel Keys & Gladys Prebehalla
  Realtime, nv *IASFM* Aug,1984
    Tales From Isaac Asimov's Science Fiction Magazine, ed. Sheila
    Williams+, Harcourt Brace Jovanovich, 1986

Morlan, A.R.
  A.R. Morlan, iv *The Horror Show* Fll,1987
  Bub and the Zomb Boys, ss *The Horror Show* Fll,1987
  The Children of the Kingdom Quiz, qz *The Horror Show* Jan,1987
  The Cuttlefish, ss *Twilight Zone* Oct,1987
  Dear D.B. ..., ss *Night Cry* v2#5,1987
  It's Alive Again! The Return of the Nit-Picky, Utterly Trivial, Totally
    Picayune Horror-Fantasy (and What the Heck, a Little Sci-Fi)
    Movie Quiz Part III, qz *The Horror Show* Fll,1987
  Just Another Bedtime Story, ss *Night Cry* v2#4,1987

Morlan, A.R. (continued)
  The Last Bedtime Story, ss *Grue* #6,1987
  The "Monster Mash" Quiz, qz *The Horror Show* Win,1987
  Night Skirt, ss *The Horror Show* Win,1987
  The On'ner, ss *Grue* #4,1987
  The Second Nit-Picky, Utterly Trivial, Totally Picayune Horror-Fantasy
    Movie Quiz -- or -- Trivial Lives, II, qz *The Horror Show* Sum,1987
  The "There Was an Old Woman" Quiz, qz *The Horror Show* Spr,1987
  Tomb of Nine Hundred Days, ss *The Horror Show* Fll,1987
  What the Janitor Found, pm *Night Cry* v2#3,1987
  The Wi'ching Well, ss *The Horror Show* Jan,1987

Morressy, John
  A Legend of Fair Women, nv *F&SF* Sep,1987
  The Quality of Murphy, nv *F&SF* Mar,1987

Morris, Chris
  Handmaids In Hell, ss **Angels in Hell**, ed. Janet Morris, Baen,1987
  Hearts and Minds, nv **Fever Season**, ed. C.J. Cherryh, DAW,1987
  Night Action, ss **Festival Moon**, ed. C.J. Cherryh, DAW,1987
  The Ransom of Hellcat, nv **Masters of Hell**, ed. Janet Morris et al,
    Baen,1987
  Snowballs in Hell, nv **Crusaders in Hell**, ed. Janet Morris, New York:
    Baen,1987

Morris, Chris & Janet Morris
  The Nature of Hell, ss **Crusaders in Hell**, ed. Janet Morris, New York:
    Baen,1987
  Sword Play, na **Festival Moon**, ed. C.J. Cherryh, DAW,1987

Morris, Janet
  Gilgamesh Redux, nv **Crusaders in Hell**, ed. Janet Morris, New York:
    Baen,1987
  Instant Karma, nv **Fever Season**, ed. C.J. Cherryh, DAW,1987
  Sea Change, nv **Masters of Hell**, ed. Janet Morris et al, Baen,1987
  Sea of Stiffs, nv **Angels in Hell**, ed. Janet Morris, Baen,1987
  Wake of the Riddler, nv **Aftermath**, ed. Robert Lynn Asprin & Lynn
    Abbey, Ace,1987

Morris, Janet & Chris Morris
  The Nature of Hell, ss **Crusaders in Hell**, ed. Janet Morris, New York:
    Baen,1987
  Sword Play, na **Festival Moon**, ed. C.J. Cherryh, DAW,1987

Morrison, Michael A.
  The American Nightmare: The Fiction of Dennis Etchison, ar *The
    Horror Show* Win,1987

Morrow, James
  Spelling God with the Wrong Blocks, ss *F&SF* May,1987
  Veritas, nv **Synergy** v1, ed. George Zebrowski,1987

Mortensen, Nancy
  The Well, ss *SF International* #2,1987

Mortum, Crematia & Kathleen E. Jurgens
  Interview with Crematia Mortum (Roberta Solomon), iv *2AM* Spr,1987

Mosiman, Billie Sue
  Final Dreams, ss *Mage* Win,1987
  Morbid Descent, ss *2AM* Sum,1987

Moudy, Walter F.
  The Survivor, nv *Amazing* May,1965
    Battlefields Beyond Tomorrow, ed. Charles G. Waugh+,
    Crown/Bonanza, 1987

Mueller, Richard
  Bless This Ship, ss *F&SF* Sep,1987

Munby, A.N.L.
  A Christmas Game, ss,1950
    Christmas Ghosts, ed. Kathryn Cramer+, Arbor House, 1987

Munster, Bill
  From the Editor, ed *Footsteps* Nov,1987

Munster, Bill & F. Paul Wilson
  An Interview with F. Paul Wilson, iv *Footsteps* Nov,1987

Munster, Bill & Gahan Wilson
  An Interview with Gahan Wilson, in *Footsteps* Nov,1987

Murphy, Pat
  Clay Devils, ss *Twilight Zone* Apr,1987
  Rachel in Love, nv *IASFM* Apr,1987
  With Four Lean Hounds, ss **Sword and Sorceress #1**, ed. Marion
    Zimmer Bradley,1984
    Young Witches & Warlocks, ed. Isaac Asimov+, Harper & Row,
    1987

Murray, Paula Helm
  Kayli's Fire, ss **Sword and Sorceress #4**, ed. Marion Zimmer
    Bradley,1987

Murray, Will
  Lester Dent and Lynn Lash: An Introduction, in
    The Sinister Ray, Lester Dent, Gryphon, 1987

Nadramia, Peggy
  conGRUEities, ed *Grue* #4,1987
  conGRUEities, ed *Grue* #5,1987
  conGRUEities, ed *Grue* #6,1987

Nagata, Linda
  Spectral Expectations, ss *Analog* Apr,1987

Nazarian, Vera
  Kihar, nv **Red Sun of Darkover**, ed. Marion Zimmer Bradley & The
    Friends of Darkover, DAW,1987

Nelms, Cheryl L.
  Don't Fuck With My Brain, pm *2AM* Fll,1987

Nelson, Cheryl Fuller
  Just a Little Souvenir, ss **Shadows #10**, ed. Charles L. Grant,1987

Nelson, K.H.
  Your Soul to Keep, ss *Space & Time* #73,1987

Nelson, Ray Faraday
  A Dream of Amerasia, ar **Philip K. Dick: The Dream Connection**, D.
    Scott Apel, Permanent Press,1987

Nesbit, Edith
  John Charrington's Wedding, ss
    The Dark Descent, ed. David G. Hartwell, Tor, 1987
  The Last of the Dragons, ss,1900
    Victorian Fairy Tales, ed. Jack Zipes, Methuen, 1987
  Man-Size in Marble, ss,1886
    Tales of the Dark 2, ed. Lincoln Child, St. Martin's, 1987
  The Prince, Two Mice and Some Kitchen-Maids, ss
    The Magic Kiss and Other Tales of Princes and Princesses, ed.
    Tony Bradman, Blackie, 1987
  The Violet Car, ss **Fear**, S. Paul: London,1910
    The Virago Book of Ghost Stories, ed. Richard Dalby, Virago, 1987

Neville, Gail
  The Resurrection, ss *Aphelion* #5,1987

Newman, Kim
  Mutant Popcorn, mr *Interzone* #20,1987
  The Next-But-One Man, ss *Interzone* #19,1987
  Patricia's Profession, ss *Interzone* #14,1985
    Interzone: The 2nd Anthology, ed. John Clute+, Simon &
    Schuster UK, 1987

Newman, R.L. & C. Taylor
  Eight Legs Hath the Spider, vi *Haunts* #9,1987

Nichols, Leigh & Dean R. Koontz
  Dean R. Koontz, iv *The Horror Show* Sum,1987

Nicholson, Geoff
  Time Travel for Fun and Profit, ss **Gollancz - Sunday Times Best SF
    Stories**, Gollancz,1987

Nicoll, Gregory
  Galileo Saw the Truth, pm *Fantasy Crossroads* Mar,1977
    There Will Be War, Vol. VI: Guns of Darkness, ed. Jerry E.
    Pournelle, Tor, 1987

Niditch, B.Z.
  Holography, pm *Ice River* Sum,1987

Nielsen, Helen
  The Room at the End of the Hall, ss *Alfred Hitchcock's Mystery
    Magazine* Oct,1973
    Alfred Hitchcock's Book of Horror Stories: Book 6, ed. Alfred
    Hitchcock, Coronet, 1987

Nisbet, Hume
  The Old Portrait, ss **Stories Weird and Wonderful**, F.V. White:
    London,1900
    Dracula's Brood, ed. Richard Dalby, Crucible, 1987
  The Vampire Maid, ss **Stories Weird and Wonderful**, F.V. White:
    London,1900
    Dracula's Brood, ed. Richard Dalby, Crucible, 1987

Niven, Larry
  The Borderland of Sol, nv *Analog* Jan,1975
    Beyond the Stars, ed. Isaac Asimov, Severn House, 1987
  Convergent Series [The Long Night], ss *F&SF* Mar,1967
    Mathenauts, ed. Rudy Rucker, Arbor House, 1987
  Neutron Star, nv *If* Oct,1966
    Great Science Fiction of the 20th Century, ed. Robert
    Silverberg+, Crown/Avenel, 1987
  The Smoke Ring [Part 1 of 4], sl *Analog* Jan,1987
  The Smoke Ring [Part 2 of 4], sl *Analog* Feb,1987
  The Smoke Ring [Part 3 of 4], sl *Analog* Mar,1987
  The Smoke Ring [Part 4 of 4], sl *Analog* Apr,1987
  There's a Wolf in My Time Machine, ss *F&SF* Jun,1971
    Robert Adams' Book of Alternate Worlds, ed. Robert Adams+,
    NAL/Signet, 1987

Nolan, William F.
  Dark Winner, ss *Whispers* #9,1976
    House Shudders, ed. Martin H. Greenberg+, DAW, 1987
  "Just Like Wild Bob", ss,1964
    Mysterious Motoring Stories, ed. William Pattrick, W.H. Allen, 1987
  My Name Is Dolly, ss **Whispers #6**, ed. Stuart David Schiff,1987
  The Return, ms *The Horror Show* Jan,1987
  The Yard, ss **Masques #2**, ed. J.N. Williamson,1987

Noonan, Bode
  Fruit Drink, ss **Red Beans and Rice**, Crossing Press,1986
    Hear the Silence, ed. Irene Zahava, Crossing Press, 1986

Norton, Andre
  Introduction, in
    Tales of the Witch World, ed. Andre Norton, Tor, 1987
  Moon Mirror, ss **Hecate's Cauldron**, ed. Susan M. Shwartz, DAW,1982
    **A Southern Fantasy: 13th World Fantasy Convention Program
    Book**, ed. Ron Lindahn+, Nashville World Fantasy Convention,
    1987
  Of the Shaping of Ulm's Heir, nv **Tales of the Witch World**, ed. Andre
    Norton, St. Martin's,1987
  Rider on a Mountain, ss **Friends of the Horseclans**, ed. Robert
    Adams & Pamela Crippen Adams, Signet,1987

Norton, Andre, Nancy Garcia & Mary Frances Zambreno
  Andre Norton Interview and Bibliography, iv *American Fantasy*
    Win,1987

Norton, Mary
  Paul's Tale, ss *Story*,1945
    Ready or Not, ed. Joan Kahn, Greenwillow, 1987

NOURSE, ALAN E.

Nourse, Alan E.
Mirror, Mirror [The Mirror], nv *Fantastic* Jun,1960
   Battlefields Beyond Tomorrow, ed. Charles G. Waugh +,
      Crown/Bonanza, 1987

Novak, Kate & Laura Hickman
   Heart of Goldmoon, na **DragonLance Tales** v3, Margaret Weis &
      Tracy Hickman, TSR,1987

Nower, Joyce
   Ephesus, pm *Ice River* Sum,1987
   On the Path to Athene Proneia, Delphi, 1984, pm *Ice River* Sum,1987

Nussbaum, Albert F.
   A Left-Handed Profession [also as "The Counterfeit Conman"], ss
      Alfred Hitchcock's Mystery Magazine Nov,1975
      Alfred Hitchcock's Book of Horror Stories: Book 6, ed. Alfred
         Hitchcock, Coronet, 1987

O'Brien, Fitz-James
   What Was It?, ss *Harper's* Mar,1859
      The Dark Descent, ed. David G. Hartwell, Tor, 1987

O'Connor, Clairr
   Ophelia's Tale, ss **Mad and Bad Fairies**, ed. Anonymous, Attic
      Press,1987

O'Connor, Flannery
   Good Country People, ss,1955
      The Dark Descent, ed. David G. Hartwell, Tor, 1987

O'Connor, William D.
   The Ghost, na Putnam: New York,1867
      Christmas Ghosts, ed. Kathryn Cramer +, Arbor House, 1987

O'Donnell, Elliott
   The Mystery of Beechcroft Farm, ss *Pearson's*,1932
      Poltergeist: Tales of Deadly Ghosts, ed. Peter Haining, Severn
         House, 1987

O'Donnell, Kevin, Jr.
   The Million Dollar Day, nv *Analog* Oct,1987

O'Donohoe, Nick
   Dagger-Flight, ss **DragonLance Tales** v2, Margaret Weis & Tracy
      Hickman, TSR,1987
   Hunting Destiny, nv **DragonLance Tales** v3, Margaret Weis & Tracy
      Hickman, TSR,1987
   Love and Ale, nv **DragonLance Tales** v1, Margaret Weis & Tracy
      Hickman, TSR,1987; *The Dragon* May,1987

O'Malley, Kathleen
   The Demon's Gift, nv **Magic in Ithkar** #4, ed. Andre Norton & Robert
      Adams,1987

O'Neill, Gene
   The Armless Conductor, ss *F&SF* Sep,1987

O'Sullivan, Vincent
   Will, ss **The Green Window**,1899
      Dracula's Brood, ed. Richard Dalby, Crucible, 1987

Oates, Joyce Carol
   Haunted, nv **The Architecture of Fear**, ed. Kathryn Cramer & Peter
      D. Pautz, Arbor House,1987
   Night-Side, nv **Night-Side**,1977
      The Dark Descent, ed. David G. Hartwell, Tor, 1987
   The Others, ss *Twilight Zone* Aug,1987

Odden, Mike
   It Speaks, ed *Minnesota Fantasy Review* #1,1987

Offutt, Andrew J.
   Homecoming, nv **Aftermath**, ed. Robert Lynn Asprin & Lynn Abbey,
      Ace,1987

Oliver, Chad
   Transformer, ss *F&SF* Nov,1954
      Isaac Asimov Presents the Great SF Stories: 16 (1954), ed. Isaac
         Asimov +, DAW, 1987

Oliver, Steven G.
   The Waters from Time, vi *Amazing* Sep,1987

Olivier, Edith
   The Night Nurse's Story, ss,1933
      The Virago Book of Ghost Stories, ed. Richard Dalby, Virago, 1987

Olson, Donald
   Kisses and Chloroform, ss *Alfred Hitchcock's Mystery Magazine*
      Jul,1974
      Alfred Hitchcock's Book of Horror Stories: Book 6, ed. Alfred
         Hitchcock, Coronet, 1987

Olson, Paul F.
   Homecoming, ss *The Horror Show* Jan,1987
   Iocus: A Retrospective, ar *The Horror Show* Spr,1987

Olson, Paul F. & J.K. Potter
   Interview with J.K. Potter, iv *The Horror Show* Jan,1987

Oltion, Jerry
   The Getaway Special, ss *Analog* Apr,1985
      **Isaac Asimov's Wonderful Worlds of Science Fiction #7: Space
         Shuttles**, ed. Isaac Asimov +, NAL/Signet, 1987
   In the Creation Science Laboratory, ss *Analog* Sep,1987
   The Love Song of Laura Morrison, ss *Analog* Aug,1987
   Neither Rain Nor Weirdness, ss *Analog* Nov,1987
   What's a Nice Girl Like You..., vi *Analog* Oct,1987

Onio
   Cartoon, ct *Twilight Zone* Oct,1987
   Cartoon, ct *Twilight Zone* Dec,1987

Onions, Oliver
   The Beckoning Fair One, nv
      The Dark Descent, ed. David G. Hartwell, Tor, 1987
   Benlian, nv **Widdershins**, Secker,1911
      Tales of the Dark 2, ed. Lincoln Child, St. Martin's, 1987
   The Master of the House, ss **The Painted Face**, Heinemann,1929
      Werewolf: Horror Stories of the Man Beast, ed. Peter Haining,
         Severn House, 1987

Ordish, Jenny
   Bundles of Joy, ss **Gollancz - Sunday Times Best SF Stories**,
      Gollancz,1987

Orr, William F.
   Euclid Alone, nv **Orbit #16**, ed. Damon Knight,1975
      Mathenauts, ed. Rudy Rucker, Arbor House, 1987

Ounsley, Simon
   Adam Found, ss *Interzone* #17,1986
      Gollancz/Sunday Times SF Competition Stories, Anonymous,
         Gollancz, 1987
   Editorial, ed *Interzone* #19,1987

Ounsley, Simon, John Clute & David Pringle
   Introduction, in
      Interzone: The 2nd Anthology, ed. John Clute +, Simon &
         Schuster UK, 1987

Owens, Barbara
   Chain, ss *F&SF* Jul,1987
   The Greenhill Gang, ss *F&SF* Feb,1987

Pace, Tom & Dan DeLong
   Cheap But Not Dirty: Proposal for a Spaceplane, ar *Analog* Mar,1987

Page, Dave
   Hawthorne and Mailer, ar *Minnesota Fantasy Review* #1,1987

Page, Gerald W.
   The Vampire in the Mirror, nv *Weirdbook* #22,1987

PAHULE, EDWARD J.

Pahule, Edward J.
Reason Enough, vi *The Horror Show* Spr,1987

Palmer, David R.
Emergence, nv *Analog* Jan 5,1981
6 Decades: The Best of Analog, ed. Stanley Schmidt, Davis, 1986

Palmer, John Phillips
The Invitation, pm *Weirdbook* #22,1987

Palwick, Susan
Ever After, nv *IASFM* Nov,1987
The Visitation, ss *Amazing* Sep,1987

Pangborn, Edgar
Angel's Egg, nv *Galaxy* Jun,1951
Great Science Fiction of the 20th Century, ed. Robert Silverberg+, Crown/Avenel, 1987
Longtooth, nv *F&SF* Jan,1970
Strange Maine, ed. Charles G. Waugh+, Tapley, 1986
The Music Master of Babylon, nv *Galaxy* Nov,1954
Isaac Asimov Presents the Great SF Stories: 16 (1954), ed. Isaac Asimov+, DAW, 1987

Pardoe, Darroll & Rosemary Pardoe
In the Footsteps of M.R. James, ar
Masters of Fantasy 3: M.R. James, M.R. James, British Fantasy Society, 1987

Pardoe, Rosemary & Richard Dalby
Introduction, in
Ghosts and Scholars, ed. Rosemary Pardoe+, Crucible, 1987

Pardoe, Rosemary & Darroll Pardoe
In the Footsteps of M.R. James, ar
Masters of Fantasy 3: M.R. James, M.R. James, British Fantasy Society, 1987

Parente, Audrey
A Step Back in Time, pm *Minnesota Fantasy Review* #1,1987

Park, John
Retrieval, ss **Tesseracts 2**, ed. Phyllis Gotlieb & Douglas Barbour, Press Porcepic: Victoria,1987

Parsons, Charmaine
Tenant Above, vi *Mage* Spr,1986
Mage FII,1987

Parsonson, Manny
Blood and Tears, nv *Space & Time* #73,1987

Partridge, Diann
Salt, ss **Red Sun of Darkover**, ed. Marion Zimmer Bradley & The Friends of Darkover, DAW,1987

Patterson, Teresa
Star Mistress, pm *Salarius* v1#4,1987

Pattrick, William
Introduction, in
Mysterious Motoring Stories, ed. William Pattrick, W.H. Allen, 1987

Paulsen, Stephen
Errand Run, vi *Aphelion* #5,1987
Logic Loop, vi *Aphelion* #5,1987

Pautz, Peter D.
Introduction, in
The Architecture of Fear, ed. Kathryn Cramer+, Arbor House, 1987

Paxson, Diana L.
Blood Dancer, ss **Sword and Sorceress** #4, ed. Marion Zimmer Bradley,1987
A Different Kind of Victory, nv **Red Sun of Darkover**, ed. Marion Zimmer Bradley & The Friends of Darkover, DAW,1987

Pearce, Philippa
Auntie, ss **Who's Afraid? and Other Strange Stories**, Kestrel/Penguin,1986
Black Eyes, ss **Black Eyes and Other Spine Chillers**, ed. Lance Salway, Pepper Press,1981
Who's Afraid? and Other Strange Stories, Morrow/Greenwillow, 1987
A Christmas Pudding Improves with Keeping, ss **Who's Afraid? and Other Strange Stories**, Kestrel/Penguin,1986
The Hirn, ss **Who's Afraid? and Other Strange Stories**, Kestrel/Penguin,1986
His Loving Sister, ss **Ghost After Ghost**, ed. Aiden Chambers, Kestrel,1982
Who's Afraid? and Other Strange Stories, Morrow/Greenwillow, 1987
Mr. Hurrel's Tallboy, ss **Who's Afraid? and Other Strange Stories**, Kestrel/Penguin,1986
A Prince in Another Place, ss **They Wait and Other Spine Chillers**, ed. Lance Salway, Pepper Press,1983
Who's Afraid? and Other Strange Stories, Morrow/Greenwillow, 1987
The Road It Went By, ss **Outsiders**, ed. Bryan Newton, Collins Educational,1985
Who's Afraid? and Other Strange Stories, Morrow/Greenwillow, 1987
Samantha and the Ghost, ss
Who's Afraid? and Other Strange Stories, Morrow/Greenwillow, 1987
Who's Afraid?, ss **Hundreds and Hundreds**, Puffin,1984
Who's Afraid? and Other Strange Stories, Morrow/Greenwillow, 1987
The Yellow Ball, ss **Who's Afraid? and Other Strange Stories**, Kestrel/Penguin,1986

Pearson, Wendy G.
The Green Man of Knowledge, ss **Tesseracts 2**, ed. Phyllis Gotlieb & Douglas Barbour, Press Porcepic: Victoria,1987

Peary, Danny
A Shaggy Dog's Tail, nv **DragonLance Tales** v2, Margaret Weis & Tracy Hickman, TSR,1987

Peattie, Elia Wilkinson
Their Dear Little Ghost, ss
Christmas Ghosts, ed. Kathryn Cramer+, Arbor House, 1987

Peck, Claudia
The Gentle Art of Making Enemies, nv **Magic in Ithkar** #4, ed. Andre Norton & Robert Adams,1987

Peeples, Mark E., Ph.D.
Huntington's Handle, ar *Analog* Oct,1987

Peirce, Hayford
Doing Well While Doing Good, ss *Analog* Aug,1975
Imperial Stars, Vol. 2: Republic and Empire, ed. Jerry E. Pournelle, Baen, 1987

Pelegrimas, Marthayn
Heavy Breathing, pm *2AM* Spr,1987
Living Donor, ss *SPWAO Showcase* #6,1987

Penn-Freeman, Margie
Tooley's Curse, pm *2AM* FII,1987

Perry, Mark C.
Cade, nv **Aftermath**, ed. Robert Lynn Asprin & Lynn Abbey, Ace,1987

Peterson, Chris & Eric Drexler
Nanotechnology, ar *Analog* mid-Dec,1987

Petherick, Simon
Introduction, in
Classic Stories of Mystery, Horror and Suspense, ed. Simon Petherick, Robert Hale, 1987

PHELPS, DONALD

Phelps, Donald
  Passionate Precision: The Fiction of Robert M. Coates, ar *Pulpsmith*
    Win,1987

Pickles, J.M.
  More Birds, ss **The Pan Book of Horror Stories #28**, Pan,1987

Pilkington, Ace G.
  Cassandra in Wonderland, pm *Amazing* May,1987
  Darwin's Oracle, pm *Amazing* Nov,1987
  Jason's Answer, pm *Amazing* Jul,1987

Pinkwater, Daniel M.
  Devil in the Drain, vi **Devil in the Drain**, E.P. Dutton,1984
    Devils and Demons, ed. Marvin Kaye, Doubleday, 1987

Piper, H. Beam
  Genesis, nv *Future* Sep,1951
    Isaac Asimov's Wonderful Worlds of Science Fiction #6:
      Neanderthals, ed. Isaac Asimov+, NAL/Signet, 1987
  Last Enemy, nv *Astounding* Aug,1950
    Robert Adams' Book of Alternate Worlds, ed. Robert Adams+,
      NAL/Signet, 1987
  Operation RSVP, ss *Amazing* Jan,1951
    Amazing Science Fiction Stories: The Wild Years 1946-1955, ed.
      Martin H. Greenberg, TSR, 1987

Poe, Edgar Allan
  The Fall of the House of Usher, ss *Burton's Gentlemen's Magazine*
    Sep,1839
    Tales of the Dark, ed. Lincoln Child, St. Martin's, 1987
    Charles Keeping's Classic Tales of the Macabre, ed. Charles
      Keeping, Blackie, 1987
    The Dark Descent, ed. David G. Hartwell, Tor, 1987
  Masque of the Red Death, ss *Graham's Lady's and Gentleman's*
    Magazine May,1842
    Cinemonsters, ed. Martin H. Greenberg, TSR, 1987
  The Tell-Tale Heart, ss *The Pioneer* Jan,1843
    Classic Stories of Mystery, Horror and Suspense, ed. Simon
      Petherick, Robert Hale, 1987
  Ulalume (unabridged), pm *American Review* Dec,1847
    Devils and Demons, ed. Marvin Kaye, Doubleday, 1987

Pohl, Frederik
  The 60/40 Stories, si
    Our Best: The Best of Frederik Pohl and C.M. Kornbluth,
      Frederik Pohl+, Baen, 1987
  Adeste Fideles, ss *Omni* Dec,1987
  Afterword, aw
    Our Best: The Best of Frederik Pohl and C.M. Kornbluth,
      Frederik Pohl+, Baen, 1987
  Biofutures: The Next Turn of the Corkscrew, ar *Twilight Zone* Oct,1987
  Chernobyl and Challenger: That Was the Year That Was, ar *Aboriginal*
    SF Sep,1987
  The Dark Shadow, ss **Universe**, ed. Byron Preiss, Bantam
    Spectra,1987
  Day Million, ss *Rogue* Feb,1966
    Great Science Fiction of the 20th Century, ed. Robert
      Silverberg+, Crown/Avenel, 1987
    Robert Silverberg's Worlds of Wonder, ed. Robert Silverberg,
      Warner, 1987
  Epilogue to The Space Merchants, si
    Our Best: The Best of Frederik Pohl and C.M. Kornbluth,
      Frederik Pohl+, Baen, 1987
  Fifty Years of Cons, ar *Amazing* Jan,1987
  The Final Stories, si
    Our Best: The Best of Frederik Pohl and C.M. Kornbluth,
      Frederik Pohl+, Baen, 1987
  The High Test, ss *IASFM* Jun,1983
    Tales From Isaac Asimov's Science Fiction Magazine, ed. Sheila
      Williams+, Harcourt Brace Jovanovich, 1986
  How to Impress an Editor, ar **L. Ron Hubbard Presents Writers of**
    the Future v3, ed. Algis Budrys, Bridge,1987
  Introduction, in
    Our Best: The Best of Frederik Pohl and C.M. Kornbluth,
      Frederik Pohl+, Baen, 1987
  My Life as a Born-Again Pig, na **Synergy** v1, ed. George
    Zebrowski,1987

Pohl, Frederik (continued)
  The Schematic Man, ss *Playboy* Jan,1969
    Mathenauts, ed. Rudy Rucker, Arbor House, 1987
  Search and Destroy, ss *Aboriginal SF* May,1987
  Stories of the Sixties, si
    Our Best: The Best of Frederik Pohl and C.M. Kornbluth,
      Frederik Pohl+, Baen, 1987
  Too Much Loosestrife, ss *Amazing* Nov,1987
  The Tunnel Under the World, nv *Galaxy* Jan,1955
    Isaac Asimov Presents the Great SF Stories: 17 (1955), ed. Isaac
      Asimov+, DAW, 1988
  The View from Mars Hill, nv *IASFM* May,1987
  What to do Until the Analyst Comes [Everybody's Happy But Me!], ss
    Imagination Feb,1956
    PsiFi: Psychological Theories and Science Fictions, ed. Jim
      Ridgway+, The British Psychological Society, 1987

Pohl, Frederik & C.M. Kornbluth
  Critical Mass, na *Galaxy* Feb,1962
    Our Best: The Best of Frederik Pohl and C.M. Kornbluth,
      Frederik Pohl+, Baen, 1987
  The Engineer, ss *Infinity* Feb,1956
    Our Best: The Best of Frederik Pohl and C.M. Kornbluth,
      Frederik Pohl+, Baen, 1987
  A Gentle Dying, ss *Galaxy* Jun,1961
    Our Best: The Best of Frederik Pohl and C.M. Kornbluth,
      Frederik Pohl+, Baen, 1987
  The Gift of Garigolli, nv *Galaxy* Aug,1974
    Our Best: The Best of Frederik Pohl and C.M. Kornbluth,
      Frederik Pohl+, Baen, 1987
  Gravy Planet, ex *Galaxy* Aug,1952
    Our Best: The Best of Frederik Pohl and C.M. Kornbluth,
      Frederik Pohl+, Baen, 1987
  Mars-Tube [as by S.D. Gottesman], ss *Astonishing Stories* Sep,1941
    Our Best: The Best of Frederik Pohl and C.M. Kornbluth,
      Frederik Pohl+, Baen, 1987
  The Meeting, ss *F&SF* Nov,1972
    Our Best: The Best of Frederik Pohl and C.M. Kornbluth,
      Frederik Pohl+, Baen, 1987
  Mute Inglorious Tam, ss *F&SF* Oct,1974
    Our Best: The Best of Frederik Pohl and C.M. Kornbluth,
      Frederik Pohl+, Baen, 1987
  Nightmare with Zeppelins, nv *Galaxy* Dec,1958
    Our Best: The Best of Frederik Pohl and C.M. Kornbluth,
      Frederik Pohl+, Baen, 1987
  The Quaker Cannon, nv *Analog* Aug,1961
    Our Best: The Best of Frederik Pohl and C.M. Kornbluth,
      Frederik Pohl+, Baen, 1987
  Trouble in Time [as by S.D. Gottesman], ss *Astonishing Stories*
    Dec,1940
    Our Best: The Best of Frederik Pohl and C.M. Kornbluth,
      Frederik Pohl+, Baen, 1987
  The World of Myrion Flowers, ss *F&SF* Oct,1961
    Our Best: The Best of Frederik Pohl and C.M. Kornbluth,
      Frederik Pohl+, Baen, 1987

Polidori, Dr. John William
  The Vampyre, ss *The New Monthly Magazine* Apr,1819
    Vampires, ed. Alan Ryan, SFBC, 1987

Pollack, Rachel
  The Protector, nv *Interzone* #16,1986
    Interzone: The 2nd Anthology, ed. John Clute+, Simon &
      Schuster UK, 1987

Pollard, J.A.
  Gone Fishing, ss **Atlantis**, ed. Isaac Asimov, Martin H. Greenberg &
    Charles G. Waugh, Signet,1988

Ponder, Michael
  Metal, Like Rain, ss *Space & Time* #73,1987

Popkes, Steven
  The Rose Garden, ss *IASFM* Aug,1987
  Stovelighter, nv *IASFM* mid-Dec,1987

PORGES, ARTHUR   **QUICK, W.T.**

Porges, Arthur
  Bank Night, ss *The Diners Club Magazine*,1966
    Alfred Hitchcock's Book of Horror Stories: Book 6, ed. Alfred
      Hitchcock, Coronet, 1987
  The Oddmedod, ss *F&SF* Jun,1987

Possony, Stefan T., Francis X. Kane & Jerry E. Pournelle
  Surprise [substantially revised, first appeared in **The Strategy of
    Technology**, 1970], ar **There Will Be War** v6, ed. Jerry E.
    Pournelle,1987

Post, Jonathan V.
  Before the Big Bang, pm *Star*Line* Nov,1986
    Rhysling Anthology 1987, ed. Anonymous, SF Poetry Assc., 1987
  Before the Big Bang: News from the Hubble Large Space Telescope,
    pm *Star*Line* Nov,1986
    Analog Jan,1987

Poster, Carol
  Sibyl, pm *Grue* #5,1987

Potter, J.K.
  Twilight Zone Gallery, il *Twilight Zone* Feb,1987

Potter, J.K. & Joe R. Lansdale
  Art of Darkness, iv *Twilight Zone* Feb,1987

Potter, J.K. & Paul F. Olson
  Interview with J.K. Potter, iv *The Horror Show* Jan,1987

Pournelle, Jerry E.
  Building Plausible Futures, ar **L. Ron Hubbard Presents Writers of
    the Future** v3, ed. Algis Budrys, Bridge,1987
  Data vs. Evidence in the Voodoo Sciences, ar *Analog* Oct,1983
    Imperial Stars, Vol. 2: Republic and Empire, ed. Jerry E.
      Pournelle, Baen, 1987
  Empire and Republic: Crisis and Future, ar **Imperial Stars** v2, ed.
    Jerry E. Pournelle,1987
  Introduction: Mercenaries and Military Virtue, in
    Hammer's Slammers, David Drake, Baen, 1987
  Introduction: The Fog of War, in **There Will Be War** v6, ed. Jerry E.
    Pournelle,1987
  Republic and Empire, ar **Imperial Stars** v2, ed. Jerry E.
    Pournelle,1987
  Uncertainty and Defense, ar **There Will Be War** v6, ed. Jerry E.
    Pournelle,1987

Pournelle, Jerry E., Francis X. Kane & Stefan T. Possony
  Surprise [substantially revised, first appeared in **The Strategy of
    Technology**, 1970], ar **There Will Be War** v6, ed. Jerry E.
    Pournelle,1987

Powell, James
  The Talking Donkey, ss *Ellery Queen's Mystery Magazine* mid-
    Dec,1987

Powell, R. Brent
  Reflections of the Past, ss *Salarius* v1#4,1987
  War Game Players, ss *Salarius* #3,1987

Powell, Talmage
  Pigeon in an Iron Lung, ss *Manhunt* Nov,1956
    Alfred Hitchcock's Book of Horror Stories: Book 6, ed. Alfred
      Hitchcock, Coronet, 1987

Powers, Tim
  Introduction, in
    The Shadow on the Doorstep/Trilobyte, James P. Blaylock+,
      Axolotl, 1987
  Night Moves, nv **Night Moves**, Tim Powers, Axolotl Press,1986
    The Year's Best Science Fiction, Fourth Annual Collection, ed.
      Gardner R. Dozois, St. Martin's, 1987

Poyer, D.C.
  Into the Sunset, nv *Analog* Jul,1986
    Imperial Stars, Vol. 2: Republic and Empire, ed. Jerry E.
      Pournelle, Baen, 1987
  Nonlethal, nv **There Will Be War** v6, ed. Jerry E. Pournelle,1987

Poyer, D.C. (continued)
  The Report on the All-Union Committee on Recent Rumors
    Concerning the Moldavian SSR, ss *Analog* mid-Dec,1987
  Turing Test, ss *Analog* Aug,1987

Prebehalla, Gladys & Daniel Keys Moran
  Realtime, nv *IASFM* Aug,1984
    Tales From Isaac Asimov's Science Fiction Magazine, ed. Sheila
      Williams+, Harcourt Brace Jovanovich, 1986

Preiss, Byron
  Frontier, pr
    The Universe, ed. Byron Preiss, Bantam Spectra, 1987

Priestley, Alma
  The Neapolitan Bedroom, ss **After Midnight Stories** #3,1987

Pringle, David
  Editorial, ed *Interzone* #20,1987
  Editorial, ed *Interzone* #21,1987
  Editorial, ed *Interzone* #22,1987
  Introduction, in
    A Touch of Sturgeon, Theodore Sturgeon, Simon & Schuster UK,
      1987

Pringle, David & J.G. Ballard
  J.G. Ballard, iv *Interzone* #22,1987

Pringle, David, John Clute & Simon Ounsley
  Introduction, in
    Interzone: The 2nd Anthology, ed. John Clute+, Simon &
      Schuster UK, 1987

Proctor, George W. & J.C. Green
  The Night of the Piasa, nv **Nightmares**, ed. Charles L. Grant,
    Playboy,1979
    Nightmares in Dixie, ed. Frank D. McSherry, Jr.+, August House,
      1987

Pronzini, Bill
  The Storm Tunnel, ss *Whispers* #23,1987

Ptacek, Kathryn
  Dead Possums, ss **Doom City**, ed. Charles L. Grant, Tor,1987

Pugmire, W.H.
  Swamp Rising, ss *Grue* #4,1987

Pugmire, W.H. & Jessica Amanda Salmonson
  "Pale, Trembling Youth", ss **Cutting Edge**, ed. Dennis Etchison,
    Doubleday,1986
    The Year's Best Horror Stories: XV, ed. Karl Edward Wagner,
      DAW, 1987

Punshon, E.R.
  The Living Stone, ss *The Cornhill Magazine* Sep,1939
    Dracula's Brood, ed. Richard Dalby, Crucible, 1987

Purdy, Andrew James
  Master of the Courts, nv *Pulpsmith* Win,1987

Purtill, Richard L.
  Something in the Blood, ss *F&SF* Aug,1986
    The Year's Best Fantasy Stories: 13, ed. Arthur W. Saha, DAW,
      1987

Quagmire, Joshua
  The Nasty Naughty Nazi Ninja Nudnik Elves, cs *Fantasy Book*
    Mar,1987

Quick, W.T.
  All the People, All the Time, ss *Analog* Jul,1987
  Cowboys and Engines, ss *Aboriginal SF* May,1987
  Cyberserker, ss *Analog* Feb,1987
  Flashbattles, ss *Analog* Sep,1987
  Safe to the Liberties of the People, ss *Analog* Jun,1987

QUILTER, DEBORAH

Quilter, Deborah
Illuminations: Crystal Update, ar *Twilight Zone* Oct,1987

Quinliven, J.O.
Beauty for Sale, nv *Horror Stories* Oct,1936
The Weirds, ed. Sheldon R. Jaffery, Starmont House, 1987

Quinn, Seabury
Fortune's Fool, nv *Weird Tales* Jul,1938
Werewolf: Horror Stories of the Man Beast, ed. Peter Haining, Severn House, 1987
The Phantom Farmhouse, nv *Weird Tales* Oct,1923
Strange Maine, ed. Charles G. Waugh+, Tapley, 1986
The Poltergeist, nv *Weird Tales* Oct,1927
Poltergeist: Tales of Deadly Ghosts, ed. Peter Haining, Severn House, 1987
Restless Souls, nv *Weird Tales* Oct,1928
Vamps, ed. Martin H. Greenberg+, DAW, 1987

Quiroga, Horacio
The Feather Pillow, ss,1907
Dracula's Brood, ed. Richard Dalby, Crucible, 1987

Radford, Elaine
Another Crow's Eyes, ss *Amazing* Nov,1987
Passing, ss *Aboriginal SF* May,1987

Rafferty, S.S.
The Death Desk, ss *Alfred Hitchcock's Mystery Magazine* Mar,1975
Alfred Hitchcock's Book of Horror Stories: Book 6, ed. Alfred Hitchcock, Coronet, 1987

Rahman, Glenn
The Butler, vi *Minnesota Fantasy Review* #1,1987

Rainbird, Phillip
True Love Grue, pm *Minnesota Fantasy Review* #1,1987

Rainey, Mark
Nightshade Crossing, ss *Minnesota Fantasy Review* #1,1987

Raisor, G.L.
The Accounting, ss *Night Cry* v2#5,1987
Cheapskate, vi *Night Cry* v2#4,1987
Identity Crisis, ss *Night Cry* v2#3,1987

Ramsland, Katherine
Nothing from Nothing Comes, ss **Masques** #2, ed. J.N. Williamson,1987

Randall, Marta
Haunted, ss *Twilight Zone* Dec,1987
Lapidary Nights, ss **Universe** #17, ed. Terry Carr,1987

Randle, Kevin
Silver and Steel, nv **DragonLance Tales** v3, Margaret Weis & Tracy Hickman, TSR,1987

raphael, dan
all the comforts of, pm *Ice River* Sum,1987

Rasmussen, William C.
Just Compensation, vi *2AM* Fll,1987

Rath, Tina
The Godmother, ss **Ghosts & Scholars** #8, ed. Rosemary Pardoe,1986
The Year's Best Horror Stories: XV, ed. Karl Edward Wagner, DAW, 1987

Rathbone, Wendy
Flashing the Black Long Streets, pm *Aboriginal SF* Sep,1987

Readers, The
Boomerangs, lt *Aboriginal SF* Feb,1987
Boomerangs, lt *Aboriginal SF* May,1987
Boomerangs, lt *Aboriginal SF* Jul,1987
Boomerangs, lt *Aboriginal SF* Sep,1987

Readers, The (continued)
Boomerangs, lt *Aboriginal SF* Nov,1987
Brass Tacks, lt *Analog* Jan,1987
Brass Tacks, lt *Analog* Feb,1987
Brass Tacks, lt *Analog* Mar,1987
Brass Tacks, lt *Analog* Apr,1987
Brass Tacks, lt *Analog* May,1987
Brass Tacks, lt *Analog* Jun,1987
Brass Tacks, lt *Analog* Jul,1987
Brass Tacks, lt *Analog* Aug,1987
Brass Tacks, lt *Analog* Sep,1987
Brass Tacks, lt *Analog* Oct,1987
Brass Tacks, lt *Analog* Nov,1987
Brass Tacks, lt *Analog* Dec,1987
Brass Tacks, lt *Analog* mid-Dec,1987
The Cauldron, lt *Fantasy Tales* #16,1986
Chamber of Horrors, lt *Horror Stories*
The Weirds, ed. Sheldon R. Jaffery, Starmont House, 1987
Forum, lt *New Pathways* Jan,1987
Forum, lt *New Pathways* Apr,1987
Forum, lt *New Pathways* Aug,1987
Inflections, lt *Amazing* Jan,1987
Inflections, lt *Amazing* Mar,1987
Inflections, lt *Amazing* May,1987
Inflections, lt *Amazing* Jul,1987
Inflections, lt *Amazing* Sep,1987
Inflections, lt *Amazing* Nov,1987
Letters, lt
The Grabinski Reader [#2, Spring 1987]
Letters, lt *American Fantasy* Sum,1987
Letters, lt *IASFM* Jan,1987
Letters, lt *IASFM* Feb,1987
Letters, lt *IASFM* Mar,1987
Letters, lt *IASFM* Apr,1987
Letters, lt *IASFM* May,1987
Letters, lt *IASFM* Jun,1987
Letters, lt *IASFM* Jul,1987
Letters, lt *IASFM* Aug,1987
Letters, lt *IASFM* Sep,1987
Letters, lt *IASFM* Oct,1987
Letters, lt *IASFM* Nov,1987
Letters, lt *IASFM* Dec,1987
Letters, lt *IASFM* mid-Dec,1987
Letters, lt *Interzone* #22,1987
Letters, lt *Twilight Zone* Apr,1987
Letters, lt *Twilight Zone* Dec,1987
Open Orbit, lt *Space & Time* #72,1987
Open Orbit, lt *Space & Time* #73,1987
Readers' Forum, lt *Tales of the Unanticipated* #2,1987
Readers' Responses, lt *Mage* Spr,1987
Real Time, lt *2AM* Spr,1987
Real Time, lt *2AM* Sum,1987
Real Time, lt *2AM* Fll,1987
Real Time, lt *2AM* Win,1987

Reamy, Tom
Beyond the Cleft, nv **Nova** #4, ed. Harry Harrison,1974
Nightmares in Dixie, ed. Frank D. McSherry, Jr.+, August House, 1987
Twilla, nv *F&SF* Sep,1974
Demons!, ed. Jack M. Dann+, Ace, 1987

Reaves, J. Michael
The Tearing of Greymare House, nv *F&SF* Mar,1983
House Shudders, ed. Martin H. Greenberg+, DAW, 1987

Reed, Chris
Second Gibraltar, ss *Back Brain Recluse* #7,1987

Reed, Chris & Michael Moorcock
Michael Moorcock, iv *Back Brain Recluse* #7,1987

Reed, Kit
The Wait [also as "To Be Taken in a Strange Country"], ss *F&SF* Apr,1958
Nightmares in Dixie, ed. Frank D. McSherry, Jr.+, August House, 1987

REED, ROBERT

ROBERTSON, DONALD FREDRICK

Reed, Robert
  Aeries, ss *Aboriginal SF* Sep,1987

Reich, David
  Black Dreams, ss *Pulpsmith* Win,1987

Reid, Carol
  Wondergirls, ss *The Horror Show* Spr,1987

Reitmeyer, David F.
  Fog, pm *IASFM* Apr,1987

Reitz, Jean
  Monsters, ss **L. Ron Hubbard Presents Writers of the Future** v3, ed.
    Algis Budrys, Bridge,1987

Relling, William, Jr.
  Blood, ss *Night Cry* v2#3,1987
  Burton's Word, ss *Whispers* #23,1987
  Infinite Man, ss *New Blood* #1,1987
  Profile: Rudyard Kipling, bg *Night Cry* v2#5,1987
  Sharper Than a Serpent's Tooth, ss *The Horror Show* Spr,1987
  Where Does Watson Road Go?, ss *Eldritch Tales* #14,1987

Relling, William, Jr. & Richard Christian Matheson
  Wonderland, ss *Night Cry* v2#5,1987

Remler, Ariel
  Illuminations: Fantasies for Sale, ar *Twilight Zone* Feb,1987
  The Sky Is a Circle: Exploring the Native American Spirit World, ar
    Twilight Zone Aug,1987
  Spirits of Shadow, ar *Twilight Zone* Aug,1987

Rendell, Ruth
  Introduction, in
    A Warning to the Curious: The Ghost Stories of M.R. James,
      M.R. James, Hutchinson, 1987
  The Vinegar Mother, nv **The Fallen Curtain**, Hutchinson,1976
    Ready or Not, ed. Joan Kahn, Greenwillow, 1987

Renton, Neil
  In Search of Yuk-Yuk, ss *The Ecphorizer* Mar,1987

Rentz, Tom
  Dreams in Stasis, pm *Mage* Win,1987
    Mage Fll,1987

Reynolds, J.B., Ferret & K.W. Jeter
  K.W. Jeter [Part 1], iv *New Pathways* Apr,1987
  K.W. Jeter [Part 2], iv *New Pathways* Aug,1987

Reynolds, Mack & Fredric Brown
  Cartoonist [Garrigan's Bems], ss *Planet Stories* May,1951
    And the Gods Laughed, Fredric Brown, Phantasia Press, 1987
  Dark Interlude, ss *Galaxy* Jan,1951
    And the Gods Laughed, Fredric Brown, Phantasia Press, 1987
  The Gamblers, nv *Startling Stories* Nov,1951
    And the Gods Laughed, Fredric Brown, Phantasia Press, 1987
  Me and Flapjack and the Martians, ss *Astounding* Dec,1952
    And the Gods Laughed, Fredric Brown, Phantasia Press, 1987
  Six-Legged Svengali, ss *Worlds Beyond* Dec,1950
    And the Gods Laughed, Fredric Brown, Phantasia Press, 1987
  The Switcheroo, ss *Other Worlds* Mar,1951
    And the Gods Laughed, Fredric Brown, Phantasia Press, 1987

Rezmerski, John Calvin
  Challengers, pm *Tales of the Unanticipated* #2,1987
  A Dream of Heredity, pm *Tales of the Unanticipated* #1,1986
    Rhysling Anthology 1987, ed. Anonymous, SF Poetry Assc., 1987

Rice, Anne
  Interview with Anne Rice, iv *American Fantasy* Spr,1987

Rice, Jane
  The Refugee, ss *Unknown* Oct,1943
    Werewolf: Horror Stories of the Man Beast, ed. Peter Haining,
      Severn House, 1987

Rich, Mark
  The Alien Reads a Romance, pm *Mage* Win,1987
  The Festival of the River, ss *Mage* Win,1985
    Mage Fll,1987
  Fortuneteller, pm *Mage* Spr,1987
  Forward from What Vanishes, pm *Amazing* Jan,1987
  In This Center Hold Solitude, pm *Mage* Win,1985
    Mage Fll,1987
  The Trace of Old Fingers, pm *2AM* Sum,1987

Richard, Stephen
  Meteors, ss **Gollancz - Sunday Times Best SF Stories**,
    Gollancz,1987

Richards, Joel
  Mencken Stuff, ss **Universe** #17, ed. Terry Carr,1987

Richards, Ramona Pope
  The Editorial Privilege, ed *Apex!* #1,1987
  In the Image of Our Fathers, ar *Apex!* #1,1987

Riddell, Mrs. J.H.
  A Strange Christmas Game, ss
    Christmas Ghosts, ed. Kathryn Cramer +, Arbor House, 1987

Ridgway, Jim & Michele Benjamin
  Commentary on Burden of Proof, ar
    PsiFi: Psychological Theories and Science Fictions, ed. Jim
      Ridgway +, The British Psychological Society, 1987
  Commentary on Come to Venus Melancholy, ar
    PsiFi: Psychological Theories and Science Fictions, ed. Jim
      Ridgway +, The British Psychological Society, 1987
  Commentary on Field Test, ar
    PsiFi: Psychological Theories and Science Fictions, ed. Jim
      Ridgway +, The British Psychological Society, 1987
  Commentary on Orr's Dreams, ar
    PsiFi: Psychological Theories and Science Fictions, ed. Jim
      Ridgway +, The British Psychological Society, 1987
  Commentary on The Question of Sex, ar
    PsiFi: Psychological Theories and Science Fictions, ed. Jim
      Ridgway +, The British Psychological Society, 1987
  Commentary on They, ar
    PsiFi: Psychological Theories and Science Fictions, ed. Jim
      Ridgway +, The British Psychological Society, 1987
  Commentary on What to Do Until the Analyst Comes, ar
    PsiFi: Psychological Theories and Science Fictions, ed. Jim
      Ridgway +, The British Psychological Society, 1987

Rilke, Rainer Maria
  Eighth Elegy [from "The Duino Elegies"], pm
    Translated by Ursula K. Le Guin.
    Buffalo Gals and Other Animal Presences, Ursula K. Le Guin,
      Capra Press, 1987

Ritchie, Anne Isabella
  Cinderella, ss **Five Old Friends and a Young Prince**, London: Smith,
    Elder,1868
    Victorian Fairy Tales, ed. Jack Zipes, Methuen, 1987

Robbins, W. Wayne
  A Beast Is Born, nv *Horror Stories* Oct,1940
    The Weirds, ed. Sheldon R. Jaffery, Starmont House, 1987

Roberson, Jennifer
  Rite of Passage, nv **Sword and Sorceress** #4, ed. Marion Zimmer
    Bradley,1987

Roberts, Keith
  Equivalent for Giles, ss **Tales from the Forbidden Planet**, ed. Roz
    Kaveney, Titan,1987
  Piper's Wait, ss **Other Edens**, ed. Christopher Evans & Robert
    Holdstock, Unwin: London,1987
  The Tiger Sweater, na *F&SF* Oct,1987

Robertson, Donald Fredrick
  The Phobos Race, ar **New Destinies** v2, ed. Jim Baen, Baen,1987

ROBESON, KENNETH

Robeson, Kenneth
King Joe Cay, na *Doc Savage* Jul,1945
  Doc Savage Omnibus #2, Bantam, 1987
Measures for a Coffin, na *Doc Savage* Jan,1946
  Doc Savage Omnibus #3, Bantam, 1987
Men of Fear, na *Doc Savage* Feb,1942
  Doc Savage Omnibus #4, Bantam, 1987
The Mindless Monsters, na *Doc Savage* Sep,1941
  Doc Savage Omnibus #2, Bantam, 1987
Mystery Island, na *Doc Savage* Aug,1941
  Doc Savage Omnibus #4, Bantam, 1987
The Pure Evil, na *Doc Savage* Mar,1948
  Doc Savage Omnibus #4, Bantam, 1987
Rock Sinister, na *Doc Savage* May,1945
  Doc Savage Omnibus #4, Bantam, 1987
The Rustling Death, na *Doc Savage* Jan,1942
  Doc Savage Omnibus #2, Bantam, 1987
The Spook of Grandpa Eben, na *Doc Savage* Dec,1941
  Doc Savage Omnibus #3, Bantam, 1987
Strange Fish, na *Doc Savage* Feb,1945
  Doc Savage Omnibus #3, Bantam, 1987
The Thing That Pursued, na *Doc Savage* Oct,1945
  Doc Savage Omnibus #2, Bantam, 1987
The Three Devils, na *Doc Savage* May,1944
  Doc Savage Omnibus #3, Bantam, 1987

Robinson, Jeanne & Spider Robinson
Stardance, na *Analog* Mar,1977
  The Dark Void, ed. Isaac Asimov, Severn House, 1987

Robinson, Kim Stanley
The Blind Geometer, na *IASFM* Aug,1987
Down and Out in the Year 2000, ss *IASFM* Apr,1986
  The Year's Best Science Fiction, Fourth Annual Collection, ed.
  Gardner R. Dozois, St. Martin's, 1987
Escape from Kathmandu, na *IASFM* Sep,1986
  Terry Carr's Best Science Fiction and Fantasy of the Year #16,
  ed. Terry Carr, Tor, 1987
The Memorial, ss **In the Field of Fire**, ed. Jeanne Van Buren Dann &
  Jack M. Dann, Tor,1987
Mother Goddess of the World, na *IASFM* Oct,1987
The Return from Rainbow Bridge, nv *F&SF* Aug,1987

Robinson, Peni
Nereid, ss *Twilight Zone* Apr,1987
  Third place winner, TZ short story contest.

Robinson, Phil
The Man-Eating Tree, ss **Under the Punkah**, Sampson Low Marsten
  Searle Rivington: London,1881
  Dracula's Brood, ed. Richard Dalby, Crucible, 1987

Robinson, Spider
By Any Other Name, na *Analog* Nov,1976
  Beyond the Stars, ed. Isaac Asimov, Severn House, 1987
Introduction, in
  Pruzy's Pot, Theodore Sturgeon, Hypatia Press, 1986

Robinson, Spider & Jeanne Robinson
Stardance, na *Analog* Mar,1977
  The Dark Void, ed. Isaac Asimov, Severn House, 1987

Rochon, Esther
Xils ["Xils", **Aurores Boreales 2** 1985], ss **Tesseracts 2**, ed. Phyllis
  Gotlieb & Douglas Barbour, Press Porcepic: Victoria,1987
  Translated by Lucille Nelson.

Rocklynne, Ross
They Fly So High, ss *Amazing* Jun,1952
  Amazing Science Fiction Stories: The Wild Years 1946-1955, ed.
  Martin H. Greenberg, TSR, 1987

Rodgers, Alan
The Boy Who Came Back from the Dead, nv **Masques** #2, ed. J.N.
  Williamson,1987

Rogal, Stan
A Little Thing, ss **Tesseracts 2**, ed. Phyllis Gotlieb & Douglas
  Barbour, Press Porcepic: Victoria,1987

Rogers, Alan
Down-Home Horrors, in *Night Cry* v2#3,1987
Introduction: Where the Dead Do Not Die, in *Night Cry* v2#5,1987

Rogers, Wayne
Sleep With Me--And Death, nv *Horror Stories* Apr,1938
  Selected Tales of Grim and Grue from the Horror Pulps, ed.
  Sheldon R. Jaffery, Bowling Green Popular Press, 1987

Roland, Paul
Beau Brummel, sg **The Curious Case of Richard Fielding and
  Other Stories**, Lary Press,1987
Cairo, sg **The Curious Case of Richard Fielding and Other Stories**,
  Lary Press,1987
The Curious Case of Richard Fielding, ss **The Curious Case of
  Richard Fielding and Other Stories**, Lary Press,1987
Death or Glory, sg **The Curious Case of Richard Fielding and Other
  Stories**, Lary Press,1987
Demon in a Glass Case, sg **The Curious Case of Richard Fielding
  and Other Stories**, Lary Press,1987
Foreword, fw
  The Curious Case of Richard Fielding and Other Stories, Lary
  Press, 1987
Ghost Ships, sg **The Curious Case of Richard Fielding and Other
  Stories**, Lary Press,1987
The Great Edwardian Airaid, sg **The Curious Case of Richard
  Fielding and Other Stories**, Lary Press,1987
Green Glass Violins, sg **The Curious Case of Richard Fielding and
  Other Stories**, Lary Press,1987
The Hanging Judge, sg **The Curious Case of Richard Fielding and
  Other Stories**, Lary Press,1987
A Hangman Waits, ss **The Curious Case of Richard Fielding and
  Other Stories**, Lary Press,1987
The Hired Executioner, ss **The Curious Case of Richard Fielding
  and Other Stories**, Lary Press,1987
In the Opium Den, sg **The Curious Case of Richard Fielding and
  Other Stories**, Lary Press,1987
Jumbee, sg **The Curious Case of Richard Fielding and Other
  Stories**, Lary Press,1987
Madame Guillotine, sg **The Curious Case of Richard Fielding and
  Other Stories**, Lary Press,1987
Madelaine, sg **The Curious Case of Richard Fielding and Other
  Stories**, Lary Press,1987
The Miracle Man, ss **The Curious Case of Richard Fielding and
  Other Stories**, Lary Press,1987
A Most Singular Specimen, ss **The Curious Case of Richard
  Fielding and Other Stories**, Lary Press,1987
Mr. Mephisto, ss **The Curious Case of Richard Fielding and Other
  Stories**, Lary Press,1987
Nocturne, ss **The Curious Case of Richard Fielding and Other
  Stories**, Lary Press,1987
Pulp, ss **The Curious Case of Richard Fielding and Other Stories**,
  Lary Press,1987
The Puppet Master, sg **The Curious Case of Richard Fielding and
  Other Stories**, Lary Press,1987
Requiem, sg **The Curious Case of Richard Fielding and Other
  Stories**, Lary Press,1987
Return to Raebourne, ss **The Curious Case of Richard Fielding and
  Other Stories**, Lary Press,1987
Stowaway, ss **The Curious Case of Richard Fielding and Other
  Stories**, Lary Press,1987
Stranger Than Strange, sg **The Curious Case of Richard Fielding
  and Other Stories**, Lary Press,1987
Twilight of the Gods, sg **The Curious Case of Richard Fielding and
  Other Stories**, Lary Press,1987

Rolt, L.T.C.
New Corner, ss *Mystery Stories* #20,1939
  Mysterious Motoring Stories, ed. William Pattrick, W.H. Allen, 1987
  Ghosts and Scholars, ed. Rosemary Pardoe +, Crucible, 1987

Rooke, Leon
Bats, ss **Tesseracts 2**, ed. Phyllis Gotlieb & Douglas Barbour, Press
  Porcepic: Victoria,1987

ROSE, RHEA

SABERHAGEN, FRED

Rose, Rhea
Squirrels in Frankfurter Highlight, ss **Tesseracts 2**, ed. Phyllis Gotlieb
& Douglas Barbour, Press Porcepic: Victoria,1987

Rose, S., (?)
Cartoon, ct *Twilight Zone* Jun,1987

Rosenbaum, Bob & Carol Serling
Life with Rod, iv *Twilight Zone* Apr,1987

Rosenberg, Joel
The Last Time, ss **Friends of the Horseclans**, ed. Robert Adams &
Pamela Crippen Adams, Signet,1987
Not for Country, Not for King, nv **New Destinies** v1, ed. Jim Baen,
Baen,1987

Rosenman, John B.
When a Rose Sings, ss *2AM* Sum,1987

Rossow, William & M. Bradley Kellogg
Reign of Fire, n. New American Library: New York,1986
Lear's Daughters, M. Bradley Kellogg +, SFBC, 1987
The Wave and the Flame, n. New American Library: New York,1986
Lear's Daughters, M. Bradley Kellogg +, SFBC, 1987

Rostand, Edmond
Don Juan's Final Night, pl
Freely revised and adapted by Marvin Kaye.
Devils and Demons, ed. Marvin Kaye, Doubleday, 1987

Roth, Harrison & Isaac Asimov
Left to Right, and Beyond, vi *Analog* Jul,1987

Rothbell, Jay
Connie Nova, ss *Pulpsmith* Win,1987

Rothman, Tony
A Memoir of Nuclear Winter, ar *Analog* Nov,1987

Rowe, Karen E.
Feminism and Fairy Tales, cr *Women's Studies* #6,1979
Don't Bet on the Prince, ed. Jack Zipes, Methuen, 1987

Rowlands, David G.
Sins of the Fathers, ss **Eye Hath Not Seen**,1981
Ghosts and Scholars, ed. Rosemary Pardoe +, Crucible, 1987

Rucker, Rudy
Bringing in the Sheaves, ss *IASFM* Jan,1987
Enlightenment Rabies, vi *New Pathways* Nov,1987
Inside Out, nv **Synergy** v1, ed. George Zebrowski,1987
Introduction, in
Mathenauts, ed. Rudy Rucker, Arbor House, 1987
The Man Who Was a Cosmic String, ss **Universe**, ed. Byron Preiss,
Bantam Spectra,1987
Message Found in a Copy of **Flatland**, ss **The 57th Franz Kafka**,
Ace,1983
Mathenauts, ed. Rudy Rucker, Arbor House, 1987
A New Golden Age, ss *Randolph-Macon Woman's College Alumnae
Bulletin* Sum,1981
Mathenauts, ed. Rudy Rucker, Arbor House, 1987
Viewpoint: Cellular Automata, ar *IASFM* Apr,1987

Rucker, Rudy & Richard Kadrey
Rudy Rucker Interview, iv *Interzone* #20,1987

Rud, Anthony M.
Ooze, nv *Weird Tales* Mar,1923
Nightmares in Dixie, ed. Frank D. McSherry, Jr. +, August House,
1987

Rudoski, Alice
If Big Brother Says So, ss *Ellery Queen's Mystery Magazine* Jul,1977
Ready or Not, ed. Joan Kahn, Greenwillow, 1987

Rusch, Kristine Kathryn
Clarion and Speculative Fiction, ar *Amazing* Nov,1987
Sing, ss *Aboriginal SF* Feb,1987

Ruskin, John
King of the Golden River, or The Black Brothers, nv,1841
Victorian Fairy Tales, ed. Jack Zipes, Methuen, 1987

Russ, Joanna
My Dear Emily, nv *F&SF* Jul,1962
The Dark Descent, ed. David G. Hartwell, Tor, 1987
Russalka or The Seacoast of Bohemia, ss **Kittatiny**, Daughters
Publishing Co.,1978
Don't Bet on the Prince, ed. Jack Zipes, Methuen, 1987
When It Changed, ss **Again, Dangerous Visions**, ed. Harlan Ellison,
Doubleday,1972
Great Science Fiction of the 20th Century, ed. Robert
Silverberg +, Crown/Avenel, 1987

Russell, Bertrand
The Queen of Sheba's Nightmare, ss **Nightmares of Eminent
Persons**, Allen & Unwin,1954
Devils and Demons, ed. Marvin Kaye, Doubleday, 1987

Russell, Eric Frank
Allamagoosa, ss *Astounding* May,1955
Isaac Asimov Presents the Great SF Stories: 17 (1955), ed. Isaac
Asimov +, DAW, 1988
Minor Ingredient, ss *Astounding* Mar,1956
Imperial Stars, Vol. 2: Republic and Empire, ed. Jerry E.
Pournelle, Baen, 1987

Russell, Ray
American Gothic, ss **Masques #2**, ed. J.N. Williamson,1987
The Cage, ss,1959
Isaac Asimov's Magical Worlds of Fantasy #8: Devils, ed. Isaac
Asimov +, NAL/Signet, 1987
I Am Returning, ss **Sardonicus**, Ballantine,1961
Devils and Demons, ed. Marvin Kaye, Doubleday, 1987
The Kolorized King Kong Kaper, ss *Whispers* #23,1987

Russo, Richard Paul
Dead Man on the Beach, ss *Twilight Zone* Jun,1987
In the Season of the Rains, ss **In the Field of Fire**, ed. Jeanne Van
Buren Dann & Jack M. Dann, Tor,1987
Mad City Beneath the Sands, ss *Twilight Zone* Oct,1987
Prayers of a Rain God, ss *F&SF* May,1987

Rutherford, Brett
Remembering Medea, pm *Haunts* #9,1987

Rutherford, Michael
The Tale and Its Master, na Spring Harbor: Delmar, NY,1986
The Year's Best Fantasy Stories: 13, ed. Arthur W. Saha, DAW,
1987

Ryan, Alan
The Bones Wizard, ss *Whispers* #21,1984
Whispers VI, ed. Stuart David Schiff, Doubleday, 1987
Following the Way, ss **Shadows #5**, ed. Charles L. Grant,1982
Vampires, ed. Alan Ryan, SFBC, 1987
The Haunted House of My Childhood, pm *Weirdbook* #22,1987
Introduction, in
Vampires, ed. Alan Ryan, SFBC, 1987

Ryan, Charles C.
Achieving Orbit, ed *Aboriginal SF* Sep,1987
On Becoming a Writer, ed *Aboriginal SF* Nov,1987
Our New Format, ed *Aboriginal SF* May,1987
Sifting for Golden Nuggets, ed *Aboriginal SF* Feb,1987

Ryman, Geoff
Love Sickness, Part 1, sl *Interzone* #20,1987
Love Sickness, Part 2, sl *Interzone* #21,1987

Rymer, James Malcolm
Varney, the Vampyre; or, The Feast of Blood, ex,1845
Vampires, ed. Alan Ryan, SFBC, 1987

Saberhagen, Fred
Adventure of the Metal Murderer, ss *Omni* Jan,1980
Saberhagen: My Best, Baen, 1987

SABERHAGEN, FRED

Saberhagen, Fred (continued)
Birthdays, na *Galaxy* Mar,1976
  Saberhagen: My Best, Baen, 1987
Earthshade, nv **The Magic May Return**, ed. Larry Niven,1981
  Saberhagen: My Best, Baen, 1987
From the Tree of Time, ss *Sorcerer's Apprentice* #14,1982
  Saberhagen: My Best, Baen, 1987
Goodlife, nv *Worlds of Tomorrow* Dec,1963
  Saberhagen: My Best, Baen, 1987
The Graphic of Dorian Gray, nv **New Destinies** v1, ed. Jim Baen,
    Baen,1987
  Saberhagen: My Best, Baen, 1987
Inhuman Error [also as "WHAT DO YOU WANT ME TO DO TO
    PROVE IM HUMAN STOP"], ss *Analog* Oct,1974
  Saberhagen: My Best, Baen, 1987
Intermission, vi **Fifty Extremely SF* Stories**, ed. Michael
    Bastraw,1982
  Saberhagen: My Best, Baen, 1987
The Long Way Home, ss *Galaxy* Jun,1961
  Saberhagen: My Best, Baen, 1987
Martha, vi *Amazing* Dec,1976
  Saberhagen: My Best, Baen, 1987
The Peacemaker [The Life Hater], ss *If* Aug,1964
  Saberhagen: My Best, Baen, 1987
Recessional, ss **Destinies** v2#4, ed. James Baen,1980
  Saberhagen: My Best, Baen, 1987
Smasher, nv *F&SF* Aug,1978
  Saberhagen: My Best, Baen, 1987
  A Very Large Array, ed. Melinda M. Snodgrass, Univ. of New
    Mexico Press, 1987
Victory, nv *F&SF* Jun,1979
  Saberhagen: My Best, Baen, 1987
WHAT DO YOU WANT ME TO DO TO PROVE IM HUMAN STOP
    [Inhuman Error], ss *Analog* Oct,1974
  Battlefields Beyond Tomorrow, ed. Charles G. Waugh+,
    Crown/Bonanza, 1987
The White Bull, nv *Fantastic* Nov,1976
  Saberhagen: My Best, Baen, 1987
Wilderness, ss *Amazing* Sep,1976
  Saberhagen: My Best, Baen, 1987
Young Girl at an Open Half-Door, ss *F&SF* Nov,1968
  Saberhagen: My Best, Baen, 1987

Saha, Arthur W.
Introduction, in
  The Year's Best Fantasy Stories: 13, ed. Arthur W. Saha, DAW,
    1987

Sakers, Don
All Fall Down, nv *Analog* May,1987
The Finagle Fiasco, ss,1983
  Mathenauts, ed. Rudy Rucker, Arbor House, 1987
The Hand of Guilt, ss *Fantasy Book* Mar,1987

Sallee, Wayne Allen
Joe Lansdale Speaks, pm *Grue* #5,1987
A Matter of Semantics, vi *Grue* #5,1987
second thoughts, pm *Grue* #5,1987
Take the "A" Train, ss *Not One of Us* Oct,1986
  The Year's Best Horror Stories: XV, ed. Karl Edward Wagner,
    DAW, 1987
The Touch, ss *Grue* #4,1987

Salmonson, Jessica Amanda
Bear at the Gate, ss **Spaceships & Spells**, ed. Jane Yolen, Martin H.
    Greenberg & Charles G. Waugh, Harper & Row,1987
Beyond the Reef, pm *Grue* #6,1987
For E.D., pm *2AM* Win,1987
The House that Knew No Hate, nv **The Architecture of Fear**, ed.
    Kathryn Cramer & Peter D. Pautz, Arbor House,1987
Strange Doings in Viktor's Village, vi *New Pathways* Jan,1987
The Trilling Princess, ss **Devils & Demons**, ed. Marvin Kaye,
    SFBC/Doubleday,1987

Salmonson, Jessica Amanda & W.H. Pugmire
"Pale, Trembling Youth", ss **Cutting Edge**, ed. Dennis Etchison,
    Doubleday,1986
  The Year's Best Horror Stories: XV, ed. Karl Edward Wagner,
    DAW, 1987

Salonia, John & Traci Salonia
The Butterflies of Betelgeuse, pm *Space & Time* #72,1987
The Imp in the Bottle, ss *Space & Time* #73,1987

Salonia, Traci & John Salonia
The Butterflies of Betelgeuse, pm *Space & Time* #72,1987
The Imp in the Bottle, ss *Space & Time* #73,1987

Salts, Katherine
Popcorn: A Matter of Survival, vi *Haunts* #9,1987

Sampson, Robert
The Scent of Roses, ss *Space & Time* #73,1987

San Souci, Robert D.
The Adventure of the German Student, ss **Short & Shivery**,
    Doubleday,1987
  From **Tales of a Traveller** (1824) by Washington Irving.
Billy Mosby's Night Ride, ss **Short & Shivery**, Doubleday,1987
  Based on "Francis Woolcott" from Charles M. Skinner's **Myths
    and Tales of Our Own Land**.
Boneless, ss **Short & Shivery**, Doubleday,1987
Brother and Sister, ss **Short & Shivery**, Doubleday,1987
  Based on a traditional African tale.
The Cegua, ss **Short & Shivery**, Doubleday,1987
  Original story based on "La Cegua" by Maximo Soto Hall.
The Deacon's Ghost, ss **Short & Shivery**, Doubleday,1987
  A retelling of "The Deacon of Myrka" from **Icelandic Legends** by
    Jon Arnason.
The Death Waltz, ss **Short & Shivery**, Doubleday,1987
  Retold from Charles M. Skinner's **Myths and Tales of Our Own
    Land**.
The Ghost of Misery Hill, ss **Short & Shivery**, Doubleday,1987
  Expanded from "The Spook of Misery Hill" in Charles M. Skinner's
    Myths and Tales of Our Own Land.
The Ghost's Cap, ss **Short & Shivery**, Doubleday,1987
  Based on an Icelandic folktale (1864).
The Ghostly Little Girl, ss **Short & Shivery**, Doubleday,1987
  Expanded from an account in **Ghostly Tales of Old Monterey** by
    Randall A. Reinstedt.
The Goblin Spider, ss **Short & Shivery**, Doubleday,1987
  A traditional Japanese story.
The Golem, ss **Short & Shivery**, Doubleday,1987
The Green Mist, ss **Short & Shivery**, Doubleday,1987
  Derived from **Legends of the Lincolnshire Cars** (1891) by M.C.
    Balfour.
The Halloween Pony, ss **Short & Shivery**, Doubleday,1987
  Based on "The Goblin Pony", a French folktale.
The Hunter in the Haunted Forest, ss **Short & Shivery**,
    Doubleday,1987
  From three Teton Sioux tales in **Myths and Legends of the
    Great Plains** by Katharine Berry Judson.
Introduction, in
  Short & Shivery, ed. Robert D. San Souci, Doubleday, 1987
Jack Frost, ss **Short & Shivery**, Doubleday,1987
  Adapted from the Russian.
Lady Eleanor's Mantle, ss **Short & Shivery**, Doubleday,1987
  Based on the story by Nathaniel Hawthorne (*Democratic Review*,
    Dec,1838).
Lavender, ss **Short & Shivery**, Doubleday,1987
  Based on an American urban legend.
The Loup-Garou, ss **Short & Shivery**, Doubleday,1987
  Based on a French-Canadian legend.
The Lovers of Dismal Swamp, ss **Short & Shivery**, Doubleday,1987
  Based on an American folktale from colonial times.
The Midnight Mass of the Dead, ss **Short & Shivery**, Doubleday,1987
  Based on Norse folklore.
Nuckelavee, ss **Short & Shivery**, Doubleday,1987
  Adapted from **Orkney Folklore and Traditions** by Walter Traill
    Dennison.
The Robber Bridegroom, ss **Short & Shivery**, Doubleday,1987
  Based on a tale from the Brothers Grimm.

SAN SOUCI, ROBERT D.

San Souci, Robert D. (continued)
　Scared To Death, ss **Short & Shivery**, Doubleday,1987
　　Based on "The Leaning Tombstone" by Margaret Rhett Martin.
　The Skeleton's Dance, ss **Short & Shivery**, Doubleday,1987
　　Based on a Japanese folktale.
　The Soldier and the Vampire, ss **Short & Shivery**, Doubleday,1987
　　Based on a traditional Russian folktale.
　Swallowed Alive, ss **Short & Shivery**, Doubleday,1987
　　Based on an account by John Bunyan (1680).
　Tailypo, ss **Short & Shivery**, Doubleday,1987
　　Based on a classic American tale.
　The Waterfall of Ghosts, ss **Short & Shivery**, Doubleday,1987
　　Based on "Yurei-Daki" (1902) by Lafcadio Hearn.
　The Witch Cat, ss **Short & Shivery**, Doubleday,1987
　　Based on an American folktale.

Sandage, Allan
　Cosmology: The Quest to Understand the Creation and Expansion of
　　the Universe, ar **Universe**, ed. Byron Preiss, Bantam Spectra,1987

Sandercombe, W. Fraser
　Just a legend, pm *Weirdbook* #22,1987

Sanders (Nippawanock), Thomas E.
　The Bridge, ss *The South Dakota Review* Spr,1975
　　Twilight Zone Aug,1987
　The Great Holy Mystery, ar *Twilight Zone* Aug,1987
　Profile: Ambrose Bierce, bg *Night Cry* v2#4,1987
　The Rock Bearers, ar *Twilight Zone* Aug,1987

Sanders, Scott Russell
　The Anatomy Lesson, ss *IASFM* Oct 26,1981
　　Tales From Isaac Asimov's Science Fiction Magazine, ed. Sheila
　　Williams +, Harcourt Brace Jovanovich, 1986

Sargent, Pamela
　Bond and Free, nv *F&SF* Jun,1974
　　The Best of Pamela Sargent, Academy Chicago, 1987
　The Broken Hoop, ss *Twilight Zone* Jun,1982
　　The Best of Pamela Sargent, Academy Chicago, 1987
　Clone Sister, nv **Eros in Orbit**, ed. Joseph Elder, Trident,1973
　　The Best of Pamela Sargent, Academy Chicago, 1987
　Fears, ss **Light Years and Dark**, ed. Michael Bishop, Berkley,1984
　　The Best of Pamela Sargent, Academy Chicago, 1987
　Gather Blue Roses, ss *F&SF* Feb,1972
　　The Best of Pamela Sargent, Academy Chicago, 1987
　Heavenly Flowers, ss *IASFM* Sep,1983
　　The Best of Pamela Sargent, Academy Chicago, 1987
　If Ever I Should Leave You [revised from *If* Feb,74], ss **Starshadows**,
　　Ace,1977
　　The Best of Pamela Sargent, Academy Chicago, 1987
　Introduction, in
　　The Best of Pamela Sargent, Academy Chicago, 1987
　The Leash, ss *Twilight Zone* Apr,1987
　The Mountain Cage, nv **Cheap Street: New Castle, VA**,1983
　　The Best of Pamela Sargent, Academy Chicago, 1987
　The Novella Race, ss **Orbit #20**, ed. Damon Knight,1978
　　The Best of Pamela Sargent, Academy Chicago, 1987
　The Old Darkness, ss *F&SF* Jul,1983
　　The Best of Pamela Sargent, Academy Chicago, 1987
　Out of Place, ss *Twilight Zone* Oct,1981
　　The Best of Pamela Sargent, Academy Chicago, 1987
　Shadows, nv **Fellowship of the Stars**, ed. Terry Carr, Simon &
　　Schuster,1974
　　The Best of Pamela Sargent, Academy Chicago, 1987
　The Shrine, ss *Twilight Zone* Dec,1982
　　The Best of Pamela Sargent, Academy Chicago, 1987
　Shrinker, nv *IASFM* Nov,1983
　　Tales From Isaac Asimov's Science Fiction Magazine, ed. Sheila
　　Williams +, Harcourt Brace Jovanovich, 1986
　The Summer's Dust, nv *F&SF* Jul,1981
　　The Best of Pamela Sargent, Academy Chicago, 1987

Sarrantonio, Al
　Bogy, ss **Whispers #6**, ed. Stuart David Schiff,1987
　Books, br *Night Cry* v2#3,1987
　Books, br *Night Cry* v2#4,1987
　Books, br *Night Cry* v2#5,1987

Sarrantonio, Al (continued)
　Fragments of Horror, ms *The Horror Show* Sum,1987
　Pigs, ss **Shadows #10**, ed. Charles L. Grant,1987

Sass, Mary
　Brain Blasters, ss *Mage* Spr,1987

Sass, R.A.
　Love is a Circle, vi *2AM* Sum,1987

Saunders, Charles R.
　Death's Friend, nv *Weirdbook* #22,1987
　Outsteppin' Fetchit, ss **Masques #2**, ed. J.N. Williamson,1987

Savage, Adrian
　The Other Side: Welcome, Chaos, ar *Twilight Zone* Oct,1987

Sawyer, Robert J.
　Uphill Climb, vi *Amazing* Mar,1987

Sawyer, Ruth
　Four Dreams of Gram Perkins, ss *The American Mercury* Oct,1926
　　Strange Maine, ed. Charles G. Waugh +, Tapley, 1986
　The Shepherds, ss,1941
　　Isaac Asimov's Magical Worlds of Fantasy #8: Devils, ed. Isaac
　　Asimov +, NAL/Signet, 1987

Saxby, Anna Lieff
　Prisoners, ss **Gollancz - Sunday Times Best SF Stories**,
　　Gollancz,1987

Saxton, Josephine
　The Cure, ss **Little Tours of Hell**, Pandora,1986
　Dinner at the Manse, ss **Little Tours of Hell**, Pandora,1986
　Falling in Love at Christmas, ss **Little Tours of Hell**, Pandora,1986
　First Day at Herradura, ss **Little Tours of Hell**, Pandora,1986
　The Golden Mile, ss **Little Tours of Hell**, Pandora,1986
　The Interferences, ss **Tales from the Forbidden Planet**, ed. Roz
　　Kaveney, Titan,1987
　Jackie Loves Food -- True, ss **Little Tours of Hell**, Pandora,1986
　A Little Tour of Hell, ss **Little Tours of Hell**, Pandora,1986
　Oily Foreign Muck, ss **Little Tours of Hell**, Pandora,1986
　The Rabbit Pie Man, ss **Little Tours of Hell**, Pandora,1986
　The Sea Urchin, ss **Little Tours of Hell**, Pandora,1986
　Souvenirs of Devon, ss **Little Tours of Hell**, Pandora,1986
　Spaghetti Halifax, ss **Little Tours of Hell**, Pandora,1986
　Tea and No Sympathy, ss **Little Tours of Hell**, Pandora,1986
　Virginia and Bread, ss **Little Tours of Hell**, Pandora,1986

Saylor, Steven
　The Pawns of Crux, ss *The Dragon* Mar,1987

Sayre, Cheryl Curry
　The Lady Who Lost Her Head, ss *Grue* #6,1987

Scarborough, Elizabeth Ann
　Milk from a Maiden's Breast, ss **Tales of the Witch World**, ed. Andre
　　Norton, St. Martin's,1987
　Song of Sorcery, n. Bantam: New York,1982
　　Songs from the Seashell Archives, Vol. 1, Bantam Spectra, 1987
　Unicorn Creed, n. Bantam: New York,1983
　　Songs from the Seashell Archives, Vol. 1, Bantam Spectra, 1987

Scarlett, Patricia
　Deity, vi *Eldritch Tales* #13,1987

Schaub, Mary H.
　Night Hound's Moon, ss **Tales of the Witch World**, ed. Andre Norton,
　　St. Martin's,1987

Schiff, Stuart David
　Editorial, ed *Whispers* #23,1987
　The End, aw *Whispers* #23,1987
　Introduction, in
　　Whispers VI, ed. Stuart David Schiff, Doubleday, 1987
　News, ar *Whispers* #23,1987

SCHMIDT, STANLEY

Schmidt, Stanley
   An Alien Viewpoint, ed *Analog* Apr,1987
   Brain Language, ed *Analog* Mar,1987
   Butterfly Futures, ed *Analog* May,1987
   Child Abuse, ed *Analog* Jun,1987
   Final Frontiers, ed *Analog* Oct,1987
   Fundamental Dilemma, ed *Analog* Jan,1987
   Great Oaks from Little Atoms, ed *Analog* Nov,1987
   The Gypsy and the Procrastinator, ed *Analog* Feb,1987
   Introduction, in
      6 Decades: The Best of Analog, ed. Stanley Schmidt, Davis, 1986
   Matters of Opinion, ed *Analog* mid-Dec,1987
   The Memetic Menace, ed *Analog* Aug,1987
   Political Standard Time, ed *Analog* Dec,1987
   The Reactionary Revolution, ed *Analog* Jul,1987

Schmitz, James H.
   Grandpa, ss *Astounding* Feb,1955
      Great Science Fiction of the 20th Century, ed. Robert
         Silverberg +, Crown/Avenel, 1987
      Isaac Asimov Presents the Great SF Stories: 17 (1955), ed. Isaac
         Asimov +, DAW, 1988
   Sleep No More, ss *Analog* Aug,1965
      6 Decades: The Best of Analog, ed. Stanley Schmidt, Davis, 1986

Schneider, Roy
   The Seed, ss *Eldritch Tales* #14,1987

Schochet
   Cartoon, ct *Twilight Zone* Oct,1987

Scholz, Carter
   Galileo Complains, ss *IASFM* Jun,1986
      Terry Carr's Best Science Fiction and Fantasy of the Year #16,
         ed. Terry Carr, Tor, 1987
   Recursion, ss **Cuts**, Drumm,1985
      New Pathways Nov,1987

Schow, David J.
   One for the Horrors, ss *Whispers* #19,1983
      Whispers VI, ed. Stuart David Schiff, Doubleday, 1987
   Pamela's Get, ss *Twilight Zone* Aug,1987
   Red Light, nv *Twilight Zone* Dec,1986
      The Year's Best Horror Stories: XV, ed. Karl Edward Wagner,
         DAW, 1987

Schreck, Dean
   Semblance, pm *Eldritch Tales* #13,1987

Schwadron
   Cartoon, ct *Twilight Zone* Dec,1987

Schwartz, Hillel
   Sleeping Beauty, ss *The Short Story Review* Win,1987

Schweitzer, Darrell
   Books: A Historical Perspective, br *Aboriginal SF* May,1987
   Books: Books Versus Careers, br *Aboriginal SF* Sep,1987
   Books: New Works from Old Masters, br *Aboriginal SF* Feb,1987
   Books: Objectivity, br *Aboriginal SF* Nov,1987
   Books: The Whole Spectrum of Fantastic Literature, br *Aboriginal SF*
      Jul,1987
   Caliban's Revenge, ss *Weirdbook* #13,1978
      Devils and Demons, ed. Marvin Kaye, Doubleday, 1987
   The Chivalry of Sir Aldingar, ss *Weirdbook* #22,1987
   H.P. Lovecraft: Still Eldritch After All These Years, ar *Amazing*
      Mar,1987
   Introduction to The Haunted Ships, ar *Fantasy Book* Mar,1987
   The Other Side: Pennies from Hell, ar *Twilight Zone* Feb,1987
   Pennies from Hell, ss *Night Cry* v2#3,1987
   The Shaper of Animals, ss *Amazing* Jul,1987
   She Just Wanted to Get out of the House, pm *Amazing* Sep,1987
   Transients, ss *Amazing* Jan,1987

Schweitzer, Darrell & John Gregory Betancourt
   The Children of Lommos, ss *Night Cry* v2#4,1987

Scott, Eleanor
   Celui-La, ss **Randalls Round**, E. Benn: London,1929
      Ghosts and Scholars, ed. Rosemary Pardoe +, Crucible, 1987
   'Will Ye No' Come Back Again?', ss **Randalls Round**, E. Benn:
      London,1929
      The Virago Book of Ghost Stories, ed. Richard Dalby, Virago, 1987

Scott, Jody
   Mushroom Roulette, ss **Tales from the Forbidden Planet**, ed. Roz
      Kaveney, Titan,1987

Scott, Sir Walter
   The Highland Widow, na **Chronicles of the Canongate**, Cadell &
      Co.,1827
      The Supernatural Short Stories of Sir Walter Scott,
         Riverrun/Calder, 1986
   My Aunt Margaret's Mirror, nv *The Keepsake*,1828
      The Supernatural Short Stories of Sir Walter Scott,
         Riverrun/Calder, 1986
   The Tapestried Chamber, ss *The Keepsake*,1828
      The Supernatural Short Stories of Sir Walter Scott,
         Riverrun/Calder, 1986
   The Two Drovers, nv **Chronicles of the Canongate**, Cadell &
      Co.,1827
      The Supernatural Short Stories of Sir Walter Scott,
         Riverrun/Calder, 1986
   Wandering Willie's Tale [from **Redgauntlet**], ex Constable:
      London,1824
      The Supernatural Short Stories of Sir Walter Scott,
         Riverrun/Calder, 1986

Scotten, W.C.
   A Matter of Condensation, ss *Analog* Jan,1987

Searles, Baird
   On Books, br *IASFM* Jan,1987
   On Books, br *IASFM* Feb,1987
   On Books, br *IASFM* Mar,1987
   On Books, br *IASFM* May,1987
   On Books, br *IASFM* Jun,1987
   On Books, br *IASFM* Aug,1987
   On Books, br *IASFM* Sep,1987
   On Books, br *IASFM* Nov,1987
   On Books, br *IASFM* mid-Dec,1987

Sears, Vickie L.
   Sticktalk, ss **Gathering Ground**, ed. Jo Cochran, J.T. Stewart &
      Mayumi Tsutakawa, Seal Press,1984
      Hear the Silence, ed. Irene Zahava, Crossing Press, 1986

Secula, S.M.
   The Missing Dumbell, ss *Haunts* #9,1987

Seidenstein, B.J.
   Road, ss *Haunts* #9,1987

Seidman, Michael
   The Dream That Follows Darkness, ss *Twilight Zone* Aug,1987

Selinsky, Deloris
   It, pm *2AM* Fll,1987

Selonke, Paul
   Beast of the Island, ss *Strange Tales of Mystery and Terror* Oct,1940
      Werewolf: Horror Stories of the Man Beast, ed. Peter Haining,
         Severn House, 1987

Serling, Carol
   Illuminations: Freedom to Imagine, ar *Twilight Zone* Apr,1987
   Introduction, in
      Rod Serling's Night Gallery Reader, ed. Carol Serling +,
         Dembner, 1987

Serling, Carol & Bob Rosenbaum
   Life with Rod, iv *Twilight Zone* Apr,1987

Serling, Rod
  The Escape Route, na **The Season to be Wary**, Little Brown:
    Boston,1967
    Rod Serling's Night Gallery Reader, ed. Carol Serling +,
    Dembner, 1987

Serraillier, Ian
  The Visitor, pm **A Second Poetry Book**, ed. John Foster, Oxford
    Univ. Press,1980
    The Ghost Story Treasury, ed. Linda Sonntag, Putnam, 1987

Severance, Carol
  Day of Strange Fortune, ss **Magic in Ithkar #4**, ed. Andre Norton &
    Robert Adams,1987
  Isle of Illusion, nv **Tales of the Witch World**, ed. Andre Norton, St.
    Martin's,1987

Sexton, Anne
  Briar Rose (Sleeping Beauty), pm **Transformations**, New York:
    Houghton Mifflin,1971
    Don't Bet on the Prince, ed. Jack Zipes, Methuen, 1987

Shahar, Eluki bes
  Light Fantastic, ss *Amazing* Mar,1987

Shalamov
  Major Pugachov's Last Battle [from **Kolyma Tales**], ar
    There Will Be War, Vol. VI: Guns of Darkness, ed. Jerry E.
    Pournelle, Tor, 1987

Shanklin, Rickey L.
  Blood of the Lamb, ss *Eldritch Tales* #13,1987

Shannon, Ed
  By the Way, ed *Minnesota Fantasy Review* #1,1987
  Internal Shadows, br *Minnesota Fantasy Review* #1,1987
  Now Appearing, vi *Minnesota Fantasy Review* #1,1987

Sharp, Evelyn
  The Spell of the Magician's Daughter, ss,1902
    Victorian Fairy Tales, ed. Jack Zipes, Methuen, 1987

Shaver, Edward F.
  Fear the Light, ss *Amazing* May,1987
  The Gods Arrive, nv *F&SF* Sep,1987

Shaw, Bob
  Burden of Proof, ss *Analog* May,1967
    PsiFi: Psychological Theories and Science Fictions, ed. Jim
    Ridgway+, The British Psychological Society, 1987
  Foreword, in
    PsiFi: Psychological Theories and Science Fictions, ed. Jim
    Ridgway+, The British Psychological Society, 1987
  Light of Other Days, ss *Analog* Aug,1966
    Great Science Fiction of the 20th Century, ed. Robert
    Silverberg+, Crown/Avenel, 1987
    Robert Silverberg's Worlds of Wonder, ed. Robert Silverberg,
    Warner, 1987

Shaw, Irwin
  Peter Two, ss *New Yorker*,1946
    Ready or Not, ed. Joan Kahn, Greenwillow, 1987

Shaw-Mathews, Patricia
  Coils, ss **Red Sun of Darkover**, ed. Marion Zimmer Bradley & The
    Friends of Darkover, DAW,1987

Shea, Michael
  The Angel of Death, nv *F&SF* Aug,1979
    Polyphemus, Arkham House, 1987
  The Autopsy, nv *F&SF* Dec,1980
    The Dark Descent, ed. David G. Hartwell, Tor, 1987
    Polyphemus, Arkham House, 1987
  Delivery, ss *F&SF* Dec,1987
  The Extra, nv *F&SF* May,1987
    Polyphemus, Arkham House, 1987
  Fat Face, nv Axolotl Press: Seattle WA,1987

Shea, Michael (continued)
  The Horror on the #33, ss *F&SF* Aug,1982
    Polyphemus, Arkham House, 1987
  The Pearls of the Vampire Queen, nv **Nifft the Lean**,1982
    Polyphemus, Arkham House, 1987
  Polyphemus, na *F&SF* Aug,1981
    Polyphemus, Arkham House, 1987
  Uncle Tuggs, nv *F&SF* May,1986
    Polyphemus, Arkham House, 1987

Sheckley, Jay
  Alien Mail to the White House, Exclusive: The Plook Letters, vi *Twilight
    Zone* Oct,1987
  Lost Soul, ss **Devils & Demons**, ed. Marvin Kaye,
    SFBC/Doubleday,1987
  Megamouse, ss *Night Cry* v2#5,1987
  The Other Side: The Zone of Silence, ar *Twilight Zone* Oct,1987
  The Other Side: Zoned Again?, ar *Twilight Zone* Aug,1987

Sheckley, Jay & Robert Sheckley
  Spectator Playoffs, ss *Night Cry* v2#3,1987

Sheckley, Robert
  The Demons, ss *Fantasy* Feb,1953
    Devils and Demons, ed. Marvin Kaye, Doubleday, 1987
  Miss Mouse and the Fourth Dimension, ss *Twilight Zone* Dec,1981
    Mathenauts, ed. Rudy Rucker, Arbor House, 1987
  The Monsters, ss *F&SF* Mar,1953
    Robert Silverberg's Worlds of Wonder, ed. Robert Silverberg,
    Warner, 1987
  Restricted Area, ss *Amazing* Jul,1953
    Amazing Science Fiction Stories: The Wild Years 1946-1955, ed.
    Martin H. Greenberg, TSR, 1987
  Shape [Keep Your Shape], nv *Galaxy* Nov,1953
    Great Science Fiction of the 20th Century, ed. Robert
    Silverberg+, Crown/Avenel, 1987

Sheckley, Robert & Jay Sheckley
  Spectator Playoffs, ss *Night Cry* v2#3,1987

Sheerin, Roisin
  Some Day My Prince Will Come, vi **Mad and Bad Fairies**, ed.
    Anonymous, Attic Press,1987

Sheffield, Charles
  Do You Really Want a Bigger U.S. Space Program?, ar **New
    Destinies** v2, ed. Jim Baen, Baen,1987
  The Dreaming Spires of Houston, ss **New Destinies** v2, ed. Jim Baen,
    Baen,1987
  Fixed Price War, ss *Analog* May,1978
    Battlefields Beyond Tomorrow, ed. Charles G. Waugh+,
    Crown/Bonanza, 1987
  The Grand Tour, ss *Analog* May,1987
  Guilt Trip, ss *Analog* Aug,1987
  Obsolete Skill, ss *F&SF* Dec,1987
  Running Out, ar **New Destinies** v2, ed. Jim Baen, Baen,1987
  Trader's Cross, nv *Analog* Mar,1987
  Trader's Partner, nv *Analog* Jul,1987
  Trapalanda, nv *IASFM* Jun,1987
  The Treasure of Odirex, na *Fantastic* Jul,1978
    **Isaac Asimov's Wonderful Worlds of Science Fiction #6:
    Neanderthals**, ed. Isaac Asimov+, NAL/Signet, 1987

Shefner, Evelyn
  The Common Body, na **Common Body, Royal Bones**, Coffee House
    Press: Minneapolis,1987
  Royal Bones, nv *Creel*
    Common Body, Royal Bones, Coffee House Press, 1987
  Troubles of a Tattooed King, ss *Carolina Quarterly*
    Common Body, Royal Bones, Coffee House Press, 1987

Sheldon, Glenn
  Accentuated Man in a Gradient Light, pm *Ice River* Sum,1987

Shelley, Mary W.
  Transformation, ss *The Keepsake*,1831
    Classic Stories of Mystery, Horror and Suspense, ed. Simon
    Petherick, Robert Hale, 1987

Shelley, Rick
  The Lizard, the Dragon, and the Eater of Souls, nv *Analog* Sep,1987

Shepard, Lucius
  Aymara, nv *IASFM* Aug,1986
    Terry Carr's Best Science Fiction and Fantasy of the Year #16,
      ed. Terry Carr, Tor, 1987
  The Black Clay Boy, ss **Whispers #6**, ed. Stuart David Schiff,1987
  Black Coral, nv **Universe #14**, ed. Terry Carr,1984
    The Jaguar Hunter, Arkham House, 1987
  Delta Sly Honey, ss **In the Field of Fire**, ed. Jeanne Van Buren Dann
      & Jack M. Dann, Tor,1987
    Twilight Zone Oct,1987
  The End of Life As We Know It, nv *IASFM* Jan,1985
    The Jaguar Hunter, Arkham House, 1987
  The Exercise of Faith, ss *Twilight Zone* Jun,1987
  The Glassblower's Dragon, ss *F&SF* Apr,1987
  How the Wind Spoke at Madaket, na *IASFM* Apr,1985
    The Jaguar Hunter, Arkham House, 1987
  The Jaguar Hunter, nv *F&SF* May,1985
    The Jaguar Hunter, Arkham House, 1987
  The Man Who Painted the Dragon Griaule, nv *F&SF* Dec,1984
    The Jaguar Hunter, Arkham House, 1987
  Mengele, ss **Universe #15**, ed. Terry Carr,1985
    The Jaguar Hunter, Arkham House, 1987
  The Night of White Bhairab, nv *F&SF* Oct,1984
    The Jaguar Hunter, Arkham House, 1987
    Demons!, ed. Jack M. Dann+, Ace, 1987
  On the Border, nv *IASFM* Aug,1987
  Pictures Made of Stone, ss *Omni* Sep,1987
  R&R, na *IASFM* Apr,1986
    The Jaguar Hunter, Arkham House, 1987
    The Year's Best Science Fiction, Fourth Annual Collection, ed.
      Gardner R. Dozois, St. Martin's, 1987
    The 1987 Annual World's Best SF, ed. Donald A. Wollheim+,
      DAW, 1987
  Salvador, ss *F&SF* Apr,1984
    The Jaguar Hunter, Arkham House, 1987
  Shades, nv **In the Field of Fire**, ed. Jeanne Van Buren Dann & Jack
      M. Dann, Tor,1987
    IASFM Dec,1987
  A Spanish Lesson, nv *F&SF* Dec,1985
    The Jaguar Hunter, Arkham House, 1987
  The Sun Spider, nv *IASFM* Apr,1987
  A Traveler's Tale, na *IASFM* Jul,1984
    The Jaguar Hunter, Arkham House, 1987
  White Trains, pm *Night Cry* v2#3,1987

Sherman, C.H.
  Tapestry, ss **Devils & Demons**, ed. Marvin Kaye,
      SFBC/Doubleday,1987

Sherman, Delia
  The Maid on the Shore, ss *F&SF* Oct,1987

Sherman, Josepha
  Danar's Hawk, ss *Fantasy Book* Mar,1987
  The Ring of Lifari, ss **Sword and Sorceress #4**, ed. Marion Zimmer
      Bradley,1987
  Zerail, ss *Fantasy Tales* #16,1986

Shiarella, Robert & William E. Kotzwinkle
  The Philosophy of Sebastian Trump or The Art of Outrage, ss **Brother
      Theodore's Chamber of Horrors**, ed. Marvin Kaye, Pinnacle,1975
    Devils and Demons, ed. Marvin Kaye, Doubleday, 1987

Shields, Ralston
  Mistress of the Blood-Drinkers, na *Horror Stories* Mar,1940
    The Weirds, ed. Sheldon R. Jaffery, Starmont House, 1987

Shiner, Edith & Lewis Shiner
  Six Flags Over Jesus, vi *IASFM* Nov,1987
  Things That Go Quack in the Night, ss *IASFM* Jan,1983
    Tales From Isaac Asimov's Science Fiction Magazine, ed. Sheila
      Williams+, Harcourt Brace Jovanovich, 1986

Shiner, Lewis
  Dancers, ss *Night Cry* v2#4,1987

Shiner, Lewis (continued)
  Introduction to "The Shadow on the Doorstep", in
    The Shadow on the Doorstep/Trilobyte, James P. Blaylock+,
      Axolotl, 1987
  Jeff Beck, ss *IASFM* Jan,1986
    The Year's Best Science Fiction, Fourth Annual Collection, ed.
      Gardner R. Dozois, St. Martin's, 1987
  The Left-Handed Muse, bg **All About Strange Monsters of the
    Recent Past**, Kansas City, MO: Ursus Imprints,1987
  Pennies from Hell, nv **Wild Cards** v2, ed. George R.R. Martin,
      Bantam,1987
  Rebels, ss *Omni* Nov,1987
  The War at Home, ss *IASFM* May,1985
    In the Field of Fire, ed. Jeanne Van Buren Dann+, Tor, 1987

Shiner, Lewis & Edith Shiner
  Six Flags Over Jesus, vi *IASFM* Nov,1987
  Things That Go Quack in the Night, ss *IASFM* Jan,1983
    Tales From Isaac Asimov's Science Fiction Magazine, ed. Sheila
      Williams+, Harcourt Brace Jovanovich, 1986

Shirley, John
  Parakeet, ss *New Pathways* Apr,1987
  Ticket to Heaven, ss *F&SF* Dec,1987

Shirley, John & Bruce Sterling
  The Unfolding, ss *Interzone* #11,1985
    Interzone: The 2nd Anthology, ed. John Clute+, Simon &
      Schuster UK, 1987

Shoemaker, Michael T.
  The Unknown Machen, pr
    Guinevere and Lancelot & Others, Arthur Machen, Purple Mouth,
      1986

Shwartz, Susan M.
  Temple to a Minor Goddess, ss *Amazing* Jan,1987

Siegel, Barbara & Scott Siegel
  The Blood Sea Monster, nv **DragonLance Tales** v1, Margaret Weis &
      Tracy Hickman, TSR,1987
  A Painter's Vision, nv **DragonLance Tales** v3, Margaret Weis & Tracy
      Hickman, TSR,1987
  The Storyteller, nv **DragonLance Tales** v2, Margaret Weis & Tracy
      Hickman, TSR,1987

Siegel, Scott & Barbara Siegel
  The Blood Sea Monster, nv **DragonLance Tales** v1, Margaret Weis &
      Tracy Hickman, TSR,1987
  A Painter's Vision, nv **DragonLance Tales** v3, Margaret Weis & Tracy
      Hickman, TSR,1987
  The Storyteller, nv **DragonLance Tales** v2, Margaret Weis & Tracy
      Hickman, TSR,1987

Sikes, Mary
  Salarius Recommends, br *Salarius* v1#4,1987

Sikes, Mary & Jon Colley
  Salarius Recommends, br *Salarius* #3,1987

Silbar, Margaret L.
  Cellular Automata, ar *Analog* Sep,1987

Silva, David B.
  Hellnotes, ed *The Horror Show* Jan,1987
  Hellnotes, ed *The Horror Show* Spr,1987
  Hellnotes, ed *The Horror Show* Sum,1987
  Hellnotes, ed *The Horror Show* Fll,1987
  Hellnotes, ed *The Horror Show* Win,1987
  Ice Sculptures, ss **Masques #2**, ed. J.N. Williamson,1987
  Matchsticks, vi *Eldritch Tales* #13,1987
  Metanoia, ss *New Blood* #1,1987
  Shifting Passions, vi *Footsteps* Nov,1987
  Watershead, vi *Grue* #5,1987

SILVERBERG, ROBERT   **SINCLAIR, KATHRYN A.**

Silverberg, Robert
  Afterword: The Valley of Neander, ar **Man Before Adam**, Robert
    Silverberg, Macrae Smith,1964
    Isaac Asimov's Wonderful Worlds of Science Fiction #6:
      Neanderthals, ed. Isaac Asimov+, NAL/Signet, 1987
  Against Babylon, nv *Omni* May,1986
    The Year's Best Science Fiction, Fourth Annual Collection, ed.
      Gardner R. Dozois, St. Martin's, 1987
    The 1987 Annual World's Best SF, ed. Donald A. Wollheim+,
      DAW, 1987
  Basileus, ss **The Best of Omni #5**,1983
    Demons!, ed. Jack M. Dann+, Ace, 1987
  Blindsight, nv *Playboy* Dec,1986
    Terry Carr's Best Science Fiction and Fantasy of the Year #16,
      ed. Terry Carr, Tor, 1987
  "Colony": I Trusted the Rug Completely, ar,1987
    Robert Silverberg's Worlds of Wonder, ed. Robert Silverberg,
      Warner, 1987
  "Common Time": With All of Love, ar,1987
    Robert Silverberg's Worlds of Wonder, ed. Robert Silverberg,
      Warner, 1987
  "Day Million": A Boy, a Girl, a Love Story, ar,1987
    Robert Silverberg's Worlds of Wonder, ed. Robert Silverberg,
      Warner, 1987
  The Fascination of the Abomination, na *IASFM* Jul,1987
    Angels in Hell, ed. Janet Morris, Baen, 1987
  "Fondly Fahrenheit": Who Am I, Which Are You?, ar,1987
    Robert Silverberg's Worlds of Wonder, ed. Robert Silverberg,
      Warner, 1987
  Foreword, fw
    Robert Silverberg's Worlds of Wonder, ed. Robert Silverberg,
      Warner, 1987
  "Four in One": Complications With Elegance, ar,1987
    Robert Silverberg's Worlds of Wonder, ed. Robert Silverberg,
      Warner, 1987
  Hardware, ss *Omni* Oct,1987
  "Home Is the Hunter": The Triumph of Honest Roger Bellamy, ar,1987
    Robert Silverberg's Worlds of Wonder, ed. Robert Silverberg,
      Warner, 1987
  "Hothouse": The Fuzzypuzzle Odyssey, ar,1987
    Robert Silverberg's Worlds of Wonder, ed. Robert Silverberg,
      Warner, 1987
  Introduction, in
    Battlefields Beyond Tomorrow, ed. Charles G. Waugh+,
      Crown/Bonanza, 1987
  Introduction: The Making of a Science-Fiction Writer, in
    Robert Silverberg's Worlds of Wonder, ed. Robert Silverberg,
      Warner, 1987
  The Iron Star, ss **Universe**, ed. Byron Preiss, Bantam Spectra,1987
  "Light of Other Days": Beyond the Radius of Capture, ar,1987
    Robert Silverberg's Worlds of Wonder, ed. Robert Silverberg,
      Warner, 1987
  "The Little Black Bag": Press Button for Triple Bypass, ar,1987
    Robert Silverberg's Worlds of Wonder, ed. Robert Silverberg,
      Warner, 1987
  Many Mansions, nv **Universe #3**, ed. Terry Carr,1973
    Robert Adams' Book of Alternate Worlds, ed. Robert Adams+,
      NAL/Signet, 1987
  "The Monsters": Don't Forget to Kill Your Wife, ar,1987
    Robert Silverberg's Worlds of Wonder, ed. Robert Silverberg,
      Warner, 1987
  Multiples, ss *Omni* Oct,1983
    The Fifth Omni Book of Science Fiction, ed. Ellen Datlow, Zebra,
      1987
  "The New Prime": Six Plots for the Price of One, ar,1987
    Robert Silverberg's Worlds of Wonder, ed. Robert Silverberg,
      Warner, 1987
  "No Woman Born": Flowing From Ring to Ring, ar,1987
    Robert Silverberg's Worlds of Wonder, ed. Robert Silverberg,
      Warner, 1987
  The Pardoner's Tale, ss *Playboy* Jun,1987
  Reflections, ar *Amazing* Jan,1987
  Reflections, ar *Amazing* Mar,1987
  Reflections, ar *Amazing* May,1987
  Reflections, ar *Amazing* Jul,1987
  Reflections, ar *Amazing* Sep,1987
  Reflections, ar *Amazing* Nov,1987

Silverberg, Robert (continued)
  "Scanners Live in Vain": Under the Wire With the Habermans, ar,1987
    Robert Silverberg's Worlds of Wonder, ed. Robert Silverberg,
      Warner, 1987
  The Secret Sharer, na *IASFM* Sep,1987
  Sundance, ss *F&SF* Jun,1969
    Great Science Fiction of the 20th Century, ed. Robert
      Silverberg+, Crown/Avenel, 1987

Silverberg, Robert & Harlan Ellison
  The Song the Zombie Sang, ss *Cosmopolitan* Dec,1970
    The Essential Ellison, Harlan Ellison, Nemo Press, 1987

Silverberg, Robert & Martin H. Greenberg
  Introduction, in
    Great Science Fiction of the 20th Century, ed. Robert
      Silverberg+, Crown/Avenel, 1987

Simak, Clifford D.
  Auk House, na **Stellar #3**, ed. Judy-Lynn del Rey,1977
    Brother and Other Stories, Severn House, 1987
  Brother, nv *F&SF* Oct,1977
    Brother and Other Stories, Severn House, 1987
  Kindergarten, nv *Astounding* Jul,1953
    Brother and Other Stories, Severn House, 1987
  Over the River and Through the Woods, ss *Amazing* May,1965
    Brother and Other Stories, Severn House, 1987
  Skirmish [Bathe Your Bearings in Blood], ss *Amazing* Dec,1950
    Amazing Science Fiction Stories: The Wild Years 1946-1955, ed.
      Martin H. Greenberg, TSR, 1987

Simmons, Dan
  E-Ticket to Namland, ss *Omni* Nov,1987

Simms, William Gilmore
  The Arm-Chair of Tustenuggee, ss
    Nightmares in Dixie, ed. Frank D. McSherry, Jr.+, August House,
      1987

Simon, Margaret B.
  Beyond Suawanee, pm *Minnesota Fantasy Review #1*,1987
  Sense of Wonder, ar *Minnesota Fantasy Review #1*,1987
  Spacer Trivia, pm *Amazing* Jul,1987

Simon, Morris
  The Wizard's Spectacles, nv **DragonLance Tales** v2, Margaret Weis &
    Tracy Hickman, TSR,1987

Simons, Walton
  If Looks Could Kill, ss **Wild Cards** v2, ed. George R.R. Martin,
    Bantam,1987

Simpson, Robert
  Children of the Night, ar *Twilight Zone* Dec,1987
  Games, gr *Twilight Zone* Aug,1987
  Illuminations: Really Weird Tales, ar *Twilight Zone* Apr,1987
  Magic in the Streets, ar *Twilight Zone* Apr,1987
  The Other Side: Children of the Night, ar *Twilight Zone* Jun,1987
  The Other Side: Dial "T" for Terror, ar *Twilight Zone* Apr,1987
  The Other Side: It Came from Across the Pond, ar *Twilight Zone*
    Aug,1987
  The Other Side: Surrealistic Wonkiness, ar *Twilight Zone* Jun,1987
  The Real Children of the Night, ar *Twilight Zone* Dec,1987

Sims, Mike
  Warm as Snow, ss **After Midnight Stories #3**,1987

Sinclair, Catherine
  Uncle David's Nonsensical Story about Giants and Fairies, ss **Holiday
    House, A Book for the Young**, London: Ward, Lock,1839
    Victorian Fairy Tales, ed. Jack Zipes, Methuen, 1987

Sinclair, Kathryn A.
  Raindance, ss **Tesseracts 2**, ed. Phyllis Gotlieb & Douglas Barbour,
    Press Porcepic: Victoria,1987

Sinclair, May
  The Token, ss **Uncanny Stories**, Hutchinson,1923
    The Virago Book of Ghost Stories, ed. Richard Dalby, Virago, 1987

Singer, Isaac Bashevis
  The Last Demon, ss **Short Friday**,1964
    Translated by Martha Glicklich and Cecil Hemley.
    Demons!, ed. Jack M. Dann+, Ace, 1987
    Devils and Demons, ed. Marvin Kaye, Doubleday, 1987

Singer, Kurt
  Poltergeist!, ss
    Poltergeist: Tales of Deadly Ghosts, ed. Peter Haining, Severn
      House, 1987

Singer, Richard
  Pop Stars, vi *Grue* #4,1987

Sjolie, Dennis John
  A Thing or Two About Razzle-Dazzle, ss *Mage* Spr,1987
    Mage Fll,1987

Skeet, Michael
  Rain, ss **Tesseracts 2**, ed. Phyllis Gotlieb & Douglas Barbour, Press
    Porcepic: Victoria,1987

Skipp, John M. & Craig Spector
  The Cleanup, ss *Night Cry* v2#4,1987
  Gentlemen, nv **The Architecture of Fear**, ed. Kathryn Cramer & Peter
    D. Pautz, Arbor House,1987

Skov, David M.
  Aversion, pm *Ouroboros* #4,1986
    Rhysling Anthology 1987, ed. Anonymous, SF Poetry Assc., 1987

Slaughter, Rick
  Delicate Immortal Meanings, ss **Gollancz - Sunday Times Best SF
    Stories**, Gollancz,1987

Smeds, Dave
  Goats, nv **In the Field of Fire**, ed. Jeanne Van Buren Dann & Jack M.
    Dann, Tor,1987
  Gullrider, ss **Sword and Sorceress** #4, ed. Marion Zimmer
    Bradley,1987
  A Hard Ride Home, ss *Mayfair* Sep,1987
  Something in the Wind, ss *Tales of the Unanticipated* #2,1987
  Termites, ss *IASFM* May,1987

Smirl, D.E.
  A Question of Belief, ss *Apex!* #1,1987

Smirl, D.E. & Jerry Meredith
  Dream in a Bottle, ss **L. Ron Hubbard Presents Writers of the
    Future** v2, ed. Algis Budrys, Bridge,1986
    The 1987 Annual World's Best SF, ed. Donald A. Wollheim+,
      DAW, 1987

Smith, Arnold
  The Face in the Fresco, ss *The London Mercury* Jun,1928
    Ghosts and Scholars, ed. Rosemary Pardoe+, Crucible, 1987

Smith, Brent R.
  Falling in Love Again, ss **The Pan Book of Horror Stories** #28,
    Pan,1987

Smith, Clark Ashton
  The Double Shadow, ss **The Double Shadow and Other Fantasies**,
    Auburn Journal: Auburn CA,1933; *Weird Tales* Feb,1939
    Isaac Asimov's Magical Worlds of Fantasy #9: Atlantis, ed. Isaac
      Asimov+, NAL/Signet, 1988
  The Plutonian Drug, ss *Amazing* Sep,1934
    Amazing Science Fiction Stories: The Wonder Years 1926-1935,
      ed. Martin H. Greenberg, TSR, 1987
  A Rendezvous in Averoigne, ss *Weird Tales* Apr,1931
    Vampires, ed. Alan Ryan, SFBC, 1987

Smith, Clark Ashton (continued)
  The Return of the Sorcerer, nv *Strange Tales of Mystery and Terror*
    Sep,1931
    Rod Serling's Night Gallery Reader, ed. Carol Serling+,
      Dembner, 1987

Smith, Cordwainer
  Alpha Ralpha Boulevard, nv *F&SF* Jun,1961
    Great Science Fiction of the 20th Century, ed. Robert
      Silverberg+, Crown/Avenel, 1987
  The Game of Rat and Dragon, nv *Galaxy* Oct,1955
    Isaac Asimov Presents the Great SF Stories: 17 (1955), ed. Isaac
      Asimov+, DAW, 1988
  Scanners Live in Vain, nv *Fantasy Book* #6,1950
    Robert Silverberg's Worlds of Wonder, ed. Robert Silverberg,
      Warner, 1987

Smith, Dean Wesley
  The Jukebox Man, ss *Night Cry* v2#5,1987

Smith, Evelyn E.
  Teragram, ss *Fantastic Universe* Jun,1955
    Young Witches & Warlocks, ed. Isaac Asimov+, Harper & Row,
      1987

Smith, Harding E.
  Quasars and Active Galaxies, ar **Universe**, ed. Byron Preiss, Bantam
    Spectra,1987

Smith, Harry
  The Ballad of Devil's Pasture, ss *Pulpsmith* Win,1987
  The Queen of the Night, pm *Pulpsmith* Win,1987

Smith, James Robert
  Things Not Seen, vi *2AM* Spr,1987

Smith, Nick
  The Life and Times of Nick Smith, pi *Salarius* v1#4,1987

Smith, Stephanie A.
  The Amber Frog, nv *IASFM* Sep,1984
    Tales From Isaac Asimov's Science Fiction Magazine, ed. Sheila
      Williams+, Harcourt Brace Jovanovich, 1986

Smith, Warren B.
  Dreams of Darkness, Dreams of Light, nv **DragonLance Tales** v1,
    Margaret Weis & Tracy Hickman, TSR,1987

SMS
  The Good Robot, cs *Interzone* #22,1987

Snellings, John H.
  First Come, First Served, ss **The Pan Book of Horror Stories** #28,
    Pan,1987

Sneyd, Steve
  The Package Tourist, ss *Back Brain Recluse* #7,1987

Snodgrass, Melinda M.
  Introduction, in
    A Very Large Array, ed. Melinda M. Snodgrass, Univ. of New
      Mexico Press, 1987
  Relative Difficulties, nv **Wild Cards** v2, ed. George R.R. Martin,
    Bantam,1987
  Requiem, ss **A Very Large Array**, ed. Melinda M. Snodgrass,
    University of New Mexico Press,1987

Snyder, Maryanne K.
  Eleanor Meets God, pm *Grue* #6,1987

Sokolov, Alexandra
  The Price of an Egg, nv **Angels in Hell**, ed. Janet Morris, Baen,1987

Solomon, Theodore
  A Hot Prospect, ss *Mage* Spr,1987

Somtow, S.P.
  ResurrecTech, nv *Night Cry* v2#3,1987

SONNEMANN, W.K.   **SPRINGER, NANCY**

Sonnemann, W.K.
   The Council of Drones, nv *Amazing* Oct,1936
      Amazing Science Fiction Stories: The War Years 1936-1945, ed.
      Martin H. Greenberg, TSR, 1987

Sontheimer, Lee Ann
   Presences, pm *2AM* Sum,1987

Soukup, Martha
   Frenchmen and Plumbers, ss *Aboriginal SF* Sep,1987
      A Very Large Array, ed. Melinda M. Snodgrass, Univ. of New
      Mexico Press, 1987
   Living in the Jungle, ss **L. Ron Hubbard Presents Writers of the
      Future** v3, ed. Algis Budrys, Bridge,1987
   Master of the Game, ss *F&SF* Nov,1987

Sourbut, Elizabeth
   The African Quota, ss **Gollancz - Sunday Times Best SF Stories**,
      Gollancz,1987

Spark, Muriel
   Alice Long's Dachshunds, na *New Yorker* Apr 1,1967
      The Stories of Muriel Spark, Bodley Head, 1987
   The Another Pair of Hands, ss *New Yorker* May 13,1985
      The Stories of Muriel Spark, Bodley Head, 1987
   Bang-Bang You're Dead, nv
      The Stories of Muriel Spark, Bodley Head, 1987
   The Black Madonna, ss
      The Stories of Muriel Spark, Bodley Head, 1987
   Come Along, Marjorie, ss
      The Stories of Muriel Spark, Bodley Head, 1987
   The Curtain Blown by the Breeze, ss
      The Stories of Muriel Spark, Bodley Head, 1987
   Daisy Overend, ss
      The Stories of Muriel Spark, Bodley Head, 1987
   The Dark Glasses, ss
      The Stories of Muriel Spark, Bodley Head, 1987
   The Dragon, ss *New Yorker* Aug 12,1985
      The Stories of Muriel Spark, Bodley Head, 1987
   The Executor, ss *New Yorker* Mar 14,1983
      The Stories of Muriel Spark, Bodley Head, 1987
   The Fathers' Daughters, ss
      The Stories of Muriel Spark, Bodley Head, 1987
   The First Year of My Life, ss *New Yorker* Jun 2,1975
      The Stories of Muriel Spark, Bodley Head, 1987
   The Fortune-Teller, ss *New Yorker* Jan 17,1983
      The Stories of Muriel Spark, Bodley Head, 1987
   The Gentile Jewesses, ss *New Yorker* Jun 22,1963
      The Stories of Muriel Spark, Bodley Head, 1987
   The House of the Famous Poet, ss *New Yorker* Apr 2,1966
      The Stories of Muriel Spark, Bodley Head, 1987
   The Leaf-Sweeper, ss,1966
      The Stories of Muriel Spark, Bodley Head, 1987
   A Member of the Family, ss *Mademoiselle* Feb,1961
      The Stories of Muriel Spark, Bodley Head, 1987
   Miss Pinkerton's Apocalypse, ss,1958
      The Stories of Muriel Spark, Bodley Head, 1987
   The Ormolu Clock, ss *New Yorker* Sep 17,1960
      The Stories of Muriel Spark, Bodley Head, 1987
   The Pawnbroker's Wife, ss
      The Stories of Muriel Spark, Bodley Head, 1987
   The Playhouse Called Remarkable, ss
      The Stories of Muriel Spark, Bodley Head, 1987
   The Portobello Road, nv *Cosmopolitan*,1958
      The Stories of Muriel Spark, Bodley Head, 1987
   'A Sad Tale's Best for Winter', ss
      The Stories of Muriel Spark, Bodley Head, 1987
   The Seraph and the Zambesi, ss
      The Stories of Muriel Spark, Bodley Head, 1987
   The Twins, ss
      The Stories of Muriel Spark, Bodley Head, 1987
   You Should Have Seen the Mess, ss
      The Stories of Muriel Spark, Bodley Head, 1987

Spears, Heather
   One, nv **Tesseracts 2**, ed. Phyllis Gotlieb & Douglas Barbour, Press
      Porcepic: Victoria,1987

Spector, Craig & John M. Skipp
   The Cleanup, ss *Night Cry* v2#4,1987
   Gentlemen, nv **The Architecture of Fear**, ed. Kathryn Cramer & Peter
      D. Pautz, Arbor House,1987

Speed, Jane
   Fair's Fair, ss *Ellery Queen's Mystery Magazine* Feb,1967
      Ready or Not, ed. Joan Kahn, Greenwillow, 1987

Speirs, Kevin
   Down Under, ss *Haunts* #9,1987

Spence, Dermot Chesson
   The Dean's Bargain, ss
      Ghosts and Scholars, ed. Rosemary Pardoe+, Crucible, 1987

Spence, Lewis
   The Horn of Vapula, ss **The Archer in the Arras**, Grant & Murray:
      London,1932
      Ghosts and Scholars, ed. Rosemary Pardoe+, Crucible, 1987

Spinrad, Hyron
   Galaxies and Clusters, ar **Universe**, ed. Byron Preiss, Bantam
      Spectra,1987

Spinrad, Norman
   Introduction, in
      **The Collected Stories of Philip K. Dick, Vol. Two: Second
         Variety**, Philip K. Dick, Underwood-Miller, 1987
   On Books: Dreamers of Space, br *IASFM* Oct,1987
   On Books: Sturgeon, Vonnegut, and Trout, br *IASFM* Apr,1987
   On Books: The Edge of the Envelope, br *IASFM* Jul,1987
   Outward Bound, nv *Analog* Mar,1964
      Imperial Stars, Vol. 2: Republic and Empire, ed. Jerry E.
      Pournelle, Baen, 1987
   Prime Time, ss *Omni* Nov,1980
      The Fifth Omni Book of Science Fiction, ed. Ellen Datlow, Zebra,
      1987

Spivack, Richard
   My Best Ever Holiday, ss **Gollancz - Sunday Times Best SF Stories**,
      Gollancz,1987

Spofford, Harriet Prescott
   Circumstance, ss *Atlantic Monthly* May,1860
      Strange Maine, ed. Charles G. Waugh+, Tapley, 1986

Springer, Nancy
   Amends, A Tale of the Sun Kings, ss *F&SF* May,1983
      Chance & Other Gestures of the Hand of Fate, Baen, 1987
   The Bard, ss **Chance & Other Gestures of the Hand of Fate**,
      Baen,1987
   The Boy Who Plaited Manes, ss *F&SF* Oct,1986
      Chance & Other Gestures of the Hand of Fate, Baen, 1987
      The Year's Best Fantasy Stories: 13, ed. Arthur W. Saha, DAW,
      1987
   Bright-Eyed Black Pony, ss **Moonsinger's Friends**, ed. Susan
      Shwartz, Bluejay,1985
      Chance & Other Gestures of the Hand of Fate, Baen, 1987
   Chance, na **Under the Wheel: Alien Stars Vol. III**, ed. Elizabeth
      Mitchell, Baen,1987
      Chance & Other Gestures of the Hand of Fate, Baen, 1987
   Come In, pm *Night Voyages Poetry Review*,1982
      Chance & Other Gestures of the Hand of Fate, Baen, 1987
   The Dog-King of Vaire, ss *Fantasy Book* Aug,1982
      Chance & Other Gestures of the Hand of Fate, Baen, 1987
   The Golden Face of Fate, na **Chance & Other Gestures of the Hand
      of Fate**, Baen,1987
   Primal Cry, nv **Chance & Other Gestures of the Hand of Fate**,
      Baen,1987
   The Prince Out of the Past, ss **Magic in Ithkar #1**, ed. Andre Norton
      & Robert Adams,1985
      Chance & Other Gestures of the Hand of Fate, Baen, 1987
   We Build a Shrine, pm **Chance & Other Gestures of the Hand of
      Fate**, Baen, 1987
   The Wolf Girl Speaks, pm *Star*Line* v5#6,1982
      Chance & Other Gestures of the Hand of Fate, Baen, 1987

ST. CLAIR, MARGARET   **STINE, G. HARRY**

St. Clair, Margaret
  The Boy Who Predicted Earthquakes, ss *Maclean's*,1950
    Rod Serling's Night Gallery Reader, ed. Carol Serling +,
      Dembner, 1987
  Brenda, ss *Weird Tales* Mar,1954
    Rod Serling's Night Gallery Reader, ed. Carol Serling +,
      Dembner, 1987
  The House in Bel Aire, ss *If* Jan,1961
    House Shudders, ed. Martin H. Greenberg +, DAW, 1987

St. Leger, Philip
  Modern History, ss **Gollancz - Sunday Times Best SF Stories**,
    Gollancz,1987

Stableford, Brian M.
  And He Not Busy Being Born..., ss *Interzone* #16,1986
    Interzone: The 2nd Anthology, ed. John Clute +, Simon &
      Schuster UK, 1987
  Layers of Meaning, ss *Interzone* #21,1987
  Sexual Chemistry, ss *Interzone* #20,1987

Staff
  Book Reviews, br *New Pathways* Jan,1987

Staig, Laurence
  Hello, Hugo, ss **Twisted Circuits**, ed. Mick Gowar, Beaver,1987

Stall, Dave
  Winged Death, ss *Minnesota Fantasy Review* #1,1987

Stamper, J.B.
  At Midnight, ss **More Tales for the Midnight Hour**,
    Apple/Scholastic,1987
  The Black Mare, ss **More Tales for the Midnight Hour**,
    Apple/Scholastic,1987
  The Collector, ss **More Tales for the Midnight Hour**,
    Apple/Scholastic,1987
  Footsteps, ss **More Tales for the Midnight Hour**,
    Apple/Scholastic,1987
  A Ghost Story, ss **More Tales for the Midnight Hour**,
    Apple/Scholastic,1987
  The Hearse, ss **More Tales for the Midnight Hour**,
    Apple/Scholastic,1987
  In the Lantern's Light, ss **More Tales for the Midnight Hour**,
    Apple/Scholastic,1987
  The Love Charm, ss **More Tales for the Midnight Hour**,
    Apple/Scholastic,1987
  The Mask, ss **More Tales for the Midnight Hour**,
    Apple/Scholastic,1987
  A Night in the Woods, ss **More Tales for the Midnight Hour**,
    Apple/Scholastic,1987
  Right Inn, ss **More Tales for the Midnight Hour**,
    Apple/Scholastic,1987
  The Shortcut, ss **More Tales for the Midnight Hour**,
    Apple/Scholastic,1987
  Trick-or-Treat, ss **More Tales for the Midnight Hour**,
    Apple/Scholastic,1987

Stanford, Derek
  Meeting Mr. Singleton, ss **After Midnight Stories** #3,1987

Stanley, John
  The Introduction: Will the Real Lefty Feep Please Rise to the
    Occasion?, in
    Lost in Time and Space with Lefty Feep, Robert Bloch, Creatures
      at Large, 1987
  Shock Supplement, mr *American Fantasy* Spr,1987
  Shock Supplement, mr *American Fantasy* Sum,1987
  Shock Supplement, mr *American Fantasy* Win,1987

Stanley, Stephen
  2087, ct *Aphelion* #5,1987

Starkey, David
  Confession, vi *Grue* #4,1987
  The Hand of God, ss *2AM* Sum,1987
  Trimmings, ss *Grue* #5,1987

Stathis, Lou
  Illuminations: Comic Relief, ar *Twilight Zone* Apr,1987
  The Other Side: Apocalyptic Voivod, ar *Twilight Zone* Dec,1987
  The Other Side: Dark Knight, ar *Twilight Zone* Jun,1987
  The Other Side: Giger Counting, ar *Twilight Zone* Dec,1987
  The Other Side: Opera of the Red Death, ar *Twilight Zone* Feb,1987
  The Other Side: Things Without Faces, ar *Twilight Zone* Jun,1987

Steakley, John
  The Swordsman Smada, nv **Friends of the Horseclans**, ed. Robert
    Adams & Pamela Crippen Adams, Signet,1987

Stein, Judith
  Why the Moon Is Small and Dark When the Sun Is Big and Shiny, ss
    Hear the Silence, ed. Irene Zahava, Crossing Press,1986

Steiner, K. Leslie
  "Return..." A Preface, pr
    The Bridge of Lost Desire, Samuel R. Delany, Arbor House, 1987

Stephenson, Bryan G.
  Dubious Pleasures, ss *Amazing* Sep,1987

Sterling, Bruce
  The Beautiful and the Sublime, nv *IASFM* Jun,1986
    The Year's Best Science Fiction, Fourth Annual Collection, ed.
      Gardner R. Dozois, St. Martin's, 1987
  Flowers for Edo, nv *IASFM* May,1987
  The Little Magic Shop, ss *IASFM* Oct,1987

Sterling, Bruce & John Shirley
  The Unfolding, ss *Interzone* #11,1985
    Interzone: The 2nd Anthology, ed. John Clute +, Simon &
      Schuster UK, 1987

Sterling, Bruce & Don Webb
  Bruce Sterling, iv *New Pathways* Aug,1987

Stevens, James A.
  Borboleta, ss *Aboriginal SF* Jul,1987

Stevens, Julie
  Century Farm, ss *Whispers* #23,1987

Stevenson, Robert Louis
  Markheim, ss *The Broken Shaft, Unwin's Annual* Chr,1885;
    Ellery Queen's Mystery Magazine Jul,1955
    Classic Stories of Mystery, Horror and Suspense, ed. Simon
      Petherick, Robert Hale, 1987
    Tales of the Dark, ed. Lincoln Child, St. Martin's, 1987
    Devils and Demons, ed. Marvin Kaye, Doubleday, 1987

Stevermer, Caroline
  Cenedwine Brocade, ss **Liavek: Wizard's Row**, ed. Will Shetterly &
    Emma Bull, Ace,1987

Stewart, Ian
  Billy the Kid, ss *Analog* Jan,1987
  Captives of the Slavestone, nv *Analog* mid-Dec,1987
  Displaced Person, na *Analog* May,1987
  The Electronic Mathematician, ar *Analog* Jan,1987

Stewart, W. Gregory
  Daedalus, pm *Star*Line* Nov,1986
    Rhysling Anthology 1987, ed. Anonymous, SF Poetry Assc., 1987

Stiegler, Marc
  The Third Alternative, nv *Analog* Nov,1987

Stine, G. Harry
  The Alternate View: Cultural Differences, ar *Analog* Sep,1987
  The Alternate View: Frontiers and Wars, ar *Analog* Jan,1987
  The Alternate View: Hardening Humans, ar *Analog* mid-Dec,1987
  The Alternate View: Overreaction, ar *Analog* Jul,1987
  The Alternate View: Stealth, ar *Analog* May,1987
  The Alternate View: The Fits and Flops of Fuzzy Logic, ar *Analog*
    Mar,1987
  The Alternate View: The Selling of Proton, ar *Analog* Nov,1987

STINE, G. HARRY

STURGEON, THEODORE

Stine, G. Harry (continued)
The Dream Is Down, ar *Analog* Feb,1987
The Space Beat: How to Stop a Space Program, ar **New Destinies**
v1, ed. Jim Baen, Baen,1987

Stith, John E.
Doing Time, ss *Aboriginal SF* Jul,1987

Stockton, Frank R.
The Great Staircase at Landover Hall, ss
Christmas Ghosts, ed. Kathryn Cramer+, Arbor House, 1987

Stoker, Bram
The Burial of the Rats, nv **Dracula's Guest**, Routledge: London,1914
Devils and Demons, ed. Marvin Kaye, Doubleday, 1987
Dracula's Guest [also as "Dracula's Daughter"], ss **Dracula's Guest**,
Routledge: London,1914
Written in 1897 as part of **Dracula**, this chapter was omitted from
the published book for reasons of length.
Vampires, ed. Alan Ryan, SFBC, 1987
Cinemonsters, ed. Martin H. Greenberg, TSR, 1987
The Judge's House, ss *Holly Leaves* Dec 5,1891
Charles Keeping's Classic Tales of the Macabre, ed. Charles
Keeping, Blackie, 1987
House Shudders, ed. Martin H. Greenberg+, DAW, 1987
The Squaw, ss,1893
Tales of the Dark, ed. Lincoln Child, St. Martin's, 1987

Stokes, Tawn
No Pets, ss **L. Ron Hubbard Presents Writers of the Future** v3, ed.
Algis Budrys, Bridge,1987

Stone, Merlin
The Plasting Project, ss **Hear the Silence**, ed. Irene Zahava, Crossing
Press,1986

Strauss, Erwin S.
SF Conventional Calendar, ms *IASFM* Jan,1987
SF Conventional Calendar, ms *IASFM* Feb,1987
SF Conventional Calendar, ms *IASFM* Mar,1987
SF Conventional Calendar, ms *IASFM* Apr,1987
SF Conventional Calendar, ms *IASFM* May,1987
SF Conventional Calendar, ms *IASFM* Jun,1987
SF Conventional Calendar, ms *IASFM* Jul,1987
SF Conventional Calendar, ms *IASFM* Aug,1987
SF Conventional Calendar, ms *IASFM* Sep,1987
SF Conventional Calendar, ms *IASFM* Oct,1987
SF Conventional Calendar, ms *IASFM* Nov,1987
SF Conventional Calendar, ms *IASFM* Dec,1987
SF Conventional Calendar, ms *IASFM* mid-Dec,1987

Strete, Craig Kee
As If Bloodied on a Hunt Before Sleep, ss *Twilight Zone* Aug,1987
The Game of Cat and Eagle, nv **In the Field of Fire**, ed. Jeanne Van
Buren Dann & Jack M. Dann, Tor,1987

Strickland, Brad
In the Hour Before Dawn, ss *F&SF* Aug,1986
The Year's Best Horror Stories: XV, ed. Karl Edward Wagner,
DAW, 1987
Oh Tin Man, Tin Man, There's No Place Like Home, ss *F&SF* May,1987

Strickland, John
Terrorstorm, ss *The Horror Show* Win,1987

Stricklin, Robert
Autograph, ss *2AM* Spr,1987

Strieber, Whitley
Perverts, ss *Whispers* #19,1983
Masters of Darkness II, ed. Dennis Etchison, Tor, 1988

Strong, Louise J.
An Unscientific Story, ss *Cosmopolitan* Feb,1903
Dracula's Brood, ed. Richard Dalby, Crucible, 1987

Stross, Charles
The Boys, ss *Interzone* #22,1987

Stuart, Don A.
Twilight, ss *Astounding* Nov,1934
6 Decades: The Best of Analog, ed. Stanley Schmidt, Davis, 1986

Stuart, Jesse
Fast-Train Ike, ss
Nightmares in Dixie, ed. Frank D. McSherry, Jr.+, August House,
1987

Stuart, Kiel
Cutting Up, ss *Muscle Training Illustrated* Sep,1987
Death Spiral, ss *Muscle Training Illustrated* Aug,1987
Green in High Hallack, ss **Tales of the Witch World**, ed. Andre
Norton, St. Martin's,1987

Stubbs, Jean
The Band in the Park, ss **Ghost Book #11**, ed. Aidan
Chambers/James Turner,1975
The Third Book of After Midnight Stories, ed. Amy Myers, Kimber,
1987

Studach, Stephen
The Black Things, pm *Eldritch Tales* #14,1987
Tomb Mate, pm *Eldritch Tales* #13,1987

Sturgeon, Jane Tannehill
Afterword, aw
Pruzy's Pot, Theodore Sturgeon, Hypatia Press, 1986

Sturgeon, Theodore
And Now the News..., ss *F&SF* Dec,1956
A Touch of Sturgeon, Simon & Schuster UK, 1987
Bright Segment, nv **Caviar**, Ballantine,1955
The Dark Descent, ed. David G. Hartwell, Tor, 1987
Dazed, nv *Galaxy* Sep,1971
Isaac Asimov's Magical Worlds of Fantasy #8: Devils, ed. Isaac
Asimov+, NAL/Signet, 1987
The Golden Helix, na *Thrilling Wonder Stories* Sum,1954
A Touch of Sturgeon, Simon & Schuster UK, 1987
Killdozer!, na *Astounding* Nov,1944
A Touch of Sturgeon, Simon & Schuster UK, 1987
Cinemonsters, ed. Martin H. Greenberg, TSR, 1987
To Marry Medusa, Baen, 1987
Memorial, ss *Astounding* Apr,1946
Battlefields Beyond Tomorrow, ed. Charles G. Waugh+,
Crown/Bonanza, 1987
Mr. Costello, Hero, nv *Galaxy* Dec,1953
A Touch of Sturgeon, Simon & Schuster UK, 1987
The Other Celia, ss *Galaxy* Mar,1957
A Touch of Sturgeon, Simon & Schuster UK, 1987
Pruzy's Pot, ss *The National Lampoon* Jun,1972
Pruzy's Pot, Theodore Sturgeon, Hypatia Press, 1986
The Sex Opposite, nv *Fantastic* Fll,1952
A Touch of Sturgeon, Simon & Schuster UK, 1987
The Skills of Xanadu, nv *Galaxy* Jul,1956
Imperial Stars, Vol. 2: Republic and Empire, ed. Jerry E.
Pournelle, Baen, 1987
Slow Sculpture, nv *Galaxy* Feb,1970
A Touch of Sturgeon, Simon & Schuster UK, 1987
Theodore Sturgeon on Philip Dick, iv Oct,1977
Philip K. Dick: The Dream Connection, D. Scott Apel, Permanent
Press, 1987
To Marry Medusa [The Cosmic Rape], n. Dell: New York pb
Aug,1958
Expanded from "To Marry Medusa" *Galaxy* Aug,58.
To Marry Medusa, Baen, 1987
A Way of Thinking, nv *Amazing* Nov,1953
Amazing Science Fiction Stories: The Wild Years 1946-1955, ed.
Martin H. Greenberg, TSR, 1987
When You Care, When You Love, nv *F&SF* Sep,1962
Great Science Fiction of the 20th Century, ed. Robert
Silverberg+, Crown/Avenel, 1987
When You're Smiling, nv *Galaxy* Jan,1955
A Touch of Sturgeon, Simon & Schuster UK, 1987
Who? [also as "Bulkhead"], nv *Galaxy* Mar,1955
Isaac Asimov Presents the Great SF Stories: 17 (1955), ed. Isaac
Asimov+, DAW, 1988

SUCHARITKUL, SOMTOW   TEPPER, SHERI S.

Sucharitkul, Somtow
Fiddling for Waterbuffaloes, nv *Analog* Apr,1986
    The Year's Best Science Fiction, Fourth Annual Collection, ed.
    Gardner R. Dozois, St. Martin's, 1987

Sullivan, Jean
Bloody Waters, ss *Eldritch Tales* #13,1987

Sullivan, Thomas
The Fence, ss **Shadows** #10, ed. Charles L. Grant,1987
The Man Who Drowned Puppies, ss **Masques** #2, ed. J.N.
    Williamson,1987
Prayerwings, nv **Doom City**, ed. Charles L. Grant, Tor,1987

Sullivan, Tim
Dinosaur on a Bicycle, nv *IASFM* Mar,1987

Summa, Alan Jude
Alan Jude Summa, bg *2AM* Win,1987
Dreams of Imagination, pm *2AM* Win,1987

Summers, Montague
The Grimoire, ss,1936
    Ghosts and Scholars, ed. Rosemary Pardoe +, Crucible, 1987
The Phantom Werewolf, ss
    Werewolf: Horror Stories of the Man Beast, ed. Peter Haining,
    Severn House, 1987

Sutton, David
Waking, ss *2AM* Win,1987

Svedbeck, Heather
After a Brief Commercial Message, ss *Twilight Zone* Apr,1987
    Second place winner, TZ short story contest.
One Special, Perfect Way, ss *2AM* Fll,1987

Swain, E.G.
The Eastern Window, ss **The Stoneground Ghost Tales**, W. Heffer:
    Cambridge,1912
    Ghosts and Scholars, ed. Rosemary Pardoe +, Crucible, 1987

Swanwick, Michael
Covenant of Souls, nv *Omni* Dec,1986
    The Year's Best Science Fiction, Fourth Annual Collection, ed.
    Gardner R. Dozois, St. Martin's, 1987
Foresight, ss *Interzone* #20,1987
Vacuum Flowers [Part 2 of 3], sl *IASFM* Jan,1987
Vacuum Flowers [Part 3 of 3], sl *IASFM* Feb,1987

Tagrin, Lawrence
Art in Space, ar *Salarius* v1#4,1987
Ice, ss *Salarius* v1#4,1987

Tarr, Judith
Piece de Resistance, nv *IASFM* Apr,1986
    The Year's Best Fantasy Stories: 13, ed. Arthur W. Saha, DAW,
    1987

Tarzia, Wade
Alandriar Goes To Earth, ss *Mage* Spr,1987
Decay in the Hero's Way, ar *Mage* Spr,1987
Message Intercepted On Hyperspatial Frequency, vi *Mage* Win,1987
    Mage Fll,1987
A Trace of Inbetween, ar *Mage* Win,1987

Tatro, Edgar F.
"War on Imagination" Feedback, lt *2AM* Spr,1987

Taylor, C. & R.L. Newman
Eight Legs Hath the Spider, vi *Haunts* #9,1987

Taylor, D.W.
Dog Meat, ss *Footsteps* Nov,1987

Taylor, Elizabeth
Poor Girl, ss **Ghost Book** #3, ed. Aidan Chambers/James
    Turner,1955
    The Virago Book of Ghost Stories, ed. Richard Dalby, Virago, 1987

Taylor, John Alfred
Bird in a Wrought Iron Cage, ss **The Chill Winds of October**, Laurel
    Arts Foundation,1986
    The Year's Best Horror Stories: XV, ed. Karl Edward Wagner,
    DAW, 1987

Taylor, Richard
Shards, pm *Ice River* Sum,1987
The Visitor, ss *2AM* Fll,1987

Taylor, Stephanie
Third Generation, ss *SF International* #2,1987

Tem, Melanie & Steve Rasnic Tem
The Sing, ss *SF International* #1,1987

Tem, Steve Rasnic
Dinosaur, ss *IASFM* May,1987
Fogwell, ss **Doom City**, ed. Charles L. Grant, Tor,1987
Ghost Signs, pm *Eldritch Tales* #14,1987
Hidey Hole, ss **Masques** #2, ed. J.N. Williamson,1987
L Is for Love, vi *Footsteps* Nov,1987
Last Dragon, ss *Amazing* Sep,1987
Leaks, ss **Whispers** #6, ed. Stuart David Schiff,1987
The Men and Women of Rivendale, ss **Night Visions** #1,1984
    Vampires, ed. Alan Ryan, SFBC, 1987
Mother Hag, ss *Grue* #5,1987
Off the Subject I: On Genre, Magical Realism, and Writing Seriously,
    ar *The Horror Show* Sum,1987
Off the Subject II: Background and Foreground, ar *The Horror Show*
    Fll,1987
Wake, ss *Eldritch Tales* #13,1987
The Woman on the Corner, ss *Whispers* #23,1987

Tem, Steve Rasnic & Melanie Tem
The Sing, ss *SF International* #1,1987

Temperley, Alan
The Abandoned Dam, nv **The Pan Book of Horror Stories** #28,
    Pan,1987

Temple, William F.
The Four-Sided Triangle, nv *Amazing* Nov,1939
    Amazing Science Fiction Stories: The War Years 1936-1945, ed.
    Martin H. Greenberg, TSR, 1987

Teng, Tais
What Avails a Psalm in the Cinders of Gehenna?, ss *SF International*
    #2,1987

Tenn, William
Child's Play, nv *Astounding* Mar,1947
    Great Science Fiction of the 20th Century, ed. Robert
    Silverberg +, Crown/Avenel, 1987
Down Among the Dead Men, nv *Galaxy* Jun,1954
    Isaac Asimov Presents the Great SF Stories: 16 (1954), ed. Isaac
    Asimov +, DAW, 1987
Mistress Sary, ss *Weird Tales* May,1947
    Young Witches & Warlocks, ed. Isaac Asimov +, Harper & Row,
    1987
She Only Goes Out at Night, ss *Fantastic Universe* Oct,1956
    Vamps, ed. Martin H. Greenberg +, DAW, 1987

Tensei, Kono
Triceratops, ss *Omni* Aug,1982
    Translated by David Lewis.
    The Fifth Omni Book of Science Fiction, ed. Ellen Datlow, Zebra,
    1987

Tepper, Sheri S.
Dervish Daughter, n. Tor: New York,1986
    The End of the Game, SFBC, 1987
Jinian Footseer, n. Tor: New York,1985
    The End of the Game, SFBC, 1987
Jinian Star-Eye, n. Tor: New York,1986
    The End of the Game, SFBC, 1987
Northshore, n. Tor: New York,1987
    The Awakeners, SFBC, 1987

TEPPER, SHERI S.   **TURTLEDOVE, HARRY**

Tepper, Sheri S. (continued)
  Southshore, n. Tor: New York,1987
  The Awakeners, SFBC, 1987

Terry, Saralee
  The Celery Stalk in the Cellar, pm **Brother Theodore's Chamber of
    Horrors**, ed. Marvin Kaye, Pinnacle,1975
  Devils and Demons, ed. Marvin Kaye, Doubleday, 1987

Thackeray, William Makepeace
  The Devil's Wager, ss,1836
  Devils and Demons, ed. Marvin Kaye, Doubleday, 1987

Thompson, Paul B. & Tonya R. Carter
  The Exiles, nv **DragonLance Tales** v3, Margaret Weis & Tracy
    Hickman, TSR,1987

Thompson, W.R.
  The Extremists, na *Analog* Jan,1987
  Health Food, ss *Analog* May,1987
  Lightning Rod, nv *Analog* Aug,1987
  Oracle, ss *Analog* Jun,1987

Tilton, Lois
  Across the Fog-Gray Sea, ss *The Dragon* Feb,1987
  The Passing of Kings, ss *The Dragon* Sep,1987

Timperley, Rosemary
  Christmas Meeting, vi,1952
    Christmas Ghosts, ed. Kathryn Cramer+, Arbor House, 1987
  The Mistress in Black, ss **Ghost Book #5**, ed. Aidan
    Chambers/James Turner,1969
    The Virago Book of Ghost Stories, ed. Richard Dalby, Virago, 1987

Tiptree, James, Jr.
  Houston, Houston, Do You Read?, na **Aurora: Beyond Equality**, ed.
    Vonda McIntyre & Susan Anderson, Fawcett,1976
    Beyond the Stars, ed. Isaac Asimov, Severn House, 1987
  How Do You Know You're Reading Philip K. Dick?, in
    **The Collected Stories of Philip K. Dick, Vol. Four: The Days of
    Perky Pat**, Philip K. Dick, Underwood-Miller, 1987
  In Midst of Life, ss *F&SF* Nov,1987
  Second Going, nv **Universe #17**, ed. Terry Carr,1987
  The Women Men Don't See, nv *F&SF* Dec,1973
    Great Science Fiction of the 20th Century, ed. Robert
    Silverberg+, Crown/Avenel, 1987
  Yanqui Doodle, nv *IASFM* Jul,1987

Toai, Doan Van & David Chanoff
  Learning from Viet Nam, ar *Encounter* Sep,1982
    There Will Be War, Vol. VI: Guns of Darkness, ed. Jerry E.
    Pournelle, Tor, 1987

Tobin, Pat
  Merovan Sea Floor and Hemispheric Maps, il
    Fever Season: Merovingen Nights #2, ed. C.J. Cherryh, DAW,
    1987
  Merovingian City Maps, il
    Fever Season: Merovingen Nights #2, ed. C.J. Cherryh, DAW,
    1987
  Merovingian City Maps and Merovin Hemispheric Maps, il **Festival
    Moon**, ed. C.J. Cherryh, DAW,1987
  Sea Floor Maps, il **Festival Moon**, ed. C.J. Cherryh, DAW,1987

Toelly, Richard
  Unborn, pm *Space & Time* #73,1987

Tolley, Michael
  Tesseractuality, br *Aphelion* #5,1987

Tolstoi, Leo
  The Tale of Ivan the Fool, nv
    Isaac Asimov's Magical Worlds of Fantasy #8: Devils, ed. Isaac
    Asimov+, NAL/Signet, 1987

Torren, Asher
  The African Woman, pm *Mage* Spr,1987
  Huayno, pm *Mage* Win,1987

Torren, Asher (continued)
  Mage Fll,1987

Travis, J.J.
  Halloween in Arkham, ss *Eldritch Tales* #13,1987

Trefil, James
  The New Physics and the Universe, ar **Universe**, ed. Byron Preiss,
    Bantam Spectra,1987

Tremayne, Peter
  The Singing Stone, ss *Fantasy Tales* #16,1986

Trewin, J.C.
  The Manse, ss **After Midnight Stories** #3,1987

Trexler, Roger Dale
  Dead Beat, ss *Minnesota Fantasy Review* #1,1987
  In Time, pm **The Dark Road and Other Poems of Darkness**,1987
  2AM Sum,1987

Tritten, Larry
  The Dead Woods, ss *F&SF* Jul,1987
  Hooray for Hollywood, vi *The Horror Show* Win,1987
  In Video Veritas, ss *F&SF* Dec,1987

Tsui, Kitty
  Why the Sea Is Salty, ss **Common Lives/Lesbian Lives**,1982
    Hear the Silence, ed. Irene Zahava, Crossing Press, 1986

Tucker, Wallace
  The Intergalactic Medium, ar **Universe**, ed. Byron Preiss, Bantam
    Spectra,1987

Tumlin, John S.
  Tiger's Hunt, ss *Aboriginal SF* May,1987

Turgenev, Ivan
  Clara Militch, nv
    The Dark Descent, ed. David G. Hartwell, Tor, 1987

Turner, George
  Not in Front of the Children, ss *Aphelion* #5,1987

Turney, C. Dell
  Portraits of a Young Artist, ss *Space & Time* #72,1987

Turtledove, Harry
  6+, na *Analog* Sep,1987
  And So to Bed, ss *Analog* Jan,1986
    The Year's Best Science Fiction, Fourth Annual Collection, ed.
    Gardner R. Dozois, St. Martin's, 1987
    Terry Carr's Best Science Fiction and Fantasy of the Year #16,
    ed. Terry Carr, Tor, 1987
  Archetypes, nv *Amazing* Nov,1985
    Agent of Byzantium, Harry Turtledove, Congdon &
    Weed/Contemporary, 1987
  Crybaby, ss *Twilight Zone* Dec,1987
  The Eyes of Argos, nv *Amazing* Jan,1986
    Agent of Byzantium, Harry Turtledove, Congdon &
    Weed/Contemporary, 1987
    There Will Be War, Vol. VI: Guns of Darkness, ed. Jerry E.
    Pournelle, Tor, 1987
  Images, nv *IASFM* Mar,1987
    Agent of Byzantium, Harry Turtledove, Congdon &
    Weed/Contemporary, 1987
  The Irvhank Effect, ss **New Destinies** v2, ed. Jim Baen, Baen,1987
  Last Favor, nv *Analog* mid-Dec,1987
  Noninterference [as by Eric G. Iverson], ss *Analog* Jul,1985
    Noninterference, Harry Turtledove, Ballantine/Del Rey, 1988
  Preface, pr
    Agent of Byzantium, Harry Turtledove, Congdon &
    Weed/Contemporary, 1987
  The Report on Bilbeis IV, na *Analog* May +2,1987
    Noninterference, Harry Turtledove, Ballantine/Del Rey, 1988
  The Report on Bilbeis IV [Part 1 of 3], sl *Analog* May,1987
  The Report on Bilbeis IV [Part 2 of 3], sl *Analog* Jun,1987
  The Report on Bilbeis IV [Part 3 of 3], sl *Analog* Jul,1987

TURTLEDOVE, HARRY   **VARLEY, JOHN**

Turtledove, Harry (continued)
  Second Survey, nv *Analog* Jul,1986
    Noninterference, Harry Turtledove, Ballantine/Del Rey, 1988
  Strange Eruptions, nv *IASFM* Aug,1986
    Agent of Byzantium, Harry Turtledove, Congdon &
      Weed/Contemporary, 1987
  Superwine, na *IASFM* Apr,1987
    Agent of Byzantium, Harry Turtledove, Congdon &
      Weed/Contemporary, 1987
  Unholy Trinity [as by Eric G. Iverson], nv *Amazing* Jul,1985
    Agent of Byzantium, Harry Turtledove, Congdon &
      Weed/Contemporary, 1987
  The Weather's Fine, ss *Playboy* Jul,1987

Tuttle, Lisa
  Birds of the Moon, ss *Fantastic* Jan,1979
    A Spaceship Built of Stone and Other Stories, Women's Press,
      1987
  A Birthday, ss **Tales from the Forbidden Planet**, ed. Roz Kaveney,
      Titan,1987
  The Bone Flute, ss *F&SF* May,1981
    A Spaceship Built of Stone and Other Stories, Women's Press,
      1987
  The Colinization of Edward Beal, ss *F&SF* Oct,1987
  The Cure, ss **Light Years and Dark**, ed. Michael Bishop, Berkley,1984
    A Spaceship Built of Stone and Other Stories, Women's Press,
      1987
  The Family Monkey, na **New Voices in Science Fiction** #1, ed.
      George R.R. Martin,1977
    A Spaceship Built of Stone and Other Stories, Women's Press,
      1987
  The Hollow Man, nv **New Voices in Science Fiction** #2, ed. George
      R.R. Martin,1979
    A Spaceship Built of Stone and Other Stories, Women's Press,
      1987
  Jamie's Grave, ss **Shadows** #10, ed. Charles L. Grant,1987
  Memories of the Body, ss *Interzone* #22,1987
  Mrs. T, ss *Amazing* Sep,1976
    A Spaceship Built of Stone and Other Stories, Women's Press,
      1987
  No Regrets, nv *F&SF* May,1985
    A Spaceship Built of Stone and Other Stories, Women's Press,
      1987
  The Other Kind, ss *IASFM* Dec,1984
    A Spaceship Built of Stone and Other Stories, Women's Press,
      1987
  The Other Room, ss *Whispers* #17,1982
    Masters of Darkness II, ed. Dennis Etchison, Tor, 1988
  A Spaceship Built of Stone, ss *IASFM* Sep,1980
    A Spaceship Built of Stone and Other Stories, Women's Press,
      1987
  Wives, ss *F&SF* Dec,1979
    A Spaceship Built of Stone and Other Stories, Women's Press,
      1987
  The Wound, ss **Other Edens**, ed. Christopher Evans & Robert
      Holdstock, Unwin: London,1987

Uglow, Jennifer
  Introduction, in
    The Virago Book of Ghost Stories, ed. Richard Dalby, Virago, 1987

unknown
  Abdullah Bulbul Amir, pm
    There Will Be War, Vol. VI: Guns of Darkness, ed. Jerry E.
      Pournelle, Tor, 1987
  Cartoon, ct *IASFM* Sep,1987
  Cartoon, ct *Twilight Zone* Feb,1987
  Cartoon, ct *Twilight Zone* Aug,1987
  Cartoon, ct *Twilight Zone* Oct,1987

Updike, John
  Jesus on Honshu, vi *New Yorker* Dec 25,1971
    Twilight Zone Jun,1987

Urquhart, Fred
  Swing High, Willie Brodie, ss **After Midnight Stories** #3,1987

Utter, Virgil
  Afterword, aw
    Prince Raynor, Henry Kuttner, Gryphon, 1987

Valentine, Mark
  The Folly, ss **14 Bellchamber Tower**, Crimson Altar Press,1987
  Madberry Hill, ss **14 Bellchamber Tower**, Crimson Altar Press,1987
  St. Michael & All Angels, ss **14 Bellchamber Tower**, Crimson Altar
      Press,1987

van Ewyck, Annemarie
  Camels for Calvin, ss *SF International* #1,1987

van Loggem, Manuel
  Touchvision, ss *SF International* #1,1987

van Vogt, A.E.
  Far Centaurus, ss *Astounding* Jan,1944
    6 Decades: The Best of Analog, ed. Stanley Schmidt, Davis, 1986

van Vogt, A.E. & Harlan Ellison
  The Human Operators, nv *F&SF* Jan,1971
    Great Science Fiction of the 20th Century, ed. Robert
      Silverberg +, Crown/Avenel, 1987

van Zandt, Kit
  Photographs, ss *Whispers* #23,1987

Vance, Jack
  The Gift of Gab, nv *Astounding* Sep,1955
    Great Science Fiction of the 20th Century, ed. Robert
      Silverberg +, Crown/Avenel, 1987
  The Miracle-Workers, na *Astounding* Jul,1958
    Battlefields Beyond Tomorrow, ed. Charles G. Waugh +,
      Crown/Bonanza, 1987
  The New Prime [Brain of the Galaxy], nv *Worlds Beyond* Feb,1951
    Robert Silverberg's Worlds of Wonder, ed. Robert Silverberg,
      Warner, 1987

Vandegrift, George
  White Mother of Shadows, nv *Terror Tales* Jan,1941
    The Weirds, ed. Sheldon R. Jaffery, Starmont House, 1987

Vander Putten, Joan
  Hooked On Love, pm *Grue* #6,1987
  Just a Little Thing, ss **Devils & Demons**, ed. Marvin Kaye,
      SFBC/Doubleday,1987
  When You Wish Upon a Corpse, ss *2AM* Win,1987

Vardeman, Robert E.
  At the Bentnail Inn, ss **Doom City**, ed. Charles L. Grant, Tor,1987
    The Crystal Clouds, n. Avon: New York pb Sep,1985
    The Jade Demons Quartet, NEL, 1987
    The Frozen Waves, n. Avon: New York pb May,1985
    The Jade Demons Quartet, NEL, 1987
    The Quaking Lands, n. Avon: New York pb Jan,1985
    The Jade Demons Quartet, NEL, 1987
  The Road of Dreams and Death, nv **Tales of the Witch World**, ed.
      Andre Norton, St. Martin's,1987
    The White Fire, n. Avon: New York pb Jan,1986
    The Jade Demons Quartet, NEL, 1987

Various Hands
  Artists' Visions of the Weird & Wondrous, il
    Fantastic Stories: Tales of the Weird and Wondrous, ed. Martin
      H. Greenberg +, TSR, 1987

Varley, John
  In the Bowl, nv *F&SF* Dec,1975
    Great Science Fiction of the 20th Century, ed. Robert
      Silverberg +, Crown/Avenel, 1987
  The Persistence of Vision, na *F&SF* Mar,1978
    The Dark Void, ed. Isaac Asimov, Severn House, 1987
  Tango Charlie and Foxtrot Romeo, na **Blue Champagne**, Dark
      Harvest,1986
    Terry Carr's Best Science Fiction and Fantasy of the Year #16,
      ed. Terry Carr, Tor, 1987

VAUGHAN, BILL

Vaughan, Bill
Here There Be Dragons, ss *Analog* Mar,1987

Vaughan, Ralph E.
Fluxed in Nova Byzantium, ss *Aboriginal SF* Nov,1987

Verniere, James
Angel Heart, mr *Twilight Zone* Apr,1987
Illuminations: Mother Was an Alien, ar *Twilight Zone* Feb,1987
Illuminations: The Man Who Would Be Spock, ar *Twilight Zone* Jun,1987
On Film, mr *Twilight Zone* Aug,1987
On Film, mr *Twilight Zone* Oct,1987
The Other Mel Brooks, ar *Twilight Zone* Aug,1987
The Other Side: Over the Edge, ar *Twilight Zone* Feb,1987
The Other Side: Weirder than Fiction, ar *Twilight Zone* Apr,1987
The Spielberg Touch, ar *Twilight Zone* Oct,1987
The Twilight Zone Review: 1986 - Film, mr *Twilight Zone* Feb,1987
The Witches of Eastwick, mr *Twilight Zone* Jun,1987

Verniere, James & Laurie Cabot
The Witch of Salem, iv *Twilight Zone* Jun,1987

Vernon, William J.
A Good Day in March, a Bearded Man, pm *Ice River* Sum,1987

Versandi, Bob
The Grandpa Urn, ss **Doom City**, ed. Charles L. Grant, Tor,1987

Vesity, Art
The First Day, ss *IASFM* Sep,1982
Tales From Isaac Asimov's Science Fiction Magazine, ed. Sheila Williams+, Harcourt Brace Jovanovich, 1986

Vinge, Joan D.
Eyes of Amber, nv *Analog* Jun,1977
The Dark Void, ed. Isaac Asimov, Severn House, 1987

Vinge, Joan D. & Vernor Vinge
The Peddler's Apprentice, nv *Analog* Aug,1975
True Names and Other Dangers, Vernor Vinge, Baen, 1987

Vinge, Vernor
The Barbarian Princess, nv *Analog* Sep,1986
Tatja Grimm's World, Baen, 1987
Bookworm, Run!, nv *Analog* Mar,1966
True Names and Other Dangers, Baen, 1987
Conquest by Default, nv *Analog* May,1968
Imperial Stars, Vol. 2: Republic and Empire, ed. Jerry E. Pournelle, Baen, 1987
Grimm's Story, na *Orbit #4*, ed. Damon Knight,1968
Tatja Grimm's World, Baen, 1987
Grimm's World, n. Berkley: New York,1969
Tatja Grimm's World, Baen, 1987
Long Shot, ss *Analog* Aug,1972
True Names and Other Dangers, Baen, 1987
True Names, na **Binary Star #5**,1981
True Names and Other Dangers, Baen, 1987
The Ungoverned, nv **Far Frontiers** v3, ed. Jerry Pournelle & Jim Baen,1985
True Names and Other Dangers, Baen, 1987

Vinge, Vernor & Joan D. Vinge
The Peddler's Apprentice, nv *Analog* Aug,1975
True Names and Other Dangers, Baen, 1987

Vinicoff, Eric
Displaced, nv *Analog* Mar,1987
Independents, ss *Analog* Apr,1987

Vinicoff, Eric & Marcia Martin
Render Unto Caesar, ss *Analog* Aug,1976
There Will Be War, Vol. VI: Guns of Darkness, ed. Jerry E. Pournelle, Tor, 1987

Viorst, Judith
...And Then The Prince Knelt Down and Tried to Put the Glass Slipper on Cinderella's Foot, pm **If I Were in Charge of the World**, New York: Atheneum,1982
Don't Bet on the Prince, ed. Jack Zipes, Methuen, 1987

Vivelo, Jackie
The Children of Winter, ss **A Trick of the Light**, Putnam,1987
A Dog Names Ransom, ss **A Trick of the Light**, Putnam,1987
The Fireside Book of Ghost Stories, ss **A Trick of the Light**, Putnam,1987
A Game of Statues, ss **A Trick of the Light**, Putnam,1987
The Girl Who Painted Raindrops, ss **A Trick of the Light**, Putnam,1987
Night Vision, ss **A Trick of the Light**, Putnam,1987
A Plague of Crowders, Or, Birds of a Feather, ss **A Trick of the Light**, Putnam,1987
Reading to Matthew, ss **A Trick of the Light**, Putnam,1987
Take Your Best Shot, ss **A Trick of the Light**, Putnam,1987

Vogel, Deborah M.
Bloodstones, vi **Sword and Sorceress #4**, ed. Marion Zimmer Bradley,1987

Volsky, Paula
The Tenancy of Mr. Eex, nv **Devils & Demons**, ed. Marvin Kaye, SFBC/Doubleday,1987

Vonarburg, Elisabeth
In the Pit ["Dans la Fosse", *Janus* 1984], ss *Solaris* Translated by Jane Brierley.
Tesseracts 2, ed. Phyllis Gotlieb+, Porcepic, 1987

Vonnegut, Kurt, Jr.
Unready to Wear, ss *Galaxy* Apr,1953
Great Science Fiction of the 20th Century, ed. Robert Silverberg+, Crown/Avenel, 1987

Wagar, W. Warren
Madonna of the Red Sun, ss **Synergy** v1, ed. George Zebrowski,1987
The Night of No Joy, nv *F&SF* Jun,1987

Wagner, Karl Edward
Blue Lady, Come Back, na **Night Visions #2**,1985
Why Not You and I?, Tor, 1987
Why Not You and I?, Dark Harvest, 1987
Endless Night, ss **The Architecture of Fear**, ed. Kathryn Cramer & Peter D. Pautz, Arbor House,1987
Into Whose Hands, nv **Whispers #4**, ed. Stuart David Schiff,1983
Why Not You and I?, Tor, 1987
Why Not You and I?, Dark Harvest, 1987
Introduction, in
The Valley So Low, Manly Wade Wellman, Doubleday, 1987
Introduction to Fat Face, in
Fat Face, Michael Shea, Axolotl, 1987
Introduction: What's in a Name?, in
The Year's Best Horror Stories: XV, ed. Karl Edward Wagner, DAW, 1987
Lacunae, ss **Cutting Edge**, ed. Dennis Etchison, Doubleday,1986
Why Not You and I?, Dark Harvest, 1987
The Last Wolf, ss *Midnight Sun #2*,1975
Why Not You and I?, Tor, 1987
Why Not You and I?, Dark Harvest, 1987
Lost Exits, ss **Why Not You and I?**, Dark Harvest,1987
Manly Wade Wellman, bg *Fantasy Tales #16*,1986
Manly Wade Wellman: A Biography, bg *The Horror Show* Spr,1987
More Sinned Against, ss **In a Lonely Place**, Scream/Press,1984
Why Not You and I?, Tor, 1987
Why Not You and I?, Dark Harvest, 1987
Neither Brute Nor Human, nv **World Fantasy Convention Program Book**,1983
Why Not You and I?, Tor, 1987
Why Not You and I?, Dark Harvest, 1987
Old Loves, ss **Night Visions #2**,1985
Why Not You and I?, Tor, 1987
Why Not You and I?, Dark Harvest, 1987
Satan's Gun, ex **World Fantasy Convention Program Book #13**,1987

WAGNER, KARL EDWARD   WATSON, IAN

Wagner, Karl Edward (continued)
  Shrapnel, ss **Night Visions #2**,1985
    Why Not You and I?, Tor, 1987
    Why Not You and I?, Dark Harvest, 1987
  Sign of the Salamander, na **John Chance Vs Dread: The Apocalypse 1**,1975
    by Curtiss Stryker, with an Introduction by Kent Allard
    Why Not You and I?, Tor, 1987
    Why Not You and I?, Dark Harvest, 1987
  Silted In, ss **Why Not You and I?**, Tor,1987
    Why Not You and I?, Dark Harvest, 1987
  Sticks, nv *Whispers* #3,1974
    The Dark Descent, ed. David G. Hartwell, Tor, 1987
  Where the Summer Ends, nv **Dark Forces**, ed. Kirby McCauley, Viking,1980
    Nightmares in Dixie, ed. Frank D. McSherry, Jr.+, August House, 1987

Wakefield, H. Russell
  Jay Walkers, ss
    Mysterious Motoring Stories, ed. William Pattrick, W.H. Allen, 1987

Waldrop, Howard
  All About Strange Monsters of the Recent Past, ss *Shayol* #4,1980
    All About Strange Monsters of the Recent Past, Ursus Imprints, 1987
  Fair Game, nv **Afterlives**, ed. Pamela Sargent & Ian Watson, New York: Vintage,1986
    The Year's Best Science Fiction, Fourth Annual Collection, ed. Gardner R. Dozois, St. Martin's, 1987
    All About Strange Monsters of the Recent Past, Ursus Imprints, 1987
  Flying Saucer Rock & Roll, ss *Omni* Jan,1985
    All About Strange Monsters of the Recent Past, Ursus Imprints, 1987
  He-We-Await, nv **All About Strange Monsters of the Recent Past**, Kansas City, MO: Ursus Imprints,1987
    IASFM mid-Dec,1987
  Helpless, Helpless, ss **Light Years and Dark**, ed. Michael Bishop, Berkley,1984
    All About Strange Monsters of the Recent Past, Ursus Imprints, 1987
  The Lions Are Asleep This Night, nv *Omni* Aug,1986
    The 1987 Annual World's Best SF, ed. Donald A. Wollheim+, DAW, 1987
    All About Strange Monsters of the Recent Past, Ursus Imprints, 1987
  Man-Mountain Gentian, ss *Omni* Sep,1983
    The Fifth Omni Book of Science Fiction, ed. Ellen Datlow, Zebra, 1987
  Night of the Cooters, ss *Omni* Apr,1987
  What Makes Heironymous Run?, ss *Shayol* #7,1985
    All About Strange Monsters of the Recent Past, Ursus Imprints, 1987

Walker, Larry
  Harbard, ss *Amazing* Jan,1987

Wallace, Edgar
  The Death Room, ss
    Poltergeist: Tales of Deadly Ghosts, ed. Peter Haining, Severn House, 1987

Walsh, Jill Paton
  Green Gravel, ss **A Quiver of Ghosts**, ed. Aiden Chambers, Bodley Head,1987

Walter, Elizabeth
  Christmas Night, nv,1975
    Christmas Ghosts, ed. Kathryn Cramer+, Arbor House, 1987
  Dual Control, ss **Dead Woman**,1975
    The Virago Book of Ghost Stories, ed. Richard Dalby, Virago, 1987

Walton, Bryce
  The Contagious Killer, ss *Alfred Hitchcock's Mystery Magazine* Jan,1966
    Alfred Hitchcock's Book of Horror Stories: Book 6, ed. Alfred Hitchcock, Coronet, 1987

Walton, Paul
  Grass Shark, ss *Twilight Zone* Jun,1987

Ward, Frank
  Smile!, ss *Amazing* Nov,1987

Warner, Bob
  Marta's Cat, vi *2AM* Spr,1987
  Supreme Being, pm *Apex!* #1,1987

Warren, Bill
  The Twilight Zone Review: 1986 - TV, mr *Twilight Zone* Feb,1987

Warren, Rosalind
  The Messenger, ss *F&SF* Jun,1987

Waters, Elisabeth
  Playfellow, ss **Red Sun of Darkover**, ed. Marion Zimmer Bradley & The Friends of Darkover, DAW,1987

Waters, Martha
  The Love Chapter [from "Journal of a Plebian Witch"], ex **Hear the Silence**, ed. Irene Zahava, Crossing Press,1986

Watkins, William Jon
  Coming of Age in Henson's Tube, ss *IASFM* Spr,1977
    Isaac Asimov's Wonderful Worlds of Science Fiction #7: Space Shuttles, ed. Isaac Asimov+, NAL/Signet, 1987
  When the Vikings Owned the Mythology, pm *Amazing* Jul,1987

Watkinson, B.F.
  Jennifer's Island, ss *Eldritch Tales* #13,1987

Watson, H.B. Marriott
  The Stone Chamber, nv **The Heart of Miranda**, John Lane: London,1899
    Dracula's Brood, ed. Richard Dalby, Crucible, 1987

Watson, Ian
  Cold Light, nv *F&SF* Apr,1986
    Evil Water, Gollancz, 1987
    Terry Carr's Best Science Fiction and Fantasy of the Year #16, ed. Terry Carr, Tor, 1987
  The Emir's Clock, ss **Other Edens**, ed. Christopher Evans & Robert Holdstock, Unwin: London,1987
  Evil Water, nv *F&SF* Mar,1987
    Evil Water, Gollancz, 1987
  The Great Atlantic Swimming Race, ss *IASFM* Mar,1986
    Evil Water, Gollancz, 1987
  Hyperzoo, ss *IASFM* mid-Dec,1987
  Immune Dreams, ss **Pulsar** #1, ed. George Hay,1978
    Mathenauts, ed. Rudy Rucker, Arbor House, 1987
  Jewels in an Angel's Wing, nv **Synergy** v1, ed. George Zebrowski,1987
  The Milk of Knowledge, ss *Aboriginal SF* Sep,1987
  The Moon and Michelangelo, nv *IASFM* Oct,1987
  On the Dream Channel Panel, ss *Amazing* Mar,1985
    Evil Water, Gollancz, 1987
  The People on the Precipice, ss *Interzone* #13,1985
    Evil Water, Gollancz, 1987
  Returning Home, ss *Omni* Dec,1982
    The Fifth Omni Book of Science Fiction, ed. Ellen Datlow, Zebra, 1987
  Salvage Rites, ss *F&SF* Jan,1987
  Skin Day, and After, ss *F&SF* Jul,1985
    Evil Water, Gollancz, 1987
  When Idaho Dived, ss **Afterwar**, ed. Janet Morris, Baen,1985
    Evil Water, Gollancz, 1987
  When the Timegate Failed, nv *Interzone* #14,1985
    Evil Water, Gollancz, 1987
    Interzone: The 2nd Anthology, ed. John Clute+, Simon & Schuster UK, 1987
  Windows, nv *IASFM* Dec,1986
    Evil Water, Gollancz, 1987
  The Wire Around the War, ss *IASFM* mid-Dec,1985
    Evil Water, Gollancz, 1987

Watt-Evans, Lawrence
  Why I Left Harry's All-Night Hamburgers, ss *IASFM* Jul,1987

Waugh, Charles G.
  Introduction: Why There Are So Many "Ladies of the Night", in
    Vamps, ed. Martin H. Greenberg+, DAW, 1987
  The Monster Matinee, in
    Cinemonsters, ed. Martin H. Greenberg, TSR, 1987

Webb, Don
  The Hag of Carmel Towers, vi *New Pathways* Jan,1987
  Kaj, vi *Grue* #5,1987
  Lesser Myths of Milwaukee, vi *New Pathways* Apr,1987
  One Hundred, ss *Ice River* Sum,1987

Webb, Don & Bruce Sterling
  Bruce Sterling, iv *New Pathways* Aug,1987

Webb, Don & Rosemary Webb
  Book Reviews, br *New Pathways* Aug,1987
  Book Reviews, br *New Pathways* Nov,1987

Webb, Mary
  Mr. Tallent's Ghost, ss,1927
    The Virago Book of Ghost Stories, ed. Richard Dalby, Virago, 1987

Webb, Rosemary & Don Webb
  Book Reviews, br *New Pathways* Aug,1987
  Book Reviews, br *New Pathways* Nov,1987

Webb, Wendy
  Law of Averages, ss **Shadows** #10, ed. Charles L. Grant,1987

Weinbaum, Stanley G.
  Shifting Seas, nv *Amazing* Apr,1937
    Amazing Science Fiction Stories: The War Years 1936-1945, ed.
      Martin H. Greenberg, TSR, 1987

Weiner, Andrew
  The Alien in the Lake, ss *IASFM* Sep,1987
  Distant Signals, ss *Twilight Zone* Jun,1984
    Tesseracts 2, ed. Phyllis Gotlieb+, Porcepic, 1987
  Fake-out, ss *Amazing* Nov,1987
  Going to Meet the Alien, nv *F&SF* Aug,1987
  Rider, nv *IASFM* Jul,1987
  Waves, nv *IASFM* Mar,1987

Weinland, Shirley
  When the Haloperidol Runs Out and the Blue Fairy Never Comes, ss
    Amazing Mar,1987

Weis, Margaret
  The Test of the Twins, ss **DragonLance Tales** v1, Margaret Weis &
    Tracy Hickman, TSR,1987

Weis, Margaret & Dezra Despain
  Raistlin's Daughter, nv **DragonLance Tales** v3, Margaret Weis &
    Tracy Hickman, TSR,1987

Weis, Margaret & Tracy Hickman
  Foreword, fw
    DragonLance Tales Vol. 2: Kender, Gully Dwarves, and Gnomes,
      ed. Margaret Weis+, TSR, 1987
    DragonLance Tales Vol. 3: Love and War, ed. Margaret Weis+,
      TSR, 1987
  The Legacy, na **DragonLance Tales** v1, Margaret Weis & Tracy
    Hickman, TSR,1987
  "Wanna Bet?", na **DragonLance Tales** v2, Margaret Weis & Tracy
    Hickman, TSR,1987

Weldon, Fay
  Breakages, ss **The Midnight Ghost Book**, ed. James Hale,1978
    The Virago Book of Ghost Stories, ed. Richard Dalby, Virago, 1987

Wellen, Edward
  Dead Ringer, na **Space Shuttles**, ed. Isaac Asimov, Martin H.
    Greenberg & Charles G. Waugh, Signet,1987
  Waswolf, ss *F&SF* Sep,1987

Wellman, Manly Wade
  Along About Sundown, ss *Whispers* Oct,1983
    The Valley So Low, Doubleday, 1987
  The Beasts That Perish, ss *Whispers* Jun,1975
    The Valley So Low, Doubleday, 1987
  Can These Bones Live?, ss *Sorcerer's Apprentice* Sum,1981
    The Valley So Low, Doubleday, 1987
  Caretaker, ss *F&SF* Oct,1977
    The Valley So Low, Doubleday, 1987
  Chastel, nv **The Year's Best Horror Stories** #7,1979
    The Valley So Low, Doubleday, 1987
  Chorazin, ss *Whispers* Oct,1978
    The Valley So Low, Doubleday, 1987
  Coven, nv *Weird Tales* Jul,1942
    Nightmares in Dixie, ed. Frank D. McSherry, Jr.+, August House,
      1987
  The Devil Is Not Mocked, ss *Unknown* Jun,1943
    Rod Serling's Night Gallery Reader, ed. Carol Serling+,
      Dembner, 1987
  The Dweller in the Temple, nv **Swords Against Darkness** #2, ed.
    Andrew J. Offutt,1977
    Isaac Asimov's Magical Worlds of Fantasy #9: Atlantis, ed. Isaac
      Asimov+, NAL/Signet, 1988
  The Ghastly Priest Doth Reign, ss *F&SF* Mar,1975
    The Valley So Low, Doubleday, 1987
  Goodman's Place, ss *F&SF* Sep,1974
    The Valley So Low, Doubleday, 1987
  Hundred Years Gone, ss *F&SF* Mar,1978
    The Valley So Low, Doubleday, 1987
  Keep Me Away, ss *Whispers* Oct,1978
    The Valley So Low, Doubleday, 1987
  Lamia, ss *Kadath* Jul,1981
    The Valley So Low, Doubleday, 1987
  Last Grave of Lill Warran, nv *Weird Tales* May,1951
    Vamps, ed. Martin H. Greenberg+, DAW, 1987
  Nobody Ever Goes There, ss **Weird Tales** #3, ed. Lin Carter,1981
    The Valley So Low, Doubleday, 1987
  One Other, ss *F&SF* Aug,1953
    Demons!, ed. Jack M. Dann+, Ace, 1987
  Owls Hoot in the Daytime, ss **Dark Forces**, ed. Kirby McCauley,
    Viking,1980
    The Valley So Low, Doubleday, 1987
  The Petey Car, ss **Superhorror**, ed. Ramsey Campbell, W.H.
    Allen,1976
    The Valley So Low, Doubleday, 1987
  Rock, Rock [The Dead Man's Chair], ss *F&SF* Oct,1973
    The Valley So Low, Doubleday, 1987
  Rouse Him Not, ss *Kadath* #5,1982
    The Valley So Low, Doubleday, 1987
  School for the Unspeakable, ss *Weird Tales* Sep,1937
    Vampires, ed. Alan Ryan, SFBC, 1987
  The Spring, ss **Shadows** #2, ed. Charles L. Grant,1979
    The Valley So Low, Doubleday, 1987
  These Doth The Lord Hate, ss *Weird Tales* Jan,1939
    The Horror Show Spr,1987
  Trill Coster's Burden, ss **Whispers** #2, ed. Stuart David Schiff,1979
    The Valley So Low, Doubleday, 1987
  Up Under the Roof, ss *Weird Tales* Oct,1938
    Pulpsmith Win,1987
  Up Under the Roof [revised from *Weird Tales* Oct,38], ss **Worse
    Things Waiting**, Carcosa: Chapel Hill NC,1973
    Masters of Darkness II, ed. Dennis Etchison, Tor, 1988
  Vandy, Vandy, ss *F&SF* Mar,1953
    The Dark Descent, ed. David G. Hartwell, Tor, 1987
  What of the Night, ss *F&SF* Mar,1980
    The Valley So Low, Doubleday, 1987
  When It Was Moonlight, ss *Unknown* Feb,1940
    Vamps, ed. Martin H. Greenberg+, DAW, 1987
  Where Did She Wander?, ss *Whispers* #23,1987
    Whispers VI, ed. Stuart David Schiff, Doubleday, 1987
    The Valley So Low, Doubleday, 1987
  The White Road, pm *Fantasy Tales* #16,1986
  Willow He Walk, ss **World Fantasy Convention Program Book**,1983
    The Valley So Low, Doubleday, 1987
  A Witch for All Seasons [as by Gans T. Field], ss *Witchcraft & Sorcery*
    #9,1973
    The Valley So Low, Doubleday, 1987

Wellman, Manly Wade (continued)
Yare, ss **New Terrors #1**, ed. Ramsey Campbell, Pan,1980
The Valley So Low, Doubleday, 1987

Wells, Catherine
The Ghost, ss **The Book of Catherine Wells**,1928
The Virago Book of Ghost Stories, ed. Richard Dalby, Virago, 1987

Wells, H.G.
The Empire of the Ants, ss *The Strand* Dec,1905
Cinemonsters, ed. Martin H. Greenberg, TSR, 1987
The Flowering of the Strange Orchid [also as "The Strange Orchid"],
ss *Pall Mall Budget* Aug,1894
Tales of the Dark 2, ed. Lincoln Child, St. Martin's, 1987
The Story of the Late Mr. Elvesham, ss *The Idler* May,1896
Charles Keeping's Classic Tales of the Macabre, ed. Charles
Keeping, Blackie, 1987
The Temptation of Harringay, ss *The St. James's Gazette* Feb,1895
Devils and Demons, ed. Marvin Kaye, Doubleday, 1987

Welsh, F.R.
First Blood, ss **The Pan Book of Horror Stories #28**, Pan,1987

Wertenbaker, G. Peyton
The Coming of the Ice, ss *Amazing* Jun,1926
Amazing Science Fiction Stories: The Wonder Years 1926-1935,
ed. Martin H. Greenberg, TSR, 1987

Westlake, Donald E.
Introduction, in
Pardon My Ghoulish Laughter, Fredric Brown, Dennis McMillan,
1987
Nackles [as by Curt Clark], ss *F&SF* Jan,1964
Twilight Zone Feb,1987

Wharton, Edith
Afterward, nv *The Century* Jan,1910
The Dark Descent, ed. David G. Hartwell, Tor, 1987
The Eyes, ss **Tales of Men and Ghosts**, Scribner: New York,1910
The Virago Book of Ghost Stories, ed. Richard Dalby, Virago, 1987

Wheeler, Deborah
Storm God, ss **Sword and Sorceress #4**, ed. Marion Zimmer
Bradley,1987
The Wasteland, ss **Red Sun of Darkover**, ed. Marion Zimmer Bradley
& The Friends of Darkover, DAW,1987

Wheeler, William H.
Editor's Note, ed *SF International* #1,1987

Whelan, Michael & Dale Johnson
Michael Whelan, iv *American Fantasy* Sum,1987

Whitbourn, John
Waiting for a Bus, ss **After Midnight Stories #3**,1987

White, D.T.
Short Are My Days of Light and Shade, ss *Aphelion* #5,1987

White, James
Custom Fitting, nv **Stellar #2**, ed. Judy-Lynn del Rey,1976
Imperial Stars, Vol. 2: Republic and Empire, ed. Jerry E.
Pournelle, Baen, 1987
The Interpreters, ss *F&SF* Mar,1987

White, Jonathan
Book Notes, br *Twilight Zone* Feb,1987
The Other Side: American Pie in the Face, ar *Twilight Zone* Apr,1987
The Other Side: Of Maus and Men, ar *Twilight Zone* Feb,1987

White, Lori Ann
Old Mickey Flip Had a Marvelous Ship, nv **L. Ron Hubbard Presents
Writers of the Future** v3, ed. Algis Budrys, Bridge,1987

White, T.H.
The Point of Thirty Miles, ss
Werewolf: Horror Stories of the Man Beast, ed. Peter Haining,
Severn House, 1987

White, Ted
Only Yesterday, ss *Amazing* Jul,1969
Nightmares in Dixie, ed. Frank D. McSherry, Jr.+, August House,
1987

Whiteaker, Marny
The Dare, ss **Red Sun of Darkover**, ed. Marion Zimmer Bradley &
The Friends of Darkover, DAW,1987

Whitehead, Henry S.
The Fireplace, ss *Weird Tales* Jan,1925
Nightmares in Dixie, ed. Frank D. McSherry, Jr.+, August House,
1987
Scar-Tissue, ss *Amazing* Jul,1946
Isaac Asimov's Magical Worlds of Fantasy #9: Atlantis, ed. Isaac
Asimov+, NAL/Signet, 1988

Whitehorn, Ingrid
The Jerra-Mee, ss *Aphelion* #5,1987

Whitlock, Dean
Containment, ss *Aboriginal SF* Feb,1987
The Million-Dollar Wound, ss *F&SF* Jan,1987
Roadkill, nv *IASFM* Nov,1987

Wiater, Stanley
Moist Dreams, ss **Masques #2**, ed. J.N. Williamson,1987

Wiater, Stanley & Piers Anthony
A Conversation with Piers Anthony, iv *Twilight Zone* Dec,1987

Wiater, Stanley & Ramsey Campbell
A Conversation With Ramsey Campbell, iv *Twilight Zone* Apr,1987

Wiggs, Susan Lilas
Sliders, ss *Grue* #6,1987

Wightman, Wayne
Cage 37, nv *F&SF* Apr,1987
In the Realm of the Heart, In the World of the Knife, ss *IASFM*
Aug,1985
Imperial Stars, Vol. 2: Republic and Empire, ed. Jerry E.
Pournelle, Baen, 1987

Wilcox, Don
The Voyage That Lasted 600 Years, nv *Amazing* Oct,1940
Amazing Science Fiction Stories: The War Years 1936-1945, ed.
Martin H. Greenberg, TSR, 1987

Wilcox, Joe
A Cell Opens, nv **Red Sun of Darkover**, ed. Marion Zimmer Bradley
& The Friends of Darkover, DAW,1987

Wilde, Jay
Death from Autophilia, ss **The Pan Book of Horror Stories #28**,
Pan,1987

Wilde, Oscar
The Happy Prince, ss **The Happy Prince and Other Tales**, London:
David Nutt,1888
Victorian Fairy Tales, ed. Jack Zipes, Methuen, 1987

Wilder, Cherry
The Decline of Sunshine, ss *Interzone* #22,1987

Wilhelm, Kate
The Disassembler, ss *F&SF* Oct,1987
Forever Yours, Anna, ss *Omni* Jul,1987
The Hounds, nv **A Shocking Thing**, ed. Damon Knight, Pocket,1974
Masters of Darkness II, ed. Dennis Etchison, Tor, 1988
The Village, ss **Bad Moon Rising**, ed. Thomas M. Disch,1973
In the Field of Fire, ed. Jeanne Van Buren Dann+, Tor, 1987

Wilhelm, Kate, Terry A. Garey, Eric M. Heideman & Damon Knight
An Interview with Kate Wilhelm and Damon Knight, iv *Tales of the
Unanticipated* #2,1987

WILHELMSEN, GEORGE

Wilhelmsen, George
  The Other Side: Land of the Rising Moon, ar *Twilight Zone* Aug,1987

Wilkerson, Cherie
  The Man Who Watched the Glaciers Run, nv **Universe #17**, ed. Terry Carr,1987
  The Moment of the Rose, ss *IASFM* Feb,1987

Wilkins, Mark
  Wartours, ss **Gollancz - Sunday Times Best SF Stories**, Gollancz,1987

Willett, F.J.
  Scare Tactics, vi *Aphelion #5*,1987
  Splitting Hares, vi *Aphelion #5*,1987

Williams, Jay
  Petronella, ss *McCalls* Jan,1973
    Don't Bet on the Prince, ed. Jack Zipes, Methuen, 1987
    The Magic Kiss and Other Tales of Princes and Princesses, ed. Tony Bradman, Blackie, 1987

Williams, Mary
  Coppard's End, ss **Haunted Waters**, Kimber,1987
  Dorothea, nv **Haunted Waters**, Kimber,1987
  Haunted Waters, n. **Haunted Waters**, Kimber,1987

Williams, Michael
  From the Yearning for War and the War's Ending, nv **DragonLance Tales** v3, Margaret Weis & Tracy Hickman, TSR,1987
  Into the Heart of the Story, nv **DragonLance Tales** v2, Margaret Weis & Tracy Hickman, TSR,1987
  Riverwind and The Crystal Staff, pm **DragonLance Tales** v1, Margaret Weis & Tracy Hickman, TSR,1987

Williams, Paul & Misha Chocholak
  Paul Williams talks to New Pathways, iv *New Pathways* Jan,1987

Williams, Randy
  Intersections, vi *2AM* Fll,1987

Williams, Walter Jon
  Dinosaurs, nv *IASFM* Jun,1987
  Ligdan and the Young Pretender, nv **There Will Be War** v6, ed. Jerry E. Pournelle,1987
  Mr. Koyama's Comet, ss **Wild Cards** v2, ed. George R.R. Martin, Bantam,1987
  Unto the Sixth Generation: Epilogue, sl **Wild Cards** v2, ed. George R.R. Martin, Bantam,1987
  Unto the Sixth Generation: Part One, sl **Wild Cards** v2, ed. George R.R. Martin, Bantam,1987
  Unto the Sixth Generation: Part Two, sl **Wild Cards** v2, ed. George R.R. Martin, Bantam,1987
  Unto the Sixth Generation: Prologue, sl **Wild Cards** v2, ed. George R.R. Martin, Bantam,1987
  Video Star, nv *IASFM* Jul,1986
    The Year's Best Science Fiction, Fourth Annual Collection, ed. Gardner R. Dozois, St. Martin's, 1987
    A Very Large Array, ed. Melinda M. Snodgrass, Univ. of New Mexico Press, 1987
  Wolf Time, nv *IASFM* Jan,1987

Williamson, Barbara
  The Thing Waiting Outside, ss *Ellery Queen's Mystery Magazine* Dec,1977
    Ready or Not, ed. Joan Kahn, Greenwillow, 1987

Williamson, Chet
  Ants, vi *Twilight Zone* Jun,1987
  Letters to Mother, ss *F&SF* Apr,1987
  Play Dead, ss *F&SF* Aug,1987
  Sen Yet Babbo & the Heavenly Host, ss *Playboy* Aug,1987

Williamson, David
  The Sandman, ss **The Pan Book of Horror Stories #28**, Pan,1987

Williamson, J.N.
  Dark Corner, br *2AM* Spr,1987

Williamson, J.N. (continued)
  Dark Corner, br *2AM* Sum,1987
  Dark Corner, br *2AM* Fll,1987
  Dark Corner, br *2AM* Win,1987
  Fragments of Horror, ms *The Horror Show* Jan,1987
  Happy Hour, ss *Twilight Zone* Feb,1987
  Introduction, in
    Masques II, ed. J.N. Williamson, Maclay & Assoc., 1987
  The Night Seasons [Part 2], sl *Night Cry* v2#3,1987
  The Night Seasons [Part 3], sl *Night Cry* v2#4,1987
  The Night Seasons [Part 4], sl *Night Cry* v2#5,1987
  Privacy Rights, ss **Whispers #6**, ed. Stuart David Schiff,1987
  Starry Coping, ss *Eldritch Tales #14*,1987
  Townkiller, ss *Grue #4*,1987
  Watchwolf, ss *Footsteps* Nov,1987
  Wordsong, ss **Masques #2**, ed. J.N. Williamson,1987

Williamson, Jack
  Introduction, in
    Amazing Science Fiction Stories: The Wonder Years 1926-1935, ed. Martin H. Greenberg, TSR, 1987
  Jamboree, ss *Galaxy* Dec,1969
    A Very Large Array, ed. Melinda M. Snodgrass, Univ. of New Mexico Press, 1987
  The Metal Man, ss *Amazing* Dec,1928
    Amazing Science Fiction Stories: The Wonder Years 1926-1935, ed. Martin H. Greenberg, TSR, 1987

Willis, Connie
  Chance, nv *IASFM* May,1986
    The Year's Best Science Fiction, Fourth Annual Collection, ed. Gardner R. Dozois, St. Martin's, 1987
  Circus Story, ss *Aboriginal SF* Feb,1987
  A Letter from the Clearys, ss *IASFM* Jul,1982
    Tales From Isaac Asimov's Science Fiction Magazine, ed. Sheila Williams+, Harcourt Brace Jovanovich, 1986
  Lord of Hosts, vi *Omni* Jun,1987
  Schwarzschild Radius, ss **Universe**, ed. Byron Preiss, Bantam Spectra,1987
  Winter's Tale, nv *IASFM* Dec,1987

Willis, Irene Cooper
  Introduction, in
    Supernatural Tales: Excursions Into Fantasy, Vernon Lee, Peter Owen, 1987

Wilson, Colin
  Active Imagination [from **The Lord of the Underworld**], ar
    The Essential Colin Wilson, Grafton, 1987
  An Autobiographical Introduction [from **Religion and the Rebel**], ar Gollancz: London,1957
    The Essential Colin Wilson, Grafton, 1987
  The Country of the Blind [from **The Outsider**], ar Gollancz: London,1956
    The Essential Colin Wilson, Grafton, 1987
  Discovery of the Vampires [from **The Mind Parasites**], ex Barker: London,1967
    The Essential Colin Wilson, Grafton, 1987
  Everyday Consciousness is a Liar [from **The New Existentialism**], ar
    The Essential Colin Wilson, Grafton, 1987
  Human Evolution [from **A Criminal History of Mankind**], ar
    The Essential Colin Wilson, Grafton, 1987
  Introduction, in
    The Essential Colin Wilson, Grafton, 1987
  The Ladder of Selves [from **Mysteries**], ar Hodder Stoughton: London,1978
    The Essential Colin Wilson, Grafton, 1987
  The Laurel and Hardy Theory of Consciousness, ar
    The Essential Colin Wilson, Grafton, 1987
  Magic - The Science of the Future [from **The Occult**], ar Random House: New York,1971
    The Essential Colin Wilson, Grafton, 1987
  The "Other Mode" [from **Frankenstein's Castle**], ar
    The Essential Colin Wilson, Grafton, 1987
  The Outsider, Twenty Years On, ar
    The Essential Colin Wilson, Grafton, 1987
  Peak Experience, ar The Schumacher Lecture,1982
    The Essential Colin Wilson, Grafton, 1987

Wilson, Colin (continued)
Personal Notes on Maslow [from **New Pathways in Psychology**], ar
   Taplinger: New York,1972
   The Essential Colin Wilson, Grafton, 1987
Postscript: The Human Condition, ar
   The Essential Colin Wilson, Grafton, 1987
A Report on the Violent Man [from **A Criminal History of Mankind**],
   ar
   The Essential Colin Wilson, Grafton, 1987
The Strange Story of Modern Philosophy [from **Beyond the
   Outsider**], ar Barker: London,1965
   The Essential Colin Wilson, Grafton, 1987
Uncle Sam [from **The World of Violence**], ex Gollancz: London,1963
   The Essential Colin Wilson, Grafton, 1987
Vision on the Eiger [from **The Black Room**], ex Weidenfeld Nicolson:
   London,1971
   The Essential Colin Wilson, Grafton, 1987

Wilson, F. Paul
Dat-Tay-Vao, ss *Amazing* Mar,1987
Doc Johnson, nv **Doom City**, ed. Charles L. Grant, Tor,1987
A Novel Preview: **Black Wind**, ex *Footsteps* Nov,1987
Traps, ss *Night Cry* v2#4,1987
The Years the Music Died, ss **Whispers** #6, ed. Stuart David
   Schiff,1987

Wilson, F. Paul & Bill Munster
An Interview with F. Paul Wilson, iv *Footsteps* Nov,1987

Wilson, Gahan
Screen, mr *Twilight Zone* Feb,1987
Screen, mr *Twilight Zone* Apr,1987
Screen, mr *Twilight Zone* Jun,1987
Screen, mr *Twilight Zone* Aug,1987
Screen, mr *Twilight Zone* Oct,1987
Screen, mr *Twilight Zone* Dec,1987

Wilson, Gahan & Bill Munster
An Interview with Gahan Wilson, in *Footsteps* Nov,1987

Wilson, Hayes
Please, No Strawberries, ss *Ellery Queen's Mystery Magazine* Mar
   10,1980
   Ready or Not, ed. Joan Kahn, Greenwillow, 1987

Wilson, Richard
Able Baker Camel, nv *Amazing* Jan,1987
The Blue Lady, ss **The Kid from Ozone Park and Other Stories**,
   Drumm,1987
Fair Morsel, vi **The Kid from Ozone Park and Other Stories**,
   Drumm,1987
The Greater Powers, ss **The Kid from Ozone Park and Other
   Stories**, Drumm,1987
Green Is the Color, ss **The Kid from Ozone Park and Other Stories**,
   Drumm,1987
Harry Protagonist, Inseminator General, ss **The Kid from Ozone Park
   and Other Stories**, Drumm,1987
IBM, My Shipmate; or, the Difference Between Orbit and Obit, pm
   Amazing Sep,1987
The Kid from Ozone Park, ss **The Kid from Ozone Park and Other
   Stories**, Drumm,1987
A Letter from a Lady, ss **The Kid from Ozone Park and Other
   Stories**, Drumm,1987
Sleeping Booty, ss **Whispers** #6, ed. Stuart David Schiff,1987
That's All, Folks, pm *Amazing* May,1987
Waiting for the Buyer, ss **The Kid from Ozone Park and Other
   Stories**, Drumm,1987

Wilson, Robert Anton
"Afterwards", aw **Philip K. Dick: The Dream Connection**, D. Scott
   Apel, Permanent Press,1987

Wilson, Robert Charles
Ballads in 3/4 Time, ss *F&SF* Apr,1987
Extras, nv *F&SF* Dec,1987

Wilson, Robin Scott
The Greening of Mrs. Edmiston, ss *F&SF* Jan,1987

Wilson, Robley, Jr.
Flaggers, ss *IASFM* Jun,1987

Winkle, Michael D.
Typo, ss *Fantasy Book* Mar,1987

Winter, Douglas E.
Movie Preview: Raising Hell with Clive Barker, mr *Twilight Zone*
   Dec,1987
Office Hours, ss **Shadows** #10, ed. Charles L. Grant,1987
Splatter, ss **Masques** #2, ed. J.N. Williamson,1987

Winter, Douglas E. & Clive Barker
Talking Terror With Clive Barker, iv *Twilight Zone* Jun,1987

Winter, Douglas E. & Charles L. Grant
A Conversation With Charles L. Grant, iv *Twilight Zone* Apr,1987

Winter-Damon, t.
Bramblebeard, pm *Mage* Win,1985
   Mage Fll,1987
if only icarus had climbed the night, pm *Fantasy Book* Mar,1987
Martyr Without Canon, pm *Grue* #4,1987

Wisman, Ken
The Finder-Keeper, ss **Shadows** #10, ed. Charles L. Grant,1987
The Philosophical Stone, ss *Interzone* #21,1987

Wismer, Donald
Safe Harbor, nv **Tin Stars**, ed. Isaac Asimov, Martin H. Greenberg &
   Charles G. Waugh, NAL/Signet,1986
   Strange Maine, ed. Charles G. Waugh+, Tapley, 1986

Witcover, Paul
The Cats of Thermidor, ss *Night Cry* v2#4,1987

Wnorowska, Diane
Seven Come Heaven?, ss **Devils & Demons**, ed. Marvin Kaye,
   SFBC/Doubleday,1987

Woeltjen, L.D.
Die Like a Man, ss **Sword and Sorceress** #4, ed. Marion Zimmer
   Bradley,1987

Wolf, Rose
Cat and Muse, ss **Magic in Ithkar** #4, ed. Andre Norton & Robert
   Adams,1987

Wolfe, Gene
All the Hues of Hell, ss **Universe**, ed. Byron Preiss, Bantam
   Spectra,1987
The Ethos of Elfland, ar *Twilight Zone* Dec,1987
The HORARS of War, ss **Nova** #1, ed. Harry Harrison,1970
   Supertanks, ed. Joe W. Haldeman+, Ace, 1987
In the House of Gingerbread, ss **The Architecture of Fear**, ed.
   Kathryn Cramer & Peter D. Pautz, Arbor House,1987
The Peace Spy, ss *IASFM* Jan,1987
Seven American Nights, na **Orbit** #20, ed. Damon Knight,1978
   The Dark Descent, ed. David G. Hartwell, Tor, 1987

Wolfe, Ron
Illuminations: A Dark and Stormy Plight, ar *Twilight Zone* Dec,1987
Illuminations: Awright, Larson! --Up Against the Wall, ar *Twilight Zone*
   Dec,1987
Illuminations: Forstchen in Maine's Eyes, ar *Twilight Zone* Aug,1987
Illuminations: Frog Heaven, ar *Twilight Zone* Apr,1987
Illuminations: Radio- Vision, ar *Twilight Zone* Aug,1987
Illuminations: TV or Not TV?, ar *Twilight Zone* Oct,1987
The Man Who Did Tricks with Glass, ss *Stardate* Apr,1986
   The Year's Best Horror Stories: XV, ed. Karl Edward Wagner,
   DAW, 1987
The Other Side: Bad-Dream Girl, ar *Twilight Zone* Aug,1987
The Other Side: Coming Soon to a Theater Somewhere, Mayby, ar
   Twilight Zone Dec,1987
The Other Side: Faces of Fear, ar *Twilight Zone* Aug,1987
The Other Side: Flies on the Screen, ar *Twilight Zone* Aug,1987
The Other Side: Grass-Roots Gore, ar *Twilight Zone* Feb,1987
The Other Side: Guilt by Association, ar *Twilight Zone* Apr,1987

WOLFE, RON

Wolfe, Ron (continued)
The Other Side: Have Yourself a Merry Little Xenophobe
  Understanding Day, ar *Twilight Zone* Aug,1987
The Other Side: Mary & Percy & Byron & Claire, ar *Twilight Zone*
  Oct,1987
The Other Side: More Hokey Holidays, ar *Twilight Zone* Oct,1987
The Other Side: Rats in the Malls, ar *Twilight Zone* Oct,1987

Wolfe, Ron & R.A. Lafferty
Counting Grandmothers: R.A. Lafferty, iv *American Fantasy* Sum,1987

Wolfenbarger, Billy
Final Dreams, pm *Grue* #5,1987
Reunion, pm *Eldritch Tales* #13,1987

Wollheim, Donald A.
Introduction, in
  The 1987 Annual World's Best SF, ed. Donald A. Wollheim +,
   DAW, 1987
The Lysenko Maze, ss *F&SF* Jul,1954
  Isaac Asimov Presents the Great SF Stories: 16 (1954), ed. Isaac
   Asimov +, DAW, 1987

Wolverton, Dave
On My Way to Paradise, na **L. Ron Hubbard Presents Writers of the
  Future** v3, ed. Algis Budrys, Bridge,1987

Wood, William
One of the Dead, nv *The Saturday Evening Post* Oct 31,1964
  House Shudders, ed. Martin H. Greenberg +, DAW, 1987

Woolrich, Cornell
Dark Melody of Madness [also as "Music from the Dark" and "Papa
  Benjamin"], nv *Dime Mystery Magazine* Jul,1935
  Nightmares in Dixie, ed. Frank D. McSherry, Jr. +, August House,
   1987
I'm Dangerous Tonight, na *All American Fiction* Nov,1937
  Isaac Asimov's Magical Worlds of Fantasy #8: Devils, ed. Isaac
   Asimov +, NAL/Signet, 1987
The Moon of Montezuma, ss *Fantastic* Nov,1952
  House Shudders, ed. Martin H. Greenberg +, DAW, 1987

Wrede, Patricia C.
The Improper Princess, ss **Spaceships & Spells**, ed. Jane Yolen,
  Martin H. Greenberg & Charles G. Waugh, Harper & Row,1987

Wright, Kit
In the Cathedral Gardens, pm **Hot Dog and Other Poems**,1981
  The Ghost Story Treasury, ed. Linda Sonntag, Putnam, 1987

Wright, T.M.
Stuff of Horror, or Gray Matter All Over the Inside of Your Skull, ar
  American Fantasy Sum,1987
A World Without Toys, ss **Shadows** #10, ed. Charles L. Grant,1987

Wu, William F.
Davi Leiko Till Midnight, ss *Twilight Zone* Oct,1987
Dead White Women, ss *Eldritch Tales* #12,1986
  The Year's Best Horror Stories: XV, ed. Karl Edward Wagner,
   DAW, 1987
On the Shadow of a Phosphor Screen, nv *IASFM* Jul,1979
  Battlefields Beyond Tomorrow, ed. Charles G. Waugh +,
   Crown/Bonanza, 1987

Wu, William F. & Robert Chilson
High Power, ss *Analog* Sep,1987
A Hog on Ice, ss *Analog* Dec,1987
No Damn Atoms, nv *Analog* Oct,1987

Wyatt, Scott
Teach the Children, pm *Minnesota Fantasy Review* #1,1987

Wylde, Thomas
The Nanny, nv *IASFM* Jul,1983
  **Isaac Asimov's Wonderful Worlds of Science Fiction #7: Space
  Shuttles**, ed. Isaac Asimov +, NAL/Signet, 1987
The Prize, ss *Night Cry* v2#5,1987

Wyndham, John
Phoney Meteor [as by John Beynon, also as "Meteor"], nv *Amazing*
  Mar,1941
  Amazing Science Fiction Stories: The War Years 1936-1945, ed.
   Martin H. Greenberg, TSR, 1987

Yarbro, Chelsea Quinn
Cabin 33, na **Shadows** #3, ed. Charles L. Grant,1980
  Vampires, ed. Alan Ryan, SFBC, 1987
Son of the Introduction: The Man Who Wrote..., in
  Lost in Time and Space with Lefty Feep, Robert Bloch, Creatures
   at Large, 1987

Yen, Johnny
Upstarts, ss **The Pan Book of Horror Stories** #28, Pan,1987

Yolen, Jane
The Ballad of the Quick Levars, sg **Liavek: Wizard's Row**, ed. Will
  Shetterly & Emma Bull, Ace,1987
City of Luck, sg **Liavek: Wizard's Row**, ed. Will Shetterly & Emma
  Bull, Ace,1987
Frog Prince, pm *F&SF* Oct,1987
Introduction, in
  Spaceships and Spells, ed. Jane Yolen +, Harper & Row, 1987
The King's Dragon, ss **Spaceships & Spells**, ed. Jane Yolen, Martin
  H. Greenberg & Charles G. Waugh, Harper & Row,1987
The Making of Dragons, pm *IASFM* Jun,1986
  Rhysling Anthology 1987, ed. Anonymous, SF Poetry Assc., 1987
The Moon Ribbon, ss **The Moon Ribbon and Other Tales**, Curtis
  Brown, Ltd.,1976
  Don't Bet on the Prince, ed. Jack Zipes, Methuen, 1987
One Old Man, with Seals, ss **Neptune Rising**, Philomel,1982
  Strange Maine, ed. Charles G. Waugh +, Tapley, 1986
Regenesis, pm *Fantasy Book* Mar,1987
Science Fiction, pm *IASFM* Jul,1987
The Uncorking of Uncle Finn, ss *F&SF* Nov,1986
  The Year's Best Fantasy Stories: 13, ed. Arthur W. Saha, DAW,
   1987
The White Babe, nv *IASFM* Jun,1987
Wolf/Child, ss *Twilight Zone* Jun,1987

Young, Robert F.
Added Inducement, ss *F&SF* Mar,1957
  Isaac Asimov's Magical Worlds of Fantasy #8: Devils, ed. Isaac
   Asimov +, NAL/Signet, 1987
A Drink of Darkness, ss *Fantastic* Jul,1962
  Fantastic Stories: Tales of the Weird and Wondrous, ed. Martin
   H. Greenberg +, TSR, 1987
The Giant, the Colleen, and the Twenty-one Cows, nv *F&SF* Jun,1987
What Bleak Land, ss *F&SF* Jan,1987

Yule, Jeffrey V.
At Night, pm *Mage* Spr,1987
A Consideration of Negative-Future Fiction, ed *Mage* Win,1987
Four Years Later..., ed *Mage* Fll,1987
Give the Reader Quality Not Quantity, ed *Mage* Spr,1985
  Mage Fll,1987
The Mage: A Retrospective, pi *Mage* Fll,1987
Science Fiction--Judging the Genre, ed *Mage* Spr,1987
  Mage Fll,1987
Serious Writing or Escapism?, ed *Mage* Win,1985
  Mage Fll,1987
William Gibson: A Cyberpunk Examined, ar *Mage* Spr,1987
Willing Suspension of Disbelief, ed *Mage* Spr,1986
  Mage Fll,1987

Zahava, Irene
Preface, pr
  Hear the Silence, ed. Irene Zahava, Crossing Press, 1986

Zahn, Timothy
Banshee, na *Analog* Sep,1987
Between a Rock and a High Place, na *Analog* Jul,1982
  **Isaac Asimov's Wonderful Worlds of Science Fiction #7: Space
  Shuttles**, ed. Isaac Asimov +, NAL/Signet, 1987
Point Man, nv **New Destinies** v1, ed. Jim Baen, Baen,1987
The President's Doll, ss *Analog* Jul,1987

ZAHN, TIMOTHY   [MISC. MATERIAL]

Zahn, Timothy (continued)
The Talisman, nv **Magic in Ithkar** #4, ed. Andre Norton & Robert Adams,1987

Zambreno, Mary Frances
Roaming Fancy, br *American Fantasy* Spr,1987
Roaming Fancy, br *American Fantasy* Sum,1987
Roaming Fancy, br *American Fantasy* Win,1987

Zambreno, Mary Frances, Nancy Garcia & Andre Norton
Andre Norton Interview and Bibliography, iv *American Fantasy* Win,1987

Zebrowski, George
Behind the Night, ss *F&SF* Apr,1987
General Jaruzelski at the Zoo, ss *Twilight Zone* Apr,1987
Godel's Doom, ss *Popular Computing* Feb,1985
Mathenauts, ed. Rudy Rucker, Arbor House, 1987
Introduction: Synergists, in **Synergy** v1, ed. George Zebrowski,1987
This Life and Later Ones, ss *Analog* Feb,1987

Zelazny, Roger
Ashes to Ashes, nv **Wild Cards** v2, ed. George R.R. Martin, Bantam,1987
Damnation Alley, na *Galaxy* Oct,1967
Supertanks, ed. Joe W. Haldeman +, Ace, 1987
For a Breath I Tarry, nv *New Worlds* Mar,1966
A Very Large Array, ed. Melinda M. Snodgrass, Univ. of New Mexico Press, 1987
Home Is the Hangman, na *Analog* Nov,1975
Beyond the Stars, ed. Isaac Asimov, Severn House, 1987
Introduction, in
The Collected Stories of Philip K. Dick, Vol. One: Beyond Lies the Wub, Philip K. Dick, Underwood-Miller, 1987
The Keys to December, ss *New Worlds* Aug,1966
Great Science Fiction of the 20th Century, ed. Robert Silverberg +, Crown/Avenel, 1987
King Solomon's Ring, ss *Fantastic* Oct,1963
Fantastic Stories: Tales of the Weird and Wondrous, ed. Martin H. Greenberg +, TSR, 1987
Permafrost, nv *Omni* Apr,1986
The 1987 Annual World's Best SF, ed. Donald A. Wollheim +, DAW, 1987
Quest's End, vi *Omni* Jun,1987
A Sketch of Their Father, in
Portraits of His Children, George R.R. Martin, Dark Harvest, 1987

Zeller, J.M.
The Hand of the Survivor, ss *Amazing* Jul,1987

Zicree, Marc Scott
Science Fiction in the Twilight Zone, ar *Twilight Zone* Oct,1987

Ziesing, Mark & Misha Chocholak
Interview with Mark Ziesing: Bookseller & Publisher, iv *New Pathways* Jan,1987

Zipes, Jack
A Fairy Tale for Our Time, ss,1985
Don't Bet on the Prince, ed. Jack Zipes, Methuen, 1987
Introduction, in
Don't Bet on the Prince, ed. Jack Zipes, Methuen, 1987
Victorian Fairy Tales, ed. Jack Zipes, Methuen, 1987
Preface, pr
Don't Bet on the Prince, ed. Jack Zipes, Methuen, 1987
Victorian Fairy Tales, ed. Jack Zipes, Methuen, 1987
A Second Gaze at Little Red Riding Hood's Trials and Tribulations, cr,1984
Don't Bet on the Prince, ed. Jack Zipes, Methuen, 1987

[Misc. Material]
1987 World Fantasy Award Nominees, bi **World Fantasy Convention Program Book** #13,1987
1st Annual Readers' Award Results, bi *IASFM* Oct,1987
About the Author, bg
Midnight Pleasures, Robert Bloch, Doubleday, 1987
About the Authors, bg
Spaceships and Spells, ed. Jane Yolen +, Harper & Row, 1987

[Misc. Material] (continued)
About the Editor, bg **Synergy** v1, ed. George Zebrowski,1987
About the Story Illustrators, bg
L. Ron Hubbard Presents Writers of the Future, Vol. III, ed. Algis Budrys, Bridge, 1987
About the Writers, bg
DragonLance Tales Vol. 2: Kender, Gully Dwarves, and Gnomes, ed. Margaret Weis +, TSR, 1987
The Analytical Laboratory, ms *Analog* Jun,1987
Appendix I: Vampire Novels, bi
Vampires, ed. Alan Ryan, SFBC, 1987
Appendix II: Vampire Movies, bi
Vampires, ed. Alan Ryan, SFBC, 1987
Appendix--Key to "I've Got a Little List", ms
Takeoff Too!, Randall Garrett, Donning/Starblaze, 1987
Art Sampler, pi *Salarius* v1#4,1987
Art Section, pi *Salarius* #3,1987
The Authors, bg
Amazing Science Fiction Stories: The Wonder Years 1926-1935, ed. Martin H. Greenberg, TSR, 1987
Amazing Science Fiction Stories: The War Years 1936-1945, ed. Martin H. Greenberg, TSR, 1987
Amazing Science Fiction Stories: The Wild Years 1946-1955, ed. Martin H. Greenberg, TSR, 1987
Bibliography, bi
Don't Bet on the Prince, ed. Jack Zipes, Methuen, 1987
Biographical Notes, bg
Magic in Ithkar 4, ed. Andre Norton +, Tor, 1987
Tales of the Witch World, ed. Andre Norton, Tor, 1987
The Complete Bibliography of F. Paul Wilson, bi *Footsteps* Nov,1987
Con-Notations, ms *Space & Time* #73,1987
Contributors, bg
Tales of the Unanticipated #2,1987
The Contributors, bg
The Universe, ed. Byron Preiss, Bantam Spectra, 1987
Tesseracts 2, ed. Phyllis Gotlieb +, Porcepic, 1987
Contributors' Notes, bg
Ice River Sum,1987
Credits, Descriptions and Comparisons of Films, bi
Cinemonsters, ed. Martin H. Greenberg, TSR, 1987
F&SF Competition: Report on Competition 42, ms *F&SF* May,1987
F&SF Competition: Report on Competition 43, ms *F&SF* Sep,1987
Film Preview: Spaceballs, pi *Twilight Zone* Aug,1987
First Annual Readers' Award Ballot, ms *IASFM* Jan,1987
For Further Reading, bi
Robert Silverberg's Worlds of Wonder, ed. Robert Silverberg, Warner, 1987
Further Reading, bi
In the Field of Fire, ed. Jeanne Van Buren Dann +, Tor, 1987
Glossary of Acronyms and Selected Terms, ms
In the Field of Fire, ed. Jeanne Van Buren Dann +, Tor, 1987
Glossary to Wandering Willie's Tale, ms
The Supernatural Short Stories of Sir Walter Scott, Sir Walter Scott, Riverrun/Calder, 1986
A Guide to Significant Works of Architectural Horror, bi
The Architecture of Fear, ed. Kathryn Cramer +, Arbor House, 1987
A Handbook for the Apprentice Magician, ms **Liavek: Wizard's Row**, ed. Will Shetterly & Emma Bull, Ace,1987
Hollywood Grapevine, ar *Twilight Zone* Jun,1987
Hollywood Grapevine, ar *Twilight Zone* Aug,1987
Hollywood Grapevine, ar *Twilight Zone* Oct,1987
Hollywood Grapevine, ar *Twilight Zone* Dec,1987
Honorable Mentions: 1986, bi
The Year's Best Science Fiction, Fourth Annual Collection, ed. Gardner R. Dozois, St. Martin's, 1987
Index, ix *Analog* Jan,1987
Index, ix *IASFM* Jan,1987
Index to City Maps, ix
Merovingen Nights: Festival Moon, ed. C.J. Cherryh, DAW, 1987
Fever Season: Merovingen Nights #2, ed. C.J. Cherryh, DAW, 1987
Index to Volume 72, ix *F&SF* Jun,1987
Index to Volume 73, ix *F&SF* Dec,1987
An Index to *Fantasy Book*, Volume 5, ix *Fantasy Book* Mar,1987

[MISC. MATERIAL]

[Misc. Material] (continued)

Issue by issue index to *Ace Mystery, Eerie Mysteries, Eerie Stories* and *Uncanny Tales*, ix
> **Selected Tales of Grim and Grue from the Horror Pulps**, ed. Sheldon R. Jaffery, Bowling Green Popular Press, 1987

List of Contributors, bg
> **Other Edens**, ed. Christopher Evans+, Unwin, 1987

Merovan Ecology, ms **Fever Season**, ed. C.J. Cherryh, DAW, 1987

Music to Read 2AM by -- Contest Winner, ms *2AM* Sum, 1987

A Note on the Authors, bg
> **Tales of the Dark 2**, ed. Lincoln Child, St. Martin's, 1987

Note on the Illustrations, ms
> **Victorian Fairy Tales**, ed. Jack Zipes, Methuen, 1987

Notes, bi
> **The Collected Stories of Philip K. Dick, Vol. Five: The Little Black Box**, Philip K. Dick, Underwood-Miller, 1987
> **The Collected Stories of Philip K. Dick, Vol. Four: The Days of Perky Pat**, Philip K. Dick, Underwood-Miller, 1987
> **The Collected Stories of Philip K. Dick, Vol. One: Beyond Lies the Wub**, Philip K. Dick, Underwood-Miller, 1987
> **The Collected Stories of Philip K. Dick, Vol. Three: The Father Thing**, Philip K. Dick, Underwood-Miller, 1987
> **The Collected Stories of Philip K. Dick, Vol. Two: Second Variety**, Philip K. Dick, Underwood-Miller, 1987

Notes, ms
> **Charles Keeping's Classic Tales of the Macabre**, ed. Charles Keeping, Blackie, 1987

Notes on Sources, bi
> **Short & Shivery**, ed. Robert D. San Souci, Doubleday, 1987

Notes on the Authors, bg
> **Strange Maine**, ed. Charles G. Waugh+, Tapley, 1986
> **Interzone: The 2nd Anthology**, ed. John Clute+, Simon & Schuster UK, 1987
> **The Virago Book of Ghost Stories**, ed. Richard Dalby, Virago, 1987

Notes on the Contributors, bg
> **The Third Book of After Midnight Stories**, ed. Amy Myers, Kimber, 1987
> **Masters of Darkness II**, ed. Dennis Etchison, Tor, 1988

Oddities & Entities, ms *American Fantasy* Spr, 1987

Oddities & Entities, ms *American Fantasy* Sum, 1987

Oddities & Entities, ms *American Fantasy* Win, 1987

Rhysling Award Winners, 1978 - 1986, bi
> **Rhysling Anthology 1987**, ed. Anonymous, SF Poetry Assc., 1987

Select Bibliography, bi
> **Victorian Fairy Tales**, ed. Jack Zipes, Methuen, 1987
> **Ghosts and Scholars**, ed. Rosemary Pardoe+, Crucible, 1987

A Selected Damon Knight Bibliography, bi *Tales of the Unanticipated* #2, 1987

A Selected Kate Wilhelm Bibliography, bi *Tales of the Unanticipated* #2, 1987

Title List: Stories

All my Doing; or Red Riding-Hood Over Again, Harriet Louisa Childe-Pemberton, nv **Fairy Tales of Every Day**, London: Christian Knowledge Society,1882

All the Birds Come Home to Roost, Harlan Ellison, ss *Playboy* Mar,1979

All the Blood Within Me, Kingsley Amis, ss *The Spectator*,1962

all the comforts of, dan raphael, pm *Ice River* Sum,1987

All the Hues of Hell, Gene Wolfe, ss **Universe**, ed. Byron Preiss, Bantam Spectra,1987

All the People, All the Time, W.T. Quick, ss *Analog* Jul,1987

All Those Enduring Old Charms, Brian W. Aldiss, vi **New Writings in SF** #23,1974

"All You Zombies-", Robert A. Heinlein, ss *F&SF* Mar,1959

Allamagoosa, Eric Frank Russell, ss *Astounding* May,1955

Allen Koszowski, Allen Koszowski, iv *The Horror Show* Fll,1987

The Alley Man, Philip Jose Farmer, na *F&SF* Jun,1959

Allsouls, Rebecca Bradley, ss **The Pan Book of Horror Stories** #28, Pan,1987

Along About Sundown, Manly Wade Wellman, ss *Whispers* Oct,1983

Along the Scenic Route [Dogfight on 101], Harlan Ellison, ss *Adam* Aug,1969

Alpha Ralpha Boulevard, Cordwainer Smith, nv *F&SF* Jun,1961

The Alternate View: Artificial Gravity: Which Way Is Up?, John G. Cramer, ar *Analog* Feb,1987

The Alternate View: Cultural Differences, G. Harry Stine, ar *Analog* Sep,1987

The Alternate View: Frontiers and Wars, G. Harry Stine, ar *Analog* Jan,1987

The Alternate View: Hardening Humans, G. Harry Stine, ar *Analog* mid-Dec,1987

The Alternate View: Laser Propulsion and the Four P's, John G. Cramer, ar *Analog* Aug,1987

The Alternate View: Overreaction, G. Harry Stine, ar *Analog* Jul,1987

The Alternate View: Recent Results, John G. Cramer, ar *Analog* Jun,1987

The Alternate View: SN1987A--Supernova Astrophysics Grows Up, John G. Cramer, ar *Analog* Dec,1987

The Alternate View: Stealth, G. Harry Stine, ar *Analog* May,1987

The Alternate View: Strings and Things, John G. Cramer, ar *Analog* Apr,1987

The Alternate View: The Fits and Flops of Fuzzy Logic, G. Harry Stine, ar *Analog* Mar,1987

The Alternate View: The Selling of Proton, G. Harry Stine, ar *Analog* Nov,1987

The Alternate View: Warm Superconductors, John G. Cramer, ar *Analog* Oct,1987

Amateurs, Leslie Fish, ss *Night Cry* v2#3,1987

The Amber Frog, Stephanie A. Smith, nv *IASFM* Sep,1984

Ambition, Barry N. Malzberg, vi *Twilight Zone* Oct,1987

Amends, A Tale of the Sun Kings, Nancy Springer, ss *F&SF* May,1983

America, Orson Scott Card, nv *IASFM* Jan,1987

America, America, America, Bruce Boston, pm *Last Wave* #5,1986

American Gothic, Ray Russell, ss **Masques** #2, ed. J.N. Williamson,1987

The American Nightmare: The Fiction of Dennis Etchison, Michael A. Morrison, ar *The Horror Show* Win,1987

The Amnesia Ballet, Jack Matthews, ss *Mundus Artium* Sum,1971

Among the Stones, Paul J. McAuley, nv *Amazing* Jan,1987

Among the Wounded, Christopher Burns, ss *Interzone* #22,1987

The Amorous Ghost, Enid Bagnold, ss **The Ghost-Book**, ed. Cynthia Asquith, Hutchinson,1926

Amos Bond, the Gunsmith, Jack Matthews, ss *Michigan Quarterly Review*

Amour Dure, Vernon Lee, nv **Hauntings, Fantastic Stories**, Heinemann: London,1890

Anachron, Damon Knight, ss *If* Jan,1954

The Analog Calendar of Upcoming Events, Anthony R. Lewis, ms *Analog* Jan,1987

The Analog Calendar of Upcoming Events, Anthony R. Lewis, ms *Analog* Feb,1987

The Analog Calendar of Upcoming Events, Anthony R. Lewis, ms *Analog* Mar,1987

The Analog Calendar of Upcoming Events, Anthony R. Lewis, ms *Analog* Apr,1987

The Analog Calendar of Upcoming Events, Anthony R. Lewis, ms *Analog* May,1987

The Analog Calendar of Upcoming Events, Anthony R. Lewis, ms *Analog* Jun,1987

The Analog Calendar of Upcoming Events, Anthony R. Lewis, ms *Analog* Jul,1987

The Analog Calendar of Upcoming Events, Anthony R. Lewis, ms *Analog* Aug,1987

The Analog Calendar of Upcoming Events, Anthony R. Lewis, ms *Analog* Sep,1987

The Analog Calendar of Upcoming Events, Anthony R. Lewis, ms *Analog* Oct,1987

The Analog Calendar of Upcoming Events, Anthony R. Lewis, ms *Analog* Nov,1987

The Analog Calendar of Upcoming Events, Anthony R. Lewis, ms *Analog* Dec,1987

The Analog Calendar of Upcoming Events, Anthony R. Lewis, ms *Analog* mid-Dec,1987

The Analytical Laboratory, [Misc. Material], ms *Analog* Jun,1987

The Anatomy Lesson, Scott Russell Sanders, ss *IASFM* Oct 26,1981

Ancient Ages, Arlan Andrews, pm *Fantasy Book* Mar,1987

Ancient Catch, Bruce Boston, pm

And He Not Busy Being Born..., Brian M. Stableford, ss *Interzone* #16,1986

And Now the News..., Theodore Sturgeon, ss *F&SF* Dec,1956

And So to Bed, Harry Turtledove, ss *Analog* Jan,1986

And the Gods Laughed, Fredric Brown, ss *Tops In Science Fiction* Fll,1953

And the Moon Be Still as Bright, Ray Bradbury, ss *Thrilling Wonder Stories* Jun,1948

...And Then The Prince Knelt Down and Tried to Put the Glass Slipper on Cinderella's Foot, Judith Viorst, pm **If I Were in Charge of the World**, New York: Atheneum,1982

And Then There Was Peace, Gordon R. Dickson, ss *If* Sep,1962

And Who Is Joah?, T.S. Huff, ss *Amazing* Nov,1987

Andre Norton Interview and Bibliography, Nancy Garcia, Andre Norton & Mary Frances Zambreno, iv *American Fantasy* Win,1987

Angel, Pat Cadigan, ss *IASFM* May,1987

Angel Heart, James Verniere, mr *Twilight Zone* Apr,1987

Angel Maker, Sara Maitland, ss

The Angel of Death, Michael Shea, nv *F&SF* Aug,1979

Angel's Egg, Edgar Pangborn, nv *Galaxy* Jun,1951

Angels (Goldengrove Unleaving), Poppy Z. Brite, ss *The Horror Show* Fll,1987

The Anger of Time, J.P. Boyd, ss *F&SF* Feb,1987

The Angle of Consciousness, Ian Miller, pi *Interzone* #21,1987

The Anorexic, Robert Frazier, pm

The Anorexic Poses for Giacometti, Robert Frazier, pm

The Anorexic Speaks Out On May Day, Robert Frazier, pm

Another Crow's Eyes, Elaine Radford, ss *Amazing* Nov,1987

Another Dead Grandfather, George Alec Effinger, ss *F&SF* Dec,1987

The Another Pair of Hands, Muriel Spark, ss *New Yorker* May 13,1985

Another Squaw?, E. Heron-Allen, ss **Some Women of the University**, Stockwell: London,1934

Another World, Ramsey Campbell, ss **Tales from the Forbidden Planet**, ed. Roz Kaveney, Titan,1987

Answer, Fredric Brown, vi **Angels and Spaceships**, Dutton,1954

Ants, Chet Williamson, vi *Twilight Zone* Jun,1987

The Apartment, Bruce Jones, ss **Twisted Tales**, San Diego: Blackthorne,1987

Apocalypse Now: The Final Climax, Michael G. Adkisson, ed *New Pathways* Nov,1987

The Apotheosis of Isaac Rosen, Jack M. Dann & Jeanne Van Buren Dann, vi *Omni* Jun,1987

The Apotheosis of Ki, Miriam Allen deFord, ss *F&SF* Dec,1956

Appendix I: Miscellaneous Notes, Marvin Kaye, ms

Appendix I: Vampire Novels, [Misc. Material], bi

Appendix II: Vampire Movies, [Misc. Material], bi

Appendix II: Who in Hell Are All These Devils? (An Infernal "Lowerarchy"), Marvin Kaye, ms

Appendix III: Selected Bibliography and Filmography, Marvin Kaye, bi

Appendix--Key to "I've Got a Little List", [Misc. Material], ms

The Apple Tree, Daphne du Maurier, nv **The Apple Tree**, Gollancz,1952

Apples, Ramsey Campbell, ss **Halloween Horrors**, ed. Alan Ryan, Doubleday,1986

Apples, L.P. Hartley, ss **The White Wand and Other Stories**, Hamilton,1954

Apples, Nina Downey Higgins, ss **Shadows** #10, ed. Charles L. Grant,1987

An Application to Succeed, Sharon Bailly, ss *Space & Time* #73,1987

The April Witch, Ray Bradbury, ss *The Saturday Evening Post* Apr 5,1952

Arachne, Lisa Mason, ss *Omni* Dec,1987

Arbitrating Neptune's Complaint, Robert Frazier, pm *Analog* mid-Dec,1985

ARCHETYPES   **BEFORE THE BIG BANG**

Archetypes, Harry Turtledove, nv *Amazing* Nov,1985

Are You Receiving Me?, David M. Charles, ss *Amazing* Nov,1987

Arena, Fredric Brown, nv *Astounding* Jun,1944

Aristotle and the Gun, L. Sprague de Camp, nv *Astounding* Feb,1958

Arithmetic of Mourning, Sharon Cumberland, pm *Pulpsmith* Win,1987

Arkham, Robert E. Howard, pm *Weird Tales* Aug,1932

The Arm-Chair of Tustenuggee, William Gilmore Simms, ss

Armageddon, Fredric Brown, ss *Unknown* Aug,1941

The Armless Conductor, Gene O'Neill, ss *F&SF* Sep,1987

Arms of the Flame Goddess, Francis James, nv *Dime Mystery Magazine* Apr,1938

An Arrow of Tempered Silver, Rayson Lorrey, ss *Fantasy Book* Mar,1987

Art and Communication, L. Ron Hubbard, ar,1977

Art and Luck, Arthur Machen, ar *The Independent* Nov 25,1933

Art and Science Fiction: Unbuilt Cities/Unrealized Dreams, Ray Bradbury, ar **Universe**, ed. Byron Preiss, Bantam Spectra,1987

Art in Space, Lawrence Tagrin, ar *Salarius* v1#4,1987

Art of Darkness, Joe R. Lansdale & J.K. Potter, iv *Twilight Zone* Feb,1987

Art Sampler, [Misc. Material], pi *Salarius* v1#4,1987

Art Section, [Misc. Material], pi *Salarius* #3,1987

Artists' Visions of the Weird & Wondrous, Various Hands, il

As If Bloodied on a Hunt Before Sleep, Craig Kee Strete, ss *Twilight Zone* Aug,1987

As in a Glass Dimly, Shane Leslie, ss

Ascian in Rose, Charles de Lint, na Axolotl Press: Seattle WA hc Apr,1987

The Ash-Tree, M.R. James, ss **Ghost Stories of an Antiquary**,1904

Ashes to Ashes, Roger Zelazny, nv **Wild Cards** v2, ed. George R.R. Martin, Bantam,1987

Ashland, Kentucky, Terence M. Green, nv *IASFM* Nov,1985

Ashputtle, Angela Carter, vi **The Virago Book of Ghost Stories**, ed. Richard Dalby, Virago,1987

The Asian Shore, Thomas M. Disch, nv **Orbit** #6, ed. Damon Knight,1970

Ask Not, Rudy Matic, ss *Night Cry* v2#5,1987

Asleep in the Arms of Mother Night, Andrew Joron, pm

Assyria, Christina Lake, ss *Interzone* #19,1987

At Midnight, J.B. Stamper, ss **More Tales for the Midnight Hour**, Apple/Scholastic,1987

At Night, Jeffrey V. Yule, pm *Mage* Spr,1987

At the Bentnail Inn, Robert E. Vardeman, ss **Doom City**, ed. Charles L. Grant, Tor,1987

At the Cross-Time Jaunter's Ball, Alexander Jablokov, nv *IASFM* Aug,1987

At the End of the Passage, Rudyard Kipling, ss *Boston Herald* Jul 20,1890

At the Feet of Karl Klodhopper, Martin Gardner, ss *Esquire* May,1948

At the Last, John Maclay, pm *Footsteps* Spr,1985

At the Mouse Circus, Harlan Ellison, ss **New Dimensions** #1, ed. Robert Silverberg/Marta Randall,1971

At the Narrow Passage, Richard C. Meredith, n. Putnam: New York,1973

At the Rummage Sale, Vicki Grove, ss *Twilight Zone* Apr,1987

Auguries, Gregory Forbes, ar *Mage* Win,1987

Auk House, Clifford D. Simak, na **Stellar** #3, ed. Judy-Lynn del Rey,1977

Aunt Susan, Joan Aiken, ss **A Goose on Your Grave**, Gollancz,1987

Auntie, Philippa Pearce, ss **Who's Afraid? and Other Strange Stories**, Kestrel/Penguin,1986

Aurin Tree, M.J. Engh, nv *IASFM* Feb,1987

"The Author of the Acacia Seeds" and Other Extracts from the Journal of the Association of Therolinguistics, Ursula K. Le Guin, ss **Fellowship of the Stars**, ed. Terry Carr, Simon & Schuster,1974

Author's Foreword, Intuition: The Guide Who Needs Steering, Hal Clement, fw

Author's Note, Leslie Halliwell, in

The Authors, [Misc. Material], bg

An Auto Mechanic Considers the Earth, Ron Houchin, pm *Pulpsmith* Win,1987

Auto Suggestion, Charles Beaumont, ss *Gamma* Sep,1965

An Autobiographical Introduction [from **Religion and the Rebel**], Colin Wilson, ar Gollancz: London,1957

Autofac, Philip K. Dick, nv *Galaxy* Nov,1955

Autograph, Robert Stricklin, ss *2AM* Spr,1987

Autoincineration of the Right Stuff, Ivan Arguelles, pm *Exquisite Corpse* May,1986

The Autopsy, Michael Shea, nv *F&SF* Dec,1980

Autumn Memories, Lisa Lepovetsky, pm *Grue* #6,1987

Aversion, David M. Skov, pm *Ouroboros* #4,1986

The Avoidance Factor, C.J. Cherryh, ar **Glass and Amber**, NESFA,1987

Axe, Lisa Lepovetsky, pm *Grue* #4,1987

Aylmer Vance and the Vampire, Alice Askew & Claude Askew, ss *The Weekly Tale-Teller*,1914

Aymara, Lucius Shepard, nv *IASFM* Aug,1986

Babel's Children, Clive Barker, nv **Clive Barker's Books of Blood** v5,1985

Baboo Mookerji's Undertaking [as by The Witness], Rudyard Kipling, vi *The Civil and Military Gazette* Sep 1,1888

Baby Town, Becky Birtha, ss **Hear the Silence**, ed. Irene Zahava, Crossing Press,1986

The Back of the Mirror, Hugh B. Cave, ss *Border Land* Oct,1987

Backdrop to Chaos, David Drake, ms **Hammer's Slammers**, Ace,1979

Backwater Time, Matt Corwin, ss *F&SF* Feb,1987

Bad Actor, Gary Brandner, ss *Alfred Hitchcock's Mystery Magazine* May,1973

Baker's Dozen, Bradley Denton, nv **Liavek: Wizard's Row**, ed. Will Shetterly & Emma Bull, Ace,1987

The Baku, Edward Bryant, nv **Night Visions** #4,1987

Balaam, Anthony Boucher, ss **9 Tales of Space and Time**, ed. Raymond J. Healey, Holt,1954

The Ballad of Devil's Pasture, Harry Smith, ss *Pulpsmith* Win,1987

The Ballad of Hastur and Cassilda, Marion Zimmer Bradley, sg **Red Sun of Darkover**, ed. Marion Zimmer Bradley & The Friends of Darkover, DAW,1987

A Ballad of Hell, John Davidson, pm

The Ballad of the Quick Levars, Jane Yolen, sg **Liavek: Wizard's Row**, ed. Will Shetterly & Emma Bull, Ace,1987

Ballade for Convention Lovers, Randall Garrett, pm,1963

Ballads in 3/4 Time, Robert Charles Wilson, ss *F&SF* Apr,1987

The Band in the Park, Jean Stubbs, ss **Ghost Book** #11, ed. Aidan Chambers/James Turner,1975

Bang-Bang You're Dead, Muriel Spark, nv

Bank Night, Arthur Porges, ss *The Diners Club Magazine*,1966

Banshee, Timothy Zahn, na *Analog* Sep,1987

The Barbarian Princess, Vernor Vinge, nv *Analog* Sep,1986

The Bard, Nancy Springer, ss **Chance & Other Gestures of the Hand of Fate**, Baen,1987

The Bare Bones: An Introduction, Clive Barker, in

Bargain, David Drake, nv **Masters of Hell**, ed. Janet Morris et al, Baen,1987

Bargains at Binsley's, Elizabeth Massie, ss *The Horror Show* Jan,1987

Barking Dogs, Terence M. Green, ss *F&SF* May,1984

The Barnyard Cock and the Weathercock, Hans Christian Andersen, vi

The Basalt, Ursula K. Le Guin, pm *Open Places* Spr,1982

Basileus, Robert Silverberg, ss **The Best of Omni** #5,1983

Basilisk, Harlan Ellison, ss *F&SF* Aug,1972

Bats, Leon Rooke, ss **Tesseracts 2**, ed. Phyllis Gotlieb & Douglas Barbour, Press Porcepic: Victoria,1987

Battle at Kahlkopolis [Battle at Kahlkhopolis], Robert Adams, nv **There Will Be War** v4, ed. Jerry E. Pournelle,1985

Battle Station, Ben Bova, na **Battle Station**, Tor,1987

Battleground, Gregory Benford & James Benford, ss *If* Jun,1971

Baudelaire's Brain, Ivan Arguelles, pm *Ice River* Sum,1987

Bayou Exterminator, Addie Lacoe, ss *Grue* #6,1987

The Beach Poet, Terry A. Garey, ed *Tales of the Unanticipated* #2,1987

Beacon, Andrew Joron, pm

The Beam, Peter Dare, ss

Bear at the Gate, Jessica Amanda Salmonson, ss **Spaceships & Spells**, ed. Jane Yolen, Martin H. Greenberg & Charles G. Waugh, Harper & Row,1987

Bear Possibility, Fredric Brown, vi *Dude* Mar,1960

A Beast Is Born, W. Wayne Robbins, nv *Horror Stories* Oct,1940

Beast of the Island, Paul Selonke, ss *Strange Tales of Mystery and Terror* Oct,1940

The Beasts That Perish, Manly Wade Wellman, ss *Whispers* Jun,1975

Beau Brummel, Paul Roland, sg **The Curious Case of Richard Fielding and Other Stories**, Lary Press,1987

The Beautiful and the Sublime, Bruce Sterling, nv *IASFM* Jun,1986

A Beautiful Disease, Andrew Joron, pm *Pig Iron* #10,1982

The Beautiful Stranger, Shirley Jackson, ss **Come Along With Me**, Viking,1968

Beauty for Sale, J.O. Quinliven, nv *Horror Stories* Oct,1936

Beauty Is the Beast, Tanith Lee, ss *American Fantasy* Fll,1986

Beaverbrook in Love, Lesley Choyce, ss *Potboiler* Spr,1983

The Beckoning Fair One, Oliver Onions, nv

Before the Big Bang, Jonathan V. Post, pm *Star*Line* Nov,1986

Before the Big Bang: News from the Hubble Large Space Telescope, Jonathan V. Post, pm *Star*Line* Nov,1986

Before the Long Journey, Stefan Grabinski, ss,1921

Behind the Night, George Zebrowski, ss *F&SF* Apr,1987

Beholder, Richard Christian Matheson, ss **Whispers #4**, ed. Stuart David Schiff,1983

Beisbol, Ben Bova, ss *Analog* Nov,1985

Belsen Express, Fritz Leiber, ss **The Second Book of Fritz Leiber**, DAW,1975

Beneath Their Blue, Blue Skins, John Forrester, nv **Spaceships & Spells**, ed. Jane Yolen, Martin H. Greenberg & Charles G. Waugh, Harper & Row,1987

Benjamin, R. Chetwynd-Hayes, nv **Dracula's Children**, Kimber,1987

Benlian, Oliver Onions, nv **Widdershins**, Secker,1911

Benny's Place, Katherine V. Forrest, ss **Dreams and Swords**, Naiad,1987

Bentley Little, William J. Grabowski & Bentley Little, iv *The Horror Show* Fll,1987

The Berserker Enters a Plea on the Death of Greater Los Angeles, Bruce Boston, pm *IASFM* May,1985

Best Friends, Robert R. McCammon, nv **Night Visions #4**,1987

The Betrayal of the Fives, Jack Matthews, ss **Ghostly Populations**, Johns Hopkins,1987

Between a Rock and a High Place, Timothy Zahn, na *Analog* Jul,1982

Between Sunset and Moonrise, R.H. Malden, ss **Nine Ghosts**, E. Arnold: London,1943

Between the Devil and the Deep Blue Sea, Michael Armstrong, nv **Crusaders in Hell**, ed. Janet Morris, New York: Baen,1987

Between the Minute and the Hour, A.M. Burrage, ss **Some Ghost Stories**,1927

Beyond Lies the Wub, Philip K. Dick, ss *Planet Stories* Jul,1952

Beyond Suawanee, Margaret B. Simon, pm *Minnesota Fantasy Review* #1,1987

Beyond That River, Paul Christopher, ss **Beyond That River**, Pal Books,1987

Beyond the Cleft, Tom Reamy, nv **Nova #4**, ed. Harry Harrison,1974

Beyond the Door, Philip K. Dick, ss *Fantastic Universe* Jan,1954

Beyond the Reef, Jessica Amanda Salmonson, pm *Grue* #6,1987

Bibliography, [Misc. Material], bi

The Bicentennial Man, Isaac Asimov, nv **Stellar** #2, ed. Judy-Lynn del Rey,1976

The Big Black and White Game, Ray Bradbury, ss *The American Mercury* Aug,1945

Big Cats, John Bark, ss **Gollancz - Sunday Times Best SF Stories**, Gollancz,1987

Big Surprise [What Was in the Box], Richard Matheson, ss *Ellery Queen's Mystery Magazine* Apr,1959

Billy Jean at Sea, Sharon N. Farber, ss *Amazing* Jul,1987

Billy Mosby's Night Ride, Robert D. San Souci, ss **Short & Shivery**, Doubleday,1987

Billy the Kid, Ian Stewart, ss *Analog* Jan,1987

Billy's Oak, Brian Lumley, ss *The Arkham Collector* Win,1970

Biofutures: The Next Turn of the Corkscrew, Frederik Pohl, ar *Twilight Zone* Oct,1987

Biographical Notes, [Misc. Material], bg

Biolog: Arlan Andrews, Jay Kay Klein, bg *Analog* Sep,1987

Biolog: David A. Hardy, Jay Kay Klein, bg *Analog* Apr,1987

Biolog: George Zebrowski, Jay Kay Klein, bg *Analog* Feb,1987

Biolog: Robert R. Chase, Jay Kay Klein, bg *Analog* Jul,1987

Bird Food, John Maclay, pm **Other Engagements**, Madison, WI: Dream House,1987

Bird in a Wrought Iron Cage, John Alfred Taylor, ss **The Chill Winds of October**, Laurel Arts Foundation,1986

The Birds, Daphne du Maurier, nv *Good Housekeeping* Oct,1952

Birds of the Moon, Lisa Tuttle, ss *Fantastic* Jan,1979

Birds of the Mutant Rain Forest, Robert Frazier, pm *IASFM* Mar,1987

A Birthday, Lisa Tuttle, ss **Tales from the Forbidden Planet**, ed. Roz Kaveney, Titan,1987

Birthdays, Fred Saberhagen, na *Galaxy* Mar,1976

The Bisara of Pooree, Rudyard Kipling, ss *The Civil and Military Gazette* Mar 4,1887

Bitch, Marion Zimmer Bradley, ss *F&SF* Feb,1987

Bite-Me-Not or, Fleur de Feu, Tanith Lee, nv *IASFM* Oct,1984

Black as a Rose, Tanith Lee, nv **Night's Sorceries**, DAW,1987

The Black Bear Bites, Robert E. Howard, ss *From Beyond the Dark Gateway* Apr,1974

Black Charlie, Gordon R. Dickson, ss *Galaxy* Apr,1954

The Black Clay Boy, Lucius Shepard, ss **Whispers #6**, ed. Stuart David Schiff,1987

Black Coral, Lucius Shepard, nv **Universe #14**, ed. Terry Carr,1984

Black Corridor, Fritz Leiber, ss *Galaxy* Dec,1967

Black Death, Bruce Jones, ss **Twisted Tales**, San Diego: Blackthorne,1987

Black Dreams, David Reich, ss *Pulpsmith* Win,1987

Black Eyes, Philippa Pearce, ss **Black Eyes and Other Spine Chillers**, ed. Lance Salway, Pepper Press,1981

The Black Hole, William J. Kaufmann, ar **Universe**, ed. Byron Preiss, Bantam Spectra,1987

Black Ice, Robert Frazier, pm

Black Jewels of the Toad, Lawrence Harding, pm *Eldritch Tales* #14,1987

Black Leonard in Negative Space, Ursula K. Le Guin, pm,1978

The Black Madonna, Muriel Spark, ss

The Black Mare, J.B. Stamper, ss **More Tales for the Midnight Hour**, Apple/Scholastic,1987

The Black Pits of Luna, Robert A. Heinlein, ss *The Saturday Evening Post* Jan 10,1948

The Black Prince, John Gordon, ss **A Quiver of Ghosts**, ed. Aiden Chambers, Bodley Head,1987

The Black Recalled, Brian Lumley, ss **World Fantasy Convention Program Book**,1983

Black Seas, Robert E. Howard, pm *Fantasy Book* Mar,1987

The Black Ship, Gerd Maximovic, ss *SF International* #2,1987

The Black Stone, Robert E. Howard, ss *Weird Tales* Nov,1931

The Black Stranger [complete version], Robert E. Howard, na *Fantasy* Mar,1953

The Black Things, Stephen Studach, pm *Eldritch Tales* #14,1987

Black Water (Suicide) [lyrics], Mercedes R. Lackey, sg **Festival Moon**, ed. C.J. Cherryh, DAW,1987

Black Water (Suicide) [music], C.J. Cherryh, sg **Festival Moon**, ed. C.J. Cherryh, DAW,1987

The Black Wedding, Garry Kilworth, ss **Other Edens**, ed. Christopher Evans & Robert Holdstock, Unwin: London,1987

The Blades, Joan Aiken, nv **Out of Time**, ed. Aidan Chambers, Bodley Head,1984

Blank?, Randall Garrett, ss *Infinity* Jun,1957

The Blast of the Book [The Five Fugitives], G.K. Chesterton, ss *The Storyteller* Oct,1933

Bleak Velocities, Gregory Benford, pm **Synergy** v1, ed. George Zebrowski,1987

Bless This Ship, Richard Mueller, ss *F&SF* Sep,1987

Blessed Are Those..., William P. Cunningham, ss *Mage* Fll,1987

Blessed Sleep, Elizabeth Massie, vi *2AM* Fll,1987

The Blind Geometer, Kim Stanley Robinson, na *IASFM* Aug,1987

Blind Man's Hood [as by Carter Dickson], John Dickson Carr, ss **The Department of Queer Complaints**, Morrow,1940

Blindsight, Robert Silverberg, nv *Playboy* Dec,1986

Blood, Fredric Brown, vi *F&SF* Feb,1955

Blood, William Relling, Jr., ss *Night Cry* v2#3,1987

Blood and Tears, Manny Parsonson, nv *Space & Time* #73,1987

Blood Brothers, Patricia Anthony, ss *Aboriginal SF* Feb,1987

Blood Dancer, Diana L. Paxson, ss **Sword and Sorceress #4**, ed. Marion Zimmer Bradley,1987

Blood Hunt, Paula Crunk & Linda Frankel, na **The Other Side of the Mirror**, ed. Marion Zimmer Bradley & The Friends of Darkover, DAW,1987

Blood Junkie, Sue Marra, pm *2AM* Win,1987

Blood of the Lamb, Rickey L. Shanklin, ss *Eldritch Tales* #13,1987

The Blood Sea Monster, Barbara Siegel & Scott Siegel, nv **DragonLance Tales** v1, Margaret Weis & Tracy Hickman, TSR,1987

Blood, Sweat and Fears, Dale Colleen Hamilton, ss **Hear the Silence**, ed. Irene Zahava, Crossing Press,1986

The Bloodsnare, Bruce Chandler Fergusson, ss *Space & Time* #72,1987

Bloodspell, A.C. Crispin, nv **Tales of the Witch World**, ed. Andre Norton, St. Martin's,1987

Bloodstones, Deborah M. Vogel, vi **Sword and Sorceress #4**, ed. Marion Zimmer Bradley,1987

Bloody Waters, Jean Sullivan, ss *Eldritch Tales* #13,1987

Blowups Happen, Robert A. Heinlein, nv *Astounding* Sep,1940

The Blue Birthmark, Martin Gardner, vi *Hence* Jul,1948

The Blue Lady, Richard Wilson, ss **The Kid from Ozone Park and Other Stories**, Drumm,1987

Blue Lady, Come Back, Karl Edward Wagner, na **Night Visions #2**,1985

The Blue Lenses, Daphne du Maurier, nv **Breaking Point**, Gollancz,1959

The Blue Lotus, Eleanor Farjeon, ss

BLUEBEARD'S EGG

Bluebeard's Egg, Margaret Atwood, nv McLelland & Stewart: Toronto,1983

The Boarded Window, Ambrose Bierce, ss **In the Midst of Life**, E.L.G. Steele: San Francisco CA,1891

Bobbie, Paul Christopher, nv **Beyond That River**, Pal Books,1987

Bogy, Al Sarrantonio, ss *Whispers #6*, ed. Stuart David Schiff,1987

Boiled Alive, Ramsey Campbell, ss *Interzone #18*,1986

A Bomb in the Head, David E. Cortesi, ss *Amazing* May,1987

Bon Appetit, Samantha Lee, vi *Fantasy Tales #16*,1986

Bond and Free, Pamela Sargent, nv *F&SF* Jun,1974

The Bonding Authority, David Drake, ms **Hammer's Slammers**, Ace,1979

The Bone Flute, Lisa Tuttle, ss *F&SF* May,1981

Boneless, Robert D. San Souci, ss **Short & Shivery**, Doubleday,1987

The Bones Wizard, Alan Ryan, ss *Whispers #21*,1984

Bonsai Man, Tom Henighan, pm **Tesseracts 2**, ed. Phyllis Gotlieb & Douglas Barbour, Press Porcepic: Victoria,1987

Boo, Yourself, Joe R. Lansdale, ss *Whispers #23*,1987

The Boogeyman, Stephen King, ss *Cavalier* Mar,1973

Boogie Man, Tappan King, ss **Devils & Demons**, ed. Marvin Kaye, SFBC/Doubleday,1987

Book Notes, Jonathan White, br *Twilight Zone* Feb,1987

The Book of Baraboo, Barry B. Longyear, na *IASFM* Mar,1980

Book Review, Crispin Burnham, br *Eldritch Tales #14*,1987

Book Reviews, Michael G. Adkisson, br *New Pathways* Apr,1987

Book Reviews, Michael G. Adkisson, br *New Pathways* Nov,1987

Book Reviews, Stan Brooks, br *Footsteps* Nov,1987

Book Reviews, Misha Chocholak, br *New Pathways* Apr,1987

Book Reviews, Misha Chocholak, br *New Pathways* Aug,1987

Book Reviews, Misha Chocholak, br *New Pathways* Nov,1987

Book Reviews, John Clute, br *Interzone #19*,1987

Book Reviews, John Clute, br *Interzone #20*,1987

Book Reviews, John Clute, br *Interzone #21*,1987

Book Reviews, John Clute, br *Interzone #22*,1987

Book Reviews, Lee Montgomerie, br *Interzone #19*,1987

Book Reviews, Lee Montgomerie, br *Interzone #20*,1987

Book Reviews, Lee Montgomerie, br *Interzone #21*,1987

Book Reviews, Lee Montgomerie, br *Interzone #22*,1987

Book Reviews, Staff, br *New Pathways* Jan,1987

Book Reviews, Don Webb & Rosemary Webb, br *New Pathways* Aug,1987

Book Reviews, Don Webb & Rosemary Webb, br *New Pathways* Nov,1987

The Book-Healer, Sandra Miesel, ss **Magic in Ithkar #4**, ed. Andre Norton & Robert Adams,1987

The Bookman's God, John Maclay, ss **Other Engagements**, Madison, WI: Dream House,1987

Books, Everett F. Bleiler, br *Twilight Zone* Feb,1987

Books, Everett F. Bleiler, br *Twilight Zone* Apr,1987

Books, Edward Bryant, br *Twilight Zone* Jun,1987

Books, Edward Bryant, br *Twilight Zone* Aug,1987

Books, Edward Bryant, br *Twilight Zone* Oct,1987

Books, Edward Bryant, br *Twilight Zone* Dec,1987

Books, Algis Budrys, br *F&SF* Jan,1987

Books, Algis Budrys, br *F&SF* Feb,1987

Books, Algis Budrys, br *F&SF* Mar,1987

Books, Algis Budrys, br *F&SF* Apr,1987

Books, Algis Budrys, br *F&SF* May,1987

Books, Algis Budrys, br *F&SF* Jun,1987

Books, Algis Budrys, br *F&SF* Jul,1987

Books, Algis Budrys, br *F&SF* Aug,1987

Books, Algis Budrys, br *F&SF* Oct,1987

Books, Algis Budrys, br *F&SF* Nov,1987

Books, Al Sarrantonio, br *Night Cry* v2#3,1987

Books, Al Sarrantonio, br *Night Cry* v2#4,1987

Books, Al Sarrantonio, br *Night Cry* v2#5,1987

Books to Look For, Orson Scott Card, br *F&SF* May,1987

Books to Look For, Orson Scott Card, br *F&SF* Jun,1987

Books to Look For, Orson Scott Card, br *F&SF* Jul,1987

Books to Look For, Orson Scott Card, br *F&SF* Aug,1987

Books to Look For, Orson Scott Card, br *F&SF* Sep,1987

Books to Look For, Orson Scott Card, br *F&SF* Oct,1987

Books to Look For, Orson Scott Card, br *F&SF* Nov,1987

Books to Look For, Orson Scott Card, br *F&SF* Dec,1987

Books: A Historical Perspective, Darrell Schweitzer, br *Aboriginal SF* May,1987

Books: Books Versus Careers, Darrell Schweitzer, br *Aboriginal SF* Sep,1987

Books: New Works from Old Masters, Darrell Schweitzer, br *Aboriginal SF* Feb,1987

Books: Objectivity, Darrell Schweitzer, br *Aboriginal SF* Nov,1987

Books: The Whole Spectrum of Fantastic Literature, Darrell Schweitzer, br *Aboriginal SF* Jul,1987

Bookworm, Run!, Vernor Vinge, nv *Analog* Mar,1966

Boomerangs, The Readers, lt *Aboriginal SF* Feb,1987

Boomerangs, The Readers, lt *Aboriginal SF* May,1987

Boomerangs, The Readers, lt *Aboriginal SF* Jul,1987

Boomerangs, The Readers, lt *Aboriginal SF* Sep,1987

Boomerangs, The Readers, lt *Aboriginal SF* Nov,1987

Borboleta, James A. Stevens, ss *Aboriginal SF* Jul,1987

The Borderland of Sol, Larry Niven, nv *Analog* Jan,1975

The Borders of Infinity, Lois McMaster Bujold, na **Free Lancers**, ed. Elizabeth Mitchell, Baen,1987

Born Again, Ben Bova, ss *Analog* May,1984

Born of Man and Woman, Richard Matheson, ss *F&SF* Sum,1950

A Bottle on the Beach, Paul Christopher, ss **Beyond That River**, Pal Books,1987

A Boy and His Dog [revised], Harlan Ellison, nv *New Worlds* Apr,1969

The Boy in the Rain, Pat Cadigan, ss *Twilight Zone* Jun,1987

The Boy Who Came Back from the Dead, Alan Rodgers, nv **Masques #2**, ed. J.N. Williamson,1987

The Boy Who Drew Cats, Lafcadio Hearn, ss,1898

The Boy Who Plaited Manes, Nancy Springer, ss *F&SF* Oct,1986

The Boy Who Predicted Earthquakes, Margaret St. Clair, ss *Maclean's*,1950

The Boy, the Dog and the Spaceship, Nicholas Fisk, ss,1974

Boylan Briggs Salutes the New Cause, Lesley Choyce, ss *The Lunatic Gazette* Dec,1982

The Boys, Charles Stross, ss *Interzone #22*,1987

Brain Blaster, Nicholas Fisk, ss **Living Fire and Other S.F. Stories**, Corgi: London,1987

Brain Blasters, Mary Sass, ss *Mage* Spr,1987

Brain Jag, Robert Chilson, ss *Analog* Jun,1987

Brain Language, Stanley Schmidt, ed *Analog* Mar,1987

The Brains of Rats, Michael Blumlein, ss *Interzone #16*,1986

Bramblebeard, t. Winter-Damon, pm *Mage* Win,1985

Brass Tacks, The Readers, lt *Analog* Jan,1987

Brass Tacks, The Readers, lt *Analog* Feb,1987

Brass Tacks, The Readers, lt *Analog* Mar,1987

Brass Tacks, The Readers, lt *Analog* Apr,1987

Brass Tacks, The Readers, lt *Analog* May,1987

Brass Tacks, The Readers, lt *Analog* Jun,1987

Brass Tacks, The Readers, lt *Analog* Jul,1987

Brass Tacks, The Readers, lt *Analog* Aug,1987

Brass Tacks, The Readers, lt *Analog* Sep,1987

Brass Tacks, The Readers, lt *Analog* Oct,1987

Brass Tacks, The Readers, lt *Analog* Nov,1987

Brass Tacks, The Readers, lt *Analog* Dec,1987

Brass Tacks, The Readers, lt *Analog* mid-Dec,1987

The Brazen Locked Room [also as "Gimmicks Three"], Isaac Asimov, ss *F&SF* Nov,1956

The Brazen Peacock, Robert E. Howard, nv *REH: Lone Star Fictioneer* Fll,1975

Break, Bruce Boston, ss **New Worlds Quarterly #7**, Moorcock/Platt/Bailey,1974

Break-Up, Richard Christian Matheson, ss **Scars**, Scream/Press,1987

Breakages, Fay Weldon, ss **The Midnight Ghost Book**, ed. James Hale,1978

Breakfast at Twilight, Philip K. Dick, ss *Amazing* Jul,1954

The Breakfast Party [League of the Living Dead], Randall Garrett, ss *Mystic* Nov,1953

Breaking into the Crystal Text, Andrew Joron, pm

Brenda, Margaret St. Clair, ss *Weird Tales* Mar,1954

Briar Rose (Sleeping Beauty), Anne Sexton, pm **Transformations**, New York: Houghton Mifflin,1971

Bride Price, Marion Zimmer Bradley, ss **The Other Side of the Mirror**, ed. Marion Zimmer Bradley & The Friends of Darkover, DAW,1987

The Bridge, Thomas E. Sanders (Nippawanock), ss *The South Dakota Review* Spr,1975

Bridles and Spurs, Arthur Machen, ar,1951

The Briefing, Randall Garrett, vi *Fantastic* Aug,1969

The Brigadier in Check -- and Mate, Sterling E. Lanier, na **The Curious Quest of Brigadier Ffellowes**, Donald M. Grant,1986

Bright Beard, Fredric Brown, vi **Nightmares and Geezenstacks**, Bantam,1961

Bright Segment, Theodore Sturgeon, nv **Caviar**, Ballantine,1955

Bright-Eyed Black Pony, Nancy Springer, ss **Moonsinger's Friends**, ed. Susan Shwartz, Bluejay,1985

Bringing in the Sheaves, Rudy Rucker, ss *IASFM* Jan,1987

Bringing It Home, Jack M. Dann & Barry N. Malzberg, ss *Twilight Zone* Feb,1987

The Broken Hoop, Pamela Sargent, ss *Twilight Zone* Jun,1982

Broken Portraiture, Bruce Boston, ss *Gallimaufry* #5,1975

The Brood, Ramsey Campbell, ss **Dark Forces**, ed. Kirby McCauley, Viking,1980

Brother, Clifford D. Simak, nv *F&SF* Oct,1977

Brother and Sister, Robert D. San Souci, ss **Short & Shivery**, Doubleday,1987

Brother Charlie, Gordon R. Dickson, nv *F&SF* Jul,1958

Brother John's Bequest, Arthur Gray, ss **Tedious Brief Tales of Granta and Gramarye**, Cambridge: Heffer,1919

Brothers, Ben Bova, ss **In the Field of Fire**, ed. Jeanne Van Buren Dann & Jack M. Dann, Tor,1987

Bruce Sterling, Bruce Sterling & Don Webb, iv *New Pathways* Aug,1987

Bruno's Revenge, Lewis Carroll, ss *Aunt Judy's Magazine*,1867

The Brushwood Boy, Rudyard Kipling, nv *The Century* Dec,1895

Bub and the Zomb Boys, A.R. Morlan, ss *The Horror Show* Fll,1987

Bubbles, David Brin, ss **Universe**, ed. Byron Preiss, Bantam Spectra,1987

Bubbling Well Road [as by The Traveler], Rudyard Kipling, vi *The Civil and Military Gazette* Jan 18,1888

Buddha at the Laundromat, Lesley Choyce, ss *New Quarterly* Sum,1982

Buffalo Gals, Won't You Come Out Tonight, Ursula K. Le Guin, nv **Buffalo Gals and Other Animal Presences**, Capra Press,1987

Buggage, Edward Bryant, ss **Night Visions** #4,1987

Build Me a Mountain, Ben Bova, ss **2020 Vision**, ed. Jerry Pournelle,1974

The Builder, Philip K. Dick, ss *Amazing* Jan,1954

Building Plausible Futures, Jerry E. Pournelle, ar **L. Ron Hubbard Presents Writers of the Future** v3, ed. Algis Budrys, Bridge,1987

The Buildings Are Falling, Tim Coats, ss *Grue* #4,1987

Bujak and the Strong Force, or God's Love, Martin Amis, nv *The London Review of Books*

The Bull, David Drake, nv *Whispers* #23,1987

Bulletin from the Galactic Center, Andrew Joron, pm

The Bully and the Beast, Orson Scott Card, na **Other Worlds** #1, ed. Roy Torgesson,1979

Bundles of Joy, Jenny Ordish, ss **Gollancz - Sunday Times Best SF Stories**, Gollancz,1987

Burden of Proof, Bob Shaw, ss *Analog* May,1967

The Bureaucratic Brain, Robert Chilson, ss *Analog* Mar,1987

The Burial of the Rats, Bram Stoker, nv **Dracula's Guest**, Routledge: London,1914

Buried Talents, Richard Matheson, ss **Masques** #2, ed. J.N. Williamson,1987

Burton's Word, William Relling, Jr., ss *Whispers* #23,1987

Business as Usual, Ron Goulart, ss *F&SF* Jul,1987

But First These Words--, Robert Bloch, ss *F&SF* May,1977

But Loyal to His Own, David Drake, nv *Galaxy* Oct,1975

But Without Orifices, Brian W. Aldiss, ss **Epoch**, ed. Roger Elwood & Robert Silverberg, Berkley,1975

The Butcher's Bill, David Drake, nv *Galaxy* Nov,1974

The Butler, Glenn Rahman, vi *Minnesota Fantasy Review* #1,1987

The Butterflies of Betelgeuse, John Salonia & Traci Salonia, pm *Space & Time* #72,1987

The Butterfly, Hans Christian Andersen, vi

Butterfly Futures, Stanley Schmidt, ed *Analog* May,1987

Buy the Rules?, Greg Gordon, gr *American Fantasy* Spr,1987

Buy the Rules?, Greg Gordon, gr *American Fantasy* Win,1987

The Buyer of Souls, John H. Knox, nv *Horror Stories* Aug,1936

Buzz-Words, Jan Mark, ss **A Quiver of Ghosts**, ed. Aiden Chambers, Bodley Head,1987

By Any Other Name, Spider Robinson, na *Analog* Nov,1976

By Crystal Light Beneath One Star, Tanith Lee, nv **Tales from the Forbidden Planet**, ed. Roz Kaveney, Titan,1987

By Invitation Only, Nancy Asire, nv **Crusaders in Hell**, ed. Janet Morris, New York: Baen,1987

By Lost Ways, Pat Cadigan, nv **Wild Cards** v2, ed. George R.R. Martin, Bantam,1987

By the Measure, Richard A. Knaak, nv **DragonLance Tales** v3, Margaret Weis & Tracy Hickman, TSR,1987

By the Way, Ed Shannon, ed *Minnesota Fantasy Review* #1,1987

By Thought Alone, William R. Fortschen, ss **There Will Be War** v6, ed. Jerry E. Pournelle,1987

By Word of Mouth, Rudyard Kipling, vi *The Civil and Military Gazette* Jun 10,1887

Cabin 33, Chelsea Quinn Yarbro, na **Shadows** #3, ed. Charles L. Grant,1980

Cadbury, the Beaver Who Lacked, Philip K. Dick, ss **The Little Black Box**, Underwood/Miller,1987

Cade, Mark C. Perry, nv **Aftermath**, ed. Robert Lynn Asprin & Lynn Abbey, Ace,1987

Cafe Royal, John Gawsworth, pm

The Cage, Ray Russell, ss,1959

Cage 37, Wayne Wightman, nv *F&SF* Apr,1987

Cairo, Paul Roland, sg **The Curious Case of Richard Fielding and Other Stories**, Lary Press,1987

Caliban's Revenge, Darrell Schweitzer, ss *Weirdbook* #13,1978

Call First, Ramsey Campbell, ss **Night Chills**, ed. Kirby McCauley, Avon,1975

Call Him Lord, Gordon R. Dickson, ss *Analog* May,1966

Call Me Fearful, Donald Franson, ss *Eldritch Tales* #14,1987

The Call of Cthulhu, H.P. Lovecraft, nv *Weird Tales* Feb,1928

The Caller of the Black, Brian Lumley, nv **The Caller of the Black**, Arkham,1971

Calling Card, Ramsey Campbell, ss,1981

Camels for Calvin, Annemarie van Ewyck, ss *SF International* #1,1987

Can These Bones Live?, Manly Wade Wellman, ss *Sorcerer's Apprentice* Sum,1981

Cancelled, Richard Christian Matheson, vi *Twilight Zone* Jun,1986

Candle in a Cosmic Wind, Joseph Manzione, nv *Analog* Aug,1987

The Candles, Hans Christian Andersen, vi

Canned Goods, Thomas M. Disch, ss *Interzone* #9,1984

Cannibals, Nancy Kress, ss *IASFM* May,1987

Canon Alberic's Scrap-Book, M.R. James, ss *National Review* Mar,1895

The Canyons of Ariel, Kenneth W. Ledbetter, nv *F&SF* Dec,1987

Captive Market, Philip K. Dick, ss *If* Apr,1955

Captives of the Slavestone, Ian Stewart, nv *Analog* mid-Dec,1987

The Car with the Green Lights, William Le Queux, ss *The Premier Magazine* Feb,1916

The Carasoyn, George MacDonald, nv **Works of Fancy and Imagination**,1871

Carefully Observed Women, Brian W. Aldiss, ss **New Writings in SF** #26,1975

Caretaker, Manly Wade Wellman, ss *F&SF* Oct,1977

Carmilla, Joseph Sheridan Le Fanu, na *The Dark Blue*,1871

Carnivores, Peter Heyrman, ss *The Horror Show* Jan,1987

Caroline, R. Chetwynd-Hayes, na **The House of Dracula**, Kimber,1987

Carthage City, Orson Scott Card, na *IASFM* Sep,1987

Cartoon, Ed Arno, ct *F&SF* Apr,1987

Cartoon, Ed Arno, ct *F&SF* Sep,1987

Cartoon, Ed Arno, ct *F&SF* Oct,1987

Cartoon, Ed Arno, ct *F&SF* Nov,1987

Cartoon, Thomas Cheney, ct *Twilight Zone* Feb,1987

Cartoon, Thomas Cheney, ct *Twilight Zone* Apr,1987

Cartoon, Thomas Cheney, ct *Twilight Zone* Jun,1987

Cartoon, Thomas Cheney, ct *Twilight Zone* Aug,1987

Cartoon, Thomas Cheney, ct *Twilight Zone* Oct,1987

Cartoon, Thomas Cheney, ct *Twilight Zone* Dec,1987

Cartoon, Gary Davison, ct *Twilight Zone* Dec,1987

Cartoon, Joseph Dawes, ct *F&SF* May,1987

Cartoon, Joseph Dawes, ct *F&SF* Sep,1987

Cartoon, Joseph Dawes, ct *F&SF* Oct,1987

Cartoon, Sandy Dean, ct *Aboriginal SF* Feb,1987

Cartoon, Joseph Farris, ct *F&SF* Feb,1987

Cartoon, Joseph Farris, ct *F&SF* Mar,1987

Cartoon, Joseph Farris, ct *F&SF* Apr,1987

Cartoon, Joseph Farris, ct *F&SF* May,1987

Cartoon, Joseph Farris, ct *F&SF* Oct,1987

Cartoon, Joseph Farris, ct *F&SF* Dec,1987

Cartoon, Feggo, ct *Twilight Zone* Jun,1987

Cartoon, Feggo, ct *Twilight Zone* Aug,1987

Cartoon, Feggo, ct *Twilight Zone* Oct,1987

Cartoon, Sidney Harris, ct *F&SF* Jan,1987

Cartoon, Sidney Harris, ct *F&SF* Jul,1987

Cartoon, Sidney Harris, ct *F&SF* Nov,1987

Cartoon, Sidney Harris, ct *F&SF* Dec,1987

Cartoon, Heiser, ct *IASFM* Oct,1987

Cartoon, Wayne Hogan, ct *Twilight Zone* Dec,1987

Cartoon, John Jonik, ct *New Yorker*,1987

Cartoon, Nurit Karlin, ct *F&SF* Oct,1987

Cartoon, L.J. Kopf, ct *F&SF* Aug,1987

Cartoon, Koster, ct *Twilight Zone* Aug,1987

Cartoon, Henry Martin, ct *F&SF* Jan,1987

Cartoon, Henry Martin, ct *F&SF* Feb,1987

Cartoon, Henry Martin, ct *F&SF* Mar,1987

Cartoon, Henry Martin, ct *F&SF* Apr,1987

Cartoon, Henry Martin, ct *F&SF* May,1987

Cartoon, Henry Martin, ct *F&SF* Jun,1987

Cartoon, Henry Martin, ct *F&SF* Jul,1987

Cartoon, Henry Martin, ct *F&SF* Aug,1987

Cartoon, Henry Martin, ct *F&SF* Sep,1987

Cartoon, Henry Martin, ct *F&SF* Nov,1987

Cartoon, Henry Martin, ct *F&SF* Dec,1987

Cartoon, Arthur Masear, ct *Twilight Zone* Jun,1987

Cartoon, Tom Mason, ct *Aboriginal SF* May,1987

Cartoon, Tom Mason, ct *Twilight Zone* Aug,1987

Cartoon, Rex May, ct *F&SF* Jan,1987

Cartoon, Rex May, ct *F&SF* Jun,1987

Cartoon, Onio, ct *Twilight Zone* Oct,1987

Cartoon, Onio, ct *Twilight Zone* Dec,1987

Cartoon, S. Rose, (?), ct *Twilight Zone* Jun,1987

Cartoon, Schochet, ct *Twilight Zone* Oct,1987

Cartoon, Schwadron, ct *Twilight Zone* Dec,1987

Cartoon, unknown, ct *IASFM* Sep,1987

Cartoon, unknown, ct *Twilight Zone* Feb,1987

Cartoon, unknown, ct *Twilight Zone* Aug,1987

Cartoon, unknown, ct *Twilight Zone* Oct,1987

Cartoonist [Garrigan's Bems], Fredric Brown & Mack Reynolds, ss *Planet Stories* May,1951

Case of Painter's Ear, John Brunner, ss **Tales from the Forbidden Planet**, ed. Roz Kaveney, Titan,1987

Casey Agonistes, Richard McKenna, ss *F&SF* Sep,1958

Cassandra, C.J. Cherryh, ss *F&SF* Oct,1978

Cassandra in Wonderland, Ace G. Pilkington, pm *Amazing* May,1987

Cassandra's Photographs, Lisa Goldstein, ss *IASFM* Aug,1987

The Castaway, Phillip C. Jennings, ss *Amazing* Mar,1987

Casting the Runes, M.R. James, nv **More Ghost Stories of an Antiquary**, Arnold,1911

Cat and Muse, Rose Wolf, ss **Magic in Ithkar #4**, ed. Andre Norton & Robert Adams,1987

Cat and the Other, Marylois Dunn, nv **Tales of the Witch World**, ed. Andre Norton, St. Martin's,1987

Cat at Play, Augustine Funnell, ss *Night Cry* v2#3,1987

Cat Burglar, Fredric Brown, vi **Nightmares and Geezenstacks**, Bantam,1961

The Cat Jumps, Elizabeth Bowen, ss **The Cat Jumps and Other Stories**,1934

Cat or Pigeon?, Gary Gygax, na **Night Arrant**, Ace/New Infinities,1987

Cat's Tale, Nancy Asire, nv **Festival Moon**, ed. C.J. Cherryh, DAW,1987

Catalyst, Rick Cook, ss *Analog* Oct,1987

The Catch, Gordon R. Dickson, ss *Astounding* Apr,1959

Catch That Zeppelin!, Fritz Leiber, ss *F&SF* Mar,1975

Catmagic, M. Lucie Chin, ss **Devils & Demons**, ed. Marvin Kaye, SFBC/Doubleday,1987

The Cats of Thermidor, Paul Witcover, ss *Night Cry* v2#4,1987

Cats Versus Rats, Gary Gygax, nv **Night Arrant**, Ace/New Infinities,1987

Catscape, Roberta Grant, nv *Amazing* Jul,1987

Caught in the Crossfire, David Drake, nv **Chrysalis #2**, ed. Roy Torgeson,1978

The Cauldron, The Readers, lt *Fantasy Tales* #16,1986

Cauldron of Rain, Fred Behrendt, pm *Space & Time* #73,1987

The Cave of Night, James E. Gunn, ss *Galaxy* Feb,1955

Cedars, John Maclay, pm *The Poet* Fll,1984

The Cegua, Robert D. San Souci, ss **Short & Shivery**, Doubleday,1987

Celebrating, Barry N. Malzberg, ss *F&SF* Aug,1987

The Celery Stalk in the Cellar, Saralee Terry, pm **Brother Theodore's Chamber of Horrors**, ed. Marvin Kaye, Pinnacle,1975

Celestian Grapevine, Bruce Boston, pm *Space & Time* #73,1987

Cell Opens, Joe Wilcox, nv **Red Sun of Darkover**, ed. Marion Zimmer Bradley & The Friends of Darkover, DAW,1987

Cellular Automata, Margaret L. Silbar, ar *Analog* Sep,1987

Celui-La, Eleanor Scott, ss **Randalls Round**, E. Benn: London,1929

Cenedwine Brocade, Caroline Stevermer, ss **Liavek: Wizard's Row**, ed. Will Shetterly & Emma Bull, Ace,1987

Century Farm, Julie Stevens, ss *Whispers* #23,1987

Ceremony, Jack M. Dann, pm **The Anthology of Speculative Poetry**, ed. Robert Frazier,1980

Ceres Situation, Rudin Moore, ss **Ultra-Vue and Selected Peripheral Visions**, self published,1987

Cetacean Dreams, Robert Frazier, pm **Light Years and Dark**, ed. Michael Bishop, Berkley,1984

Chain, Barbara Owens, ss *F&SF* Jul,1987

Chains of Air, Web of Aether, Philip K. Dick, nv **Stellar #5**, ed. Judy-Lynn del Rey,1980

Challengers, John Calvin Rezmerski, pm *Tales of the Unanticipated* #2,1987

Chamber of Horrors, The Readers, lt *Horror Stories*

Chance, Nancy Springer, na **Under the Wheel: Alien Stars Vol. III**, ed. Elizabeth Mitchell, Baen,1987

Chance, Connie Willis, nv *IASFM* May,1986

A Change of Ownership, L.P. Hartley, ss

The Changed Man and the King of Words, Orson Scott Card, nv *Omni* Dec,1982

The Changeling Hunt, Robert R. Chase, nv *Analog* Jul,1987

The Changeling Uncovered, Bruce Boston, pm *IASFM* Jan,1987

Chapterhouse Dune, Frank Herbert, n. Gollancz: London,1985

Character Assassination, H.J. Cording, ss *Haunts* #9,1987

Charlie Among the Elves, Edward H. Knatchbull-Hugessen, ss **Moonshine**, London: Macmillan,1871

Charlie and the Chocolate Factory, Roald Dahl, n. Knopf: New York,1964

Charlie and the Great Glass Elevator, Roald Dahl, n. Knopf: New York,1972

Chastel, Manly Wade Wellman, nv **The Year's Best Horror Stories #7**,1979

Cheap But Not Dirty: Proposal for a Spaceplane, Dan DeLong & Tom Pace, ar *Analog* Mar,1987

Cheapskate, G.L. Raisor, vi *Night Cry* v2#4,1987

Chernobyl and Challenger: That Was the Year That Was, Frederik Pohl, ar *Aboriginal SF* Sep,1987

Child Abuse, Stanley Schmidt, ed *Analog* Jun,1987

Child's Play, William Tenn, nv *Astounding* Mar,1947

The Children of Lommos, John Gregory Betancourt & Darrell Schweitzer, ss *Night Cry* v2#4,1987

The Children of Noah, Richard Matheson, ss *Alfred Hitchcock's Mystery Magazine* Mar,1957

The Children of the Kingdom Quiz, A.R. Morlan, qz *The Horror Show* Jan,1987

Children of the Night, Tanith Lee, na **Night's Sorceries**, DAW,1987

Children of the Night, Robert Simpson, ar *Twilight Zone* Dec,1987

The Children of the Sea, Patricia Matthews, ss *F&SF* Feb,1987

Children of the Stars, Bruce Jones, nv **Twisted Tales**, San Diego: Blackthorne,1987

The Children of Winter, Jackie Vivelo, ss **A Trick of the Light**, Putnam,1987

Children's Books, Gregory Forbes, br *Mage* Sum,1985

Children's Lesson at Loines Observatory, Robert Frazier, pm *IASFM* Dec,1984

The Children, They Laugh So Sweetly, Charles L. Grant, ss *F&SF* Oct,1985

The Chimney, Ramsey Campbell, ss **Whispers #1**, ed. Stuart David Schiff,1977

The Chivalry of Sir Aldingar, Darrell Schweitzer, ss *Weirdbook* #22,1987

Chorazin, Manly Wade Wellman, ss *Whispers* Oct,1978

A Christian in Wonderland, Orson Scott Card, ar *Apex!* #1,1987

The Christmas Banquet, Nathaniel Hawthorne, nv *Democratic Review* Dec,1843

A Christmas Game, A.N.L. Munby, ss,1950

Christmas Meeting, Rosemary Timperley, vi,1952

Christmas Night, Elizabeth Walter, nv,1975

A Christmas Pudding Improves with Keeping, Philippa Pearce, ss **Who's Afraid? and Other Strange Stories**, Kestrel/Penguin,1986

Christmas Reunion, Sir Andrew Caldecott, ss **Not Exactly Ghosts**, E. Arnold: London,1946

A Christmas Tree, Charles Dickens, ss

The Chromium Fence, Philip K. Dick, ss *Imagination* Jul,1955

The Chrononaut Visits the Famous Pair During Their First Experiment, Robert Frazier, pm *IASFM* Jul,1987

Chrysalis, Ray Bradbury, ss *Amazing* Jul,1946

Chrysalis, Gregory Kusnick, ss *Analog* mid-Dec,1987

The Church of the Lord's Universe, David Drake, ms **Hammer's Slammers**, Ace,1979

Cinderella, Tony Bradman, ss **The Magic Kiss and Other Tales of Princes and Princesses**, Tony Bradman, Blackie,1987

Cinderella, Anne Isabella Ritchie, ss **Five Old Friends and a Young Prince**, London: Smith, Elder,1868

Cinderella and the Glass Slipper, George Cruikshank, ss,1854

THE CIRCULAR LIBRARY OF STONES

The Circular Library of Stones, Carol Emshwiller, ss *Omni* Feb,1987
Circumstance, Harriet Prescott Spofford, ss *Atlantic Monthly* May,1860
Circus Story, Connie Willis, ss *Aboriginal SF* Feb,1987
The Citadel of Darkness, Henry Kuttner, nv *Strange Stories* Aug,1939
The City [Purpose], Ray Bradbury, ss *Startling Stories* Jul,1950
The City and the Stars, Arthur C. Clarke, n. Harcourt Brace: New York,1956
City of Luck, Jane Yolen, sg **Liavek: Wizard's Row**, ed. Will Shetterly & Emma Bull, Ace,1987
City of Sleep, Helen Hughes, ss *Pulpsmith* Win,1987
Clara Militch, Ivan Turgenev, nv
Clarimonda, Theophile Gautier, nv **One of Cleopatra's Nights and Other Fantastic Romances**, B. Worthington: New York,1882
Clarion and Speculative Fiction, Kristine Kathryn Rusch, ar *Amazing* Nov,1987
Class of '61, Neal Barrett, Jr., ss *IASFM* Oct,1987
Classified Ads, Donald R. Burleson, ss *The Horror Show* Spr,1987
Clawing at the Moon, Janice Dillard, pm *Footsteps* Nov,1987
Clay Devils, Pat Murphy, ss *Twilight Zone* Apr,1987
The Clean Up Your Own Mess, A Crazy Alien, ms *Aboriginal SF* Sep,1987
The Cleanup, John M. Skipp & Craig Spector, ss *Night Cry* v2#4,1987
Clear to Eternity, Bruce Boston, pm *Amazing* Jul,1987
Clive Barker Interview, Clive Barker, Nancy Garcia & Robert T. Garcia, iv *American Fantasy* Win,1987
The Cloak, Robert Bloch, ss *Unknown* May,1939
Cloak and Stagger, Gordon R. Dickson, nv *Future* Fll,1957
The Cloak and the Staff, Gordon R. Dickson, nv *Analog* Aug,1980
The Clockwork Woman, Ann R. Brown, ss **Magic in Ithkar** #4, ed. Andre Norton & Robert Adams,1987
Cloddy Hans, Hans Christian Andersen, ss
Clone Sister, Pamela Sargent, nv **Eros in Orbit**, ed. Joseph Elder, Trident,1973
Close Encounters with Michael Bishop, Michael Bishop & Misha Chocholak, iv *New Pathways* Jan,1987
Closer than a Brother, Jan Mark, ss **Twisted Circuits**, ed. Mick Gowar, Beaver,1987
Closing the Loop, John Kilgore, ss *Space & Time* #72,1987
Closing Time, George R.R. Martin, ss *IASFM* Nov,1982
Clove's Essence, William Borden, ss *Pulpsmith* Win,1987
The Cobbler, Roger Robert Lovin, ss *F&SF* Dec,1987
Cobwebs, Ray Brown, nv *Analog* Aug,1987
Code in the Head, Randall Garrett, ss *Future* #29,1956
The Coelura, Anne McCaffrey, na Underwood-Miller: Columbia, PA,1983
Coils, Patricia Shaw-Mathews, ss **Red Sun of Darkover**, ed. Marion Zimmer Bradley & The Friends of Darkover, DAW,1987
Cold Christmas, Dick Davies, cs *The Horror Show* Jan,1987
The Cold Equations, Tom Godwin, nv *Astounding* Aug,1954
Cold Light, Ian Watson, nv *F&SF* Apr,1986
Cold Print, Ramsey Campbell, ss **Tales of the Cthulhu Mythos**, ed. August Derleth, Arkham,1969
cold rust grit: end of dreams, Joe W. Haldeman, pm *IASFM* mid-Dec,1987
The Colinization of Edward Beal, Lisa Tuttle, ss *F&SF* Oct,1987
The Collar, Hans Christian Andersen, vi
Collector, Bill Congreve, ss *Aphelion* #5,1987
The Collector, J.B. Stamper, ss **More Tales for the Midnight Hour**, Apple/Scholastic,1987
Colony, Philip K. Dick, ss *Galaxy* Jun,1953
"Colony": I Trusted the Rug Completely, Robert Silverberg, ar,1987
The Colour out of Space [also as "Monster of Terror"], H.P. Lovecraft, nv *Amazing* Sep,1927
Colt .24, Rick Hautala, ss **Devils**, ed. Isaac Asimov, Martin H. Greenberg & Charles G. Waugh, Signet,1987
Come Along, Marjorie, Muriel Spark, ss
'Come Follow!', Sheila Hodgson, ss **Ghosts & Scholars** #4, ed. Rosemary Pardoe,1982
Come In, Nancy Springer, pm *Night Voyages Poetry Review*,1982
Come Into Animal Presence, Denise Levertov, pm,1961
Come Into the Garden, Mawdsley, Leslie Halliwell, nv **A Demon Close Behind**, Robert Hale,1987
Come to Venus Melancholy, Thomas M. Disch, ss *F&SF* Nov,1965
Come Where My Love Lies Dreaming, Bob Leman, ss **Shadows** #10, ed. Charles L. Grant,1987
Comeback, Robert Bloch, ss *Previews* Oct,1984
Comes the Bad Time, Bentley Little, ss *The Horror Show* Win,1987
Comes the Revolution [from **The Future of Flight**], Dean Ing, ar,1985

A CONVERSATION WITH RAMSEY CAMPBELL

Coming of Age in Henson's Tube, William Jon Watkins, ss *IASFM* Spr,1977
The Coming of the Ice, G. Peyton Wertenbaker, ss *Amazing* Jun,1926
Commentary on Burden of Proof, Michele Benjamin & Jim Ridgway, ar
Commentary on Come to Venus Melancholy, Michele Benjamin & Jim Ridgway, ar
Commentary on Field Test, Michele Benjamin & Jim Ridgway, ar
Commentary on Orr's Dreams, Michele Benjamin & Jim Ridgway, ar
Commentary on The Question of Sex, Michele Benjamin & Jim Ridgway, ar
Commentary on They, Michele Benjamin & Jim Ridgway, ar
Commentary on What to Do Until the Analyst Comes, Michele Benjamin & Jim Ridgway, ar
Committee of the Whole, Frank Herbert, nv *Galaxy* Apr,1965
The Common Body, Evelyn Shefner, na **Common Body, Royal Bones**, Coffee House Press: Minneapolis,1987
Common Time, James Blish, ss *Science Fiction Quarterly* Aug,1953
"Common Time": With All of Love, Robert Silverberg, ar,1987
Community Service, Judith R. Behunin, vi *Footsteps* Nov,1987
The Commuter, Philip K. Dick, ss *Amazing* Sep,1953
Commuters, Richard Christian Matheson, ss **Scars**, Scream/Press,1987
The Companion, Ramsey Campbell, ss **Frights**, ed. Kirby McCauley, St. Martins,1976
The Complete Bibliography of F. Paul Wilson, [Misc. Material], bi *Footsteps* Nov,1987
"Complete disorder is impossible.", Robert Frazier, pm
The Computer Cried Charge!, George R.R. Martin, ss *Amazing* Jan,1976
The Computer Game, Phil Cartwright, ss **Twisted Circuits**, ed. Mick Gowar, Beaver,1987
Con-Notations, [Misc. Material], ms *Space & Time* #73,1987
Concerning Titus Crow, Brian Lumley, in
The Concrete Mixer, Ray Bradbury, ss *Thrilling Wonder Stories* Apr,1949
A Condition of Release, L.P. Hartley, ss **The White Wand and Other Stories**, Hamilton,1954
Conestoga History, James B. Johnson, ss *Analog* May,1987
Confession, David Starkey, vi *Grue* #4,1987
A Confession Found in a Prison in the Time of Charles the Second, Charles Dickens, ss
Confession of Innocence, Melissa Mia Hall, ss **Doom City**, ed. Charles L. Grant, Tor,1987
conGRUEities, Peggy Nadramia, ed *Grue* #4,1987
conGRUEities, Peggy Nadramia, ed *Grue* #5,1987
conGRUEities, Peggy Nadramia, ed *Grue* #6,1987
Connie Nova, Jay Rothbell, ss *Pulpsmith* Win,1987
Conquest by Default, Vernor Vinge, nv *Analog* May,1968
Conrad and the Dragon, L.P. Hartley, nv
The Conscience of the King, Nancy Asire & C.J. Cherryh, na **Angels in Hell**, ed. Janet Morris, Baen,1987
A Consideration of Negative-Future Fiction, Jeffrey V. Yule, ed *Mage* Win,1987
The Conspicuous Turtle, Martin Gardner, ss *Esquire* Apr,1947
Conspiracy of Noise, Paul Di Filippo, nv *F&SF* Nov,1987
Constant Father, Charles L. Grant, ss **World Fantasy Convention Program Book** #13,1987
Constitution for Utopia [Constitution], John W. Campbell, Jr., ed *Analog* Mar,1961
Contact [Earthmen Bearing Gifts], Fredric Brown, vi *Galaxy* Jun,1960
The Contagious Killer, Bryce Walton, ss *Alfred Hitchcock's Mystery Magazine* Jan,1966
Containment, Dean Whitlock, ss *Aboriginal SF* Feb,1987
Contaminated People, Sergio Gaut vel Hartman, ss *SF International* #2,1987
Contention, Karen Joy Fowler, ss **Artificial Things**, New York: Bantam,1986
Contest Information, [Misc. Material], ms
Contributors, [Misc. Material], bg
The Contributors, [Misc. Material], bg
Contributors' Notes, [Misc. Material], bg
Convergent Series [The Long Night], Larry Niven, ss *F&SF* Mar,1967
Conversation Piece, Richard Christian Matheson, ss **Whispers** #2, ed. Stuart David Schiff,1979
A Conversation with a Silence, Ursula K. Le Guin, pm,1986
A Conversation With Charles L. Grant, Charles L. Grant & Douglas E. Winter, iv *Twilight Zone* Apr,1987
A Conversation with Piers Anthony, Piers Anthony & Stanley Wiater, iv *Twilight Zone* Dec,1987
A Conversation With Ramsey Campbell, Ramsey Campbell & Stanley Wiater, iv *Twilight Zone* Apr,1987

The Cookie Lady, Philip K. Dick, ss *Fantasy Fiction* Jun,1953
Cool Air, H.P. Lovecraft, ss *Tales Of Magic and Mystery* Mar,1928
Coon Dawgs, Edward Bryant, ss **Trilobyte/The Shadow on the Doorstep**, Edward Bryant & James P. Blaylock, Seattle: Axolotl,1987
Coppard's End, Mary Williams, ss **Haunted Waters**, Kimber,1987
Cordoba to Die, Diane de Avalle-Arce, ss *Apex! #1*,1987
The Corner Cupboard, L.P. Hartley, ss
Cornstalk Riddles, Joseph Payne Brennan, pm *Grue #4*,1987
The Coronet, L. Sprague de Camp, ss *F&SF* Nov,1976
Corpse, Harlan Ellison, ss *F&SF* Jan,1972
Corpses on Parade, Edith Jacobson & Ejler Jacobson, nv *Dime Mystery Magazine* Apr,1938
The Cosmic Poachers, Philip K. Dick, ss *Imagination* Jul,1953
Cosmology: The Quest to Understand the Creation and Expansion of the Universe, Allan Sandage, ar **Universe**, ed. Byron Preiss, Bantam Spectra,1987
Cosmos, Mary Heckler, pm *Weirdbook #22*,1987
The Cotillon, L.P. Hartley, ss
Cottage Tenant, Frank Belknap Long, nv *Fantastic* Apr,1975
The Council of Drones, W.K. Sonnemann, nv *Amazing* Oct,1936
Counting Grandmothers: R.A. Lafferty, R.A. Lafferty & Ron Wolfe, iv *American Fantasy* Sum,1987
The Country of the Blind [from **The Outsider**], Colin Wilson, ar Gollancz: London,1956
The Country Wife, William J. Grabowski, vi *Haunts #9*,1987
The Courage of Friends, Paul Edwards, ss **Friends of the Horseclans**, ed. Robert Adams & Pamela Crippen Adams, Signet,1987
Court of Enquiry, Kingsley Amis, ss *The Spectator*,1956
The Courting of Dinah Shadd, Rudyard Kipling, nv *Macmillan's* Mar,1890
Cousin Jo, S.B. Dieckman, ss *Haunts #9*,1987
Coven, Manly Wade Wellman, nv *Weird Tales* Jul,1942
Covenant, Jaime MacPherson, ss *Apex! #1*,1987
Covenant of Souls, Michael Swanwick, nv *Omni* Dec,1986
Covenant With a Dragon, Susan Casper, ss **In the Field of Fire**, ed. Jeanne Van Buren Dann & Jack M. Dann, Tor,1987
Coventry, Robert A. Heinlein, na *Astounding* Jul,1940
Cowboys and Engines, W.T. Quick, ss *Aboriginal SF* May,1987
The Cravin', Carl Jacobi, pm *Ski-U-Mah* May,1930
Craving, Gary William Crawford, pm *Grue #5*,1987
The Crawlers, Philip K. Dick, ss *Imagination* Jul,1954
Credibility, John Kessel, nv **In the Field of Fire**, ed. Jeanne Van Buren Dann & Jack M. Dann, Tor,1987
Credits, Descriptions and Comparisons of Films, [Misc. Material], bi
Crime of Passion, Bill Dodds, ss *Aphelion #5*,1987
The Crimson Blind, Henrietta D. Everett, ss **The Death-Mask, and Other Ghosts**, Philip Allan: London,1920
Critical Mass, C.M. Kornbluth & Frederik Pohl, na *Galaxy* Feb,1962
Cross Purposes, George MacDonald, nv **Dealing With Fairies**,1867
The Crossways, L.P. Hartley, ss
Crouch End, Stephen King, nv **New Tales of the Cthulhu Mythos**, Arkham,1980
The Crowd, Ray Bradbury, ss *Weird Tales* May,1943
The Crown Derby Plate, Marjorie Bowen, ss,1952
The Crown of Laurel, Ursula K. Le Guin, pm,1987
Crown of Thorns, Edward P. Hughes, ss **There Will Be War** v6, ed. Jerry E. Pournelle,1987
The Cruel Sky, Arthur C. Clarke, ss *Boy's Life* Jul +1,1967
Crusade, Arthur C. Clarke, ss **The Farthest Reaches**, ed. Joseph Elder, Trident,1968
Crusaders in Love, Bill Kerby, nv **Crusaders in Hell**, ed. Janet Morris, New York: Baen,1987
Cry Havoc, Davis Grubb, ss *Ellery Queen's Mystery Magazine* Aug,1976
Cry Wolf, Basil Copper, ss **Vampires, Werewolves and Other Monsters**, ed. Roger Elwood,1974
Crybaby, Harry Turtledove, ss *Twilight Zone* Dec,1987
Crying in the Rain, Tanith Lee, ss **Other Edens**, ed. Christopher Evans & Robert Holdstock, Unwin: London,1987
Crystal, Charles L. Grant, ss *F&SF* Aug,1986
The Crystal Clouds, Robert E. Vardeman, n. Avon: New York pb Sep,1985
The Crystal Crypt, Philip K. Dick, ss *Planet Stories* Jan,1954
Cubeworld, Henry R. Gross, nv **Mathenauts**, ed. Rudy Rucker, Arbor House,1987
Cultural Conflict, David Drake, nv **Destinies** v1#2, ed. James Baen,1979
Cultural Exchange, Keith Laumer, nv *If* Sep,1962

A Cultural Side-Effect, Brian W. Aldiss, ss **Final Stage**, ed. Edward L. Ferman & Barry N. Malzberg, Charterhouse,1974
Cum Grano Salis [as by David Gordon], Randall Garrett, nv *Astounding* May,1959
The Cure, Josephine Saxton, ss **Little Tours of Hell**, Pandora,1986
The Cure, Lisa Tuttle, ss **Light Years and Dark**, ed. Michael Bishop, Berkley,1984
Curiosity, Don Herron, pm *Eldritch Tales #13*,1987
The Curious Case of Richard Fielding, Paul Roland, ss **The Curious Case of Richard Fielding and Other Stories**, Lary Press,1987
A Curious Experience, Norah Lofts, ss *Woman's Journal*,1971
The Curse of the Catafalques, F. Anstey, ss
The Curse of the Crimson God, Robert E. Howard, nv **Swords of Shahrazar**, Futura/Orbit,1976
Curse of the Demon's Wife, Bruce Boston, pm *IASFM* Aug,1987
Cursed Be the City, Henry Kuttner, nv *Strange Stories* Apr,1939
The Curtain Blown by the Breeze, Muriel Spark, ss
Custom Fitting, James White, nv **Stellar #2**, ed. Judy-Lynn del Rey,1976
Cuthbert, R. Chetwynd-Hayes, nv **Dracula's Children**, Kimber,1987
Cutting Up, Kiel Stuart, ss *Muscle Training Illustrated* Sep,1987
The Cuttlefish, A.R. Morlan, ss *Twilight Zone* Oct,1987
Cyberserker, W.T. Quick, ss *Analog* Feb,1987
Cycle, Bruce Jones, ss **Twisted Tales**, San Diego: Blackthorne,1987
Cyclopean Hours August 27, 1883, Robert Frazier, pm *IASFM* Aug,1987
Daddy, Earl Godwin, ss **Shadows #7**, ed. Charles L. Grant,1984
Daddy's Big Girl, Ursula K. Le Guin, ss *Omni* Jan,1987
Daedalus, W. Gregory Stewart, pm *Star*Line* Nov,1986
Daemon, John Devin, pm *Amazing* Jul,1987
Daemon, James Patrick Kelly, ss *F&SF* Nov,1987
The Daffodil Returns the Smile, Brian W. Aldiss, ss **New Writings in SF #26**,1975
Dagger-Flight, Nick O'Donohoe, ss **DragonLance Tales** v2, Margaret Weis & Tracy Hickman, TSR,1987
Daisy Overend, Muriel Spark, ss
Damnation Alley, Roger Zelazny, na *Galaxy* Oct,1967
Damned Funny [as by Eugene D. Goodwin], Marvin Kaye, ss **Fiends and Creatures**, ed. Marvin Kaye, Popular Library,1975
The Damned Thing, Ambrose Bierce, ss **Can Such Things Be?**, Cassell: New York,1893
Dan'l Boone Kilt a Saucer Here, Peter Edler, ss *Pulpsmith* Win,1987
Danar's Hawk, Josepha Sherman, ss *Fantasy Book* Mar,1987
Dance at the Gym, Marion Zimmer Bradley, ss *The San Francisco Chronicle* Sep 17,1987
Dance of the Bloodless Ones, Francis James, nv *Terror Tales* Jul,1937
Dance of the Damned, Arthur J. Burks, nv *Horror Stories* Aug,1936
Dance of the Spirit Untouched, Elizabeth Massie, ss *Footsteps* Nov,1987
Dancers, Lewis Shiner, ss *Night Cry* v2#4,1987
Dandelion Wine, Ray Bradbury, co Doubleday: Garden City, NY,1957
Dandelion Wine, Ray Bradbury, ss *Gourmet* Jun,1953
Daniel White for the Greater Good, Harlan Ellison, ss *Rogue* Mar,1961
The Dare, Marny Whiteaker, ss **Red Sun of Darkover**, ed. Marion Zimmer Bradley & The Friends of Darkover, DAW,1987
The Darfsteller, Walter M. Miller, Jr., na *Astounding* Jan,1955
Darghud's Doll, Brian Lumley, ss **The Horror at Oakdene and Others**, Arkham,1977
The Dark Boy, August Derleth, ss *F&SF* Feb,1957
Dark Corner, J.N. Williamson, br *2AM* Spr,1987
Dark Corner, J.N. Williamson, br *2AM* Sum,1987
Dark Corner, J.N. Williamson, br *2AM* Fll,1987
Dark Corner, J.N. Williamson, br *2AM* Win,1987
The Dark Glasses, Muriel Spark, ss
Dark Interlude, Fredric Brown & Mack Reynolds, ss *Galaxy* Jan,1951
The Dark King, C.J. Cherryh, ss **The Year's Best Fantasy Stories #3**,1977
Dark Melody of Madness [also as "Music from the Dark" and "Papa Benjamin"], Cornell Woolrich, nv *Dime Mystery Magazine* Jul,1935
The Dark Ones, Richard Christian Matheson, vi *Twilight Zone* Jun,1982
The Dark Shadow, Frederik Pohl, ss *Universe*, ed. Byron Preiss, Bantam Spectra,1987
Dark Stretch of Road, John Maclay, ss *Grue #3*,1986
Dark Winner, William F. Nolan, ss *Whispers #9*,1976
Dark, Dark, Jack Matthews, ss *The Antioch Review* Spr,1984
The Darkfishers, John Gregory Betancourt, ss *Aboriginal SF* Jul,1987
The Darkwater Hall Mystery, Kingsley Amis, ss *Playboy*,1978
The Darkworld Contract, Kurt Hyatt Heinrich, ss *Space & Time #72*,1987
The Darning Needle, Hans Christian Andersen, ss
Darwin's Oracle, Ace G. Pilkington, pm *Amazing* Nov,1987

Dat-Tay-Vao, F. Paul Wilson, ss *Amazing* Mar,1987

Data vs. Evidence in the Voodoo Sciences, Jerry E. Pournelle, ar *Analog* Oct,1983

Date with an Angel, Nancy Garcia, mr *American Fantasy* Spr,1987

The Daughter of the Magician, Tanith Lee, na **Night's Sorceries**, DAW,1987

Davi Leiko Till Midnight, William F. Wu, ss *Twilight Zone* Oct,1987

A Day at the Beach With Picasso, Jeff Hopp, cs *Space & Time* #72,1987

The Day Boy and the Night Girl, George MacDonald, nv,1879

A Day in the Life, Christopher Ewart, ss **L. Ron Hubbard Presents Writers of the Future** v3, ed. Algis Budrys, Bridge,1987

Day Million, Frederik Pohl, ss *Rogue* Feb,1966

"Day Million": A Boy, a Girl, a Love Story, Robert Silverberg, ar,1987

The Day Mr. Computer Fell out of its Tree, Philip K. Dick, ss **The Little Black Box**, Underwood/Miller,1987

Day of Strange Fortune, Carol Severance, ss **Magic in Ithkar** #4, ed. Andre Norton & Robert Adams,1987

The Day of the Jester, Leslie Halliwell, ss **A Demon Close Behind**, Robert Hale,1987

The Day the Nurk Field Collapsed, Lesley Choyce, ss **The Dream Auditor**, Indivisible Books,1986

The Days of Perky Pat, Philip K. Dick, nv *Amazing* Dec,1963

Dazed, Theodore Sturgeon, nv *Galaxy* Sep,1971

De Marigny's Clock, Brian Lumley, ss **The Caller of the Black**, Arkham,1971

De-Programming Rose Ellen, Mort Castle, vi *2AM* Sum,1987

The Deacon's Ghost, Robert D. San Souci, ss **Short & Shivery**, Doubleday,1987

Dead Beat, Roger Dale Trexler, ss *Minnesota Fantasy Review* #1,1987

Dead End, Richard Christian Matheson, ss **Shadows** #2, ed. Charles L. Grant,1979

A Dead Finger, Sabine Baring-Gould, ss **A Book of Ghosts**, Methuen: London,1904

The Dead Hand, William Wilkie Collins, nv

Dead in the West (Part 4 of 4), Joe R. Lansdale, sl *Eldritch Tales* #13,1987

Dead Letter, Fredric Brown, vi **Nightmares and Geezenstacks**, Bantam,1961

The Dead Man, Fritz Leiber, nv *Weird Tales* Nov,1950

Dead Man on the Beach, Richard Paul Russo, ss *Twilight Zone* Jun,1987

Dead Man's Tie, Jack C. Haldeman, II, ss *Twilight Zone* Feb,1987

The Dead Past, Isaac Asimov, nv *Astounding* Apr,1956

Dead Possums, Kathryn Ptacek, ss **Doom City**, ed. Charles L. Grant, Tor,1987

Dead Ringer, Edward Wellen, na **Space Shuttles**, ed. Isaac Asimov, Martin H. Greenberg & Charles G. Waugh, Signet,1987

Dead White Women, William F. Wu, ss *Eldritch Tales* #12,1986

The Dead Woods, Larry Tritten, ss *F&SF* Jul,1987

The Deadly "Nackles" Affair, Harlan Ellison, ar *Twilight Zone* Feb,1987

Deal with the D.E.V.I.L., Theodore R. Cogswell, vi *Fantasy Book* Dec,1981

Dean R. Koontz, Dean R. Koontz & Leigh Nichols, iv *The Horror Show* Sum,1987

The Dean's Bargain, Dermot Chesson Spence, ss

Dear D.B. ..., A.R. Morlan, ss *Night Cry* v2#5,1987

Dear Illusion, Kingsley Amis, ss *Covent Garden Stories* #1,1972

Death and the Ugly Woman, Bruce D. Arthurs, ss **Sword and Sorceress** #4, ed. Marion Zimmer Bradley,1987

Death by Misadventure, Elijah Ellis, ss *Alfred Hitchcock's Mystery Magazine* Jan,1964

The Death Desk, S.S. Rafferty, ss *Alfred Hitchcock's Mystery Magazine* Mar,1975

Death Flight, John Maclay, vi *Night Cry* v2#4,1987

Death from Autophilia, Jay Wilde, ss **The Pan Book of Horror Stories** #28, Pan,1987

A Death in the Day of, Gary A. Braunbeck, ss *The Horror Show* Win,1987

Death Is a White Rabbit, Fredric Brown, nv *Strange Detective Mysteries* Jan,1942

Death of a Vampire, Fredric Brown, nv *Strange Detective Mysteries* May,1943

The Death of Halpin Frayser, Ambrose Bierce, ss **Can Such Things Be?**, Cassell: New York,1893

Death on the Mountain, Fredric Brown, vi **Nightmares and Geezenstacks**, Bantam,1961

Death or Glory, Paul Roland, sg **The Curious Case of Richard Fielding and Other Stories**, Lary Press,1987

The Death Room, Edgar Wallace, ss

Death Spiral, Kiel Stuart, ss *Muscle Training Illustrated* Aug,1987

Death Tolls the Bell, Hugh B. Cave, nv *Terror Tales* Jul,1935

The Death Waltz, Robert D. San Souci, ss **Short & Shivery**, Doubleday,1987

Death's Friend, Charles R. Saunders, nv *Weirdbook* #22,1987

Death's Master, Tanith Lee, n. DAW: New York,1979

Deathangel, Mercedes R. Lackey, nv **Festival Moon**, ed. C.J. Cherryh, DAW,1987

Deathbed, Richard Christian Matheson, vi **Masques** #2, ed. J.N. Williamson,1987

The Deathbird, Harlan Ellison, nv *F&SF* Mar,1973

Deathmarch in Disneyland, Vance Aandahl, nv *F&SF* Jul,1987

Deathstroke, James Anderson, ss *Eldritch Tales* #14,1987

Deathtracks, Dennis Etchison, ss **Death**, ed. Stuart David Schiff, Playboy,1982

Deborah's Children, Grant D. Callin, ss *Analog* Sep,1983

Decay in the Hero's Way, Wade Tarzia, ar *Mage* Spr,1987

Decisive Warfare: Retrospect and Prospect, Reginald Bretnor, ar **There Will Be War** v6, ed. Jerry E. Pournelle,1987

The Decline of Sunshine, Cherry Wilder, ss *Interzone* #22,1987

The Deep End, Robert R. McCammon, ss **Night Visions** #4,1987

The Deep Range, Arthur C. Clarke, n. Harcourt Brace: New York,1957

The Deep Range, Arthur C. Clarke, ss **Star Science Fiction Stories** #3, ed. Frederik Pohl, Ballantine,1954

Defeat at the Hands of Alien Scholars, Bruce Boston, pm *Star*Line*,1979

The Defenders, Philip K. Dick, nv *Galaxy* Jan,1953

Definitions of Honor, Richard A. Knaak, nv **DragonLance Tales** v2, Margaret Weis & Tracy Hickman, TSR,1987

Deity, Patricia Scarlett, vi *Eldritch Tales* #13,1987

Delenda Est, Poul Anderson, nv *F&SF* Dec,1955

A Delicate Adjustment, Elizabeth N. Moon, na *Analog* Feb,1987

Delicate Immortal Meanings, Rick Slaughter, ss **Gollancz - Sunday Times Best SF Stories**, Gollancz,1987

Delilah and the Space-Rigger, Robert A. Heinlein, ss *Blue Book* Dec,1949

Delirium's Mistress, Tanith Lee, n. DAW: New York,1986

Delivery, Michael Shea, ss *F&SF* Dec,1987

Delta Sly Honey, Lucius Shepard, ss **In the Field of Fire**, ed. Jeanne Van Buren Dann & Jack M. Dann, Tor,1987

Delusion's Master, Tanith Lee, n. DAW: New York,1981

Demon in a Glass Case, Paul Roland, sg **The Curious Case of Richard Fielding and Other Stories**, Lary Press,1987

The Demon Lover, Anonymous, pm

The Demon Lover, Elizabeth Bowen, ss **The Demon Lover**, J. Cape,1945

Demon Luck, Craig Shaw Gardner, ss **Magic in Ithkar** #4, ed. Andre Norton & Robert Adams,1987

The Demon's Gift, Kathleen O'Malley, nv **Magic in Ithkar** #4, ed. Andre Norton & Robert Adams,1987

The Demons, Robert Sheckley, ss *Fantasy* Feb,1953

The Demythologised Lycanthrope, James Farlow, ss

Denizens, Bruce Boston, pm

Dennis Etchison, Dennis Etchison & William J. Grabowski, iv *The Horror Show* Win,1987

Depression Seance, Bruce Boston, nv *Fiction Magazine* #9,1976

Dept. of "What Was the Question?" Dept., Harlan Ellison, ms **The Essential Ellison**, Nemo Press,1987

The Depths, Ramsey Campbell, nv **Dark Companions**, Macmillan,1982

Der Golem, G.N. Gabbard, pm *2AM* Win,1987

Dervish Daughter, Sheri S. Tepper, n. Tor: New York,1986

Descendant, Iain Banks, nv **Tales from the Forbidden Planet**, ed. Roz Kaveney, Titan,1987

A Detached Interpretation of Voyager's Greeting to Extraterrestrials, John Devin, pm *Amazing* Mar,1987

The Devil, Isaac Asimov, in

The Devil and Daniel Webster [also as "All That Money Can Buy"], Stephen Vincent Benet, ss *The Saturday Evening Post* Oct 24,1936

The Devil and the Trombone, Martin Gardner, ss *The Record Changer* May,1948

The Devil in Exile, Brian Cleeve, ss,1968

Devil in the Drain, Daniel M. Pinkwater, vi **Devil in the Drain**, E.P. Dutton,1984

The Devil Is Not Mocked, Manly Wade Wellman, ss *Unknown* Jun,1943

The Devil Was Sick, Bruce Elliott, ss *F&SF* May,1951

Devil's Advocate, Patricia Anne Buard, ss **Red Sun of Darkover**, ed. Marion Zimmer Bradley & The Friends of Darkover, DAW,1987

The Devil's Wager, William Makepeace Thackeray, ss,1836

The Devilish Rat, Edward Page Mitchell, ss *The Sun* Jan 27,1878

Devolution, Edmond Hamilton, ss *Amazing* Dec,1936

The Devourer, Leonard Carpenter, pm *2AM* Spr,1987

Dial "F" for Frankenstein, Arthur C. Clarke, ss *Playboy* Jan,1965

Diamond Jim, Lisa St. Aubin de Teran, ss **The Virago Book of Ghost Stories**, ed. Richard Dalby, Virago,1987

The Diary of Mr. Poynter, M.R. James, nv **A Thin Ghost**, Longmans, Green,1919

Dick Whittington and Her Cat, Anne Killean, ss **Mad and Bad Fairies**, ed. Anonymous, Attic Press,1987

Die Like a Man, L.D. Woeltjen, ss **Sword and Sorceress #4**, ed. Marion Zimmer Bradley,1987

Die--Nasty, Robert Bloch, ss **Midnight Pleasures**, Doubleday,1987

A Different Kind of Victory, Diana L. Paxson, nv **Red Sun of Darkover**, ed. Marion Zimmer Bradley & The Friends of Darkover, DAW,1987

Different Path, P.J. Buchanan, nv **Red Sun of Darkover**, ed. Marion Zimmer Bradley & The Friends of Darkover, DAW,1987

Dig Me No Grave, Robert E. Howard, ss *Weird Tales* Feb,1937

Digressions from the Second Person Future, John Barnes, ss *IASFM* Jan,1987

Diner, Neal Barrett, Jr., ss *Omni* Nov,1987

Dinner at Dawn, Ray Bradbury, ss *Everywoman's Magazine* Feb,1954

Dinner at the Manse, Josephine Saxton, ss **Little Tours of Hell**, Pandora,1986

Dinosaur, Steve Rasnic Tem, ss *IASFM* May,1987

Dinosaur on a Bicycle, Tim Sullivan, nv *IASFM* Mar,1987

Dinosaurs, Walter Jon Williams, nv *IASFM* Jun,1987

The Direction of the Road, Ursula K. Le Guin, ss **Orbit #12**, ed. Damon Knight,1973

The Disassembler, Kate Wilhelm, ss *F&SF* Oct,1987

Discovery of the Vampires [from **The Mind Parasites**], Colin Wilson, ex Barker: London,1967

Displaced, Eric Vinicoff, nv *Analog* Mar,1987

Displaced Person, Ian Stewart, na *Analog* May,1987

Distant Signals, Andrew Weiner, ss *Twilight Zone* Jun,1984

Do You Really Want a Bigger U.S. Space Program?, Charles Sheffield, ar **New Destinies** v2, ed. Jim Baen, Baen,1987

Doc Johnson, F. Paul Wilson, nv **Doom City**, ed. Charles L. Grant, Tor,1987

Doctor Doom Conducting, Howard V. Hendrix, vi *Aboriginal SF* Sep,1987

Doctor's Dozen, Bruce Boston, ss *The Portland Review*,1981

Dog Meat, D.W. Taylor, ss *Footsteps* Nov,1987

A Dog Names Ransom, Jackie Vivelo, ss **A Trick of the Light**, Putnam,1987

Dog, Cat, and Baby, Joe R. Lansdale, vi **Masques #2**, ed. J.N. Williamson,1987

The Dog-King of Vaire, Nancy Springer, ss *Fantasy Book* Aug,1982

Doing Colfax, Edward Bryant, ss **Night Visions #4**,1987

Doing Time, John E. Stith, ss *Aboriginal SF* Jul,1987

Doing Well While Doing Good, Hayford Peirce, ss *Analog* Aug,1975

The Doll's Ghost, F. Marion Crawford, ss **Wandering Ghosts**, Macmillan,1911

The Doll's House, Hester Gorst, ss **Horrors**, ed. Anonymous, Philip Allan: London,1933

Dolls, Ramsey Campbell, nv **The Mayflower Book of Black Magic Stories #4**, ed. Michael Parry,1976

Dolphin's Way, Gordon R. Dickson, ss *Analog* Jun,1964

The Dome, Fredric Brown, ss *Thrilling Wonder Stories* Aug,1951

The Dome of Many Colors, Martin Gardner, ss *The University of Kansas City Review* Win,1944

Don Juan's Final Night, Edmond Rostand, pl

Don't Drink the Sky at Myrmidon, Bruce Boston, pm *IASFM* Jan,1984

Don't Fuck With My Brain, Cheryl L. Nelms, pm *2AM* Fll,1987

Don't Look Now, Daphne du Maurier, na,1970

The Donkey Prince, Angela Carter, ss,1970

Donor, James E. Gunn, nv *Fantastic* Nov,1960

Doom City, Robert R. McCammon, ss **Doom City**, ed. Charles L. Grant, Tor,1987

Dooniveh, the Moon, Tanith Lee, na **Night's Sorceries**, DAW,1987

Dop*elgan*er, Garry Kilworth, ss *Interzone #21*,1987

Doppler Effects, Robert Frazier, pm *IASFM* Feb,1985

Dora, Paul Christopher, ss **Beyond That River**, Pal Books,1987

Dorothea, Mary Williams, nv **Haunted Waters**, Kimber,1987

Double Gross-Out at the Uh-Oh Saloon, Dick Davies, cs *The Horror Show* Sum,1987

The Double Shadow, Clark Ashton Smith, ss **The Double Shadow and Other Fantasies**, Auburn Journal: Auburn CA,1933

Double Whammy, Robert Bloch, ss *Fantastic* Feb,1970

Doughfoot Sanctum, James William Holzer, ss **There Will Be War** v6, ed. Jerry E. Pournelle,1987

Down Among the Dead Men, William Tenn, nv *Galaxy* Jun,1954

Down and Out in the Year 2000, Kim Stanley Robinson, ss *IASFM* Apr,1986

Down by the Sea Wreck, Frederick Hohing, ss *Ice River* Sum,1987

Down in the Dark, Ardath Mayhar, ss *The Horror Show* Sum,1987

Down in the Darkness, Dean R. Koontz, nv *The Horror Show* Sum,1986

Down Under, Kevin Speirs, ss *Haunts #9*,1987

Down, Satan!, Clive Barker, ss **Clive Barker's Books of Blood** v4,1985

Down-Home Horrors, Alan Rogers, in *Night Cry* v2#3,1987

Dr Horder's Room, Patrick Carleton, ss **Thrills**, Anon (Charles Birkin), Philip Allan,1935

Dr. Birdmouse, Reginald Bretnor, ss *Fantastic* Apr,1962

Dr. Locrian's Asylum, Thomas Ligotti, ss *Grue #5*,1987

Dracula's Guest [also as "Dracula's Daughter"], Bram Stoker, ss **Dracula's Guest**, Routledge: London,1914

Draculain Genealogical Table, R. Chetwynd-Hayes, ms

Dragon, Ann Cathey, pm *Salarius* v1#4,1987

The Dragon, Muriel Spark, ss *New Yorker* Aug 12,1985

A Dragon for Seyour Chan, Paul J. McAuley, ss *Interzone #19*,1987

Dragon Meat, Robert Don Hughes, ss *The Dragon* Apr,1987

Dragon Moon, Henry Kuttner, na *Weird Tales* Jan,1941

Dramatis Personae, Lynn Abbey, pr

The Draw, Jerome Bixby, ss *Amazing* Mar,1954

Dread, Clive Barker, nv **Clive Barker's Books of Blood** v2,1984

A Dream at Noonday, Gardner R. Dozois, ss **Orbit #7**, ed. Damon Knight,1970

The Dream Auditor, Lesley Choyce, ss **The Dream Auditor**, Indivisible Books,1986

Dream Baby, Bruce McAllister, nv **In the Field of Fire**, ed. Jeanne Van Buren Dann & Jack M. Dann, Tor,1987

Dream in a Bottle, Jerry Meredith & D.E. Smirl, ss **L. Ron Hubbard Presents Writers of the Future** v2, ed. Algis Budrys, Bridge,1986

The Dream Is Down, G. Harry Stine, ar *Analog* Feb,1987

A Dream of Amerasia, Ray Faraday Nelson, ar **Philip K. Dick: The Dream Connection**, D. Scott Apel, Permanent Press,1987

A Dream of Castles, Frances Garfield, ss **World Fantasy Convention Program Book #13**,1987

The Dream of Duncan Parrenness, Rudyard Kipling, ss *The Civil and Military Gazette* Dec 25,1884

A Dream of Heredity, John Calvin Rezmerski, pm *Tales of the Unanticipated #1*,1986

A Dream of Theobold, Gary William Crawford, pm *Eldritch Tales #13*,1987

Dream Tables, Robert Frazier, pm

The Dream That Follows Darkness, Michael Seidman, ss *Twilight Zone* Aug,1987

Dream Webs, Bruce Boston, pm *Night Cry* v2#3,1987

The Dream-Woman [The Ostler], William Wilkie Collins, nv *Household Words* Chr,1855

Dreaming Is a Private Thing, Isaac Asimov, ss *F&SF* Dec,1955

The Dreaming Spires of Houston, Charles Sheffield, ss **New Destinies** v2, ed. Jim Baen, Baen,1987

Dreams in Stasis, Tom Rentz, pm *Mage* Win,1987

Dreams of Darkness, Dreams of Light, Warren B. Smith, nv **DragonLance Tales** v1, Margaret Weis & Tracy Hickman, TSR,1987

Dreams of Imagination, Alan Jude Summa, pm *2AM* Win,1987

Dreamtigers, Robert Frazier, pm *Amazing* Mar,1987

The Dreitarbund, Rudyard Kipling, vi *The Civil and Military Gazette* Oct 22,1887

Dress of White Silk, Richard Matheson, ss *F&SF* Oct,1951

The Drifting Snow [as by Stephen Grendon], August Derleth, ss *Weird Tales* Feb,1934

The Driftwood in the Fox's Den, Mark Calcamuggio, ss *Space & Time #72*,1987

Drink My Blood ["Drink My Red Blood", also as "Blood Son"], Richard Matheson, ss *Imagination* Apr,1951

A Drink of Darkness, Robert F. Young, ss *Fantastic* Jul,1962

Driving the Spikes, Harlan Ellison, ar *Los Angeles*,1983

The Drones are Willing..., A Crazy Alien, ms *Aboriginal SF* Jul,1987

The Drop of Water, Hans Christian Andersen, vi

Drummer's Star, Edward Bryant, ss **Trilobyte/The Shadow on the Doorstep**, Edward Bryant & James P. Blaylock, Seattle: Axolotl,1987

Drummer's Star, Edward Bryant, ss **Trilobyte/The Shadow on the Doorstep**, Seattle: Axolotl,1987

Dual Control, Elizabeth Walter, ss **Dead Woman**,1975

Dubious Pleasures, Bryan G. Stephenson, ss *Amazing* Sep,1987

Duel, Richard Matheson, nv *Playboy* Apr,1971

The Dung Beetle, Hans Christian Andersen, ss

Dust, Richard Christian Matheson, ss **Scars**, Scream/Press,1987
The Dust-Cloud, E.F. Benson, ss **The Room in the Tower and Other Stories**, London: Mills Boon,1912
Dutchman, Jack McDevitt, nv *IASFM* Feb,1987
The Dutchman's Ghost Town, Andrew M. Greeley, nv *F&SF* Feb,1987
The Dwarf Who Knew Too Much, Harry Dolan, ss *Mage* Win,1987
The Dweller in the Temple, Manly Wade Wellman, nv **Swords Against Darkness #2**, ed. Andrew J. Offutt,1977
DX, Joe W. Haldeman, ss **In the Field of Fire**, ed. Jeanne Van Buren Dann & Jack M. Dann, Tor,1987
E Gubling Dow, Gordon R. Dickson, ss *Satellite* May,1959
E-Ticket to Namland, Dan Simmons, ss *Omni* Nov,1987
The Earth is Flat and We're All Like to Drown, Garry Kilworth, ss **Tales from the Forbidden Planet**, ed. Roz Kaveney, Titan,1987
The Earth Men, Ray Bradbury, ss *Thrilling Wonder Stories* Aug,1948
Earthshade, Fred Saberhagen, nv **The Magic May Return**, ed. Larry Niven,1981
An Easter Treasure, Edward Bryant, ss **Trilobyte/The Shadow on the Doorstep**, Edward Bryant & James P. Blaylock, Seattle: Axolotl,1987
The Eastern Window, E.G. Swain, ss **The Stoneground Ghost Tales**, W. Heffer: Cambridge,1912
Echoes, Richard Christian Matheson, ss *The Horror Show* Win,1986
Ecowareness, Harlan Ellison, ss *Sideshow* Sep,1974
Ed White, Spacewalking, June 3, 1965, Robert Frazier, pm *IASFM* May,1985
Edges, Gregg Keizer, ss *Omni* Jun,1983
Editor's Foreword, Mick Gowar, in
Editor's Note, William H. Wheeler, ed *SF International* #1,1987
The Editor's Page, Gordon Linzner, ed *Space & Time* #72,1987
The Editor's Page, Gordon Linzner, ed *Space & Time* #73,1987
Editorial, W. Paul Ganley, ed *Weirdbook* #22,1987
Editorial, Nancy Garcia & Robert T. Garcia, ed *American Fantasy* Spr,1987
Editorial, Nancy Garcia & Robert T. Garcia, ed *American Fantasy* Sum,1987
Editorial, Nancy Garcia & Robert T. Garcia, ed *American Fantasy* Win,1987
Editorial, Dennis Mallonee, ed *Fantasy Book* Mar,1987
Editorial, Peter McNamara, ed *Aphelion* #5,1987
Editorial, Simon Ounsley, ed *Interzone* #19,1987
Editorial, David Pringle, ed *Interzone* #20,1987
Editorial, David Pringle, ed *Interzone* #21,1987
Editorial, David Pringle, ed *Interzone* #22,1987
Editorial, Stuart David Schiff, ed *Whispers* #23,1987
The Editorial Privilege, Ramona Pope Richards, ed *Apex!* #1,1987
Eel Island Shoals, John M. Ford, sg **Liavek: Wizard's Row**, ed. Will Shetterly & Emma Bull, Ace,1987
The Eels, Shelton Arnel Johnson, pm *Amazing* Mar,1987
The Egg, Leonard Carpenter, pm *Eldritch Tales* #13,1987
The Egret, Michael Bishop, ss *Playboy* Jun,1987
The Egyptian Diamond, Randall Garrett, pm *Amazing* Mar,1961
Eight Legs Hath the Spider, R.L. Newman & C. Taylor, vi *Haunts* #9,1987
Eight Poems from **Songs from a White Heart**, Jack M. Dann, ar *Twilight Zone* Aug,1987
Eighth Elegy [from "The Duino Elegies"], Rainer Maria Rilke, pm
The Eighth Planet, Sara Maitland, ss
The Elder, Poppy Z. Brite, ss *The Horror Show* Jan,1987
The Eldritch Eye, Gary A. Braunbeck, ss *Eldritch Tales* #14,1987
Eldritch Lair, Crispin Burnham, ed *Eldritch Tales* #13,1987
Eldritch Lair, Crispin Burnham, ed *Eldritch Tales* #14,1987
Eldritch Lair - Dungeon Level, Charles L. Baker, ed *Eldritch Tales* #13,1987
Eleanor Meets God, Maryanne K. Snyder, pm *Grue* #6,1987
The Electric Ant, Philip K. Dick, nv *F&SF* Oct,1969
The Electronic Mathematician, Ian Stewart, ar *Analog* Jan,1987
Elegy for Cygnus X-1, Shelton Arnel Johnson, pm *Amazing* Nov,1987
Elegy to a Dead Satellite: Luna, Elton Andrews, pm *Amazing* Nov,1987
Element of Doubt, A.L. Barker, ss **After Midnight Stories** #3,1987
Elixir for the Emperor, John Brunner, ss *Fantastic* Nov,1964
Elizabeth Massie, Elizabeth Massie, iv *The Horror Show* Fll,1987
Ellen, in Her Time, Charles L. Grant, ss **The Architecture of Fear**, ed. Kathryn Cramer & Peter D. Pautz, Arbor House,1987
Elysium Horizon, Leo Bigley, ss *Mage* Spr,1987
Embroidery, Ray Bradbury, ss *Marvel* Nov,1951
Emergence, David R. Palmer, nv *Analog* Jan 5,1981
The Emir's Clock, Ian Watson, ss **Other Edens**, ed. Christopher Evans & Robert Holdstock, Unwin: London,1987

The Emperor's New Cloths, Hans Christian Andersen, ss
Empire and Republic: Crisis and Future, Jerry E. Pournelle, ar **Imperial Stars** v2, ed. Jerry E. Pournelle,1987
The Empire of the Ants, H.G. Wells, ss *The Strand* Dec,1905
The Empire Strikes Back, Donald F. Glut, n. Ballantine: New York,1980
An Empty Gift, Steve Benson, ss *Analog* Dec,1983
The Empty House, Algernon Blackwood, ss **The Empty House**, Eveleigh Nash,1906
The Empty Schoolroom, Pamela Hansford Johnson, ss **The Uncertain Element**, ed. Kay Dick, Jarrolds: London,1950
En La Noche [Torrid Sacrifice], Ray Bradbury, ss *Cavalier* Nov,1952
Encased in the Amber of Probabilities, Robert Frazier, pm *IASFM* Mar,1987
The Enchanted Kiss, O. Henry, ss
Encounter, Stephen Leigh, nv **Destinies** v1#3, ed. James Baen,1979
The End, Stuart David Schiff, aw *Whispers* #23,1987
The End [Nightmare in Time], Fredric Brown, vi *Dude* May,1961
The End of a Summer's Day, Ramsey Campbell, ss **Demons By Daylight**,1973
The End of Life As We Know It, Lucius Shepard, nv *IASFM* Jan,1985
The End of Silence, Joan Aiken, ss **A Quiver of Ghosts**, ed. Aiden Chambers, Bodley Head,1987
The End of Summer, Algis Budrys, nv *Astounding* Nov,1954
The End of the Hunt, Uwe Luserke, ss *SF International* #1,1987
Ender's Game, Orson Scott Card, na *Analog* Aug,1977
Endless Night, Karl Edward Wagner, ss **The Architecture of Fear**, ed. Kathryn Cramer & Peter D. Pautz, Arbor House,1987
The Enemy Stars, Poul Anderson, n. J.B. Lippincott,1959
The Engine of Samoset Erastus Hale and One Other, Unknown, Avram Davidson, ss *Amazing* Jul,1987
The Engineer, C.M. Kornbluth & Frederik Pohl, ss *Infinity* Feb,1956
Enigma 2: Diagrams for Three Stories, Brian W. Aldiss, gp **Final Stage**, ed. Edward L. Ferman & Barry N. Malzberg, Charterhouse,1974
Enigma 3: The Aperture Moment, Brian W. Aldiss, gp **Epoch**, ed. Roger Elwood & Robert Silverberg, Berkley,1975
Enigma 4: The Eternal Theme of Exile, Brian W. Aldiss, gp **New Writings in SF** #23,1974
Enlightenment Rabies, Rudy Rucker, vi *New Pathways* Nov,1987
Enoch, Robert Bloch, ss *Weird Tales* Sep,1946
Enter a Pilgrim, Gordon R. Dickson, ss *Analog* Aug,1974
Entity Trap [From These Ashes], Fredric Brown, ss *Amazing* Aug,1950
The Entrance Exam, Mary Carey, ss **The Witch Book**, ed. Anonymous, Rand McNally,1976
Entropanto, Gerry McCarthy, ss **Gollancz - Sunday Times Best SF Stories**, Gollancz,1987
Entropy Comix, Michael G. Adkisson, cs *New Pathways* Apr,1987
Entropy Comix, Michael G. Adkisson, cs *New Pathways* Aug,1987
Ephesus, Joyce Nower, pm *Ice River* Sum,1987
Epilogue, Ray Bradbury, aw **The Illustrated Man**,1951
Epilogue to The Space Merchants, Frederik Pohl, si
Epiphany, Arlan Andrews, ss *Analog* Sep,1987
An Episode in the Death of Philip K. Dick, Michael Bishop, vi *New Pathways* Aug,1987
An Episode of Cathedral History, M.R. James, ss **A Thin Ghost**, Longmans, Green,1919
Epitaph by an Alien in Yellow Moonlight, Jack R. Hill, pm *Amazing* Sep,1987
Equator, Brian W. Aldiss, n. Brown, Watson: London,1958
Equivalent for Giles, Keith Roberts, ss **Tales from the Forbidden Planet**, ed. Roz Kaveney, Titan,1987
Eradication's Rise, Christina Kiplinger, pm *Fantasy Tales* #16,1986
Erasure, Robert Frazier, pm *Amazing* Nov,1987
Eric and the Red Blotches, C. Bruce Hunter, vi *Eldritch Tales* #14,1987
Ernesta [from "Mundane's World"], Judy Grahn, ex **Hear the Silence**, ed. Irene Zahava, Crossing Press,1986
Erotophobia, Harlan Ellison, ss *Penthouse* Aug,1971
Errand Run, Stephen Paulsen, vi *Aphelion* #5,1987
Escape from Kathmandu, Kim Stanley Robinson, na *IASFM* Sep,1986
The Escape Route, Rod Serling, na **The Season to be Wary**, Little Brown: Boston,1967
Escape to Akureyri, Leslie Halliwell, nv **A Demon Close Behind**, Robert Hale,1987
Esoteric References, Robert T. Garcia, br *American Fantasy* Sum,1987
Etchings of Her Memories, Richard A. Lupoff, ss *Amazing* Mar,1987
"The eternal form eludes us.", Robert Frazier, pm
The Eternal Theme of Exile, Brian W. Aldiss, vi **New Writings in SF** #23,1974
Ethics and the Work Place, Joey Froehlich, pm *Apex!* #1,1987

THE ETHOS OF ELFLAND

The Ethos of Elfland, Gene Wolfe, ar *Twilight Zone* Dec,1987
Euclid Alone, William F. Orr, nv **Orbit** #16, ed. Damon Knight,1975
Eudoric's Unicorn, L. Sprague de Camp, ss **The Year's Best Fantasy Stories** #3,1977
Euroshima Mon Amour/Radical Kisses, Andrew Darlington, pm *The Mentor* Jan,1986
Eve Times Four, Poul Anderson, nv *Fantastic* Apr,1960
The Evening and the Morning and the Night, Octavia E. Butler, nv *Omni* May,1987
An Evening In, Vicki Ann Heydron, ar **Moments of Love**, New York: Bantam,1979
Evening Primrose, John Collier, ss,1940
Event Horizon, Andrew Joron, pm
Ever After, Susan Palwick, nv *IASFM* Nov,1987
Evert Sparrow That Falls, Rebecca Lee, ss *Aboriginal SF* Nov,1987
Every Garbage Dump Has One, Michael C. McPherson, vi *Haunts* #9,1987
Everybody Needs a Little Love, Robert Bloch, ss **Masques** #1, ed. J.N. Williamson,1984
Everyday Consciousness is a Liar [from **The New Existentialism**], Colin Wilson, ar
Everything but Freedom, Marion Zimmer Bradley, na **The Other Side of the Mirror**, ed. Marion Zimmer Bradley & The Friends of Darkover, DAW,1987
Everything to Live For, Charles L. Grant, ss **Whispers** #6, ed. Stuart David Schiff,1987
The Evil Prince, Hans Christian Andersen, vi
Evil Water, Ian Watson, nv *F&SF* Mar,1987
Evileye, Dean Ing, ss **Far Frontiers** v2, ed. Jerry Pournelle & Jim Baen,1985
The Evolution of the Death Murals, Bruce Boston, pm *IASFM* Sep,1985
The Ex-Khan, Robert Lynn Asprin, ss **Angels in Hell**, ed. Janet Morris, Baen,1987
The Executor, Muriel Spark, ss *New Yorker* Mar 14,1983
The Exercise of Faith, Lucius Shepard, ss *Twilight Zone* Jun,1987
Exhibit Piece, Philip K. Dick, ss *If* Aug,1954
Exiled of Worlds, Robert Frazier & Andrew Joron, pm *Amazing* Sep,1987
The Exiles, Tonya R. Carter & Paul B. Thompson, nv **DragonLance Tales** v3, Margaret Weis & Tracy Hickman, TSR,1987
The Exiles [The Mad Wizards of Mars], Ray Bradbury, ss *Maclean's* Sep 15,1949
The Exit Door Leads In, Philip K. Dick, ss *Rolling Stone College Papers* #1,1979
The Exit to San Breta, George R.R. Martin, ss *Fantastic* Feb,1972
Expedition, Fredric Brown, vi *F&SF* Feb,1957
Expendable, Philip K. Dick, ss *F&SF* Jul,1953
Experiment, Fredric Brown, vi *Galaxy* Feb,1954
The Experiment, M.R. James, ss
Expert Witness, Michael C. McPherson, vi *2AM* Win,1987
Expiration Policy, Laurence M. Janifer, ss *Analog* Nov,1983
Explanatory Notes, Michael Cox, ms
Explorers We, Philip K. Dick, ss *F&SF* Jan,1959
The Extra, Michael Shea, nv *F&SF* May,1987
Extras, Robert Charles Wilson, nv *F&SF* Dec,1987
An Extraterrestrial, Ish, Mike Curry, pm *Amazing* May,1987
The Extremists, W.R. Thompson, na *Analog* Jan,1987
The Eye Above the Mantel, Frank Belknap Long, ss *The United Amateur*,1921
An Eye for an Eye, Peter Heyrman, ss *Night Cry* v2#5,1987
Eye for Eye, Orson Scott Card, na *IASFM* Mar,1987
The Eye of Klagg, Donald Briyles, vi *Eldritch Tales* #13,1987
The Eye of the Sibyl, Philip K. Dick, ss **Philip K. Dick: The Dream Connection**, D. Scott Apel, Permanent Press,1987
The Eyes, Edith Wharton, ss **Tales of Men and Ghosts**, Scribner: New York,1910
The Eyes Have It, Philip K. Dick, ss *(The Original) Science Fiction Stories* #1,1953
Eyes of Amber, Joan D. Vinge, nv *Analog* Jun,1977
The Eyes of Argos, Harry Turtledove, nv *Amazing* Jan,1986
The Eyes of the Gods, Richard Corwin, ss **Sword and Sorceress** #4, ed. Marion Zimmer Bradley,1987
F&SF Competition: Report on Competition 42, [Misc. Material], ms *F&SF* May,1987
F&SF Competition: Report on Competition 43, [Misc. Material], ms *F&SF* Sep,1987
F&SF Crossword, Dorothy Davis, pz *F&SF* Feb,1987
The Fable Alludes to You, Hans Christian Andersen, vi
The Fable of the Farmer and the Fox, John Brunner, vi *Omni* Jun,1987

The Fable of the Three Princes, Isaac Asimov, nv **Spaceships & Spells**, ed. Jane Yolen, Martin H. Greenberg & Charles G. Waugh, Harper & Row,1987
The Face, L.P. Hartley, nv
Face Down in Gloria Swanson's Swimming Pool, Harlan Ellison, ar *Los Angeles*,1978
The Face in the Fresco, Arnold Smith, ss *The London Mercury* Jun,1928
The Facts of Life, Christopher Evans, ss **Other Edens**, ed. Christopher Evans & Robert Holdstock, Unwin: London,1987
The Faded Sun: Kesrith, C.J. Cherryh, n. DAW: New York,1978
The Faded Sun: Kutath, C.J. Cherryh, n. DAW: New York,1980
The Faded Sun: Shon'Jir, C.J. Cherryh, n. DAW: New York,1979
Faerie Tale: The Thing Beneath the Bridge, Raymond E. Feist, ex *Twilight Zone* Dec,1987
Fahrenheit 451, Ray Bradbury, n. Ballantine: New York,1953
Fair Game, Philip K. Dick, ss *If* Sep,1959
Fair Game, Howard Waldrop, nv **Afterlives**, ed. Pamela Sargent & Ian Watson, New York: Vintage,1986
Fair Morsel, Richard Wilson, vi **The Kid from Ozone Park and Other Stories**, Drumm,1987
Fair's Fair, Jane Speed, ss *Ellery Queen's Mystery Magazine* Feb,1967
A Fairy Tale for Our Time, Jack Zipes, ss,1985
Faith of Our Fathers, Philip K. Dick, nv **Dangerous Visions**, ed. Harlan Ellison, Doubleday,1967
Faith of Tarot, Piers Anthony, n. Berkley: New York,1980
Faith of the Progeny, Bruce Boston, pm *Bifrost*
The Faithful Companion at Forty, Karen Joy Fowler, ss *IASFM* Jul,1987
The Faithless, Bruce Boston, pm
Fake-out, Andrew Weiner, ss *Amazing* Nov,1987
The Fall, Mark Gorton, ss **Gollancz - Sunday Times Best SF Stories**, Gollancz,1987
A Fall from Grace, Sara Maitland, ss **Weddings and Funerals**, Latourette/Maitland, Brilliance,1984
Fall In at the Double, L.P. Hartley, ss
The Fall of Flatbush Smith, Martin Gardner, vi *Esquire* Sep,1947
A Fall of Moondust, Arthur C. Clarke, n. Harcourt Brace & World: New York,1961
The Fall of the House of Usher, Edgar Allan Poe, ss *Burton's Gentlemen's Magazine* Sep,1839
Falling Free [Part 1 of 4], Lois McMaster Bujold, sl *Analog* Dec,1987
Falling Free [Part 2 of 4], Lois McMaster Bujold, sl *Analog* mid-Dec,1987
Falling in Love Again, Brent R. Smith, ss **The Pan Book of Horror Stories** #28, Pan,1987
Falling in Love at Christmas, Josephine Saxton, ss **Little Tours of Hell**, Pandora,1986
Family Dentistry, Donald R. Burleson, ss *F&SF* Aug,1987
The Family Monkey, Lisa Tuttle, na **New Voices in Science Fiction** #1, ed. George R.R. Martin,1977
The Famous Hospitality of Dao'i, J.J. Hunt, pm *IASFM* Sep,1987
The Fantastic Battlefield, Roland J. Green, ar *Amazing* Jan,1987
Fantasy Book Reviews, John Gregory Betancourt, br *Fantasy Book* Mar,1987
Far Centaurus, A.E. van Vogt, ss *Astounding* Jan,1944
Farewells on the Melon Bridge, Rob Hollis Miller, pm *New Pathways* Jan,1987
The Fascination of the Abomination, Robert Silverberg, na *IASFM* Jul,1987
Fast Forward to the Past, Polly Frost, ss *New Yorker* Jul 6,1987
Fast-Train Ike, Jesse Stuart, ss
Fat Face, Michael Shea, nv Axolotl Press: Seattle WA,1987
The Fat Man, Joe R. Lansdale, ss *The Horror Show* Jan,1987
Fatal Error, Fredric Brown, vi **Nightmares and Geezenstacks**, Bantam,1961
Fate and the Dreamer, Millea Kenin, ss **Sword and Sorceress** #4, ed. Marion Zimmer Bradley,1987
The Fate of Aoife and the Children of Aobh, Mary Dorcey, ss **Mad and Bad Fairies**, ed. Anonymous, Attic Press,1987
The Fate of Madame Cabanel, Eliza Lynn Linton, ss **With a Silken Thread**, Chatto & Windus: London,1880
Father Macclesfield's Tale, Robert Hugh Benson, ss **A Mirror of Shalott**, Pitman: London,1907
Father Meuron's Tale, Robert Hugh Benson, ss **A Mirror of Shalott**, Pitman: London,1907
The Father-Thing, Philip K. Dick, ss *F&SF* Dec,1954
The Fathers' Daughters, Muriel Spark, ss
Faust Forward, Marc Laidlaw, ss *F&SF* Mar,1987
Fear the Light, Edward F. Shaver, ss *Amazing* May,1987
Fearing's Fall, Leonard Carpenter, ss *Amazing* Sep,1987

FOR FURTHER READING

For Further Reading, [Misc. Material], bi
For Leonard, Darko, and Burton Watson, Ursula K. Le Guin, pm,1982
For Mars, Vote NO, Ben Bova, ed *Analog* Sep,1987
For Spacers Snarled in the Hair of Comets, Bruce Boston, pm *IASFM* Apr,1984
For Ted, Ursula K. Le Guin, pm **Wild Angels**, Capra Press,1975
For the Blood Is the Life, F. Marion Crawford, ss **Wandering Ghosts**, Macmillan,1911
For the Love of Mother, Paul Christopher, ss **Beyond That River**, Pal Books,1987
For Thus Do I Remember Carthage, Michael Bishop, ss **Universe**, ed. Byron Preiss, Bantam Spectra,1987
Forays into Derleth Country, Steve Eng, ar *Eldritch Tales* #13,1987
Forbidden Knowledge, Kathryn Cramer, ss **Mathenauts**, ed. Rudy Rucker, Arbor House,1987
Force Majeur, Katherine V. Forrest, ss **Dreams and Swords**, Naiad,1987
Forecast for a Burning Planet, Bruce Boston, pm **Nuclear Futures**, Velocities Chapbook Series,1987
The Foreign Hand-Tie [as by David Gordon], Randall Garrett, nv *Analog* Dec,1961
Foresight, Michael Swanwick, ss *Interzone* #20,1987
The Forest of Time, Michael F. Flynn, na *Analog* Jun,1987
The Forever Summer, Ronald Anthony Cross, nv *IASFM* Mar,1983
Forever Yours, Anna, Kate Wilhelm, ss *Omni* Jul,1987
Foreword, Poul Anderson, fw
Foreword, Michael Bishop, fw
Foreword, Ben Bova, fw
Foreword, Algis Budrys, fw
Foreword, Michael Cox, in
Foreword, Steven Owen Godersky, fw
Foreword, Tracy Hickman & Margaret Weis, fw
Foreword, Stephen King, fw
Foreword, Paul Roland, fw
Foreword, Bob Shaw, in
Foreword, Robert Silverberg, fw
Foreword: You Are Here, Phyllis Gotlieb, fw
The Forge of God, Greg Bear, ex Tor: New York Sep,1987
Forgetfullness, Isaac Asimov, ed *IASFM* Jun,1987
Fortune's Fool, Seabury Quinn, nv *Weird Tales* Jul,1938
The Fortune-Teller, Muriel Spark, ss *New Yorker* Jan 17,1983
Fortuneteller, Mark Rich, pm *Mage* Spr,1987
Forum, The Readers, lt *New Pathways* Jan,1987
Forum, The Readers, lt *New Pathways* Apr,1987
Forum, The Readers, lt *New Pathways* Aug,1987
Forward from What Vanishes, Mark Rich, pm *Amazing* Jan,1987
Foster, You're Dead, Philip K. Dick, nv **Star Science Fiction Stories #3**, ed. Frederik Pohl, Ballantine,1954
Found Poem, Ursula K. Le Guin, pm,1986
Four Brands of Impossible, Norman Kagan, nv *F&SF* Sep,1964
Four Cat Poems, Ursula K. Le Guin, si
Four Dreams of Gram Perkins, Ruth Sawyer, ss *The American Mercury* Oct,1926
Four in One, Damon Knight, nv *Galaxy* Feb,1953
"Four in One": Complications With Elegance, Robert Silverberg, ar,1987
Four Years Later..., Jeffrey V. Yule, ed *Mage* Fll,1987
The Four-Sided Triangle, William F. Temple, nv *Amazing* Nov,1939
The Fox and the Forest [To the Future], Ray Bradbury, ss *Colliers* May 13,1950
Fractured Dimensions, Daniel J. Hay, ss *Salarius* #3,1987
A Fragment of a Novel, George Gordon, Lord Byron, uw,1816
Fragments of Horror, Dennis Etchison, ms *The Horror Show* Win,1987
Fragments of Horror, Ray Garton, ms *The Horror Show* Fll,1987
Fragments of Horror, Robert R. McCammon, ms *The Horror Show* Spr,1987
Fragments of Horror, Al Sarrantonio, ms *The Horror Show* Sum,1987
Fragments of Horror, J.N. Williamson, ms *The Horror Show* Jan,1987
Frank Utpatel: Wood Engraver, Rodger Gerberding, bg *Mage* Win,1987
Frat Rat Bash, Edward Bryant, ss **Night Visions #4**,1987
Free Day, Peg Kerr, ss **Tales of the Unanticipated #2**,1987
Free With This Box!, Harlan Ellison, ss *The Saint* Mar,1958
Freedom From Fear, Ben Bova, ed *Analog* Nov,1984
Freeforall, Margaret Atwood, ss *The Toronto Star Weekly* Sep 20,1986
Freezeframe, Gregory Benford, ss *Interzone* #17,1986
Frenchmen and Plumbers, Martha Soukup, ss *Aboriginal SF* Sep,1987
Friction in War [from **On War**], Karl von Clausewitz, ar
A Friend in Need, W. Somerset Maugham, ss,1925
A Friend of the Family, David Kubicek, ss *Space & Time* #72,1987
Friend's Best Man, Jonathan Carroll, ss *F&SF* Jan,1987

The Friendly Man, Gordon R. Dickson, ss *Astounding* Feb,1951
The Friends of Plonk, Kingsley Amis, ss *Town*,1964
The Frog Prince, Anne Cooper, ss **Mad and Bad Fairies**, ed. Anonymous, Attic Press,1987
Frog Prince, Jane Yolen, pm *F&SF* Oct,1987
from A Life of Copernicus, Paul Merchant, pm *Ice River* Sum,1987
From Alabamy, with Hate [March to Montgomery], Harlan Ellison, ar *Knight* Sep,1965
From Competition 4: Story Leads from the Year's Worst Fantasy and SF, Harlan Ellison, ms *F&SF* Apr,1973
From Competition 8: Near-Miss SF Titles, Harlan Ellison, ms *F&SF* Sep,1974
From Competition 23: Unwieldy SF Titles, Harlan Ellison, ms *F&SF* Feb,1980
From Competition 26: Imaginary Collaborations, Harlan Ellison, ms *F&SF* Mar,1981
From Competition 39: Complete the Following Sentence..., Harlan Ellison, ms *F&SF* Mar,1986
From Out of the Past, Randall D. Larson, ss *Eldritch Tales* #13,1987
From the Editor, Bill Munster, ed *Footsteps* Nov,1987
From the Mouths of Lizards, Bruce Boston, pm
From the Tree of Time, Fred Saberhagen, ss *Sorcerer's Apprentice* #14,1982
From the Yearning for War and the War's Ending, Michael Williams, nv **DragonLance Tales** v3, Margaret Weis & Tracy Hickman, TSR,1987
Frontier, Byron Preiss, pr
The Frozen Cardinal, Michael Moorcock, ss **Other Edens**, ed. Christopher Evans & Robert Holdstock, Unwin: London,1987
The Frozen Waves, Robert E. Vardeman, n. Avon: New York pb May,1985
The Fruit at the Bottom of the Bowl [Touch and Go], Ray Bradbury, ss *Detective Book* Nov,1948
Fruit Drink, Bode Noonan, ss **Red Beans and Rice**, Crossing Press,1986
A Fruitless Assignment, Ambrose Bierce, ss
The FTL Addict Fixes, Bruce Boston, pm *Velocities*,1983
Fullwood's Web, Graham Charnock, ss **Other Edens**, ed. Christopher Evans & Robert Holdstock, Unwin: London,1987
Fun and Games, Irmtraud Kremp, ss *SF International* #2,1987
Fundamental Dilemma, Stanley Schmidt, ed *Analog* Jan,1987
The Fungoid Intruder, Leonard Carpenter, pm *2AM* Win,1987
Further Reading, [Misc. Material], bi
The Future of the Jovian System, Gregory Benford, ss **The Planets**, ed. Byron Preiss, Bantam,1985
G. Wayne Miller, G. Wayne Miller, iv *The Horror Show* Fll,1987
Galactic Checks and Balances: An Introduction to **The Forge of God**, Greg Bear, is *Twilight Zone* Oct,1987
Galatea, Isaac Asimov, ss *IASFM* mid-Dec,1987
Galaxies and Clusters, Hyron Spinrad, ar **Universe**, ed. Byron Preiss, Bantam Spectra,1987
A Galaxy Called Rome, Barry N. Malzberg, nv *F&SF* Jul,1975
Galileo Complains, Carter Scholz, ss *IASFM* Jun,1986
Galileo Saw the Truth, Gregory Nicoll, pm *Fantasy Crossroads* Mar,1977
The Gallery of Masks, David Busby, nv *F&SF* Aug,1987
The Gamblers, Fredric Brown & Mack Reynolds, nv *Startling Stories* Nov,1951
The Game of Cat and Eagle, Craig Kee Strete, nv **In the Field of Fire**, ed. Jeanne Van Buren Dann & Jack M. Dann, Tor,1987
The Game of Magical Death, Doug Hornig, ss *F&SF* Mar,1987
The Game of Rat and Dragon, Cordwainer Smith, ss *Galaxy* Oct,1955
A Game of Statues, Jackie Vivelo, ss **A Trick of the Light**, Putnam,1987
The Game of Time and Pain, Samuel R. Delany, na **The Bridge of Lost Desire**, Arbor House,1987
A Game of Unchance, Philip K. Dick, ss *Amazing* Jul,1964
Game Players, Tanith Lee, ss **Night's Sorceries**, DAW,1987
Game Review, Jim Massin, gr *Salarius* v1#4,1987
Games, Robert Simpson, gr *Twilight Zone* Aug,1987
Gaming, Matthew J. Costello, gr *IASFM* Jan,1987
Gaming, Matthew J. Costello, gr *IASFM* Feb,1987
Gaming, Matthew J. Costello, gr *IASFM* Mar,1987
Gaming, Matthew J. Costello, gr *IASFM* Apr,1987
Gaming, Matthew J. Costello, gr *IASFM* May,1987
Gaming, Matthew J. Costello, gr *IASFM* Jun,1987
Gaming, Matthew J. Costello, gr *IASFM* Jul,1987
Gaming, Matthew J. Costello, gr *IASFM* Aug,1987
Gaming, Matthew J. Costello, gr *IASFM* Sep,1987
Gaming, Matthew J. Costello, gr *IASFM* Oct,1987
Gaming, Matthew J. Costello, gr *IASFM* Nov,1987

GAMING   **GONE FISHING**

Gaming, Matthew J. Costello, gr *IASFM* Dec,1987
Gaming, Matthew J. Costello, gr *IASFM* mid-Dec,1987
Garage Sale, Lois McMaster Bujold, vi *American Fantasy* Spr,1987
Garage Sale, Bentley Little, ss *Space & Time* #72,1987
The Garbage Collector, Ray Bradbury, ss *The Nation* Oct,1953
A Garden of Blackred Roses, Charles L. Grant, nv **Dark Forces**, ed. Kirby McCauley, Viking,1980
The Garden of Paradise, Hans Christian Andersen, ss
The Gardener, Rudyard Kipling, ss **Debits and Credits**, London: Macmillan,1926
The Gardener and the Lord and Lady, Hans Christian Andersen, ss
Gardens and Fountains, Tony Bowerman, ss **Gollancz - Sunday Times Best SF Stories**, Gollancz,1987
The Gate Key, Hans Christian Andersen, ss
The Gate of Ghosts, Karen Joy Fowler, nv **Artificial Things**, New York: Bantam,1986
Gather Blue Roses, Pamela Sargent, ss *F&SF* Feb,1972
Gather Round the Flowing Bowler, Robert Bloch, ss *Fantastic Adventures* May,1942
The Geezenstacks, Fredric Brown, ss *Weird Tales* Sep,1943
Gemini, Tanith Lee, nv **Chrysalis #9**, ed. Roy Torgeson,1981
General Jaruzelski at the Zoo, George Zebrowski, ss *Twilight Zone* Apr,1987
The Generous Gambler, Charles Pierre Baudelaire, vi
Genesis, H. Beam Piper, nv *Future* Sep,1951
Genre-Love and the Magic of Words: John Maclay, William J. Grabowski & John Maclay, iv *2AM* Fll,1987
The Gentile Jewesses, Muriel Spark, ss *New Yorker* Jun 22,1963
The Gentle Art of Making Enemies, Claudia Peck, nv **Magic in Ithkar #4**, ed. Andre Norton & Robert Adams,1987
A Gentle Dying, C.M. Kornbluth & Frederik Pohl, ss *Galaxy* Jun,1961
Gentlemen, John M. Skipp & Craig Spector, nv **The Architecture of Fear**, ed. Kathryn Cramer & Peter D. Pautz, Arbor House,1987
Gentlemen, Be Seated!, Robert A. Heinlein, ss *Argosy* May,1948
The Getaway Special, Jerry Oltion, ss *Analog* Apr,1985
Getting Down with Lionel Fenn, Lionel Fenn, iv *American Fantasy* Sum,1987
Getting Home, F.M. Busby, nv *F&SF* Apr,1974
The Ghastly Priest Doth Reign, Manly Wade Wellman, ss *F&SF* Mar,1975
The Ghost, William D. O'Connor, na Putnam: New York,1867
The Ghost, Catherine Wells, ss **The Book of Catherine Wells**,1928
Ghost Alarm, Nicholas Fisk, ss,1986
Ghost and the Skeleton, Anonymous, pm
Ghost Breakers, Fredric Brown, nv *Thrilling Detective* Jul,1944
The Ghost Car, Ken Batten, ss *Ghost Stories* Oct,1928
The Ghost Dance, Robert Faulcon, n. Arrow Books: London,1983
The Ghost Lemurs of Madagascar, William S. Burroughs, ss *Omni* Apr,1987
The Ghost of First Crow, Jack Matthews, ss *Niobe*
The Ghost of Misery Hill, Robert D. San Souci, ss **Short & Shivery**, Doubleday,1987
The Ghost of the Model T, Betsy Emmons, ss *Weird Tales* Nov,1942
Ghost Ships, Paul Roland, sg **The Curious Case of Richard Fielding and Other Stories**, Lary Press,1987
Ghost Signs, Steve Rasnic Tem, pm *Eldritch Tales* #14,1987
The Ghost Stories of M.R. James, Richard Dalby, ar
A Ghost Story, J.B. Stamper, ss **More Tales for the Midnight Hour**, Apple/Scholastic,1987
Ghost Story Competition, M.R. James, ms *The Spectator* Chr,1930
The Ghost Train, Sydney J. Bounds, ss
The Ghost's Cap, Robert D. San Souci, ss **Short & Shivery**, Doubleday,1987
The Ghostly Little Girl, Robert D. San Souci, ss **Short & Shivery**, Doubleday,1987
Ghostly Populations, Jack Matthews, ss **Ghostly Populations**, Johns Hopkins,1987
The Ghostly Rental, Henry James, nv *Scribner's* Sep,1876
Ghosts - Treat Them Gently, M.R. James, ar *London Evening News* Apr 17,1931
The Ghosts at Grantley, Leonard Kip, nv
Ghosts of Night and Morning, Marvin Kaye, ss *Night Cry* v2#5,1987
The Giant's Heart, George MacDonald, nv
The Giant, the Colleen, and the Twenty-one Cows, Robert F. Young, nv *F&SF* Jun,1987
The Gift, Pat Forde, nv *Analog* Dec,1987
The Gift, Katherine V. Forrest, ss **Dreams and Swords**, Naiad,1987
The Gift, Joe W. Haldeman, pm **Dealing in Futures**, Viking,1985
A Gift from the Culture, Iain Banks, ss *Interzone* #20,1987

The Gift of Gab, Jack Vance, nv *Astounding* Sep,1955
The Gift of Garigolli, C.M. Kornbluth & Frederik Pohl, nv *Galaxy* Aug,1974
A Gift of Prophecy, C.J. Cherryh, ss **Glass and Amber**, NESFA,1987
Gilbert, R. Chetwynd-Hayes, nv **The House of Dracula**, Kimber,1987
Gilgamesh Redux, Janet Morris, nv **Crusaders in Hell**, ed. Janet Morris, New York: Baen,1987
Gipsies, Arthur Machen, ar *The Academy and Literature* Dec 9,1911
The Girl in the Mirror, Margot Arnold, ss,1976
The Girl in the Tau-Dream, Brian W. Aldiss, ss **Final Stage**, ed. Edward L. Ferman & Barry N. Malzberg, Charterhouse,1974
The Girl Who Died for Art, and Lived, Eric Brown, ss *Interzone* #22,1987
The Girl Who Painted Raindrops, Jackie Vivelo, ss **A Trick of the Light**, Putnam,1987
The Girl Who Trod on the Loaf, Hans Christian Andersen, ss
The Girl with the Hungry Eyes, Fritz Leiber, ss **The Girl With the Hungry Eyes**, ed. Donald A. Wollheim, Avon,1949
Give the Reader Quality Not Quantity, Jeffrey V. Yule, ed *Mage* Spr,1985
Glam's Story, Eleanor Arnason, ss *Tales of the Unanticipated* #2,1987
Glass, Nancy Kress, ss *IASFM* Sep,1987
Glass, John Maclay, pm *Footsteps* Spr,1985
Glass Cloud, James Patrick Kelly, na *IASFM* Jun,1987
The Glass Flower, George R.R. Martin, nv *IASFM* Sep,1986
The Glassblower's Dragon, Lucius Shepard, ss *F&SF* Apr,1987
Glimmer, Glimmer, George Alec Effinger, ss *Playboy* Nov,1987
A Glimpse of the Ankou, Kevin J. Anderson, ss *The Horror Show* Win,1987
The Gloconda, Harlan Ellison, ss *The Cleveland News*,1949
A Glorious Triumph for the People, E. Michael Blake, ss **There Will Be War v6**, ed. Jerry E. Pournelle,1987
Glossanalia [Glossolalia], Arlan Andrews, ss *Analog* Jul,1982
Glossary of Acronyms and Selected Terms, [Misc. Material], ms
Glossary to Wandering Willie's Tale, [Misc. Material], ms
Glowworm, Harlan Ellison, ss *Infinity* Feb,1956
The Gnarly Man, L. Sprague de Camp, nv *Unknown* Jun,1939
Gnawing, G. Wayne Miller, ss *The Horror Show* Spr,1987
Goats, Dave Smeds, nv **In the Field of Fire**, ed. Jeanne Van Buren Dann & Jack M. Dann, Tor,1987
The Goblin Spider, Robert D. San Souci, ss **Short & Shivery**, Doubleday,1987
God Bless Them, Gordon R. Dickson, nv **The Best of Omni #3**,1982
God Emperor of Dune, Frank Herbert, n. Gollancz: London,1981
God of Self, G. Wayne Miller, ss *The Horror Show* Fll,1987
God of Tarot, Piers Anthony, n. Berkley: New York,1979
The God of the Razor, Joe R. Lansdale, ss *Grue* #5,1987
God's Eyes, Michael Armstrong, nv **Masters of Hell**, ed. Janet Morris et al, Baen,1987
God's Hour, Michael Bishop, vi *Omni* Jun,1987
Godel's Doom, George Zebrowski, ss *Popular Computing* Feb,1985
The Godmother, Tina Rath, ss **Ghosts & Scholars #8**, ed. Rosemary Pardoe,1986
The Gods Arrive, Edward F. Shaver, nv *F&SF* Sep,1987
The Gods of the Copybook Headings, Rudyard Kipling, pm
The Gods of the Gaps, Gregory Benford, na **Crusaders in Hell**, ed. Janet Morris, New York: Baen,1987
Going to Meet the Alien, Andrew Weiner, nv *F&SF* Aug,1987
The Golden Apples of the Sun, Ray Bradbury, co Doubleday: Garden City, NY,1953
The Golden Apples of the Sun, Ray Bradbury, ss *Planet Stories* Nov,1953
The Golden Face of Fate, Nancy Springer, na **Chance & Other Gestures of the Hand of Fate**, Baen,1987
The Golden Helix, Theodore Sturgeon, na *Thrilling Wonder Stories* Sum,1954
The Golden Key, George MacDonald, nv **Dealing With Fairies**,1867
The Golden Kite, the Silver Wind, Ray Bradbury, ss *Epoch* Win,1953
The Golden Lump, Nicholas Fisk, nv **Living Fire and Other S.F. Stories**, Corgi: London,1987
The Golden Man, Philip K. Dick, nv *If* Apr,1954
The Golden Mile, Josephine Saxton, ss **Little Tours of Hell**, Pandora,1986
The Golden Opportunity of Lefty Feep, Robert Bloch, nv *Fantastic Adventures* Nov,1942
The Golden Rope, Tanith Lee, nv **Red As Blood**, DAW,1983
Goldfish in My Head, David C. Kopaska-Merkel, pm *Night Cry* v2#4,1987
The Golem, Robert D. San Souci, ss **Short & Shivery**, Doubleday,1987
Gone Fishing, J.A. Pollard, ss **Atlantis**, ed. Isaac Asimov, Martin H. Greenberg & Charles G. Waugh, Signet,1988

THE GOOD ALWAYS COME BACK   **THE HAPPY AUTUMN FIELDS**

The Good Always Come Back, Richard Christian Matheson, ss *Twilight Zone* Apr,1986

Good Country People, Flannery O'Connor, ss,1955

Good Dancing, Sailor!, Martin Gardner, ss *The University of Kansas City Review* Spr,1946

A Good Day in March, a Bearded Man, William J. Vernon, pm *Ice River* Sum,1987

A Good Knight's Tale, Harold Bakst, nv **DragonLance Tales** v3, Margaret Weis & Tracy Hickman, TSR,1987

Good Lady Ducayne, Mary Elizabeth Braddon, nv *The Strand* Feb,1896

Good Neighbor, Bruce Jones, ss **Twisted Tales**, San Diego: Blackthorne,1987

The Good Robot, SMS, cs *Interzone* #22,1987

Good-By, Grandma, Ray Bradbury, ss *The Saturday Evening Post* May 25,1957

Goodbye Houston Street, Goodbye, Richard Kadrey, ss *Interzone* #19,1987

Goodlife, Fred Saberhagen, nv *Worlds of Tomorrow* Dec,1963

Goodman's Place, Manly Wade Wellman, ss *F&SF* Sep,1974

Goosebumps, Richard Christian Matheson, ss **Scars**, Scream/Press,1987

Gopher in the Gilly, Harlan Ellison, ss **Stalking the Nightmare**,1982

Goslin Day, Avram Davidson, ss *Orbit* #6, ed. Damon Knight,1970

The Goulart Archipelago, Ron Goulart, ar *Twilight Zone* Feb,1987

Graduation, Richard Christian Matheson, ss *Whispers* #10,1977

Grail, Harlan Ellison, nv *Twilight Zone* Apr,1981

The Grand Tour, Charles Sheffield, ss *Analog* May,1987

The Grande Trouvaille, Arthur Machen, ar,1923

Grandpa, James H. Schmitz, ss *Astounding* Feb,1955

The Grandpa Urn, Bob Versandi, ss **Doom City**, ed. Charles L. Grant, Tor,1987

Granny's Birthday, Fredric Brown, vi *Alfred Hitchcock's Mystery Magazine* Jun,1960

The Graphic of Dorian Gray, Fred Saberhagen, nv **New Destinies** v1, ed. Jim Baen, Baen,1987

Grass Shark, Paul Walton, ss *Twilight Zone* Jun,1987

Grave Angels, Richard Kearns, nv *F&SF* Apr,1986

The Graveyard Rats, Henry Kuttner, ss *Weird Tales* Mar,1936

Gravity Has Always Been Our Enemy, Roger L. Dutcher, pm *IASFM* Oct,1987

Gravy Planet, C.M. Kornbluth & Frederik Pohl, ex *Galaxy* Aug,1952

Gray Ghost: A Reminiscence, R.A. Lafferty, ss,1987

Gray Matter, Stephen King, ss *Cavalier* Oct,1973

Gray Nights, William P. Cunningham, vi *Mage* Win,1985

The Great Atlantic Swimming Race, Ian Watson, ss *IASFM* Mar,1986

The Great C, Philip K. Dick, ss *Cosmos SF&F* Sep,1953

The Great Counterfeit Memory Sin-Drome, Andrew Darlington, ss *Back Brain Recluse* #7,1987

The Great Edwardian Airaid, Paul Roland, sg **The Curious Case of Richard Fielding and Other Stories**, Lary Press,1987

The Great Fire, Ray Bradbury, ss *Seventeen* Mar,1949

The Great Holy Mystery, Thomas E. Sanders (Nippawanock), ar *Twilight Zone* Aug,1987

Great Lost Discoveries I - Invisibility, Fredric Brown, vi *Gent* Feb,1961

Great Lost Discoveries II - Invulnerability, Fredric Brown, vi *Gent* Feb,1961

Great Lost Discoveries III - Immortality, Fredric Brown, vi *Gent* Feb,1961

Great Oaks from Little Atoms, Stanley Schmidt, ed *Analog* Nov,1987

The Great Staircase at Landover Hall, Frank R. Stockton, ss

The Great Wide World Over There [Cora and the Great Wide World Over There], Ray Bradbury, ss *Maclean's* Aug 15,1952

The Greater Powers, Richard Wilson, ss **The Kid from Ozone Park and Other Stories**, Drumm,1987

The Green Building, Gordon R. Dickson, ss *Satellite* Dec,1956

Green Glass Violins, Paul Roland, sg **The Curious Case of Richard Fielding and Other Stories**, Lary Press,1987

Green Gravel, Jill Paton Walsh, ss **A Quiver of Ghosts**, ed. Aiden Chambers, Bodley Head,1987

The Green Hills of Earth, Robert A. Heinlein, ss *The Saturday Evening Post* Feb 8,1947

Green in High Hallack, Kiel Stuart, ss **Tales of the Witch World**, ed. Andre Norton, St. Martin's,1987

Green Is the Color, John M. Ford, na **Liavek: Wizard's Row**, ed. Will Shetterly & Emma Bull, Ace,1987

Green Is the Color, Richard Wilson, ss **The Kid from Ozone Park and Other Stories**, Drumm,1987

The Green Machine, Ray Bradbury, ss *Argosy (UK)* Mar,1951

The Green Man of Knowledge, Wendy G. Pearson, ss **Tesseracts 2**, ed. Phyllis Gotlieb & Douglas Barbour, Press Porcepic: Victoria,1987

The Green Mist, Robert D. San Souci, ss **Short & Shivery**, Doubleday,1987

The Green Morning, Ray Bradbury, ss **The Martian Chronicles**,1950

Green Tea, Joseph Sheridan Le Fanu, nv *All the Year Round* Oct 23,1869

Green Wine for Dreaming, Ray Bradbury, ss **Dandelion Wine**, Ray Bradbury, Doubleday,1957

The Green Woman, Meghan B. Collins, ss *Ms.*,1982

The Greenhill Gang, Barbara Owens, ss *F&SF* Feb,1987

The Greening of Mrs. Edmiston, Robin Scott Wilson, ss *F&SF* Jan,1987

The Griffin, Edward T. Babinski, pm *Apex!* #1,1987

Grimm's Story, Vernor Vinge, na *Orbit* #4, ed. Damon Knight,1968

Grimm's World, Vernor Vinge, n. Berkley: New York,1969

The Grimoire, Montague Summers, ss,1936

Grinning Moon, Frederick J. Mayer, pm *Eldritch Tales* #14,1987

Grow Your Own Baby, Ferret & Mink Mole, cs *New Pathways* Nov,1987

Guardian, Leslie Fish, sg *Festival Moon*, ed. C.J. Cherryh, DAW,1987

Guardian Angel, Arthur C. Clarke, nv *New Worlds* Win,1950

Guest-Room in Hell, Leon Byrne, ss *Horror Stories* Oct,1936

A Guide to Significant Works of Architectural Horror, [Misc. Material], bi

Guilt Trip, Charles Sheffield, ss *Analog* Aug,1987

Guinevere and Lancelot, Arthur Machen, ss,1926

The Guitarist, Grace Hallworth, ss **Mouth Open Story Jump Out**, Methuen,1984

Gullrider, Dave Smeds, ss **Sword and Sorceress #4**, ed. Marion Zimmer Bradley,1987

The Gun, Philip K. Dick, ss *Planet Stories* Sep,1952

A Gun for Grandfather, F.M. Busby, ss *Future* Fll,1957

The Gun That Didn't Go Bang, Nicholas Fisk, nv **Living Fire and Other S.F. Stories**, Corgi: London,1987

The Guy, Ramsey Campbell, ss **Demons By Daylight**,1973

Gwyneth Jones Interview, Gwyneth Jones & Paul Kincaid, iv *Interzone* #19,1987

The Gypsy and the Procrastinator, Stanley Schmidt, ed *Analog* Feb,1987

H.P. Lovecraft: Problems in Critical Recognition, Peter Cannon, ar *Mage* Win,1987

H.P. Lovecraft: Still Eldritch After All These Years, Darrell Schweitzer, ar *Amazing* Mar,1987

Hackers in the Dewey, R.D. Davis, vi *Mage* Win,1987

The Hag of Carmel Towers, Don Webb, vi *New Pathways* Jan,1987

Haiku, Ann Cathey, pm *Salarius* v1#4,1987

Hail and Farewell, Ray Bradbury, ss *Today* Mar 29,1953

The Hairy Parents, A. Bertram Chandler, ss *Void* #2,1975

Haiti the Shepherd, Ambrose Bierce, ss **In the Midst of Life**, E.L.G. Steele: San Francisco CA,1891

Half Past Dead, John J. Miller, nv **Wild Cards** v2, ed. George R.R. Martin, Bantam,1987

Hall of Mirrors, Fredric Brown, ss *Galaxy* Dec,1953

Halley's Passing, Michael McDowell, ss *Twilight Zone* Jun,1987

Halloween in Arkham, J.J. Travis, ss *Eldritch Tales* #13,1987

The Halloween Pony, Robert D. San Souci, ss **Short & Shivery**, Doubleday,1987

The Halls of Doom, Herbert Jerry Baker, ss *Eldritch Tales* #14,1987

Hammer's Slammers, David Drake, co Ace: New York pb Apr,1979

The Hand of God, David Starkey, ss *2AM* Sum,1987

The Hand of Guilt, Don Sakers, ss *Fantasy Book* Mar,1987

The Hand of the Survivor, J.M. Zeller, ss *Amazing* Jul,1987

A Handbook for the Apprentice Magician, [Misc. Material], ms **Liavek: Wizard's Row**, ed. Will Shetterly & Emma Bull, Ace,1987

The Handbug, H.W. Baichtal, ss *Tales of the Unanticipated* #2,1987

Handmaids In Hell, Chris Morris, ss **Angels in Hell**, ed. Janet Morris, Baen,1987

The Hands, Ramsey Campbell, ss **Cutting Edge**, ed. Dennis Etchison, Doubleday,1986

The Hanging Judge, Paul Roland, sg **The Curious Case of Richard Fielding and Other Stories**, Lary Press,1987

The Hanging Stranger, Philip K. Dick, ss *Science Fiction Adventures* Dec,1954

Hangman, David Drake, na **Hammer's Slammers**, Ace,1979

A Hangman Waits, Paul Roland, ss **The Curious Case of Richard Fielding and Other Stories**, Lary Press,1987

Hanuman, Stephen Earl, ss **Gollancz - Sunday Times Best SF Stories**, Gollancz,1987

The Happiness Machine [also as "The Time Machine"], Ray Bradbury, ss *The Saturday Evening Post* Sep 14,1957

The Happy Autumn Fields, Elizabeth Bowen, ss **The Demon Lover**, J. Cape,1945

HAPPY BIRTHDAY UNIVERSE!

Happy Birthday Universe! [Bonne Fete Univers!], Alain Bergeron, nv *Solaris* #65,1986
Happy Birthday, Kim White, Kathe Koja, ss *SF International* #1,1987
The Happy Family, Hans Christian Andersen, vi
Happy Hour, J.N. Williamson, ss *Twilight Zone* Feb,1987
The Happy Prince, Oscar Wilde, ss **The Happy Prince and Other Tales**, London: David Nutt,1888
Harbard, Larry Walker, ss *Amazing* Jan,1987
A Hard Ride Home, Dave Smeds, ss *Mayfair* Sep,1987
Hard? Science? Fiction?, Gregory Benford, br *Amazing* Jul,1987
Hardshell, Dean R. Koontz, nv **Night Visions** #4,1987
Hardware, Robert Silverberg, ss *Omni* Oct,1987
Harlan Ellison's I, Robot, Isaac Asimov, ar *IASFM* Nov,1987
Harlan Ellison's Watching, Harlan Ellison, mr *F&SF* Feb,1987
Harlan Ellison's Watching, Harlan Ellison, mr *F&SF* Apr,1987
Harlan Ellison's Watching, Harlan Ellison, mr *F&SF* May,1987
Harlan Ellison's Watching, Harlan Ellison, mr *F&SF* Jul,1987
Harlan Ellison's Watching, Harlan Ellison, mr *F&SF* Sep,1987
Harlan Ellison's Watching, Harlan Ellison, mr *F&SF* Oct,1987
Harmonica Song, Dan Duncan, pm **There Will Be War** v6, ed. Jerry E. Pournelle,1987
Harmony of Fear, John Brower, mr *Minnesota Fantasy Review* #1,1987
Harry Protagonist, Inseminator General, Richard Wilson, ss **The Kid from Ozone Park and Other Stories**, Drumm,1987
Harvest, John Maclay, vi *Dementia* #1,1986
Harvests, Nancy Varian Berberick, nv **DragonLance Tales** v1, Margaret Weis & Tracy Hickman, TSR,1987
Hatrack River, Orson Scott Card, nv *IASFM* Aug,1986
Haunted, Edward Bryant, ss **Night Visions** #4,1987
Haunted, Joyce Carol Oates, nv **The Architecture of Fear**, ed. Kathryn Cramer & Peter D. Pautz, Arbor House,1987
Haunted, Marta Randall, ss *Twilight Zone* Dec,1987
The Haunted and the Haunters, Sir Edward George Bulwer-Lytton, Lord Lytton, nv *Blackwood's* Aug,1859
The Haunted Bungalow, Charles Duff, ss
Haunted City of the Moon, Joey Froehlich, pm *Eldritch Tales* #13,1987
The Haunted House of My Childhood, Alan Ryan, pm *Weirdbook* #22,1987
The Haunted Saucepan, Margery Lawrence, ss **Nights of the Round Table**, Hutchinson: London,1926
The Haunted Ships, Allan Cunningham, nv **Traditional Tales of the English and Scottish Peasantry**, London: Taylor & Hessey,1822
Haunted Subalterns, Rudyard Kipling, ss *The Civil and Military Gazette* May 27,1887
Haunted Waters, Mary Williams, n. **Haunted Waters**, Kimber,1987
The Haunting, Margaret Mahy, ex J.M. Dent: London,1982
The Haunting of Joshua Tree, Leslie Halliwell, ss **A Demon Close Behind**, Robert Hale,1987
Hawk Among the Sparrows, Dean McLaughlin, na *Analog* Jul,1968
Hawthorne and Mailer, Dave Page, ar *Minnesota Fantasy Review* #1,1987
He Stepped on the Devil's Tail, Winston K. Marks, ss *Fantastic Universe* Feb,1955
He-We-Await, Howard Waldrop, nv **All About Strange Monsters of the Recent Past**, Kansas City, MO: Ursus Imprints,1987
Head in His Hands, Carl Jacobi, ss *Thrilling Mystery Stories* Nov,1937
The Healing, Sandy Boucher, nv **Hear the Silence**, ed. Irene Zahava, Crossing Press,1986
Health Food, W.R. Thompson, ss *Analog* May,1987
Hearing Is Believing, Ramsey Campbell, ss **Shadows** #4, ed. Charles L. Grant,1981
The Hearse, J.B. Stamper, ss **More Tales for the Midnight Hour**, Apple/Scholastic,1987
The Heart of Darkness, Gary Gygax, nv **Night Arrant**, Ace/New Infinities,1987
Heart of Goldmoon, Laura Hickman & Kate Novak, na **DragonLance Tales** v3, Margaret Weis & Tracy Hickman, TSR,1987
Heart of Stone, Peter Heyrman, ss *The Horror Show* Sum,1987
Heart Throb, Sara Maitland, ss **Passion Fruit**, Winterson, Pandora,1986
Hearth Cat and Winter Wren, Nancy Varian Berberick, nv **DragonLance Tales** v2, Margaret Weis & Tracy Hickman, TSR,1987
Hearts and Minds, Chris Morris, nv **Fever Season**, ed. C.J. Cherryh, DAW,1987
The Heavenly Blue Answer, Ronald Anthony Cross, ss **In the Field of Fire**, ed. Jeanne Van Buren Dann & Jack M. Dann, Tor,1987
Heavenly Flowers, Pamela Sargent, ss *IASFM* Sep,1983
Heavy Breathing, Marthayn Pelegrimas, pm *2AM* Spr,1987
Hegemony, Andrew Joron, pm

Heinrich; or, The Love of Gold, Alfred Crowquill, ss **Fairy Footsteps; or Lessons from Legends**, London: H. Lea,1860
Heir Apparent, Robert Bloch, ss **Tales of the Witch World**, ed. Andre Norton, St. Martin's,1987
Heir to the Kingdom, John Maclay, ss *Australian Horror & Fantasy Magazine*
The Heirs of Earth, Paul J. McAuley, nv *Amazing* May,1987
The Helium Farewell, Joe Clifford Faust, ss *Haunts* #9,1987
Hell, Richard Christian Matheson, ss **Scars**, Scream/Press,1987
A Hell of a Story, H.R.F. Keating, ss *Ellery Queen's Mystery Magazine* Jun,1982
Hell to Pay, Randall Garrett, nv *Beyond Fantasy Fiction* Mar,1954
Hell-Bent [contest story], Ford McCormack, ss *F&SF* Jun,1951
Hellbike, George Foy, ss **Masters of Hell**, ed. Janet Morris et al, Baen,1987
Hellnotes, David B. Silva, ed *The Horror Show* Jan,1987
Hellnotes, David B. Silva, ed *The Horror Show* Spr,1987
Hellnotes, David B. Silva, ed *The Horror Show* Sum,1987
Hellnotes, David B. Silva, ed *The Horror Show* Fll,1987
Hellnotes, David B. Silva, ed *The Horror Show* Win,1987
Hello, Hugo, Laurence Staig, ss **Twisted Circuits**, ed. Mick Gowar, Beaver,1987
Hellraiser, Cory Glaberson & Stephen Jones, mr *American Fantasy* Win,1987
Helpless, Helpless, Howard Waldrop, ss **Light Years and Dark**, ed. Michael Bishop, Berkley,1984
Hemingway in Space, Kingsley Amis, ss *Punch* Dec,1960
Henry Kuttner: An Introduction, L. Sprague de Camp, in
Herbert George Morley Roberts Wells, Esq., Arthur C. Clarke, ed *If* Dec,1967
Herbert West--Reanimator ["Grewsome Tales", *Home Brew*: Feb-Jul 1922], H.P. Lovecraft, gp *Weird Tales* Mar,1942
'Here He Lies Where He Longed to Be', Winifred Galbraith, vi *The Spectator* Chr,1930
Here There Be Dragons, Bill Vaughan, ss *Analog* Mar,1987
Heredity, David H. Keller, M.D., ss *The Vortex* #2,1947
Heretics of Dune, Frank Herbert, n. Gollancz: London,1984
Hermes to the Ages, Frederick D. Gottfried, nv *Analog* Jan,1980
Hermione Gould, Paul Christopher, nv **Beyond That River**, Pal Books,1987
Hero, Joe W. Haldeman, na *Analog* Jun,1972
A Hero of the Spican Conflict, Bruce Boston, pm *Aboriginal SF* Nov,1987
Heroes of Audio: Jane Schonberger, Scott Jenkins, bg *American Fantasy* Sum,1987
Heroes of Audio: Mike McDonough, Scott Jenkins, bg *American Fantasy* Win,1987
Heroics, James Patrick Kelly, ss *IASFM* Nov,1987
Hide and Go Seek, Nancy Varian Berberick, nv **DragonLance Tales** v3, Margaret Weis & Tracy Hickman, TSR,1987
Hide and Seek, Gerard Klein, vi,1973
Hidey Hole, Steve Rasnic Tem, ss **Masques** #2, ed. J.N. Williamson,1987
A High Dive, L.P. Hartley, ss
High Power, Robert Chilson & William F. Wu, ss *Analog* Sep,1987
High Road of Lost Men, Brad Linaweaver, nv **Friends of the Horseclans**, ed. Robert Adams & Pamela Crippen Adams, Signet,1987
The High Test, Frederik Pohl, ss *IASFM* Jun,1983
High-Tech Insolence, Russell Baker, vi *New York Times* May 18,1986
Highbrow, Neal Barrett, Jr., ss *IASFM* Jul,1987
The Highest Treason, Randall Garrett, nv *Analog* Jan,1961
The Highland Widow, Sir Walter Scott, na **Chronicles of the Canongate**, Cadell & Co.,1827
The Highway [as by Leonard Spalding], Ray Bradbury, ss *Copy* Spr,1950
Hilda's Letter, L.P. Hartley, nv **The White Wand and Other Stories**, Hamilton,1954
Hilifter, Gordon R. Dickson, ss *Analog* Feb,1963
The Hired Executioner, Paul Roland, ss **The Curious Case of Richard Fielding and Other Stories**, Lary Press,1987
The Hirn, Philippa Pearce, ss **Who's Afraid? and Other Strange Stories**, Kestrel/Penguin,1986
His Loving Sister, Philippa Pearce, ss **Ghost After Ghost**, ed. Aiden Chambers, Kestrel,1982
His Master's Voice, Andrew Joron, pm
Hit Me, Rudin Moore, nv **Ultra-Vue and Selected Peripheral Visions**, self published,1987
The Hitch-Hiker, Roald Dahl, ss **Henry Sugar and Other Stories**, 1977,1977

Hitchhiker, Sheila Finch, ss *Amazing* Sep,1987

Hobbyist, Fredric Brown, vi *Playboy* May,1961

Hobson's Choice, Alfred Bester, ss *F&SF* Aug,1952

Hog, David Drake, ss **World Fantasy Convention Program Book** #13,1987

A Hog on Ice, Robert Chilson & William F. Wu, ss *Analog* Dec,1987

Hogfoot Right and Bird-Hands, Garry Kilworth, ss **Other Edens**, ed. Christopher Evans & Robert Holdstock, Unwin: London,1987

A Hole in the Sun, Roger MacBride Allen, nv *Analog* Apr,1987

Holiday, Richard Christian Matheson, ss *Twilight Zone* Feb,1982

The Hollow, Bruce Jones, ss **Twisted Tales**, San Diego: Blackthorne,1987

The Hollow Man, Lisa Tuttle, nv **New Voices in Science Fiction #2**, ed. George R.R. Martin,1979

Hollywood Grapevine, Anonymous, ar *Twilight Zone* Apr,1987

Hollywood Grapevine, [Misc. Material], ar *Twilight Zone* Jun,1987

Hollywood Grapevine, [Misc. Material], ar *Twilight Zone* Aug,1987

Hollywood Grapevine, [Misc. Material], ar *Twilight Zone* Oct,1987

Hollywood Grapevine, [Misc. Material], ar *Twilight Zone* Dec,1987

Hollywood Revisited: The Body Snatchers, Robert Frazier, pm *IASFM* Feb,1987

Holography, B.Z. Niditch, pm *Ice River* Sum,1987

Holy Quarrel, Philip K. Dick, nv *Worlds of Tomorrow* May,1966

Home for Dinner, Mollie L. Burleson, ss *Eldritch Tales* #13,1987

Home Is the Hangman, Roger Zelazny, na *Analog* Nov,1975

Home Is the Hunter, Henry Kuttner, ss *Galaxy* Jul,1953

"Home Is the Hunter": The Triumph of Honest Roger Bellamy, Robert Silverberg, ar,1987

Home, Sweet Home, L.P. Hartley, ss

Homecoming, C.J. Cherryh, ss *Shayol* Dec,1979

Homecoming, Andrew J. Offutt, nv **Aftermath**, ed. Robert Lynn Asprin & Lynn Abbey, Ace,1987

Homecoming, Paul F. Olson, ss *The Horror Show* Jan,1987

Homer's Whistle, Joan Aiken, ss **They Wait and Other Spine Chillers**, ed. Lance Salway, Pepper Press,1983

The Homework Horror, Greg Cox, ss *Amazing* May,1987

Honeycomb, Esther M. Friesner, nv **Magic in Ithkar #4**, ed. Andre Norton & Robert Adams,1987

Honeymoon in Hell, Fredric Brown, nv *Galaxy* Nov,1950

Honorable Mentions: 1986, [Misc. Material], bi

The Hood Maker, Philip K. Dick, ss *Imagination* Jun,1955

The Hoodoo, Rudin Moore, na **Ultra-Vue and Selected Peripheral Visions**, self published,1987

Hooked On Love, Joan Vander Putten, pm *Grue* #6,1987

Hooray for Hollywood, Larry Tritten, vi *The Horror Show* Win,1987

The HORARS of War, Gene Wolfe, ss **Nova #1**, ed. Harry Harrison,1970

The Horla, Guy de Maupassant, nv *Gil Blas* Oct 26,1886

The Horn of Vapula, Lewis Spence, ss **The Archer in the Arras**, Grant & Murray: London,1932

The Horrible Horns, Martin Gardner, ss *London Mystery Magazine* Dec,1950

The Horror at His Heels, Wyatt Blassingame, ss *Horror Stories* Aug,1936

The Horror at Hops Cottage, Leslie Halliwell, ss **A Demon Close Behind**, Robert Hale,1987

Horror House of Blood, Ramsey Campbell, ss **The Height of the Scream**,1976

The Horror on the #33, Michael Shea, ss *F&SF* Aug,1982

Horse Camp, Ursula K. Le Guin, ss *New Yorker* Aug 25,1986

The Horse on the Escalator, Martin Gardner, ss *Esquire* Oct,1946

Horse Race, Fredric Brown, vi **Nightmares and Geezenstacks**, Bantam,1961

The Horsehair Trunk [The Secret Darkness], Davis Grubb, ss *Ellery Queen's Mystery Magazine* Oct,1956

The Horseman, Sam Gafford, vi *Eldritch Tales* #14,1987

Horses of Light, Bruce Boston, pm

The Hospice, Robert Aickman, nv **Cold Hand in Mine**, Scribner's,1975

A Hot Prospect, Theodore Solomon, ss *Mage* Spr,1987

Hothouse, Brian W. Aldiss, nv *F&SF* Feb,1961

"Hothouse": The Fuzzypuzzle Odyssey, Robert Silverberg, ar,1987

The Hound, H.P. Lovecraft, ss *Weird Tales* Feb,1924

The Hounds, Kate Wilhelm, nv **A Shocking Thing**, ed. Damon Knight, Pocket,1974

The House, Fredric Brown, vi *Fantastic* Aug,1960

The House, Andre Maurois, vi,1931

The House and the Brain, Sir Edward George Bulwer-Lytton, Lord Lytton, nv *Blackwood's* Aug,1859

The House in Bel Aire, Margaret St. Clair, ss *If* Jan,1961

The House in the Tree, Gary Gygax, nv **Night Arrant**, Ace/New Infinities,1987

The House of the Famous Poet, Muriel Spark, ss *New Yorker* Apr 2,1966

House of Weapons, Gordon R. Dickson, na **Far Frontiers** v2, ed. Jerry Pournelle & Jim Baen,1985

The House on the Headland, Kingsley Amis, ss *The Times*,1979

The House Surgeon, Rudyard Kipling, nv *Harper's* Sep + 1,1909

The House that Knew No Hate, Jessica Amanda Salmonson, nv **The Architecture of Fear**, ed. Kathryn Cramer & Peter D. Pautz, Arbor House,1987

The House That Lacked a Bogle, Sorche Nic Leodhas, ss,1981

House--with Ghost, August Derleth, ss **Lonesome Places**, Arkham: Sauk City, WI,1962

The House-Party, Emma S. Duffin, vi *The Spectator* Chr,1930

Houseguests, Nancy Asire, nv **Masters of Hell**, ed. Janet Morris et al, Baen,1987

Houston, Houston, Do You Read?, James Tiptree, Jr., na **Aurora: Beyond Equality**, ed. Vonda McIntyre & Susan Anderson, Fawcett,1976

How Do You Know You're Reading Philip K. Dick?, James Tiptree, Jr., in

How Exciting!, Isaac Asimov, in

How It Happened, Arthur Conan Doyle, ss *The Strand* Sep,1913

How Love Came to Professor Guildea, Robert S. Hichens, nv **Tongues of Conscience**,1900

How the Wind Spoke at Madaket, Lucius Shepard, na *IASFM* Apr,1985

How to Impress an Editor, Frederik Pohl, ar **L. Ron Hubbard Presents Writers of the Future** v3, ed. Algis Budrys, Bridge,1987

How to Sound Like an Expert, Gregory Benford, ar **L. Ron Hubbard Presents Writers of the Future** v3, ed. Algis Budrys, Bridge,1987

The Howling Man [as by C.B. Lovehill], Charles Beaumont, ss *Rogue* Nov,1959

Huayno, Asher Torren, pm *Mage* Win,1987

Hugh Cave: An Appreciation, Don Hutchinson, bg *Border Land* Oct,1987

Human Evolution [from **A Criminal History of Mankind**], Colin Wilson, ar

Human Is, Philip K. Dick, ss *Startling Stories* Win,1955

A Human Nerve Cell, Robert Frazier, pm

The Human Operators, Harlan Ellison & A.E. van Vogt, nv *F&SF* Jan,1971

Human Remains, Bruce Boston, pm *Star*Line* v5#4,1982

Humorists in a Strange Land, Robert Coulson, br *Amazing* May,1987

Hundred Years Gone, Manly Wade Wellman, ss *F&SF* Mar,1978

Hunger, David Martin, ss *New Pathways* Jan,1987

The Hunter in the Haunted Forest, Robert D. San Souci, ss **Short & Shivery**, Doubleday,1987

Hunter's Moon, Poul Anderson, nv *Analog* Nov,1978

The Hunter: A.D. 20,000, Andrew Joron, pm *Amazing* Nov,1982

Hunting Destiny, Nick O'Donohoe, nv **DragonLance Tales** v3, Margaret Weis & Tracy Hickman, TSR,1987

The Hunting Lodge, Randall Garrett, nv *Astounding* Jul,1954

Hunting Machine, Carol Emshwiller, ss *(The Original) Science Fiction Stories* May,1957

The Hunting of the Snark, Lewis Carroll, n.,1978

Huntington's Handle, Mark E. Peeples, Ph.D., ar *Analog* Oct,1987

Hurricane Haze, Margaret Atwood, nv

Hush, Dear Conscience, C.B. Gilford, ss *Alfred Hitchcock's Mystery Magazine* May,1974

The Hyperbolic Super-Blitz, Norris D. Hertzog, vi *Heart of Texas Commodore Home User Group Newsletter* Jan,1986

Hyperzoo, Ian Watson, ss *IASFM* mid-Dec,1987

A Hypothetical Lizard, Alan Moore, nv **Liavek: Wizard's Row**, ed. Will Shetterly & Emma Bull, Ace,1987

I am myself, Denise Dumars, pm *Grue* #4,1987

I Am Returning, Ray Russell, ss **Sardonicus**, Ballantine,1961

I Bid You Welcome, Denise Dumars, pm *Weirdbook* #22,1987

"I died for a while...", Jack M. Dann, pm **The Anthology of Speculative Poetry**, ed. Robert Frazier,1980

I Have No Mouth, and I Must Scream, Harlan Ellison, ss *If* Mar,1967

I Hope I Shall Arrive Soon [Frozen Journey], Philip K. Dick, ss *Playboy* Dec,1980

I Made You, Walter M. Miller, Jr., ss *Astounding* Mar,1954

The I of the Beholder, Joe Fischetti, ss *Analog* Oct,1987

I Praise My Nativity, Robert E. Howard, pm *Fantasy Book* Mar,1987

I See You Never, Ray Bradbury, vi *New Yorker* Nov 8,1947

I Spy Strangers, Kingsley Amis, ss **My Enemy's Enemy**, London: Gollancz,1962

I Was a Teenage Reptile, Ferret & Mink Mole, cs *New Pathways* Aug,1987

I'M DANGEROUS TONIGHT

I'm Dangerous Tonight, Cornell Woolrich, na *All American Fiction* Nov,1937

I'm Going to Get You, F.M. Busby, ss *Fantastic* Mar,1974

I'm Scared, Jack Finney, ss *Colliers* Sep 15,1951

I've Got a Little List, Randall Garrett, pm *F&SF* Nov,1953

I, Robot: The Movie [Part 1 of 3], Harlan Ellison, sl *IASFM* Nov,1987

I, Robot: The Movie [Part 2 of 3], Harlan Ellison, sl *IASFM* Dec,1987

I, Robot: The Movie [Part 3 of 3], Harlan Ellison, sl *IASFM* mid-Dec,1987

I, Rocket, Ray Bradbury, ss *Amazing* May,1944

IBM, My Shipmate; or, the Difference Between Orbit and Obit, Richard Wilson, pm *Amazing* Sep,1987

Ice, Lawrence Tagrin, ss *Salarius* v1#4,1987

The Ice Dragon, George R.R. Martin, nv **Dragons of Light**, ed. Orson Scott Card, Ace,1980

Ice Dreams, Sharon N. Farber, ss *IASFM* Mar,1987

Ice Sculptures, David B. Silva, ss **Masques #2**, ed. J.N. Williamson,1987

Identity Crisis, G.L. Raisor, ss *Night Cry* v2#3,1987

Ideological Defeat, Christopher Anvil, nv *Analog* Sep,1972

Idiot Solvant, Gordon R. Dickson, ss *Analog* Jan,1962

If Big Brother Says So, Alice Rudoski, ss *Ellery Queen's Mystery Magazine* Jul,1977

If Damon Comes, Charles L. Grant, ss **The Year's Best Horror Stories #6**,1978

If Ever I Should Leave You [revised from *If* Feb,74], Pamela Sargent, ss **Starshadows**, Ace,1977

If Gravity Were Like Weather, Bruce Boston, pm *Star*Line*,1982

If Looks Could Kill, Walton Simons, ss **Wild Cards** v2, ed. George R.R. Martin, Bantam,1987

If Not Us, Then Who?, Jack Matthews, ss **Ghostly Populations**, Johns Hopkins,1987

if only icarus had climbed the night, t. Winter-Damon, pm *Fantasy Book* Mar,1987

If the Driver Vanishes..., Peter T. Garratt, ss *Interzone* #13,1985

If There Were No Benny Cemoli, Philip K. Dick, ss *Galaxy* Dec,1963

If This Goes On-, Robert A. Heinlein, na *Astounding* Feb,1940

If This Is Winnetka, You Must Be Judy, F.M. Busby, nv **Universe #5**, ed. Terry Carr,1974

If You Take My Hand, My Son, Mort Castle, ss **Masques #2**, ed. J.N. Williamson,1987

The Ifs of History, Isaac Asimov, in

An Illuminated Manuscript, Andrew Joron, pm

Illumination, Ray Bradbury, ss *Reporter* May 16,1957

Illuminations: A Dark and Stormy Plight, Ron Wolfe, ar *Twilight Zone* Dec,1987

Illuminations: A Little Night Music, Tappan King, ar *Twilight Zone* Feb,1987

Illuminations: An Audience with the King, Tyson Blue, ar *Twilight Zone* Aug,1987

Illuminations: Awright, Larson! --Up Against the Wall, Ron Wolfe, ar *Twilight Zone* Dec,1987

Illuminations: Bad Feng-Shui Killed Bruce Lee, Mark Arnold, ar *Twilight Zone* Jun,1987

Illuminations: Building a Better Egg, Allan Maurer, ar *Twilight Zone* Dec,1987

Illuminations: Comic Relief, Lou Stathis, ar *Twilight Zone* Apr,1987

Illuminations: Computer Rosetta Stone, Allan Maurer, ar *Twilight Zone* Dec,1987

Illuminations: Crystal Revelations, Christopher Karwowski, ar *Twilight Zone* Jun,1987

Illuminations: Crystal Update, Deborah Quilter, ar *Twilight Zone* Oct,1987

Illuminations: Dreamland, Tappan King, ar *Twilight Zone* Dec,1987

Illuminations: Eternal Evil, Tappan King, ar *Twilight Zone* Oct,1987

Illuminations: Expeditions to the Unknown, Mark Arnold, ar *Twilight Zone* Jun,1987

Illuminations: Fantasies for Sale, Ariel Remler, ar *Twilight Zone* Feb,1987

Illuminations: First Pooch Sees Ghost, Mark Arnold, ar *Twilight Zone* Aug,1987

Illuminations: Forstchen in Maine's Eyes, Ron Wolfe, ar *Twilight Zone* Aug,1987

Illuminations: Freedom to Imagine, Carol Serling, ar *Twilight Zone* Apr,1987

Illuminations: Frog Heaven, Ron Wolfe, ar *Twilight Zone* Apr,1987

Illuminations: I Sing the Body Eclectic, Mark Arnold, ar *Twilight Zone* Oct,1987

Illuminations: Latin Lama, Tappan King, ar *Twilight Zone* Oct,1987

Illuminations: Leaps of Faith, Tappan King, ar *Twilight Zone* Jun,1987

Illuminations: Magic Underfoot, Tappan King, ar *Twilight Zone* Aug,1987

Illuminations: Many Happy Returns, Tyson Blue, ar *Twilight Zone* Aug,1987

Illuminations: Mother Was an Alien, James Verniere, ar *Twilight Zone* Feb,1987

Illuminations: Painting the Town Red, Christopher Karwowski, ar *Twilight Zone* Feb,1987

Illuminations: Prophet of the "Damned", Peter R. Emshwiller, ar *Twilight Zone* Oct,1987

Illuminations: Radio Sci-Fi, Christopher Karwowski, ar *Twilight Zone* Apr,1987

Illuminations: Radio- Vision, Ron Wolfe, ar *Twilight Zone* Aug,1987

Illuminations: Really Weird Tales, Robert Simpson, ar *Twilight Zone* Apr,1987

Illuminations: Red SF, Peter R. Emshwiller, ar *Twilight Zone* Feb,1987

Illuminations: Starmagic, Christopher Karwowski, ar *Twilight Zone* Apr,1987

Illuminations: Strange Hangups, Christopher Karwowski, ar *Twilight Zone* Jun,1987

Illuminations: The Creature from the Silt in the Black Lagoon, Tappan King, ar *Twilight Zone* Oct,1987

Illuminations: The Man Who Would Be Spock, James Verniere, ar *Twilight Zone* Jun,1987

Illuminations: The Return of Lefty Feep, Anonymous, br *Twilight Zone* Aug,1987

Illuminations: TV or Not TV?, Ron Wolfe, ar *Twilight Zone* Oct,1987

Illuminations: TZ Meets the '80s, Christopher Karwowski, ar *Twilight Zone* Feb,1987

Illuminations: You May Be Typecast, Allan Maurer, ar *Twilight Zone* Dec,1987

The Illustrated Man, Ray Bradbury, co Doubleday: Garden City, NY,1951

Illustrations, Allen Koszowski, il *The Horror Show* Fll,1987

An Image in Twisted Silver, Charles L. Grant, ss *Twilight Zone* Apr,1987

Images, Harry Turtledove, nv *IASFM* Mar,1987

Imagine, a Proem, Fredric Brown, pm *F&SF* May,1955

IMAGO, Mary Kittredge, ss *Aboriginal SF* May,1987

The Imitation Demon, Robert Kuttner, ss *Weird Tales* Sep,1954

The Immobility Crew, Brian W. Aldiss, ss **Final Stage**, ed. Edward L. Ferman & Barry N. Malzberg, Charterhouse,1974

The Immortal Dog, Jack Matthews, ss *Jeopardy*

The Immortals, Martin Amis, ss

Immune Dreams, Ian Watson, ss **Pulsar #1**, ed. George Hay,1978

The Imp in the Bottle, John Salonia & Traci Salonia, ss *Space & Time* #73,1987

Imp to Nymph, Piers Anthony, ss **World Fantasy Convention Program Book #13**,1987

Imperfect Catch, Nathan A. Bucklin, ss *Tales of the Unanticipated* #2,1987

The Impossible Planet, Philip K. Dick, ss *If* Oct,1953

The Impossible Smile [as by Jael Cracken], Brian W. Aldiss, na *Science Fantasy* May + 1,1965

Impostor, Philip K. Dick, ss *Astounding* Jun,1953

Improbable Bestiary: The Bandersnatch (Frumius carrollii), F. Gwynplaine MacIntyre, pm *Amazing* Nov,1987

The Improper Princess, Patricia C. Wrede, ss **Spaceships & Spells**, ed. Jane Yolen, Martin H. Greenberg & Charles G. Waugh, Harper & Row,1987

In a Dark, Dark Box, Jane Hollowood, ss **Spooky**, ed. Pamela Lonsdale,1987

In a Land of Sand and Ruin and Gold, David Langford, ss **Other Edens**, ed. Christopher Evans & Robert Holdstock, Unwin: London,1987

In a Thousand Years, Hans Christian Andersen, vi

In Alien Tongues, C.J. Cherryh, ar *Sorcerer's Apprentice* WiS,1981

In Days of Cataclysm, Bruce Boston, pm

In Lonely Lands, Harlan Ellison, ss *Fantastic Universe* Jan,1959

In Memoriam: Manly Wade Wellman, Crispin Burnham, bg *Eldritch Tales* #13,1987

In Midst of Life, James Tiptree, Jr., ss *F&SF* Nov,1987

In Praise of Sociobiology, Dr. John Gribbin & Mary Gribbin, ar **New Destinies** v1, ed. Jim Baen, Baen,1987

In Search of the Rattlesnake Plantain, Margaret Atwood, ss *Harper's* Aug,1986

In Search of Yuk-Yuk, Neil Renton, ss *The Ecphorizer* Mar,1987

In the Bag, Ramsey Campbell, ss **Cold Fear**, ed. Hugh Lamb, W.H. Allen,1987

In the Beginning There Was Humming [from "What Dinah Thought"], Deena Metzger, ex **Hear the Silence**, ed. Irene Zahava, Crossing Press,1986

IN THE BONE

In the Bone, Gordon R. Dickson, nv *If* Oct,1966

In the Bowl, John Varley, nv *F&SF* Dec,1975

In the Cathedral Gardens, Kit Wright, pm **Hot Dog and Other Poems**,1981

In the Country of the Blind (Part 1 of 2), Michael F. Flynn, sl *Analog* Oct,1987

In the Country of the Blind (Part 2 of 2), Michael F. Flynn, sl *Analog* Nov,1987

In the Creation Science Laboratory, Jerry Oltion, ss *Analog* Sep,1987

In the Duck Yard, Hans Christian Andersen, ss

In the Eyes of the Pilot, Bruce Boston, pm *Amazing* Mar,1987

In the Footsteps of M.R. James, Darroll Pardoe & Rosemary Pardoe, ar

In the Garden of the State, Bruce Boston, pm *Amazing* May,1987

In the Hour Before Dawn, Brad Strickland, ss *F&SF* Aug,1986

In the House of Gingerbread, Gene Wolfe, ss **The Architecture of Fear**, ed. Kathryn Cramer & Peter D. Pautz, Arbor House,1987

In the House of Suddhoo, Rudyard Kipling, ss *The Civil and Military Gazette* Apr 30,1886

In the Image of Our Fathers, Ramona Pope Richards, ar *Apex!* #1,1987

In the Kingdom at Morning, Stephen L. Burns, nv *Analog* Feb,1987

In the Lantern's Light, J.B. Stamper, ss **More Tales for the Midnight Hour**, Apple/Scholastic,1987

In the Lost Lands, George R.R. Martin, ss **Amazons** #2, ed. Jessica Amanda Salmonson,1982

In the Memory Room, Michael Bishop, ss **The Architecture of Fear**, ed. Kathryn Cramer & Peter D. Pautz, Arbor House,1987

In the Name of the Father, Edward P. Hughes, nv *F&SF* Sep,1980

In the News, Thomas M. Disch, pm *Night Cry* v2#5,1987

In the Old Places, A. Arthur Griffin, pm *Weirdbook* #22,1987

In the Opium Den, Paul Roland, sg **The Curious Case of Richard Fielding and Other Stories**, Lary Press,1987

In the Pit ["Dans la Fosse", *Janus* 1984], Elisabeth Vonarburg, ss *Solaris*

In the Realm of the Heart, In the World of the Knife, Wayne Wightman, ss *IASFM* Aug,1985

In the Season of the Rains, Richard Paul Russo, ss **In the Field of Fire**, ed. Jeanne Van Buren Dann & Jack M. Dann, Tor,1987

In the Sickbay, R.V. Branham, nv **L. Ron Hubbard Presents Writers of the Future** v3, ed. Algis Budrys, Bridge,1987

In the Tank, Ardath Mayhar, ss **Masques** #2, ed. J.N. Williamson,1987

In the Temple of Terror, Brian Lumley, nv *Weirdbook* #22,1987

In the Tower, Jack McDevitt, nv *Universe* #17, ed. Terry Carr,1987

In the Tube, Paul Christopher, vi **Beyond That River**, Pal Books,1987

In the Twilight Zone, Tappan King, ed *Twilight Zone* Feb,1987

In the Twilight Zone, Tappan King, ed *Twilight Zone* Apr,1987

In the Twilight Zone, Tappan King, ed *Twilight Zone* Jun,1987

In the Twilight Zone, Tappan King, ed *Twilight Zone* Aug,1987

In the Twilight Zone, Tappan King, ed *Twilight Zone* Oct,1987

In the Twilight Zone, Tappan King, ed *Twilight Zone* Dec,1987

In The Wilderness, John Maclay, ss *Etchings & Odysseys* #7,1985

In This Center Hold Solitude, Mark Rich, pm *Mage* Win,1985

In Time, Roger Dale Trexler, pm **The Dark Road and Other Poems of Darkness**,1987

In Video Veritas, Larry Tritten, ss *F&SF* Dec,1987

Inception, Brian Lumley, ss **The Compleat Crow**, Ganley,1987

An Incident in the City, A.F. Kidd, ss **Ghosts & Scholars** #1, ed. Rosemary Pardoe,1979

Incorporation, Richard Christian Matheson, ss **Scars**, Scream/Press,1987

The Incredible Bomber, Fredric Brown, nv *G-Man Detective* Mar,1942

The Indefatigable Frog, Philip K. Dick, ss *Fantastic Story* Jul,1953

Independents, Eric Vinicoff, ss *Analog* Apr,1987

Index, [Misc. Material], ix *Analog* Jan,1987

Index, [Misc. Material], ix *IASFM* Jan,1987

Index to City Maps, [Misc. Material], ix

Index to Volume 72, [Misc. Material], ix *F&SF* Jun,1987

Index to Volume 73, [Misc. Material], ix *F&SF* Dec,1987

Index to Weird Menace Pulps, Robert Kenneth Jones, ix **The Weird Menace**, Opar Press,1972

An Index to *Fantasy Book*, Volume 5, [Misc. Material], ix *Fantasy Book* Mar,1987

An Indian Ghost in England, Rudyard Kipling, ss *The Pioneer* Dec 10,1885

Indian Summer, Philip Gladwin, ss **Gollancz - Sunday Times Best SF Stories**, Gollancz,1987

The Indian's Grave, Ross McKay, ss **After Midnight Stories** #3,1987

Infinite Man, William Relling, Jr., ss *New Blood* #1,1987

Infinite Resources, Randall Garrett, ss *F&SF* Jul,1954

The Infinites, Philip K. Dick, ss *Planet Stories* May,1953

Inflections, The Readers, lt *Amazing* Jan,1987

Inflections, The Readers, lt *Amazing* Mar,1987

Inflections, The Readers, lt *Amazing* May,1987

Inflections, The Readers, lt *Amazing* Jul,1987

Inflections, The Readers, lt *Amazing* Sep,1987

Inflections, The Readers, lt *Amazing* Nov,1987

Influencing the Hell Out of Time and Teresa Golowitz, Parke Godwin, ss *Twilight Zone* Jan,1982

Information in War [from **On War**], Karl von Clausewitz, ar

Inheritance, Annette S. Crouch, ss *Grue* #6,1987

Inheritor, David Drake, na **Aftermath**, ed. Robert Lynn Asprin & Lynn Abbey, Ace,1987

Inhuman Error [also as "WHAT DO YOU WANT ME TO DO TO PROVE IM HUMAN STOP"], Fred Saberhagen, ss *Analog* Oct,1974

Inky, Jayge Carr, ss *Whispers* #23,1987

An Inopportune Visit, Paul Bowles, ss *Threepenny Review* Spr,1987

Inside Out, Rudy Rucker, ss *Synergy* v1, ed. George Zebrowski,1987

Insight at Flame Lake, Martin Amis, ss *Vanity Fair*

Instant Karma, Janet Morris, nv **Fever Season**, ed. C.J. Cherryh, DAW,1987

Intellectual Cliches, Isaac Asimov, ed *IASFM* Feb,1987

The Interdisciplinary Viewpoint of Science Fiction, Michael G. Adkisson, ar *New Pathways* Apr,1987

Interesting Times, Christopher Anvil, ss *Analog* Dec,1987

Interference, L.P. Hartley, ss

The Interferences, Josephine Saxton, ss **Tales from the Forbidden Planet**, ed. Roz Kaveney, Titan,1987

The Intergalactic Medium, Wallace Tucker, ar **Universe**, ed. Byron Preiss, Bantam Spectra,1987

Interim, Ray Bradbury, vi **The Martian Chronicles**,1950

The Interloper, Ramsey Campbell, ss **Demons By Daylight**,1973

Intermission, Robert Coover, ss *Playboy* Feb,1987

Intermission, Fred Saberhagen, vi **Fifty Extremely SF* Stories**, ed. Michael Bastraw,1982

Internal Shadows, Ed Shannon, br *Minnesota Fantasy Review* #1,1987

The Interpreters, James White, ss *F&SF* Mar,1987

The Interrogation, Dean R. Koontz, ss *The Horror Show* Sum,1987

Intersections, Randy Williams, vi *2AM* Fll,1987

Interstellar Tract, Bruce Boston, pm **Nuclear Futures**, Velocities Chapbook Series,1987

Interview with a Gentleman Farmer, Bruce Boston, ss *City Miner* #1,1976

Interview with Anne Rice, Anne Rice, iv *American Fantasy* Spr,1987

Interview with Bill Froehlich, Bill Froehlich & Cory Glaberson, iv *American Fantasy* Win,1987

Interview with Crematia Mortum (Roberta Solomon), Kathleen E. Jurgens & Crematia Mortum, iv *2AM* Spr,1987

An Interview with F. Paul Wilson, Bill Munster & F. Paul Wilson, iv *Footsteps* Nov,1987

An Interview with Gahan Wilson, Bill Munster & Gahan Wilson, in *Footsteps* Nov,1987

Interview with J.K. Potter, Paul F. Olson & J.K. Potter, iv *The Horror Show* Jan,1987

Interview with Joe R. Lansdale, William J. Grabowski & Joe R. Lansdale, iv *The Horror Show* Jan,1987

An Interview with Kate Wilhelm and Damon Knight, Terry A. Garey, Eric M. Heideman, Damon Knight & Kate Wilhelm, iv *Tales of the Unanticipated* #2,1987

Interview with Mark Ziesing: Bookseller & Publisher, Misha Chocholak & Mark Ziesing, iv *New Pathways* Jan,1987

An Interview with Robert McCammon, Rodney A. Labbe & Robert R. McCammon, iv *Footsteps* Nov,1987

Interview with Robert R. McCammon, William J. Grabowski & Robert R. McCammon, iv *The Horror Show* Spr,1987

Intimations of Mortality, Isaac Asimov, ed *IASFM* Mar,1987

Into Gold, Tanith Lee, nv *IASFM* Mar,1986

Into My Parlor, Randall Garrett, vi **Takeoff Too!**, Norfolk, VA: Donning/Starblaze,1987

Into the Heart of the Story, Michael Williams, nv **DragonLance Tales** v2, Margaret Weis & Tracy Hickman, TSR,1987

Into the Sunset, D.C. Poyer, nv *Analog* Jul,1986

Into Whose Hands, Karl Edward Wagner, nv **Whispers** #4, ed. Stuart David Schiff,1983

Introdiction to Glowworm, Harlan Ellison, is *Unearth* Win,1977

Introduction, Robert Adams, in

Introduction, Brian W. Aldiss, in

Introduction, Kingsley Amis, in

Introduction, Poul Anderson, in

Introduction, Isaac Asimov, in

INTRODUCTION

Introduction, Robert Lynn Asprin, in
Introduction, Clive Barker, in
Introduction, Robert Bloch, in
Introduction, Marion Zimmer Bradley, in
Introduction, John Brunner, in
Introduction, Algis Budrys, in
Introduction, F.M. Busby, in
Introduction, Ramsey Campbell, in
Introduction, Terry Carr, in
Introduction, Lord David Cecil, in
Introduction, R. Chetwynd-Hayes, in
Introduction, Lincoln Child, in
Introduction, John Clute, Simon Ounsley & David Pringle, in
Introduction, Michael Cox, in
Introduction, Richard Dalby, in
Introduction, Richard Dalby & Rosemary Pardoe, in
Introduction, Jack M. Dann & Jeanne Van Buren Dann, in
Introduction, Ellen Datlow, in
Introduction, Thomas M. Disch, in
Introduction, Gardner R. Dozois, in
Introduction, David Drake, in
Introduction, Dennis Etchison, in
Introduction, Christopher Evans & Robert P. Holdstock, in
Introduction, Charles L. Grant, in
Introduction, Roger Lancelyn Green, in
Introduction, Martin H. Greenberg & Robert Silverberg, in
Introduction, James E. Gunn, in
Introduction, Peter Haining, in
Introduction, Joe W. Haldeman, in
Introduction, David G. Hartwell, in
Introduction, Michael Hayes, in
Introduction, Vicki Ann Heydron, in
Introduction, Joan Kahn, in
Introduction, Roz Kaveney, in
Introduction, Marvin Kaye, in
Introduction, Charles Keeping, in
Introduction, Damon Knight, in
Introduction, Ursula K. Le Guin, in
Introduction, Miroslaw Lipinski, in
Introduction, Francis Lyall, in
Introduction, Frank D. McSherry, Jr., in
Introduction, Andre Norton, in
Introduction, William Pattrick, in
Introduction, Peter D. Pautz, in
Introduction, Simon Petherick, in
Introduction, Frederik Pohl, in
Introduction, Tim Powers, in
Introduction, David Pringle, in
Introduction, Ruth Rendell, in
Introduction, Spider Robinson, in
Introduction, Rudy Rucker, in
Introduction, Alan Ryan, in
Introduction, Arthur W. Saha, in
Introduction, Robert D. San Souci, in
Introduction, Pamela Sargent, in
Introduction, Stuart David Schiff, in
Introduction, Stanley Schmidt, in
Introduction, Carol Serling, in
Introduction, Robert Silverberg, in
Introduction, Melinda M. Snodgrass, in
Introduction, Norman Spinrad, in
Introduction, Jennifer Uglow, in
Introduction, Karl Edward Wagner, in
Introduction, Donald E. Westlake, in
Introduction, J.N. Williamson, in
Introduction, Jack Williamson, in
Introduction, Irene Cooper Willis, in
Introduction, Colin Wilson, in
Introduction, Donald A. Wollheim, in
Introduction, Jane Yolen, in
Introduction, Roger Zelazny, in
Introduction, Jack Zipes, in
Introduction (from Notes and Queries), Arthur Machen, in,1926
Introduction (from The Dragon of the Alchemists), Arthur Machen, in,1926
Introduction to "The Shadow on the Doorstep", Lewis Shiner, in
Introduction to Fat Face, Karl Edward Wagner, in
Introduction to the 1987 Edition, Arthur C. Clarke, in

Introduction to The Haunted Ships, Darrell Schweitzer, ar *Fantasy Book* Mar,1987
Introduction: "Horror and the Hearth of Darkness", Martin H. Greenberg, in
Introduction: Honeymoons and Geezenstacks and Fredric William Brown, Richard A. Lupoff, in
Introduction: Knave's World, Laurence M. Janifer, in
Introduction: Mercenaries and Military Virtue, Jerry E. Pournelle, in
Introduction: Neanderthal Man, Isaac Asimov, in
Introduction: Shuttles, Isaac Asimov, in
Introduction: Sublime Rebel, Terry Dowling, in
Introduction: Synergists, George Zebrowski, in **Synergy** v1, ed. George Zebrowski,1987
Introduction: The Fog of War, Jerry E. Pournelle, in **There Will Be War** v6, ed. Jerry E. Pournelle,1987
Introduction: The Keeper of the Night, Tappan King, in *Night Cry* v2#4,1987
Introduction: The Lost City, Isaac Asimov, in
Introduction: The Making of a Science-Fiction Writer, Robert Silverberg, in
Introduction: The Spirit of Christmas, David G. Hartwell, in
Introduction: What Again?, Isaac Asimov, in
Introduction: What's in a Name?, Karl Edward Wagner, in
Introduction: Where the Dead Do Not Die, Alan Rogers, in *Night Cry* v2#5,1987
Introduction: Why There Are So Many "Ladies of the Night", Charles G. Waugh, in
The Introduction: Will the Real Lefty Feep Please Rise to the Occasion?, John Stanley, in
Intruder, Richard Christian Matheson, ss *Gallery* Sep,1986
Investing in Futures, Kingsley Amis, ss **The Compleat Imbiber**, ed. Cyril Ray,1986
Invisible Boy, Ray Bradbury, ss *Mademoiselle* Nov,1945
The Invisible Empire, Arthur Knight, ar *Pulpsmith* Win,1987
The Invitation, John Phillips Palmer, pm *Weirdbook* #22,1987
Iocus: A Retrospective, Paul F. Olson, ar *The Horror Show* Spr,1987
Irene, Good Night, Barbara W. Durkin, ss *Whispers* #23,1987
The Irish Fairy Tale, Frances Molloy, vi **The Female Line: Northern Irish Writers**
Irma, R. Chetwynd-Hayes, nv **Dracula's Children**, Kimber,1987
Iron [Part 2], Poul Anderson, sl **New Destinies** v1, ed. Jim Baen, Baen,1987
Iron Butterflies, Mona A. Clee, ss *Twilight Zone* Dec,1987
The Iron Star, Robert Silverberg, ss **Universe**, ed. Byron Preiss, Bantam Spectra,1987
The Irvhank Effect, Harry Turtledove, ss **New Destinies** v2, ed. Jim Baen, Baen,1987
Ishbar, The Trueborn, George Florance-Guthridge, ss *Pulpsmith* Win,1987
The Island, L.P. Hartley, ss **The Travelling Grave and Other Stories**, Arkham,1948
Isle of Illusion, Carol Severance, nv **Tales of the Witch World**, ed. Andre Norton, St. Martin's,1987
The Isle of the Torturers, Steve Eng, pm *Eldritch Tales* #14,1987
Isolation Area, Ben Bova, nv *F&SF* Oct,1984
Issue by issue index to *Ace Mystery*, *Eerie Mysteries*, *Eerie Stories* and *Uncanny Tales*, [Misc. Material], ix
It, Deloris Selinsky, pm *2AM* Fll,1987
It Came from the Slushpile, Bruce Bethke, ss *Aboriginal SF* Jul,1987
"It is a circle.", Jack M. Dann, pm *Twilight Zone* Aug,1987
It Speaks, Mike Odden, ed *Minnesota Fantasy Review* #1,1987
"It was a good day to die...", Jack M. Dann, pm *Twilight Zone* Aug,1987
It Wasn't a Half-Bad Year, Charles L. Grant, br *Amazing* Sep,1987
It's Alive Again! The Return of the Nit-Picky, Utterly Trivial, Totally Picayune Horror-Fantasy (and What the Heck, a Little Sci-Fi) Movie Quiz Part III, A.R. Morlan, qz *The Horror Show* Fll,1987
It's Great to be Back!, Robert A. Heinlein, ss *The Saturday Evening Post* Jul 26,1947
It's Quite True, Hans Christian Andersen, vi
IT, Out of Darkest Jungle, Gordon R. Dickson, ss *Fantastic* Dec,1964
An Item of Supporting Evidence, Brian Lumley, ss *The Arkham Collector* Win,1970
J.G. Ballard, J.G. Ballard & David Pringle, iv *Interzone* #22,1987
Jack Frost, Robert D. San Souci, ss **Short & Shivery**, Doubleday,1987
Jackbird, Bruce Boston, ss *Gallimaufry* #3,1974
Jackie Loves Food -- True, Josephine Saxton, ss **Little Tours of Hell**, Pandora,1986
Jacob's Ladder, M. Shayne Bell, nv *The Leading Edge* #10,1985

THE JAGUAR HUNTER

The Jaguar Hunter, Lucius Shepard, nv *F&SF* May,1985

Jailhouse Blues, Dragan R. Filipovic, ss *SF International* #2,1987

Jamboree, Jack Williamson, ss *Galaxy* Dec,1969

James, Gordon R. Dickson, ss *F&SF* May,1955

James Blish and Michael Sherman's "The Duplicated Man", Randall Garrett, pm *Future* #29,1956

James P. Crow, Philip K. Dick, ss *Planet Stories* May,1954

The Jameson Satellite, Neil R. Jones, nv *Amazing* Jul,1931

Jamie Burke and the Queen of England, Sasha Miller, ss *F&SF* Jun,1987

Jamie's Grave, Lisa Tuttle, ss **Shadows** #10, ed. Charles L. Grant,1987

Japanese Tea, Terence M. Green, ss **Alien Worlds**, ed. Paul Collins, Void,1979

Jason's Answer, Ace G. Pilkington, pm *Amazing* Jul,1987

Jay Walkers, H. Russell Wakefield, ss

Jaycee, Fredric Brown, vi *F&SF*,1955

Jeff Beck, Lewis Shiner, ss *IASFM* Jan,1986

The Jefferson Orbit, Ben Bova, ar **Far Frontiers** v1, ed. Jerry Pournelle & Jim Baen,1985

Jeffty Is Five, Harlan Ellison, ss *F&SF* Jul,1977

Jendick's Swamp, Joseph Payne Brennan, ss **Doom City**, ed. Charles L. Grant, Tor,1987

Jennifer's Island, B.F. Watkinson, ss *Eldritch Tales* #13,1987

Jerk the Giant Killer, Robert Bloch, nv *Fantastic Adventures* Oct,1942

The Jerra-Mee, Ingrid Whitehorn, ss *Aphelion* #5,1987

Jessie, Katherine V. Forrest, nv **Dreams and Swords**, Naiad,1987

Jessie's Friend, Bruce Jones, ss **Twisted Tales**, San Diego: Blackthorne,1987

Jesus on Honshu, John Updike, vi *New Yorker* Dec 25,1971

Jewels in an Angel's Wing, Ian Watson, nv **Synergy** v1, ed. George Zebrowski,1987

Jinian Footseer, Sheri S. Tepper, n. Tor: New York,1985

Jinian Star-Eye, Sheri S. Tepper, n. Tor: New York,1986

Joe Lansdale Speaks, Wayne Allen Sallee, pm *Grue* #5,1987

Johannes Kepler and His Cosmic Mystery, Robert Frazier, pm *IASFM* Mar,1983

John Borkowski: An Appreciation, Irwin M. Chapman, bg *2AM* Fll,1987

John Charrington's Wedding, Edith Nesbit, ss

John Crowley Interview, John Crowley & Gregory Feeley, iv *Interzone* #21,1987

John Dee's Song, Michael Moorcock, pm *Back Brain Recluse* #7,1987

John Mortonson's Funeral, Ambrose Bierce, vi *Night Cry* v2#4,1987

The Joke, Fredric Brown, ss **Nightmares and Geezenstacks**, Bantam,1961

The Joker [as by anonymous], Rudyard Kipling, ss *The Pioneer* Jan 1,1889

The Jolly Corner, Henry James, nv

Jon's World, Philip K. Dick, nv **Time to Come**, ed. August Derleth, Farrar,1954

Jonathon, D.J. Cipriani, III, vi *Mage* Spr,1987

Jube: Five, George R.R. Martin, sl **Wild Cards** v2, ed. George R.R. Martin, Bantam,1987

Jube: Four, George R.R. Martin, sl **Wild Cards** v2, ed. George R.R. Martin, Bantam,1987

Jube: One, George R.R. Martin, sl **Wild Cards** v2, ed. George R.R. Martin, Bantam,1987

Jube: Seven, George R.R. Martin, sl **Wild Cards** v2, ed. George R.R. Martin, Bantam,1987

Jube: Six, George R.R. Martin, sl **Wild Cards** v2, ed. George R.R. Martin, Bantam,1987

Jube: Three, George R.R. Martin, sl **Wild Cards** v2, ed. George R.R. Martin, Bantam,1987

Jube: Two, George R.R. Martin, sl **Wild Cards** v2, ed. George R.R. Martin, Bantam,1987

The Judge's House, Bram Stoker, ss *Holly Leaves* Dec 5,1891

Judgment Call, John Kessel, nv *F&SF* Oct,1987

Juggernaut, Dorothy K. Broster, ss **Couching at the Door**, Heinemann: London,1942

The Jukebox Man, Dean Wesley Smith, ss *Night Cry* v2#5,1987

July 16, 1945, 5:29:45 AM, Mountain War Time, Robert Frazier, pm *IASFM* Oct,1986

Jumbee, Paul Roland, sg **The Curious Case of Richard Fielding and Other Stories**, Lary Press,1987

The Jumpers, Hans Christian Andersen, vi

Junior Partner, Ron Goulart, ss *Fantastic* Sep,1962

Jury Duty, Batton Lash, cs *American Fantasy* Spr,1987

Just a legend, W. Fraser Sandercombe, pm *Weirdbook* #22,1987

Just a Little Souvenir, Cheryl Fuller Nelson, ss **Shadows** #10, ed. Charles L. Grant,1987

LADY WITH UNICORN

Just a Little Thing, Joan Vander Putten, ss **Devils & Demons**, ed. Marvin Kaye, SFBC/Doubleday,1987

Just Another Bedtime Story, A.R. Morlan, ss *Night Cry* v2#4,1987

Just Another Day at the Weather Service, Elizabeth N. Moon, vi *Analog* Nov,1987

Just Compensation, William C. Rasmussen, vi *2AM* Fll,1987

Just Like Their Masters, Mona A. Clee, ss **Shadows** #10, ed. Charles L. Grant,1987

"Just Like Wild Bob", William F. Nolan, ss,1964

Just Waiting, Ramsey Campbell, ss *Twilight Zone* Dec,1983

K.W. Jeter, Les Escott & K.W. Jeter, iv *Interzone* #22,1987

K.W. Jeter [Part 1], Ferret, K.W. Jeter & J.B. Reynolds, iv *New Pathways* Apr,1987

K.W. Jeter [Part 2], Ferret, K.W. Jeter & J.B. Reynolds, iv *New Pathways* Aug,1987

Kaj, Don Webb, vi *Grue* #5,1987

Kaleidoscope, Ray Bradbury, ss *Thrilling Wonder Stories* Oct,1949

Kaleidoscope of Dust, Andrew Joron, pm

Kanaloa, W.S. Merwin, pm *New Yorker* Apr 13,1987

Karl, R. Chetwynd-Hayes, nv **The House of Dracula**, Kimber,1987

Kathleen Jurgens interviews Commander USA, Commander USA & Kathleen E. Jurgens, iv *2AM* Fll,1987

Kayli's Fire, Paula Helm Murray, ss **Sword and Sorceress** #4, ed. Marion Zimmer Bradley,1987

Keep Me Away, Manly Wade Wellman, ss *Whispers* Oct,1978

Keep Out, Fredric Brown, ss *Amazing* Mar,1954

Ken's Mystery, Julian Hawthorne, nv **David Poindexter's Disappearance**, Appleton,1888

The Keys to December, Roger Zelazny, ss *New Worlds* Aug,1966

Kid Charlemagne, Paul Di Filippo, ss *Amazing* Sep,1987

The Kid from Ozone Park, Richard Wilson, ss **The Kid from Ozone Park and Other Stories**, Drumm,1987

Kihar, Vera Nazarian, nv **Red Sun of Darkover**, ed. Marion Zimmer Bradley & The Friends of Darkover, DAW,1987

Killdozer!, Theodore Sturgeon, na *Astounding* Nov,1944

The Killing Bottle, L.P. Hartley, nv

Kindergarten, Clifford D. Simak, nv *Astounding* Jul,1953

King Joe Cay, Kenneth Robeson, na *Doc Savage* Jul,1945

King of the Cyber Rifles, George Alec Effinger, ss *IASFM* mid-Dec,1987

The King of the Elves, Philip K. Dick, nv *Beyond Fantasy Fiction* Sep,1953

King of the Golden River, or The Black Brothers, John Ruskin, nv,1841

The King of the Hill, Paul J. McAuley, ss *Interzone* #14,1985

King Solomon's Ring, Roger Zelazny, ss *Fantastic* Oct,1963

The King's Dragon, Jane Yolen, ss **Spaceships & Spells**, ed. Jane Yolen, Martin H. Greenberg & Charles G. Waugh, Harper & Row,1987

Kingdom Come, Bruce McAllister, ss *Omni* Feb,1987

Kinsman, Ben Bova, ex *Omni* Sep,1979

Kinsman, Ben Bova, n. Quantum Science Fiction, The Dial Press: New York,1979

Kisses and Chloroform, Donald Olson, ss *Alfred Hitchcock's Mystery Magazine* Jul,1974

Kitten Kaboodle and Sidney Australia, Harvey Jacobs, ss *F&SF* Jun,1987

Kleinism, Arthur L. Klein, ms *Amazing* Jan,1987

Kleinism, Arthur L. Klein, ms *Amazing* Mar,1987

Kleinisms, Arthur L. Klein, ms *Amazing* Jul,1987

The Knife, John Maclay, ss *Crosscurrents* Fll,1984

A Knocking in the Wall, August Derleth, ss *Weird Tales* Jul,1951

Knox, Harlan Ellison, ss *Crawdaddy* Mar,1974

The Kolorized King Kong Kaper, Ray Russell, ss *Whispers* #23,1987

Kool Running, Paul Collins, ss *SF International* #1,1987

Korowaar, Mary Elizabeth Counselman, ss

Krarg Enters, Dennis Hamley, ss **Twisted Circuits**, ed. Mick Gowar, Beaver,1987

Krash-Bangg Joe and the Pineal-Zen Equation, Eric Brown, ss *Interzone* #21,1987

L Is for Love, Steve Rasnic Tem, vi *Footsteps* Nov,1987

Lacunae, Karl Edward Wagner, ss **Cutting Edge**, ed. Dennis Etchison, Doubleday,1986

The Ladder of Selves [from **Mysteries**], Colin Wilson, ar Hodder Stoughton: London,1978

The Ladies of Mandrigyn, Barbara Hambly, n. Ballantine: New York pb Mar,1984

Lady Eleanor's Mantle, Robert D. San Souci, ss **Short & Shivery**, Doubleday,1987

The Lady Who Lost Her Head, Cheryl Curry Sayre, ss *Grue* #6,1987

Lady with Unicorn, Sara Maitland, ss **The Virago Book of Ghost Stories**, ed. Richard Dalby, Virago,1987

Lake George in High August, John Robert Bensink, ss **Masques** #2, ed. J.N. Williamson,1987

The Lame King, Joan Aiken, ss **A Goose on Your Grave**, Gollancz,1987

Lamia, Manly Wade Wellman, ss *Kadath* Jul,1981

The Lamp [also as "The Lamp from Atlantis"], L. Sprague de Camp, nv *F&SF* Mar,1975

Landmarks of the Laboratory, Ray Clark Dickson, pm *Pulpsmith* Win,1987

Landscape in Black, Thomas Glave, Jr., pm *Pulpsmith* Win,1987

The Language of the Sea, Carolyn Ives Gilman, nv **L. Ron Hubbard Presents Writers of the Future** v3, ed. Algis Budrys, Bridge,1987

The Lansdale House of Horror, Joe R. Lansdale, mr *The Horror Show* Jan,1987

Lapidary Nights, Marta Randall, ss **Universe** #17, ed. Terry Carr,1987

Larger Than Oneself, Robert Aickman, nv,1966

Laser Propulsion, Ben Bova, ar,1984

The Last Bedtime Story, A.R. Morlan, ss *Grue* #6,1987

The Last Command, Arthur C. Clarke, ss *Bizarre Mystery* Nov,1965

The Last Cruise of the Judas Iscariot, Edward Page Mitchell, ss *The Sun* Apr 16,1882

The Last Demon, Isaac Bashevis Singer, ss **Short Friday**,1964

The Last Department, Rudyard Kipling, pm

Last Dragon, Steve Rasnic Tem, ss *Amazing* Sep,1987

Last Enemy, H. Beam Piper, nv *Astounding* Aug,1950

The Last Evolution, John W. Campbell, Jr., ss *Amazing* Aug,1932

Last Favor, Harry Turtledove, nv *Analog* mid-Dec,1987

The Last Gays of Parpheii, Karen B. Heath, vi *Salarius* v1#4,1987

Last Grave of Lill Warran, Manly Wade Wellman, nv *Weird Tales* May,1951

The Last Lords of Gardonal, William Gilbert, ss *Argosy* Jul +3,1867

The Last Martian, Fredric Brown, ss *Galaxy* Oct,1950

The Last Night of the World, Ray Bradbury, ss *Esquire* Feb,1951

The Last Objective, Paul A. Carter, nv *Astounding* Aug,1946

The Last of the Dragons, Edith Nesbit, ss,1900

The Last of the Masters, Philip K. Dick, nv *Orbit* #5,1954

The Last One of the Season, Mercedes R. Lackey, ss *American Fantasy* Win,1987

The Last Shuttle, Isaac Asimov, ss,1981

The Last Specimen, Joan Aiken, ss

The Last Super Bowl, George R.R. Martin, nv *Gallery* Feb,1975

The Last Time, Joel Rosenberg, ss **Friends of the Horseclans**, ed. Robert Adams & Pamela Crippen Adams, Signet,1987

The Last Trip, Archie Binns, ss *Weird Tales* Aug,1925

The Last Wolf, Karl Edward Wagner, ss *Midnight Sun* #2,1975

The Last, the Very Last [also as "The Time Machine"], Ray Bradbury, ss *Reporter* Jun 2,1955

The Laurel and Hardy Theory of Consciousness, Colin Wilson, ar

Lavender, Robert D. San Souci, ss **Short & Shivery**, Doubleday,1987

Law of Averages, Wendy Webb, ss **Shadows** #10, ed. Charles L. Grant,1987

The Lawns of Summer, Ray Bradbury, ss *Nation's Business* Feb,1952

Layers of Meaning, Brian M. Stableford, ss *Interzone* #21,1987

The Leading Edge, Anonymous, br **New Destinies** v1, ed. Jim Baen, Baen,1987

The Leading Edge, Roland J. Green, br **New Destinies** v2, ed. Jim Baen, Baen,1987

The Leaf-Sweeper, Muriel Spark, ss,1966

Leakage, Wim Burkunk, ss *SF International* #1,1987

Leaks, Steve Rasnic Tem, ss **Whispers** #6, ed. Stuart David Schiff,1987

Learning Curve, David Drake, nv **Angels in Hell**, ed. Janet Morris, Baen,1987

Learning from Viet Nam, David Chanoff & Doan Van Toai, ar *Encounter* Sep,1982

The Learning of Eeshta, F.M. Busby, ss *If* Oct,1973

The Leash, Pamela Sargent, ss *Twilight Zone* Apr,1987

The Leather Funnel, Arthur Conan Doyle, ss *The Strand* Jun,1903

Leave Them Raving, David Daniel, vi *The Horror Show* Jan,1987

The Left Eye of God, Ardath Mayhar, vi *Salarius* v1#4,1987

Left or Right?, Martin Gardner, ss *Esquire*,1951

Left to Right, Isaac Asimov, vi *Analog* Jan,1987

Left to Right, and Beyond, Isaac Asimov & Harrison Roth, vi *Analog* Jul,1987

The Left-Handed Muse, Lewis Shiner, bg **All About Strange Monsters of the Recent Past**, Kansas City, MO: Ursus Imprints,1987

A Left-Handed Profession [also as "The Counterfeit Conman"], Albert F. Nussbaum, ss *Alfred Hitchcock's Mystery Magazine* Nov,1975

Legacy, Terence M. Green, ss *F&SF* Mar,1985

The Legacy, Tracy Hickman & Margaret Weis, na **DragonLance Tales** v1, Margaret Weis & Tracy Hickman, TSR,1987

The Legal Problems of a Thieves' World, Darwin Bromley, ar *American Fantasy* Spr,1987

A Legend of Fair Women, John Morressy, nv *F&SF* Sep,1987

The Legend of Joe Lee, John D. MacDonald, ss *Cosmopolitan* Oct,1964

The Legend of Madame Krasinska, Vernon Lee, nv **Vanitas**, Heinemann: London,1892

Legitimate Lady, or I Stash My Cash Behind My Golden Door, Bill Costley, vi *Pulpsmith* Win,1987

The Lesser Magic, Gregory Kusnick, nv *Analog* Apr,1987

Lesser Myths of Milwaukee, Don Webb, vi *New Pathways* Apr,1987

Lester Dent and Lynn Lash: An Introduction, Will Murray, in

Let Loose, Mary Cholmondeley, ss,1898

'Let us Now Praise Unknown Women and Our Mothers who Begat Us', Sara Maitland, ss **Stepping Out**, Oosthuizen,1986

Lethe Dreams, Bentley Little, ss *Night Cry* v2#3,1987

A Letter from a Lady, Richard Wilson, ss **The Kid from Ozone Park and Other Stories**, Drumm,1987

A Letter from Bubba: Extraterrestrials, Hollis Fletcher, ss *Amazing* Jul,1987

A Letter from the Clearys, Connie Willis, ss *IASFM* Jul,1982

Letter from Tomorrow, Poul Anderson, ss *Analog* Aug,1987

Letter to a Grandchild, Robert Frazier, pm *IASFM* Apr,1987

A Letter to Patricia Warrick from Philip Dick, Philip K. Dick, lt Sep 11,1978

A Letter to Scott Apel from Philip Dick, Philip K. Dick, lt Aug 8,1980

Letters, The Readers, lt

Letters, The Readers, lt *American Fantasy* Sum,1987

Letters, The Readers, lt *IASFM* Jan,1987

Letters, The Readers, lt *IASFM* Feb,1987

Letters, The Readers, lt *IASFM* Mar,1987

Letters, The Readers, lt *IASFM* Apr,1987

Letters, The Readers, lt *IASFM* May,1987

Letters, The Readers, lt *IASFM* Jun,1987

Letters, The Readers, lt *IASFM* Jul,1987

Letters, The Readers, lt *IASFM* Aug,1987

Letters, The Readers, lt *IASFM* Sep,1987

Letters, The Readers, lt *IASFM* Oct,1987

Letters, The Readers, lt *IASFM* Nov,1987

Letters, The Readers, lt *IASFM* Dec,1987

Letters, The Readers, lt *IASFM* mid-Dec,1987

Letters, The Readers, lt *Interzone* #22,1987

Letters, The Readers, lt *Twilight Zone* Apr,1987

Letters, The Readers, lt *Twilight Zone* Dec,1987

Letters From Home, Karen Joy Fowler, ss **In the Field of Fire**, ed. Jeanne Van Buren Dann & Jack M. Dann, Tor,1987

Letters from Laura, Mildred Clingerman, ss *F&SF* Oct,1954

Letters to Mother, Chet Williamson, ss *F&SF* Apr,1987

Lewis and Clark and After, Ursula K. Le Guin, pm *The Seattle Review* Sum,1987

Liberty Port, David Drake, na **Free Lancers**, ed. Elizabeth Mitchell, Baen,1987

The Liberty Watchers, Sidney Bernard, ar *Pulpsmith* Win,1987

The Lieutenant and the Folksinger, Ben Bova, ss **Maxwell's Demons**,1978

Life, Piers Anthony, ss *Twilight Zone* Dec,1987

The Life and Times of Nick Smith, Nick Smith, pi *Salarius* v1#4,1987

Life Assurance, Lynn Abbey, nv **Fever Season**, ed. C.J. Cherryh, DAW,1987

Life Hutch, Harlan Ellison, ss *If* Apr,1956

A Life in the Day of, Robert R. McCammon, ss **Night Visions** #4,1987

Life with Rod, Bob Rosenbaum & Carol Serling, iv *Twilight Zone* Apr,1987

Life-Line, Robert A. Heinlein, ss *Astounding* Aug,1939

Lifeguard, Doug Beason, nv **New Destinies** v1, ed. Jim Baen, Baen,1987

Ligdan and the Young Pretender, Walter Jon Williams, nv **There Will Be War** v6, ed. Jerry E. Pournelle,1987

Light Fantastic, Eluki bes Shahar, ss *Amazing* Mar,1987

The Light of Darkness, Arthur C. Clarke, ss *Playboy* Jun,1966

Light of Other Days, Bob Shaw, ss *Analog* Aug,1966

"Light of Other Days": Beyond the Radius of Capture, Robert Silverberg, ar,1987

The Light Princess, George MacDonald, nv

Light Reading, John Devin, pm *Amazing* Jan,1987

Lightning Rod, W.R. Thompson, nv *Analog* Aug,1987

LIGHTS OUT

Lights Out [from **Swan Song**], Robert R. McCammon, ex Pocket: New York,1987

Like Clockwork, Stephen Gallagher, ss *F&SF* Mar,1987

Like Shadows in the Dark, Stephen Gallagher, ss **Shadows** #10, ed. Charles L. Grant,1987

Lilith's, Ramsey Campbell, ss **The Mayflower Book of Black Magic Stories** #5, ed. Michael Parry,1976

Limb Still Kicking from a Stillborn Novel, Bruce Boston, ss *Gallimaufry* #7,1976

Limits, David Lunde, pm *IASFM* Feb,1986

Lineage, John F. Moore, vi *Salarius* v1#4,1987

The Lion, the Witch and the Wardrobe, C.S. Lewis, n. The Blakiston Co.: Philadelphia,1950

The Lions Are Asleep This Night, Howard Waldrop, nv *Omni* Aug,1986

Liquid Assets, Dean Ing, ss **Destinies** v1#4, ed. James Baen,1979

The Liquor Cabinet of Dr. Malikudzu, Marc Laidlaw, ss *Night Cry* v2#4,1987

List of Contributors, [Misc. Material], bg

Listen to the Music in My Hands, Charles L. Grant, ss *Twilight Zone* Feb,1987

Litany for Dictatorships, Stephen Vincent Benet, pm

The Litter, James Kisner, ss **Masques** #2, ed. J.N. Williamson,1987

The Little Black Bag, C.M. Kornbluth, nv *Astounding* Jul,1950

"The Little Black Bag": Press Button for Triple Bypass, Robert Silverberg, ar,1987

The Little Black Box, Philip K. Dick, nv *Worlds of Tomorrow* Aug,1964

The Little Blue Pill, Michael Lubow, ss *Playboy* Apr,1987

Little Claus and Big Claus, Hans Christian Andersen, ss

The Little Creeps, Walter M. Miller, Jr., nv *Amazing* Dec,1951

Little Daylight, George MacDonald, ss **Works of Fancy and Imagination**,1871

Little Doors, Paul Di Filippo, nv *Night Cry* v2#5,1987

A Little Elevator Music, Dennis Holmberg, ss *2AM* Spr,1987

A Little Further Up the Fox..., George M. Ewing, nv *IASFM* Apr,1987

Little Green Men, Barry B. Longyear, ss **Spaceships & Spells**, ed. Jane Yolen, Martin H. Greenberg & Charles G. Waugh, Harper & Row,1987

The Little Lamb, Fredric Brown, ss *Manhunt* Aug,1953

Little Magazine That Could, Eric M. Heideman, ed *Tales of the Unanticipated* #2,1987

The Little Magic Shop, Bruce Sterling, ss *IASFM* Oct,1987

The Little Man Who Wasn't All There, Robert Bloch, ss *Fantastic Adventures* Aug,1942

The Little Match Girl, Hans Christian Andersen, vi

The Little Mermaid, Hans Christian Andersen, nv

The Little Movement, Philip K. Dick, ss *F&SF* Nov,1952

Little Myth Marker, Robert Lynn Asprin, n. The Donning Company/Publishers: Norfolk & Virginia Beach, VA,1985

A Little of What You Fancy, Mary Catherine McDaniel, ss **L. Ron Hubbard Presents Writers of the Future** v3, ed. Algis Budrys, Bridge,1987

Little People, Colleen Drippe', ss *Apex!* #1,1987

A Little Piece of Home, Dorothy Davies, ss *SF International* #1,1987

The Little Puppy That Could, Martin Amis, nv *The Literary Review*

Little Red Riding Hood, Olga Broumas, pm **Beginning With O**, New Haven, CT: Yale Univ. Press,1977

A Little Something for Us Tempunauts, Philip K. Dick, nv **Final Stage**, ed. Edward L. Ferman & Barry N. Malzberg, Charterhouse,1974

A Little Thing, Stan Rogal, ss **Tesseracts 2**, ed. Phyllis Gotlieb & Douglas Barbour, Press Porcepic: Victoria,1987

A Little Tour of Hell, Josephine Saxton, ss **Little Tours of Hell**, Pandora,1986

Little White Mongrel, Paul Christopher, ss **Beyond That River**, Pal Books,1987

The Living Dead [also as "Underground"], Robert Bloch, ss *Ellery Queen's Mystery Magazine* Apr,1967

Living Donor, Marthayn Pelegrimas, ss *SPWAO Showcase* #6,1987

Living Fire, Nicholas Fisk, ss **Living Fire and Other S.F. Stories**, Corgi: London,1987

Living in a World of Maps, Orson Scott Card, aw

Living in the Jungle, Martha Soukup, ss **L. Ron Hubbard Presents Writers of the Future** v3, ed. Algis Budrys, Bridge,1987

The Living Mist [also as "We, the Mist"], Ralph Milne Farley, nv *Amazing* Aug,1940

The Living Stone, E.R. Punshon, ss *The Cornhill Magazine* Sep,1939

The Lizard, the Dragon, and the Eater of Souls, Rick Shelley, nv *Analog* Sep,1987

Lizzie Borden Took an Axe, Robert Bloch, ss *Weird Tales* Nov,1946

Lo, How an Oak E'er Blooming, Suzette Haden Elgin, ss *F&SF* Feb,1986

Lob's Girl, Joan Aiken, ss

Local Colour, Arthur Machen, ar *Literature* Apr 23,1898

A Lock of Satan's Hair, Fredric Brown, nv *Dime Mystery Magazine* Jan,1943

Locking Up, John Maclay, ss *Night Cry* v2#1,1986

The Locusts, Ray Bradbury, vi **The Martian Chronicles**,1950

Logic Loop, Stephen Paulsen, vi *Aphelion* #5,1987

Logic of Empire, Robert A. Heinlein, nv *Astounding* Mar,1941

The Logical Life, Hal Clement, ss **Stellar** #1, ed. Judy-Lynn del Rey,1974

The Loneliness of the Long-Distance Writer, Lesley Choyce, ss *Orion* v1#2,1982

The Lonely Songs of Laren Dorr, George R.R. Martin, nv *Fantastic* May,1976

Lonelyache, Harlan Ellison, ss *Knight* Jul,1964

Long Knives, J.R. Dunn, nv **L. Ron Hubbard Presents Writers of the Future** v3, ed. Algis Budrys, Bridge,1987

The Long Rain [Death-by-Rain], Ray Bradbury, ss *Planet Stories* Sum,1950

The Long Remembering, Poul Anderson, ss *F&SF* Nov,1957

Long Shot, Vernor Vinge, ss *Analog* Aug,1972

The Long Watch, Robert A. Heinlein, ss *American Legion Magazine* Dec,1949

The Long Way Home, Fred Saberhagen, ss *Galaxy* Jun,1961

The Long Years [also as "Dwellers in Silence"], Ray Bradbury, ss *Maclean's* Sep 15,1948

Long, Long Ago, R. Chetwynd-Hayes, nv **Tales from the Shadows**, Kimber,1986

The Longest Science-Fiction Story Ever Told, Arthur C. Clarke, ss **The Wind from the Sun**, HBJ,1972

Longtooth, Edgar Pangborn, nv *F&SF* Jan,1970

Loony Toon, Bentley Little, vi *The Horror Show* Fll,1987

Lord of Hosts, Connie Willis, vi *Omni* Jun,1987

Lord of the Worms, Brian Lumley, na *Weirdbook* #17,1983

Lord Toede's Disastrous Hunt, Harold Bakst, nv **DragonLance Tales** v2, Margaret Weis & Tracy Hickman, TSR,1987

Loren Eiseley's Time Passages, Robert Frazier, pm *IASFM* mid-Dec,1982

Losing Souls to California Dreaming, Roger L. Dutcher, pm *IASFM* Sep,1987

Lost Eons, Lawrence Harding, pm *Space & Time* #72,1987

Lost Exits, Karl Edward Wagner, ss **Why Not You and I?**, Dark Harvest,1987

Lost Face, Jack London, ss *New York Herald* Dec 13,1908

Lost in Translation, Dean Ing, ss **Far Frontiers** v1, ed. Jerry Pournelle & Jim Baen,1985

The Lost Legion, Rudyard Kipling, ss *The Strand* May,1892

The Lost Secret, Laurence M. Janifer, nv **The Best of Omni** #5,1983

Lost Soul, Jay Sheckley, ss **Devils & Demons**, ed. Marvin Kaye, SFBC/Doubleday,1987

The Lost Years of Cosmology, Dr. John Gribbin, ar *Analog* Dec,1987

Lot No. 249, Arthur Conan Doyle, nv *Harper's* Sep,1892

Louis, R. Chetwynd-Hayes, nv **The House of Dracula**, Kimber,1987

Loulou; or The Domestic Life of the Language, Margaret Atwood, nv *Science Fiction Story-Reader*

The Loup-Garou, Robert D. San Souci, ss **Short & Shivery**, Doubleday,1987

Love (Ash I), Poppy Z. Brite, ss *The Horror Show* Fll,1987

Love and Ale, Nick O'Donohoe, nv **DragonLance Tales** v1, Margaret Weis & Tracy Hickman, TSR,1987

Love and the Tiddlywinks, Martin Gardner, vi *Esquire* Sep,1949

Love at the 99th Percentile, Christopher Gilbert, ss *F&SF* Nov,1987

Love Bytes, Nicholas Fisk, ss **Twisted Circuits**, ed. Mick Gowar, Beaver,1987

The Love Chapter [from "Journal of a Plebian Witch"], Martha Waters, ex **Hear the Silence**, ed. Irene Zahava, Crossing Press,1986

The Love Charm, J.B. Stamper, ss **More Tales for the Midnight Hour**, Apple/Scholastic,1987

Love Comes to the Middleman, Marc Laidlaw, ss **Mathenauts**, ed. Rudy Rucker, Arbor House,1987

Love in Bloom, Laurence M. Janifer, ss *Analog* mid-Dec,1984

Love is a Circle, R.A. Sass, vi *2AM* Sum,1987

Love Laughs at Locks, Gary Gygax, nv **Night Arrant**, Ace/New Infinities,1987

Love Sickness, Part 1, Geoff Ryman, sl *Interzone* #20,1987

Love Sickness, Part 2, Geoff Ryman, sl *Interzone* #21,1987

A Love Song for Jerry Falwell, Harlan Ellison, ar,1984

The Love Song of Laura Morrison, Jerry Oltion, ss *Analog* Aug,1987

Love That Universe, Arthur C. Clarke, ss *Escapade*,1961

LOVE-STARVED

Love-Starved, Charles L. Grant, ss *F&SF* Aug,1979

Loved Ones, Rane Arroyo, pm *Ice River* Sum,1987

Loveman's Comeback, Ramsey Campbell, nv **More Devil's Kisses**, ed. Linda Lovecraft, Corgi,1977

Lover, Leslie Halliwell, pm **A Demon Close Behind**, Robert Hale,1987

Lovers, Kevin Lenihan, ss *The Horror Show* Win,1987

The Lovers of Dismal Swamp, Robert D. San Souci, ss **Short & Shivery**, Doubleday,1987

The Loves of Lady Coldpence, Martin Gardner, ss *Esquire* Mar,1948

Luella Miller, Mary E. Wilkins Freeman, ss **The Wind in the Rose-Bush and Other Stories of the Supernatural**, Doubleday,1903

The Luggage Store, Ray Bradbury, vi **The Martian Chronicles**,1950

Lullaby for My Dyke and Her Cat, Sara Maitland, ss

Luminaries, Bruce Boston, pm **Aliens & Lovers**, ed. Millea Kenin, Unique Graphics,1983

Lumisland, Mary Caraker, ss *F&SF* Sep,1987

A Lunar Cycle, Peg Libertus, pm *Aboriginal SF* Feb,1987

Lunatic Bridge, Pat Cadigan, nv **The Omni Book of Science Fiction #5**, ed. Ellen Datlow,1987

Lunch at Etienne's, Nancy Etchemendy, ss *F&SF* Nov,1987

The Lycanthropist, Catherine Crowe, ss,1850

The Lysenko Maze, Donald A. Wollheim, ss *F&SF* Jul,1954

M.R. James on Ghost Stories, M.R. James, ar

M.Y.T.H. Inc. Link, Robert Lynn Asprin, n. The Donning Company/Publishers: Norfolk & Virginia Beach, VA,1986

The Machine Age, Paul Gooding, ss **Gollancz - Sunday Times Best SF Stories**, Gollancz,1987

The Machine Man of Ardathia, Francis Flagg, ss *Amazing* Nov,1927

The Machine That Won the War, Isaac Asimov, ss *F&SF* Oct,1961

Mackintosh Willy, Ramsey Campbell, ss **Shadows #2**, ed. Charles L. Grant,1979

Mad City Beneath the Sands, Richard Paul Russo, ss *Twilight Zone* Oct,1987

The Mad Poet's Magic Fails, Lisa Lepovetsky, pm *2AM* Spr,1987

Madame Guillotine, Paul Roland, sg **The Curious Case of Richard Fielding and Other Stories**, Lary Press,1987

Madberry Hill, Mark Valentine, ss **14 Bellchamber Tower**, Crimson Altar Press,1987

Madelaine, Paul Roland, sg **The Curious Case of Richard Fielding and Other Stories**, Lary Press,1987

A Madman, Maurice Level, vi

Madonna of the Red Sun, W. Warren Wagar, ss **Synergy** v1, ed. George Zebrowski,1987

A Madonna of the Trenches, Rudyard Kipling, ss *London Pall Mall Magazine* Sep,1924

Maelstrom II, Arthur C. Clarke, ss *Playboy* Apr,1965

Mage Reviews, Mage Staff, br *Mage* Spr,1987

Mage Reviews, Mage Staff, br *Mage* Win,1987

The Mage: A Retrospective, Jeffrey V. Yule, pi *Mage* Fll,1987

Maggie's Bite, Laurence Housman, ss,1947

The Magic, Frank LoProto, vi *2AM* Fll,1987

Magic - The Science of the Future [from **The Occult**], Colin Wilson, ar Random House: New York,1971

The Magic Fishbone, Charles Dickens, ss *Our Young Folks*,1868

Magic in a World of Magic, Anne Cameron, nv **Hear the Silence**, ed. Irene Zahava, Crossing Press,1986

Magic in the Streets, Robert Simpson, ar *Twilight Zone* Apr,1987

The Magic Kiss, Tony Bradman, ss **The Magic Kiss and Other Tales of Princes and Princesses**, Tony Bradman, Blackie,1987

Magic Lantern Show, Cory Glaberson, mr *American Fantasy* Spr,1987

Magic Lantern Show, Cory Glaberson, mr *American Fantasy* Sum,1987

Magic Lantern Show, Cory Glaberson, mr *American Fantasy* Win,1987

Magic Matter, Robert L. Forward, ar **New Destinies** v1, ed. Jim Baen, Baen,1987

The Magic of the Past, Brian W. Aldiss, nv **The Magic of the Past**, Kerosina,1987

Magic Trick, Ruth Berman, pm *Minnesota Fantasy Review #1*,1987

The Maid on the Shore, Delia Sherman, ss *F&SF* Oct,1987

Major Pugachov's Last Battle [from **Kolyma Tales**], Shalamov, ar

The Making of Dragons, Jane Yolen, pm *IASFM* Jun,1986

The Making of Revelation, Part I, Philip Jose Farmer, nv **After the Fall**, ed. Robert Sheckley, Ace,1980

A Malady of Magicks, Craig Shaw Gardner, n. Ace: New York pb Feb,1986

Malagan and the Lady of Rascas, Michael de Larrabeiti, ss **Elsewhere** v3, ed. Terri Winding & Mark Allan Arnold,1984

Malf, Dean Ing, nv **Analog Annual**, ed. Ben Bova, Pyramid,1976

The Malice of Inanimate Objects, M.R. James, ss *The Masquerade* Jun,1933

The Man, Ray Bradbury, ss *Thrilling Wonder Stories* Feb,1949

The Man and the Snake, Ambrose Bierce, ss **In the Midst of Life**, E.L.G. Steele: San Francisco CA,1891

The Man Eater, Ursula K. Le Guin, pm,1986

The Man I'll Never Be, Doug Beason, ss *Amazing* May,1987

The Man in the Underpass, Ramsey Campbell, ss **The Year's Best Horror Stories #3**,1975

Man o' Dreams, Will F. McMorrow, ss *Argosy All-Story Weekly* Jan 5,1929

Man of Distinction, Fredric Brown, ss *Thrilling Wonder Stories* Feb,1951

Man of Parts, Horace L. Gold, ss **9 Tales of Space and Time**, ed. Raymond J. Healey, Holt,1954

The Man on the Mushroom, Harlan Ellison, in **Ellison Wonderland**, Paperback Library,1974

The Man Who Came Back, Edward D. Hoch, nv *Alfred Hitchcock's Mystery Magazine* May,1973

The Man Who Collected Bloch, Phillip C. Heath, ss *Eldritch Tales #13*,1987

The Man Who Cried "Wolf!", Robert Bloch, ss *Weird Tales* May,1945

The Man Who Devoured Literature, George Alec Effinger, ss *Twilight Zone* Apr,1987

The Man Who Did Tricks with Glass, Ron Wolfe, ss *Stardate* Apr,1986

The Man Who Drowned Puppies, Thomas Sullivan, ss **Masques #2**, ed. J.N. Williamson,1987

The Man Who Never Grew Young, Fritz Leiber, ss **Night's Black Agents**, Arkham,1947

The Man Who Painted the Dragon Griaule, Lucius Shepard, nv *F&SF* Dec,1984

The Man Who Saw the Future, Edmond Hamilton, ss *Amazing* Oct,1930

The Man Who Sold the Moon, Robert A. Heinlein, nv **The Man Who Sold the Moon**, Shasta,1950

The Man Who Walked on the Moon, J.G. Ballard, ss *Interzone #13*,1985

The Man Who Was a Cosmic String, Rudy Rucker, ss **Universe**, ed. Byron Preiss, Bantam Spectra,1987

The Man Who Was Heavily into Revenge, Harlan Ellison, ss *Analog* Aug,1978

The Man Who Wasn't There, Anonymous, pm

The Man Who Watched the Glaciers Run, Cherie Wilkerson, nv **Universe #17**, ed. Terry Carr,1987

The Man Who Wrote Shakespeare, E. Bertrand Loring, ss *F&SF* Jan,1987

The Man with the Dundreary Weepers, Leslie Halliwell, ss **A Demon Close Behind**, Robert Hale,1987

The Man with the Strange Head, Miles J. Breuer, M.D., ss *Amazing* Jan,1927

The Man-Eating Tree, Phil Robinson, ss **Under the Punkah**, Sampson Low Marsten Searle Rivington: London,1881

Man-Mountain Gentian, Howard Waldrop, ss *Omni* Sep,1983

Man-Size in Marble, Edith Nesbit, ss,1886

Manaspill, Dean Ing, na **The Magic May Return**, ed. Larry Niven,1981

Mandikini, Gregory Benford, ss **Universe**, ed. Byron Preiss, Bantam Spectra,1987

Mandrake, Caralyn Inks, nv **Magic in Ithkar #4**, ed. Andre Norton & Robert Adams,1987

Mandrake, Kelvin I. Jones, ss **After Midnight Stories #3**,1987

Mandy Larkin, Katherine V. Forrest, ss **Dreams and Swords**, Naiad,1987

The Mangler, Stephen King, nv *Cavalier* Dec,1972

Manly Wade Wellman, Karl Edward Wagner, bg *Fantasy Tales #16*,1986

Manly Wade Wellman: A Biography, Karl Edward Wagner, bg *The Horror Show* Spr,1987

The Manse, J.C. Trewin, ss **After Midnight Stories #3**,1987

Many Mansions, Robert Silverberg, nv **Universe #3**, ed. Terry Carr,1973

Marcus, R. Chetwynd-Hayes, nv **Dracula's Children**, Kimber,1987

Marie Curie Contemplating the Role of Women Scientists in the Glow of a Beaker, Robert Frazier, pm *IASFM* mid-Dec,1987

Marikova, R. Chetwynd-Hayes, nv **The House of Dracula**, Kimber,1987

Marion's Wall, Jack Finney, n. Simon & Schuster: New York,1973

Marionettes, Inc., Ray Bradbury, ss *Startling Stories* Mar,1949

The Mark of the Beast, Rudyard Kipling, ss *The Pioneer* Jul 12,1890

Markheim, Robert Louis Stevenson, ss *The Broken Shaft, Unwin's Annual Chr*,1885

Marriages, John Maclay, pm *Scavenger's Newsletter*

Mars-Tube [as by S.D. Gottesman], C.M. Kornbluth & Frederik Pohl, ss *Astonishing Stories* Sep,1941

Marsyas in Flanders, Vernon Lee, ss,1900

Marta's Cat, Bob Warner, vi *2AM* Spr,1987

Martha, Fred Saberhagen, vi *Amazing* Dec,1976

THE MARTIAN

The Martian [Impossible], Ray Bradbury, ss *Super Science Stories* Nov,1949

The Martian Chronicles, Ray Bradbury, co Doubleday: Garden City, NY,1950

Martians Come in Clouds, Philip K. Dick, ss *Fantastic Universe* Jun,1954

Martyr Without Canon, t. Winter-Damon, pm *Grue* #4,1987

The Mask, J.B. Stamper, ss **More Tales for the Midnight Hour**, Apple/Scholastic,1987

Masks, Jeff Johnston, ss *2AM* Spr,1987

Mason's Life, Kingsley Amis, ss *The Sunday Times*,1972

Masque of the Red Death, Edgar Allan Poe, ss *Graham's Lady's and Gentleman's Magazine* May,1842

Master of the Courts, Andrew James Purdy, nv *Pulpsmith* Win,1987

Master of the Game, Martha Soukup, ss *F&SF* Nov,1987

The Master of the House, Oliver Onions, ss **The Painted Face**, Heinemann,1929

The Master of Time, J. John Chevalier, ss *Space & Time* #73,1987

Masters of the Void, Paul Christopher, ss **Beyond That River**, Pal Books,1987

Matchsticks, David B. Silva, vi *Eldritch Tales* #13,1987

"A mathematical formula is a hymn of the universe.", Robert Frazier, pm **Perception Barriers**, BPW&P: Berkeley CA,1987

Mathematician, Bruce Boston, pm *Star*Line*,1978

The Mathenauts, Norman Kagan, nv *If* Jul,1964

The Mating of the Storm Birds, Bruce Boston, pm **Aliens & Lovers**, ed. Millea Kenin, Unique Graphics,1983

A Matter of Condensation, W.C. Scotten, ss *Analog* Jan,1987

A Matter of Semantics, Wayne Allen Sallee, vi *Grue* #5,1987

A Matter of Trust, A Crazy Alien, ms *Aboriginal SF* Nov,1987

Matters of Opinion, Stanley Schmidt, ed *Analog* mid-Dec,1987

Maureen Birnbaum on the Art of War, George Alec Effinger, nv **Friends of the Horseclans**, ed. Robert Adams & Pamela Crippen Adams, Signet,1987

Maurice and Mog, James Herbert, ss **Masques #2**, ed. J.N. Williamson,1987

Max Weber's War, Robert A. Frezza, ss *Amazing* Jan,1987

Maxie Silas, Augustine Funnell, ss *F&SF* Jun,1987

The Maxwell Equations, Anatoly Dnieprov, ss **Destination: Amaltheia**, ed. Richard Dixon, Moscow: Foreign Languages Publishing House,1963

May's Lion, Ursula K. Le Guin, ss *The Little Magazine* v14#1,1983

Maybe a Love Poem for my Friend, Sara Maitland, pm

The Maze and the Monster, Edward D. Hoch, ss *The Magazine of Horror* Aug,1963

Mazes, Ursula K. Le Guin, ss **Epoch**, ed. Roger Elwood & Robert Silverberg, Berkley,1975

Me 'n' Isaac at the Movies, Harlan Ellison, ar *IASFM* Nov,1987

Me and Flapjack and the Martians, Fredric Brown & Mack Reynolds, ss *Astounding* Dec,1952

Me Pal Jonesy, Dick Davies, cs *The Horror Show* Spr,1987

Me, Tree, Morgan Llywelyn, ss **Devils & Demons**, ed. Marvin Kaye, SFBC/Doubleday,1987

The Meadow, Ray Bradbury, ss **Best One Act Plays**,1948

Measures for a Coffin, Kenneth Robeson, na *Doc Savage* Jan,1946

Meddler, Philip K. Dick, ss *Future* Oct,1954

The Meeting, C.M. Kornbluth & Frederik Pohl, ss *F&SF* Nov,1972

Meeting Mr. Singleton, Derek Stanford, ss **After Midnight Stories #3**,1987

A Meeting with Medusa, Arthur C. Clarke, na *Playboy* Dec,1971

Megamouse, Jay Sheckley, ss *Night Cry* v2#5,1987

A Member of the Family, Muriel Spark, ss *Mademoiselle* Feb,1961

Members Only, Bruce Jones, nv **Twisted Tales**, San Diego: Blackthorne,1987

Memento Mori, Joseph Kosiewska, ss *Pulpsmith* Win,1987

The Memetic Menace, Stanley Schmidt, ed *Analog* Aug,1987

Memetics and the Modular Mind--Modeling the Development of Social Movements, H. Keith Henson, ar *Analog* Aug,1987

A Memoir of Nuclear Winter, Tony Rothman, ar *Analog* Nov,1987

The Memorial, Kim Stanley Robinson, ss **In the Field of Fire**, ed. Jeanne Van Buren Dann & Jack M. Dann, Tor,1987

Memorial, Theodore Sturgeon, ss *Astounding* Apr,1946

Memorial Service, Leslie Halliwell, ss **A Demon Close Behind**, Robert Hale,1987

Memories of the Body, Lisa Tuttle, ss *Interzone* #22,1987

Memory, Isaac Asimov, ed *IASFM* Dec,1987

A Memory of John W. Campbell, Randall Garrett, bg,1968

The Men and Women of Rivendale, Steve Rasnic Tem, ss **Night Visions #1**,1984

Men of Fear, Kenneth Robeson, na *Doc Savage* Feb,1942

The Menace from Earth, Robert A. Heinlein, ss *F&SF* Aug,1957

Menage a Super-Trois, Felix C. Gotschalk, ss *F&SF* May,1987

Mencken Stuff, Joel Richards, ss **Universe #17**, ed. Terry Carr,1987

Mengele, Lucius Shepard, ss **Universe #15**, ed. Terry Carr,1985

The Mercenary, Antonio Bellomi, ss *SF International* #2,1987

Merchant Dying, Paul A. Gilster, ss *Aboriginal SF* Jul,1987

Mercy Worse Than None, John Brunner, nv **Aftermath**, ed. Robert Lynn Asprin & Lynn Abbey, Ace,1987

Merlina and the Colored Ice, Martin Gardner, ss *A.D.* Fll,1951

Mermaids, Fred Croft, pm *Eldritch Tales* #13,1987

Merovan Ecology, [Misc. Material], ms **Fever Season**, ed. C.J. Cherryh, DAW,1987

Merovan Sea Floor and Hemispheric Maps, Pat Tobin, il

Merovingian Ecology, Mercedes R. Lackey, ms **Festival Moon**, ed. C.J. Cherryh, DAW,1987

Merovingian City Maps, Pat Tobin, il

Merovingian City Maps and Merovin Hemispheric Maps, Pat Tobin, il **Festival Moon**, ed. C.J. Cherryh, DAW,1987

Merry May, Ramsey Campbell, nv **Scared Stiff**, Los Angeles: Scream/Press,1987

Message Found in a Copy of **Flatland**, Rudy Rucker, ss **The 57th Franz Kafka**, Ace,1983

A Message from Charity, William M. Lee, ss *F&SF* Nov,1967

Message Intercepted On Hyperspatial Frequency, Wade Tarzia, vi *Mage* Win,1987

The Messenger, Rosalind Warren, ss *F&SF* Jun,1987

Messiah, John Gregory Betancourt, ss *Amazing* May,1987

The Metal Man, Jack Williamson, ss *Amazing* Dec,1928

Metal, Like Rain, Michael Ponder, ss *Space & Time* #73,1987

Metanoia, David B. Silva, ss *New Blood* #1,1987

Meteors, Stephen Richard, ss **Gollancz - Sunday Times Best SF Stories**, Gollancz,1987

The Mezzotint, M.R. James, ss **Ghost Stories of an Antiquary**,1904

MHD, Ben Bova, ar **Battle Station**, Tor,1987

Michael Moorcock, Michael Moorcock & Chris Reed, iv *Back Brain Recluse* #7,1987

Michael Whelan, Dale Johnson & Michael Whelan, iv *American Fantasy* Sum,1987

The Middle Toe of the Right Foot, Ambrose Bierce, ss **In the Midst of Life**, E.L.G. Steele: San Francisco CA,1891

Middle Woman, Orson Scott Card, ss

Midnight Hobo, Ramsey Campbell, ss **Nightmares**, ed. Charles L. Grant, Playboy,1979

The Midnight Mass of the Dead, Robert D. San Souci, ss **Short & Shivery**, Doubleday,1987

A Midnight Visitor, John Kendrick Bangs, ss *Harper's Weekly* Dec 10,1892

Midnights, Charles L. Grant, br *American Fantasy* Spr,1987

Midnights, Charles L. Grant, br *American Fantasy* Sum,1987

Midnights, Charles L. Grant, br *American Fantasy* Win,1987

Milk from a Maiden's Breast, Elizabeth Ann Scarborough, ss **Tales of the Witch World**, ed. Andre Norton, St. Martin's,1987

The Milk of Knowledge, Ian Watson, ss *Aboriginal SF* Sep,1987

Millennium, Ben Bova, n. Random House: New York,1976

Millennium, Fredric Brown, vi *F&SF* Mar,1955

The Million Dollar Day, Kevin O'Donnell, Jr., nv *Analog* Oct,1987

The Million-Dollar Wound, Dean Whitlock, ss *F&SF* Jan,1987

The Million-Year Picnic, Ray Bradbury, ss *Planet Stories* Sum,1946

The Mindless Monsters, Kenneth Robeson, na *Doc Savage* Sep,1941

Mindrace, James B. Livingstone, pm *Mage* Spr,1986

Mindsword, Robert Randolph Medcalf, Jr., pm *Space & Time* #72,1987

The Mindworm, C.M. Kornbluth, ss *Worlds Beyond* Dec,1950

Minor Ingredient, Eric Frank Russell, ss *Astounding* Mar,1956

The Minority Report, Philip K. Dick, ss *Fantastic Universe* Jan,1956

Minuke, Nigel Kneale, ss *Harper's* Sep,1950

Minutes of the Last Meeting at Olduvai, Steven R. Boyett, vi *Aboriginal SF* Nov,1987

The Miracle Man, Paul Roland, ss **The Curious Case of Richard Fielding and Other Stories**, Lary Press,1987

Miracle of the Flowers, David R. Bunch, ss *Pulpsmith* Win,1987

The Miracle of the Lily, Clare Winger Harris, nv *Amazing* Apr,1928

The Miracle-Workers, Jack Vance, na *Astounding* Jul,1958

The Mirror Monster, Stephen Meade, ss *Night Cry* v2#3,1987

The Mirror of Nitocris, Brian Lumley, ss **The Caller of the Black**, Arkham,1971

Mirror of Prometheus, Andrew Joron, pm

Mirror Trick, Janet Fox, ss *Tales of the Unanticipated* #2,1987

MIRROR, MIRROR

Mirror, Mirror [The Mirror], Alan E. Nourse, nv *Fantastic* Jun,1960

Misadjustment, Philip K. Dick, ss *Science Fiction Quarterly* Feb,1957

Misconception, F.M. Busby, ss *Vertex* Apr,1975

Misfit, Robert A. Heinlein, ss *Astounding* Nov,1939

Miss Attila the Hun, Dean R. Koontz, nv **Night Visions** #4,1987

Miss Cornelius, W.F. Harvey, ss **The Beast With Five Fingers**, J.M. Dent,1928

Miss de Mannering of Asham, F.M. Mayor, ss **The Room Opposite**, Longmans, Green: London,1935

Miss Manning's Angelic Moment, Sara Maitland, ss

Miss Mouse and the Fourth Dimension, Robert Sheckley, ss *Twilight Zone* Dec,1981

Miss Pinkerton's Apocalypse, Muriel Spark, ss,1958

The Missing Dumbell, S.M. Secula, ss *Haunts* #9,1987

Mist-Thoughts (Lyrics), Mercedes R. Lackey, sg **Fever Season**, ed. C.J. Cherryh, DAW,1987

Mist-Thoughts (Music), C.J. Cherryh, sg **Fever Season**, ed. C.J. Cherryh, DAW,1987

The Mistress in Black, Rosemary Timperley, ss **Ghost Book** #5, ed. Aidan Chambers/James Turner,1969

Mistress of the Blood-Drinkers, Ralston Shields, na *Horror Stories* Mar,1940

Mistress Sary, William Tenn, ss *Weird Tales* May,1947

Mitkey Rides Again, Fredric Brown, nv *Planet Stories* Nov,1950

Mobius, Richard Christian Matheson, ss **Scars**, Scream/Press,1987

Moby Dick II; or The Missile Whale, Patricia Highsmith, ss **Tales of Natural and Unnatural Catastrophes**, Bloomsbury,1987

Modern History, Philip St. Leger, ss **Gollancz - Sunday Times Best SF Stories**, Gollancz,1987

Moist Dreams, Stanley Wiater, ss **Masques** #2, ed. J.N. Williamson,1987

The Mold of Yancy, Philip K. Dick, nv *If* Aug,1955

The Mole Men Want Your Eyes, Frederick C. Davis, na *Horror Stories* Apr,1938

Mom, Harlan Ellison, nv *Silver Foxes* Aug,1976

The Moment of the Magician, Alan Dean Foster, n. Phantasia: West Bloomfield, MI hc Sep,1984

The Moment of the Rose, Cherie Wilkerson, ss *IASFM* Feb,1987

The Monkey, Stephen King, nv *Gallery* Nov,1980

The Monkey Treatment, George R.R. Martin, nv *F&SF* Jul,1983

Monkshood Manor, L.P. Hartley, ss **The White Wand and Other Stories**, Hamilton,1954

Monster, Nicholas Fisk, ss,1984

The Monster and the Moon, Bruce Boston, ss *Fiction Magazine* #4,1973

The "Monster Mash" Quiz, A.R. Morlan, qz *The Horror Show* Win,1987

The Monster Matinee, Charles G. Waugh, in

Monster Squad, Anonymous, mr *American Fantasy* Sum,1987

Monsters, Jean Reitz, ss **L. Ron Hubbard Presents Writers of the Future** v3, ed. Algis Budrys, Bridge,1987

The Monsters, Robert Sheckley, ss *F&SF* Mar,1953

"The Monsters": Don't Forget to Kill Your Wife, Robert Silverberg, ar,1987

Mood Wendigo, Thomas A. Easton, ss *Analog* May,1980

The Moon and Michelangelo, Ian Watson, nv *IASFM* Oct,1987

Moon and the Devil, Lawrence C. Connolly, ss *The Horror Show* Spr,1987

Moon Boats Taken from the Earth, Joey Froehlich, pm *Space & Time* #72,1987

Moon Mirror, Andre Norton, ss **Hecate's Cauldron**, ed. Susan M. Shwartz, DAW,1982

The Moon of Montezuma, Cornell Woolrich, ss *Fantastic* Nov,1952

Moon of Popping Trees, R. Garcia y Robertson, nv *Amazing* Sep,1987

The Moon Ribbon, Jane Yolen, ss **The Moon Ribbon and Other Tales**, Curtis Brown, Ltd.,1976

Moon Rise, Anke M. Kriske, pm *Grue* #6,1987

Moonbase Orientation Manual I: Transport and Manufacturing, Ben Bova, ar *Analog* Jun,1987

Moonbase Orientation Manual II: Research and Recreation, Ben Bova, ar *Analog* Jul,1987

Moondo Bizarro, Phillip C. Jennings, nv **New Destinies** v2, ed. Jim Baen, Baen,1987

Moonflower, Melissa Mia Hall, ss **Shadows** #10, ed. Charles L. Grant,1987

Moonlighter, David S. Garnett, ss **Other Edens**, ed. Christopher Evans & Robert Holdstock, Unwin: London,1987

The Moonlit Road, Ambrose Bierce, ss **Can Such Things Be?**, Cassell: New York,1893

Moonwatcher, Steve Bowkett, pm *Star*Line* Sep,1986

Moral Fibre, Kingsley Amis, ss *Esquire*,1958

Moral Technology, Paul Heapy, ss **Gollancz - Sunday Times Best SF Stories**, Gollancz,1987

Morbid Descent, Billie Sue Mosiman, ss *2AM* Sum,1987

More Birds, J.M. Pickles, ss **The Pan Book of Horror Stories** #28, Pan,1987

More Sinned Against, Karl Edward Wagner, ss **In a Lonely Place**, Scream/Press,1984

Mortality, Rick Cook, ss *Analog* Jan,1987

The Most Incredible Thing, Hans Christian Andersen, ss

A Most Singular Specimen, Paul Roland, ss **The Curious Case of Richard Fielding and Other Stories**, Lary Press,1987

Mother by Protest [also as "Trespass"], Richard Matheson, nv *Fantastic* Oct,1953

Mother Goddess of the World, Kim Stanley Robinson, na *IASFM* Oct,1987

Mother Hag, Steve Rasnic Tem, ss *Grue* #5,1987

Mother Moon, Ann Cathey, pm *Salarius* v1#4,1987

Mother Was an Alien, Katherine V. Forrest, ss **Dreams and Swords**, Naiad,1987

Moulder of Monsters, G.T. Fleming-Roberts, ss *Terror Tales* Jul,1937

Mount St. Helens/Omphalos, Ursula K. Le Guin, pm **Wild Angels**, Capra Press,1975

The Mountain Cage, Pamela Sargent, nv Cheap Street: New Castle, VA,1983

Mountaineers Are Always Free, Avram Davidson, ss *F&SF* Oct,1987

Mouse, Fredric Brown, ss *Thrilling Wonder Stories* Jun,1949

The Mouser Goes Below, Fritz Leiber, ss *Whispers* #23,1987

Movie Preview: Raising Hell with Clive Barker, Douglas E. Winter, mr *Twilight Zone* Dec,1987

Moving Day, R. Chetwynd-Hayes, ss **After Midnight Stories** #3,1987

Moxon's Master, Ambrose Bierce, ss **Can Such Things Be?**, Cassell: New York,1893

Mr. Blandfoot's Picture, L.P. Hartley, nv **The White Wand and Other Stories**, Hamilton,1954

Mr. Costello, Hero, Theodore Sturgeon, nv *Galaxy* Dec,1953

Mr. Humphreys and His Inheritance, M.R. James, nv **More Ghost Stories of an Antiquary**, Arnold,1911

Mr. Hurrel's Tallboy, Philippa Pearce, ss **Who's Afraid? and Other Strange Stories**, Kestrel/Penguin,1986

Mr. Justice Harbottle, Joseph Sheridan Le Fanu, nv *Belgravia* Jan,1872

Mr. Koyama's Comet, Walter Jon Williams, ss **Wild Cards** v2, ed. George R.R. Martin, Bantam,1987

Mr. Mephisto, Paul Roland, ss **The Curious Case of Richard Fielding and Other Stories**, Lary Press,1987

Mr. Nobody, Anonymous, pm

Mr. Right, Richard Christian Matheson, vi *Whispers* #21,1984

Mr. Spaceship, Philip K. Dick, nv *Imagination* Jan,1953

Mr. Tallent's Ghost, Mary Webb, ss,1927

Mr. Valdoom's Backyard, John Wayne Burt, ss *Space & Time* #73,1987

Mr. Wizard, R.D. Davis, ss *Mage* Spr,1987

Mrs. Carteret Receives, L.P. Hartley, co,1971

Mrs. Carteret Receives, L.P. Hartley, nv

Mrs. T, Lisa Tuttle, ss *Amazing* Sep,1976

Mugger, Richard Christian Matheson, ss **Scars**, Scream/Press,1987

Mulligan [from **Stained Glass Rain**], Bruce Boston, ex *Berkeley Poets' Co-op* #2,1971

Multiple Origami, J.B. Allen, ss *Amazing* Jul,1987

Multiples, Robert Silverberg, ss *Omni* Oct,1983

A Multitude of Monsters, Craig Shaw Gardner, n. Ace: New York pb Sep,1986

The Mummy Murders, Lester Dent, na *Detective Dragnet* Dec,1932

Murder in Ten Easy Lessons, Fredric Brown, ss *Ten Detective Aces* May,1945

The Murderer, Ray Bradbury, ss *Argosy (UK)* Jun,1953

The Murderer's Song, Michael Moorcock, nv **Tales from the Forbidden Planet**, ed. Roz Kaveney, Titan,1987

Murderers Walk, Garry Kilworth, ss **Other Edens**, ed. Christopher Evans & Robert Holdstock, Unwin: London,1987

Mushroom Roulette, Jody Scott, ss **Tales from the Forbidden Planet**, ed. Roz Kaveney, Titan,1987

Mushrooms, Paul Christopher, nv **Beyond That River**, Pal Books,1987

Music, Christopher Karwowski, ar *Twilight Zone* Jun,1987

The Music Box, Sue Marra, pm *2AM* Spr,1987

The Music Master of Babylon, Edgar Pangborn, nv *Galaxy* Nov,1954

Music to Read 2AM by -- Contest Winner, [Misc. Material], ms *2AM* Sum,1987

A Musical Interlude [chapter 4 of **The Vampire Tapestry**], Suzy McKee Charnas, ex Simon & Schuster: New York,1980

The Musicians, Ray Bradbury, vi **The Martian Chronicles**,1950
Mutant Popcorn, Nick Lowe, mr *Interzone* #19,1987
Mutant Popcorn, Nick Lowe, mr *Interzone* #21,1987
Mutant Popcorn, Kim Newman, mr *Interzone* #20,1987
Mute Inglorious Tam, C.M. Kornbluth & Frederik Pohl, ss *F&SF* Oct,1974
MX Knows Best, Gordon R. Dickson, nv *Saturn* Jul,1957
My Aunt Margaret's Mirror, Sir Walter Scott, nv *The Keepsake*,1828
My Best Ever Holiday, Richard Spivack, ss **Gollancz - Sunday Times Best SF Stories**, Gollancz,1987
My Country 'Tis Not Only of Thee, Brian W. Aldiss, nv **In the Field of Fire**, ed. Jeanne Van Buren Dann & Jack M. Dann, Tor,1987
My Dead Dog, Bobby, Joe R. Lansdale, vi *The Horror Show* Sum,1987
My Dear Emily, Joanna Russ, nv *F&SF* Jul,1962
My Enemy's Enemy, Kingsley Amis, ss *Encounter*,1955
My Eyes, My Eyes Are Melting, Keith Allen Daniels, pm *Star*Line* Jan,1986
My Father, Harlan Ellison, ar *Los Angeles Free Press*,1972
My Favorite Murder, Ambrose Bierce, ss
My Life as a Born-Again Pig, Frederik Pohl, na **Synergy** v1, ed. George Zebrowski,1987
My Mother, Harlan Ellison, ar *Saint Louis Literary Supplement*,1976
My Name Is Dolly, William F. Nolan, ss **Whispers** #6, ed. Stuart David Schiff,1987
My Own True Ghost Story, Rudyard Kipling, ss *The Week's News* Feb 25,1888
Myron Chester and the Toads, James P. Blaylock, ss *IASFM* Feb,1987
The Mysterious Cemetery, Patricia Highsmith, ss **Tales of Natural and Unnatural Catastrophes**, Bloomsbury,1987
A Mysterious House, Algernon Blackwood, ss *Belgravia* Jul,1889
The Mysterious Mansion, Honore de Balzac, ss
Mysterious Smith, Martin Gardner, ss **The No-Sided Professor**, Prometheus,1987
The Mysterious Stranger, Anonymous, nv *Odds and Ends*,1860
Mystery Island, Kenneth Robeson, na *Doc Savage* Aug,1941
The Mystery of Beechcroft Farm, Elliott O'Donnell, ss *Pearson's*,1932
A Mystery of the Campagna, Anne Crawford, nv *Unwins's Annual*,1887
Myth-ing Persons, Robert Lynn Asprin, n. The Donning Company/Publishers: Norfolk & Virginia Beach, VA,1984
Nabuti: Warm Welcome to a UN Committee, Patricia Highsmith, ss **Tales of Natural and Unnatural Catastrophes**, Bloomsbury,1987
Nackles, Harlan Ellison, pl *Twilight Zone* Feb,1987
Nackles [as by Curt Clark], Donald E. Westlake, ss *F&SF* Jan,1964
Naiads, John Gawsworth, pm
Name and Number, Brian Lumley, nv *Kadath* Jul,1982
The Naming of Names, Ray Bradbury, vi **The Martian Chronicles**,1950
Nanny, Philip K. Dick, ss *Startling Stories* Spr,1955
Nanny, Michael P. Kube-McDowell, nv *Analog* Nov,1987
The Nanny, Thomas Wylde, nv *IASFM* Jul,1983
Nanotechnology, Eric Drexler & Chris Peterson, ar *Analog* mid-Dec,1987
Napkin Engineering, Roald Hoffman, pm *The Manhattan Review* Fll,1986
Narcissus Flower, Gerben Hellinga, Jr., ss *SF International* #2,1987
Narrow Escape from a Sauna, A Crazy Alien, ms *Aboriginal SF* Feb,1987
Nasty, Fredric Brown, vi *Playboy* Apr,1959
The Nasty Naughty Nazi Ninja Nudnik Elves, Joshua Quagmire, cs *Fantasy Book* Mar,1987
Nativity of Thought, Bruce Boston, pm
The Natural Way, Janet Lorimer, ss *2AM* Spr,1987
Naturally, Fredric Brown, vi *Beyond Fantasy Fiction* Sep,1954
The Nature of Hell, Chris Morris & Janet Morris, ss **Crusaders in Hell**, ed. Janet Morris, New York: Baen,1987
The Navigator, Andrew Joron, pm
Nazca Lines, Roger L. Dutcher & Robert Frazier, pm *IASFM* May,1987
The Neapolitan Bedroom, Alma Priestley, ss **After Midnight Stories** #3,1987
The Near Departed, Richard Matheson, vi **Masques** #2, ed. J.N. Williamson,1987
Necros, Brian Lumley, ss **After Midnight Stories** #2,1986
A Neighbour's Landmark, M.R. James, ss *The Eton Chronic* Mar 17,1924
Neighbourhood Watch, Greg Egan, ss *Aphelion* #5,1987
The Neighbours, Meg Buxton, ss **After Midnight Stories** #3,1987
Neither Brute Nor Human, Karl Edward Wagner, nv **World Fantasy Convention Program Book**,1983
Neither Rain Nor Weirdness, Jerry Oltion, ss *Analog* Nov,1987
Neither Rest nor Refuge, Ardath Mayhar, ss **Tales of the Witch World**, ed. Andre Norton, St. Martin's,1987
Neither Your Jenny Nor Mine, Harlan Ellison, ss *Knight* Apr,1964
Nellthu, Anthony Boucher, vi *F&SF* Aug,1955

A Neo-Canterbury Tale: The Hog Driver's Tale, James S. Dorr, pm *Fantasy Book* Jun,1986
Nereid, Peni Robinson, ss *Twilight Zone* Apr,1987
Nerilka's Story, Anne McCaffrey, n. Bantam: New York hc Mar,1986
Nerve, Jack M. Dann, pm *Twilight Zone* Aug,1987
Nesting Instinct, Scott Baker, nv **The Architecture of Fear**, ed. Kathryn Cramer & Peter D. Pautz, Arbor House,1987
Nestled, Jeremy Forsyth, ss *New Blood* #1,1987
Neutron Star, Larry Niven, nv *If* Oct,1966
The Neutron Tide, Arthur C. Clarke, ss *Galaxy* May,1970
The New Atlantis, Ursula K. Le Guin, na **The New Atlantis**, ed. Robert Silverberg,1975
A New Christmas Carol, Arthur Machen, vi,1924
New Corner, L.T.C. Rolt, ss *Mystery Stories* #20,1939
A New Golden Age, Rudy Rucker, ss *Randolph-Macon Woman's College Alumnae Bulletin* Sum,1981
The New Mother, Lucy Lane Clifford, ss,1882
The New Physics and the Universe, James Trefil, ar **Universe**, ed. Byron Preiss, Bantam Spectra,1987
The New Prime [Brain of the Galaxy], Jack Vance, nv *Worlds Beyond* Feb,1951
"The New Prime": Six Plots for the Price of One, Robert Silverberg, ar,1987
New Rose Hotel, William Gibson, ss *Omni* Jul,1984
The New Season, Robert Bloch, ss **Masques** #2, ed. J.N. Williamson,1987
New Writers, Isaac Asimov, ed *IASFM* Jan,1987
New York Night, John Maclay, ss **Other Engagements**, Madison, WI: Dream House,1987
News, Stuart David Schiff, ar *Whispers* #23,1987
The Next-But-One Man, Kim Newman, ss *Interzone* #19,1987
Ni Venos, Doktoro Zamenof, Ni Venos!, Harry Harrison, ss **Tales from the Forbidden Planet**, ed. Roz Kaveney, Titan,1987
Nicaragua: A Speech to My Former Comrades on the Left, David Horowitz, ar *Commentary* Jun,1986
The Night, Ray Bradbury, ss *Weird Tales* Jul,1946
Night Action, Chris Morris, ss **Festival Moon**, ed. C.J. Cherryh, DAW,1987
The Night Before Christmas, Robert Bloch, nv **Dark Forces**, ed. Kirby McCauley, Viking,1980
Night Fears, L.P. Hartley, ss
Night Firing--1967, John Maclay, pm *Fungi* #9,1986
Night Flight, Bruce Boston, pm *Star*Line*,1978
Night Hound's Moon, Mary H. Schaub, ss **Tales of the Witch World**, ed. Andre Norton, St. Martin's,1987
A Night in the Netherhells, Craig Shaw Gardner, n. Ace: New York pb Jun,1987
A Night in the Woods, J.B. Stamper, ss **More Tales for the Midnight Hour**, Apple/Scholastic,1987
The Night Is Freezing Fast, Thomas F. Monteleone, ss **Masques** #2, ed. J.N. Williamson,1987
Night Meeting, Ray Bradbury, ss **The Martian Chronicles**,1950
Night Moves, Tim Powers, nv **Night Moves**, Tim Powers, Axolotl Press,1986
The Night Nurse's Story, Edith Olivier, ss,1933
The Night of Delicate Terrors, Harlan Ellison, ss *The Paper: A Chicago Weekly* Apr 8,1961
The Night of No Joy, W. Warren Wagar, nv *F&SF* Jun,1987
Night of the Cooters, Howard Waldrop, ss *Omni* Apr,1987
The Night of the Piasa, J.C. Green & George W. Proctor, nv **Nightmares**, ed. Charles L. Grant, Playboy,1979
The Night of the Trolls, Keith Laumer, na *Worlds of Tomorrow* Oct,1963
The Night of White Bhairab, Lucius Shepard, nv *F&SF* Oct,1984
The Night People, Jack Finney, n. Doubleday: Garden City, NY,1977
Night Ride, Nancy Asire, nv **Fever Season**, ed. C.J. Cherryh, DAW,1987
Night Ride, Bruce Boston, pm *Night Cry* v2#3,1987
The Night Seasons [Part 2], J.N. Williamson, sl *Night Cry* v2#3,1987
The Night Seasons [Part 3], J.N. Williamson, sl *Night Cry* v2#4,1987
The Night Seasons [Part 4], J.N. Williamson, sl *Night Cry* v2#5,1987
Night Skirt, A.R. Morlan, ss *The Horror Show* Win,1987
Night Vision, Jackie Vivelo, ss **A Trick of the Light**, Putnam,1987
Night's Daughter, Day's Desire, Tanith Lee, nv **Night's Sorceries**, DAW,1987
Night's Master, Tanith Lee, n. DAW: New York,1978
Night's Sorceries, Tanith Lee, n. DAW: New York,1987
Night-Side, Joyce Carol Oates, nv **Night-Side**,1977

NIGHTFRIEND

Nightfriend, John F. Carr & Roland J. Green, nv **Friends of the Horseclans**, ed. Robert Adams & Pamela Crippen Adams, Signet,1987

The Nightingale, Hans Christian Andersen, ss

Nightmare Collector, Bruce Boston, pm *Night Cry* v2#3,1987

Nightmare in Blue, Fredric Brown, vi *Dude* May,1961

Nightmare in Gray, Fredric Brown, vi *Dude* May,1961

Nightmare in Green, Fredric Brown, vi **Nightmares and Geezenstacks**, Bantam,1961

Nightmare in Red, Fredric Brown, vi *Dude* May,1961

Nightmare in White, Fredric Brown, vi **Nightmares and Geezenstacks**, Bantam,1961

Nightmare in Yellow, Fredric Brown, vi *Dude* May,1961

Nightmare on Elm Street 3, Wes Craven, Robert Englund & Heather Langencamp, iv *The Horror Show* Spr,1987

Nightmare with Zeppelins, C.M. Kornbluth & Frederik Pohl, nv *Galaxy* Dec,1958

Nightmares, Anonymous, ar *The Horror Show* Jan,1987

Nightmares, Anonymous, ar *The Horror Show* Spr,1987

Nightmares, Anonymous, ar *The Horror Show* Sum,1987

Nightmares, Anonymous, ar *The Horror Show* Fll,1987

Nightmares, Anonymous, ar *The Horror Show* Win,1987

The Nightrunners, Joe R. Lansdale, ex Dark Harvest: Niles, IL hc Sep,1987

Nightshade Crossing, Mark Rainey, ss *Minnesota Fantasy Review* #1,1987

Nightskin, John Brizzolara, ss *Twilight Zone* Feb,1987

The Nine Lessons and Carols, Lanyon Jones, ss **After Midnight Stories** #3,1987

Nine Words in Winter, Caralyn Inks, ss **Tales of the Witch World**, ed. Andre Norton, St. Martin's,1987

The Nisse at the Sausagemonger's, Hans Christian Andersen, ss

No Brother, No Friend, Richard C. Meredith, n. Doubleday: Garden City, NY,1976

No Damn Atoms, Robert Chilson & William F. Wu, nv *Analog* Oct,1987

No End in Sight, Patricia Highsmith, ss **Tales of Natural and Unnatural Catastrophes**, Bloomsbury,1987

No Flowers for Henry, Hugh B. Cave, ss *Whispers* #23,1987

No Hiding Place, Jack L. Chalker, nv **Stellar** #3, ed. Judy-Lynn del Rey,1977

No Longer the Stars, Bruce Boston, pm **Nuclear Futures**, Velocities Chapbook Series,1987

No Matter What They Say, Sometimes It Is Too Late, Gregory N. Krolczyk, vi *2AM* Win,1987

No Particular Night or Morning, Ray Bradbury, ss **The Illustrated Man**,1951

No Pets, Tawn Stokes, ss **L. Ron Hubbard Presents Writers of the Future** v3, ed. Algis Budrys, Bridge,1987

No Regrets, Lisa Tuttle, nv *F&SF* May,1985

No War, or Battle's Sound [Or Battle's Sound], Harry Harrison, nv *If* Oct,1968

No Woman Born, C.L. Moore, nv *Astounding* Dec,1944

"No Woman Born": Flowing From Ring to Ring, Robert Silverberg, ar,1987

No-Sided Professor, Martin Gardner, ss *Esquire* Jan,1947

Nobelist Schimmelhorn, Reginald Bretnor, nv *F&SF* May,1987

Nobody Bothers Gus [as by Paul Janvier], Algis Budrys, ss *Astounding* Nov,1955

Nobody Ever Goes There, Manly Wade Wellman, ss **Weird Tales** #3, ed. Lin Carter,1981

Nobody Spoke or Waved Goodbye, Brian W. Aldiss, vi **New Writings in SF** #23,1974

Nocturne, Robert Bloch, ss **Greystone Bay**, ed. Charles L. Grant, Tor,1985

Nocturne, Paul Roland, ss **The Curious Case of Richard Fielding and Other Stories**, Lary Press,1987

Noninterference [as by Eric G. Iverson], Harry Turtledove, ss *Analog* Jul,1985

Nonlethal, D.C. Poyer, nv **There Will Be War** v6, ed. Jerry E. Pournelle,1987

The Noonday Witch, Dorothy J. Heydt, nv **Sword and Sorceress** #4, ed. Marion Zimmer Bradley,1987

Nora Says "Check.", Martin Gardner, ss *Esquire* Jan,1948

Norby and the Invaders, Isaac Asimov & Janet Asimov, n. Walker: New York,1985

Norby and the Lost Princess, Isaac Asimov & Janet Asimov, n. Walker: New York,1985

Norg Gleeble Gop, Alan Dean Foster, ss *F&SF* Aug,1987

OFF THE SUBJECT II: BACKGROUND AND FOREGROUND

North Scarning [The Older Evil], Brian W. Aldiss, ss *The Illustrated London News* Dec,1986

Northshore, Sheri S. Tepper, n. Tor: New York,1987

Nostalgia, John Maclay, pm *Footsteps* Nov,1987

...Not a Prison Make, Joseph P. Martino, nv *Analog* Sep,1966

Not After Midnight, Daphne du Maurier, na

Not By Its Cover, Philip K. Dick, ss *Famous Science Fiction* Sum,1968

Not for Country, Not for King, Joel Rosenberg, nv **New Destinies** v1, ed. Jim Baen, Baen,1987

Not in Front of the Children, George Turner, ss *Aphelion* #5,1987

Not Just Traces of Me, G. Wayne Miller, vi *The Horror Show* Sum,1987

Not Yet the End, Fredric Brown, vi *Captain Future* Win,1941

A Note on the Authors, [Misc. Material], bg

Note on the Illustrations, [Misc. Material], ms

Note to the Reader, Daphne du Maurier, pr

Notes, [Misc. Material], bi

Notes, [Misc. Material], ms

Notes on Sources, [Misc. Material], bi

Notes on the Authors, [Misc. Material], bg

Notes on the Contributors, [Misc. Material], bg

Nothing from Nothing Comes, Katherine Ramsland, ss **Masques** #2, ed. J.N. Williamson,1987

Nothing There, G. Wayne Miller, ss *The Horror Show* Fll,1987

Noughts and Crosses, L.P. Hartley, ss

The Novel of the White Powder [also as "The White Powder"], Arthur Machen, nv **The Three Impostors**, John Lane,1895

A Novel Preview: **Black Wind**, F. Paul Wilson, ex *Footsteps* Nov,1987

The Novella Race, Pamela Sargent, ss **Orbit** #20, ed. Damon Knight,1978

Novelty Act, Philip K. Dick, nv *Fantastic* Feb,1964

Now Appearing, Ed Shannon, vi *Minnesota Fantasy Review* #1,1987

Nuckelavee, Robert D. San Souci, ss **Short & Shivery**, Doubleday,1987

Nuclear Autumn, Ben Bova, ss **Far Frontiers** v2, ed. Jerry Pournelle & Jim Baen,1985

Nuclear FX, Ferret & Mink Mole, cs *New Pathways* Jan,1987

Nuclear FX, Ferret & Mink Mole, cs *New Pathways* Aug,1987

Nuclear FX, Ferret & Mink Mole, cs *New Pathways* Nov,1987

La Nuit des Chiens, Leslie Halliwell, ss **A Demon Close Behind**, Robert Hale,1987

Null-O, Philip K. Dick, ss *If* Dec,1958

Number 13, M.R. James, ss **Ghost Stories of an Antiquary**,1904

The Nuptial Flight of Warbirds, Algis Budrys, nv *Analog* May,1978

Nutrimancer, Marc Laidlaw, ss *IASFM* Aug,1987

O Captain, My Captain, Katherine V. Forrest, na **Dreams and Swords**, Naiad,1987

O Civile, Sister M. Anne Arkee, O.S.F., pm *Amazing* Mar,1987

Oath-Bound, Pauline Griffin, nv **Tales of the Witch World**, ed. Andre Norton, St. Martin's,1987

Oathbreaker, Marion Zimmer Bradley, nv **The Other Side of the Mirror**, ed. Marion Zimmer Bradley & The Friends of Darkover, DAW,1987

Obsidian Sphinx, Morris Liebson, pm *Amazing* Sep,1987

Obsolete, Richard Christian Matheson, ss **Scars**, Scream/Press,1987

Obsolete Skill, Charles Sheffield, ss *F&SF* Dec,1987

Occidental Injury, Arlan Andrews, vi *Analog* Oct,1987

Occupant, Kim Antieau, ss **Doom City**, ed. Charles L. Grant, Tor,1987

October 31, Andy Honeycutt, ss *Haunts* #9,1987

Oddities & Entities, [Misc. Material], ms *American Fantasy* Spr,1987

Oddities & Entities, [Misc. Material], ms *American Fantasy* Sum,1987

Oddities & Entities, [Misc. Material], ms *American Fantasy* Win,1987

The Oddmedod, Arthur Porges, ss *F&SF* Jun,1987

Of Ancient Swords and Evil Mist, James R. Heidbrink, ss **Tales of the Witch World**, ed. Andre Norton, St. Martin's,1987

Of Children in the Foliage, Terence M. Green, ss **Aurora: New Canadian Writing 1979**, ed. Morris Wolfe, Doubleday Canada,1979

Of Law and Magic, C.J. Cherryh, nv **Moonsinger's Friends**, ed. Susan Shwartz, Bluejay,1985

Of Mice and Otis, F.M. Busby, ss *Amazing* Mar,1972

Of Mist, and Grass, and Sand, Vonda N. McIntyre, nv *Analog* Oct,1973

Of the People, Gordon R. Dickson, ss *F&SF* Dec,1955

Of the Shaping of Ulm's Heir, Andre Norton, nv **Tales of the Witch World**, ed. Andre Norton, St. Martin's,1987

Of Withered Apples, Philip K. Dick, ss *Cosmos SF&F* Jul,1954

The Off Season, Ray Bradbury, ss *Thrilling Wonder Stories* Dec,1948

Off the Subject I: On Genre, Magical Realism, and Writing Seriously, Steve Rasnic Tem, ar *The Horror Show* Sum,1987

Off the Subject II: Background and Foreground, Steve Rasnic Tem, ar *The Horror Show* Fll,1987

OFFICE HOURS   **THE OTHER SIDE: APOCALYPTIC VOIVOD**

Office Hours, Douglas E. Winter, ss **Shadows** #10, ed. Charles L. Grant,1987

The Ogre, Avram Davidson, ss *If* Jul,1959

The Ogre Courting, Juliana Horatia Ewing, ss *Aunt Judy's Magazine*,1871

Oh Say Can You See--, Robert Bloch, ss **Analog Yearbook** #1,1978

Oh Tin Man, Tin Man, There's No Place Like Home, Brad Strickland, ss *F&SF* May,1987

Oh, to Be a Blobel!, Philip K. Dick, ss *Galaxy* Feb,1964

"Oh, Wakan Tanka...", Jack M. Dann, pm *Twilight Zone* Aug,1987

"Oh, Whistle, and I'll Come to You, My Lad", M.R. James, nv **Ghost Stories of an Antiquary**,1904

Oil of Dog, Ambrose Bierce, ss

Oily Foreign Muck, Josephine Saxton, ss **Little Tours of Hell**, Pandora,1986

The Old Darkness, Pamela Sargent, ss *F&SF* Jul,1983

Old Garfield's Heart, Robert E. Howard, ss *Weird Tales* Dec,1933

Old Loves, Karl Edward Wagner, ss *Night Visions* #2,1985

The Old Man and the Cherry Tree, Kevin J. Anderson, ss *Grue* #3,1986

Old Man Gloom, Martin Gardner, ss *Esquire* Nov,1950

Old Mickey Flip Had a Marvelous Ship, Lori Ann White, nv **L. Ron Hubbard Presents Writers of the Future** v3, ed. Algis Budrys, Bridge,1987

The Old Ones, Ray Bradbury, vi **The Martian Chronicles**,1950

The Old Ones, Andrew Joron, pm

The Old Poet, Joan Aiken, ss **A Goose on Your Grave**, Gollancz,1987

The Old Portrait, Hume Nisbet, ss **Stories Weird and Wonderful**, F.V. White: London,1900

The Old Woman Upstairs, Elizabeth Engstrom, ss *2AM* Win,1987

Olida, Bob Leman, nv *F&SF* Apr,1987

Ollie's Hands, Dean R. Koontz, ss *Infinity* #4, ed. Robert Hoskins,1972

The Olympic Runner, Dennis Etchison, nv *Fantasy Tales* #16,1986

Omega, Amelia Reynolds Long, ss *Amazing* Jul,1932

On a Clear Day, Edward Lodi, vi *2AM* Fll,1987

On Becoming a Writer, Charles C. Ryan, ed *Aboriginal SF* Nov,1987

On Books, Baird Searles, br *IASFM* Jan,1987

On Books, Baird Searles, br *IASFM* Feb,1987

On Books, Baird Searles, br *IASFM* Mar,1987

On Books, Baird Searles, br *IASFM* May,1987

On Books, Baird Searles, br *IASFM* Jun,1987

On Books, Baird Searles, br *IASFM* Aug,1987

On Books, Baird Searles, br *IASFM* Sep,1987

On Books, Baird Searles, br *IASFM* Nov,1987

On Books, Baird Searles, br *IASFM* mid-Dec,1987

On Books: Dreamers of Space, Norman Spinrad, br *IASFM* Oct,1987

On Books: Sturgeon, Vonnegut, and Trout, Norman Spinrad, br *IASFM* Apr,1987

On Books: The Edge of the Envelope, Norman Spinrad, br *IASFM* Jul,1987

On Exhibit, Janet Aulisio, il *Amazing* Jan,1987

On Exhibit, Peter Botsis, il *Amazing* Nov,1987

On Exhibit, Bob Eggleton, il *Amazing* Sep,1987

On Exhibit, Stephen E. Fabian, il *Amazing* Mar,1987

On Exhibit, Hank Jankus, il *Amazing* May,1987

On Exhibit, John Lakey, il *Amazing* Jul,1987

On Film, James Verniere, mr *Twilight Zone* Aug,1987

On Film, James Verniere, mr *Twilight Zone* Oct,1987

On Gaming, Matthew J. Costello, gr *Analog* Jan,1987

On Gaming, Matthew J. Costello, gr *Analog* Feb,1987

On Gaming, Matthew J. Costello, gr *Analog* Mar,1987

On Gaming, Matthew J. Costello, gr *Analog* Apr,1987

On Gaming, Matthew J. Costello, gr *Analog* May,1987

On Gaming, Matthew J. Costello, gr *Analog* Jun,1987

On Gaming, Matthew J. Costello, gr *Analog* Jul,1987

On Gaming, Matthew J. Costello, gr *Analog* Aug,1987

On Gaming, Matthew J. Costello, gr *Analog* Sep,1987

On Gaming, Matthew J. Costello, gr *Analog* Oct,1987

On Gaming, Matthew J. Costello, gr *Analog* Nov,1987

On Gaming, Matthew J. Costello, gr *Analog* Dec,1987

On Gaming, Matthew J. Costello, gr *Analog* mid-Dec,1987

On Golden Seas, Arthur C. Clarke, ss *Omni* May,1987

On Ice, Barry N. Malzberg, ss *Amazing* Jan,1973

On My Way to Paradise, Dave Wolverton, na **L. Ron Hubbard Presents Writers of the Future** v3, ed. Algis Budrys, Bridge,1987

On No Account, My Love, Elizabeth Jenkins, ss **Ghost Book** #3, ed. Aidan Chambers/James Turner,1955

On the Boardwalk, John Maclay, ss **Other Engagements**, Madison, WI: Dream House,1987

On the Border, Lucius Shepard, nv *IASFM* Aug,1987

On the Dream Channel Panel, Ian Watson, ss *Amazing* Mar,1985

On the Leads, Sabine Baring-Gould, ss **A Book of Ghosts**, Methuen: London,1904

On the Path to Athene Proneia, Delphi, 1984, Joyce Nower, pm *Ice River* Sum,1987

On the Shadow of a Phosphor Screen, William F. Wu, nv *IASFM* Jul,1979

On Weaponry, Arthur C. Clarke, ar *Analog* mid-Dec,1987

The On'ner, A.R. Morlan, ss *Grue* #4,1987

Once Upon a Chair, Paul Christopher, nv **Beyond That River**, Pal Books,1987

Once Upon a Unicorn, F.M. Busby, ss *Fantastic* Apr,1973

One, Heather Spears, nv **Tesseracts 2**, ed. Phyllis Gotlieb & Douglas Barbour, Press Porcepic: Victoria,1987

One April Day, William P. Dillon, ss *Grue* #4,1987

One for the Horrors, David J. Schow, ss *Whispers* #19,1983

One for the Road, Stephen King, ss *Maine* Mar,1977

One Hundred, Don Webb, ss *Ice River* Sum,1987

One is One and All Alone, Nicholas Fisk, ss **Living Fire and Other S.F. Stories**, Corgi: London,1987

One Life, Furnished in Early Poverty, Harlan Ellison, ss *Orbit* #8, ed. Damon Knight,1970

One More Martini, Martin Gardner, ss *Esquire* Feb,1950

One of the Dead, William Wood, nv *The Saturday Evening Post* Oct 31,1964

One Old Man, with Seals, Jane Yolen, ss **Neptune Rising**, Philomel,1982

One Other, Manly Wade Wellman, ss *F&SF* Aug,1953

One Special, Perfect Way, Heather Svedbeck, ss *2AM* Fll,1987

One Spring in Wyoming, Charles L. Grant, ss *Aboriginal SF* Feb,1987

One Summer Night, Ambrose Bierce, vi **Can Such Things Be?**, Cassell: New York,1893

The One Thing to Fear, John Maclay, ss *Footsteps* Fll,1986

One Way Street, Jerome Bixby, ss *Amazing* Jan,1954

One-Trick Dog, Bruce Boston, vi *IASFM* May,1987

The Only One, David S. Garnett, ss *Interzone* #22,1987

Only Yesterday, Ted White, ss *Amazing* Jul,1969

Oom, Martin Gardner, vi *The Journal of Science-Fiction* Fll,1951

Ooze, Anthony M. Rud, nv *Weird Tales* Mar,1923

Open Orbit, The Readers, lt *Space & Time* #72,1987

Open Orbit, The Readers, lt *Space & Time* #73,1987

An Open Window, Robert E. Howard, pm *Weird Tales* Sep,1932

Open-Ended Universe, Ruth Berman, pm *Amazing* Jul,1986

Operation Balsam; or Touch-Me-Not, Patricia Highsmith, ss **Tales of Natural and Unnatural Catastrophes**, Bloomsbury,1987

Operation RSVP, H. Beam Piper, ss *Amazing* Jan,1951

Ophelia's Tale, Clairr O'Connor, ss **Mad and Bad Fairies**, ed. Anonymous, Attic Press,1987

Or All the Seas with Oysters, Avram Davidson, ss *Galaxy* May,1958

...Or Your Money Back [as by David Gordon], Randall Garrett, ss *Astounding* Sep,1959

Oracle, W.R. Thompson, ss *Analog* Jun,1987

Ordeal in Space, Robert A. Heinlein, ss *Town & Country* May,1948

The Order of the Peacock Angel, Cooper McLaughlin, nv *F&SF* Jan,1987

The Original 11 Observations of Methuselah, Robert Frazier, pm *IASFM* Aug,1987

The Ormolu Clock, Muriel Spark, ss *New Yorker* Sep 17,1960

An Ornament to His Profession, Charles L. Harness, nv *Analog* Feb,1966

The Orphan, Neil W. Hiller, ss *F&SF* May,1987

Orpheus with Clay Feet [as by Jack Dowland], Philip K. Dick, ss *Escapade*,1964

Orr's Dreams [from **The Lathe of Heaven**], Ursula K. Le Guin, ex Scribners: New York,1971

The Other Celia, Theodore Sturgeon, ss *Galaxy* Mar,1957

The Other Eye of Polyphemus, Harlan Ellison, ss *Cosmos* Nov,1977

The Other Foot, Ray Bradbury, ss *New Story* Mar,1951

The Other Kind, Lisa Tuttle, ss *IASFM* Dec,1984

The Other Mel Brooks, James Verniere, ar *Twilight Zone* Aug,1987

The "Other Mode" [from **Frankenstein's Castle**], Colin Wilson, ar

The Other Room, Lisa Tuttle, ss *Whispers* #17,1982

The Other Side, Ramsey Campbell, ss *Twilight Zone* Apr,1987

The Other Side of the Mirror, Patricia Floss, na **The Other Side of the Mirror**, ed. Marion Zimmer Bradley & The Friends of Darkover, DAW,1987

The Other Side: American Pie in the Face, Jonathan White, ar *Twilight Zone* Apr,1987

The Other Side: Apocalyptic Voivod, Lou Stathis, ar *Twilight Zone* Dec,1987

The Other Side: Bad-Dream Girl, Ron Wolfe, ar *Twilight Zone* Aug,1987
The Other Side: Baffling Seneca Guns, Allan Maurer, ar *Twilight Zone* Dec,1987
The Other Side: Chaos, Inc., Richard Kadrey, ar *Twilight Zone* Feb,1987
The Other Side: Children of the Night, Robert Simpson, ar *Twilight Zone* Jun,1987
The Other Side: Coming Soon to a Theater Somewhere, Mayby, Ron Wolfe, ar *Twilight Zone* Dec,1987
The Other Side: Dark Knight, Lou Stathis, ar *Twilight Zone* Jun,1987
The Other Side: Dial "T" for Terror, Robert Simpson, ar *Twilight Zone* Apr,1987
The Other Side: Elephant Parts, Tappan King, ar *Twilight Zone* Oct,1987
The Other Side: Faces of Fear, Ron Wolfe, ar *Twilight Zone* Aug,1987
The Other Side: Flies on the Screen, Ron Wolfe, ar *Twilight Zone* Aug,1987
The Other Side: Giger Counting, Lou Stathis, ar *Twilight Zone* Dec,1987
The Other Side: Gore-Gonzola, Mark Arnold, ar *Twilight Zone* Jun,1987
The Other Side: Grass-Roots Gore, Ron Wolfe, ar *Twilight Zone* Feb,1987
The Other Side: Guilt by Association, Ron Wolfe, ar *Twilight Zone* Apr,1987
The Other Side: Have Yourself a Merry Little Xenophobe Understanding Day, Ron Wolfe, ar *Twilight Zone* Aug,1987
The Other Side: Horrible Twisted Things Crawling, Mark Arnold, ar *Twilight Zone* Jun,1987
The Other Side: In God We Rust, Mark Arnold, ar *Twilight Zone* Apr,1987
The Other Side: It Came from Across the Pond, Robert Simpson, ar *Twilight Zone* Aug,1987
The Other Side: King Kong Lived, Peter R. Emshwiller, ar *Twilight Zone* Apr,1987
The Other Side: Land of the Rising Moon, George Wilhelmsen, ar *Twilight Zone* Aug,1987
The Other Side: Mary & Percy & Byron & Claire, Ron Wolfe, ar *Twilight Zone* Oct,1987
The Other Side: More Hokey Holidays, Ron Wolfe, ar *Twilight Zone* Oct,1987
The Other Side: Now Revealed: Money-Making Secrets of the Shockmeisters, Esther M. Friesner, ar *Twilight Zone* Dec,1987
The Other Side: Of Maus and Men, Jonathan White, ar *Twilight Zone* Feb,1987
The Other Side: Opera of the Red Death, Lou Stathis, ar *Twilight Zone* Feb,1987
The Other Side: Over the Edge, James Verniere, ar *Twilight Zone* Feb,1987
The Other Side: Pennies from Hell, Darrell Schweitzer, ar *Twilight Zone* Feb,1987
The Other Side: Queen Tut, Paul Learn, ar *Twilight Zone* Feb,1987
The Other Side: Rats in the Malls, Ron Wolfe, ar *Twilight Zone* Oct,1987
The Other Side: Surrealistic Wonkiness, Robert Simpson, ar *Twilight Zone* Jun,1987
The Other Side: The Zone of Silence, Jay Sheckley, ar *Twilight Zone* Oct,1987
The Other Side: Things Without Faces, Lou Stathis, ar *Twilight Zone* Jun,1987
The Other Side: Vanishing Hitchikers and Dead Cats, Tyson Blue, ar *Twilight Zone* Oct,1987
The Other Side: Watch Horror Movies and Get Rich, Allan Maurer, ar *Twilight Zone* Dec,1987
The Other Side: Weirder than Fiction, James Verniere, ar *Twilight Zone* Apr,1987
The Other Side: Welcome, Chaos, Adrian Savage, ar *Twilight Zone* Oct,1987
The Other Side: Zoned Again?, Jay Sheckley, ar *Twilight Zone* Aug,1987
Other Voices, Alan Brennert, is *Twilight Zone* Oct,1987
The Other Woman, Ramsey Campbell, nv **The Devil's Kisses**, ed. Linda Lovecraft, Corgi,1976
The Other World, Murray Leinster, na *Startling Stories* Nov,1949
The Others, Joyce Carol Oates, ss *Twilight Zone* Aug,1987
Ouija, Paul Haberman, vi *Grue* #4,1987
Our Christmas Spirit, George A. McIntyre, ss *Fantasy Tales* #16,1986
Our Galaxy, Eric J. Chaisson, ar **Universe**, ed. Byron Preiss, Bantam Spectra,1987
"Our Little Miss", Harlan Ellison, ar *Los Angeles Free Press*,1970
Our New Format, Charles C. Ryan, ed *Aboriginal SF* May,1987
Our Patrol, Randall Garrett, sg,1978
Ouroboros, John J. Miller, nv **A Very Large Array**, ed. Melinda M. Snodgrass, University of New Mexico Press,1987
Out in the Garden, Philip K. Dick, ss *Fantasy Fiction* Aug,1953
Out of Copyright, Ramsey Campbell, ss *Whispers* #15,1982

Out of Darkness, Lillian Stewart Carl, ss *IASFM* Apr,1987
Out of Place, Pamela Sargent, ss *Twilight Zone* Oct,1981
Out of the Cradle, Mary Caraker, nv *F&SF* Jul,1987
The Outpost Undiscovered By Tourists, Harlan Ellison, ss *F&SF* Jan,1982
The Outsider, Twenty Years On, Colin Wilson, ar
Outsteppin' Fetchit, Charles R. Saunders, ss **Masques** #2, ed. J.N. Williamson,1987
Outward Bound, Norman Spinrad, nv *Analog* Mar,1964
Over His Head, Bruce Jones, ss **Twisted Tales**, San Diego: Blackthorne,1987
Over the River, P. Schuyler Miller, ss *Unknown* Apr,1941
Over the River and Through the Woods, Clifford D. Simak, ss *Amazing* May,1965
Overproof [as by Jonathan Blake Mackenzie], Randall Garrett, nv *Analog* Oct,1965
A Overruling Passion, Galad Elflandsson, nv **Doom City**, ed. Charles L. Grant, Tor,1987
Overseas Call, Robert Frazier, pm *IASFM* Oct,1987
Owls Hoot in the Daytime, Manly Wade Wellman, ss **Dark Forces**, ed. Kirby McCauley, Viking,1980
The Package Tourist, Steve Sneyd, ss *Back Brain Recluse* #7,1987
Pages from a Young Girl's Journal, Robert Aickman, nv *F&SF* Feb,1973
Pains and Pleasures, L.P. Hartley, ss
Paint the Meadows with Delight, Pamela Dean, nv **Liavek: Wizard's Row**, ed. Will Shetterly & Emma Bull, Ace,1987
A Painter's Vision, Barbara Siegel & Scott Siegel, nv **DragonLance Tales** v3, Margaret Weis & Tracy Hickman, TSR,1987
The Pair of Them, Thomas M. Disch, pm *Night Cry* v2#5,1987
Palace Revolution [Gambler's World], Keith Laumer, nv *If* Nov,1961
Palaces on Pluto?, Andrew Joron, pm *Amazing* Nov,1986
"Pale, Trembling Youth", W.H. Pugmire & Jessica Amanda Salmonson, ss **Cutting Edge**, ed. Dennis Etchison, Doubleday,1986
Palindrome, Thomas M. Disch, ss *Omni* Sep,1987
Pamela's Get, David J. Schow, ss *Twilight Zone* Aug,1987
The Pampas Clump, L.P. Hartley, ss
The Panama Mechanism, Leo Bigley, ss *Mage* Spr,1986
Panspermia, Andrew Joron, pm
Paper Moon, Garry Kilworth, ss *Omni* Jan,1987
Paradise, E. Veronica Figueirido, ss *SF International* #2,1987
Paradise Paddock, L.P. Hartley, ss
Parakeet, John Shirley, ss *New Pathways* Apr,1987
The Parasite, Arthur Conan Doyle, nv *Harper's Weekly* Nov 10,1894
Parasite Mansion, Mary Elizabeth Counselman, nv *Weird Tales* Jan,1942
Pardon My Ghoulish Laughter, Fredric Brown, ss *Strange Detective Mysteries* Feb,1942
The Pardoner's Tale, Robert Silverberg, ss *Playboy* Jun,1987
Particles of a Wave. An Afterword, Sara Maitland, aw
Partly Murphy, Henry Melton, ss *Analog* May,1987
Partners (Lyrics), Mercedes R. Lackey, sg **Fever Season**, ed. C.J. Cherryh, DAW,1987
Partners (Music), C.J. Cherryh, sg **Fever Season**, ed. C.J. Cherryh, DAW,1987
Passing, Elaine Radford, ss *Aboriginal SF* May,1987
The Passing of Kings, Lois Tilton, ss *The Dragon* Sep,1987
The Passing of the Elves, Keith Allen Daniels, pm *2AM* Win,1987
Passionate Precision: The Fiction of Robert M. Coates, Donald Phelps, ar *Pulpsmith* Win,1987
Past Light, Robert Frazier, pm *IASFM* Jun,1986
The Past of Mrs Pickering, Leslie Halliwell, nv **A Demon Close Behind**, Robert Hale,1987
The Paths of the Perambulator, Alan Dean Foster, n. Phantasia: West Bloomfield, MI hc Nov,1985
Patricia's Profession, Kim Newman, ss *Interzone* #14,1985
Patterns, Pat Cadigan, ss *Omni* Aug,1987
Paul Williams talks to New Pathways, Misha Chocholak & Paul Williams, iv *New Pathways* Jan,1987
Paul's Tale, Mary Norton, ss *Story*,1945
Pawn in Play, C.J. Cherryh, nv **Masters of Hell**, ed. Janet Morris et al, Baen,1987
The Pawnbroker's Wife, Muriel Spark, ss
The Pawns of Crux, Steven Saylor, ss *The Dragon* Mar,1987
Pay for the Printer, Philip K. Dick, ss *Satellite* Oct,1956
Paycheck, Philip K. Dick, nv *Imagination* Jun,1953
The Peace Spy, Gene Wolfe, ss *IASFM* Jan,1987
Peacebringer [Sword of Peace], Ward Moore, nv *Amazing* Mar,1950
The Peacemaker [The Life Hater], Fred Saberhagen, ss *If* Aug,1964
Peak Experience, Colin Wilson, ar The Schumacher Lecture,1982
The Pear-Shaped Man, George R.R. Martin, ss *Omni* Oct,1987

PEARLS OF RAIN

Pearls of Rain, David C. Kopaska-Merkel, pm *Night Cry* v2#4,1987
The Pearls of the Vampire Queen, Michael Shea, nv **Nifft the Lean**,1982
The Peculiar Such Thing, Virginia Hamilton, ss **The People Could Fly: American Black Folktales**, Knopf,1985
The Peddler's Apprentice, Joan D. Vinge & Vernor Vinge, nv *Analog* Aug,1975
The Pedestrian, Ray Bradbury, ss *Reporter* Aug 7,1951
Pen and Inkwell, Hans Christian Andersen, vi
Pennies from Hell, Darrell Schweitzer, ss *Night Cry* v2#3,1987
Pennies from Hell, Lewis Shiner, nv **Wild Cards** v2, ed. George R.R. Martin, Bantam,1987
People of the Dark, Robert E. Howard, nv *Strange Tales of Mystery and Terror* Jun,1932
The People on the Precipice, Ian Watson, ss *Interzone* #13,1985
Per Far L'Amore, L.P. Hartley, ss
Perception Barriers, Robert Frazier, pm *IASFM* Dec,1985
The Perfect Gift, Jean Darling, ss *Night Cry* v2#4,1987
Permafrost, Roger Zelazny, nv *Omni* Apr,1986
Perpetuity Blues, Neal Barrett, Jr., nv *IASFM* May,1987
The Persistence of Vision, John Varley, na *F&SF* Mar,1978
A Persistent Woman, Marjorie Bowen, vi **Dark Ann, and Other Stories**, John Lane: London,1927
Personal Notes on Maslow [from **New Pathways in Psychology**], Colin Wilson, ar Taplinger: New York,1972
Perspectives in SF, C.J. Cherryh, ed **Glass and Amber**, NESFA,1987
perverse love, mel buffington, pm *Ice River* Sum,1987
Perverts, Whitley Strieber, ss *Whispers* #19,1983
Peter Two, Irwin Shaw, ss *New Yorker*,1946
The Petey Car, Manly Wade Wellman, ss **Superhorror**, ed. Ramsey Campbell, W.H. Allen,1976
Petronella, Jay Williams, ss *McCalls* Jan,1973
The Phantom Farmhouse, Seabury Quinn, nv *Weird Tales* Oct,1923
Phantom Fingers, Robert S. Carr, ss *Weird Tales* May,1927
The Phantom Rickshaw, Rudyard Kipling, ss *Quartette* Chr,1885
The Phantom Werewolf, Montague Summers, ss
Phil as I Knew Him, D. Scott Apel, in
Philip K. Dick in Interview, D. Scott Apel, Kevin C. Briggs & Philip K. Dick, iv **Philip K. Dick: The Dream Connection**, D. Scott Apel, Permanent Press,1987
Philip K. Dick: The Dream Connection, D. Scott Apel, ar **Philip K. Dick: The Dream Connection**, D. Scott Apel, Permanent Press,1987
The Philosophical Stone, Ken Wisman, ss *Interzone* #21,1987
The Philosophy of Sebastian Trump or The Art of Outrage, William E. Kotzwinkle & Robert Shiarella, ss **Brother Theodore's Chamber of Horrors**, ed. Marvin Kaye, Pinnacle,1975
The Phobos Race, Donald Fredrick Robertson, ar **New Destinies** v2, ed. Jim Baen, Baen,1987
Phone Repairs, Nancy Kress, ss *IASFM* Dec,1986
Phoney Meteor [as by John Beynon, also as "Meteor"], John Wyndham, nv *Amazing* Mar,1941
The Photofinish: On Attending a Lecture at Fermi Lab, Rev. Benedict Auer, O.S.B., pm *Amazing* Jul,1987
Photographs, Kit van Zandt, ss *Whispers* #23,1987
Pick-Up, Peter Heyrman, vi *Twilight Zone* Dec,1987
Pickman's Model, H.P. Lovecraft, ss *Weird Tales* Oct,1927
Picture, Robert Bloch, ss **Shadows** #1, ed. Charles L. Grant,1978
Pictures Made of Stone, Lucius Shepard, ss *Omni* Sep,1987
Piece de Resistance, Judith Tarr, nv *IASFM* Apr,1986
The Pied Piper Fights the Gestapo, Robert Bloch, ss *Fantastic Adventures* Jun,1942
Pierrot on the Moon, Michael Moorcock, pm *Back Brain Recluse* #7,1987
Pigeon in an Iron Lung, Talmage Powell, ss *Manhunt* Nov,1956
Pigeons from Hell, Robert E. Howard, nv *Weird Tales* May,1938
The Piggy Bank, Hans Christian Andersen, vi
Pigs, Al Sarrantonio, ss **Shadows** #10, ed. Charles L. Grant,1987
Pipe Dream, Ann Cathey, pm *Salarius* #3,1987
Piper in the Woods, Philip K. Dick, ss *Imagination* Feb,1953
Piper's Wait, Keith Roberts, ss **Other Edens**, ed. Christopher Evans & Robert Holdstock, Unwin: London,1987
Place of Meeting, Charles Beaumont, ss *Orbit* #2,1954
A Place to Stay for a Little While, Jim Aikin, nv *IASFM* Jun,1986
placebo, mel buffington, pm *Ice River* Sum,1987
A Plague of Crowders, Or, Birds of a Feather, Jackie Vivelo, ss **A Trick of the Light**, Putnam,1987
A Plague on Your Houses, Mercedes R. Lackey, nv **Fever Season**, ed. C.J. Cherryh, DAW,1987
Plan 10 from Zone R-3, Polly Frost, ss *New Yorker* Apr 13,1987

THE PREACHER BEHIND THE WALL

Planet for Transients, Philip K. Dick, ss *Fantastic Universe* Oct,1953
The Plasting Project, Merlin Stone, ss **Hear the Silence**, ed. Irene Zahava, Crossing Press,1986
Plausibility, Isaac Asimov, ed *IASFM* Sep,1987
Play Dead, Chet Williamson, ss *F&SF* Aug,1987
Play's the Thing, Bob Booth, nv **Doom City**, ed. Charles L. Grant, Tor,1987
Playback, Arthur C. Clarke, ss *Playboy* Dec,1966
Playfellow, Elisabeth Waters, ss **Red Sun of Darkover**, ed. Marion Zimmer Bradley & The Friends of Darkover, DAW,1987
The Playground, Ray Bradbury, ss *Esquire* Oct,1953
The Playhouse Called Remarkable, Muriel Spark, ss
Playing for Keeps, Jack C. Haldeman, II, ss *IASFM* May,1982
Please Do Not Touch, L.P. Hartley, ss
Please, No Strawberries, Hayes Wilson, ss *Ellery Queen's Mystery Magazine* Mar 10,1980
Pliny's Commentaries, Ned Huston, nv **Universe** #17, ed. Terry Carr,1987
The Plutonian Drug, Clark Ashton Smith, ss *Amazing* Sep,1934
The Pocket Song, Randall Garrett, ss,1977
Podolo, L.P. Hartley, ss **The Travelling Grave and Other Stories**, Arkham,1948
The Poets' War, Bruce Boston, ss *City Miner* #7,1977
Point Man, Timothy Zahn, nv **New Destinies** v1, ed. Jim Baen, Baen,1987
The Point of Thirty Miles, T.H. White, ss
Point Zero, Terence M. Green, ss *F&SF* May,1986
Policy [The Madman from Earth], Keith Laumer, nv *If* Mar,1962
Political Standard Time, Stanley Schmidt, ed *Analog* Dec,1987
The Poltergeist, Seabury Quinn, nv *Weird Tales* Oct,1927
Poltergeist III, Jay Bonansinga, mr *American Fantasy* Sum,1987
Poltergeist!, Kurt Singer, ss
Polyphemus, Michael Shea, na *F&SF* Aug,1981
Poor Girl, Elizabeth Taylor, ss **Ghost Book** #3, ed. Aidan Chambers/James Turner,1955
Poor Little Warrior!, Brian W. Aldiss, ss *F&SF* Apr,1958
Pop Stars, Richard Singer, vi *Grue* #4,1987
Popcorn: A Matter of Survival, Katherine Salts, vi *Haunts* #9,1987
Poppa Was a Catcher, Steven Gould, na **New Destinies** v2, ed. Jim Baen, Baen,1987
Poppy Z. Brite, Poppy Z. Brite & William J. Grabowski, iv *The Horror Show* Fll,1987
Popsy, Stephen King, ss **Masques** #2, ed. J.N. Williamson,1987
Popular's Weird Menace Pulps, Robert Kenneth Jones, ar **The Weird Menace**, Opar Press,1972
The Porcelain Salamander, Orson Scott Card, ss **Unaccompanied Sonata**,1981
Porcinity's Palace, Walter F. Mercadel, ss *Space & Time* #73,1987
Portfolio, Frank Kelly Freas, pi **World Fantasy Convention Program Book** #13,1987
Portfolio, Ron Lindahn & Val Lakey Lindahn, pi **World Fantasy Convention Program Book** #13,1987
The Portobello Road, Muriel Spark, nv *Cosmopolitan*,1958
Portraits of a Young Artist, C. Dell Turney, ss *Space & Time* #72,1987
Portraits of His Children, George R.R. Martin, nv *IASFM* Nov,1985
Post-Historic Pastorale, Andrew Joron, pm
Postmarked: the Crab Nebula, Robert Frazier, pm
Postscript: The Human Condition, Colin Wilson, ar
Pot-Boil Blues, John M. Ford, sg **Liavek: Wizard's Row**, ed. Will Shetterly & Emma Bull, Ace,1987
Potential, Isaac Asimov, ss *IASFM* Feb,1983
Pots, C.J. Cherryh, nv **Afterwar**, ed. Janet Morris, Baen,1985
The Potted Princess, Rudyard Kipling, ss *St. Nicholas Magazine*,1893
Potter's Gray, Joan Aiken, ss **Up the Chimney Down and Other Stories**,1984
Power Times One, J. Michael Matuszewicz, ss *IASFM* Feb,1983
Powerguns, David Drake, ms **Hammer's Slammers**, Ace,1979
Powerhouse, Ray Bradbury, ss *Charm* Mar,1948
Pranks, Robert Bloch, ss **Halloween Horrors**, ed. Alan Ryan, Doubleday,1986
The Prayer, L.P. Hartley, ss
A Prayer for One's Enemy, Harlan Ellison, nv *Cad* Mar,1966
Prayers of a Rain God, Richard Paul Russo, ss *F&SF* May,1987
Prayers of Steel, Misha Chocholak, vi *Ice River* Sum,1987
Prayerwings, Thomas Sullivan, nv **Doom City**, ed. Charles L. Grant, Tor,1987
The Pre-Persons, Philip K. Dick, nv *F&SF* Oct,1974
The Preacher Behind the Wall, George Case, ss *Space & Time* #72,1987

PRECIOUS ARTIFACT

Precious Artifact, Philip K. Dick, ss *Galaxy* Oct,1964
Predators, Edward Bryant, ss **Night Visions** #4,1987
Preface, Gretta M. Anderson, pr *2AM* Spr,1987
Preface, Gretta M. Anderson, pr *2AM* Sum,1987
Preface, Gretta M. Anderson, pr *2AM* Fll,1987
Preface, Gretta M. Anderson, pr *2AM* Win,1987
Preface, D. Scott Apel, pr
Preface, Arthur C. Clarke, pr
Preface, Richard Dalby, pr
Preface, Philip K. Dick, pr
Preface, Dennis Etchison, pr
Preface, Martin Gardner, pr
Preface, Dean Ing, pr
Preface, Sheldon R. Jaffery, pr
Preface, Harry Turtledove, pr
Preface, Irene Zahava, pr
Preface, Jack Zipes, pr
Preface (from Afterglow), Arthur Machen, pr,1924
Presences, Lee Ann Sontheimer, pm *2AM* Sum,1987
A Present for Pat, Philip K. Dick, ss *Startling Stories* Jan,1954
Preserves, Jon Cohen, ss *Twilight Zone* Feb,1987
The Preserving Machine, Philip K. Dick, ss *F&SF* Jun,1953
President Buck Jones Rallies and Waves the Flag, Patricia Highsmith, nv **Tales of Natural and Unnatural Catastrophes**, Bloomsbury,1987
The President's Doll, Timothy Zahn, ss *Analog* Jul,1987
Pretty Boy Crossover, Pat Cadigan, ss *IASFM* Jan,1986
Pretty Maggie Moneyeyes, Harlan Ellison, nv *Knight* May,1967
The Prevaricator, Carlos Baker, ss **The Talismans and Other Stories**,1976
The Price of an Egg, Alexandra Sokolov, nv **Angels in Hell**, ed. Janet Morris, Baen,1987
The Price of Cabbages, Brian W. Aldiss, nv **Other Edens**, ed. Christopher Evans & Robert Holdstock, Unwin: London,1987
The Price of the Absolute, L.P. Hartley, ss **The White Wand and Other Stories**, Hamilton,1954
Pride and Primacy, Randall Garrett, ss *If* Apr,1974
Pride of the Fleet, Bruce Jones, ss **Swords Against Darkness** #1, ed. Andrew J. Offutt,1977
The Priests, Leonard Carpenter, pm *Eldritch Tales* #14,1987
Primal Cry, Nancy Springer, nv **Chance & Other Gestures of the Hand of Fate**, Baen,1987
Primary, Ben Bova, ss *IASFM* Feb,1985
Primatives, Robin Wayne Bailey & Robert Chilson, nv *Amazing* Jul,1987
Prime Time, Norman Spinrad, ss *Omni* Nov,1980
Prince Alberic and the Snake Lady, Vernon Lee, na **Pope Jacynth and Other Fantastic Tales**, Grant Richards: London,1904
Prince Amilec, Tanith Lee, ss **Princess Hynchatti and Some Other Surprises**, London: Macmillan,1972
Prince Caspian, C.S. Lewis, n. The Blakiston Co.: Philadelphia,1951
A Prince in Another Place, Philippa Pearce, ss **They Wait and Other Spine Chillers**, ed. Lance Salway, Pepper Press,1983
The Prince Out of the Past, Nancy Springer, ss **Magic in Ithkar** #1, ed. Andre Norton & Robert Adams,1985
The Prince's Birthday, Keith Minnion, ss *The Dragon* Jun,1987
The Prince's Dream, Jean Ingelow, ss **The Little Wonder-Horn**, London: Henry S. King,1872
The Prince, Two Mice and Some Kitchen-Maids, Edith Nesbit, ss
The Princess and Her Future, Tanith Lee, ss **Red As Blood**, DAW,1983
The Princess and the Bear, Orson Scott Card, nv **The Berkley Showcase** v1, ed. Victoria Schochet & John W. Silbersack,1980
The Princess and the Clown, Margaret Mahy, ss **Mahy Magic**, Dent,1986
The Princess and the Pea, Hans Christian Andersen, vi
The Princess Nobody, Andrew Lang, ss,1884
Princess of Darkness, Frederick Cowles, ss **Dracula's Brood**, ed. Richard Dalby, Crucible,1987
Princess Thirty Moonbeams and the Hard Luck Bargaining Kit, Lesley Choyce, ss **The Dream Auditor**, Indivisible Books,1986
The Princess Who Stood On Her Own Two Feet, Jeanne Desy, ss **Stories for Free Children**, ed. Letty Pogrebin, New York: McGraw Hill,1982
The Prisoner of Chillon, James Patrick Kelly, nv *IASFM* Jun,1986
Prisoners, Anna Lieff Saxby, ss **Gollancz - Sunday Times Best SF Stories**, Gollancz,1987
Privacy Rights, J.N. Williamson, ss **Whispers** #6, ed. Stuart David Schiff,1987
Private Conversation [lyrics], Mercedes R. Lackey, sg **Festival Moon**, ed. C.J. Cherryh, DAW,1987

Private Conversation [music], C.J. Cherryh, sg **Festival Moon**, ed. C.J. Cherryh, DAW,1987
Private Eye, Henry Kuttner, nv *Astounding* Jan,1949
Private Eye Oglesby [as "Crunchy Wunchy's First Case"], Martin Gardner, ss *London Mystery Magazine* Feb,1951
A Private Ghost, Joyce Cary, ss **Spring Song and Other Stories**, Michael Joseph,1960
Privileged Information, Lesley Choyce, ss **The Dream Auditor**, Indivisible Books,1986
The Prize, Thomas Wylde, ss *Night Cry* v2#5,1987
Prize Ship, Philip K. Dick, ss *Thrilling Wonder Stories* Win,1954
Proallognostication, Andrew Giesler, vi *Analog* Nov,1987
Proctor Valley, Dale Hoover, ss *Grue* #6,1987
The Prodigal, Tanith Lee, nv **Night's Sorceries**, DAW,1987
Professor and Colonel, Ruth Berman, ss **Mathenauts**, ed. Rudy Rucker, Arbor House,1987
Profile: Ambrose Bierce, Thomas E. Sanders (Nippawanock), bg *Night Cry* v2#4,1987
Profile: John Gawsworth, Steve Eng, bg *Night Cry* v2#3,1987
Profile: Rudyard Kipling, William Relling, Jr., bg *Night Cry* v2#5,1987
Progeny, Philip K. Dick, ss *If* Nov,1954
prognostication, Keith Allen Daniels, pm *Grue* #4,1987
Project: Earth, Philip K. Dick, ss *Imagination* Dec,1953
Projections, Bentley Little, ss *The Horror Show* Jan,1987
Prologue, Robert Adams, pr
Prologue: The Illustrated Man, Ray Bradbury, ss **The Illustrated Man**,1951
Prominant Author, Philip K. Dick, ss *If* May,1954
The Promise, Mary Fenoglio, nv **Red Sun of Darkover**, ed. Marion Zimmer Bradley & The Friends of Darkover, DAW,1987
Promised Star, Ira Herman, ss *Amazing* Nov,1987
Promises, Sara Maitland, ss
Proof, F.M. Busby, ss *Amazing* Sep,1972
prophylaxis, mel buffington, pm *Ice River* Sum,1987
The Protector, Rachel Pollack, nv *Interzone* #16,1986
Protocol [The Yllian Way], Keith Laumer, nv *If* Jan,1962
The Prowler in the City at the Edge of the World, Harlan Ellison, nv **Dangerous Visions**, ed. Harlan Ellison, Doubleday,1967
Pruzy's Pot, Theodore Sturgeon, ss *The National Lampoon* Jun,1972
Psi-Man Heal My Child! [also as "Psi-Man"], Philip K. Dick, nv *Imaginative Tales* Nov,1955
Psi-Rec: Priest of Roses, Paladin of Swords, the War Within, Peter Dillingham, pm **There Will Be War** v6, ed. Jerry E. Pournelle,1987
Psicopath [as by Darrell T. Langart], Randall Garrett, ss *Analog* Oct,1960
The Puiss of Krrlik, F.M. Busby, ss *Fantastic* Apr,1972
Pulp, Paul Roland, ss **The Curious Case of Richard Fielding and Other Stories**, Lary Press,1987
Pulsebeat, J.B. Cather, nv *Analog* Dec,1987
Pumpkin, Robert Bloch, nv *Twilight Zone* Dec,1984
Punk Funeral, Peggy Dembicer, pm *Grue* #6,1987
Punky and the Yale Man, Harlan Ellison, nv *Knight* Jan,1966
The Puppet Master, Paul Roland, sg **The Curious Case of Richard Fielding and Other Stories**, Lary Press,1987
The Pure Evil, Kenneth Robeson, na *Doc Savage* Mar,1948
The Pure Product, John Kessel, nv *IASFM* Mar,1986
The Purple Hour, Paul Christopher, ss **Beyond That River**, Pal Books,1987
The Purple Pterodactyls, L. Sprague de Camp, ss *F&SF* Aug,1976
Pushbutton War, Joseph P. Martino, ss *Analog* Aug,1960
Puzzle Pages, Gaye Beer & Ben Daily, pz *Salarius* v1#4,1987
Puzzle Pages, Ben Daily, pz *Salarius* #3,1987
The Pylon, L.P. Hartley, ss
Pyramids, Paul Christopher, ss **Beyond That River**, Pal Books,1987
QTL, Arlan Andrews, vi *Analog* Feb,1987
The Quaker Cannon, C.M. Kornbluth & Frederik Pohl, nv *Analog* Aug,1961
The Quaking Lands, Robert E. Vardeman, n. Avon: New York pb Jan,1985
The Quality of Murphy, John Morressy, nv *F&SF* Mar,1987
Quarantine, Arthur C. Clarke, vi *IASFM* Spr,1977
The Quarry, Gordon R. Dickson, ss *Astounding* Sep,1958
Quasars and Active Galaxies, Harding E. Smith, ar **Universe**, ed. Byron Preiss, Bantam Spectra,1987
Quasars, Black Holes, and Maarten Schmidt's Bad Day at the Office, Robert Frazier, pm *Arc* Spr,1985
The Queen of Air and Darkness, Poul Anderson, na *F&SF* Apr,1971

THE QUEEN OF LOWER SAIGON

The Queen of Lower Saigon, Barry N. Malzberg, ss **In the Field of Fire**, ed. Jeanne Van Buren Dann & Jack M. Dann, Tor,1987

The Queen of Sheba's Nightmare, Bertrand Russell, ss **Nightmares of Eminent Persons**, Allen & Unwin,1954

The Queen of the Night, Harry Smith, pm *Pulpsmith* Win,1987

The Queen's Looking Glass, Sandra M. Gilbert & Susan Gubar, cr **The Mad Woman in the Attic**, New Haven, CT: Yale Univ. Press,1979

Quest for an Unnamed Place, Jack Matthews, ss *Kansas Quarterly*

Quest's End, Roger Zelazny, vi *Omni* Jun,1987

A Question of Belief, D.E. Smirl, ss *Apex!* #1,1987

A Question of Re-Entry, J.G. Ballard, nv *Fantastic* Mar,1963

The Question of Sex [from **The Left Hand of Darkness**], Ursula K. Le Guin, ex Ace: New York,1969

A Quiet Day at the Fair, Sharon Green, nv **Magic in Ithkar** #4, ed. Andre Norton & Robert Adams,1987

A Quire of Foolscap, Carl Jacobi, ss *Whispers* #23,1987

A Quotella for Ted Sturgeon, Robert Frazier, pm *IASFM* Jan,1986

R&R, Lucius Shepard, na *IASFM* Apr,1986

The Rabbit Pie Man, Josephine Saxton, ss **Little Tours of Hell**, Pandora,1986

Rachaela, Poul Anderson, nv *Fantasy Fiction* Jun,1953

Rachel in Love, Pat Murphy, nv *IASFM* Apr,1987

Radionda, Dennis Jordan, ss *Grue* #5,1987

Rags from Riches, Christopher Anvil, ss *Amazing* Nov,1987

Rain, Michael Skeet, ss **Tesseracts 2**, ed. Phyllis Gotlieb & Douglas Barbour, Press Porcepic: Victoria,1987

Raindance, Kathryn A. Sinclair, ss **Tesseracts 2**, ed. Phyllis Gotlieb & Douglas Barbour, Press Porcepic: Victoria,1987

Raistlin's Daughter, Dezra Despain & Margaret Weis, nv **DragonLance Tales** v3, Margaret Weis & Tracy Hickman, TSR,1987

Ramsey Campbell Interview, Ramsey Campbell, Nancy Garcia & Robert T. Garcia, iv *American Fantasy* Win,1987

The Random Man, Marc Laidlaw, vi *IASFM* Jul,1984

Rank Injustice, Keith Laumer, nv **New Destinies** v1, ed. Jim Baen, Baen,1987

Franklin Felano Doosevelt, Martin Gardner, ss **The No-Sided Professor**, Prometheus,1987

The Ransom of Hellcat, Chris Morris, nv **Masters of Hell**, ed. Janet Morris et al, Baen,1987

Rapunzel, Sara Henderson Hay, pm **Story Hour**, Fayetteville: Univ. of Arkansas Press,1982

Rat Boy, Paul Lake, ss *F&SF* May,1987

Rats, M.R. James, ss

The Rats in the Walls, H.P. Lovecraft, ss *Weird Tales* Mar,1924

Rautavaara's Case, Philip K. Dick, ss *Omni* Oct,1980

The Reach [Do the Dead Sing?], Stephen King, ss *Yankee* Nov,1981

Reach Out and Scorch Someone, H.R. Felgenhauer, pm *Mage* Win,1987

Reaching for Paradise, Brad Miner, nv **Angels in Hell**, ed. Janet Morris, Baen,1987

The Reactionary Revolution, Stanley Schmidt, ed *Analog* Jul,1987

Reactionary Utopias, Gregory Benford, ar **Far Frontiers** v4, ed. Jerry Pournelle & Jim Baen,1986

Readers' Forum, The Readers, lt *Tales of the Unanticipated* #2,1987

Readers' Responses, The Readers, lt *Mage* Spr,1987

Reading to Matthew, Jackie Vivelo, ss **A Trick of the Light**, Putnam,1987

The Real, William Meyer, pm *Pulpsmith* Win,1987

The Real Children of the Night, Robert Simpson, ar *Twilight Zone* Dec,1987

Real Time, The Readers, lt *2AM* Spr,1987

Real Time, The Readers, lt *2AM* Sum,1987

Real Time, The Readers, lt *2AM* Fll,1987

Real Time, The Readers, lt *2AM* Win,1987

The Real World, F.M. Busby, ss *Fantastic* Dec,1972

Realtime, Daniel Keys Moran & Gladys Prebehalla, nv *IASFM* Aug,1984

Reason Enough, Edward J. Pahule, vi *The Horror Show* Spr,1987

Rebel's Quest, F.M. Busby, n. Bantam: New York,1984

Rebel's Seed, F.M. Busby, n. Bantam: New York,1986

Rebels, Lewis Shiner, ss *Omni* Nov,1987

Rebound [The Power], Fredric Brown, vi *Galaxy* Apr,1960

Recall Mechanism, Philip K. Dick, ss *If* Jul,1959

Recessional, Fredric Brown, vi *Dude* Mar,1960

Recessional, Fred Saberhagen, ss **Destinies** v2#4, ed. James Baen,1980

The Reckoning, John Maclay, vi **Other Engagements**, Madison, WI: Dream House,1987

Recommended Reading, Terry Carr, bi

THE REPORT ON THE ALL-UNION COMMITTEE ON RECENT...

The Recurring Smash [as by S.T.], Rudyard Kipling, vi *The Civil and Military Gazette* Oct 13,1887

Recursion, Carter Scholz, ss **Cuts**, Drumm,1985

Recycle, John Maclay, pm *SPWAO Showcase* #5,1985

Red, Richard Christian Matheson, vi *Night Cry* v1#6,1986

Red as Blood, Tanith Lee, ss *F&SF* Jul,1979

The Red House, Rane Arroyo, pm *Ice River* Sum,1987

Red Light, David J. Schow, nv *Twilight Zone* Dec,1986

Red Paint, David Barker, ss *The Horror Show* Sum,1987

The Red Shoes, Hans Christian Andersen, ss

Red Zone, Brian Hodge, ss *The Horror Show* Win,1987

Redeemer's Riddle, Stephen L. Burns, nv **Sword and Sorceress** #4, ed. Marion Zimmer Bradley,1987

The Reel Stuff: A Witchin' Summer, Jessie Horsting, mr *Aboriginal SF* May,1987

The Reel Stuff: Dog Days, Jessie Horsting, mr *Aboriginal SF* Jul,1987

The Reel Stuff: The Good, the Bad and the Maybes, Jessie Horsting, mr *Aboriginal SF* Feb,1987

The Reference Library, Thomas A. Easton, br *Analog* Jan,1987

The Reference Library, Thomas A. Easton, br *Analog* Feb,1987

The Reference Library, Thomas A. Easton, br *Analog* Mar,1987

The Reference Library, Thomas A. Easton, br *Analog* Apr,1987

The Reference Library, Thomas A. Easton, br *Analog* May,1987

The Reference Library, Thomas A. Easton, br *Analog* Jun,1987

The Reference Library, Thomas A. Easton, br *Analog* Jul,1987

The Reference Library, Thomas A. Easton, br *Analog* Aug,1987

The Reference Library, Thomas A. Easton, br *Analog* Sep,1987

The Reference Library, Thomas A. Easton, br *Analog* Oct,1987

The Reference Library, Thomas A. Easton, br *Analog* Nov,1987

The Reference Library, Thomas A. Easton, br *Analog* Dec,1987

The Reference Library, Thomas A. Easton, br *Analog* mid-Dec,1987

Refill, John Maclay, pm *Twisted* #1,1985

Reflections, Robert Silverberg, ar *Amazing* Jan,1987

Reflections, Robert Silverberg, ar *Amazing* Mar,1987

Reflections, Robert Silverberg, ar *Amazing* May,1987

Reflections, Robert Silverberg, ar *Amazing* Jul,1987

Reflections, Robert Silverberg, ar *Amazing* Sep,1987

Reflections, Robert Silverberg, ar *Amazing* Nov,1987

Reflections of the Past, R. Brent Powell, ss *Salarius* v1#4,1987

Reflections on Yarbro's **False Dawn**, James A. Lee, br *2AM* Win,1987

The Refugee, Jane Rice, ss *Unknown* Oct,1943

Regenesis, Jane Yolen, pm *Fantasy Book* Mar,1987

Reign of Fire, M. Bradley Kellogg & William Rossow, n. New American Library: New York,1986

The Reincarnated Queens of England, Menke Katz, pm *Pulpsmith* Win,1987

Relative Difficulties, Melinda M. Snodgrass, nv **Wild Cards** v2, ed. George R.R. Martin, Bantam,1987

Relative Distances, Robert Frazier, pm *Amazing* Mar,1987

The Reluctant Dragon, Kenneth Grahame, ss **Dream Days**, London: John Lane,1898

Remember the Alamo!, T.R. Fehrenbach, ss *Analog* Dec,1961

Remembering Medea, Brett Rutherford, pm *Haunts* #9,1987

Renaissance Man, Lesley Choyce, ss **The Dream Auditor**, Indivisible Books,1986

Render Unto Caesar, Marcia Martin & Eric Vinicoff, ss *Analog* Aug,1976

Rendezvous, Bruce Jones, nv **Twisted Tales**, San Diego: Blackthorne,1987

A Rendezvous in Averoigne, Clark Ashton Smith, ss *Weird Tales* Apr,1931

Rendezvous with Rama, Arthur C. Clarke, n. Gollancz: London,1973

Rent-a-Joke, Marjorie Darke, ss **Twisted Circuits**, ed. Mick Gowar, Beaver,1987

Rent-a-Womb vs. The Mighty Right, Patricia Highsmith, ss **Tales of Natural and Unnatural Catastrophes**, Bloomsbury,1987

The Repairer of Reputations, Robert W. Chambers, nv **The King in Yellow**, New York & Chicago: F. Tennyson Neely,1895

"Repent, Harlequin!" Said the Ticktockman, Harlan Ellison, ss *Galaxy* Dec,1965

The Report on Bilbeis IV, Harry Turtledove, na *Analog* May +2,1987

The Report on Bilbeis IV [Part 1 of 3], Harry Turtledove, sl *Analog* May,1987

The Report on Bilbeis IV [Part 2 of 3], Harry Turtledove, sl *Analog* Jun,1987

The Report on Bilbeis IV [Part 3 of 3], Harry Turtledove, sl *Analog* Jul,1987

The Report on the All-Union Committee on Recent Rumors Concerning the Moldavian SSR, D.C. Poyer, ss *Analog* mid-Dec,1987

A Report on the Violent Man [from **A Criminal History of Mankind**], Colin Wilson, ar

Repossession, David Campton, ss **Whispers** #6, ed. Stuart David Schiff,1987

Republic and Empire, Jerry E. Pournelle, ar **Imperial Stars** v2, ed. Jerry E. Pournelle,1987

Requiem, Robert A. Heinlein, ss *Astounding* Jan,1940

Requiem, Paul Roland, sg **The Curious Case of Richard Fielding and Other Stories**, Lary Press,1987

Requiem, Melinda M. Snodgrass, ss **A Very Large Array**, ed. Melinda M. Snodgrass, University of New Mexico Press,1987

Requiem For a Universe, Poul Anderson, ss **Universe**, ed. Byron Preiss, Bantam Spectra,1987

Rescue Party, Arthur C. Clarke, nv *Astounding* May,1946

Resonance Ritual, Paula May, ss **L. Ron Hubbard Presents Writers of the Future** v3, ed. Algis Budrys, Bridge,1987

Rest Stops in the Sawing of a Log, Robert Frazier, pm

Restless Souls, Seabury Quinn, nv *Weird Tales* Oct,1928

Restricted Area, Robert Sheckley, ss *Amazing* Jul,1953

The Resurgence of Miss Ankle-Strap Wedgie, Harlan Ellison, ss **Love Ain't Nothing But Sex Misspelled**, Trident,1968

ResurrecTech, S.P. Somtow, nv *Night Cry* v2#3,1987

The Resurrection, Gail Neville, ss *Aphelion* #5,1987

Retirement [Even Death Gets Tired], Ron Leming, ss *Outlaw Biker* Mar,1986

Retreat, S.R. Compton, pm *Star*Line* Sep,1986

Retreat Syndrome, Philip K. Dick, ss *Worlds of Tomorrow* Jan,1965

Retrieval, John Park, ss **Tesseracts 2**, ed. Phyllis Gotlieb & Douglas Barbour, Press Porcepic: Victoria,1987

Retroflex, F.M. Busby, vi *Vertex* Oct,1974

Retrograde Analysis, William Ballard, ss *Analog* Dec,1987

The Return, Marjory E. Lambe, ss *Hutchinson's Mystery Story Magazine* Mar,1924

The Return, Katharine E. Matchette, ss *Apex!* #1,1987

The Return, William F. Nolan, ms *The Horror Show* Jan,1987

The Return from Rainbow Bridge, Kim Stanley Robinson, nv *F&SF* Aug,1987

Return Match, Philip K. Dick, ss *Galaxy* Feb,1967

The Return of Imray [The Recrudescence of Imray], Rudyard Kipling, ss **Mine Own People**, New York: Hurst & Co.,1891

Return of the Jedi, James Kahn, n. Ballantine: New York,1983

The Return of the Sorcerer, Clark Ashton Smith, nv *Strange Tales of Mystery and Terror* Sep,1931

Return to an Unknown City, Jack Matthews, ss *Mississippi Valley Review*

Return to Raebourne, Paul Roland, ss **The Curious Case of Richard Fielding and Other Stories**, Lary Press,1987

"Return..." A Preface, K. Leslie Steiner, pr

Returning Home, Ian Watson, ss *Omni* Dec,1982

Reunion, Arthur C. Clarke, ss **Infinity** #2, ed. Robert Hoskins,1971

Reunion, Billy Wolfenbarger, pm *Eldritch Tales* #13,1987

A Revel in Rel Mord, Gary Gygax, na **Night Arrant**, Ace/New Infinities,1987

Revelations in Black, Carl Jacobi, ss *Weird Tales* Apr,1933

A Rewarding Experience, L.P. Hartley, ss **The White Wand and Other Stories**, Hamilton,1954

Rhysling Award Winners, 1978 - 1986, [Misc. Material], bi

A Ribbon for Margaret's Doll, Dragan R. Filipovic, ss *SF International* #1,1987

Rider, Andrew Weiner, nv *IASFM* Jul,1987

A Rider on a Blue Horse Waits Outside the Hospital Wall, Conger Beasley, Jr., vi *Ice River* Sum,1987

Rider on a Mountain, Andre Norton, ss **Friends of the Horseclans**, ed. Robert Adams & Pamela Crippen Adams, Signet,1987

Right Inn, J.B. Stamper, ss **More Tales for the Midnight Hour**, Apple/Scholastic,1987

The Right Shuttle, Alan Dean Foster, ar *Amazing* May,1987

Rika's World, Sue Moorhouse, ss **Gollancz - Sunday Times Best SF Stories**, Gollancz,1987

The Ring of Hans Carvel, Fredric Brown, vi **Nightmares and Geezenstacks**, Bantam,1961

The Ring of Lifari, Josepha Sherman, ss **Sword and Sorceress** #4, ed. Marion Zimmer Bradley,1987

The Ring with the Velvet Ropes, Edward D. Hoch, ss **With Malice Toward All**, ed. Robert L. Fish,1968

Rising Generation, Ramsey Campbell, ss *Night Cry* v2#5,1987

Rising Waters, Patricia Ferrara, ss *F&SF* Jul,1987

Rite of Passage, Jennifer Roberson, nv **Sword and Sorceress** #4, ed. Marion Zimmer Bradley,1987

Ritual, Arthur Machen, ss,1937

The Rivalry, Richard Easton, ss *The Virginia Quarterly Review* Win,1987

Riverwind and The Crystal Staff, Michael Williams, pm **DragonLance Tales** v1, Margaret Weis & Tracy Hickman, TSR,1987

The Roaches, Thomas M. Disch, ss *Escapade* Oct,1965

Road, B.J. Seidenstein, ss *Haunts* #9,1987

The Road It Went By, Philippa Pearce, ss **Outsiders**, ed. Bryan Newton, Collins Educational,1985

Road Map, F.M. Busby, ss **Clarion** #3, ed. Robert Scott Wilson,1973

The Road of Dreams and Death, Robert E. Vardeman, nv **Tales of the Witch World**, ed. Andre Norton, St. Martin's,1987

Roadkill, Dean Whitlock, nv *IASFM* Nov,1987

The Roads Must Roll, Robert A. Heinlein, nv *Astounding* Jun,1940

Roaming Fancy, Mary Frances Zambreno, br *American Fantasy* Spr,1987

Roaming Fancy, Mary Frances Zambreno, br *American Fantasy* Sum,1987

Roaming Fancy, Mary Frances Zambreno, br *American Fantasy* Win,1987

Roaring Tower, Stella Gibbons, ss **Roaring Tower**,1937

The Robber Bridegroom, Robert D. San Souci, ss **Short & Shivery**, Doubleday,1987

Robert, Stanley Ellin, ss *Sluth Mystery Magazine* Oct,1958

Robot AL-76 Goes Astray, Isaac Asimov, ss *Amazing* Feb,1942

The Rock Bearers, Thomas E. Sanders (Nippawanock), ar *Twilight Zone* Aug,1987

Rock Sinister, Kenneth Robeson, na *Doc Savage* May,1945

Rock, Rock [The Dead Man's Chair], Manly Wade Wellman, ss *F&SF* Oct,1973

The Rocket [Outcast of the Stars], Ray Bradbury, ss *Super Science Stories* Mar,1950

The Rocket Man, Ray Bradbury, ss *Maclean's* Mar 1,1951

Rocket Summer, Ray Bradbury, vi **The Martian Chronicles**,1950

The Rocking-Horse Winner, D.H. Lawrence, ss **The Ghost-Book**, ed. Cynthia Asquith, Hutchinson,1926

Rokuro-Kubi, Lafcadio Hearn, ss **Kwaidan**,1904

Roman Charity, L.P. Hartley, nv

Roman Headstone, John Gawsworth, pm

Romance, Isaac Asimov, ss *IASFM* Jul,1987

Romantic/Science Fiction, C.J. Cherryh, sp *Archon* 2 (convention),1978

Roog, Philip K. Dick, ss *F&SF* Feb,1953

Room 1786, Terence M. Green, ss *Leisure Ways* Nov,1982

The Room at the End of the Hall, Helen Nielsen, ss *Alfred Hitchcock's Mystery Magazine* Oct,1973

The Room in the Castle, Ramsey Campbell, ss **The Inhabitant of the Lake**, Arkham,1964

The Room in the Tower, E.F. Benson, ss **The Room in the Tower and Other Stories**, London: Mills Boon,1912

Roomers, Bruce Jones, ss **Twisted Tales**, San Diego: Blackthorne,1987

Roomie, David Daniel, ss *2AM* Win,1987

The Rooted Lover, Laurence Housman, ss **A Farm in Fairyland**, London: Kegan Paul,1894

The Roots of Fantasy, Gregory Forbes, ar *Mage* Spr,1985

Rope Trick, Fredric Brown, vi *Adam* May,1959

The Rose Elf, Hans Christian Andersen, ss

A Rose for Emily, William Faulkner, ss *The Forum* Apr,1930

The Rose Garden, M.R. James, ss **More Ghost Stories of an Antiquary**, Arnold,1911

The Rose Garden, Steven Popkes, ss *IASFM* Aug,1987

Roses of Ashes, Scott E. Green, pm *Eldritch Tales* #14,1987

Rouse Him Not, Manly Wade Wellman, ss *Kadath* #5,1982

Royal Bones, Evelyn Shefner, nv *Creel*

Rubber Dinosaurs and Wooden Elephants, L. Sprague de Camp, ar *Analog* mid-Dec,1987

The Rubber Room, Robert Bloch, ss **New Terrors** #2, ed. Ramsey Campbell, Pan,1980

Rude Awakening, Thomas M. Disch, vi *Omni* May,1987

Rudolph, R. Chetwynd-Hayes, nv **Dracula's Children**, Kimber,1987

Rudy Rucker Interview, Richard Kadrey & Rudy Rucker, iv *Interzone* #20,1987

The Rule of Names, Ursula K. Le Guin, ss *Fantastic* Apr,1964

Rules of Conduct, Michael Mirolla, ss **Tesseracts 2**, ed. Phyllis Gotlieb & Douglas Barbour, Press Porcepic: Victoria,1987

Runaround [Starvation], Fredric Brown, ss *Astounding* Sep,1942

Runaway, Orson Scott Card, nv *IASFM* Jun,1987

Running It Back, Susan Johnson, mr *American Fantasy* Spr,1987

Running It Back, Susan Johnson, mr *American Fantasy* Win,1987

Running Out, Charles Sheffield, ar **New Destinies** v2, ed. Jim Baen, Baen,1987

Runt, Bentley Little, ss *The Horror Show* Spr,1987

Russalka or The Seacoast of Bohemia, Joanna Russ, ss **Kittatiny**, Daughters Publishing Co.,1978

Rustle of Wings, Fredric Brown, ss *F&SF* Aug,1953

The Rustling Death, Kenneth Robeson, na *Doc Savage* Jan,1942

S.O.S., Kathinka Lannoy, ss *SF International* #2,1987

S.R.O. [as by Ellis Hart], Harlan Ellison, ss *Amazing* Mar,1957

'A Sad Tale's Best for Winter', Muriel Spark, ss

Safe Harbor, Donald Wismer, nv **Tin Stars**, ed. Isaac Asimov, Martin H. Greenberg & Charles G. Waugh, NAL/Signet,1986

Safe to the Liberties of the People, W.T. Quick, ss *Analog* Jun,1987

The Saga of Machine Gun Joe, Harlan Ellison, vi *Sundial* Jan,1955

Saga of the Crimson Knight [Part 2], John Carbonaro & Ann Cathey, sl *Salarius* #3,1987

The Saint and the Vicar, Cecil Binney, ss **50 Years of Ghost Stories**, ed. Anonymous, Hutchinson: London,1935

The Saints and Sinners Run, Becky Birtha, ss **Hear the Silence**, ed. Irene Zahava, Crossing Press,1986

Salarius Recommends, Jon Colley & Mary Sikes, br *Salarius* #3,1987

Salarius Recommends, Mary Sikes, br *Salarius* v1#4,1987

Sales Pitch, Philip K. Dick, ss *Future* Jun,1954

Sallie C., Neal Barrett, Jr., ss **Best of the West**, ed. Western Writers of America, Garden City, NY: Doubleday,1986

Salt, Diann Partridge, ss **Red Sun of Darkover**, ed. Marion Zimmer Bradley & The Friends of Darkover, DAW,1987

The Salt Garden, Margaret Atwood, nv *Ms.* Sep,1984

Salvador, Lucius Shepard, ss *F&SF* Apr,1984

Salvage Rites, Ian Watson, ss *F&SF* Jan,1987

Samantha and the Ghost, Philippa Pearce, ss

The Samaritan Rule, Laurence M. Janifer, ss *Analog* Mar,1984

Sanctity, R.M. Lamming, ss **Other Edens**, ed. Christopher Evans & Robert Holdstock, Unwin: London,1987

Sanctuary, Kim Antieau, ss **Shadows** #9, ed. Charles L. Grant,1986

Sandmagic, Orson Scott Card, nv **Swords Against Darkness** #4, ed. Andrew J. Offutt,1979

The Sandman, David Williamson, ss **The Pan Book of Horror Stories** #28, Pan,1987

Satan's Gun, Karl Edward Wagner, ex **World Fantasy Convention Program Book** #13,1987

Satisfaction Guaranteed, Isaac Asimov, ss *Amazing* Apr,1951

Satisfaction Guaranteed, P.E. Cunningham, ss *F&SF* Jun,1987

Saturnin Sektor, Stefan Grabinski, ss,1920

Savages [from "Concealed Savages of Tudor England"], Arthur Machen, ar *The American Mercury* Feb,1936

Saving Grace, Orson Scott Card, ss *Night Cry* v2#5,1987

Saving Time, Russell M. Griffin, na *F&SF* Feb,1987

Savitri and Satyavan, Madhur Jaffrey, ss **Seasons of Splendour**, Pavilion,1985

Scanners Live in Vain, Cordwainer Smith, nv *Fantasy Book* #6,1950

"Scanners Live in Vain": Under the Wire With the Habermans, Robert Silverberg, ar,1987

The Scar, Ramsey Campbell, ss *Startling Mystery Stories* Sum,1969

The Scar, Dennis Etchison, ss *The Horror Show* Win,1987

Scar-Tissue, Henry S. Whitehead, ss *Amazing* Jul,1946

Scare Tactics, F.J. Willett, vi *Aphelion* #5,1987

Scared To Death, Robert D. San Souci, ss **Short & Shivery**, Doubleday,1987

Scarlet Ibis, Margaret Atwood, nv

Scarrowfell, Robert P. Holdstock, nv **Other Edens**, ed. Christopher Evans & Robert Holdstock, Unwin: London,1987

The Scent of Roses, Robert Sampson, ss *Space & Time* #73,1987

Schalken the Painter, Joseph Sheridan Le Fanu, ss *Dublin University Magazine* May,1839

The Schematic Man, Frederik Pohl, ss *Playboy* Jan,1969

School for the Unspeakable, Manly Wade Wellman, ss *Weird Tales* Sep,1937

The School Friend, Robert Aickman, nv,1964

A School Story, M.R. James, ss **More Ghost Stories of an Antiquary**, Arnold,1911

Schrodinger's Cat, Ursula K. Le Guin, ss **Universe** #5, ed. Terry Carr,1974

Schwarzschild Radius, Connie Willis, ss **Universe**, ed. Byron Preiss, Bantam Spectra,1987

Science Fiction, Jane Yolen, pm *IASFM* Jul,1987

Science Fiction & Fantasy Cover Art, Gregory Forbes, ar *Mage* Win,1985

Science Fiction in the Twilight Zone, Marc Scott Zicree, ar *Twilight Zone* Oct,1987

The Science Fiction World, Mervyn R. Binns, ar *Aphelion* #5,1987

Science Fiction--Judging the Genre, Jeffrey V. Yule, ed *Mage* Spr,1987

Science: A Sacred Poet, Isaac Asimov, ar *F&SF* Sep,1987

Science: Asking the Right Question, Isaac Asimov, ar *F&SF* Nov,1987

Science: Beginning With Bone, Isaac Asimov, ar *F&SF* May,1987

Science: Brightening Stars, Isaac Asimov, ar *F&SF* Jul,1987

Science: New Stars, Isaac Asimov, ar *F&SF* Jun,1987

Science: Opposite!, Isaac Asimov, ar *F&SF* Jan,1987

Science: Sail On! Sail On!, Isaac Asimov, ar *F&SF* Feb,1987

Science: Super-Exploding Stars, Isaac Asimov, ar *F&SF* Aug,1987

Science: The Incredible Shrinking Planet, Isaac Asimov, ar *F&SF* Mar,1987

Science: The Light-Bringer, Isaac Asimov, ar *F&SF* Apr,1987

Science: The Road to Humanity, Isaac Asimov, ar *F&SF* Dec,1987

Science: The Very Error of the Moon, Isaac Asimov, ar *F&SF* Oct,1987

Scottish Prayer, Anonymous, pm

Scout's Honor, Joanne Mitchell, ss *Aboriginal SF* Nov,1987

Screen, Gahan Wilson, mr *Twilight Zone* Feb,1987

Screen, Gahan Wilson, mr *Twilight Zone* Apr,1987

Screen, Gahan Wilson, mr *Twilight Zone* Jun,1987

Screen, Gahan Wilson, mr *Twilight Zone* Aug,1987

Screen, Gahan Wilson, mr *Twilight Zone* Oct,1987

Screen, Gahan Wilson, mr *Twilight Zone* Dec,1987

Scylla and Charybdis, John Gawsworth, vi **New Tales of Horror By Eminent Authors**, ed. Anonymous, Hutchinson,1934

Sea Change, Scott Baker, ss *F&SF* Mar,1986

Sea Change, C.J. Cherryh, ss **Elsewhere** v1, ed. Terri Winding & Mark Allan Arnold,1981

Sea Change, Janet Morris, nv **Masters of Hell**, ed. Janet Morris et al, Baen,1987

Sea Floor Maps, Pat Tobin, il **Festival Moon**, ed. C.J. Cherryh, DAW,1987

Sea of Stiffs, Janet Morris, nv **Angels in Hell**, ed. Janet Morris, Baen,1987

The Sea Urchin, Josephine Saxton, ss **Little Tours of Hell**, Pandora,1986

Seal-Self, Sara Maitland, ss

Sealed Orders [Retief of the Red-Tape Mountain], Keith Laumer, nv *If* May,1962

Search and Destroy, Frederik Pohl, ss *Aboriginal SF* May,1987

Searchlight, Robert A. Heinlein, vi *Scientific American* Aug,1962

Season of Disbelief, Ray Bradbury, ss *Colliers* Nov 25,1950

The Season of Sitting, Ray Bradbury, ar *Charm* Aug,1951

Seaton's Aunt, Walter de la Mare, nv **The Riddle and Other Stories**, London: Selwyn and Blount,1923

Second Chance, Fredric Brown, vi **Nightmares and Geezenstacks**, Bantam,1961

Second Chance, Jack Finney, ss **The Third Level**, New York: Rinehart & Co.,1957

A Second Gaze at Little Red Riding Hood's Trials and Tribulations, Jack Zipes, cr,1984

Second Gibraltar, Chris Reed, ss *Back Brain Recluse* #7,1987

Second Going, James Tiptree, Jr., nv **Universe** #17, ed. Terry Carr,1987

The Second Kind of Loneliness, George R.R. Martin, ss *Analog* Dec,1972

The Second Nit-Picky, Utterly Trivial, Totally Picayune Horror-Fantasy Movie Quiz -- or -- Trivial Lives, II, A.R. Morlan, qz *The Horror Show* Sum,1987

Second Sight, Ramsey Campbell, ss **Masques** #2, ed. J.N. Williamson,1987

Second Spring, Theodore Mathieson, nv *The Saint* Jun,1959

Second Survey, Harry Turtledove, nv *Analog* Jul,1986

The Second Third of C, Neil Ferguson, ss *Interzone* #19,1987

second thoughts, Wayne Allen Sallee, pm *Grue* #5,1987

Second Variety, Philip K. Dick, nv *Space Science Fiction* May,1953

The Second Wave, Matthew J. Costello, ar *Amazing* Mar,1987

The Secret [The Secret of the Men in the Moon], Arthur C. Clarke, ss *This Week* Aug 11,1963

The Secret Hour, Jack Matthews, ss *Premiere*

The Secret Sharer, Robert Silverberg, na *IASFM* Sep,1987

Secret Under Antarctica, Gordon R. Dickson, n. Holt, Rinehart & Winston: New York,1963

Secret Under the Caribbean, Gordon R. Dickson, n. Holt, Rinehart & Winston: New York,1964

Secret Under the Sea, Gordon R. Dickson, n. Henry Holt,1960

Secret Worship, Algernon Blackwood, nv **John Silence**,1908

The Seductress, Ramsey Campbell, nv **The Mayflower Book of Black Magic Stories** #6, ed. Michael Parry,1976

See Now, a Pilgrim, Gordon R. Dickson, na *Analog* Sep,1985

The Seed, Roy Schneider, ss *Eldritch Tales* #14,1987

Seeing Is Believing (But Love Is Blind), Lynn Abbey, nv **Aftermath**, ed. Robert Lynn Asprin & Lynn Abbey, Ace,1987

Seeing the World, Ramsey Campbell, ss **Shadows** #7, ed. Charles L. Grant,1984

Select Bibliography, [Misc. Material], bi

Selected Bibliography, Richard Dalby, bi

A Selected Damon Knight Bibliography, [Misc. Material], bi *Tales of the Unanticipated* #2,1987

A Selected Kate Wilhelm Bibliography, [Misc. Material], bi *Tales of the Unanticipated* #2,1987

Selected Readings, Andrew Fraknoi, bi

Selena's Song, Elyse Guttenberg, ss **Spaceships & Spells**, ed. Jane Yolen, Martin H. Greenberg & Charles G. Waugh, Harper & Row,1987

Semblance, Dean Schreck, pm *Eldritch Tales* #13,1987

Sen Yet Babbo & the Heavenly Host, Chet Williamson, ss *Playboy* Aug,1987

The Sending of Dana Da, Rudyard Kipling, ss *The Week's News* Feb 11,1888

A Senoi Dream, Malcolm Ashworth, ss **Gollancz - Sunday Times Best SF Stories**, Gollancz,1987

Sense of Wonder, Margaret B. Simon, ar *Minnesota Fantasy Review* #1,1987

Sentences, Richard Christian Matheson, ss **Death**, ed. Stuart David Schiff, Playboy,1982

Sentry, Fredric Brown, vi *Galaxy* Feb,1954

The Seraph and the Zambesi, Muriel Spark, ss

Serious Writing or Escapism?, Jeffrey V. Yule, ed *Mage* Win,1985

Serpent's Egg, R.A. Lafferty, n.,1987

Service Call, Philip K. Dick, ss *(The Original) Science Fiction Stories* Jul,1955

The Settlers, Ray Bradbury, vi **The Martian Chronicles**,1950

Seven American Nights, Gene Wolfe, na **Orbit** #20, ed. Damon Knight,1978

Seven Bird and Beast Poems, Ursula K. Le Guin, si

Seven Come Heaven?, Diane Wnorowska, ss **Devils & Demons**, ed. Marvin Kaye, SFBC/Doubleday,1987

Seventh Sense, Robert Haisty, ss *Omni* Sep,1983

The Sex Opposite, Theodore Sturgeon, nv *Fantastic* Fll,1952

Sexual Chemistry, Brian M. Stableford, ss *Interzone* #20,1987

SF Conventional Calendar, Erwin S. Strauss, ms *IASFM* Jan,1987

SF Conventional Calendar, Erwin S. Strauss, ms *IASFM* Feb,1987

SF Conventional Calendar, Erwin S. Strauss, ms *IASFM* Mar,1987

SF Conventional Calendar, Erwin S. Strauss, ms *IASFM* Apr,1987

SF Conventional Calendar, Erwin S. Strauss, ms *IASFM* May,1987

SF Conventional Calendar, Erwin S. Strauss, ms *IASFM* Jun,1987

SF Conventional Calendar, Erwin S. Strauss, ms *IASFM* Jul,1987

SF Conventional Calendar, Erwin S. Strauss, ms *IASFM* Aug,1987

SF Conventional Calendar, Erwin S. Strauss, ms *IASFM* Sep,1987

SF Conventional Calendar, Erwin S. Strauss, ms *IASFM* Oct,1987

SF Conventional Calendar, Erwin S. Strauss, ms *IASFM* Nov,1987

SF Conventional Calendar, Erwin S. Strauss, ms *IASFM* Dec,1987

SF Conventional Calendar, Erwin S. Strauss, ms *IASFM* mid-Dec,1987

SF: From Secret Movement to Big Business, Brian W. Aldiss, ar *Aboriginal SF* May,1987

Shade and the Elephant Man, Emily Devenport, ss *Aboriginal SF* May,1987

Shades, Lucius Shepard, nv **In the Field of Fire**, ed. Jeanne Van Buren Dann & Jack M. Dann, Tor,1987

The Shadow, Marion Zimmer Bradley, nv **Red Sun of Darkover**, ed. Marion Zimmer Bradley & The Friends of Darkover, DAW,1987

The Shadow Kingdom, Robert E. Howard, nv *Weird Tales* Aug,1929

The Shadow of Space, Philip Jose Farmer, nv *If* Nov,1967

The Shadow of the Beast, Robert E. Howard, ss **The Shadow of the Beast**, Glenn Lord,1977

Shadow of the Immortal (Part 2 of 3), Charles L. Baker, sl *Eldritch Tales* #13,1987

Shadow of the Immortal (Part 3 of 3), Charles L. Baker, sl *Eldritch Tales* #14,1987

The Shadow on the Doorstep, James P. Blaylock, ss *IASFM* May,1986

The Shadow on the Wall, L.P. Hartley, ss

The Shadow Watchers, Dick Baldwin, ss **Fiends and Creatures**, ed. Marvin Kaye, Popular Library,1975

The Shadows, George MacDonald, nv

Shadows, Pamela Sargent, nv **Fellowship of the Stars**, ed. Terry Carr, Simon & Schuster,1974

The Shadowy Third, Ellen Glasgow, ss *Scribner's* Dec,1916

A Shaggy Dog's Tail, Danny Peary, nv **DragonLance Tales** v2, Margaret Weis & Tracy Hickman, TSR,1987

Shalamari, Marc Laidlaw, ss *IASFM* Dec,1987

Shambleau, C.L. Moore, nv *Weird Tales* Nov,1933

Shape [Keep Your Shape], Robert Sheckley, nv *Galaxy* Nov,1953

The Shaper of Animals, Darrell Schweitzer, ss *Amazing* Jul,1987

Shards, Richard Taylor, pm *Ice River* Sum,1987

Shards of Honor, Lois McMaster Bujold, n. Baen: New York,1986

Shared Secrets: Inside the World of Shared Worlds, Nancy Garcia, ar *American Fantasy* Spr,1987

Sharing, Mort Castle, vi *Grue* #4,1987

Shark, Edward Bryant, nv *Orbit* #12, ed. Damon Knight,1973

Sharper than a Serpent's Tooth, C.J. Cherryh, nv **Crusaders in Hell**, ed. Janet Morris, New York: Baen,1987

Sharper Than a Serpent's Tooth, William Relling, Jr., ss *The Horror Show* Spr,1987

Shattered Like a Glass Goblin, Harlan Ellison, ss *Orbit* #4, ed. Damon Knight,1968

She Closed Her Eyes, Craig Shaw Gardner, nv **Doom City**, ed. Charles L. Grant, Tor,1987

She Comes When You're Leaving, Bruce Boston, ss *Berkeley Poets' Co-op* #9,1975

She Just Wanted to Get out of the House, Darrell Schweitzer, pm *Amazing* Sep,1987

She Only Goes Out at Night, William Tenn, ss *Fantastic Universe* Oct,1956

She Told Me, Honor, Brian Cronwall, pm *Tales of the Unanticipated* #2,1987

She Unnames Them, Ursula K. Le Guin, vi *New Yorker* Jan 21,1985

The Sheeted Dead, Charles L. Grant, ss **In the Field of Fire**, ed. Jeanne Van Buren Dann & Jack M. Dann, Tor,1987

Shell Game, Philip K. Dick, ss *Galaxy* Sep,1954

Shelob's Dreme, Thomas M. Egan, pm *Eldritch Tales* #13,1987

The Shepherdess and the Chimney Sweep, Hans Christian Andersen, ss

The Shepherds, Ruth Sawyer, ss,1941

Shift, Nancy Holder, nv **Doom City**, ed. Charles L. Grant, Tor,1987

Shifting Passions, David B. Silva, vi *Footsteps* Nov,1987

Shifting Seas, Stanley G. Weinbaum, nv *Amazing* Apr,1937

The Shining Ones, Arthur C. Clarke, ss *Playboy* Aug,1964

Shipwrecked on Destiny Five, Andrew Joron, pm *IASFM* May,1985

Shipwright, Donald Kingsbury, na *Analog* Apr,1978

Shiva Shiva, Ronald Anthony Cross, nv *F&SF* Sep,1987

Shock Supplement, John Stanley, mr *American Fantasy* Spr,1987

Shock Supplement, John Stanley, mr *American Fantasy* Sum,1987

Shock Supplement, John Stanley, mr *American Fantasy* Win,1987

The Shore, Ray Bradbury, vi **The Martian Chronicles**,1950

Short Are My Days of Light and Shade, D.T. White, ss *Aphelion* #5,1987

The Short Happy Life of the Brown Oxford, Philip K. Dick, ss *F&SF* Jan,1954

The Short Happy Lives of Eustace Weaver I, Fredric Brown, vi *Ellery Queen's Mystery Magazine* Jun,1961

The Short Happy Lives of Eustace Weaver II, Fredric Brown, vi *Ellery Queen's Mystery Magazine* Jun,1961

The Short Happy Lives of Eustace Weaver III, Fredric Brown, vi *Ellery Queen's Mystery Magazine* Jun,1961

The Short Ones, Raymond E. Banks, nv *F&SF* Mar,1955

The Shortcut, J.B. Stamper, ss **More Tales for the Midnight Hour**, Apple/Scholastic,1987

Should Old Acquaintance... [Part 2], Mercedes R. Lackey, sl *Fantasy Book* Mar,1987

Should Old Acquaintance... [Part 3], Mercedes R. Lackey, sl *Fantasy Book* Mar,1987

The Show, Bentley Little, ss *The Horror Show* Fll,1987

Showdown, Jack Creek, ss *2AM* Win,1987

Shrapnel, Karl Edward Wagner, ss **Night Visions** #2,1985

The Shrine, Robert Faulcon, n. Arrow Books: London,1984

The Shrine, Pamela Sargent, ss *Twilight Zone* Dec,1982

The Shrine of Temptation, Judith Merril, ss *Fantastic* Apr,1962

Shrinker, Pamela Sargent, nv *IASFM* Nov,1983

Sibyl, Carol Poster, pm *Grue* #5,1987

Sibyl Sits In, Martin Gardner, vi *The Record Changer* Oct,1948

Sifting for Golden Nuggets, Charles C. Ryan, ed *Aboriginal SF* Feb,1987

The Sightseers, Ben Bova, vi **Future City**, ed. Roger Elwood, Trident,1973

SIGN OF THE SALAMANDER

Sign of the Salamander, Karl Edward Wagner, na **John Chance Vs Dread: The Apocalypse 1**,1975

The Signalman [from "Mugby Junction"], Charles Dickens, ss *All the Year Round* Chr,1866

Signals, Charles L. Harness, na **Synergy** v1, ed. George Zebrowski,1987

Significant Moments in the Life of My Mother, Margaret Atwood, ss *Queen's Quarterly*

The Signing of Tulip, F.M. Busby, ss *Vertex* Jun,1975

Silence, Leonid Andreyev, ss **Silence**, Leonid Andreyev,1910

Silence Falls on Mecca's Walls, Robert E. Howard, pm **Cthulhu: The Mythos and Kindred Horrors**, New York: Baen,1987

Silent Night, Ben Bova, ss *IASFM* Dec,1987

The Silent Towns, Ray Bradbury, ss *Charm* Mar,1949

Silted In, Karl Edward Wagner, ss **Why Not You and I?**, Tor,1987

Silver and Steel, Kevin Randle, nv **DragonLance Tales** v3, Margaret Weis & Tracy Hickman, TSR,1987

The Silver Box, Louise Lawrence, nv **A Quiver of Ghosts**, ed. Aiden Chambers, Bodley Head,1987

The Silver Clock, L.P. Hartley, ss

The Silver Leopard, Robert Lawson, ss **Spaceships & Spells**, ed. Jane Yolen, Martin H. Greenberg & Charles G. Waugh, Harper & Row,1987

The Silver Walks, William Gibson, ss *High Times* Nov,1987

Simonetta Perkins, L.P. Hartley, na,1925

Sing, Kristine Kathryn Rusch, ss *Aboriginal SF* Feb,1987

The Sing, Melanie Tem & Steve Rasnic Tem, ss *SF International* #1,1987

Singing Nightmares, Joey Froehlich, pm *Grue* #5,1987

The Singing Stone, Peter Tremayne, ss *Fantasy Tales* #16,1986

Single Combat, Joseph Green, ss *New Worlds* Aug,1964

The Singular Death of Morton, Algernon Blackwood, ss *The Tramp* Dec,1910

The Sinister Ray, Lester Dent, nv *Detective Dragnet* Mar,1932

Sins of the Fathers, David G. Rowlands, ss **Eye Hath Not Seen**,1981

Sir Dominick's Bargain [revised from "The Fortunes of Sir Robert Ardagh" *Dublin University Magazine* Mar,1838], Joseph Sheridan Le Fanu, ss *All the Year Round*,1872

siseneG, Arthur C. Clarke, vi *Analog* May,1984

Sister of Midnight, Shariann Lewitt, ss **Friends of the Horseclans**, ed. Robert Adams & Pamela Crippen Adams, Signet,1987

The Sisters, John Maclay, ss **Other Engagements**, Madison, WI: Dream House,1987

Six Flags Over Jesus, Edith Shiner & Lewis Shiner, vi *IASFM* Nov,1987

Six-Legged Svengali, Fredric Brown & Mack Reynolds, ss *Worlds Beyond* Dec,1950

The Sixth Ship, Martin Gardner, ss *Our Navy* Sep,1951

Sixtus VI, Pope of the Red Slipper, Patricia Highsmith, nv **Tales of Natural and Unnatural Catastrophes**, Bloomsbury,1987

The Skeleton's Dance, Robert D. San Souci, ss **Short & Shivery**, Doubleday,1987

A Sketch of Their Father, Roger Zelazny, in

The Skills of Xanadu, Theodore Sturgeon, nv *Galaxy* Jul,1956

Skin Day, and After, Ian Watson, ss *F&SF* Jul,1985

Skin Deep, Emily Devenport, ss *Aboriginal SF* Sep,1987

Skiophanes' Proof, Luke Andreski, ss **Gollancz - Sunday Times Best SF Stories**, Gollancz,1987

Skirmish [Bathe Your Bearings in Blood], Clifford D. Simak, ss *Amazing* Dec,1950

The Skull, Philip K. Dick, ss *If* Sep,1952

The Skull of the Marquis de Sade, Robert Bloch, nv *Weird Tales* Sep,1945

The Sky Is a Circle: Exploring the Native American Spirit World, Ariel Remler, ar *Twilight Zone* Aug,1987

The Sky Is Burning, Harlan Ellison, ss *If* Aug,1958

Skylab Done It, George Alec Effinger, nv *F&SF* Mar,1987

Sleep No More, James H. Schmitz, ss *Analog* Aug,1965

Sleep With Me--And Death, Wayne Rogers, nv *Horror Stories* Apr,1938

Sleeping Beauty, Hillel Schwartz, ss *The Short Story Review* Win,1987

Sleeping Booty, Richard Wilson, ss *Whispers* #6, ed. Stuart David Schiff,1987

Sleeping Out, Ursula K. Le Guin, pm,1985

Sleipner, Late Thurinda, Rudyard Kipling, ss *The Week's News* May 12,1888

Sliders, Susan Lilas Wiggs, ss *Grue* #6,1987

Sliding Rock, Terry Boren, ss **A Very Large Array**, ed. Melinda M. Snodgrass, University of New Mexico Press,1987

Slow Roll In Neutral, Scott E. Green, pm *Eldritch Tales* #13,1987

Slow Sculpture, Theodore Sturgeon, nv *Galaxy* Feb,1970

The Slype House, A.C. Benson, ss **The Isles of Sunset**, Isbister: London,1904

SOMETHING IN THE WIND

Small Heirlooms, M. John Harrison, ss **Other Edens**, ed. Christopher Evans & Robert Holdstock, Unwin: London,1987

Small Miracle, Randall Garrett, ss *Amazing* Jun,1959

A Small Miracle of Fishhooks and Straight Pins, David R. Bunch, ss *Fantastic* Jun,1961

Small Press Reviews, Irwin M. Chapman, br *2AM* Spr,1987

Small Press Reviews, Irwin M. Chapman, br *2AM* Sum,1987

Small Press Reviews, Irwin M. Chapman, br *2AM* Fll,1987

Small Press Reviews, Irwin M. Chapman, br *2AM* Win,1987

Small Talk, James Kisner, ss *Grue* #4,1987

Small Town, Philip K. Dick, ss *Amazing* May,1954

Smasher, Fred Saberhagen, nv *F&SF* Aug,1978

The Smile on the Face of the Kite, Leslie Halliwell, nv **A Demon Close Behind**, Robert Hale,1987

Smile!, Frank Ward, ss *Amazing* Nov,1987

Smoke Ghost, Fritz Leiber, ss *Unknown* Oct,1941

The Smoke Ring [Part 1 of 4], Larry Niven, sl *Analog* Jan,1987

The Smoke Ring [Part 2 of 4], Larry Niven, sl *Analog* Feb,1987

The Smoke Ring [Part 3 of 4], Larry Niven, sl *Analog* Mar,1987

The Smoke Ring [Part 4 of 4], Larry Niven, sl *Analog* Apr,1987

The Smoking Mirror, R.E. Klein, ss *Space & Time* #73,1987

Smoking-Room Story, Leslie Halliwell, ss **A Demon Close Behind**, Robert Hale,1987

The Snail and the Rosebush, Hans Christian Andersen, vi

Snake-Eyes, Tom Maddox, nv *Omni* Apr,1986

A Snitch in Time, Robert Bloch, ss **Lost in Time and Space with Lefty Feep**, Creatures at Large,1987

Snorkeling in the River Lethe, Rory Harper, ss *Amazing* Jan,1987

Snow, Bentley Little, ss *Grue* #4,1987

The Snow Apples, Gwyneth Jones, ss **Tales from the Forbidden Planet**, ed. Roz Kaveney, Titan,1987

Snow Horse, Joan Aiken, ss

The Snow Queen, Hans Christian Andersen, nv,1844

Snow White, The Merseyside Fairy Story Collective, ss *Spare Rib* #51,1972

Snowballs in Hell, Chris Morris, nv **Crusaders in Hell**, ed. Janet Morris, New York: Baen,1987

Snowblind, Marc Laidlaw, ss *Twilight Zone* Feb,1987

The Snowman, Hans Christian Andersen, ss

Snowsong, Nancy Varian Berberick, nv **DragonLance Tales** v2, Margaret Weis & Tracy Hickman, TSR,1987

The Snuff-Box, Terry Jones, ss **Fairy Tales**, Terry Jones, Pavilion,1981

Snulbug, Anthony Boucher, ss *Unknown* Dec,1941

So Beautiful She Was, A.M. Decker, pm *Minnesota Fantasy Review* #1,1987

So Long Old Girl, Martin Gardner, pm,1945

So Shall Ye Reap, George Alec Effinger, ss *Analog* Aug,1987

Soap, Keith Haviland, ss **Gollancz - Sunday Times Best SF Stories**, Gollancz,1987

Soldier [Soldier from Tomorrow], Harlan Ellison, ss *Fantastic Universe* Oct,1957

The Soldier and the Vampire, Robert D. San Souci, ss **Short & Shivery**, Doubleday,1987

Soldier, Sailor, Bruce Boston, nv *Fiction Magazine* #7,1974

Sole Survivor, Jonathan Lowe, pm *Eldritch Tales* #13,1987

The Solid Muldoon, Rudyard Kipling, ss *The Week's News* Jun 2,1888

Soliloquy, Denise Dumars, pm *Grue* #6,1987

Solo, Holmes Miller, ss *Grue* #5,1987

Soluble-Fish ["Poisson-Soluble", **Aurores Boreales 2** 1985], Joel Champetier, vi *Solaris* #59,1985

Some Common Misunderstandings about Ghosts, Ronald Frame, ss **A Quiver of Ghosts**, ed. Aiden Chambers, Bodley Head,1987

Some Concrete Notions About Demons, Bruce Boston, ss *The Magazine of Speculative Poetry* #5,1987

Some Day My Prince Will Come, Roisin Sheerin, vi **Mad and Bad Fairies**, ed. Anonymous, Attic Press,1987

'Some Day My Prince Will Come': Female Acculturation through the Fairy Tale, Marcia K. Lieberman, cr *College English* #34,1972

Some Kinds of Life [as by Richard Phillips], Philip K. Dick, ss *Fantastic Universe* Oct,1953

Some Terrible Letters from Scotland, James Hogg, ss

Somehow, I Don't Think We're In Kansas, Toto [revised], Harlan Ellison, ar *Genesis*,1974

Someone Else's House, Lee Chisholm, nv *IASFM* Mar,1979

Someone in the Lift, L.P. Hartley, ss

Something in the Blood, Richard L. Purtill, ss *F&SF* Aug,1986

Something in the Wind, Dave Smeds, ss *Tales of the Unanticipated* #2,1987

SOMETHING STRANGE   THE STORYTELLER

Something Strange, Kingsley Amis, nv *The Spectator*,1960
Son of a Witch, Robert Bloch, nv *Fantastic Adventures* Sep,1942
Son of the Introduction: The Man Who Wrote..., Chelsea Quinn Yarbro, in
The Son of the Mighty Casey [as by Nitram Rendrag], Martin Gardner, pm **The Annotated Casey at the Bat**, ed. Martin Gardner, Clarkson Potter,1967
A Song of a Pitiful Poor Gawdawful Thing, Batton Lash, cs *American Fantasy* Win,1987
Song of Sorcery, Elizabeth Ann Scarborough, n. Bantam: New York,1982
The Song the Zombie Sang, Harlan Ellison & Robert Silverberg, ss *Cosmopolitan* Dec,1970
The Songbirds of Pain, Garry Kilworth, ss **The Songbirds of Pain**, Gollancz,1984
Sonic Curiosity, Matt Howarth, cs *New Pathways* Jan,1987
Sonic Curiosity, Matt Howarth, cs *New Pathways* Apr,1987
Sonic Curiosity, Matt Howarth, cs *New Pathways* Aug,1987
Sonic Curiosity, Matt Howarth, cs *New Pathways* Nov,1987
The Sonic Flowerfall of Primes, Andrew Joron, pm *New Worlds* #216,1982
Sophy Mason Comes Back, E.M. Delafield, ss *Time & Tide*,1930
A Sort of Sun Spot, Bartholomew Blockley, ss **Gollancz - Sunday Times Best SF Stories**, Gollancz,1987
Sorworth Place, Russell Kirk, nv *F&SF* Nov,1962
Sound and the Electric Ear Drum, S.A. Kelly, pm *Amazing* Nov,1987
The Sound and the Fury, Scott Jenkins, ar *American Fantasy* Sum,1987
The Sound and the Fury, Scott Jenkins, ar *American Fantasy* Win,1987
A Sound of Thunder, Ray Bradbury, ss *Colliers* Jun 28,1952
Soup from a Sausage Stick, Hans Christian Andersen, ss
Southshore, Sheri S. Tepper, n. Tor: New York,1987
Souvenir, Philip K. Dick, ss *Fantastic Universe* Oct,1954
Souvenirs of Devon, Josephine Saxton, ss **Little Tours of Hell**, Pandora,1986
The Space Beat: How to Stop a Space Program, G. Harry Stine, ar **New Destinies** v1, ed. Jim Baen, Baen,1987
Space Flight, Isaac Asimov, ed *IASFM* May,1987
Space Jockey, Robert A. Heinlein, ss *The Saturday Evening Post* Apr 26,1947
Space Station, Ben Bova, ar,1985
Space Weapons, Ben Bova, ar *Amazing* Jul,1985
Spacer Trivia, Margaret B. Simon, pm *Amazing* Jul,1987
A Spaceship Built of Stone, Lisa Tuttle, ss *IASFM* Sep,1980
A Spaceship Named McGuire, Randall Garrett, nv *Analog* Jul,1961
Spaghetti Halifax, Josephine Saxton, ss **Little Tours of Hell**, Pandora,1986
A Spanish Lesson, Lucius Shepard, nv *F&SF* Dec,1985
Speaking Wolf, Ardath Mayhar, ss *Pulpsmith* Win,1987
The Speckled Gantry, Joseph Green & Patrice Milton, ss **Destinies** v1#2, ed. James Baen,1979
Spectator Playoffs, Jay Sheckley & Robert Sheckley, ss *Night Cry* v2#3,1987
The Specter General, Theodore R. Cogswell, na *Astounding* Jun,1952
Spectral Expectations, Linda Nagata, ss *Amazing* Apr,1987
Speech Sounds, Octavia E. Butler, ss *IASFM* mid-Dec,1983
Spell of Binding, Richard Cornell, ss **Sword and Sorceress** #4, ed. Marion Zimmer Bradley,1987
The Spell of the Magician's Daughter, Evelyn Sharp, ss,1902
Spelling God with the Wrong Blocks, James Morrow, ss *F&SF* May,1987
Spider King, Will Johnson, pm *Space & Time* #72,1987
Spider Love, L. Sprague de Camp, ss *F&SF* Nov,1977
The Spielberg Touch, James Verniere, ar *Twilight Zone* Oct,1987
Spiral Sands [Spiral Winds], Garry Kilworth, ss *Interzone* #9,1984
Spirit of the Night, Tom Maddox, nv *IASFM* Sep,1987
The Spirit Way, Leigh Ann Hussey, ss *The Dragon* Dec,1987
Spirits of Shadow, Ariel Remler, ar *Twilight Zone* Aug,1987
Spitting in the Wind, Lynn Abbey, nv **Masters of Hell**, ed. Janet Morris et al, Baen,1987
Splatter, Douglas E. Winter, ss **Masques** #2, ed. J.N. Williamson,1987
Splitting Hares, F.J. Willett, vi *Aphelion* #5,1987
The Spoiled Wife, Robert Bloch, ss **Chrysalis** #3, ed. Roy Torgeson,1978
The Sponge, Steph Miller, pm *Space & Time* #72,1987
The Spook of Grandpa Eben, Kenneth Robeson, na *Doc Savage* Dec,1941
The Spring, Manly Wade Wellman, ss **Shadows** #2, ed. Charles L. Grant,1979
Spring Song of the Frogs, Margaret Atwood, ss

Springs Eternal, David Drake, nv **Crusaders in Hell**, ed. Janet Morris, New York: Baen,1987
The Squaw, Bram Stoker, ss,1893
Squirrels in Frankfurter Highlight, Rhea Rose, ss **Tesseracts 2**, ed. Phyllis Gotlieb & Douglas Barbour, Press Porcepic: Victoria,1987
St. Michael & All Angels, Mark Valentine, ss **14 Bellchamber Tower**, Crimson Altar Press,1987
Stability, Philip K. Dick, ss **Beyond Lies the Wub**, Underwood/Miller,1987
Stages, Ramsey Campbell, nv **Scared Stiff**, Los Angeles: Scream/Press,1987
Stakeout, Batton Lash, cs *American Fantasy* Sum,1987
The Stalking, Robert Faulcon, n. Arrow Books: London,1983
The Stalls of Barchester Cathedral, M.R. James, ss *Contemporary Review* v97#35,1910
Stand-By [also as "Top Standby Job"], Philip K. Dick, ss *Amazing* Oct,1963
Standard Procedure, Colleen Drippe', ss *2AM* Spr,1987
Standing Down, David Drake, nv **Hammer's Slammers**, Ace,1979
The Star, Arthur C. Clarke, ss *Infinity* Nov,1955
The Star Drifter Grounded, Bruce Boston, pm *Star*Line*,1979
Star Mistress, Teresa Patterson, pm *Salarius* v1#4,1987
The Star Mouse, Fredric Brown, ss *Planet Stories* Spr,1942
Star Rebel, F.M. Busby, n. Bantam: New York,1984
Star Wars, George Lucas, n. Ballantine: New York,1976
Starbirth and Maturity, Martin Cohen, ar **Universe**, ed. Byron Preiss, Bantam Spectra,1987
Stardance, Jeanne Robinson & Spider Robinson, na *Analog* Mar,1977
Stardust, Harvey Jacobs, ss *Omni* Aug,1987
A Starpilot Muses on the Universal Tidal Pool, Robert Frazier, pm *IASFM* Aug,1986
Starry Coping, J.N. Williamson, ss *Eldritch Tales* #14,1987
A Starship Commander, McPheeter, Mike Curry, pm *Amazing* Sep,1987
Startide Rising, David Brin, n. Bantam: New York pb Sep,1983
The Statement of Randolph Carter, H.P. Lovecraft, ss *The Vagrant* May,1920
Static, David Daniel, ss *The Horror Show* Jan,1987
A Statistical Proposition, A Crazy Alien, ms *Aboriginal SF* May,1987
Statues, Ray Bradbury, ss **Dandelion Wine**, Ray Bradbury, Doubleday,1957
Status Symbol, Hal Clement, nv **Intuit**, NESFA,1987
Stay Out of Innsmouth, John Buettner, pm *Eldritch Tales* #14,1987
The Steadfast Tin Soldier, Hans Christian Andersen, ss
A Step Back in Time, Audrey Parente, pm *Minnesota Fantasy Review* #1,1987
The Step Beyond, John Maclay, ss **Darkness on the Edge of Town**, an,1985
Stevie and the Dark [The Dark Came Out to Play], Zenna Henderson, ss *Imagination* May,1952
Sticks, Karl Edward Wagner, nv *Whispers* #3,1974
Sticktalk, Vickie L. Sears, ss **Gathering Ground**, ed. Jo Cochran, J.T. Stewart & Mayumi Tsutakawa, Seal Press,1984
Stiffened in a Banquet Dish, Peggy Sue Alberhasky, pm *Grue* #5,1987
A Still from the Mead Collection, Robert Frazier, pm *IASFM* Jan,1984
The Still Waters, Lester del Rey, ss *Fantastic* Apr,1955
Stinkers, J.L. Comeau, ss *Grue* #6,1987
The Stone Chamber, H.B. Marriott Watson, nv **The Heart of Miranda**, John Lane: London,1899
The Stone Coffin, B, ss *Magdalene Collage Magazine* Dec,1913
A Stone's Throw Away, Roger E. Moore, ss **DragonLance Tales** v1, Margaret Weis & Tracy Hickman, TSR,1987
Stories of the Sixties, Frederik Pohl, si
Storm God, Deborah Wheeler, ss **Sword and Sorceress** #4, ed. Marion Zimmer Bradley,1987
The Storm Tunnel, Bill Pronzini, ss *Whispers* #23,1987
Stormtower, Andrew Joron, pm
A Story About Death, Judith Gorog, ss **A Taste for Quiet**, Putnam,1982
The Story Mac Told, Jack Matthews, ss *Western Humanities Review*
The Story of a King's Daughter, Mary Louisa Molesworth, ss **Christmas-Tree Land**, London: Macmillan,1884
The Story of Emer, Joni Crone, ss **Mad and Bad Fairies**, ed. Anonymous, Attic Press,1987
The Story of the Goblins Who Stole a Sexton, Charles Dickens, ss
The Story of the Late Mr. Elvesham, H.G. Wells, ss *The Idler* May,1896
The Story to End All Stories for Harlan Ellison's Anthology **Dangerous Visions**, Philip K. Dick, vi *Niekas* FII,1968
The Storyteller, Barbara Siegel & Scott Siegel, nv **DragonLance Tales** v2, Margaret Weis & Tracy Hickman, TSR,1987

Stovelighter, Steven Popkes, nv *IASFM* mid-Dec,1987

Stowaway, Paul Roland, ss **The Curious Case of Richard Fielding and Other Stories**, Lary Press,1987

Strands, Janet Fox, ss *Grue #6*,1987

The Strange Affair at Upton Strangewold, Frederick Cowles, ss **Ghosts & Scholars**, ed. Rosemary Pardoe,1987

A Strange Christmas Game, Mrs. J.H. Riddell, ss

Strange Doings in Viktor's Village, Jessica Amanda Salmonson, vi *New Pathways* Jan,1987

Strange Eden, Philip K. Dick, ss *Imagination* Dec,1954

Strange Eruptions, Harry Turtledove, nv *IASFM* Aug,1986

Strange Fish, Kenneth Robeson, na *Doc Savage* Feb,1945

Strange Memories of Death, Philip K. Dick, ss *Interzone #8*,1984

The Strange Ride of Morrowbie Jukes, Rudyard Kipling, nv *Quartette* Chr,1885

The Strange Story of Modern Philosophy [from **Beyond the Outsider**], Colin Wilson, ar Barker: London,1965

Strange Wine, Harlan Ellison, ss *Amazing* Jun,1976

The Stranger, Gordon R. Dickson, ss *Imagination* May,1952

The Stranger, Martin Gardner, vi **The No-Sided Professor**, Prometheus,1987

Stranger Station, Damon Knight, nv *F&SF* Dec,1956

Stranger Than Strange, Paul Roland, sg **The Curious Case of Richard Fielding and Other Stories**, Lary Press,1987

Strangers on Paradise [Strangers in Paradise], Damon Knight, ss *F&SF* Apr,1986

The Stray, Susan Casper & Gardner R. Dozois, ss *Twilight Zone* Dec,1987

Stuck With It, Hal Clement, nv **Stellar #2**, ed. Judy-Lynn del Rey,1976

Stuff of Horror, or Gray Matter All Over the Inside of Your Skull, T.M. Wright, ar *American Fantasy* Sum,1987

Subatomic Particles, Michael J. Brutvan, ss *Mage* Win,1987

Succubi, Michael R. Collings, pm *Footsteps* Nov,1987

The Sum of the Parts, Dorothy J. Heydt, nv **Red Sun of Darkover**, ed. Marion Zimmer Bradley & The Friends of Darkover, DAW,1987

The Sumach, Ulric Daubeny, ss **The Elemental**, Routledge: London,1919

Summation: 1986, Gardner R. Dozois, in

Summer in the Air [also as "The Sound of Summer Running"], Ray Bradbury, ss *The Saturday Evening Post* Feb 18,1956

The Summer Night [The Spring Night], Ray Bradbury, vi *Arkham Sampler* Win,1948

The Summer People, Shirley Jackson, ss *Charm*,1950

The Summer's Dust, Pamela Sargent, nv *F&SF* Jul,1981

A Summons, L.P. Hartley, ss **The White Wand and Other Stories**, Hamilton,1954

Sun and Shadow, Ray Bradbury, ss *Reporter* Mar 17,1953

The Sun Spider, Lucius Shepard, nv *IASFM* Apr,1987

Sundance, Robert Silverberg, ss *F&SF* Jun,1969

Sunday Review, Bruce Boston, vi *City Miner #3*,1976

Sunday Special, Paul Christopher, ss **Beyond That River**, Pal Books,1987

The Sunrise, Margaret Atwood, nv

Sunset, John Maclay, pm *Twisted #2*,1985

The Sunshine Club, Ramsey Campbell, ss **The Dodd, Mead Gallery of Horror**, ed. Charles L. Grant, Dodd Mead,1983

Superiority, Arthur C. Clarke, ss *F&SF* Aug,1951

Supernovae: Creative Cataclysms in the Galaxy, David J. Helfand, ar **Universe**, ed. Byron Preiss, Bantam Spectra,1987

Supertanks, David Drake, ms **Hammer's Slammers**, Ace,1979

Superwine, Harry Turtledove, na *IASFM* Apr,1987

The Supramarket, Leanne Frahm, ss **Doom City**, ed. Charles L. Grant, Tor,1987

The Supremacy of Bacteria [revised from *IASFM* Aug,83], Robert Frazier, pm **Light Years and Dark**, ed. Michael Bishop, Berkley,1984

Supreme Being, Bob Warner, pm *Apex! #1*,1987

A Surface Raid, Philip K. Dick, ss *Fantastic Universe* Jul,1955

Surprise [substantially revised, first appeared in **The Strategy of Technology**, 1970], Francis X. Kane, Stefan T. Possony & Jerry E. Pournelle, ar **There Will Be War** v6, ed. Jerry E. Pournelle,1987

Survey Team, Philip K. Dick, ss *Fantastic Universe* May,1954

Surviving, Judith Moffett, nv *F&SF* Jun,1986

Survivor, Katherine V. Forrest, ss **Dreams and Swords**, Naiad,1987

The Survivor, Walter F. Moudy, nv *Amazing* May,1965

Survivors, Isaac Asimov, ed *IASFM* Nov,1987

Susan's Plant, Nicholas Fisk, nv **Living Fire and Other S.F. Stories**, Corgi: London,1987

Susi's Lovely World, Eduardo Julio Carletti, ss *SF International #2*,1987

Susie Q2, Terence M. Green, ss *IASFM* Aug,1983

The Swagger Stick, Laurence M. Janifer, nv **Knave & the Game**, Doubleday,1987

Swallowed Alive, Robert D. San Souci, ss **Short & Shivery**, Doubleday,1987

Swamp Rising, W.H. Pugmire, ss *Grue #4*,1987

The Swan, Ray Bradbury, ss *Cosmopolitan* Sep,1954

Swan Song, William J. Grabowski, br *The Horror Show* Spr,1987

Swan Song, Robert R. McCammon, ex Pocket: New York Jun,1987

Sweet Chariot, Catherine Cooke & John P. Cooke, ss *Space & Time #72*,1987

Sweet Dreams, Beverly Brunelle, ss *Haunts #9*,1987

Sweet Freedom! and a Picnic on the White House Lawn, Patricia Highsmith, ss **Tales of Natural and Unnatural Catastrophes**, Bloomsbury,1987

The Sweethearts (The Top of the Ball), Hans Christian Andersen, vi

Swept and Garnished, Rudyard Kipling, ss *London Pall Mall Magazine* Jan,1915

The Swineherd, Hans Christian Andersen, ss

Swing High, Willie Brodie, Fred Urquhart, ss **After Midnight Stories #3**,1987

The Switcheroo, Fredric Brown & Mack Reynolds, ss *Other Worlds* Mar,1951

A Sword in Hand, Leigh Ann Hussey, nv *Fantasy Book* Mar,1987

The Sword of Parmagon, Harlan Ellison, ss *The Cleveland News*,1949

Sword Play, Chris Morris & Janet Morris, na **Festival Moon**, ed. C.J. Cherryh, DAW,1987

The Sword That Wept, Sandra Miesel, ss *Amazing* Sep,1987

The Swords, Robert Aickman, nv,1976

Swords of Shahrazar [also as "The Treasure of Shaibar Kahn"], Robert E. Howard, na *Top-Notch* Oct,1934

The Swordsman Smada, John Steakley, nv **Friends of the Horseclans**, ed. Robert Adams & Pamela Crippen Adams, Signet,1987

Symbolism in Science Fiction, Ben Bova, ar *The Writer* Jun,1984

Symphony in Ursa Major, James Brunet, ss *Aboriginal SF* Jul,1987

Syndicated Television: What Is It, Anyway?, Anonymous, ar *Twilight Zone* Dec,1987

Tabby Lorenzo, Ursula K. Le Guin, pm,1984

Table of Orginization and Equipment, Hammer's Regiment, David Drake, ms **Hammer's Slammers**, Ace,1979

Tableau with Three Ghostly Women, Jack Matthews, ss *Chariton Review*,1979

The "Tagore" Letter, Philip K. Dick, lt Sep 23,1981

Tailypo, Robert D. San Souci, ss **Short & Shivery**, Doubleday,1987

Take Me, For Instance, Hugh B. Cave, ss *Whispers #5*,1974

Take Off Your Cap When a Funeral Passes, Leslie Halliwell, ss **A Demon Close Behind**, Robert Hale,1987

Take the "A" Train, Wayne Allen Sallee, ss *Not One of Us* Oct,1986

Take Two, Bill Kerby, nv **Masters of Hell**, ed. Janet Morris et al, Baen,1987

Take Your Best Shot, Jackie Vivelo, ss **A Trick of the Light**, Putnam,1987

Take Your Choice, Sakyo Komatsu, ss *SF International #1*,1987

Taking Stock, Jack Matthews, ss **Ghostly Populations**, Johns Hopkins,1987

Taking the Night Train, Thomas F. Monteleone, nv *Night Voyages* Spr,1981

The Tale and Its Master, Michael Rutherford, na Spring Harbor: Delmar, NY,1986

A Tale at Rilling's Inn, Nancy Varian Berberick, ss *Amazing* Mar,1987

The Tale of Gorgik [long version], Samuel R. Delany, na *IASFM* Sum,1979

The Tale of Happiton, Douglas Hofstadter, ss **Metamagical Themas**, Basic Books,1985

A Tale of Heroes, Mercedes R. Lackey, nv **Sword and Sorceress #4**, ed. Marion Zimmer Bradley,1987

The Tale of Ivan the Fool, Leo Tolstoi, nv

The Tale of Rumor and Desire, Samuel R. Delany, na *Callaloo* Spr,1987

The Tale of the Valiant Demoiselle, Sara Maitland, nv

Tales from the Original Gothic, John M. Ford, ss **The Architecture of Fear**, ed. Kathryn Cramer & Peter D. Pautz, Arbor House,1987

The Talisman, Hans Christian Andersen, vi

The Talisman, Robert Faulcon, n. Arrow Books: London,1983

The Talisman, Timothy Zahn, nv **Magic in Ithkar #4**, ed. Andre Norton & Robert Adams,1987

The Talking Donkey, James Powell, ss *Ellery Queen's Mystery Magazine* mid-Dec,1987

TALKING TERROR WITH CLIVE BARKER   **THREE ROCK POEMS**

Talking Terror With Clive Barker, Clive Barker & Douglas E. Winter, iv
    Twilight Zone Jun,1987
Tangents, Greg Bear, ss *Omni* Jan,1986
Tango Charlie and Foxtrot Romeo, John Varley, na **Blue Champagne**,
    Dark Harvest,1986
Tank, Francis E. Izzo, ss *IASFM* Mar,1979
The Tank and Its Wife, Arsen Darnay, ss *Analog* Jan,1978
The Tank Lords, David Drake, na **Far Frontiers** v6, ed. Jerry Pournelle
    & Jim Baen,1986
Tanning, John Maclay, ss *Etchings & Odysseys* #5,1984
The Tapestried Chamber, Sir Walter Scott, ss *The Keepsake*,1828
Tapestry, C.H. Sherman, ss **Devils & Demons**, ed. Marvin Kaye,
    SFBC/Doubleday,1987
Tarfu's Last Show, Bruce Boston, ss **Future Pastimes**, ed. Scott
    Edelstein, Aurora,1977
Target: Berlin!, George Alec Effinger, nv **New Dimensions** #6, ed.
    Robert Silverberg/Marta Randall,1976
Tattler, Michael Arthur Betts, mr *The Horror Show* Jan,1987
Tattler, Michael Arthur Betts, mr *The Horror Show* Sum,1987
Tattler, Michael Arthur Betts, mr *The Horror Show* Fll,1987
Tattler, Michael Arthur Betts, mr *The Horror Show* Win,1987
Tattler, Michael Arthur Betts & Wes Craven, mr *The Horror Show*
    Spr,1987
Tattler, William J. Grabowski, br *The Horror Show* Jan,1987
Tattler, William J. Grabowski, br *The Horror Show* Spr,1987
Tattler, William J. Grabowski, br *The Horror Show* Sum,1987
Tattler, William J. Grabowski, br *The Horror Show* Fll,1987
Tattler, William J. Grabowski, br *The Horror Show* Win,1987
Tattoos, Jack M. Dann, nv *Omni* Nov,1986
The Taxpayer, Ray Bradbury, vi **The Martian Chronicles**,1950
Tea and No Sympathy, Josephine Saxton, ss **Little Tours of Hell**,
    Pandora,1986
Tea Leaves, Rebecca Bradley, ss **The Pan Book of Horror Stories** #28,
    Pan,1987
Teach the Children, Scott Wyatt, pm *Minnesota Fantasy Review* #1,1987
The Teapot, Hans Christian Andersen, vi
The Tearing of Greymare House, J. Michael Reaves, nv *F&SF* Mar,1983
The Technique, Chris Lacher, ss *Eldritch Tales* #14,1987
Teeth Marks, Edward Bryant, ss *F&SF* Jun,1979
Telecommunion, Andrew Joron, pm
Telefuture, Ben Bova, ar *Omni* Feb,1985
Telephone, Laurence M. Janifer, vi *Analog* Jun,1987
Telephone Ghosts, Robert Frazier, pm *Pig Iron* #10,1982
Television, Robin Bromley, ar *Twilight Zone* Jun,1987
Tell Me All About Yourself, F.M. Busby, ss **New Dimensions** #3, ed.
    Robert Silverberg/Marta Randall,1973
The Tell-Tale Heart, Edgar Allan Poe, ss *The Pioneer* Jan,1843
Telltale Tics and Tremors, Harlan Ellison, ar *Unearth* Fll,1977
Temple to a Minor Goddess, Susan M. Shwartz, ss *Amazing* Jan,1987
The Temporary King, Paul J. McAuley, nv *F&SF* Jan,1987
The Temptation of Harringay, H.G. Wells, ss *The St. James's Gazette*
    Feb,1895
Tempus Non Fugit, Gordon R. Dickson, nv *(The Original) Science
    Fiction Stories* Mar,1957
Ten Times Black, J. Hunter Daves, ss *Grue* #5,1987
The Tenancy of Mr. Eex, Paula Volsky, nv **Devils & Demons**, ed. Marvin
    Kaye, SFBC/Doubleday,1987
Tenant Above, Charmaine Parsons, vi *Mage* Spr,1986
Teragram, Evelyn E. Smith, ss *Fantastic Universe* Jun,1955
Termites, Dave Smeds, ss *IASFM* May,1987
A Terran Odyssey, Philip K. Dick, nv **The Little Black Box**,
    Underwood/Miller,1987
Terrorstorm, John Strickland, ss *The Horror Show* Win,1987
Tesseractuality, Michael Tolley, br *Aphelion* #5,1987
The Test, Katherine V. Forrest, ss **Dreams and Swords**, Naiad,1987
The Test, Richard Matheson, ss *F&SF* Nov,1954
Test for Tyrants, Edward P. Hughes, ss **New Destinies** v2, ed. Jim
    Baen, Baen,1987
Test in Orbit, Ben Bova, ss *Analog* Sep,1965
The Test of the Twins, Margaret Weis, ss **DragonLance Tales** v1,
    Margaret Weis & Tracy Hickman, TSR,1987
The Testament of Geoffrey, J. Brian Clarke, ss *Analog* May,1987
Testing..., Laurence M. Janifer, ss *Analog* Nov,1980
Tetrahedron Letters, Andrew Joron, pm *The Portland Review*,1979
Thang, Martin Gardner, vi *Comment* Fll,1948
Thanotopolis Revisited, Lesley Choyce, ss **The Dream Auditor**,
    Indivisible Books,1986
That Fearful Symmetry, Algis Budrys, vi *Twilight Zone* Apr,1987

That Hell-Bound Train, Robert Bloch, ss *F&SF* Sep,1958
That Thing in There, Ardath Mayhar, ss *Eldritch Tales* #13,1987
That's All, Folks, Richard Wilson, pm *Amazing* May,1987
Thatcher's Bluff, James Anderson, ss *Haunts* #9,1987
"The ground has a face...", Jack M. Dann, pm **The Anthology of
    Speculative Poetry**, ed. Robert Frazier,1980
"The medicine man tells me...", Jack M. Dann, pm *Twilight Zone*
    Aug,1987
Their Dear Little Ghost, Elia Wilkinson Peattie, ss
Theodore Sturgeon on Philip Dick, Theodore Sturgeon, iv Oct,1977
There Shall Be No Darkness, James Blish, nv *Thrilling Wonder Stories*
    Apr,1950
There Was an Old Lady..., Eleanor Arnason, pm *Tales of the
    Unanticipated* #2,1987
The "There Was an Old Woman" Quiz, A.R. Morlan, qz *The Horror Show*
    Spr,1987
There Will Come Soft Rains, Ray Bradbury, ss *Colliers* May 6,1950
There's a Long, Long Trail A-Winding, Russell Kirk, nv **Frights**, ed. Kirby
    McCauley, St. Martins,1976
There's a Phantom in My Word-Processor, Bev Jafek, ss *Pulpsmith*
    Win,1987
There's a Wolf in My Time Machine, Larry Niven, ss *F&SF* Jun,1971
There's Magic in Shakespeare, Reginald Bretnor, nv *Night Cry*
    v2#4,1987
There's No Fool... [as by David Gordon], Randall Garrett, ss
    Astounding Aug,1956
Thermo, Robert Hays, pm *Amazing* Nov,1987
These Doth The Lord Hate, Manly Wade Wellman, ss *Weird Tales*
    Jan,1939
These Shall Not Be Lost, Everett B. Cole, nv *Astounding* Jan,1953
They, Robert A. Heinlein, ss *Unknown* Apr,1941
They Fly So High, Ross Rocklynne, ss *Amazing* Jun,1952
They Wait, Jan Mark, ss **They Wait and Other Spine Chillers**, ed.
    Lance Salway, Pepper Press,1983
"They", Rudyard Kipling, nv *Scribner's* Aug,1904
The Thick Red Moment, Harlan Ellison, ar *The Los Angeles Weekly
    News*,1981
Thieves' World, Nancy Garcia, ar *American Fantasy* Spr,1987
The Thin People, Brian Lumley, ss *Whispers* #23,1987
The Thing in the Cellar, David H. Keller, M.D., ss *Weird Tales* Mar,1932
The Thing on the Roof, Robert E. Howard, ss *Weird Tales* Feb,1932
A Thing or Two About Razzle-Dazzle, Dennis John Sjolie, ss *Mage*
    Spr,1987
The Thing That Pursued, Kenneth Robeson, na *Doc Savage* Oct,1945
The Thing Waiting Outside, Barbara Williamson, ss *Ellery Queen's
    Mystery Magazine* Dec,1977
Things Not Seen, James Robert Smith, vi *2AM* Spr,1987
Things That Go Quack in the Night, Edith Shiner & Lewis Shiner, ss
    IASFM Jan,1983
Thinkability, Martin Amis, ms
The Third Alternative, Marc Stiegler, nv *Analog* Nov,1987
The Third Expedition, Ray Bradbury, ss *Planet Stories* Fll,1948
Third Generation, Stephanie Taylor, ss *SF International* #2,1987
Third Wind, Richard Christian Matheson, ss **Masques** #1, ed. J.N.
    Williamson,1984
This Life and Later Ones, George Zebrowski, ss *Analog* Feb,1987
This Old Man, Charles L. Grant, ss *Night Cry* v2#3,1987
This Time, Ramsey Campbell, ss **Night Visions** #3,1986
This Too Is Science:, John Devin, pm *Amazing* May,1987
Thomas Canty, Thomas Cantry & Greg Ketter, pi *American Fantasy*
    Spr,1987
The Thought, L.P. Hartley, ss **The Travelling Grave and Other Stories**,
    Arkham,1948
Thought Experiment, Andrew Joron, pm
Thoughts on VALIS, Philip K. Dick, lt Mar 5,1979
A Thousand Faces, Bruce Boston, pm
Three Coins in Clockwork Fountains [Three Coins in Enigmatic
    Fountains], Brian W. Aldiss, gp **New Writings in SF** #26,1975
The Three Cowboys, Martin Gardner, vi *Humpty Dumpty's Magazine*
    Jan,1959
Three Day Magic, Charlotte Armstrong, na *F&SF* Sep,1952
Three Days, Tanith Lee, nv **Shadows** #7, ed. Charles L. Grant,1984
The Three Devils, Kenneth Robeson, na *Doc Savage* May,1944
Three Little Owls, Fredric Brown, vi **Nightmares and Geezenstacks**,
    Bantam,1961
Three Miles Up, Elizabeth Jane Howard, ss **We Are for the Dark**, Cape:
    London,1951
Three Rock Poems, Ursula K. Le Guin, si

THREE SPRITES

Three Sprites, Thomas M. Disch, pm *Night Cry* v2#4,1987
Three Tinks on the House, F.M. Busby, ss *Vertex* Jun,1973
Three Were Chosen [Chapters 5&6], J.C. Jarik, sl *Salarius* #3,1987
Three Were Chosen [Chapters 7&8], J.C. Jarik, sl *Salarius* v1#4,1987
Three, or Four, for Dinner, L.P. Hartley, ss
Three-Part Puzzle, Gordon R. Dickson, ss *Analog* Jun,1962
Through the Fifth Dimension, Konrad R. Fialkowski, ss *SF International* #1,1987
Through the Looking Glass, Lewis Carroll, n.,1972
Through Time & Space with Ferdinand Feghoot I, Grendel Briarton, vi *Amazing* Jul,1987
Through Time & Space with Ferdinand Feghoot i, Grendel Briarton, vi *Amazing* Mar,1987
Thumbelina the Left Wing Fairy, Joni Crone, ss **Mad and Bad Fairies**, ed. Anonymous, Attic Press,1987
The Thunderer, Alan Dean Foster, ss *F&SF* Apr,1987
Thursday Evenings, E.F. Benson, ss
Thy Sting, Damien Broderick, vi *Omni* Jun,1987
Ticket to Heaven, John Shirley, ss *F&SF* Dec,1987
Ties of Faith, Gillian FitzGerald, nv **Friends of the Horseclans**, ed. Robert Adams & Pamela Crippen Adams, Signet,1987
Tiger Green, Gordon R. Dickson, nv *If* Nov,1965
The Tiger Sweater, Keith Roberts, na *F&SF* Oct,1987
Tiger's Hunt, John S. Tumlin, ss *Aboriginal SF* May,1987
Tight Little Stitches in a Dead Man's Back, Joe R. Lansdale, nv **Nukes**, ed. John Maclay, Maclay,1986
Till Death Do Us Part, Terence M. Green, ss *F&SF* Dec,1981
Time and Chance, Eric M. Heideman, nv **L. Ron Hubbard Presents Writers of the Future** v3, ed. Algis Budrys, Bridge,1987
The Time Disease, Martin Amis, ss *Granta*
The Time of His Life, Larry Eisenberg, ss *F&SF* Apr,1968
Time of Need, F.M. Busby, ss *Vertex* Aug,1974
The Time of the Eye, Harlan Ellison, ss *The Saint* May,1959
The Time of the Transference, Alan Dean Foster, n. Phantasia: West Bloomfield, MI hc Aug,1986
Time Travel for Fun and Profit, Geoff Nicholson, ss **Gollancz - Sunday Times Best SF Stories**, Gollancz,1987
Time Windows, Lori Allen, ss *F&SF* Jun,1987
Time Wounds All Heels, Robert Bloch, ss *Fantastic Adventures* Apr,1942
Time's House, Bruce Boston, pm *IASFM* Sep,1983
Time's Rub, Gregory Benford, ss Cheap Street: New Castle, VA,1984
Timed Exposure, Richard Christian Matheson, ss **Scars**, Scream/Press,1987
Timerider, Doris Egan, nv *Amazing* Mar,1986
The Tinderbox, Hans Christian Andersen, ss,1835
Tiny Devils, Patricia Jeres, pm *New Pathways* Jan,1987
Tired Old Man, Harlan Ellison, ss *Mike Shane Mystery Magazine* Jan,1976
The Tissue-Culture King, Julian Huxley, ss *Yale Review*,1926
Tit for Tat, Justin Leiber, ss *Amazing* Jul,1987
Tithing Night, Louise Cooper, ss **Tales from the Forbidden Planet**, ed. Roz Kaveney, Titan,1987
To a Cockroach, John Maclay, pm *Scavenger's Newsletter* Apr,1985
To Be Blind, Paul Christopher, ss **Beyond That River**, Pal Books,1987
To Grab Power, Hayden Howard, ss *If* Jan,1971
To Hell with the Stars, Jack McDevitt, ss *IASFM* Dec,1987
To Marry Medusa [The Cosmic Rape], Theodore Sturgeon, n. Dell: New York pb Aug,1958
To Not Return, Steve Eng, pm *Space & Time* #73,1987
To Rebuild the Eyrie, Sasha Miller, nv **Tales of the Witch World**, ed. Andre Norton, St. Martin's,1987
To See the Sun, Kingsley Amis, ss
To Serve the Master, Philip K. Dick, ss *Imagination* Feb,1956
To Sleep Perchance To Dream, Matt McGregor, ss *Minnesota Fantasy Review* #1,1987
To Sooth the Savage Beast, Elizabeth Massie, ss *The Horror Show* Fll,1987
To Touch a Star, Ben Bova, ss **Universe**, ed. Byron Preiss, Bantam Spectra,1987
To Trap a Demon, Ardath Mayhar, ss **Magic in Ithkar** #4, ed. Andre Norton & Robert Adams,1987
Toad, Singular, Juleen Brantingham, ss **Whispers** #6, ed. Stuart David Schiff,1987
Toadstool Sinfonia, Laurence M. Janifer, ss *Analog* Jul,1980
The Token, May Sinclair, ss **Uncanny Stories**, Hutchinson,1923
Tomb Mate, Stephen Studach, pm *Eldritch Tales* #13,1987
The Tomb of His Ancestors, Rudyard Kipling, nv *McClure's* Dec,1897
Tomb of Nine Hundred Days, A.R. Morlan, ss *The Horror Show* Fll,1987

The Tombs: An Excerpt from **Memos from Purgatory**, Harlan Ellison, ar **Memos from Purgatory**, Harlan Ellison, Regency,1961
The Tongueless Horror, Wyatt Blassingame, nv *Dime Mystery Magazine* Apr,1934
Tongues, Bruce Boston, pm
A Tonic, L.P. Hartley, ss **The White Wand and Other Stories**, Hamilton,1954
Tony and the Beetles [also as "Retreat from Rigel"], Philip K. Dick, ss *Orbit* #2,1953
Too Far, Fredric Brown, vi *F&SF* Sep,1955
Too Much Loosestrife, Frederik Pohl, ss *Amazing* Nov,1987
Too Much Trouble, Kingsley Amis, ss **Penguin Modern Stories** #11,1972
Tooley's Curse, Margie Penn-Freeman, pm *2AM* Fll,1987
Torrey Pines Reserve, Ursula K. Le Guin, pm **Hard Words & Other Poems**, Harper & Row,1981
Totem, Ursula K. Le Guin, pm **Hard Words & Other Poems**, Harper & Row,1981
The Totem Pole, Robert Bloch, ss *Weird Tales* Aug,1939
The Touch, Wayne Allen Sallee, ss *Grue* #4,1987
Touchvision, Manuel van Loggem, ss *SF International* #1,1987
The Tour of the Sleeping Steamboat, Jack Matthews, ss *The Carleton Miscellany*
Tourist Spots for Time Travelers, Robert Frazier, pm *IASFM* Dec,1986
Tourney, Brian W. Aldiss, ss **Tales from the Forbidden Planet**, ed. Roz Kaveney, Titan,1987
Toward a Distant Train, Jack Matthews, ss *Southwest Review*
The Tower, Aidan Chambers, ss **A Quiver of Ghosts**, ed. Aiden Chambers, Bodley Head,1987
The Tower, John Maclay, ss *Etchings & Odysseys* #9,1986
Townkiller, J.N. Williamson, ss *Grue* #4,1987
A Toy Princess, Mary De Morgan, ss **On a Pincushion**, London: Seeley, Jackson & Halliday,1877
Trace, Jerome Bixby, ss,1961
A Trace of Inbetween, Wade Tarzia, ar *Mage* Win,1987
The Trace of Old Fingers, Mark Rich, pm *2AM* Sum,1987
Track of a Legend, Cynthia Felice, ss *Omni* Dec,1982
Trackdown, John F. Moore, ss *Aboriginal SF* Feb,1987
Tracking Through the Mutant Rain Forest, Robert Frazier, pm *IASFM* May,1987
The Tractate Middoth, M.R. James, ss **More Ghost Stories of an Antiquary**, Arnold,1911
Trader's Cross, Charles Sheffield, nv *Analog* Mar,1987
Trader's Partner, Charles Sheffield, nv *Analog* Jul,1987
Training Ground, Nancy Kress, nv **Liavek: Wizard's Row**, ed. Will Shetterly & Emma Bull, Ace,1987
The Transfer, Algernon Blackwood, ss *Country Life* Dec 9,1911
Transformation, Mary W. Shelley, ss *The Keepsake*,1831
Transformer, Chad Oliver, ss *F&SF* Nov,1954
Transients, Darrell Schweitzer, ss *Amazing* Jan,1987
Transit of Earth, Arthur C. Clarke, ss *Playboy* Jan,1971
Trapalanda, Charles Sheffield, nv *IASFM* Jun,1987
Traps, F. Paul Wilson, ss *Night Cry* v2#4,1987
Trave, Shirley Meier, ss **Magic in Ithkar** #4, ed. Andre Norton & Robert Adams,1987
Traveler's Report on Florida's World Famous 'Alligator Alley', Mink Mole, fa *New Pathways* Nov,1987
A Traveler's Tale, Lucius Shepard, na *IASFM* Jul,1984
Travelling Grave, L.P. Hartley, co Arkham House: Sauk City, WI,1948
The Travelling Grave, L.P. Hartley, ss
The Treasure of Abbot Thomas, M.R. James, ss **Ghost Stories of an Antiquary**,1904
The Treasure of Odirex, Charles Sheffield, na *Fantastic* Jul,1978
The Treasures of Tartary, Robert E. Howard, nv *Thrilling Adventures* Jan,1935
Treaty in Tartessos, Karen Anderson, ss *F&SF* May,1963
The Tree and the Harp, George Mackay Brown, ss **A Quiver of Ghosts**, ed. Aiden Chambers, Bodley Head,1987
The Tree on the Mountain [from "What Dinah Thought"], Deena Metzger, ex **Hear the Silence**, ed. Irene Zahava, Crossing Press,1986
The Tree-Wife of Arketh, Syn Ferguson, ss **Sword and Sorceress** #4, ed. Marion Zimmer Bradley,1987
Tricentennial, Joe W. Haldeman, ss *Analog* Jul,1976
Triceratops, Kono Tensei, ss *Omni* Aug,1982
Trick-or-Treat, J.B. Stamper, ss **More Tales for the Midnight Hour**, Apple/Scholastic,1987
Trill Coster's Burden, Manly Wade Wellman, ss **Whispers** #2, ed. Stuart David Schiff,1979

THE TRILLING PRINCESS

The Trilling Princess, Jessica Amanda Salmonson, ss **Devils & Demons**, ed. Marvin Kaye, SFBC/Doubleday,1987

Trimmings, David Starkey, ss *Grue* #5,1987

Triptych, Garry Kilworth, gp **Other Edens**, ed. Christopher Evans & Robert Holdstock, Unwin: London,1987

Triptych, Sara Maitland, ss

The Trolley, Ray Bradbury, ss *Good Housekeeping* Jul,1955

Trouble at the Jade Towers, Patricia Highsmith, nv **Tales of Natural and Unnatural Catastrophes**, Bloomsbury,1987

Trouble in Time [as by S.D. Gottesman], C.M. Kornbluth & Frederik Pohl, ss *Astonishing Stories* Dec,1940

The Trouble with Bubbles, Philip K. Dick, ss *If* Sep,1953

Troubles of a Tattooed King, Evelyn Shefner, ss *Carolina Quarterly*

Truce, Anne Eliot Crompton, ss **Spaceships & Spells**, ed. Jane Yolen, Martin H. Greenberg & Charles G. Waugh, Harper & Row,1987

Truck Driver, Robert Chilson, ss *Analog* Jan,1972

Trucks, Stephen King, ss *Cavalier* Jun,1973

True Love Grue, Phillip Rainbird, pm *Minnesota Fantasy Review* #1,1987

True Love: Groping for the Holy Grail [How I Survived the Great Videotape Matchmaker], Harlan Ellison, ar *Los Angeles*,1978

True Magic, Robert A. Metzger, ss *Aboriginal SF* Nov,1987

True Names, Vernor Vinge, na **Binary Star** #5,1981

True Revelation of the Apparition of One Mrs. Veal, Daniel Defoe, ar,1706

True Sight, Ann Cathey, pm *Salarius* #3,1987

Trust Me, Joseph Lyons, ss **The Architecture of Fear**, ed. Kathryn Cramer & Peter D. Pautz, Arbor House,1987

Truth and Fiction, Isaac Asimov, ed *IASFM* Apr,1987

The Tunnel under the World, Frederik Pohl, nv *Galaxy* Jan,1955

Turing Test, D.C. Poyer, ss *Analog* Aug,1987

Turning Forty, John Maclay, pm **Other Engagements**, Madison, WI: Dream House,1987

The Turning Wheel, Philip K. Dick, nv *(The Original) Science Fiction Stories* #2,1954

Twenty-One Minutes, Rudy Kremberg, ss *Haunts* #9,1987

Twice-Killed Corpse, Fredric Brown, nv *Ten Detective Aces* Mar,1942

Twig, Gordon R. Dickson, nv *Stellar* #1, ed. Judy-Lynn del Rey,1974

Twilight, Don A. Stuart, ss *Astounding* Nov,1934

Twilight of the Dawn, Dean R. Koontz, nv **Night Visions** #4,1987

Twilight of the Gods, Paul Roland, sg **The Curious Case of Richard Fielding and Other Stories**, Lary Press,1987

Twilight Zone Gallery, J.K. Potter, il *Twilight Zone* Feb,1987

The Twilight Zone Gallery: The Art of Jeffrey Jones, Bernard Abrams & Jeffrey Jones, pi *Twilight Zone* Aug,1987

The Twilight Zone Gallery: The Art of Jim Burns, Jeffrey Jones & Tappan King, pi *Twilight Zone* Oct,1987

The Twilight Zone Movie Trial: An Opinion, Anonymous, ms *Twilight Zone* Aug,1987

The Twilight Zone Review: 1986 - Fiction, Edward Bryant, br *Twilight Zone* Feb,1987

The Twilight Zone Review: 1986 - Film, James Verniere, mr *Twilight Zone* Feb,1987

The Twilight Zone Review: 1986 - TV, Bill Warren, mr *Twilight Zone* Feb,1987

Twilla, Tom Reamy, nv *F&SF* Sep,1974

Twinned Stars: Newton & Halley, Robert Frazier, pm **Perception Barriers**, BPW&P: Berkeley CA,1987

Twins, David Case, ss *Fantasy Tales* #16,1986

The Twins, Muriel Spark, ss

Twistbuck's Game, Gary Gygax, nv **Night Arrant**, Ace/New Infinities,1987

The Two Drovers, Sir Walter Scott, nv **Chronicles of the Canongate**, Cadell & Co.,1827

Two for the River, L.P. Hartley, co,1961

Two for the River, L.P. Hartley, ss

Two Gentlemen of the Trade, Robert Lynn Asprin, ss **Festival Moon**, ed. C.J. Cherryh, DAW,1987

The Two Vaynes, L.P. Hartley, ss **The White Wand and Other Stories**, Hamilton,1954

Two Virgins, Hans Christian Andersen, vi

Two Walkers Across the Time Flats, Andrew Joron, pm

Two Yards of Dragon, L. Sprague de Camp, nv **Flashing Swords!** #3, ed. Lin Carter,1976

Typo, Michael D. Winkle, ss *Fantasy Book* Mar,1987

The Ugly Duckling, Hans Christian Andersen, ss

The Ugly Little Boy [Lastborn], Isaac Asimov, na *Galaxy* Sep,1958

Uglypuss, Margaret Atwood, nv

Ulalume (unabridged), Edgar Allan Poe, pm *American Review* Dec,1847

Ultimate Getaways, Mark Arnold, ar *Twilight Zone* Oct,1987

Ultra-Vue, Rudin Moore, n. **Ultra-Vue and Selected Peripheral Visions**, self published,1987

Unborn, Richard Toelly, pm *Space & Time* #73,1987

Uncertainty and Defense, Jerry E. Pournelle, ar **There Will Be War** v6, ed. Jerry E. Pournelle,1987

Uncle David's Nonsensical Story about Giants and Fairies, Catherine Sinclair, ss **Holiday House, A Book for the Young**, London: Ward, Lock,1839

Uncle Dobbin's Parrot Fair, Charles de Lint, nv *IASFM* Nov,1987

Uncle Green-Eye, B.J. Martinez, ss *F&SF* Mar,1987

Uncle Sam [from **The World of Violence**], Colin Wilson, ex Gollancz: London,1963

Uncle Sherm (A Fantasy), Charlotte Brown Hammond, ss *Grue* #4,1987

Uncle Tuggs, Michael Shea, nv *F&SF* May,1986

The Uncommon Prayer Book, M.R. James, ss **A Warning to the Curious**,1925

Uncommon Sense, Hal Clement, ss *Astounding* Sep,1945

The Uncorking of Uncle Finn, Jane Yolen, ss *F&SF* Nov,1986

The Undead, Robert Bloch, ss **The Book Sail 16th Anniversary Catalog**,1984

Under a Hungry Moon, Jeannette M. Hopper, ss *Footsteps* Nov,1987

Under Her Skin, Susan Casper, ss *Amazing* Mar,1987

Under Siege, George R.R. Martin, nv *Omni* Oct,1985

Under the Carpet, Philip Lorimer, ss **The Pan Book of Horror Stories** #28, Pan,1987

Under the Hammer, David Drake, nv *Galaxy* Oct,1974

The Undertaker Reflects, John Maclay, pm *Fungi* #12,1986

Unearthing Suite, Margaret Atwood, ss

A Unfiltered Man, Robert A. Metzger, ss *Aboriginal SF* Sep,1987

The Unfolding, John Shirley & Bruce Sterling, ss *Interzone* #11,1985

The Unforgiven, John Maclay, pm *Weirdbook* #20,1985

Unfortunately, Fredric Brown, vi *F&SF* Oct,1958

The Ungoverned, Vernor Vinge, nv **Far Frontiers** v3, ed. Jerry Pournelle & Jim Baen,1985

Unholy Trinity [as by Eric G. Iverson], Harry Turtledove, nv *Amazing* Jul,1985

Unicorn Creed, Elizabeth Ann Scarborough, n. Bantam: New York,1983

Unicorn Tapestry, Suzy McKee Charnas, na **New Dimensions** #11, ed. Robert Silverberg/Marta Randall,1980

Unification, Isaac Asimov, ed *IASFM* Aug,1987

Universe--The Ultimate Artifact?, Richard D. Meisner, ar *Analog* Apr,1987

The Universe: An Introduction, Andrew Fraknoi, in

University Field Observation Guide for the Planet Earth or U.F.O. Handbook, Arthur B. Burnett, ss *Salarius* #3,1987

Unknown, Isaac Asimov, ed *IASFM* Oct,1987

Unknown Drives, Richard Christian Matheson, ss **Nightmares**, ed. Charles L. Grant, Playboy,1979

The Unknown Machen, Michael T. Shoemaker, pr

The Unlimited Draw of Tick Boileau, Rudyard Kipling, ss *Quartette* Chr,1885

Unmistakably the Finest, Scott Bradfield, nv *Interzone* #8,1984

Unready to Wear, Kurt Vonnegut, Jr., ss *Galaxy* Apr,1953

The Unreconstructed M, Philip K. Dick, nv *(The Original) Science Fiction Stories* Jan,1957

An Unscientific Story, Louise J. Strong, ss *Cosmopolitan* Feb,1903

Unsound Variations, George R.R. Martin, na *Amazing* Jan,1982

Unto the Sixth Generation: Epilogue, Walter Jon Williams, sl **Wild Cards** v2, ed. George R.R. Martin, Bantam,1987

Unto the Sixth Generation: Part One, Walter Jon Williams, sl **Wild Cards** v2, ed. George R.R. Martin, Bantam,1987

Unto the Sixth Generation: Part Two, Walter Jon Williams, sl **Wild Cards** v2, ed. George R.R. Martin, Bantam,1987

Unto the Sixth Generation: Prologue, Walter Jon Williams, sl **Wild Cards** v2, ed. George R.R. Martin, Bantam,1987

Unworthy of the Angel, Stephen R. Donaldson, nv **Nine Visions**, Seabury Press,1983

Up in Smoke, Arthur Winfield Knight, pm *2AM* Fll,1987

Up the Garden Path, L.P. Hartley, ss **The White Wand and Other Stories**, Hamilton,1954

Up Under the Roof, Manly Wade Wellman, ss *Weird Tales* Oct,1938

Up Under the Roof [revised from *Weird Tales* Oct,38], Manly Wade Wellman, ss **Worse Things Waiting**, Carcosa: Chapel Hill NC,1973

Uphill Climb, Robert J. Sawyer, vi *Amazing* Mar,1987

The Uplift War, David Brin, n. Phantasia: West Bloomfield, MI hc Apr,1987

Upon Hearing New Evidence That Meteors Caused the Great Extinctions, Robert Frazier, pm *Amazing* Jan,1987

UPON THE DULL EARTH   **WAR AND/OR PEACE**

Upon the Dull Earth, Philip K. Dick, nv *Beyond Fantasy Fiction* Sep,1954

The Upper Berth, F. Marion Crawford, nv *The Broken Shaft, Unwin's Annual*,1886

Upstarts, Johnny Yen, ss **The Pan Book of Horror Stories** #28, Pan,1987

Uroboros, Bruce Boston, pm *Fungi* #11,1986

The Use of Archaeology in Worldbuilding, C.J. Cherryh, ar *SFWA Bulletin*,1978

User-Friendly, John Gordon, ss **Twisted Circuits**, ed. Mick Gowar, Beaver,1987

Usher II [Carnival of Madness], Ray Bradbury, ss *Thrilling Wonder Stories* Apr,1950

Vacuum Flowers [Part 2 of 3], Michael Swanwick, sl *IASFM* Jan,1987

Vacuum Flowers [Part 3 of 3], Michael Swanwick, sl *IASFM* Feb,1987

Valerie, Harlan Ellison, ss *Los Angeles Free Press* Nov 3,1972

The Valley of the Worm, Robert E. Howard, ss *Weird Tales* Feb,1934

Vampire, Richard Christian Matheson, ss **Cutting Edge**, ed. Dennis Etchison, Doubleday,1986

The Vampire Cat of Nabeshima, Bernhardt J. Hurwood, ss **Monsters Galore**, ed. Bernhardt J. Hurwood, Fawcett,1965

The Vampire in the Mirror, Gerald W. Page, nv *Weirdbook* #22,1987

The Vampire Maid, Hume Nisbet, ss **Stories Weird and Wonderful**, F.V. White: London,1900

The Vampyre, Vasile Alecsandrai, pm *English Illustrated Magazine* Nov,1886

The Vampyre, Dr. John William Polidori, ss *The New Monthly Magazine* Apr,1819

Vandy, Vandy, Manly Wade Wellman, ss *F&SF* Mar,1953

The Vanishing American, Charles Beaumont, ss *F&SF* Aug,1955

The Variable Man, Philip K. Dick, na *Space Science Fiction* Sep,1953

Varney, the Vampyre; or, The Feast of Blood, James Malcolm Rymer, ex,1845

Vaster Than Empires and More Slow, Ursula K. Le Guin, nv **New Dimensions** #1, ed. Robert Silverberg/Marta Randall,1971

Vehicles for Future Wars [also as "Military Vehicles: Into the Third Millennium"], Dean Ing, ar **Destinies** v1#4, ed. James Baen,1979

Vehicular Man, Andrew Joron, pm

The Veldt [The World the Children Made], Ray Bradbury, ss *The Saturday Evening Post* Sep 23,1950

Veneers of Sleep, Robert Frazier, pm **Alternate Lives**,1986

Vengeance Fleet [Vengeance, Unlimited], Fredric Brown, vi *Super Science Stories* Jul,1950

The Vengeance of Ulios [The Avenger from Atlantis], Edmond Hamilton, nv *Weird Tales* Jul,1935

Venus, Our Very Favourite Star, M. Travis Lane, pm **Tesseracts 2**, ed. Phyllis Gotlieb & Douglas Barbour, Press Porcepic: Victoria,1987

Vergil and the Caged Bird, Avram Davidson, ss *Amazing* Jan,1987

Veritas, James Morrow, nv **Synergy** v1, ed. George Zebrowski,1987

The Verts Get a Nuke, Michael Armstrong, ss *F&SF* Aug,1987

The Very Best Defense, Laurence M. Janifer, nv *ROM*

The Very Last Day of a Good Woman [The Last Day], Harlan Ellison, ss *Rogue* Nov,1958

The Very Last Party at #13 Mallory Way, L.E. Carroll, nv **L. Ron Hubbard Presents Writers of the Future** v3, ed. Algis Budrys, Bridge,1987

A Very Present Help, L.P. Hartley, nv

Vestiges of Time, Richard C. Meredith, n. Doubleday: Garden City, NY,1978

The Vexation of Percival Lowell's Sight, Robert Frazier, pm *IASFM* Jul,1984

Victim, Lee Barwood, pm *Weirdbook* #22,1987

Victory, Fred Saberhagen, nv *F&SF* Jun,1979

Video, Welch D. Everman, ar *Twilight Zone* Feb,1987

Video, Welch D. Everman, ar *Twilight Zone* Jun,1987

Video Star, Walter Jon Williams, nv *IASFM* Jul,1986

The View from Mars Hill, Frederik Pohl, nv *IASFM* May,1987

View from the Abscissa, Bruce Boston, pm

Viewpoint: A Few Small Press Magazines, Colleen Drippe', br *Apex!* #1,1987

Viewpoint: Cellular Automata, Rudy Rucker, ar *IASFM* Apr,1987

A Vignette, M.R. James, ss *The London Mercury* v35,1936

The Viking's Stone, Brian Lumley, ss **The Horror at Oakdene and Others**, Arkham,1977

Vilcabamba, Carol Emshwiller, ss *Twilight Zone* Aug,1987

The Village, Kate Wilhelm, ss **Bad Moon Rising**, ed. Thomas M. Disch,1973

The Villain, Ken Doggett, ss *Space & Time* #72,1987

The Vinegar Mother, Ruth Rendell, nv **The Fallen Curtain**, Hutchinson,1976

The Violet Car, Edith Nesbit, ss **Fear**, S. Paul: London,1910

A Virgil Finlay Portfolio, Harry Dolan & Virgil Finlay, pi *Mage* Spr,1987

The Virgin from Kalamazoo, Martin Gardner, vi *Men Only* Jun,1951

The Virgin of the Seven Daggers, Vernon Lee, nv **For Maurice, Five Unlikely Stories**, John Lane: London,1927

Virginia and Bread, Josephine Saxton, ss **Little Tours of Hell**, Pandora,1986

A Vision of Honor, Sharon Green, nv **Friends of the Horseclans**, ed. Robert Adams & Pamela Crippen Adams, Signet,1987

Vision of Tarot, Piers Anthony, n. Berkley: New York,1980

Vision on the Eiger [from **The Black Room**], Colin Wilson, ex Weidenfeld Nicolson: London,1971

The Visionary Land, Jack Matthews, ss *Michigan Quarterly Review*

The Visitation, Greg Bear, vi *Omni* Jun,1987

Visitation, Tom Henighan, pm **Tesseracts 2**, ed. Phyllis Gotlieb & Douglas Barbour, Press Porcepic: Victoria,1987

The Visitation, Susan Palwick, ss *Amazing* Sep,1987

The Visitor, Ray Bradbury, ss *Startling Stories* Nov,1948

The Visitor, Ian Serraillier, pm **A Second Poetry Book**, ed. John Foster, Oxford Univ. Press,1980

The Visitor, Richard Taylor, ss *2AM* Fll,1987

A Visitor from Down Under, L.P. Hartley, ss **The Ghost-Book**, ed. Cynthia Asquith, Hutchinson,1926

Visitors, Jack M. Dann, ss *IASFM* Oct,1987

Vital Signs, Dean Ing, na **Destinies** v2#3, ed. James Baen,1980

The Voice from the Ether, Lloyd Arthur Eshbach, nv *Amazing* May,1931

The Voice in the Garden, Harlan Ellison, vi *Lighthouse* Jun,1967

The Voice in the Night, William Hope Hodgson, ss *Blue Book* Nov,1907

The Voice of God, Winifred Holtby, ss **Truth Is Not Sober**,1934

The Voice of the Beach, Ramsey Campbell, nv *Fantasy Tales* Sum,1982

Voices in the Earth, Alan Brennert, ss *Twilight Zone* Oct,1987

Voices in the Wind, Elizabeth S. Helfman, ss **Spaceships & Spells**, ed. Jane Yolen, Martin H. Greenberg & Charles G. Waugh, Harper & Row,1987

Voodoo, Fredric Brown, vi *Beyond Fantasy Fiction* Sep,1954

Vox Sanguinis, Andrew Joron, pm

The Voyage of the Dawn Treader, C.S. Lewis, n. The Blakiston Co.: Philadelphia,1952

The Voyage That Lasted 600 Years, Don Wilcox, nv *Amazing* Oct,1940

W.S., L.P. Hartley, ss **Ghost Book** #2, ed. Aidan Chambers/James Turner,1952

Wailing Well, M.R. James, ss,1927

The Wait [also as "To Be Taken in a Strange Country"], Kit Reed, ss *F&SF* Apr,1958

Wait a Minute!, Rudin Moore, ss **Ultra-Vue and Selected Peripheral Visions**, self published,1987

Waiting for a Bus, John Whitbourn, ss **After Midnight Stories** #3,1987

Waiting for Sunlight, Paul Christopher, ss **Beyond That River**, Pal Books,1987

Waiting for the Buyer, Richard Wilson, ss **The Kid from Ozone Park and Other Stories**, Drumm,1987

Waiting for the Hunger, Nina Kiriki Hoffman, ss **Doom City**, ed. Charles L. Grant, Tor,1987

Waiting for the Universe to Begin, Brian W. Aldiss, ss **Epoch**, ed. Roger Elwood & Robert Silverberg, Berkley,1975

The Waiting Game, Bruce Jones, ss **Twisted Tales**, San Diego: Blackthorne,1987

The Waiting-Room, Phyllis Bottome, ss **Strange Fruit**,1928

The Waits, L.P. Hartley, ss

Wake, Steve Rasnic Tem, ss *Eldritch Tales* #13,1987

Wake of the Riddler, Janet Morris, nv **Aftermath**, ed. Robert Lynn Asprin & Lynn Abbey, Ace,1987

Waking, David Sutton, ss *2AM* Win,1987

The Walker Behind, Marion Zimmer Bradley, ss *F&SF* Jul,1987

Walking on Water, Margaret Atwood, ss

Wall of Crystal, Eye of Night, Algis Budrys, nv *Galaxy* Dec,1961

Wallflower, Mark Baricevic, ss *2AM* Fll,1987

Waltz of the Flowers, Paul Collins & Trevor Donohue, ss *Aphelion* #5,1987

The Wanderer, Eva Jones, vi *Mage* Win,1985

Wandering Willie's Tale [from **Redgauntlet**], Sir Walter Scott, ex Constable: London,1824

"Wanna Bet?", Tracy Hickman & Margaret Weis, na **DragonLance Tales** v2, Margaret Weis & Tracy Hickman, TSR,1987

Want Ad, Bruce Boston, pm *Star*Line* 1981

War and/or Peace, Lee Montgomerie, ss *Interzone* #11,1985

The War at Home, Lewis Shiner, ss *IASFM* May,1985

War Game, Philip K. Dick, ss *Galaxy* Dec,1959

War Game Players, R. Brent Powell, ss *Salarius* #3,1987

War of the Unseen Worlds, Leslie Fish, nv **Fever Season**, ed. C.J. Cherryh, DAW,1987

"War on Imagination" Feedback, Edgar F. Tatro, lt *2AM* Spr,1987

War Veteran, Philip K. Dick, nv *If* Mar,1955

The War with the Fnools, Philip K. Dick, ss *Galaxy* Feb,1969

Warm as Snow, Mike Sims, ss **After Midnight Stories** #3,1987

A Warning to the Curious, M.R. James, ss *The London Mercury* Aug,1925

The Warrior's Apprentice, Lois McMaster Bujold, n. Baen: New York,1986

Wartours, Mark Wilkins, ss **Gollancz - Sunday Times Best SF Stories**, Gollancz,1987

Was Frankenstein Simply Einstein Being Frank? or Scientists in Science Fiction, Gregory Benford, ar **New Destinies** v2, ed. Jim Baen, Baen,1987

The Wasteland, Deborah Wheeler, ss **Red Sun of Darkover**, ed. Marion Zimmer Bradley & The Friends of Darkover, DAW,1987

Waswolf, Edward Wellen, ss *F&SF* Sep,1987

Watch Doll, William D. Cottrell, ss *Whispers* #23,1987

Watch Out!, Bruce Coville, ss **Spaceships & Spells**, ed. Jane Yolen, Martin H. Greenberg & Charles G. Waugh, Harper & Row,1987

A Watcher by the Dead, Ambrose Bierce, ss **In the Midst of Life**, E.L.G. Steele: San Francisco CA,1891

The Watchers, Ray Bradbury, vi **The Martian Chronicles**,1950

Watchwolf, J.N. Williamson, ss *Footsteps* Nov,1987

The Water Ghost of Harrowby Hall, John Kendrick Bangs, ss *Harper's Weekly* Jun 27,1891

The Waterfall of Ghosts, Robert D. San Souci, ss **Short & Shivery**, Doubleday,1987

The Waters from Time, Steven G. Oliver, vi *Amazing* Sep,1987

Watershead, David B. Silva, vi *Grue* #5,1987

Waterspider, Philip K. Dick, nv *If* Jan,1964

The Wave and the Flame, M. Bradley Kellogg & William Rossow, n. New American Library: New York,1986

The Wave We Ride, Bruce Boston, pm

Waves, Andrew Weiner, nv *IASFM* Mar,1987

Way in the Middle of the Air, Ray Bradbury, ss *Other Worlds* Jul,1950

A Way of Thinking, Theodore Sturgeon, nv *Amazing* Nov,1953

The Ways of Love, Poul Anderson, nv **Destinies** v1#2, ed. James Baen,1979

Wayward Children, Richard A. Knaak, nv **DragonLance Tales** v1, Margaret Weis & Tracy Hickman, TSR,1987

We Also Walk Dogs, Robert A. Heinlein, ss *Astounding* Jul,1941

We Build a Shrine, Nancy Springer, pm **Chance & Other Gestures of the Hand of Fate**, Baen,1987

We Can Remember It for You Wholesale, Philip K. Dick, nv *F&SF* Apr,1966

"We cannot escape humility.", Robert Frazier, pm *F&SF* Nov,1983

We Have Always Lived in the Forest, Nancy Holder, ss **Shadows** #10, ed. Charles L. Grant,1987

We Who Are His Followers, G. Wayne Miller, ss *The Horror Show* Win,1987

The Weapon, Fredric Brown, ss *Astounding* Apr,1951

Weasling Out, Phyllis Eisenstein, ss *Whispers* #23,1987

The Weather With Morgana, Stephen L. Burns, ss *2AM* Sum,1987

The Weather's Fine, Harry Turtledove, ss *Playboy* Jul,1987

The Webbed Axis, Andrew Joron, pm

A Wedding Chest, Vernon Lee, ss **Pope Jacynth and Other Fantastic Tales**, Grant Richards: London,1904

The Weeping Oak, Charles de Lint, ss **Sword and Sorceress** #4, ed. Marion Zimmer Bradley,1987

Weigh Station, Richard Kostelanetz, br *Pulpsmith* Win,1987

The Weird Doom of Floyd Scrilch, Robert Bloch, ss *Fantastic Adventures* Jul,1942

Weird LAWKI, Stephen L. Gillett, Ph.D., ar *Amazing* Jul,1987

The Weird Occurrence in Odd Alley, Gary Gygax, na **Night Arrant**, Ace/New Infinities,1987

The Weirds, Sheldon R. Jaffery, in

The Well, Nancy Mortensen, ss *SF International* #2,1987

Well Bottled at Slab's, John Gregory Betancourt, ss *The Dragon* Oct,1987

The Well-Meaning Mayor, Leslie Charteris, ss,1935

Were-Hunter, Mercedes R. Lackey, nv **Tales of the Witch World**, ed. Andre Norton, St. Martin's,1987

The Werewolf and the Vampire, R. Chetwynd-Hayes, nv **The Monster Club**,1975

Werewolfgirl, Robert Randolph Medcalf, Jr., pm *Eldritch Tales* #13,1987

The Werwolves, Henry Beaugrand, ss *The Century* Aug,1898

West, Orson Scott Card, na **Free Lancers**, ed. Elizabeth Mitchell, Baen,1987

West Texas, Ursula K. Le Guin, pm,1980

Wet Behind the Ears, Jack C. Haldeman, II, ss *IASFM* Oct,1982

Wet Magic, Henry Kuttner, na *Unknown* Feb,1943

What Are You Going to Be When You Grow Up?, Gregory Benford, nv **Spaceships & Spells**, ed. Jane Yolen, Martin H. Greenberg & Charles G. Waugh, Harper & Row,1987

What Avails a Psalm in the Cinders of Gehenna?, Tais Teng, ss *SF International* #2,1987

What Bleak Land, Robert F. Young, ss *F&SF* Jan,1987

What Brothers Are For, Patricia Anthony, ss *Aboriginal SF* Nov,1987

WHAT DO YOU WANT ME TO DO TO PROVE IM HUMAN STOP [Inhuman Error], Fred Saberhagen, ss *Analog* Oct,1974

What If..., Isaac Asimov, ss *Fantastic* Sum,1952

What is Going on in The Oaks Around the Barn, Ursula K. Le Guin, pm,1986

What Is the Universe?, Isaac Asimov, ar **Universe**, ed. Byron Preiss, Bantam Spectra,1987

What It Said, Russell Hoban, ss *Sanity* Jan,1987

What Makes Heironymous Run?, Howard Waldrop, ss *Shayol* #7,1985

What of the Night, Manly Wade Wellman, ss *F&SF* Mar,1980

What Papa Does Is Always Right, Hans Christian Andersen, ss

What Should an SF Novel Be About?, Brian W. Aldiss, ar *Fantasy Review* Apr,1986

What the Dead Men Say, Philip K. Dick, na *Worlds of Tomorrow* Jun,1964

What the Janitor Found, A.R. Morlan, pm *Night Cry* v2#3,1987

What the Large Night Left, Genine Hannes, pm *Ice River* Sum,1987

What to do Until the Analyst Comes [Everybody's Happy But Me!], Frederik Pohl, ss *Imagination* Feb,1956

What Was It?, Fitz-James O'Brien, ss *Harper's* Mar,1859

What'll We Do with Ragland Park?, Philip K. Dick, nv *Amazing* Nov,1963

What's a Nice Girl Like You..., Jerry Oltion, vi *Analog* Oct,1987

The Wheelbarrow Thief, Laurence M. Janifer, nv *ROM*

When a Rose Sings, John B. Rosenman, ss *2AM* Sum,1987

When Idaho Dived, Ian Watson, ss **Afterwar**, ed. Janet Morris, Baen,1985

When It Changed, Joanna Russ, ss **Again, Dangerous Visions**, ed. Harlan Ellison, Doubleday,1972

When It Was Moonlight, Manly Wade Wellman, ss *Unknown* Feb,1940

When Jaquerel Walked With Shadows, Janet Fox, ss *Weirdbook* #22,1987

When the Air Gets Thick and Sweet, Lisa Kucharski, pm *Ice River* Sum,1987

When the Haloperidol Runs Out and the Blue Fairy Never Comes, Shirley Weinland, ss *Amazing* Mar,1987

When the Timegate Failed, Ian Watson, nv *Interzone* #14,1985

When the Twerms Came, Arthur C. Clarke, vi *Playboy* May,1972

When the Vikings Owned the Mythology, William Jon Watkins, pm *Amazing* Jul,1987

When You Care, When You Love, Theodore Sturgeon, nv *F&SF* Sep,1962

When You Wish Upon a Corpse, Joan Vander Putten, ss *2AM* Win,1987

When You're Smiling, Theodore Sturgeon, nv *Galaxy* Jan,1955

Where Did She Wander?, Manly Wade Wellman, ss *Whispers* #23,1987

Where Does Watson Road Go?, William Relling, Jr., ss *Eldritch Tales* #14,1987

Where not to buy Cufflinks in Stockholm, Leslie Halliwell, ss **A Demon Close Behind**, Robert Hale,1987

Where the Heart Is, Ramsey Campbell, ss **The Architecture of Fear**, ed. Kathryn Cramer & Peter D. Pautz, Arbor House,1987

Where the Summer Ends, Karl Edward Wagner, nv **Dark Forces**, ed. Kirby McCauley, Viking,1980

Where There's a Will, Richard Matheson & Richard Christian Matheson, ss **Dark Forces**, ed. Kirby McCauley, Viking,1980

The Whimper of Whipped Dogs, Harlan Ellison, nv **Bad Moon Rising**, ed. Thomas M. Disch,1973

The Whining, Ramsey Campbell, ss **The Hounds of Hell**, ed. Michel Parry, Gollancz,1974

The Whirlpool Rapids, Margaret Atwood, ss *Toronto Globe and Mail*

The Whisperer, John Marsh, ss **After Midnight Stories** #3,1987

The White Babe, Jane Yolen, nv *IASFM* Jun,1987

The White Bull, Fred Saberhagen, nv *Fantastic* Nov,1976

THE WHITE DONKEY

The White Donkey, Ursula K. Le Guin, ss *TriQuarterly* #49,1980

The White Fire, Robert E. Vardeman, n. Avon: New York pb Jan,1986

White Mother of Shadows, George Vandegrift, nv *Terror Tales* Jan,1941

The White Road, Charles de Lint, nv **Tales of the Witch World**, ed. Andre Norton, St. Martin's,1987

The White Road, Manly Wade Wellman, pm *Fantasy Tales* #16,1986

White Trains, Lucius Shepard, pm *Night Cry* v2#3,1987

The White Wand, L.P. Hartley, co,1954

The White Wand, L.P. Hartley, nv **The White Wand and Other Stories**, Hamilton,1954

Whitewash, Rose Macaulay, ss **Ghost Book** #2, ed. Aidan Chambers/James Turner,1952

Who Goes There? [as by Don A. Stuart], John W. Campbell, Jr., na *Astounding* Aug,1938

Who or What was It?, Kingsley Amis, ss *Playboy*,1972

Who Walks at Night, John Maclay, ss *The Horror Show* Sum,1986

Who Will Speak for Earth? An Essay on Extraterrestrial Intelligence and Contact, Donald Goldsmith, ar **Universe**, ed. Byron Preiss, Bantam Spectra,1987

Who's a Clever Boy?, James Gibbins, ss **Gollancz - Sunday Times Best SF Stories**, Gollancz,1987

Who's Afraid?, Philippa Pearce, ss **Hundreds and Hundreds**, Puffin,1984

Who's Who in the British Horror Scene, R.S. Hadji, ar *American Fantasy* Win,1987

Who? [also as "Bulkhead"], Theodore Sturgeon, nv *Galaxy* Mar,1955

The Whole Town's Sleeping, Ray Bradbury, ss *McCalls* Sep,1950

Whooo-ooo Flupper!, Nicholas Fisk, ss,1986

Why I Left Harry's All-Night Hamburgers, Lawrence Watt-Evans, ss *IASFM* Jul,1987

Why the Moon Is Small and Dark When the Sun Is Big and Shiny, Judith Stein, ss **Hear the Silence**, ed. Irene Zahava, Crossing Press,1986

Why the Sea Is Salty, Kitty Tsui, ss **Common Lives/Lesbian Lives**,1982

The Wi'ching Well, A.R. Morlan, ss *The Horror Show* Jan,1987

The Wicked Stepmother's Lament, Sara Maitland, ss **More Tales I Tell My Mother**, Journeyman,1987

A Wicked Voice, Vernon Lee, nv **Hauntings, Fantastic Stories**, Heinemann: London,1890

The Widow Renounced, Bruce Boston, pm *Night Cry* v2#3,1987

The Wife's Story, Ursula K. Le Guin, ss **The Compass Rose**, Harper & Row,1982

The Wilder One, Harlan Ellison, vi *Sundial* Jan,1955

The Wilderness, Ray Bradbury, ss *F&SF* Nov,1952

Wilderness, Fred Saberhagen, ss *Amazing* Sep,1976

Will, Vincent O'Sullivan, ss **The Green Window**,1899

Will Little Note, Nor Long Remember, Jack Clemons, nv *Amazing* Nov,1987

'Will Ye No' Come Back Again?', Eleanor Scott, ss **Randalls Round**, E. Benn: London,1929

The William Carlos Williams Variations, Robert Frazier, pm *Arc* Spr,1985

William Gibson: A Cyberpunk Examined, Jeffrey V. Yule, ar *Mage* Spr,1987

Willing Suspension of Disbelief, Jeffrey V. Yule, ed *Mage* Spr,1986

Willow, C.J. Cherryh, nv **Hecate's Cauldron**, ed. Susan M. Shwartz, DAW,1982

Willow He Walk, Manly Wade Wellman, ss **World Fantasy Convention Program Book**,1983

The Willow Platform, Joseph Payne Brennan, ss *Whispers* #1,1973

The Willows, Algernon Blackwood, nv **The Listener and Other Stories**,1907

Willows, Candas Jane Dorsey, ss **Tesseracts 2**, ed. Phyllis Gotlieb & Douglas Barbour, Press Porcepic: Victoria,1987

Willy Wonka and the L. Walker Biofair, Elizabeth Massie, ss *The Horror Show* Fll,1987

The Wind from the Sun [Sunjammer], Arthur C. Clarke, nv *Boy's Life* Mar,1964

The Wind on Haunted Hill, Ruskin Bond, ss

Windham's Folly, G. Wayne Miller, ss *Space & Time* #73,1987

The Window, Ray Bradbury, ss *Colliers* Aug 5,1950

Windows, Ian Watson, nv *IASFM* Dec,1986

Wing Quack Flap, Joan Aiken, ss **Cold Feet**, Jean Richardson, Hodder & Stoughton,1985

Winged Death, Dave Stall, ss *Minnesota Fantasy Review* #1,1987

The Wings of a Bat, Lawrence Harding, pm *Grue* #5,1987

Winter Downs, Ursula K. Le Guin, pm **Hard Words & Other Poems**, Harper & Row,1981

Winter Gathering, Ann K. Kotowicz, ss *Twilight Zone* Apr,1987

Winter in America, Paul Di Filippo, ss *New Pathways* Aug,1987

Winter in America: Fact or Fiction?, Michael G. Adkisson, ar *New Pathways* Aug,1987

The Winter Market, William Gibson, nv *Vancouver* Nov,1985

Winter's Chill, George R.R. Martin, nv **Wild Cards** v2, ed. George R.R. Martin, Bantam,1987

Winter's King, Ursula K. Le Guin, nv **Orbit** #5, ed. Damon Knight,1969

Winter's Tale, Connie Willis, nv *IASFM* Dec,1987

Winterscape, Tom Hansen, pm *Pulpsmith* Win,1987

Wiping the Slate Clean, G. Wayne Miller, ss **Masques** #2, ed. J.N. Williamson,1987

The Wire Around the War, Ian Watson, ss *IASFM* mid-Dec,1985

Wireless, Rudyard Kipling, ss *Scribner's* Aug,1902

The Wish, Roald Dahl, ss,1948

The Wish House, Rudyard Kipling, ss *McClure's* Oct 15,1924

A Wish Named Arnold, Charles de Lint, ss **Spaceships & Spells**, ed. Jane Yolen, Martin H. Greenberg & Charles G. Waugh, Harper & Row,1987

Wishbone, Anne Gay, ss **Gollancz - Sunday Times Best SF Stories**, Gollancz,1987

The Witch Cat, Robert D. San Souci, ss **Short & Shivery**, Doubleday,1987

A Witch for All Seasons [as by Gans T. Field], Manly Wade Wellman, ss *Witchcraft & Sorcery* #9,1973

Witch Girl, Elizabeth Coatsworth, ss

Witch Mother, Christopher Gilbert, ss *Night Cry* v2#3,1987

The Witch of Salem, Laurie Cabot & James Verniere, iv *Twilight Zone* Jun,1987

The Witch-Hunt, Mairin Johnston, ss **Mad and Bad Fairies**, ed. Anonymous, Attic Press,1987

The Witches of Eastwick, James Verniere, mr *Twilight Zone* Jun,1987

The Witches of Wenshar, Barbara Hambly, n. Ballantine: New York pb Jul,1987

Witchwood, Mike Hurley, ss *Haunts* #9,1987

With a Little Help From His Friends, Victor Milan, nv **Wild Cards** v2, ed. George R.R. Martin, Bantam,1987

With Four Lean Hounds, Pat Murphy, ss **Sword and Sorceress** #1, ed. Marion Zimmer Bradley,1984

With Morning Comes Mistfall, George R.R. Martin, ss *Analog* May,1973

Witheling End, L.P. Hartley, ss **The White Wand and Other Stories**, Hamilton,1954

The Withered Arm, Thomas Hardy, nv *Blackwood's* Jan,1888

Within the Walls of Tyre, Michael Bishop, nv *Weirdbook* #13,1978

Wives, Lisa Tuttle, ss *F&SF* Dec,1979

The Wizard of the Wood, Harry Davidov, pm *Fantasy Book* Jun,1986

The Wizard's Spectacles, Morris Simon, nv **DragonLance Tales** v2, Margaret Weis & Tracy Hickman, TSR,1987

The Wolf Girl, Guy Endore, ss *Argosy* Dec,1920

The Wolf Girl Speaks, Nancy Springer, pm *Star*Line* v5#6,1982

Wolf Time, Walter Jon Williams, nv *IASFM* Jan,1987

Wolf/Child, Jane Yolen, ss *Twilight Zone* Jun,1987

Wolfland, Tanith Lee, nv *F&SF* Oct,1980

Wolfshead, Robert E. Howard, nv *Weird Tales* Apr,1926

The Wolves of God, Algernon Blackwood, ss **The Wolves of God**, Cassell,1921

The Woman in Black, Dennis Etchison, ss *Whispers* #21,1984

The Woman on the Corner, Steve Rasnic Tem, ss *Whispers* #23,1987

The Woman Who Is the Midnight Wind, Terence M. Green, ss **Tesseracts**, ed. Judith Merril, Press Porcepic: Victoria,1985

Woman with a Hole in the Center of Her Chest, Conger Beasley, Jr., vi *New Pathways* Aug,1987

The Women Men Don't See, James Tiptree, Jr., nv *F&SF* Dec,1973

Won By a Fall, L.P. Hartley, ss

The Wonderful Day [Miracle on Main Street], Robert Arthur, nv *Argosy Weekly* Jul 6,1940

Wondergirls, Carol Reid, ss *The Horror Show* Spr,1987

Wonderland, Richard Christian Matheson & William Relling, Jr., ss *Night Cry* v2#5,1987

Wooden Tony, Lucy Lane Clifford, ss **The Last Touches and Other Stories**, London: Adam & Charles Black,1892

The Woodland of Zarad-Thra, Robin Wayne Bailey, nv **Sword and Sorceress** #4, ed. Marion Zimmer Bradley,1987

The Woodrow Wilson Dime, Jack Finney, n. Simon & Schuster: New York,1968

A Word from Our Sponsor, Fredric Brown, ss *Other Worlds* Sep,1951

Wordfinder, Adele Geras, ss **Twisted Circuits**, ed. Mick Gowar, Beaver,1987

THE WORDS THAT COUNT   ZOMBIQUE

The Words That Count, Ramsey Campbell, ss **The Height of the Scream**,1976

Wordsong, J.N. Williamson, ss **Masques** #2, ed. J.N. Williamson,1987

Wordware, Charles Ardai, gr *Twilight Zone* Dec,1987

Working Stiff, Paul Curtis, ss *Fantasy Book* Mar,1987

The World in the Rock, Kara Dalkey, ss **Liavek: Wizard's Row**, ed. Will Shetterly & Emma Bull, Ace,1987

The World Next Door, Brad Ferguson, ss *IASFM* Sep,1987

The World of E.E. "Doc" Smith, Randall Garrett, ar *The Comics Journal*,1978

The World of Myrion Flowers, C.M. Kornbluth & Frederik Pohl, ss *F&SF* Oct,1961

A World of Talent, Philip K. Dick, nv *Galaxy* Oct,1954

The World She Wanted, Philip K. Dick, ss *Science Fiction Quarterly* May,1953

A World Without Toys, T.M. Wright, ss **Shadows** #10, ed. Charles L. Grant,1987

World's End, John Gawsworth, pm

Worldwreckers, Laurence M. Janifer, ss *Analog* Oct,1987

Worms of the Earth, Robert E. Howard, nv *Weird Tales* Nov,1932

The Wound, Lisa Tuttle, ss **Other Edens**, ed. Christopher Evans & Robert Holdstock, Unwin: London,1987

A Wrecker's Tale, Bruce Boston, pm *The Magazine of Speculative Poetry* Sum,1985

Writing With Percission: Cooking Salmon in the Dishwasher: Nontraditional Computer Use for Science Fiction and Fantasy Writers, Part 1, Dan Goodman, ar *Tales of the Unanticipated* #2,1987

Xax Xox, Ferret, cs *New Pathways* Nov,1987

The Xeelee Flower, S.M. Baxter, ss *Interzone* #19,1987

Xessex, Katherine V. Forrest, ss *F&SF* Feb,1983

Xils ["Xils", **Aurores Boreales 2** 1985], Esther Rochon, ss **Tesseracts 2**, ed. Phyllis Gotlieb & Douglas Barbour, Press Porcepic: Victoria,1987

Xmas Over, Ursula K. Le Guin, pm *Clinton Street Quarterly*,1984

Xorinda the Witch, Andrew M. Greeley, ss *American Fantasy* Sum,1987

Yanqui Doodle, James Tiptree, Jr., nv *IASFM* Jul,1987

The Yard, Colleen Drippe', ss *Grue* #6,1987

The Yard, William F. Nolan, ss **Masques** #2, ed. J.N. Williamson,1987

Yare, Manly Wade Wellman, ss **New Terrors** #1, ed. Ramsey Campbell, Pan,1980

The Year of the Quiet Computer, Brian W. Aldiss, ss **New Writings in SF** #26,1975

The Years the Music Died, F. Paul Wilson, ss **Whispers** #6, ed. Stuart David Schiff,1987

Yellachile's Cage, Robert R. McCammon, ss **World Fantasy Convention Program Book** #13,1987

The Yellow Ball, Philippa Pearce, ss **Who's Afraid? and Other Strange Stories**, Kestrel/Penguin,1986

The Yellow Sign, Robert W. Chambers, nv **The King in Yellow**, New York & Chicago: F. Tennyson Neely,1895

The Yellow Wallpaper, Charlotte Perkins Gilman, ss *New England Magazine* Jan,1892

Yelloweye, Steve Barnes, nv **Friends of the Horseclans**, ed. Robert Adams & Pamela Crippen Adams, Signet,1987

Yesterday House, Fritz Leiber, nv *Galaxy* Aug,1952

Yesterday's Child, Thomas F. Monteleone, ss *Grue* #5,1987

Ylla [I'll Not Look for Wine], Ray Bradbury, ss *Maclean's* Jan 1,1950

You Can Go Now, Dennis Etchison, ss *Mike Shane Mystery Magazine* Sep,1980

You Can't Take It With You, C.J. Henderson, ss *Eldritch Tales* #14,1987

You Could Be Wrong, Robert Bloch, ss *Amazing* Mar,1955

You Got It, Terry Carr, ss *F&SF* May,1987

You Should Have Seen the Mess, Muriel Spark, ss

The Yougoslaves, Robert Bloch, nv *Night Cry* v1#5,1986

Young Girl at an Open Half-Door, Fred Saberhagen, ss *F&SF* Nov,1968

Young Goodman Brown, Nathaniel Hawthorne, ss *New England Magazine* Apr,1835

Your Appointment Will Be Yesterday, Philip K. Dick, ss *Amazing* Aug,1966

Your Mind is a Mirror, Joan Aiken, ss **A Goose on Your Grave**, Gollancz,1987

Your Soul to Keep, K.H. Nelson, ss *Space & Time* #73,1987

Yours Truly, Jack the Ripper, Robert Bloch, ss *Weird Tales* Jul,1943

Zena, R. Chetwynd-Hayes, nv **Dracula's Children**, Kimber,1987

Zerail, Josepha Sherman, ss *Fantasy Tales* #16,1986

Zero Gee, Ben Bova, nv **Again, Dangerous Visions**, ed. Harlan Ellison, Doubleday,1972

Zero Hour, Ray Bradbury, ss *Planet Stories* Fll,1947

Zombie Bride, Robert Randolph Medcalf, Jr., pm *Eldritch Tales* #14,1987

Zombique, Joseph Payne Brennan, ss *Alfred Hitchcock's Mystery Magazine* Oct,1972

Contents List

14 BELLCHAMBER TOWER

*14 Bellchamber Tower Mark Valentine (Crimson Altar Press No ISBN, Nov,87 [1987], £1.30, 35pp, pb) Three stories about psychic investigator Ralph Tyler. Illustrated by Stella Hender.
Contents:
   3 St. Michael & All Angels, ss *
  15 The Folly, ss *
  25 Madberry Hill, ss *

*The 1987 Annual World's Best SF Donald A. Wollheim & Arthur W. Saha, ed. (DAW 0-88677-203-6, Jun,87 [May,87], $3.95, 303pp, pb) Anthology of "bests" from 1986 with 10 stories, including several Hugo and Nebula nominees. Has the Nebula-winning novella, "R&R" by Lucius Shepard. Recommended. (CNB)
Contents:
  vii Introduction, Donald A. Wollheim, in
  11 Permafrost, Roger Zelazny, nv Omni Apr,1986
  36 Timerider, Doris Egan, nv Amazing Mar,1986
  82 Pretty Boy Crossover, Pat Cadigan, ss IASFM Jan,1986
  94 R&R, Lucius Shepard, na IASFM Apr,1986
 181 Lo, How an Oak E'er Blooming, Suzette Haden Elgin, ss F&SF Feb,1986
 191 Dream in a Bottle, Jerry Meredith & D.E. Smirl, ss L. Ron Hubbard Presents Writers of the Future v2, ed. Algis Budrys, Bridge,1986
 206 Into Gold, Tanith Lee, nv IASFM Mar,1986
 240 The Lions Are Asleep This Night, Howard Waldrop, nv Omni Aug,1986
 263 Against Babylon, Robert Silverberg, nv Omni May,1986
 286 Strangers on Paradise [Strangers in Paradise], Damon Knight, ss F&SF Apr,1986

+2001: A Space Odyssey/The City and the Stars/The Deep Range/ A Fall of Moondust/Rendezvous With Rama Arthur C. Clarke (Octopus/Heinemann 0-905712-82-X, 1987 [Nov,87], $11.98, 747pp, hc) Omnibus edition of the above titles. First U.S. edition.
Contents:
  7 2001: A Space Odyssey, n. New American Library: New York,1968
 139 The City and the Stars, n. Harcourt Brace: New York,1956 Revised and expanded from Against the Fall of Night (Gnome 1953).
 305 The Deep Range, n. Harcourt Brace: New York,1957 Expanded from "The Deep Range", Star Science Fiction Stories #3, Frederik Pohl ed., Ballantine 1954.
 449 A Fall of Moondust, n. Harcourt Brace & World: New York,1961
 601 Rendezvous with Rama, n. Gollancz: London,1973

*The 28th Pan Book of Horror Stories Clarence Paget, ed. (Pan 0-330-30133-0, Nov,87, £1.95, 156pp, pb) Original horror anthology.
Contents:
  7 The Abandoned Dam, Alan Temperley, nv *
  50 Tea Leaves, Rebecca Bradley, ss *
  53 Upstarts, Johnny Yen, ss *
  58 First Come, First Served, John H. Snellings, ss *
  70 Gray Matter, Stephen King, ss Cavalier Oct,1973
  82 Final Call for Passenger Paul, Christopher Fowler, ss *
  94 The Sandman, David Williamson, ss *
  98 More Birds, J.M. Pickles, ss *
 112 Death from Autophilia, Jay Wilde, ss *
 118 Under the Carpet, Philip Lorimer, ss *
 130 First Blood, F.R. Welsh, ss *
 142 Allsouls, Rebecca Bradley, ss *
 147 Falling in Love Again, Brent R. Smith, ss *

*2AM [v.1 #3, Spring 1987] Gretta M. Anderson, ed. (2AM Publications, $3.95, 58pp, 8.5 x 11 pb)
Contents:
  4 Preface, Gretta M. Anderson, pr *
  5 Film Reviews, Jon Holsinger, mr *
 10 The Music Box, Sue Marra, pm *
 11 Dark Corner, J.N. Williamson, br *
 15 The Natural Way, Janet Lorimer, ss *
 21 Interview with Crematia Mortum (Roberta Solomon), Kathleen E. Jurgens & Crematia Mortum, iv *
 25 Masks, Jeff Johnston, ss *
 27 Heavy Breathing, Marthayn Pelegrimas, pm *
 29 Autograph, Robert Stricklin, ss *
 33 A Little Elevator Music, Dennis Holmberg, ss *
 36 The Mad Poet's Magic Fails, Lisa Lepovetsky, pm *

 39 Marta's Cat, Bob Warner, vi *
 41 The Devourer, Leonard Carpenter, pm *
 43 Standard Procedure, Colleen Drippe', ss *
 49 Real Time, The Readers, lt *
 51 Things Not Seen, James Robert Smith, vi *
 53 "War on Imagination" Feedback, Edgar F. Tatro, lt *
 55 Small Press Reviews, Irwin M. Chapman, br *

*2AM [v.1 #4, Summer 1987] Gretta M. Anderson, ed. (2AM Publications, $3.95, 46pp, 8.5 x 11 pb)
Contents:
  4 Preface, Gretta M. Anderson, pr *
  5 Dark Corner, J.N. Williamson, br *
  7 In Time, Roger Dale Trexler, pm The Dark Road and Other Poems of Darkness,1987
  8 Film Reviews, Jon Holsinger, mr *
 13 Love is a Circle, R.A. Sass, vi *
 15 De-Programming Rose Ellen, Mort Castle, vi *
 17 The Hand of God, David Starkey, ss *
 19 The Trace of Old Fingers, Mark Rich, pm *
 21 Morbid Descent, Billie Sue Mosiman, ss *
 24 Presences, Lee Ann Sontheimer, pm *
 25 Music to Read 2AM by -- Contest Winner, ms *
 27 When a Rose Sings, John B. Rosenman, ss *
 35 The Weather With Morgana, Stephen L. Burns, ss *
 43 Small Press Reviews, Irwin M. Chapman, br *
 46 Real Time, The Readers, lt *

*2AM [v.2 #1, Fall 1987] Gretta M. Anderson, ed. (2AM Publications, $3.95, 46pp, 8.5 x 11 pb)
Contents:
  4 Preface, Gretta M. Anderson, pr *
  5 John Borkowski: An Appreciation, Irwin M. Chapman, bg *
  6 Film Reviews, Jon Holsinger, mr *
  8 Up in Smoke, Arthur Winfield Knight, pm *
  9 Dark Corner, J.N. Williamson, br *
 13 One Special, Perfect Way, Heather Svedbeck, ss *
 17 Intersections, Randy Williams, vi *
 18 Kathleen Jurgens interviews Commander USA, Kathleen E. Jurgens & Commander USA, iv *
 21 Finders Keepers, Kathleen Chaddock, vi *
 23 Real Time, The Readers, lt *
 24 The Visitor, Richard Taylor, ss *
 29 Blessed Sleep, Elizabeth Massie, vi *
 31 Wallflower, Mark Baricevic, ss *
 35 Genre-Love and the Magic of Words: John Maclay, William J. Grabowski & John Maclay, iv *
 36 It, Deloris Selinsky, pm *
 37 Don't Fuck With My Brain, Cheryl L. Nelms, pm *
 37 The Hyperbolic Super-Blitz, Norris D. Hertzog, vi Heart of Texas Commodore Home User Group Newsletter Jan,1986
 39 Small Press Reviews, Irwin M. Chapman, br *
 42 Tooley's Curse, Margie Penn-Freeman, pm *
 43 Just Compensation, William C. Rasmussen, vi *
 45 The Magic, Frank LoProto, vi *
 46 On a Clear Day, Edward Lodi, vi *

*2AM [v.2 #2, Winter 1987] Gretta M. Anderson, ed. (2AM Publications, $3.95, 46pp, 8.5 x 11 pb)
Contents:
  4 Preface, Gretta M. Anderson, pr *
  5 Alan Jude Summa, Alan Jude Summa, bg *
  6 Film Reviews, Jon Holsinger, mr *
  9 Dark Corner, J.N. Williamson, br *
 13 The Old Woman Upstairs, Elizabeth Engstrom, ss *
 17 When You Wish Upon a Corpse, Joan Vander Putten, ss *
 20 Der Golem, G.N. Gabbard, pm *
 21 Real Time, The Readers, lt *
 23 Waking, David Sutton, ss *
 27 Roomie, David Daniel, ss *
 29 Dreams of Imagination, Alan Jude Summa, pm *
 30 No Matter What They Say, Sometimes It Is Too Late, Gregory N. Krolczyk, vi *
 31 Small Press Reviews, Irwin M. Chapman, br *
 34 The Fungoid Intruder, Leonard Carpenter, pm *
 35 Blood Junkie, Sue Marra, pm *
 37 Showdown, Jack Creek, ss *
 39 The Passing of the Elves, Keith Allen Daniels, pm *
 41 Expert Witness, Michael C. McPherson, vi *

2AM

43 Reflections on Yarbro's **False Dawn**, James A. Lee, br *
45 Final Exam, Doug Beason, vi *
46 For E.D., Jessica Amanda Salmonson, pm *

*3 By Finney Jack Finney (Simon & Schuster Fireside 0-671-64048-8, Jul,87, $10.95, 416pp, tp) Omnibus edition of **The Woodrow Wilson Dime** (1968), **Marion's Wall** (1973), and **The Night People** (1977).
Contents:
> **The Woodrow Wilson Dime**, n. Simon & Schuster: New York,1968
> **Marion's Wall**, n. Simon & Schuster: New York,1973
> **The Night People**, n. Doubleday: Garden City, NY,1977

*6 Decades: The Best of Analog Stanley Schmidt, ed. (Davis no ISBN, 1986, free to subscribers, 128pp, pb) Anthology of 6 science fiction stories sent free to new subscribers of *Analog*.
Contents:
6 Introduction, Stanley Schmidt, in
7 Twilight, Don A. Stuart, ss *Astounding* Nov,1934
20 Far Centaurus, A.E. van Vogt, ss *Astounding* Jan,1944
35 The Dead Past, Isaac Asimov, nv *Astounding* Apr,1956
68 Sleep No More, James H. Schmitz, ss *Analog* Aug,1965
81 Of Mist, and Grass, and Sand, Vonda N. McIntyre, nv *Analog* Oct,1973
96 Emergence, David R. Palmer, nv *Analog* Jan 5,1981

*Aboriginal SF [v.1 #3, Feb.-March 1987] Charles C. Ryan, ed. (Aboriginal SF, $2.50, 32pp, 11.25 x 17 tb)
Contents:
3 Narrow Escape from a Sauna, A Crazy Alien, ms *
3 Sifting for Golden Nuggets, Charles C. Ryan, ed *
4 Boomerangs, The Readers, lt *
5 Aborigines: Devolution and Disappearances, Laurel Lucas, bg *
6 Sing, Kristine Kathryn Rusch, ss *
8 The Reel Stuff: The Good, the Bad and the Maybes, Jessie Horsting, mr *
9 Blood Brothers, Patricia Anthony, ss *
12 Books: New Works from Old Masters, Darrell Schweitzer, br *
13 Cartoon, Sandy Dean, ct *
16 Containment, Dean Whitlock, ss *
17 One Spring in Wyoming, Charles L. Grant, ss *
19 A Lunar Cycle, Peg Libertus, pm *
23 Cartoon, Sandy Dean, ct *
24 Trackdown, John F. Moore, ss *
25 Circus Story, Connie Willis, ss *

*Aboriginal SF [v.1 #4, May-June 1987] Charles C. Ryan, ed. (Aboriginal SF, $2.50, 64pp, 8 x 10.5 pb)
Contents:
3 A Statistical Proposition, A Crazy Alien, ms *
5 Our New Format, Charles C. Ryan, ed *
6 SF: From Secret Movement to Big Business, Brian W. Aldiss, ar *
7 Cartoon, Tom Mason, ct *
8 Search and Destroy, Frederik Pohl, ss *
14 Books: A Historical Perspective, Darrell Schweitzer, br *
16 Tiger's Hunt, John S. Tumlin, ss *
24 Shade and the Elephant Man, Emily Devenport, ss *
32 The Reel Stuff: A Witchin' Summer, Jessie Horsting, mr *
37 Aborigines: A NATO Alliance?, Laurel Lucas, bg *
40 IMAGO, Mary Kittredge, ss *
45 Boomerangs, The Readers, lt *
48 Cowboys and Engines, W.T. Quick, ss *
56 Passing, Elaine Radford, ss *
62 Cartoon, Tom Mason, ct *

*Aboriginal SF [v.1 #5, July-Aug. 1987] Charles C. Ryan, ed. (Aboriginal SF, $2.50, 64pp, 8 x 10.5 pb)
Contents:
4 Merchant Dying, Paul A. Gilster, ss *
8 Borboleta, James A. Stevens, ss *
12 The Drones are Willing..., A Crazy Alien, ms *
13 Books: The Whole Spectrum of Fantastic Literature, Darrell Schweitzer, br *
16 Doing Time, John E. Stith, ss *
24 The Darkfishers, John Gregory Betancourt, ss *
30 Aborigines: Plan 9 From Roslindale, Laurel Lucas, bg *
32 The Reel Stuff: Dog Days, Jessie Horsting, mr *
38 Boomerangs, The Readers, lt *
40 Symphony in Ursa Major, James Brunet, ss *

ALFRED HITCHCOCK'S BOOK OF HORROR STORIES: BOOK 6

56 It Came from the Slushpile, Bruce Bethke, ss *

*Aboriginal SF [v.1 #6, Sept.-Oct. 1987] Charles C. Ryan, ed. (Aboriginal SF, $2.50, 64pp, 8 x 10.5 pb)
Contents:
6 The Clean Up Your Own Mess, A Crazy Alien, ms *
7 Achieving Orbit, Charles C. Ryan, ed *
8 The Milk of Knowledge, Ian Watson, ss *
16 Aeries, Robert Reed, ss *
23 Chernobyl and Challenger: That Was the Year That Was, Frederik Pohl, ar *
24 Frenchmen and Plumbers, Martha Soukup, ss *
26 Books: Books Versus Careers, Darrell Schweitzer, br *
30 Aborigines: NASA Experiments With SF, Laurel Lucas, bg *
32 A Unfiltered Man, Robert A. Metzger, ss *
37 Boomerangs, The Readers, lt *
40 Skin Deep, Emily Devenport, ss *
47 Flashing the Black Long Streets, Wendy Rathbone, pm *
56 Doctor Doom Conducting, Howard V. Hendrix, vi *

*Aboriginal SF [v.2 #1, Nov.-Dec. 1987] Charles C. Ryan, ed. (Aboriginal SF, $2.50, 64pp, 8 x 10.5 pb)
Contents:
4 A Matter of Trust, A Crazy Alien, ms *
5 On Becoming a Writer, Charles C. Ryan, ed *
6 Aborigines: Nature Versus Nurture, Laurel Lucas, bg *
8 Evert Sparrow That Falls, Rebecca Lee, ss *
16 True Magic, Robert A. Metzger, ss *
22 Books: Objectivity, Darrell Schweitzer, br *
24 What Brothers Are For, Patricia Anthony, ss *
31 A Hero of the Spican Conflict, Bruce Boston, pm *
32 Fluxed in Nova Byzantium, Ralph E. Vaughan, ss *
36 Minutes of the Last Meeting at Olduvai, Steven R. Boyett, vi *
48 Scout's Honor, Joanne Mitchell, ss *
62 Boomerangs, The Readers, lt *

*Agent of Byzantium Harry Turtledove (Congdon & Weed/ Contemporary 0-86553-183-8, Apr,87, $15.95, 246pp, hc) Historical alternate-world (14th century) quasi-novel. The stories originally appeared in *Amazing* and *Isaac Asimov's SF Magazine*. They feature Basil Argyros, agent of the Empire. All are good by themselves, but they need bridging material to make them work as a novel. Although 15 years are said to elapse in the book, one gets little feeling of this; they could have taken place within months of each other. Still, the book is enjoyable and worth reading. (TM)
Contents:
v The Ifs of History, Isaac Asimov, in
ix Preface, pr
1 The Eyes of Argos, nv *Amazing* Jan,1986
39 Strange Eruptions, nv *IASFM* Aug,1986
75 Unholy Trinity [as by Eric G. Iverson], nv *Amazing* Jul,1985
113 Archetypes, nv *Amazing* Nov,1985
145 Images, nv *IASFM* Mar,1987
189 Superwine, na *IASFM* Apr,1987

*Alchemical Texts Bruce Boston (Ocean View no ISBN, 1985, $3.00, 18pp, ph) Poetry collection chapbook. In **The Bruce Boston Omnibus**.
Contents:
5 The Alchemist Among Us, pm
6 The Alchemist Is Born in a Sudden Changing of Seasons, pm
7 The Alchemist in Transit, pm
9 The Alchemist Discovers a Universal Solvent, pm *IASFM* Dec,1984
10 The Alchemist in Place, pm
12 The Alchemist Takes a Lover in the Infinite Variety of Fire, pm
14 A Thousand Faces, pm
16 Tongues, pm

Alfred Hitchcock's Book of Horror Stories: Book 6 Alfred Hitchcock, ed. (Coronet 0-340-41115-5, Jul,87, £2.25, 190pp, pb) Reprint (Davis 1981, as 1st half of **Tales to Make Your Hair Stand on End**) horror anthology. Actually edited by Eleanor Sullivan.
Contents:
9 Hush, Dear Conscience, C.B. Gilford, ss *Alfred Hitchcock's Mystery Magazine* May,1974
33 Death by Misadventure, Elijah Ellis, ss *Alfred Hitchcock's Mystery Magazine* Jan,1964
48 The Death Desk, S.S. Rafferty, ss *Alfred Hitchcock's Mystery Magazine* Mar,1975

AMAZING SCIENCE FICTION STORIES

```
 68 Kleinisms, Arthur L. Klein, ms *
 71 A Letter from Bubba: Extraterrestrials, Hollis Fletcher, ss *
 74 On Exhibit, John Lakey, il *
 78 Catscape, Roberta Grant, nv *
101 The Hand of the Survivor, J.M. Zeller, ss *
108 Weird LAWKI, Stephen L. Gillett, Ph.D., ar *
119 Billy Jean at Sea, Sharon N. Farber, ss *
129 When the Vikings Owned the Mythology, William Jon Watkins,
     pm *
130 Multiple Origami, J.B. Allen, ss *
135 Daemon, John Devin, pm *
136 Primatives, Robin Wayne Bailey & Robert Chilson, nv *
159 Inflections, The Readers, lt *
161 Spacer Trivia, Margaret B. Simon, pm *
```

Amazing Science Fiction Stories [v.62 #3, September 1987] Patrick Lucien Price, ed. (TSR, $1.75, 162pp, pb)
Contents:
```
  6 Reflections, Robert Silverberg, ar *
 10 Fearing's Fall, Leonard Carpenter, ss *
 30 Kid Charlemagne, Paul Di Filippo, ss *
 47 The Visitation, Susan Palwick, ss *
 53 Epitaph by an Alien in Yellow Moonlight, Jack R. Hill, pm *
 57 It Wasn't a Half-Bad Year, Charles L. Grant, br *
 64 Last Dragon, Steve Rasnic Tem, ss *
 82 Moon of Popping Trees, R. Garcia y Robertson, nv *
111 The Waters from Time, Steven G. Oliver, vi *
113 IBM, My Shipmate; or, the Difference Between Orbit and Obit,
     Richard Wilson, pm *
114 On Exhibit, Bob Eggleton, il *
118 The Sword That Wept, Sandra Miesel, ss *
131 A Starship Commander, McPheeter, Mike Curry, pm *
132 Dubious Pleasures, Bryan G. Stephenson, ss *
139 Obsidian Sphinx, Morris Liebson, pm *
140 Hitchhiker, Sheila Finch, ss *
158 Exiled of Worlds, Andrew Joron & Robert Frazier, pm *
159 Inflections, The Readers, lt *
161 She Just Wanted to Get out of the House, Darrell Schweitzer, pm *
```

Amazing Science Fiction Stories [v.62 #4, November 1987] Patrick Lucien Price, ed. (TSR, $1.75, 162pp, pb)
Contents:
```
  6 Reflections, Robert Silverberg, ar *
 12 And Who Is Joah?, T.S. Huff, ss *
 28 Another Crow's Eyes, Elaine Radford, ss *
 37 Erasure, Robert Frazier, pm *
 38 Are You Receiving Me?, David M. Charles, ss *
 48 Elegy to a Dead Satellite: Luna, Elton Andrews, pm *
 49 Adolescence and Adulthood in Science Fiction, Orson Scott Card,
     ar *
 59 Smile!, Frank Ward, ss *
 64 Promised Star, Ira Herman, ss *
 71 Darwin's Oracle, Ace G. Pilkington, pm *
 72 Too Much Loosestrife, Frederik Pohl, ss *
 90 On Exhibit, Peter Botsis, il *
 95 Improbable Bestiary: The Bandersnatch (Frumius carrollii), F.
     Gwynplaine MacIntyre, pm *
 96 Fake-out, Andrew Weiner, ss *
111 Elegy for Cygnus X-1, Shelton Arnel Johnson, pm *
112 Clarion and Speculative Fiction, Kristine Kathryn Rusch, ar *
121 Sound and the Electric Ear Drum, S.A. Kelly, pm *
122 Rags from Riches, Christopher Anvil, ss *
128 Will Little Note, Nor Long Remember, Jack Clemons, nv *
159 Thermo, Robert Hays, pm *
160 Inflections, The Readers, lt *
```

Amazing Science Fiction Stories: The War Years 1936-1945 Martin H. Greenberg, ed. (TSR 0-88038-440-9, May,87, $3.95, 331pp, pb) Anthology of 10 sf stories, with an introduction by Isaac Asimov. Available in the UK for £2.50.
Contents:
```
  7 Introduction, Isaac Asimov, in
 11 Robot AL-76 Goes Astray, Isaac Asimov, ss Amazing Feb,1942
 29 Devolution, Edmond Hamilton, ss Amazing Dec,1936
 49 The Four-Sided Triangle, William F. Temple, nv Amazing Nov,1939
 79 The Voyage That Lasted 600 Years, Don Wilcox, nv Amazing
     Oct,1940
119 Adam Link's Vengeance, Eando Binder, nv Amazing Feb,1940
```

```
157 The Living Mist [also as "We, the Mist"], Ralph Milne Farley, nv
     Amazing Aug,1940
197 Phoney Meteor [as by John Beynon, also as "Meteor"], John
     Wyndham, nv Amazing Mar,1941
229 The Council of Drones, W.K. Sonnemann, nv Amazing Oct,1936
279 Shifting Seas, Stanley G. Weinbaum, nv Amazing Apr,1937
311 I, Rocket, Ray Bradbury, ss Amazing May,1944
333 The Authors, bg
```

Amazing Science Fiction Stories: The Wild Years 1946-1955 Martin H. Greenberg, ed. (TSR 0-88038-441-7, Aug,87, $3.95, 318pp, pb) Anthology of 12 stories from *Amazing*.
Contents:
```
  5 Introduction, Robert Bloch, in
 11 You Could Be Wrong, Robert Bloch, ss Amazing Mar,1955
 29 Breakfast at Twilight, Philip K. Dick, ss Amazing Jul,1954
 51 Operation RSVP, H. Beam Piper, ss Amazing Jan,1951
 63 Satisfaction Guaranteed, Isaac Asimov, ss Amazing Apr,1951
 83 Restricted Area, Robert Sheckley, ss Amazing Jul,1953
105 Peacebringer [Sword of Peace], Ward Moore, nv Amazing
     Mar,1950
139 The Little Creeps, Walter M. Miller, Jr., nv Amazing Dec,1951
191 The Draw, Jerome Bixby, ss Amazing Mar,1954
215 A Way of Thinking, Theodore Sturgeon, nv Amazing Nov,1953
251 Skirmish [Bathe Your Bearings in Blood], Clifford D. Simak, ss
     Amazing Dec,1950
275 They Fly So High, Ross Rocklynne, ss Amazing Jun,1952
297 Chrysalis, Ray Bradbury, ss Amazing Jul,1946
319 The Authors, bg
```

Amazing Science Fiction Stories: The Wonder Years 1926-1935 Martin H. Greenberg, ed. (TSR 0-88038-439-5, Mar,87 [Feb,87], $3.95, 316pp, pb) Anthology of stories from the first decade of *Amazing*, with an introduction by Jack Williamson. UK price £2.50.
Contents:
```
  7 Introduction, Jack Williamson, in
 11 The Metal Man, Jack Williamson, ss Amazing Dec,1928
 27 The Jameson Satellite, Neil R. Jones, nv Amazing Jul,1931
 57 The Man Who Saw the Future, Edmond Hamilton, ss Amazing
     Oct,1930
 77 The Machine Man of Ardathia, Francis Flagg, ss Amazing
     Nov,1927
 97 The Tissue-Culture King, Julian Huxley, ss Yale Review,1926;
     Amazing Aug,1927
127 The Voice from the Ether, Lloyd Arthur Eshbach, nv Amazing
     May,1931
165 The Coming of the Ice, G. Peyton Wertenbaker, ss Amazing
     Jun,1926
185 The Miracle of the Lily, Clare Winger Harris, nv Amazing Apr,1928
209 The Man with the Strange Head, Miles J. Breuer, M.D., ss
     Amazing Jan,1927
223 Omega, Amelia Reynolds Long, ss Amazing Jul,1932
241 The Plutonian Drug, Clark Ashton Smith, ss Amazing Sep,1934
257 The Last Evolution, John W. Campbell, Jr., ss Amazing Aug,1932
281 The Colour out of Space [also as "Monster of Terror"], H.P.
     Lovecraft, nv Amazing Sep,1927
318 The Authors, bg
```

American Fantasy [v.2 #2, Winter 1987] Robert T. Garcia & Nancy Garcia, eds. (Robert & Nancy Garcia, $4.95, 64pp, 8.5 x 11 pb)
Contents:
```
  4 Editorial, Nancy Garcia & Robert T. Garcia, ed *
  6 Oddities & Entities, ms *
  8 Midnights, Charles L. Grant, br *
 11 Shock Supplement, John Stanley, mr *
 13 Roaming Fancy, Mary Frances Zambreno, br *
 18 The Sound and the Fury, Scott Jenkins, ar *
 19 Heroes of Audio: Mike McDonough, Scott Jenkins, bg *
 20 All in Favor, W.T. Lowe, vi *
 22 Andre Norton Interview and Bibliography, Nancy Garcia, Mary
     Frances Zambreno & Andre Norton, iv *
 26 Hellraiser, Cory Glaberson & Stephen Jones, mr *
 30 Alan Moore Interview, Neil Gaiman & Alan Moore, iv *
 36 Ramsey Campbell Interview, Nancy Garcia, Robert T. Garcia &
     Ramsey Campbell, iv *
 42 Clive Barker Interview, Nancy Garcia, Robert T. Garcia & Clive
     Barker, iv *
 49 Who's Who in the British Horror Scene, R.S. Hadji, ar *
 52 The Last One of the Season, Mercedes R. Lackey, ss *
```

ANALOG SCIENCE FICTION/SCIENCE FACT

129 On Gaming, Matthew J. Costello, gr *
130 The Analytical Laboratory, ms *
132 Safe to the Liberties of the People, W.T. Quick, ss *
147 The Alternate View: Recent Results, John G. Cramer, ar *
152 Brain Jag, Robert Chilson, ss *
164 Oracle, W.R. Thompson, ss *
178 The Reference Library, Thomas A. Easton, br *
186 Brass Tacks, The Readers, lt *
192 The Analog Calendar of Upcoming Events, Anthony R. Lewis, ms *

Analog Science Fiction/Science Fact [v.107 # 7, July 1987] Stanley Schmidt, ed. (Davis, $2.00, 192pp, pb)
Contents:
    4 The Reactionary Revolution, Stanley Schmidt, ed *
   14 The Changeling Hunt, Robert R. Chase, nv *
   48 Biolog: Robert R. Chase, Jay Kay Klein, bg *
   49 Moonbase Orientation Manual II: Research and Recreation, Ben Bova, ar *
   70 The President's Doll, Timothy Zahn, ss *
   85 On Gaming, Matthew J. Costello, gr *
   86 Trader's Partner, Charles Sheffield, nv *
  116 Left to Right, and Beyond, Harrison Roth & Isaac Asimov, vi *
  119 All the People, All the Time, W.T. Quick, ss *
  128 The Alternate View: Overreaction, G. Harry Stine, ar *
  130 The Report on Bilbeis IV [Part 3 of 3], Harry Turtledove, sl *
  179 The Reference Library, Thomas A. Easton, br *
  187 Brass Tacks, The Readers, lt *
  192 The Analog Calendar of Upcoming Events, Anthony R. Lewis, ms *

Analog Science Fiction/Science Fact [v.107 # 8, August 1987] Stanley Schmidt, ed. (Davis, $2.00, 192pp, pb)
Contents:
    4 The Memetic Menace, Stanley Schmidt, ed *
   12 The Love Song of Laura Morrison, Jerry Oltion, ss *
   29 Memetics and the Modular Mind--Modeling the Development of Social Movements, H. Keith Henson, ar *
   44 Candle in a Cosmic Wind, Joseph Manzione, nv *
   78 Guilt Trip, Charles Sheffield, ss *
   89 Letter from Tomorrow, Poul Anderson, ss *
   96 Lightning Rod, W.R. Thompson, nv *
  122 On Gaming, Matthew J. Costello, gr *
  123 Turing Test, D.C. Poyer, ss *
  128 So Shall Ye Reap, George Alec Effinger, ss *
  142 The Alternate View: Laser Propulsion and the Four P's, John G. Cramer, ar *
  146 Cobwebs, Ray Brown, nv *
  181 The Reference Library, Thomas A. Easton, br *
  188 Brass Tacks, The Readers, lt *
  192 The Analog Calendar of Upcoming Events, Anthony R. Lewis, ms *

Analog Science Fiction/Science Fact [v.107 # 9, September 1987] Stanley Schmidt, ed. (Davis, $2.00, 192pp, pb)
Contents:
    4 For Mars, Vote NO, Ben Bova, ed *
   16 6+, Harry Turtledove, na *
   68 Cellular Automata, Margaret L. Silbar, ar *
   81 On Gaming, Matthew J. Costello, gr *
   82 Banshee, Timothy Zahn, na *
  123 Epiphany, Arlan Andrews, ss *
  129 Biolog: Arlan Andrews, Jay Kay Klein, bg *
  130 The Lizard, the Dragon, and the Eater of Souls, Rick Shelley, nv *
  150 The Alternate View: Cultural Differences, G. Harry Stine, ar *
  154 Flashbattles, W.T. Quick, ss *
  159 The Reference Library, Thomas A. Easton, br *
  166 In the Creation Science Laboratory, Jerry Oltion, ss *
  173 High Power, Robert Chilson & William F. Wu, ss *
  187 Brass Tacks, The Readers, lt *
  192 The Analog Calendar of Upcoming Events, Anthony R. Lewis, ms *

Analog Science Fiction/Science Fact [v.107 #10, October 1987] Stanley Schmidt, ed. (Davis, $2.00, 192pp, pb)
Contents:
    4 Final Frontiers, Stanley Schmidt, ed *
   10 In the Country of the Blind (Part 1 of 2), Michael F. Flynn, sl *
   70 Occidental Injury, Arlan Andrews, vi *

ANALOG SCIENCE FICTION/SCIENCE FACT

   72 Huntington's Handle, Mark E. Peeples, Ph.D., ar *
   85 On Gaming, Matthew J. Costello, gr *
   86 No Damn Atoms, Robert Chilson & William F. Wu, nv *
  108 What's a Nice Girl Like You..., Jerry Oltion, vi *
  110 The I of the Beholder, Joe Fischetti, ss *
  125 The Alternate View: Warm Superconductors, John G. Cramer, ar *
  130 Worldwreckers, Laurence M. Janifer, ss *
  144 Catalyst, Rick Cook, ss *
  150 The Million Dollar Day, Kevin O'Donnell, Jr., nv *
  179 The Reference Library, Thomas A. Easton, br *
  187 Brass Tacks, The Readers, lt *
  192 The Analog Calendar of Upcoming Events, Anthony R. Lewis, ms *

Analog Science Fiction/Science Fact [v.107 #11, November 1987] Stanley Schmidt, ed. (Davis, $2.00, 192pp, pb)
Contents:
    4 Great Oaks from Little Atoms, Stanley Schmidt, ed *
   14 Nanny, Michael P. Kube-McDowell, nv *
   53 A Memoir of Nuclear Winter, Tony Rothman, ar *
   74 Just Another Day at the Weather Service, Elizabeth N. Moon, vi *
   76 The Third Alternative, Marc Stiegler, nv *
  109 On Gaming, Matthew J. Costello, gr *
  110 Proallognostication, Andrew Giesler, vi *
  112 Neither Rain Nor Weirdness, Jerry Oltion, ss *
  127 The Alternate View: The Selling of Proton, G. Harry Stine, ar *
  131 The Reference Library, Thomas A. Easton, br *
  136 In the Country of the Blind (Part 2 of 2), Michael F. Flynn, sl *
  186 Brass Tacks, The Readers, lt *
  192 The Analog Calendar of Upcoming Events, Anthony R. Lewis, ms *

Analog Science Fiction/Science Fact [v.107 #12, December 1987] Stanley Schmidt, ed. (Davis, $2.00, 192pp, pb)
Contents:
    6 Political Standard Time, Stanley Schmidt, ed *
   12 Falling Free [Part 1 of 4], Lois McMaster Bujold, sl *
   68 The Lost Years of Cosmology, Dr. John Gribbin, ar *
   82 The Gift, Pat Forde, nv *
  103 On Gaming, Matthew J. Costello, gr *
  104 Interesting Times, Christopher Anvil, ss *
  117 The Alternate View: SN1987A--Supernova Astrophysics Grows Up, John G. Cramer, ar *
  122 A Hog on Ice, Robert Chilson & William F. Wu, ss *
  137 The Analog Calendar of Upcoming Events, Anthony R. Lewis, ms *
  138 Retrograde Analysis, William Ballard, ss *
  152 Pulsebeat, J.B. Cather, nv *
  177 The Reference Library, Thomas A. Easton, br *
  185 Brass Tacks, The Readers, lt *

Analog Science Fiction/Science Fact [v.107 #13, Mid-December 1987] Stanley Schmidt, ed. (Davis, $2.00, 192pp, pb)
Contents:
    4 Matters of Opinion, Stanley Schmidt, ed *
   14 Last Favor, Harry Turtledove, nv *
   46 On Weaponry, Arthur C. Clarke, ar *
   48 Nanotechnology, Chris Peterson & Eric Drexler, ar *
   61 On Gaming, Matthew J. Costello, gr *
   62 Falling Free [Part 2 of 4], Lois McMaster Bujold, sl *
  102 The Report on the All-Union Committee on Recent Rumors Concerning the Moldavian SSR, D.C. Poyer, ss *
  117 Rubber Dinosaurs and Wooden Elephants, L. Sprague de Camp, ar *
  126 The Alternate View: Hardening Humans, G. Harry Stine, ar *
  130 Chrysalis, Gregory Kusnick, ss *
  148 Captives of the Slavestone, Ian Stewart, nv *
  179 The Reference Library, Thomas A. Easton, br *
  187 Brass Tacks, The Readers, lt *
  192 The Analog Calendar of Upcoming Events, Anthony R. Lewis, ms *

*And the Gods Laughed Fredric Brown (Phantasia Press 0-932096-47-6, Oct,87 [Sep,87], $19.00, 431pp, hc) Collection of fantasy and sf stories, with an introduction by Richard A. Lupoff. Over 70 stories -- 6 written in collaboration with Mack Reynolds. It contains the complete text of two earlier collections, **Nightmares and Geezenstacks** (1961) and **Honeymoon in Hell** (1958), plus additional stories. There is a signed, limited, boxed 475-copy edition ($50) with bound signed sheets left over from an earlier book.
Contents:

Andersen's Fairy Tales Hans Christian Andersen (NAL/Signet Classic 0-451-52107-2, Jun,87 [May,87], $3.95, 381pp, pb) Reissue (NAL/Signet 1966) selection from **The Snow Queen and Other Tales**; selected, translated, and with an afterword by Pat Shaw Iverson. Illustrations by Sheila Greenwald.
Contents:

*Angels in Hell Janet Morris, ed. (Baen 0-671-65360-1, Oct,87 [Sep,87], $3.50, 307pp, pb) Shared-world fantasy original anthology, in the "Heroes in Hell" series. 8 stories.
Contents:

APEX!

Apex! [#1] Ramona Pope Richards, ed. (Dragon's Tale Enterprises, $3.50, 44pp, 8.5x11 pb)
Contents:
  3 The Editorial Privilege, Ramona Pope Richards, ed *
  5 Covenant, Jaime MacPherson, ss *
  8 A Christian in Wonderland, Orson Scott Card, ar *
 10 A Question of Belief, D.E. Smirl, ss *
 16 Viewpoint: A Few Small Press Magazines, Colleen Drippe', br *
 18 Little People, Colleen Drippe', ss *
 27 In the Image of Our Fathers, Ramona Pope Richards, ar *
 30 The Griffon, Edward T. Babinski, pm *
 31 Ethics and the Work Place, Joey Froehlich, pm *
 31 Supreme Being, Bob Warner, pm *
 32 Cordoba to Die, Diane de Avalle-Arce, ss *
 38 The Return, Katharine E. Matchette, ss *

Aphelion [# 5, Summer 86/87] Peter McNamara, ed. (Aphelion Publications, A$5.95, 76pp, 8.5 x 11 pb)
Contents:
  1 Editorial, Peter McNamara, ed *
  3 Neighbourhood Watch, Greg Egan, ss *
  9 Scare Tactics, F.J. Willett, vi *
  9 The Adventure of the Unearthly Spy, Rick Kennett, vi *
  9 Errand Run, Stephen Paulsen, vi *
 10 Not in Front of the Children, George Turner, ss *
 18 2087, Stephen Stanley, ct *
 19 Crime of Passion, Bill Dodds, ss *
 24 2087, Stephen Stanley, ct *
 25 Short Are My Days of Light and Shade, D.T. White, ss *
 26 Logic Loop, Stephen Paulsen, vi *
 26 Splitting Hares, F.J. Willett, vi *
 27 Waltz of the Flowers, Paul Collins & Trevor Donohue, ss *
 31 2087, Stephen Stanley, ct *
 32 The Jerra-Mee, Ingrid Whitehorn, ss *
 34 2087, Stephen Stanley, ct *
 35 Tesseractuality, Michael Tolley, br *
 38 The Science Fiction World, Mervyn R. Binns, ar *
 42 Alexia and Graham Bell, Rosaleen Love, ss *
 44 Collector, Bill Congreve, ss *
 50 The Resurrection, Gail Neville, ss *
 57 2087, Stephen Stanley, ct *
 58 For as Long as You Burn, Terry Dowling, nv *

The Architecture of Fear Kathryn Cramer & Peter D. Pautz, eds. (Arbor House 0-87795-921-8, Oct,87 [Sep,87], $18.95, 304pp, hc) Original anthology with 14 horror stories by Gene Wolfe, Ramsey Campbell, Charles L. Grant, and others.
Contents:
 xi Introduction, Peter D. Pautz, in
  1 In the House of Gingerbread, Gene Wolfe, ss *
 20 Where the Heart Is, Ramsey Campbell, ss *
 30 Ellen, in Her Time, Charles L. Grant, ss *
 41 Nesting Instinct, Scott Baker, nv *
 84 Endless Night, Karl Edward Wagner, ss *
 94 Trust Me, Joseph Lyons, ss *
 97 The Fetch, Robert Aickman, nv Intrusions,1980
144 Visitors, Jack M. Dann, ss IASFM Oct,1987
158 Gentlemen, John M. Skipp & Craig Spector, nv *
188 Down in the Darkness, Dean R. Koontz, nv The Horror Show Sum,1986
214 Haunted, Joyce Carol Oates, nv *
237 In the Memory Room, Michael Bishop, ss *
249 Tales from the Original Gothic, John M. Ford, ss *
269 The House that Knew No Hate, Jessica Amanda Salmonson, nv *
299 Afterword: Houses of the Mind, Kathryn Cramer, aw
303 A Guide to Significant Works of Architectural Horror, bi

Ascian in Rose Charles de Lint (Axolotl 0-939879-10-7, Apr,87 [Mar,87], $30.00, 84pp, hc) Fantasy novella set in the same world as the novel Moonheart. Limited to 300 signed copies (also fifty leatherbound, $65.00).
Contents:
    Ascian in Rose, na *

The Awakeners Sheri S. Tepper (SFBC #11277, Sep,87, $6.98, hc) Omnibus edition of sf duology Northshore (Tor 1987) and Southshore (Tor 1987). They really form one novel, so this could be considered the first complete edition.

BATTLEFIELDS BEYOND TOMORROW: SCIENCE FICTION WAR...

Contents:
    Northshore, n. Tor: New York,1987
    Southshore, n. Tor: New York,1987

Back Brain Recluse [# 7] Chris Reed, ed. (Back Brain Recluse, 40p, 38pp, 6x8 pb)
Contents:
  4 The Package Tourist, Steve Sneyd, ss *
 10 Michael Moorcock, Chris Reed & Michael Moorcock, iv *
 14 John Dee's Song, Michael Moorcock, pm *
 20 Pierrot on the Moon, Michael Moorcock, pm *
 24 Second Gibraltar, Chris Reed, ss *
 32 The Great Counterfeit Memory Sin-Drome, Andrew Darlington, ss *

Battle Station Ben Bova (Tor 0-812-53202-3, Oct,87 [Sep,87], $3.50, 304pp, pb) Collection of fiction and non-fiction.
Contents:
 xi Foreword, fw
  1 Battle Station, na *
 60 Space Weapons, ar Amazing Jul,1985
 76 Nuclear Autumn, ss Far Frontiers v2, ed. Jerry Pournelle & Jim Baen,1985
 82 Freedom From Fear, ed Analog Nov,1984
 89 Beisbol, ss Analog Nov,1985
101 The Jefferson Orbit, ar Far Frontiers v1, ed. Jerry Pournelle & Jim Baen,1985
114 Isolation Area, nv F&SF Oct,1984
146 Space Station, ar,1985
164 Primary, ss IASFM Feb,1985
175 MHD, ar *
192 Born Again, ss Analog May,1984
211 Laser Propulsion, ar,1984
216 The Sightseers, vi Future City, ed. Roger Elwood, Trident,1973
221 Telefuture, ar Omni Feb,1985
236 Foeman [Foeman, Where Do You Flee?], na Galaxy Jan,1969
296 Symbolism in Science Fiction, ar The Writer Jun,1984

Battlefields Beyond Tomorrow: Science Fiction War Stories Charles G. Waugh & Martin H. Greenberg, eds. (Crown/Bonanza 0-517-64105-4, Dec,87, $8.98, 650pp, hc) Anthology of 25 sf stories with an introduction by Robert Silverberg. An "instant remainder" book.
Contents:
 ix Introduction, Robert Silverberg, in
  1 Superiority, Arthur C. Clarke, ss F&SF Aug,1951
 10 Single Combat, Joseph Green, ss New Worlds Aug,1964
 26 Committee of the Whole, Frank Herbert, nv Galaxy Apr,1965
 41 Ender's Game, Orson Scott Card, na Analog Aug,1977
 75 Hero, Joe W. Haldeman, na Analog Jun,1972
125 The Survivor, Walter F. Moudy, nv Amazing May,1965
149 The Last Objective, Paul A. Carter, nv Astounding Aug,1946
173 WHAT DO YOU WANT ME TO DO TO PROVE IM HUMAN STOP [Inhuman Error], Fred Saberhagen, ss Analog Oct,1974
190 Hangman, David Drake, na Hammer's Slammers, Ace,1979
235 The Night of the Trolls, Keith Laumer, na Worlds of Tomorrow Oct,1963
277 The Nuptial Flight of Warbirds, Algis Budrys, nv Analog May,1978
312 Mirror, Mirror [The Mirror], Alan E. Nourse, nv Fantastic Jun,1960
340 The Miracle-Workers, Jack Vance, na Astounding Jul,1958
398 Memorial, Theodore Sturgeon, ss Astounding Apr,1946
410 Shark, Edward Bryant, nv Orbit #12, ed. Damon Knight,1973
426 ...Not a Prison Make, Joseph P. Martino, nv Analog Sep,1966
448 Hawk Among the Sparrows, Dean McLaughlin, na Analog Jul,1968
491 No War, or Battle's Sound [Or Battle's Sound], Harry Harrison, nv If Oct,1968
509 The Defenders, Philip K. Dick, nv Galaxy Jan,1953
529 In the Name of the Father, Edward P. Hughes, nv F&SF Sep,1980
545 On the Shadow of a Phosphor Screen, William F. Wu, nv IASFM Jul,1979
575 The Specter General, Theodore R. Cogswell, na Astounding Jun,1952
621 Fixed Price War, Charles Sheffield, ss Analog May,1978
633 The Long Watch, Robert A. Heinlein, ss American Legion Magazine Dec,1949
646 The Machine That Won the War, Isaac Asimov, ss F&SF Oct,1961

THE BEST OF PAMELA SARGENT

*The Best of Pamela Sargent Pamela Sargent (Academy Chicago 0-89733-242-3, Oct,87, $15.95, 322pp, hc) Collection of 14 sf stories plus a foreword by Michael Bishop and an introduction by Pamela Sargent. Edited by Martin H. Greenberg.
Contents:
   ix Foreword, Michael Bishop, fw
  xxi Introduction, in
    1 Gather Blue Roses, ss *F&SF* Feb,1972
    8 Clone Sister, nv **Eros in Orbit**, ed. Joseph Elder, Trident,1973
   37 If Ever I Should Leave You [revised from *If* Feb,74], ss **Starshadows**, Ace,1977
   54 Bond and Free, nv *F&SF* Jun,1974
   82 Shadows, nv **Fellowship of the Stars**, ed. Terry Carr, Simon & Schuster,1974
  130 The Novella Race, ss **Orbit #20**, ed. Damon Knight,1978
  148 The Summer's Dust, nv *F&SF* Jul,1981
  197 Out of Place, ss *Twilight Zone* Oct,1981
  314 The Broken Hoop, ss *Twilight Zone* Jun,1982
  233 The Shrine, ss *Twilight Zone* Dec,1982
  248 The Old Darkness, ss *F&SF* Jul,1983
  268 The Mountain Cage, nv Cheap Street: New Castle, VA,1983
  290 Heavenly Flowers, ss *IASFM* Sep,1983
  306 Fears, ss **Light Years and Dark**, ed. Michael Bishop, Berkley,1984

*The Best of the Mage [# 8, Fall 1987] Jeffrey V. Yule, ed. (Colgate University, $2.50, 64pp, 8.5 x 11 pb)
Contents:
    3 Four Years Later..., Jeffrey V. Yule, ed *
    4 The Festival of the River, Mark Rich, ss *Mage* Win,1985
    9 Huayno, Asher Torren, pm *Mage* Win,1987
   10 Bramblebeard, t. Winter-Damon, pm *Mage* Win,1985
   11 The Panama Mechanism, Leo Bigley, ss *Mage* Spr,1986
   17 In This Center Hold Solitude, Mark Rich, pm *Mage* Win,1985
   18 The Wanderer, Eva Jones, vi *Mage* Win,1985
   20 Give the Reader Quality Not Quantity, Jeffrey V. Yule, ed *Mage* Spr,1985
   20 Serious Writing or Escapism?, Jeffrey V. Yule, ed *Mage* Win,1985
   21 Willing Suspension of Disbelief, Jeffrey V. Yule, ed *Mage* Spr,1986
   21 Science Fiction--Judging the Genre, Jeffrey V. Yule, ed *Mage* Spr,1987
   22 A Thing or Two About Razzle-Dazzle, Dennis John Sjolie, ss *Mage* Spr,1987
   28 Tenant Above, Charmaine Parsons, vi *Mage* Spr,1986
   30 The Mage: A Retrospective, Jeffrey V. Yule, pi *
   38 Hackers in the Dewey, R.D. Davis, vi *Mage* Win,1987
   41 The Fictive World View of H.P. Lovecraft, Donald R. Burleson, ar *Mage* Spr,1986
   45 Mindrace, James B. Livingstone, pm *Mage* Spr,1986
   46 The Dwarf Who Knew Too Much, Harry Dolan, ss *Mage* Win,1987
   53 Gray Nights, William P. Cunningham, vi *Mage* Win,1985
   55 Blessed Are Those..., William P. Cunningham, ss *
   59 The Roots of Fantasy, Gregory Forbes, ar *Mage* Spr,1985
   59 Children's Books, Gregory Forbes, br *Mage* Sum,1985
   60 Science Fiction & Fantasy Cover Art, Gregory Forbes, ar *Mage* Win,1985
   61 Dreams in Stasis, Tom Rentz, pm *Mage* Win,1987
   62 Message Intercepted On Hyperspatial Frequency, Wade Tarzia, vi *Mage* Win,1987

*Beyond that River Paul Christopher (Pal Books 3-925942-00-9, Nov,87 [Dec,87], £4.95, 288pp, pb) Original horror collection.
Contents:
    5 Once Upon a Chair, nv *
   37 Sunday Special, ss *
   45 Bobbie, nv *
   73 Little White Mongrel, ss *
   83 For the Love of Mother, ss *
   95 Dora, ss *
  111 A Bottle on the Beach, ss *
  125 The Purple Hour, ss *
  137 Masters of the Void, ss *
  149 Pyramids, ss *
  159 To Be Blind, ss *
  169 Beyond That River, ss *
  185 Waiting for Sunlight, ss *
  195 Hermione Gould, nv *
  233 Mushrooms, nv *
  285 In the Tube, vi *

Beyond the Stars Isaac Asimov, ed. (Severn House 0-7278-1374-9, Feb,87, £8.95, 320pp, hc) Reprint (Doubleday 1985 as first half of **The Hugo Winners: Volume 4**) sf anthology. [First U.K. edition]
Contents:
      Introduction: What Again?, Isaac Asimov, in
    5 Home Is the Hangman, Roger Zelazny, na *Analog* Nov,1975
   70 The Borderland of Sol, Larry Niven, nv *Analog* Jan,1975
  116 Catch That Zeppelin!, Fritz Leiber, ss *F&SF* Mar,1975
  141 By Any Other Name, Spider Robinson, na *Analog* Nov,1976
  200 Houston, Houston, Do You Read?, James Tiptree, Jr., na **Aurora: Beyond Equality**, ed. Vonda McIntyre & Susan Anderson, Fawcett,1976
  259 The Bicentennial Man, Isaac Asimov, nv **Stellar #2**, ed. Judy-Lynn del Rey,1976
  302 Tricentennial, Joe W. Haldeman, ss *Analog* Jul,1976

*Bluebeard's Egg Margaret Atwood (Cape 0-224-02245-8, Jun,87, £10.95, 281pp, hc) Collection of stories, some with elements of fantasy.
Contents:
   11 Significant Moments in the Life of My Mother, ss *Queen's Quarterly*
   31 Hurricane Haze, nv
   61 Loulou; or The Domestic Life of the Language, nv *Science Fiction Story-Reader*
   83 Uglypuss, nv
  111 The Whirlpool Rapids, ss *Toronto Globe and Mail*; *Red Book Magazine* Nov,1986
  120 Walking on Water, ss From Chateleine
  131 Bluebeard's Egg, nv McLelland & Stewart: Toronto,1983
  165 Spring Song of the Frogs, ss From Company
  179 Scarlet Ibis, nv
  201 The Salt Garden, nv *Ms.* Sep,1984
  229 In Search of the Rattlesnake Plantain, ss *Harper's* Aug,1986
  241 The Sunrise, nv
  263 Unearthing Suite, ss

*The Book of Spells Sara Maitland (Michael Joseph 0-7181-2755-2, Sep,87, £9.95, 174pp, hc) Collection of short stories (mainly original) about magic.
Contents:
    1 Angel Maker, ss
   11 The Eighth Planet, ss
   23 Seal-Self, ss
   33 Heart Throb, ss **Passion Fruit**, Winterson, Pandora,1986
   45 Maybe a Love Poem for my Friend, pm
   47 The Tale of the Valiant Demoiselle, nv
   73 Promises, ss
   83 Miss Manning's Angelic Moment, ss
   91 Lullaby for My Dyke and Her Cat, ss
  101 Triptych, ss
  121 Flower Garden, ss
  135 A Fall from Grace, ss **Weddings and Funerals**, Latourette/Maitland, Brilliance,1984
  147 The Wicked Stepmother's Lament, ss **More Tales I Tell My Mother**, Journeyman,1987
  155 'Let us Now Praise Unknown Women and Our Mothers who Begat Us', ss **Stepping Out**, Oosthuizen,1986
  165 Particles of a Wave. An Afterword, aw

*Border Land [Special World Fantasy Convention Issue, Oct. 1987] R.S. Hadji, ed. (Artimus Publications, free at convention, 12pp, 8.5 x 11 pb)
Contents:
    3 Take Me, For Instance, Hugh B. Cave, ss *Whispers #5*,1974
    6 The Back of the Mirror, Hugh B. Cave, ss *
    9 Hugh Cave: An Appreciation, Don Hutchinson, bg *

*The Bridge of Lost Desire Samuel R. Delany (Arbor House 0-87795-931-5, Nov,87 [Oct,87], $17.95, 310pp, hc) Collection of 2 original stories and one extensively revised piece, in the "Neveryona" fantasy series, plus an appendix by the author's alter ego, K. Leslie Steiner.
Contents:
    1 The Game of Time and Pain, na *
  137 The Tale of Rumor and Desire, na *Callaloo* Spr,1987
  235 The Tale of Gorgik [long version], na *IASFM* Sum,1979
  297 "Return..." A Preface, K. Leslie Steiner, pr

BROTHER AND OTHER STORIES

*Brother and Other Stories Clifford D. Simak (Severn House 0-7278-1417-6, Apr,87 [Mar,87], £8.95, 165pp, hc) A new collection of Simak's short stories, edited by Francis Lyall. This has a 1986 copyright date, but has only just appeared.
Contents:
1 Introduction, Francis Lyall, in
7 Brother, nv *F&SF* Oct,1977
31 Over the River and Through the Woods, ss *Amazing* May,1965
42 Auk House, na **Stellar** #3, ed. Judy-Lynn del Rey,1977
109 Kindergarten, nv *Astounding* Jul,1953

*Buffalo Gals and Other Animal Presences Ursula K. Le Guin (Capra Press 0-88496-270-9, Sep,87 [Aug,87], $15.95, 196pp, hc) Collection of stories and poetry about animals (and plants and minerals) -- sf, fantasy, and associational. The title story is a fine original. (FCM) *PW* described the book and Le Guin as "a mixture of prodigious talent and stubborn polemic, which has alternately exhilarated and exasperated sf readers since the '60s" -- a perfect summing-up (CNB).
Contents:
9 Introduction, in
14 Come Into Animal Presence, Denise Levertov, pm,1961
17 Buffalo Gals, Won't You Come Out Tonight, nv *
55 Three Rock Poems, si
56 The Basalt, pm *Open Places* Spr,1982
56 Flints, pm,1986
57 Mount St. Helens/Omphalos, pm **Wild Angels**, Capra Press,1975
61 Mazes, ss **Epoch**, ed. Roger Elwood & Robert Silverberg, Berkley,1975
67 The Wife's Story, ss **The Compass Rose**, Harper & Row,1982
75 Five Vegetable Poems, si
76 Torrey Pines Reserve, pm **Hard Words & Other Poems**, Harper & Row,1981
77 Lewis and Clark and After, pm *The Seattle Review* Sum,1987
77 West Texas, pm,1980
78 Xmas Over, pm *Clinton Street Quarterly*,1984
78 The Crown of Laurel, pm,1987
84 The Direction of the Road, ss **Orbit** #12, ed. Damon Knight,1973
92 Vaster Than Empires and More Slow, nv **New Dimensions** #1, ed. Robert Silverberg/Marta Randall,1971
131 Seven Bird and Beast Poems, si
132 What is Going on in The Oaks Around the Barn, pm,1986
133 For Ted, pm **Wild Angels**, Capra Press,1975
132 Found Poem, pm,1986
132 Totem, pm **Hard Words & Other Poems**, Harper & Row,1981
135 Winter Downs, pm **Hard Words & Other Poems**, Harper & Row,1981
135 The Man Eater, pm,1986
136 Sleeping Out, pm,1985
140 The White Donkey, ss *TriQuarterly* #49,1980
143 Horse Camp, ss *New Yorker* Aug 25,1986
151 Four Cat Poems, si
152 Tabby Lorenzo, pm,1984
152 Black Leonard in Negative Space, pm,1978
153 A Conversation with a Silence, pm,1986
154 For Leonard, Darko, and Burton Watson, pm,1982
158 Schrodinger's Cat, ss **Universe** #5, ed. Terry Carr,1974
167 "The Author of the Acacia Seeds" and Other Extracts from the Journal of the Association of Therolinguistics, ss **Fellowship of the Stars**, ed. Terry Carr, Simon & Schuster,1974
179 May's Lion, ss *The Little Magazine* v14#1,1983
191 Eighth Elegy [from "The Duino Elegies"], Rainer Maria Rilke, pm Translated by Ursula K. Le Guin.
194 She Unnames Them, vi *New Yorker* Jan 21,1985

*Cardography Orson Scott Card (Hypatia Press 0-940-84102-9, Mar,87, $17.95, 183pp, hc) Collection of 5 fantasy stories plus an introduction by David Hartwell plus a new afterword (and maps) by Card. Limited to 750 + 194 + 56 copies in various limited, signed states.
Contents:
Introduction, David G. Hartwell, in
The Bully and the Beast, na **Other Worlds** #1, ed. Roy Torgesson,1979
The Porcelain Salamander, ss **Unaccompanied Sonata**,1981
Sandmagic, nv **Swords Against Darkness** #4, ed. Andrew J. Offutt,1979
Middle Woman, ss
The Princess and the Bear, nv **The Berkley Showcase** v1, ed. Victoria Schochet & John W. Silbersack,1980
Living in a World of Maps, aw

CHARLES KEEPING'S CLASSIC TALES OF THE MACABRE

*Casting the Runes and Other Ghost Stories M.R. James (World's Classics 0-19-281719-1, Apr,87 [Jun,87], £3.95, 352pp, pb) Collection of ghost stories, edited by Michael Cox.
Contents:
xi Introduction, Michael Cox, in
1 Canon Alberic's Scrap-Book, ss *National Review* Mar,1895
14 The Mezzotint, ss **Ghost Stories of an Antiquary**,1904
26 Number 13, ss **Ghost Stories of an Antiquary**,1904
43 Count Magnus, ss **Ghost Stories of an Antiquary**,1904
57 "Oh, Whistle, and I'll Come to You, My Lad", nv **Ghost Stories of an Antiquary**,1904
78 The Treasure of Abbot Thomas, ss **Ghost Stories of an Antiquary**,1904
97 A School Story, ss **More Ghost Stories of an Antiquary**, Arnold,1911
105 The Rose Garden, ss **More Ghost Stories of an Antiquary**, Arnold,1911
117 The Tractate Middoth, ss **More Ghost Stories of an Antiquary**, Arnold,1911
135 Casting the Runes, nv **More Ghost Stories of an Antiquary**, Arnold,1911
157 The Stalls of Barchester Cathedral, ss *Contemporary Review* v97#35,1910
172 Mr. Humphreys and His Inheritance, nv **More Ghost Stories of an Antiquary**, Arnold,1911
199 The Diary of Mr. Poynter, nv **A Thin Ghost**, Longmans, Green,1919
210 An Episode of Cathedral History, ss **A Thin Ghost**, Longmans, Green,1919
228 The Uncommon Prayer Book, ss **A Warning to the Curious**,1925
242 A Neighbour's Landmark, ss *The Eton Chronic* Mar 17,1924
257 A Warning to the Curious, ss *The London Mercury* Aug,1925
275 Rats, ss
281 The Experiment, ss
288 The Malice of Inanimate Objects, ss *The Masquerade* Jun,1933
293 A Vignette, ss *The London Mercury* v35,1936
299 Explanatory Notes, Michael Cox, ms
337 M.R. James on Ghost Stories, ar

*Chance & Other Gestures of the Hand of Fate Nancy Springer (Baen 0-671-65337-7, Sep,87 [Aug,87], $3.50, 240pp, pb) Collection of 8 stories and three poems; the second half of the title work is a new continuation. Grim, effective fantasy and horror (FCM).
Contents:
1 Chance, na **Under the Wheel: Alien Stars Vol. III**, ed. Elizabeth Mitchell, Baen,1987
67 The Golden Face of Fate, na *
125 The Wolf Girl Speaks, pm *Star*Line* v5#6,1982
127 The Boy Who Plaited Manes, ss *F&SF* Oct,1986
145 The Bard, ss *
155 Bright-Eyed Black Pony, ss **Moonsinger's Friends**, ed. Susan Shwartz, Bluejay,1985
175 Come In, pm *Night Voyages Poetry Review*,1982
177 The Prince Out of the Past, ss **Magic in Ithkar** #1, ed. Andre Norton & Robert Adams,1985
189 Amends, A Tale of the Sun Kings, ss *F&SF* May,1983
205 The Dog-King of Vaire, ss *Fantasy Book* Aug,1982
217 We Build a Shrine, pm *
219 Primal Cry, nv *

*Charles Keeping's Classic Tales of the Macabre Charles Keeping, ed. (Blackie 0-216-92147-3, Sep,87 [Nov,87], £8.95, 172pp, hc) Horror/occult anthology. Illustrated throughout by Charles Keeping.
Contents:
7 Introduction, Charles Keeping, in
9 The Judge's House, Bram Stoker, ss *Holly Leaves* Dec 5,1891
27 The Fall of the House of Usher, Edgar Allan Poe, ss *Burton's Gentlemen's Magazine* Sep,1839
46 The Story of the Late Mr. Elvesham, H.G. Wells, ss *The Idler* May,1896
63 Lot No. 249, Arthur Conan Doyle, nv *Harper's* Sep,1892
95 The Withered Arm, Thomas Hardy, nv *Blackwood's* Jan,1888
124 "Oh, Whistle, and I'll Come to You, My Lad", M.R. James, nv **Ghost Stories of an Antiquary**,1904
143 The Statement of Randolph Carter, H.P. Lovecraft, ss *The Vagrant* May,1920
150 Between the Minute and the Hour, A.M. Burrage, ss **Some Ghost Stories**,1927
164 Notes, ms

COMMON BODY, ROYAL BONES

*The Compleat Crow Brian Lumley (Ganley 0-932445-21-7, Jul,87 [Jun;87], $7.50, 191pp, tp) Collection, a gathering of the "Titus Crow" psychic detective horror stories, illustrated by Stephen E. Fabian. Hardcover and deluxe signed editions have been announced, but we have not seen them.
Contents:

*The Complete Adventures of Charlie and Mr. Willy Wonka Roald Dahl (Unwin Hyman 0-04-440074-8, Oct,87 [Nov,87], £9.95, 316pp, hc) Omnibus of the two Charlie books. This is the first omnibus edition that includes the Michael Foreman illustration
Contents:

*The Complete Alice and The Hunting of the Snark Lewis Carroll (Salem House 0-88162-228-1, Apr,87 [Mar,87], $24.95, 344pp, hc) Omnibus art book. Although the text is not new, the interest here is in the profuse illustrations by Ralph Steadman. The 8.5" x 11" size helps too. The three illustrated volumes have appeared separately: **Alice in Wonderland** (1967), **Through the Looking Glass** (1972), and **The Hunting of the Snark** (1978).
Contents:

+ **The Complete Short Stories of L.P. Hartley** L.P. Hartley (Beaufort 0-8253-0353-2, 1986 [Oct,87], $24.95, 760pp, hc) Omnibus edition of a novella plus four earlier collections: "Simonetta Perkins" (1925); **The Travelling Grave** (1948); **The White Wand** (1954); **Two for the River** (1961); and **Mrs. Carteret Receives** (1971). Many of the 51 stories are fantasy. (**The Travelling Grave** was originally published by Arkham House). This edition has a 1986 date, but was not seen until 1987. First U.S. edition (Hamilton 1973).
Contents:

THE COMPLETE SUPERNATURAL STORIES OF RUDYARD...

*The Complete Supernatural Stories of Rudyard Kipling Rudyard Kipling (W.H. Allen 0-491-03285-4, Jan,87, £12.95, 427pp, hc) Collection of supernatural stories, edited by Peter Haining.
Contents:

THE DARK DESCENT

*Dark Feasts Ramsey Campbell (Robinson 0-948164-47-6, Sep,87 [Aug,87], £9.95, 339pp, hc) Horror collection.
Contents:

THE DEVIL'S ADVOCATE: AN AMBROSE BIERCE READER

The Dark Void Isaac Asimov, ed. (Severn House 0-7278-1424-9, Jun,87 [Jul,87], £9.95, 239pp, hc) Reprint (Doubleday 1985 as second half of **The Hugo Winners: Volume 4**) sf anthology. [First U.K. edition]
Contents:

*A Demon Close Behind Leslie Halliwell (Robert Hale 0-7090-2932-2, Apr,87 [Jul,87], £10.95, 240pp, hc) Original ghost collection.
Contents:

*Demons! Jack M. Dann & Gardner R. Dozois, eds. (Ace 0-441-14264-8, Jul,87 [Jun,87], $3.50, 283pp, pb) Anthology of 14 fantasy stories about demons.
Contents:

*The Devil's Advocate: An Ambrose Bierce Reader Ambrose Bierce (Chronicle 0-87701-401-9, Dec,87 [Nov,87], $22.50, 327pp, hc) A selection of stories, newspaper columns, letters, poetry, and excerpts from books. Edited by Brian St. Pierre. A Trade paperback edition (0-87701-476-0, $12.95) was announced but not seen. Stories indexed are from the section "Stories of the Supernatural."
Contents:

DEVILS AND DEMONS

THE DREAM AUDITOR

*Dreams and Swords** Katherine V. Forrest (Naiad 0-941483-03-7, Sep,87, $8.95, 175pp, tp) Collection of 10 lesbian-oriented stories, mostly sf and horror. 9 of the stories are apparently originals.
Contents:

*Earthclan** David Brin (SFBC #11624, Dec,87, $9.98, 985pp, hc) Omnibus edition of **Startide Rising** and **The Uplift War**.
Contents:

*Echoes of Valor** Karl Edward Wagner, ed. (Tor 0-812-55750-6, Feb,87 [Jan,87], $2.95, 286pp, pb) Anthology of 3 novelettes by Robert E. Howard, Fritz Leiber, and Henry Kuttner. The Howard Conan story, "The Black Stranger", appears here complete for the first time. The Leiber, "Adept's Gambit", a Grey Mouser/Fafhrd tale, appears here in its original 1947 form, which is different from its later book versions.
Contents:

*Einstein's Monsters** Martin Amis (Cape 0-224-02435-3, Apr,87 [May,87], £5.95, 127pp, hc) Collection of stories, including some sf. Simultaneous with American edition.
Contents:

Eldritch Tales No. 13 [v.4 #1] Crispin Burnham, ed. (Yith Press, $6.00, 123pp, 5.2 x 7.5 pb)
Contents:

Eldritch Tales No. 14 [v.4 #2] Crispin Burnham, ed. (Yith Press, $6.00, 112pp, 5.2 x 7.5 pb)
Contents:

*The End of the Game** Sheri S. Tepper (SFBC #105205, Jan,87, $7.98, 529pp, hc) Omnibus edition of the "Jinian" fantasy trilogy and the third trilogy in the "True Game" deklogy sans uno.
Contents:

*The Enemy Stars** Poul Anderson (Baen 0-671-65339-3, Jul,87 [Jun,87], $2.95, 218pp, pb) Contains the novel **The Enemy Stars** (Lippincott 1959) plus a novelette coda, "The Ways of Love" (1979).
Contents:

The Essential Colin Wilson Colin Wilson (Grafton 0-586-06865-1, Feb,87, £4.95, 336pp, tp) Reprint (Harrap 1985) collection of non-fiction and fiction including some occult and sf.
Contents:

THE ESSENTIAL COLIN WILSON

*The **Essential Ellison** Harlan Ellison (Nemo Press 0-914261-01-0,
Aug,87 [Jul,87], $29.95, 1019pp, hc) Collection of many, many stories
and essays, edited by Terry Dowling, Richard Delap, and Gil Lamont.
This is ment as a 35-year retrospective (it's taken 3 years to publish) of
Ellison's work, from his early 1949 juvenilia to his work in the '80s. It's
not a "best of", but a "warts and all" collection, divided into 15 sections
with introductions to each one by one of the various editors. The texts
of every item have been "corrected", but not rewritten. It isn't a book
you sit down and *read* as much as you browse it. It isn't even
reviewable except as a book-length study of Ellison's life. It's a well
made book despite its size, and should stand up to years of use -- even
throwing across a room. A bargain at twice the price. Recommended.
(CNB) A limited edition ($60) was announced, but has apparently not
appeared yet.
Contents:

FAHRENHEIT 451/THE ILLUSTRATED MAN/DANDELION...

***Evil Water** Ian Watson (Gollancz 0-575-03953-1, Mar,87 [Aug,87],
£10.95, 200pp, hc) Sf collection.
Contents:

***The Exploits of Ebenezvm** Craig Shaw Gardner (SFBC #11588,
Nov,87, $6.98, 437pp, hc) Humorous fantasy omnibus of **A Malady of
Magics**, **A Multitude of Monsters**, and **A Night in the Netherhells**.
Contents:

***The Faded Sun Trilogy** C.J. Cherryh (Methuen 0-413-14310-4, Apr,87,
£3.95, 756pp, pb) Omnibus of three sf novels.
Contents:

+**Fahrenheit 451/The Illustrated Man/Dandelion Wine/The Golden
Apples of the Sun/The Martian Chronicles** Ray Bradbury (Octopus/
Heinemann 1-85256-023-1, 1987 [Nov,87], $11.98, 798pp, hc)
Omnibus edition of 5 novels. First U.S. edition.
Contents:

FAHRENHEIT 451/THE ILLUSTRATED MAN/DANDELION...

147 The Other Foot, ss *New Story* Mar,1951
159 The Highway [as by Leonard Spalding], ss *Copy* Spr,1950
162 The Man, ss *Thrilling Wonder Stories* Feb,1949
172 The Long Rain [Death-by-Rain], ss *Planet Stories* Sum,1950
185 The Rocket Man, ss *Maclean's* Mar 1,1951
194 The Fire Balloons [In This Sign], ss *Imagination* Apr,1951
210 The Last Night of the World, ss *Esquire* Feb,1951
214 The Exiles [The Mad Wizards of Mars], ss *Maclean's* Sep 15,1949; *F&SF* WiS,1950
226 No Particular Night or Morning, ss **The Illustrated Man**,1951
234 The Fox and the Forest [To the Future], ss *Colliers* May 13,1950
247 The Visitor, ss *Startling Stories* Nov,1948
259 The Concrete Mixer, ss *Thrilling Wonder Stories* Apr,1949
276 Marionettes, Inc., ss *Startling Stories* Mar,1949
282 The City [Purpose], ss *Startling Stories* Jul,1950
289 Zero Hour, ss *Planet Stories* Fll,1947
298 The Rocket [Outcast of the Stars], ss *Super Science Stories* Mar,1950
307 Epilogue, aw **The Illustrated Man**,1951
309 **Dandelion Wine**, co Doubleday: Garden City, NY,1957
313 Illumination, ss *Reporter* May 16,1957
319 Dandelion Wine, ss *Gourmet* Jun,1953
321 Summer in the Air [also as "The Sound of Summer Running"], ss *The Saturday Evening Post* Feb 18,1956
330 The Season of Sitting, ar *Charm* Aug,1951
334 The Night, ss *Weird Tales* Jul,1946
342 The Lawns of Summer, ss *Nation's Business* Feb,1952
345 The Happiness Machine [also as "The Time Machine"], ss *The Saturday Evening Post* Sep 14,1957
356 Season of Disbelief, ss *Colliers* Nov 25,1950
365 The Last, the Very Last [also as "The Time Machine"], ss *Reporter* Jun 2,1955
372 The Green Machine, ss *Argosy (UK)* Mar,1951
378 The Trolley, ss *Good Housekeeping* Jul,1955
381 Statues, ss **Dandelion Wine**, Ray Bradbury, Doubleday,1957
401 The Window, ss *Colliers* Aug 5,1950
408 The Swan, ss *Cosmopolitan* Sep,1954
421 The Whole Town's Sleeping, ss *McCalls* Sep,1950
437 Good-By, Grandma, ss *The Saturday Evening Post* May 25,1957
443 Dinner at Dawn, ss *Everywoman's Magazine* Feb,1954
460 Green Wine for Dreaming, ss **Dandelion Wine**, Ray Bradbury, Doubleday,1957
483 **The Golden Apples of the Sun**, co Doubleday: Garden City, NY,1953
485 The Fog Horn [The Beast from 20,000 Fathoms], ss *The Saturday Evening Post* Jun 23,1951
491 The Pedestrian, ss *Reporter* Aug 7,1951; *F&SF* Feb,1952
495 The April Witch, ss *The Saturday Evening Post* Apr 5,1952
504 The Wilderness, ss *F&SF* Nov,1952
512 The Fruit at the Bottom of the Bowl [Touch and Go], ss *Detective Book* Nov,1948; *Ellery Queen's Mystery Magazine* Jan,1953
521 Invisible Boy, ss *Mademoiselle* Nov,1945
529 The Flying Machine, ss **The Golden Apples of the Sun**, Doubleday,1953
533 The Murderer, ss *Argosy (UK)* Jun,1953
540 The Golden Kite, the Silver Wind, ss *Epoch* Win,1953
544 I See You Never, vi *New Yorker* Nov 8,1947
547 Embroidery, ss *Marvel* Nov,1951
550 The Big Black and White Game, ss *The American Mercury* Aug,1945
560 A Sound of Thunder, ss *Colliers* Jun 28,1952
571 The Great Wide World Over There [Cora and the Great Wide World Over There], ss *Maclean's* Aug 15,1952
581 Powerhouse, ss *Charm* Mar,1948
589 En La Noche [Torrid Sacrifice], ss *Cavalier* Nov,1952
593 Sun and Shadow, ss *Reporter* Mar 17,1953
600 The Meadow, ss **Best One Act Plays**,1948
613 The Garbage Collector, ss *The Nation* Oct,1953
617 The Great Fire, ss *Seventeen* Mar,1949
623 Hail and Farewell, ss *Today* Mar 29,1953
629 The Golden Apples of the Sun, ss *Planet Stories* Nov,1953
635 **The Martian Chronicles**, co Doubleday: Garden City, NY,1950
637 Rocket Summer, vi **The Martian Chronicles**,1950
638 Ylla [I'll Not Look for Wine], vi *Maclean's* Jan 1,1950
649 The Summer Night [The Spring Night], vi *Arkham Sampler* Win,1948
651 The Earth Men, ss *Thrilling Wonder Stories* Aug,1948
663 The Taxpayer, vi **The Martian Chronicles**,1950
665 The Third Expedition, ss *Planet Stories* Fll,1948

679 And the Moon Be Still as Bright, ss *Thrilling Wonder Stories* Jun,1948
701 The Settlers, vi **The Martian Chronicles**,1950
702 The Green Morning, ss **The Martian Chronicles**,1950
706 The Locusts, vi **The Martian Chronicles**,1950
707 Night Meeting, ss **The Martian Chronicles**,1950
714 The Shore, vi **The Martian Chronicles**,1950
715 Interim, vi **The Martian Chronicles**,1950
715 The Musicians, vi **The Martian Chronicles**,1950
717 Way in the Middle of the Air, ss *Other Worlds* Jul,1950
728 The Naming of Names, vi **The Martian Chronicles**,1950
729 Usher II [Carnival of Madness], ss *Thrilling Wonder Stories* Apr,1950
742 The Old Ones, vi **The Martian Chronicles**,1950
743 The Martian [Impossible], ss *Super Science Stories* Nov,1949
754 The Luggage Store, vi **The Martian Chronicles**,1950
755 The Off Season, ss *Thrilling Wonder Stories* Dec,1948
765 The Watchers, vi **The Martian Chronicles**,1950
766 The Silent Towns, ss *Charm* Mar,1949
775 The Long Years [also as "Dwellers in Silence"], ss *Maclean's* Sep 15,1948
785 There Will Come Soft Rains, ss *Colliers* May 6,1950
790 The Million-Year Picnic, ss *Planet Stories* Sum,1946

***Fantastic Stories: Tales of the Weird and Wondrous** Martin H. Greenberg & Patrick L. Price, eds. (TSR 0-88038-521-9, May,87, $7.95, 253pp, tp) Anthology of 16 stories from the magazine, with an introduction by James E. Gunn plus a selection of color cover reproductions.
Contents:
 7 Introduction, James E. Gunn, in
 11 Double Whammy, Robert Bloch, ss *Fantastic* Feb,1970
 21 A Drink of Darkness, Robert F. Young, ss *Fantastic* Jul,1962
 33 A Question of Re-Entry, J.G. Ballard, nv *Fantastic* Mar,1963
 59 The Exit to San Breta, George R.R. Martin, ss *Fantastic* Feb,1972
 70 The Shrine of Temptation, Judith Merril, ss *Fantastic* Apr,1962
 85 Dr. Birdmouse, Reginald Bretnor, ss *Fantastic* Apr,1962
 97 Eve Times Four, Poul Anderson, nv *Fantastic* Apr,1960
 126 The Rule of Names, Ursula K. Le Guin, ss *Fantastic* Apr,1964
ins. Artists' Visions of the Weird & Wondrous, Various Hands, il
 135 The Still Waters, Lester del Rey, ss *Fantastic* Apr,1955
 144 A Small Miracle of Fishhooks and Straight Pins, David R. Bunch, ss *Fantastic* Jun,1961
 148 Novelty Act, Philip K. Dick, nv *Fantastic* Feb,1964
 174 What If..., Isaac Asimov, ss *Fantastic* Sum,1952
 186 Elixir for the Emperor, John Brunner, ss *Fantastic* Nov,1964
 202 King Solomon's Ring, Roger Zelazny, ss *Fantastic* Oct,1963
 220 Junior Partner, Ron Goulart, ss *Fantastic* Sep,1962
 229 Donor, James E. Gunn, nv *Fantastic* Nov,1960

*Fantasy Book [v.5 #5, March 1987] Dennis Mallonee & Nick Smith, eds. (Fantasy Book Enterprises, $3.95, 64pp, 8.5 x 11 pb)
Contents:
 2 Should Old Acquaintance... [Part 2], Mercedes R. Lackey, sl *
 10 Typo, Michael D. Winkle, ss *
 15 Danar's Hawk, Josepha Sherman, ss *
 21 Regenesis, Jane Yolen, pm *
 22 A Sword in Hand, Leigh Ann Hussey, nv *
 30 if only icarus had climbed the night, t. Winter-Damon, pm *
 31 An Arrow of Tempered Silver, Rayson Lorrey, ss *
 34 Black Seas, Robert E. Howard, pm *
 35 Working Stiff, Paul Curtis, ss *
 38 The Hand of Guilt, Don Sakers, ss *
 42 An Index to *Fantasy Book*, Volume 5, ix *
 43 Editorial, Dennis Mallonee, ed *
 43 I Praise My Nativity, Robert E. Howard, pm *
 44 Introduction to The Haunted Ships, Darrell Schweitzer, ar *
 44 The Haunted Ships, Allan Cunningham, nv **Traditional Tales of the English and Scottish Peasantry**, London: Taylor & Hessey,1822
 49 Fantasy Book Reviews, John Gregory Betancourt, br *
 50 Should Old Acquaintance... [Part 3], Mercedes R. Lackey, sl *
 59 Ancient Ages, Arlan Andrews, pm *
 60 The Nasty Naughty Nazi Ninja Nudnik Elves, Joshua Quagmire, cs *

*Fantasy Tales [v.8 #16, Winter 1986] Stephen Jones, ed. (Stephen Jones, 90p + 18p p&p/$3.00 + $1.00 p&p, 53pp, 6"x8" pb)

FANTASY TALES

Contents:
3 The Olympic Runner, Dennis Etchison, nv *
14 Manly Wade Wellman, Karl Edward Wagner, bg *
16 The White Road, Manly Wade Wellman, pm *
17 Red, Richard Christian Matheson, vi *Night Cry* v1#6,1986
19 The Singing Stone, Peter Tremayne, ss *
27 After the Funeral, Hugh B. Cave, ss *
33 Twins, David Case, ss *
37 Zerail, Josepha Sherman, ss *
42 Eradication's Rise, Christina Kiplinger, pm *
44 Our Christmas Spirit, George A. McIntyre, ss *
48 Bon Appetit, Samantha Lee, vi *
51 The Cauldron, The Readers, lt *

***Fat Face** Michael Shea (Axolotl 0-939879-13-1, May,87, $30.00, 36pp, hc) A Chthulhu Mythos horror novelette, with an introduction by Karl Edward Wagner. Limited edition of 300, signed by Shea and Wagner. There are also 50 leatherbound copies, for $65.00.
Contents:
Introduction to Fat Face, Karl Edward Wagner, in
1 Fat Face, nv *

***Fever Dream** Ray Bradbury (St. Martin's 0-312-57285-9, Nov,87 [Oct,87], $6.95, 32pp, hc) Juvenile fantasy story. A 1948 Bradbury fantasy tale with new illustrations by Darrel Anderson (each with a "glow in the dark" detail).
Contents:
Fever Dream, ss *Weird Tales* Sep,1948

***Fever Season: Merovingen Nights #2** C.J. Cherryh, ed. (DAW 0-88677-224-9, Oct,87 [Sep,87], $3.50, 297pp, pb) Shared world original anthology, second in the series. C.J. Cherryh writes all the connections between the stories, weaving them into a quasi-novel.
Contents:
11 Fever Season, C.J. Cherryh, ss *
29 Hearts and Minds, Chris Morris, nv *
59 Fever Season (reprised), C.J. Cherryh, ms *
71 A Plague on Your Houses, Mercedes R. Lackey, nv *
105 Fever Season (reprised), C.J. Cherryh, ms *
109 War of the Unseen Worlds, Leslie Fish, nv *
139 Fever Season (reprised), C.J. Cherryh, ms *
149 Night Ride, Nancy Asire, nv *
179 Fever Season (reprised), C.J. Cherryh, ms *
193 Life Assurance, Lynn Abbey, nv *
231 Fever Season (final reprise), C.J. Cherryh, ms *
241 Instant Karma, Janet Morris, nv *
271 Fever Season (Lyrics), Mercedes R. Lackey, sg *
271 Fever Season (Music), C.J. Cherryh, sg *
273 Mist-Thoughts (Lyrics), Mercedes R. Lackey, sg *
273 Mist-Thoughts (Music), C.J. Cherryh, sg *
275 Partners (Lyrics), Mercedes R. Lackey, sg *
275 Partners (Music), C.J. Cherryh, sg *
277 Index to City Maps, ix
280 Merovingian City Maps, Pat Tobin, il
285 Merovan Ecology, ms *
298 Merovan Sea Floor and Hemispheric Maps, Pat Tobin, il

***The Fifth Omni Book of Science Fiction** Ellen Datlow, ed. (Zebra 0-8217-2050-3, Apr,87 [Mar,87], $3.95, 381pp, pb) Anthology of sf from *Omni* plus one original story by Pat Cadigan.
Contents:
1 Introduction, Ellen Datlow, in
13 Multiples, Robert Silverberg, ss *Omni* Oct,1983
41 Man-Mountain Gentian, Howard Waldrop, ss *Omni* Sep,1983
67 Returning Home, Ian Watson, ss *Omni* Dec,1982
85 Triceratops, Kono Tensei, ss *Omni* Aug,1982
Translated by David Lewis.
103 New Rose Hotel, William Gibson, ss *Omni* Jul,1984
121 Adagio, Barry B. Longyear, nv *Omni* Sep,1984
161 Track of a Legend, Cynthia Felice, ss *Omni* Dec,1982
179 Prime Time, Norman Spinrad, ss *Omni* Nov,1980
201 Edges, Gregg Keizer, ss *Omni* Jun,1983
227 The Songbirds of Pain, Garry Kilworth, ss **The Songbirds of Pain**, Gollancz,1984; *Omni* Aug,1985
245 The Changed Man and the King of Words, Orson Scott Card, nv *Omni* Dec,1982
293 400 Boys, Marc Laidlaw, ss *Omni* Nov,1982
315 Seventh Sense, Robert Haisty, ss *Omni* Sep,1983
331 Lunatic Bridge, Pat Cadigan, nv *

***Firefight 2000** Dean Ing (Baen 0-671-65648-1, Jun,87 [May,87], $2.95, 247pp, pb) Collection of stories and speculative articles.
Contents:
1 Preface, pr
5 Fleas, ss **Destinies** v1#3, ed. James Baen,1979
11 Firefight 2000, ar *
23 Manaspill, na **The Magic May Return**, ed. Larry Niven,1981
69 Malf, nv **Analog Annual**, ed. Ben Bova, Pyramid,1976
99 Comes the Revolution [from **The Future of Flight**], ar,1985
109 Liquid Assets, ss **Destinies** v1#4, ed. James Baen,1979
129 Lost in Translation, ss **Far Frontiers** v1, ed. Jerry Pournelle & Jim Baen,1985
155 Evileye, ss **Far Frontiers** v2, ed. Jerry Pournelle & Jim Baen,1985
167 Vehicles for Future Wars [also as "Military Vehicles: Into the Third Millennium"], ar **Destinies** v1#4, ed. James Baen,1979
199 Vital Signs, na **Destinies** v2#3, ed. James Baen,1980

***Footsteps** [#8, November 1987] Bill Munster, ed. (Bill Munster, $4.95, 84pp, 7 x 10 pb) F. Paul Wilson Special Erotic Horror Edition
Contents:
2 From the Editor, Bill Munster, ed *
6 An Interview with F. Paul Wilson, Bill Munster & F. Paul Wilson, iv *
15 The Complete Bibliography of F. Paul Wilson, bi *
19 A Novel Preview: **Black Wind**, F. Paul Wilson, ex *
27 Dance of the Spirit Untouched, Elizabeth Massie, ss *
35 Shifting Passions, David B. Silva, vi *
37 Under a Hungry Moon, Jeannette M. Hopper, ss *
43 An Interview with Gahan Wilson, Bill Munster & Gahan Wilson, in *
50 Book Reviews, Stan Brooks, br *
59 Clawing at the Moon, Janice Dillard, pm *
60 Watchwolf, J.N. Williamson, ss *
64 Dog Meat, D.W. Taylor, ss *
70 Community Service, Judith R. Behunin, vi *
74 Succubi, Michael R. Collings, pm *
76 L Is for Love, Steve Rasnic Tem, vi *
79 Nostalgia, John Maclay, pm *
80 An Interview with Robert McCammon, Rodney A. Labbe & Robert R. McCammon, iv *

***Force Fields** Andrew Joron (Starmont House 0-930261-86-0, Apr,87, $8.95, 55pp, tp) Collection of sf poetry, illustrated by Richard Herman.
Contents:
1 Breaking into the Crystal Text, pm
2 His Master's Voice, pm
3 Shipwrecked on Destiny Five, pm *IASFM* May,1985
6 Agency, pm
8 A Beautiful Disease, pm *Pig Iron* #10,1982
10 The Webbed Axis, pm
14 Event Horizon, pm
15 Mirror of Prometheus, pm
17 Vehicular Man, pm
18 Tetrahedron Letters, pm *The Portland Review*,1979
21 The Hunter: A.D. 20,000, pm *Amazing* Nov,1982
23 Post-Historic Pastorale, pm
26 Asleep in the Arms of Mother Night, pm
28 Thought Experiment, pm
29 Two Walkers Across the Time Flats, pm
30 Hegemony, pm
32 Kaleidoscope of Dust, pm
34 Panspermia, pm
36 The Old Ones, pm
37 All Equations are Lesion's Equal, pm
39 Beacon, pm
40 The Navigator, pm
43 Bulletin from the Galactic Center, pm
44 Stormtower, pm
46 Palaces on Pluto?, pm *Amazing* Nov,1986
47 Vox Sanguinis, pm
49 Telecommunion, pm
50 The Sonic Flowerfall of Primes, pm *New Worlds* #216,1982
55 An Illuminated Manuscript, pm

***Free Lancers** Elizabeth Mitchell, ed. (Baen 0-671-65352-0, Sep,87 [Aug,87], $2.95, 248pp, pb) Original anthology with works by Orson Scott Card, David Drake, and Lois McMaster Bujold; all involve mercenaries of sorts (the Card very loosely). An excellent gathering -- highly recommended (FCM & TM).
Contents:
1 West, Orson Scott Card, na *

256 The Eastern Window, E.G. Swain, ss **The Stoneground Ghost Tales**, W. Heffer: Cambridge,1912
264 Select Bibliography, bi

*Glass and Amber C.J. Cherryh (NESFA 0-915368-34-X, Feb,87, 212pp, hc) Collection of minor stories and articles, some original. Issued to commemorate Cherryh's appearance as Boskone 24 Guest of Honor. Limited to 1,000 copies, of which the first 225 are signed and boxed (and sold out at the con -- ISBN -89-7). The regular post-con list price has apparently not been set yet.
Contents:

1 Of Law and Magic, nv **Moonsinger's Friends**, ed. Susan Shwartz, Bluejay,1985
36 Homecoming, ss *Shayol* Dec,1979
41 Romantic/Science Fiction, sp Archon 2 (convention),1978; *Lan's Lantern* Jun,1980
52 The Dark King, ss **The Year's Best Fantasy Stories #3**,1977
65 Perspectives in SF, sp *
71 Sea Change, ss **Elsewhere** v1, ed. Terri Winding & Mark Allan Arnold,1981
92 The Avoidance Factor, ar *
99 A Gift of Prophecy, ss *
123 The Use of Archaeology in Worldbuilding, ar *SFWA Bulletin*,1978
135 Willow, nv **Hecate's Cauldron**, ed. Susan M. Shwartz, DAW,1982
164 In Alien Tongues, ar *Sorcerer's Apprentice* WiS,1981
172 Pots, nv **Afterwar**, ed. Janet Morris, Baen,1985

*Gollancz/Sunday Times SF Competition Stories Anonymous, ed. (Gollancz 0-575-04074-2, Aug,87, £10.95, 200pp, hc) Collection of best stories entered for the recent Gollancz & Sunday Times SF Short Story Competition. Actually edited by Malcolm Edwards.
Contents:

7 Moral Technology, Paul Heapy, ss *
14 Big Cats, John Bark, ss *
21 Prisoners, Anna Lieff Saxby, ss *
28 A Senoi Dream, Malcolm Ashworth, ss *
35 Delicate Immortal Meanings, Rick Slaughter, ss *
42 Adam Found, Simon Ounsley, ss *Interzone #17*,1986
49 Soap, Keith Haviland, ss *
58 Meteors, Stephen Richard, ss *
64 Bundles of Joy, Jenny Ordish, ss *
72 Skiophanes' Proof, Luke Andreski, ss *
82 Time Travel for Fun and Profit, Geoff Nicholson, ss *
91 A Sort of Sun Spot, Bartholomew Blockley, ss *
98 Wartours, Mark Wilkins, ss *
104 Wishbone, Anne Gay, ss *
114 The Fall, Mark Gorton, ss *
125 The African Quota, Elizabeth Sourbut, ss *
133 Modern History, Philip St. Leger, ss *
141 Who's a Clever Boy?, James Gibbins, ss *
148 Entropanto, Gerry McCarthy, ss *
154 Gardens and Fountains, Tony Bowerman, ss *
163 Rika's World, Sue Moorhouse, ss *
169 Indian Summer, Philip Gladwin, ss *
176 My Best Ever Holiday, Richard Spivack, ss *
184 Hanuman, Stephen Earl, ss *
192 The Machine Age, Paul Gooding, ss *

*A Goose on Your Grave Joan Aiken (Gollancz 0-575-03985-X, May,87 [Dec,87], £6.95, 159pp, hc) Collection of stories, many of them fantasy or supernatural.
Contents:

7 Your Mind is a Mirror, ss *
24 Wing Quack Flap, ss **Cold Feet**, Jean Richardson, Hodder & Stoughton,1985
41 Snow Horse, ss
53 Potter's Gray, ss **Up the Chimney Down and Other Stories**,1984
70 The Old Poet, ss *
81 Lob's Girl, ss
95 The Last Specimen, ss
107 The Lame King, ss *
118 Homer's Whistle, ss **They Wait and Other Spine Chillers**, ed. Lance Salway, Pepper Press,1983
133 The Blades, nv **Out of Time**, ed. Aidan Chambers, Bodley Head,1984
151 Aunt Susan, ss *

*The Grabinski Reader [#2, Spring 1987] Miroslaw Lipinski, ed. (Teawood Publications, $2.50, 16pp, 7 x 8.5 pb)

Contents:

2 Introduction, Miroslaw Lipinski, in
4 Saturnin Sektor, Stefan Grabinski, ss,1920
10 Before the Long Journey, Stefan Grabinski, ss,1921
16 Letters, The Readers, lt

Great Science Fiction of the 20th Century Robert Silverberg & Martin H. Greenberg, eds. (Crown/Avenel 0-517-64124-0, 1987 [Nov,87], $8.98, 726pp, hc) Anthology. This is an "instant remainder" of **The Arbor House Treasury of Modern Science Fiction**, omitting one story, "The Marching Morons" by C.M. Kornbluth.
Contents:

vi Introduction, Robert Silverberg & Martin H. Greenberg, in
1 Angel's Egg, Edgar Pangborn, nv *Galaxy* Jun,1951
33 Rescue Party, Arthur C. Clarke, nv *Astounding* May,1946
57 Shape [Keep Your Shape], Robert Sheckley, nv *Galaxy* Nov,1953
71 Alpha Ralpha Boulevard, Cordwainer Smith, nv *F&SF* Jun,1961
97 Winter's King, Ursula K. Le Guin, nv **Orbit #5**, ed. Damon Knight,1969
115 Or All the Seas with Oysters, Avram Davidson, ss *Galaxy* May,1958
125 Common Time, James Blish, ss *Science Fiction Quarterly* Aug,1953
145 When You Care, When You Love, Theodore Sturgeon, nv *F&SF* Sep,1962
181 The Shadow of Space, Philip Jose Farmer, nv *If* Nov,1967
205 "All You Zombies-", Robert A. Heinlein, ss *F&SF* Mar,1959
217 I'm Scared, Jack Finney, ss *Colliers* Sep 15,1951
229 Child's Play, William Tenn, nv *Astounding* Mar,1947
255 Grandpa, James H. Schmitz, ss *Astounding* Feb,1955
275 Private Eye, Henry Kuttner, nv *Astounding* Jan,1949
301 Sundance, Robert Silverberg, ss *F&SF* Jun,1969
315 In the Bowl, John Varley, nv *F&SF* Dec,1975
343 Kaleidoscope, Ray Bradbury, ss *Thrilling Wonder Stories* Oct,1949
353 Unready to Wear, Kurt Vonnegut, Jr., ss *Galaxy* Apr,1953
365 Wall of Crystal, Eye of Night, Algis Budrys, nv *Galaxy* Dec,1961
385 Day Million, Frederik Pohl, ss *Rogue* Feb,1966
391 Hobson's Choice, Alfred Bester, ss *F&SF* Aug,1952
405 The Gift of Gab, Jack Vance, nv *Astounding* Sep,1955
451 The Man Who Never Grew Young, Fritz Leiber, ss **Night's Black Agents**, Arkham,1947
459 Neutron Star, Larry Niven, nv *If* Oct,1966
475 Impostor, Philip K. Dick, ss *Astounding* Jun,1953
489 The Human Operators, Harlan Ellison & A.E. van Vogt, nv *F&SF* Jan,1971
507 Poor Little Warrior!, Brian W. Aldiss, ss *F&SF* Apr,1958
513 When It Changed, Joanna Russ, ss **Again, Dangerous Visions**, ed. Harlan Ellison, Doubleday,1972
521 The Bicentennial Man, Isaac Asimov, nv **Stellar #2**, ed. Judy-Lynn del Rey,1976
557 Hunting Machine, Carol Emshwiller, ss *(The Original) Science Fiction Stories* May,1957
563 Light of Other Days, Bob Shaw, ss *Analog* Aug,1966
571 The Keys to December, Roger Zelazny, ss *New Worlds* Aug,1966
593 Of Mist, and Grass, and Sand, Vonda N. McIntyre, nv *Analog* Oct,1973
613 A Galaxy Called Rome, Barry N. Malzberg, nv *F&SF* Jul,1975
631 Stranger Station, Damon Knight, nv *F&SF* Dec,1956
653 The Time of His Life, Larry Eisenberg, ss *F&SF* Apr,1968
661 The Women Men Don't See, James Tiptree, Jr., nv *F&SF* Dec,1973
687 The Queen of Air and Darkness, Poul Anderson, na *F&SF* Apr,1971

*Grue [#4, 1987] Peggy Nadramia, ed. (Hell's Kitchen Productions, $4.00, 88pp, 5.5 x 8.5 pb)
Contents:

3 conGRUEities, Peggy Nadramia, ed *
7 Snow, Bentley Little, ss *
15 Martyr Without Canon, t. Winter-Damon, pm *
17 Axe, Lisa Lepovetsky, pm *
18 First Plane I See Tonight, John C. Broaddus, ss *
23 Townkiller, J.N. Williamson, ss *
30 Sharing, Mort Castle, vi *
31 Small Talk, James Kisner, ss *
34 prognostication, Keith Allen Daniels, pm *
35 The Buildings Are Falling, Tim Coats, ss *
40 I am myself, Denise Dumars, pm *
41 One April Day, William P. Dillon, ss *
46 Confession, David Starkey, vi *
49 Swamp Rising, W.H. Pugmire, ss *
54 Ouija, Paul Haberman, vi *

GRUE

55 Uncle Sherm (A Fantasy), Charlotte Brown Hammond, ss *
66 Cornstalk Riddles, Joseph Payne Brennan, pm *
69 The On'ner, A.R. Morlan, ss *
79 Pop Stars, Richard Singer, vi *
80 The Touch, Wayne Allen Sallee, ss *

*Grue [#5, 1987] Peggy Nadramia, ed. (Hell's Kitchen Productions, $4.00, 88pp, 5.5 x 8.5 pb)
Contents:
  3 conGRUEities, Peggy Nadramia, ed *
  5 The God of the Razor, Joe R. Lansdale, ss *
15 Joe Lansdale Speaks, Wayne Allen Sallee, pm *
16 Radionda, Dennis Jordan, ss *
29 Yesterday's Child, Thomas F. Monteleone, ss *
36 Craving, Gary William Crawford, pm *
37 Trimmings, David Starkey, ss *
43 second thoughts, Wayne Allen Sallee, pm *
46 Ten Times Black, J. Hunter Daves, ss *
54 Sibyl, Carol Poster, pm *
55 Kaj, Don Webb, vi *
57 Singing Nightmares, Joey Froehlich, pm *
57 aborted dream, Opie R. Houston, pm *
59 A Matter of Semantics, Wayne Allen Sallee, vi *
61 Mother Hag, Steve Rasnic Tem, ss *
67 The Wings of a Bat, Lawrence Harding, pm *
68 Solo, Holmes Miller, ss *
75 Watershead, David B. Silva, vi *
78 Final Dreams, Billy Wolfenbarger, pm *
79 Dr. Locrian's Asylum, Thomas Ligotti, ss *
87 Stiffened in a Banquet Dish, Peggy Sue Alberhasky, pm *

*Grue [#6, 1987] Peggy Nadramia, ed. (Hell's Kitchen Productions, $4.00, 88pp, 5.5 x 8.5 pb)
Contents:
  3 conGRUEities, Peggy Nadramia, ed *
  5 Hooked On Love, Joan Vander Putten, pm *
  6 Sliders, Susan Lilas Wiggs, ss *
13 Beyond the Reef, Jessica Amanda Salmonson, pm *
14 The Last Bedtime Story, A.R. Morlan, ss *
21 Soliloquy, Denise Dumars, pm *
22 Strands, Janet Fox, ss *
31 Stinkers, J.L. Comeau, ss *
43 Punk Funeral, Peggy Dembicer, pm *
46 Proctor Valley, Dale Hoover, ss *
59 The Lady Who Lost Her Head, Cheryl Curry Sayre, ss *
64 The Yard, Colleen Drippe', ss *
73 Autumn Memories, Lisa Lepovetsky, pm *
74 Bayou Exterminator, Addie Lacoe, ss *
80 Moon Rise, Anke M. Kriske, pm *
81 Inheritance, Annette S. Crouch, ss *
88 Eleanor Meets God, Maryanne K. Snyder, pm *

*Guinevere and Lancelot & Others Arthur Machen (Purple Mouth 0-9603300-2-X, Dec,86 [Feb,87], $10.00, 47pp, tp) Collection of essays and stories, edited by Michael T. Shoemaker and Cuyler W. Brooks, Jr., illustrated by Steve Fabian.
Contents:
vii The Unknown Machen, Michael T. Shoemaker, pr
  1 Introduction (from Notes and Queries), in,1926
  7 Guinevere and Lancelot, ss,1926
16 Savages [from "Concealed Savages of Tudor England"], ar The American Mercury Feb,1936
17 Gipsies, ar The Academy and Literature Dec 9,1911
21 Ritual, ss,1937
25 Introduction (from The Dragon of the Alchemists), in,1926
29 The Grande Trouvaille, ar,1923
32 Bridles and Spurs, ar,1951
36 Local Colour, ar Literature Apr 23,1898
40 Art and Luck, ar The Independent Nov 25,1933
43 Preface (from Afterglow), pr,1924

*Hammer's Slammers David Drake (Baen 0-671-65632-5, Apr,87 [Mar,87], $3.50, 318pp, pb) Collection with Hammer's Slammers (Ace 1979) plus the short novel "The Tank Lords".
Contents:
  7 Hammer's Slammers, co Ace: New York pb Apr,1979
  7 Introduction: Mercenaries and Military Virtue, Jerry E. Pournelle, in
13 But Loyal to His Own, nv Galaxy Oct,1975
46 Supertanks, ms Hammer's Slammers, Ace,1979

50 The Butcher's Bill, nv Galaxy Nov,1974
78 The Church of the Lord's Universe, ms Hammer's Slammers, Ace,1979
82 Under the Hammer, nv Galaxy Oct,1974
107 Powerguns, ms Hammer's Slammers, Ace,1979
112 Cultural Conflict, nv Destinies v1#2, ed. James Baen,1979
134 Backdrop to Chaos, ms Hammer's Slammers, Ace,1979
138 Caught in the Crossfire, nv Chrysalis #2, ed. Roy Torgeson,1978
156 The Bonding Authority, ms Hammer's Slammers, Ace,1979
160 Hangman, na Hammer's Slammers, Ace,1979
233 Table of Orginization and Equipment, Hammer's Regiment, ms Hammer's Slammers, Ace,1979
237 Standing Down, nv Hammer's Slammers, Ace,1979
261 The Tank Lords, na Far Frontiers v6, ed. Jerry Pournelle & Jim Baen,1986

*Haunted Waters Mary Williams (Kimber 0-7183-0650-3, Oct,87, £9.50, 190pp, hc) Original ghost collection.
Contents:
  7 Haunted Waters, n. *
123 Coppard's End, ss *
131 The Eyes to See, ss Ghosts in Country Villages, ed. Val Baker, Kimber,1983
147 Dorothea, nv *

*Haunts [# 9/10, Fall 1987] Joseph K. Cherkes, ed. (Nightshade, $3.25, 84pp, 5.5 x 8.5 pb)
Contents:
  3 October 31, Andy Honeycutt, ss *
  7 Every Garbage Dump Has One, Michael C. McPherson, vi *
10 Twenty-One Minutes, Rudy Kremberg, ss *
20 The Country Wife, William J. Grabowski, vi *
24 Popcorn: A Matter of Survival, Katherine Salts, vi *
26 Road, B.J. Seidenstein, ss *
30 Thatcher's Bluff, James Anderson, ss *
35 Cousin Jo, S.B. Dieckman, ss *
39 Character Assassination, H.J. Cording, ss *
49 Witchwood, Mike Hurley, ss *
55 Remembering Medea, Brett Rutherford, pm *
56 Eight Legs Hath the Spider, C. Taylor & R.L. Newman, vi *
58 Down Under, Kevin Speirs, ss *
63 The Missing Dumbell, S.M. Secula, ss *
68 Sweet Dreams, Beverly Brunelle, ss *
76 The Helium Farewell, Joe Clifford Faust, ss *
84 Final Words: A Letter From the Editor, Joseph K. Cherkes, aw *

*Hear the Silence: Stories of Myth, Magic and Renewal Irene Zahava, ed. (Crossing Press 0-89594-212-7, Sep,86 [Jan,87], $22.95, 194pp, hc) Original anthology of feminist sf and fantasy stories of spirituality and self-renewal; 11 of the stories are original, 4 are reprints. Several are pieces of novels in progress. Published in 1986 but not seen until 1987.
Contents:
ix Preface, Irene Zahava, pr
  1 Magic in a World of Magic, Anne Cameron, nv *
34 In the Beginning There Was Humming [from "What Dinah Thought"], Deena Metzger, ex *
39 Baby Town, Becky Birtha, ss *
56 Why the Sea Is Salty, Kitty Tsui, ss Common Lives/Lesbian Lives,1982
73 Blood, Sweat and Fears, Dale Colleen Hamilton, ss *
89 Fruit Drink, Bode Noonan, ss Red Beans and Rice, Crossing Press,1986
97 The Healing, Sandy Boucher, nv *
120 Sticktalk, Vickie L. Sears, ss Gathering Ground, ed. Jo Cochran, J.T. Stewart & Mayumi Tsutakawa, Seal Press,1984
127 The Saints and Sinners Run, Becky Birtha, ss *
137 The Plasting Project, Merlin Stone, ss *
146 Why the Moon Is Small and Dark When the Sun Is Big and Shiny, Judith Stein, ss *
152 Ernesta [from "Mundane's World"], Judy Grahn, ex *
168 The Love Chapter [from "Journal of a Plebian Witch"], Martha Waters, ex *
179 The Tree on the Mountain [from "What Dinah Thought"], Deena Metzger, ex *
192 She Unnames Them, Ursula K. Le Guin, vi New Yorker Jan 21,1985

A HERON CAUGHT IN WEEDS   THE HORROR SHOW

*A Heron Caught in Weeds Keith Roberts (Kerosina 0-948893-09-5, Apr,87, £3.95, 46pp, tp) Poetry collection, edited by Jim Goddard. Limited to 350 copies in this form.
Contents:
    5 Introduction, ms
    9 Grainne, pm
   13 Calais Encounter, pm
   14 Home Thoughts from a Coach, pm
   15 De Profundis, Pro Temporis, pm
   16 A Civic Problem, Observed, pm
   17 Spanbroekmolen, pm
   18 Hill 60, pm
   19 Sanctuary Wood, pm
   20 Tyne Cot, pm
   21 Ypres, 1980, pm
   22 At Hellfire Corner, pm
   23 The Last Resort, pm
   24 A L'enfant Sauvage, pm
   25 Envoi, pm
   29 A Para, pm
   30 A Wykehamist, pm
   31 A Technical Author, pm
   32 A Language Tutor, pm
   33 A Marine Engineer, pm
   37 Sham Hill, pm
   39 Ave Atque Vale, pm
   40 Friday, June 4th: Henley, 1982, pm
   41 A Downland Haunting, pm
   42 The Raising of the Mary Rose, pm
   43 The Iron Child, pm
   44 Ghost at the Rose, pm
   45 Verulam, pm
   46 Behind the Organ Case, pm

*The Horror Show [v.5 #1, January 1987] David B. Silva, ed. (Phantasm Press, $3.95, 72pp, 8.5 x 11 pb)
Contents:
    3 Hellnotes, David B. Silva, ed *
    5 Bargains at Binsley's, Elizabeth Massie, ss *
    9 Fragments of Horror, J.N. Williamson, ms *
   11 Carnivores, Peter Heyrman, ss *
   16 Interview with Joe R. Lansdale, William J. Grabowski & Joe R. Lansdale, iv *
   20 The Lansdale House of Horror, Joe R. Lansdale, mr *
   23 The Fat Man, Joe R. Lansdale, ss *
   27 Cold Christmas, Dick Davies, cs *
   28 Leave Them Raving, David Daniel, vi *
   31 Projections, Bentley Little, ss *
   35 Interview with J.K. Potter, Paul F. Olson & J.K. Potter, iv *
   39 Tattler, William J. Grabowski, br *
   43 Nightmares, Anonymous, ar *
   45 The Elder, Poppy Z. Brite, ss *
   49 The Wi'ching Well, A.R. Morlan, ss *
   53 Tattler, Michael Arthur Betts, mr *
   56 The Return, William F. Nolan, ms *
   60 The Children of the Kingdom Quiz, A.R. Morlan, qz *
   63 Homecoming, Paul F. Olson, ss *
   69 Static, David Daniel, ss *

*The Horror Show [v.5 #2, Spring 1987] David B. Silva, ed. (Phantasm Press, $3.95, 72pp, 8.5 x 11 pb)
Contents:
    3 Hellnotes, David B. Silva, ed *
    5 Swan Song, Robert R. McCammon, ex Pocket: New York Jun,1987
    9 Interview with Robert R. McCammon, William J. Grabowski & Robert R. McCammon, iv *
   12 Swan Song, William J. Grabowski, br *
   13 Fragments of Horror, Robert R. McCammon, ms *
   17 Runt, Bentley Little, ss *
   21 Me Pal Jonesy, Dick Davies, cs *
   23 Classified Ads, Donald R. Burleson, ss *
   26 These Doth The Lord Hate, Manly Wade Wellman, ss *Weird Tales* Jan,1939
   29 Manly Wade Wellman: A Biography, Karl Edward Wagner, bg *
   32 Tattler, William J. Grabowski, br *
   36 Iocus: A Retrospective, Paul F. Olson, ar *
   39 Sharper Than a Serpent's Tooth, William Relling, Jr., ss *
   44 Moon and the Devil, Lawrence C. Connolly, ss *

   53 Tattler, Michael Arthur Betts & Wes Craven, mr *
   50 Nightmare on Elm Street 3, Wes Craven, Heather Langencamp & Robert Englund, iv *
   57 Gnawing, G. Wayne Miller, ss *
   63 Reason Enough, Edward J. Pahule, vi *
   65 Wondergirls, Carol Reid, ss *
   69 Nightmares, Anonymous, ar *
   70 The "There Was an Old Woman" Quiz, A.R. Morlan, qz *

*The Horror Show [v.5 #3, Summer 1987] David B. Silva, ed. (Phantasm Press, $3.95, 64pp, 8.5 x 11 pb)
Contents:
    3 Hellnotes, David B. Silva, ed *
    5 The Interrogation, Dean R. Koontz, ss *
   16 Not Just Traces of Me, G. Wayne Miller, vi *
   18 Tattler, William J. Grabowski, br *
   22 Dean R. Koontz, Leigh Nichols & Dean R. Koontz, iv *
   24 Fragments of Horror, Al Sarrantonio, ms *
   29 The Nightrunners, Joe R. Lansdale, ex Dark Harvest: Niles, IL hc Sep,1987
   32 Down in the Dark, Ardath Mayhar, ss *
   35 My Dead Dog, Bobby, Joe R. Lansdale, vi *
   36 Red Paint, David Barker, ss *
   41 Off the Subject I: On Genre, Magical Realism, and Writing Seriously, Steve Rasnic Tem, ar *
   43 Double Gross-Out at the Uh-Oh Saloon, Dick Davies, cs *
   44 Tattler, Michael Arthur Betts, mr *
   48 Heart of Stone, Peter Heyrman, ss *
   52 Ollie's Hands, Dean R. Koontz, ss **Infinity** #4, ed. Robert Hoskins,1972
   60 Nightmares, Anonymous, ar *
   62 The Second Nit-Picky, Utterly Trivial, Totally Picayune Horror-Fantasy Movie Quiz -- or -- Trivial Lives, II, A.R. Morlan, qz *

*The Horror Show [v.5 #4, Fall 1987] David B. Silva, ed. (Phantasm Press, $3.95, 80pp, 8.5 x 11 pb)
Contents:
    3 Hellnotes, David B. Silva, ed *
    5 Love (Ash I), Poppy Z. Brite, ss *
    8 Poppy Z. Brite, William J. Grabowski & Poppy Z. Brite, iv *
   11 Angels (Goldengrove Unleaving), Poppy Z. Brite, ss *
   19 The Show, Bentley Little, ss *
   22 Bentley Little, William J. Grabowski & Bentley Little, iv *
   25 Loony Toon, Bentley Little, vi *
   29 Willy Wonka and the L. Walker Biofair, Elizabeth Massie, ss *
   35 Elizabeth Massie, Elizabeth Massie, iv *
   37 To Sooth the Savage Beast, Elizabeth Massie, ss *
   40 Allen Koszowski, Allen Koszowski, iv *
   41 Illustrations, Allen Koszowski, il *
   43 Bub and the Zomb Boys, A.R. Morlan, ss *
   48 A.R. Morlan, A.R. Morlan, iv *
   51 Tomb of Nine Hundred Days, A.R. Morlan, ss *
   56 Tattler, William J. Grabowski, br *
   60 Nightmares, Anonymous, ar *
   63 Nothing There, G. Wayne Miller, ss *
   66 G. Wayne Miller, G. Wayne Miller, iv *
   69 God of Self, G. Wayne Miller, ss *
   73 Off the Subject II: Background and Foreground, Steve Rasnic Tem, ar *
   74 Fragments of Horror, Ray Garton, ms *
   76 Tattler, Michael Arthur Betts, mr *
   79 It's Alive Again! The Return of the Nit-Picky, Utterly Trivial, Totally Picayune Horror-Fantasy (and What the Heck, a Little Sci-Fi) Movie Quiz Part III, A.R. Morlan, qz *

*The Horror Show [v.5 #5, Winter 1987] David B. Silva, ed. (Phantasm Press, $3.95, 72pp, 8.5 x 11 pb)
Contents:
    3 Hellnotes, David B. Silva, ed *
    5 The Scar, Dennis Etchison, ss *
   11 Red Zone, Brian Hodge, ss *
   15 Dennis Etchison, William J. Grabowski & Dennis Etchison, iv *
   23 Comes the Bad Time, Bentley Little, ss *
   26 A Death in the Day of, Gary A. Braunbeck, ss *
   29 Lovers, Kevin Lenihan, ss *
   33 The American Nightmare: The Fiction of Dennis Etchison, Michael A. Morrison, ar *
   37 Tattler, William J. Grabowski, br *
   41 Fragments of Horror, Dennis Etchison, ms *

ISAAC ASIMOV PRESENTS THE GREAT SF STORIES: 17...

228 Allamagoosa, Eric Frank Russell, ss *Astounding* May,1955
243 The Vanishing American, Charles Beaumont, ss *F&SF* Aug,1955
254 The Game of Rat and Dragon, Cordwainer Smith, nv *Galaxy* Oct,1955
270 The Star, Arthur C. Clarke, ss *Infinity* Nov,1955
277 Nobody Bothers Gus [as by Paul Janvier], Algis Budrys, ss *Astounding* Nov,1955
292 Delenda Est, Poul Anderson, nv *F&SF* Dec,1955
333 Dreaming Is a Private Thing, Isaac Asimov, ss *F&SF* Dec,1955

*Isaac Asimov's Magical Worlds of Fantasy #8: Devils Isaac Asimov, Martin H. Greenberg & Charles G. Waugh, eds. (NAL/Signet 0-451-14865-7, Jun,87 [May,87], $3.50, 351pp, pb) Anthology of 18 fantasy stories.
Contents:
9 The Devil, Isaac Asimov, in
13 I'm Dangerous Tonight, Cornell Woolrich, na *All American Fiction* Nov,1937
91 The Devil in Exile, Brian Cleeve, ss,1968
105 The Cage, Ray Russell, ss,1959
113 The Tale of Ivan the Fool, Leo Tolstoi, nv
143 The Shepherds, Ruth Sawyer, ss,1941
151 He Stepped on the Devil's Tail, Winston K. Marks, ss *Fantastic Universe* Feb,1955
167 Rustle of Wings, Fredric Brown, ss *F&SF* Aug,1953
173 That Hell-Bound Train, Robert Bloch, ss *F&SF* Sep,1958
189 Added Inducement, Robert F. Young, ss *F&SF* Mar,1957
197 The Devil and Daniel Webster [also as "All That Money Can Buy"], Stephen Vincent Benet, ss *The Saturday Evening Post* Oct 24,1936
213 Colt .24, Rick Hautala, ss *
225 The Making of Revelation, Part I, Philip Jose Farmer, nv **After the Fall**, ed. Robert Sheckley, Ace,1980
243 The Howling Man [as by C.B. Lovehill], Charles Beaumont, ss *Rogue* Nov,1959
261 Trace, Jerome Bixby, ss,1961
265 Guardian Angel, Arthur C. Clarke, nv *New Worlds* Win,1950
309 The Devil Was Sick, Bruce Elliott, ss *F&SF* Apr,1951
321 Deal with the D.E.V.I.L., Theodore R. Cogswell, vi *Fantasy Book* Dec,1981
325 Dazed, Theodore Sturgeon, nv *Galaxy* Sep,1971

*Isaac Asimov's Magical Worlds of Fantasy #9: Atlantis Isaac Asimov, Martin H. Greenberg & Charles G. Waugh, eds. (NAL/Signet 0-451-15144-5, Jan,88 [Dec,87], $3.95, 349pp, pb) Anthology of 11 fantasy stories.
Contents:
9 Introduction: The Lost City, Isaac Asimov, in
15 Treaty in Tartessos, Karen Anderson, ss *F&SF* May,1963
23 The Vengeance of Ulios [The Avenger from Atlantis], Edmond Hamilton, nv *Weird Tales* Jul,1935
61 Scar-Tissue, Henry S. Whitehead, ss *Amazing* Jul,1946
77 The Double Shadow, Clark Ashton Smith, ss **The Double Shadow and Other Fantasies**, Auburn Journal: Auburn CA,1933; *Weird Tales* Feb,1939
95 The Dweller in the Temple, Manly Wade Wellman, nv **Swords Against Darkness** #2, ed. Andrew J. Offutt,1977
123 Gone Fishing, J.A. Pollard, ss *
129 The Lamp [also as "The Lamp from Atlantis"], L. Sprague de Camp, nv *F&SF* Mar,1975
153 The Shadow Kingdom, Robert E. Howard, nv *Weird Tales* Aug,1929
193 The New Atlantis, Ursula K. Le Guin, na **The New Atlantis**, ed. Robert Silverberg,1975
225 Dragon Moon, Henry Kuttner, na *Weird Tales* Jan,1941
273 The Brigadier in Check -- and Mate, Sterling E. Lanier, na **The Curious Quest of Brigadier Ffellowes**, Donald M. Grant,1986

*Isaac Asimov's Science Fiction Magazine [v.11 # 1, January 1987] Gardner R. Dozois, ed. (Davis, $2.00, 192pp, pb)
Contents:
4 New Writers, Isaac Asimov, ed *
9 Letters, The Readers, lt *
18 Gaming, Matthew J. Costello, gr *
22 America, Orson Scott Card, nv *
54 The Peace Spy, Gene Wolfe, ss *
63 The Changeling Uncovered, Bruce Boston, pm *
64 Wolf Time, Walter Jon Williams, nv *
94 Digressions from the Second Person Future, John Barnes, ss *

103 Bringing in the Sheaves, Rudy Rucker, ss *
110 Vacuum Flowers [Part 2 of 3], Michael Swanwick, sl *
180 On Books, Baird Searles, br *
187 Index, ix *
191 First Annual Readers' Award Ballot, ms *
192 SF Conventional Calendar, Erwin S. Strauss, ms *

*Isaac Asimov's Science Fiction Magazine [v.11 # 2, February 1987] Gardner R. Dozois, ed. (Davis, $2.00, 192pp, pb)
Contents:
4 Intellectual Cliches, Isaac Asimov, ed *
9 Letters, The Readers, lt *
21 Gaming, Matthew J. Costello, gr *
22 Aurin Tree, M.J. Engh, nv *
58 The Fights of Spring, Isaac Asimov, ss *
70 Dutchman, Jack McDevitt, nv *
92 The Moment of the Rose, Cherie Wilkerson, ss *
101 Myron Chester and the Toads, James P. Blaylock, ss *
110 Vacuum Flowers [Part 3 of 3], Michael Swanwick, sl *
182 The Gift, Joe W. Haldeman, pm **Dealing in Futures**, Viking,1985
184 On Books, Baird Searles, br *
191 Hollywood Revisited: The Body Snatchers, Robert Frazier, pm *
192 SF Conventional Calendar, Erwin S. Strauss, ms *

*Isaac Asimov's Science Fiction Magazine [v.11 # 3, March 1987] Gardner R. Dozois, ed. (Davis, $2.00, 192pp, pb)
Contents:
4 Intimations of Mortality, Isaac Asimov, ed *
10 Letters, The Readers, lt *
20 Gaming, Matthew J. Costello, gr *
22 Images, Harry Turtledove, nv *
62 Dinosaur on a Bicycle, Tim Sullivan, nv *
83 Encased in the Amber of Probabilities, Robert Frazier, pm *
84 Waves, Andrew Weiner, nv *
116 Birds of the Mutant Rain Forest, Robert Frazier, pm *
118 Ice Dreams, Sharon N. Farber, ss *
134 Eye for Eye, Orson Scott Card, na *
184 On Books, Baird Searles, br *
192 SF Conventional Calendar, Erwin S. Strauss, ms *

*Isaac Asimov's Science Fiction Magazine [v.11 # 4, April 1987] Gardner R. Dozois, ed. (Davis, $2.00, 192pp, pb)
Contents:
4 Truth and Fiction, Isaac Asimov, ed *
9 Letters, The Readers, lt *
20 Gaming, Matthew J. Costello, gr *
22 Viewpoint: Cellular Automata, Rudy Rucker, ar *
36 The Sun Spider, Lucius Shepard, nv *
70 Rachel in Love, Pat Murphy, nv *
96 Letter to a Grandchild, Robert Frazier, pm *
98 A Little Further Up the Fox..., George M. Ewing, nv *
117 Fog, David F. Reitmeyer, pm *
118 Out of Darkness, Lillian Stewart Carl, ss *
130 Superwine, Harry Turtledove, na *
179 On Books: Sturgeon, Vonnegut, and Trout, Norman Spinrad, br *
192 SF Conventional Calendar, Erwin S. Strauss, ms *

*Isaac Asimov's Science Fiction Magazine [v.11 # 5, May 1987] Gardner R. Dozois, ed. (Davis, $2.00, 192pp, pb)
Contents:
4 Space Flight, Isaac Asimov, ed *
9 Letters, The Readers, lt *
17 Gaming, Matthew J. Costello, gr *
20 Flowers for Edo, Bruce Sterling, nv *
50 Nazca Lines, Roger L. Dutcher & Robert Frazier, pm *
52 Perpetuity Blues, Neal Barrett, Jr., nv *
80 Termites, Dave Smeds, ss *
96 Angel, Pat Cadigan, ss *
111 One-Trick Dog, Bruce Boston, vi *
114 The View from Mars Hill, Frederik Pohl, nv *
134 Dinosaur, Steve Rasnic Tem, ss *
146 Cannibals, Nancy Kress, nv *
183 Tracking Through the Mutant Rain Forest, Robert Frazier, pm *
184 On Books, Baird Searles, br *
192 SF Conventional Calendar, Erwin S. Strauss, ms *

*Isaac Asimov's Science Fiction Magazine [v.11 # 6, June 1987] Gardner R. Dozois, ed. (Davis, $2.00, 192pp, pb)

SAAC ASIMOV'S SCIENCE FICTION MAGAZINE

Isaac Asimov's Science Fiction Magazine [v.11 # 7, July 1987]
Gardner R. Dozois, ed. (Davis, $2.00, 192pp, pb)

Isaac Asimov's Science Fiction Magazine [v.11 # 8, August 1987]
Gardner R. Dozois, ed. (Davis, $2.00, 192pp, pb)

Isaac Asimov's Science Fiction Magazine [v.11 # 9, September 1987]
Gardner R. Dozois, ed. (Davis, $2.00, 192pp, pb)

Isaac Asimov's Science Fiction Magazine [v.11 #10, October 1987]
Gardner R. Dozois, ed. (Davis, $2.00, 192pp, pb)

ISAAC ASIMOV'S WONDERFUL WORLDS OF SCIENCE...

Isaac Asimov's Science Fiction Magazine [v.11 #11, November 1987]
Gardner R. Dozois, ed. (Davis, $2.00, 192pp, pb)

Isaac Asimov's Science Fiction Magazine [v.11 #12, December 1987]
Gardner R. Dozois, ed. (Davis, $2.00, 192pp, pb)

Isaac Asimov's Science Fiction Magazine [v.11 #13, Mid-December
1987] Gardner R. Dozois, ed. (Davis, $2.00, 192pp, pb)

***Isaac Asimov's Wonderful Worlds of Science Fiction #6:
Neanderthals*** Isaac Asimov, Martin H. Greenberg & Charles G.
Waugh, eds. (NAL/Signet 0-451-14716-2, Feb,87 [Jan,87], $3.95,
351pp, pb) Anthology of 11 stories and an article.

*Isaac Asimov's Wonderful Worlds of Science Fiction #7: Space Shuttles Isaac Asimov, Martin H. Greenberg & Charles G. Waugh, eds. (NAL/Signet 0-451-15017-1, Oct,87 [Sep,87], $3.95, 384pp, pb) Anthology of 14 stories.
Contents:

*Jackbird: Tales of Illusion & Identity Bruce Boston (Berkeley Poets' Workshop & Press no ISBN, 1976, $2.00, 88pp, tp) Collection of six stories. In **The Bruce Boston Omnibus**.
Contents:

*The Jade Demons Quartet Robert E. Vardeman (NEL 0-450-41351-9, Nov,87 [Oct,87], £4.95, 829pp, tp) Fantasy omnibus.
Contents:

*The Jaguar Hunter Lucius Shepard (Arkham House 0-87054-154-4, May,87 [Mar,87], $21.95, 404pp, hc) Collection of 11 stories by the best of the new writers. Most of these were awards nominees. Highly recommended. (CNB)
Contents:

*The Kid From Ozone Park & Other Stories Richard Wilson (Drumm 0-936055-32-4, Aug,87 [Jul,87], $3.50, 62pp, pb) Small pamphlet collection of 8 original stories, put together by the author before his death in March 1987. Drumm Booklet #27.
Contents:

*The Kinsman Saga Ben Bova (Tor 0-312-93028-3, Oct,87 [Sep,87], $17.95, 566pp, hc) Sf novel. A slight rewrite of Bova's two best books, **Millennium** (1976) and **Kinsman** (1979), his excellent series about the space program, near-future politics, and SDI(!). The rewrite adds more characterization and motivation, but events have turned these into parallel world books, destroying most of their original power. (CNB)
Contents:

*Knave & the Game Laurence M. Janifer (Doubleday 0-385-15238-8, Aug,87, $12.95, 173pp, hc) Collection of 9 sf stories about adventurer Gerald Knave.
Contents:

*L. Ron Hubbard Presents Writers of the Future, Vol. III Algis Budrys, ed. (Bridge 0-88404-245-6, Apr,87, $4.50, 429pp, pb) Original anthology of 14 stories plus essays by Pohl, Benford, Pournelle, and Hubbard. Later releases of the first edition have a sticker on the back cover correcting a typo in the ISBN.
Contents:

*Lear's Daughters M. Bradley Kellogg & William Rossow (SFBC #107003, Apr,87, $8.98, 725pp, hc) Omnibus edition of **The Wave and the Flame** and **Reign of Fire** (both NAL 1986), a two-part sf novel set on a fascinating planet with a bizarre weather pattern (Rossow provided scientific input). Highly recommended. (FCM)
Contents:

*Liavek: Wizard's Row Will Shetterly & Emma Bull, eds. (Ace 0-441-48190-6, Sep,87 [Aug,87], $2.95, 212pp, pb) Shared-world original anthology, third in the series. 8 stories, plus appendices of songs and background material.
Contents:

LIAVEK: WIZARD'S ROW

The Light Princess and Other Stories George MacDonald (Kelpies 0-86241-164-5, Oct,87, £1.95, 288pp, pb) Reprint (Gollancz 1961) juvenile fantasy collection.
Contents:

*Little Tours of Hell Josephine Saxton (Methuen/Pandora 0-86358-095-5, Dec,86 [Aug,87], $8.95, 146pp, tp) Collection of 14 stories with elements of horror and humor, "Tall Tales of Food and Holidays". This is the 1986 British edition from Routledge & Kegan Paul/Pandora, now available in the U.S. through Methuen. A hardcover at $19.95 is also listed; not seen.
Contents:

*Living Fire and Other S.F. Stories Nicholas Fisk (Corgi 0-552-52453-0, Aug,87, £1.95, 188pp, pb) Original sf collection.
Contents:

*Lost in Time and Space with Lefty Feep Robert Bloch (Creatures at Large 0-940064-01-4, Apr,87 [Mar,87], $12.95, 258pp, tp) Collection of 9 humorous sf stories, one original, about a racetrack tout. Introduction by Chelsea Quinn Yarbro. The paperback is limited to 5,000 copies, and a 250-copy hardcover edition (-02-2, $40) was announced but not seen.
Contents:

THE MAGAZINE OF FANTASY & SCIENCE FICTION

*Mad and Bad Fairies Anonymous, ed. (Attic Press 0-946211-40-X, Jul,87 [Oct,87], £3.50, 60pp, tp) Anthology of feminist fairy tales. Volume 3 in the "Fairytales for Feminists" series.
Contents:

*The Magazine of Fantasy & Science Fiction [v.72 #1, January 1987] Edward L. Ferman, ed. (Mercury Press, $1.75, 162pp, pb)
Contents:

*The Magazine of Fantasy & Science Fiction [v.72 #2, February 1987] Edward L. Ferman, ed. (Mercury Press, $1.75, 162pp, pb)
Contents:

*The Magazine of Fantasy & Science Fiction [v.72 #3, March 1987] Edward L. Ferman, ed. (Mercury Press, $1.75, 162pp, pb)
Contents:

THE MAGAZINE OF FANTASY & SCIENCE FICTION

THE MAGAZINE OF FANTASY & SCIENCE FICTION

THE MAGAZINE OF FANTASY & SCIENCE FICTION

48 Cartoon, Joseph Farris, ct *
49 The Cobbler, Roger Robert Lovin, ss *
70 Cartoon, Sidney Harris, ct *
71 The Canyons of Ariel, Kenneth W. Ledbetter, nv *
93 Obsolete Skill, Charles Sheffield, ss *
104 Cartoon, Henry Martin, ct *
105 Another Dead Grandfather, George Alec Effinger, ss *
120 Delivery, Michael Shea, ss *
128 Science: The Road to Humanity, Isaac Asimov, ar *
140 Ticket to Heaven, John Shirley, ss *
160 Index to Volume 73, ix *

The Mage [# 6, Winter 1987] Jeffrey V. Yule, ed. (Colgate University, $2.00, 52pp, 8.5 x 11 pb)
Contents:
3 A Consideration of Negative-Future Fiction, Jeffrey V. Yule, ed *
5 Message Intercepted On Hyperspatial Frequency, Wade Tarzia, vi *
8 The Dwarf Who Knew Too Much, Harry Dolan, ss *
15 Auguries, Gregory Forbes, ar *
16 The Alien Reads a Romance, Mark Rich, pm *
17 Hackers in the Dewey, R.D. Davis, vi *
19 Huayno, Asher Torren, pm *
20 Frank Utpatel: Wood Engraver, Rodger Gerberding, bg *
32 Final Dreams, Billie Sue Mosiman, ss *
35 Reach Out and Scorch Someone, H.R. Felgenhauer, pm *
36 A Trace of Inbetween, Wade Tarzia, ar *
39 H.P. Lovecraft: Problems in Critical Recognition, Peter Cannon, ar *
44 Subatomic Particles, Michael J. Brutvan, ss *
49 Mage Reviews, Mage Staff, br *
51 Dreams in Stasis, Tom Rentz, pm *

The Mage [# 7, Spring 1987] Jeffrey V. Yule, ed. (Colgate University, $2.50, 68pp, 8.5 x 11 pb)
Contents:
3 Science Fiction--Judging the Genre, Jeffrey V. Yule, ed *
4 A Thing or Two About Razzle-Dazzle, Dennis John Sjolie, ss *
10 Brain Blasters, Mary Sass, ss *
13 Decay in the Hero's Way, Wade Tarzia, ar *
15 Mr. Wizard, R.D. Davis, ss *
23 At Night, Jeffrey V. Yule, pm *
24 Jonathon, D.J. Cipriani, III, vi *
26 A Virgil Finlay Portfolio, Harry Dolan & Virgil Finlay, pi *
36 Mage Reviews, Mage Staff, br *
39 Fortuneteller, Mark Rich, pm *
40 A Hot Prospect, Theodore Solomon, ss *
47 The African Woman, Asher Torren, pm *
48 William Gibson: A Cyberpunk Examined, Jeffrey V. Yule, ar *
51 Elysium Horizon, Leo Bigley, ss *
58 Alandriar Goes To Earth, Wade Tarzia, ss *
62 Readers' Responses, The Readers, lt *

Magic in Ithkar 4 Andre Norton & Robert Adams, eds. (Tor 0-812-54719-5, Jul,87 [Jun,87], $3.50, 278pp, pb) Original anthology of 15 stories, latest in the "Ithkar" shared world fantasy series.
Contents:
1 Prologue, Robert Adams, pr
9 The Clockwork Woman, Ann R. Brown, ss *
19 First Do No Harm, Mildred Downey Broxon, ss *
39 Honeycomb, Esther M. Friesner, nv *
61 Demon Luck, Craig Shaw Gardner, ss *
73 A Quiet Day at the Fair, Sharon Green, nv *
97 Mandrake, Caralyn Inks, nv *
119 To Trap a Demon, Ardath Mayhar, ss *
131 Trave, Shirley Meier, ss *
147 The Book-Healer, Sandra Miesel, ss *
167 The Demon's Gift, Kathleen O'Malley, nv *
189 The Gentle Art of Making Enemies, Claudia Peck, nv *
215 Day of Strange Fortune, Carol Severance, ss *
235 Cat and Muse, Rose Wolf, ss *
253 The Talisman, Timothy Zahn, nv *
275 Biographical Notes, bg

The Magic Kiss and Other Tales of Princes and Princesses Tony Bradman, ed. (Blackie 0-216-92015-9, Aug,87 [Dec,87], £6.95, 94pp, hc) Anthology of short stories about princes and princesses.
Contents:
7 The Magic Kiss, Tony Bradman, ss *

MASTERS OF DARKNESS II

17 Savitri and Satyavan, Madhur Jaffrey, ss **Seasons of Splendour**, Pavilion,1985
29 The Blue Lotus, Eleanor Farjeon, ss
35 The Snuff-Box, Terry Jones, ss **Fairy Tales**, Terry Jones, Pavilion,1981
43 Petronella, Jay Williams, ss *McCalls* Jan,1973
57 The Princess and the Clown, Margaret Mahy, ss **Mahy Magic**, Dent,1986
65 The Prince, Two Mice and Some Kitchen-Maids, Edith Nesbit, ss
85 Cinderella, Tony Bradman, ss *

*The **Magic of the Past** Brian W. Aldiss (Kerosina 0-948893-13-3, Aug,87, £4.50, 48pp, tp) Original sf collection.
Contents:
5 Introduction, in
9 North Scarning [The Older Evil], ss *The Illustrated London News* Dec,1986
22 The Magic of the Past, nv *

***Masques II** J.N. Williamson, ed. (Maclay & Assoc. 0-940776-24-3, Jun,87 [Jul,87], $19.95, 221pp, hc) Original anthology of 27 horror stories, including work by Stephen King, Ramsey Campbell, and Richard Matheson. Issued in silver boards without dust wrapper.
Contents:
7 Introduction, J.N. Williamson, in
13 Popsy, Stephen King, ss *
25 Second Sight, Ramsey Campbell, ss *
31 The Yard, William F. Nolan, ss *
39 The New Season, Robert Bloch, ss *
46 The Near Departed, Richard Matheson, vi *
49 Ice Sculptures, David B. Silva, ss *
59 Wiping the Slate Clean, G. Wayne Miller, ss *
66 The Litter, James Kisner, ss *
77 Splatter, Douglas E. Winter, ss *
86 Deathbed, Richard Christian Matheson, vi *
88 American Gothic, Ray Russell, ss *
103 Moist Dreams, Stanley Wiater, ss *
107 Dog, Cat, and Baby, Joe R. Lansdale, vi *
109 Nothing from Nothing Comes, Katherine Ramsland, ss *
118 If You Take My Hand, My Son, Mort Castle, ss *
127 Maurice and Mog, James Herbert, ss *
135 Fish Story, Dennis Hamilton, ss *
146 Outsteppin' Fetchit, Charles R. Saunders, ss *
152 In the Tank, Ardath Mayhar, ss *
158 Hidey Hole, Steve Rasnic Tem, ss *
163 The Night Is Freezing Fast, Thomas F. Monteleone, ss *
172 Buried Talents, Richard Matheson, ss *
179 Lake George in High August, John Robert Bensink, ss *
183 Wordsong, J.N. Williamson, ss *
190 The Man Who Drowned Puppies, Thomas Sullivan, ss *
196 The Boy Who Came Back from the Dead, Alan Rodgers, nv *

***Masters in Hell** Janet Morris, ed. (Baen 0-671-65379-2, Dec,87 [Nov,87], $3.50, 280pp, pb) Original anthology in the "Heroes in Hell" shared world fantasy series, with 9 stories.
Contents:
1 The Ransom of Hellcat, Chris Morris, nv *
21 Take Two, Bill Kerby, nv *
59 Hellbike, George Foy, ss *
77 Houseguests, Nancy Asire, nv *
119 Spitting in the Wind, Lynn Abbey, nv *
149 God's Eyes, Michael Armstrong, nv *
183 Bargain, David Drake, nv *
211 Pawn in Play, C.J. Cherryh, nv *
251 Sea Change, Janet Morris, nv *

***Masters of Darkness II** Dennis Etchison, ed. (Tor 0-812-51764-4, Jan,88 [Dec,87], $3.95, 338pp, pb) Anthology of 15 horror stories, an "author's choice" selection with afterwords by the authors.
Contents:
x Preface, Dennis Etchison, pr
1 Up Under the Roof [revised from *Weird Tales* Oct,38], Manly Wade Wellman, ss **Worse Things Waiting**, Carcosa: Chapel Hill NC,1973
10 The Other Room, Lisa Tuttle, ss *Whispers* #17,1982
26 A Garden of Blackred Roses, Charles L. Grant, nv **Dark Forces**, ed. Kirby McCauley, Viking,1980
57 Cottage Tenant, Frank Belknap Long, nv *Fantastic* Apr,1975

MASTERS OF DARKNESS II

95 The Hounds, Kate Wilhelm, nv **A Shocking Thing**, ed. Damon Knight, Pocket,1974
129 Zombique, Joseph Payne Brennan, ss *Alfred Hitchcock's Mystery Magazine* Oct,1972
143 Taking the Night Train, Thomas F. Monteleone, nv *Night Voyages* Spr,1981
166 Black Corridor, Fritz Leiber, ss *Galaxy* Dec,1967
183 Strangers on Paradise [Strangers in Paradise], Damon Knight, ss *F&SF* Apr,1986
206 Gemini, Tanith Lee, nv **Chrysalis #9**, ed. Roy Torgeson,1981
231 Glimmer, Glimmer, George Alec Effinger, ss *Playboy* Nov,1987
242 Perverts, Whitley Strieber, ss *Whispers* #19,1983
259 On Ice, Barry N. Malzberg, ss *Amazing* Jan,1973
270 The Monkey Treatment, George R.R. Martin, nv *F&SF* Jul,1983
312 Casey Agonistes, Richard McKenna, ss *F&SF* Sep,1958
328 Notes on the Contributors, bg

*Masters of Fantasy 3: M.R. James M.R. James (British Fantasy Society no ISBN, May,87 [1987], £0.90, 24pp, pb) Ghost collection. Edited by Richard Dalby. Volume 10 in the BFS Booklet series. [Not seen]
Contents:
3 Introduction, Richard Dalby, in
4 The Ghost Stories of M.R. James, Richard Dalby, ar
10 Ghosts - Treat Them Gently, ar *London Evening News* Apr 17,1931
13 In the Footsteps of M.R. James, Rosemary Pardoe & Darroll Pardoe, ar
16 A School Story, ss **More Ghost Stories of an Antiquary**, Arnold,1911
21 Selected Bibliography, Richard Dalby, bi

*Mathenauts: Tales of Mathematical Wonder Rudy Rucker, ed. (Arbor House 0-87795-891-2, Jun,87 [May,87], $18.95, 300pp, hc) Anthology of sf stories dealing with (or taking off from) mathematical concepts.
Contents:
xi Introduction, Rudy Rucker, in
1 1 to 999 [One in a Thousand], Isaac Asimov, ss *Gallery* Sep,1981
8 Four Brands of Impossible, Norman Kagan, nv *F&SF* Sep,1964
37 Tangents, Greg Bear, ss *Omni* Jan,1986
54 A New Golden Age, Rudy Rucker, ss *Randolph-Macon Woman's College Alumnae Bulletin* Sum,1981
62 Professor and Colonel, Ruth Berman, ss *
69 The Maxwell Equations, Anatoly Dnieprov, ss **Destination: Amaltheia**, ed. Richard Dixon, Moscow: Foreign Languages Publishing House,1963
108 Left or Right?, Martin Gardner, ss *Esquire*,1951
112 Immune Dreams, Ian Watson, ss **Pulsar** #1, ed. George Hay,1978
125 Forbidden Knowledge, Kathryn Cramer, ss *
136 Godel's Doom, George Zebrowski, ss *Popular Computing* Feb,1985
146 The Tale of Happiton, Douglas Hofstadter, ss **Metamagical Themas**, Basic Books,1985
158 The Finagle Fiasco, Don Sakers, ss,1983
162 Convergent Series [The Long Night], Larry Niven, ss *F&SF* Mar,1967
168 No-Sided Professor, Martin Gardner, ss *Esquire* Jan,1947; *F&SF* Feb,1951
179 Euclid Alone, William F. Orr, nv **Orbit** #16, ed. Damon Knight,1975
211 Love Comes to the Middleman, Marc Laidlaw, ss *
216 Miss Mouse and the Fourth Dimension, Robert Sheckley, ss *Twilight Zone* Dec,1981
225 The Feeling of Power, Isaac Asimov, ss *If* Feb,1958
235 Cubeworld, Henry R. Gross, nv *
257 The Schematic Man, Frederik Pohl, ss *Playboy* Jan,1969
263 Time's Rub, Gregory Benford, ss Cheap Street: New Castle, VA,1984
276 Message Found in a Copy of **Flatland**, Rudy Rucker, ss **The 57th Franz Kafka**, Ace,1983
286 The Mathenauts, Norman Kagan, nv *If* Jul,1964

*Merovingen Nights: Festival Moon C.J. Cherryh, ed. (DAW 0-88677-192-7, Apr,87 [Mar,87], $3.50, 300pp, pb) Shared-world sf original anthology based on the background of Cherryh's **Angel With the Sword**.
Contents:
15 Festival Moon, C.J. Cherryh, ss *
28 First Night Cruise, Leslie Fish, nv *
66 Festival Moon (reprised), C.J. Cherryh, vi *

MORE TALES FOR THE MIDNIGHT HOUR

71 Two Gentlemen of the Trade, Robert Lynn Asprin, ss *
85 Festival Moon (reprised), C.J. Cherryh, vi *
89 Cat's Tale, Nancy Asire, nv *
114 Festival Moon (reprised), C.J. Cherryh, vi *
118 Deathangel, Mercedes R. Lackey, nv *
150 Festival Moon (reprised), C.J. Cherryh, vi *
153 Sword Play, Janet Morris & Chris Morris, na *
213 Festival Moon (reprised), C.J. Cherryh, vi *
217 First-Bath, Lynn Abbey, nv *
253 Festival Moon (reprised), C.J. Cherryh, vi *
255 Night Action, Chris Morris, ss *
270 Festival Moon (final reprise), C.J. Cherryh, vi *
277 Sea Floor Maps, Pat Tobin, il *
280 Merovingen Ecology, Mercedes R. Lackey, ms *
287 Index to City Maps, ix
290 Merovingian City Maps and Merovin Hemispheric Maps, Pat Tobin, il *
297 Guardian, Leslie Fish, sg *
299 Black Water (Suicide) [lyrics], Mercedes R. Lackey, sg *
299 Black Water (Suicide) [music], C.J. Cherryh, sg *
300 Private Conversation [lyrics], Mercedes R. Lackey, sg *
300 Private Conversation [music], C.J. Cherryh, sg *

*Midnight Pleasures Robert Bloch (Doubleday 0-385-19439-0, Apr 17,87 [Mar,87], $12.95, 177pp, hc) Collection of 14 stories.
Contents:
1 The Rubber Room, ss **New Terrors** #2, ed. Ramsey Campbell, Pan,1980
17 The Night Before Christmas, nv **Dark Forces**, ed. Kirby McCauley, Viking,1980
41 Pumpkin, nv *Twilight Zone* Dec,1984
62 The Spoiled Wife, ss **Chrysalis** #3, ed. Roy Torgeson,1978
72 Oh Say Can You See--, ss **Analog Yearbook** #1,1978
90 But First These Words--, ss *F&SF* May,1977
98 Picture, ss **Shadows** #1, ed. Charles L. Grant,1978
106 The Undead, ss **The Book Sail 16th Anniversary Catalog**,1984
111 Comeback, ss *Previews* Oct,1984
118 Nocturne, ss **Greystone Bay**, ed. Charles L. Grant, Tor,1985
126 Die--Nasty, ss *
132 Pranks, ss **Halloween Horrors**, ed. Alan Ryan, Doubleday,1986
146 Everybody Needs a Little Love, ss **Masques** #1, ed. J.N. Williamson,1984
165 The Totem Pole, ss *Weird Tales* Aug,1939
179 About the Author, bg

*Minnesota Fantasy Review [v.1 #1, October 1987] Ed Shannon & Mike Odden, eds. (Ed Shannon & Mike Odden, $5.00, 48pp, 8.5 x 11 pb)
Contents:
4 It Speaks, Mike Odden, ed *
4 By the Way, Ed Shannon, ed *
5 Now Appearing, Ed Shannon, vi *
7 Nightshade Crossing, Mark Rainey, ss *
15 Winged Death, Dave Stall, ss *
20 The Butler, Glenn Rahman, vi *
21 Korowaar, Mary Elizabeth Counselman, ss
26 Dead Beat, Roger Dale Trexler, ss
29 To Sleep Perchance To Dream, Matt McGregor, ss *
34 Head in His Hands, Carl Jacobi, ss *Thrilling Mystery Stories* Nov,1937
41 So Beautiful She Was, A.M. Decker, pm *
41 The Cravin', Carl Jacobi, pm *Ski-U-Mah* May,1930
41 A Step Back in Time, Audrey Parente, pm *
41 True Love Grue, Phillip Rainbird, pm *
43 Beyond Suawanee, Margaret B. Simon, pm *
43 Teach the Children, Scott Wyatt, pm *
45 Magic Trick, Ruth Berman, pm *
31 Sense of Wonder, Margaret B. Simon, ar *
39 Hawthorne and Mailer, Dave Page, ar *
42 Internal Shadows, Ed Shannon, br *
44 Harmony of Fear, John Brower, mr *

*More Tales for the Midnight Hour J.B. Stamper (Scholastic Apple 0-590-41184-5, Oct,87, $2.50, 117pp, pb) Original collection of 13 juvenile horror stories.
Contents:
1 The Shortcut, ss *
8 Trick-or-Treat, ss *
19 The Hearse, ss *

MORE TALES FOR THE MIDNIGHT HOUR

28 At Midnight, ss *
37 The Black Mare, ss *
46 The Love Charm, ss *
58 The Mask, ss *
65 Right Inn, ss *
77 The Collector, ss *
86 A Ghost Story, ss *
93 In the Lantern's Light, ss *
100 Footsteps, ss *
108 A Night in the Woods, ss *

A Mysterious House Algernon Blackwood (Tragara Press 0-948189-15-0, Jul,87 [Aug,87], £9.00, 24pp, tp) Reprint (*Belgravia* July 1889) of Blackwood's first published short story, with an introduction by Richard Dalby. A limited edition of 125 copies, of which 100 are for sale. [Not seen]
Contents:
A Mysterious House, ss *Belgravia* Jul,1889

*Mysterious Motoring Stories William Pattrick, ed. (W.H. Allen 0-491-03643-4, Feb,87, £10.95, 224pp, hc) Anthology of supernatural stories about cars. Reprinted (Star 1987) as **Duel and Other Horror Stories of the Road**.
Contents:
7 Introduction, William Pattrick, in
11 The Car with the Green Lights, William Le Queux, ss *The Premier Magazine* Feb,1916
29 The Dust-Cloud, E.F. Benson, ss **The Room in the Tower and Other Stories**, London: Mills Boon,1912
43 How It Happened, Arthur Conan Doyle, ss *The Strand* Sep,1913
49 The Last Trip, Archie Binns, ss *Weird Tales* Aug,1925
59 The Demon Lover, Elizabeth Bowen, ss **The Demon Lover**, J. Cape,1945
69 Jay Walkers, H. Russell Wakefield, ss
83 The Ghost of the Model T, Betsy Emmons, ss *Weird Tales* Nov,1942
91 The Ghost Car, Ken Batten, ss *Ghost Stories* Oct,1928
109 New Corner, L.T.C. Rolt, ss *Mystery Stories* #20,1939
123 "Just Like Wild Bob", William F. Nolan, ss,1964
133 Auto Suggestion, Charles Beaumont, ss *Gamma* Sep,1965
149 Duel, Richard Matheson, nv *Playboy* Apr,1971
175 Second Chance, Jack Finney, ss **The Third Level**, New York: Rinehart & Co.,1957
193 Trucks, Stephen King, ss *Cavalier* Jun,1973
211 The Hitch-Hiker, Roald Dahl, ss **Henry Sugar and Other Stories**, 1977,1977

*Myth Alliances Robert Lynn Asprin (SFBC #11114, Jul,87 [Aug,87], $6.98, 375pp, hc) Omnibus edition of three books in the humorous fantasy series.
Contents:
Myth-ing Persons, n. The Donning Company/Publishers: Norfolk & Virginia Beach, VA,1984
Little Myth Marker, n. The Donning Company/Publishers: Norfolk & Virginia Beach, VA,1985
M.Y.T.H. Inc. Link, n. The Donning Company/Publishers: Norfolk & Virginia Beach, VA,1986

*Nerilka's Story & The Coelura Anne McCaffrey (Bantam UK 0-593-01043-4, Jan,87, £8.95, 192pp, hc) Omnibus edition of two fantasy novellas.
Contents:
7 **Nerilka's Story**, n. Bantam: New York hc Mar,1986
135 The Coelura, na Underwood-Miller: Columbia, PA,1983

*New Destinies, Vol. 1/Spring 1987 Jim Baen, ed. (Baen 0-671-65628-7, Mar,87 [Feb,87], $2.95, 288pp, pb) Original anthology/magazine, Vol.1/Spring 1987, incorporating the preceding Baen anthology **Far Frontiers** and concluding a Poul Anderson novella serialized there; it also has other fiction and non-fiction, including an unsigned review column.
Contents:
6 Point Man, Timothy Zahn, nv *
43 Magic Matter, Robert L. Forward, ar *
70 Iron [Part 2], Poul Anderson, sl *
126 Not for Country, Not for King, Joel Rosenberg, nv *
156 In Praise of Sociobiology, Dr. John Gribbin & Mary Gribbin, ar *
170 Lifeguard, Doug Beason, nv *

NEW PATHWAYS INTO SCIENCE FICTION AND FANTASY

192 The Space Beat: How to Stop a Space Program, G. Harry Stine, ar *
210 The Graphic of Dorian Gray, Fred Saberhagen, nv *
232 Rank Injustice, Keith Laumer, nv *
281 The Leading Edge, Anonymous, br *

*New Destinies, Vol. 2/Fall 1987 Jim Baen, ed. (Baen 0-671-65346-6, Aug,87 [Jul,87], $2.95, 232pp, pb) Original anthology of stories and essays.
Contents:
5 Running Out, Charles Sheffield, ar *
27 Do You Really Want a Bigger U.S. Space Program?, Charles Sheffield, ar *
47 The Dreaming Spires of Houston, Charles Sheffield, ss *
61 Moondo Bizarro, Phillip C. Jennings, nv *
83 Was Frankenstein Simply Einstein Being Frank? or Scientists in Science Fiction, Gregory Benford, ar *
103 The Phobos Race, Donald Fredrick Robertson, ar *
119 Test for Tyrants, Edward P. Hughes, ss *
135 The Leading Edge, Roland J. Green, br *
147 The Irvhank Effect, Harry Turtledove, ss *
163 Poppa Was a Catcher, Steven Gould, na *

*New Pathways Into Science Fiction And Fantasy [v.1 #6, Jan/Feb 1987] Michael G. Adkisson, ed. (MGA Services, $2.50, 38pp, 8.5 x 11 pb)
Contents:
4 Forum, The Readers, lt *
5 Book Reviews, Staff, br *
6 Close Encounters with Michael Bishop, Misha Chocholak & Michael Bishop, iv *
12 Enigma 2: Diagrams for Three Stories, Brian W. Aldiss, gp **Final Stage**, ed. Edward L. Ferman & Barry N. Malzberg, Charterhouse,1974
The Girl in the Tau-Dream; ss
The Immobility Crew; ss
A Cultural Side-Effect; ss
22 Sonic Curiosity, Matt Howarth, cs *
23 The Hag of Carmel Towers, Don Webb, vi *
25 Sonic Curiosity, Matt Howarth, cs *
26 Paul Williams talks to New Pathways, Misha Chocholak & Paul Williams, iv *
29 Interview with Mark Ziesing: Bookseller & Publisher, Misha Chocholak & Mark Ziesing, iv *
32 Strange Doings in Viktor's Village, Jessica Amanda Salmonson, vi *
34 Hunger, David Martin, ss *
37 Farewells on the Melon Bridge, Rob Hollis Miller, pm *
37 Tiny Devils, Patricia Jeres, pm *
38 Nuclear FX, Ferret & Mink Mole, cs *

*New Pathways Into Science Fiction And Fantasy [v.1 #7, April/May 1987] Michael G. Adkisson, ed. (MGA Services, $2.50, 38pp, 8.5 x 11 pb)
Contents:
4 Forum, The Readers, lt *
6 Book Reviews, Misha Chocholak, br *
6 Entropy Comix, Michael G. Adkisson, cs *
8 The Interdisciplinary Viewpoint of Science Fiction, Michael G. Adkisson, ar *
9 Book Reviews, Michael G. Adkisson, br *
10 Sonic Curiosity, Matt Howarth, cs *
11 K.W. Jeter [Part 1], J.B. Reynolds, Ferret & K.W. Jeter, iv *
15 Thoughts on **VALIS**, Philip K. Dick, lt Mar 5,1979
Excerpted from a letter to John B. Ross.
17 Enigma 3: The Aperture Moment, Brian W. Aldiss, gp **Epoch**, ed. Roger Elwood & Robert Silverberg, Berkley,1975
Waiting for the Universe to Begin; ss
But Without Orifices; ss
Aimez-Vous Holman Hunt?; ss
26 Lesser Myths of Milwaukee, Don Webb, vi *
28 Parakeet, John Shirley, ss *
34 The Aka Fragments [Part 1], David Memmott, sl *

*New Pathways Into Science Fiction And Fantasy [v.1 #8, August 1987] Michael G. Adkisson, ed. (MGA Services, $2.50, 38pp, 8.5 x 11 pb)
Contents:
4 Forum, The Readers, lt *
5 Book Reviews, Don Webb & Rosemary Webb, br *

OTHER ENGAGEMENTS

  43 The Undertaker Reflects, pm *Fungi* #12,1986
  44 The Step Beyond, ss **Darkness on the Edge of Town**, an,1985
  50 Night Firing--1967, pm *Fungi* #9,1986
  52 The Reckoning, vi *
  55 Tanning, ss *Etchings & Odysseys* #5,1984
  60 At the Last, pm *Footsteps* Spr,1985
  61 Harvest, vi *Dementia* #1,1986
  65 Refill, pm *Twisted* #1,1985
  67 On the Boardwalk, ss *
  73 Bird Food, pm *
  74 Who Walks at Night, ss *The Horror Show* Sum,1986
  81 Marriages, pm *Scavenger's Newsletter*
  82 The Knife, ss *Crosscurrents* Fll,1984
  88 In The Wilderness, ss *Etchings & Odysseys* #7,1985
  93 Cedars, pm *The Poet* Fll,1984
  94 The Tower, ss *Etchings & Odysseys* #9,1986
  99 The Unforgiven, pm *Weirdbook* #20,1985
101 The One Thing to Fear, ss *Footsteps* Fll,1986
108 To a Cockroach, pm *Scavenger's Newsletter* Apr,1985
109 The Bookman's God, ss *
116 Sunset, pm *Twisted* #2,1985
118 The Flood, ss *The Horror Show* Fll,1986

*The Other Side of the Mirror Marion Zimmer Bradley & The Friends of Darkover (DAW 0-88677-185-4, Feb,87 [Jan,87], $3.50, 303pp, pb) Shared-world anthology of "Darkover" stories. There are 5 stories here. Three of them are by Bradley and apparently appear for the first time. One is a 40,000 word novella. This is the most interesting and best of the "Darkover" anthologies. (CNB)
Contents:
  9 Introduction, Marion Zimmer Bradley, in
 13 The Other Side of the Mirror, Patricia Floss, na *
 80 Bride Price, Marion Zimmer Bradley, ss *
 94 Everything but Freedom, Marion Zimmer Bradley, na *
209 Oathbreaker, Marion Zimmer Bradley, nv *
233 Blood Hunt, Linda Frankel & Paula Crunk, na *

*Our Best: The Best of Frederik Pohl and C.M. Kornbluth Frederik Pohl & C.M. Kornbluth (Baen 0-671-65620-1, Feb,87 [Jan,87], $2.95, 286pp, pb) Collection of 12 collaborative stories, with new introductions by Pohl.
Contents:
  7 Introduction, Frederik Pohl, in
 13 Stories of the Sixties, Frederik Pohl, si
 17 Critical Mass, na *Galaxy* Feb,1962
 63 The World of Myrion Flowers, ss *F&SF* Oct,1961
 73 The Engineer, ss *Infinity* Feb,1956
 83 A Gentle Dying, ss *Galaxy* Jun,1961
 93 Nightmare with Zeppelins, nv *Galaxy* Dec,1958
105 The Quaker Cannon, nv *Analog* Aug,1961
139 The 60/40 Stories, Frederik Pohl, si
143 Trouble in Time [as by S.D. Gottesman], ss *Astonishing Stories* Dec,1940
165 Mars-Tube [as by S.D. Gottesman], ss *Astonishing Stories* Sep,1941
201 Epilogue to The Space Merchants, Frederik Pohl, si
205 Gravy Planet, ex *Galaxy* Aug,1952
219 The Final Stories, Frederik Pohl, si
221 Mute Inglorious Tam, ss *F&SF* Oct,1974
235 The Gift of Garigolli, nv *Galaxy* Aug,1974
269 The Meeting, ss *F&SF* Nov,1972
285 Afterword, Frederik Pohl, aw

Pardon My Ghoulish Laughter Fredric Brown (Dennis McMillan 0-9609986-6-7, Oct,87, $5.95, 163pp, tp) Reprint (Dennis McMillan 1986) collection of mystery stories, all involving vampires, voodoo, etc.; but only one is actually sf or fantasy. There is an introduction by Donald E. Westlake.
Contents:
  5 Introduction, Donald E. Westlake, in
  9 The Incredible Bomber, nv *G-Man Detective* Mar,1942
 29 Death Is a White Rabbit, nv *Strange Detective Mysteries* Jan,1942
 51 Death of a Vampire, nv *Strange Detective Mysteries* May,1943
 77 Pardon My Ghoulish Laughter, ss *Strange Detective Mysteries* Feb,1942
 91 Twice-Killed Corpse, nv *Ten Detective Aces* Mar,1942
111 A Lock of Satan's Hair, nv *Dime Mystery Magazine* Jan,1943
131 Ghost Breakers, nv *Thrilling Detective* Jul,1944

The Past Through Tomorrow Vol. 1 Robert A. Heinlein (NEL 0-450-05463-2, Sep,87, £2.95, 320pp, pb) Reissue (Putnam 1967, in one volume) sf collection. Part of the "Future History" series.
Contents:
  9 Introduction, Damon Knight, in
 17 Life-Line, ss *Astounding* Aug,1939
 37 The Roads Must Roll, nv *Astounding* Jun,1940
 75 Blowups Happen, nv *Astounding* Sep,1940
123 The Man Who Sold the Moon, nv **The Man Who Sold the Moon**, Shasta,1950
215 Delilah and the Space-Rigger, ss *Blue Book* Dec,1949
229 Space Jockey, ss *The Saturday Evening Post* Apr 26,1947
247 Requiem, ss *Astounding* Jan,1940
265 The Long Watch, ss *American Legion Magazine* Dec,1949
279 Gentlemen, Be Seated!, ss *Argosy* May,1948
289 The Black Pits of Luna, ss *The Saturday Evening Post* Jan 10,1948
303 It's Great to be Back!, ss *The Saturday Evening Post* Jul 26,1947

The Past Through Tomorrow Vol. 2 Robert A. Heinlein (NEL 0-450-04005-4, Sep,87, £2.95, 347pp, pb) Reissue (Putnam 1967, in one volume) sf collection. Part of the "Future History" series.
Contents:
  9 Introduction, Damon Knight, in
 17 We Also Walk Dogs, ss *Astounding* Jul,1941
 41 Searchlight, vi *Scientific American* Aug,1962
 45 Ordeal in Space, ss *Town & Country* May,1948
 61 The Green Hills of Earth, ss *The Saturday Evening Post* Feb 8,1947
 73 Logic of Empire, nv *Astounding* Mar,1941
119 The Menace from Earth, ss *F&SF* Aug,1957
143 If This Goes On-, na *Astounding* Feb,1940
279 Coventry, na *Astounding* Jul,1940
327 Misfit, ss *Astounding* Nov,1939

*Perception Barriers Robert Frazier (BPW&P 0-917658-25-6, Aug,87, $5.95, 46pp, tp) Book of poetry, much of it sf-oriented.
Contents:
  7 "Complete disorder is impossible.", pm
  8 Perception Barriers, pm *IASFM* Dec,1985
  9 The Anorexic, pm
 10 The Anorexic Speaks Out On May Day, pm
 11 The Anorexic Poses for Giacometti, pm
 12 Children's Lesson at Loines Observatory, pm *IASFM* Dec,1984
 13 Postmarked: the Crab Nebula, pm
 14 Doppler Effects, pm *IASFM* Feb,1985
 15 Relative Distances, pm *Amazing* Mar,1987
 16 A Human Nerve Cell, pm
 17 Rest Stops in the Sawing of a Log, pm
 19 "The eternal form eludes us.", pm
 20 Ed White, Spacewalking, June 3, 1965, pm *IASFM* May,1985
 21 Loren Eiseley's Time Passages, pm *IASFM* mid-Dec,1982
 22 The Vexation of Percival Lowell's Sight, pm *IASFM* Jul,1984
 23 Johannes Kepler and His Cosmic Mystery, pm *IASFM* Mar,1983
 24 The First Spacewoman: An Inquiry, pm *IASFM* mid-Dec,1984
 25 Twinned Stars: Newton & Halley, pm *
 26 A Still from the Mead Collection, pm *IASFM* Jan,1984
 27 Marie Curie Contemplating the Role of Women Scientists in the Glow of a Beaker, pm *IASFM* mid-Dec,1983
 28 Quasars, Black Holes, and Maarten Schmidt's Bad Day at the Office, pm *Arc* Spr,1985
 29 Dream Tables, pm
 30 "We cannot escape humility.", pm *F&SF* Nov,1983
 31 The Supremacy of Bacteria [revised from *IASFM* Aug,83], pm **Light Years and Dark**, ed. Michael Bishop, Berkley,1984
 32 Arbitrating Neptune's Complaint, pm *Analog* mid-Dec,1985
 33 A Quotella for Ted Sturgeon, pm *IASFM* Jan,1986
 34 "A mathematical formula is a hymn of the universe.", pm *
 35 A Starpilot Muses on the Universal Tidal Pool, pm *IASFM* Aug,1986
 36 The William Carlos Williams Variations, pm *Arc* Spr,1985
 37 Cetacean Dreams, pm **Light Years and Dark**, ed. Michael Bishop, Berkley,1984
 38 Telephone Ghosts, pm *Pig Iron* #10,1982
 40 Flash Sleep, pm **Night Visions**,1981
 42 Black Ice, pm
 43 July 16, 1945, 5:29:45 AM, Mountain War Time, pm *IASFM* Oct,1986
 44 Past Light, pm *IASFM* Jun,1986

PULPSMITH

*A Quiver Of Ghosts** Aidan Chambers, ed. (Bodley Head 0-370-31008-X, Mar,87 [Sep,87], £3.95, 137pp, tp) Original juvenile ghost anthology.
Contents:

*Ready or Not: Here Come Fourteen Frightening Stories!** Joan Kahn, ed. (Greenwillow 0-688-07167-8, Aug,87 [Oct,87], $11.75, 159pp, hc) Young adult anthology of 14 horror stories. Most, but not all, are supernatural.
Contents:

*The Rebel Dynasty, Volume I** F.M. Busby (Bantam Spectra 0-553-26954-2, Dec,87 [Nov,87], $4.95, 443pp, pb) Omnibus of two space opera novels, **Star Rebel** (Bantam 1984) and **Rebel's Quest** (Bantam 1984), in the "Holzein Dynasty" series. Busby writes some of the best modern space opera. Recommended. (CNB)
Contents:

*The Rebel Dynasty, Volume II** F.M. Busby (Bantam Spectra 0-553-26988-7, Jan,88 [Dec,87], $4.95, 475pp, pb) Omnibus edition of **The Alien Debt** (Bantam 1984) and **Rebel's Seed** (Bantam 1986), two parts of the "Holzein Dynasty" space opera series.
Contents:

*Red Sun of Darkover** Marion Zimmer Bradley & The Friends of Darkover (DAW 0-88677-230-3, Nov,87 [Oct,87], $3.95, 287pp, pb) Original shared world anthology of Darkover stories including two pieces by Bradley.
Contents:

*Retief: Envoy to New Worlds** Keith Laumer (Baen 0-671-65635-X, Apr,87 [Mar,87], $2.95, 245pp, pb) Collection of Retief stories which includes the six stories from **Envoy to New Worlds** (Ace 1963) plus "Rank Injustice" (which first appeared in **New Destinies** earlier this year). To add to the confusion, five of the six **Envoy** stories appeared along with a short novel as **Retief Unbound** (Ace 1979).
Contents:

*Rhysling Anthology 1987** Anonymous, ed. (SF Poetry Assc. no ISBN, Sep,87, $2.00, 30pp, ph) Anthology of sf poetry, finalists for the 1987 Rhysling Awards.
Contents:

*Robert Adams' Book of Alternate Worlds** Robert Adams, Pamela Crippen Adams & Martin H. Greenberg, eds. (NAL/Signet 0-451-14894-0, Jul,87 [Jun,87], $3.95, 366pp, pb) Anthology of 9 alternate-world stories, both sf and fantasy.
Contents:

ROD SERLING'S THE TWILIGHT ZONE MAGAZINE

Rod Serling's The Twilight Zone Magazine [v.7 #2, June 1987] Tappan King, ed. (TZ Publications, $2.50, 102pp, pb)
Contents:

Rod Serling's The Twilight Zone Magazine [v.7 #3, August 1987] Tappan King, ed. (TZ Publications, $2.50, 102pp, pb)
Contents:

ROD SERLING'S THE TWILIGHT ZONE MAGAZINE

Rod Serling's The Twilight Zone Magazine [v.7 #4, October 1987] Tappan King, ed. (TZ Publications, $2.50, 102pp, pb)
Contents:

ROD SERLING'S THE TWILIGHT ZONE MAGAZINE

SCARED STIFF: TALES OF SEX AND DEATH

SCARS

SHADOWS 10

*Scars** Richard Christian Matheson (Scream/Press 0-910489-15-7, Aug,87 [Oct,87], $20.00, 168pp, hc) Collection of 27 fantasy and horror stories, including 9 originals. Foreword by Stephen King, introduction by Dennis Etchison, and illustrations by Harry O. Morris.
Contents:
    i Foreword, Stephen King, fw
    v Introduction, Dennis Etchison, in
    1 Third Wind, ss **Masques** #1, ed. J.N. Williamson,1984
  11 The Good Always Come Back, ss *Twilight Zone* Apr,1986
  17 Sentences, ss **Death**, ed. Stuart David Schiff, Playboy,1982
  29 Unknown Drives, ss **Nightmares**, ed. Charles L. Grant, Playboy,1979
  35 Timed Exposure, ss *
  39 Obsolete, ss *
  41 Red, vi *Night Cry* v1#6,1986
  45 Beholder, ss **Whispers** #4, ed. Stuart David Schiff,1983
  53 Dead End, ss **Shadows** #2, ed. Charles L. Grant,1979
  63 Commuters, ss *
  67 Graduation, ss *Whispers* #10,1977
  83 Conversation Piece, ss **Whispers** #2, ed. Stuart David Schiff,1979
  91 Echoes, ss *The Horror Show* Win,1986
  95 Incorporation, ss *
  99 Hell, ss *
 105 Break-Up, ss *
 109 Mr. Right, vi *Whispers* #21,1984
 113 Cancelled, vi *Twilight Zone* Jun,1986
 123 Mugger, ss *
 127 The Dark Ones, vi *Twilight Zone* Jun,1982
 129 Holiday, ss *Twilight Zone* Feb,1982
 137 Vampire, ss **Cutting Edge**, ed. Dennis Etchison, Doubleday,1986
 141 Intruder, ss *Gallery* Sep,1986
 145 Dust, ss *
 149 Goosebumps, ss *
 157 Mobius, ss *
 161 Where There's a Will, Richard Christian Matheson & Richard Matheson, ss **Dark Forces**, ed. Kirby McCauley, Viking,1980

*The Second Great Dune Trilogy** Frank Herbert (Gollancz 0-575-04018-1, Apr,87, £10.95, 1111pp, hc) Omnibus edition of the last three "Dune" novels.
Contents:
    7 **God Emperor of Dune**, n. Gollancz: London,1981
 355 **Heretics of Dune**, n. Gollancz: London,1984
 737 **Chapterhouse Dune**, n. Gollancz: London,1985

*Secrets of the Deep** Gordon R. Dickson (Critic's Choice 0-931773-29-6, Oct,85 [Apr,87], $2.95, 288pp, pb) Omnibus of 3 juvenile sf adventure books. This actually first appeared in 10/85, but we missed listing it.
Contents:
    Secret Under the Sea, n. Henry Holt,1960
    Secret Under Antarctica, n. Holt, Rinehart & Winston: New York,1963
    Secret Under the Caribbean, n. Holt, Rinehart & Winston: New York,1964

*Selected Tales of Grim and Grue from the Horror Pulps** Sheldon R. Jaffery, ed. (Bowling Green Popular Press 0-87972-392-0, Aug,87 [Oct,87], $15.95, 195pp, tp) Anthology of 8 stories from the horror pulps, offset from the magazines -- including illos and ads. There is also an index to Weird Menace pulps and an article about them. Also announced in hardcover; not seen.
Contents:
xiii Preface, Sheldon R. Jaffery, pr
    1 Popular's Weird Menace Pulps, Robert Kenneth Jones, ar **The Weird Menace**, Opar Press,1972
    9 Index to Weird Menace Pulps, Robert Kenneth Jones, ix **The Weird Menace**, Opar Press,1972
  35 Issue by issue index to *Ace Mystery, Eerie Mysteries, Eerie Stories* and *Uncanny Tales*, ix
  40 Arms of the Flame Goddess, Francis James, nv *Dime Mystery Magazine* Apr,1938
  64 Death Tolls the Bell, Hugh B. Cave, nv *Terror Tales* Jul,1935
  96 The Buyer of Souls, John H. Knox, nv *Horror Stories* Aug,1936
 116 The Tongueless Horror, Wyatt Blassingame, nv *Dime Mystery Magazine* Apr,1934
 134 Sleep With Me--And Death, Wayne Rogers, nv *Horror Stories* Apr,1938

 153 Moulder of Monsters, G.T. Fleming-Roberts, ss *Terror Tales* Jul,1937
 164 Dance of the Damned, Arthur J. Burks, nv *Horror Stories* Aug,1936
 180 Corpses on Parade, Edith Jacobson & Ejler Jacobson, nv *Dime Mystery Magazine* Apr,1938

*Serpent's Egg** R.A. Lafferty (Morrigan 1-870338-15-4, Aug,87, £27.50, 177pp, hc) Fantasy novel mixing Lafferty's quirky Catholic fundamentalism with clones, robots, and a strange unknown sentient race on a future Earth. 250 copy limited edition, includes an extra story.
Contents:
    1 **Serpent's Egg**, n.,1987
 167 Gray Ghost: A Reminiscence, ss,1987

*SF International** [No. 1, January/February 1987] William H. Wheeler, ed. (Andromeda Press, $2.50, 96pp, 5.25 x 8.25 pb)
Contents:
    4 Editor's Note, William H. Wheeler, ed *
    5 The Sing, Steve Rasnic Tem & Melanie Tem, ss *
  14 The End of the Hunt, Uwe Luserke, ss *
  22 A Little Piece of Home, Dorothy Davies, ss *
  26 Leakage, Wim Burkunk, ss *
     Translated by Annemarie van Ewyck.
  33 Take Your Choice, Sakyo Komatsu, ss *
     Translated by Shiro Tamura & Grania Davis.
  47 Kool Running, Paul Collins, ss *
  55 Camels for Calvin, Annemarie van Ewyck, ss *
  64 Happy Birthday, Kim White, Kathe Koja, ss *
  71 Touchvision, Manuel van Loggem, ss *
  77 A Ribbon for Margaret's Doll, Dragan R. Filipovic, ss *
     Translated by Mire Adzic.
  84 Through the Fifth Dimension, Konrad R. Fialkowski, ss *
     Translated by Stanley G. Rud.

*SF International** [No. 2, March/April 1987] William H. Wheeler, ed. (Andromeda Press, $2.50, 110pp, 5.25 x 8.25 pb)
Contents:
    5 Third Generation, Stephanie Taylor, ss *
  25 What Avails a Psalm in the Cinders of Gehenna?, Tais Teng, ss *
  40 Susi's Lovely World, Eduardo Julio Carletti, ss *
  47 Fun and Games, Irmtraud Kremp, ss *
  55 S.O.S., Kathinka Lannoy, ss *
  60 Jailhouse Blues, Dragan R. Filipovic, ss *
  67 Contaminated People, Sergio Gaut vel Hartman, ss *
  75 Narcissus Flower, Gerben Hellinga, Jr., ss *
  79 The Mercenary, Antonio Bellomi, ss *
  88 Paradise, E. Veronica Figueiredo, ss *
  95 The Well, Nancy Mortensen, ss *
 104 The Black Ship, Gerd Maximovic, ss *

*The Shadow on the Doorstep/Trilobyte** James P. Blaylock & Edward Bryant (Axolotl 0-939879-16-6, Aug,87, $30.00, 14 + 27pp, hc) Back-to-back "double" with a short story by Blaylock (originally published in *Asimov's*) and 3 very short stories by Bryant (these appear to be original despite a 1986 copyright). Signed, limited edition of 300 copies; a deluxe leatherbound was also announced at $65.00.
Contents:
    Introduction to "The Shadow on the Doorstep", Lewis Shiner, in
    1 The Shadow on the Doorstep, James P. Blaylock, ss *IASFM* May,1986
    Introduction, Tim Powers, in
    1 An Easter Treasure, Edward Bryant, ss **Trilobyte/The Shadow on the Doorstep**, Edward Bryant & James P. Blaylock, Seattle: Axolotl,1987
    9 Coon Dawgs, Edward Bryant, ss **Trilobyte/The Shadow on the Doorstep**, Edward Bryant & James P. Blaylock, Seattle: Axolotl,1987
  17 Drummer's Star, Edward Bryant, ss **Trilobyte/The Shadow on the Doorstep**, Edward Bryant & James P. Blaylock, Seattle: Axolotl,1987

*Shadows 10** Charles L. Grant, ed. (Doubleday 0-385-23893-2, Oct,87, $12.95, 178pp, hc) Original anthology of 14 horror stories.
Contents:
 vii Introduction, Charles L. Grant, in
    1 Jamie's Grave, Lisa Tuttle, ss *
  17 Apples, Nina Downey Higgins, ss *
  26 A World Without Toys, T.M. Wright, ss *

SHADOWS 10   SPACE & TIME

SPACE & TIME

114 Open Orbit, The Readers, lt *

Space & Time [#73, Winter 1988] Gordon Linzner, ed. (Space & Time, $4.00, 120pp, 5.5 x 8.5 pb)
Contents:
  2 The Editor's Page, Gordon Linzner, ed *
  4 Your Soul to Keep, K.H. Nelson, ss *
 12 Blood and Tears, Manny Parsonson, nv *
 30 To Not Return, Steve Eng, pm *
 31 An Application to Succeed, Sharon Bailly, ss *
 36 The Master of Time, J. John Chevalier, ss *
 43 Celestian Grapevine, Bruce Boston, pm *
 44 Metal, Like Rain, Michael Ponder, ss *
 54 Windham's Folly, G. Wayne Miller, ss *
 60 Unborn, Richard Toelly, pm *
 61 The Imp in the Bottle, John Salonia & Traci Salonia, ss *
 76 Cauldron of Rain, Fred Behrendt, pm *
 83 Porcinity's Palace, Walter F. Mercadel, ss *
 88 Con-Notations, ms *
 89 The Smoking Mirror, R.E. Klein, ss *
102 Mr. Valdoom's Backyard, John Wayne Burt, ss *
114 Open Orbit, The Readers, lt *
116 The Scent of Roses, Robert Sampson, ss *

A Spaceship Built of Stone and Other Stories Lisa Tuttle (Women's Press 0-7043-4084-4, Aug,87, £4.50, 192pp, tp) Sf collection.
Contents:
  1 No Regrets, nv *F&SF* May,1985
 25 Wives, ss *F&SF* Dec,1979
 35 The Family Monkey, na **New Voices in Science Fiction** #1, ed. George R.R. Martin,1977
 77 Mrs. T, ss *Amazing* Sep,1976
 87 The Bone Flute, ss *F&SF* May,1981
105 A Spaceship Built of Stone, ss *IASFM* Sep,1980
123 The Cure, ss **Light Years and Dark**, ed. Michael Bishop, Berkley,1984
135 The Hollow Man, nv **New Voices in Science Fiction** #2, ed. George R.R. Martin,1979
165 The Other Kind, ss *IASFM* Dec,1984
183 Birds of the Moon, ss *Fantastic* Jan,1979

Spaceships and Spells Jane Yolen, Martin H. Greenberg & Charles G. Waugh, eds. (Harper & Row 0-06-026796-8, Nov,87, $12.95, 182pp, hc) Original anthology of 13 juvenile sf and fantasy stories.
Contents:
  3 Introduction, Jane Yolen, in
  5 A Wish Named Arnold, Charles de Lint, ss *
 16 The Improper Princess, Patricia C. Wrede, ss *
 36 Watch Out!, Bruce Coville, ss *
 41 The Silver Leopard, Robert Lawson, ss *
 47 Truce, Anne Eliot Crompton, ss *
 59 The Fable of the Three Princes, Isaac Asimov, nv *
 85 Little Green Men, Barry B. Longyear, ss *
 92 Selena's Song, Elyse Guttenberg, ss *
107 The King's Dragon, Jane Yolen, ss *
111 Voices in the Wind, Elizabeth S. Helfman, ss *
123 Beneath Their Blue, Blue Skins, John Forrester, nv *
145 Bear at the Gate, Jessica Amanda Salmonson, ss *
149 What Are You Going to Be When You Grow Up?, Gregory Benford, nv *
180 About the Authors, bg

Spellsinger's Scherzo Alan Dean Foster (SFBC #10611, May,87, $7.98, 661pp, hc) Second omnibus of three novels in the "Spellsinger" fantasy series.
Contents:
   The Moment of the Magician, n. Phantasia: West Bloomfield, MI hc Sep,1984
   The Paths of the Perambulator, n. Phantasia: West Bloomfield, MI hc Nov,1985
   The Time of the Transference, n. Phantasia: West Bloomfield, MI hc Aug,1986

The Stalking Robert Faulcon (Arrow 0-09-930440-6, Jul,87, £3.50, 400pp, pb) Omnibus edition of the first two books in the "Night Hunter" series. Billed as "Robert Holdstock writing as Robert Faulcon".
Contents:
  1 **The Stalking**, n. Arrow Books: London,1983
201 **The Talisman**, n. Arrow Books: London,1983

The Star Wars Trilogy George Lucas, Donald F. Glut & James Kahn (Ballantine/Del Rey 0-345-34806-0, May,87, $8.95, 471pp, tp) Omnibus of the three film novelizations from *Star Wars*, a "special tenth-anniversary edition."
Contents:
   Star Wars, George Lucas, n. Ballantine: New York,1976
   The Empire Strikes Back, Donald F. Glut, n. Ballantine: New York,1980
   Return of the Jedi, James Kahn, n. Ballantine: New York,1983

The Stories of Muriel Spark Muriel Spark (Bodley Head 0-370-31020-9, Apr,87 [Oct,87], £12.95, 314pp, hc) Collection of short stories, some with a supernatural element.
Contents:
  1 The Portobello Road, nv *Cosmopolitan*,1958
 21 The Curtain Blown by the Breeze, ss
 34 The Black Madonna, ss
 52 Bang-Bang You're Dead, nv
 77 The Seraph and the Zambesi, ss
 85 The Twins, ss
 94 The Playhouse Called Remarkable, ss
104 The Pawnbroker's Wife, ss
111 Miss Pinkerton's Apocalypse, ss,1958
121 'A Sad Tale's Best for Winter', ss
127 The Leaf-Sweeper, ss,1966
133 Daisy Overend, ss
141 You Should Have Seen the Mess, ss
147 Come Along, Marjorie, ss
158 The Ormolu Clock, ss *New Yorker* Sep 17,1960
167 The Dark Glasses, ss
180 A Member of the Family, ss *Mademoiselle* Feb,1961
192 The House of the Famous Poet, ss *New Yorker* Apr 2,1966
200 The Fathers' Daughters, ss
211 Alice Long's Dachshunds, na *New Yorker* Apr 1,1967
263 The First Year of My Life, ss *New Yorker* Jun 2,1975
270 The Gentile Jewesses, ss *New Yorker* Jun 22,1963
277 The Executor, ss *New Yorker* Mar 14,1983
285 The Fortune-Teller, ss *New Yorker* Jan 17,1983
295 The Another Pair of Hands, ss *New Yorker* May 13,1985
305 The Dragon, ss *New Yorker* Aug 12,1985

Strange Maine Charles G. Waugh, Martin H. Greenberg & Frank D. McSherry, Jr., eds. (Tapley 0-912769-10-6, Oct,86 [Jan,87], $9.95, 295pp, tp) Anthology of sf, fantasy, and horror stories set in Maine, with works by King, Leiber, Pangborn, etc.
Contents:
  7 The Children of Noah, Richard Matheson, ss *Alfred Hitchcock's Mystery Magazine* Mar,1957
 23 The Phantom Farmhouse, Seabury Quinn, nv *Weird Tales* Oct,1923
 45 Longtooth, Edgar Pangborn, nv *F&SF* Jan,1970
 77 One for the Road, Stephen King, ss *Maine* Mar,1977
 93 Four Dreams of Gram Perkins, Ruth Sawyer, ss *The American Mercury* Oct,1926
105 Circumstance, Harriet Prescott Spofford, ss *Atlantic Monthly* May,1860
115 The Last Cruise of the Judas Iscariot, Edward Page Mitchell, ss *The Sun* Apr 16,1882
123 The Prevaricator, Carlos Baker, ss **The Talismans and Other Stories**,1976
137 One Old Man, with Seals, Jane Yolen, ss **Neptune Rising**, Philomel,1982
145 Safe Harbor, Donald Wismer, nv **Tin Stars**, ed. Isaac Asimov, Martin H. Greenberg & Charles G. Waugh, NAL/Signet,1986
165 Mood Wendigo, Thomas A. Easton, ss *Analog* May,1980
177 Death Is a White Rabbit, Fredric Brown, nv *Strange Detective Mysteries* Jan,1942
195 Yesterday House, Fritz Leiber, nv *Galaxy* Aug,1952
219 Three Day Magic, Charlotte Armstrong, na *F&SF* Sep,1952
    A shorter version was first printed in 1948.
293 Notes on the Authors, bg

The Stranger Gordon R. Dickson (Tor 0-812-53579-0, Mar,87 [Feb,87], $2.95, 254pp, pb) Sf collection of 14 stories, mostly from the Fifties and early Sixties.
Contents:
  9 God Bless Them, nv **The Best of Omni** #3,1982
 41 James, ss *F&SF* May,1955
 48 E Gubling Dow, ss *Satellite* May,1959

THE STRANGER   TAKEOFF TOO!

The Supernatural Short Stories of Sir Walter Scott Sir Walter Scott (Riverrun/Calder 0-7145-4086-2, Oct,86 [Jan,87], $8.95, 217pp, tp) Reprint (Calder 1977) collection of ghost stories edited by Michael Hayes. Published in 1986; missed. This is a universal edition, published in England with names of UK, US, and Canadian publishers; distributed in the US by Kampmann.
Contents:

*****Supernatural Tales: Excursions Into Fantasy** Vernon Lee (Peter Owen 0-7206-0680-2, Feb,87, £10.95, 222pp, hc) Collection of 6 supernatural stories set in different periods in Italian history. This is a pseudonym for Violet Paget. Available in the US from DuFour Editions for $18.95.
Contents:

*****Supertanks** Joe W. Haldeman, Martin H. Greenberg & Charles G. Waugh, eds. (Ace 0-441-79106-9, Apr,87 [Mar,87], $3.50, 262pp, pb) Anthology of 10 sf tank stories including the shorter (and better) version of **Damnation Alley** by Roger Zelazny.
Contents:

*****Sword and Sorceress IV** Marion Zimmer Bradley, ed. (DAW 0-88677-210-9, Jul,87 [Jun,87], $3.50, 285pp, pb) Original anthology of 18 fantasy stories, by both seasoned professionals and new writers.
Contents:

Swords of Shahrazar Robert E. Howard (Ace 0-441-79237-5, Nov,87 [Oct,87], $2.95, 165pp, pb) Reprint (Berkley 1978) collection of 5 quasi-fantasy/adventure stories. An expansion of an earlier 3-story collection under the same title (Orbit 1976).
Contents:

*****Synergy; New Science Fiction: Vol. 1** George Zebrowski, ed. (Harcourt Brace Jovanovich 0-15-687700-7, Nov,87, $5.95, 234pp, tp) Original anthology of 6 stories, a poem, and an article on sf. The centerpiece is a novella by Frederik Pohl, "My Life as a Born-Again Pig".
Contents:

*****Takeoff Too!** Randall Garrett (Donning/Starblaze 0-89865-455-6, Apr,87, $7.95, 311pp, tp) A second volume of sf parodies and pastiches, following **Takeoff**. Introduction and afterword by Vicki Ann Heydron, who made the selections and tells why.
Contents:

TAKEOFF TOO!

281 Our Patrol, sg,1978
282 ...Or Your Money Back [as by David Gordon], ss *Astounding* Sep,1959
300 I've Got a Little List, pm *F&SF* Nov,1953
302 An Evening In, Vicki Ann Heydron, ar **Moments of Love**, New York: Bantam,1979
307 Appendix--Key to "I've Got a Little List", ms

*Tales From Isaac Asimov's Science Fiction Magazine Sheila Williams & Cynthia Manson, eds. (Harcourt Brace Jovanovich 0-15-284209-8, Oct,86 [Mar,87], $15.95, 298pp, hc) Young-adult anthology of 17 stories from *Asimov's*; introduction by Isaac Asimov. This has a 1986 copyright, but we did not see it until 1987.
Contents:
 vii Introduction, Isaac Asimov, in
  1 The Amber Frog, Stephanie A. Smith, nv *IASFM* Sep,1984
 23 The Anatomy Lesson, Scott Russell Sanders, ss *IASFM* Oct 26,1981
 31 The First Day, Art Vesity, ss *IASFM* Sep,1982
 43 The Forever Summer, Ronald Anthony Cross, nv *IASFM* Mar,1983
 75 The High Test, Frederik Pohl, ss *IASFM* Jun,1983
 91 A Letter from the Clearys, Connie Willis, ss *IASFM* Jul,1982
107 Playing for Keeps, Jack C. Haldeman, II, ss *IASFM* May,1982
115 Potential, Isaac Asimov, ss *IASFM* Feb,1983
127 Power Times One, J. Michael Matuszewicz, ss *IASFM* Feb,1983
137 The Random Man, Marc Laidlaw, vi *IASFM* Jul,1984
143 Realtime, Gladys Prebehalla & Daniel Keys Moran, nv *IASFM* Aug,1984
193 Shrinker, Pamela Sargent, nv *IASFM* Nov,1983
221 Someone Else's House, Lee Chisholm, nv *IASFM* Mar,1979
243 Speech Sounds, Octavia E. Butler, ss *IASFM* mid-Dec,1983
263 Tank, Francis E. Izzo, ss *IASFM* Mar,1979
273 Things That Go Quack in the Night, Lewis Shiner & Edith Shiner, ss *IASFM* Jan,1983
289 Wet Behind the Ears, Jack C. Haldeman, II, ss *IASFM* Oct,1982

*Tales from the Flat Earth: Night's Daughter Tanith Lee (SFBC #11345, Oct,87, $14.98, 2 vols, 601pp, hc) Omnibus edition of two books in the "Flat Earth" fantasy series, **Delirium's Mistress** (DAW 1986) and **Night's Sorceries** (DAW 1987). Part of a two-volume set.
Contents:
  1 **Delirium's Mistress**, n. DAW: New York,1986
355 **Night's Sorceries**, n. DAW: New York,1987

*Tales from the Flat Earth: The Lords of Darkness Tanith Lee (SFBC #11360, Oct,87, $14.98, 2 vol.s, 726pp, hc) Omnibus edition of 3 books from the "Flat Earth" fantasy series: **Night's Master** (DAW 1978), **Death's Master** (DAW 1979), and **Delusion's Master** (DAW 1981). Part of a two-volume set.
Contents:
  1 **Night's Master**, n. DAW: New York,1978
193 **Death's Master**, n. DAW: New York,1979
541 **Delusion's Master**, n. DAW: New York,1981

*Tales from the Forbidden Planet Roz Kaveney, ed. (Titan 1-85286-004-9, Aug,87, £4.95, 256pp, tp) Original sf anthology. This is supposedly published on 29th October, but was made available for the Worldcon and is now in most specialist shops.
Contents:
  9 Introduction, Roz Kaveney, in
 13 Tourney, Brian W. Aldiss, ss *
 27 Equivalent for Giles, Keith Roberts, ss *
 45 The Interferences, Josephine Saxton, ss *
 65 The Earth is Flat and We're All Like to Drown, Garry Kilworth, ss *
 75 Tithing Night, Louise Cooper, ss *
 95 Another World, Ramsey Campbell, ss *
111 By Crystal Light Beneath One Star, Tanith Lee, nv *
133 Descendant, Iain Banks, nv *
159 Mushroom Roulette, Jody Scott, ss *
173 A Birthday, Lisa Tuttle, ss *
187 Ni Venos, Doktoro Zamenof, Ni Venos!, Harry Harrison, ss *
199 The Snow Apples, Gwyneth Jones, ss *
215 A Case of Painter's Ear, John Brunner, ss *
231 The Murderer's Song, Michael Moorcock, nv *

*Tales of Narnia C.S. Lewis (Collins 0-00-184294-3, Dec,87, £4.95, 543pp, hc) Juvenile fantasy omnibus. Printed for, and distributed by, W.H. Smith only.

Contents:
  7 **The Lion, the Witch and the Wardrobe**, n. The Blakiston Co.: Philadelphia,1950
174 **Prince Caspian**, n. The Blakiston Co.: Philadelphia,1951
357 **The Voyage of the Dawn Treader**, n. The Blakiston Co.: Philadelphia,1952

*Tales of Natural and Unnatural Catastrophes Patricia Highsmith (Bloomsbury 0-7475-0097-5, Dec,87, £11.95, 189pp, hc) Original literary sf/occult collection.
Contents:
  9 The Mysterious Cemetery, ss *
 20 Moby Dick II; or The Missile Whale, ss *
 34 Operation Balsam; or Touch-Me-Not, ss *
 53 Nabuti: Warm Welcome to a UN Committee, ss *
 67 Sweet Freedom! and a Picnic on the White House Lawn, ss *
 82 Trouble at the Jade Towers, nv *
107 Rent-a-Womb vs. The Mighty Right, ss *
127 No End in Sight, ss *
140 Sixtus VI, Pope of the Red Slipper, nv *
162 President Buck Jones Rallies and Waves the Flag, nv *

*Tales of the Dark Lincoln Child, ed. (St. Martin's 0-312-90339-1, Jul,87 [Jun,87], $3.50, 184pp, pb) Anthology of 10 horror stories.
Contents:
 vii Introduction, Lincoln Child, in
  1 The Fall of the House of Usher, Edgar Allan Poe, ss *Burton's Gentlemen's Magazine* Sep,1839
 19 The Signalman [from "Mugby Junction"], Charles Dickens, ss *All the Year Round* Chr,1866
 33 Green Tea, Joseph Sheridan Le Fanu, nv *All the Year Round* Oct 23,1869
 63 The Squaw, Bram Stoker, ss,1893
 75 Markheim, Robert Louis Stevenson, ss *The Broken Shaft, Unwin's Annual* Chr,1885; *Ellery Queen's Mystery Magazine* Jul,1955
 91 The Upper Berth, F. Marion Crawford, nv *The Broken Shaft, Unwin's Annual*,1886
113 The Yellow Wallpaper, Charlotte Perkins Gilman, ss *New England Magazine* Jan,1892
129 "They", Rudyard Kipling, nv *Scribner's* Aug,1904
152 The Yellow Sign, Robert W. Chambers, nv **The King in Yellow**, New York & Chicago: F. Tennyson Neely,1895
172 The Voice in the Night, William Hope Hodgson, ss *Blue Book* Nov,1907

*Tales of the Dark 2 Lincoln Child, ed. (St. Martin's 0-312-90769-9, Sep,87 [Aug,87], $3.50, 181pp, pb) Anthology of 9 late-19th and early-20th-century supernatural stories.
Contents:
 vii Introduction, Lincoln Child, in
  1 The Dead Hand, William Wilkie Collins, nv
 28 The Damned Thing, Ambrose Bierce, ss **Can Such Things Be?**, Cassell: New York,1893; *Weird Tales* Sep,1923
 39 Man-Size in Marble, Edith Nesbit, ss,1886
 56 The Leather Funnel, Arthur Conan Doyle, ss *The Strand* Jun,1903
 71 Mr. Humphreys and His Inheritance, M.R. James, nv **More Ghost Stories of an Antiquary**, Arnold,1911
103 The Novel of the White Powder [also as "The White Powder"], Arthur Machen, nv **The Three Impostors**, John Lane,1895
124 The Flowering of the Strange Orchid [also as "The Strange Orchid"], H.G. Wells, nv *Pall Mall Budget* Aug,1894
134 The Empty House, Algernon Blackwood, ss **The Empty House**, Eveleigh Nash,1906
155 Benlian, Oliver Onions, nv **Widdershins**, Secker,1911
178 A Note on the Authors, bg

*Tales of the Unanticipated [#2, Spring 1987] Eric M. Heideman, ed. (Minnesota Science Fiction Society, $2.50, 48pp, 8.5 x 11 pb)
Contents:
  2 Little Magazine That Could, Eric M. Heideman, ed *
  3 The Beach Poet, Terry A. Garey, ed *
  4 Contributors, bg
  5 Readers' Forum, The Readers, lt *
  6 Writing With Percission: Cooking Salmon in the Dishwasher: Nontraditional Computer Use for Science Fiction and Fantasy Writers, Part 1, Dan Goodman, ar *
  8 Glam's Story, Eleanor Arnason, ss *
 14 Mirror Trick, Janet Fox, ss *
 18 Free Day, Peg Kerr, ss *

TALES OF THE UNANTICIPATED

*Tales of the Witch World Andre Norton, ed. (Tor 0-312-94475-6, Sep,87 [Aug,87], $15.95, 343pp, hc) Original shared-world anthology set in Norton's Witch World.
Contents:

*Tarot Piers Anthony (Ace 0-441-79841-1, Nov,87 [Oct,87], $8.95, 616pp, tp) Omnibus edition of a fantasy trilogy: **God of Tarot** (Jove 1979), **Vision of Tarot** (Berkley 1980), and **Faith of Tarot** (Berkley 1980); they're combined, with new, continuous chapter numbering.
Contents:

*Tatja Grimm's World Vernor Vinge (Baen 0-671-65336-9, Jul,87 [Jun,87], $3.50, 277pp, pb) Collects 3 Tatja stories. The last 2 were previously published together as **Grimm's World** (Berkley 1969).
Contents:

*Terry Carr's Best Science Fiction and Fantasy of the Year #16 Terry Carr, ed. (Tor 0-312-93025-9, Sep,87 [Aug,87], $17.95, 402pp, hc) Anthology of 11 stories, plus a summary of the sf year by *Locus* editor Charles N. Brown.
Contents:

*Tesseracts 2 Phyllis Gotlieb & Douglas Barbour, eds. (Porcepic 0-88878-270-5, Nov,87, C$9.95, 295pp, tp) Mostly original anthology of 23 Canadian sf stories, including some appearing in English for the first time.

THERE WILL BE WAR, VOL. VI: GUNS OF DARKNESS

Contents:

*Test of Honor Lois McMaster Bujold (SFBC #10681, May,87, $7.98, 473pp, hc) Omnibus edition of related sf adventure novels.
Contents:

*There Will Be War, Vol. VI: Guns of Darkness Jerry E. Pournelle, ed. (Tor 0-812-54961-9, Jun,87 [May,87], $3.95, 406pp, pb) Anthology of both fiction and non-fiction work on war; 12 of the 24 items are original.
Contents:

*Thieves' World 10: Aftermath Robert Lynn Asprin & Lynn Abbey, eds. (Ace 0-441-80597-3, Nov,87 [Oct,87], $3.50, 273pp, pb) Original anthology of 6 stories, latest in the "Thieves' World" fantasy shared world series.
Contents:
    x Dramatis Personae, Lynn Abbey, pr
    1 Introduction, Robert Lynn Asprin, in
    5 Cade, Mark C. Perry, nv *
  54 Wake of the Riddler, Janet Morris, nv *
  95 Inheritor, David Drake, na *
168 Mercy Worse Than None, John Brunner, nv *
199 Seeing Is Believing (But Love Is Blind), Lynn Abbey, nv *
233 Homecoming, Andrew J. Offutt, nv *

*The Third Book of After Midnight Stories Amy Myers, ed. (Kimber 0-7183-0667-8, Oct,87, £9.50, 208pp, hc) Original ghost/occult anthology.
Contents:
    9 The Thin People, Brian Lumley, ss *Whispers* #23,1987
  22 The Neapolitan Bedroom, Alma Priestley, ss *
  40 Moving Day, R. Chetwynd-Hayes, ss *
  57 Element of Doubt, A.L. Barker, ss *
  70 The Manse, J.C. Trewin, ss *
  84 Waiting for a Bus, John Whitbourn, ss *
  93 The Band in the Park, Jean Stubbs, ss **Ghost Book** #11, ed. Aidan Chambers/James Turner,1975
110 The Indian's Grave, Ross McKay, ss *
118 Warm as Snow, Mike Sims, ss *
129 Meeting Mr. Singleton, Derek Stanford, ss *
140 The Neighbours, Meg Buxton, ss *
154 The Whisperer, John Marsh, ss *
169 Mandrake, Kelvin I. Jones, ss *
182 Swing High, Willie Brodie, Fred Urquhart, ss *
198 The Nine Lessons and Carols, Lanyon Jones, ss *
205 Notes on the Contributors, bg

*Timeliner Trilogy Richard C. Meredith (Arrow 0-09-951690-X, Aug,87, £3.95, 712pp, pb) Sf omnibus. Volume 14 in the Venture SF series. [First U.K. edition]
Contents:
    1 **At the Narrow Passage**, n. Putnam: New York,1973
241 **No Brother, No Friend**, n. Doubleday: Garden City, NY,1976
477 **Vestiges of Time**, n. Doubleday: Garden City, NY,1978

*To Marry Medusa Theodore Sturgeon (Baen 0-671-65370-9, Dec,87 [Nov,87], $2.95, 251pp, pb) Collection of two stories, "To Marry Medusa" (1958) and "Killdozer" (1944). The former is actually a reprint of **The Cosmic Rape** (Dell 1958) instead of "To Marry Medusa" (*Galaxy* 1958). The magazine version was much shorter.
Contents:
    1 **To Marry Medusa** [**The Cosmic Rape**], n. Dell: New York pb Aug,1958
        Expanded from "To Marry Medusa" *Galaxy* Aug,58.
165 Killdozer!, na *Astounding* Nov,1944

*A Touch of Sturgeon Theodore Sturgeon (Simon & Schuster UK 0-671-65526-4, Aug,87 [Jul,87], £10.95, 235pp, hc) Collection of 8 stories. Published in Britain only, by the British arm of Simon & Schuster. Available in U.S. as an import. Selected and introduced by David Pringle.
Contents:
 vii Introduction, David Pringle, in
    1 Killdozer!, na *Astounding* Nov,1944
  63 The Sex Opposite, nv *Fantastic* Fll,1952
  87 Mr. Costello, Hero, nv *Galaxy* Dec,1953
110 The Golden Helix, na *Thrilling Wonder Stories* Sum,1954
159 When You're Smiling, nv *Galaxy* Jan,1955
183 And Now the News..., ss *F&SF* Dec,1956
201 The Other Celia, ss *Galaxy* Mar,1957
217 Slow Sculpture, nv *Galaxy* Feb,1970

*A Trick of the Light Jackie Vivelo (Putnam 0-399-21468-2, Oct,87, $13.95, 124pp, hc) Collection of 9 juvenile mystery/horror stories, subtitled "Stories to Read at Dusk".
Contents:
    9 Reading to Matthew, ss *
  25 The Girl Who Painted Raindrops, ss *
  41 A Dog Names Ransom, ss *
  59 Night Vision, ss *

  71 A Game of Statues, ss *
  83 The Children of Winter, ss *
  95 The Fireside Book of Ghost Stories, ss *
107 A Plague of Crowders, Or, Birds of a Feather, ss *
117 Take Your Best Shot, ss *

*True Names and Other Dangers Vernor Vinge (Baen 0-671-65363-6, Nov,87 [Oct,87], $2.95, 275pp, pb) Collection of 5 stories (one a collaboration with Joan D. Vinge), plus author's notes.
Contents:
    1 Bookworm, Run!, nv *Analog* Mar,1966
  47 True Names, na **Binary Star** #5,1981
144 The Peddler's Apprentice, Vernor Vinge & Joan D. Vinge, nv *Analog* Aug,1975
198 The Ungoverned, nv **Far Frontiers** v3, ed. Jerry Pournelle & Jim Baen,1985
255 Long Shot, ss *Analog* Aug,1972

*Twisted Circuits Mick Gowar, ed. (Beaver 0-09-943400-8, Jan,87, £1.75, 144pp, pb) Original juvenile sf anthology.
Contents:
    7 Editor's Foreword, Mick Gowar, in
    9 Closer than a Brother, Jan Mark, ss *
  25 Love Bytes, Nicholas Fisk, ss *
  41 User-Friendly, John Gordon, ss *
  55 Krarg Enters, Dennis Hamley, ss *
  73 Rent-a-Joke, Marjorie Darke, ss *
  93 Wordfinder, Adele Geras, ss *
108 The Computer Game, Phil Cartwright, ss *
125 Hello, Hugo, Laurence Staig, ss *

*Twisted Tales Bruce Jones (Blackthorne 0-932629-73-3, Sep,87 [Aug,87], $9.95, 243pp, tp) Collection of 13 horror stories, mostly originals, illustrated by Richard Corben. There's also supposed to be a mass market edition (not seen).
Contents:
    1 The Waiting Game, ss *
  19 Roomers, ss *
  33 The Hollow, ss *
  53 Pride of the Fleet, ss **Swords Against Darkness** #1, ed. Andrew J. Offutt,1977
  71 Jessie's Friend, ss *
  87 Over His Head, ss *
103 Black Death, ss *
115 Cycle, ss *
131 Good Neighbor, ss *
145 Children of the Stars, nv *
171 The Apartment, ss *
183 Rendezvous, nv *
213 Members Only, nv *

*Ultra-Vue and Selected Peripheral Visions Rudin Moore (self published no ISBN, Aug,87 [Jul,87], price unknown, 389pp, tp) Collection of five original fantasy stories. Order from Gary Smith (Rudin Moore), 715 SW Bay St., Newport OR 97365.
Contents:
    1 A Ceres Situation, ss *
  17 Hit Me, nv *
  41 Wait a Minute!, ss *
  51 The Hoodoo, na *
101 **Ultra-Vue**, n. *

*The Universe Byron Preiss, ed. (Bantam Spectra 0-553-05227-6, Nov,87 [Oct,87], $27.95, 333pp, hc) Original anthology of sf stories, science articles, and illustrations by numerous space artists.
Contents:
    7 Frontier, Byron Preiss, pr
  12 The Universe: An Introduction, Andrew Fraknoi, in
  20 What Is the Universe?, Isaac Asimov, ar *
  25 Art and Science Fiction: Unbuilt Cities/Unrealized Dreams, Ray Bradbury, ar *
  34 Our Galaxy, Eric J. Chaisson, ar *
  48 Mandikini, Gregory Benford, ss *
  68 Starbirth and Maturity, Martin Cohen, ar *
  81 To Touch a Star, Ben Bova, ss *
  98 Supernovae: Creative Cataclysms in the Galaxy, David J. Helfand, ar *
115 The Iron Star, Robert Silverberg, ss *
136 The Black Hole, William J. Kaufmann, ar *

A WARNING TO THE CURIOUS: THE GHOST STORIES OF...

Way of the Pilgrim Gordon R. Dickson (Ace 0-441-87486-X, May,87 [Apr,87], $16.95, 341pp, hc) Sf novel of Earth conquered by giant aliens.
Contents:

Weirdbook 22 [Summer 1987] W. Paul Ganley, ed. (W. Paul Ganley, $6.00, 62pp, pb)
Contents:

The Weirds Sheldon R. Jaffery, ed. (Starmont House 0-930261-92-5, Apr,87, $9.95, 173pp, tp) Anthology of facsimiles of stories, illustrations, and some ads from "the era of the shudder-pulps." These have all been taken from *Terror Stories* and *Horror Stories*. There is a historical introduction on the era.
Contents:

Werewolf: Horror Stories of the Man Beast Peter Haining, ed. (Severn House 0-7278-1465-6, Sep,87 [Oct,87], £9.95, 250pp, hc) Horror anthology.
Contents:

WHO'S AFRAID? AND OTHER STRANGE STORIES

Whispers [#23/24, v.6 #3-4, October 1987] Stuart David Schiff, ed. (Stuart David Schiff, $8.95, 176pp, pb)
Contents:

Whispers VI Stuart David Schiff, ed. (Doubleday 0-385-19927-9, Jul,87, $12.95, 181pp, hc) Original anthology of 15 horror stories.
Contents:

+**Who's Afraid? and Other Strange Stories** Philippa Pearce (Morrow/ Greenwillow 0-688-06895-2, Apr 20,87 [Apr,87], $10.25, 152pp, hc) Collection of young-adult "spooky stories." First U.S. edition (Kestrel Penguin 1986).
Contents:

WHO'S AFRAID? AND OTHER STRANGE STORIES

  121 The Hirn, ss *
  137 The Yellow Ball, ss *

***Why Not You and I?** Karl Edward Wagner (Tor 0-812-52708-9, Sep,87 [Aug,87], $3.95, 306pp, pb) Collection of 9 horror stories, one as by "Curtiss Stryker".
Contents:
    1 Into Whose Hands, nv **Whispers** #4, ed. Stuart David Schiff,1983
   32 Old Loves, ss **Night Visions** #2,1985
   52 More Sinned Against, ss **In a Lonely Place**, Scream/Press,1984
   73 Shrapnel, ss **Night Visions** #2,1985
   86 The Last Wolf, ss *Midnight Sun* #2,1975
   99 Neither Brute Nor Human, nv **World Fantasy Convention Program Book**,1983
  138 Sign of the Salamander, na **John Chance Vs Dread: The Apocalypse 1**,1975
       by Curtiss Stryker, with an Introduction by Kent Allard
  221 Blue Lady, Come Back, na **Night Visions** #2,1985
  295 Silted In, ss *

***Why Not You and I?** Karl Edward Wagner (Dark Harvest 0-913165-25-5, Nov,87 [Oct,87], $34.95, 240pp, hc) Collection of 11 horror stories. It contains all of the stories from the September '87 Tor book of the same title, plus two additional stories, "Lacunae" and "Lost Exits". Full page illustrations by Ron & Val Lakey Lindahn. Limited to 300 signed numbered boxed copies.
Contents:
    1 Neither Brute Nor Human, nv **World Fantasy Convention Program Book**,1983
   27 Into Whose Hands, nv **Whispers** #4, ed. Stuart David Schiff,1983
   48 Old Loves, ss **Night Visions** #2,1985
   62 More Sinned Against, ss **In a Lonely Place**, Scream/Press,1984
   76 Shrapnel, ss **Night Visions** #2,1985
   85 The Last Wolf, ss *Midnight Sun* #2,1975
   95 Sign of the Salamander, na **John Chance Vs Dread: The Apocalypse 1**,1975
       by Curtiss Stryker, with an Introduction by Kent Allard
  149 Blue Lady, Come Back, na **Night Visions** #2,1985
  198 Lacunae, ss **Cutting Edge**, ed. Dennis Etchison, Doubleday,1986
  209 Lost Exits, ss *
  217 Silted In, ss **Why Not You and I?**, Tor,1987

***Wild Cards II: Aces High** George R.R. Martin, ed. (Bantam Spectra 0-553-26464-8, Apr,87 [Mar,87], $3.95, 390pp, pb) Original anthology/braided sf mega-novel, part of a series. There are 9 or 10 connected stories, but no contents page.
Contents:
    3 Pennies from Hell, Lewis Shiner, nv *
   33 Jube: One, George R.R. Martin, sl *
   40 Unto the Sixth Generation: Prologue, Walter Jon Williams, sl *
   43 Jube: Two, George R.R. Martin, sl *
   51 Ashes to Ashes, Roger Zelazny, nv *
   81 Unto the Sixth Generation: Part One, Walter Jon Williams, sl *
  112 Unto the Sixth Generation: Part Two, Walter Jon Williams, sl *
  141 Jube: Three, George R.R. Martin, sl *
  149 If Looks Could Kill, Walton Simons, ss *
  168 Jube: Four, George R.R. Martin, sl *
  173 Unto the Sixth Generation: Epilogue, Walter Jon Williams, sl *
  175 Winter's Chill, George R.R. Martin, nv *
  209 Jube: Five, George R.R. Martin, sl *
  219 Relative Difficulties, Melinda M. Snodgrass, nv *
  260 With a Little Help From His Friends, Victor Milan, nv *
  302 Jube: Six, George R.R. Martin, sl *
  307 By Lost Ways, Pat Cadigan, nv *
  344 Mr. Koyama's Comet, Walter Jon Williams, ss *
  349 Half Past Dead, John J. Miller, nv *
  382 Jube: Seven, George R.R. Martin, sl *

***The Wind From the Sun** Arthur C. Clarke (NAL/Signet 0-451-14754-5, Mar,87 [Feb,87], $3.50, 244pp, pb) A slightly revised edition (3 new vignettes plus a new introduction) of the earlier collection (Harcourt Brace Jovanovich 1972). Even NAL doesn't really consider it a new book, and lists it as the 9th printing of the earlier work. Nevertheless, Clarke completists should note the three new "stories."
Contents:
  vii Preface, pr
   ix Introduction to the 1987 Edition, in
    1 The Food of the Gods, ss *Playboy* May,1964
    7 Maelstrom II, ss *Playboy* Apr,1965

THE YEAR'S BEST HORROR STORIES: XV

   27 The Shining Ones, ss *Playboy* Aug,1964
   50 The Wind from the Sun [Sunjammer], nv *Boy's Life* Mar,1964
   77 The Secret [The Secret of the Men in the Moon], ss *This Week* Aug 11,1963
   85 The Last Command, ss *Bizarre Mystery* Nov,1965
   88 Dial "F" for Frankenstein, ss *Playboy* Jan,1965
   97 Reunion, ss *Infinity* #2, ed. Robert Hoskins,1971
  100 Playback, ss *Playboy* Dec,1966
  104 The Light of Darkness, ss *Playboy* Jun,1966
  113 The Longest Science-Fiction Story Ever Told, ss **The Wind from the Sun**, HBJ,1972
  115 Herbert George Morley Roberts Wells, Esq., ed *If* Dec,1967
  119 Love That Universe, ss *Escapade*,1961
  124 Crusade, ss **The Farthest Reaches**, ed. Joseph Elder, Trident,1968
  131 The Cruel Sky, ss *Boy's Life* Jul + 1,1967
  157 The Neutron Tide, ss *Galaxy* May,1970
  160 Transit of Earth, ss *Playboy* Jan,1971
  179 A Meeting with Medusa, na *Playboy* Dec,1971
  240 When the Twerms Came, vi *Playboy* May,1972
  242 Quarantine, vi *IASFM* Spr,1977
  244 siseneG, vi *Analog* May,1984

***The Woman Who Is the Midnight Wind** Terence M. Green (Pottersfield Press 0-919001-33-5, Apr,87 [Mar,87], C$9.95, 137pp, tp) Collection of 10 stories by a Canadian sf writer.
Contents:
    7 Ashland, Kentucky, nv *IASFM* Nov,1985
   32 Barking Dogs, ss *F&SF* May,1984
   48 Legacy, ss *F&SF* Mar,1985
   53 The Woman Who Is the Midnight Wind, ss **Tesseracts**, ed. Judith Merril, Press Porcepic: Victoria,1985
   66 Room 1786, ss *Leisure Ways* Nov,1982
   69 Japanese Tea, ss **Alien Worlds**, ed. Paul Collins, Void,1979
   84 Susie Q2, ss *IASFM* Aug,1983
  101 Till Death Do Us Part, ss *F&SF* Dec,1981
  117 Point Zero, ss *F&SF* May,1986
  130 Of Children in the Foliage, ss **Aurora: New Canadian Writing 1979**, ed. Morris Wolfe, Doubleday Canada,1979

***The Year Before Yesterday** Brian W. Aldiss (Franklin Watts 0-531-15040-2, Apr,87 [Mar,87], $16.95, 227pp, hc) Sf alternate world novel composed of **Equator** (Brown, Watson 1958) and "The Impossible Smile" (*Science Fantasy* May & June 1965 as by Jael Cracken) plus a new framework.
Contents:
    Equator, n. Brown, Watson: London,1958
    The Impossible Smile [as by Jael Cracken], na *Science Fantasy* May + 1,1965

***The Year's Best Fantasy Stories: 13** Arthur W. Saha, ed. (DAW 0-88677-233-8, Nov,87 [Oct,87], $2.95, 238pp, pb) Anthology of 11 stories from 1986 plus an introduction/summation of the year in fantasy.
Contents:
   11 Introduction, Arthur W. Saha, in
   15 Beauty Is the Beast, Tanith Lee, ss *American Fantasy* Fll,1986
   31 Something in the Blood, Richard L. Purtill, ss *F&SF* Aug,1986
   47 Piece de Resistance, Judith Tarr, nv *IASFM* Apr,1986
   70 Long, Long Ago, R. Chetwynd-Hayes, nv **Tales from the Shadows**, Kimber,1986
   96 The Old Man and the Cherry Tree, Kevin J. Anderson, ss *Grue* #3,1986
  104 Phone Repairs, Nancy Kress, ss *IASFM* Dec,1986
  119 The Tale and Its Master, Michael Rutherford, na Spring Harbor: Delmar, NY,1986
  167 Sanctuary, Kim Antieau, ss **Shadows** #9, ed. Charles L. Grant,1986
  180 The Uncorking of Uncle Finn, Jane Yolen, ss *F&SF* Nov,1986
  188 A Place to Stay for a Little While, Jim Aikin, nv *IASFM* Jun,1986
  223 The Boy Who Plaited Manes, Nancy Springer, ss *F&SF* Oct,1986

***The Year's Best Horror Stories: XV** Karl Edward Wagner, ed. (DAW 0-88677-226-5, Oct,87 [Sep,87], $3.50, 300pp, pb) Anthology of 18 horror stories from 1986.
Contents:
   11 Introduction: What's in a Name?, Karl Edward Wagner, in
   14 The Yougoslaves, Robert Bloch, nv *Night Cry* v1#5,1986

THE YEAR'S BEST HORROR STORIES: XV

*****The Year's Best Science Fiction, Fourth Annual Collection** Gardner R. Dozois, ed. (St. Martin's 0-312-00709-4, May,87 [Apr,87], $19.95, 602pp, hc) Anthology of 27 of the best stories of 1986. Dozois does an excellent job. Recommended. (CNB)
Contents:

*****Young Witches & Warlocks** Isaac Asimov, Martin H. Greenberg & Charles G. Waugh, eds. (Harper & Row 0-06-020183-5, Jul,87, $11.95, 207pp, hc) Juvenile anthology of fantasy stories.
Contents:

[SF IN NON-GENRE PUBLICATIONS]

*[SF in Non-Genre Publications]
Contents:

The Little Blue Pill, Michael Lubow, ss *Playboy* Apr,1987
The Pardoner's Tale, Robert Silverberg, ss *Playboy* Jun,1987
The Egret, Michael Bishop, ss *Playboy* Jun,1987
The Weather's Fine, Harry Turtledove, ss *Playboy* Jul,1987
Sen Yet Babbo & the Heavenly Host, Chet Williamson, ss *Playboy*
    Aug,1987
Glimmer, Glimmer, George Alec Effinger, ss *Playboy* Nov,1987
Dance at the Gym, Marion Zimmer Bradley, ss *The San Francisco*
    Chronicle Sep 17,1987
Sleeping Beauty, Hillel Schwartz, ss *The Short Story Review*
    Win,1987
What It Said, Russell Hoban, ss *Sanity* Jan,1987
Living Donor, Marthayn Pelegrimas, ss *SPWAO Showcase* #6,1987
The Rivalry, Richard Easton, ss *The Virginia Quarterly Review*
    Win,1987

Appendices

1987 Book Summary

It was another record year for science fiction publishing -- the third in a row. Total books published rose to 1675 -- up 12% from the year before. Even more astonishing, it was all in new books (+21%). Reprints actually declined by 1%. A record 177 publishers produced sf and fantasy books. The trade paperback reprint was down 40% -- clearly a format whose time has gone. Trade paperback originals, however, were up 16%, and new mass market books were up by 30% to a record 534 titles. The interesting comparison is that new titles have doubled in a decade, while reissues have remained the same. See graph #1 for a look at this. The leveling off of reprints is especially interesting.

What do we count and not count? Our monthly book list is the basis, of course. Everything counted has appeared there, but not everything appearing there is counted. We exclude foreign books unless they're worldwide editions with an American distributor. We exclude non-sf books by sf authors, science books, non-fiction with only a passing reference to sf, pamphlets, and chapbooks. The list includes 1986 books we did not see until 1987, and 1988 dated books we saw in 1987. When there are simultaneous hardcover and paperback editions, we count both. If we see only one edition, we only count one edition, even though we note the possible existence of the other one in our descriptions. Limited editions with multiple bindings and states are

Cumulative Book Survey

Year	Type	HARDBOUND		TRADE PB		MASS MKT PB		ALL BOOKS		%NEW
1977	New	220	(+18%)			225	(-21%)	445	(-5%)	
	Reprint	95	(-41%)			441	(+36%)	536	(+11%)	
	Total	315	(-9%)			666	(+10%)	981	(+3%)	45%
1978	New	239	(+9%)			289	(+28%)	528	(+19%)	
	Reprint	173	(+82%)			488	(+11%)	661	(+23%)	
	Total	412	(+31%)			777	(+17%)	1189	(+21%)	44%
1979	New	320	(+34%)			365	(+26%)	685	(+30%)	
	Reprint	132	(-24%)			47	(-3%)	603	(-9%)	
	Total	452	(+10%)			836	(+8%)	1288	(+8%)	53%
1980	New	264	(-18%)	43		323		630	(-8%)	
	Reprint	106	(-20%)	62		386		554	(-8%)	
	Total	370	(-18%)	105		709		1184	(-8%)	53%
1981	New	247	(-6%)	35	(-19%)	297	(-8%)	579	(-8%)	
	Reprint	77	(-27%)	54	(-13%)	343	(-11%)	474	(-14%)	
	Total	324	(-12%)	89	(-15%)	640	(-10%)	1053	(-11%)	55%
1982	New	246	(--)	49	(+40%)	277	(-7%)	572	(-1%)	
	Reprint	70	(-9%)	61	(+13%)	344	(--)	475	(--)	
	Total	316	(-2%)	110	(+24%)	621	(-3%)	1047	(-1%)	55%
1983	New	252	(+2%)	69	(+41%)	260	(-6%)	581	(+2%)	
	Reprint	80	(+14%)	61	(--)	363	(+5%)	504	(+6%)	
	Total	332	(+5%)	130	(+18%)	623	(--)	1085	(+4%)	54%
1984	New	270	(+7%)	69	(--)	274	(+5%)	613	(+6%)	
	Reprint	92	(+15%)	76	(+25%)	395	(+9%)	563	(+12%)	
	Total	362	(+9%)	145	(+12%)	669	(+7%)	1176	(+8%)	52%
1985	New	305	(+13%)	78	(+13%)	332	(+21%)	715	(+17%)	
	Reprint	84	(-9%)	106	(+39%)	427	(+8%)	617	(+10%)	
	Total	389	(+7%)	184	(+27%)	759	(+13%)	1332	(+13%)	54%
1986	New	338	(+11%)	97	(+24%)	411	(+24%)	846	(+18%)	
	Reprint	100	(+19%)	100	(-6%)	456	(+7%)	656	(+6%)	
	Total	438	(+13%)	197	(+7%)	867	(+14%)	1502	(+13%)	56%
1987	New	380	(+12%)	112	(+16%)	534	(+30%)	1026	(+21%)	
	Reprint	92	(-8%)	60	(-40%)	497	(+9%)	649	(-1%)	
	Total	472	(+8%)	172	(-12%)	1031	(+19%)	1675	(+12%)	61%

CHART 1: ORIGINAL BOOKS

1987		1987	1986	1985	1984	1983	1982	1981
298	SF Novels	29.0%	34.7%	34.8%	32.4%	32.4%	32.2%	32.3%
352	Fantasy/Hor.	34.3%	31.0%	24.8%	28.1%	25.4%	22.6%	23.5%
(256)	Fantasy	[24.9%	23.9%	23.2%	25.3%	22.0%]		
(96)	Horror	[9.4%	7.2%	1.5%	2.8%	3.5%]		
96	Anthologies	9.4%	8.5%	9.0%	9.3%	9.2%	11.0%	12.8%
76	Collections	7.4%	7.9%	6.7%	8.8%	7.0%	10.8%	9.7%
74	Novelizations	7.0%	2.6%	5.5%	4.9%	6.4%	5.1%	4.5%
69	Ref/History	6.7%	8.1%	10.3%	10.3%	10.1%	8.4%	6.4%
31	Art/Humor	3.0%	3.5%	3.9%	3.3%	1.2%	3.1%	1.0%
25	Omnibus	2.4%	2.6%	2.8%	1.8%	3.1%	3.0%	2.2%
7	Misc.	0.7%	0.9%	2.2%	1.1%	5.1%	3.8%	7.6%

CHART 2: TOP PUBLISHERS -- TOTAL BOOKS

	1987	1986	1985	1984	1983	1982	1981
Putnam/Berkley/Ace	200	212	237	255	222	221	202
Tor	144	137	102	55	47	31	19
Ballantine/Del Rey/etc.	132	105	100	104	108	92	94
Bantam	80	70	77	71	58	42	57
DAW	71	63	85	80	69	67	64
Baen	69	64	57	28	-	-	-
NAL/Signet	65	58	45	28	30	33	25
SFBC	64	59	63	55	61	59	56
Simon & Schuster/Pocket	59	50	38	59	88	81	79
Dell/Delacorte	58	28	21	13	5	14	30
Warner/Pop. Lib. Questar	55	51	29	11	23	10	8

CHART 3: TOP PUBLISHERS -- ORIGINAL BOOKS

	1987	1986	1985	1984	1983	1982	1981	1980
Putnam/Berkley/Ace	119	82	92	84	87	65	84	90
Tor	77	74	54	28	29	24	14	-
Ballantine/Del Rey etc.	57	50	41	40	45	43	32	33
Bantam	51	34	28	30	20	23	26	26
Warner/Pop. Lib.	43	34	18	6	6	7	2	6
Baen	41	43	32	17	-	-	-	-
Simon&Schus./Pocket	39	32	20	29	44	45	49	44
Avon	38	24	17	14	3	8	14	20
DAW	34	29	41	39	42	37	39	38
NAL/Signet	28	34	24	16	16	20	14	15
St. Martin's	27	8	8	11	6	10	7	14
Arbor House	21	24	10	-	6	6	6	3

CHART 4: RECOMMENDED READING

	1987	1986	1985	1984	1983	1982	1981
Tor	16	12	14	1	2	2	-
Bantam	16	9	12	6	5	7	7
Putnam/Berkley/Ace	13	15	22	20	17	12	18
Ballantine/Del Rey	12	10	12	12	10	13	9
Arbor House	9	8	7	3	1	0	2
Doubleday	8	9	7	4	7	7	9
DAW	8	6	9	9	12	9	14
Warner/Pop. Lib.	7	5	4	-	-	1	-
S&S/Pocket	6	-	-	-	-	-	-
Baen	5	10	8	6	-	-	-

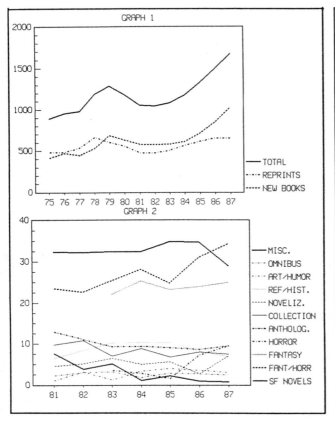

PUBLISHER	HARDCOVER		PAPERBACK		TRADE PB		TOTAL
Total Books Published 1987	New	Reprint	New	Reprint	New	Reprint	
Putnam/Berkley/Ace/etc.	23	-	94	81	2	-	200
Tor	19	1	55	66	3	-	144
Ballantine/Del Rey/etc.	10	1	45	74	2	-	132
Bantam	11	-	38	28	2	1	80
DAW	-	-	34	37	-	-	71
Baen	2	-	39	28	-	-	69
NAL/Signet/Onyx/Plume	4	-	23	37	1	-	65
SFBC	14	50	-	-	-	-	64
Avon	-	-	37	26	1	-	64
S&S/Pocket/etc.	7	1	30	18	2	1	59
Dell/Delacorte	5	-	16	29	-	8	58
Warner/Popular Library	5	-	33	12	5	-	55
St. Martin's	17	1	9	11	1	1	40
Macmillan/Atheneum/etc.	27	1	-	2	1	-	31
Zebra	-	-	23	7	-	-	30
Harper & Row	13	-	-	6	1	6	26
Doubleday	20	1	-	-	1	1	23
Arbor House	20	1	-	-	1	-	22
Viking/Penguin	7	2	1	5	1	5	21
TSR/Windwalker	-	-	14	-	5	-	19
Leisure	-	-	16	3	-	-	19
Carroll & Graf	1	-	1	9	1	1	13
Donning Starblaze	1	-	-	-	10	2	13
Starmont	-	2	-	-	9	1	12
Morrow/Greenwillow	10	2	-	-	-	-	12
Critics' Choice/Bart	-	-	5	6	-	-	11
Franklin Watts/Orchard	10	1	-	-	-	-	11
HBJ/Harvest	6	1	-	1	2	1	11
Scholastic/Apple/Point	-	-	6	4	-	-	10
Houghton Mifflin	5	4	-	-	-	-	9
Quality Paperback Book Club	-	-	-	-	-	9	9
Greenwood	8	-	-	-	-	-	8
Dutton/Philomel	6	1	-	-	-	-	7
ABC-Clio/Windrush/etc.	-	7	-	-	-	-	7
Bridge	5	-	1	-	-	-	6
Crown/Avenel /Bonanza/Harmony	5	1	-	-	-	-	6
Underwood-Miller	6	-	-	-	-	-	6
Congdon & Weed/ Contemporary	6	-	-	-	-	-	6
Methuen/Arkana/Pandora	1	-	-	-	4	-	5
Paperjacks	-	-	3	2	-	-	5
Walker Millennium	5	-	-	-	-	-	5
Random House/Knopf	4	-	-	-	-	1	5
135 misc. publishers	98	14	11	5	57	22	207
TOTAL 177 publishers	**381**	**92**	**534**	**497**	**112**	**60**	**1676**

counted only once unless there are textual differences. Rewritten books are counted as new, but books with minor revisions are counted as reprints. We count first American editions as new books even though we may have mentioned an earlier British one. Omnibus volumes are new even if everything in them has appeared before. If a book is broken down into more volumes, it's considered a reprint unless there is new material.

The difference between "trade" and mass market paperback remains a headache. We have gone back to size as the only criterion. Trade paperbacks are bigger.

The 1026 new books are broken down in Chart 1 by subject. There were 298 sf novels, up slightly from 294 the year before, although their percentage of the total dropped. The fantasy/horror combination finally passed sf. There were 352 novels, up from 263 last year. Horror showed the largest growth and will be broken out completely next year. See Graph #2 for a visual look at this information.

The 298 sf novels can be broken down as follows: Juveniles: 38; First Novels: 36 (up from 27 last year); Romance Sf: 3; Post-Holocaust Survivalist Adventure: 37; Translation: 3; Literary Sf: 3; Sf horror: 6. The biggest jump was in the survivalist novels (only 18 last year). The sf horror category is relatively new. These books are not counted in the fantasy/horror category. 123, or 41%, of the sf novels were parts of series or set in an already used universe.

There were 256 fantasy novels (not counting horror), up from 202 last year. Yes, fantasy is still growing. The breakdown is as follows: Juvenile: 52; First Novels: 23; Romance: 6; Ghost Stories: 10; Translations: 7; Literary Fantasy: 15. 123, or 48%, were parts of series — not much different from the sf figures.

In the horror category, 8 of the 96 were parts of series, and 1 was

a first novel.

The number of novelizations was way up (to 74 from 22 last year) because we count anything written from a "bible" or a continuation of someone else's work as a novelization. Thus, the total includes 12 "Robotech" novels, 10 "Star Trek" novels, 3 Conans, 5 "Dungeons and Dragons" scenarios, Charles Platt's sequel to a Piers Anthony series, "Thieves' World" novels, "Hell" novels, and the various novels based on worlds of Asimov, Zelazny, and Clarke.

The 96 anthologies (up from 72 last year) included 35 with mostly original stories — 13 fantasy, 6 horror, and 16 sf. 18 of them were shared-world series.

There were 72 collections — up from 67 last year. 18 were horror and 12 had original stories. 7 had linked stories and were quasi-novels.

There was exactly the same number of reference books published as the year before: 69. The rest of the categories were essentially the same.

The percentages information in Chart 1 allows you to compare the relative categories year by year. Horror has grown phenomenally in the last two years and will probably continue. The novelization category will probably also continue to grow, as more series are written in other authors' backgrounds. See graph 2 for a visual look at all this.

Charts 2 and 3 give the top publishers for total and original books. There have only been minor changes in order since last year. DAW passed Baen in total books again; Dell/Delacorte came back on the list thanks to a strong juvenile reprint program; Pocket is back up there (almost to the Timescape days) thanks to "Star Trek", horror, and some of the strangest juvenile series around. Only the leader, Berkley Publishing, did fewer total books this year, and they more than made up for it by doing many more new books. Their percentage of new books to total went from 39% to 60% — second only to Bantam's 64% among the leading publishers. The downside of the Berkley original expansion is the dropping of more than 100 Ace titles from their backlist. Baen Books published more titles but fewer originals as their backlist reissue program started. St. Martin's, besides buying Tor, started an agressive sf program of their own. NAL dropped significantly in new title production because of a low inventory. It should improve next year.

The leading publisher of hardcover originals, Macmillan/Atheneum/MacElderry/Scribners/etc., didn't do enough total titles to make the chart, but they published 27 original juveniles in the sf or fantasy field, followed by more traditional sf hardcover publishers Putnam's (23), Arbor House (20), Doubleday (20), and Tor (19).

It's difficult to make any judgement about relative quality of publishers, so of course we've tried it in Chart 4, which shows the number of *Locus* Recommended books (see pages 406-408). Tor and Bantam come higher than original and total book leader Berkley. The surprise to me is the upsurge in S&S/Pocket and the fewer Baen titles even though they went down in original books published. S&S has been moving into the "big" book field with Barker, Bradley, McCammon, and their sf list in the U.K. Perhaps someday they'll even have an sf imprint again. We recommended a record 165 books this year — about 16% of the total published. 55 publishers had titles on the final list.

Chart 5 should show which publishers dominated which recommended category and the rates of recommended to published books. As usual, it is left as an exercise to the reader.

Finally, Charts 6 and 7 attempt to show something about commercial success. They show "bestseller month" per publisher. We keep the chains separate from the Locus list because the buying patterns are different. Del Rey still leads both lists, but not by the commanding number they had several years ago. They've improved their standing on the *Locus* list from 18.4% to 20.1%, as usual split about evenly between hardcovers and paperbacks. TSR, thanks to "Dragonlance", and Bridge, thanks to L. Ron Hubbard's dekalogy, have seriously cut into Del Rey's domination in Waldenbooks and B. Dalton's. Neither publisher has done well in the specialty stores which form the major basis for the Locus list.

Putnam/Berkley improved their standing on the *Locus* list from 17.5% to 18.2%, thanks to the new Ace/Putnam hardcovers. They lost out in the chains, dropping from 12% to 8.6% because of TSR, Bridge, and Pocket's "Star Trek" program. "Star Trek"

improved Pocket's bestseller standing on both lists. Tor dropped quite a bit on both lists — from 13.6% to 11.2% on the *Locus* list, and from 7.8 to a dismal 2.4% on the chain list, in spite of having many more recommended books this year. Bantam improved quite a bit on the *Locus* list, but was almost knocked off the chain list, dropping from 7.3% to 3.4%. Arbor House hung onto fifth place in the *Locus* list and increased its percentage from 6.8% to 8.5%. (Note: on the lists, trade paperbacks are considered hardcover. The "pb" column is for mass market paperbacks only.) The major bestseller changes this year are at the chains, where Bridge dominated the hardcover list, TSR the trade paperback list, and Pocket's "Star Trek" series the mass market paperback list.

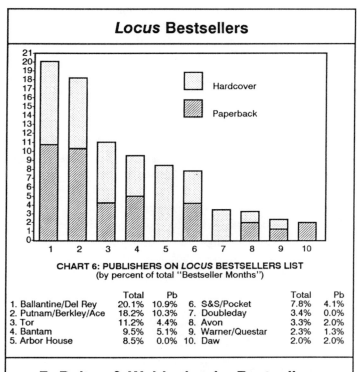

CHART 6: PUBLISHERS ON *LOCUS* BESTSELLERS LIST
(by percent of total "Bestseller Months")

	Total	Pb			Total	Pb
1. Ballantine/Del Rey	20.1%	10.9%	6.	S&S/Pocket	7.8%	4.1%
2. Putnam/Berkley/Ace	18.2%	10.3%	7.	Doubleday	3.4%	0.0%
3. Tor	11.2%	4.4%	8.	Avon	3.3%	2.0%
4. Bantam	9.5%	5.1%	9.	Warner/Questar	2.3%	1.3%
5. Arbor House	8.5%	0.0%	10.	Daw	2.0%	2.0%

B. Dalton & Waldenbooks Bestsellers

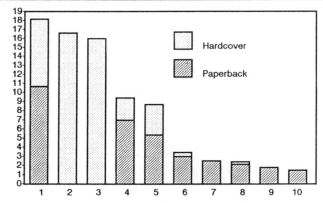

CHART 7: B. DALTON & WALDENBOOKS BESTSELLERS
(by percent of total "Bestseller Months")

	Total	Pb			Total	Pb
1. Ballantine/Del Rey	18.1%	10.7%	6.	Bantam	3.4%	3.0%
2. TSR	16.5%	0.0%	7.	Daw	2.5%	2.5%
3. Bridge	16.0%	0.0%	8.	Tor	2.4%	2.2%
4. S&S/Pocket	9.4%	7.0%	9.	NAL/Signet	1.8%	1.8%
5. Putnam/Berkley/Ace	8.6%	5.4%	10.	Avon	1.7%	1.7%

1987 Magazine Summary

Not much that was good happened in the professional magazine field in 1987. *Night Cry* and *Far Frontiers* disappeared (the latter was replaced by **Destinies**, which we consider an anthology series instead of a magazine). Circulations were mostly flat, with variations up or down under 5%. Another announced magazine, *sf*, was cancelled almost immediately. There were some interesting developments in the semiprofessional and fanzine fields (see below). In other words, it was the same as usual.

Amazing

This was Patrick Lucien Price's first full year as editor. Martin H. Greenberg is Editorial Consultant, and there is a bewildering, ever-changing array of assistant editors and editorial assistants. The closest thing to an editorial is an opinion page by Robert Silverberg. The circulation remained awful. The publisher can easily double or triple the circulation by doing a direct mail campaign or a subscription drive through Publishers Clearing House. They are still unconvinced it is worth it. The magazine has good, varied covers -- although too many were very dark. The non-fiction to fiction ratio seems too high, although I appreciate some of the critical articles. It was an ok year for the magazine. It needs more readers to survive.

Analog

As usual, the best work in *Analog* was the longer material — serials by Niven, Turtledove, and Bujold, plus novellas by many others. The magazine looks good and has the easiest to read text, thanks to its two-column format. *Analog* has the highest circulation of the all-fiction magazines, and some of the best artwork.

Asimov's

For the first time since 1983, the overall circulation of *Asimov's* didn't drop, although it now has the worst newsstand circulation of any of the professional magazines ever. It had the most well written fiction and some of the best science fiction stories published during 1987. It also had some of the worst covers, some of the best critical essays (by Norman Spinrad), a fascinating look at **I, Robot** by Harlan Ellison, and the most non-sf stories in a science fiction magazine. Easily the most lively of the magazines. It should, however, be renamed *Gardner Dozois' Almost Science Fiction Magazine*, to abide by truth in advertising.

F&SF

The circulation dropped again and is now the lowest it has ever been. The magazine went through a redesign with the October issue, but the cover design — the one item which should be radically different — is nearly unchanged. I may or may not get used to the thin, airy type inside. Orson Scott Card has been added as a book recommender — not quite a reviewer. The high points in the magazine are in the fantasy short stories. *Asimov's* seems to have taken over the powerful novelettes that

used to be here. Still an excellent magazine which should have a much higher circulation.

Night Cry

There were only 3 1987 issues of *Night Cry* before the magazine was suspended. The publisher apparently felt it was not worth the investment to try and build a subscription list the way they did with *Twilight Zone*. I'm not sure I disagree. A pure horror digest magazine may be too specialized.

The Twilight Zone

Although the circulation dropped slightly, it was a good year for the magazine. It looks excellent, has interesting, varied, contents, and just needs more promotion to build circulation. Associate Editor (and *Night Cry* editor) Alan Rodgers has left to pursue a full-time writing career.

Omni

There were 29 fiction pieces in *Omni* this year, thanks to a theme collection of 8 short-shorts. The circulation went up less than 1%, but that's still 7,000 copies. *Omni* is a magazine that prints one or two sf stories each issue and is *very* successful. I don't think they would be as successful if they did more fiction, and suspect the fiction is the last thing read — if it's read at all.

Quality

On the *Locus* Recommended Reading List for short fiction (see page 35), there are 41 stories from *IASFM* — more than all the other magazines put together! *F&SF* had 16 recommended stories, *Omni* 9 (but *Omni* only published 28 stories!), *Analog* 3, *Amazing* 3, *Interzone* 2, and *Night Cry* 1.

Conclusions

The professional sf magazines are probably doomed. The golden era of the all-fiction magazine ran from 1900 to 1950, with only the sf and mystery digests surviving into the present. Most of today's readers grew up with the paperback book, and go there first for entertainment. They buy short fiction in collections and anthologies and are mostly uninterested in the personality and continuity that are the mainstays of magazines. Even among *Locus* readers, less than half read any of the sf magazines. But in the long run, we're all dead anyway, so the problem is how to apply geriatrics and cosmetics to the magazine field now. Paperback publishers have found that price is *not* a major consideration in buying books. In fact, readers expect to pay more for better material. The magazines should be priced the same as paperbacks — $3.50 on an average, $3.95 if they have something special. There should be something special almost every issue — special anniversary issue, special author issue, special awards issue, etc. *Analog*, *Twilight Zone*, and *Omni* deliver what they promise on the cover. *Asimov's* and *F&SF* desperately need new cover packages. The magazines should also steal a leaf from the successful **Writers of the Future** and stress contests, prizes, new!

improved! writers!, etc. People don't *read* a magazine until after they pick it up and buy it. Quality contents will keep readers, but advertising, glitzy covers (metallic ink, embossing, etc.) and hype are needed to get them there in the first place. As shown by the circulation graphs, newsstand sales are dismal and getting worse. The problem is that subscription drives don't seem to impress people who are unfamiliar with the magazine. You convert newsstand buyers to subscribers, and your newsstand distribution drops. Perhaps more giveaways and freebies of back issues would help. I'm also a fan of the mixed media, large size, multi-graphic package. *Omni* and *TZ* come close. A large-size fantasy/horror magazine might also work. Will anybody try it? After all, all it takes is money.

The Semi-Professional Magazines

We define Semi-Professional magazines as fiction magazines which have no national newsstand circulation (but do have bookstore sales), have circulation under 10,000, but are otherwise professional. They have color covers, publish primarily fiction, pay at least 2 cents a word on acceptance, have circulation in the thousands, not hundreds, and appear at least quarterly. Others are irregular serials, small press magazines, or fanzines.

Interzone is the most interesting of them. It had four excellent issues in 1987. Alas, after more than five years, it still apparently has a circulation under 3,000. It's supported by a British Arts Council grant and run on a volunteer basis, but it needs and deserves more readers.

Aboriginal Sf produced 5 issues in 1987 and switched from an 11" x 17" tabloid format to an 8.5" x 11" size. They published half a dozen short stories per issue plus the usual magazine features. They're doing well and plan to go to slick paper in 1988, raising the single-copy price to $3.00. The editor seems happy with the

way things are going now, and says there are another 1,500 subscriptions not yet entered. They print 11,000 copies of each issue and, as you can see by the figures, sell about half. The 11" x 17" format didn't work because of display problems and a reluctance by advertisers to try a new size. If *Abo* can raise its paid circulation to 10,000, we'll move it to the professional category even without newsstand distribution.

Fantasy Book published one 1987 issue before suspending publication. The editors vow to return, but I'd be somewhat surprised. After 5 years, they still only had a 2,500-copy circulation. The magazine was obviously going nowhere.

Aphelion, an Australian semi-pro magazine, threw in the towel after the fifth issue.

Whispers amd *Fantasy Tales* each produced one excellent issue in 1987 and are thus classified as "irregular serials."

Weird Tales was revived but is dated 1988 so will be discussed next year, even though it appeared in October 1987.

Another 1988 dated magazine which came out late in 1987 was *Argos F&SF*. It was an unannounced surprise — and a very pleasant one, with a near-professional look. We'll see what the next year brings.

American Fantasy is an oddity in that it doesn't have a coherent approach to subject matter. There's a bit of fiction, some interviews, some artwork, some reviews, etc. The reproduction is excellent, but it has more of the feel of a scrapbook than a magazine. It produced three issues dated 1987.

Small Press, etc.

Laserjet printing and computer typesetting have brought forth a number of small press and/or amateur fiction magazines/ fanzines. Most of the new ones have been in the horror field — apparently fertile ground for new writers. See our monthly magazine lists for information on *The Horror Show*, *Grue*, *2 AM*,

---

CURRENT PUBLICATION DATA FOR ACTIVE PROFESSIONAL FICTION MAGAZINES

Amazing Stories — Bimonthly, $1.75 per copy.
Patrick L. Price — editor.
Editorial address — P.O. Box 110, Lake Geneva WI 53147.
Subscriptions — $9 per year (6 issues) in U.S. & Canada;
    $25 surface mail, $50 air mail, elsewhere.

Analog — 13 issues/year, $2.00 per copy.
Stanley Schmidt — editor.
Editorial address — 380 Lexington Ave., New York NY
    10017.
Subscription address — P.O. Box 1936, Marion OH 43305.
Subscriptions — $19.50 per year in U.S.; $24.20 elsewhere.

Isaac Asimov's SF Magazine — 13 issues/ year, $2.00 per
    copy.
Gardner Dozois — editor.
Editorial address — 380 Lexington Ave., New York NY 10017.
Subscription address — Box 1933, Marion OH 43305.
Subscriptions — $19.50 per year in U.S.; $24.20 elsewhere.

Fantasy & Science Fiction — Monthly, $1.75 per copy.
Edward L. Ferman — editor.
Editorial address — Box 56, Cornwall CT 06753.
Subscription address — same.
Subscriptions — $19.50 per year in U.S.; $23.50 elsewhere.

Omni — Monthly, $3.00 per copy.
Ellen Datlow — fiction editor.
Editorial address — 1965 Broadway, New York NY 10023.
Subscription address — Box 3026, Harlan IA 51537.
Subscriptions — $24.00 per year in U.S.; $28.00 elsewhere.

Twilight Zone — Bimonthly, $2.50 per copy.
Tappan King — editor.
Editorial address — 800 Second Ave., New York NY 10017.
Subscription address — P.O. Box 252, Mount Morris IL
    61054.
Subscriptions — $15.50 per year (6 issues) in U.S.; $18.50
    elsewhere.

Eldritch Tales, etc. On the science fiction side, *New Pathways* was the most consistently interesting.

The critical field almost improved in 1987. *Short Form*, a critical fanzine on short fiction, had one issue out of 4 scheduled. *Science Fiction Eye* managed 2 late issues out of 3 announced. *Thrust* went quarterly but failed to produce a fourth issue. All have vowed, older and wiser, to do better next year. They all discovered that putting out a regularly scheduled magazine is a full-time job.

Fantasy Review, sold to a professional newsletter publisher, was suspended. The field is only open to fanatics who don't care about profits.

The resurrected *Australian Science Fiction Review* produced 6 thin, scrappy issues. It's still looking for a coherent voice. I don't think it's possible for a collectively edited magazine.

The British semi-academic magazine *Foundation* produced 3 issues and was easily the best in the field. The two straight academic journals, *Science Fiction Studies* and *Extrapolation*, each produced 3 issues of varying interest.

—*Charles N. Brown*

PROFESSIONAL MAGAZINES
ISSUES PUBLISHED (ALL FICTION ONLY)

TITLE	1987
Amazing	6
Analog	13
Fantasy & Science Fiction	12
Isaac Asimov's SF Magazine	13
Night Cry	3
The Twilight Zone	6
Total Issues Published	53

TOTAL ISSUES

Year	Fiction Titles	Issues
1987	6	53
1986	7	57
1985	7	58
1984	5	50
1983	5	50
1982	7	61
1981	8	59
1980	8	49
1979	9	57
1978	10	55
1977	13	73
1976	10	71
1975	10	89
1974	13	109
1973	13	88
1972	10	72
1971	22	82

TEN YEAR CIRCULATION FIGURES

Year	Subscriptions	Newsstand Sales	Returns	%Newsstand Sale	Paid Circulation	Paid Circ. Change
Aboriginal SF						
1987	4,021	883	168	84%	4,904	--
Amazing						
1978	1,522	21,262	42,096	34%	22,784	-11.4%
1979	1,397	20,935	43,188	33%	22,332	-1.9%
1980	900	16,439	48,661	25%	17,339	-22.4%
1981	750	17,034	34,489	33%	17,784	+2.5%
1982	900	10,600	31,000	25%	11,500	-35.0%
1983	1,236	10,050	22,913	30%	11,286	-1.8%
1984	1,861	9,069	17,545	34%	10,931	-3.1%
1985	2,252	10,071	16,233	38%	12,323	+12.7%
1986	2,416	10,767	17,116	39%	13,183	+7.0%
1987	2,603	11,074	18,998	37%	13,677	+3.7%
Analog						
1978	49,820	54,792	66,117	45%	104,612	-3.7%
1979	45,000	45,000	------	---	90,000	-14.0%
1980	59,000	45,000	------	---	104,000	+14.1%
1981	53,846	38,548	70,951	35%	92,394	-11.2%
1982	65,171	34,731	61,023	36%	99,902	+8.1%
1983	81,971	27,838	58,583	32%	109,809	+9.9%
1984	74,124	22,613	62,162	27%	96,739	-11.9%
1985	75,967	21,217	60,653	26%	97,184	+0.5%
1986	78,123	20,000	51,809	28%	98,123	+1.0%
1987	77,844	19,365	46,587	29%	97,209	-0.9%
Isaac Asimov's Science Fiction Magazine						
1978	42,095	66,748	83,742	44%	108,843	--
1979	46,330	48,429	93,402	34%	94,759	-12.9%
1980	59,000	30,000	------	---	89,000	-6.1%
1981	79,164	23,905	70,303	25%	103,069	+15.8%
1982	66,445	19,200	48,674	28%	85,645	-16.9%
1983	88,818	16,369	41,191	28%	105,187	+22.8%
1984	83,931	12,105	44,216	21%	96,036	-8.7%
1985	71,915	11,933	37,365	24%	83,848	-12.7%
1986	69,011	10,378	30,389	25%	79,389	-5.3%
1987	71,356	9,970	29,244	25%	81,326	+2.4%
The Magazine of Fantasy & Science Fiction						
1978	34,676	23,242	44,316	34%	57,900	0%
1979	36,775	20,953	45,854	31%	57,728	-3.0%
1980	40,272	21,799	42,382	34%	62,071	+7.5%
1981	41,132	19,101	39,085	33%	60,233	-3.0%
1982	44,865	16,863	32,850	34%	61,721	+2.5%
1983	47,799	14,507	26,103	36%	62,306	+0.9%
1984	44,164	13,819	21,808	39%	57,983	-6.9
1985	40,072	14,177	21,972	39%	54,249	-6.4%
1986	42,672	13,798	17,790	44%	56,470	+4.1%
1987	39,878	13,012	16,011	45%	52,890	-6.3%
Locus						
1977	2,809	379	3	99%	3,188	+27.3%
1978	3,235	601	5	99%	3,836	+20.3%
1979	3,480	1,015	7	99%	4,495	+17.2%
1980	3,592	1,336	29	98%	4,928	+9.6%
1981	3,670	1,253	60	95%	4,924	--
1982	3,836	1,292	13	99%	5,128	+4.1%
1983	4,047	1,891	58	97%	5,938	+15.8%
1984	4,319	2,472	64	97%	6,791	+14.3%
1985	4,440	2,820	89	97%	7,260	+6.9%
1986	4,413	2,909	91	97%	7,322	+0.9%
1987	4,590	3,066	176	95%	7,656	+4.6%
Omni						
1979	89,218	670,630	268,423	71%	759,848	--
1980	172,238	670,801	314,318	68%	843,039	+10.9%
1981	211,755	552,155	426,727	56%	763,910	-9.4%
1982	205,078	548,098	384,100	59%	753,176	-1.4%
1983	318,179	478,908	325,745	60%	797,087	+5.8%
1984	467,971	369,029	371,448	50%	837,00	+5.0%
1985	566,191	337,358	231,116	59%	903,549	+8.0%
1986	621,239	281,775	281,885	50%	903,014	--
1987	625,530	284,705	276,089	51%	910,235	+0.8%
Rod Serling's The Twilight Zone Magazine						
1981	1,859	52,196	137,423	28%	54,055	--
1982	6,145	46,561	116,141	29%	52,706	-2.5%
1983	25,237	37,168	99,024	27%	62,405	+18.4%
1984	94,317	31,325	83,369	27%	126,111	+102.1%
1985	73,799	26,971	76,555	26%	100,770	-20.1%
1986	68,252	26,550	75,546	26%	94,802	-5.9%
1987	63,840	24,471	78,692	24%	88,31	-6.8%

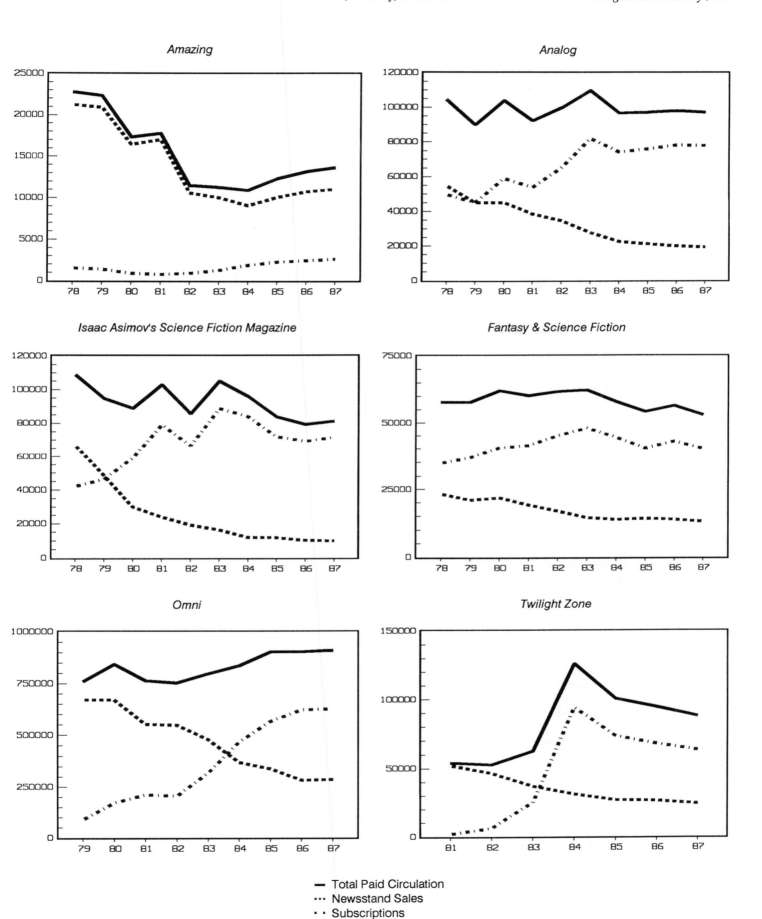

Total Paid Circulation
Newsstand Sales
Subscriptions

Cinema Summary by Frank M. Robinson

This year's film grosses hit new highs but had mixed results as far as science fiction and fantasy films went. Total grosses hit around $4.2 billion, with the number of feature films totalling 511 – the highest such total since 1970. Unfortunately, only two films in the Top 10 were fantasy or science fiction-oriented, though six of the top 25 qualified.

But first, a discussion of what constitutes the "Top 10". *Variety* and *USA Today* list only those films released in the calendar year. *The Hollywood Reporter* lists those in the calendar year plus Christmas releases from the year before. The latter seems fairer to me – Christmas releases, usually major blockbusters, seldom make enough in the last few weeks of their calendar year to be listed in the Top 10 and are then excluded from the following year's Top 10 since they were released the year before. Which means some of our largest-grossing films never make it into the Top 10. Makes no sense to me, so from now on I'll be including Christmas releases from the year before.

The only sf and fantasy films to make the Top 10 this year were *The Golden Child* (number 4 at $79.8 million gross), an Eddie Murphy thriller and the first recent film to capitalize on Hollywood's current fascination with the inscrutable East, and *The Witches of Eastwick* (number 9 at $63.7 million), starring Jack Nicholson as the Devil, with Cher, Susan Sarandon, and Michelle Pfeiffer as his willing but eventually rebellious handmaidens.

Top grossing film of the year was *Beverly Hills Cop II* ($153.6 million), followed by *Platoon* ($137.9 million), *Fatal Attraction* ($123.5 million), *The Untouchables* ($76.2 million), *The Secret of My Success* ($67 million), *Stakeout* ($65.4 million), *Lethal Weapon* ($65.1 million), and *Three Men and a Baby* ($59.5 million). *Three Men and a Baby* and *Fatal Attraction* were still in release – and among the Top 10 – and their final tallies will be considerably higher.

The Golden Child and *Platoon* were Christmas releases from last year and will not show up on a number of Top 10 lists. For those who are curious, *Star Trek IV: The Voyage Home*, which was *not* a Christmas release, earned more than $30 million of its total gross in 1987. Final tally: $110,000,000.

Once past the top slots, science fiction and fantasy showed surprising strength, with eight films grossing $30 million or more. Arnold Schwarzenegger was a one-man movie studio all by himself, joining Eddie Murphy, Michael Douglas, Jack Nicholson, and Michael J. Fox in his ability to carry a film at the box office. *Predator*, pitting Schwarzenegger's character against an almost invisible alien in South American jungles, grossed $57 million, while *The Running Man* (from the book by Richard Bachman aka Stephen King) pulled in $34.2 million. The film was still in release, and the final gross should reach $40 million or more.

Surprise hit of the year was *Robocop* ($53.4 million), directed by Paul Verhoeven, a Dutch director best known for *Spetters* and *Soldier of Orange*. *Robocop* was Verhoeven's first attempt at directing an American-style science fiction thriller. The results were stunning – and on a low budget, at that.

It's also worth noting the new James Bond, Timothy Dalton, who appeared in the latest in the series, *The Living Daylights* ($51.1 million). There's probably no actor alive who could take over Sean Connery's old role, but Dalton comes close -- much closer than Roger Moore. *The Living Daylights* features far fewer gad-gets, and is the least science fiction-oriented of the later Bond films, so it's not listed among my second eight.

(Classifying the Bond films with science fiction and fantasy films is probably not justifiable, at least not in this case. But classification is more of a problem with *The Believers* – $18.5 million – which *Variety* called an "occult thriller," and *Angel Heart* – $17 million – dealing with, among other things, voodoo in New Orleans.)

Nightmare on Elm Street 3: Dream Warriors clocked in at $44 million. The film had knock-out special effects, didn't take itself too seriously and, perhaps as a result, received the most critical acclaim of any in the series. *Little Shop of Horrors* ended up its run with a gross of $38.7 million, a figure probably resented by dentists everywhere. *Mannequin*, a film about a store window dummy that comes to life, was a close $38 million.

Mel Brooks satirized *Star Wars* in *Spaceballs*, which grossed $36.7 million; it might have done better if Brooks had released it before *Star Wars* had become a cultural icon. *Like Father, Like Son* pulled in $34.4 million, while vampires in Santa Cruz turned out to be a popular theme for *The Lost Boys*, $32.1 million. It made a star out of Keifer Sutherland, the leader of the boys. *Harry and the Hendersons* grossed a modest $27 million. An Amblin production, it proved that it takes the Spielberg touch to breathe life into an E.T. – or a Bigfoot – and that said touch can't be passed on to his disciples.

Biggest disappointment of the year was the very modest showing of *The Princess Bride* at $26.9 million. Still in release, it's unlikely that the final gross will go much above $30 million (though it's guaranteed to do better in the cassette market than *Harry*, even at an announced $89.95 for the tape. Wait a month or two and buy the disc.) Critically acclaimed, it was also my personal favorite for best science fiction or fantasy film of the year.

Another disappointment was *Innerspace*, at $25.9 million. Featuring Dennis Quaid and an ingratiating Martin Short, the film misfired on almost all fronts.

There were nine films that grossed $10 million or better, most of them made on small budgets, which may break even in the cassette market. *Hello Again* ($19.5 million) proved that Shelly Long should have remained behind the bar at *Cheers*, while *Masters of the Universe* ($17 million) proved that the Saturday morning serials don't always translate to the big screen. *Project X* ($16.1 million) proved that a gaggle of talented chimps can easily upstage one of the most talented actors in the business, Matthew Broderick.

Superman IV ($15.3 million) never got off the ground, though it did better than the dozen or so horror films on the list. Clive Barker's *Hellraiser* grossed $14 million, *The Gate* did $13.4 million, John Carpenter's *Prince of Darkness* $12.9 million, *Creep Show II* $12.3 million, *Batteries Not Included* – another entry from Amblin – $10 million (it's still in release, and the final gross will be much higher), *The Hidden* (starring Kyle MacLachlan of *Dune* and *Blue Velvet*) $9.2 million, and *Teen Wolf Too* $7.5 million (the original grossed well only because of Michael J. Fox).

The remaining non-hits (I don't promise that I've got them all): *Witchboard* ($7.4 million), *House II: The Second Story* ($5.3 million), *Made in Heaven* ($4.5 million), *King Kong Lives* ($4.3 million), *My Demon Lover* ($3.9 million), *The Monster Squad*

($3.8 million), **Allan Quatermain and the Lost City of Gold** ($3.7 million), **The Evil Dead** ($3.6 million), **Near Dark** ($2.9 million), **Hello, Mary Lou: Prom Night II** ($2.6 million), **The Kindred** ($2.4 million), **Date with an Angel** ($1.7 million), and finally, **Making Mr. Right** ($1.7 million — shockingly disappointing, since it starred brilliant Broadway and screen actor John Malkovich).

Films that did so poorly we were unable to find any grosses for them at all included **Gothic**, **Graveyard Shift**, and **I Was a Teenage Zombie**. I'm sure there were others that fell between the cracks at the box office, but space and time preclude their appearing here. For these films, as well as for the other low gross-ers, cassette and disc sales may make some of them profitable, especially if initial budgets were low.

If we add up absolutely everything listed above, we come up with $840 million, or approximately 20% of the total box office gross of $4.2 billion. Of the Top 10, science fiction and fantasy accounted for a little more than 16%. That's a far cry from last year's 28% of the Top Ten gross, though the genre's share of the entire gross for the year was up.

No **Star Trek**, no **Aliens**, little in the Top 10 that the genre could claim as its own — the only reason why **The Golden Child** did well was because of the presence of Eddie Murphy. (To a lesser extent, the same is probably true of **The Witches of Eastwick**, with Jack Nicholson, and the Arnold Schwarzenegger films.) But next year...there'll be George Lucas' **Willow**, and the betting right now is that it will be a box office smash. **Aliens III** won't show up until 1989 (to be followed by **Aliens IV**, this one starring Sigourney Weaver, who only has a walk-on in **III**.) God knows when **Baron Munchausen** will make it to the screens, or **Star Trek V**, but 1988 is bound to hold some pleasant surprises.

Critically, a number of films rated rave reviews in both the popular and the trade press, including **The Princess Bride**, **The Witches of Eastwick**, **The Believers**, **Angel Heart**, **Near Dark**, **Project X**, **Hellraiser**, and **Robocop**.

I loved them all.

On other fronts in the film business, John Landis, director of the film **Twilight Zone: The Movie**, and four co-defendants were found innocent in the **TZ** case, which had dragged on for months. Landis and his co-defendants had been accused of involuntary manslaughter in the deaths of actor Vic Morrow and two child actors, Renee Chen and Myca Dinh Le. Morrow and one child had been decapitated, the other child crushed, by a helicopter that crashed during a night shoot on the movie. If convicted, Landis could have faced six years in prison.

If the new release market was slightly soft for sf and fantasy, the genre continued to shine in the afterburner markets of cassette and disc. All the "sell-through" tapes — tapes priced at $29.95 or below so the market is the home purchaser rather than the renter — did well. That includes **Top Gun**, **Star Trek IV**, **Crocodile Dundee**, **Indiana Jones and the Temple of Doom**, **An American Tail**, and a number of Disney titles — **Lady and the Tramp**, etc.

On disc, the genre was represented as well as it was on tape, or even more so. Pioneer released the list of the top 50 best-selling American laser disc titles, and science fiction and fantasy led all the rest by a wide margin. The Top 10 best selling laser discs: **The Empire Strikes Back**, **Star Wars**, **Return of the Jedi**, **Raiders of the Lost Ark**, **Top Gun**, **Star Trek II: The Wrath of Khan**, **Aliens**, **Ghostbusters**, **Alien**, and **Indiana Jones and the Temple of Doom**. That's 9 out of 10 for sf and fantasy — and 24 out of the top 50.

(It's also one of the reasons why I mention the disc format as much as I do — it's obviously popular among science fiction fans and professionals.)

What didn't happen this year that was supposed to: The advent of CD-V, the introduction of the gold-tinted compact disc containing 20 minutes of music and a five-minute video. I'm told it's definately on the way, but I'll believe it when I see it. What did happen was the introduction of Super-VHS (with ED-Beta soon to follow) and the growth in popularity of the large-screen tv set. The latter is just in time for the high-definition tape formats on both tape and disc.

Television seemed on the verge of finally discovering the genre in a big way. **Star Trek: The Next Generation** went into syndication in 230 markets, representing 96% coverage. Ratings-wise, **STTNG** (at 10.3) was Number 4, just after the **World Wrestling Federation** and just before the **Oprah Winfrey Show**. Rumors of dissension on the show didn't seem to hurt its popularity at all. (The leading syndicated show was **Wheel of Fortune** at 17.)

Another syndicated show doing well (and also from Paramount) was **Friday the 13th**. An hour show, it was surprisingly well scripted. Despite the title, the show had little in common with the movies of the same name. Promised for the near future (and once again from Paramount): **War of the Worlds**.

Network tv produced one surprise in **Beauty and the Beast**, a show which ended up on the Top 10 lists of many critics. By year's end, it was lodged in the middle 40s in the ratings, and moving up as the word spread. **Alf**, the cute (to some) alien from outer space on NBC, was a Top 10 show (much to my surprise), but **The Charmings**, a modern reprise of the characters in **Sleeping Beauty**, was in the 60s. **Werewolf** continued to turn in top-quality shows for the Fox network, but Fox had yet to really establish any of its shows. Nevertheless, **Werewolf** was third in the Fox lineup, and this against competition (at least in the Bay Area) from **Family Ties** and **Murder She Wrote**.

The class casualty of the season: **Max Headroom** was cancelled by ABC. Despite critical acclaim and satirical immortality in political cartoons and especially "Doonesbury", the program never caught on with general viewers; its following was enthusiastic but small.

Rumors of science fiction or fantasy shows for television continued to proliferate, but no start dates were listed for any of them.

So, how did 1987 do when it came to science fiction and fantasy? Not bad, not bad at all. Not that many in the Top 10, but a surprising number of middle earners. More than a foothold on television, and gangbusters in the cassette and disc markets.

There's too much guaranteed money to be made in the afterburner market for science fiction and fantasy to be ignored when it comes to feature films. So the prediction for 1988 is: More of the same. A few in the Top 10, heavy representation in the middle list, with inexpensive horror and slasher films holding down the bottom, buried among which will be the occasional gem.

—*Frank M. Robinson*

Sources for this article include the weekly Variety, The Hollywood Reporter, Video, *and* Video Review. *Many thanks to tipsters David Gerrold, Chris Bunch, and Allan Cole for items throughout the year.*

Recommended Reading

Our 1987 Recommended Reading List (see pages 406-408) is, as usual, a consensus put together by the *Locus* staff, reviewers, and outsiders. This year's preliminary short fiction list was based on recommendations by Amy Thomson and Mark Kelly. Other contributors included Gardner Dozois, Art Saha, Debbie Notkin, Faren Miller, Michael Swanwick, Orson Scott Card, and Ellen Datlow. I put together the basic list of books from our reviewers' comments, comments from reviewers in other magazines, and bestseller lists. Our reviewers then did some adding and subtracting.

We also used the preliminary Nebula nomination list, but ran into some problems because of differences in eligibility. The Locus Awards are for work which first appeared in 1987. The Nebula nominations process allows authors to withdraw works in favor of later editions even if they've not been scheduled yet. Since the nominations are carried over until the new edition appears, it has become popular for authors to withdraw their hardcover editions in favor of future paperbacks. Nearly all the leading Nebula nominated novels are 1985 and 1986 books first appearing in paper. They are not eligible for the Locus or Hugo Awards. The Nebula list also counts first *American* publication only. The leading Nebula novella nominee, "The Unconquered Country" by Geoff Ryman, appeared in *Interzone* in 1984, won the World Fantasy Award in 1985, appeared in expanded form as a British book in 1986, and finally as a Bantam paperback in 1987. We've used the Nebula list as a backup, but not as heavily as in past years.

Any story or book recommended by more than one source became part of the final list. Others were added by argument, fiat, or because it seemed reasonable at the time. The comments by reviewers that follow were written before the final list was decided on and mention items not on it or ineligible because of prior publication. We've left in the publisher's name or magazine citation where the item is *not* on the final list, and dispensed with it if the item appears there with full citations. Although we try to limit work to that published in 1987, there are exceptions. We use magazine dates instead of month published, because it would be much too confusing otherwise. We also will relist work dated January 1987 if our recommenders insist, even though it was mostly published in November and December 1986. Thus, **When Gravity Fails** by George Alec Effinger, which we listed last year, is listed again. **The Penguin World Omnibus of Science Fiction** and **Don't Bet on the Prince** appeared in England in 1986, but we did not see them until 1987.

The line between sf and fantasy is very thin. We decided by vote. I consider graphic novels as primarily artwork and list them as such. I had no idea where to put **Cvltvre Made Stvpid**, which had several recommendations even though I don't consider it sf or fantasy related. It's obviously realistic non-fiction.

—C.N. Brown

It was a year of quirky individualism in both sf and fantasy. While the big names of sf kept right on going (new novels from Clarke, Heinlein, Niven, Pohl, etc.), and hard sf's heirs apparent (the triumvirate of Bear, Benford, and Brin) staked their claims, no current movement, literary or mirror-shaded, showed signs of dominating science fiction. Gibson, Sterling, Shirley, published no book-length works; Kim Stanley Robinson was equally silent. Only Lucius Shepard consolidated his advance on the heights with **Life During Wartime**, more a compendium of previous works than a new statement.

The most successful exploration of Cyberpunk sensibilities, George Alec Effinger's *neo-noir* **When Gravity Fails**, made it onto our 1986 list but bears an official 1987 date, so it merits another recommendation. This year's borderline book, the superb **An Alien Light** by Nancy Kress, (Arbor House) will be back on my list for 1988. Among other selections, the two standouts are Mike McQuay's eloquent, surprising **Memories**, and George Turner's powerful **The Sea and Summer** (US edition from Arbor House later this year). The near-future also forms a dark backdrop for unexpected heroes in Richard Bowker's **Dover Beach** and Lisa Goldstein's **A Mask for the General**. Like Effinger, Bowker imports elements of the detective novel. Another genre-bender, Stephen King's **The Tommyknockers**, combines off-the-wall sf with King's trademark Down East horror. Julian May's **Intervention** rescues Earth from the brink of annihilation with great panache, preparing the way for more tales of the Galactic Milieu. Space opera, one of the few refuges for optimism in today's sf, made a notable comeback in 1987, with the promising starts of new series by Jack Vance (**Araminta Station**) and Iain M. Banks (**Consider Phlebas**), along with two fine first novels, Christopher Hinz's **Liege-Killer** and C.S. Friedman's **In Conquest Born**. Sheri S. Tepper's **After Long Silence** brought music to the fore, in a spectacular exercise in planet-building.

The year's best fantasies belied the field's reputation as a wasteland of endless series and juvenile power trips. Orson Scott Card, pre-eminent in sf for 1986, switched to alternate history and an unusual brand of all-American fantasy in **Seventh Son**, beginning a series which should be anything but predictable. The gonzo high spirits and warped romanticism of California wild men Tim Powers (**On Stranger Tides**), K.W. Jeter (**Infernal Devices**), and James P. Blaylock (**Land of Dreams**) continued to resist definition as a movement, either sf or fantasy, unless you adopt their own tongue-in-cheek term, "steam punk." Each of these novels was a well-publicized hardcover original, representing a breakthrough for all three authors.

Popular horror novelists made successful forays into fantasy: Clive Barker in **Weaveworld**, the ubiquitous Stephen King in his second "Dark Tower" book, **The Drawing of the Three**, and Robert R. McCammon in the post-apocalyptic sf/fantasy/horror blend of **Swan Song**. Science fiction and Shakespearian romantic comedy made an even stranger entrance into fantasy in Richard Grant's delightful **Rumors of Spring**. (Could Grant be the long-awaited modern successor to those sly enchanters Pratt and de Camp?)

Literary fantasists John Crowley and Jonathan Carroll served up the dazzling but enigmatic **Aegypt** and the haunting dreamquest **Bones of the Moon**. Kirk Mitchell revived rambunctious writers from the past century in **Never the Twain**, while R.A. MacAvoy's **The Grey Horse** interweaves magic with the complex reality of 19th-century Ireland. Other excellent fantasies range from the surreal futurism of Richard Bowes' **Feral Cell** (Questar) to the humor of Terry Pratchett's charming **Equal Rites**, and the mature sword and sorcery of Barbara Hambly's **The Witches of Wenshar**.

Every year ushers in a promising new crop of first novelists. Newcomers abounded in 1987. Aside from those already mentioned (Friedman, Hinz), sf found a diversity of fresh talents in Michael Armstrong (**After the Zap**), Rebecca Ore (**Becoming Alien**), H.M. Saint (**Memoirs of an Invisible Man**), and Paul Park (**Soldiers of Paradise**). First fantasies include variations on tradition from Bruce Fergusson (**The Shadow of His Wings**) and Midori Snyder (**Soulstring**), the haunted pre-history of **Reindeer Moon** by noted anthropologist Elizabeth Marshall Thomas, and even more individualistic novels by Ellen Kushner (**Swordspoint**) and Dave Duncan (**A Rose-Red City**).

Short fiction continues to find a good home in collections and anthologies, with the small presses bringing some of the best. To name just a few, Capra, Arkham House, Ursus, and Hypatia deserve congratulations for giving us Ursula K. Le Guin's **Buffalo Gals...**, Michael Shea's **Polyphemus**, Howard Waldrop's **All About Strange Monsters...**, and Orson Scott Card's **Cardography**. Highlights from larger publishers include **Night's Sorceries** by Tanith Lee, **Evil Water** by Ian Watson, and **The Bridge of Lost Desire** by Samuel R. Delany. Britain produced two fine anthologies, **Interzone** and **Other Edens**. While I didn't have a chance to read most of the American gatherings, I did enjoy the original stories in **Free Lancers** edited by Elizabeth Mitchell.

There's a daunting amount of worthwhile fiction still being produced. All I can say is — take a look through the *Locus* Recommended List, then plunge in!   —*Faren Miller*

1987 was not a good year for science fiction. The death of Terry Carr deprived the field of an editor who changed the medium and the way authors used it. His impeccable taste is gone. Would a novel like Mike McQuay's **Memories** (although published elsewhere) have been possible had it not been for Carr's groundwork over the years? It remains a high spot, and not just of my 1987 reading. There may be books which take the high ground and become widely acknowledged classics, but there are also those that, for their intimacy, do not so much command respect as summon up great affection. The other novel that sticks in my mind, for entirely different reasons, is Robert A. Heinlein's **To Sail Beyond the Sunset**. Surely there is no other author in science fiction who can kick up a fuss so easily as Heinlein, unless it be John Norman. **To Sail** somehow managed to be an absolutely outrageous piece of work and, at the same time, a wonderful ensemble number celebrating the twilight of a long and remarkable career. Another Old Master showed just what could be done, when Frederik Pohl published the fourth(!) and concluding novel of the Heechee series, **Annals of the Heechee**. It is a satisfying conclusion to a richly textured, vastly conceived work, which ranges from the tortured psyche of a fantastically lucky neurotic to the Big Bang itself.

Gregory Benford's **Great Sky River** continues what is surely one of the more important science fiction works in progress, his meditation on the role of organic life and machine-based intelligence in the Universe. It is a little surprising, but a summary of the other novels published during 1987 shows many that deserve reading. **The Time Wanderers** by the Strugatsky brothers (Richardson & Steirman) and **Death Arms** by K.W. Jeter (Morrigan) continue to stand out. However entertaining David Brin's **The Uplift War** was, it verged dangerously on being just too silly. Despite this, there is a lot of storytelling potential left in Brin's concept, so I'll be in line along with everyone else when the next installment is issued. Greg Bear's **The Forge of God** is exciting to read for what it might have been. Somewhere along the way, however, the book got away from him. I prefer to think of it as a great unfinished work of art. As the summaries by the other reviewers show, there was a large number of other excellent novels that I didn't get a crack at, either when they came out or afterward. Don't let my loss be yours, since some of them look every bit as satisfying as anything I was able to read.

What I did read was Lucius Shepard. With two books, he became the hottest "new" author around since John Varley. Bantam felt so strongly about his fixup novel, **Life During Wartime**, they did it as a mainstream book. Although it had some rough spots, it also had some wonderful writing. Arkham House published the first collection of his stories, **The Jaguar Hunter**, perhaps the most important one they have done since their early Lovecraft and Bradbury collections. It was *good*.

Speaking of collections, get a copy of Howard Waldrop's **All About Strange Monsters of the Recent Past** if you still can. Recognition of this uniquely gifted (if that is the operative word) writer, in the form of such a small press, beautifully crafted collection, has been all too long in coming. It is also hard not to miss **The Essential Ellison**. Although moderately priced, it is big enough, literally, to be the cornerstone of an Ellison library. Also don't ignore the monumental **The Collected Stories of Philip K. Dick**, an enormous undertaking which delivers all that the title promises. In a year when the small presses tended toward unrewarding collections, Phantasia did us a favor by bringing that master of the short-short story Fredric Brown back into print. Their collection of his stories, **And the Gods Laughed**, was a pleasant surprise.

As seems to be the case these days, the year saw the publication of a number of important, useful, entertaining, or otherwise readable books about the field. The one that comes most easily to mind is **Anatomy of Wonder** in its third, vastly revised, edition, with extensive coverage of foreign science fiction and reference materials. There was also what will probably be the only major study of James Blish, **Imprisoned in a Tesseract**. It is an important book about an important author. It would also be hard to ignore Michael Moorcock's provocative **Wizardry and Wild Romance** and John J. Pierce's historical survey, **Foundations of Science Fiction**.

Last, but not least, there is the indescribable but hilarious **Cvltvre Made Stvpid** by Tom Weller. He's done it twice now. Can he go for #3?   —*Dan Chow*

1987 was a bumper year for sf and fantasy. As always, there were more books than the year before; in this case, many of them were memorable. Strong Hugo contenders should include Brin's **The Uplift War**, Niven, Pournelle, and Barnes' **The Legacy of Heorot**, and Effinger's **When Gravity Fails**. For the first time, we're likely to see a comic book on the novel list, one which might just win; Alan Moore's **Watchmen**. Despite *Locus*'s insistence on calling it an art book, it's sf, and a novel by word count: it's well over the minimum without even taking the pictures into account. If fantasy was likely to win, I'd expect to see Carroll's **Bones of the Moon** and Baker's **Weaveworld** on the list. I was enchanted by several novels I wouldn't have read if not for *Locus*, most notable among them **The Secret Ascension** by Michael Bishop, which is the best Philip K. Dick to be published recently. First novels worth noting: Heather Gladney's odd Japanese-Arabic fantasy **Teot's War**, Loren MacGregor's space opera **The Net**, Emma Bull's entry in the modern fantasy sweepstakes **War for the Oaks**.

Disturbing Trends abound. As a bookseller, I'm quite aware of how long books stay in print, and it's not very long. At least one of the books on the Recommended Reading List, Patricia Geary's **Strange Toys**, is already unavailable from the publisher despite strong critical acclaim. To some extent this can be blaimed on the lamentable Thor Power Tool decision if the IRS, but it also reflects more of a worry about short-term profits than was common in the book industry ten years ago. It's a continuing trend; and it's aided and abetted by the power of the large chain bookstores. In the past, if one publisher didn't like your work, you could always find another to look at it; now, if the chains don't like your work, you have a lot more trouble selling your book. And what the chains like is very different from what fans like. Compare the *Locus* bestseller list with the Walden and Dalton lists that are published right next to it.

The small press publishers have been growing, too. Since most of their books aren't carried by the chains, perhaps there's some hope there. But look at what they publish: small editions of the books that the mainstream won't do in hardcover, signed editions that consist of the mainstream publisher's sheets bound in tacky materials, or short pieces. And almost none of them is set up to publish writers who do not already have a following. Chris Drumm and Jeff Connor have each tried to do works by less well known writers, but they're exceptions. Also lamentable is a lack of design sense: one publisher did a short story collection with a table of contents with no page numbers; another apparently sets books on an IBM Selectric; another has no idea of how to use white space; all supposedly produce "quality" editions, but none have any sense of what quality is. It's not the paper, it's not the binding, and it's not the printing, gang: it's how you put it all together that makes something worthwhile. Even the classy small publishers like Underwood-Miller have taken to doing a minimal job: where an index or bibliography would make a book much more useful, it's no longer automatically there. I think this will affect the resale market: many of these books will never be worth much more than the buyer paid for them, and in some cases signed editions are going for less at auction than the publisher's original price.

Every so often a mainstream publisher will produce a nice limited edition, and it shows what can be done by someone who cares. A short plug for a gorgeous one: The Collins edition of Baker's **Weaveworld**. Slipcased, with a leather spine, all edges gilt, a gold pattern on the inside edge of the boards, marbled endpapers, and a suite of illustrations by Barker found only in this edition, this book is a delight for those who like well-designed, well-made books. It also carries a high pricetag: Copies are going for about $300.

    —*Tom Whitmore*

Lucius Shepard had another good year, Robert Silverberg and Ursula K. Le Guin are still in peak form, and Pat Murphy, Karen Joy Fowler, and Bruce Sterling all wrote ferociously good stories. None of this is *news*. Let's forget Benford and Wolfe and Willis for a moment and go rooting about in the obscurer corners of the field. Let's look for the unexpected. What follows is a brief, eccentric, biased and unbalanced look at several short works worth getting excited over, arguing about, voting for, and possibly even reading.

The joke is that Neal Barrett, Jr. stood too close to Howard Waldrop one day and mutated. The truth is that Barrett, who's been producing respectable sf for years, has gone abruptly and irreversibly gonzo. Witness this year's "Perpetuity Blues", wherein secret agents fight the Communist Conspiracy undercover in Montgomery Wards, New Yorkers tie celery to cats, and trailer camp aliens introduce us to the concept of interdimensional tofu. Or "Highbrow", in which future generations devote their lives to the creation of an enormous statue of Richard Nixon. Or "Diner", or "Class of '61" (*Asimov's* 10/87), which prove that Barrett's strange sensibilities can be applied to serious themes with equal success. Discovering Neal Barrett, Jr. is like first becoming aware of Howard Waldrop or R.A. Lafferty. This man is something special, and he's on a roll.

Harry Turtledove continued the adventures of Basil Argyros, agent of Byzantium, with "Images" (*IASFM* 3/87) and "Superwine". People who know tell me this alternate history series is meticulously researched, but what really makes these stories special is the dazzling demonstration of how some very basic technology — the printing press, gunpowder, innoculation — could have been discovered long before it actually happened, and the careful demonstration of the effects of said technology on the culture. This is hard science fiction at its most praiseworthy, and especially difficult to pull off as Turtledove has, with flair, conviction, and a strong plot sense. Terrific stuff.

Those of us who love and admire William S. Burroughs' work have long wondered what it would be like if he were required to adhere to the same rules as the rest of us. Would a conventional WSB story be as good as his innovative work? Would it even be worth reading? Somehow Ellen Datlow of *Omni* managed to coax exactly that story out of him, and it's a delight. "The Ghost Lemurs of Madagascar" relates the encounter of Captain Mission, pirate, Utopian, and agent of panic, with the sad and timeless hidden mysteries of the world. For the scholastically minded, this story places Burroughs smack-dab in the Romantic descent (a position acknowledged with a nod to Defoe), and for others it can serve as a window into his *oeuvre*. More importantly, it's gorgeously written (I could quote you whole paragraphs), and genuinely moving. So yes, Burroughs can write. I knew it all along.

Finally, it's been a banner year for Pat Cadigan fans: In addition to her first novel, she's had three extremely strong stories out. "Angel" is a tough-and-tender story of transcendence and life on the street — the sort of thing Cadigan does better than anyone. "Patterns" (*Omni* 8/87) is a very weird look at the neur-oreality of television, a topic I wish more writers would tackle, and has the year's single best opening line. And in "Lunatic Fringe" (**Omni SF V** also incorporated into **Mindplayers**) Deadpan Ally once again explores the heart of human darkness. It's worth noting that she has stories in *three* magazines in January of 1988 — and if *Omni*'s "Headset" is merely crisp and authoritative, and *F&SF*'s "Two" is only wonderfully written, touching and horrifying all at once, "My Brother's Keeper" in *Asimov's* is the single most chilling thing I've read in a long time. If you haven't tried Cadigan yet, you're still drinking that sissy kid stuff.

Much more happened this year, but you'll have to learn it from somebody else, someone who's had the stamina and moral character to actually read every piece of short genre fiction published this year. Me, I very carefully skipped at least one story from each magazine and anthology that fell into my hands. Don't call and ask why I left your story out. I only read for pleasure nowadays.   —*Michael Swanwick*

The field of short fiction was in a state of vigorous fermentation in 1987. Out of nearly 800 pieces of short fiction I read, (somewhere near 80-90% of the original short fiction published this year), there were over 80 stories I recommended for the *Locus* list of recommended short fiction.

My favorite is Octavia Butler's "The Evening and the Morning and the Night". It is about a woman with a hereditary disease that causes madness and self-induced mutilation. The protagonist deals with her parents' grotesque death and her own fear of the disease. What sets this gutsy, powerful work above the others is its unflinching look at some of the least discussed fears of this culture; madness, disability, and disfigurement. An excellent story skillfully rendered by a woman working at the top of her craft.

"Rachel in Love" by Pat Murphy is another excellent novelette, currently running high in the Nebula ratings. It too is extremely well-written, and powerful. It concerns a young girl in a chimpanzee's body. When her father dies, Rachel is captured and taken to a chimp primate lab, where she is caged, and kept for breeding purposes. Like "The Evening and the Morning and the Night", this story's central themes are powerful and painful to read. Both are well written and moving. Both deserve awards and acclaim.

Vietnam was a trendy story topic this year. **In The Field of Fire**, the acclaimed anthology, had two extremely powerful novelettes, "Shades" by Lucius Shepard, and "Dream Baby" by Bruce McAllister. "Shades" is a riveting story about a Vietnam vet who goes back to Vietnam to cover a story about the ghost of one of the men in his outfit who was killed in action. If you want escapist

fiction, look elsewhere. Shepard doesn't pull any punches. It's painstakingly detailed, vividly described and absolutely unputdownable. "Dream Baby" is about a nurse who begins to have clairvoyant dreams about soldiers who are going to die. She is scooped up by a special team of psychic talents run by Intelligence and used to predict the deaths of the soldiers on the team. I found "Dream Baby" more chilling than "Shades" due to its tight, unrelenting focus on the nurse's violent reaction to the trauma of the war.

Ian Watson's "The Moon and Michaelangelo" is another favorite. A stone carver, brought along on an expedition to study a primitive culture of lemur-like aliens who live in a city of beautiful stone carvings, finds a transcendent form of immortality in this mysterious and luminous novelette. The solution to the mysterious alien sculpture is at once so surprising and so compellingly beautiful that this story stands head and shoulders above most of the rest of this year's crop of sf.

"Cage 37" by Wayne Wightman is full of surprises. The novelette has a completely unpredictable plot and two engaging, well-rendered teenage protagonists. The ending is also beautiful and more profound than the piece's screwball comedic tone leads one to expect.

Bruce Sterling's "Flowers of Edo" blends so many of my favorite elements into one story that it would be just plain impossible for me to dislike it. There's the wonderful, revolutionary upheavals of Japan's early Meiji Restoration period, when feudal Japan opened up to the West; there's the remaining traces of Japan's floating world, and the vivid art and imagination of the wood-block print artist Yoshitoshi Taiso. This work succeeds through its myriad surprising details. Sterling distills the essence of the Meiji Period into an excellent piece of fiction. My fondness for this story may be due to rank favoritisim, but the story values make it worthy of a high recommendation to the community of sf readers.

Most of the stories I am recommending this year are serious stories full of sturm und drang und angst. Delia Sherman's "The Maid on the Shore" (*F&SF* 10/87) is a simple, sturdy, folk tale. It has the familiar, warm feel of a childhood keepsake. But "The Maid on the Shore" is also fresh and original, with characters and plot twists wholly its own. All too often seemingly simple tales like this get passed over for glitzy stories with lots of stylistic chrome on their bumpers and very little humanity behind their mirror-shades. We forget that straightforward tales of simple magic are often the ones that get remembered.

Richard Paul Russo's "Prayers of a Rain God" (*F&SF* 5/87) is a moving story about an ex-astronaut who begins dreaming that aliens are praying to him to send rain. The deftness and feeling with which Russo handles his characters make this piece special.

"The Circular Library of Stones" by Carol Emshwiller concerns an old woman who is excavating stones left behind by a mysterious civilization. She must choose between life in a nursing home, or death and the discovery of her excavations. Emshwiller beautifully delineates the fine line between visionary inspiration and madness with spare, elegant prose.

Mona Clee's "Iron Butterfly" (*TZ* 12/87) is about a suicidal woman who meets the spirit of Mary Pickford in a darkened and dilapidated movie house, and is given the courage to survive. The endurance and pluck of Clee's characters make this story something special. "By Crystal Light Beneath One Star" is one of Tanith Lee's best and most challenging stories. Set in a timeless world that functions as a place of exile for political prisoners, this recursive piece is very different from the fantasy stories Lee is better known for. I hope that some enterprising editor makes it more widely available to an American audience.

Horror fiction ususally seems to involve someone getting killed or mutilated in some new and vivid technicolor fashion. Roger Robert Lovin's "The Cobbler" (*F&SF* 12/87), about a leprechaun and an immortal man in the vieux carre of New Orleans, is a wolf in borzoi's clothing. The witty, urbane tone of the story gives no hint of the grisly ending.

Novellas were, as usual, sparse and hard to find. Geoff Ryman had two strong entries, "The Unconquered Country", a folkish tale about an alternate Cambodia, and "Love Sickness" (*Interzone* 20-21), a quirky love story between an actress and a genetically altered Woolie who is a musical genius. These two powerful yet disparate novellas highlight Ryman's power and versatility as a writer. I hope more of his excellent fiction sees publication on this side of the Atlantic.

Kim Stanley Robinson also came out with two fine novellas, "Mother Goddess of the World" and "The Blind Geometer" . "Mother Goddess" is a wild chase across the Himalayas by a couple of crazed moutaineers, a Buddhist saint, and a determined cameraman. Robinson renders Everest with a dazzle that leaves one gasping for breath, blinded by the snowy briliance of his prose. "The Blind Geometer" captures the internal landscape of the mathematician of the title, who finds himself the subject of a complicated espionage scheme. Whether or not the author presents an accurate portrayal of blindness, I cannot say, but Robinson has succeeded in creating an intiguingly alien inner world of the blind-from-birth protagonist. The plot strains the suspenders of disbelief a bit more than is ideal, but overall, it's a damn fine story.

Robert Silverberg's excellent novella "The Secret Sharer" rounds out my list of favorite stories. This may be literary heresy, but I prefer the Silverberg story to the original Conrad piece. It is an excellent example of the kind of thought experiments that science fiction does so well. Using the literary devices of science fiction, Silverberg is able to explore Conrad's themes in more depth. I recommend the reading and comparison of these two fine stories as an exercise to the reader.

1987 saw the death of several of the field's finest writers. Less noticeable were the many fine new writers who sold their first stories. Many of the more impressive debuts came in *Amazing Stories,* which premiered Robert Frazier with "Dreamtigers" (3/87), Dean Whitlock's "The Million Dollar Wound", David E. Cortesi's "A Bomb in the Head", J.M. Zeller with "The Hand of the Survivor" (7/87), Roberta Grant's "Catscape" (7/87), and R. Garcia y Robertson with "The Moon of Popping Trees". Lisa Mason's "Arachne" (*Omni* 12/87) was a first sale, as was Eric Brown's "Krash Bangg Joe and the Pineal-Zen Equation". Then there were the splashy first appearances of the **Writers of the Future** crew, including Paula May, and Mary Catherine McDaniels. Other notable debuts include: Shirley Weinland's "When the Haloperidol Runs Out and the Blue Fairy Never Comes" (*Amazing* 3/87), Delia Sherman's "Maid on the Shore" (*F&SF* 10/87), and Matt Corwin's "Backwater Time" (*F&SF* 2/87) .

          —Amy Thomson

I read less this past year, due to limited time and inclination (past a certain point this reading becomes mind-numbing). I started sending *Locus* recommendations almost ten years ago, when interest in short fiction seemed to be in decline and good stories were being overlooked; *Locus*'s lists for 1977 were short and combined the short story and novelette categories. Things have changed. *Locus* has a regular short fiction reviewer, and there is a whole magazine devoted to reviewing short fiction, Orson Scott Card's *Short Form* (though I have yet to see the second issue). Short fiction isn't necessarily better than it was ten years ago, but it's getting more attention.

There were at least 800 stories published in 1987, and that's just in the professional magazines and books. The figure would be considerably higher if the various semi-professional publications *Locus* receives were counted.. There were more shared-world/braided-novel anthologies this year, and it was a relatively good year for straight sf anthologies, with **In the Field of Fire, Universe 17, Synergy #1, The Universe,** and **Other Edens** standing out.

1987 was dominated by *Asimov's* (which might more accurately be titled *Gardner Dozois's Speculative Fiction Magazine*), where two of my favorite novellas were published, Kim Robinson's "The Blind Geometer" and Robert Silverberg's "The Secret Sharer". Robinson's story is only incidentally sf (the hero has some futuristic gizmos and his work may have application to particle beam weapons), but is a fascinating intellectual stew of mathematics, music, and perception, from the perspective of being blind. Silverberg's far future tale is a compelling story with well-drawn characters, and also features something hard to find in sf these days, vivid imagination combined with expressive writing. The opening pages especially, where Silverberg describes the huge starship, are quite wonderful.

Another outstanding novella, perhaps the best story this year, is Geoff Ryman's "Love Sickness". A story of forbidden and frustrated love in a future when knowledge and attitudes are communicated with viruses, it is rich with invention: Rolfa, a seven-foot tall "Woolie" (genetically bred to live in Antarctica) who covertly composes music to score Dante; Joe the Postperson, who carries messages with his viral memory; Marye's ability to "hear" music as she reads a score; and a production of "Love's Labour's Lost" in which the director's job is to reproduce the correct version as remembered by the viruses. This story won't be eligible for the Nebula award until it is reprinted in the U.S. (the same reason Ryman's 1984 "The Unconquered Country" is only now a Nebula nominee), but "Love Sickness" is certainly eligible now for the *Locus* and Hugo awards; don't miss it.

Kim Stanley Robinson also wrote my favorite fantasy, "The Return from Rainbow Bridge". In plot a standard *Twilight Zone/*

F&SF situation — ordinary person has an equivocal experience with the strange — this story is elevated above the majority both by Robinson's vivid writing and by his acute sense of the meaning of the experience. Not content with the usual tease of most such stories (did it or didn't it happen?), Robinson knows how such an incident can transform a life, and how important the event is, whether or not it was "really" as perceived.

Cyberpunk (for lack of a more convenient word; John Shirley prefers "the Movement") was diffuse in 1987. The best example was Michael Swanwick's colorful novel **Vacuum Flowers**, a book I now suggest to people along with **Neuromancer** and **Schismatrix** to show them what cyberpunk is all about. "The Movement's" inner circle seemed to spend more time this year bickering about political correctness or the true meaning of the word "wetware" than publishing stories. Meanwhile, other writers adapted cyberprops to their own ends and produced good stories, notably Effinger's **When Gravity Fails** and Silverberg's "The Pardoner's Tale". A prototypical c.p. story this year was Walter Jon Williams' "Wolf Time" (*Asimov's* 1/87), a tale of interplanetary operatives and the potential of DNA encoding. Williams stretched further with "Dinosaurs", a parable about aliens who are more human than the overly-evolved human who brings their doom. New writer Eric Brown debuted with "Krash-Bangg Joe and the Pineal-Zen Equation", a story about telepathy and private eyes and many other things, with the exhuberance and flavor and third-worldliness of cyberpunk. Another new writer, Lisa Mason, applied cyberspace to the legal system in "Arachne" (*Omni* 12/87). These few examples didn't constitute much of a trend in 1987, but they did stand out above the flatness and failed imagination of much other supposedly futuristic sf. My favorite bad example this year was a cover story in *Analog* ("formerly *Astounding*") which offered a solution to the problem of adequate child-care for working families, and took us to an alien planet to do it. It was, indeed, not very astounding. The core cyberpunk movement may be dissolving, but one can hope that its ideas continue to spread.

Several other novellas are worth mentioning, including James Patrick Kelly's "Glass Cloud", a more conventional (i.e. non-cyberpunk) portrayal of the near future, concerning a visiting alien race and the New Age-ish religion it inspires. A different sort of religious impulse is explored in Orson Scott Card's "Eye for Eye", which concerns a backwoods tribe of Biblical zealots jealously perpetuating its psychokinetic powers. And Russell Griffin's "Saving Time" (*F&SF* 2/87) is a hilarious time travel tale of attempting to meddle with history.

Orson Scott Card had an especially fine year. In addition to "Eye for Eye", his Alvin Maker series, beginning with the novel **Seventh Son**, carried on with "Carthage City" and "Runaway" (*Asimov's* 9/87). Both stories are independent in themselves, though they may be excerpts from forthcoming novels. Another story, "America", is part of a separate series, similar in flavor, related to the future of Utah. Card excels in portraying characters with strong convictions in regional settings.

Connie Willis wrote two of the most unusual stories this year: "Schwarzchild Radius", in which the expected physics lesson is realized as an experience at the Russian front of World War I; and "Winter's Tale", a clever solution (fantasy only by courtesy, as an alternate history) to the Shakespeare identity problem, up to and including the strange bit in Will's will about the second-best bed.

Lucius Shepard had a varied year, publishing two strong Vietnam stories, "Shades" and "Delta Sly Honey"; "Pictures Made of Stone" (*Omni* 9/87), just as powerful by virtue of brevity; "The Glassblower's Dragon", a fragile fantasy sustained by the strength of Shepard's prose; and "On the Border", a mix of near-future sf and desert magic.

And Alice Sheldon left us with three very different James Tiptree, Jr. stories, the violent war story "Yanqui Doodle", an amusing parable about gods and man, "Second Going"; and the grimly ironic "In Midst of Life", in which a man who kills himself out of boredom finds a purpose in the afterlife.

Pat Murphy's "Rachel in Love" is one of the best novelettes of the year, a prime example of a writer achieving great effects with a standard idea, in this case mind transference from human to chimp. It is a poignant and moving story, especially in those moments when the memories of the lost little girl flutter to the surface of the maturing chimp's awareness.

Other exceptional novelettes include Bruce Sterling's "Flowers of Edo", a well-researched tale of fires and demons in historical Tokyo, with hints of ironic prophecy such as those that gave "Dinner in Audoghast" its pungency. Octavia Butler's "The Evening and the Morning and the Night" is a careful confrontation with the effects of a violent disease, with no easy answers. And Howard Waldrop's "He-We-Await" is another well-researched tale, this about an Egyptian dynasty resurrected in the 20th century.

Other noteworthy short stories include Pat Cadigan's "Angel", a bluesy, inner-city sort of story that surprised me by resolving into sf, not fantasy. Marta Randall's "Lapidary Nights" is a very neat and compact revenge tale with an exotic setting. In "For Thus I Remember Carthage", Michael Bishop explains 20th-century cosmology to a 5th-century Augustine with the virtuosic invention of new Latin- and Chinese-inspired terminology: this is a story to set alongside Sterling's historical fantasies mentioned above. Karen Joy Fowler's "The Faithful Companion at Forty" (left out of last year's collection **Artificial Things** after being present in the galleys) presents the droll maunderings of the famous masked man's sidekick, now middle-aged and feeling neglected. Kate Wilhelm's "Forever Yours, Anna" is an economical tale of graphology and time travel. And Michael Swanwick's "Foresight" (*Interzone* 20) is a tour de force about the time after a mysterious Event when people's memories operate in reverse order — they remember only their futures — an effect which Swanwick simulates by telling the story in reverse order; it's dizzying.

—Mark R. Kelly

1987 Recommended Reading List

Novels -- Science Fiction

The Forge of God, Greg Bear (Tor)
Great Sky River, Gregory Benford (Bantam Spectra)
The Secret Ascension, Michael Bishop (Tor)
Dover Beach, Richard Bowker (Bantam Spectra)
The Uplift War, David Brin (Phantasia/Bantam)
Dawn, Octavia E. Butler (Warner)
2061: Odyssey Three, Arthur C. Clarke (Del Rey)
Still River, Hal Clement (Del Rey)
Way of The Pilgrim, Gordon R. Dickson (Ace)
When Gravity Fails, George Alec Effinger (Arbor/Bantam)
A Mask For The General, Lisa Goldstein (Bantam Spectra)
Rumors of Spring, Richard Grant (Bantam Spectra)
To Sail Beyond The Sunset, Robert A. Heinlein (Ace Putnam)
The Doomed Planet, L. Ron Hubbard (Bridge)
Dark Seeker, K.W. Jeter (Tor)
The Tommyknockers, Stephen King (Putnam)
Intervention, Julian May (Houghton Mifflin)

Fool's Run, Patricia A. McKillip (Warner)
Memories, Mike McQuay (Bantam Spectra)
The Smoke Ring, Larry Niven (Del Rey)
The Legacy of Heorot, Larry Niven, Jerry Pournelle, and Steven Barnes (Gollancz/Simon & Schuster)
The Annals of the Heechee, Frederik Pohl (Del Rey)
Life During Wartime, Lucius Shepard (Bantam)
Little Heroes, Norman Spinrad (Bantam Spectra)
Vacuum Flowers, Michael Swanwick (Arbor House)
After Long Silence, Sheri S. Tepper (Bantam Spectra)
The Awakeners, Sheri S. Tepper (Tor, 2 vols., **Northshore, Southshore**; SFBC Complete)
The Sea and Summer, George Turner (Faber & Faber)
Araminta Station, Jack Vance (Underwood-Miller/Tor)
Code Blue -- Emergency, James White (Del Rey)
Voice of the Whirlwind, Walter Jon Williams (Tor)
The Urth of the New Sun, Gene Wolfe (Tor)

Novels -- Fantasy

Being A Green Mother, Piers Anthony (Del Rey)
Weaveworld, Clive Barker (Poseidon/Collins)
Land of Dreams, James P. Blaylock (Arbor House)
The Firebrand, Marion Zimmer Bradley (Simon & Schuster)
Aegypt, John Crowley (Bantam Spectra)
Seventh Son, Orson Scott Card (Tor)
Bones of the Moon, Jonathan Carroll (Century/Arbor House)
A Man Rides Through, Stephen R. Donaldson (Del Rey)
Guardians of the West, David Eddings (Del Rey)
Daughter of The Empire, Raymond E. Feist and Janny Wurts (Doubleday)
Strange Toys, Patricia Geary (Bantam Spectra)
The Hour of the Thin Ox, Colin Greenland (Unwin Hyman)

The Witches of Wenshar, Barbara Hambly (Del Rey)
Infernal Devices, K.W. Jeter (St. Martin's Press)
Darkspell, Katharine Kerr (Doubleday)
The Dark Tower II: The Drawing of the Three, Stephen King (Grant)
The Grey Horse, R.A. MacAvoy (Bantam Spectra)
Swan Song, Robert R. McCammon (Pocket)
Never the Twain, Kirk Mitchell (Ace)
On Stranger Tides, Tim Powers (Ace)
Equal Rites, Terry Pratchett (Gollancz)
Lincoln's Dreams, Connie Willis (Bantam Spectra)
Sign Of Chaos, Roger Zelazny (Arbor House)

First Novels

After The Zap, Michael Armstrong (Popular Library Questar)
The Man Who Pulled Down the Sky, John Barnes (Congdon & Weed)
The American Book of the Dead, Stephen Billias (Popular Library Questar)
The Movement of Mountains, Michael Blumlein (St. Martin's Press)
War for the Oaks, Emma Bull (Ace)
Mindplayers, Pat Cadigan (Bantam Spectra)
A Rose-Red City, Dave Duncan (Del Rey)
A Death of Honor, Joe Clifford Faust (Del Rey)
The Shadow of His Wings, Bruce Fergusson (Arbor House)
In Conquest Born, C.S. Friedman (DAW)
Teot's War, Heather Gladney (Ace)
Liege-Killer, Christopher Hinz (St. Martin's Press)
The Brentwood Witches, Brenda Jordan (Ace)
Swordspoint, Ellen Kushner (Allen & Unwin/Arbor)

Arrows Of The Queen, Mercedes Lackey (DAW)
The Net, Loren J. MacGregor (Ace)
The Architects of Hyperspace, Thomas R. McDonough (Avon)
Pennterra, Judith Moffett (Congdon & Weed)
Frame of Reference, Jerry Oltion (Popular Library Questar)
Becoming Alien, Rebecca Ore (Tor)
Soldiers of Paradise, Paul Park (Arbor House)
Napoleon Disentimed, Hayford Peirce (Tor)
The Leeshore, Robert Reed (Donald I. Fine)
Memoirs of an Invisible Man, H.M. Saint (Atheneum)
Soulstring, Midori Snyder (Ace)
Wild Card Run, Sara Stamey (Berkley)
Reindeer Moon, Elizabeth Marshall Thomas (Houghton Mifflin)
Station Gehenna, Andrew Weiner (Congdon & Weed)
Ambient, Jack Womack (Weidenfeld & Nicolson)

Anthologies

The Penguin World Omnibus of Science Fiction, Brian Aldiss and Sam J. Lundwall, eds. (Penguin)
The Great SF Stories: 16, Isaac Asimov and Martin Greenberg, eds. (DAW)
New Destinies Vol II, Jim Baen, ed. (Baen)
Sword and Sorceress IV, Marion Zimmer Bradley, ed. (DAW)
Writers of the Future Volume III, Algis Budrys, ed. (Bridge)
Universe 17, Terry Carr, ed. (Doubleday)
Terry Carr's Best Science Fiction and Fantasy of the Year #16 Terry Carr, ed. (Tor)
The Architecture of Fear, Kathryn Cramer and Peter D. Pautz, eds. (Arbor House)
Interzone, The Second Anthology, J. Clute, D. Pringle and S. Ousley, eds. (Simon & Schuster UK)
In the Field of Fire, Jeanne Van Buren Dann and Jack Dann, eds. (Tor)
The Fifth Omni Book of Science Fiction, Ellen Datlow, ed. (Zebra)
The Year's Best Science Fiction, Fourth Annual Collection, Gardner Dozois, ed. (St. Martin's Press)
Other Edens, Christopher Evans & Robert Holdstock, eds. (Unwin)

Shadows 10, Charles L. Grant, ed. (Doubleday)
The Dark Descent, David G. Hartwell, ed. (Tor)
Tales From The Forbidden Planet, Roz Kaveny, ed. (Titan)
Devils & Demons, Marvin Kaye, ed. (Doubleday)
Free Lancers, Elizabeth Mitchell, ed. (Baen)
Tales of the Witch World, Andre Norton, ed. (Tor)
The Universe, Byron Preiss, ed. (Bantam Spectra)
Vampires, Alan Ryan, ed. (Doubleday)
The Year's Best Fantasy Stories #13, Arthur Saha, ed. (DAW)
Whispers VI, Stuart David Schiff, ed. (Doubleday)
Robert Silverberg's Worlds of Wonder, Robert Silverberg, ed. (Warner)
Masques II, J.N. Williamson, ed. (Maclay & Associates)
The 1987 Annual World's Best SF, Donald A. Wollheim, ed. (DAW)
The Year's Best Horror Stories XV, Karl Edward Wagner, ed. (DAW)
Synergy: New Science Fiction, Vol.1, George Zebrowski, ed. (Harcourt Brace Jovanovich)
Don't Bet on the Prince, Jack Zipes, ed. (Methuen)

Short Story Collections

And The Gods Laughed, Fredric Brown (Phantasia Press)
Getting Home, F.M. Busby (Ace)
Scared Stiff, Tales of Sex and Death, Ramsey Campbell (Scream/Press)
Cardography, Orson Scott Card (Hypatia)
The Bridge of Lost Desire, Samuel R. Delany (Arbor House)
The Collected Stories of Philip K. Dick, Volumes I through V,
     Philip K. Dick (Underwood-Miller)
The Essential Ellison, Harlan Ellison (The Nemo Press)
Night's Sorceries, Tanith Lee (DAW)
Buffalo Gals and Other Animal Presences, Ursula K. Le Guin
     (Capra Press)
Portraits of His Children, George R.R. Martin (Dark Harvest)

The Best of Pamela Sargent, (Academy Chicago)
Polyphemus, Michael Shea (Arkham House)
The Jaguar Hunter, Lucius Shepard (Arkham House)
Chance and Other Gestures of the Hand of Fate, Nancy Springer (Baen)
A Touch of Sturgeon, Theodore Sturgeon (Simon & Schuster UK)
True Names...and Other Dangers, Vernor Vinge (Baen)
Why Not You and I?, Karl Edward Wagner (Tor/Dark Harvest)
All About Strange Monsters of the Recent Past, Howard Waldrop (Ursus)
Evil Water, Ian Watson (Gollancz)
The Valley So Low: Southern Mountain Stories, Manly Wade Wellman
     (Doubleday)

ART/HUMOR

Watchmen, Alan Moore and Dave Gibbons (Warner)
The Raging Tide: Or, The Black Doll's Imbroglio, Edward Gorey
     (Beaufort)
Cvltvre Made Stvpid, Tom Weller (Houghton Mifflin)
Michael Whelan's Worlds of Wonder, Michael Whelan (Del Rey)
A Closer Look, Patrick Woodroffe (Harmony)

BIBLIOGRAPHY

Anatomy of Wonder, 3rd Edition Neil Barron, ed. (R.R. Bowker)
Science Fiction, Fantasy, & Horror 1986, Charles N. Brown
     & William G. Contento, (Locus Press)
Science Fiction and Fantasy Reference Index, Vols I & II, H.W. Hall,
     (Gale)

CRITICISM & HISTORY

The Tale That Wags the God, James Blish (Advent)

NonFiction

The Definitive Time Machine, Harry M. Geduld (Visions)
Imprisoned in a Tesseract: The Life of James Blish, David Ketterer
     (Kent State)
The Battle of Brazil, Jack Mathews (Crown)
Wizardry and Wild Romance, Michael Moorcock (Gollancz)
The Maker of Dune: Insights of a Maker of Science Fiction, Frank Herbert,
     edited by Tim O'Reilly (Berkley)
Foundations of Science Fiction, John J. Pierce (Greenwood)
Mary Shelley, Muriel Spark (Dutton)
Intersections, Fantasy and Science Fiction, George E. Slusser &
     Eric S. Rabin, eds. (Southern Illinois University Press)
Robert Heinlein, Leon Stover (Twayne)
Mind in Motion, The Fiction of Philip K. Dick, Patricia S. Warrick
     (Southern Illinois University Press)
How To Write Tales of Horror, Fantasy & Science Fiction,
     J.N. Williamson, ed. (Writer's Digest)

Novellas

"The Blind Geometer", Kim Stanley Robinson (*IASFM* 8/87)
"Mother Goddess of the World", Kim Stanley Robinson (*IASFM* 10/87)
"Love Sickness", Geoff Ryman (*Interzone* #20-21)
"The Secret Sharer", Robert Silverberg (*IASFM* 9/87)
"Displaced Person", Ian Stewart (*Analog* 5/87)
"Superwine", Harry Turtledove (*IASFM* 4/87)

"The Borders of Infinity", Lois McMaster Bujold (**Freelancers**)
"Eye for Eye", Orson Scott Card (*IASFM* 3/87)
"The Forest of Time", Michael Flynn (*Analog* 6/87)
"Fugue State", John M. Ford (**Under the Wheel**)
"Saving Time", Russell Griffin (*F&SF* 2/87)
"Glass Cloud", James Patrick Kelly (*IASFM* 6/87)

Novelettes

"Ever After", Susan Palwick (*IASFM* 11/87)
"Adeste Fideles", Frederik Pohl (*Omni* 12/87)
"My Life as a Born-Again Pig", Frederik Pohl (**Synergy 1**)
"The Return from Rainbow Bridge", Kim Stanley Robinson (*F&SF* 8/87)
"Fat Face", Michael Shea (Axolotl Press)
"Trapalanda", Charles Sheffield (*IASFM* 6/87)
"On the Border", Lucius Shepard (*IASFM* 8/87)
"Shades", Lucius Shepard (**In the Field of Fire** *IASFM* 12/87)
"The Sun Spider", Lucius Shepard (*IASFM* 4/87)
"Goats", Dave Smeds (**In the Field of Fire**)
"Flowers of Edo", Bruce Sterling (*IASFM* 5/87)
"Second Going", James Tiptree, Jr. (**Universe 17**)
"Yanqui Doodle", James Tiptree, Jr. (*IASFM* 7/87)
"He-We-Await", Howard Waldrop (**All About Strange Monsters...**
     IASFM Mid-12/87)
"The Moon and Michaelangelo", Ian Watson (*IASFM* 10/87)
"Going to Meet the Alien", Andrew Weiner (*F&SF* 8/87)
"Waves", Andrew Weiner (*IASFM* 4/87)
"Cage 37", Wayne Wightman (*F&SF* 4/87)
"Dinosaurs", Walter Jon Williams (*IASFM* 6/87)
"Winter's Tale", Connie Willis (*IASFM* 12/87)
"Extras", Robert Charles Wilson (*F&SF* 12/87)

"The Price of Cabbages", Brian Aldiss (**Other Edens**)
"A Hole in the Sun", Roger MacBride Allen (*Analog* 4/87)
"Descendent", Iain Banks (**Forbidden Planet**)
"Perpetuity Blues", Neal Barrett, Jr. (*IASFM* 5/87)
"Mandikini", Gregory Benford (**The Universe**)
"Krash-Bangg Joe and the Pineal-Zen Equation", Eric Brown
     (*Interzone* #21)
"The Evening and the Morning and the Night", Octavia E. Butler
     (*Omni* 5/87)
"America", Orson Scott Card (*IASFM* 1/87)
"Runaway", Orson Scott Card (*IASFM* 6/87)
"Uncle Dobbin's Parrot Fair", Charles de Lint (*IASFM* 11/87)
"Conspiracy of Noise", Paul Di Filippo (*F&SF* 11/87)
"Skylab Done It", George Alec Effinger (*F&SF* 3/87)
"Moon of Popping Trees", R. Garcia y Robertson (*Amazing* 9/87)
"At the Cross-Time Jaunter's Ball", Alexander Jablokov (*IASFM* 8/87)
"Buffalo Gals Won't You Come Out Tonight", Ursula K. Le Guin
     (**Buffalo Gals...**/*F&SF* 11/87)
"The Pear-Shaped Man", George R.R. Martin (*Omni* 10/87)
"Dream Baby", Bruce McAllister (**In the Field of Fire** *IASFM* 10/87)
"Among the Stones", Paul J. McAuley (*Amazing* 1/87)
"Dutchman", Jack McDevitt (*IASFM* 2/87)
"Rachel in Love", Pat Murphy (*IASFM* 4/87)

Short Stories

"Diner", Neal Barrett, Jr. (*Omni* 11/87)
"Highbrow", Neal Barrett, Jr. (*IASFM* 7/87)
"For Thus Do I Remember Carthage", Michael Bishop (**The Universe**)
"The Ghost Lemurs of Madagascar", William S. Burroughs (*Omni* 4/87)
"Angel", Pat Cadigan (*IASFM* 5/87)
"Friend's Best Man", Jonathan Carroll (*F&SF* 1/87)
"A Bomb in the Head", David E. Cortesi (*Amazing* 5/87)
"The Circular Library of Stones", Carol Emshwiller (*Omni* 2/87)
"The World Next Door", Brad Ferguson (*IASFM* 9/87)
"The Faithful Companion at Forty", Karen Joy Fowler (*IASFM* 7/87)
"Maxie Silas", Augustine Funnell (*F&SF* 6/87)
"Cassandra's Photographs", Lisa Goldstein (*IASFM* 8/87)
"Daemon", James Patrick Kelly (*F&SF* 11/87)
"Heroics", James Patrick Kelly (*IASFM* 11/87)
"Glass", Nancy Kress (*IASFM* 9/87)
"The Liquor Cabinet of Dr. Malikudzu", Marc Laidlaw
    (*Night Cry* Summer '87)
"Nutrimancer", Marc Laidlaw (*IASFM* 8/87)
"By Crystal Light Beneath One Star", Tanith Lee (**Forbidden Planet**)
"Crying in the Rain", Tanith Lee (**Other Edens**)
"Kingdom Come", Bruce McAllister (*Omni* 2/87)
"To Hell With the Stars", Jack McDevitt (*IASFM* 12/87)

"The Rose Garden", Steven Popkes (*IASFM* 8/87)
"Lapidary Nights", Marta Randall (**Universe 17**)
"Pamela's Get", David Schow (*TZ* 8/87)
"Delta Sly Honey", Lucius Shepard (**In the Field of Fire** *TZ* 10/87)
"The Glassblower's Dragon", Lucius Shepard (*F&SF* 4/87)
"The Iron Star", Robert Silverberg (**The Universe**)
"The Pardoner's Tale", Robert Silverberg (*Playboy* 6/87)
"Termites", Dave Smeds (*IASFM* 5/87)
"The Little Magic Shop", Bruce Sterling (*IASFM* 10/87)
"Oh Tin Man, Tin Man, There's No Place Like Home", Brad Strickland
    (*F&SF* 5/87)
"In Midst of Life", James Tiptree, Jr. (*F&SF* 11/87)
"The Wound", Lisa Tuttle (**Other Edens**)
"Night of the Cooters", Howard Waldrop (*Omni* 4/87)
"Why I Left Harry's All-Night Hamburgers", Lawrence Watt-Evans
    (*IASFM* 7/87)
"The Alien in the Lake", Andrew Weiner (*IASFM* 9/87)
"The Million-Dollar Wound", Dean Whitlock (*F&SF* 1/87)
"Forever Yours, Anna", Kate Wilhelm (*Omni* 7/87)
"Schwarzschild Radius", Connie Willis (**The Universe**)
"What Bleak Land", Robert F. Young (*F&SF* 1/87)

Major Awards

Hugo Awards

Best Novel - Speaker for the Dead, Orson Scott Card (Tor/ Century)

Also Nominated: **The Ragged Astronauts**, Bob Shaw (Gollancz/ Baen); **Count Zero**, William Gibson (IASFM Jan-Mar,1986/ Gollancz/Arbor House); **Marooned in Realtime**, Vernor Vinge (*Analog* May-Aug,1986/Bluejay); **Black Genesis**, L. Ron Hubbard (Bridge/New Era)

Best Novella - "Gilgamesh in the Outback", Robert Silverberg (*IASFM* Jul,1986/**Rebels in Hell**)

Also Nominated: "Escape from Kathmandu", Kim Stanley Robinson (*IASFM* Sep,1986); "R&R", Lucius Shepard (*IASFM* Apr,1986); "Spice Pogrom", Connie Willis (*IASFM* Oct,1986); "Eifelheim", Michael Flynn (*Analog* Nov,1986)

Best Novelette - "Permafrost", Roger Zelazny (*Omni* Apr,1986)

Also Nominated: "Thor Meets Captain America", David Brin (*F&SF* Jul,1986); "The Winter Market", William Gibson (*Vancouver Magazine* Nov,1985/*Interzone* 15,1986/*Stardate* Mar,1986/**Burning Chrome**); "Hatrack River", Orson Scott Card (*IASFM* Aug,1986); "The Barbarian Princess", Vernor Vinge (*Analog* Sep,1986)

Best Short Story - "Tangents", Greg Bear (*Omni* Jan,1986)

Also Nominated: "Robot Dreams", Isaac Asimov (**Robot Dreams**/ *IASFM* mid-Dec,1986); "The Boy Who Plaited Manes", Nancy Springer (*F&SF* Oct,1986); "Still Life", David S. Garnett (*F&SF* Mar,1986); "Rat", James Patrick Kelly (*F&SF* Jun,1986)

Best Non-Fiction - Trillion Year Spree, Brian Aldiss w/ David Wingrove (Gollancz/Atheneum)

Also Nominated: **The Dark Knight Returns**, Frank Miller (Warner/ Titan); **Industrial Light and Magic**, Thomas G. Smith (Del Rey); **Science Fiction in Print: 1985**, Charles N. Brown & William G. Contento (Locus Press); **Only Apparently Real**, Paul Williams (Arbor House)

Best Dramatic Presentation - *Aliens*

Also Nominated: *Star Trek 4: The Voyage Home*; *The Fly*; *Little Shop of Horrors*; *Labyrinth*

Best Semi-Prozine - *Locus*, ed. Charles N. Brown

Also Nominated: *Interzone*, ed. Simon Ounsley and David Pringle; *Science Fiction Chronicle*, ed. Andrew Porter; *Science Fiction Review*, ed. Richard E. Geis; *Fantasy Review*, ed. Robert Collins

Best Professional Artist - Jim Burns

Also Nominated: Frank Kelly Freas; Don Maitz; Barclay Shaw; Tom Kidd; J.K. Potter

Best Professional Editor - Terry Carr

Also Nominated: Gardner Dozois; David Hartwell; Ed Ferman; Stanley Schmidt

Best Fan Writer - Dave Langford

Also Nominated: Patrick Nielsen Hayden; Simon Ounsley; Mike Glyer; D. West; Arthur Hlavaty

Best Fan Artist - Brad Foster

Also Nominated: Arthur ATom Thomson; Stu Shiffman; Taral; Steve Fox

Best Fanzine - *Ansible*, ed. Dave Langford

Also Nominated: *File 770*, ed. Mike Glyer; *Lan's Lantern*, ed.

George Laskowski; *Texas SF Inquirer*, ed. Pat Mueller; *Trapdoor*, ed. Robert Lichtman

The John W. Campbell Award - Karen Joy Fowler

Also Nominated: Lois McMaster Bujold; Katharine Eliska Kimbriel; Rebecca Brown Ore; Leo Frankowski; Robert Touzalin Reed

Locus Awards

Best Science Fiction Novel - Speaker for the Dead, Orson Scott Card (Tor)

Best Fantasy Novel - Soldier of the Mist, Gene Wolfe (Tor)

Best First Novel - The Hercules Text, Jack McDevitt (Ace)

Best Non-Fiction - Trillion Year Spree, Brian Aldiss with David Wingrove (Gollancz/Atheneum)

Best Novella - "R&R", Lucius Shepard (*IASFM* Apr,1986)

Best Novelette - "Thor Meets Captain America", David Brin (*F&SF* Jul,1986)

Best Short Story - "Robot Dreams", Isaac Asimov (**Robot Dreams**/*IASFM* mid-Dec,1986)

Best Collection - Blue Champagne, John Varley (Dark Harvest)

Best Anthology - The Year's Best Science Fiction, Third Annual Collection, ed. Gardner Dozois (Bluejay)

Best Artist - Michael Whelan

Best Magazine - *The Magazine of Fantasy and Science Fiction*

Best Publisher - Ballantine/Del Rey

Locus Best All-Time Awards

Best All-Time Science Fiction Novel - Dune, Frank Herbert (Chilton 1965)

Best All-Time Fantasy Novel - The Lord of the Rings, J.R.R. Tolkien (Allen & Unwin 1954)

Best All-Time Science Fiction Author - Robert A. Heinlein

Best All-Time Fantasy Author - J.R.R. Tolkien

Nebula Awards

Best Novel - Speaker for the Dead, Orson Scott Card (Tor)

Also Nominated: **Free Live Free**, Gene Wolfe (Ziesing/Tor); **The Handmaid's Tale**, Margaret Atwood (Houghton Mifflin); **The Journal of Nicholas the American**, Leigh Kennedy (Atlantic Monthly); **This Is the Way the World Ends**, James Morrow (Holt)

Best Novella - "R&R", Lucius Shepard (*IASFM* Apr,1986)

Also Nominated: "Dydeetown Girl", F. Paul Wilson (**Far Frontiers IV**); "Escape from Kathmandu", Kim Stanley Robinson (*IASFM* Sep,1986); "Gilgamesh in the Outback", Robert Silverberg (*IASFM* Jul,1986/**Rebels in Hell**); "Newton Sleep", Gregory Benford (*F&SF* Jan,1986/**Heroes in Hell**)

Best Novelette - "The Girl Who Fell Into the Sky", Kate Wilhelm (*IASFM* Oct,1986)

Also Nominated: "Aymara", Lucius Shepard (*IASFM* Aug,1986); "Hatrack River", Orson Scott Card (*IASFM* Aug,1986); "Listening to Brahms", Suzy McKee Charnas (*Omni* Apr,1986); "Permafrost", Roger Zelazny (*Omni* Apr,1986); "Surviving", Judith Moffett (*F&SF* Jun,1986); "The Winter Market", William Gibson (*Vancouver Magazine* Nov,1985/*Interzone* 15,1986/*Stardate* Mar,1986/**Burning Chrome**)

Best Short Story - "Tangents", Greg Bear (*Omni* Jan,1986)

Also Nominated: "The Boy Who Plaited Manes", Nancy Springer (*F&SF* Oct,1986); "The Lions Are Asleep This Night", Howard Waldrop (*Omni* Aug,1986); "Pretty Boy Crossover", Pat Cadigan (*IASFM* Jan,1986); "Rat", James Patrick Kelly (*F&SF* Jun,1986); "Robot Dreams", Isaac Asimov (**Robot Dreams**/*IASFM* mid-Dec,1986)

Grand Master Award - Isaac Asimov

World Fantasy Awards

Best Novel - **Perfume**, Patrick Suskind (Knopf/Pocket)

Also Nominated: **Talking Man**, Terry Bisson (Arbor House/ Avon); **The Pet**, Charles L. Grant (Tor); **It**, Stephen King (Viking/NAL); **Strangers**, Dean R. Koontz (Putnam/Berkley); **The Tricksters**, Margaret Mahy (Dent/Atheneum); **Soldier of the Mist**, Gene Wolfe (Tor)

Best Novella - "Hatrack River", Orson Scott Card (*IASFM* May,1986)

Also Nominated: "The Hellbound Heart", Clive Barker (**Night Visions 3**); "Night Moves", Tim Powers (Axolotl Press); "The Night Seasons", J.N. Williamson (*Night Cry* Winter,1986); "Chance", Connie Willis (*IASFM* May,1986)

Best Short Story - "Red Light", David J. Schow (*Twilight Zone* Dec,1986)

Also Nominated: "The Brains of Rats", Michael Blumlein (*Interzone* 16,1986); "They're Coming for You", Les Daniels (**Cutting Edge**); "The End of the Whole Mess", Stephen King (*Omni* Oct,1986); "Tight Little Stitches in a Dead Man's Back", Joe R. Lansdale (**Nukes**); "The Rise and Fall of Father Alex", Amyas Naegele (*F&SF* Oct,1986); "The Boy Who Plaited Manes", Nancy Springer (*F&SF* Oct,1986); "Pain", Whitley Strieber (**Cutting Edge**)

Best Anthology/Collection - **Tales of the Quintana Roo**, James Tiptree, Jr. (Arkham House)

Also Nominated: **Cutting Edge**, ed. Dennis Etchison (Doubleday); **Dreams of Dark and Light**, Tanith Lee (Arkham House); **Night Visions 3**, ed. George R.R. Martin (Dark Harvest); **Liavek: The Players of Luck**, ed. Will Shetterly & Emma Bull (Ace); **Black Wine**, ed. Douglas E. Winter (Dark Harvest); **Merlin's Booke**, Jane Yolen (Ace/SteelDragon)

Best Artist - Robert Gould

Also Nominated: Chris Van Allsburg; Steve Gervais; J.K. Potter

Special Award--Professional - Jane Yolen

Also Nominated: Donald M. Grant (Grant); David G. Hartwell (Arbor); The Editors of *Interzone*; Jack Sullivan (**The Penguin Encyclopedia of Horror and the Supernatural**); Terry Windling (Ace); Jane Yolen (**Favorite Tales from Around the World**)

Special Award--Non-Professional - Jeff Conner (Scream/Press)

Special Award--Non-Professional - W. Paul Ganley (*Weirdbook* / Weirdbook Press)

Also Nominated: Steven Jones and David Sutton (*Fantasy Tales*); David B. Silva (*The Horror Show*)

Life Achievement Award - Jack Finney

Special Award - Andre Norton

Other Awards

Ballantine/Del Rey/Fawcett Tolkien Essay Contest

Winner - Judy Holiday Kroeger

British Fantasy Awards

Best Novel - **It**, Stephen King (Hodder & Striughton)

Best Short Fiction - "The Olympic Runner", Dennis Etchison

Best Small Press - *Fantasy Tales*, ed. Stephen Jones and David Sutton

Best Film - *Aliens*

Best Artist - J.K. Potter

Special Award - Clarles L. Grant

British SF Association Awards

Best Novel - **The Ragged Astronauts**, Bob Shaw (Gollancz)

Also Nominated: **Schismatrix**, Bruce Sterling (Penguin); **Queen of the States**, Josephine Saxton, (Women's Press); **Count Zero** - William Gibson (*IASFM* Jan-Mar,1986/Gollancz/ Arbor House)

Blood Music, Greg Bear (Gollancz)

Best Short Story - "Kaeti and the Hangman", Keith Roberts (**Kaeti & Company**)

Also Nominated: "Jingling Geordie's Hole", Ian Watson (*Interzone* 17,1986); "And He Not Busy Being Born", Brian Stableford (*Interzone* 16,1986); "The Winter Market", William Gibson (*Vancouver Magazine* Nov,1985/*Interzone* 15,1986/ *Stardate* Mar,1986/**Burning Chrome**)

Best Media Production - *Aliens*

Also Nominated: *Reanimator*; *Overdrawn at the Memory Bank* (tv film); *Mr. Pye* (tv); *Dr. Who: Trial of a Timelord* (tv)

Best Artwork - "The Clocktower Girl", Keith Roberts (**Kaeti & Company**/*Vector* 132)

Also Nominated: "Screaming of the Beetle", SMS (*Interzone* 18,1986); Peter Lion (cover, *Interzone* 15, 1986); Jim Burns (cover, *Interzone* 16,1986); John Avon (cover, *Interzone* 17,1986)

John W. Campbell Memorial Award

First Place - **A Door into Ocean**, Joan Slonczewski (Arbor House/Avon)

Second Place - **This Is the Way the World Ends**, James Morrow (Holt)

Third Place - **Speaker for the Dead**, Orson Scott Card (Tor)

Casper Awards, Canadian SF & Fantasy Achievement Awards

Best Work in English - **The Wandering Fire**, Guy Gavriel Kay (Collins)

Also Nominated: Michael Coney, for lifetime achievement; **Yarrow**, Charles De Lint (Ace); **A Hidden Place**, Robert Charles Wilson (Bantam); **Lifter**, Crawford Killian (Ace)

Best Work in French - "La Carte du Tendre", Elisabeth Vonarburg (Aimer)

Also Nominated: "Bonne Fete Univers", Alain Bergeron (*Solaris* 65); "Salut le Monde", Claude-Michel Prevost (*Solaris* 70); **Coquillage**, Esther Rochon

Fan Achievement - Elisabeth Vonarburg

Also Nominated: Robert Runte; Fran Skene

Arthur C. Clark Award
Best Science Fiction Novel Published in the United Kingdom
Winner - **The Handmaid's Tale**, Margaret Atwood (Cape)
Also Nominated: **Eon**, Greg Bear (Gollancz); **Stars in My Pocket Like Grains of Sand**, Samuel R. Delany (Grafton); **Escape Plans**, Gwyneth Jones (Allen & Unwin); **The Memory of Whiteness**, Kim Stanley Robinson (Futura/Macdonald); **Queen of the States**, Josephine Saxton, (Women's Press); **The Ragged Astronauts**, Bob Shaw (Gollancz); **Green Eyes**, Lucius Shepard (Chatto & Windus)

Compton Crook Award - Best Novel
Nominees: **Shards of Honor**, Lois McMaster Bujold (Baen); **The Game of Fox and Lion**, Robert R. Chase (Del Rey); **The Cross-Time Engineer**, Leo Frankowski (Del Rey); **A Hidden Place**, Robert Charles Wilson (Bantam); **The Doomsday Effect**, Thomas Wren (Baen)

William Crawford Award
Best First Fantasy Novel - Judith Tarr, **The Hound and the Falcon** (Bluejay 1986)
Also Nominated: Greg Bear, **The Infinity Concerto/The Serpent Mage** (/Berkley 1986); Timothy Findley, **Not Wanted on the Voyage** (Penguin Canada 1984); Paul Hazel, "The Finnbranch Trilogy"; Guy Gavriel Kay, "The Fionavar Tapestry"; Dan Simmons, **Sonl of Kali** (Bluejay 1985); Tad Williams, **Tailchaser's Song** (Daw 1985)

Daedalus Awards
Life Achievement - Andre Norton
Short Fiction, Horror - Steve Rasnic Tem
Short Fiction, Fantasy - Jane Yolen
Short Fiction, Science Fiction - Tim Sullivan
Novel, Horror - **It**, Stephen King (Viking)
Novel, Fantasy - **The Shattered Horse**, Somtow Sucharitkul (Tor, as by S.P. Somtow)
Novel, Science Fiction - **Radio Free Albemuth**, Philip K. Dick (Arbor House 1985)
Zeus Award - Gardner Dozois

Davis Publications Awards, 1986
Isaac Asimov's Science Fiction Magazine:
Best Short Story - "Robot Dreams", Isaac Asimov (**Robot Dreams**/*IASFM* mid-Dec,1986)
Best Novelette - "Prisoner of Chillon", James Patrick Kelly (*IASFM* Jun,1986)
Best Novella - "Spice Pogrom", Connie Willis (*IASFM* Oct,1986)
Analog Science Fiction Science Fact:
Best Cover Artist - Tom Kidd, for **Marooned in Real Time** by Vernor Vinge
Best Science Fact - "The Long Stern Chase: A Speculative Exercise", Rick Cook (*Analog* Jul,1986)
Best Short Story - "Phreak Encounter", Roger Macbride Allen (*Analog* May,1986)
Best Novella - "Eifelheim", Michael Flynn (*Analog* Nov,1986)

Philip K. Dick Award
Best Original Paperback Novel - **Homunculus**, James Blaylock (Ace)
Runners-up - **The Hercules Text**, Jack McDevitt (Ace); **Artificial Things**, Karen Joy Fowler (Bantam); **A Hidden Place**, Robert Charles Wilson (Bantam)

J. Lloyd Eaton Award
Best Scholarly Book on SF and Fantasy - Tie: **Scientific Romance in Britain: 1890-1950**, Brian Stableford (Fourth Estate 1985); **Some Kinds of Paradise: The Emergence of American Science Fiction**, Thomas D. Clareson (Greenwood 1985)

Gigamesh Awards (Spain)
Best Fantasy Novel - Death's Master, Tanith Lee (Martinez Roca)
Best Fantasy Short Story (tie) - "House of Thieves" and "The Bazaar of the Bazarre", Fritz Leiber (**Swords Against Death**)
Best Horror Anthology/Collection (tie) - **Songs the Dead Men Sing**, George R.R. Martin (Martinez Roca) and **Clive Barker's Books of Blood 1** (Planeta)
Best Horror Short Story (tie) - "Down Among the Dead Men", Gardner Dozois and Jack Dann (**The Dodd, Mead Gallery of Horror**, Martinez Roca), "The Midnight Meat Train", and "In the Hills, the Cities", Both by Clive Barker (**Books of Blood 1**, Planeta)
Best Fanzine - *Transito*
Special Award - *Cuasar* (Argentine fanzine)
Special Award - Els Libres de Glauco (Spanish publisher in Catalan) for the series "L'Arca" (devoted to the grand masters of fantastic literature)
Special Award - Albert Sole for his translation of Tanith Lee's **Night's Master**

Kurd Lasswitz Awards
Best Novel - **Die Wallfahrer** (The Pilgrim), Carl Amery
Best Novella - "Umkreisungen" (Orbits), Karl Michael Armer
Best Short Story - "Play Future", Rainer Erler
Best Translator - Lore Strassl
Best Artist - Klaus Holitzka
Best Film/TV Play - *"News-Bericht Uber die reise in Eine Strahlende Zukunft"* (News Report on a Voyage into a "Beaming" Future), Rainer Erler
Best Radio Play - *"Totenfloss"* (Raft of the Dead), Harald Mueller
Special Award - *Science Fiction Media* (news magazine)
Best Foreign Novel Translated into German - **Elleander Morning**, Jerry Yulsman

Libertarian Futurist Society
Prometheus Award - **Marooned in Realtime**, Vernor Vinge (*Analog* May-Aug,1986/Bluejay)
Also Nominated: **Circuit**, Melinda Snodgrass (Berkley); **A Door into Ocean**, Joan Sloczewski (Avon); **The Handmaid's Tale**, Margaret Atwood (Fawcett)
Hall of Fame Winners - **Stranger in a Strange Land**, Robert A. Heinlein and **Anthem**, Ayn Rand

Rhysling Awards for SF Poetry

Best Long Poem - "Daedalus", W. Gregory Stewart (*Star*Line* Nov-Dec,1986)

Best Short Poem (tie) - "Before the Big Bang", Jonathan V. Post (*Star*Line* Nov-Dec,1986/*Analog* Jan,1987) and "A Dream of Heredity", John Calvin Rezmerski (*Tales of the Unanticipated* Fall,1986)

Rosny-Aine Award (French)

Best Novel - **La Ville au Fond de l'Oeil**, Francis Berthelot (Denoel)

Also Nominated: **Operation Serrure Carnivore**, Serge Brussolo; **La Malediction de l'Ephemere**, Richard Canal; **Marilyn Monroe et les Samourais du Pere Noel**, Pierre Stolze; **Phenix**, Bernard Simonay

Best Short Story - "Memoire Vive, Memoire Morte", Gerald Klein (**Demain les Puces**, Denole)

Also Nominated: "Blafarde ta peau, rouge ton regard", Roland Wagner; "Nouveaux apercus sur la Bete du Devonshire", Richard Nolane; "Les murailles du milieu", Pierre Giuliani; "Carte blanche", Sylvie Laine

SF & Fantasy Workshop Awards

Best Short Story Editor - Edward L. Ferman, *F&SF*

Best Book Editor - Susan Allison, Editor-in-Chief, The Berkley Publishing Group

Science Fiction Book Club Award

First Place - **Killashandra**, Anne McCaffrey

Second Place - **Ender's War**, Orson Scott Card

Third Place - **The Summer Tree**, Guy Gavriel Kay

Seiun Award (Japanese Hugo)

Best Novel - **Prism**, Chohei Kambayashi

Best Novelette - "Martian Railroad 19", Kosyu Tani

Best Translated Novel - **Neuromancer**, William Gibson

Best Translated Novelette - "PRESS ENTER ■", John Varley

Best Dramatic Presentation - *Brazil*

Best Comics - "Urusei-yatyura", Rumiko Takahashi

Best Artist - Michiaki Satoh

Best Nonfiction - "Dr. Ishihara's SF Laboratory", Dr. Fujio Ishihara

Takumi Shibano Award - Ken Yamaoka

Small Press Writers & Artists Orginization Awards

Best Magazine/Editor - Peggy Nadramia, *Grue*

Best Writer - Colleen Drippe'

Best Artist - Allen Koszowski

Best Poet - D.M. Vosk

Best Nonfiction Writer - Joe Lansdale

Best Comic Writer/Artist - Larry Dickinson

Dale Donaldson Memorial Award - W. Paul Ganley and David B. Silva (tie)

W.H. Smith Illustration Awards

First Place - Ralph Steadman, **I, Leonardo** (Cape)

Second Place - Justin Todd, **Alice in Wonderland** and **Through the Looking Glass** (Gollancz)

Theodore Sturgeon Memorial Award

First Place - "Surviving", Judith Moffett (*F&SF* Jun,1986)

Second Place - Tie: "Elephant", Susan Palwick (*IASFM* Nov,1986) and "The Grave Angels", Richard Kearns (*F&SF* Apr,1986)

Honorable Mention - "Pretty Boy Crossover", Pat Cadigan (*IASFM* Jan,1986); "The Lions Are Asleep This Night", Howard Waldrop (*Omni* Aug,1986)

World SF Awards

Harry Harrison Award ("for improving the status of sf internationally") - Carlo Pagetti (Italy), Wolfgang Jeschke (West Germany)

Karel Award (for translation) - Annarita Guarnieri (Italy), Wiktor Bukato (Poland)

President's Award ("for independence of thought in sf") - Patrick Parrinder (U.K.), Arkady & Boris Strugatsky (U.S.S.R.)

Special President's Award ("for achievements in the sf field") - Tom Olander (Finland); Elisabeth Gille, Pierre Barbet, Jacques Goimard (France); Peter Kuczka (Hungary); Lino Aldani (Italy); Adam Hollanek (Poland); Neil Barron, Charles N. Brown, Marshall B. Tymn (U.S.)

Writers Guild of America Awards for Outstanding Achievement in Television and Radio Writing

Anthology Episode/Single Program category: *"Paladin of the Lost Hour"*, Harlan Ellison (**The Twilight Zone**); *"The Last Defender of Camelot"*, George R.R. Martin (**The Twilight Zone**); *"Her Pilgrim Soul"*, Alan Brennert (**The Twilight Zone**); *"The Doll"*, Richard Matheson (**Amazing Stories**)

Writers of the Future Contest, 1986

Grand Prize Winner: "On My Way to Paradise", Dave Wolverton

First Quarter:

First Place - "Time and Chance", Eric M. Heideman

Second Place - "The Very Last Party At #13 Mallory Way", L.E. Carroll

Third Place - "In the Sickbay", R.V. Branham

Second Quarter:

First Place - "Jacob's Ladder", M. Shayne Bell

Second Place - "The Language of the Sea", Carolyn Ives Gilman

Third Place - "Old Mickey Flip Had a Marvelous Ship", Lori Ann White

Third Quarter:

First Place - "Living in the Jungle", Martha Soukup

Second Place - "No Pets", Tawn Stokes

Third Place - "Monsters", Jean Reitz

Fourth Quarter:

Second Place - "Long Knives", J.R. Dunn

Third Place - "A Little of What You Fancy", Mary Catherine McDaniel

Finalists: "A Day in the Life", Christopher Ewart; "Resonance Ritual", Paula May

Necrology

Frank Andrasovsky, May 1987, Co-Founder of Cleveland SF Society
Frank Arnold, January 3, 1914 - November 14, 1987, British SF Fan
Charles Lee Barrett, M.D., age 77, February 7, 1987, Collector
Walter M. Baumhofer, age 82, September 23, 1987, Artist
Alfred Bester, December 18, 1913 - September 30, 1987, Writer
Dimitri Bilenkin, 1933 - July 27, 1987, Soviet SF Writer
E. Nelson Bridwell, age 55, January 23, 1987, Comics Writer
Ron Busch, September 25, 1928 - August 12, 1987, Publisher
Erskine Caldwell, age 83, April 11, 1987, Writer
Dr. Archibald F. Carr, Jr., age 77, May 21, 1987, Writer
Terry Carr, February 19, 1937 - April 7, 1987, Writer, Editor
Theodore R. Cogswell, March 10, 1918 - February 3, 1987, Writer
Mari Beth (Wheeler) Colvin, age 65, October 19, 1987, Fan
Vernell Corriell, age 68, January 14, 1987, Fan
Humberto Costantini, age 63, June 7, 1987, Argentinian Satirist, Playwright, Poet
Marguerite Lofft de Angeli, age 98, Writer/Illustrator of Children's Books
Richard Delap, July 20, 1942 - October 26, 1987, Reviewer, Editor
Maude Dickson, age 96, February 2, 1987, Mother of Gordon R. Dickson
Carola Edmond, June 14, 1987, British Editor
Polly Freas, January 24, 1987, Wife of Illustrator Frank Kelly Freas
James Friend, age 55, December 1, 1987, Educator
Randall Garrett, December 16, 1927 - December 31, 1987, Writer
Roger Lancelyn Green, November 2, 1918 - October 8, 1987, British Critic, Writer
Lawrence Lyle Heinlein, age 86, January 17, 1987, Brother of Robert A. Heinlein
Gail Kaufman, age early 40s, April 1987, Fan
Paul Hugo Little, age 72, June 22, 1987, Pulp Writer
Joseph LoBrutto, age 12, May 18, 1987, Son of Doubleday Editor Pat LoBrutto
Alistair MacLean, age 64, February 2, 1987, Writer
Cecil Madden, age 84, death announced May 28, 1987, British Radio and Television Producer
Bea Mahaffey, August 24, 1928 - March 28, 1987, Editor
George Markstein, age 57, January 15, 1987, British Writer, TV Scriptwriter
Richard Marquand, age 49, September 5, 1987, British Director
Harold Matson, age 89, January 5, 1987, Literary Agent
Hugh (Mac) McCaffrey, age 63, April 19, 1987, Brother of Anne McCaffrey
C.L. Moore, January 24, 1911 - April 4, 1987, Writer
Arch Oboler, December 6, 1909 - March 19, 1987, Writer
G. Edward Pendray, May 19, 1901 - September 5, 1987, Scientist, Writer
Ray Puechner, August 12, 1935 - July 17, 1987, Literary Agent
Richard Ben Sapir, July 27, 1936 - January 27, 1987, Writer
Eugen Semitjov, age 64, June 13, 1987, Swedish SF Writer, Space Artist
Ron Smith, age about 50, November 5, 1987, Editor, Writer
James Tiptree, Jr. (Alice B. Sheldon), August 24, 1915 - May 19, 1987, Writer
Patrick Troughton, March 25, 1920 - March 28, 1987, Actor
Donald A. Wandrei, age 79, October 15, 1987, Writer
Anthony West, August 14, 1914 - December 27, 1987, Writer
Richard Wilson, September 23, 1920 - March 29, 1987, Writer
Marguerite Yourcenar, June 3, 1903 - December 18, 1987, Writer

ABC-Clio
2040 Alameda Padre Serra
Box 4397
Santa Barbara CA 93103-1788

Academy Chicago
425 N. Michigan Ave.
Chicago IL 60611

The Acolyte Press
P.O. Box 12731
1100 AS Amsterdam 20
The Netherlands

Adama Books
306 W. 38th St.
New York NY 10018

Advent: Publishers, Inc.
P.O. Box A3228
Chicago IL 60690

Aeolus Publications
Box 2643
Vista CA 92084

Alyson Publications
40 Plympton St.
Boston MA 02118

Amador Publishers
Box 12335
Albuquerque NM 87195

Andrion Books
128 East 56th Street
New York NY 10022

Ansatz Press
75 Fairview Ave. #2D
New York NY 10040

Ansunda Publications
P.O. Box 158
Harris IA 51345

ANZ Religious Publications
P.O. Box 619, Kenmore Station
Boston MA 02215

Arco Publishing
215 Park Ave. South
New York NY 10003

Ardis Publishers
2901 Heatherway
Ann Arbor MI 48104

Arkham House
P.O. Box 546
Sauk City WI 53583

Asiapac Books & Educational Aids
Blk 163, Bukit Merah Central
#03-3599
Singapore 0315, Malaysia

August House
Box 3223
Little Rock AR 72203

The Axolotl Press
3915 First Avenue N.E.
Seattle, WA 98105

Beacon Press
25 Beacon St.
Boston MA 02108

Beccon Publications
75 Rosslyn Ave.
Harold Wood
Essex RM3 0RG
UK.

Berkeley Poets Workshop & Press
Box 459
Berkeley CA 94701

Bethany House
6820 Auto Club Rd.
Minneapolis MN 55438

Blackthorne Publishing, Inc.
786 Blackthorne Ave.
El Cajon CA 92020

Borgo Press
P.O. Box 2845
San Bernardino CA 92406

R.R. Bowker Co.
245 W. 17 St.
New York NY 10011

Bowling Green University
Popular Press
Bowling Green OH 43403

Bud Plant, Inc.
Box 1886
Grass Valley CA 95945

Canyon Press
162 Ruby Avenue
San Carlos, CA 94070

Capra Press
Box 2068
Santa Barbara CA 93120

Carcanet Press Ltd.
208-212 Corn Exchange Bldgs.
Manchester M4 3BQ, UK

Carcanet/U.S.
108 E. 31st St.
New York NY 10016

Citadel Press
120 Enterprise Ave.
Secaucus NJ 07094

Coffee House Press
P.O. Box 10870
Minneapolis MN 55458

Comico
1547 DeKalb St.
Norristown PA 19401

Corroboree Press
2729 Bloomington Ave. S.
Minneapolis MN 55407

Creatures at Large
P.O. Box 687
1082 Grand Teton Drive
Pacifica CA 94044

The Crossing Press
P.O. Box 640
Trumansburg NY 14886

Crossway Books
9825 W. Roosevelt Rd
Westchester IL 60153

John Daniel, Publisher
P.O. Box 21922
Santa Barbara CA 93121

Dark Harvest
Box 941
Arlington Heights IL 60006

David & Charles Inc.
North Pomfret VT 05053

Dillon Press Inc.
242 Portland Ave. S.
Minneapolis MN 55415

The Donning Co.
5659 Virginia Beach Blvd.
Norfolk VA 23502

Dragon Press
P.O. Box 78
Pleasantville NY 10570

Dream House
P.O. Box 864
Madison WI 53701

Dream/Press
Box 8531
Santa Cruz CA 95061

Dufour Editions
Box 449
Chester Springs PA 19425-0049

Ebony Books
GPO Box 1294L
Melbourne, VIC 3001
Australia

Eclipse Comics
Box 1099
Forestville CA 95436

M. Evans & Co.
216 East 49th St.
New York NY 10017

Facts on File
460 Park Ave. S.
New York NY 10016

Falcon Books,
Gibbs M. Smith, Inc.
P.O. Box 667
Layton UT 84041

Fandata Publications
7761 Asterella Ct.
Springfield VA 22152-3133

Fandom Computer Services
P.O. Box 4278
San Bernardino CA 92409

Fandom Unlimited Enterprises
Box 70868
Sunnyvale CA 94086

Fantagraphics Books
1800 Bridgegate St.
Suite #101
Westlake Village CA 91361

FASA Corp.
Box 6930
Chicago IL 60680

First Comics, Inc.
435 N. La Salle St.
Chicago IL 60610

Flatiron Distributors
175 Fifth Ave, Suite 814
New York NY 10010

Fragments West
3908 E. 4th St
Long Beach CA 90814

Gale Research Co.
Book Tower
Detroit MI 48226

W. Paul Ganley
P.O. Box 149, Amherst Branch
Buffalo NY 14226

Garland Publishing
136 Madison Ave.
New York NY 10016

Donald M. Grant
Publisher, Inc.
West Kingston RI 02892

Greenwood Press
88 Post Road West
Box 5007
Westport CT 06881

Gregg Press
70 Lincoln St.
Boston MA 02111

Gryphon Books
P.O. Box 209
Brooklyn NY 11228

Hale & Iremonger Pty Ltd
GPO Box 2552
Sydney NSW
Australia

G.K. Hall & Co.
70 Lincoln St.
Boston MA 02111

Harvard University Press
79 Garden St.
Cambridge MA 02138

Highland Press
P.O. Box 861
Oak Park IL 60303

Hill House
P.O. Box 1783,
Grand Central Station
New York NY 10017

Hopkins,
Fandom Computer Services
P.O. Box 4278
San Bernardino CA 92409

The House of Collectibles
201 E. 50th St.
New York NY 10022

Hypatia Press
86501 Central Road
Eugene OR 97402

Imagine, Inc.
Box 9674
Pittsburgh PA 15226

Indiana University Press
10th & Morton Sts.
Bloomington IN 47405

Inland Book Co.
22 Hemingway Ave.
East Haven CT 06512.

Integrated Dist. Services
250 Commercial St.
Manchester NH 03101

International Polygonics Ltd.
Box 1563
New York NY 10159

InterVarsity Press
Box F
Downers Grove IL 60515

Irwin Publishing
409 King St. W. #401
Toronto, Ont. M5V 1K1
Canada

Johns Hopkins Univ. Press
701 West 40th St., Suite 275
Baltimore MD 21211

Jwindz Publishing
3812 E. 55th St.
Minneapolis MN 55417

The Kent State Univ. Press
Kent OH 44242

Kerosina Publications
27 Hampton Rd.
Worcester Park
Surrey KT4 8EU
U.K.

Kinnell Publications
43 Kingsfield Ave.
North Harrow
Mddx. HA2 6AQ
UK.

Laissez Faire Produktion AB
Rasundavagen 129
S-171 30 Solna
Sweden
(checks to John-Henri Holmberg)

Land of Enchantment
P.O. Box 5360
Plymouth MI 48170

Lerner Publications Co.
241 First Avenue N.
Minneapolis MN 55401

Locus Press
Box 13305
Oakland CA 94661

Loompanics Unlimited
P.O. Box 1197
Port Townsend WA 98368

Louisiana State University Press
Baton Rouge LA 70893

Maclay & Associates
P.O. Box 16253
Baltimore MD 21210

Macmillan Canada
146 Front St. W. #685
Toronto, Ont. M5S 1G2
Canada

Madrona Publishers
Dept. X
Box 22667
Seattle WA 98122

McFarland & Co., Inc.
Box 611
Jefferson NC 28640

MCFI
Box 46
MIT Branch P.O.
Cambridge MA 02139

Dennis McMillan Publications
1995 Calais Dr. #3
Miami Beach FL 33141

McPherson & Co.
Box 1126
Kingston NY 12401

Meckler Publishing
11 Ferry Lane West
Westport CT 06880

Merrimack Publishers' Circle
47 Pelham Rd.
Salem NH 03079

Mercury House
300 Montgomery St.
San Francisco CA 94104

Methuen, Inc.
29 W. 35th St.
New York NY 10001.

Misfit Press, Howard DeVore
4705 Weddel
Dearborn MI 48125

Moonfire Productions
Box 1952
Wrightwood CA 92397

Morrigan Publications
84 Ivy Avenue
Southdown, Bath
Avon BA2 1AN
United Kingdom

Morrison, Raven-Hill Publishers
8555 Sunset Blvd.
Los Angeles CA 90069

Morton Falls Publishing Co.
Rt. 9, Box 810-S
Canyon Lake TX 78130

The Naiad Press, Inc.
Box 10543
Tallahassee FL 32302

NBM Publishing
35-53 70th St.
Jackson Heights NY 11372

The Nemo Press
1205 Harney St.
Omaha NE 68102

NESFA Press
Box G, MIT Station
Cambridge MA 02139

The New Establishment Press
447 Roycroft Blvd
Amherst NY 14226

New Media Publishing, Inc.
3530 Mound View Ave.
Studio City CA 91604

New Victoria Publishers
Box 27
Norwich VT 05055

Newcastle Publishing Co.
PO Box 7589
Van Nuys CA 91409

Northwestern Univ. Press
1735 Benson Ave.
Evanston IL 60201

Ocean View Books
Box 4148
Mountain View CA 94040

Octavia Press
3546 Edison Rd.
Cleveland OH 44121

Ohio University Press
Scott Quadrangle
Athens OH 45701

Oriflamme Publishing Ltd
60 Charteris Road
London N4 3AB
U.K.

The Oryx Press
2214 N Central at Encanto
Phoenix AZ 85004

Paragon House
90 Fifth Ave.
New York NY 10011

Peachtree Publishers Ltd.
494 Armour Circle N.E.
Atlanta GA 30324

Phantasia Press
5536 Crispin Way
West Bloomfield MI 48033

Philtrum Publishing Co.
Box 1186
Bangor ME 04401

Pictorial Legends
c/o The Event Company
435 Holland Ave.
Los Angeles CA 90042

Pottersfield Press
RR2
Porters Lake,
Nova Scotia B6J 2S0
Canada

Press Porcepic
235-560 Johnson St.
Victoria, BC Canada V8W 3C6

Pressworks Publishing Inc.
P.O. Box 12606
Dallas TX 75225

Prestige Art Galleries
3909 West Howard St.
Skokie IL 60076

Princeton Univ. Press
3175 Princeton Pike
Lawrenceville NJ 06848

Prometheus Books
700 E. Amherst St.
Buffalo NY 14215

Purple Mouth Press
713 Paul St.
Newport News VA 23605

Purple Prose Press
400 Napoleon Rd #402
Bowling Green OH 43402

Queensland University Press
5 S. Union St.
Lawrence MA 01843

Ragweed Press
Box 2023
Charlottetown, P.E.I.
C1A 7N7
Canada

Re/Search
20 Romolo St., Suite B
San Francisco CA 94133

Rosemill House
920 Cajon Street
Redlands CA 92373

Routledge & Kegan Paul
9 Park St
Boston MA 02108

Rune Press
P.O. Box 8297
Lake St. Sta.
Minneapolis MN 55406

Salem House
462 Boston St.
Topsfield MA 01983

Scarecrow Press, Inc.
52 Liberty St.
P.O. Box 656
Metuchen NJ 08840

School Street Press
P.O. Box 558
Hastings-on-Hudson NY 10706

Science Fiction Poetry Association
2012 Pyle Road
Schenectady, NY 12303

Scolar Press
2430 Bancroft Way
Berkeley CA 94704

SCREAM/PRESS   MARK V. ZIESING

Scream/Press
Box 481146
Los Angeles CA 90048

The Seal Press
312 S. Washington
Seattle, WA 98104

Serconia Press
P.O. Box 1786
Seattle WA 98111

Seven Suns Publications
Castle Estate, Route 1
Fairfield IA 52556

Shambhala Publications
314 Dartmouth St.
Boston MA 02116

Shaw Associates
625 Baltimore Way
Suite 1406
Coral Gables FL 33134

The Shoestring Press
P.O. Box 4327
995 Sherman Ave.
Hamden CT 06514

Southern Illinois Univ. Press
P.O. Box 3697
Carbondale IL 62902

Space & Time
138 W. 70th St., #4B
New York NY 10023-4432

Spinsters/Aunt Lute Book Co.
Box 410687
San Francisco CA 94141

Spring Harbor Press
P.O. Box 346
Delmar NY 12054

St. James Press
425 N. Michigan Ave.
Chicago IL 60611

St. Luke's Press
Mid-Memphis Tower
1407 Union Ave., Suite 401
Memphis TN 38104

Starmont House
P.O. Box 851
Mercer Island WA 98040

SteelDragon Press
Box 7253, Powderhorn Station
Minneapolis MN 55407

The Strange Company
P.O. Box 864
Madison WI 53701

Strawberry Hill Press
2594 15th Ave.
San Francisco CA 94127

Sun & Moon Press
6363 Wilshire Blvd., Suite 115
Los Angeles CA 90048

Lance Tapley, Publisher
86 Winthrop St.
P.O. Box 2439
Augusta ME 04330

Terminus Publishing Co.
Box 13418
Philadelphia PA 19101

Titan Books
P.O. Box 250
London E3 4RT
England

Tough Dove Books
Box 548
Little River CA 95456

Oswald Train, Publisher
Box 1891
Philadelphia PA 19105

Twaci Press
P.O. Box 87, M.I.T. Branch P.O.
Cambridge MA 02139

Twayne Publishers
G.K. Hall & Co.
70 Lincoln St.
Boston MA 02111

2 AM Publications
Box 6754
Rockford IL 61125

UMI Research Press
P.O. Box 1467
Ann Arbor MI 48106

Underwood-Miller
515 Chestnut St.
Columbia PA 17512

Unicorn Publishing House
1148 Parsippany Blvd
Parsippany NJ 07054

University of Chicago Press
5801 S. Ellis Ave.
Chicago IL 60637

The University of Georgia Press
Athens GA 30602

University of Illinois Press
54 E. Gregory Dr.
Champaign IL 61820

University of Iowa Press
Iowa City IA 52242

Univ. of Queensland Press (USA)
250 Commercial St.
Manchester NH 03101

University Press of America
4720 Boston Way
Lanham MD 20706

University Press of New England
17 1/2 Lebanon St.
Hanover NH 03755

United Mythologies Press
Box 390, Station A
Weston, Ont. M9N 3N1
Canada

Frederick Ungar Publishing Co.
36 Cooper Sq.
New York NY 10013

Ursus Imprints
5539 Jackson
Kansas City MO 64130

Wayne State Univ. Press
The Leonard N. Simons Bldg.
5959 Woodward Ave.
Detroit MI 48202

Weirdbook Press
Box 149, Amherst Branch
Buffalo, NY 14226-0149

Willowisp Press
401 E. Wilson Bridge Rd.
Worthington OH 43085

The Women's Press
124 Shoreditch High St.
London E1 6JE
U.K.

World Fantasy Convention
Box 27201
Tempe AZ 85282

Writer's Digest Books
9933 Alliance Rd.
Cincinnati OH 45242

Xanadu Publications
5 Uplands Rd
London N8 9NN
U.K.

Yankee Books
Main Street
Dublin NH 03444

Mark V. Ziesing
P.O. Box 806
Willimantic CT 06226

Abbreviations

*	first edition	Jul	July	
+	first American edition	Jun	June	
ad	adaptation	*LASL News*	*Los Alamos Scientific Laboratory News*	
ai	author's introduction to story	lp	large paperback, 8 ½" x 11"	
Amazing	*Amazing Stories / Amazing Science Fiction*	lt	letter	
an	anthology	Mar	March	
Apr	April	May	May	
ar	article	mg	magazine	
Aug	August	mr	movie review	
aw	afterword	ms	miscellaneous	
bg	biography	n.	novel	
bi	bibliographic material	na	novella	
br	book review	nf	non-fiction	
bx	boxed set of books	Nov	November	
CBS	Columbia Broadcasting System	nv	novelette	
CFC	Carolyn F. Cushman	oa	original anthology	
Chr	Christmas issue	oc	original collection	
CNB	Charles N. Brown	Oct	October	
co	collection of stories by one author	om	omnibus edition	
cr	criticism	pb	paperback	
cs	comic strip	ph	pamphlet/chapbook	
ct	cartoon	pi	pictorial	
da	anthology, one half of a double	pl	play	
dc	collection, one half of a double	pm	poem	
Dec	December	pp	number of pages	
dg	digest size magazine	pr	preface	
dn	novel, one half of a double	PSP	Phil Stephensen-Payne	
ec	edited collection	pt	photography	
ed	editorial	pz	puzzle	
ex	extract	qp	quality paperback	
F&SF	*The Magazine of Fantasy & Science Fiction*	qz	quiz	
fa	facetious article	sa	story adaptation of a play/screenplay	
FCM	Faren C. Miller	*Saint*	*The Saint Detective Magazine / The Saint Mystery Magazine*	
Feb	February			
Fll	Fall/Autumn	Sep	September	
fw	foreword	sf	special feature	
gc	graphic collection	SFBC	Science Fiction Book Club: Garden City, NY	
gn	graphic novel	sg	song	
gp	group of related stories	si	section introduction	
gr	game review	sl	serial segment	
hc	hardcover	sp	speech	
hu	humor	Spr	Spring	
IASFM	*Isaac Asimov's Science Fiction Magazine*	sr	story review	
ibc	inside back cover	ss	short story	
If	*IF / Worlds of If Science Fiction*	Sum	Summer	
ifc	inside front cover	tb	tabloid	
il	illustration	tc	title change	
Impulse	*Impulse / SF Impulse*	TM	Trevin Matlock	
in	introduction	tp	trade paperback	
ins	insert	tr	translation	
is	introduction to story	U.K.	United Kingdom	
ISBN	international standard book number	uw	unfinished work	
iv	interview	v	volume	
ix	index	vi	vignette	
Jan	January	Win	Winter	
JF	Jo Fletcher	WiS	Winter-Spring	